WORDSWORTH CLASSICS
OF WORLD LITERATURE
General Editor: Tom Griffith

THE ILIAD

THE ODYSSEY

D0351197

Chapman's Homer

The Iliad
The Odyssey

❖

Translated by George Chapman

With an Introduction by Jan Parker

WORDSWORTH CLASSICS
OF WORLD LITERATURE

For my husband
ANTHONY JOHN RANSON
with love from your wife, the publisher.
Eternally grateful for your unconditional love,
not just for me but for our children,
Simon, Andrew and Nichola Trayler

Readers who are interested in other titles from
Wordsworth Editions are invited to visit our website at
www.wordsworth-editions.com

For our latest list and a full mail-order service, contact
Bibliophile Books, 5 Thomas Road, London E14 7BN
Tel: +44 (0)20 7515 9222 Fax: +44 (0)20 7538 4115
E-mail: orders@bibliophilebooks.com

This edition published 2000 by Wordsworth Editions Limited
8B East Street, Ware, Hertfordshire SG12 9HJ

ISBN 13:   978 1 84022 117 6

Text © Wordsworth Editions Limited 2000
Introduction © Jan Parker 2002

Wordsworth® is a registered trademark of
Wordsworth Editions Limited,
the company founded by Michael Trayler in 1987

Typeset in Great Britain by Antony Gray
Printed and bound by Clays Ltd, St Ives plc

CONTENTS

GENERAL INTRODUCTION

Chapman's Translation

> With Poesie to open Poesie
>
> CHAPMAN 'To the Reader'

Hector bidding farewell to his wife and baby son . . . Odysseus bound to the mast listening to the Sirens . . . heroes exhanging spear thrusts or vaunting words . . . Penelope at the loom . . . Achilles dragging Hector's body round the gates of Troy – scenes from Homer have been reportrayed in every generation. The questions about mortality and identity that Homer's heroes ask, the bonds of love and fellowship that motivate them, have gripped audiences for three millennia.

The task of bringing Homer's text alive to an audience is a challenging one – for the translator now as for the 'Sons of Homer' who performed the epics entire to audiences in classical Greece. Both have to deliver richness and variety of voice and tone, have to excite and engage at dramatic moments, yet focus attention on telling details, on quiet reflection. Both have to interest in a story passed down from father to son, from generation to generation, yet seemingly told now for the first time.

Chapman's *Iliad* and *Odyssey* stand in their own right as great English epic poems. They also stand as two of the liveliest and most readable translations of Homer. The language is Shakespeare's, not ours; it represents a past golden age of heroes and adventurers – just so did Homer's Greek represent to the Classical Greeks the heroes of the legendary Trojan War.

Chapman's translation is the first into English, written in the vibrant English of Shakespeare's circle – stories of warfare and adventure written for those with 'Elizabethan' heroic expectations. As a poet Chapman crafted Elizabethan language into a formal yet supple flowing verse form that is a joy to read; there is a freshness that makes vivid the everyday natural and craftsman's world as well as the worlds of the battlefield and of Mount Olympus. As a Renaissance playwright translating Homer while Shakespeare was writing *Hamlet*, he engaged with the idea of the hero, both as supremely inspiring ('What a piece of work is a man') and as tragically fragile ('this quintessence of dust'). As a Humanist thinker he could convey the human and heroic condition from the perspectives of both man and [pre-Christian] god.

As the first translation it was influential – the first books of the *Iliad* were almost certainly drawn on by Shakespeare in writing *Troilus and Cressida* – but most importantly it was new-fashioned. The newness of the experience of reading classical texts fuelled new ideas of what it is to engage with and communicate them: Chapman's desire was to be shaped by as well as shape his translation of Homer. Every later translator saw himself in a line of pious transmission and had either to struggle with a sense of inadequacy or consciously react against the great tradition. Chapman is free to respond freshly to the text, to take liberties, even: he expands the text of Penelope's great speech to Odysseus to point up the emotional intensity of this central moment. His poetry has none of the formal 'classicism', rotundity and high nobility of eighteenth-century poets or the post-heroic flatness of modern translations; his couplets are not shaped, in the way that Pope's Homer's 'heroic couplets' are – a shaping that imparts a conscious nobility even to rapid, everyday details – but are free-flowing, open, rhyming lines. It is worth the odd expansion or difficult progression of words to be free of the false reverence and false 'heroism' of later translations.

Homer is difficult to translate because of his breadth and depth of tone – breadth in his variety of voices and heroic registers, depth in the layers of the past ages – both Dark Age and Golden Age societies – that go to make up the final versions we know as the *Iliad* and *Odyssey*. Chapman's translation is particularly good at conveying both breadth and depth – Chapman can move from sensitive emotional perceptions to high drama; he can (almost uniquely) follow Homer in endowing the everyday world the heroes inhabit with a sheen of graceful materiality – every spear, every ship is described as special in its utility, every tree or animal vivid in its particularity. This is the skill of a craftsman poet, who can delight in the well-wroughtness of a ship, door or spear as much as a well-fabricated tale; the skill of an epic poet who can bring a past, lost world to life by painting bright details overlaid neither with synthetic pastel nor with nostalgic dark tones.

There cannot be a perfect translation, except that built up in the individual reader's mind. But there can be a translation that helps the reader to engage with Homer, and Chapman's is arguably the best. Driving his poetry is the excitement of the Renaissance discovery of classical civilisation as at once vital and distant; his artistry enables the reader to engage with a masterpiece which is still today simultaneously vivid and classic. It is this excitement and vitality that most mark out the experience of reading Chapman's *Homer*, as testified to by Keats:

> Oft of one wide expanse have I been told
> That deep browed Homer ruled as his demesne;
> Yet never did I breathe its pure serene
> Till I heard CHAPMAN speak out loud and bold.

Chapman and Homer

CHAPMAN – the Elizabethan dramatist George Chapman's *Seven Books of the Iliads of Homer Prince of Poets,* published in 1598, was the first translation of Homer from Greek into English. The seven Books: 1, 2, 7–11, appeared as Shakespeare was writing *Hamlet*; his *Iliad* was revised, completed and published in 1610–1, his *Odyssey* in 1614–5.

HOMER – the traditional name for the final composer/shaper[s] (perhaps in the eighth century BC, perhaps in northern, Greek-speaking Asia Minor) of the oral stories about Achilles, Troy and Odysseus. These stories perhaps go back to a historical trade war between the allies of Mycenaean Greece and Troy some time between the fifteenth and twelfth centuries BC. The fluid oral sections may have gradually become set into a traditional, accepted text; at some point the text was written down. The *Iliad* and *Odyssey* may have been composed by different people, though they were later treated as associated. The texts were stabilised for performance in Athens in the late sixth century BC.

After the settled societies of Mycenaean Greece and Asia Minor – the historical kingdoms of 'Mycenaean' Sparta, Pylos, Mycenae and Troy-Hissarlik – came a period of depopulation. During this period, popularly called 'The Dark Ages', a different ethnic group invaded Greece. They laid claim to the land they had taken over by investigating and preserving the hero cults of the previous population. Throughout this period, it is presumed, the hero stories of the Mycenaean period were preserved, performed and eventually, with the development of writing, recorded.

Note about Names

Chapman uses the Latin form of the Greek gods' names – Jupiter or Jove for Zeus, Juno for Hera, Vulcan for Hephaistus, Venus for Aphrodite. He frequently uses patronymics for the heroes – Laertides, Aeacides for Odysseus, Achilles etc. The Glossary of Proper Names (p. LXXIX) lists the various forms with the usual Greek equivalents; for clarity, the introduction uses the commonly known Greek form of name for both gods and heroes.

INTRODUCTION TO THE ILIAD

> Achilles' baneful wrath resound, O goddess – that impos'd
> Infinite sorrows on the Greeks, and many brave souls loos'd
> From breasts heroic . . .

The *Iliad* opens with an invitation to join the audience, to hear the deeds of heroes retold, their deaths recounted. The teller of tales invokes the Muse who saw the events, to ensure that this is a true record of the deaths of the 'brave souls': the only reward for the tragedy of heroes' deaths is that their deeds are recorded and remembered down the generations.

What did they die for? For Achilles' anger, for Agamemnon's stupid intransigence, for Paris' passion, for the gods' malevolence, for no reason except they were in the wrong place at the wrong time . . . The *Iliad* is a record of deaths: of the tragedy of the death of Sarpedon, whose warm personality sounds through the stories from the Trojan camp, and of Patroclus, whose gentle kindness sounds through those from the Greek side; of pity for the many young men whose first adult act is to enter the battle where they find death not glory.

But each hero's deeds are also woven into a tapestry of life – scenes from Mount Olympus, where the gods meet, feast and enjoy immortal bliss; scenes of animals, farm life and nature worked in miniature as similes; scenes from the ordinary life 'back home', worked on to Achilles' shield as a replacement for and a reminder of the world he will now never see again. The battlefield is seen from the combatants' viewpoint – decisive encounters that don't materialise, death strokes that go astray, triumphant advances that suddenly leave the victor vulnerable: the tiny chance events that save or destroy. But the battlefield is also a tragic stage – each action set against a backcloth of patterns, possibilities and judgements made by the poet and by the gods. The geography of Troy is marked out by the gods – Troy citadel and the Greek ships are targets that may be attacked only when History and Destiny permit; when Hector or Patroclus get carried away they seem to bring on themselves not just death but doom.

The theme of the poem is the consequences of the terrible anger of Achilles. He is extreme – the one who fights best, cares most for his honour, is least able to accept the abrogation of the 'heroic code', is least able to accept the human condition. It is his extremity that renders him a hero – not in the sense of a shining example but in the sense of having the stature to test and demonstrate the limits of what it is to be human. The question for most of the *Iliad* is whether the extremity of Achilles' anger renders him *in*human; Book 24 ends in tears of compassion, as Achilles joins with the father of his bitterest enemy in weeping over Hector's body, acknowledging that he too will soon be only a lifeless corpse and a name.

The battlefield is seen with all the intensity of those who have decided to exchange long life for glory, but also with the flippancy of the gods who see human affairs as childish. There is the sadness of those such as Achilles' mother or Hector's wife – who watch the battle from afar and await the consequences; there is also the remoteness of the immortals, for whom mortals are like leaves on a tree – they fall each autumn and are replaced each spring. One of the reasons for reading the *Iliad* is that it sets prowess against these other perspectives – the heroes are driven to greater feats because otherwise their lives will have been as unindividuated as those leaves on the tree; Achilles weeps for the pain his death will cause his father and the immortal grief it will bring his goddess mother. Yet the power of the life force, the energy and charge of the story and the storytelling do not allow the heroes to give up. His deeds are heroic because they are done in the teeth of the knowledge that death is all around and that the only immortality is the remembrance of later generations.

The heroes round the wall of Troy do not fight out of loyalty to a cause – Achilles and Sarpedon as allies remind their respective Greek and Trojan generals that they are fighting because they agreed to, not out of personal involvement. They fight, as Sarpedon reminds his second-in-command Glaucus, because it is their place to do so and because, as heroes, that is the only respectable arena in which to prove and define themselves. Audiences in the past have been drawn to the poem for the same reason as postwar readers now are put off by it – as a glorification of war and of the definition of a man as a skilled fighting machine. Both reactions over-simplify the epic poem, which reflects, and reflects on, every kind of attitude to war and death. Both reactions are wrong in thinking the poem shows heroes who have something to live and die for – the heroes, rather, are all too clear that what they give their lives for can be seen as now glorious and now foolish and deluded. The *Iliad* is a multifaceted account of the human condition – which is to strive for life and individuation while facing tragedy and nothingness.

Chapman's Heroes

As the performers of fifth-century Athens had to re-create a past 'age of heroes' for their audience, so every translator has to transmit Homer to an audience distanced in time and in social values. To engage with Homer is to be drawn away from contemporary culture in reimagining the past. Such engagement leads to highlighting knots in the text that seem both central and strange: cruxes, such as that of the nature and values of the heroes in the *Iliad*, that have to be interpreted by the modern reader. Twentieth-century translations tend to the anti-heroic, giving Achilles a brooding self-centredness and making Agamemnon a petty, querulous tyrant. Pope, on the contrary, ennobles both. Chapman, with an eye to the Elizabethan court, is attuned to the problem of the hero in society and gives both parties stature, strong though different characters and dignified, individualised voices. This comes out in the way he renders the quarrel that leads   to Achilles' wrath: when Nestor, the wise counsellor, tries to intercede between Agamemnon's royal temper and Achilles' hurt pride, saying that Achilles must be mollified because he is their only safeguard, Agamemnon is made to reply:

> 'All this, good father,' said the king, 'is comely and good right,
> But this man breaks all such bounds; he affects, past all men, height;
> All would in his power hold, all make his subjects; give to all
> His hot will for a temperate law.'

Achilles' version of the rupture is in Book 9, when his friends, suffering at the hands of the Trojans, beg him to return to help them. Though warm in his reception of them, he refuses the Greeks' request in a powerful and moving speech finely rendered by Chapman – Agamemnon's slight was no petty insult but a tearing down of the whole value system by which Achilles had lived and with which he daily faced danger and death:

> 'Their suit is wretchedly enforc'd to free their own despairs,
> And my life never shall be hir'd with thankless, desperate pray'rs;
> For never had I benefit, that ever foil'd the foe:
> Ev'n share hath he that keeps his tent and he to field doth go;
> With equal honour cowards die, and men most valiant,
> The much performer, and the man that can of nothing vaunt.
> No overplus I ever found, when with my mind's most strife
> To do them good, to dangerous fight I have expos'd my life.
> But ev'n as to unfeather'd birds the careful dam brings meat,
> Which when she hath bestow'd, herself hath nothing left to eat:
> So when my broken sleeps have drawn the nights t'extremest length,
> And ended many bloody days with still employed strength . . .
> I have been robb'd before their eyes . . . '

Chapman understands the importance of a hero's honour, understands the conflict between the hero's duty to himself and, as a leader of men, his duty to his companions and allies. He examines Achilles and Hector as political leaders not as individuated 'heroes'; their regret for their falling out with Agamemnon and Polydamas respectively are stressed by Chapman as political rather than personal lessons. Compared to a twentieth-century individualistic sense of the hero, these are figures shaped by their society's demands. Both Achilles' and Hector's tragedy, Chapman brings out, is that they are brought down by the conflicting demands of what is due to themselves and what should be suppressed in their duty of care to others: Achilles is affected by his attempt to divorce his personal loyalty to Patroclus and his Myrmidons from the claims on him of his comrades-in-arms – Ajax, Diomedes etc. Meanwhile Hector's rashness in going against Polydamas' advice is shown as personal rather than tactical; his death at Achilles' hands is brought on at least in part through his sense that he has let down those he has been trained to regard, the people of Troy. He is a prince, not a hero, and his rush to assert himself as a hero is a mistake that destroys him.

Chapman's understanding of these issues may be informed by Renaissance, Roman-derived ideas on the Stoic hero's need to align state and private duty; it may be informed by his knowledge of Elizabethan rather than Greek society (although his notes show his competence in Greek, it is not clear how comprehensive a Greek scholar he was). In any case, the result is that he holds up to his heroes exemplary models, by whose standards the heroes fail. The point of contact with Greek society is that Homer's heroes also have a consciousness (*aidos*) by which they judge their own behaviour: Hector, for example, examines himself on his reasons for not fleeing Achilles and concludes that he is inhibited by his failing as a leader of men and by the elders watching him. The Greek text, in emphasising his *aidos,* his sensibility of what is expected of him, carries a strong sense that at the last he is in some way crippled by this consciousness. In a sense, therefore, Chapman engages with the problem of the hero in society in the same way as the heroes themselves do.

The Story of the *Iliad*

The *Iliad* is one of the stories of 'Ilium' – Troy. It is the story of the tragic consequences of Achilles' 'baneful wrath'. The story is set in the ninth year of the war fought by the Greeks against the Trojans for harbouring Paris and the runaway wife Helen. The King of Mycenae, Agamemnon, and his brother Menelaus, the wronged husband, lead a coalition of forces under their various chiefs from all round Greece against Hector, son of King Priam of Troy. Hector too leads allies – from Greek-speaking Asia Minor, and from

North of the Troad (the Dardanelles) – including the sympathetically portrayed Sarpedon.

The main story, of the consequences of Agamemnon's insult to the best Greek fighter, Achilles, and Achilles' withdrawal, starts Book 1. The story broadens to include Mount Olympus where the gods feast unconcerned, to the women and old men in Troy, to the heroes and casualties of the battlefield. The main story comes back in Book 9, when Agamemnon, realising that he cannot manage without Achilles, sends a delegation to soothe Achilles' hurt pride. The rest of the tragedy comes from Achilles' refusal to be soothed. In Book 13, Patroclus begs Achilles to let him appear in Achilles' armour to give heart to the Greeks; he throws caution to the wind, and Book 16 has his and Sarpedon's tragic deaths. The rest of the epic concerns Achilles' incapacity to deal with the death of his beloved friend Patroclus – with his insane vengeful rage as he tries to find appropriate compensation for the death. Even human sacrifice and the killing of Patroclus' killer Hector are insufficient: he carries on violating Hector's dead body. In Book 23 he has to accept that the only thing he can do for Patroclus is to bury him with fine funeral games, games over which he presides, negotiating and rewarding rival claims to excellence. The *Iliad* finishes with the frail Priam's visit to 'man-slaying' Achilles to beg back the body of Hector. They join in tears of common grief, in a shared sense of tragic pity, as Priam weeps over the hands that killed his son and Achilles over the reminder of his own father, soon to weep over *his* son now doomed to die at Troy.

Book 1

The trouble starts with a girl. The Greek commander Agamemnon is reluctant to give his prize, the beautiful Chryseis, back to her father, Phoebus Apollo's priest. When Apollo forces his hand by sending a plague on the Greek camp, and he is compelled to give the girl back, he angrily demands compensation from his chiefs. He takes Achilles' girl, Briseis, against all propriety. This rouses Achilles' 'baneful wrath', the theme of the poem, not just because he cares for the 'bride of his spear'. Achilles is incensed by the injustice of losing his prize, given to him as a mark of his exertion and risk-taking in a battle fought to get back someone else's wife – Helen. Achilles is checked by Athene from killing Agamemnon but neither she nor the old and wise Nestor can persuade him to heal the rift. All he sees is that to continue to fight would be to continue to bring honour to the man who insulted him. Achilles withdraws to his tent; Agamemnon says he can do very well without him, but of course he cannot. Achilles is the best fighter among the Greeks and his stature is demonstrated by how badly the war goes without him.

There is a parallel falling out among the powers that be on Mount Olympus, where Hera, Queen of the Gods, accuses Zeus of dallying with Achilles' mother Thetis. (Thetis has come to him to beg for the gods' help in demonstrating the Greeks' need for Achilles and, in ritual supplication, has thrown her arms round Zeus' knees.) There is a pettishness and bluster similar to Agamemnon's about Zeus' assertion of authority when he is in the wrong. But when he blusters, the mountain shakes – the King of the Gods may not have moral authority but he has tremendous power.

The insult to Achilles' honour brings death and tragedy to Greeks and Trojans alike – it is literally a deadly insult. The insult to the Queen is quickly resolved by the clowning of their crippled son Hephaestus. Since the gods are immortal, nothing has lasting or grave consequences for them.

Book 2

Agamemnon is shown up in Book 1 as forgetful of the responsibilities of command and of his duty to keep together and reward the forces he has summoned to avenge, as Achilles pointed out, a domestic wrong. He is exposed further in Book 2. Having received a 'pernicious' dream from Zeus that, after nine years of vain effort, he is about to capture Troy, he decides to test the army by reporting that the dream advised flight. The army delightedly takes up the proposition that they return to their homes and families and it needs all the guile and oratory of Odysseus to dissuade them from setting sail.

This book gives the background to the main story of the *Iliad* – the baneful wrath of Achilles and the sorrows and heroic deaths it caused. There is, unusually, a sense of the ordinary men, those 'without a name', who have become caught up in their chiefs' feud. Their concerns are voiced by the base Thersites but also by Agamemnon and Odysseus. There is a strong evocation of the past nine years of fruitless effort, of wear and tear on men and equipment,

'. . . now our vessels rotten grow.
Our tackling fails; our wives, young sons, sit in their doors and long
For our arrival . . . '

In the Catalogue of Forces there are also glimpses of other *Iliad*s, other stories that would have been part of the Trojan War cycle of poems, and of other poets. The poet's shaping of the narrative is also clearly visible in this book – in Zeus's sending of a false dream and Agamemnon's false reporting of it. This play of ironies is framed by a narratorial comment –

O fool, he thought to take in that next day old Priam's town,
Not knowing what affairs Jove had in purpose . . .

The poet does know both what Zeus purposes and the outcome of the war.

From his perspective he can criticise those with more limited vision. The poet is the servant of the Muses who 'are present here, are wise, and all things know' and who provide a true report of all the forces at Troy. The poet is the 'servant of Fame' – of report – in several senses: he is dependent on the tradition passed down through generations of poets, shaping, adding and refining the stories. He is also the servant of fame in being the one channel of immortality available for the heroes on both sides of the Trojan War – immortality of fame in epic song.

There is another invocation: 'But now the man that overshined them all, Sing, muse'. Achilles' claim to be best is borne out in the muse's reckoning – 'Great Ajax for strength passed all the peers of war While vex'd Achilles was away, but he surpass'd him far.' The scene shifts to Hector at Troy, surrounded by the auxiliary leaders 'of special excellence', finishing with Sarpedon and Glaucus who are the major and most sympathetic characters on the Trojan side. At the very end of the list comes Amphimachus, never again mentioned, who is given a brief biography that both serves as his epitaph and his pathetic, momentary fame. He came to the battlefield dressed in the gold that marked him out to be a target and so doomed him:

> The fool Amphimachus, to field, brought gold to be his wrack,
> Proud-girl-like that doth ever bear her dower on her back;
> Which wise Achilles mark'd, slew him, and took his gold, in strife
> At Xanthus' flood; so little Death did fear his golden life.

We suddenly remember what Achilles excels *at*.

Book 3

As Book 1 gave a character sketch of the main characters in the Greek camp – Achilles caring for his honour above all, Agamemnon weak and egotistical, Nestor old, respected, drawing on the past – so Book 3 introduces the telling characteristics of those on the Trojan side. Book 3 introduces the cause of the war – the beautiful Paris, who seduced Helen away from her Spartan home. He is set against his brother Hector, the brave leader of the Trojans. Hector is ever vigilant about his own honour and that of his allies – part of his job as war leader is to sting the heroic consciousness of his leaders, spurring them on. Paris, however, is one person untouched by others' sense of him, by others' heroic values, by his brother's reproaches. He is unwilling to face up to Menelaus, the wronged husband, though it was his abduction of Helen (his reward for awarding Aphrodite the goddesses' beauty prize) that started the Trojan War. Menelaus spies Paris lounging and makes for him like 'a serpent . . . her blue neck, swoln with poison raised, and her sting out'. Paris is scared, but unrepentant. He:

Shrunk in his beauties. Which beheld by Hector, he let go
This bitter check on him: 'Accurs'd! Made but in beauty's scorn,
Impostor, woman's man! O heav'n, that thou hadst ne'er been born
                                        . . . O wretch! Not dare to stay
Weak Menelaus! But 'twas well . . .

Your harp's sweet touch, curl'd locks, fine shape, and gifts so exquisite,
Giv'n thee by Venus, would have done your fine dames little good,
When blood and dust had ruffled them . . .
                                        . . . thou well deserv'st
A coat of tombstone, not of steel, in which for form thou serv'st.'
To this thus Paris spake (for form that might inhabit heav'n):
'Hector, because thy sharp reproof is out of justice giv'n,
I take it well . . .
Yet I, less practis'd than thyself in these extremes of war,
May well be pardon'd, though less bold; in these your worth exceeds,
In others, mine. Nor is my mind of less force to the deeds
Requir'd in war, because my form more flows in gifts of peace.
Reproach not therefore the kind gifts of golden Cyprides.' [Venus]

Helen is equally beautiful, as even the old men of Troy, chattering in the
sun like grasshoppers, are moved to admit:

Those wise and almost wither'd men found this heat in their years
That they were forc'd (though whispering) to say: 'What man
                                                        can blame
The Greeks and Trojans to endure for so admired a dame,
So many miseries, and so long? In her sweet countenance shine
Looks like the goddesses . . .'

Unlike Paris, however, she *does* have a pronounced sense of responsibility
for coming to Troy. She looks down from the walls of Troy to see her fate
decided, picking out for King Priam those Greek fighters who are left after
nearly ten years, and is stricken with anguish.

Menelaus challenges Paris to a duel to the death – a simple settlement of
the war. Menelaus prays to Zeus protector of marriage and guest bonds; he
wounds Paris but not seriously, his sword breaks and he takes Paris by the
throat; Aphrodite breaks his grip and wafts Paris from the battlefield to
Helen's bedroom. The proper, dignified solution has been frustrated by the
gods. In extraordinary and outspoken human defiance, Helen refuses to be
a pawn, refuses to go to Paris's bed and suggests to Aphrodite that she
herself go instead. But the gods cannot be defied . . .

Book 4

Book 4 opens on Mount Olympus with Zeus asking, over a cup of nectar, whether the gods should plant 'war and combat' or 'impartial friendship' between the two sides. With Hera and Athene, the losers, still feuding with the winner of the judgment of Paris, Aphrodite, the vote is for continued war. The chilling deal is that Zeus will allow Troy to be destroyed provided he can destroy Hera's favourite cities next time he has a mind to.

On the ground, the mêlée continues, once the gods tempt an all-too-vain Pandarus into breaking the truce. The history and the craftsmanship of the bow he uses is described in loving detail, a haven of pastoral calm before the fateful arrow hits. The skin wound it inflicts on Menelaus is likened to the delicate staining of precious ivory – from a visual similarity a glowing miniature is painted of a very different world.

The rest of the book follows Agamemnon, seen in a more sympathetic light as he cares for his brother and puts heart into his troops. Battle is joined, like rivers in spate. Men die, after a short biography – like Simoisius, whose parents' marriage and his birth are celebrated:

> Sweet was that birth of his
> To his kind parents, and his growth did all their care employ;
> And yet those rites of piety, that should have been his joy
> To pay their honour'd years again, in as affectionate sort,
> He could not graciously perform, his sweet life was so short.

In dying he is likened to a poplar lying with curly leaves by the fen, felled by a wheelwright. He is given his moment in the history, his death is graced by a telling image before he becomes, like all the others, a victim to be despoiled, a victory to be vaunted.

Book 5

Book 5 is the book of Diomedes' preeminence – his time for glory both on the battlefield and in the epic. Pallas Athene ('the Maid') grants him the vision to recognise immortals fighting on the battlefield so he can avoid them or, in the case of the gods of war and love (Ares, Aphrodite), take them on. Others, without it, attribute to some god or fate the chance happenings of battle: Pandarus, sure of his aim, attributes his failure to hit Menelaus to

> 'Some great immortal, that conveys his shoulders in a cloud,
> Goes by and puts by every dart at his bold breast bestow'd.'

Diomedes is preeminent, more than human, until warned by Apollo that he has gone too far: the god

> . . . exceeding wrathful grew,
>
> And asked him: 'What! Not yield to gods? Thy equals learn to know:
> The race of gods is far above men creeping here below.'

Far above, perhaps, but not more dignified – Ares lets out an unmartial bellow when stabbed by Diomedes.

Diomedes thinks it ignoble to shrink from fighting Aeneas and Pandarus; rather he sees them, and especially their horses, as an opportunity to win the two assets that establish the status of the hero – 'exquisite prize' and 'exceeding renown'. Diomedes sometimes seems a very straightforward hero!

The gods, in disguise, play at Trojans and Greeks; when they get tired or hurt they can go home to have everything made better. Aphrodite's mother strokes her grazed hand and soothes her by promising that Diomedes shall be punished for his 'insolence' in wounding her, a goddess, by being childless:

> 'Diomed . . .
> Not knowing he that fights with heav'n hath never long to live,
> And for this deed, he never shall have a child about his knee
> To call him father . . .'
> This said, with both her hands she cleans'd the tender back and palm
> Of all the sacred blood they lost; and, never using balm,
> The pain ceas'd, and the wound was cured . . .

Not for gods the pain, suffering, heroism or bravery of risking death, the sacrifice of leaving, as Sarpedon has done, everything that makes life worth living:

> 'For far hence Asian Lycia lies, where gulfy Xanthus flows
> And where my lov'd wife, infant son, and treasure nothing scant,
> I left behind me . . .'

Responding to a call to arms, Sarpedon is doomed never to see them again.

Book 6

The battle continues, with no sign of Zeus's plan, agreed with Thetis in Book 1, to give the Trojans dominance – a dominance that would make clear to the Greeks how much they need Achilles back. The battle is a matter of individual duels, preceded by the ritual exchange of names and lineage. In battle, as in any contest, the glory of the victor rests in part on the stature and credentials of his opponent. It is the name and lineage which give each individual an identity, to combat the gods' perspective, voiced by Apollo in Book 21, that men are no more worth quarrelling over than leaves that flourish for a time and are then replaced by others.

Diomedes is here asked

>   'Why dost thou so explore,'
> Said Glaucus, 'of what race I am? When like the race of leaves
> The race of man is, that deserves no question, nor receives
> My being any other breath. The wind in autumn strows
> The earth with old leaves, then the spring the woods with new endows,
> And so death scatters men on earth, so life puts out again . . . '

But in his narrative of the history that marks Glaucus out as an individual, he unexpectedly establishes common ground with his foe, Diomedes. The meeting ends not in death but with an exchange of armour in token of a historic bond of hospitality between them. (The observance of this bond leads to Glaucus being tricked out of his gold armour!)

Hector goes back to Troy to organise prayers to Athene. The move to the non-combatants' world – old men, women and children – in Troy emphasises both the bulwark that Hector is and the price paid by the dependants of those who lose the heroic duels that are going on outside. The non-combatants at that moment include Paris, who says he has been debating the merits of heroic battle, but will now join in and fight. Hector wards off the words of his mother and Helen, his dependants, as distractions and presses on to find his wife Andromache. In the most moving scene of the *Iliad*, he laments the fate that she will suffer, made worse because of her and her captor's knowledge that she was the wife of the worthiest of the Trojans. His heroic stature will, after his death, be a matter of suffering not pride to those he leaves behind. Their baby cries in fear, not at the terrible future but at Hector's helmet – the horse-hair crest he thinks grows from his father's head. Hector tenderly reassures him and swings him through the air, and Andomache smiles through her tears. Hector prays for his son's glorious future (a heartfelt wish that will be unfulfilled – the conquering Greeks will dash his brains out to crush the seed of Hector). He pities her, reminding her that no man escapes his fate:

>   ' . . . and fate, whose wings can fly?
> Noble, ignoble, fate controls: once born, the best must die.'

Both must resume their work. He collects Paris for battle while his household mourns for him:

> On went his helm; his princess home, half cold with kindly fears,
> When every fear turn'd back her looks, and every look shed tears.

Book 7

Hector challenges the Greeks to name a champion to meet him in single combat, ironically envisaging the mound on the shore of the Hellespont, that will stand for all time to be a monument to his and his victim's heroic deeds:

> 'Survivors sailing the black sea may thus his name renew:
> "This is his monument, whose blood long since did fates imbrue,
> Whom passing far in fortitude, illustrious Hector slew."
> This shall posterity report, and my fame never die.'

The irony is the poet's. The *Iliad* ends with the making of a burial mound – Hector's: he will be Achilles' victim. Posterity will be the immortal report of his death, in this, the *Iliad*.

The Greeks discuss who to put up; the ranking is plain and is confirmed by the voice of the poet. Nestor voices his scorn, recalling a similar situation from his youth when he had been the victor though the youngest. In response nine come forward; the lot chooses Ajax, who speaks the traditional pre-combat words of menace, which Hector counters by saying that he is not a novice, and laying out the rules of engagement. It is a good fight, it seems, for when night intervenes the two separate in mutual respect and exchange of gifts.

Attempts to resolve the issues underlying the war – Paris's flouting of the sacred bond of guest-friendship and the taking of Helen and her treasures as 'spoil' – continue when the Trojan council proposes to give both back. Paris refuses to return Helen but will return the possessions with interest. The Greeks refuse. A truce is arranged to allow for the burial of the dead, and the Greeks build a defensive wall, which offends the gods; Zeus comforts Poseidon by foretelling the time when it will be obliterated by the sea. The physical survival of landmarks is, from the gods' perspective, a fragile thing.

Book 8

Book 7 ends with Zeus's threatening thunder over the Greek camp. Book 8 starts with his terrifying threats to the immortals: he is the strongest of the gods, and his strength will be terrible to anyone who interferes with his newly-resumed plan to allow the Trojans to dominate. Gracious when obeyed, he smiles at Athene and sits in triumph overlooking Troy.

The fighting in the previous books has been reported, either from the combatants' point of view or from the gods', as individual charges and combats. Now there is a new sense of the overall geography of the battle-field, with three zones. The first is the city of Troy, with the non-combatants and dependants – the Greek goal; the second the plain in front of the walls where the day's fighting goes on, which the Trojans are now encouraged by the gods to dominate; the third the area behind the new Greek earth wall and ditch, the camp and the Greek ships in the harbour – the Trojan goal. Zeus's will (decided in Book 1 when, at Thetis' request, he nodded his ambrosial head, and now activated) is expressed by the golden scales which turn against the Greeks; the thunderclaps are perceived by the two sides as deterring or encouraging. Now Zeus's will is in operation, the still-continuing Greek successes are marked as a tragic flouting of the gods. This marking out of the territory into permitted and forbidden areas also applies to the Trojans, because Zeus's will operates in partnership with the fates. Since they have decreed that Troy will fall, the new-found Trojan confidence is also ironised as heedless of the eventual tragedy ahead: Hector's words ring rashly:

> 'I know benevolent Jupiter did by his beck profess
> Conquest and high renown to me, and to the Greeks distress.
> O fools, to raise such silly forts, not worth the least account,
> Nor able to resist our force! With ease our horse may mount
> Quite over all their hollow dyke; but when their fleet I reach,
> Let Memory to all the world a famous bonfire teach:
> For I will all their ships inflame, with whose infestive smoke
> (Fear-shrunk, and hidden near their keels) the conquer'd
>
> > > Greeks shall choke.'

Hector's derision of the Greeks' dyke is ironised (as often, with Hector) by the audience's knowledge that Troy, not the Greek ships, will finally be destroyed. So the Trojans, despite their god-assisted advance, have a no-go area, a zone which it is now overweening and hubristic to occupy: the camp and ships beyond the dyke.

This tragic 'charging' of the geography of Troy with danger zones changes the perspective from which fights are seen: from now on, indiv-iduals seem not so much to go out to fight as to meet their fate.

Book 9

Zeus's plan has the immediate effect of depressing Agamemnon; he again proposes returning home. Diomedes and Nestor dissuade him, instead persuading him to try to undo his spurning of the Greeks' best fighter. Agamemnon acknowledges his folly and sends them, with Odysseus, as envoys to Achilles, to offer generous restitution and recompense. The envoys are warmly greeted by Achilles and Patroclus as Achilles' 'best esteemed friends'. In the name of that affection, Odysseus appeals to Achilles to save the Greek ships from Hector – out of pity for their plight even if he cannot bring himself to relent towards Agamemnon and accept the recompense offered. He tempts him with winning 'triumphant glory' for himself by killing Hector. Achilles however is impervious. The whole basis on which he has been exerting and endangering himself has, he says, been destroyed:

'With equal honour cowards die, and men most valiant,
The much performer, and the man that can of nothing vaunt.'

The destiny, the reward of the best and the worst, have been equalised; the reciprocity in the relations between Agamemnon and those he leads has gone; none of the respect for bonds that underpinned the summoning of the army remains; there is therefore no reason left to fight the Trojans. No amount of material recompense can wipe out the outrage inflicted by Agamemnon. Material possessions cannot be weighed against a man's life, especially not against Achilles' life. He has a uniquely definite, unchancy, choice-dependent fate: either a short life with glory but no homecoming or a long life without glory.

'The one, that if I here remain t'assist our victory,
My safe return shall never live, my fame shall never die:
If my return obtain success, much of my fame decays,
But death shall linger his approach, and I live many days.'

Achilles' speech is overpowering; only Phoenix, his old tutor, can respond. He tells a long tale of restitution refused until it was withdrawn and the work done for no reward. This elicits the blunt statement that Achilles no longer needs the honour granted by human society, and that someone who loves him should therefore hate those whom he hates, sharing affections and honours alike.

Ajax sees that Achilles is not to be moved even by his friends, that he clings to his anger – though society provides recompense even for the killing of a brother or child, let alone the abduction of a slave girl. Achilles assents with his reason but cannot tolerate the outrage. His reply is that until he himself and his men are affected, he will not fight: a slight shift in position which shows that he feels, even while rejecting, the force of his friends' need for him (a sensitivity that Patroclus will appeal to in Book 16, with tragic results). Odysseus takes the answer back, while Phoenix stays the night. Diomedes outspokenly condemns Agamemnon for pleading with Achilles, as it has only made him more obdurate and full of pride. Achilles will fight again, he predicts, when his fighting spirit and the god drive him to.

Book 10

Book 10 is a night interlude with a different atmosphere to other books. It is darker and more antiquarian in its interest in ancient arms. Because of this, and because its events are not referred to in other books, it has been thought an addition.

Agamemnon, Menelaus and Nestor all awake in the middle of the night and rouse the Greek leaders. Nestor senses that the Greek position is at a critical point and proposes a reconnaissance of the Trojan intentions; those who undertake it are to be richly rewarded with 'fame of all men canopied with heaven' and a choice gift. Diomedes chooses Odysseus as the best companion once Agamemnon, almost comically protective of his brother in this dangerous exploit, has hastily stipulated that Diomedes should not take rank into account. Odysseus puts on his Mycenaean boar's tusk helmet, and with a prayer to Athene they set out.

Meanwhile Hector also calls for a scout to win honour and Achilles' horses by establishing the Greeks' position and morale. Dolon volunteers, but runs straight into Odysseus and Diomedes. He offers a ransom for his release; Odysseus reassures him and asks him for information. Dolon gives it; when they have what they need, despite a ritual plea for mercy, they kill him out of hand. They capture the wonderful horses of Rhesus while indulging in a blood bath. They return in triumph with the horses which, strangely, are never again mentioned.

Book 11

Books 11 to 18 cover the grim and bloody fighting on a single day, a day when Zeus's promise to Thetis to show the Greeks how much they need her son is dreadfully fulfilled.

The battle starts with the sides facing each other like two lines of reapers who:

> Bear down the furrows speedily, and thick their handfuls fall:
> So at the joining of the hosts ran slaughter through them all.

Agamemnon has his *aristeia*, his time of preeminence, killing two sons of Priam whom Achilles had previously captured and ransomed:

> And as a lion having found the furrow of a hind,
> Where she had calv'd two little twins, at will and ease doth grind
> The joints snatch'd in his solid jaws, and crusheth into mist
> Their tender lives, their dam, though near, not able to resist,
> But shook with vehement fear herself, flies through the oaken chase
> From that fell savage, drown'd in sweat, and seeks some covert place:
> So when with most unmatched strength the Grecian general bent
> 'Gainst these two princes, none durst aid their native king's descent.

Other victims include two sons of an opponent of Menelaus, despite their ritual plea for mercy, and Iphidamas, who 'straight his bridal chamber left' on his wedding night to win glory at Troy.

Hector, on the watch, waits until Agamemnon is wounded: as Zeus told him, it is now his turn to be preeminent. Odysseus and Diomedes perceive that the tide is with the Trojans but fight hard until they too are wounded. Ajax fights valiantly until he has to retreat 'As when a dull mill ass comes near a goodly field of corn' but is slowly driven back by children guarding the crop. In this simile, as in others, the point of similarity – stubbornness, strength, imperturbability when threatened by lesser foes, the insensibility and dignity of the movement – is embroidered into an evocative picture of real life in the non-heroic world, so that the initial comparison is only the starting point of the interest of the scene.

Achilles, who has not returned home as he threatened but is watching from the stern of his ship, sends Patroclus to establish who is wounded; it is the invaluable healer, Machaon. He goes to Nestor, who is drinking from a cup similar to one actually found at Mycenae ('Nestor's cup'), but Patroclus refuses to sit down because he must get back to Achilles. Nestor regales him with a long tale about his exploits when he was young, with the implication that glory is enjoyed when it is won among companions and celebrated in public, not privately dwelt on. Nestor reminds Patroclus, presumably still standing, of their fathers' advice – Achilles' that he be always preeminent in battle, Patroclus' that as the elder he should counsel Achilles. Nestor suggests that he reason with him or, fatally, that he at least stand in for Achilles to help the losing Greeks. Patroclus, moved by Nestor's words, then sees for himself the crisis among the Greeks. He is appealed to by the wounded Eurypylus, whom he tends; he does not get back to Achilles until Book 16.

Book 12

The wall around the Greek camp that offended the gods is attacked by the Trojans, although the poet reveals that it will not fall until after the taking of Troy, when Apollo and Poseidon will turn the rivers on it. Hector, his triumphs ironised as always by the sense that he is bringing his own doom down on himself, follows the advice of the cautious Polydamas to attack on foot, but quarrels recklessly with him over whether to follow an omen. The two Ajaxes meanwhile encourage all the different ranks of Greek fighters, drawn together in this emergency.

Sarpedon encourages his friend Glaucus to join him in making a full assault on the wall. He reminds him that the preeminent position they enjoy at home comes from their being preeminent in battle. (Sarpedon has several times reminded Hector that he has no common cause with him: he has left his wife and child to be an ally to take part in the 'glory-giving battle'.) He continues, surprisingly to modern ears, to say that if they were immortal the last thing he would ask of his friend would be to undergo the pain and risk of battle; but as death will come the only option is to stake and risk their mortality to gain immortal glory. This central statement of what drives the hero is remarkably free of aggression or delight in battle for its own sake:

> 'Glaucus, say, why are we honour'd more
> Than other men of Lycia in place, with greater store
> Of meats and cups, with goodlier roofs, delightsome gardens, walks,
> More lands and better, so much wealth that court and country talks
> Of us and our possessions . . . Come, be we great in deed
> As well as look; shine not in gold, but in the flames of fight,
> That so our neat-arm'd Lycians may say: "See, these are right
> Our kings, our rulers; these deserve to eat and drink the best;
> These govern not ingloriously: these thus exceed the rest,
> Do more than they command to do." O friend, if keeping back
> Would keep back age from us, and death, and that we might not wrack
> In this life's human sea at all, but that deferring now
> We shunn'd death ever, nor would I half this vain valour show,
> Nor glorify a folly so, to wish thee to advance:
> But since we must go, though not here, and that, besides the chance
> Propos'd now, there are infinite fates of other sort in death,
> Which (neither to be fled nor 'scaped) a man must sink beneath,
> Come, try we if this sort be ours: and either render thus
> Glory to others, or make them resign the like to us.'

Sarpedon and Glaucus on the Trojan side and Ajax and Teucer on the Greek side of the wall all do valiant deeds; the contest is evenly matched, like neighbours disputing a field boundary. Zeus's scales, likened to those of a poor spinster weighing her day's work of weaving, are evenly balanced until gradually they turn in favour of Hector, who breaks through the wall.

Book 13

Zeus's attention elsewhere, Poseidon rallies the two Ajaxes and the Greeks, the more so after his grandson is killed by Hector. As a contrast to the god-inspired delight in battle voiced by the Ajaxes there is an interchange between Meriones and Idomeneus. These, catching each other unawares away from the fighting, loudly declare their valour and distance themselves from the signs and wounds of a coward; they then put their declarations into bloody practice. Idomeneus is preeminent until he comes up against Aeneas; the fighting is evenly matched thereafter, until Hector and the two Ajaxes confront each other. In this long and bloody book, men who are winning their bride-price, are beloved sons-in-law, have been hospitable, are caring or sweetly graceful, who are lovers of innocent pursuits, beloved of their parents, all die, bloodily and graphically – or like trees, felled and left.

Book 14

Nestor and the Greek leaders not on the field discuss the situation, showing their usual characteristics: Agamemnon for the third time proposes withdrawing, Odysseus roundly condemns the suggestion, Diomedes single- mindedly proposes that they return to the battlefield even though he is himself wounded.

Hera has been watching Poseidon's championship of the Greeks while Zeus's back was turned; she comes up with a more radical plan of deception and disobedience. She goes to the pro-Trojan Aphrodite and persuades her to give her the girdle of desirability, the *kestos*, ostensibly to reunite the two gods Oceanus and Tethys. She then bribes the reluctant god of sleep to keep Zeus comatose after she has seduced him, so that she can affect the battle before Troy, and Poseidon can encourage the Greeks. Fully equipped, she visits Zeus, who is overwhelmed with desire for her greater than that he has felt for any goddess or woman – even his seven greatest conquests, all of which he details for her. Underneath their embrace spring soft flowers; the consequences of their union will be Trojan dead.

Book 15

When Zeus awakes to see Hector wounded and the Trojans in flight, with Poseidon in pursuit, he threatens to repeat his former violence to Hera. Hera escapes the charge on a technicality. Zeus, pleased at her submission, prophesies what is to happen: the deaths of Patroclus, Hector and his own son Sarpedon, all as the consequences of the supplication of Thetis. Ares angrily demurs, pleading the need to avenge his son regardless of the consequences. Athene reasons with him. By now some other mortal, better or stronger than his son, will have been or will soon be killed. It is a hard thing to rescue all the generations of mortals.

Iris is sent to make Poseidon comply, with the reminder that Zeus is more powerful and older than Poseidon and that the Furies side with the elder born: Poseidon denies him the precedence if not the power, but is persuaded of the rightness of her case. He yields, provided Zeus does not in the end spare Troy.

Apollo is sent down to hearten and inspire Hector. The Trojans despatch many Greeks; with Apollo's help, they wreck the Greek bastions like a child playing on a beach. As sandcastles to wanton boys are the bulwarks of men to the gods:

> And then, as he had chok'd their dyke, he tumbled down their wall.
> And look how easily any boy, upon the sea-ebb'd shore,
> Makes with a little sand a toy, and cares for it no more,
> But as he rais'd it childishly, so in his wanton vein,
> Both with his hands and feet he pulls and spurns it down again.

The terrified Greeks pray to Zeus; he thunders, which omen the Trojans take as favourable to them.

Patroclus meanwhile has been attending to Eurypylus, but on seeing the Trojans swarm over the ramparts and threaten the Greek ships, he sees that the time has come to put Nestor's suggestion to Achilles. The shape of the battle becomes tauter, and Hector makes straight for Ajax. Teucer, Ajax's brother, goes to his aid but as he fires his arrow his newly-twisted string breaks. All see this as a mark of divine interference: Teucer and Ajax attribute it to some pro-Trojan god, the poet and Hector to Zeus.

Both Hector and Ajax speak rousingly to their forces: Hector of Zeus's plan and the honour of defending their families, Ajax of the imminence of the crisis and the respect that serves both glory and self-preservation. Hector, in his Zeus-granted hour of glory, rages like a murderous lion. Respect, fear, and Nestor's exhortations to think of their fathers, are the only things that keep the Greeks from scattering.

Ajax, like a display rider, leaps agilely from ship to ship to fight and encourage the Greeks, while Hector like an eagle darts for one ship, to fight at close quarters. The book ends with Ajax being forced slowly back and calling for a last-ditch effort, while Hector in Zeus's name, calls for fire to burn the Greek ships.

Book 16

With Hector on the point of defeating the Greeks, so going against the fate-ordained end by firing their ships and trapping them without the means to escape, Book 16 picks up Patroclus' story from Book 11. In tears, he returns to the waiting Achilles to report the plight of the Greeks:

> 'Wherefore weeps my friend
> So like a girl, who, though she sees her mother cannot tend
> Her childish humours, hangs on her, and would be taken up,
> Still viewing her with tear-drown'd eyes, when she has made
>
> her stoop?'

Patroclus begs for Achilles' arms, 'since any shadow seen' of Achilles will hearten the Greeks and frighten the Trojans. The poet marks the significance of this, the request that brings tragedy on Patroclus, Hector, numerous Trojans and Achilles himself:

> Thus foolish man he su'd
> For his sure death.

Achilles consents, but only if Patroclus goes no further than warding off the immediate danger from the Greek, and his own, ships. This will enhance Achilles' glory; to go beyond would diminish it and bring him up against the gods.

Meanwhile Ajax is being battered by the Trojans, by the will of Zeus and by Hector. As the fire approaches his own ships, Achilles helps to muster the Myrmidons, who pour out like a pack of ravening, slavering wolves, with Patroclus at their head. Achilles, after careful ritual, prays to Zeus that his dear friend may be successful, sufficient and prudent:

> 'But fight he ne'er so well,
> No further let him trust his fight, but, when he shall repel
> Clamour and danger from our fleet, vouchsafe a safe retreat
> To him and all his companies, with fames and arms complete.'

Zeus grants one prayer and denies the other. The Myrmidons, like angry wasps stirred up by idle children, fall on the 'amazed' Trojans and force them back. Patroclus is preeminent in the fighting; over many from both sides close 'blood-red death and strong destiny'. Sarpedon resolves to stem the retreat by standing against Patroclus; they face each other like vultures. Zeus, watching, sees that Sarpedon, his son, is destined to die, as he had outlined in Book 15. Much moved at the reality he considers intervening. Hera points out that to go against a mortal's marked fate would disrupt the boundary between mortal and immortal. Rather, Zeus must accept that the proper end, the reward, for a mortal is to have due burial and a physical memorial, a focus for the commemoration that dead heroes receive. Zeus weeps bloody tears for his son.

Sarpedon dies, like a tree felled or a bull savaged, clawing in the dust. He adjures Glaucus, already wounded, to fight over his body. Glaucus is overwhelmed with grief and pain, and prays to Apollo; he calls on the Trojan leaders to avenge him, their mainstay. Against the raging Trojans line up Patroclus and the Ajaxes, burning to strip Sarpedon's body which soon becomes buried under weapons and fighting, like a milk pail covered by flies.

Hector sees that the scales are turning against him and loses heart, leaving the Myrmidons to despoil the corpse, which is spirited away by Sleep and Death. But the scales are turning too against Patroclus. In the grip of passion, he forgets Achilles' injunction, 'which had he kept, had kept black death from him', and chases the Trojans not only away from the ships but right across the battle zone up to the walls of Troy. The poet asks him, as though he could be the narrator of his doom, who else he took with him to his death. Patroclus is like 'one of heaven' as he attacks the walls of Troy; on his fourth assault Apollo tells him to cease what exceeds his fate. Patroclus gives way, and Apollo goes to Hector to tempt him to triumph over him.

Patroclus, 'so near his own grave death', mocks the dying fall of Hector's charioteer and fights Hector over the body, while Trojans and Greeks contest for dominance as 'winds strive to make a lofty wood Bow to their greatness'. Bodies fall like trees; the Greeks come out on top, 'past meas-ure'. Three times Patroclus charges and wins superhuman victories; then the end of his life appears as, unseen, dreadful Apollo himself strikes him. Achilles' helmet is taken up by Hector, 'whose death was near', and 'in confusion, thus dismay'd' Patroclus is then wounded by a passing Trojan. Hector sees his advantage and delivers the final blow: 'on thee shall vultures prey, Poor wretch, nor shall thy mighty friend afford thee any aid', even though he no doubt told you not to come home before 'hewing great Hector's breast'. The dying Patroclus answers that he has been beaten by the gods, not by him, together with destiny which will shortly wait on him in the shape of Achilles:

> 'And this one thing more concerns thee; note it then:
> Thou shalt not long survive thyself; nay, now Death calls for thee,
> And violent Fate; Achilles' lance shall make this good for me.'

With these words, his soul flies away, 'sorrowing for his sad fate, to leave him young'. Hector refuses to accept the words as prophetic and takes Achilles' armour.

Book 17

Menelaus bestrides the body, and there kills Euphorbus, a lovely young man:

> . . . all with gore
> His locks, that like the Graces were, and which he ever wore
> In gold and silver ribands wrapp'd, were piteously wet.

Euphorbus was the first to wound Patroclus. His death, however, is described in a long pathetic simile – like an olive tree with spreading branches curled with snowy flowers, watered with delicious springs, which is uprooted by a sudden gale.

Apollo recalls Hector from chasing Achilles' divine horses. Menelaus debates whether to withdraw from facing Hector and the god, which would be prudent, but the hasty abandonment of Patroclus' corpse and arms would offend the Greeks. He makes a 'lion-like retreat' and eventually returns with Ajax to the now despoiled body of Patroclus.

Glaucus meanwhile upbraids Hector for abandoning Sarpedon's corpse and showing ingratitude to his allies. He demands they get Patroclus' body inside Troy to use as barter for Sarpedon's armour. Hector rebuts the charge and assumes Achilles' divine armour. Zeus, addressing him as the poet addressed Patroclus, strengthens him for what will be his final battle, granting him:

> 'Those arms, in glory of thy acts, thou shalt have that frail blaze
> Of excellence that neighbours death, a strength ev'n to amaze.'

Hector calls on all the allies and offers half the spoils and equal glory to whoever gets Patroclus' body inside the walls. They rush to obey, the fighting very fierce until the ground runs with blood: 'Silly fools, Ajax prevented this, By raising ramparts to his friend with half their carcasses.' The bloody struggle over the body continues like that to stretch and cure a fat-drenched ox-hide. The body, like the whole expedition, has become something that cannot be given up without loss of honour, even when the cost is high.

Achilles' mother conceals Patroclus' death from him; Achilles' horses stand like statues on a tomb in grief for him. Zeus pities them, as deathless creatures involved with mortals and subject, like Thetis, to a grief that too is deathless.

The bitter fighting continues; the Trojans have the advantage. Finally, however, the Ajaxes start to clear a path for Patroclus' body as, the myth goes, Odysseus would later clear a path for Achilles'. Patroclus' death foreshadows and in some ways brings about Achilles'. There is a strong sense that by borrowing and dying in Achilles' armour, his warrior's skin and identity, he has ensured the death of the man he was impersonating.

Book 18

Achilles, waiting in fearful anticipation, guesses that Patroclus is dead, even before news is brought. Patroclus is his beloved, is his responsibility. He has died because Achilles refused to help their friends; he has died in Achilles' armour and in Achilles' stead. Achilles cannot cope with the loss and is overborne by rage and grief.

His grief reaches Thetis, who comes to him as she did, tragically as it has turned out, in Book 1. The favour showed him by Zeus, at her request, has had a terrible outcome. He is doomed if he kills Hector, yet must wreak vengeance for his friend. He regrets, but lays aside, the wrath that caused his inaction and Patroclus' death; she laments for the best of sons, now doomed to an early death. He too is aware of the everlasting grief brought on her by his death but he does not now seek to evade it.

'And if such fate expect my life, where death strikes, I will lie.
Meantime I wish a good renown. . . But any further stay
(Which your much love perhaps may wish) assay not to persuade;
All vows are kept, all pray'rs heard, now free way for fight is made.'

She offers the only comfort she can – new armour so that he can go back into battle to find the vengeance and renown that is all his short life can now offer him.

The struggle over the body is suddenly resolved when Achilles shows himself – a sight that brings panic to the Trojans even though he is unarmed. The Greeks bring the body back, a warrior's cortège; the sun sets in mark of the disjointedness and extremity of the death:

>   . . . his friends, with all remorse,
> Marching about it. His great friend, dissolving then in tears
> To see his truly-lov'd return'd so hors'd upon a hearse,
> Whom with such horse and chariot he set out safe and whole,
> Now wounded with unpitying steel, now sent without a soul,
> Never again to be restor'd, never receiv'd but so,
> He follow'd mourning bitterly. The sun (yet far to go)
> Juno commanded to go down, who in his pow'r's despite
> Sunk to the ocean, over earth dispersing sudden night.

On the Trojan side Polydamas, as always, counsels caution and retrenchment. Hector, antipathetic to him and his advice, is unwilling to give up the day's advances, is unwilling to 'retreat to Troy's old prison' even if it means a trial of strength with Achilles. The Trojans, 'fools', applaud this worse counsel: 'Minerva robb'd them of their brains, to like the ill advice'. As often, a god is shown as externally influencing a course of action which is equally pictured as determined by the psychology of the individuals.

Achilles spends the night in grief-stricken reminiscence, in tending the corpse, and in vowing vengeance and offerings: Hector and twelve Trojan princes as human sacrifice.

Hephaestus agrees to forge divine armour for him to replace that which was despoiled from Patroclus, to do him honour for the rest of his short life and so that other men wonder at it when he comes to meet his fate. On the wonderful shield is depicted the cosmos and two cities:

>   The one did nuptials celebrate,
> Observing at them solemn feasts; the brides from forth their bow'rs
> With torches usher'd through the streets; a world of paramours
> Excited by them, youths and maids in lovely circles danc'd,
> To whom the merry pipe and harp their spritely sounds advanc'd.

Also depicted is an arbitration over a blood price – such things can be mediated in the non-military world – and the second city at war, with gods helping the defenders. Elsewhere a pastoral scene is disturbed by an ambush, agricultural scenes of ploughing and harvest, herding of cattle, with a bull the prey of lions, and of sheep. The last scenes, like the first, are of festivities, a dance floor with finely dressed young people, revolving in song and dance, and the Ocean encircling everything.

When it is finished, Thetis takes the shield, with the rest of the shining armour, to Achilles, who will never again see everyday human scenes such as those depicted.

Book 19

Achilles, terrifying and radiant with passion, takes and delights in the armour. He gives Patroclus' body treatment suited to a hero and gathers his forces; he publically remits his anger against Agamemnon and sorrows for all the dead who have fallen because of their strife. Agamemnon publicly acknowledges that he was in the wrong but 'not I but destinies, And Jove himself, and black Erinnys' [Fury] are responsible, who inflicted delusion; he likens himself to Zeus, who was similarly deluded by Hera in order to gain precedence for Eurystheus rather than Heracles. However, he acknowledges that it is for him to make amends, as proposed before by the envoys in Book 9. This time Achilles does not spurn them; they are for Agamemnon to give or not, as he thinks fit, but the important task now is to get back to the fighting.

Achilles vows not to eat or drink until he has avenged Patroclus; he cannot attend to such things until he has discharged the fury in his heart. Pragmatic Odysseus advises that Achilles' mind should be set at rest by an oath sworn by Agamemnon that he has not touched Briseis and that the troops should eat first. Many men die; the best thing is to bury them, mourn them and then eat and drink to have strength to carry on fighting. Achilles is subverting the wise order of things. After a sacrifice, the council ends with Achilles musing on the delusions that led to his anger and conflict with Agamemnon, and whether it was Zeus' plan to bring destruction on so many Greeks.

Briseis, brought back by the Myrmidons, is overcome with weeping to see the body of Patroclus; she remembers his unfailing kindness from the day when Achilles, having killed her husband and three brothers, captured her – and his promise that Achilles would heal the wound he had made by marrying her and that he would preside over their wedding feast. The women around share her laments, overtly for Patroclus but each also for herself. Achilles' mind too turns to his own griefs. He thinks of the past, and of his father and his son Neoptolemus who will not see him again. Athene takes pity on him and instils nectar to keep him from fainting.

Armed in his new armour he goes out to his horses and exhorts them to look after him better than they did Patroclus – to bring him safely from the battlefield. One horse answers, in human speech, absolving them from blame for his death which is now shortly to come.

Book 20

The return of Achilles compels the attention even of the gods. Zeus calls an assembly to revoke his decree of non-interference, a formal mirroring of the assembly of the Greeks in Book 19. He fears that Achilles will go beyond fate and storm Troy, and so allows the gods free rein to favour whichever side they wish: Hera, Pallas Athene, Poseidon, Hermes and Hephaestus to the Greeks; Ares, Phoebus Apollo, Artemis and Aphrodite to the Trojans. His plan seems now to have been fulfilled.

Achilles' first major encounter is with Aeneas, whom he taunts with being marginalised by king Priam and with the reminder of a previous encounter when the gods saved him. Aeneas replies that he is well able to exchange insults, like a child or a fishwife, but now is the time for action, not taunts. Achilles' five-fold shield protects him from a deadly thrust. Poseidon intervenes, perceiving that Aeneas will lose the encounter in the false confidence given by Apollo's words – though the god 'did never mean To add to his great words his guard against the ruin then Summoned against him . . . What fool is he!' Poseidon saves Aeneas for his destined end – to be the progenitor of a mighty [Roman] race who will dominate Troy in generations to come. Achilles is disgusted to find his foe evaporate.

Apollo warns Hector not to confront Achilles, but when Achilles cuts down his latest victim, Polydorus, 'exquisite of foot' – Hector's youngest brother and Priam's favourite – he can bear it no longer and goes for him. Hector, like Aeneas, replies shortly to Achilles' taunts and throws his spear. Three times Athene blows it away from Achilles and turns it back to Hector's feet. Three times Achilles' deadly charge is lost in the mist in which Apollo surrounds Hector. After the fourth, Achilles turns to slaughter lesser men.

One young man is killed as he is reaching out to Achilles' knees:

> With free submission. . . O poor fool, to sue to him . . .
> In his hot fury. He was none of these remorseful men,
> Gentle and affable, but fierce at all times, and mad then.

As inhuman fire, so Achilles sweeps everywhere with his spear, 'inaccessible' (ie refusing pleas for mercy); as oxen crush corn on the threshing floor, so Achilles tramples dead men.

> Thus to be magnified,
> His most inaccessible hands in human blood he dyed.

Book 21

Achilles chases the Trojans up to the river Xanthus and pollutes the water with blood,

> Twelve fair young princes then
> He chose of all to take alive, to have them freshly slain
> On that most solemn day of wreak, resolv'd on for his friend.

He hands them over like startled fawns, bound, and resumes his killing. A young man – Priam's young son Lycaon – is unable to escape Achilles. His recent history is recounted in the same way as many previous young victims, serving both to give a sense of reality and potential to the life that is going to be cut short, and as a memorial of that life. But the biography this time is relevant – he has been captured before by Achilles who has accepted ransom for him; he is therefore protected from harm at Achilles' hands by the sacred obligation of host to protect the guest from harm. Achilles is bemused to see in the river a youth he has consigned either to the sea or to a land far away; Lycaon is terrified. He runs under Achilles' spear thrust to grab his knees in supplication: the ritual gesture of submission that should be respected. He pleads for respect for his position and for the bond, for pity for his mother (not the same one as Hector's) whose other son Achilles has just slain, for mercy.

Achilles is without mercy. No longer is he prepared to ransom or spare Trojans, especially not a son of Priam's.

> 'Die, die, my friend. What tears are these? What sad looks spoil thy face?
> Patroclus died, that far pass'd thee: nay, seest thou not beside
> Myself, ev'n I, a fair young man, and rarely magnified . . .
> Death, and as violent a fate, must overtake ev'n me.'

Lycaon stops trying to ward off the inevitable; Achilles kills him and tosses him into the river with a dreadful taunt:

> 'Go, feed fat the fish with loss
> Of thy left blood; they clean will suck thy green wounds, and this saves
> Thy mother tears upon thy bed . . .
> . . . perish then, till cruell'st death hath laid
> All at the red feet of Revenge for my slain friend . . .'

This butchery offends the divine river, choked with his corpses; Achilles will move the site of his killing but it will not stop until he or Hector has the mastery.

Achilles, like something more than mortal, sweeps down on more Trojans. The river calls to Apollo and his fellow river to bury him and his arms, his renown lost forever, in their depths; Achilles fights on, carried along by the billowing, debris-filled flood. Hera intervenes by sending Hephaestus to burn up the river. Scamandrus, his waters seething, gives up his supernatural battle with Achilles. Hephaestus is called off by Hera; 'it was not fit A god should suffer so for men.'

Athene and Ares, still feeling quarrelsome, fight childishly among themselves. Ares [god of war!] is worsted and has to be comforted by Aphrodite. Hera now sets Athene on and smiles to see how Athene pushes the goddess of love in the chest, sending her flying on top of Ares. Poseidon exhorts Apollo to join in the rough and tumble, but Apollo refuses to fight for 'wretched men that flourish for a time Like leaves'. In the middle of laughing at the gods, we are reminded of the human condition and of why Achilles, like Glaucus in Book 6, risks everything for 'his renown'.

Artemis calls her brother Apollo a coward, Hera calls her a shameless hussy and boxes her ears, which sends her crying and telling tales to her father, Zeus.

Away from this playground scrapping, the not-so-wretched 'Rabid Achilles with his lance, still glory being the goad That pricked his fury', carries on killing Trojans as they flee to Troy. Priam orders the gates to be opened for them and Apollo goes to their aid.

Agenor is sent to hold up Achilles; when he sees him, he debates whether there is any escape route. He concludes that there is none, and that his only chance is to fight, since Achilles is, after all mortal. He challenges him: 'Thy hope is too great, Peleus' son . . . fool' to hope to take Troy before it is destined. He succeeds in hitting him, but is spirited away before a return blow. Apollo in Agenor's form distracts Achilles, leading him up hill and down dale, while the Trojans get safely into the city.

Book 22

Book 22 brings the combat to the death between the preeminent fighters on the two sides, a resolution set up yet frustrated by the unresolved duels in Books 3 and 7. The combat is between Achilles, of the Greeks the most single-minded and best fighter, caring only for his honour, and Hector, the bulwark of Troy. The events of the *Iliad* have however complicated and undermined the two heroes' standing. Hector by his rash, ill-tempered decision has endangered many Trojans; Achilles by standing on his honour and refusing Agamemnon's reparation has allowed many friends and Patroclus to go to their deaths. A sense of personal tragedy pervades the confrontation. Hector, who cares only for his honour as a hero and protector of his family and Troy, has made a fatal misjudgement, has exposed himself to their censure. Achilles, who cares only for his own personal honour and his own men, has compromised both by his intransigence. Hector, spurred on before by the consciousness of those watching from the walls of Troy, is now shackled by it; Achilles, who declared that he cared nothing for the aims of the war but only for his integrity and heroic name, has become an inhuman, vengeful force.

Gods and Hector's dependants look down on him, as he decides to stand his ground rather than retreat through the closing gates: he waits like a venom-filled

> . . . dragon, when she sees a traveller bent upon
> Her breeding den . . . sits him firm, and at his nearest pace
> Wraps all her cavern in her folds, and thrusts a horrid face
> Out at his entry . . .

But when Achilles comes,

> . . . now near
> His Mars-like presence terribly came brandishing his spear.
> His right arm shook it, his bright arms, like day, came glittering on
> Like fire-light, or the light of heav'n shot from the rising sun.
> This sight outwrought discourse, cold fear shook Hector from his
>   stand.
> No more stay now, all ports were left, he fled in fear the hand
> Of that fear-master, who, hawk-like, air's swiftest passenger,
> That holds a timorous dove in chase, and with command doth bear
> His fiery onset; the dove hastes, the hawk comes whizzing on,
> This way and that he turns and winds, and cuffs the pigeon;
> And till he truss it, his great spirit lays hot charge on his wing:
> So urg'd Achilles Hector's flight, so still fear's point did sting
> His troubled spirit; his knees wrought hard; along the wall he flew . . .
> The gods beheld them, all much mov'd; and Jove said: 'O ill sight!
> A man I love much I see forc'd in most unworthy flight . . .'

Zeus debates, as when he saw Sarpedon going to his death, whether to intervene. Athene's reply is the same as Hera's was then: alter Fate? Do it then, but all the rest of us gods shall not approve. Zeus retracts, Athene flies down. Hector runs as if in a nightmare, not able to outpace his pursuer, Achilles keeping between him and the gates. Three times they circuit the walls, while Achilles prevents Greeks from interfering, lest they detract from his full glory. On the fourth, Zeus sets their 'two fates of bitter death' into his golden scales, and Hector's is the heavier. Apollo forsakes Hector; Athene goes to him, disguised as his brother come to help, and they turn to face Achilles.

Hector tries to reach an agreement that the winner will not defile the loser's body, but will return it respectfully. Achilles rejects these 'fair and temperate terms', saying that no conditions can be laid down between them, any more than between predator and prey. Hector should look to his 'hunger for slaughter': Athene will ensure that he pays with his life for the friends he slew.

Achilles casts his spear and misses; Hector seizes on this sign that Achilles is not after all an instrument of the gods and taunts him. He throws his spear, which misses, and turns to his brother 'Deiphobus' for a replacement. He sees that he is alone, and knows that the gods have cheated him and summoned him deathwards. There is no way out. But he can at least die nobly. He draws his sword and swoops like an eagle.

Hector is protected by the armour he stripped from Patroclus; only the neck is vulnerable; Achilles strikes and Hector drops in the dust. Achilles vaunts over him, 'fool' to think himself safe when he killed Patroclus:

'. . . the dogs and fowls in foulest use
Shall tear thee up, thy corse expos'd to all the Greeks abuse.'
He, fainting, said: 'Let me implore, ev'n by thy knees and soul,
And thy great parents, do not see a cruelty so foul
Inflicted on me: brass and gold receive at any rate,
And quit my person, that the peers and ladies of our state
May tomb it . . .'

Achilles, implacable, refuses to countenance the humane request of returning his body for burial; rather, 'rage would let me eat thee raw'. He rehearses his refusal to ransom his body to his parents so they can 'hold solemnities of death'. Rather he will deface his corpse. Hector's dying words prophesy Achilles' imminent death; Achilles replies that he will bear his fate. He strips the armour; the Greeks, rushing to see the naked body of their main enemy, comment on its softness as they repeatedly spear it.

Achilles remembers Patroclus. He sends the young men back to sing of their triumph and the imminent downfall of Troy. He devises a terrible, unworthy treatment for the corpse – dragging it by pierced ankles behind his chariot, to the distress of Hector's mother and father. In anguish, they lament, Priam desperate to beg the body from Achilles, Hecuba foreseeing her life of suffering. But Andromache, who mourned him while he was still alive, does not know of his death; she is preparing a bath for his return when she hears the cries. Seeing how he is being treated, she faints and her wedding coronet falls from her head. When she recovers, she laments for herself and bewails the harsh treatment her fatherless son will experience.

Book 23

Book 23 is about the proper treatment of the dead – about the splendid funeral games, the tomb, the ritual of remembrance and celebration of the dead's fame. But for Achilles these are not sufficient to come to terms with Patroclus' death. He has to find some compensation to offer him: Trojan dead, twelve princes as a human sacrifice, Hector's death, despoliation and degradation, his own going without food, drink, washing and shaving. The Achilles who refused compensation from Agamemnon for the slight to his honour, because possessions, 'though lost, may come again', but the soul, 'once gone, never more To her frail mansion any man can her lost pow'rs restore', now seeks to offer recompense:

'Now I pay to thy late overthrow
All my revenges vow'd before. Hector lies slaughter'd here
Dragg'd at my chariot, and our dogs shall all in pieces tear
His hated limbs. Twelve Trojan youths, born of their noblest strains,
I took alive; and yet enrag'd, will empty all their veins
Of vital spirits, sacrific'd before thy heap of fire.'

His fury comes from not being able to find anything sufficient. His sleep is disturbed by the ghost of Patroclus, complaining that he is prevented from taking up his proper place among the dead, asking not for revenge but for speedy burial, and that their ashes should in due course lie together in a single urn. Achilles tries to embrace him, but the spirit slips away and Achilles awakes in sorrow.

Preparations for the funeral are completed. There is a chariot procession and a ritual offering of locks of hair. Achilles cuts the lock which was dedicated for a safe return to the river of his home – Patroclus' death means he will not now return.

The chief mourners stay to build a huge pyre, and the body is wrapped in the fat of sacrificial animals and laid on it. Achilles kills the twelve young nobles, and the pyre is lit with supernatural fire. A tomb, which will also house Achilles, is made over the urn holding the cremated bones, and the funeral games begin.

Achilles provides prizes from his store – cauldrons, tripods, horses, women and iron – for the best in each of the events. In these funeral games, foreshadowing his own, he will preside over others' demonstrations of prowess rather than demonstrate his own excellence. The first is the chariot race, to be run around a mark in the ground that may be a grave marker now long forgotten [so fragile, it seems, is the hero's renown]. Nestor gives his son, Antilochus, advice on how to use his skill to excel, even though his horses are not the best – to such good effect that he is second. Diomedes, the favourite, is helped by the gods to come in first. Achilles judges that the best man came in last, because he was fouled, and proposes to award him second place. Antilochus hotly disputes the justice of this. [Achilles of all people should think before taking someone's publicly awarded prize away from him!] Achilles smiles and diplomatically awards an extra prize of spoil he himself has taken. But then Menelaus objects that Antilochus beat him by cunning, not by being intrinsically better: he judges that he himself deserves second prize because he is superior in power and greatness. When Antilochus submissively owns his inferiority, Menelaus graciously allows him to keep second prize. The unawarded fifth prize Achilles presents to Nestor, as he is no longer able to compete. Nestor remembers with relish the prizes he won when he was in his prime. So the difficult negotiation of who is best is played out and this time resolved, with prizes not lives at stake. Achilles has been reintegrated into society.

The next contest is boxing. Epeius claims to be the best at boxing, even though he falls short in battle. He proves to be right. In the next competition, wrestling, Odysseus and Greater Ajax are the contestants [as they will to be for the arms of Achilles]. They are locked together for so long that the onlookers get restive, and they make a final attempt to throw each other. Odysseus remembers his craftiness and trips Ajax, but Achilles intervenes to award the prize equally.

The foot race is next, in which, like the chariot race, Achilles would be preeminent if he had entered. Odysseus is lying second to the lesser Ajax when after a prayer to Athene, Ajax slips in some dung. Everyone laughs, but he still comes in second. Antilochus ruefully accepts being beaten by a much older man, reminding everyone of Achilles' speed. Achilles repays the compliment by an extra prize.

The fifth contest is a gladiatorial duel over the armour of Sarpedon, with a sword to the man who gets in a vital thrust. Achilles awards the contest to Diomedes before serious injury.

The single prize for the discus is a precious five year supply of iron. Ajax comes second for the third time. Meriones steals the archery prize from Teucer by an extraordinary shot. The spear throwing is settled without a contest by Achilles, who acknowledges Agamemnon as the best without his having to compete. This compliment completes the games and Achilles' reconciliation with the commanders.

Book 24

Alone, Achilles weeps for Patroclus, unable to sleep for memories. At dawn, he harnesses the horses and drags Hector's corpse round Patroclus' tomb before sleeping, 'but with Hector's corse his rage had never done'. The gods take pity on the violated body. Apollo condemns Achilles for being excessive, for lacking both restraining shame and the capacity to endure that is part of man's lot. He is angering the gods and dishonouring the earth. Thetis, unable to face the gods in sorrow for a mortal, is summoned by Zeus to hear that Hector's body must be ransomed. She tells Achilles, while Iris goes to Priam to reassure him and offer Hermes as guide. Priam asks his wife, Hecuba, what he should do, as if the message from the gods were immaterial and his earlier intention to beg the body from Achilles had come back to him. This, like many other turning-points in the action, is prompted in parallel both by the gods' intervention and by the individual's nature. Hecuba scorns his proposal, saying that Achilles is savage and will neither pity nor respect him. But Priam is determined. He goes with an omen, and Hermes as guide, into the enemy camp.

Trembling, he enters Achilles' tent and in supplication grasps

> . . . fast holding the bent knee
> Of Hector's conqueror, and kiss'd that large man-slaught'ring hand,
> That much blood from his sons had drawn.

He speaks to him as a suppliant, reminding him of his father and offering gifts beyond number.

'Achilles, fear the gods,
Pity an old man, like thy sire, different in only this,
That I am wretcheder, and bear that weight of miseries
That never man did, my curs'd lips enforc'd to kiss that hand
That slew my children.'

His words stirs a passion of grieving for his own father in Achilles, who cries
now for him, now for Patroclus. A tragic sympathy binds the two bitter
enemies: they grieve for their common, human lot. He sets the old man on
his feet: 'Sit, And settle we our woes, though huge, for nothing profits it.
Cold mourning wastes but our lives' heats.' Achilles describes the way the
gods spin life for unfortunate mortals, lying in unhappiness while the gods
themselves have no sorrows. There are two urns at the door of Zeus, from
which he dispenses evils and blessings. Peleus was given all blessings, but
only one son:

'One blossom but myself; and I, shaken as soon as blown.
Nor shall I live to cheer his age, and give nutrition
To him that nourish'd me . . . Thyself that did enjoy
(As we have heard) a happy life . . . but when the gods did turn
Thy blest state to partake with bane, war and the bloods of men
Circled thy city, never clear – sit down and suffer then,
Mourn not inevitable things; thy tears can spring no deeds
To help thee, nor recall thy son . . . '
'Give me no seat, great seed of Jove, when yet unransomed
Hector lies riteless in thy tents; but deign with utmost speed
His resignation, that these eyes may see his person freed,
And thy grace satisfied with gifts. Accept what I have brought.'

This request provokes Achilles, though already minded to give Hector
back. He masters himself and thoughtfully orders that the corpse be
washed, anointed and dressed, himself lifting the body on to the litter. He
weeps, then:

Cried out for anger, and thus pray'd: 'O friend, do not except
Against this favour to our foe (if in the deep thou hear),
And that I give him to his sire; he gave fair ransom.'

He provides food for them both. As even Niobe ate when she was worn
out with grieving for the loss of her children, so must they. They gaze at
each other in wonder, Priam at Achilles' beauty and grace, Achilles at
Priam's dignity and power of speech. Priam asks for a bed, worn out as he is
with lack of food and sleep; Achilles orders two to be made, asking Priam
how long a truce he would like for the proper celebration of Hector's
funeral. Eleven days is agreed.

Priam returns with Hector's body, which is lamented by Cassandra, Andromache, Hecuba and finally Helen, who remembers that he was always kind to her. During the truce they mourn for Hector, until on the eleventh day they build a grave barrow over the bones.

And so horse-taming Hector's rites gave up his soul to rest.

INTRODUCTION TO THE ODYSSEY

> Much have I travelled in the realms of gold,
> And many goodly states and kingdoms seen;
> Round many western islands have I been
> Which bards in fealty to Apollo hold.
> Oft of one wide expanse have I been told
> That deep-browed Homer ruled as his demesne;
> Yet never did I breathe its pure serene
> Till I heard CHAPMAN speak out loud and bold:
> Then felt I like some watcher of the skies
> When a new planet swims into his ken;
> Or like stout Cortez when with eagle eyes
> He stared at the Pacific – and all his men
> Looked at each other with a wild surmise –
> Silent upon a peak in Darien.

JOHN KEATS

The *Odyssey* is the story of all-experiencing Odysseus (Ulysses as Chapman, following Latin usage, called him) who insisted on hearing the Sirens sing – the adventurer among monsters, the lover of goddesses, the traveller flung on foreign shores, the teller of tales. It is the story of Odysseus' travels, his visits to every sort of human and monstrous society, from those who eat fruit dropping from the trees to those who work a double agricultural shift; from the Aeolians who give divine gifts to their guest – Aeolus' bag of winds to get them home – to the Cyclops whose guest gift is to eat the guest last. It is also the story of the hero's return from Troy, being gradually stripped of his men and his standing, the victim of fate and the gods. He is driven to return home not because home is better than the delights of the Lotus eaters or of Calypso – Ithaca is rocky, only good for goats – but because it is where he belongs. Odysseus is stripped even of his name, but he still has a wife, son and father on Ithaca.

Calypso is blunt about their inferior charms – she is a divinely beautiful goddess who can offer him immortality and lordship of her domain; Odysseus agrees that his wife

> 'In wit is far inferior to thee,
> In feature, stature, all the parts of show,
> She being a mortal, an immortal thou,
> Old ever growing, and yet never old.
> Yet her desire shall all my days see told,
> Adding the sight of my returning day,
> And natural home.'

Odysseus, gone nearly two decades, may still see Ithaca as his 'natural home' but the opening books show that he is on the edge of being displaced. His son is no longer a child but is coming into man's estate; his wife, pursued by suitors presuming on his death, is being forced to give up her status as his wife and create an independent identity for herself. Odysseus' identity is not sitting for him back home, waiting with his wife and son to be reclaimed; it must be forged anew in his relationships with an adolescent son and a newly independent, courted woman. The major part of the *Odyssey* is not about one-eyed monsters and clashing rocks, it is about the recognition of others and by Odysseus of who he is.

That recognition is complex and subtle – only for the old dog on the dungheap is recognition easy, only for him is his master the same person as he was twenty years ago. The idea of 'the return home', the *nostos* (the word that gives us nostalgia – the pain of longing for home and the past) which runs through the poem is rendered complex by setting it against questions of identity and of stability of personality. Odysseus is self-conscious; there are levels of thought, acuity and strategy in his projection of himself that deepen everything he does, every speech he makes, every tale he tells. His story is that of the ultimate story-teller (his actions at Troy and the accounts of his travels are nearly all presented within the narrative, by himself or a bard). The *Odyssey* is full of archetypal stories: various societies that are mirror images of the norm; various women who seduce or bewitch men; sailors' tales – whirlpools and clashing rocks, nine-headed monsters and sacred cattle, wicked witches and sirens. The frame for the telling of these stories is the court of Nausicaa – the young princess dreaming (literally) of marriage who goes down to the shore and finds and saves a shipwrecked man. He is gradually discovered to be a great hero of Troy; her father offers him her hand and holds betrothal games at which the hero triumphs. There cannot be a fairy tale ending however, because the unknown hero has a life and wife elsewhere. In becoming part of Odysseus' story Nausicaa, Calypso, Polyphemus the Cyclops and the rest, lose their control of the ending of their stories; they become figures in a story of one man's encounter with myth.

Chapman's *Odyssey*

Odysseus' characteristic quality in Homer is to be *polytropos, poikilometis* – multifaceted, various-minded. The many sides of Odysseus' (or Ulysses') story have fascinated story-tellers from the time of Homer to the twentieth century's James Joyce and Derek Walcott. Odysseus is the most represented as well as the most variously represented figure of European literature. In Greek tragedy he is the devious, amoral politician; in the Troy Tales popular in the Roman world he is a figure of romance; a long-established moralising tradition was concerned to interpret his story as exemplary (Odysseus bound to the mast a type of Christ's crucifixion): his wanderings as expiatory and exemplifying the Roman and Christian virtues of patience, fortitude and prudence.

Chapman revered Odysseus and revelled in the richness and resonance of his stories. He responded to and could convey all the different sides of Odysseus – his craftiness and inventiveness, his ability to survive, his extraordinary venturesomeness, his passion and his careful reserve. He can render with wonderful ease the many shades of Odysseus' experiences – the moments of searing emotion, such as when Odysseus tries to embrace his mother's shade in the Underworld:

> ' . . . when I had great desire to prove
> My arms the circle where her soul did move.
> Thrice prov'd I, thrice she vanish'd like a sleep,
> Or fleeting shadow, which struck much more deep
> The wounds my woes made, and made ask her why
> She would my love to her embraces fly,
> And not vouchsafe that ev'n in hell we might
> Pay pious Nature her unalter'd right.'

and moments of high fantasy: the Sirens

> ' . . . sit amidst a mead,
> And round about it runs a hedge or wall
> Of dead men's bones, their wither'd skins and all
> Hung all upon it . . . '

the strange landscapes, such as Calypso's magic isle:

> A grove grew
> In endless spring about her cavern round,
> With odorous cypress, pines and poplars, crown'd,
> Where hawks, sea-owls and long-tongu'd bitterns bred,
> And other birds their shady pinions spread –
> All fowls maritimal; none roosted there
> But those whose labours in the water were.

> A vine did all the hollow cave embrace,
> Still green, yet still ripe bunches gave it grace.
> Four fountains, one against another, pour'd
> Their silver streams, and meadows all enflow'r'd
> With sweet balm-gentle and blue violets hid,
> That deck'd the soft breast of each fragrant mead.

Ithaca is a starker setting than the Phaeacia and Mycenae of the earlier books, both physically (Ithaca is economically and materially a Dark Age society) and morally – Odysseus is disguised as a beggar, bringing bloody revenge on the suitors. Chapman is at home in both settings – in both he moves from sensitive emotional perceptions to high drama; he is extraordinary in being able to follow Homer in endowing the everyday world of Ithaca with a sheen of graceful materiality. Chapman, like Homer and like Odysseus, delights in both a well-crafted door and a well-fabricated tale.

One description stands out as an example – Odysseus' description of his making of the marriage bed out of a living olive tree. This is the central moment of the *Odyssey*, the final proof that Odysseus is who he is, the final recognition of Odysseus by Penelope after doubt, trickery and disguise. It is significant that Odysseus is recognised by his description of his act of craftsmanship; the bed, immovable, stands as the symbol of Odysseus' return to the centre of his household, never to be dislodged; the olive tree stands for shelter and resource for generations past and future. All this resonates in Chapman's description of the 'masterpiece, a wonder done By me and none but me.'

> 'There was an olive tree that had his growth
> Amidst a hedge, and was of shadow proud,
> Fresh, and the prime age of his verdure show'd,
> His leaves and arms so thick that to the eye
> It showed a column for solidity.
> To this had I a comprehension
> To build my bridal bow'r; which all of stone,
> Thick as the tree of leaves, I rais'd, and cast
> A roof about it nothing meanly grac'd,
> Put glu'd doors to it, that op'd art enough.
> Then from the olive every broad leav'd bough
> I lopp'd away, then fell'd the tree, and then
> Went over it both with my axe and plane,
> Both govern'd by my line. And then I hew'd
> My curious bedstead out; in which I shew'd
> Work of no common hand. All this begun,
> I could not leave till to perfection
> My pains had brought it; took my wimble, bor'd

> The holes as fitted, and did last afford
> The varied ornament which showed no want
> Of silver, gold, and polished elephant.
> An ox hide dyed in purple then I threw
> Above the cords . . . '

Homer, and Chapman, are master story-tellers of an age now gone, an age of heroes and craft traditions now lost. Both inlay into the everyday, material world descriptions of the miraculous fashioning of the heirlooms from that heroic past. When Telemachus visits Sparta, Menelaus offers him a guest gift:

> 'Of all my house-gifts then, that up I lay
> For treasure there, I will bestow on thee
> The fairest, and the greatest price to me.
> I will bestow on thee a rich carv'd cup,
> Of silver all, but all the brims wrought up
> With finest gold: it was the only thing
> That the heroical Sidonian king
> Presented to me, when we were to part
> At his receipt of me, and 'twas the art
> Of that great artist that of heav'n is free –
> And yet ev'n this will I bestow on thee.'

It seems likely that Homer not so much wrote as stitched together the *Odyssey*: bound Dark Age and Golden Age reflections into a multi-layered, beautifully crafted whole. Chapman had the versatility, responsiveness and poetic craft to convey those many layers and to set within and against them a variegated, various-minded, heroic Odysseus:

> A much-sustaining, patient, heav'nly man
> Whose genius turns through many ways to truth.

Chapman, drawing on the creative energy, language and ethos of an age opening itself up to the masterpieces of the past, felt particularly in tune with Homer. Coleridge said that Chapman's translations were as Homer would have written if he had lived in Elizabethan England; Chapman's translations make one feel moreover that Homer would have *enjoyed* living in Elizabethan England – that he would have felt at home and that his works would have been richly and popularly appreciated. Chapman's Homer was not performed at the Globe, but maybe that omission can be rectified . . .

Books 1–4

The opening books of the *Odyssey* deal not with Odysseus himself but with what his absence means to those left behind. Odysseus has lost the battle to bring his men safe home from Troy and is alone with the nymph Calypso, who has trapped him in her caves. The story opens as the deadlock and inactivity on Calypso's island and on Ithaca are about to be broken by the gods' intervention – Odysseus is about to be released from his very pleasant gaol and go home.

On Ithaca Odysseus' baby son of nearly twenty years ago is about to enter manhood. Both he and his mother Penelope are trapped by Odysseus' disappearance – he is neither son nor king, she neither wife nor widow: they cannot move on until they hear news of Odysseus' safety or death. In the absence of a head of the household a swarm of suitors have settled in the house, devouring Telemachus' inheritance. From the perspective of Mount Olympus, the home of the gods, it is clear that it is time the stalemate is broken.

Hermes is dispatched to order Calypso to release Odysseus while Athene, disguised as Odysseus' old friend Mentas, goes to Telemachus to give him self-confidence. Her very arrival prompts Telemachus' first adult respons-ible act – looking up from musing on his absent father, he notes with displeasure that a guest is not being attended to. He hastens to greet and entertain him, as is proper to the master of the household. The goddess sits down to advise him, recommending that he set out to find what has happened to his father. In the course of talking to the goddess Telemachus grows from a despondent, unsure child to a young adult, encouraged by Athene/Mentas to take action in the same way that Apollo impelled the young Orestes to avenge his father King Agamemnon.

His new maturity is immediately evident to Penelope, who is told to look to her handiwork and leave discussion to the men, and especially to him who is now master of the house:

> 'Go you then in, and take your work in hand,
> Your web, and distaff, and your maids command
> To ply their fit work. Words to men are due,
> And those reproving counsels you pursue –
> And most to me of all men, since I bear
> The rule of all things that are manag'd here.'

Book 1 ends with Telemachus speaking sharply to the suitors, Book 2 starts with him exerting himself over the Assembly, called for the first time since Odysseus went away.

The suitors are minor lords of Ithaca and of surrounding areas. Those eligible to come to the Ithacan assembly protest against Telemachus'

complaints that for nearly four years they have eaten up house and home –
it is Penelope, they claim, who is causing the delay:

> 'Your mother, first in craft, is first in cause.
> Three years are past, and near the fourth now draws,
> Since first she mock'd the peers Achaian.
> All she made hope, and promis'd every man,
> Sent for us ever, left love's show in nought,
> But in her heart conceal'd another thought.'

She has refused to remarry until she has woven a shroud for her father-in-
law:

> 'Laertes the heroë, it shall deck
> His royal corse, since I should suffer check
> In ill report of every common dame,
> If one so rich should show in death his shame.'

A proper sentiment in a noble lady – concern for propriety and for her good
name. But for three years she has woven by day and unpicked her work by
night, showing herself to be cunning and resourceful, a worthy partner of
Odysseus the 'resourceful/tricky-minded' spinner of tales. Her cunning has
increased her desirability and reputation, making the suitors even more
desperate to win a lady so wise, skilled and beautiful. If Odysseus manages
to return, he comes back to a wife who has come to be valued in her own
right, desired and famous for qualities developed in the twenty years of his
absence.

Telemachus, helped by Athene, assembles stores and a team of young
bloods and takes command of a ship to search for definite news of his
father. He goes secretly, but by the time he returns he will have assumed
the status and learned the manners and duties of a prince: when Odysseus
returns he, too, will be a force to be reckoned with.

The emotions and character of the adolescent Telemachus are tellingly
charted. At the start of the Book 1 he is despondent and unselfconfident,
feeling his position to be hard. Athene/Mentas gives him a sense of the
stature of his absent father and the courage to act as one favoured by the
gods. His speeches in the Assembly in Book 2, the first of his manhood,
swing from self-assertive to self-pitying and back to decisive. When in Book
3 he arrives in Pylos in the Peloponnese at King Nestor's palace, he is too
embarrassed to approach his host because he doesn't know what to say. He
is so overawed by the splendour of the Spartan palace in Book 4 that he
whispers to his companion that it seems like the court of the king of the
gods. However, from the old hero Nestor and from the powerful king of
Sparta, Menelaus, and his wife Helen of Troy, he learns how to behave, how
to sacrifice and pray to the gods, to celebrate a feast, to entertain guests and

to talk fittingly to his father's peers. He is also given a powerful sense of his father as a public man for the first time – of his cleverness, skill in speaking and effectiveness in council, of his strength, leadership and craftiness, of the impression he made on the great ones at Troy over the years of fighting. Finally, in his diplomacy in asking for a different, more wieldy parting gift from Menelaus, he is proclaimed to be his father's son. He has journeyed to find out about his father; in so doing he has found out about himself.

The world of Ithaca where there isn't enough grain or grass to pasture a horse, of adolescence, of drunken guests outstaying their welcome, offer portraits of a real world. Menelaus' court at Sparta provides a bridge into the heroic world of Troy: the wooden horse, the beautiful, divine Helen with potions that can give insensibility to the most terrible human tragedy, King Menelaus who only managed to return home after a fight with the Old Man of the Sea. The *Odyssey* constantly juxtaposes the real world of human relationships and human tragedy with the heroic and fabulous world of stories – stories which are in the main told by the heroes themselves.

Books 5–8

Book 4 ends on a dramatic note, with the suitors waiting in ambush to kill the returning Telemachus and clear the obstacle to Odysseus' throne and bed. The scene then shifts to Odysseus detained by the nymph Calypso, spending nights of love with the goddess and days of weeping for home. Hermes, alighting to tell Calypso of the gods' decision to help Odysseus return home, is enchanted by the beauties of the place – fountains playing in four directions, the all-important vine flourishing, sweet meadows and a luxurious variety of trees and birds. Yet Odysseus weeps for rocky Ithaca and his aging wife: he has been offered a paradise, the love of an ever young nymph and immortality, but he has turned them all down. Instead he will brave the dangers of the sea and the sea god's continued vendetta against him in the hope of returning home.

Calypso does not want to let him go – she complains of sexism on Olympus, such that gods can take any number of human lovers but goddesses' love affairs are punished and abruptly terminated. But she accepts Zeus's decree and shows Odysseus how to build a raft – he must use his famous resourcefulness to fashion his own means of escape from his desert island. When Poseidon's anger catches up with him and his raft is broken beneath him by the tempest, Odysseus reaches, literally, rock bottom: rather than dying nameless and tombless he wishes he had died at Troy:

> In which despair he thus spake: 'Woe is me!
> What was I born to, man of misery! . . .
> Then had I been allotted to have died,
> By all the Greeks with funerals glorified

> (Whence death, encouraging good life, had grown),
> Where now I die by no man mourn'd nor known.'

But somehow, resourceful even now, he manages to grab hold of a spar and with the help of an amulet given him by the sea goddess Leucothea he makes it to within sight of land. His joy at seeing land is described by a telling, touching simile of human love:

> The winds grew calm, and clear was all the air,
> Not one breath stirring. Then he might descry,
> Rais'd by the high seas, clear, the land was nigh.
> And then, look how to good sons that esteem
> Their father's life dear (after pains extreme . . .)
> When on their pray'rs they see descend at length
> Health from the heav'ns, clad all in spirit and strength,
> The sight is precious: so since here should end
> Ulysses' toils . . . for his own sake to see
> The shores, the woods so near, such joy had he.

All journeys in the *Odyssey* are significant; this one takes Odysseus away from the nurture of the nymph who wanted to keep him for ever (whose name means the Hider or Burier) and strips him of everything but his life. He left Troy with ships and men which were successively lost; this last battle with the sea casts him naked and half-dead on the shore of Phaeacia. Like an exhausted animal, he buries himself in leaves and saves his last spark of energy like a man saving the seed of fire by covering the last embers in ash.

The first half of the *Odyssey* falls into three parts – Telemachus growing up and Odysseus turning down Calypso, immortality and a home in paradise (1–4); Odysseus as the unknown stranger in Phaeacia (5–8); and Odysseus telling his adventures among savages and immortals, who endanger his safe return to Ithaca either by threats or blandishment (9–12). Phaeacia is a half-way house between the exotic worlds, dangers and excitements of his adventures and the very domestic world and relationship problems of Ithaca. Like Calypso's though, the princess Nausicaa's hospitality, in offering an alternative home for the hero, poses a threat.

Nausicaa decides to go down to the beach with her maids to wash the palace clothes so they are fine and clean for the wedding she has been dreaming of. Her youth, beauty and innocence, her wheedling of her 'dear father' are charmingly painted, as is her adolescent embarrassment at mentioning her forthcoming marriage. Yet when, while playing a ball game on the beach, she is faced with a battered, naked, rime-covered sailor, she acts with nobility and mature grace. Her acute consciousness of her attraction to Odysseus and of the impropriety of being alone with him, she turns into a thoughtful strategy to get him received and tended by her mother, Queen Arete. Odysseus is saved from death from exposure and exhaustion by the care of a lovely girl.

Book 7 paints a full picture of the court of King Alcinous of Phaeacia. The Phaeacians used to live near the Cyclopes; harassed by them they moved, and now live 'far apart by themselves, very dear to the gods': they are a powerful, independent and carefree people who are wary of strangers. They have automata of gold and silver designed by the blacksmith god Hephaestus – guard dogs and young serving men – and lush grass and fruit continuously ripened by the West wind independent of the seasons. They have the skill of seamanship to take Odysseus home if he can persuade them to – the sea god Poseidon is Alcinous' grandfather. However, Odysseus is hated by Poseidon, who will punish those who help him, so he must keep his identity secret. He must be accepted, but not too much – he cannot stay to marry Nausicaa but must not slight her. As Telemachus needed all his wits to deal with tricky social situations on his journey, so his father needs all his. Athene looks after both father and son in much the same way – encouraging them by appearing in disguise as a helpmeet, giving them a sheen of vigour and grace. But whereas the point of Telemachus' journey was to establish his identity, to be accepted as his father's son, Odysseus has to avoid his identity becoming known prematurely. So the stories of the Trojan war to which both are treated by their hosts serve very different purposes: Telemachus gains a sense of his father as a hero at Troy, and of his cunning and subtlety when he hears the story of the Trojan Horse, but Odysseus has to hide his face, acutely conscious of his tears and the heroic sensibility aroused by hearing his fame as a hero resung.

Both Telemachus and Odysseus feel a complex response when hearing the bard sing of Odysseus and the Trojan war: as a hero passed into history, into song – 'heroised'. It is positive for Telemachus, who had seen his father's absence only as a problem or a source of potential shame. For Odysseus the effect of hearing of his own deeds and now dead companions as passed into song is to induce overwhelming grief. Vergil writes of a similar upwelling of feeling in Aeneas when he sees Troy depicted on temple doors in the backwoods of Africa – *sunt lacrimae rerum et mentem mortalia tangunt* – 'tears in the nature of things, the mind touched by human mortality'. To be heroised is not to be adored as a living star but to be canonised – accepted as part of that community of dead heroes whose deeds will be sung at feasts throughout the generations. It is a reminder that the only sort of participation in life for the hero is that of his fame on men's lips. Odysseus hears his deeds canonised in a way that distances him from them. In the same way, the sublimely comic story of Hephaestus entangling his wife and her lover in a net distances the laughing human audience from the gods, confirming them in their status as mortals, alive now round the feast hearth.

Odysseus in Phaeacia needs the two skills of the hero – effectiveness in council and effectiveness in contest. Both are tested when he is challenged to take part in a mini festival games, put on for his entertainment after the feasting and song. Odysseus is conscious that he is out of condition and out of training and that it would be neither fitting nor politic for a married man begging safe passage home to shine in a contest designed to test and demonstrate the prowess of young men. He declines, but is abused as one more concerned with profit than excellence; his fighting spirit roused by the insult, he makes a fearfully long discus throw. Behind the story motif – the unknown hero challenged to demonstrate his mettle – is the vivid placing of Odysseus, the hero-survivor of war, storm and hostile cultures against this people who live apart, priding themselves on their seafaring, dancing and athleticism. Accepted for what he is, as worthy of guest-friendship, he is given gifts, promised return, and given a final feast. He now can reveal his identity, an identity introduced to the Phaeacians by the bard who at Odysseus' request sings again of Troy, this time of the wooden horse. In Books 9–12 Odysseus will become his own bard, telling the tale of his adventures.

Books 9–10

Odysseus' tales are both delightful and resonant with significance, as befits a master story-teller: throughout the *Odyssey* listeners take pleasure in and are moved by the stories they hear and by the subtle timing and placing of stories for effect. The Cyclops, Scylla and Charybdis, the lotus eaters, the enchantress Circe who turns Odysseus' men into swine – are stories well known and delighted in through generations. Odysseus shapes them into well-constructed narrative – the lotus eaters (threat to the return through enchantment); the Cyclops Polyphemus (a man-eating monster in a cave); Aeolus (wind god's island, safe return vitiated by Odysseus' men who open the bag of winds while Odysseus sleeps); the Laestrygonians (man-eating giants) – form the first set, which are neatly paralleled by the second set: the Sirens (threat to the return through enchantment); Scylla (a man-eating monster in a cave) and the whirlpool Charybdis; Helios (sun god's island, safe return vitiated by Odysseus' men who kill the sacred cattle, Odysseus sleeps); Scylla and Charybdis again. Between the two sets comes the major figure of Circe, who first detains him as her lover and then sends him on his way (via the Underworld), a figure paralleled by Calypso who finally sends him on his way to Ithaca via Phaeacia.

In the course of his travels he visits every sort of location on the earth and under it – clashing rocks, a floating island, a whirlpool, the Underworld. He experiences every sort of society – people who live in caves (Calypso, Cyclops), in a hall in a forest (Circe); pastoralists who don't practise agriculture (the Cyclopes), who feed off flowery blossoms (the lotus eaters), who work a day shift and a night shift (the Laestrygonians), whose fruit ripens regardless of season (the Phaeacians); those who practise incest (Aeolus), who don't have assemblies, laws or ships to travel (the Cyclopes), who are served by automata (the Phaeacians). In each new place Odysseus has to find out whether the inhabitants are 'of rude disdain, churlish and tyrannous or . . . pious and hospitable' – what kind of society, what kind of agriculture, what kind of laws. And, most importantly, whether they respect the god-validated universal law of hospitality, whereby strangers must be cared for, entertained and given guest presents. Odysseus finds out in this instance that the Cyclopes are anything but pious and hospitable – Polyphemus' offer of a guest gift to Odysseus is to eat him last.

The satisfaction of the symmetry and order of the well-crafted tale is appropriate to Odysseus the crafty, various-minded, the resourceful. Perhaps because of the teller, perhaps because the tales, themselves archetypal folk and sailors' motifs, seem to signify more than lies on the surface, the story of the journey of Odysseus intrigues the mind as well as satisfies the ears. The Sirens do not just sing sailors to their deaths on the rocks, as mermaids do in many cultures – they entice by promising knowledge of 'Whatsoever all the earth can show'; by the ability to see, inter alia, 'wide Troy' and 'whatsoever there The Grecians and the Trojans both sustain'd By those high issues that the gods ordain'd.' The sailor is lured not by song but by access to the material from which they can make immortal song, an access that only the all-seeing, omniscient Muses have.

Similarly, the pleasure of the childlike joke of Odysseus calling himself 'No-man', so that the Cyclops yells 'No-man hath giv'n me death', is deepened by the running questioning of who Odysseus is now he is no longer one of the famous heroes at Troy. To the Greeks and Trojans of the *Iliad* Odysseus' name, his reputation for prowess and cunning, was his identity. But in the worlds he now inhabits anonymity is safer – the consequence of his vaunting his triumph over the Cyclops by shouting out to him from a safe distance that 'No-man' was a pseudonym is that the victory and, it turns out, Poseidon's punishment, can be fixed firmly to 'Odysseus'. As he travels he is gradually stripped of his companions from Troy: to the Cyclops, Circe and Calypso he is a human body; he goes down to the underworld away from all living creatures and ends up alone, naked, dependent on Calypso (the goddess) and then Nausicaa and Arete (the maid and the mother). There is development as well as symmetry in the stories – there is a unifying onward thrust of narrative as Odysseus moves from being the hero at Troy and leader of men to a leader of a small band using his wits to get out of one situation after another until he ends up on Calypso and Nausicaa's island as 'but a man'.

There is a strong thread running through the *Odyssey* that memory and recognition are the two stable markers of identity. So the lotus eaters are as dangerous as Poseidon to him, because they have the power to make men forget home. The magic root given to Odysseus by Hermes protects him from being turned into an animal with human consciousness (horror of horrors – remembrance without outward form) but does not protect him from the power of Circe's bed, which entices him to forget about home. Unlike Calypso, who wants to keep him as her husband as well as lover and is willing to change him into an immortal in order to do it, the bond between Circe and Odysseus is explicitly and solely sexual – he needs protection from the gods to prevent her unmanning him when he is naked; he needs to master her in bed before she will release his companions from her spell. The sexual union of Circe and Odysseus is a form of self-forgetfulness – his men have to remind him of home. Losing himself sexually is followed by a visit to the Land of the Dead: a linking of sex   and death. In the Underworld Circe's spell of forgetfulness will be finally broken, his identity and purpose reasserted: he is recognised as Odysseus by his former companions at Troy, and is vividly reminded of his home by meeting the shades of his parents. It is this theme of Odysseus' loss and reinvention of his identity that binds the well-loved tales into the *Odyssey* as a whole. They take their place between Telemachus' search for identity at the start and the final books, which deal with the complex process of Odysseus gaining recognition and a renewed identity on Ithaca.

Book 11 – The Underworld

Odysseus, unbeknown to him, has a new ghost to follow, his companion Elpenor who broke his neck in the night. This is a narrative reworking of the traditional human sacrifice needed as a prelude to raiding the Halls of Death; no golden bough but blood and the promise of more sacrifice make Odysseus able to talk to the dead. The first, very personal encounters are with Elpenor and with his mother, neither of whom he expected to see here. But, prudent as ever, he keeps his mother away from the blood until he has consulted the great prophet Tiresias. From him he learns of the need to punish the suitors in his palace; that his return will be made very hard because he has offended Poseidon by tricking and blinding his Cyclops son. Finally he learns how to make peace with Poseidon by travelling inland until he can find a people who know nothing of the sea (a society more difficult for a Greek to imagine than all the monsters he has encountered!) and about his own death – from the sea, in prosperous old age.

Many of the scenes are vivid stories from myth – of women who bore the gods' children, of men who suffer in the afterlife for sins committed on earth. But the majority of the encounters are woven into Odysseus' story – the dead souls warn him about women long left to plan revenge on absent husbands (Clytemnestra – will Penelope really be different?), teach him lessons about judgment and punishment (Minos, Tityus, Tantalus, Sisyphus), about suffering and endurance (Heracles), all of which he will draw on when he returns to Ithaca.

In an extremely moving scene with his mother he also learns about death itself – he tried to embrace her but she evaded his grasp:

> . . . thrice she vanish'd like a sleep,
> Or fleeting shadow, which struck much more deep
> The wounds my woes made, and made ask her why
> She would my love to her embraces fly.

She who gave him life shows him the insubstantiality and irreversibility of death. This lesson is strengthened by Achilles (who in the *Iliad* is obsessed by heroism, the risking of death for eternal glory) saying

> 'I rather wish to live in earth a swain,
> Or serve a swain for hire, that scarce can gain
> Bread to sustain him, than, that life once gone,
> Of all the dead sway the imperial throne.'

Human life looks different from the Underworld; only Telamonian Ajax is intransigent, keeping enmity in death as he did in life.

Book 12

The Underworld divides the two parallel sets of Odysseus' adventures, the latter informed by his experiences there. In the Underworld Odysseus gains knowledge and sense of self; he also gains distance on the heroic ethic that powered the society in Troy. Instead, he can see punishment and retribution at work; from Books 11–14 we see him put what he has learned into sometimes harsh practice.

As Odysseus approaches each new world there is the challenge and danger of what customs, what practices, will be current there. The later set of adventures are a darker version of the earlier: the Sirens of Book 12 offer not just happy forgetfulness of self and home, as the lotus eaters did, but access to the record of the hero's doing that only the Muses, who can see and record everything, hold:

> 'Come here, thou worthy of a world of praise,
> That dost so high the Grecian glory raise,
> Ulysses! Stay thy ship, and that song hear
> That none pass'd ever but it bent his ear,
> But left him ravish'd, and instructed more
> By us, than any ever heard before.
> For we know all things whatsoever were

> In wide Troy labour'd; whatsoever there
> The Grecians and the Trojans both sustain'd
> By those high issues that the gods ordain'd.
> And whatsoever all the earth can show
> T'inform a knowledge of desert, we know.'

To turn that down is to turn down all remaining access to the [now lost] heroic world of Troy. Odysseus the all-experiencing does not turn anything down easily – following Circe's warning he has blocked up his men's ears but allowed himself, lashed to the mast, to hear the blandishments. His men are oblivious both of the Sirens and Odysseus' pleas to be freed, and all survive. In this second set of adventures Odysseus asserts his cunning and uses experiences gained in the Cyclops' cave to cheer his crew through; he conceals the human 'toll' Scylla will extort and, despite Circe's advice, he arms himself to do battle with her on their behalf. His comment on his pain at their death shows the emotional range he now possesses:

> Six friends had Scylla snatch'd out of our keel,
> In whom most loss did force and virtue feel.
> When looking to my ship, and lending eye
> To see my friends' estates, their heels turn'd high,
> And hands cast up, I might discern, and hear
> Their calls to me for help, when now they were
> To try me in their last extremities.
> And as an angler . . . for surprise
> Of little fish. . . hoists them high
> Up to the air, then slightly hurls them by,
> When helpless sprawling on the land they lie:
> So easily Scylla to her rock had rapt
> My woeful friends, and so unhelp'd entrapp'd
> Struggling they lay beneath her violent rape,
> Who in their tortures, desp'rate of escape,
> Shriek'd as she tore, and up their hands to me
> Still threw for sweet life. I did never see,
> In all my suff'rance ransacking the seas,
> A spectacle so full of miseries.

The adventures end with Charybdis stripping Odysseus of his last remaining companions, leaving him clinging to a fig tree. He is described as waiting for the whirlpool to vomit back a spar from his wrecked ship like a judge listening to civil cases:

> At length time frees him from their civil wars,
> When glad he riseth and to dinner goes:
> So time, at length, releas'd with joys my woes.

Stripped of his last warrior companions, experienced, cunning and vengeful from his various adventures, he moves now to civil rather than heroic life.

After finishing the long story of his adventures, Odysseus accomplishes the final part of his journey swiftly and painlessly, with gifts and in a ship provided by the Phaeacians. The transition is almost magical; as at other crucial times he falls asleep 'bound so fast it scarce gave way to breath . . . next of all to death' but this time the punishment falls after his safe landing – Poseidon turns the Phaeacian ship to stone.

Books 13–14

Telemachus at Menelaus' court was told of his father's heroic world and Odysseus' stature within it. But what will Odysseus' stature be in the non-heroic world of barren, suitor-infested Ithaca? How will his son, or anyone else, recognise the man who left nearly twenty years ago? And in what sense, if at all, can he be identified (and identify himself) as the same man?

Pallas Athene's first act is to disguise his homeland, to complicate and delay Odysseus' recognition and announcement of his identity:

> . . . to make strange the more
> His safe arrival, lest upon his shore
> He should make known his face, and utter all
> That might prevent th'event that was to fall.
> Which she prepar'd so well that not his wife,
> Presented to him, should perceive his life –
> No citizen, no friend, till righteous fate
> Upon the wooers' wrongs were consummate.

Odysseus' first contact on Ithaca is with the disguised Athene; checking his immediate joy that he is home he conceals his identity in a long 'Cretan' tale (the Cretans were famous for their lies). Athene is overjoyed at his trickiness, his subtlety, his alikeness to her, his desire to test Penelope rather than rush to her arms :

> 'Thou of men art far,
> For words and counsels, the most singular,
> But I above the gods in both may boast . . .
> Another man, that so long miseries
> Had kept from his lov'd home, and thus return'd
> To see his house, wife, children, would have burn'd
> In headlong lust to visit . . . '

Athene tells him that Penelope is constant and equally cunning in keeping herself free from the suitors; that Telemachus is safely returned from a journey that has won him renown on his own account. She will help and glory in the bloodletting of the suitors that Odysseus will initiate:

> 'I hope the bloods
> And brains of some of these that waste thy goods
> Shall strew thy goodly pavements. Join we then . . . '

Athene disguises him as an old beggar and sends him off to an elderly, faithful swineherd, Eumaeus, who receives him with the simple hospitality due to wanderers.

From Eumaeus' words we get a stark (Dark Age?) account of the suitors' offences – they are eating too much in a poor country with not enough food – literally eating up Telemachus' inheritance. In this world Odysseus' fluency can be turned to good account – his lying tale succeeds in begging a cloak, but he is warned that news of Odysseus, such as that for which beggars have up till now been rewarded, will no longer be believed or recompensed at the palace.

Book 15

Athene goes to Sparta to bring Telemachus home – the trap set in Book 4 by the suitors, who have gone unchecked while Telemachus was a boy and Odysseus absent, is now gradually closing in on the suitors themselves. Athene represents to the newly-mature Telemachus that his mother may not always remain locked in the past – with his adulthood comes the possibility of her independence; she may choose to reward the most persistent of her suitors . . . Telemachus skilfully negotiates his departure and his parting gifts (including a robe from Helen for his future bride). He arrived like a boy but leaves as hero among heroes.

On his return journey he accepts the supplication of a fugitive: he is now able, in his own right as the man in charge, to offer sacred guest-friendship and his protection.

Meanwhile Odysseus has asked Eumaeus for news of his mother and father – news he already has from the Underworld is now told to him on earth. This elicits memories of Eumaeus' childhood, which Odysseus asks him to tell properly. In a vivid reference to the world of those who listened to Homer's stories, Eumaeus agrees – there's nothing else to do in the long evenings other than listen to stories or sleep the clock round. Besides, tales are a way of turning pain to good – the suffering is metamorphosed into pleasure as the story is recounted for men's delight.

> We two . . . will our bosoms cheer
> With memories and tales of our annoys.
> Betwixt his sorrows every human joys,
> He most, who most hath felt and furthest err'd.'

After Eumaeus' life story, the narrative shifts back to Telemachus, who avoids the suitors' trap and makes his way to Eumaeus – a return elevated by portents and by Athene's guidance.

Book 16

Eumaeus' is the halfway house between shore and palace, the intermediary between father and son. There is no simple coming together between this boy who has had to grow up without a father and this man whose identity and qualities have been those of an individual hero – they have to negotiate a relationship while learning to establish their new identities on Ithaca.

The first sign of Telemachus' place is the fawning of Eumaeus' dogs (the dogs that were ready to attack Odysseus). Telemachus belongs here; he calls Eumaeus 'Atta' – a respectful and intimate term. Similes in Homer are used frequently to point to an unusual yet striking similarity (Odysseus clinging to the rocky shore in Phaeacia like an octopus). But when Eumaeus greets Telemachus Homer says:

> There breath'd no kind-soul'd father that was fill'd
> Less with his son's embraces, that had liv'd
> Ten years in far-off earth, now new retriev'd,
> His only child too, gotten in his age,
> And for whose absence he had felt the rage
> Of griefs upon him . . .

The point of this simile is that it is a simile – Eumaeus is *not* Telemachus's adoring father; the simile wonders at the gap between the emotions of the biological father, who demonstrates none of the natural sentiment of the simile and who observes his son coolly from the shadows, and the kind, tearful old man who has served as his emotional base all these years.

Looking after Odysseus is a problem for Telemachus, aware that the household structures of his youth are disintegrating and that events at the palace are moving too fast for him to be able to receive and protect a guest. Odysseus questions him about his helplessness and almost reproaches him (a very acute and timeless exchange between aging father and fully-grown son: 'I could have done something about it at your age . . . '). Athene intervenes by rejuvenating him, to Telemachus' astonishment: he now thinks Odysseus to be a visiting deity. This Odysseus brusquely denies, abruptly revealing who he is:

>   'I hold
> No deified state. Why put you thus on me
> A god's resemblance? I am only he
> That bears thy father's name.'

Odysseus, the all-enduring, is suddenly overwhelmed at the suffering his absence has caused Telemachus, and weeping tries to embrace him. Telemachus keeps his distance, still taking him to be a god in disguise come to test him – in his wariness showing himself truly to be his father's son. When he does finally believe, they weep together like birds whose fledglings have been stolen away from them by man – shedding common tears for the loss of the years spent separately.

Those years are lost, but they can establish a bond of common purpose: to rid the palace of the suitors and to bring the household to trial. Odysseus answers Telemachus with 'the truth' about his journey (as distinct from the Cretan tales he tells everyone else, even Athene!) and sends him back to the palace to put the first part of their secret plan into action. Here he must endure, as his father has had to do, whatever ill-treatment the suitors mete out.

The narrative switches to the suitors, whose ambush of Telemachus has been unsuccessful. They too talk of things coming to a crisis: Telemachus' coming-of-age brings the need for Penelope to finally make a choice.

The book ends with Eumaeus' return from the palace. A great deal has happened in his absence, although Athene reverses Odysseus' rejuvenation so the scene in the hut appears the same. Telemachus and Odysseus are now bound in common secret knowledge – Eumaeus is uncertain about the figures he has seen in the 'ambush' ship:

> The prince smil'd, and knew
> They were the wooers, casting secret view
> Upon his father.

Book 17

Book 17 starts with Telemachus' return to Penelope who has been worrying about him – an emotional return vividly anticipated from the adolescent's point of view: he must go, he says to

> 'My mother . . .   . . . who, till her eyes
> Mine own eyes witness, varies tears and cries
> Through all extremes . . . '

Penelope does indeed create the 'scene' Telemachus feared:

> Her kind embraces, with effusion
> Of loving tears; kiss'd both his lovely eyes,
> His cheeks, and forehead; and gave all supplies
> With this entreaty: 'Welcome, sweetest light . . . '

Telemachus uses his new assurance to hold her off ('Move me not now'), telling her to collect her womenfolk to see to the ritual thanksgiving while he goes to call an assembly and see to his suppliant, the seer

Theoclymenus. He does relent later, telling her the high points of his trip and assuring her that Odysseus is alive but detained. Theoclymenus reinforces this message, saying that Odysseus is not only alive but already on Ithaca. For the first time, Penelope does not turn down the possibility.

The theme of the avenger in disguise occupies the centre of this and the next book. In incident after incident Odysseus is abused and ill treated, although his bodily strength beneath the shabby disguise causes many a suitor to rue the insult. The motif of the poor stranger who appears in a household and who eventually throws off the disguise, rewards the worthy and generous and punishes the uncivil, is a common folk motif; the stranger is often (as Telemachus and one of the suitors suspected) a god in disguise. Odysseus' real qualities of cunning, endurance and bodily strength can be displayed as a beggar as much as a king – this is a different world from the *Iliad*, where the noble are all brave and all beautiful, and only the low-born, foul-mouthed Thersites is ugly. In this world, Odysseus can harp on a commonality between the highest and the lowest in both being subservient to the needs of the belly. Here Odysseus is recognisably himself whether fighting a beggars' duel, standing up to the suitors' blows or begging his food with cunning stories.

The folk story of the disguised judge is interwoven with the narrative of the double process of recognition: of Odysseus being recognised as himself and of Odysseus learning who he now is, in the non-Iliadic world of Ithaca. On his first journey into town he sees his old dog, Argus, whom he trained for the chase before leaving for Troy, now lying on a dunghill dying of old age and neglect. The mistreatment of the once fine, prized hunting dog is distressing, a symbol of the waste by the suitors of Odysseus' royal goods, and points to the sort of treatment anyone helpless will receive at their hands. Infinitely moving is the old dog's summoning of his very last energy to wag his tail and prick his ears in recognition of his long absent master, before dying. For the dog, the recognition is simple, the relationship stable – no words or explanation are needed; the relationship between master and hound unchanged by twenty years. For others, Odysseus has to establish himself, to be recognised not *as* anything but *for* what he now is.

The centrepiece of Books 17–20 is the private meeting between Penelope and the still disguised Odysseus – a meeting prefigured by the nurse's recognition of Odysseus from a scar that marked him from childhood. As with Argus, the recognition is simple – Odysseus for her is in some sense the same as the boy she suckled, who went on his first boar hunt, the scar a witness to the continuity. Odysseus prevents her from telling Penelope. Penelope's recognition will be fuller, more complex and more difficult to achieve.

At the end of Book 17 the long-awaited meeting between Penelope and Odysseus is anticipated but is then, dramatically, postponed for a whole book. In the meantime there is a mock duel between Odysseus and Irus for the position of 'official' beggar, with the suitors putting forward Irus as their 'champion'. Irus, like Argus, is an illustration of the rottenness of the palace as now infested by the suitors; his downfall is welcomed as just, prefiguring the more general punishment Odysseus will mete out, and the episode is a lively burlesque of a heroic encounter.

Books 18–20

Odysseus' return coincides with and precipitates the new independence of both his son and his wife; Penelope's reaction both to her son's maturity and to the now more authoritative reports of Odysseus' safety is carefully described. Homeric psychology maps easily onto modern – any modern novel could convincingly translate the scene where Athene put it in the heart of Penelope that after years of waiting and mourning she should now smarten herself up and show herself to the suitors in order that she should demonstrate her desirability to her husband and son . . . and herself:

> Who laughing yet, to show her humour bore
> No serious appetite to that light show,
> She told Eurynome, that not till now
> She ever knew her entertain desire
> To please her wooers' eyes, but oft on fire
> She set their hate, in keeping from them still;
> Yet now she pleas'd t'appear . . .

Although Penelope and her nurse Eurynome are frank about the ravages worked by time and dull grief, a beauty bath and facial and a revivifying sleep contribute, with Athene's help, to her radiant appearance. Penelope says several times that Odysseus took with him her bloom and value as a woman (*arete*), but both are now restored: wearing

> So thin a veil, that through it quite there shone
> A grace so stol'n, it pleas'd above the clear,
> And sunk the knees of every wooer there,
> Their minds so melted in love's vehement fires,
> That to her bed she heighten'd all desires.

As a man demonstrates his *arete* in contest, in battle, in the assembly and by the gifts that accrue, so a woman demonstrates hers by the dowry she can command, by the gifts she can inspire. Odysseus, from his beggar's seat, sees both her and the suitors' reaction. He is going to have to compete against the others to [re]win Penelope, a wife whose status and desirability have been reasserted.

Penelope's state of mind is sensitively described. Coming round from her beauty sleep, she had wished she could stay in that soft sleep for ever and never awake to the grief and longing that has been her life for twenty years; when she is fully awake it is as if she is reborn to another life. She acknowledges her son's beard as a *rite de passage* for her too: she offers to marry but demands proper wooing gifts. Although she says she cannot believe reports that Odysseus is alive and coming back, in Book 19 she dreams of his return. But it is an ambivalent dream – he is the eagle that slaughters the geese of the household (the suitors) – geese that she 'joy'd to see' and for whose death she cries and sorrows. Odysseus' return may be a consummation devoutly to be wished, but it is also a threat to her newly-found status as a woman.

Penelope's consciousness of Odysseus is shown by her concern for him after his 'duel': she upbraids Telemachus for not taking better care of a stranger guest. Telemachus is now assured enough to feign helplessness when it will serve his and his father's cause. For the first time, too, he speaks out against the suitors' carousing – he sends them to their homes to sleep it off and himself goes to bed, leaving the palace quiet for Odysseus' and Penelope's meeting, in the half-shadows of the empty hall. In one last delay, Odysseus has to fight for his place once more, this time against the wicked maidservant Melantho. Penelope joins him in condemning the woman; when it comes, Odysseus' purge will extend to the servants who have consorted with the suitors as well as the suitors themselves.

When Penelope and Odysseus finally come together their exchanges are in character but strike common resonances – Odysseus addresses her as one whose fame goes up to heaven, as like a king ruling as a lord (Odysseus elsewhere has cried like a woman who long missed her husband). He is too full of grief to tell his tale; Penelope represents herself, again, as one whose *arete* has been destroyed by longing. She explains the trick with which she has kept her suitors at bay for years: she has made the weaving of a shroud for her father-in-law the defining act which has to be completed before leaving Odysseus' household for a new one. In a device worthy of 'Odysseus, full of tricks', weaving all day she has each night unpicked her work. In answer, Odysseus embarks on another 'Cretan' tale, where he claims to have entertained Odysseus. He thus establishes a bond between himself and Odysseus, one that moves Penelope to tears.

> Thus many tales Ulysses told his wife,
> At most but painting, yet most like the life;
> Of which her heart such sense took through her ears,
> It made her weep as she would turn to tears.
> And as from off the mountains melts the snow. . .
> So down her fair cheeks her kind tears did glide,
> Her miss'd lord mourning, set so near her side.

Odysseus himself is near to tears, but conceals them. Despite her emotional sympathy with the stranger, Penelope decides to test him by asking him to describe Odysseus' clothes and appearance. Odysseus of course can describe exactly the outfit Penelope made for him, can describe how he looked when she last saw him.

> When all these signs she knew for chiefly true,
> Desire of moan upon her beauties grew,
> And yet, ev'n that desire suffic'd, she said:
> 'Till this, my guest, a wretched state array'd
> Your ill-us'd person, but from this hour forth
> You shall be honour'd, and find all the worth
> That fits a friend . . . '

He has passed the test, and through his beggarly appearance she has accepted him as an worthy link to her husband. He tries to offer one further bond with Odysseus – he says he has seen his stockpile of rich gifts amassed on the way home. (He would have been home long before but has travelled to accrue wealth: a harsh statement but one which likens him to a suitor amassing wedding gifts . . .) Penelope however will not accept such proof of his survival. But the story has turned her mind away from Odysseus as he left, the young hero, to Odysseus as he must be now, battered by experience and like the man in front of her. She orders Odysseus' old nurse to bathe him:

> 'Euryclea, rise, and wash the feet of one
> That is of one age with your sovereign gone,
> Such hands, such feet hath, though of alter'd grace.
> Much grief in men will bring on change apace.'

Euryclea imagines the man in front of her as Odysseus and weeps for both. Her recognition of the scar brings to her and us a vivid evocation of his naming ceremony and young manhood. Like fond carers through the ages she sees the man but remembers and is bonded to the boy; like sons through the ages Odysseus is conscious of everything in his identity that is not continuous with his early self; he threatens her and prevents her from revealing who he is to Penelope.

Penelope keeps Odysseus with her until late, confiding in him her indecision and her unwillingness to have confidence in the prediction of Odysseus' return and reclaiming of his own. While talking to him a bond is established; she decides to set up a bridal contest – her new husband must match her old in shooting an arrow through a line of twelve crossed axes. Both, separately yet similarly, pass a turbulent night.

Books 21–22

Book 21 is a tense, exciting, self-contained book – the trial of the bow. Penelope takes out and weeps over this attribute of Odysseus, now a symbol of his power and loss. Its history points to its significance – an heirloom given to Odysseus before its owner was murdered while Heracles' guest; so potent a symbol and so precious that Odysseus left it behind when he went to Troy. The suitors are ambivalent about the test – worried that they might fail, might prove themselves inferior to Odysseus, yet secretly hopeful of being the bow's master. The narrator points to the baselessness of their hope – they will die by the bow, long eager to revenge abuse of hospitality, safely back in its rightful owner's hands.

Telemachus highlights the significance of this trial of men – he describes his mother's many attractions and tries to string the bow in order that he might replace his father as his mother's lord and guardian. As he is about to succeed he glances at Odysseus – through tact, cunning and/or inhibition he then pretends to be too young and weak. All except the two leading suitors try and fail; Odysseus reveals his identity to two more faithful servants and shows his scar as a proof of identity, a sign. The chief suitor tries and fails, acknowledging the ignominy of being so demonstrably weaker than Odysseus. The final contestant consoles him and himself with pointing out that this fateful day is that of Apollo the archer – of course they will fail (and Odysseus succeed) on such a day. When the bow is lain aside Odysseus' proposition that he just try his strength with the bow (he is carefully not entering the competition but transforming the feat into the prelude to his revenge) is met with outrage and the accusation that he is drunk. A warning story of the vengeance wreaked by a centaur when his animal passions were aroused by alcohol misfires, pointing as it does to the terrible fury Odysseus will with justice wreak on them.

There is continued tension between Telemachus, Penelope and Odysseus: Penelope's continued interest in standing up for the beggar encourages him to try to string the bow and promises rich rewards. Telemachus leaps to assert his authority over the bow and tells her to take her distaff and go back to the women's quarters where she belongs. He has had it in his power to win her himself: he now feels able to stand as an independent man in front of his mother (and perhaps of his father). The stringing of the bow has indeed been a test of manhood. The book finishes with the long-anticipated sight: Odysseus easily stringing his great bow and sending an arrow surely through the twelve crossed axeheads.

With Book 22 comes the vengeance – a complete cleansing of the suitors and their consorts, completed by Odysseus purifying the palace with fire and brimstone. The deaths are described with delight in the skill and appropriateness of the shot or stroke and perhaps with a certain bloodthirstiness that, despite its battlefield setting, is less a feature of the *Iliad*.

Antinous is shot through the throat in the act of drinking and in falling overturns the banquet table – a fitting start to the punishment of the suitors' greed. He is killed by Odysseus in the guise of the stranger-beggar who has been insulted and buffeted; then Odysseus declares who he is and kills the other suitors as the returning, vengeful lord. Now Telemachus can act without guile as his father's helpmeet – he helps Odysseus arm and together with the two loyal retainers, gets access to the armoury. Melanthius the collaborator is, literally, strung up – dangling from the roof timbers all night, he waits to be finished off and mutilated. Odysseus' henchmen repay the insults to their master – the suitor who threw an ox-hoof at Odysseus now has an answering 'guest gift' – death.

Some sue for mercy – Liodes the suitors' diviner pleads non-involvement but is denied on the grounds that he must have wished for Odysseus' death in his wish to wed and bed his wife:

> 'If you be priest amongst them, as you plead,
> Yet you would marry, and with my wife too,
> And have descent by her. For all that woo
> Wish to obtain – which they should never do,
> Dames' husbands living. You must therefore pray,
> Of force and oft, in court here, that the day
> Of my return for home might never shine;
> The death to me wish'd therefore shall be thine.'

Odysseus comes as avenger, as bringer of justice, as punisher of those who sought to replace him.

The poet Phemius has a more persuasive suit and is allowed by the poet Homer to make it very powerfully: the bard is in charge of heroes' reputations and Odysseus' fame is in his and his brethren's hands. He is allowed to live, when Telemachus vouches that he sang for the suitors under duress. Chapman makes Telemachus appeal for clemency as a prince to a king:

> This did the prince's sacred virtue hear,
> And to the king, his father, said: 'Forbear
> To mix the guiltless with the guilty's blood.'

With Athene's help, all the rest are killed like fish caught in a net; Odysseus is covered in gore like a lion feeding on an ox. In a ghastly episode, the twelve maidservants who have been consorting with the suitors are made to clean up the slaughter in the hall and then are led out and killed by being strung up by the neck as a pigeon 'in any grove caught with a . . . net, With struggling pinions 'gainst the ground doth beat Her tender body'; their feet soon stop kicking. In blackly comic contrast, the old Nurse refuses to fetch fire and brimstone to cleanse the gore of the mass killing until she has first brought Odysseus a cloak: it is not proper that the Master should go round in rags. The book ends with the faithful women servants embracing him in joy at having him back, a recognition which brings tears to his eyes:

> And plied him so with all their loving graces
> That tears and sighs took up his whole desire;
> For now he knew their hearts to him entire.

Book 23

Book 23 is the final twisting together of the stories of the *Odyssey* – of Odysseus' final and completing recognition by his wife, of Telemachus' establishment as a grown son within a two-parent household, of Odysseus' final narration of his adventures – to his wife.

Now only Penelope, sunk in the deepest sleep she has known since Odysseus' loss, does not know of Odysseus' return. Euryclea flies upstairs with the speed of youth; Penelope is only with difficulty convinced that it might indeed be Odysseus: even the scar, she points out, might be faked by a god!

This reserve, this caution, this insistence on putting the stranger to the test, is what marks Penelope as Odysseus' 'other half'. Precisely because it is how Odysseus would have acted, he is both amused and understanding; in answer to Telemachus' anger at his mother's 'flint hard heart' he says:

> 'Take
> Your mother from the prease, that she may make
> Her own proofs of me . . . But now, because I go
> So poorly clad, she takes disdain to know
> So loath'd a creature for her loved lord.

For Penelope, least of all, is the recognition that of simple continuity of identity – she has to accept him back. Chapman's understanding and sensitivity makes the exchange between them one of the most moving parts of his *Odyssey* (he embroiders Penelope's speech by adding the parts in brackets):

> Like an immortal from the bath he rose,
> And to his wife did all his grace dispose,
> Encount'ring thus her strangeness: 'Cruel dame,
> Of all that breathe, the gods past steel and flame
> Have made thee ruthless. Life retains not one
> Of all dames else . . . as twenty years
> To miss her husband, drown'd in woes and tears,
> And, at his coming, keep aloof . . .

> [Penelope replied]
> ['Your mean appearance made not me retire,
> Nor this your rich show makes me now admire,
> Nor moves at all; for what is all to me,
> If not my husband? All his certainty
> I knew at parting; but, so long apart,
> The outward likeness holds no full desert
> For me to trust to.] Go, nurse, see address'd
> A soft bed for him, and the single rest
> Himself affects so. Let it be the bed
> That stands within our bridal chamber-stead
> Which he himself made. Bring it forth from thence,
> And see it furnished with magnificence.'

This is a test (the bed, as the real Odysseus well knew, was immovably constructed round a living olive tree) worthy of Odysseus the cunning – a trick that he recognises and wonders at:

> This said she to assay him, and did stir
> Ev'n his establish'd patience, and to her;
> Whom thus he answer'd: 'Woman, your words prove
> My patience strangely. Who is it can move
> My bed out of his place? . . .
> For in the fixture of the bed is shown
> A masterpiece, a wonder; and 'twas done
> By me, and none but me.'

Penelope has held out against hope ever since the first signs that Odysseus was alive and returning, has refused to believe even when told that he had killed the suitors, has demanded proof even when he stood in front of her. Now the last barrier is removed:

> This sunk her knees and heart to hear so true
> The signs she urg'd; and first did tears ensue
> Her rapt assurance; then she ran and spread
> Her arms around his neck, kissed oft his head . . .

Meanwhile, Telemachus is given a job to do: he is to arrange the festivities of his mother's wedding, to create the impression that Penelope has accepted the suitor who succeeded in the bow competition (as, in a sense, she has).

The book ends with Penelope and Odysseus making love:

> The king and queen then now, as newly wed,
> Resum'd the old laws of th'embracing bed.

and exchanging stories – it is as if all the suffering and losses are redeemed by becoming the means of intimacy:

> The bride and bridegroom having ceas'd to keep
> Observed love-joys, from their fit delight
> They turn'd to talk. The queen did then recite
> What she had suffer'd . . . Great Ulysses then,
> What ever slaughters he had made of men,
> What ever sorrows he himself sustain'd,
> Repeated amply; and her ears remain'd
> With all delight attentive to their end.

Book 24

There are still some loose threads to be resolved in Book 24 – Melanthius' story is woven into those of the other heroes of Troy by the narrative following the souls of the suitors down to the Underworld. Here the dead heroes are given voice by the narrator and can talk to one another as if for the first time. Agamemnon tells Achilles about Achilles' funeral and contrasts it sadly with the way his own dead body was treated. There has been a running contrast between Odysseus' story and that of Agamemnon and Menelaus: Telemachus adjured to live up to Orestes' example in ridding his household of rivals to his absent father's bed; Penelope in her constancy compared favourably with Clytemnestra; in her prudence and chastity with Helen. Now, the news of Odysseus' avenging homecoming being brought by the suitors to Agamemnon in the Underworld, these stories are stitched together; the end of Odysseus' story told to the heroes of Troy forms a fitting conclusion to both the *Iliad* and the *Odyssey*.

There is one last thread – Odysseus has yet to be accepted by his father, Laertes, living in the country like a poor peasant. As always, Odysseus observes, tests out and deceives before telling his father who he is; the shock nearly kills the broken-down old man. As with Penelope, though, the habitual distance between himself and those to whom he tells 'Cretan tales' is disturbed by his emotions –

> Him when Ulysses saw consum'd with age,
> And all the ensigns on him that the rage
> Of grief presented, he brake out in tears;
>   . . . his mind
> Had much contention, if to yield to kind,
> Make straight way to his father, kiss, embrace,
> Tell his return . . .

but he keeps to his plan to tell how he entertained Odysseus, years ago. Laertes presumes his son dead:

> This a cloud of grief
> Cast over all the forces of his life.
> With both his hands the burning dust he swept
> Up from the earth, which on his head he heap'd,
> And fetch'd a sigh, as in it life were broke.

The effect on Odysseus of his father's distress is physical; he drops his pretence and reveals himself. As with Penelope, the declaration is too sudden a turn to be believed – Laertes needs physical proof and identification. Odysseus shows him the scar, the mark of his boyhood hunting trip with his grandfather, and reminisces about the planting of the trees which Laertes gave him, now full-grown. Laertes is rejuvenated, metaphorically and actually, and takes his place as a hero among his people. The *Odyssey* ends with the three generations of heroes reunited, facing the suitors' vengeful kin, before Athene intervenes to end the the killing. Laertes tells Telemachus to be worthy of his lineage; Telemachus, now a proven warrior, replies with vigour:

> The old king sprung for joy to hear his spirit,
> And said: 'O lov'd immortals, what a day
> Do your clear bounties to my life display!
> I joy, past measure, to behold my son
> And [grandson] close in such contention
> Of virtues martial.'

The household is complete.

JAN PARKER
The Open University

FURTHER READING

Vergil reimagined and resituated the *Odyssey* in his *Aeneid* books 1–6, the *Iliad* in books 7–12. There are many modern poetic translations of which that of C. Day Lewis (Oxford 1998) is my favourite. Dryden's classic translation is available in Wordsworth Classics of World Literature, edited by James Morwood.

James Joyce's *Ulysses*, Derek Walcott's *Omeros* (Faber 1990) and Christopher Logue's *Kings* (Faber 1991) are the outstanding versions of Homer for the 20th century.

Homer inspired many later dramatists: Aeschylus' *Agamemnon*, Euripides' *Trojan Women*, *Helen* and *Iphigeneia in Aulis* all explore the issues surrounding the Greek expedition; Sophocles' *Ajax* and *Philoctetes* both take Odysseus (for better and worse) as the archetypal survivor. Shakespeare's *Troilus and Cressida* combines material from the Troy romances (as used by Chaucer in his *Troilus and Criseyde*) with material from Chapman's *Seven Books of the Iliad*.

Claudio Monteverdi's *Return of Ulysses*, The Dance Theatre of Harlem's *Troy Games* and Michael Tippett's *King Priam* all use Homeric themes to powerful musical and dramatic effect.

For more on Homer, history and archaeology see *Homer: Readings and Images*, ed. C. Emlyn-Jones and L. Hardwick (Duckworth 1992).

For more on the oral performance, see Greg Nagy's stimulating *Poetry as Performance* (Cambridge 1999).

For comprehensive and definitive answers to all Homeric questions, see *New Companion to Homer*, ed. B. B. Powell and I. A. Morris (Brill 1997).

For Chapman's contribution to the epic tradition see Colin Burrow's *From Epic to Romance* (Cambridge 1996).

NOTE ON LINE NUMBERING

Chapman's text is numbered in the margin, every ten lines. The line numbers in square brackets at the top of the page refer to the Greek texts of the *Iliad* and the *Odyssey*.

GLOSSARY OF UNFAMILIAR WORDS

abode (verb) foretell
abodes (noun) omens
accited summoned
aesture swelling tide
affected beloved
apaid satisfied
approve prove, try
areeds advises
arew in a row
artires ligaments [arteries]
bace run
bedfere bed companion
beeves cows
besogne base fellow, commoner
bever evening meal
bewray display
blanch whiten, make to look good
blore blast
bracks broken, torn parts
bray chew up
cantles portions
carquenet/carcanet necklace
cast pair [of eagles]
cates delicacies
champain level country
conceit concept, idea, impression
cope covering
cote outstrip
curets cuirass
curious careful, painstaking
currie quarry
disperple sprinkle

dite winnow
diversory wayside inn
dorp village
doubt redoubt, barrier
dubbed smeared
emprese enterprise
err wander
error wandering
expiscating enquiring into
fautour guardian
fell'ffs outer-parts of wheel
fere mate, companion
fil'd defiled
flaw wave, roller
flea flay
froes women
frontless shameless
froofe augur handle
giggots quarter joints
gull (verb) to swallow
hoice hoist
humorous damp
illation deduction
immane huge, cruel
inform animate
insecution pursuit
intended attended
lien lain
luster cave, den, hide
mall beat
mate oppose
maund basket
mere pure, whole
muse animal run

nave   central part of wheel

neat   oxen

nephew   grandson

or . . . or . . .   either . . . or . . .

owes   owns

paise   weight, balance

penia   poverty

perse   pierce

pile   weapon tip

plain   complain

poitril   breast-piece

port   impressive demeanour

prease   press

procinct   preparation

proin   prune

proller   vagabond

proof   trial, attempt

prove   try, attempt

quaint   neat

queach   thicket

quite   put a stop to

race   raze, destroy

ranch'd   wrenched

rate   weight, valuation

reduce   lead back

reflect   turn back

rock   distaff and wool

rub   blockage

saker   falcon

say   assay, sample

scoles   scales

sere(s)   talon(s)

sewer   server

she   showy appearance

shent   disgraceful

skall   scale

sod (verb)   past tense of seethe

sort   lot, number

stale   stem

state   prince or royal entry

stitches   furrows

strake   metal rim

strooted   swelled

surcuidrie/surquedy
    overweening pride

taint   thrust

tappish   seek cover

thrumbs   tufts

tyring   tearing at

ure   use

utter passage   passage out, exit

wan (noun)   wand/winnower

yare   quick, ready

yote   soak

GLOSSARY OF NAMES

Latinised Gods' Names

Athenia, Minerva Pallas Athene
Diana Artemis
Dis Pluto, Hades
Jove, Jupiter Zeus
Juno Hera

Mars Ares
Neptune Poseidon
Venus Aphrodite
Vulcan Hephaestus

Proper Names, Patronymics, Alternative Forms of Men and Gods

Achaia Greece
Achive Greek
Aeacides Achilles, grandson of Aeacus
Ajaces Ajax the Greater and Ajax the Lesser
Alexander Paris
Anchisiades Aeneas, son of Anchises
Arcesiades' seed Odysseus/ Ulysses, son of Laertes son of Arcesius
Argicides Hermes/Mercury, slayer of Argus
Atrides Agamemnon and Menelaus, sons of Atreus
Boreas North-west wind
Ceston Aphrodite's/Venus' enchanted girdle
Cynthia Artemis/Diana
Cyprides Aphrodite/Venus
Dardan Trojan
Dardanides Priam

Deucalides Idomeneus, son of Deucalion
Dis Pluto, god of the underworld
Ephaistus Hephaestus/Vulcan
Erebus region of the underworld
Erectheus
Eris Strife
Eristhius, Erecthius, Erectheus Erechtheus, founder of Athens
Erinnys Fury
Eurus East wind
Hymen god of marriage
Iaons Ionians/Athenians
Icarius' seed Penelope
Ilion/Ilians Troy, Trojans
Ilithyae/Lucina/Eileithyia goddess of labour and child-birth
Ithacus Odysseus/Ulysses
Jove's divine son Hercules
Jove's seed various(!) including Athene/Minerva, Prayers,

Aphrodite/Venus, Ares/Mars,
Apollo, Artemis/Diana, Hebe
Lacedaemon Sparta
Laertiades/Laertes' son
Odysseus/Ulysses
Laomedon's son Priam
Latona Leto, mother of Apollo
and Artemis/Diana
Lotophagi Lotus eaters
Lucina/Eileithyia goddess of
labour and childbirth,
Maid Athene/Minerva
Menoetiades/Menoetius' son
Patroclus
Mulciber Hephaestus/Vulcan
Neleides Nestor, son of Neleus
Nereus' seed Thetis
Nestorides Pisistratus, son of
Nestor
Notus South wind
Oileus *Iliad* Bk 9: Trojan killed
by Agamemnon. Elsewhere:
father of Ajax Oïliades
Oïliades Ajax the Lesser, son of
Oïleus
Pallas Athene/Minerva
**Panthaedes/Panthoedes/Panthus'
son** Polydamas

Parcas Fates
Pelias Achilles' spear
Pelides Achilles, son of Peleus
Pergamus Troy citadel
Phoebe Artemis
Phoebus Apollo, the sun
Pluto/Dis god of the underworld
Priamides Hector, son of Priam
Saturnia Hera/Juno, daughter
of Saturn
Saturnides Zeus/Jove/Jupiter,
son of Saturn
Smintheus Apollo
Stygian of the Styx, river of the
underworld
Telemachus' father Odysseus/
Ulysses
Telamonius Ajax, son of
Telamon, Ajax the Greater
Tellus the Earth
Thaumantia Iris, rainbow
messenger goddess
Thetis' son Achilles
Tritonia Athene/Minerva
Tydides/Tydeus' son Diomedes
Tyndaris Helen
Venus' son Aeneas
Zephyr West wind

THE ILIAD

BOOK ONE

The Argument

Apollo's priest to th' Argive fleet doth bring
Gifts for his daughter prisoner to the king;
For which her tender'd freedom he entreats.
But, being dismiss'd with contumelious threats,
At Phoebus' hands, by vengeful prayer, he seeks
To have a plague inflicted on the Greeks.
Which had, Achilles doth a council cite,
Embold'ning Chalcas, in the king's despite,
To tell the truth why they were punish'd so:
From hence their fierce and deadly strife did grow,
For wrong in which Aeacides so raves,
That goddess Thetis, from her throne of waves
Ascending heaven, of Jove assistance won,
To plague the Greeks by absence of her son;
And make the general himself repent,
To wrong so much his army's ornament.
This found by Juno, she with Jove contends;
Till Vulcan, with heaven's cup, the quarrel ends.

Another Argument

Alpha the prayer of Chryses sings:
The army's plague: the strife of kings.

BOOK ONE

ACHILLES' baneful wrath – resound, O goddess – that impos'd
Infinite sorrows on the Greeks, and many brave souls loos'd
From breasts heroic; sent them far, to that invisible cave
That no light comforts; and their limbs to dogs and vultures gave:
To all which Jove's will gave effect; from whom first strife begun
Betwixt Atrides, king of men, and Thetis' godlike son.
    What god gave Eris their command, and op'd that fighting vein?
Jove's and Latona's son: who, fir'd against the king of men
For contumely shown his priest, infectious sickness sent
To plague the army, and to death by troops the soldiers went –   10
Occasion'd thus: Chryses, the priest, came to the fleet to buy
For presents of unvalu'd price, his daughter's liberty:
The golden sceptre and the crown of Phoebus in his hands,
Proposing; and made suit to all, but most to the commands
Of both th' Atrides, who most rul'd. 'Great Atreus' sons,' said he,
'And all ye well-greav'd Greeks, the gods, whose habitations be
In heavenly houses, grace your powers with Priam's razed town,
And grant ye happy conduct home: to win which wish'd renown
Of Jove, by honouring his son (far-shooting Phoebus), deign
For these fit presents to dissolve the ransomable chain   20
Of my lov'd daughter's servitude.' The Greeks entirely gave
Glad acclamations, for sign that their desires would have
The grave priest reverenc'd, and his gifts of so much price embrac'd.
The general yet bore no such mind, but viciously disgrac'd
With violent terms the priest; and said: 'Dotard! Avoid our fleet;
Where ling'ring be not found by me, nor thy returning feet
Let ever visit us again, lest nor thy godhead's crown
Nor sceptre save thee! Her thou seek'st I still will hold mine own
Till age deflow'r her. In our court at Argos, far transferr'd
From her lov'd country, she shall ply her web, and see prepar'd   30
With all fit ornaments my bed. Incense me then no more;
But if thou wilt be safe, begone.' This said, the sea-beat shore
(Obeying his high will) the priest trod off with haste and fear;
And walking silent, till he left far off his enemies' ear,
Phoebus, fair-hair'd Latona's son, he stirr'd up with a vow

To this stern purpose: 'Hear, thou god that bear'st the silver bow,
That Chrysa guard'st, rul'st Tenedos with strong hand, and the round
Of Cilla most divine dost walk – O Sminthius! If crown'd
With thankful offerings thy rich fane I ever saw, or fir'd
Fat thighs of oxen and of goats to thee, this grace desir'd   40
Vouchsafe to me: pains for my tears, let these rude Greeks repay,
Forc'd with thy arrows.' Thus he pray'd, and Phoebus heard him pray;
And vex'd at heart, down from the tops of steep heaven stoop'd; his bow
And quiver cover'd round, his hands did on his shoulders throw;
And of the angry deity the arrows as he mov'd
Rattled about him. Like the night he rang'd the host, and rov'd
(Apart the fleet set) terribly: with his hard-loosing hand
His silver bow twang'd; and his shafts did first the mules command
And swift hounds; then the Greeks themselves his deadly arrows shot.
The fires of death went never out: nine days his shafts flew hot   50
About the army; and the tenth, Achilles called a court
Of all the Greeks: heaven's white-arm'd queen (who everywhere cut short,
Beholding her lov'd Greeks, by death) suggested it; and he –
All met in one – arose, and said: 'Atrides, now I see
We must be wandering again, flight must be still our stay
(If flight can save us now); at once sickness and battle lay
Such strong hand on us. Let us ask some prophet, priest, or prove
Some dream-interpreter (for dreams are often sent from Jove)
Why Phoebus is so much incens'd; if unperformed vows
He blames in us, or hecatombs; and if these knees he bows   60
To death, may yield his graves no more: but offering all supply
Of savours burnt from lambs and goats, avert his fervent eye,
And turn his temperate.' Thus, he sate: and then stood up to them
Chalcas, surnam'd Thestorides, of augurs the supreme:
(He knew things present, past, to come; and rul'd the equipage
Of th' Argive fleet to Ilion for his prophetic rage
Given by Apollo:) who, well-seen in th' ill they felt, propos'd
This to Achilles: 'Jove's belov'd, would thy charge see disclos'd
The secret of Apollo's wrath? Then covenant and take oath
To my discovery – that with words and powerful actions both,   70
Thy strength will guard the truth in me, because I well conceive
That he whose empire governs all, whom all the Grecians give
Confirm'd obedience, will be mov'd; and then you know the state
Of him that moves him, when a king hath once mark'd for his hate
A man inferior: though that day his wrath seems to digest
Th' offence he takes, yet evermore he rakes up in his breast
Brands of quick anger, till revenge hath quench'd to his desire
The fire reserved. Tell me, then, if whatsoever ire

Suggests in hurt of me to him, thy valour will prevent?'
   Achilles answer'd: 'All thou know'st speak, and be confident: 80
For by Apollo, Jove's belov'd (to whom performing vows,
O Chalcas, for the state of Greece, thy spirit prophetic shows
Skills that direct us), not a man of all these Grecians here –
I living, and enjoying the light shot through this flowery sphere –
Shall touch thee with offensive hands, though Agamemnon be
The man in question, that doth boast the mightiest empery
Of all our army.' Then took heart the prophet, unreprov'd,
And said: 'They are not unpaid vows, nor hecatombs, that mov'd
The god against us: his offence is for his priest impair'd
By Agamemnon, that refus'd the present he preferr'd,   90
And kept his daughter. This is cause why heaven's Far-darter darts
These plagues amongst us; and this still will empty in our hearts
His deathful quiver, uncontain'd, till to her loved sire
The black-eyed damsel be resign'd; no redemptory hire
Took for her freedom – not a gift – but all the ransom quit,
And she convey'd, with sacrifice, till her enfranchis'd feet
Tread Chrysa under: then the god, so pleas'd, perhaps we may
Move to remission.' Thus, he sate; and up, the great in sway,
Heroic Agamemnon rose, eagerly bearing all:
His mind's seat overcast with fumes: an anger general   100
Fill'd all his faculties; his eyes sparkled like kindling fire,
Which sternly cast upon the priest, thus vented he his ire:
   'Prophet of ill! For never good came from thee towards me
Not to a word's worth: evermore thou took'st delight to be
Offensive in thy auguries, which thou continuest still,
Now casting thy prophetic gall, and vouching all our ill
(Shot from Apollo) is impos'd since I refus'd the price
Of fair Chryseis' liberty; which would in no worth rise
To my rate of herself: which moves my vows to have her home,
Past Clytemnestra loving her, that grac'd my nuptial room   110
With her virginity and flower: nor ask her merits less,
For person, disposition, wit, and skill in housewif'ries.
And yet, for all this, she shall go, if more conducible
That course be than her holding here. I rather wish the weal
Of my lov'd army than the death. Provide yet instantly
Supply for her, that I alone of all our royalty
Lose not my winnings: 'tis not fit: ye see all – I lose mine
Forc'd by another – see as well, some other may resign
His prize to me.' To this replied the swift-foot, god-like son
Of Thetis, thus: 'King of us all in all ambition,   120
Most covetous of all that breathe, why should the great-soul'd Greeks

Supply thy lost prize out of theirs? Nor what thy avarice seeks
Our common treasury can find; so little it doth guard
Of what our raz'd towns yielded us, of all which most is shar'd,
And given our soldiers: which again to take into our hands
Were ignominious and base. Now then, since god commands,
Part with thy most-lov'd prize to him: not any one of us
Exacts it of thee; yet we all, all loss thou suffer'st thus
Will treble – quadruple in gain, when Jupiter bestows
The sack of well-wall'd Troy on us; which by his word he owes.'   130

   'Do not deceive yourself with wit,' he answer'd, 'god-like man,
Though your good name may colour it, 'tis not your swift foot can
Outrun me here; nor shall the gloss set on it with the god
Persuade me to my wrong. Wouldst thou maintain in sure abode
Thine own prize, and slight me of mine? Resolve this: if our friends,
As fits in equity my worth, will right me with amends,
So rest it; otherwise, myself will enter personally
On thy prize, that of Ithacus, or Ajax, for supply:
Let him on whom I enter rage. But come, we'll order these
Hereafter, and in other place. Now put to sacred seas   140
Our black sail; in it rowers put, in it fit sacrifice;
And to these I will make ascend my so much envied prize,
Bright-cheek'd Chryseis. For conduct of all which, we must choose
A chief out of our counsellors; thy service we must use,
Idomeneus; Ajax, thine; or thine, wise Ithacus;
Or thine, thou terriblest of men, thou son of Peleus:
Which fittest were, that thou might'st see these holy acts perform'd
For which thy cunning zeal so pleads; and he, whose bow thus storm'd
For our offences, may be calm'd.' Achilles with a frown
Thus answer'd: 'O thou impudent! Of no good but thine own   150
Ever respectful, but of that with all craft covetous:
With what heart can a man attempt a service dangerous –
Or at thy voice be spirited to fly upon a foe –
Thy mind thus wretched? For myself, I was not injur'd so
By any Trojan, that my powers should bid them any blows;
In nothing bear they blame of me: Phthia, whose bosom flows
With corn and people, never felt impair of her increase
By their invasion: hills enow, and far-resounding seas,
Pour out their shades and deeps between: but thee, thou frontless man,
We follow, and thy triumphs make, with bonfires of our bane: 160
Thine, and thy brother's vengeance sought, thou dog's eyes, of this Troy
By our expos'd lives; whose deserts thou neither dost employ
With honour nor with care. And now, thou threat'st to force from me
The fruit of my sweat, which the Greeks gave all: and though it be –

Compar'd with thy part, then snatch'd up – nothing, nor ever is
At any sack'd town; but of fight, the fetcher in of this,
My hands have most share: in whose toils when I have emptied me
Of all my forces, my amends in liberality –
Though it be little – I accept, and turn pleas'd to my tent:
And yet that little, thou esteem'st too great a continent   170
In thy incontinent avarice. For Phthia therefore now
My course is, since 'tis better far, than here t' endure that thou
Should'st still be ravishing my right, draw my whole treasure dry – '
    'And add, dishonour,' he replied: 'if thy heart serve thee, flee;
Stay not for my cause; other here will aid and honour me:
If not, yet Jove I know is sure; that counsellor is he
That I depend on: as for thee, of all our Jove-kept kings
Thou still art most mine enemy: strifes, battles, bloody things,
Make thy blood feasts still. But if strength, that these moods build upon,
Flow in thy nerves, god gave thee it; and so 'tis not thine own,   180
But in his hands still: what then lifts thy pride in this so high?
Home with thy fleet, and myrmidons; use there their empery:
Command not here. I weigh thee not, nor mean to magnify
Thy rough-hewn rages; but instead I thus far threaten thee:
Since Phoebus needs will force from me Chryseis, she shall go;
My ships and friends shall waft her home: but I will imitate so
His pleasure, that mine own shall take, in person, from thy tent
Bright-cheek'd Briseis; and so tell thy strength how eminent
My power is, being compar'd with thine: all other making fear
To vaunt equality with me, or in this proud kind bear   190
Their beards against me.' Thetis' son at this stood vex'd, his heart
Bristled his bosom, and two ways drew his discursive part,
If from his thigh his sharp sword drawn, he should make room about
Atrides' person, slaught'ring him, or sit his anger out,
And curb his spirit. While these thoughts striv'd in his blood and mind,
And he his sword drew, down from heaven Athenia stoop'd, and shin'd
About his temples: being sent by th' ivory-wristed queen
Saturnia, who out of her heart had ever loving been
And careful for the good of both. She stood behind, and took
Achilles by the yellow curls, and only gave her look   200
To him; appearance not a man of all the rest could see.
He, turning back his eye, amaze strook every faculty:
Yet straight he knew her by her eyes, so terrible they were,
Sparkling with ardour, and thus spake: 'Thou seed of Jupiter,
Why com'st thou? To behold his pride that boasts our empery?
Then witness with it my revenge, and see that insolence die
That lives to wrong me.' She replied, 'I come from heaven to see

Thine anger settled, if thy soul will use her sovereignty
In fit reflection. I am sent from Juno, whose affects
Stand heartily inclin'd to both: come, give us both, respects;   210
And cease contention: draw no sword; use words, and such as may
Be bitter to his pride, but just; for trust in what I say,
A time shall come, when thrice the worth of that he forceth now,
He shall propose for recompense of these wrongs: therefore throw
Reins on thy passions, and serve us.' He answer'd: 'Though my heart
Burn in just anger, yet my soul must conquer th' angry part,
And yield you conquest: who subdues his earthy part for heaven,
Heaven to his prayers subdues his wish.' This said, her charge was given
Fit honour: in his silver hilt he held his able hand,
And forc'd his broad sword up; and up to heaven did re-ascend   220
Minerva, who, in Jove's high roof that bears the rough shield, took
Her place with other deities. She gone, again forsook
Patience his passion, and no more his silence could confine
His wrath, that this broad language gave: 'Thou ever steep'd in wine!
Dog's face, with heart but of a hart, that nor in th' open eye
Of fight dar'st thrust into a press, nor with our noblest lie
In secret ambush. These works seem too full of death for thee:
Tis safer far in th' open host to dare an injury
To any crosser of thy lust. Thou subject-eating king!
Base spirits thou govern'st, or this wrong had been the last foul thing   230
Thou ever author'dst: yet I vow, and by a great oath swear,
Even by this sceptre, that as this never again shall bear
Green leaves or branches, nor increase with any growth his size,
Nor did since first it left the hills, and had his faculties
And ornaments bereft with iron; which now to other end
Judges of Greece bear, and their laws, receiv'd from Jove, defend
(For which my oath to thee is great): so, whensoever need
Shall burn with thirst of me thy host, no prayers shall ever breed
Affection in me to their aid, though well-deserved woes
Afflict thee for them, when to death man-slaught'ring Hector throws   240
Whole troops of them, and thou torment'st thy vex'd mind with conceit
Of thy rude rage now, and his wrong that most deserv'd the right
Of all thy army.' Thus: he threw his sceptre gainst the ground,
With golden studs stuck, and took seat. Atrides' breast was drown'd
In rising choler. Up to both sweet-spoken Nestor stood,
The cunning Pylian orator; whose tongue pour'd forth a flood
Of more than honey-sweet discourse (two ages were increas'd
Of divers-languag'd men, all born in his time and deceas'd,
In sacred Pylos, where he reign'd amongst the third ag'd men):
He, well-seen in the world, advis'd, and thus express'd it then.   250

'O gods! Our Greek earth will be drown'd in just tears; rapeful Troy,
Her king, and all his sons, will make as just a mock, and joy
Of these disjunctions, if of you, that all our host excel
In counsel and in skill of fight, they hear this: come, repel
These young men's passions; y'are not both, put both your years in one,
So old as I: I liv'd long since, and was companion
With men superior to you both, who yet would ever hear
My counsels with respect. Mine eyes yet never witness were,
Nor ever will be, of such men as then delighted them –
Perithous, Exadius, and god-like Polyphem,   260
Ceneus, and Dryas prince of men, Aegean Theseus,
A man like heaven's immortals form'd; all, all most vigorous,
Of all men that even those days bred; most vigorous men, and fought
With beasts most vigorous – mountain beasts! – (for men in strength were nought
Match'd with their forces) – fought with them, and bravely fought them down.
Yet even with these men I convers'd, being call'd to the renown
Of their societies, by their suites, from Pylos far, to fight
In th' Asian kingdom; and I fought to a degree of might
That help'd even their mights, against such, as no man now would dare
To meet in conflict: yet even these my counsels still would hear,   270
And with obedience crown my words. Give you such palm to them;
'Tis better than to wreathe your wrath. Atrides, give not stream
To all thy power, nor force his prize; but yield her still his own,
As all men else do. Nor do thou, encounter with thy crown,
Great son of Peleus, since no king that ever Jove allow'd
Grace of a sceptre, equals him. Suppose thy nerves endow'd
With strength superior, and thy birth a very goddess gave,
Yet he of force is mightier, since what his own nerves have,
Is amplied with just command of many other. King of men,
Command thou then thyself; and I with my prayers will obtain   280
Grace of Achilles to subdue his fury: whose parts are
Worth our intreaty, being chief check to all our ill in war.'
   'All this, good father,' said the king, 'is comely and good right,
But this man breaks all such bounds; he affects past all men, height;
All would in his power hold; all make his subjects; give to all
His hot will for a temperate law: all which he never shall
Persuade at my hands. If the gods have given him the great style
Of ablest soldier, made they that his licence to revile
Men with vile language?' Thetis' son prevented him, and said:
   'Fearful and vile I might be thought, if the exactions laid   290
By all means on me I should bear. Others command to this,
Thou shalt not me; or if thou dost, far my free spirit is
From serving thy command. Beside this I affirm – afford

Impression of it in thy soul – I will not use my sword
On thee or any for a wench, unjustly though thou tak'st
The thing thou gav'st; but all things else that in my ship thou mak'st
Greedy survey of, do not touch without my leave; or do –
Add that act's wrong to this, that these may see that outrage too –
And then comes my part; then be sure thy blood upon my lance
Shall flow in vengeance.' These high terms these two at variance　　　300
Us'd to each other; left their seats, and after them arose
The whole court. To his tents and ships, with friends and soldiers, goes
Angry Achilles. Atreus' son the swift ship launch'd, and put
Within it twenty chosen row'rs; within it likewise shut
The hecatomb, t'appease the god: then caus'd to come aboard
Fair-cheek'd Chryseis. For the chief, he in whom Pallas pour'd
Her store of counsels, Ithacus, aboard went last, and then
The moist ways of the sea they sail'd. And now the king of men
Bade all the host to sacrifice. They sacrific'd, and cast
The offal of all to the deeps; the angry god they grac'd　　　310
With perfect hecatombs: some bulls, some goats, along the shore
Of the unfruitful sea, inflam'd. To heaven the thick fumes bore
Enwrapped savours. Thus, though all the politic king made shew
Respects to heaven, yet he himself all that time did pursue
His own affections. The late jar, in which he thunder'd threats
Against Achilles, still he fed; and his affections' heats
Thus vented to Talthibius and grave Eurybates,
Heralds, and ministers of trust, to all his messages:

　　'Haste to Achilles tent; where take Briseis' hand, and bring
Her beauties to us: if he fail to yield her, say your king　　　320
Will come himself, with multitudes that shall the horribler
Make both his presence, and your charge, that so he dares defer.'

　　This said, he sent them with a charge of hard condition.
They went unwillingly, and trod the fruitless sea's shore; soon
They reach'd the navy and the tents, in which the quarter lay
Of all the myrmidons, and found the chief Chief in their sway,
Set at his black bark in his tent. Nor was Achilles glad
To see their presence; nor themselves in any glory had
Their message, but with reverence stood, and fear'd th' offended king:
Ask'd not the dame, nor spake a word. He, yet well knowing the thing
That caus'd their coming, grac'd them thus: 'Heralds, ye men that bear
The messages of men and gods, y'are welcome, come ye near:
I nothing blame you, but your king: 'tis he I know doth send
You for Briseis, she is his. Patroclus, honour'd friend,
Bring forth the damsel, and these men let lead her to their lord;
But, heralds, be you witnesses before the most ador'd,

Before us mortals, and before your most ungentle king,
Of what I suffer: that if war ever hereafter bring
My aid in question, to avert any severest bane
It brings on others, I am 'scus'd to keep mine aid in wane,   340
Since they mine honour. But your king, in tempting mischief, raves;
Nor sees at once by present things the future: how like waves
Ills follow ills; injustices being never so secure
In present times, but after-plagues even then are seen as sure –
Which yet he sees not; and so soothes his present lust, which check'd,
Would check plagues future; and he might, in succouring right, protect
Such as fight for his right at fleet; they still in safety fight
That fight still justly.' This speech us'd, Patroclus did the rite
His friend commanded, and brought forth Briseis from her tent,
Gave her the heralds, and away to th' Achive ships they went: 350
She sad and scarce for grief could go; her love all friends forsook,
And wept for anger. To the shore of th' old sea, he, betook
Himself alone, and casting forth upon the purple sea
His wet eyes, and his hands to heaven advancing, this sad plea
Made to his mother: 'Mother! Since you brought me forth to breathe
So short a life, Olympius had good right to bequeath
My short life, honour: yet that right he doth in no degree,
But lets Atrides do me shame, and force that prize from me
That all the Greeks gave.' This with tears he utter'd, and she heard –
Set with her old sire in his deeps – and instantly appear'd   360
Up from the gray sea like a cloud; sate by his side, and said:
    'Why weeps my son? What grieves thee? Speak; conceal not what hath laid
Such hard hand on thee; let both know.' He, sighing like a storm,
Replied: 'Thou dost know; why should I things known again inform?
We march'd to Thebes, the sacred town of king Eëtion,
Sack'd it, and brought to fleet the spoil; which every valiant son
Of Greece indifferently shar'd. Atrides had for share
Fair-cheek'd Chryseis: after which, his priest, that shoots so far,
Chryses, the fair Chryseis' sire, arriv'd at th' Achive fleet
With infinite ransom, to redeem the dear imprison'd feet   370
Of his fair daughter. In his hands he held Apollo's crown
And golden sceptre, making suit to every Grecian son,
But most the sons of Atreus (the other's orderers).
Yet they least heard him; all the rest receiv'd with reverend ears
The motion: both the priest and gifts gracing, and holding worth
His wish'd acceptance. Atreus' son, yet (vex'd) commanded forth
With rude terms Phoebus' reverend priest: who angry, made retreat,
And pray'd to Phoebus; in whose grace he standing passing great,
Got his petition. The god an ill shaft sent abroad,

That tumbled down the Greeks in heaps. The host had no abode   380
That was not visited. We ask'd a prophet that well knew
The cause of all, and from his lips Apollo's prophecies flew,
Telling his anger. First myself exhorted to appease
The anger'd god, which Atreus' son did at the heart displease;
And up he stood – us'd threats – perform'd. The black-ey'd Greeks sent home
Chryseis to her sire, and gave his god a hecatomb:
Then, for Briseis, to my tents Atrides' heralds came,
And took her that the Greeks gave all. If then thy powers can frame
Wreak for thy son, afford it; scale Olympus, and implore
Jove, if by either word or fact thou ever didst restore   390
Joy to his griev'd heart, now to help. I oft have heard thee vaunt
In court of Peleus, that alone thy hand was conversant
In rescue from a cruel spoil the black-cloud-gathering Jove,
Whom other godheads would have bound (the power whose pace doth move
The round earth, heaven's great queen, and Pallas): to whose bands
Thou cam'st with rescue, bringing up him with the hundred hands
To great Olympus whom the gods call Briaraeus, men
Aegaeon; who his sire surpass'd, and was as strong again;
And in that grace sat glad by Jove: th' immortals stood dismay'd
At his ascension, and gave free passage to his aid.   400
Of all this tell Jove; kneel to him, embrace his knee, and pray,
If Troy's aid he will ever deign, that now their forces may
Beat home the Greeks to fleet and sea, embruing their retreat
In slaughter, their pains paying the wreak of their proud sovereign's heat;
And that far-ruling king may know from his poor soldier's harms
His own harm falls: his own and all in mine, his best in arms.'

    Her answer she pour'd out in tears: 'O me, my son,' said she,
'Why brought I up thy being at all, that brought thee forth to be
Sad subject of so hard a fate? O would to heaven, that since
Thy fate is little, and not long, thou might'st without offence   410
And tears perform it! But to live thrall to so stern a fate
As grants thee least life, and that least so most unfortunate,
Grieves me t' have given thee any life. But what thou wishest now,
If Jove will grant, I'll up and ask: Olympus crown'd with snow
I'll climb: but sit thou fast at fleet; renounce all war, and feed
Thy heart with wrath, and hope of wreak; till which come, thou shalt need
A little patience: Jupiter went yesterday to feast
Amongst the blameless Aethiops, in th' Ocean's deepen'd breast,
All gods attending him: the twelfth, high heaven again he sees,
And then his brass-pav'd court I'll scale, cling to his pow'rful knees, 420
And doubt not but to win thy wish.' Thus, made she her remove,
And left wrath tyring on her son, for his enforced love.

Ulysses, with the hecatomb, arriv'd at Chrysa's shore:
And when amidst the hav'n's deep mouth they came to use the oar,
They straight struck sail: then roll'd them up, and on the hatches threw.
The top-mast to the kelsine then with halyards down they drew;
They brought the ship to port with oars; then forked anchor cast;
And 'gainst the violence of storm, for drifting made her fast.

   All come ashore, they all expos'd the holy hecatomb
To angry Phoebus; and with it, Chryseis welcom'd home: 430
Whom to her sire, wise Ithacus, that did at th' altar stand,
For honour, led; and, speaking thus, resign'd her to his hand:
'Chryses, the mighty king of men, great Agamemnon, sends
Thy lov'd seed by my hands to thine; and to thy god commends
A hecatomb, which my charge is to sacrifice, and seek
Our much-sigh mix'd-woe, his recure, invok'd by every Greek.

   Thus he resign'd her, and her sire receiv'd her highly joy'd.
About the well-built altar then they orderly employ'd
The sacred offering: wash'd their hands, took salt cakes, and the priest,
With hands held up to heaven, thus pray'd: 'O thou that all things seest,
Fautour of Chrysa, whose fair hand doth guardfully dispose
Celestial Cilia, governing in all pow'r Tenedos –
O hear thy priest! And as thy hand, in free grace to my prayers
Shot fervent plague-shafts through the Greeks, now hearten their affairs
With health renew'd; and quite remove th' infection from their blood.'

   He pray'd; and to his pray'rs again the god propitious stood.
All, after pray'r, cast on salt cakes; drew back, kill'd, flay'd the beeves,
Cut out and dubb'd with fat their thighs, fair dress'd with doubled leaves;
And on them all the sweetbreads prick'd. The priest, with small sere wood
Did sacrifice, pour'd on red wine; by whom the young men stood,   450
And turn'd, in five ranks, spits; on which (the legs enough) they eat
The inwards; then in giggots cut the other fit for meat,
And put to fire; which roasted well they drew: the labour done,
They serv'd the feast in that fed all to satisfaction.

   Desire of meat and wine thus quench'd, the youths crown'd cups of wine,
Drunk off, and fill'd again to all. That day was held divine,
And spent in paeans to the Sun, who heard with pleased ear;
When whose bright chariot stoop'd to sea, and twilight hid the clear,
All soundly on their cables slept, even till the night was worn:
And when the lady of the light, the rosy-finger'd Morn,   460
Rose from the hills, all fresh arose, and to the camp retir'd.
Apollo with a fore-right wind their swelling bark inspir'd:
The top-mast hoisted, milk-white sails on his round breast they put;
The mizens strooted with the gale, the ship her course did cut
So swiftly, that the parted waves against her ribs did roar;

Which coming to the camp, they drew aloft the sandy shore:
Where, laid on stocks, each soldier kept his quarter as before.
   But Peleus' son, swift-foot Achilles, at his swift ships sate
Burning in wrath, nor ever came to councils of estate
That make men honour'd; never trod the fierce embattled field;   470
But kept close, and his lov'd heart pin'd: what fight and cries could yield,
Thirsting at all parts to the host. And now since first he told
His wrongs to Thetis, twelve fair morns their ensigns did unfold,
And then the ever-living gods mounted Olympus, Jove
First in ascension. Thetis then remember'd well to move
Achilles motion: rose from the sea, and by the morn's first light,
The great heaven and Olympus climb'd; where in supremest height
Of all that many-headed hill, she saw the far-seen son
Of Saturn, set from all the rest, in his free seat alone:
Before whom (on her own knees fall'n) the knees of Jupiter   480
Her left hand held, her right his chin; and thus she did prefer
Her son's petition: 'Father Jove! If ever I have stood
Aidful to thee in word or work, with this implored good
Requite my aid, renown my son, since in so short a race
(Past others) thou confin'st his life: an insolent disgrace
Is done him by the king of men; he forc'd from him a prize
Won with his sword. But thou, O Jove, that art most strong, most wise,
Honour my son for my sake; add strength to the Trojans side
By his side's weakness, in his want; and see Troy amplified
In conquest, so much, and so long, till Greece may give again   490
The glory reft him; and the more illustrate the free reign
Of his wrong'd honour.' Jove at this sate silent, not a word
In long space pass'd him. Thetis still hung on his knee, implor'd
The second time his help, and said: 'Grant, or deny my suit,
Be free in what thou doest; I know thou canst not sit thus mute
For fear of any; speak, deny, that so I may be sure,
Of all heaven's goddesses, 'tis I that only must endure
Dishonour by thee.' Jupiter, the great cloud-gatherer, griev'd
With thought of what a world of griefs this suit ask'd, being achiev'd,
Swell'd, sigh'd, and answer'd: 'Works of death thou urgest; O at this   500
Juno will storm, and all my powers inflame with contumelies.
Ever she wrangles, charging me in ear of all the gods
That I am partial still; that I add the displeasing odds
Of my aid to the Ilians. Begone then, lest she see:
Leave thy request to my care: yet, that trust may hearten thee
With thy desire's grant, and my power to give it act approve
How vain her strife is, to thy prayer my eminent head shall move;
Which is the great sign of my will with all th' immortal states;

Irrevocable; never fails; never without the rates
Of all powers else: when my head bows, all heads bow with it still   510
As their first mover, and gives power to any work I will.'
    He said; and his black eyebrows bent; above his deathless head
Th' ambrosian curls flow'd; great heaven shook, and both were severed,
Their counsels broken. To the depth of Neptune's kingdom, div'd
Thetis from heaven's height: Jove arose, and all the gods receiv'd
(All rising from their thrones) their sire, attending to his court:
None sate when he arose; none delay'd the furnishing his port
Till he came near: all met with him, and brought him to his throne.
    Nor sate great Juno ignorant, when she beheld alone
Old Nereus' silver-footed seed with Jove, that she had brought   520
Counsels to heaven; and straight her tongue had teeth in it, that wrought
This sharp invective: 'Who was that (thou craftiest counsellor
Of all the gods), that so apart some secret did implore?
Ever apart from me, thou lov'st to counsel and decree
Things of more close trust, than thou think'st are fit t'impart to me:
Whatever thou determin'st, I must ever be denied
The knowledge of it by thy will.' To her speech thus replied
The father both of men and gods: 'Have never hope to know
My whole intentions, though my wife: it fits not, nor would show
Well to thine own thoughts: but what fits thy woman's ear to hear,   530
Woman, nor man, nor god shall know before it grace thine ear:
Yet what apart from men and gods I please to know, forbear
T'examine, or inquire of that.' She with the cow's fair eyes,
Respected Juno, this return'd: 'Austere king of the skies,
What hast thou utter'd! When did I before this time inquire,
Or sift thy counsels? Passing close you are still; your desire
Is serv'd with such care, that I fear you can scarce vouch the deed
That makes it public; being seduc'd by this old sea-god's seed,
That could so early use her knees, embracing thine. I doubt
The late act of thy bowed head, was for the working out   540
Of some boon she ask'd; that her son, thy partial hand would please
With plaguing others.' 'Wretch!' said he, 'thy subtle jealousies
Are still exploring: my designs can never 'scape thine eye,
Which yet thou never canst prevent. Thy curiosity
Makes thee less car'd for at my hands, and horrible the end
Shall make thy humour. If it be what thy suspects intend,
What then? 'Tis my free will it should: to which let way be given
With silence; curb your tongue in time, lest all the gods in heaven
Too few be and too weak to help thy punish'd insolence,
When my inaccessible hands shall fall on thee.' The sense   550
Of this high threat'ning made her fear, and silent she sate down,

Humbling her great heart. All the gods in court of Jove did frown
At this offence giv'n: amongst whom heav'n's famous artizan,
Ephaistus, in his mother's care this comely speech began
    'Believe it, these words will breed wounds beyond our powers to bear,
If thus for mortals ye fall out. Ye make a tumult here
That spoils our banquet. Evermore worst matters put down best.
But, mother, though yourself be wise, yet let your son request
His wisdom's audience. Give good terms to our lov'd father Jove,
For fear he take offence again, and our kind banquet prove   560
A wrathful battle. If he will, the heavenly light'ner can
Take you and toss you from your throne; his power Olympian
Is so surpassing. Soften then with gentle speech his spleen,
And drink to him; I know his heart will quickly down again.'
    This said, arising from his throne, in his lov'd mother's hand
He put the double-handled cup, and said: 'Come, do not stand
On these cross humours; suffer, bear, though your great bosom grieve,
And lest blows force you, all my aid not able to relieve
Your hard condition, though these eyes behold it, and this heart
Sorrow to think it; 'tis a task too dangerous to take part   570
Against Olympius. I myself the proof of this still feel:
When other gods would fain have help'd, he took me by the heel,
And hurl'd me out of heaven: all day I was in falling down;
At length in Lemnos I struck earth: the likewise falling sun
And I, together set: my life almost set too: yet there
The Sintii cheer'd and took me up.' This did to laughter cheer
White-wristed Juno, who now took the cup of him, and smil'd.
The sweet peace-making draught went round, and lame Ephaistus fil'd
Nectar to all the other gods. A laughter never left,
Shook all the blessed deities, to see the lame so deft   580
At that cup service. All that day even till the sun went down,
They banqueted; and had such cheer as did their wishes crown.
Nor had they music less divine: Apollo there did touch
His most sweet harp; to which with voice, the Muses pleas'd as much.
But when the sun's fair light was set – each godhead to his house
Address'd for sleep, where every one with art most curious,
By heaven's great both-foot-halting god a several roof had built –
Even he to sleep went by whose hand heaven is with lightning gilt,
High Jove, where he had us'd to rest, when sweet sleep seiz'd his eyes;
By him the golden-thron'd queen slept, the queen of deities.   590

THE END OF THE FIRST BOOK

BOOK TWO

The Argument

Jove calls a vision up from Somnus' den,
To bid Atrides muster up his men.
The King – to Greeks dissembling his desire –
Persuades them to their country to retire.
By Pallas' will, Ulysses stays their flight,
And wise old Nestor heartens them to fight.
They take their meat: which done, to arms they go
And march in good array against the foe.
So those of Troy: when Iris from the sky,
Of Saturn's son performs the embassy.

Another Argument

Beta the dream and synod cites;
And catalogues the naval knights.

BOOK TWO

THE OTHER GODS, and knights at arms, all night slept; only Jove
Sweet slumber seiz'd not: he discours'd how best he might approve
His vow made for Achilles' grace; and make the Grecians find
His miss in much death. All ways cast, this counsel serv'd his mind
With most allowance: to dispatch a harmful dream to greet
The king of men; and gave this charge: 'Go to the Achive fleet,
Pernicious dream, and being arriv'd in Agamemnon's tent,
Deliver truly all this charge: command him to convent
His whole host arm'd before these towers; for now Troy's broad-way'd town
He shall take in: the heaven-hous'd gods are now indifferent grown;   10
Juno's request hath won them: Troy now under imminent ills
At all parts labours.' This charge heard the vision straight fulfils;
The ships reach'd, and Atrides' tent in which he found him laid;
Divine sleep pour'd about his powers. He stood above his head
Like Nestor (grac'd of old men most), and this did intimate:

'Sleeps the wise Atreus' tame-horse son? A counsellor of state
Must not the whole night spend in sleep: to whom the people are
For guard committed, and whose life stands bound to so much care.
Now hear me then (Jove's messenger), who though far off from thee,
Is near thee yet in love and care; and gives command by me,   20
To arm thy whole host. Thy strong hand the broad-way'd town of Troy
Shall now take in: no more the gods dissentiously employ
Their high-hous'd powers: Juno's suit hath won them all to her;
And ill fates overhang these towers, address'd by Jupiter.
Fix in thy mind this; nor forget to give it action, when
Sweet sleep shall leave thee.' Thus, he fled; and left the king of men
Repeating in discourse his dream; and dreaming still, awake,
Of power, not ready yet for act. O fool! He thought to take
In that next day old Priam's town, not knowing what affairs
Jove had in purpose; who prepar'd, by strong light, sighs and cares   30
For Greeks and Trojans. The dream gone, his voice still murmured
About the king's ears: who sate up, put on him in his bed
His silken inner weed, fair, new, and then in haste arose;
Cast on his ample mantle, tied to his soft feet fair shoes;
His silver-hilted sword he hung about his shoulders, took

His father's sceptre never stain'd; which then abroad he shook,
And went to fleet. And now great heaven goddess Aurora scal'd,
To Jove and all gods bringing light, when Agamemnon call'd
His heralds, charging them aloud to call to instant court
The thick-hair'd Greeks. The heralds call'd, the Greeks made quick resort.
The council chiefly he compos'd of old great minded men,
At Nestor's ships, the Pylian king: all there assembled, then
Thus Atreus' son began the court: 'Hear, friends: a dream divine
Amidst the calm night in my sleep did through my shut eyes shine,
Within my fantasy: his form did passing naturally
Resemble Nestor: such attire, a stature just as high,
He stood above my head, and words thus fashion'd did relate:

   "Sleeps the wise Atreus'-tame-horse son? A counsellor of state
Must not the whole night spend in sleep: to whom the people are
For guard committed, and whose life stands bound to so much care.   50
Now hear me then (Jove's messenger), who though far off from thee,
Is near thee yet in love and care; and gives command by me,
To arm thy whole host. Thy strong hand the broad-way'd town of Troy
Shall now take in: no more the gods dissentiously employ
Their high-hous'd powers: Saturnia's suit hath won them all to her;
And ill fates over-hang these towers, address'd by Jupiter.
Fix in thy mind this." This express'd, he took wing, and away;
And sweet sleep left me: let us then by all our means assay
To arm our army; I will first (as far as fits our right)
Try their addictions, and command with full sail'd ships our flight: 60
Which if they yield to, oppose you.' He sate, and up arose
Nestor, of sandy Pylos king: who, willing to dispose
Their counsel to the public good, propos'd this to the state:

   'Princes and councillors of Greece, if any should relate
This vision but the king himself, it might be held a tale,
And move the rather our retreat: but since our general
Affirms he saw it, hold it true; and all our best means make
To arm our army.' This speech us'd, he first the council brake:
The other sceptre-hearing states arose too, and obey'd
The people's rector. Being abroad, the earth was overlaid   70
With flockers to them that came forth: as when of frequent bees
Swarms rise out of a hollow rock, repairing the degrees
Of their egression endlessly, with ever rising new
From forth their sweet nest; as their store, still as it faded, grew,
And never would cease sending forth her clusters to the spring,
They still crowd out so, this flock here, that there, belabouring
The loaded flowers: so from the ships and tents the army's store
Troop'd to these princes, and the court, along th' unmeasur'd shore:

Amongst whom Jove's ambassadress, Fame in her virtue shin'd,
Exciting greediness to hear. The rabble thus inclin'd,   80
Hurried together; uproar seiz'd the high court; earth did groan
Beneath the settling multitude: tumult was there alone.
Thrice three vociferous heralds rose to check the rout, and get
Ear to their Jove-kept governors, and instantly was set
The huge confusion: every man set fast, the clamour ceas'd.
Then stood divine Atrides up, and in his hand compress'd
His sceptre, th' elaborate work of fiery Mulciber:
Who gave it to Saturnian Jove; Jove to his messenger;
His messenger, Argicides, to Pelops, skill'd in horse;
Pelops to Atreus, chief of men; he dying, gave it course   90
To Prince Thyestes, rich in herds; Thyestes to the hand
Of Agamemnon render'd it, and with it the command
Of many isles, and Argos all. On this he leaning, said
   'O friends, great sons of Danaus, servants of Mars, Jove laid
A heavy curse on me, to vow, and bind it with the bent
Of his high forehead, that (this Troy of all her people spent)
I should return, yet now to mock our hopes built on his vow,
And charge ingloriously my flight: when such an overthrow
Of brave friends I have authored. But to his mightiest will
We must submit us, that hath raz'd and will be razing still   100
Men's footsteps from so many towns: because his power is most,
He will destroy most. But how vile, such and so great an host
Will show to future times, that match'd with lesser numbers far,
We fly, not putting on the crown of our so long-held war:
Of which there yet appears no end. Yet should our foes and we
Strike truce, and number both our powers, Troy taking all that be
Her arm'd inhabitants, and we in tens should all sit down
At our truce banquet, every ten allow'd one of the town
To fill his feast-cup, many tens would their attendant want:
So much I must affirm our power exceeds th' inhabitant.   110
But their auxiliary bands, those brandishers of spears,
(From many cities drawn) are they that are our hinderers,
Not suff'ring well-rais'd Troy to fall. Nine years are ended now
Since Jove our conquest vow'd, and now our vessels rotten grow.
Our tackling fails; our wives, young sons, sit in their doors and long
For our arrival: yet the work that should have wreak'd our wrong,
And made us welcome, lies unwrought. Come then, as I bid all
Obey, and fly to our lov'd home: for now, nor ever, shall
Our utmost take in broad-way'd Troy.' This said, the multitude
Was all for home; and all men else, that what this would conclude   120
Had not discover'd. All the crowd was shov'd about the shore,

In sway, like rude and raging waves rous'd with the fervent blore
Of th' east and south winds, when they break from Jove's clouds, and are borne
On rough backs of th' Icarian seas: or like a field of corn
High grown, that Zephyr's vehement gusts bring easily underneath,
And make the stiff up-bristled ears do homage to his breath:
For even so easily, with the breath Atrides us'd, was sway'd
The violent multitude. To fleet with shouts, and disarray'd,
All rush'd; and with a fog of dust their rude feet dimm'd the day;
Each cried to other, 'Cleanse our ships; come, launch, aboard, away.'   130
The clamour of the runners home reach'd heaven; and then past fate,
The Greeks had left Troy, had not then the goddess of estate
Thus spoke to Pallas: 'O foul shame! Thou untam'd seed of Jove,
Shall thus the sea's broad back be charg'd with these our friends' remove,
Thus leaving Argive Helen here? Thus Priam grac'd? Thus Troy?
In whose fields, far from their lov'd own, for Helen's sake, the joy
And life of so much Grecian birth is vanish'd! Take thy way
T' our brass-arm'd people, speak them fair, let not a man obey
The charge now given, nor launch one ship.' She said, and Pallas did
As she commanded: from the tops of heaven's steep hill she slid,   140
And straight the Greeks' swift ships she reach'd: Ulysses (like to Jove
In gifts of counsel) she found out; who to that base remove
Stirr'd not a foot, nor touch'd a ship, but griev'd at heart to see
That fault in others. To him close, the blue-eyed deity
Made way, and said: 'Thou wisest Greek, divine Laertes' son,
Thus fly ye homewards to your ships? Shall all thus headlong run?
Glory to Priam thus ye leave, glory to all his friends,
If thus ye leave her here, for whom so many violent ends
Have clos'd your Greek eyes, and so far from their so loved home.
Go to these people, use no stay; with fair terms overcome   150
Their foul endeavour: not a man, a flying sail let hoice.'
    Thus spake she, and Ulysses knew 'twas Pallas by her voice:
Ran to the runners; cast from him his mantle, which his man
And herald, grave Eurybates, the Ithacensian
That follow'd him, took up. Himself to Agamemnon went,
His incorrupted sceptre took, his sceptre of descent,
And with it went about the fleet. What prince, or man of name,
He found flight-given, he would restrain with words of gentlest blame:
    'Good sir, it fits not you to fly, or fare as one afraid;
You should not only stay yourself, but see the people stayed.   160
You know not clearly – though you heard the king's words – yet his mind:
He only tries men's spirits now, and whom his trials find
Apt to this course, he will chastise. Nor you, nor I, heard all
He spake in council; nor durst press too near our general,

Lest we incens'd him to our hurt. The anger of a king
Is mighty: he is kept of Jove, and from Jove likewise spring,
His honours; which out of the love of wise Jove, he enjoys.'
Thus he the best sort us'd: the worst, whose spirits brake out in noise,
He cudgell'd with his sceptre, chid, and said: 'Stay, wretch; be still,
And hear thy betters; thou art base, and both in power and skill   170
Poor and unworthy, without name in counsel or in war.
We must not all be kings: the rule is most irregular
Where many rule: one lord, one king, propose to thee; and he
To whom wise Saturn's son hath giv'n both law and empery,
To rule the public, is that king.' Thus ruling, he restrain'd
The host from flight: and then again the council was maintain'd
With such a concourse, that the shore rang with the tumult made:
As when the far-resounding sea doth in his rage invade
His sandy confines, whose sides groan with his involved wave,
And make his own breast echo sighs. All sate, and audience gave;   180
Thersites only would speak all. A most disorder'd store
Of words he foolishly pour'd out; of which his mind held more
Than it could manage: any thing with which he could procure
Laughter, he never could contain. He should have yet been sure
To touch no kings: t' oppose their states becomes not jesters' parts.
But he the filthiest fellow was of all that had deserts
In Troy's brave siege: he was squint-ey'd, and lame of either foot;
So crook-back'd, that he had no breast; sharp-headed, where did shoot
(Here and there 'spers'd) thin mossy hair. He most of all envied
Ulysses and Aeacides, whom still his spleen would chide: 190
Nor could the sacred king himself avoid his saucy vein;
Against whom, since he knew the Greeks did vehement hates sustain,
(Being angry for Achilles wrong) he cried out, railing thus:

     'Atrides, why complain'st thou now? What would'st thou more of us?
Thy tents are full of brass, and dames; the choice of all are thine,
With whom we must present thee first, when any towns resign
To our invasion. Want'st thou then, besides all this, more gold
From Troy's knights to redeem their sons, whom to be dearly sold,
I or some other Greek must take? Or would'st thou yet again
Force from some other lord his prize, to soothe the lusts that reign   200
In thy encroaching appetite? It fits no prince to be
A prince of ill, and govern us, or lead our progeny
By rape to ruin. O base Greeks, deserving infamy,
And ills eternal! Greekish girls, not Greeks ye are: come, flee
Home with our ships; leave this man here to perish with his preys,
And try if we help'd him or not: he wrong'd a man that weighs
Far more than he himself in worth; he forc'd from Thetis' son

And keeps his prize still: nor think I, that mighty man hath won
The style of wrathful worthily; he's soft, he's too remiss,
Or else, Atrides, his had been thy last of injuries.'   210
   Thus he the people's pastor chid: but straight stood up to him
Divine Ulysses; who with looks exceeding grave and grim,
This bitter check gave: 'Cease, vain fool, to vent thy railing vein
On kings thus, though it serve thee well: nor think thou canst restrain,
With that thy railing faculty, their wills in least degree;
For not a worse of all this host, came with our king than thee,
To Troy's great siege: then do not take into that mouth of thine
The names of kings; much less revile the dignities that shine
In their supreme states: wresting thus this motion for our home,
To soothe thy cowardice; since ourselves yet know not what will come   220
Of these designments: if it be our good to stay, or go:
Nor is it that thou stand'st on; thou revil'st our general so,
Only because he hath so much, not given by such as thou,
But our heroes. Therefore this thy rude vein makes me vow,
(Which shall be curiously observ'd) if ever I shall hear
This madness from thy mouth again, let not Ulysses bear
This head, nor be the father call'd of young Telemachus,
If to thy nakedness I take and strip thee not, and thus
Whip thee to fleet from council; send with sharp stripes weeping hence,
This glory thou affect'st – to rail.' This said, his insolence   230
He settled with his sceptre; struck his back and shoulders so,
That bloody wales rose; he shrunk round, and from his eyes did flow
Moist tears, and looking filthily, he sate, fear'd, smarted, dried
His blubber'd cheeks; and all the press, though griev'd to be denied
Their wish'd retreat for home, yet laugh'd delightsomely, and spake
Either to other: 'O ye gods, how infinitely take
Ulysses' virtues in our good! Author of counsels, great
In ordering armies, how most well this act became his heat,
To beat from council this rude fool. I think his saucy spirit
Hereafter will not let his tongue abuse the sov'reign merit,   240
Exempt from such base tongues as his.' Thus spake the people: then
The city-razer Ithacus stood up to speak again,
Holding his sceptre. Close to him gray-eyed Minerva stood;
And like a herald, silence caus'd, that all the Achive brood
(From first to last) might hear and know the counsel; when (inclin'd
To all their good) Ulysses said: 'Atrides, now I find
These men would render thee the shame of all men; nor would pay
Their own vows to thee, when they took their free and honour'd way
From Argos hither, that till Troy were by their brave hands rac'd,
They would not turn home: yet like babes, and widows, now they haste   250

To that base refuge. 'Tis a spite to see men melted so
In womanish changes. Though 'tis true, that if a man do go
Only a month to sea, and leave his wife far off, and he
Tortur'd with winter's storms, and toss'd with a tumultuous sea,
Grows heavy, and would home; us then, to whom the thrice three year
Hath fill'd his revoluble orb since our arrival here,
I blame not to wish home much more: yet all this time to stay,
Out of our judgments, for our end, and now to take our way
Without it, were absurd and vile. Sustain then, friends; abide
The time set to our object: try if Calchas prophesied   260
True of the time or not. We know, ye all can witness well,
(Whom these late death-conferring fates have fail'd to send to hell)
That when in Aulis all our fleet assembled with a freight
Of ills to Ilion and her friends, beneath the fair grown height,
A platane bore, about a fount, whence crystal water flow'd,
And near our holy altar, we upon the gods bestow'd
Accomplish'd hecatombs; and there appear'd a huge portent,
A dragon with a bloody scale, horrid to sight, and sent
To light by great Olympius; which crawling from beneath
The altar, to the platane climb'd; and ruthless crash'd to death   270
A sparrow's young, in number eight, that in a top-bough lay
Hid under leaves: the dam the ninth, that hover'd every way,
Mourning her lov'd birth; till at length, the serpent watching her,
Her wing caught, and devour'd her too. This dragon, Jupiter
(That brought him forth) turn'd to a stone, and made a powerful mean
To stir our zeals up, that admir'd when of a fact so clean
Of all ill as our sacrifice, so fearful an ostent
Should be the issue. Calchas then thus prophesied th' event:
"Why are ye dumb-struck, fair-hair'd Greeks? Wise Jove is he hath shown
This strange ostent to us. 'Twas late, and passing lately done,   280
But that grace it foregoes to us, for suffering all the state
Of his appearance (being so slow), nor time shall end, nor fate.
As these eight sparrows, and the dam (that made the ninth) were eat
By this stern serpent, so nine years we are t' endure the heat
Of ravenous war, and in the tenth, take in this broad-way'd town."
    Thus he interpreted this sign; and all things have their crown
As he interpreted, till now. The rest then, to succeed,
Believe as certain: stay we all, till that most glorious deed
Of taking this rich town, our hands are honour'd with.' This said,
The Greeks gave an unmeasur'd shout; which back the ships repaid   290
With terrible echoes, in applause of that persuasion
Divine Ulysses us'd; which yet held no comparison
With Nestor's next speech, which was this: 'O shameful thing! Ye talk

Like children all, that know not war. In what air's region walk
Our oaths, and covenants? Now I see, the fit respects of men
Are vanish'd quite; our right hands given, our faiths, our counsels vain,
Our sacrifice with wine; all fled, in that profaned flame
We made to bind all: for thus still, we vain persuasions frame,
And strive to work our end with words, not joining stratagemes
And hands together, though thus long the power of our extremes   300
Hath urg'd us to them. Atreus' son, firm as at first hour stand:
Make good thy purpose; talk no more in councils, but command
In active field. Let two or three, that by themselves advise,
Faint in their crowning; they are such as are not truly wise.
They will for Argos ere they know if that which Jove hath said
Be false or true. I tell them all, that high Jove bow'd his head
As first we went aboard our fleet, for sign we should confer
These Trojans their due fate and death; almighty Jupiter
All that day darting forth his flames, in an unmeasur'd light,
On our right hands; let therefore none once dream of coward flight,   310
Till (for his own) some wife of Troy he sleeps withal, the rape
Of Helen wreaking, and our sighs, enforc'd for her escape.
If any yet dare dote on home, let his dishonour'd haste
His black and well-built bark but touch, that (as he first disgrac'd
His country's spirit) fate and death may first his spirit let go.
But be thou wise, king, do not trust thyself, but others. Know
I will not use an abject word: see all thy men array'd
In tribes and nations, that tribes tribes, nations may nations aid:
Which doing, thou shalt know what chiefs, what soldiers play the men,
And what the cowards: for they all will fight in several then,   320
Easy for note. And then shalt thou, if thou destroy'st not Troy,
Know if the prophecies defect, or men thou dost employ
In their approv'd arts, want in war, or lack of that brave heat
Fit for the vent'rous spirits of Greece, was cause to thy defeat.'

    To this the king of men replied: 'O father, all the sons
Of Greece thou conquer'st in the strife of consultations.
I would to Jove, Athenia, and Phoebus, I could make
(Of all) but ten such counsellors; then instantly would shake
King Priam's city, by our hands laid hold on, and laid waste.
But Jove hath order'd I should grieve, and to that end hath cast   330
My life into debates past end. Myself and Thetis' son
(Like girls) in words fought for a girl, and I th' offence begun:
But if we ever talk as friends, Troy's thus deferred fall
Shall never vex us more one hour. Come then, to victuals all,
That strong Mars all may bring to field; each man his lance's steel
See sharpen'd well, his shield well lin'd, his horses meated well,

His chariot carefully made strong, that these affairs of death
We all day may hold fiercely out: no man must rest, or breath.
The bosoms of our targeters must all be steep'd in sweat.
The lancer's arm must fall dissolv'd; our chariot-horse with heat   340
Must seem to melt. But if I find one soldier take the chace,
Or stir from fight, or fight not still, fix'd in his enemy's face,
Or hid a-shipboard, all the world for force nor price shall save
His hated life; but fowls amid dogs be his abhorred grave.'

He said, and such a murmur rose, as on a lofty shore
The waves make when the south wind comes, and tumbles them before
Against a rock, grown near the strand, which diversly beset
Is never free, but here and there with varied uproars beat.

All rose then, rushing to the fleet, perfum'd their tents, and eat,
Each off'ring to th' immortal gods, and praying to 'scape the heat   350
Of war and death. The king of men an ox of five years' spring
T' almighty Jove slew; call'd the peers, first Nestor, then the king
Idomenaeus; after them, th' Ajaces, and the son
Of Tydeus; Ithacus the sixth, in counsel paragon
To Jove himself – All these he had, but at-a-martial-cry
Good Menelaus, since he saw his brother busily
Employ'd at that time, would not stand on invitation,
But of himself came. All about the off'ring overthrown
Stood round, took salt-cakes, and the king himself thus pray'd for all:

'O Jove, most great, most glorious, that in that starry hall   360
Sitt'st drawing dark clouds up to air, let not the sun go down,
Darkness supplying it, till my hands the palace and the town
Of Priam overthrow and burn, the arms on Hector's breast
Dividing, spoiling with my sword thousands (in interest
Of his bad quarrel) laid by him in dust, and eating earth.'

He pray'd; Jove heard him not, but made more plentiful the birth
Of his sad toils; yet took his gifts. Prayers past, cakes on they threw:
The ox then, to the altar drawn, they kill'd, and from him drew
His hide; then cut him up; his thighs (in two hewn) dubb'd with fat;
Prick'd on the sweetbreads; and with wood, leafless, and kindled at   370
Apposed fire, they burn the thighs; which done, the inwards, slit,
They broil'd on coals and eat. The rest in giggots cut, they spit,
Roast cunningly, draw, sit and feast: nought lack'd to leave allay'd
Each temperate appetite; which serv'd, Nestor began and said:

'Atrides, most grac'd king of men, now no more words allow,
Nor more defer the deed Jove vows. Let heralds summon now
The brazen-coated Greeks, and us range everywhere the host,
To stir a strong war quickly up.' This speech no syllable lost;
The high-voic'd heralds instantly he charg'd to call to arms

The curl'd-head Greeks; they call'd; the Greeks straight answer'd their alarms.
The Jove-kept kings about the king all gather'd, with their aid
Rang'd all in tribes and nations. With them the gray-eyed maid
Great Aegis (Jove's bright shield) sustain'd, that can be never old,
Never corrupted, fring'd about with serpents forg'd of gold,
As many as suffic'd to make an hundred fringes, worth
An hundred oxen; every snake all sprawling, all set forth
With wondrous spirit. Through the host with this the goddess ran
In fury, casting round her eyes, and furnish'd every man
With strength, exciting all to arms, and fight incessant. None
Now liked their lov'd homes like the wars. And as a fire upon   390
A huge wood, on the heights of hills, that far off hurls his light,
So the divine brass shin'd on these, thus thrusting on for fight:
Their splendour through the air reach'd heaven: and as about the flood
Caïster, in an Asian mead, flocks of the airy brood,
Cranes, geese, or long-neck'd swans, here, there, proud of their pinions fly,
And in their falls lay out such throats, that with their spiritful cry
The meadow shrieks again: so here, these many-nation'd men
Flow'd over the Scamandrian field, from tents and ships: the din
Was dreadful, that the feet of men and horse beat out of earth.
And in the flourishing mead they stood, thick as the odorous birth   400
Of flow'rs, or leaves bred in the spring; or thick as swarms of flies
Throng then to sheep-cotes, when each swarm his erring wing applies
To milk 'dew'd on the milk-maid's pails: all eagerly dispos'd
To give to ruin the Ilians. And as in rude heaps clos'd,
Though huge goatherds are at their food, the goatherds easily yet
Sort into sundry herds, so here the chiefs in battle set,
Here tribes, here nations, ordering all. Amongst whom shin'd the king,
With eyes like lightning-loving Jove; his forehead answering,
In breast like Neptune; Mars in waist: and as a goodly bull
Most eminent of all a herd, most strong, most masterful,   410
So Agamemnon Jove that day made overheighten clear
That heav'n-bright army, and preferr'd to all th' heroës there.

   Now tell me, Muses, you that dwell in heavenly roofs (for you
Are goddesses, are present here, are wise, and all things know;
We only trust the voice of fame, know nothing), who they were
That here were captains of the Greeks. Commanding princes here,
The multitude exceed my song, though fitted to my choice
Ten tongues were, harden'd palates ten, a breast of brass, a voice
Infract and trump-like: that great work, unless the seed of Jove
(The deathless Muses) undertake, maintains a pitch above   420
All mortal powers. The princes then, and navy that did bring
Those so inenarrable troops; and all their soils, I sing.

THE CATALOGUE OF THE GRECIAN SHIPS AND CAPTAINS

Peneleus and Leitus, all that Boeotia bred,
Arcesilaus, Clonius and Prothoaenor led –
Th' inhabitants of Hyria, and stony Aulida,
Schaene, Schole, the hilly Eteon, and holy Thespia;
Of Graea, and great Micalesse, that hath the ample plain
Of Harma, and Ilesius, and all that did remain
In Erith, and in Eleon; in Hylen, Peteona,
In fair Ocalea, and the town well-builded Medeona;   430
Capas, Eutresis, Thisbe that for pigeons doth surpass;
Of Coroneia, Haliart, that hath such store of grass;
All those that in Platea dwelt, that Glissa did possess;
And Hypothebs, whose well-built walls are rare and fellowless,
In rich Onchestus' famous wood to watery Neptune vow'd;
And Arne, where the vine-trees are, with vigorous bunches bow'd;
With them that dwelt in Mydea, and Nissa most divine;
All those whom utmost Anthedon did wealthily confine.
From all these coasts in general full fifty sail were sent,
And six score strong Boeotian youths in every burthen went.   440
But those who in Aspledon dwelt, and Mynian Orchomen,
God Mars's sons did lead (Ascalaphus and Iahmen),
Who in Azidon Actor's house did of Astioche come;
The bashful maid, as she went up into the higher room,
The war-god secretly compress'd: in safe conduct of these,
Did thirty hollow-bottom'd barks divide the wavy seas.

Brave Schedius and Epistrophus the Phocian captains were,
Naubolida, Iphitus' sons, all proof 'gainst any fear;
With them the Cyparisians went, and bold Pythonians,
Men of religious Chrysa's soil, and fat Daulidians,   450
Panopaeans, Anemores, and fierce Hyampolists;
And those that dwell where Cephisus casts up his silken mists;
The men that fair Lylea held near the Cephisian spring:
All which did forty sable barks to that designment bring.
About th' entoil'd Phocensian fleet had these their sail assign'd,
And near to the sinister wing the arm'd Boeotians shin'd.

Ajax the less, Oïleus' son, the Locrians led to war,
Not like to Ajax Telamon, but lesser man by far:
Little he was, and ever wore a breastplate made of lin;
But for the manage of his lance he general praise did win.   460
The dwellers of Caliarus, of Bessa, Opoën,
The youths of Cynus, Scarphis, and Augias, lovely men;

Of Tarphis, and of Thronius, near flood Boagrius' fall:
Twice twenty martial barks of these, less Ajax sail'd withal.

Who near Euboea's blessed soil their habitations had,
Strength-breathing Abants, who their seats in sweet Euboea made;
The Astiaeans rich in grapes, the men of Chalcida,
The Cerinths bordering on the sea; of rich Eretria,
Of Dyon's highly-seated town, Charistus, and of Styre;
All these the Duke Alphenor led, a flame of Mars's sire,   470
Surnam'd Chalcodontiades, the mighty Abants' guide,
Swift men of foot, whose broad-set backs their trailing hair did hide,
Well seen in fight, and soon could pierce with far extended darts
The breastplates of their enemies, and reach their dearest hearts.
Forty black men of war did sail in this Alphenor's charge.

The soldiers that in Athens dwelt – a city builded large –
The people of Erecthius, whom Jove-sprung Pallas fed,
And plenteous-feeding Tellus brought out of her flow'ry bed,
Him Pallas placed in her rich fane, and every ended year,
Of bulls and lambs th' Athenian youths please him with off'rings there.   480
Mighty Menestheus, Peteus' son, had their divided care:
For horsemen and for targeters, none could with him compare,
Nor put them into better place, to hurt or to defend,
But Nestor – for he elder was – with him did sole contend:
With him came fifty sable sail. And out of Salamine
Great Ajax brought twelve sail that with th' Athenians did combine.

Who did in fruitful Argos dwell, or strong Hyrintha keep,
Hermion, or in Asinen whose bosom is so deep;
Trazena, Elion, Epidaure where Bacchus crowns his head,
Egina, and Mazeta's soil, did follow Diomed   490
And Sthenelus, the dear-lov'd suit of famous Capaneus,
Together with Eurialus, heir of Mecistaeus,
The king of Talaeonides; past whom in deeds of war,
The famous soldier Diomed of all was held by far;
Four score black ships did follow these. The men fair Mycene held –
The wealthy Corinth, Cleon that for beauteous sight excell'd,
Araethirea's lovely seat, and in Ornia's plain,
And Sicyona where at first did king Adrastus reign;
High-seated Genoëssa's towers, and Hyperisius;
That dwelt in fruitful Pellenen, and in divine Aegius,   500
With all the sea-side borderers, and wide Helice's friends –
To Agamemnon every town her native birth commends,
In double fifty sable barks. With him a world of men
Most strong and full of valour went: and he in triumph then
Put on his most resplendent arms, since he did overshine

The whole heroic host of Greece, in pow'r of that design.

    Who did in Lacedaemon's rule th' unmeasur'd concave hold,
High Phare's, Sparta's, Messe's towers, for doves so much extoll'd;
Bryseia's and Augia's grounds, strong Laa, Oetylon,
Amyclas, Helo's harbour-town that Neptune beats upon: 510
All these did Menelaus lead (his brother, that in cries
Of war was famous); sixty ships convey'd these enemies
To Troy in chief, because their king was chiefly injur'd there,
In Helen's rape, and did his best to make them buy it dear.

    Who dwelt in Pylos' sandy soil, and Arene the fair,
In Thryon near Alphaeus' flood, and Aepy full of air,
In Cyparisseus, Amphygen, and little Peteleon,
The town where all the Illiots dwelt, and famous Doreon,
Where all the Muses – opposite in strife of poesy,
To ancient Thamyris of Thrace – did use him cruelly   520
(He coming from Eurytus' court, the wise Oechalian king),
Because he proudly durst affirm he could more sweetly sing
Than that Pierean race of Jove; who, angry with his vaunt,
Bereft his eyesight, and his song that did the ear enchant,
And of his skill to touch his harp disfurnished his hand:
All these in ninety hollow keels grave Nestor did command.

    The richly blest inhabitants of the Arcadian land
Below Cyllene's mount (that by Epyrus' tomb did stand)
Where dwelt the bold near-fighting men: who did in Phaeneus live,
And Orchomen where flocks of sheep the shepherds clust'ring drive   530
In Rype and in Stratie the fair Mantinean town,
And strong Enispe that for height is ever weather-blown;
Tegea, and in Stymphalus, Parrhasia strongly wall'd;
All these Alcaeus' son to field (king Agapenor) call'd,
In sixty barks he brought them on, and every bark well mann'd
With fierce Arcadians, skill'd to use the utmost of a band.
King Agamemnon on these men did well-built ships bestow,
To pass the gulfy purple sea, that did no sea rites know.

    They who in Hermin, Buphrasis, and Elis did remain,
What Olen's cliffs, Alisius, and Myrsin did contain,   540
Were led to war by twice two dukes; and each ten ships did bring,
Which many venturous Epians did serve for burthening,
Beneath Alphimacus his charge, and valiant Talphius
(Son of Euritus Actor one, the next of Cteatus);
Diores Amarincides the third ships did employ,
The fourth divine Polixenus (Agasthenis's joy).

    The king of fair Angeiades, who from Dulichius came,
And from Euchinaus' sweet isles which hold their holy frame

By ample Elis region – Meges Phelides led:

Whom Duke Phyleus, Jove's belov'd, begat; and whilom fled   550

To large Dulichius, for the wrath that fir'd his father's breast.

Twice twenty ships with ebon sails were in his charge address'd.

    The warlike men of Cephale, and those of Ithaca,

Woody Neritus, and the men of wet Crocilia;

Sharp Aegilipha, Samos' isle, Zacynthus (sea-inclos'd) –

Epyrus, and the men that hold the continent oppos'd;

All these did wise Ulysses lead, in counsel peer to Jove:

Twelve ships he brought, which in their course vermilion sterns did move.

    Thoas, Andremon's well-spoke son, did guide th' Aetolians well,

Those that in Pleuron, Olenon, and strong Pylene dwell,   560

Great Calcis that by sea-side stands, and stony Calydon;

(For now no more of Oeneus' sons surviv'd; they all were gone:

No more his royal self did live, no more his noble son

The golden Meleager now, their glasses all were run.)

All things were left to him in charge; the Aetolians' chief he was,

And forty ships to Trojan wars the seas within him did pass.

    The royal soldier Idomen did lead the Cretans stout:

The men of Gnossus, and the town Cortima wall'd about,

Of Lictus, and Myletus' towers, of white Lycastus' state,

Of Phestus and of Rhistias the cities fortunate,   570

And all the rest inhabiting the hundred towns of Crete;

Whom warlike Idomen did lead, co-partner in the fleet,

With kill-man Merion: eighty ships with them did Troy invade.

    Tlepolemus Heraclides, right strong and bigly made,

Brought nine tall ships of war from Rhodes, which haughty Rhodians mann'd;

Who dwelt in three dissever'd parts of that most pleasant land,

Which Lyndus and Jalissus were, and bright Camyrus, call'd.

Tlepolemus commanded these, in battle unappall'd:

Whom fair Astioche brought forth, by force of Hercules;

Led out of Ephyr with his hand, from river Selleës,   580

When many towns of princely youths he levell'd with the ground.

Tlepolem in his father's house (for building much renown'd)

Brought up to headstrong state of youth, his mother's brother slew,

The flower of arms, Lycymnius, that somewhat aged grew:

Then straight he gather'd him a fleet, assembling bands of men,

And fled by sea, to shun the threats that were denounced then,

By other sons and nephews of th' Alciden fortitude;

He in his exile came to Rhodes, driven in with tempests rude.

The Rhodians were distinct in tribes, and great with Jove did stand,

The king of men and gods, who gave much treasure to their land.   590

    Nireus out of Syma's haven three well-built barks did bring:

Nireus, fair Aglaia's son, and Charopes, the king:
Nireus was the fairest man that to fair Ilion came
Of all the Greeks, save Peleus' son, who passed for general frame.
But weak this was, not fit for war, and therefore few did guide.

    Who did in Cassus, Nisyrus, and Crapathus abide,
In Co, Euripilus's town, and in Calydna's soils,
Phydippus and bold Antiphus did guide to Trojan toils
(The sons of crowned Thessalus, deriv'd from Hercules);
Who went with thirty hollow ships well order'd to the seas.   600

    Now will I sing the sackful troops Pelasgian Argos held,
That in deep Alus, Alope, and soft Trechina dwell'd;
In Pthya, and in Hellade where live the lovely dames,
The Myrmidons, Helenians, and Achives, rob'd of fames –
All which the great Aeacides in fifty ships did lead.
For these forgot war's horrid voice, because they lack'd their head,
That would have brought them bravely forth; but now at fleet did he,
That wind-like user of his feet, fair Thetis' progeny,
Wroth for bright-cheek'd Briseis' loss, whom from Lyrnessus' spoils
(His own exploit) he brought away as trophy of his toils,   610
When that town was depopulate; he sunk the Theban tow'rs,
Myneta and Epistrophus he sent to Pluto's bow'rs,
Who came of king Evenus' race, great Helepiades:
Yet now he idly lives enrag'd, but soon must leave his ease.

    Of those that dwelt in Phylace, and flow'ry Pyrrason,
The wood of Ceres, and the soil that sheep are fed upon –
Iten, and Antron built by sea, and Pteleus full of grass –
Protesilaus while he liv'd the worthy captain was:
Whom now the sable earth detains. His tear-torn-faced spouse
He woeful left in Phylace, and his half-finish'd house: 620
A fatal Dardan, first his life of all the Greeks bereft,
As he was leaping from his ship; yet were his men unleft
Without a chief, for though they wish'd to have no other man
But good Protesilay their guide, Podarces yet began
To govern them (Iphitis' son, the son of Philacus),
Most rich in sheep, and brother to short-liv'd Protesilaus:
Of younger birth, less and less strong; yet serv'd he to direct
The companies, that still did more their ancient duke affect.
Twice twenty jetty sails with him the swelling stream did take.

    But those that did in Pheres dwell at the Baebreian lake   630
In Baebe, and in Glaphira, Iaolcus builded fair;
In thrice six ships to Pergamus did through the seas repair,
With old Admetes' tender son, Eumelus, whom he bred
Of Alceste, Pelius' fairest child of all his female seed.

The soldiers that before the siege Methone's vales did hold,
Thaumaciae, flow'ry Melibae, and Olison the cold,
Duke Philoctetes governed (in darts, of finest sleight);
Seven vessels in his charge convey'd their honourable freight,
By fifty rowers in a bark, most expert in the bow:
But he in sacred Lemnos lay, brought miserably low   640
By torment of an ulcer grown with Hydra's poison'd blood;
Whose sting was such, Greece left him there in most impatient mood:
Yet thought they on him at his ship, and choos'd to head his men
Medon, Oïleus' bastard son, brought forth to him by Rhen.

From Thricce, bleak Ithomen's cliffs, and hapless Oechaly –
Euritus' city rul'd by him in wilful tyranny –
In charge of Aesculapius' sons (physician highly prais'd)
Machaon, Podalirius, were thirty vessels rais'd.

Who near Hiperia's fountain dwelt, and in Ormenius,
The snowy tops of Titannus, and in Asterius,   650
Evemon's son, Euripilus, did lead into the field:
Whose towns did forty black-sail'd ships to that encounter yield.

Who Gyrton and Argissa held, Orthen and Elon's seat,
And chalky Oloössine, were led by Polypete,
The issue of Perithous, the son of Jupiter.
Him the Athenian Theseus' friend, Hypodamy did bear,
When he the bristled savages did give Ramnusia,
And drove them out of Pelius, as far as Athica.
He came not single, but with him, Leonteus Coron's son,
An arm of Mars: and Coron's life Ceneus' seed begun.   660
Twice twenty ships attended these.
                                        Guneus next did bring
From Cyphus twenty sail and two, the Enians following,
And fierce Peraebi, that about Dodone's frozen mould
Did plant their houses; and the men that did the meadows hold,
Which Titoresius decks with flowers, and his sweet current leads
Into the bright Peneius, that hath the silver heads;
Yet with his admirable stream doth not his waves commix,
But glides aloft on it like oil: for 'tis the flood of Styx,
By which th' immortal gods do swear. Teuthredon's honour'd birth,
Prothous, led the Magnets forth, who near the shady earth   670
Of Pelius and Peneion dwelt; forty revengeful sail
Did follow him. These were the dukes and princes of avail
That came from Greece. But now the man that overshin'd them all,
Sing, muse, and their most famous steeds to my recital call,
That both th' Atrides followed; fair Pheretiedes
The bravest mares did bring by much; Eumelius manag'd these:

Swift of their feet as birds of wings, both of one hair did shine,
Both of an age, both of a height, as measur'd by a line:
Whom silver-bow'd Apollo bred in the Pierean mead,
Both slick and dainty, yet were both in war of wondrous dread.   680
   Great Ajax Telamon for strength past all the peers of war,
While vex'd Achilles was away; but he surpass'd him far.
The horse that bore that faultless man were likewise past compare:
Yet lay he at the crook'd-stern'd ships, and fury was his fare,
For Atreus' son's ungracious deed: his men yet pleas'd their hearts
With throwing of the holed stone, with hurling of their darts,
And shooting fairly on the shore. Their horse at chariots fed
On greatest parsley, and on sedge that in the fens is bred.
His princes' tents their chariots held, that richly cover'd were.
His princes, amorous of their chief, walk'd storming here and there   690
About the host, and scorn'd to fight: their breaths as they did pass
Before them flew as if a fire fed on the trembling grass:
Earth under-groan'd their high-rais'd feet, as when offended Jove,
In Arime, Typhoeius with rattling thunder drove
Beneath the earth: (in Arime men say the grave is still,
Where thunder tomb'd Typhoeius, and is a monstrous hill:)
And as that thunder made earth groan, so groan'd it as they past,
They trod with such hard-set-down steps, and so exceeding fast.
   To Troy, the rainbow-girded dame right heavy news relates
From Jove, as all to council drew in Priam's palace-gates,   700
Resembling Priam's son in voice, Polytes, swift of feet –
In trust whereof as sentinel, to see when from the fleet
The Grecians sallied, he was set upon the lofty brow
Of aged Esietes' tomb – and this did Iris show:
   'O Priam, thou art always pleas'd with indiscreet advice,
And fram'st thy life to times of peace, when such a war doth rise
As threats inevitable spoil; I never did behold
Such and so mighty troops of men, who trample on the mould
In number like Autumnus' leaves, or like the marine sand,
All ready round about the walls to use a ruining hand.   710
Hector, I therefore charge thee most, this charge to undertake:
A multitude remain in Troy will fight for Priam's sake,
Of other lands and languages; let every leader then
Bring forth well arm'd into the field his several bands of men.'
   Strong Hector knew a deity gave charge to this assay,
Dismiss'd the council straight; like waves, clusters to arms do sway,
The ports are all wide open set, out rush'd the troops in swarms,
Both horse and foot; the city rung with sudden-cried alarms.
   A column stands without the town, that high his head doth raise,

A little distant, in a plain trod down with divers ways;   720
Which men do Batieia call, but the immortals name
Myrinne's famous sepulchre (the wondrous active dame):
Here were th' auxiliary bands that came in Troy's defence,
Distinguish'd under several guides of special excellence.

The duke of all the Trojan power great helm-deck'd Hector was,
Which stood of many mighty men, well skill'd in darts of brass.
Aeneas of commixed seed (a goddess with a man,
Anchises with the queen of love) the troops Dardanian
Led to the field; (his lovely sire in Ida's lower shade
Begat him of sweet Cypridis;) he solely was not made   730
Chief leader of the Dardan powers; Antenor's valiant sons,
Archilochus and Acamas, were join'd companions.

Who in Zelia dwelt beneath the sacred foot of Ide –
That drank of black Aesepus stream, and wealth made full of pride –
The Aphnii, Lycaon's son, whom Phoebus gave his bow,
Prince Pandarus did lead to field.
                                Who Adrestinus owe,
Apesus' city, Pitaei, and mount Tereiës,
Adrestus and stout Amphius led, who did their sire displease
(Merops Percosius), that excell'd all Troy in heavenly skill
Of future-searching prophecy: for much against his will   740
His sons were agents in those arms: whom since they disobey'd,
The fates, in letting slip their threads, their hasty valours stay'd.

Who in Percotes, Practius, Arisba, did abide,
Who Sestus and Abydus bred, Hyrtacides did guide,
Prince Asius Hyrtacides, that through great Selees' force,
Brought from Arisba to that fight the great and fiery horse.

Pyleus and Hypothous the stout Pelasgians led,
Of them Larissa's fruitful soil before had nourished:
These were Pelasgian Pithus' sons, son of Teutamidas.

The Thracian guides were Pyrous, and valiant Acamas,   750
Of all that the impetuous flood of Hellespont enclos'd.

Euphemus the Ciconian troops in his command dispos'd,
Who from Trezenias Ceades right nobly did descend.

Pyrechmes did the Peons rule that crooked bows do bend:
From Axius out of Amidon, he had them in command,
From Axius, whose most beauteous stream still overflows the land.

Pylemen with the well arm'd heart the Paphlagonians led,
From Enes, where the race of mules fit for the plough is bred;
The men that broad Cytorus' bounds, and Sesamus enfold,
About Parthenius' lofty flood (in houses much extoll'd),   760
From Cromna and Aegialus, the men that arms did bear,

And Eurithymus situate high, Pylemen's soldiers were.
　Epistrophus and Dius did the Halizonians guide,
Far-fetch'd from Alybe, where first the silver mines were tried.
　Chronius and Augur Eunomus the Mysians did command,
Who could not with his auguries the strength of death withstand,
But suffer'd it beneath the stroke of great Aeacides,
In Xanthus, where he made more souls dive to the Stygian seas.
　Phorcys, and fair Ascanius, the Phrygians brought to war,
Well train'd for battle, and were come out of Ascania far.　　　　770
　With Methles, and with Antiphus (Pylemen's sons) did fight
The men of Mezon, whom the fen Gygaea brought to light;
And those Maeonians that beneath the mountain Tmolus sprung.
　The rude unletter'd Caribae, that barbarous were of tongue,
Did under Naustes' colours march, and young Amphimachus
(Nomyon's famous sons); to whom the mountain Phthirorus,
That with the famous wood is crown'd, Miletus, Micales
That hath so many lofty marks for men that love the seas,
The crooked arms Meander bow'd with his so snaky flood,
Resign'd for conduct the choice youth of all their martial brood.　　780
The fool Amphimachus, to field, brought gold to be his wrack,
Proud-girl-like that doth ever bear her dower upon her back,
Which wise Achilles mark'd, slew him, and took his gold, in strife
At Xanthus' flood; so little Death did fear his golden life.
　Sarpedon led the Lycians, and Glaucus unreprov'd,
From Lycia, and the gulfy flood of Xanthus far remov'd.

THE END OF THE SECOND BOOK

BOOK THREE

The Argument

Paris, betwixt the hosts, to single fight
Of all the Greeks, dares the most hardy knight:
King Menelaus doth accept his brave,
Conditioning that he again should have
Fair Helena, with all she brought to Troy,
If he subdu'd; else Paris should enjoy
Her, and her wealth, in peace. Conquest doth grant
Her dear wreath to the Grecian combatant:
But Venus to her champion's life doth yield
Safe rescue, and conveys him from the field
Into his chamber, and for Helen sends;
Whom much her lover's foul disgrace offends.
Yet Venus still for him makes good her charms,
And ends the second combat in his arms.

Another Argument

Gamma the single fight doth sing
'Twixt Paris and the Spartan king.

BOOK THREE

WHEN EVERY least commander's will best soldiers had obey'd,
    And both the hosts were rang'd for fight, the Trojans would have fray'd
    The Greeks with noises, crying out, in coming rudely on
At all parts, like the cranes that fill with harsh confusion
Of brutish clangour all the air, and in ridiculous war
(Eschewing the unsuffer'd storms shot from the winter's star)
Visit the ocean, and confer the pigmy soldiers death.
The Greeks charg'd silent, and like men, bestow'd their thrifty breath
In strength of far-resounding blows, still entertaining care
Of either's rescue, when their strength did their engagements dare.   10
And as upon a hill's steep top, the south wind pours a cloud,
To shepherds thankless, but by thieves that love the night, allow'd,
A darkness letting down, that blinds a stone's cast off men's eyes,
Such darkness from the Greeks' swift feet (made all of dust) did rise.
But ere stern conflict mix'd both strengths, fair Paris stept before
The Trojan host: athwart his back a panther's hide he wore,
A crooked bow, and sword, and shook two brazen-headed darts,
With which well arm'd, his tongue provok'd the best of Grecian hearts
To stand with him in single fight. Whom, when the man wrong'd most
Of all the Greeks, so gloriously saw stalk before the host,   20
As when a lion is rejoic'd, with hunger half forlorn,
That finds some sweet prey (as a hart, whose grace lies in his horn,
Or sylvan goat) which he devours, though never so pursu'd
With dogs and men: so Sparta's king exulted when he view'd
The fair-faced Paris so expos'd to his so thirsted wreak –
Whereof his good cause made him sure – the Grecian front did break,
And forth he rush'd, at all parts arm'd; leapt from his chariot,
And royally prepar'd for charge. Which seen, cold terror shot
The heart of Paris, who retir'd as headlong from the king,
As in him he had shunn'd his death; and as a hilly spring   30
Presents a serpent to a man, full underneath his feet,
Her blue neck, swoln with poison, rais'd, and her sting out, to greet
His heedless entry; suddenly his walk he altereth,
Starts back amaz'd, is shook with fear, and looks as pale as death:
So Menelaus Paris scar'd; so that divine-fac'd foe

Shrunk in his beauties. Which beheld by Hector, he let go
This bitter check at him. 'Accurs'd! Made but in beauty's scorn,
Impostor, woman's man! O heav'n, that thou hadst ne'er been born!
Or, being so manless, never liv'd to bear man's noblest state,
The nuptial honour; which I wish, because it were a fate   40
Much better for thee than this shame; this spectacle doth make
A man a monster. Hark! How loud the Greeks laugh, who did take
Thy fair form for a continent of parts as fair; a rape
Thou mad'st of nature, like their queen. No soul, an empty shape
Takes up thy being: yet how spite to every shade of good
Fills it with ill: for as thou art, thou couldst collect a brood
Of others like thee, and far hence fetch'd ill enough to us,
Even to thy father: all these friends make those foes mock them thus,
In thee; for whose ridiculous sake, so seriously they lay
All Greece and fate upon their necks. O wretch! Not dare to stay   50
Weak Menelaus! But 'twas well, for in him thou hadst tried
What strength lost beauty can infuse; and with the more grief died,
To feel thou robb'st a worthier man, to wrong a soldier's right.
Your harp's sweet touch, curl'd locks, fine shape, and gifts so exquisite,
Giv'n thee by Venus, would have done your fine dames little good,
When blood and dust had ruffled them; and had as little stood
Thyself in stead; but what thy care of all these in thee flies,
We should inflict on thee ourselves; infectious cowardice
In thee hath terrified our host; for which thou well deserv'st
A coat of tombstone, not of steel, in which for form thou serv'st.   60
    To this thus Paris spake (for form, that might inhabit heav'n):
'Hector, because thy sharp reproof is out of justice giv'n,
I take it well: but though thy heart, inur'd to these affrights,
Cuts through them as an axe through oak, that more us'd more excites
The workman's faculty, whose art can make the edge go far;
Yet I, less practis'd than thyself in these extremes of war,
May well be pardon'd, though less bold: in these your worth exceeds,
In others, mine: nor is my mind of less force to the deeds
Requir'd in war, because my form more flows in gifts of peace.
Reproach not therefore the kind gifts of golden Cyprides;   70
All heaven's gifts have their worthy price, as little to be scorn'd,
As to be won with strength, wealth, state; with which to be adorn'd,
Some men would change state, wealth or strength. But if your martial heart
Wish me to make my challenge good, and hold it such a part
Of shame to give it over thus, cause all the rest to rest;
And 'twixt both hosts, let Sparta's king and me perform our best
For Helen and the wealth she brought: and he that overcomes,
Or proves superior any way, in all your equal dooms,

Let him enjoy her utmost wealth, keep her, or take her home;
The rest strike leagues of endless date, and hearty friends become: 80
You dwelling safe in gleby Troy, the Greeks retire their force
T' Achaia, that breeds fairest dames, and Argos, fairest horse.'
    He said, and his amendful words did Hector highly please,
Who rush'd betwixt the fighting hosts, and made the Trojans cease,
By holding up in midst his lance: the Grecians noted not
The signal he for parley used, but at him fiercely shot,
Hurl'd stones, and still were levelling darts. At last the king of men,
Great Agamemnon, cried aloud: 'Argives! For shame, contain;
Youths of Achaia, shoot no more: the fair-helm'd Hector shows
As he desir'd to treat with us.' This said, all ceas'd from blows,   90
And Hector spake to both the hosts: 'Trojans, and hardy Greeks,
Hear now what he that stirr'd these wars for their cessation seeks;
He bids us all, and you, disarm, that he alone may fight
With Menelaus, for us all; for Helen and her right,
With all the dow'r she brought to Troy; and he that wins the day,
Or is in all the art of arms superior any way,
The queen, and all her sorts of wealth, let him at will enjoy;
The rest strike truce, and let love seal firm leagues 'twixt Greece and Troy.'
    The Greek host wonder'd at this brave; silence flew everywhere;
At last spake Sparta's warlike king: 'Now also give me ear,   100
Whom grief gives most cause of reply; I now have hope to free
The Greeks and Trojans of all ills they have sustain'd for me
And Alexander, that was cause I stretch'd my spleen so far:
Of both then, which is nearest fate, let his death end the war;
The rest immediately retire, and greet all homes in peace.
Go then (to bless your champion, and give his powers success),
Fetch for the earth, and for the sun (the gods on whom ye call)
Two lambs, a black one and a white, a female and a male;
And we another for ourselves will fetch, and kill to Jove:
To sign which rites bring Priam's force, because we well approve   110
His sons perfidious, envious (and out of practis'd bane
To faith, when she believes in them) Jove's high truce may profane;
All young men's hearts are still unstaid; but in those well-weigh'd deeds
An old man will consent to pass things past, and what succeeds
He looks into, that he may know how best to make his way
Through both the fortunes of a fact – and will the worst obey.'
    This granted, a delightful hope both Greeks and Trojans fed
Of long'd-for rest from those long toils their tedious war had bred.
Their horses then in rank they set, drawn from their chariots round,
Descend themselves, took off their arms, and plac'd them on the ground,
Near one another; for the space 'twixt both the hosts was small.

Hector two heralds sent to Troy, that they from thence might call
King Priam; and to bring the lambs, to rate the truce they swore.
But Agamemnon to the fleet Talthibius sent before,
To fetch their lamb, who nothing slackt the royal charge was given.
    Iris, the rainbow, then came down, ambassadress from heaven,
To white-arm'd Helen: she assum'd at every part the grace
Of Helen's last love's sister's shape, who had the highest place
In Helen's love; and had to name, Laodice, most fair
Of all the daughters Priam had; and made the nuptial pair,   130
With Helicaon, royal sprout of old Antenor's seed.
She found queen Helena at home, at work about a weed,
Wov'n for herself: it shin'd like fire, was rich, and full of size,
The work of both sides being alike, in which she did comprise
The many labours warlike Troy and brass-arm'd Greece endur'd
For her fair sake, by cruel Mars and his stern friends procur'd.
Iris came in in joyful haste, and said, 'O come with me,
Lov'd nymph, and an admired sight of Greeks and Trojans see,
Who first on one another brought a war so full of tears:
Even thirsty of contentious war now every man forbears,   140
And friendly by each other sits, each leaning on his shield,
Their long and shining lances pitch'd fast by them in the field.
Paris and Sparta's king alone must take up all the strife,
And he that conquers only call fair Helena his wife.'
    Thus spake the thousand-colour'd dame; and to her mind commends
The joy to see her first espous'd, her native tow'rs and friends,
Which stirr'd a sweet desire in her, to serve the which she hied:
Shadow'd her graces with white veils, and (though she took a pride
To set her thoughts at gaze, and see in her clear beauty's flood,
What choice of glory swam to her), yet tender womanhood   150
Season'd with tears her joys to see more joys the more offence,
And that perfection could not flow from earthly excellence.
    Thus went she forth, and took with her her women most of name,
Aethra (Pitthaeus' lovely birth) and Clymene, whom fame
Hath for her fair eyes memoris'd. They reach'd the Scaean tow'rs,
Where Priam sat to see the fight, with all his counsellors;
Panthous, Larnpus, Clitius, and stout Hycetaon,
Thimaetes, wise Antenor, and profound Ucalegon:
All grave old men, and soldiers they had been, but for age
Now left the wars; yet counsellors they were exceeding sage.   160
And as in well grown woods, on trees, cold spiny grasshoppers
Sit chirping, and send voices out that scarce can pierce our ears
For softness, and their weak faint sounds, so talking on the tow'r,
These seniors of the people sat: who when they saw the pow'r

Of beauty in the queen ascend, ev'n those cold-spirited peers,
Those wise and almost wither'd men found this heat in their years,
That they were forc'd (though whispering) to say: 'What man can blame
The Greeks and Trojans to endure for so admir'd a dame,
So many miseries, and so long? In her sweet countenance shine
Looks like the goddesses: and yet (though never so divine)   170
Before we boast, unjustly still, of her enforced prize,
And justly suffer for her sake, with all our progenies,
Labour and ruin, let her go: the profit of our land
Must pass the beauty.' Thus, though these could bear so fit a hand
On their affections, yet when all their gravest powers were us'd,
They could not choose but welcome her, and rather they accus'd
The gods than beauty; for thus spake the most fam'd king of Troy:
'Come, loved daughter, sit by me, and take the worthy joy
Of thy first husband's sight, old friends and Princes near allied;
And name me some of these brave Greeks, so manly beautified.   180
Come: do not think I lay the wars endur'd by us on thee –
The gods have sent them, and the tears in which they swam to me.
Sit then, and name this goodly Greek, so tall, and broadly spread,
Who than the rest, that stand by him, is higher by the head;
The bravest man I ever saw, and most majestical:
His only presence makes me think him king amongst them all.'
    The fairest of her sex replied: 'Most rev'rend father-in-law,
Most lov'd, most fear'd, would some ill death had seiz'd me, when I saw
The first mean, why I wrong'd you thus; that I had never lost
The sight of these my ancient friends; of him that lov'd me most,   190
Of my sole daughter, brothers both; with all those kindly mates,
Of one soil, one age borne with me, though under different fates:
But these boons envious stars deny; the memory of these
In sorrow pines those beauties now, that then did too much please;
Nor satisfy they your demand, to which I thus reply:
That's Agamemnon, Atreus' son, the great in empery;
A king, whom double royalty doth crown, being great and good,
And one that was my brother-in-law, when I contain'd my blood,
And was more worthy, if at all I might be said to be,
My being being lost so soon, in all that honour'd me.'   200
    The good old king admir'd, and said: 'O Atreus' blessed son!
Born unto joyful destinies, that hast the empire won
Of such a world of Grecian youths as I discover here.
I once march'd into Phrygia, that many vines doth bear,
Where many Phrygians I beheld, well skill'd in use of horse,
That of the two men, like two gods, were the commanded force –
Otroeus, and great Migdonus – who on Sangarius' sands

Set down their tents, with whom myself, for my assistant bands,
Was number'd as a man in chief; the cause of war was then
Th' Amazon dames, that in their facts affected to be men.   210
In all, there was a mighty pow'r, which yet did never rise
To equal these Achaian youths, that have the sable eyes.'
Then (seeing Ulysses next) he said: 'Lov'd daughter, what is he,
That lower than great Atreus' son seems by the head to me?
Yet in his shoulders and big breast presents a broader show;
His armour lies upon the earth; he up and down doth go,
To see his soldiers keep their ranks, and ready have their arms,
If, in this truce, they should be tried by any false alarms:
Much like a well-grown bell-wether or feltred ram he shows,
That walks before a wealthy flock of fair white-fleeced ewes.'   220
    High Jove and Leda's fairest seed to Priam thus replies:
'This is the old Laertes' son, Ulysses, call'd the wise;
Who, though unfruitful Ithaca was made his nursing seat,
Yet knows he every sort of sleight, and is in counsels great.
    The wise Antenor answer'd her: 'Tis true, renowned dame;
For some times past wise Ithacus to Troy a legate came,
With Menelaus, for your cause: to whom I gave receipt
As guests, and welcom'd to my house, with all the love I might.
I learn'd the wisdoms of their souls, and humours of their blood:
For when the Trojan council met, and these together stood,   230
By height of his broad shoulders had Atrides eminence;
Yet set, Ulysses did exceed, and bred more reverence.
And when their counsels and their words they wove in one, the speech
Of Atreus' son was passing loud, small, fast, yet did not reach
To much, being naturally born Laconical: nor would
His humour lie for anything, or was (like th' other) old;
But when the prudent Ithacus did to his counsels rise,
He stood a little still, and fix'd upon the earth his eyes,
His sceptre moving neither way, but held it formally,
Like one that vainly doth affect. Of wrathful quality,   240
And frantic (rashly judging him) you would have said he was;
But when out of his ample breast he gave his great voice pass,
And words that flew about our ears like drifts of winter's snow,
None thenceforth might contend with him, though nought admir'd for show.'
    The third man aged Priam mark'd, was Ajax Telamon:
Of whom he ask'd: 'What lord is that so large of limb and bone,
So rais'd in height, that to his breast I see there reacheth none?
    To him the goddess of her sex, the large-veil'd Helen, said:
'That lord is Ajax Telamon, a bulwark in their aid.
On th' other side stands Idomen, in Crete of most command,   250

And round about his royal sides his Cretan captains stand.
Oft hath the warlike Spartan king giv'n hospitable due
To him within our Lacene court, and all his retinue.
And now the other Achive dukes I generally discern;
All which I know, and all their names could make thee quickly learn.
Two princes of the people yet I nowhere can behold:
Castor, the skilful knight on horse, and Pollux, uncontroll'd
For all stand-fights, and force of hand; both at a burthen bred,
My natural brothers: either here they have not followed
From lovely Sparta, or arriv'd within the sea-borne fleet,   260
In fear of infamy for me in broad field shame to meet.'

    Nor so, for holy Tellus' womb inclos'd those worthy men,
In Sparta their beloved soil. The voiceful heralds then
The firm agreement of the gods through all the city ring:
Two lambs, and spirit-refreshing wine (the fruit of earth) they bring,
Within a goat-skin bottle clos'd; Idaeus also brought
A massy glittering bowl, and cups, that all of gold were wrought;
Which bearing to the king, they cried: 'Son of Laomedon,
Rise, for the well-rode peers of Troy and brass-arm'd Greeks in one
Send to thee to descend the field, that they firm vows may make;   270
For Paris and the Spartan king must fight for Helen's sake,
With long arm'd lances; and the man that proves victorious,
The woman, and the wealth she brought, shall follow to his house;
The rest knit friendship, and firm leagues; we safe in Troy shall dwell;
In Argos and Achaia they, that do in dames excel.'

    He said, and Priam's aged joints with chilled fear did shake;
Yet instantly he had his men his chariot ready make.
Which soon they did, and he ascends: he takes the reins, and guide
Antenor calls, who instantly mounts to his royal side,
And through the Scaean ports to field, the swift-foot horse they drive.   280
And when at them of Troy and Greece the aged lords arrive,
From horse, on Troy's well-feeding soil, 'twixt both the hosts they go.
When straight up rose the king of men, up rose Ulysses too;
The heralds in their richest coats repeat (as was the guise)
The true vows of the gods (term'd theirs, since made before their eyes);
Then in a cup of gold they mix the wine that each side brings,
And next pour water on the hands of both the kings of kings.
Which done, Atrides drew his knife, that evermore he put
Within the large sheath of his sword, with which away he cut
The wool from both fronts of the lambs, which (as a rite in use   290
Of execration to their heads, that brake the plighted truce)
The heralds of both hosts did give the peers of both. And then
With hands and voice advanc'd to heav'n, thus pray'd the king of men:

'O Jove, that Ida dost protect, and hast the titles won,
Most glorious, most invincible; and thou all-seeing Sun,
All-hearing, all-recomforting; floods, earth, and pow'rs beneath,
That all the perjuries of men chastise ev'n after death,
Be witnesses, and see perform'd the hearty vows we make;
If Alexander shall the life of Menelaus take,
He shall from henceforth Helena, with all her wealth, retain;   300
And we will to our household gods hoist sail, and home again.
If by my honour'd brother's hand be Alexander slain,
The Trojans then shall his forc'd queen with all her wealth restore,
And pay convenient fine to us and ours for evermore.
If Priam and his sons deny to pay this, thus agreed,
When Alexander shall be slain, for that perfidious deed,
And for the fine, will I fight here till dearly they repay,
By death and ruin, the amends that falsehood keeps away.
    This said, the throats of both the lambs cut with his royal knife,
He laid them panting on the earth, till (quite depriv'd of life)   310
The steel had robb'd them of their strength. Then golden cups they crown'd,
With wine out of a cistern drawn; which pour'd upon the ground,
They fell upon their humble knees to all the deities,
And thus pray'd one of both the hosts, that might do sacrifice:
    'O Jupiter, most high, most great, and all the deathless pow'rs,
Who first shall dare to violate the late sworn oaths of ours,
So let the bloods and brains of them, and all they shall produce,
Flow on the stain'd face of the earth, as now this sacred juice:
And let their wives with bastardies brand all their future race.'
Thus pray'd they: but with wish'd effects their pray'rs Jove did not grace.
When Priam said: 'Lords of both hosts, I can no longer stay
To see my lov'd son try his life; and so must take my way
To wind-exposed Ilion: Jove yet and heav'n's high states
Know only, which of these must now pay tribute to the Fates.'
    Thus putting in his coach the lambs, he mounts and reins his horse,
Antenor to him, and to Troy both take their speedy course.
    Then Hector, Priam's martial son, stepp'd forth, and met the ground,
With wise Ulysses, where the blows of combat must resound.
Which done, into a helm they put two lots, to let them know
Which of the combatants should first his brass-pil'd javelin throw.   330
When all the people standing by, with hands held up to heav'n,
Pray'd Jove, the conquest might not be by force or fortune giv'n,
But that the man, who was in right the author of most wrong,
Might feel his justice, and no more these tedious wars prolong,
But sinking to the house of death, leave them (as long before)
Link'd fast in leagues of amity, that might dissolve no more.

Then Hector shook the helm that held the equal dooms of chance,
Look'd back, and drew; and Paris first had lot to hurl his lance.

The soldiers all sat down enrank'd, each by his arms and horse,
That then lay down, and cool'd their hoofs. And now th' allotted course
Bids fair-hair'd Helen's husband arm: who first makes fast his greaves
With silver buckles to his legs, then on his breast receives
The curets that Lycaon wore (his brother), but made fit
For his fair body; next his sword he took, and fasten'd it
(All damask'd) underneath his arm; his shield then grave and great
His shoulders wore, and on his head his glorious helm he set
Topp'd with a plume of horse's hair, that horribly did dance,
And seem'd to threaten as he mov'd. At last he takes his lance,
Exceeding big, and full of weight, which he with ease could use.

In like sort, Sparta's warlike king himself with arms indues.				350
Thus arm'd at either army both, they both stood bravely in,
Possessing both hosts with amaze: they came so chin to chin,
And with such horrible aspects, each other did salute.

A fair large field was made for them: where wraths – for hugeness – mute,
And mutual, made them mutually at either shake their darts
Before they threw: then Paris first with his long javelin parts;
It smote Atrides' orby targe, but ran not through the brass:
For in it (arming well the shield) the head reflected was.

Then did the second combatant apply him to his spear;
Where ere he threw, he thus besought almighty Jupiter:				360

'O Jove! Vouchsafe me now revenge, and that my enemy,
For doing wrong so undeserv'd, may pay deservedly
The pains he forfeited; and let these hands inflict those pains,
By conquering, ay, by conquering dead, him on whom life complains:
That any now, or any one of all the brood of men
To live hereafter, may with fear from all offence abstain,
Much more from all such foul offence to him that was his host,
And entertain'd him, as the man whom he affected most.'

This said, he shook, and threw his lance; which struck through Paris' shield,
And with the strength he gave to it, it made the curets yield,				370
His coat of mail, his breast, and all, and drove his entrails in,
In that low region, where the guts in three small parts begin:
Yet he, in bowing of his breast, prevented sable death.
This taint he follow'd with his sword, drawn from a silver sheath:
Which lifting high, he struck his helm, full where his plume did stand,
On which it piecemeal brake, and fell from his unhappy hand.
At which he sighing stood, and star'd upon the ample sky;
And said: 'O Jove, there is no god giv'n more illiberally
To those that serve thee than thyself; why have I pray'd in vain?

I hop'd my hand should have reveng'd the wrongs I still sustain   380
On him that did them, and still dares their foul defence pursue;
And now my lance hath miss'd his end, my sword in shivers flew,
And he 'scapes all. With this again he rush'd upon his guest,
And caught him by the horse-hair plume that dangled on his crest,
With thought to drag him to the Greeks: which he had surely done,
And so besides the victory had wondrous glory won,
Because the needle-painted lace, with which his helm was tied
Beneath his chin, and so about his dainty throat implied,
Had strangled him; but that in time, the Cyprian seed of Jove
Did break the string, with which was lin'd that which the needle wove,
And was the tough thong of a steer; and so the victor's palm
Was (for so full a man at arms) only an empty helm
That then he swung about his head, and cast among his friends,
Who scrambled, and took 't up with shouts. Again then he intends
To force the life-blood of his foe, and ran on him amain,
With shaken javelin; when the queen, that lovers loves, again
Attended, and now ravish'd him from that encounter quite,
With ease, and wondrous suddenly; for she (a goddess) might.
She hid him in a cloud of gold, and never made him known,
Till in his chamber, fresh and sweet, she gently set him down,   400
And went for Helen, whom she found in Scaea's utmost height,
To which whole swarms of city dames had climb'd to see the sight.

  To give her errand good success, she took on her the shape
Of beldame Graea, who was brought by Helen in her rape,
From Lacedaemon, and had trust in all her secrets still,
Being old; and had (of all her maids) the main bent of her will;
And spun for her her finest wool: like her, love's empress came,
Pull'd Helen by the heavenly veil, and softly said: 'Madame,
My lord calls for you, you must needs make all your kind haste home;
He's in your chamber, stays, and longs, sits by your bed; pray come,   410
'Tis richly made, and sweet, but he more sweet, and looks so clear,
So fresh, and movingly attir'd, that (seeing) you would swear
He came not from the dusty fight, but from a courtly dance,
Or would to dancing.' This she made a charm for dalliance,
Whose virtue Helen felt, and knew, by her so radiant eyes,
White neck, and most enticing breasts, the deified disguise.

  At which amaz'd, she answer'd her: 'Unhappy deity,
Why lov'st thou still in these deceits to wrap my phantasy?
Or whither yet (of all the towns given to their lust beside,
In Phrygia, or Maeonia) com'st thou to be my guide?   420
If there (of divers languag'd men) thou hast, as here in Troy,
Some other friend, to be my shame, since here thy latest joy,

By Menelaus now subdu'd, by him shall I be borne
Home to his court, and end my life in triumphs of his scorn.
And to this end, would thy deceits my wanton life allure?
Hence, go thyself to Priam's son, and all the ways abjure
Of gods, or godlike minded dames, nor ever turn again
Thy earth-affecting feet to heav'n, but for his sake sustain
Toils here; guard, grace him endlessly, till he requite thy grace
By giving thee my place with him; or take his servant's place,   430
If all dishonourable ways your favours seek to serve
His never-pleas'd incontinence: I better will deserve
Than serve his dotage now. What shame were it for me to feed
This lust in him; all honour'd dames would hate me for the deed:
He leaves a woman's love so sham'd, and shows so base a mind
To feel nor my shame nor his own; griefs of a greater kind
Wound me, than such as can admit such kind delights so soon.'
    The goddess, angry that (past shame) her mere will was not done,
Replied: 'Incense me not, you wretch, lest (once incens'd) I leave
Thy curs'd life to as strange a hate, as yet it may receive   440
A love from me; and lest I spread through both hosts such despite,
For those plagues they have felt for thee, that both abjure thee quite,
And setting thee in midst of both, turn all their wraths on thee,
And dart thee dead, that such a death may wreak thy wrong of me.'
    This struck the fair dame with such fear, it took her speech away,
And (shadow'd in her snowy veil) she durst not but obey;
And yet, to shun the shame she fear'd, she vanish'd undescried
Of all the Trojan ladies there; for Venus was her guide.
    Arriv'd at home, her women both fell to their work in haste;
When she that was of all her sex the most divinely grac'd   450
Ascended to a higher room, though much against her will,
Where lovely Alexander was, being led by Venus still.
The laughter-loving dame discern'd her mov'd mind, by her grace;
And for her mirth sake set a stool full before Paris face,
Where she would needs have Helen sit; who, though she durst not choose
But sit, yet look'd away for all the goddess pow'r could use,
And us'd her tongue too, and to chide whom Venus sooth'd so much;
And chid, too, in this bitter kind. 'And was thy cowardice such
(So conquer'd) to be seen alive? O would to god thy life
Had perish'd by his worthy hand, to whom I first was wife.   460
Before this, thou wouldst glorify thy valour and thy lance,
And past my first love's boast them far: go once more, and advance
Thy braves against his single power: this foil might fall by chance.
Poor conquer'd man; 'twas such a chance as I would not advise
Thy valour should provoke again: shun him, thou most unwise,

Lest next, thy spirit sent to hell, thy body be his prize.'

   He answer'd: 'Pray thee, woman, cease to chide and grieve me thus:
Disgraces will not ever last; look on their end; on us
Will other gods, at other times, let fall the victor's wreath,
As on him Pallas put it now. Shall our love sink beneath   470
The hate of fortune? In love's fire let all hates vanish. Come,
Love never so inflam'd my heart; no, not when bringing home
Thy beauty's so delicious prize, on Cranaë's blest shore
I long'd for, and enjoy'd thee first.' With this he went before,
She after, to th' odorous bed. While these to pleasure yield,
Perplex'd Atrides, savage-like, ran up and down the field,
And every thickest troop of Troy, and of their far-call'd aid,
Search'd for his foe, who could not be by any eye betray'd;
Nor out of friendship (out of doubt) did they conceal his sight,
All hated him so like their deaths, and ow'd him such despite.   480

   At last thus spake the king of men: 'Hear me, ye men of Troy,
Ye Dardans and the rest, whose pow'rs you in their aids employ,
The conquest on my brother's part, ye all discern is clear:
Do you then Argive Helena, with all her treasure here,
Restore to us, and pay the mulct that by your vows is due;
Yield us an honour'd recompense, and all that should accrue
To our posterities, confirm; that when you render it,
Our acts may here be memoris'd.' This all Greeks else thought fit.

THE END OF THE THIRD BOOK

BOOK FOUR

The Argument

The gods in council at the last decree
That famous Ilion shall expugned be.
And that their own continued faults may prove
The reasons that have so incensed Jove,
Minerva seeks, with more offences done
Against the lately injur'd Atreus' son –
A ground that clearest would make seen their sin –
To have the Lycian Pandarus begin.
He ('gainst the truce with sacred covenants bound)
Gives Menelaus a dishonour'd wound.
Machaon heals him. Agamemnon then
To mortal war incenseth all his men:
The battles join, and in the heat of light,
Cold death shuts many eyes in endless night.

Another Argument

In *Delta* is the gods' assize;
The truce is broke; wars freshly rise.

BOOK FOUR

WITHIN THE FAIR-PAV'D court of Jove, he and the gods conferr'd
    About the sad events of Troy: amongst whom minister'd
    Bless'd Hebe, nectar. As they sat and did Troy's tow'rs behold,
They drank, and pledg'd each other round, in full-crown'd cups of gold.
The mirth at whose feast was begun by great Saturnides,
In urging a begun dislike amongst the goddesses,
But chiefly in his solemn queen, whose spleen he was dispos'd
To tempt yet further, knowing well what anger it inclos'd,
And how wives' angers should be used. On which (thus pleas'd) he play'd:
   'Two goddesses there are that still give Menelaus aid,   10
And one that Paris loves. The two that sit from us so far
(Which Argive Juno is, and she that rules in deeds of war)
No doubt are pleas'd to see how well the late-seen fight did frame:
And yet upon the adverse part, the laughter-loving dame
Made her pow'r good too for her friend. For though he were so near
The stroke of death in th' other's hopes, she took him from them clear:
The conquest yet is questionless the martial Spartan king's;
We must consult then what events shall crown these future things,
If wars and combats we shall still with even successes strike,
Or as impartial friendship plant on both parts. If ye like   20
The last, and that it will as well delight as merely please
Your happy deities, still let stand old Priam's town in peace,
And let the Lacedaemon king again his queen enjoy.'
   As Pallas and heaven's queen sat close, complotting ill to Troy,
With silent murmurs they receiv'd this ill-lik'd choice from Jove.
'Gainst whom was Pallas much incens'd, because the queen of love
Could not without his leave relieve in that late point of death
The son of Priam, whom she loath'd; her wrath yet fought beneath
Her supreme wisdom, and was curb'd: but Juno needs must ease
Her great heart with her ready tongue, and said: 'What words are these,   30
Austere, and too much Saturn's son? Why wouldst thou render still
My labours idle, and the sweat of my industrious will
Dishonour with so little power? My chariot horse are tir'd
With posting to and fro for Greece, and bringing banes desir'd
To people-must'ring Priamus, and his perfidious sons:

Yet thou protect'st, and join'st with them whom each just deity shuns.
Go on, but ever go resolv'd all other gods have vow'd
To cross thy partial course for Troy, in all that makes it proud.'
     At this, the cloud-compelling Jove a far-fetch'd sigh let fly,
And said: 'Thou fury! What offence of such impiety   40
Hath Priam or his sons done thee, that with so high a hate
Thou shouldst thus ceaselessly desire to raze and ruinate
So well a builded town as Troy? I think, hadst thou the pow'r,
Thou wouldst the ports and far-stretch'd walls fly over, and devour
Old Priam and his issue quick, and make all Troy thy feast;
And then at length I hope thy wrath and tired spleen would rest:
To which run on thy chariot, that nought be found in me
Of just cause to our future jars. In this yet strengthen thee,
And fix it in thy memory fast, that if I entertain
As peremptory a desire to level with the plain   50
A city where thy loved live, stand not betwixt my ire
And what it aims at, but give way, when thou hast thy desire,
Which now I grant thee willingly, although against Troy will:
For not beneath the ample sun, and heaven's star-bearing hill,
There is a town of earthly men so honour'd in my mind
As sacred Troy, nor of earth's kings as Priam and his kind,
Who never let my altars lack rich feast of off'rings slain,
And their sweet savours: for which grace I honour them again.'
     Dread Juno, with the cow's fair eyes, replied: 'Three towns there are
Of great and eminent respect, both in my love and care: 60
Mycenae, with the broad highways; and Argos, rich in horse;
And Sparta; all which three destroy, when thou envy'st their force:
I will not aid them, nor malign thy free and sovereign will;
For if I should be envious, and set against their ill,
I know my envy were in vain, since thou art mightier far:
But we must give each other leave, and wink at either's war.
I likewise must have pow'r to crown my works with wished end,
Because I am a deity, and did from thence descend,
Whence thou thyself, and th' elder born: wise Saturn was our sire,
And thus there is a two-fold cause that pleads for my desire,   70
Being sister, and am call'd thy wife: and more, since thy command
Rules all gods else, I claim therein a like superior hand.
All wrath before then now remit, and mutually combine
In either's empire; I thy rule, and thou illustrate mine.
So will the other gods agree, and we shall all be strong.
And first (for this late plot) with speed let Pallas go among
The Trojans, and some one of them entice to break the truce,
By off'ring in some treacherous wound the honour'd Greeks abuse.'

   The father both of men and gods agreed; and Pallas sent
With these wing'd words to both the hosts: 'Make all haste, and invent   80
Some mean by which the men of Troy, against the truce agreed,
May stir the glorious Greeks to arms, with some inglorious deed.'
   Thus charg'd he her with haste, that did before in haste abound;
Who cast herself from all the heights with which steep heaven is crown'd:
And as Jove brandishing a star (which man a comet calls)
Hurls out his curled hair abroad, that from his brand exhals
A thousand sparks, to fleets at sea, and every mighty host,
Of all presages and ill-haps a sign mistrusted most:
So Pallas fell 'twixt both the camps, and suddenly was lost;
When through the breasts of all that saw she struck a strong amaze,   90
With viewing in her whole descent her bright and ominous blaze.
When straight one to another turn'd, and said: 'Now thund'ring Jove
(Great arbiter of peace and arms) will either 'stablish love
Amongst our nations, or renew such war as never was.'
   Thus either army did presage, when Pallas made her pass
Amongst the multitude of Troy; who now put on the grace
Of brave Laodocus, the flow'r of old Antenor's race,
And sought for Lycian Pandarus, a man that being bred
Out of a faithless family, she thought was fit to shed
The blood of any innocent, and break the covenant sworn.   100
He was Lycaon's son, whom Jove into a wolf did turn
For sacrificing of a child, and yet in arms renown'd,
As one that was inculpable: him Pallas standing found,
And round about him his strong troops that bore the shady shields:
He brought them from Aesepus flood, let through the Lycian fields.
Whom standing near, she whisper'd thus: 'Lycaon's warlike son,   5
Shall I despair at thy kind hands to have a favour done?
Nor dar'st thou let an arrow fly upon the Spartan king?
It would be such a grace to Troy, and such a glorious thing,
That every man would give his gift; but Alexander's hand   110
Would load thee with them, if he could discover from his stand
His foe's pride struck down with thy shaft, and he himself ascend
The flaming heap of funeral: come, shoot him, princely friend.
But first invoke the god of light, that in thy land was born,
And is in archers' art the best that ever sheaf hath worn;
To whom a hundred first-ew'd lambs vow thou in holy fire,
When safe to sacred Zelia's tow'rs thy zealous steps retire.'
   With this, the mad-gift-greedy man Minerva did persuade:
Who instantly drew forth a bow, most admirably made
Of th' antler of a jumping goat, bred in a steep up-land;   120
Which archer-like (as long before he took his hidden stand,

The evick skipping from a rock) into the breast he smote,
And headlong fell'd him from his cliff. The forehead of the goat
Held out a wondrous goodly palm, that sixteen branches brought:
Of all which, join'd, an useful bow a skilful bowyer wrought;
Which pick'd and polish'd, both the ends he hid with horns of gold.
And this bow, bent, he close laid down, and bad his soldiers hold
Their shields before him, lest the Greeks, discerning him, should rise
In tumults ere the Spartan king could be his arrow's prize.
Mean space, with all his care he choos'd, and from his quiver drew   130
An arrow, feather'd best for flight, and yet that never flew;
Strong headed, and most apt to pierce; then took he up his bow,
And nock'd his shaft, the ground whence all their future grief did grow.
When praying to his god the sun, that was in Lycia bred,
And king of archers, promising that he the blood would shed
Of full an hundred first fallen lambs, all offer'd to his name,
When to Zelia's sacred walls from rescu'd Troy he came –
He took his arrow by the nock, and to his bended breast
The oxy sinew close he drew, even till the pile did rest
Upon the bosom of the bow; and as that savage prise   140
His strength constrain'd into an orb – as if the wind did rise –
The coming of it made a noise, the sinew-forged string
Did give a mighty twang, and forth the eager shaft did sing
(Affecting speediness of flight) amongst the Achive throng.
Nor were the blessed heavenly powr's unmindful of thy wrong,
O Menelaus; but in chief Jove's seed, the Pillager,
Stood close before, and slack'd the force the arrow did confer,
With as much care and little hurt as doth a mother use,
And keep off from her babe, when sleep doth through his pow'rs diffuse
His golden humour; and th' assaults of rude and busy flies   150
She still checks with her careful hand: for so the shaft she plies,
That on the buttons made of gold which made his girdle fast,
And where his curets double were, the fall of it she plac'd.
And thus much proof she put it to: the buckle made of gold,
The belt it fast'ned, bravely wrought, his curets double fold,
And last, the charmed plate he wore which help'd him more than all,
And 'gainst all darts and shafts bestow'd, was to his life a wall –
So (through all these) the upper skin the head did only race;
Yet forth the blood flow'd, which did much his royal person grace,
And show'd upon his ivory skin, as doth a purple dye   160
Laid (by a dame of Caria, or lovely Maeony)
On ivory, wrought in ornaments to deck the cheeks of horse,
Which in her marriage room must lie: whose beauties have such force,
That they are wish'd of many knights; but are such precious things,

That they are kept for horse that draw the chariots of kings:
Which horse, so deck'd, the charioteer esteems a grace to him.
Like these in grace the blood upon thy solid thighs did swim,
O Menelaus, down thy calves and ankles to the ground:
For nothing decks a soldier so, as doth an honour'd wound.
Yet fearing he had far'd much worse, the hair stood up on end   170
On Agamemnon, when he saw so much black blood descend.
And stiff'ned with the like dismay was Menelaus too:
But seeing th' arrow's stale without, and that the head did go
No further than it might be seen, he call'd his spirits again:
Which Agamemnon marking not, but thinking he was slain,
He grip't his brother by the hand, and sigh'd as he would break,
Which sigh the whole host took from him; who thus at last did speak:
    'O dearest brother, is't for this – that thy death must be wrought –
Wrought I this truce? For this hast thou the single combat fought
For all the army of the Greeks? For this hath Ilion sworn,   180
And trod all faith beneath their feet? Yet all this hath not worn
The right we challeng'd out of force; this cannot render vain
Our stricken right hands, sacred wine, nor all our off'rings slain:
For though Olympius be not quick in making good our ill,
He will be sure as he is slow; and sharplier prove his will.
Their own hands shall be ministers of those plagues they despise
Which shall their wives and children reach, and all their progenies.
For both in mind and soul I know that there shall come a day
When Ilion – Priam – all his pow'r shall quite be worn away,
When heav'n-inhabiting Jove shall shake his fiery shield at all,   190
For this one mischief. This I know, the world cannot recall.
But be all this, all my grief still for thee will be the same,
Dear brother, if thy life must here put out his royal flame:
I shall to sandy Argos turn with infamy my face,
And all the Greeks will call for home: old Priam and his race
Will flame in glory, Helena untouch'd be still their prey,
And thy bones in our enemies' earth our cursed fates shall lay;
Thy sepulchre be trodden down, the pride of Troy desire
(Insulting on it). Thus, O thus, let Agamemnon's ire
In all his acts be expiate, as now he carries home   200
His idle army, empty ships, and leaves here overcome
Good Menelaus. When this brave breaks in their hated breath,
Then let the broad earth swallow me, and take me quick to death.'
    'Nor shall this ever chance,' said he, 'and therefore be of cheer,
Lest all the army, led by you, your passions put in fear:
The arrow fell in no such place as death could enter at;
My girdle, curets doubled here, and my most trusted plate,

Objected all 'twixt me and death, the shaft scarce piercing one.'
'Good brother,' said the king, 'I wish it were no further gone;
For then our best in medicines skill'd shall ope and search the wound,   210
Applying balms to ease thy pains, and soon restore thee sound.'
This said, divine Talthybius he call'd, and bad him haste
Machaon (Aesculapius' son), who most of men was grac'd
With physic's sovereign remedies, to come and lend his hand
To Menelaus, shot by one well skill'd in the command
Of bow and arrows; one of Troy, or of the Lycian aid,
'Who much hath glorified our foe, and us as much dismay'd.'
     He heard and hasted instantly, and cast his eyes about
The thickest squadrons of the Greeks, to find Machaon out.
He found him standing guarded well with well-arm'd men of Thrace,   220
With whom he quickly join'd, and said: 'Man of Apollo's race,
Haste – for the king of men commands – to see a wound impress'd
In Menelaus (great in arms) by one instructed best
In th' art of archery, of Troy, or of the Lycian bands,
That them with much renown adorns, us with dishonour brands.
     Machaon much was mov'd with this, who with the herald flew
From troop to troop alongst the host, and soon they came in view
Of hurt Atrides, circled round with all the Grecian kings,
Who all gave way; and straight he draws the shaft, which forth he brings
Without the forks; the girdle then, plate, curets, off he plucks,   230
And views the wound; when first from it the clotter'd blood he sucks,
Then medicines, wondrously compos'd, the skilful leech applied,
Which loving Chiron taught his sire; he from his sire had tried.
     While these were thus employ'd to ease the Atrean martialist,
The Trojans arm'd, and charg'd the Greeks; the Greeks arm and resist.
Then not asleep, nor maz'd with fear, nor shifting off the blows,
You could behold the king of men, but in full speed he goes
To set a glorious fight on foot: and he examples this
With toiling, like the worst, on foot; who therefore did dismiss
His brass-arm'd chariot, and his steeds, with Ptolomeus' son,   240
(Son of Pyraides) their guide, the good Eurymedon;
'Yet,' said the king, 'attend with them, lest weariness should seize
My limbs, surcharg'd with ordering troops so thick and vast as these.'
     Eurymedon then rein'd his horse, that trotted neighing by;
The king a footman – and so scow'rs the squadrons orderly.
     Those of his swiftly-mounted Greeks that in their arms were fit,
Those he put on with cheerful words, and bad them not remit
The least spark of their forward spirits, because the Trojans durst
Take these abhorr'd advantages, but let them do their worst:
For they might be assur'd that Jove would patronise no lies,   250

And that who with the breach of truce would hurt their enemies,
With vultures should be torn themselves; that they should raze their town,
Their wives, and children at their breast, led vassals to their own.

But such as he beheld hang off from that increasing fight,
Such would he bitterly rebuke, and with disgrace excite:
'Base Argives, blush ye not to stand, as made for butts to darts?
Why are ye thus discomfited like hinds that have no hearts?
Who wearied with a long-run field, are instantly emboss'd,
Stand still, and in their beastly breasts is all their courage lost:
And so stand you struck with amaze, nor dare to strike a stroke.   260
Would ye the foe should nearer yet your dastard spleens provoke,
Even where on Neptune's foamy shore our navies lie in sight,
To see if Jove will hold your hands, and teach ye how to fight?'

Thus he (commanding) rang'd the host, and passing many a band,
He came to the Cretensian troops, where all did armed stand
About the martial Idomen; who bravely stood before
In vanguard of his troops, and match'd for strength a savage boar,
Meriones, his charioteer, the rearguard bringing on.
Which seen to Atreus' son, to him it was a sight alone,
And Idomen's confirmed mind with these kind words he seeks: 270
'O Idomen! I ever lov'd thy self past all the Greeks,
In war, or any work of peace, at table, every where;
For when the best of Greece besides mix ever at our cheer
My good old ardent wine with small, and our inferior mates
Drink even that mix'd wine measur'd too, thou drink'st without those rates
Our old wine neat, and evermore thy bowl stands full like mine,
To drink still when and what thou wilt. Then rouse that heart of thine,
And whatsoever heretofore thou hast assum'd to be,
This day be greater.' To the king in this sort answer'd he:

'Atrides, what I ever seem'd, the same at every part   280
This day shall show me at the full, and I will fit thy heart.
But thou should'st rather cheer the rest, and tell them they in right
Of all good war must offer blows, and should begin the fight
(Since Troy first brake the holy truce) and not indure these braves,
To take wrong first, and then be dar'd to the revenge it craves:
Assuring them that Troy in fate must have the worse at last,
Since first, and 'gainst a truce, they hurt, where they should have embrac'd.'

This comfort and advice did fit Atrides' heart indeed;
Who still through new-rais'd swarms of men held his laborious speed,
And came where both th' Ajaces stood; whom like the last he found   290
Arm'd, casqued, and ready for the fight. Behind them hid the ground
A cloud of foot, that seem'd to smoke. And as a goatherd spies,
On some hill's top, out of the sea, a rainy vapour rise,

Driv'n by the breath of Zephyrus, which though far off he rest,
Comes on as black as pitch, and brings a tempest in his breast,
Whereat he frighted drives his herds apace into a den:
So dark'ning earth with darts and shields show'd these with all their men.

    This sight with like joy fir'd the king, who thus let forth the flame,
In crying out to both the dukes: 'O you of equal name,
I must not cheer, nay, I disclaim all my command of you;   300
Yourselves command with such free minds, and make your soldiers show,
As you nor I led, but themselves. O would our father Jove,
Minerva, and the God of Light, would all our bodies move
With such brave spirits as breathe in you: then Priam's lofty town
Should soon be taken by our hands, for ever overthrown.'

    Then held he on to other troops, and Nestor next beheld,
The subtle Pylian orator, range up and down the field,
Embattelling his men at arms, and stirring all to blows;
Points every legion out his chief, and every chief he shows
The forms and discipline of war: yet his commanders were   310
All expert, and renowned men: great Pelagon was there,
Alastor, manly Chromius, and Hemon worth a throne,
And Byas that could armies lead. With these he first put on
His horse troops with their chariots: his foot (of which he choos'd
Many, the best and ablest men, and which he ever us'd
As rampire to his general power) he in the rear dispos'd.
The slothful, and the least in spirit, he in the midst inclos'd,
That such as wanted noble wills, base need might force to stand.
His horse troops, that the vanguard had, he strictly did command
To ride their horses temperately, to keep their ranks, and shun   320
Confusion, lest their horsemanship and courage made them run
(Too much presum'd on) much too far, and (charging so alone)
Engage themselves in th' enemy's strength, where many fight with one.
'Who his own chariot leaves to range, let him not freely go,
But straight unhorse him with a lance: for 'tis much better so.
And with this discipline,' said he, 'this form, these minds, this trust,
Our ancestors have walls and towns laid level with the dust.'

    Thus prompt, and long inur'd to arms, this old man did exhort;
And this Atrides likewise took in wondrous cheerful sort;
And said: 'O father, would to heav'n that as thy mind remains   330
In wonted vigour, so thy knees could undergo our pains.
But age, that all men overcomes, hath made his prize on thee;
Yet still I wish that some young man, grown old in mind, might be
Put in proportion with thy years; and thy mind, young in age,
Be fitly answer'd with his youth, that still where conflicts rage,
And young men us'd to thirst for fame, thy brave exampling hand

Might double our young Grecian spirits, and grace our whole command.'
   The old knight answer'd: 'I myself could wish, O Atreus' son,
I were as young as when I slew brave Ereuthalion;
But gods at all times give not all their gifts to mortal men.   340
If then I had the strength of youth, I miss'd the counsels then
That years now give me, and now years want that main strength of youth;
Yet still my mind retains her strength (as you now said the sooth),
And would be where that strength is us'd, affording counsels sage
To stir youth's minds up; 'tis the grace and office of our age.
Let younger sinews, men sprung up whole ages after me,
And such as have strength, use it, and as strong in honour be.'
   The king, all this while comforted, arriv'd next where he found
Well-rode Menestheus (Peteus' son) stand still, environ'd round
With his well-train'd Athenian troops; and next to him he spied   350
The wise Ulysses, deedless too, and all his bands beside
Of strong Cephalians; for as yet th' alarm had not been heard
In all their quarters, Greece and Troy were then so newly stirr'd,
And then first mov'd, as they conceiv'd; and they so look'd about
To see both hosts give proof of that they yet had cause to doubt.
   Atrides seeing them stand so still, and spend their eyes at gaze,
Began to chide: 'And why,' said he, 'dissolv'd thus in amaze,
Thou son of Peteus, Jove-nurs'd king, and thou in wicked sleight,
A cunning soldier, stand ye off? Expect ye that the fight
Should be by other men begun? 'Tis fit the foremost band   360
Should show you there; you first should front who first lifts up his hand.
First you can hear, when I invite the princes to a feast,
When first, most friendly, and at will ye eat and drink the best;
Yet in the fight most willingly ten troops ye can behold
Take place before ye.' Ithacus at this his brows did fold,
And said: 'How hath thy violent tongue broke through thy set of teeth
To say that we are slack in fight, and to the field of death
Look others should enforce our way, when we were busied then,
Ev'n when thou speak'st, against the foe to cheer and lead our men?
But thy eyes shall be witnesses, if it content thy will,   370
And that (as thou pretend'st) these cares do so affect thee still:
The father of Telemachus (whom I esteem so dear,
And to whom as a legacy I'll leave my deeds done here)
Even with the foremost band of Troy hath his encounter dar'd,
And therefore are thy speeches vain, and had been better spar'd.'
   He, smiling, since he saw him mov'd, recall'd his words, and said:
'Most generous Laertes' son, most wise of all our aid,
I neither do accuse thy worth, more than thyself may hold
Fit (that inferiors think not much – being slack – to be controll'd),

Nor take I on me thy command: for well I know thy mind   380
Knows how sweet gentle counsels are, and that thou stand'st inclin'd,
As I myself, for all our good. On then: if now we spake
What hath displeas'd, another time we full amends will make:
And gods grant that thy virtue here may prove so free and brave,
That my reproofs may still be vain, and thy deservings grave.'
   Thus parted they; and forth he went, when he did leaning find,
Against his chariot, near his horse, him with a mighty mind,
Great Diomedes (Tydeus' son) and Sthenelus, the seed
Of Capaneius, whom the king seeing likewise out of deed,
Thus cried he out on Diomed: 'O me! In what a fear   390
The wise great warrior, Tydeus' son, stands gazing everywhere
For others to begin the fight! It was not Tydeus' use
To be so daunted, whom his spirit would evermore produce
Before the foremost of his friends in these affairs of fright,
As they report that have beheld him labour in a fight.
For me, I never knew the man, nor in his presence came,
But excellent above the rest he was in general fame.
And one renown'd exploit of his I am assur'd is true;
He came to the Mycenian court, without arms, and did sue
At godlike Polinices' hands, to have some worthy aid   400
To their designs, that 'gainst the walls of sacred Thebes were laid.
He was great Polinices' guest, and nobly entertain'd:
And of the kind Mycenian state what he requested gain'd,
In mere consent: but when they should the same in act approve,
By some sinister prodigies, held out to them by Jove,
They were discourag'd; thence he went, and safely had his pass
Back to Aesopus' flood, renown'd for bulrushes and grass.
Yet, once more their ambassador the Grecian peers address,
Lord Tydeus to Eteocles; to whom being given access,
He found him feasting with a crew of Cadmeans in his hall;   410
Amongst whom, though an enemy, and only one to all,
To all yet he his challenge made at every martial feat,
And eas'ly foil'd all, since with him Minerva was so great.
The rank-rode Cadmeans, much incens'd with their so foul disgrace,
Lodg'd ambuscados for their foe, in some well-chosen place,
By which he was to make return. Twice five-and-twenty men,
And two of them great captains too, the ambush did contain.
The names of those two men of rule were Maeon, Haemon's son,
And Lycophontes, Keep-field call'd, the heir of Autophon,
By all men honour'd like the gods: yet these and all their friends   420
Were sent to hell by Tydeus' hand, and had untimely ends,
He trusting to the aid of gods, reveal'd by augury;

Obeying which one chief he sav'd, and did his life apply
To be the heavy messenger of all the others' deaths;
And that sad message, with his life, to Maeon he bequeaths.
So brave a knight was Tydeus: of whom a son is sprung,
Inferior far in martial deeds, though higher in his tongue.'

　　All this Tydides silent heard, aw'd by the reverend king;
Which stung hot Sthenelus with wrath, who thus put forth his sting:

　　'Atrides, when thou know'st the truth, speak what thy knowledge is,
And do not lie so; for I know, and I will brag in this,
That we are far more able men than both our fathers were;
We took the seven-fold ported Thebes, when yet we had not there
So great help as our fathers had, and fought beneath a wall
(Sacred to Mars) by help of Jove, and trusting to the fall
Of happy signs from other gods; by whom we took the town
Untouch'd, our fathers perishing there by follies of their own:
And therefore never more compare our fathers' worth with ours.'

　　Tydides frown'd at this, and said: 'Suppress thine anger's pow'rs,
Good friend, and hear why I refrain'd: thou seest I am not mov'd　　　　440
Against our general, since he did but what his place behov'd,
Admonishing all Greeks to fight; for if Troy prove our prize,
The honour and the joy is his: if here our ruin lies,
The shame and grief for that as much is his in greatest kinds;
As he then his charge, weigh we ours: which is our dauntless minds.'

　　Thus, from his chariot, amply arm'd, he jump'd down to the ground:
The armour of the angry king so horribly did sound,
It might have made his bravest foe let fear take down his braves.
And as when with the west wind's flaws the sea thrusts up her waves,
One after other, thick and high, upon the groaning shores;　　　　450
First in herself loud, but oppos'd with banks and rocks, she roars,
And, all her back in bristles set, spits every way her foam:
So after Diomed instantly the field was overcome
With thick impressions of the Greeks, and all the noise that grew
(Ordering and cheering up their men) from only leaders flew.
The rest went silently away, you could not hear a voice,
Nor would have thought in all their breasts they had one in their choice,
Their silence uttering their awe of them that them controll'd;
Which made each man keep bright his arms, march, fight still where he should.
The Trojans, like a sort of ewes penn'd in a rich man's fold,　　　　460
Close at his door, till all be milk'd, and never baaing hold,
Hearing the bleating of their lambs, did all their wide host fill
With shouts and clamours; nor observ'd one voice, one baaing still
But show'd mix'd tongues from many a land of men call'd to their aid.
Rude Mars had th' ordering of their spirits; of Greeks, the learned Maid.

But Terror follow'd both the hosts, and Flight, and furious Strife
(The sister and the mate of Mars), that spoil of human life;
And never is her rage at rest; at first she is but small,
Yet after, but a little fed, she grows so vast and tall,
That while her feet move here in earth, her forehead is in heaven: 470
And this was she that made even then both hosts so deadly given.
Through every troop she stalk'd, and stirr'd rough sighs up as she went:
But when in one field both the foes her fury did content,
And both came under reach of darts, then darts and shields oppos'd
To darts and shields; strength answer'd strength; then swords and targets clos'd
With swords and targets, both with pikes, and then did tumult rise
Up to her height; then conquerors' boasts mix'd with the conquer'd's cries.
Earth flow'd with blood. And as from hills rain-waters headlong fall,
That all ways eat huge ruts, which, met in one bed, fill a vall
With such a confluence of streams, that on the mountain grounds   480
Far off, in frighted shepherds' ears, the bustling noise rebounds:
So grew their conflicts, and so show'd their scuffling to the ear,
With flight and clamour still commix'd, and all effects of fear.
    And first renown'd Antilochus slew (fighting in the face
Of all Achaia's foremost bands, with an undaunted grace)
Echepolus Thalysiades: he was an armed man,
Whom on his hair-plum'd helmet's crest the dart first smote, then ran
Into his forehead, and there stuck, the steel pile making way
Quite through his skull; a hasty night shut up his latest day.
His fall was like a light-rac'd tow'r, like which lying there dispread,   490
King Elephenor (who was son to Chalcodon, and led
The valiant Abants), covetous that he might first possess
His arms, laid hands upon his feet, and hal'd him from the press
Of darts and javelins hurl'd at him. The action of the king
When great-in-heart Agenor saw, he made his javelin sing
To th' other's labour; and along as he the trunk did wrest,
His side (at which he bore his shield, in bowing of his breast)
Lay naked, and receiv'd the lance that made him lose his hold
And life together; which in hope of that he lost, he sold.
But for his sake the fight grew fierce; the Trojans and their foes   500
Like wolves on one another rush'd, and man for man it goes.
    The next of name that serv'd his fate great Ajax Telamon
Preferr'd so sadly; he was heir to old Anthemion,
And deck'd with all the flow'r of youth, the fruit of which yet fled,
Before the honour'd nuptial torch could light him to his bed;
His name was Symoisius: for some few years before,
His mother walking down the hill of Ida, by the shore
Of silver Symois, to see her parents' flocks, with them

She feeling suddenly the pains of child-birth, by the stream
Of that bright river brought him forth; and so (of Symois) 510
They call'd him Symoisius. Sweet was that birth of his
To his kind parents, and his growth did all their care employ;
And yet those rites of piety, that should have been his joy
To pay their honour'd years again, in as affectionate sort,
He could not graciously perform, his sweet life was so short,
Cut off with mighty Ajax' lance. For as his spirit put on,
He struck him at his breast's right pap, quite through his shoulder-bone;
And in the dust of earth he fell, that was the fruitful soil
Of his friends' hopes; but where he sow'd he buried all his toil.
And as a poplar shot aloft, set by a river side, 520
In moist edge of a mighty fen, his head in curls implied,
But all his body plain and smooth; to which a wheelwright puts
The sharp edge of his shining axe, and his soft timber cuts
From his innative root, in hope to hew out of his bole
The fell'ffs, or out-parts of a wheel, that compass in the whole,
To serve some goodly chariot; but being big and sad,
And to be hal'd home through the bogs, the useful hope he had
Sticks there; and there the goodly plant lies withering out his grace:
So lay by Jove-bred Ajax' hand Anthemion's forward race,
Nor could through that vast fen of toils be drawn to serve the ends 530
Intended by his body's pow'rs, nor cheer his aged friends.
　　But now the gay-arm'd Antiphus (a son of Priam) threw
His lance at Ajax through the press, which went by him, and flew
On Leucus, wise Ulysses' friend; his groin it smote, as fain
He would have drawn into his spoil the carcass of the slain,
By which he fell, and that by him; it vex'd Ulysses' heart,
Who thrust into the face of fight, well arm'd at every part,
Came close, and look'd about to find an object worth his lance;
Which when the Trojans saw him shake, and he so near advance,
All shrunk. He threw, and forth it shin'd, nor fell but where it fell'd: 540
His friend's grief gave it angry pow'r, and deadly way it held
Upon Democoön, who was sprung of Priam's wanton force,
Came from Abydus, and was made the master of his horse;
Through both his temples struck the dart; the wood of one side shew'd,
The pile out of the other look'd, and so the earth he strew'd
With much sound of his weighty arms. Then back the foremost went,
Ev'n Hector yielded; then the Greeks gave worthy clamours vent,
Effecting then their first dumb pow'rs; some drew the dead, and spoil'd,
Some follow'd, that in open flight Troy might confess it foil'd.
Apollo, angry at the sight, from top of Ilion cried: 550
'Turn head, ye well-rode peers of Troy, feed not the Grecians' pride;

They are not charm'd against your points, of steel nor iron fram'd;
Nor lights the fair-hair'd Thetis' son, but sits at fleet inflam'd.'
  So spake the dreadful god from Troy. The Greeks, Jove's noblest seed
Encourag'd to keep on the chace: and where fit spirit did need,
She gave it, marching in the midst. Then flew the fatal hour
Back on Diores, in return of Ilion's sun-burn'd pow'r,
Diores Amarincides, whose right leg's ankle-bone
And both the sinews, with a sharp and handful-charging stone,
Pirus Imbrasides did break, that led the Thracian bands,   560
And came from Aenos; down he fell, and up he held his hands
To his lov'd friends; his spirit wing'd to fly out of his breast,
With which not satisfied, again Imbrasides address'd
His javelin at him, and so ripp'd his navel, that the wound,
As endlessly it shut his eyes, so open'd on the ground,
It pour'd his entrails. As his foe went then suffic'd away,
Thoas Aetolius threw a dart that did his pile convey
Above his nipple, through his lungs; when (quitting his stern part)
He clos'd with him, and from his breast first drawing out his dart,
His sword flew in, and by the midst it wip'd his belly out,   570
So took his life, but left his arms: his friends so flock'd about,
And thrust forth lances of such length, before their slaughter'd king,
Which, though their foe were big and strong, and often brake the ring
Forg'd of their lances, yet (enforc'd) he left th' affected prize;
The Thracian and Epeian dukes laid close with closed eyes,
By either other, drown'd in dust; and round about the plain
All hid with slaughter'd carcasses, yet still did hotly reign
The martial planet, whose effects had any eye beheld
Free and unwounded (and were led by Pallas through the field,
To keep off javelins, and suggest the least fault could be found),   580
He could not reprehend the fight, so many strew'd the ground.

THE END OF THE FOURTH BOOK

BOOK FIVE

The Argument

King Diomed (by Pallas' spirit inspir'd
With will and power) is for his acts admir'd:
Mere men, and men deriv'd from deities,
And deities themselves, he terrifies;
Add wounds to terrors; his inflamed lance
Draws blood from Mars, and Venus; in a trance
He casts Aeneas with a weighty stone;
Apollo quickens him, and gets him gone:
Mars is recur'd by Paeon, but by Jove
Rebuk'd, for authoring breach of human love.

Another Argument

In *Epsilon*, heav'n's blood is shed
By sacred rage of Diomed.

BOOK FIVE

THEN PALLAS breath'd in Tydeus' son: to render whom supreme
    To all the Greeks, at all his parts, she cast a hotter beam
    On his high mind, his body fill'd with much superior might,
And made his complete armour cast a far more complete light.
From his bright helm and shield did burn a most unwearied fire,
Like rich Autumnus' golden lamp, whose brightness men admire
Past all the other host of stars, when with his cheerful face,
Fresh wash'd in lofty ocean waves, he doth the skies enchase.
    To let whose glory lose no sight, still Pallas made him turn
Where tumult most express'd his power, and where the fight did burn.   10
    An honest and a wealthy man inhabited in Troy –
Dares the priest of Mulciber, who two sons did enjoy,
Idaeus and bold Phegeus, well seen in every fight:
These (singled from their troops, and hors'd) assail'd Minerva's knight,
Who rang'd from fight to fight, on foot; all hasting mutual charge
(And now drawn near), first Phegeus threw a javelin swift and large;
Whose head the king's left shoulder took, but did no harm at all:
Then rush'd he out a lance at him, that had no idle fall,
But in his breast stuck 'twixt the paps, and struck him from his horse.
Which stern sight when Idaeus saw (distrustful of his force   20
To save his slaughter'd brother's spoil), it made him headlong leap
From his fair chariot, and leave all: yet had not 'scap'd the heap
Of heavy funeral, if the god, great president of fire,
Had not in sudden clouds of smoke (and pity of his sire,
To leave him utterly unheir'd) giv'n safe pass to his feet.
He gone, Tydides sent the horse and chariot to the fleet.
    The Trojans seeing Dares' sons, one slain, the other fled,
Were struck-amaz'd: the blue-ey'd Maid (to grace her Diomed
In giving free way to his power) made this so ruthful fact
A fit advantage to remove the war-god out of act,   30
Who rag'd so on the Ilion side; she grip't his hand and said:
'Mars, Mars, thou ruiner of men, that in the dust hast laid
So many cities, and with blood thy godhead dost distain,
Now shall we cease to show our breasts as passionate as men,
And leave the mixture of our hands, resigning Jove his right –

As rector of the gods – to give the glory of the fight
Where he affecteth, lest he force what we should freely yield?
He held it fit, and went with her from the tumultuous field,
Who set him in an herby seat, on broad Scamander's shore.
He gone, all Troy was gone with him; the Greeks drave all before,   40
And every leader slew a man; but first the king of men
Deserv'd the honour of his name, and led the slaughter then,
And slew a leader, one more huge than any man he led,
Great Odius, duke of Halizons; quite from his chariot's head
He struck him with a lance to earth, as first he flight address'd;
It took his forward-turned back, and look'd out of his breast:
His huge trunk sounded, and his arms did echo the resound.
    Idomenaeus to the death did noble Phaestus wound,
The son of Maeon Borus, that from cloddy Terna came:
Who, taking chariot, took his wound, and tumbled with the same   50
From his attempted seat; the lance through his right shoulder strook,
And horrid darkness struck through him: the spoil his soldiers took.
    Atrides-Menelaus slew (as he before him fled)
Scamandrius, son of Strophius, that was a huntsman bred;
A skilful huntsman, for his skill Diana's self did teach,
And made him able with his dart, infallibly to reach
All sorts of subtlest savages, which many a woody hill
Bred for him, and he much preserv'd – and all to show his skill.
Yet not the dart-delighting queen taught him to shun this dart,
Nor all his hitting so far off (the mast'ry of his art):   60
His back receiv'd it, and he fell upon his breast withal:
His body's ruin, and his arms, so sounded in his fall,
That his affrighted horse flew off, and left him like his life.
    Meriones slew Phereclus, whom she that ne'er was wife,
Yet goddess of good housewives, held in excellent respect,
For knowing all the witty things that grace an architect,
And having pow'r to give it all the cunning use of hand:
Harmonides his sire built ships, and made him understand
(With all the practice it requir'd) the frame of all that skill.
He built all Alexander's ships, that author'd all the ill   70
Of all the Trojans and his own, because he did not know
The oracles advising Troy, for fear of overthrow,
To meddle with no sea affair but live by tilling land.
This man Meriones surpris'd, and drave his deadly hand
Through his right hip; the lance's head ran through the region
About the bladder, underneath th' in-muscles, and the bone;
He (sighing) bow'd his knees to death, and sacrific'd to earth.
    Phylides stay'd Pedaeus' flight, Antenor's bastard birth,

Whom virtuous Theano his wife, to please her husband, kept
As tenderly as those she lov'd. Phylides near him stept,   80
And in the fountain of the nerves did drench his fervent lance,
At his head's back-part; and so far the sharp head did advance,
It cleft the organ of his speech, and th' iron, cold as death,
He took betwixt his grinning teeth, and gave the air his breath.

Eurypilus the much renown'd, and great Evemon's son,
Divine Hypsenor slew, begot by stout Dolopion
And consecrate Scamander's priest; he had a god's regard
Amongst the people: his hard flight the Grecian follow'd hard,
Rush'd in so close, that with his sword he on his shoulder laid
A blow that his arm's brawn cut off; nor there his vigour stay'd,   90
But drave down, and from off his wrist it hew'd his holy hand,
That gush'd out blood, and down it dropp'd upon the blushing sand;
Death with his purple finger shut – and violent fate – his eyes.

Thus fought these, but distinguish'd well, Tydides so implies
His fury, that you could not know whose side had interest
In his free labours, Greece or Troy. But as a flood increas'd
By violent and sudden show'rs, let down from hills like hills
Melted in fury, swells and foams, and so he overfills
His natural channel, that besides both hedge and bridge resigns
To his rough confluence, far spread, and lusty flourishing vines   100
Drown'd in his outrage: Tydeus' son so overran the field,
Strew'd such as flourish'd in his way, and made whole squadrons yield.

When Pandarus, Lycaon's son, beheld his ruining hand
With such resistless insolence make lanes through every band,
He bent his gold-tipp'd bow of horn, and shot him (rushing in)
At his right shoulder, where his arms were hollow; forth did spin
The blood, and down his curets ran; then Pandarus cried out:
'Rank-riding Trojans, now rush in: now, now, I make no doubt
Our bravest foe is mark'd for death; he cannot long sustain
My violent shaft, if Jove's fair son did worthily constrain   110
My foot from Lycia.' Thus he brav'd, and yet his violent shaft
Struck short with all his violence; Tydides life was sav'd;
Who yet withdrew himself behind his chariot and steeds,
And call'd to Sthenelus: 'Come, friend, my wounded shoulder needs
Thy hand to ease it of this shaft.' He hasted from his seat
Before the coach, and drew the shaft: the purple wound did sweat,
And drown his shirt of mail in blood, and as it bled he pray'd:

'Hear me, of Jove Aegiochus thou most unconquer'd Maid,
If ever in the cruel field thou hast assistful stood
Or to my father or myself, now love, and do me good;   120
Give him into my lance's reach that thus hath giv'n a wound

To him thou guard'st, preventing me, and brags that never more
I shall behold the cheerful sun.' Thus did the king implore.
The goddess heard, came near, and took the weariness of fight
From all his nerves and lineaments, and made them fresh and light,
And said: 'Be bold, O Diomed, in every combat shine;
The great shield-shaker Tydeus' strength (that knight, that sire of thine)
By my infusion breathes in thee. And from thy knowing mind
I have remov'd those erring mists that made it lately blind,
That thou may'st difference gods from men, and therefore use thy skill   130
Against the tempting deities, if any have a will
To try if thou presum'st of that as thine, that flows from them,
And so assum'st above thy right. Where thou discern'st a beam
Of any other heavenly power than she that rules in love,
That calls thee to the change of blows, resist not, but remove;
But if that goddess be so bold (since she first stirr'd this war),
Assault and mark her from the rest, with some infamous scar.'
    The blue-eyed goddess vanished, and he was seen again
Amongst the foremost; who before though he were prompt and fain
To fight against the Trojans powers, now on his spirits were call'd   140
With thrice the vigour – lion-like, that hath been lately gall'd
By some bold shepherd in a field, where his curl'd flocks were laid,
Who took him as he leap'd the fold; not slain yet, but appay'd
With greater spirit, comes again, and then the shepherd hides
(The rather for the desolate place) and in his coate abides,
His flocks left guardless; which amaz'd, shake and shrink up in heaps;
He ruthless freely takes his prey, and out again he leaps:
So sprightly, fierce, victorious, the great heroë flew
Upon the Trojans, and at once he two commanders slew,
Hypenor and Astynous; in one his lance he fix'd   150
Full at the nipple of his breast, the other smote betwixt
The neck and shoulder with his sword; which was so well laid on,
It swept his arm and shoulder off. These left, he rush'd upon
Abbas and Polyëidus, of old Eurydamas
The hapless sons; who could by dreams tell what would come to pass:
Yet when his sons set forth to Troy, the old man could not read
By their dreams what would chance to them; for both were stricken dead
By great Tydides. After these, he takes into his rage
Xanthus, and Thoön, Phenops' sons, born to him in his age;
The good old man even pin'd with years, and had not one son more   160
To heir his goods; yet Diomed took both, and left him store
Of tears and sorrows in their steads, since he could never see
His sons leave those hot wars alive: so this the end must be
Of all his labours; what he heap'd, to make his issue great,

Authority heir'd, and with her seed fill'd his forgotten seat.
Then snatch'd he up two Priamists that in one chariot stood,
Echemon and fair Chromius; as feeding in a wood
Oxen or steers are, one of which a lion leaps upon,
Tears down, and wrings in two his neck: so sternly Tydeus' son
Threw from their chariot both these hopes of old Dardanides,   170
Then took their arms, and sent their horse to those that ride the seas.

Aeneas, seeing the troops thus toss'd, broke through the heat of fight
And all the whizzing of the darts, to find the Lycian knight,
Lycaon's son; whom having found, he thus bespake the peer:

'O Pandarus! Where's now thy bow? Thy deathful arrows, where?
In which no one in all our host but gives the palm to thee;
Nor in the sun-lov'd Lycian greens, that breed our archery,
Lives any that exceeds thyself. Come, lift thy hands to Jove,
And send an arrow at this man, if but a man he prove,
That wins such god-like victories, and now affects our host   180
With so much sorrow: since so much of our best blood is lost
By his high valour, I have fear some god in him doth threat,
Incens'd for want of sacrifice; the wrath of god is great.'

Lycaon's famous son replied: 'Great counsellor of Troy,
This man so excellent in arms, I think is Tydeus' joy;
I know him by his fiery shield, by his bright three-plum'd casque,
And by his horse; nor can I say, if or some god doth mask
In his appearance, or he be whom I nam'd Tydeus' son:
But without god the things he does for certain are not done.
Some great immortal, that conveys his shoulders in a cloud,   190
Goes by and puts by every dart at his bold breast bestow'd,
Or lets it take with little hurt; for I myself let fly
A shaft that shot him through his arms, but had as good gone by:
Yet which I gloriously affirm'd, had driven him down to hell.
Some god is angry, and with me; for far hence, where I dwell,
My horse and chariots idle stand, with which some other way
I might repair this shameful miss: eleven fair chariots stay
In old Lycaon's court, new made, new trimm'd to have been gone,
Curtain'd and arrast under foot, two horse to every one,
That eat white barley and black oats, and do no good at all: 200
And these Lycaon (that well knew how these affairs would fall)
Charg'd, when I set down this design, I should command with here;
And gave me many lessons more, all which much better were
Than any I took forth myself. The reason I laid down
Was but the sparing of my horse, since in a sieged town
I thought our horse-meat would be scant, when they were us'd to have
Their manger full; so I left them, and like a lackey slave

Am come to Ilion, confident in nothing but my bow,
That nothing profits me; two shafts I vainly did bestow
At two great princes, but of both, my arrows neither slew;   210
Nor this, nor Atreus' younger son: a little blood I drew,
That serv'd but to incense them more. In an unhappy star
I therefore from my armoury have drawn those tools of war,
That day when for great Hector's sake, to amiable Troy
I came to lead the Trojan bands. But if I ever joy
(In safe return) my country's sight, my wives, my lofty tow'rs,
Let any stranger take this head, if to the fiery pow'rs
This bow, these shafts, in pieces burst, by these hands be not thrown,
Idle companions that they are, to me and my renown.'
    Aeneas said: 'Use no such words; for any other way   220
Than this, they shall not now be us'd: we first will both assay
This man with horse and chariot. Come then, ascend to me,
That thou mayst try our Trojan horse, how skill'd in field they be,
And in pursuing those that fly, or flying being pursu'd,
How excellent they are of foot: and these, if Jove conclude
The 'scape of Tydeus again, and grace him with our flight,
Shall serve to bring us safely off. Come, I'll be first shall fight:
Take thou these fair reins and this scourge; or (if thou wilt) fight thou,
And leave the horses' care to me.' He answer'd: 'I will now
Descend to fight; keep thou the reins, and guide thyself thy horse,   230
Who with their wonted manager will better wield the force
Of the impulsive chariot, if we be driven to fly,
Than with a stranger; under whom they will be much more shy,
And fearing my voice, wishing thine, grow resty; nor go on
To bear us off, but leave engag'd mighty Tydeus' son,
Themselves and us. Then be thy part thy one-hoof'd horses' guide;
I'll make the fight, and with a dart receive his utmost pride.'
    With this the gorgeous chariot both thus prepar'd ascend,
And make full way at Diomed; which noted by his friend:
'Mine own most loved mind,' said he, 'two mighty men of war   240
I see come with a purpos'd charge: one's he that hits so far
With bow and shaft, Lycaon's son; the other fames the brood
Of great Anchises, and the queen that rules in amorous blood,
Aeneas, excellent in arms: come up, and use your steeds,
And look not war so in the face, lest that desire that feeds
Thy great mind be the bane of it.' This did with anger sting
The blood of Diomed, to see his friend, that chid the king
Before the fight, and then preferr'd his ableness, and his mind,
To all his ancestors in fight, now come so far behind.
Whom thus he answer'd: 'Urge no flight, you cannot please me so: 250

Nor is it honest in my mind to fear a coming foe,
Or make a flight good, though with fight; my powers are yet entire,
And scorn the help-tire of a horse; I will not blow the fire
Of their hot valours with my flight, but cast upon the blaze
This body borne upon my knees. I entertain amaze?
Minerva will not see that shame; and since they have begun,
They shall not both elect their ends, and he that 'scapes shall run,
Or stay and take the other's fate; and this I leave for thee:
If amply wise Athenia give both their lives to me,
Rein our horse to their chariot hard, and have a special heed   260
To seize upon Aeneas' steeds, that we may change their breed,
And make a Grecian race of them that have been long of Troy;
For these are bred of those brave beasts, which for the lovely boy
That waits now on the cup of Jove, Jove, that far-seeing god,
Gave Tros the king in recompense, the best that ever trod
The sounding centre, underneath the morning and the sun.
Anchises stole the breed of them, for where their sires did run,
He closely put his mares to them, and never made it known
To him that heir'd them, who was then the king Laomedon.
Six horses had he of that race, of which himself kept four,   270
And gave the other two his son; and these are they that scour
The field so bravely towards us, expert in charge and flight:
If these we have the power to take, our prize is exquisite,
And our renown will far exceed.' While these were talking thus,
The fir'd horse brought th' assailants near, and thus spake Pandarus:
    'Most suff'ring-minded Tydeus' son, that hast of war the art,
My shaft that struck thee, slew thee not; I now will prove a dart.'
This said, he shook, and then he threw, a lance, aloft and large,
That in Tydides' curets stuck, quite driving through his targe;
Then bray'd he out so wild a voice that all the field might hear: 280
'Now have I reach'd thy root of life, and by thy death shall bear
Our praise's chief prize from the field.' Tydides undismay'd
Replied: 'Thou err'st, I am not touch'd; but more charge will be laid
To both your lives before you part; at least the life of one
Shall satiate the throat of Mars.' This said – his lance was gone:
Minerva led it to his face, which at his eye ran in,
And as he stoop'd struck through his jaws, his tongue's root, and his chin.
Down from the chariot he fell, his gay arms shin'd and rung,
The swift horse trembled, and his soul for ever charm'd his tongue.
    Aeneas with his shield and lance leapt swiftly to his friend,   290
Afraid the Greeks would force his trunk; and that he did defend,
Bold as a lion of his strength: he hid him with his shield,
Shook round his lance, and horribly did threaten all the field

With death, if any durst make in. Tydides rais'd a stone
With his one hand, of wondrous weight, and pour'd it mainly on
The hip of Anchisiades, wherein the joint doth move
The thigh ('tis call'd the buckle-bone), which all in sherds it drove,
Brake both the nerves, and with the edge cut all the flesh away.
It stagger'd him upon his knees, and made th' heroë stay
His struck-blind temples on his hand, his elbow on the earth;   300
And there this prince of men had died, if she that gave him birth
(Kiss'd by Anchises on the green, where his fair oxen fed,
Jove's loving daughter) instantly had not about him spread
Her soft embraces, and convey'd within her heavenly veil
(Us'd as a rampire 'gainst all darts, that did so hot assail)
Her dear-lov'd issue from the field. Then Sthenelus in haste
(Remembering what his friend advis'd) from forth the press made fast
His own horse to their chariot, and presently laid hand
Upon the lovely-coated horse Aeneas did command.
Which bringing to the wond'ring Greeks, he did their guard commend   310
To his belov'd Deiphylus (who was his inward friend,
And of his equals one to whom he had most honour shown),
That he might see them safe at fleet: then stept he to his own,
With which he cheerfully made in, to Tydeus' mighty race.
He, mad with his great enemy's rape, was hot in desperate chace
Of her that made it with his lance, arm'd less with steel than spite,
Well knowing her no deity that had to do in fight –
Minerva his great patroness, nor she that raceth towns,
Bellona, but a goddess weak, and foe to men's renowns.
Her through a world of fight pursu'd at last he overtook,   320
And thrusting up his ruthless lance, her heavenly veil he strook
(That ev'n the Graces wrought themselves, at her divine command)
Quite through, and hurt the tender back of her delicious hand:
The rude point piercing through her palm, forth flow'd th' immortal blood
(Blood such as flows in blessed gods, that eat no human food,
Nor drink of our inflaming wine, and therefore bloodless are,
And call'd immortals); out she cried, and could no longer bear
Her lov'd son, whom she cast from her; and in a sable cloud,
Phoebus receiving, hid him close from all the Grecian crowd,
Lest some of them should find his death. Away flew Venus then,   330
And after her cried Diomed: 'Away, thou spoil of men,
Though sprung from all-preserving Jove; these hot encounters leave:
Is 't not enough that silly dames thy sorceries should deceive,
Unless thou thrust into the war, and rob a soldier's right?
I think a few of these assaults will make thee fear the fight,
Wherever thou shalt hear it nam'd.' She, sighing, went her way

Extremely griev'd, and with her griefs her beauties did decay,
And black her ivory body grew. Then from a dewy mist
Brake swift-foot Iris to her aid, from all the darts that hiss'd
At her quick rapture; and to Mars they took their plaintive course,　　340
And found him on the fight's left hand; by him his speedy horse
And huge lance, lying in a fog. The queen of all things fair
Her loved brother on her knees besought with instant prayer,
His golden-riband-bound-man'd horse to lend her up to heav'n;
For she was much griev'd with a wound a mortal man had giv'n,
Tydides, that 'gainst Jove himself durst now advance his arm.

　　He granted, and his chariot (perplex'd with her late harm)
She mounted, and her waggoness was she that paints the air;
The horse she rein'd and with a scourge importun'd their repair,
That of themselves out-flew the wind, and quickly they ascend　　350
Olympus, high seat of the gods. Th' horse knew their journey's end,
Stood still, and from their chariot the windy-footed dame
Dissolv'd, and gave them heavenly food; and to Dione came
Her wounded daughter; bent her knees; she kindly bade her stand,
With sweet embraces help'd her up, strok'd her with her soft hand,
Call'd kindly by her name, and ask'd: 'What god hath been so rude,
Sweet daughter, to chastise thee thus, as if thou wert pursu'd
Even to the act of some light sin, and deprehended so?
For otherwise, each close escape is in the great let go.'

　　She answer'd: 'Haughty Tydeus' son hath been so insolent,　　360
Since he whom most my heart esteems of all my lov'd descent
I rescu'd from his bloody hand: now battle is not giv'n
To any Trojans by the Greeks, but by the Greeks to heav'n.'

　　She answer'd: 'Daughter, think not much, though much it grieve thee: use
The patience, whereof many gods examples may produce,
In many bitter ills receiv'd, as well that men sustain
By their inflictions, as by men repaid to them again.
Mars suffer'd much more than thyself by Ephialtes' pow'r
And Otus', Aloeus' sons, who in a brazen tow'r
And in inextricable chains, cast that war-greedy god;　　370
Where twice six months and one he liv'd; and there the period
Of his sad life perhaps had clos'd, if his kind stepdame's eye
(Fair Erebaea) had not seen, who told it Mercury;
And he by stealth enfranchis'd him, though he could scarce enjoy
The benefit of franchisement, the chains did so destroy
His vital forces with their weight. So Juno suffer'd more,
When with a three-fork'd arrow's head Amphitryon's son did gore
Her right breast, past all hope of cure. Pluto sustain'd no less
By that self man, and by a shaft of equal bitterness,

Shot through his shoulder at hell gates; and there amongst the dead   380
(Were he not deathless) he had died: but up to heaven he fled
(Extremely tortur'd) for recure, which instantly he won
At Paeon's hand, with sovereign balm; and this did Jove's great son,
Unblest, great-high-deed-daring man, that car'd not doing ill,
That with his bow durst wound the gods! But by Minerva's will
Thy wound the foolish Diomed was so profane to give,
Not knowing he that fights with heav'n hath never long to live;
And for this deed, he never shall have child about his knee
To call him father, coming home. Besides, hear this from me,
Strength-trusting man, though thou be strong, and art in strength a tow'r,   390
Take heed a stronger meet thee not, and that a woman's pow'r
Contains not that superior strength, and lest that woman be
Adrastus' daughter, and thy wife, the wise Aegiale,
When – from this hour not far – she wakes, even sighing with desire
To kindle our revenge on thee with her enamouring fire,
In choosing her some fresh young friend, and so drown all thy fame,
Won here in war, in her court-peace, and in an opener shame.'
    This said, with both her hands she cleans'd the tender back and palm
Of all the sacred blood they lost; and, never using balm,
The pain ceas'd, and the wound was cur'd of this kind queen of love.   400
    Juno and Pallas seeing this, assay'd to anger Jove
And quit his late made mirth with them about the loving dame,
With some sharp jest, in like sort built upon her present shame.
Gray-ey'd Athenia began, and ask'd the Thunderer,
If – nothing moving him to wrath – she boldly might prefer
What she conceiv'd to his conceit: and staying no reply,
She bade him view the Cyprian fruit he lov'd so tenderly;
Whom she thought hurt, and by this means, intending to suborn
Some other lady of the Greeks (whom lovely veils adorn)
To gratify some other friend of her much-loved Troy,   410
As she embrac'd and stirr'd her blood to the Venerean joy,
The golden clasp those Grecian dames upon their girdles wear,
Took hold of her delicious hand, and hurt it, she had fear.
    The Thunderer smil'd, and call'd to him love's golden Arbitress
And told her those rough works of war were not for her access:
She should be making marriages, embracings, kisses, charms;
Stern Mars and Pallas had the charge of those affairs in arms.
    While these thus talk'd, Tydides' rage still thirsted to achieve
His prize upon Anchises' son, though well he did perceive
The Sun himself protected him: but his desires (enflam'd   420
With that great Trojan prince's blood, and arms so highly fam'd)
Not that great god did reverence. Thrice rush'd he rudely on,

And thrice betwixt his darts and death the Sun's bright target shone:
But when upon the fourth assault (much like a spirit) he flew,
The far-off working deity exceeding wrathful grew,
And ask'd him: 'What! Not yield to gods? Thy equals learn to know:
The race of gods is far above men creeping here below.'

   This drave him to some small retreat: he would not tempt more near
The wrath of him that struck so far, whose power had now set clear
Aeneas from the stormy field, within the holy place   430
Of Pergamus; where, to the hope of his so sovereign grace,
A goodly temple was advanc'd, in whose large inmost part
He left him, and to his supply inclin'd his mother's heart
(Latona) and the dart-pleas'd queen, who cur'd and made him strong.

   The silver-bow'd-fair god then threw in the tumultuous throng
An image, that in stature, look and arms he did create
Like Venus' son; for which the Greeks and Trojans made debate,
Laid loud strokes on their ox-hide shields and bucklers easily borne –
Which error Phoebus pleas'd to urge on Mars himself in scorn:

   'Mars, Mars,' said he, 'thou plague of men, smear'd with the dust and blood
Of humans and their ruin'd walls, yet thinks thy godhead good
To fright this fury from the field, who next will fight with Jove?
First, in a bold approach he hurt the moist palm of thy love:
And next (as if he did affect to have a deity's pow'r)
He held out his assault on me.'

                    This said, the lofty tow'r
Of Pergamus he made his seat; and Mars did now excite
The Trojan forces, in the form of him that led to fight
The Thracian troops, swift Acamas. 'O Priam's sons,' said he,
'How long the slaughter of your men can ye sustain to see?
Even till they brave you at your gates? Ye suffer beaten down   450
Aeneas, great Anchises' son, whose prowess we renown
As much as Hector's: fetch him off from this contentious prease.'

   With this, the strength and spirits of all his courage did increase:
And yet Sarpedon seconds him, with this particular taunt
Of noble Hector: 'Hector, where is thy unthankful vaunt,
And that huge strength on which it built? That thou, and thy allies,
With all thy brothers (without aid of us or our supplies,
And troubling not a citizen) the city safe would hold ?
In all which friends' and brothers' helps, I see not, nor am told,
Of any one of their exploits; but – all held in dismay   460
Of Diomed, like a sort of dogs that at a lion bay,
And entertain no spirit to pinch – we, your assistants here,
Fight for the town as you help'd us; and I (an aiding peer,
No citizen) even out of care that doth become a man

For men and children's liberties, add all the aid I can –
Not out of my particular cause; far hence my profit grows,
For far hence Asian Lycia lies, where gulfy Xanthus flows
And where my lov'd wife, infant son, and treasure nothing scant,
I left behind me (which I see those men would have, that want:
And therefore they that have, would keep) yet I – as I would lose   470
Their sure fruition – cheer my troops, and with their lives propose
Mine own life, both to general fight, and to particular cope
With this great soldier, though I say I entertain no hope
To have such gettings as the Greeks, nor fear to lose like Troy.
Yet thou (even Hector) deedless stand'st, and car'st not to employ
Thy town-born friends, to bid them stand, to fight and save their wives,
Lest as a fowler casts his nets upon the silly lives
Of birds of all sorts, so the foe your walls and houses hales,
One with another, on all heads; or such as 'scape their falls
Be made the prey and prize of them (as willing overthrown,   480
That holp not for you with their force) and so this brave-built town
Will prove a chaos. That deserves in thee so hot a care
As should consume thy days and nights, to hearten and prepare
Th' assistant princes: pray their minds to bear their fat-brought toils,
To give them worth with worthy fight, in victories and foils
Still to be equal, and thyself, exampling them in all,
Need no reproofs nor spurs. All this in thy free choice should fall.'
    This stung great Hector's heart; and yet, as every generous mind
Should silent bear a just reproof, and show what good they find
In worthy counsels, by their ends put into present deeds,   490
Not stomach nor be vainly sham'd, so Hector's spirit proceeds
And from his chariot, wholly arm'd, he jump'd upon the sand,
On foot so toiling through the host, a dart in either hand,
And all hands turn'd against the Greeks; the Greeks despis'd their worst,
And, thick'ning their instructed powers, expected all they durst.
    Then with the feet of horse and foot the dust in clouds did rise:
And as in sacred floors of barns, upon corn-winnowers flies
The chaff, driven with an opposite wind, when yellow Ceres dites,
Which all the diters' feet, legs, arms, their heads and shoulders whites:
So look'd the Grecians gray with dust, that struck the solid heav'n,   500
Rais'd from returning chariots and troops together driv'n.
Each side stood to their labours firm: fierce Mars flew through the air,
And gather'd darkness from the fight, and with his best affair
Obey'd the pleasure of the Sun, that wears the golden sword,
Who bade him raise the spirits of Troy, when Pallas ceas'd t' afford
Her helping office to the Greeks. And then his own hands wrought,
Which (from his fane's rich chancel, cur'd) the true Aeneas brought,

And plac'd him by his peers in field, who did with joy admire
To see him both alive and safe, and all his pow'rs entire,
Yet stood not sifting how it chanc'd: another sort of task,   510
Then stirring th' idle sieve of news, did all their forces ask,
Inflam'd by Phoebus, harmful Mars, and Eris, eag'rer far.
The Greeks had none to hearten them; their hearts rose with the war,
But chiefly Diomed, Ithacus, and both th' Ajaces us'd
Stirring examples and good words: their own fames had infus'd
Spirit enough into their bloods to make them neither fear
The Trojans force nor Fate itself, but still expecting were
When most was done, what would be more; their ground they still made good.
And in their silence and set pow'rs, like fair still clouds they stood,
With which Jove crowns the tops of hills in any quiet day,   520
When Boreas and the ruder winds (that use to drive away
Air's dusky vapours, being loose, in many a whistling gale)
Are pleasingly bound up and calm, and not a breath exhale:
So firmly stood the Greeks, nor fled, for all the Ilions' aid.

Atrides yet coasts through the troops, confirming men so staid:
'O friends,' said he, 'hold up your minds; strength is but strength of will;
Rev'rence each other's good in fight, and shame at things done ill.
Where soldiers show an honest shame, and love of honour lives
That ranks men with the first in fight, death fewer liveries gives
Than life, or than where Fame's neglect makes cowards fight at length;
Flight neither doth the body grace, nor shows the mind hath strength.'
He said, and swiftly through the troops a mortal lance did send,
That reft a standard-bearer's life, renown'd Aeneas' friend,
Deicoön Pergasides, whom all the Trojans lov'd
As he were one of Priam's sons, his mind was so approv'd
In always fighting with the first. The lance his target took,
Which could not interrupt the blow that through it clearly strook,
And in his belly's rim was sheath'd, beneath his girdle-stead.
He sounded, falling – and his arms with him resounded – dead.

Then fell two princes of the Greeks by great Aeneas' ire,   540
Diocleus' sons, Orsilochus and Crethon, whose kind sire
In bravely-builded Phaera dwelt, rich, and of sacred blood;
He was descended lineally from great Alphaeus flood,
That broadly flows through Pylos fields: Alphaeus did beget
Orsilochus, who in the rule of many men was set,
And that Orsilochus begat the rich Diocleus:
Diocleus sire to Crethon was, and this Orsilochus.
Both these, arriv'd at man's estate, with both th' Atrides went,
To honour them in th' Ilion wars; and both were one way sent,
To death as well as Troy, for death hid both in one black hour.   550

As two young lions (with their dam sustain'd but to devour)
Bred on the tops of some steep hill, and in the gloomy deep
Of an inaccessible wood, rush out, and prey on sheep,
Steers, oxen, and destroy men's stalls so long that they come short,
And by the owners' steel are slain: in such unhappy sort
Fell these beneath Aeneas' power. When Menelaus view'd
Like two tall fir-trees these two fall, their timeless falls he rued
And to the first fight, where they lay, a vengeful force he took;
His arms beat back the sun in flames, a dreadful lance he shook:
Mars put the fury in his mind, that by Aeneas' hands   560
(Who was to make the slaughter good) he might have strew'd the sands.
Antilochus (old Nestor's son) observing he was bent
To urge a combat of such odds, and knowing – the event
Being ill on his part – all their pains (alone sustain'd for him)
Err'd from their end, made after hard, and took them in the trim
Of an encounter; both their hands and darts advanc'd, and shook,
And both pitch'd in full stand of charge; when suddenly the look
Of Anchisiades took note of Nestor's valiant son,
In full charge too; which two to one made Venus' issue shun
The hot adventure, though he were a soldier well approv'd.   570
Then drew they off their slaughter'd friends; who given to their belov'd,
They turn'd where fight show'd deadliest hate, and there mix'd with the dead
Pylemen, that the targeteers of Paphlagonia led,
A man like Mars; and with him fell good Mydon that did guide
His chariot, Atymnus' son. The prince Pylemen died
By Menelaus, Nestor's joy slew Mydon; one before,
The other in the chariot: Atrides' lance did gore
Pylemen's shoulder in the blade: Antilochus did force
A mighty stone up from the earth, and, as he turn'd his horse,
Struck Mydon's elbow in the midst: the reins of ivory   580
Fell from his hands into the dust: Antilochus let fly
His sword withal, and rushing in a blow so deadly laid
Upon his temples, that he groan'd, tumbled to earth, and stay'd
A mighty while preposterously (because the dust was deep)
Upon his neck and shoulders there, even till his foe took keep
Of his priz'd horse, and made them stir; and then he prostrate fell:
His horse Antilochus took home. When Hector had heard tell
(Amongst the uproar) of their deaths, he laid out all his voice,
And ran upon the Greeks: behind came many men of choice,
Before him march'd great Mars himself, match'd with his female mate,   590
The dread Bellona: she brought on (to fight for mutual fate)
A tumult that was wild and mad: he shook a horrid lance,
And now led Hector, and anon, behind would make the chance.

  This sight when great Tydides saw, his hair stood up on end:
And him, whom all the skill and power of arms did late attend,
Now like a man in counsel poor, that travelling goes amiss,
And having pass'd a boundless plain, not knowing where he is,
Comes on the sudden where he sees a river rough, and raves,
With his own billows ravished into the king of waves,
Murmurs with foam, and frights him back: so he, amaz'd, retir'd,   600
And thus would make good his amaze: 'O friends, we all admir'd
Great Hector as one of himself well-darting, bold in war
When some god guards him still from death, and makes him dare so far;
Now Mars himself, form'd like a man, is present in his rage;
And therefore, whatsoever cause importunes you to wage
War with these Trojans, never strive, but gently take your rod,
Lest in your bosoms for a man ye ever find a god.'
  As Greece retir'd, the pow'r of Troy did much more forward press;
And Hector two brave men of war sent to the fields of peace:
Menesthes, and Anchialus; one chariot bare them both.   610
Their fall made Ajax Telamon ruthful of heart, and wroth;
Who light'ned out a lance that smote Amphius Selages,
That dwelt in Paedos, rich in lands, and did huge goods possess:
But Fate to Priam and his sons conducted his supply.
The javelin on his girdle struck, and pierced mortally
His belly's lower part; he fell; his arms had looks so trim
That Ajax needs would prove their spoil; the Trojans pour'd on him
Whole storms of lances, large and sharp, of which a number stuck
In his rough shield; yet from the slain he did his javelin pluck,
But could not from his shoulders force the arms he did affect,   620
The Trojans with such drifts of darts the body did protect,
And wisely Telamonius fear'd their valorous defence,
So many, and so strong of hand, stood in with such expense
Of deadly prowess; who repell'd (though big, strong, bold he were)
The famous Ajax, and their friend did from his rapture bear.
  Thus this place fill'd with strength of fight; in th' army's other press,
Tlepolemus, a tall big man, the son of Hercules,
A cruel destiny inspir'd, with strong desire to prove
Encounter with Sarpedon's strength, the son of cloudy Jove;
Who coming on to that stern end, had chosen him his foe: 630
Thus Jove's great nephew and his son 'gainst one another go.
Tlepolemus – to make his end more worth the will of fate –
Began as if he had her pow'r, and show'd the mortal state
Of too much confidence in man, with this superfluous brave:
'Sarpedon, what necessity or needless humour drave
Thy form to these wars? Which in heart I know thou dost abhor,

A man not seen in deeds of arms, a Lycian counsellor.
They lie that call thee son to Jove, since Jove bred none so late.
The men of elder times were they, that his high power begat,
Such men as had Herculean force; my father Hercules   640
Was Jove's true issue; he was bold, his deeds did well express
They sprung out of a lion's heart. He whilom came to Troy
(For horse, that Jupiter gave Tros for Ganimed, his boy)
With six ships only, and few men, and tore the city down,
Left all her broad ways desolate, and made the horse his own:
For thee, thy mind is ill dispos'd, thy body's pow'rs are poor,
And therefore are thy troops so weak; the soldier evermore
Follows the temper of his chief, and thou pull'st down a side.
But say thou art the son of Jove, and hast thy means supplied
With forces fitting his descent, the pow'rs that I compel   650
Shall throw thee hence, and make thy head run ope the gates of hell.'
    Jove's Lycian issue answer'd him: 'Tlepolemus, 'tis true –
Thy father holy Ilion in that sort overthrew;
Th' injustice of the king was cause, that where thy father had
Us'd good deservings to his state, he quitted him with bad.
Hesione, the joy and grace of king Laomedon,
Thy father rescu'd from a whale, and gave to Telamon
In honour'd nuptials (Telamon, from whom your strongest Greek
Boasts to have issu'd); and this grace might well expect the like:
Yet he gave taunts for thanks, and kept against his oath his horse. 660
And therefore both thy father's strength and justice might enforce
The wreak he took on Troy: but this and thy cause differ far;
Sons seldom heir their fathers' worths, thou canst not make his war:
What thou assum'st from him is mine, to be on thee impos'd.'
    With this, he threw an ashen dart, and then Tlepolemus loos'd
Another from his glorious hand: both at one instant flew;
Both struck; both wounded; from his neck Sarpedon's javelin drew
The life-blood of Tlepolemus; full in the midst it fell,
And what he threaten'd, th' other gave: that darkness, and that hell.
Sarpedon's left thigh took the lance; it pierc'd the solid bone,   670
And with his raging head ran through; but Jove preserv'd his son.
The dart yet vex'd him bitterly, which should have been pull'd out,
But none consider'd then so much, so thick came on the rout,
And fill'd each hand so full of cause to ply his own defence;
'Twas held enough (both fall'n) that both were nobly carried thence.
    Ulysses knew th' events of both, and took it much to heart
That his friend's enemy should 'scape, and in a twofold part
His thoughts contended, if he should pursue Sarpedon's life,
Or take his friend's wreak on his men. Fate did conclude this strife,

By whom 'twas otherwise decreed than that Ulysses' steel   680
Should end Sarpedon. In this doubt Minerva took the wheel
From fickle Chance, and made his mind resolve to right his friend
With that blood he could surest draw. Then did Revenge extend
Her full power on the multitude. Then did he never miss;
Alastor, Halius, Chromius, Noemon, Pritanis,
Alcander, and a number more, he slew, and more had slain,
If Hector had not understood; whose pow'r made in amain,
And struck fear through the Grecian troops, but to Sarpedon gave
Hope of full rescue; who thus cried: 'O Hector! Help and save
My body from the spoil of Greece, that to your loved town   690
My friends may see me borne: and then let earth possess her own,
In this soil, for whose sake I left my country's; for no day
Shall ever show me that again, nor to my wife display
And young hope of my name, the joy of my much thirsted sight:
All which I left for Troy; for them let Troy then do this right.'
    To all this Hector gives no word, but greedily he strives
With all speed to repel the Greeks, and shed in floods their lives,
And left Sarpedon: but what face soever he put on
Of following the common cause, he left this prince alone,
For his particular grudge, because so late he was so plain   700
In his reproof before the host, and that did he retain;
However, for example sake he would not show it then,
And for his shame too, since 'twas just. But good Sarpedon's men
Ventur'd themselves, and forc'd him off, and set him underneath
The goodly beech of Jupiter, where now they did unsheath
The ashen lance: strong Pelagon, his friend, most lov'd, most true,
Enforc'd it from his maimed thigh: with which his spirit flew,
And darkness over-flew his eyes; yet with a gentle gale,
That round about the dying prince cool Boreas did exhale,
He was revived, recomforted, that else had griev'd and died.   710
    All this time flight drave to the fleet the Argives, who applied
No weapon 'gainst the proud pursuit, nor ever turn'd a head;
They knew so well that Mars pursu'd, and dreadful Hector led.
Then who was first, who last, whose lives the iron Mars did seize,
And Priam's Hector? Helenus, surnamed Oenopides;
Good Teuthras, and Orestes skill'd in managing of horse;
Bold Oenomaus, and a man renown'd for martial force,
Trechus, the great Aetolian chief, Oresbius, that did wear
The gaudy mitre, studied wealth extremely, and dwelt near
Th' Athlantic lake Cephisides, in Hyla, by whose seat   720
The good men of Boeotia dwelt. This slaughter grew so great,
It flew to heaven: Saturnia discern'd it, and cried out

To Pallas: 'O unworthy sight, to see a field so fought,
And break our words to Sparta's king, that Ilion should be rac'd,
And he return reveng'd, when thus we see his Greeks disgrac'd,
And bear the harmful rage of Mars! Come, let us use our care,
That we dishonour not our pow'rs.' Minerva was as yare
As she, at the despite of Troy. Her golden-bridled steeds
Then Saturn's daughter brought abroad, and Hebe, she proceeds
T' address her chariot instantly; she gives it either wheel   730
Beam'd with eight spokes of sounding brass; the axle-tree was steel,
The fell'ffs incorruptible gold, their upper hands of brass,
Their matter most unvalued, their work of wondrous grace.
The naves in which the spokes were driv'n were all with silver bound;
The chariot's seat two hoops of gold and silver strength'ned round,
Edg'd with a gold and silver fringe; the beam that look'd before
Was massy silver, on whose top geres all of gold it wore,
And golden poitrils. Juno mounts, and her hot horses rein'd,
That thirsted for contention, and still of peace complain'd.
    Minerva wrapt her in the robe that curiously she wove,   740
With glorious colours, as she sate on th' azure floor of Jove;
And wore the arms that he puts on, bent to the tearful field,
About her broad-spread shoulders hung his huge and horrid shield,
Fring'd round with ever-fighting snakes; through it was drawn to life
The miseries and deaths of fight; in it frown'd bloody Strife;
In it shin'd sacred Fortitude; in it fell Pursuit flew;
In it the monster Gorgon's head, in which held out to view
Were all the dire ostents of Jove; on her big head she plac'd
His four-plum'd glittering casque of gold, so admirably vast
It would an hundred garrisons of soldiers comprehend.   750
Then to her shining chariot her vigorous feet ascend,
And in her violent hand she takes his grave, huge, solid lance,
With which the conquests of her wrath she useth to advance
And overturn whole fields of men, to show she was the seed
Of him that thunders. Then heaven's queen, to urge her horses speed,
Takes up the scourge, and forth they fly; the ample gates of heaven
Rung, and flew open of themselves, the charge whereof is given,
With all Olympus and the sky, to the distinguish'd Hours,
That clear or hide it all in clouds, or pour it down in show'rs.
This way their scourge-obeying horse made haste, and soon they won   760
The top of all the topful heavens, where aged Saturn's son
Sate sever'd from the other gods; then stay'd the white-arm'd queen
Her steeds, and ask'd of Jove, if Mars did not incense his spleen
With his foul deeds, in ruining so many and so great
In the command and grace of Greece, and in so rude a heat.

At which, she said, Apollo laugh'd, and Venus, who still sue
To that mad god for violence, that never justice knew;
For whose impiety she ask'd if with his wished love
Herself might free the field of him. He bade her rather move
Athenia to the charge she sought, who us'd of old to be   770
The bane of Mars, and had as well the gift of spoil as he.

    This grace she slack'd not, but her horse scourg'd, that in nature flew
Betwixt the cope of stars and earth: and how far at a view
A man into the purple sea may from a hill descry,
So far a high-neighing horse of heaven at every jump would fly.

    Arriv'd at Troy, where broke in curls the two floods mix their force,
Scamander and bright Simois, Saturnia stay'd her horse,
Took them from chariot, and a cloud of mighty depth diffus'd
About them; and the verdant banks of Simois produc'd
In nature what they eat in heaven. Then both the goddesses   780
March'd like a pair of timorous doves, in hasting their access
To th' Argive succour. Being arriv'd, where both the most and best
Were heap'd together (showing all like lions at a feast
Of new-slain carcasses; or boars, beyond encounter strong);
There found they Diomed; and there, 'midst all th' admiring throng,
Saturnia put on Stentor's shape, that had a brazen voice,
And spake as loud as fifty men; like whom she made a noise,
And chid the Argives: 'O ye Greeks, in name and outward rite
But princes only, not in act: what scandal, what despite
Use ye to honour! All the time the great Aeacides   790
Was conversant in arms, your foes durst not a foot address
Without their ports, so much they fear'd his lance that all controll'd;
And now they out-ray to your fleet.' This did with shame make bold
The general spirit and power of Greece; when, with particular note
Of their disgrace, Athenia made Tydeus issue hote.
She found him at his chariot, refreshing of his wound
Inflicted by slain Pandarus; his sweat did so abound,
It much annoy'd him underneath the broad belt of his shield;
With which – and tired with his toil – his soul could hardly yield
His body motion. With his hand he lifted up the belt,   800
And wip'd away that clotter'd blood the fervent wound did melt.
Minerva lean'd against his horse, and near their withers laid
Her sacred hand, then spake to him: 'Believe me, Diomed,
Tydeus exampled not himself in thee his son; not great,
But yet he was a soldier, a man of so much heat
That in his embassy for Thebes, when I forbad his mind
To be too vent'rous, and when feasts his heart might have declin'd,
With which they welcom'd him, he made a challenge to the best,

And foil'd the best; I gave him aid, because the rust of rest
That would have seiz'd another mind he suffer'd not, but us'd   810
The trial I made like a man, and their soft feasts refus'd.
Yet when I set thee on, thou faint'st; I guard thee, charge, exhort
That – I abetting thee – thou shouldst be to the Greeks a fort,
And a dismay to Ilion; yet thou obey'st in nought,
Afraid, or slothful, or else both: henceforth renounce all thought
That ever thou wert Tydeus' son.' He answer'd her: 'I know
Thou art Jove's daughter; and for that in all just duty owe
Thy speeches rev'rence, yet affirm ingenuously that fear
Doth neither hold me spiritless, nor sloth. I only bear
Thy charge in zealous memory, that I should never war   820
With any blessed deity, unless (exceeding far
The limits of her rule) the queen, that governs chamber sport,
Should press to field; and her thy will enjoin'd my lance to hurt.
But he whose pow'r hath right in arms, I knew in person here,
Besides the Cyprian deity, and therefore did forbear,
And here have gather'd in retreat these other Greeks you see,
With note and rev'rence of your charge.' 'My dearest mind,' said she,
'What then was fit is chang'd: 'tis true, Mars hath just rule in war –
But just war; otherwise he raves, not fights; he's alter'd far.
He vow'd to Juno and myself that his aid should be us'd   830
Against the Trojans; whom it guards, and therein he abus'd
His rule in arms, infring'd his word, and made his war unjust:
He is inconstant, impious, mad. Resolve then; firmly trust
My aid of thee against his worst, or any deity:
Add scourge to thy free horse, charge home: he fights perfidiously.'

This said, as that brave king, her knight, with his horse-guiding friend,
Were set before the chariot, for sign he should descend,
That she might serve for waggoness, she pluck'd the wagg'ner back,
And up into his seat she mounts: the beechen tree did crack
Beneath the burthen; and good cause, it bore so large a thing: 840
A goddess so replete with power, and such a puissant king.

She snatch'd the scourge up and the reins, and shut her heavenly look
In Hell's vast helm, from Mars's eyes; and full career she took
At him, who then had newly slain the mighty Periphas,
Renown'd son to Ochesius, and far the strongest was
Of all th' Aetolians; to whose spoil the bloody god was run.
But when this man-plague saw th' approach of god-like Tydeus' son,
He let his mighty Periphas lie, and in full charge he ran
At Diomed, and he at him; both near, the god began,
And (thirsty of his blood) he throws a brazen lance, that bears   850
Full on the breast of Diomed, above the reins and gears;

But Pallas took it on her hand, and struck the eager lance
Beneath the chariot. Then the knight of Pallas doth advance,
And cast a javelin off at Mars; Minerva sent it on,
That (where his arming girdle girt) his belly graz'd upon,
Just at the rim, and ranch'd the flesh: the lance again he got,
But left the wound; that stung him so, lie laid out such a throat
As if nine or ten thousand men had bray'd out all their breaths
In one confusion, having felt as many sudden deaths.
The roar made both the hosts amaz'd. Up flew the god to heav'n,   860
And with him was through all the air as black a tincture driv'n
To Diomed's eyes, as when the earth half chok'd with smoking heat
Of gloomy clouds, that stifle men, and pitchy tempests' threat,
Usher'd with horrid gusts of wind: with such black vapours plum'd,
Mars flew t' Olympus, and broad heav'n, and there his place resum'd.
Sadly he went and sat by Jove, show'd his immortal blood,
That from a mortal-man-made wound pour'd such an impious flood;
And weeping pour'd out these complaints: 'O Father, storm'st thou not
To see us take these wrongs from men? Extreme griefs we have got
Ev'n by our own deep counsels held, for gratifying them;   870
And thou, our council's president, conclud'st in this extreme
Of fighting ever: being rul'd by one that thou hast bred –
One never well, but doing ill, a girl so full of head
That though all other gods obey, her mad moods must command
By thy indulgence, nor by word nor any touch of hand
Correcting her; thy reason is, she is a spark of thee
And therefore she may kindle rage in men 'gainst gods, and she
May make men hurt gods, and those gods that are besides thy seed:
First in the palm's height Cyprides; then runs the impious deed
On my hurt person; and could life give way to death in me,   880
Or had my feet not fetch'd me off, heaps of mortality
Had kept me consort.'
                    Jupiter, with a contracted brow,
Thus answer'd Mars: 'Thou many minds, inconstant changeling thou,
Sit not complaining thus by me, whom most of all the gods
Inhabiting the starry hill I hate: no periods
Being set to thy contentions, brawls, fights, and pitching fields –
Just of thy mother Juno's moods: stiff-neck'd, and never yields,
Though I correct her still, and chide; nor can forbear offence,
Though to her son; this wound I know tastes of her insolence.
But I will prove more natural; thou shalt be cur'd because   890
Thou com'st of me: but hadst thou been so cross to sacred laws,
Being born to any other god, thou hadst been thrown from heav'n
Long since, as low as Tartarus, beneath the giants driv'n.'

This said, he gave his wound in charge to Paeon, who applied
Such sov'reign medicines, that as soon the pain was qualified,
And he recur'd: as nourishing milk, when runnet is put in,
Runs all in heaps of tough thick curd, though in his nature thin:
Even so soon his wound's parted sides ran close in his recure;
For he – all deathless – could not long the parts of death endure.
Then Hebe bath'd, and put on him fresh garments, and he sate   900
Exulting by his sire again, in top of all his state;
So, having from the spoils of men made his desir'd remove,
Juno and Pallas reascend the starry court of Jove.

THE END OF THE FIFTH BOOK

BOOK SIX

The Argument

The gods now leaving an indifferent field,
The Greeks prevail, the slaughter'd Trojans yield:
Hector, by Helenus' advice, retires
In haste to Troy, and Hecuba desires
To pray Minerva to remove from fight
The son of Tydeus, her affected knight;
And vow to her for favour of such price
Twelve oxen should be slain in sacrifice.
In mean space Glaucus and Tydides meet
And either other with remembrance greet
Of old love 'twixt their fathers, which inclines
Their hearts to friendship; who change arms for signs
Of a continued love for either's life.
Hector, in his return, meets with his wife,
And taking in his armed arms his son,
He prophesies the fall of Ilion.

Another Argument

In *Zeta*, Hector prophesies;
Prays for his son; wills sacrifice.

BOOK SIX

THE STERN FIGHT freed of all the gods, conquest with doubtful wings
 Flew on their lances: every way the restless field she flings
 Betwixt the floods of Symois and Xanthus, that confin'd
All their affairs at Ilion, and round about them shin'd.
 The first that weigh'd down all the field of one particular side
Was Ajax, son of Telamon, who like a bulwark plied
The Greeks protection, and of Troy the knotty orders brake;
Held out a light to all the rest, and show'd them how to make
Way to their conquest. He did wound the strongest man of Thrace,
The tallest and the biggest set, Eussorian Acamas: 10
His lance fell on his casque's plum'd top in stooping; the fell head
Drove through his forehead to his jaws; his eyes night shadowed.
 Tydides slew Teuthranides Axilus, that did dwell
In fair Arisba's well-built tow'rs: he had of wealth a well,
And yet was kind and bountiful; he would a traveller pray
To be his guest; his friendly house stood in the broad highway,
In which he all sorts nobly us'd; yet none of them would stand
'Twixt him and death, but both himself and he that had command
Of his fair horse, Calisius, fell lifeless on the ground.
Euryalus Opheltius and Dresus dead did wound,   20
Nor ended there his fiery course, which he again begins,
And ran to it successfully, upon a pair of twins,
Aesepus and bold Pedasus, whom good Bucolion,
That first call'd father (though base born) renown'd Laomedon,
On Nais *Abarbaraea* got, a nymph that as she fed
Her curled flocks Bucolion woo'd, and mix'd in love and bed.
Both these were spoil'd of arms and life by Mecistiades.
 Then Polypaetes for stern death Astialus did seize.
Ulysses slew Percosius; Teucer, Aretaön;
Antilochus (old Nestor's joy) Ablerus; the great son   30
Of Atreus, and king of men, Elatus, whose abode
He held at upper Pedasus, where Satnius' river flow'd.
The great heroë Leïtus stay'd Philacus in flight
From further life: Eurypilus Melanthius reft of light.
 The brother to the king of men Adrestus took alive,

Whose horse, affrighted with the flight, their driver now did drive
Amongst the low-grown tamarisk trees, and at an arm of one
The chariot in the draught-tree brake, the horse brake loose, and ron
The same way other fliers fled, contending all to town:
Himself close at the chariot wheel upon his face was thrown,   40
And there lay flat, roll'd up in dust. Atrides inwards drave,
And holding at his breast his lance, Adrestus sought to save
His head by losing of his feet and trusting to his knees:
On which the same parts of the king he hugs, and offers fees
Of worthy value for his life, and thus pleads their receipt:
'Take me alive, O Atreus' son, and take a worthy weight
Of brass, elaborate iron, and gold: a heap of precious things
Are in my father's riches hid, which when your servant brings
News of my safety to his ears, he largely will divide
With your rare bounties.' Atreus' son thought this the better side,   50
And meant to take it, being about to send him safe to fleet:
Which when, far off, his brother saw, he wing'd his royal feet,
And came in threat'ning, crying out: 'O soft heart! What's the cause
Thou spar'st these men thus? Have not they observ'd these gentle laws
Of mild humanity to thee, with mighty argument
Why thou shouldst deal thus, in thy house, and with all precedent
Of honour'd guest rites entertain'd? Not one of them shall fly
A bitter end for it from heav'n, and much less (dotingly)
'Scape our revengeful fingers: all, ev'n th' infant in the womb,
Shall taste of what they merited, and have no other tomb   60
Than raz'd Ilion, nor their race have more fruit than the dust.'
This just cause turn'd his brother's mind, who violently thrust
The prisoner from him; in whose guts the king of men impress'd
His ashen lance; which (pitching down his foot upon the breast
Of him that upwards fell) he drew; then Nestor spake to all:
  'O friends, and household men of Mars, let not your pursuit fall
With those ye fell, for present spoil; nor, like the king of men,
Let any 'scape unfell'd; but on, dispatch them all, and then
Ye shall have time enough to spoil.' This made so strong their chace
That all the Trojans had been hous'd, and never turn'd a face,   70
Had not the Priamist Helenus (an augur most of name)
Will'd Hector and Aeneas thus: 'Hector! Anchises' fame!
Since on your shoulders, with good cause, the weighty burden lies
Of Troy and Lycia, being both of noblest faculties,
For counsel, strength of hand, and apt to take chance at her best
In every turn she makes, stand fast, and suffer not the rest,
By any way search'd out for 'scape, to come within the ports,
Lest, fled into their wives' kind arms, they there be made the sports

Of the pursuing enemy: exhort and force your bands
To turn their faces; and while we employ our ventur'd hands,   80
Though in a hard condition, to make the other stay,
Hector, go thou to Ilion, and our queen mother pray,
To take the richest robe she hath, the same that's chiefly dear
To her court fancy; with which gem, assembling more to her
Of Troy's chief matrons, let all go (for fear of all our fates)
To Pallas' temple; take the key, unlock the heavy gates,
Enter, and reach the highest tow'r, where her Palladium stands,
And on it put the precious veil, with pure and rev'rend hands,
And vow to her, besides the gift, a sacrificing stroke
Of twelve fat heifers of a year, that never felt the yoke   90
(Most answering to her maiden state), if she will pity us,
Our town, our wives, our youngest joys; and him that plagues them thus
Take from the conflict, Diomed, that fury in a fight,
That true son of great Tydeus, that cunning lord of flight;
Whom I esteem the strongest Greek, for we have never fled
Achilles (that is prince of men, and whom a goddess bred)
Like him, his fury flies so high, and all men's wraths commands.'

    Hector intends his brother's will, but first through all his bands
He made quick way, encouraging; and all, to fear afraid,
All turn'd their heads, and made Greece turn. Slaughter stood still dismay'd
On their parts, for they thought some god, fall'n from the vault of stars,
Was rush'd into the Ilians' aid, they made such dreadful wars.

    Thus Hector, toiling in the waves, and thrusting back the flood
Of his ebb'd forces, thus takes leave: 'So, so, now runs your blood
In his right current: forwards now, Trojans, and far-call'd friends;
Awhile hold out, till for success to this your brave amends
I haste to Ilion, and procure our counsellors and wives
To pray, and offer hecatombs, for their states in our lives.'

    Then fair-helm'd Hector turn'd to Troy, and as he trod the field,
The black bull's hide that at his back he wore about his shield   110
(In the extreme circumference) was with his gait so rock'd
That, being large, it both at once his neck and ankles knock'd.

    And now betwixt the hosts were met Hippolochus' brave son
Glaucus, who in his very look hope of some wonder won,
And little Tydeus' mighty heir, who seeing such a man
Offer the field (for usual blows), with wondrous words began:

    What art thou, strong'st of mortal men, that putt'st so far before,
Whom these fights never show'd mine eyes? They have been evermore
Sons of unhappy parents born, that came within the length
Of this Minerva-guided lance, and durst close with the strength   120
That she inspires in me. If heav'n be thy divine abode,

And thou a deity thus inform'd, no more with any god
Will I change lances; the strong son of Drius did not live
Long after such a conflict dar'd, who godlessly did drive
Nisaeus' nurses through the hill made sacred to his name,
And called Nisseius: with a goad he punch'd each furious dame,
And made them every one cast down their green and leafy spears.
This th' homicide Lycurgus did; and those ungodly fears
He put the froes in seized their god. Even Bacchus he did drive
From his Nisseius, who was fain, with huge exclaims, to dive   130
Into the ocean: Thetis there in her bright bosom took
The flying deity, who so fear'd Lycurgus' threats, he shook.
For which the freely living gods so highly were incens'd
That Saturn's great son struck him blind, and with his life dispens'd
But small time after: all because th' immortals lov'd him not
Nor lov'd him since he striv'd with them: and this end hath begot
Fear in my powers to fight with heaven. But if the fruits of earth
Nourish thy body, and thy life be of our human birth,
Come near, that thou mayst soon arrive on that life-bounding shore,
To which I see thee hoist such sail.' 'Why dost thou so explore,'   140
Said Glaucus, 'of what race I am? When like the race of leaves
The race of man is, that deserves no question, nor receives
My being any other breath. The wind in autumn strows
The earth with old leaves, then the spring the woods with new endows,
And so death scatters men on earth, so life puts out again
Man's heavy issue. But my race, if (like the course of men)
Thou seek'st in more particular terms, 'tis this (to many known):
In midst of Argos, nurse of horse, there stands a walled town,
Ephyre, where the mansion-house of Sysiphus did stand –
Of Sysiphus Aeölides, most wise of all the land.   150
Glaucus was son to him, and he begat Bellerophon,
Whose body heaven indued with strength, and put a beauty on,
Exceeding lovely. Praetus yet his cause of love did hate,
And banish'd him the town; (he might – he rul'd the Argive state;
The virtue of the one Jove plac'd beneath the others pow'r.)
His exile grew since he denied to be the paramour
Of fair Anteia, Praetus' wife, who felt a raging fire
Of secret love to him; but he, whom wisdom did inspire
As well as prudence (one of them advising him to shun
The danger of a princess' love, the other not to run   160
Within the danger of the gods, the act being simply ill),
Still entertaining thoughts divine, subdu'd the earthly still.
She, rul'd by neither of his wits, preferr'd her lust to both;
And, false to Praetus, would seem true, with this abhorr'd untroth:

'Praetus, or die thyself,' said she, 'or let Bellerophon die;
He urg'd dishonour to thy bed: which since I did deny,
He thought his violence should grant, and sought thy shame by force.'
The king, incens'd with her report, resolv'd upon her course,
But doubted how it should be run: he shunn'd his death direct,
Holding a way so near not safe, and plotted the effect　　　　　　170
By sending him with letters seal'd (that, opened, touch his life)
To Rheuns king of Lycia, and father to his wife.
He went, and happily he went: the gods walk'd all his way.
And being arriv'd in Lycia, where Xanthus doth display
The silver ensigns of his waves, the king of that broad land
Receiv'd him with a wondrous free and honourable hand.
Nine days he feasted him, and kill'd an ox in every day,
In thankful sacrifice to heaven, for his fair guest; whose stay,
With rosy fingers brought the world the tenth well-welcom'd morn:
And then the king did move to see the letters he had borne　　　　180
From his lov'd son-in-law; which seen, he wrought thus their contents.
Chymaera, the invincible, he sent him to convince,
Sprung from no man, but mere divine; a lion's shape before,
Behind a dragon's, in the midst a goat's shagg'd form she bore,
And flames of deadly fervency flew from her breath and eyes:
Yet her he slew; his confidence in sacred prodigies
Render'd him victor. Then he gave his second conquest way,
Against the famous Solymi, when (he himself would say
Reporting it) he enter'd on a passing vigorous fight.
His third huge labour he approv'd against a woman's spite,　　　190
That fill'd a field of Amazons: he overcame them all.
Then set they on him sly Deceit, when Force had such a fall:
An ambush of the strongest men that spacious Lycia bred,
Was lodg'd for him; whom he lodg'd sure: they never rais'd a head.
His deeds thus showing him deriv'd from some celestial race,
The king detain'd, and made amends, with doing him the grace
Of his fair daughter's princely gift; and with her, for a dow'r,
Gave half his kingdom; and to this, the Lycians on did pour
More than was given to any king: a goodly planted field,
In some parts thick of groves and woods; the rest rich crops did yield.　　200
This field, the Lycians futurely (of future wand'rings there
And other errors of their prince, in the unhappy rear
Of his sad life) the Errant call'd. The princess brought him forth
Three children (whose ends griev'd him more, the more they were of worth):
Isander, and Hippolochus, and fair Laodomy,
With whom ev'n Jupiter himself left heav'n itself to lie,
And had by her the man at arms, Sarpedon, call'd divine.

The gods then left him, lest a man should in their glories shine,
And set against him; for his son, Isandrus, in a strife
Against the valiant Solymi, Mars reft of light and life;   210
Leodamië (being envied of all the goddesses)
The golden-bridle-handling queen – the maiden patroness –
Slew with an arrow: and for this he wand'red evermore
Alone through his Aleian field, and fed upon the core
Of his sad bosom, flying all the loath'd consorts of men.
Yet had he one surviv'd to him, of those three childeren,
Hippolochus, the root of me: who sent me here with charge
That I should always bear me well, and my deserts enlarge
Beyond the vulgar, lest I sham'd my race, that far excell'd
All that Ephyra's famous towers or ample Lycia held.   220
This is my stock; and this am I.' This cheer'd Tydides' heart;
Who pitch'd his spear down, lean'd, and talk'd in this affectionate part:
    'Certes – in thy great ancestor, and in mine own – thou art
A guest of mine, right ancient; king Oeneus twenty days
Detain'd with feasts Bellerophon, whom all the world did praise;
Betwixt whom mutual gifts were given: my grandsire gave to thine
A girdle of Phoenician work, impurpled wondrous fine.
Thine gave a two-neck'd jug of gold, which though I use not here,
Yet still it is my gem at home. But if our fathers were
Familiar, or each other knew, I know not, since my sire   230
Left me a child, at siege of Thebes, where he left his life's fire.
But let us prove our grandsires' sons, and be each other's guests.
To Lycia when I come, do thou receive thy friend with feasts;
Peloponnesus, with the like, shall thy wish'd presence greet.
Mean space, shun we each other here, though in the press we meet.
There are enow of Troy beside, and men enough renown'd,
To right my pow'rs, whomever heav'n shall let my lance confound.
So are there of the Greeks for thee: kill who thou canst; and now
For sign of amity 'twixt us, and that all these may know
We glory in th' hospitious rites our grandsires did commend,   240
Change we our arms before them all.' From horse then both descend,
Join hands, give faith, and take; and then did Jupiter elate
The mind of Glaucus, who to show his rev'rence to the state
Of virtue in his grandsire's heart, and gratulate beside
The offer of so great a friend, exchanged in that good pride
Curets of gold for those of brass that did on Diomed shine:
One of a hundred oxen's price, the other but of nine.

    By this had Hector reach'd the ports of Scaea, and the tow'rs.
About him flock'd the wives of Troy, the children, paramours,
Inquiring how their husbands did, their fathers, brothers, loves.   250

He stood not then to answer them, but said: 'It now behoves
Ye should go all t' implore the aid of heaven in a distress
Of great effect, and imminent.' Then hasted he access
To Priam's goodly builded court, which round about was run
With walking porches, galleries, to keep off rain and sun.
Within, of one side, on a row of sundry colour'd stones,
Fifty fair lodgings were built out, for Priam's fifty sons,
And for as fair sort of their wives; and in the opposite view
Twelve lodgings of like stone, like height, were likewise built arew,
Where, with their fair and virtuous wives, twelve princes, son-in-law	260
To honourable Priam, lay. And here met Hecuba
(The loving mother) her great son, and with her needs must be
The fairest of her female race, the bright Laodice.
The queen grip't hard her Hector's hand, and said: 'O worthiest son,
Why leav'st thou field? Is't not because the cursed nation
Afflict our countrymen and friends? They are their moans that move
Thy mind to come and lift thy hands – in his high tow'r – to Jove.
But stay a little, that myself may fetch our sweetest wine,
To offer first to Jupiter; then that these joints of thine
May be refresh'd: for (woe is me) how thou art toil'd and spent!	270
Thou for our city's general state, thou for our friends far sent,
Must now the press of fight endure, now solitude to call
Upon the name of Jupiter, thou only for us all.
But wine will something comfort thee: for to a man dismay'd
With careful spirits, or too much with labour overlaid,
Wine brings much rescue, strength'ning much the body and the mind.'
	The great helm-mover thus receiv'd the auth'ress of his kind:
My royal mother, bring no wine, lest rather it impair
Than help my strength, and make my mind forgetful of th' affair
Committed to it. And to pour it out in sacrifice –	280
I fear with unwash'd hands to serve the pure-liv'd deities;
Nor is it lawful, thus imbrued with blood and dust, to prove
The will of heav'n, or offer vows to cloud-compelling Jove.
I only come to use your pains, assembling other dames,
Matrons, and women honour'd most, with high and virtuous names,
With wine and odours, and a robe most ample, most of price,
And which is dearest in your love, to offer sacrifice
In Pallas' temple, and to put the precious robe ye bear
On her Palladium; vowing all twelve oxen of a year,
Whose necks were never rung with yoke, shall pay her grace their lives,	290
If she will pity our sieg'd town, pity ourselves, our wives,
Pity our children, and remove from sacred Ilion
The dreadful soldier Diomed. And when yourselves are gone

About this work, myself will go to call into the field
(If he will hear me) Helen's love, whom would the earth would yield,
And headlong take into her gulf, ev'n quick before mine eyes.
For then my heart, I hope, would cast her load of miseries;
Borne for the plague he hath been born, and bred to the deface
(By great Olympius) of Troy, our sire, and all our race.'

   This said, grave Hecuba went home, and sent her maids about   300
To bid the matrons: she herself descended, and search'd out
(Within a place that breath'd perfumes) the richest robe she had,
Which lay with many rich ones more, most curiously made
By women of Sydonia, which Paris brought from thence,
Sailing the broad sea, when he made that voyage of offence,
In which he brought home Helena. That robe transferr'd so far
(That was the undermost) she took – it glitter'd like a star –
And with it went she to the fane, with many ladies more,
Amongst whom fair-cheek'd Theano unlock'd the folded door,
Chaste Theano, Antenor's wife, and of Cisseüs' race,   310
Sister to Hecuba, both born to that great king of Thrace.
Her th' Ilians made Minerva's priest; and her they follow'd all
Up to the temple's highest tow'r, where on their knees they fall,
Lift up their hands, and fill the fane with ladies' piteous cries.
Then lovely Theano took the veil, and with it she implies
The great Palladium, praying thus: 'Goddess of most renown
In all the heav'n of goddesses! Great guardian of our town,
Reverend Minerva! Break the lance of Diomed; cease his grace;
Give him to fall in shameful flight, headlong, and on his face,
Before our ports of Ilion, that instantly we may   320
Twelve unyok'd oxen of a year in this thy temple slay
To thy sole honour; take their bloods, and banish our offence;
Accept Troy's zeal, her wives, and save our infants' innocence.'

   She pray'd, but Pallas would not grant. Mean space was Hector come
Where Alexander's lodgings were, that many a goodly room
Had, built in them by architects, of Troy's most curious sort –
And where no lodgings but a house, nor no house but a court,
Or had all these contain'd in them; and all within a tow'r,
Next Hector's lodgings and the king's. The lov'd of heaven's chief pow'r
(Hector) here ent'red. In his hand a goodly lance he bore,   330
Ten cubits long; the brazen head went shining in before,
Help'd with a burnish'd ring of gold. He found his brother then
Amongst the women, yet prepar'd to go amongst the men:
For in their chamber he was set, trimming his arms, his shield,
His curets, and was trying how his crooked bow would yield
To his straight arms. Amongst her maids was set the Argive queen,

Commanding them in choicest works. When Hector's eye had seen
His brother thus accompanied, and that he could not bear
The very touching of his arms, but where the women were,
And when the time so needed men, right cunningly he chid.   340
That he might do it bitterly, his cowardice he hid
(That simply made him so retir'd) beneath an anger, feign'd
In him by Hector, for the hate the citizens sustain'd
Against him for the foil he took in their cause, and again,
For all their general foils in his. So Hector seems to plain
Of his wrath to them, for their hate, and not his cowardice,
As that were it that shelt'red him in his effeminacies,
And kept him in that dangerous time from their fit aid in fight;
For which he chid thus: 'Wretched man! So timeless is thy spite,
That 'tis not honest; and their hate is just, 'gainst which it bends.'   350
War burns about the town for thee; for thee our slaughter'd friends
Besiege Troy with their carcasses, on whose heaps our high walls
Are overlook'd by enemies; the sad sounds of their falls
Without are echo'd with the cries of wives and babes within;
And all for thee: and yet for them thy honour cannot win
Head of thine anger; thou shouldst need no spirit to stir up thine,
But thine should set the rest on fire, and with a rage divine
Chastise impartially the best, that impiously forbears.
Come forth, lest thy fair tow'rs and Troy be burn'd about thine ears.'

Paris acknowledg'd (as before) all just that Hector spake,   360
Allowing justice, though it were for his injustice sake:
And where his brother put a wrath upon him by his art,
He takes it (for his honour's sake) as sprung out of his heart,
And rather would have anger seem his fault than cowardice;
And thus he answer'd: 'Since – with right – you join'd check with advice,
And I hear you, give equal ear: it is not any spleen
Against the town, as you conceive, that makes me so unseen,
But sorrow for it; which to ease, and by discourse digest
Within myself, I live so close. And yet, since men might wrest
My sad retreat, like you, my wife with her advice inclin'd   370
This my addression to the field, which was mine own free mind,
As well as th' instance of her words: for though the foil were mine,
Conquest brings forth her wreaths by turns: stay then this haste of thine
But till I arm, and I am made a consort for thee straight;
Or go, I'll overtake thy haste.' Helen stood at receipt,
And took up all great Hector's powers, t' attend her heavy words;
By which had Paris no reply; this vent her grief affords:

'Brother (if I may call you so, that had been better born
A dog, than such a horrid dame as all men curse and scorn,

A mischief-maker, a man-plague), O would to god the day   380
That first gave light to me had been a whirlwind in my way,
And borne me to some desert hill, or hid me in the rage
Of earth's most far-resounding seas, ere I should thus engage
The dear lives of so many friends: yet since the gods have been
Helpless foreseers of my plagues, they might have likewise seen
That he they put in yoke with me, to bear out their award,
Had been a man of much more spirit; and, or had nobler dar'd
To shield mine honour with this deed, or with his mind had known
Much better the upbraids of men, that so he might have shown
(More like a man) some sense of grief for both my shame and his.   390
But he is senseless, nor conceives what any manhood is;
Nor now, nor ever after will: and therefore hangs, I fear,
A plague above him. But come near, good brother; rest you here,
Who, of the world of men, stands charg'd with most unrest for me –
Vile wretch – and for my lover's wrong: on whom a destiny
So bitter is impos'd by Jove, that all succeeding times
Will put – to our unended shames – in all men's mouths our crimes.'
     He answer'd: 'Helen, do not seek to make me sit with thee:
I must not stay, though well I know thy honour'd love of me.
My mind calls forth to aid our friends, in whom my absence breeds   400
Longings to see me: for whose sakes, importune thou to deeds
This man by all means, that your care may make his own make hast,
And meet me in the open town, that all may see at last
He minds his lover. I myself will now go home, and see
My household, my dear wife and son, that little hope of me.
For, sister, 'tis without my skill if I shall ever more
Return and see them, or to earth her right in me restore:
The gods may stoop me, by the Greeks.' This said, he went to see
The virtuous princess, his true wife, white-arm'd Andromache.
She, with her infant son and maid, was climb'd the tow'r, about   410
The sight of him that sought for her, weeping and crying out.
Hector, not finding her at home, was going forth, retir'd,
Stood in the gate, her woman call'd, and curiously inquir'd
Where she was gone, bad tell him true, if she were gone to see
His sisters, or his brothers' wives, or whether she should be
At temple with the other dames, t' implore Minerva's ruth.
     Her woman answer'd: since he ask'd, and urg'd so much the truth,
The truth was she was neither gone to see his brothers' wives,
His sisters, nor t' implore the ruth of Pallas on their lives,
But (she advertis'd of the bane Troy suffer'd, and how vast   420
Conquest had made herself for Greece) like one distraught, made haste
To ample Ilion with her son and nurse; and all the way

Mourn'd, and dissolv'd in tears for him. Then Hector made no stay,
But trod her path, and through the streets, magnificently built,
All the great city past, and came where (seeing how blood was spilt)
Andromache might see him come; who made as he would pass
The ports without saluting her, not knowing where she was.
She, with his sight, made breathless haste to meet him: she, whose grace
Brought him withal so great a dow'r, she that of all the race
Of king Aëtion, only liv'd: Aëtion, whose house stood   430
Beneath the mountain *Placius*, environ'd with the wood
Of Theban Hippoplace, being court to the Cilician land.
She ran to Hector, and with her, tender of heart and hand,
Her son, borne in his nurse's arms: when like a heavenly sign,
Compact of many golden stars, the princely child did shine
Whom Hector call'd Scamandrius, but whom the town did name
Astyanax, because his sire did only prop the same.
Hector, though grief bereft his speech, yet smil'd upon his joy.
Andromache cried out, mix'd hands, and to the strength of Troy
Thus wept forth her affection: 'O noblest in desire!   440
Thy mind, inflam'd with others' good, will set thyself on fire:
Nor pitiest thou thy son, nor wife, who must thy widow be
If now thou issue: all the field will only run on thee.
Better my shoulders underwent the earth, than thy decease;
For then would earth bear joys no more, then comes the black increase
Of griefs (like Greeks on Ilion). Alas! What one survives
To be my refuge? One black day bereft seven brothers' lives,
By stern Achilles; by his hand my father breath'd his last,
His high-wall'd rich Cilician Thebes sack'd by him, and laid wast:
The royal body yet he left unspoil'd – religion charm'd   450
That act of spoil – and all in fire he burn'd him complete arm'd,
Built over him a royal tomb, and to the monument
He left of him th' Oreades (that are the high descent
Of Aegis-bearing Jupiter), another of their own
Did add to it, and set it round with elms, by which is shown
(In theirs) the barrenness of death: yet might it serve beside
To shelter the said monument from all the ruffinous pride
Of storms and tempests, us'd to hurt things of that noble kind.
The short life yet my mother liv'd, he sav'd, and serv'd his mind
With all the riches of the realm; which not enough esteem'd,   460
He kept her prisoner, whom small time, but much more wealth redeem'd:
And she in sylvan Hyppoplace Cilicia rul'd again,
But soon was over-rul'd by death: Diana's chaste disdain
Gave her a lance, and took her life. Yet all these gone from me,
Thou amply render'st all; thy life makes still my father be,

My mother, brothers: and besides thou art my husband too,
Most lov'd, most worthy. Pity then, dear love, and do not go;
For thou gone, all these go again: pity our common joy,
Lest – of a father's patronage, the bulwark of all Troy –
Thou leav'st him a poor widow's charge. Stay, stay then, in this tow'r,   470
And call up to the wild fig-tree all thy retired pow'r:
For there the wall is easiest scal'd, and fittest for surprise,
And there th' Ajaces, Idomen, th' Atrides, Diomed, thrice
Have both survey'd and made attempt, I know not if induc'd
By some wise augury, or the fact was naturally infus'd
Into their wits, or courages.' To this, great Hector said:
'Be well assur'd, wife, all these things in my kind cares are weigh'd.
But what a shame and fear it is, to think how Troy would scorn
(Both in her husbands and her wives, whom long-train'd gowns adorn)
That I should cowardly fly off! The spirit I first did breathe   480
Did never teach me that; much less, since the contempt of death
Was settled in me, and my mind knew what a worthy was;
Whose office is to lead in fight, and give no danger pass
Without improvement. In this fire must Hector's trial shine;
Here must his country, father, friends, be in him made divine.
And such a stormy day shall come (in mind and soul I know)
When sacred Troy shall shed her tow'rs, for tears of overthrow,
When Priam, all his birth and pow'r, shall in those tears be drown'd.
But neither Troy's posterity so much my soul doth wound,
Priam, nor Hecuba herself, nor all my brothers' woes   490
(Who though so many, and so good, must all be food for foes)
As thy sad state, when some rude Greek shall lead thee weeping hence,
These free days clouded, and a night of captive violence
Loading thy temples; out of which thine eyes must never see,
But spin the Greek wives webs of task, and their fetch-water be
To Argos, from Messeides, or clear Hyperia's spring:
Which, howsoever thou abhorr'st, Fate's such a shrewish thing
She will be mistress; whose curst hands, when they shall crush out cries
From thy oppressions, being beheld by other enemies,
Thus they will nourish thy extremes: "This dame was Hector's wife,   500
A man, that at the wars of Troy did breathe the worthiest life
Of all their army." This again will rub thy fruitful wounds,
To miss the man that to thy bands could give such narrow bounds.
But that day shall not wound mine eyes; the solid heap of night
Shall interpose, and stop mine ears, against thy plaints and plight.'
     This said, he reach'd to take his son: who of his arms afraid,
And then the horse-hair plume, with which he was so overlaid,
Nodded so horribly, he cling'd back to his nurse, and cried.

Laughter affected his great sire, who doff'd and laid aside
His fearful helm, that on the earth cast round about it light;   510
Then took and kiss'd his loving son, and (balancing his weight
In dancing him) these loving vows to living Jove he us'd,
And all the other bench of gods: 'O you that have infus'd
Soul to this infant, now set down this blessing on his star.
Let his renown be clear as mine, equal his strength in war;
And make his reign so strong in Troy, that years to come may yield
His facts this fame, when rich in spoils, he leaves the conquer'd field
Sown with his slaughters: these high deeds exceed his father's worth,
And let this echo'd praise supply the comforts to come forth
Of his kind mother, with my life.' This said, th' heroic sire   520
Gave him his mother; whose fair eyes fresh streams of love's salt fire
Billow'd on her soft cheeks, to hear the last of Hector's speech,
In which his vows compris'd the sum of all he did beseech
In her wish'd comfort. So she took into her odorous breast
Her husband's gift; who, mov'd to see her heart so much oppress'd,
He dried her tears, and thus desir'd: 'Afflict me not, dear wife,
With these vain griefs. He doth not live that can disjoin my life
And this firm bosom, but my fate; and fate, whose wings can fly?
Noble, ignoble, fate controls: once born, the best must die.
Go home, and set thy huswifery on these extremes of thought,   530
And drive war from them with thy maids; keep them from doing nought:
These will be nothing; leave the cares of war to men, and me,
In whom of all the Ilian race they take their high'st degree.'

    On went his helm; his princess home, half cold with kindly fears,
When every fear turn'd back her looks, and every look shed tears,
To slaught'ring Hector's house, soon reach'd; her many women there
Wept all to see her. In his life, great Hector's funerals were –
Never look'd any eye of theirs to see their lord safe home,
Scap'd from the gripes and pow'rs of Greece. And now was Paris come
From his high tow'rs; who made no stay, when once he had put on   540
His richest armour, but flew forth: the flints he trod upon
Sparkled with lustre of his arms; his long-ebb'd spirits now flow'd
The higher for their lower ebb. And as a fair steed proud
With full-given mangers, long tied up, and now his head-stall broke,
He breaks from stable, runs the field, and with an ample stroke
Measures the centre, neighs, and lifts aloft his wanton head,
About his shoulders shakes his crest, and where he hath been fed,
Or in some calm flood wash'd, or stung with his high plight, he flies
Amongst his females, strength puts forth, his beauty beautifies,
And like life's mirror, bears his gait: so Paris from the tow'r   550
Of lofty Pergamus came forth; he show'd a sun-like pow'r

In carriage of his goodly parts, address'd now to the strife,
And found his noble brother near the place he left his wife.
Him thus respected he salutes: 'Right worthy, I have fear
That your so serious haste to field my stay hath made forbear,
And that I come not as you wish.' He answer'd: 'Honour'd man,
Be confident, for not myself nor any others can
Reprove in thee the work of fight, at least, not any such
As is an equal judge of things: for thou hast strength as much
As serves to execute a mind very important. But   560
Thy strength too readily flies off: enough will is not put
To thy ability. My heart is in my mind's strife, sad,
When Troy (out of her much distress she and her friends have had
By thy procurement) doth deprave thy nobleness in mine ears.
But come, hereafter we shall calm these hard conceits of theirs,
When from their ports the foe expuls'd, high Jove to them hath giv'n
Wish'd peace, and us free sacrifice to all the powers of heav'n.'

THE END OF THE SIXTH BOOK

BOOK SEVEN

The Argument

Hector, by Helenus' advice, doth seek
Adventurous combat on the boldest Greek.
Nine Greeks stand up, acceptants every one,
But lot selects strong Ajax Telamon.
Both, with high honour, stand th' important fight,
Till heralds part them by approached night.
Lastly, they grave the dead: the Greeks erect
A mighty wall, their navy to protect;
Which angers Neptune. Jove, by hapless signs,
In depth of night, succeeding woes divines.

Another Argument

In *Eta*, Priam's strongest son
Combats with Ajax Telamon.

BOOK SEVEN

THIS SAID, brave Hector through the ports, with Troy's bane-bringing knight,
 Made issue to th' insatiate field, resolv'd to fervent fight.
 And as the weather-wielder sends to seamen prosperous gales,
When with their sallow polish'd oars, long lifted from their falls,
Their wearied arms, dissolv'd with toil, can scarce strike one stroke more,
Like those sweet winds appear'd these lords to Trojans tir'd before.
Then fell they to the works of death. By Paris' valour fell
King Areithous' hapless son, that did in Arna dwell,
Menesthius, whose renowned sire a club did ever bear,
And of Philomedusa got (that had her eyes so clear)   10
This slaughter'd issue. Hector's dart struck Eioneus dead;
Beneath his good steel casque it pierc'd above his gorget stead.
Glaucus (Hyppolochus's son) that led the Lycian crew,
Iphinous-Dexiades with sudden javelin slew,
As he was mounting to his horse: his shoulders took the spear,
And ere he sate, in tumbling down his pow'rs dissolved were.
 When gray-ey'd Pallas had perceiv'd the Greeks so fall in fight,
From high Olympus' top she stoop'd, and did on Ilion light.
Apollo to encounter her to Pergamus did fly,
From whence he (looking to the field) wish'd Trojans victory.   20
At Jove's broad beech these godheads met, and first Jove's son objects:
'Why, burning in contention thus, do thy extreme affects
Conduct thee from our peaceful hill? Is it to oversway
The doubtful victory of fight, and give the Greeks the day?
Thou never pitiest perishing Troy, yet now let me persuade,
That this day no more mortal wounds may either side invade.
Hereafter, till the end of Troy, they shall apply the fight,
Since your immortal wills resolve to overturn it quite.'
 Pallas replied: 'It likes me well; for this came I from heav'n:
But to make either army cease, what order shall be giv'n?'   30
He said: 'We will direct the spirit that burns in Hectors breast
To challenge any Greek to wounds, with single pow'rs impress'd;
Which Greeks (admiring) will accept, and make some one stand out,
So stout a challenge to receive with a defence as stout.'
It is confirm'd, and Helenus (King Priam's loved seed)

By augury discern'd th' event that these two pow'rs decreed,
And greeting Hector ask'd him this: 'Wilt thou be once advis'd?
I am thy brother, and thy life with mine is ev'nly prised.
Command the rest of Troy and Greece to cease this public fight,
And what Greek bears the greatest mind, to single strokes excite.   40
I promise thee that yet thy soul shall not descend to fates;
So heard I thy survival cast by the celestial states.'
Hector with glad allowance gave his brother's counsel ear,
And, fronting both the hosts, advanc'd just in the midst his spear.
The Trojans instantly surcease, the Greeks Atrides stay'd.
The god that bears the silver bow and war's triumphant Maid,
On Jove's beech like two vultures sat, pleas'd to behold both parts
Flow in to hear, so sternly arm'd with huge shields, helms and darts,
And such fresh horror as you see driven through the wrinkled waves
By rising Zephyr, under whom the sea grows black, and raves;   50
Such did the hasty gathering troops of both hosts make, to hear;
Whose tumult settled, 'twixt them both thus spake the challenger:
   'Hear, Trojans, and ye well-arm'd Greeks, what my strong mind (diffus'd
Through all my spirits) commands me speak; Saturnius hath not us'd
His promis'd favour for our truce, but studying both our ills,
Will never cease till Mars by you his ravenous stomach fills
With ruin'd Troy, or we consume your mighty sea-borne fleet.
Since then the general peers of Greece in reach of one voice meet,
Amongst you all, whose breast includes the most impulsive mind,
Let him stand forth as combatant, by all the rest design'd.   60
Before whom thus I call high Jove to witness of our strife:
If he with home-thrust iron can reach th' exposure of my life,
Spoiling my arms, let him at will convey them to his tent,
But let my body be return'd, that Troy's two-sex'd descent
May waste it in the funeral pile: if I can slaughter him
(Apollo honouring me so much), I'll spoil his conquer'd limb,
And bear his arms to Ilion, where in Apollo's shrine
I'll hang them, as my trophies due; his body I'll resign
To be disposed by his friends in flamy funerals,
And honour'd with erected tomb, where Hellespontus falls   70
Into Aegaeum, and doth reach ev'n to your naval road,
That when our beings in the earth shall hide their period,
Survivors sailing the black sea may thus his name renew:
"This is his monument, whose blood long since did fates imbrue,
Whom passing far in fortitude, illustrious Hector slew."
This shall posterity report, and my fame never die.'
   This said, dumb silence seiz'd them all; they shamed to deny,
And fear'd to undertake. At last did Menelaus speak,

Check'd their remissness, and so sigh'd, as if his heart would break:
'Ah me, but only threat'ning Greeks, not worthy Grecian names!   80
This more and more, not to be borne, makes grow our huge defames,
If Hector's honourable proof be entertain'd by none.
But you are earth and water all, which – symboliz'd in one –
Have fram'd your faint unfiery spirits: ye sit without your hearts,
Grossly inglorious: but myself will use acceptive darts,
And arm against him, though you think I am 'gainst too much odds:
But conquest's garlands hang aloft amongst th' immortal gods.'

   He arm'd, and gladly would have fought; but, Menelaus, then
By Hector's far more strength thy soul had fled th' abodes of men,
Had not the kings of Greece stood up, and thy attempt restrain'd,   90
And ev'n the king of men himself that in such compass reign'd,
Who took him by the bold right hand, and sternly pluck'd him back:
'Mad brother, 'tis no work for thee, thou seek'st thy wilful wrack:
Contain, though it despite thee much, nor for this strife engage
Thy person with a man more strong, and whom all fear t' enrage:
Yea whom Aeacides himself in men-renowning war
Makes doubt t' encounter, whose huge strength surpasseth thine by far.
Sit thou then by thy regiment; some other Greek will rise
(Though he be dreadless, and no war will his desires suffice,
That makes this challenge to our strength) our valours to avow: 100
To whom, if he can 'scape with life, he will be glad to bow.'

   This drew his brother from his will; who yielded, knowing it true,
And his glad soldiers took his arms; when Nestor did pursue
The same reproof he set on foot, and thus supplied his turn:
'What huge indignity is this! How will our country mourn!
Old Peleus, that good king, will weep, that worthy counsellor,
That trumpet of the Myrmidons, who much did ask me for
All men of name that went to Troy; with joy he did inquire
Their valour and their towardness, and I made him admire.
But that ye all fear Hector now, if his grave ears shall hear,   110
How will he lift his hands to heaven, and pray that death may bear
His grieved soul into the deep! O would to heaven's great king,
Minerva, and the god of light, that now my youthful spring
Did flourish in my willing veins as when at Phaea's tow'rs,
About the streams of Jardanus, my gather'd Pylean pow'rs
And dart-employ'd Arcadians fought near raging Celadon;
Amongst whom first of all stood forth great Ereuthalion,
Who th' arms of Areïthous wore – brave Areïthous,
And, since he still fought with a club, surnam'd Clavigerus;
All men and fair-girt ladies both for honour call'd him so.   120
He fought not with a keep-off spear, or with a far-shot bow,

But with a massy club of iron he broke through armed bands:
And yet Lycurgus was his death, but not with force of hands;
With sleight (encount'ring in a lane, where his club wanted sway)
He thrust him through his spacious waist, who fell, and upwards lay,
In death not bowing his face to earth: his arms he did despoil,
Which iron Mars bestow'd on him; and those in Mars's toil
Lycurgus ever after wore. But when he aged grew,
Enforc'd to keep his peaceful house, their use he did renew
On mighty Ereuthalion's limbs, his soldier, loved well;   130
And with these arms he challeng'd all that did in arms excel:
All shook, and stood dismay'd, none durst his adverse champion make.
Yet this same forward mind of mine of choice would undertake
To fight with all his confidence; though youngest enemy
Of all the army we conduct, yet I fought with him, I:
Minerva made me so renown'd, and that most tall strong peer
I slew; his big bulk lay on earth, extended here and there,
As it were covetous to spread the centre everywhere.
O that my youth were now as fresh, and all my pow'rs as sound;
Soon should bold Hector be impugn'd: yet you that most are crown'd   140
With fortitude of all our host, ev'n you methinks are slow,
Not free and set on fire with lust t' encounter such a foe.'

   With this, nine royal princes rose: Atrides for the first;
Then Diomed; th' Ajaces then, that did th' encounter thirst;
King Idomen and his consorts; Mars-like Meriones
(Evemon's son); Euripilus; and Andremonides
(Whom all the Grecians Thoas call'd, sprung of Andremon's blood);
And wise Ulysses; every one propos'd for combat stood.

   Again Gerenius Nestor spake: 'Let lots be drawn by all;
His hand shall help the well-arm'd Greeks on whom the lot doth fall,   150
And to his wish shall he be help'd, if he escape with life
The harmful danger-breathing fit of his adventurous strife.'

   Each mark'd his lot, and cast it in to Agamemnon's casque;
The soldiers pray'd, held up their hands, and this of Jove did ask
(With eyes advanc'd to heav'n): 'O Jove, so lead the herald's hand
That Ajax or great Tydeus' son may our wish'd champion stand;
Or else the king himself, that rules the rich Mycenian land.'

   This said, old Nestor mix'd the lots: the foremost lot survey'd
With Ajax Telamon was sign'd, as all the soldiers pray'd;
One of the heralds drew it forth, who brought and show'd it round,   160
Beginning at the right hand first, to all the most renown'd:
None knowing it, every man denied, but when he forth did pass
To him which mark'd and cast it in, which famous Ajax was,
He stretch'd his hand, and into it the herald put the lot,

Who (viewing it) th' inscription knew; the duke denied not,
But joyfully acknowledg'd it, and threw it at his feet,
And said: 'O friends, the lot is mine, which to my soul is sweet.
For now I hope my fame shall rise in noble Hector's fall.
But whilst I arm myself, do you on great Saturnius call;
But silently, or to yourselves, that not a Trojan hear –   170
Or openly, if you think good, since none alive we fear.
None with a will, if I will not, can my bold powers affright,
At least for plain fierce swinge of strength, or want of skill in fight:
For I will well prove that my birth, and breed in Salamine,
Was not all consecrate to meat, or mere effects of wine.'
    This said, the well-giv'n soldiers pray'd; up went to heav'n their eyne:
'O Jove, that Ida dost protect, most happy, most divine,
Send victory to Ajax' side; fame grace his goodly limb:
Or if thy love bless Hector's life, and thou hast care of him,
Bestow on both like power, like fame.' This said, in bright arms shone   180
The good strong Ajax: who, when all his war attire was on,
March'd like the hugely figur'd Mars, when angry Jupiter,
With strength on people proud of strength sends him forth to infer
Wreakful contention, and comes on with presence full of fear:
So th' Achive rampire, Telamon, did 'twixt the hosts appear –
Smil'd, yet of terrible aspect; on earth with ample pace
He boldly stalk'd, and shook aloft his dart with deadly grace.
It did the Grecians good to see, but heartquakes shook the joints
Of all the Trojans. Hector's self felt thoughts with horrid points
Tempt his bold bosom: but he now must make no counterflight,   190
Nor (with his honour) now refuse, that had provok'd the fight.
Ajax came near; and like a tow'r his shield his bosom barr'd –
The right side brass, and seven ox-hides within it quilted hard;
Old Tychius, the best currier that did in Hyla dwell,
Did frame it for exceeding proof, and wrought it wondrous well.
With this stood he to Hector close, and with this brave began:
'Now, Hector, thou shalt clearly know, thus meeting man to man,
What other leaders arm our host besides great Thetis' son
Who with his hardy lion's heart hath armies overrun.
But he lies at our crook'd-stern'd fleet, a rival with our king   200
In height of spirit; yet to Troy he many knights did bring,
Coequal with Aeacides, all able to sustain
All thy bold challenge can import: begin then, words are vain.'
    The helm-grac'd Hector answer'd him: 'Renowned Telamon,
Prince of the soldiers come from Greece, assay not me, like one
Young and immartial, with great words – as to an Amazon dame.
I have the habit of all fights, and know the bloody frame

Of every slaughter: I well know the ready right hand charge,
I know the left, and every sway of my secureful targe;
I triumph in the cruelty of fixed combat fight,   210
And manage horse to all designs. I think then with good right,
I may be confident as far as this my challenge goes,
Without being taxed with a vaunt borne out with empty shows.
But being a soldier so renown'd, I will not work on thee
With least advantage of that skill I know doth strengthen me
(And so with privity of sleight win that for which I strive),
But at thy best, ev'n open strength, if my endeavours thrive.'
    Thus sent he his long javelin forth; it struck his foe's huge shield
Near to the upper skirt of brass, which was the eighth it held.
Six folds th' untamed dart struck through, and in the seventh tough hide   220
The point was check'd. Then Ajax threw: his angry lance did glide
Quite through his bright orbicular targe, his curace, shirt of mail,
And did his manly stomach's mouth with dangerous taint assail:
But in the bowing of himself, black death too short did strike.
Then both to pluck their javelins forth encount'red, lion-like,
Whose bloody violence is increas'd by that raw food they eat –
Or boars, whose strength wild nourishment doth make so wondrous great.
Again Priamides did wound in midst his shield of brass,
Yet pierc'd not through the upper plate, the head reflected was:
But Ajax, following his lance, smote through his target quite,   230
And stay'd bold Hector rushing in; the lance held way outright,
And hurt his neck; out gush'd the blood. Yet Hector ceas'd not so,
But in his strong hand took a flint (as he did backwards go),
Black, sharp and big, laid in the field; the sevenfold targe it smit
Full on the boss, and round about the brass did ring with it.
But Ajax a far greater stone lift up, and (wreathing round,
With all his body laid to it) he sent it forth to wound,
And gave unmeasur'd force to it: the round stone broke within
His rundled target: his lov'd knees to languish did begin,
And he lean'd, stretch'd out on his shield; but Phoebus rais'd him straight.   240
Then had they laid on wounds with swords, in use of closer fight,
Unless the heralds (messengers of gods and godlike men),
The one of Troy, the other Greece, had held betwixt them then
Imperial sceptres: then the one, Idaeus, grave and wise,
Said to them: 'Now no more, my sons; the sov'reign of the skies
Doth love you both; both soldiers are, all witness with good right,
But now night lays her mace on earth; 'tis good t' obey the night.'
    'Idaeus,' Telamon replied, 'to Hector speak, not me:
He that call'd all our Achive peers to station fight, 'twas he.
If he first cease, I gladly yield.' Great Hector then began: 250

'Ajax, since Jove to thy big form made thee so strong a man,
And gave thee skill to use thy strength, so much that for thy spear
Thou art most excellent of Greece, now let us fight forbear.
Hereafter we shall war again, till Jove our herald be,
And grace with conquest which he will; heav'n yields to night – and we.
Go thou and comfort all thy fleet, all friends and men of thine,
As I in Troy my favourers, who in the fane divine
Have offer'd orisons for me: and come, let us impart
Some ensigns of our strife, to show each other's suppled heart,
That men of Troy and Greece may say, thus their high quarrel ends;   260
Those that encount'ring were such foes, are now – being separate – friends.'
He gave a sword, whose handle was with silver studs through driven,
Scabbard and all, with hangers rich. By Telamon was given
A fair well-glossed purple waist. Thus Hector went to Troy,
And after him a multitude, fill'd with his safety's joy,
Despairing he could ever 'scape the puissant fortitude
And unimpeached Ajax' hands. The Greeks like joy renew'd
For their reputed victory, and brought him to the king,
Who to the great Saturnides preferr'd an offering:
An ox that fed on five fair springs; they flay'd and quart'red him,   270
And then (in pieces cut) on spits they roasted every limb;
Which neatly dress'd they drew it off: work done, they fell to feast:
All had enough, but Telamon the king fed past the rest
With good large pieces of the chine. Thus thirst and hunger stay'd,
Nestor, whose counsels late were best, vows new, and first he said:
'Atrides, and my other lords, a sort of Greeks are dead,
Whose black blood near Scamander's stream inhuman Mars hath shed:
Their souls to hell descended are. It fits thee then our king
To make our soldiers cease from war, and by the day's first spring,
Let us ourselves (assembled all) the bodies bear to fire,   280
With mules and oxen near our fleet, that when we home retire,
Each man may carry to the sons of fathers slaughter'd here
Their honour'd bones: one tomb for all, for ever, let us rear,
Circling the pile without the field; at which we will erect
Walls, and a ravelin, that may safe our fleet and us protect.
And in them let us fashion gates, solid, and barr'd about,
Through which our horse and chariots may well get in and out.
Without all, let us dig a dike, so deep it may avail
Our forces 'gainst the charge of horse and foot, that come t' assail:
And thus th' attempts that I see swell in Troy's proud heart shall fail.'   290
    The kings do his advice approve: so Troy doth court convent
At Priam's gate, in th' Ilion tow'r, fearful and turbulent.
Amongst all wise Antenor spake: 'Trojans and Dardan friends,

And peers assistants, give good ear to what my care commends
To your consents, for all our good: resolve; let us restore
The Argive Helen, with her wealth, to him she had before:
We now defend but broken faiths. If, therefore, ye refuse,
No good event can I expect of all the wars we use.'

He ceas'd, and Alexander spake, husband to th' Argive queen:
'Antenor, to mine ears thy words harsh and ungracious been;   300
Thou canst use better if thou wilt, but if these truly fit
Thy serious thoughts, the gods with age have reft thy graver wit.
To warlike Trojans I will speak: I clearly do deny
To yield my wife, but all her wealth I'll render willingly,
Whatever I from Argos brought, and vow to make it more
(Which I have ready in my house) if peace I may restore.'

Priam, surnam'd Dardanides, godlike in counsels grave,
In his son's favour well advis'd, this resolution gave:
'My royal friends of every state, there is sufficient done,
For this late council we have call'd, in th' offer of my son.   310
Now then let all take needful food; then let the watch be set,
And every court of guard held strong: so when the morn doth wet
The high rais'd battlements of Troy, Idaeus shall be sent
To th' Argive fleet, and Atreus' sons, t' unfold my son's intent,
From whose fact our contention springs, and (if they will) obtain
Respite from heat of fight, till fire consume our soldiers slain:
And after, our most fatal war let us importune still,
Till Jove the conquest have dispos'd to his unconquer'd will.'

All heard, and did obey the king, and (in their quarters all
That were to set the watch that night) did to their suppers fall.   320
Idaeus in the morning went, and th' Achive peers did find
In counsel at Atrides' ship: his audience was assign'd,
And in the midst of all the kings the vocal herald said:

'Atrides, my renowned king, and other kings his aid,
Propose by me, in their commands, the offers Paris makes
(From whose joy all our woes proceed); he princely undertakes
That all the wealth he brought from Greece (would he had died before!)
He will, with other added wealth, for your amends restore:
But famous Menelaus' wife he still means to enjoy,
Though he be urg'd the contrary by all the peers of Troy.   330
And this besides I have in charge, that if it please you all,
They wish both sides may cease from war, that rites of funeral
May on their bodies be perform'd that in the fields lie slain,
And after, to the will of Fate, renew the fight again.

All silence held at first; at last, Tydides made reply:
'Let no man take the wealth, or dame; for now a child's weak eye

May see the imminent black end of Priam's empery.'
   This sentence, quick and briefly given, the Greeks did all admire.
Then said the king: 'Herald, thou hear'st in him the voice entire
Of all our peers, to answer thee, for that of Priam's son.   340
But, for our burning of the dead, by all means I am won
To satisfy thy king therein, without the slend'rest gain
Made of their spoiled carcasses; but freely (being slain)
They shall be all consum'd with fire: to witness which I cite
High thund'ring Jove, that is the king of Juno's bed's delight.'
   With this, he held his sceptre up to all the sky-thron'd pow'rs,
And grave Idaeus did return to sacred Ilion's tow'rs,
Where Ilians and Dardanians did still their counsels ply,
Expecting his return: he came, and told his legacy.
All, whirlwind like, assembled then; some bodies to transport,   350
Some to hew trees. On th' other part, the Argives did exhort
Their soldiers to the same affairs. Then did the new-fir'd sun
Smite the broad fields, ascending heaven, and th' ocean smooth did run,
When Greece and Troy mix'd in such peace, you scarce could either know;
Then wash'd they off their blood and dust, and did warm tears bestow
Upon the slaughter'd, and in cars convey'd them from the field.
Priam commanded none should mourn, but in still silence yield
Their honour'd carcasses to fire, and only grieve in heart.
All burn'd, to Troy Troy's friends retire; to fleet, the Grecian part.
Yet doubtful night obscur'd the earth, the day did not appear,   360
When round about the funeral pile the Grecians gather'd were;
The pile they circled with a tomb, and by it rais'd a wall,
High tow'rs to guard the fleet and them, and in the midst of all
They built strong gates, through which the horse and chariots passage had.
Without the rampire a broad dike long and profound they made,
On which they pallisadoes pitch'd; and thus the Grecians wrought.
Their huge works in so little time were to perfection brought,
That all gods by the Lightner set the frame thereof admir'd;
'Mongst whom the earthquake-making god this of their king inquir'd:
'Father of gods, will any man, of all earth's grassy sphere,   370
Ask any of the gods' consents to any actions there,
If thou wilt see the shag-hair'd Greeks with headstrong labours frame
So huge a work, and not to us due off'rings first enflame?
As far as white Aurora's dews are sprinkled through the air,
Fame will renown the hands of Greece for this divine affair.
Men will forget the sacred work the Sun and I did raise
For King Laomedon; bright Troy and this will bear the praise.'
   Jove was extremely mov'd with him, and said: 'What words are these,
Thou mighty shaker of the earth, thou lord of all the seas?

Some other god, of far less power, might hold conceits, dismay'd   380
With this rare Grecian stratagem, and thou rest well apaid;
For it will glorify thy name as far as light extends,
Since, when these Greeks shall see again their native soil and friends
(The bulwark batter'd), thou mayst quite devour it with thy waves,
And cover with thy fruitless sands this fatal shore of graves,
That what their fiery industries have so divinely wrought
In raising it – in razing it, thy pow'r will prove it nought.
    Thus spake the gods among themselves: set was the fervent sun,
And now the great work of the Greeks was absolutely done.
Then slew they oxen in their tents, and strength with food reviv'd,   390
When out of Lemnos a great fleet of odorous wine arriv'd,
Sent by Euneus, Jason's son, born of Hypsiphile.
The fleet contain'd a thousand tun, which must transported be
To Atreus' sons, as he gave charge, whose merchandise it was.
The Greeks bought wine for shining steel, and some for sounding brass,
Some for ox-hides, for oxen some, and some for prisoners.
A sumptuous banquet was prepar'd, and all that night the peers
And fair-hair'd Greeks consum'd in feast: so Trojans, and their aid.
And all the night Jove thunder'd loud: pale fear all thoughts dismay'd.
While they were gluttonous in earth, Jove wrought their banes in heav'n: 400
They pour'd full cups upon the ground, and were to offerings driv'n,
Instead of quaffings: and to drink none durst attempt, before
In solemn sacrifice they did almighty Jove adore.
Then to their rests they all repair'd: bold zeal their fear bereav'd,
And sudden sleep's refreshing gift securely they receiv'd.

THE END OF THE SEVENTH BOOK

BOOK EIGHT

The Argument

When Jove to all the gods had giv'n command,
That none to either host should helpful stand,
To Ida he descends; and sees from thence
Juno and Pallas haste the Greeks' defence:
Whose purpose his command, by Iris given,
Doth intervent. Then came the silent even;
When Hector charg'd fires should consume the night,
Lest Greeks in darkness took suspected flight.

Another Argument

In *Theta* gods a council have;
Troy's conquest; glorious Hector's brave.

BOOK EIGHT

THE CHEERFUL LADY of the light, deck'd in her saffron robe,
Dispers'd her beams through every part of this enflow'red globe,
When thund'ring Jove a court of gods assembled by his will,
In top of all the topful heights that crown th' Olympian hill.
    He spake, and all the gods gave ear: 'Hear how I stand inclin'd,
That god nor goddess may attempt t' infringe my sov'reign mind,
But all give suffrage, that with speed I may these discords end.
What god soever I shall find endeavour to defend
Or Troy or Greece, with wounds to heav'n he sham'd shall reascend,
Or (taking him with his offence) I'll cast him down as deep   10
As Tartarus (the brood of night), where Barathrum doth steep
Torment in his profoundest sinks, where is the floor of brass,
And gates of iron; the place for depth as far doth hell surpass
As heav'n for height exceeds the earth. Then shall he know from thence
How much my pow'r, past all the gods, hath sov'reign eminence.
Endanger it the whiles and see; let down our golden chain,
And at it let all deities their utmost strengths constrain,
To draw me to the earth from heaven. You never shall prevail,
Though with your most contention ye dare my state assail:
But when my will shall be dispos'd to draw you all to me,   20
Even with the earth itself, and seas, ye shall enforced be.
Then will I to Olympus' top our virtuous engine bind,
And by it everything shall hang, by my command inclin'd:
So much I am supreme to gods, to men supreme as much.'
The gods sat silent, and admir'd, his dreadful speech was such.
    At last his blue-ey'd daughter spake: 'O great Saturnides!
O father, O heaven's highest king, well know we the excess
Of thy great power, compar'd with all: yet the bold Greeks' estate
We needs must mourn, since they must fall beneath so hard a fate:
For if thy grave command enjoin, we will abstain from fight.   30
But to afford them such advice as may relieve their plight,
We will, with thy consent, be bold, that all may not sustain
The fearful burthen of thy wrath, and with their shames be slain.'
He smil'd, and said: 'Be confident, thou art belov'd of me:
I speak not this with serious thoughts, but will be kind to thee.'

This said, his brass-hoof'd winged horse he did to chariot bind,
Whose crests were fring'd with manes of gold; and golden garments shin'd
On his rich shoulders; in his hand he took a golden scourge,
Divinely fashion'd, and with blows their willing speed did urge,
Mid way betwixt the earth and heaven. To Ida then he came,   40
Abounding in delicious springs, and nurse of beasts untame,
Where on the mountain Gargarus men did a fane erect
To his high name, and altars sweet, and there his horse he check'd,
Dissolv'd them from his chariot, and in a cloud of jet
He cover'd them, and on the top took his triumphant seat,
Beholding Priam's famous town, and all the fleet of Greece.
The Greeks took breakfast speedily, and arm'd at every piece;
So Trojans, who though fewer far, yet all to fight took arms:
Dire need enforc'd them to avert their wives' and children's harms.
All gates flew open; all the host did issue, foot and horse,   50
In mighty tumult: straight one place adjoin'd each adverse force.
Then shields with shields met, darts with darts, strength against strength oppos'd:
The boss-pik'd targets were thrust on, and thunder'd as they clos'd
In mighty tumult; groan for groan, and breath for breath did breath,
Of men then slain, and to be slain: earth flow'd with fruits of death.
While the fair morning's beauty held and day increas'd in height,
Their javelins mutually made death transport an equal freight:
But when the hot meridian point bright Phoebus did ascend,
Then Jove his golden balances did equally extend,
And of long-rest-conferring death, put in two bitter fates   60
For Troy and Greece; he held the midst: the day of final dates
Fell on the Greeks: the Greeks' hard lots sunk to the flow'ry ground,
The Trojans leapt as high as heaven; then did the claps resound
Of his fierce thunder, lightning leapt amongst each Grecian troop:
The sight amaz'd them, pallid fear made boldest stomachs stoop.
Then Idomen durst not abide; Atrides went his way,
And both th' Ajaces: Nestor yet against his will did stay
(That grave protector of the Greeks), for Paris with a dart
Enrag'd one of his chariot horse; he smote the upper part
Of all his skull, ev'n where the hair, that made his foretop, sprung;   70
The hurt was deadly, and the pain so sore the courser stung
(Pierc'd to the brain) he stamp'd and plung'd; one on another bears,
Entangled round about the beam; then Nestor cut the gears
With his new-drawn authentic sword: meanwhile the fiery horse
Of Hector brake into the press, with their bold ruler's force:
Then good old Nestor had been slain, had Diomed not espy'd,
Who to Ulysses, as he fled, importunately cried:
'Thou that in counsels dost abound, O Laertiades,

Why fliest thou? Why thus coward-like shunn'st thou the honour'd press?
Take heed thy back take not a dart; stay, let us both intend　　　　　80
To drive this cruel enemy from our dear aged friend.'
He spake; but wary Ithacus would find no patient ear,
But fled forthright, even to the fleet. Yet though he single were,
Brave Diomed mix'd amongst the fight, and stood before the steeds
Of old Neleides, whose estate thus kingly he areeds:
　　'O father, with these youths in fight thou art unequal plac'd:
Thy willing sinews are unknit, grave age pursues thee fast,
And thy unruly horse are slow; my chariot therefore use,
And try how ready Trojan horse can fly him that pursues,
Pursue the flier, and every way perform the varied fight:　　　　　90
I forc'd them from Anchises' son, well skill'd in cause of flight.
Then let my squire lead hence thy horse: mine thou shalt guard, whilst I
(By thee advanc'd) assay the fight, that Hector's self may try
If my lance dote with the defects that fail best minds in age,
Or find the palsy in my hands, that doth thy life engage.'
　　This noble Nestor did accept, and Diomed's two friends,
Eurymedon that valour loves, and Sthenelus, ascends
Old Nestor's coach. Of Diomed's horse Nestor the charge sustains,
And Tydeus' son took place of fight; Neleides held the reins,
And scourg'd the horse, who swiftly ran direct in Hector's face,　　　100
Whom fierce Tydides bravely charg'd; but – he turn'd from the chace –
His javelin Eniopeus smit, mighty Thebaeus' son,
And was great Hector's charioteer; it through his breast did run,
Near to his pap; he fell to earth, back flew his frighted horse,
His strength and soul were both dissolv'd. Hector had deep remorse
Of his mishap, yet left he him, and for another sought;
Not long his steeds did want a guide, for straight good fortune brought
Bold Archeptolemus, whose life did from Iphytis spring:
He made him take the reins and mount. Then souls were set on wing,
Then high exploits were undergone, then Trojans in their walls　　　110
Had been infolded like meek lambs, had Jove wink'd at their falls –
Who hurl'd his horrid thunder forth, and made pale lightnings fly
Into the earth, before the horse that Nestor did apply.
A dreadful flash burnt through the air, that savour'd sulphur-like,
Which down before the chariot the dazzled horse did strike:
The fair reins fell from Nestor's hand, who did in fear entreat
Renown'd Tydides into flight to turn his fury's heat.
'For know'st thou not,' said he, 'our aid is not supplied from Jove?
This day he will give fame to Troy; which, when it fits his love,
We shall enjoy: let no man tempt his unresisted will,　　　　　120
Though he exceed in gifts of strength, for he exceeds him still.'

'Father', replied the king, ''tis true; but both my heart and soul
Are most extremely griev'd to think how Hector will control
My valour with his vaunts in Troy, that I was terror-sick
With his approach: which when he boasts let earth devour me quick.'

  'Ah, warlike Tydeus son!' said he, 'what needless words are these?
Though Hector should report thee faint, and amorous of thy ease,
The Trojans, nor the Trojan wives, would never give him trust,
Whose youthful husbands thy free hand hath smother'd so in dust.'
This said, he turn'd his one-hoof'd horse to flight, and troop did take,   130
When Hector and his men with shouts did greedy pursuit make,
And pour'd on darts, that made air sigh; then Hector did exclaim:
'O Tydeus' son, the kings of Greece do most renown thy name
With highest place, feasts and full cups; who now will do thee shame.
Thou shalt be like a woman us'd, and they will say: "Depart,
Immartial minion, since to stand Hector thou hast no heart."
Nor canst thou scale our turrets' tops, nor lead the wives to fleet
Of valiant men, that wife-like fear'st my adverse charge to meet.'

  This two ways mov'd him: still to fly, or turn his horse and fight.
Thrice thrust he forward to assault, and every time the fright   140
Of Jove's fell thunder drave him back, which he propos'd for sign
(To show the change of victory) Trojans should victors shine.
Then Hector comforted his men: 'All my adventurous friends,
Be men, and of your famous strength think of the honour'd ends.
I know benevolent Jupiter did by his beck profess
Conquest and high renown to me, and to the Greeks distress.
O fools, to raise such silly forts, not worth the least account,
Nor able to resist our force! With ease our horse may mount
Quite over all their hollow dike; but when their fleet I reach,
Let Memory to all the world a famous bonfire teach: 150
For I will all their ships inflame, with whose infestive smoke
(Fear-shrunk, and hidden near their keels) the conquer'd Greeks shall choke.'

  Then cherish'd he his famous horse: 'O Xanthus!' now said he,
'And thou Podargus, Aethon too, and Lampus, dear to me,
Make me some worthy recompense for so much choice of meat,
Giv'n you by fair Andromache, bread of the purest wheat,
And with it, for your drink, mix'd wine, to make ye wished cheer,
Still serving you before myself (her husband young and dear) –
Pursue, and use your swiftest speed, that we may take for prize
The shield of old Neleides, which Fame lifts to the skies,   160
Even to the handles telling it to be of massy gold;
And from the shoulders let us take of Diomed the bold,
The royal curace Vulcan wrought with art so exquisite.
These if we make our sacred spoil, I doubt not but this night

Ev'n to their navy to enforce the Greeks' unturned flight.'
This Juno took in high disdain, and made Olympus shake,
As she but stirr'd within her throne; and thus to Neptune spake:

'O Neptune, what a spite is this? Thou god so huge in power,
Afflicts it not thy honour'd heart, to see rude spoil devour
These Greeks that have in Helice and Aege off'red thee   170
So many and so wealthy gifts? Let them the victors be.
If we, that are the aids of Greece, would beat home these of Troy,
And hinder broad-ey'd Jove's proud will, it would abate his joy.'

He, angry, told her she was rash, and he would not be one
Of all the rest should strive with Jove, whose power was match'd by none.
Whiles they conferr'd thus, all the space the trench contain'd before
(From that part of the fort that flank'd the navy-anchoring shore)
Was fill'd with horse and targeteers, who there for refuge came,
By Mars-swift Hector's power engaged, Jove gave his strength the same:
And he with spoilful fire had burn'd the fleet, if Juno's grace   180
Had not inspir'd the king himself to run from place to place,
And stir up every soldier's power to some illustrious deed.
First visiting their leaders' tents, his ample purple weed
He wore, to show all who he was; and did his station take
At wise Ulysses' sable barks, that did the battle make
Of all the fleet, from whence his speech might with more ease be driv'n
To Ajax' and Achilles' ships, to whose chief charge were giv'n
The vanguard and the rearguard both – both for their force of hand
And trusty bosoms. There arriv'd, thus urg'd he to withstand
Th' insulting Trojans: 'O what shame, ye empty-hearted lords,   190
Is this to your admired forms! Where are your glorious words,
In Lemnos vaunting you the best of all the Grecian host?
"We are the strongest men," ye said, "we will command the most,
Eating most flesh of high-horn'd beeves, and drinking cups full crown'd,
And every man a hundred foes – two hundred – will confound!"
Now all our strength, dar'd to our worst, one Hector cannot tame,
Who presently with horrid fire will all our fleet inflame.
O Father Jove, hath ever yet thy most unsuffer'd hand
Afflicted with such spoil of souls the king of any land,
And taken so much fame from him – when I did never fail   200
(Since under most unhappy stars this fleet was under sail)
Thy glorious altars, I protest, but above all the gods
Have burnt fat thighs of beeves to thee, and pray'd to raze th' abodes
Of rape-defending Ilion? Yet grant, almighty Jove,
One favour – that we may at least with life from hence remove,
Not under such inglorious hands the hands of death employ,
And where Troy should be stoop'd by Greece, let Greece fall under Troy.'

To this ev'n weeping king did Jove remorseful audience give,
And shook great heav'n to him for sign his men and he should live.
Then quickly cast he off his hawk, the eagle prince of air,   210
That perfects his unspotted vows; who seiz'd in her repair
A sucking hind calf, which she truss'd in her enforcive seres,
And by Jove's altar let it fall, amongst th' amazed peers,
Where the religious Achive kings with sacrifice did please
The author of all oracles, divine Saturnides.
    Now when they knew the bird of Jove, they turn'd courageous head.
When none (though many kings put on) could make his vaunt, he led
Tydides to renew'd assault, or issu'd first the dike,
Or first did fight: but far the first, stone dead his lance did strike
Arm'd Agelaus, by descent surnam'd Phradmonides;   220
He turn'd his ready horse to flight, and Diomed's lance did seize
His back betwixt his shoulder-blades, and look'd out at his breast;
He fell, and his arms rang his fall. Th' Atrides next address'd
Themselves to fight; th' Ajaces next, with vehement strength endued;
Idomeneus, and his friend stout Merion, next pursued;
And after these Euripelus, Evemon's honour'd race:
The ninth, with backward, wreathed bow, had little Teucer place;
He still fought under Ajax' shield, who sometimes held it by,
And then he look'd his object out, and let his arrow fly;
And whomsoever, in the press he wounded, him he slew,   230
Then under Ajax' seven-fold shield he presently withdrew:
He far'd like an unhappy child, that doth to mother run
For succour, when he knows full well he some shrewd turn hath done.
What Trojans then were to their deaths by Teucer's shafts impress'd?
Hapless Orsylochus was first, Ormenus, Ophelest,
Detor, and hardy Cronius, and Lycophon divine;
And Amopaon that did spring from Polyemon's line,
And Menalippus: all, on heaps, he tumbled to the ground.
The king rejoic'd to see his shafts the Phrygian ranks confound;
Who straight came near, and spake to him: 'O Teucer, lovely man,   240
Strike still so sure, and be a grace to every Grecian,
And to thy father Telamon, who took thee kindly home
(Although not by his wife his son) and gave thee foster room,
Ev'n from thy childhood; then to him, though far from hence remov'd,
Make good fame reach, and to thyself I vow what shall be prov'd:
If he that dreadful Aegis bears, and Pallas, grant to me
Th' expugnance of well-builded Troy, I first will honour thee
Next to myself with some rich gift, and put it in thy hand:
A three-foot vessel, that for grace in sacred fanes doth stand,
Or two horse and a chariot, or else a lovely dame,   250

That may ascend on bed with thee, and amplify thy name.'
　　Teucer right nobly answer'd him: 'Why, most illustrious king,
I being thus forward of myself, dost thou adjoin a sting?
Without which, all the power I have I cease not to employ:
For from the place where we repuls'd the Trojans towards Troy,
I all the purple field have strew'd with one or other slain:
Eight shafts I shot, with long steel heads, of which not one in vain;
All were in youthful bodies fix'd, well skill'd in war's constraint.
Yet this wild dog, with all my aim, I have no power to taint.'
This said, another arrow forth from his stiff string he sent　　　　　260
At Hector, whom he long'd to wound, but still amiss it went:
His shaft smit fair Gorgythion, of Priam's princely race,
Who in Aepina was brought forth (a famous town in Thrace)
By Castianira, that for form was like celestial breed.
And as a crimson poppy flower, surcharged with his seed,
And vernal humours failing thick, declines his heavy brow,
So, of one side, his helmet's weight his fainting head did bow.
Yet Teucer would another shaft at Hector's life dispose,
So fain he such a mark would hit, but still beside it goes;
Apollo did avert the shaft: but Hector's charioteer,　　　　　270
Bold Archeptolemus, he smit, as he was rushing near
To make the fight: to earth he fell, his swift horse back did fly,
And there were both his strength and soul exil'd eternally.
Huge grief for Hector's slaughter'd friend pinch'd in his mighty mind:
Yet was he forc'd to leave him there, and his void place resign'd
To his sad brother, that was by, Cebriones: whose ear
Receiving Hector's charge, he straight the weighty reins did bear;
And Hector from his shining coach, with horrid voice, leap'd on,
To wreak his friend on Teucer's hand, and up he took a stone,
With which he at the archer ran; who from his quiver drew　　　　　280
A sharp-pil'd shaft, and nock'd it sure: but in great Hector flew
With such fell speed, that in his draught he his right shoulder strook,
Where 'twixt his neck and breast the joint his native closure took:
The wound was wondrous full of death, his string in sunder flees;
His numbed hand fell strengthless down, and he upon his knees.
Ajax neglected not to aid his brother thus depress'd,
But came and sav'd him with his shield; and two more friends, address'd
To be his aid, took him to fleet: Mecistius, Echius' son,
And gay Alastor. Teucer sigh'd, for all his service done.
　　Then did Olympius with fresh strength the Trojan powers revive,　　　　　290
Who to their trenches once again the troubled Greeks did drive.
Hector brought terror with his strength, and ever fought before.
As when some highly stomach'd hound, that hunts a sylvan boar

Or kingly lion, loves the haunch, and pincheth oft behind,
Bold of his feet, and still observes the game to turn inclin'd,
Not utterly dissolv'd in flight: so Hector did pursue,
And whosoever was the last he ever did subdue.
They fled, but when they had their dike and palisadoes pass'd
(A number of them put to sword), at ships they stay'd at last.
Then mutual exhortations flew, then – all with hands and eyes   300
Advanc'd to all the gods – their plagues wrung from them open cries.
Hector with his four rich-man'd horse, assaulting always rode;
The eyes of Gorgon burnt in him, and war's vermilion god.
The goddess that all goddesses for snowy arms out-shin'd,
Thus spake to Pallas, to the Greeks with gracious ruth inclin'd:
    'O Pallas, what a grief is this? Is all our succour past
To these our perishing Grecian friends – at least, withheld at last –
Ev'n now, when one man's violence must make them perish all,
In satisfaction of a fate so full of funeral?
Hector Priamides now raves, no more to be endur'd,   310
That hath already on the Greeks so many harms inur'd.'
    The azure goddess answer'd her: 'This man had surely found
His fortitude and life dissolv'd, even on his father's ground,
By Grecian valour, if my sire, infested with ill moods,
Did not so dote on these of Troy, too jealous of their bloods:
And ever an unjust repulse stands to my willing pow'rs,
Little rememb'ring what I did in all the desperate hours
Of his affected Hercules: I ever rescu'd him,
In labours of Euristheus, untouch'd in life or limb,
When he (heav'n knows) with drowned eyes look'd up for help to heav'n;
Which ever, at command of Jove, was by my suppliance giv'n.
But had my wisdom reach'd so far, to know of this event,
When to the solid-ported depths of hell his son was sent,
To hale out hateful Pluto's dog from darksome Erebus,
He had not scap'd the streams of Styx, so deep and dangerous.
Yet Jove hates me, and shows his love in doing Thetis' will,
That kiss'd his knees, and strok'd his chin, pray'd, and importun'd still,
That he would honour with his aid her city-razing son,
Displeas'd Achilles: and for him our friends are thus undone.
But time shall come again, when he, to do his friends some aid,   330
Will call me his Glaucopides, his sweet and blue-ey'd maid.
Then harness thou thy horse for me, that his bright palace gates
I soon may enter, arming me, to order these debates.
And I will try if Priam's son will still maintain his cheer,
When in the crimson paths of war I dreadfully appear;
For some proud Trojans shall be sure to nourish dogs and fowls,

And pave the shore with fat and flesh, depriv'd of lives and souls.'
  Juno prepar'd her horse, whose manes ribands of gold enlac'd:
Pallas her parti-colour'd robe on her bright shoulders cast,
Divinely wrought with her own hands, in th' entry of her sire;   340
Then put she on her ample breast her under-arming tire,
And on it her celestial arms; the chariot straight she takes,
With her huge heavy violent lance, with which she slaughter makes
Of armies, fatal to her wrath. Saturnia whipp'd her horse,
And heaven gates, guarded by the Hours, op'd by their proper force:
Through which they flew. Whom when Jove saw (set near th' Idalian springs),
Highly displeas'd, he Iris call'd, that hath the golden wings,
And said: 'Fly, Iris, turn them back, let them not come at me:
Our meetings – severally dispos'd – will nothing gracious be.
Beneath their o'erthrown chariot I'll shiver their proud steeds,   350
Hurl down themselves, their waggon break, and for their stubborn deeds
In ten whole years they shall not heal the wounds I will impress
With horrid thunder, that my maid may know when to address
Arms 'gainst her father. For my wife, she doth not so offend;
'Tis but her use to interrupt whatever I intend.
Iris, with this, left Ida's hills, and up t' Olympus flew,
Met near heav'n-gates the goddesses, and thus their haste withdrew:
  'What course intend you? Why are you wrapp'd with your fancies' storm?
Jove likes not ye should aid the Greeks, but threats – and will perform –
To crush in pieces your swift horse, beneath their glorious yokes,   360
Hurl down yourselves, your chariot break; and those empoison'd strokes
His wounding thunder shall imprint in your celestial parts,
In ten full springs ye shall not cure, that she that tames proud hearts
(Thyself, Minerva) may be taught to know for what, and when,
Thou dost against thy father fight; for sometimes childeren
May with discretion plant themselves against their fathers' wills –
But not where humours only rule, in works beyond their skills.
For Juno, she offends him not, nor vexeth him so much;
For 'tis her use to cross his will, her impudence is such:
The habit of offence in this she only doth contract,   370
And so grieves or incenseth less, though ne'er the less her fact.
But thou most griev'st him, dogged dame, whom he rebukes in time,
Lest silence should pervert thy will, and pride too highly climb
In thy bold bosom; desperate girl, if seriously thou dare
Lift thy unwieldy lance 'gainst Jove, as thy pretences are.'
  She left them, and Saturnia said: 'Ah me! Thou seed of Jove,
By my advice we will no more unfit contention move
With Jupiter, for mortal men; of whom, let this man die
And that man live, whoever he pursues with destiny.

And let him (plotting all events) dispose of either host,   380
As he thinks fittest for them both, and may become us most.'
     Thus turn'd she back, and to the Hours her rich-man'd horse resign'd,
Who them t' immortal mangers bound; the chariot they inclin'd
Beneath the crystal walls of heaven; and they in golden thrones
Consorted, other deities, replete with passions.
Jove, in his bright-wheel'd chariot, his fiery horse now beats
Up to Olympus, and aspir'd the gods' eternal seats.
Great Neptune loos'd his horse, his car upon the altar plac'd,
And heavenly-linen coverings did round about it cast.
The far-seer us'd his throne of gold: the vast Olympus shook   390
Beneath his feet; his wife and maid apart their places took,
Nor any word afforded him. He knew their thoughts, and said:
'Why do you thus torment yourselves? You need not sit dismay'd
With the long labours you have us'd, in your victorious fight,
Destroying Trojans, 'gainst whose lives you heap such high despite.
Ye should have held your glorious course; for be assur'd, as far
As all my pow'rs, by all means urg'd, could have sustain'd the war,
Not all the host of deities should have retir'd my hand
From vow'd inflictions on the Greeks – much less you two withstand.
But you, before you saw the fight, much less the slaughter there,   400
Had all your goodly lineaments possess'd with shaking fear,
And never had your chariot borne their charge to heav'n again,
But thunder should have smit you both, had you one Trojan slain.'
     Both goddesses let fall their chins upon their ivory breasts,
Set next to Jove, contriving still afflicted Troy's unrests:
Pallas for anger could not speak; Saturnia, contrary,
Could not for anger hold her peace, but made this bold reply:
     'Not-to-be-suff'red Jupiter! What need'st thou still enforce
Thy matchless power? We know it well. But we must yield remorse
To them that yield us sacrifice: nor need'st thou thus deride   410
Our kind obedience, nor our griefs, but bear our powers applied
To just protection of the Greeks, that anger tomb not all
In Troy's foul gulf of perjury, and let them stand should fall.'
     'Grieve not,' said Jove, 'at all done yet: for if thy fair eyes please,
This next red morning they shall see the great Saturnides
Bring more destruction to the Greeks; and Hector shall not cease
Till he have roused from the fleet swift-foot Aeacides,
In that day when before their ships, for his Patroclus slain,
The Greeks in great distress shall fight, for so the Fates ordain.
I weigh not thy displeased spleen, though to th' extremest bounds   420
Of earth and seas it carry thee, where endless night confounds
Japet, and my dejected sire, who sit so far beneath,

They never see the flying sun, nor hear the winds that breathe,
Near to profoundest Tartarus: nor thither if thou went,
Would I take pity of thy moods, since none more impudent.'
   To this she nothing did reply. And now Sol's glorious light
Fell to the sea, and to the land drew up the drowsy night.
The Trojans griev'd at Phoebus' fall, which all the Greeks desir'd:
And sable night (so often wish'd) to earth's firm throne aspir'd.
   Hector intending to consult, near to the gulfy flood,   430
Far from the fleet, led to a place pure and exempt from blood,
The Trojans' forces: from their horse all lighted, and did hear
Th' oration Jove-lov'd Hector made; who held a goodly spear,
Eleven full cubits long; the head was brass, and did reflect
A wanton light before him still; it round about was deck'd
With strong hoops of new-burnish'd gold. On this he lean'd, and said:
   'Hear me, my worthy friends of Troy, and you our honour'd aid:
A little since I had conceit we should have made retreat,
By light of the inflamed fleet, with all the Greeks' escheat;
But darkness hath prevented us, and sav'd, with special grace,   440
These Achives and their shore-hal'd fleet. Let us then render place
To sacred Night, our suppers dress, and from our chariot free
Our fair-man'd horse, and meat them well: then let there convoy'd be,
From forth the city presently, oxen and well-fed sheep,
Sweet wine, and bread. And fell much wood, that all night we may keep
Plenty of fires, even till the light bring forth the lovely morn;
And let their brightness glaze the skies, that night may not suborn
The Greeks' escape, if they for flight the sea's broad back would take:
At least they may not part with ease, but as retreat they make,
Each man may bear a wound with him, to cure when he comes home,   450
Made with a shaft or sharp'ned spear, and others fear to come,
With charge of lamentable war, 'gainst soldiers bred in Troy.
Then let our heralds through the town their offices employ,
To warn the youth yet short of war, and time-white fathers, past,
That in our god-built tow'rs they see strong courts of guard be plac'd
About the walls; and let our dames, yet flourishing in years,
That, having beauties to keep pure, are most inclin'd to fears –
Since darkness in distressful times more dreadful is than light –
Make lofty fires in every house: and thus, the dangerous night
Held with strong watch, if th' enemy have ambuscadoes laid   460
Near to our walls, and therefore seem in flight the more dismay'd,
Intending a surprise, while we are all without the town,
They every way shall be impugn'd to every man's renown.
Perform all this, brave Trojan friends: what now I have to say
Is all express'd; the cheerful morn shall other things display.

It is my glory (putting trust in Jove and other gods)
That I shall now expulse these dogs, fates sent to our abodes,
Who bring ostents of destiny, and black their threat'ning fleet.
But this night let us hold strong guards: to-morrow we will meet
(With fierce-made war) before their ships; and I'll make known to all   470
If strong Tydides from their ships can drive me to their wall,
Or I can pierce him with my sword, and force his bloody spoil.
The wished morn shall show his power, if he can shun his foil,
I running on him with my lance. I think when day ascends,
He shall lie wounded with the first, and by him many friends.
O that I were as sure to live immortal, and sustain
No frailties with increasing years, but evermore remain
Ador'd like Pallas, or the Sun, as all doubts die in me,
That heav'n's next light shall be the last the Greeks shall ever see.'
     This speech all Trojans did applaud; who from their traces loos'd   480
Their sweating horse, which severally with headstals they repos'd,
And fast'ned by their chariots; when others brought from town
Fat sheep and oxen instantly; bread, wine; and hewed down
Huge store of wood: the winds transferr'd into the friendly sky
Their supper's savour, to the which they sat delightfully,
And spent all night in open field; fires round about them shin'd –
As when about the silver moon, when air is free from wind,
And stars shine clear, to whose sweet beams high prospects, and the brows
Of all steep hills and pinnacles, thrust up themselves for shows,
And ev'n the lowly valleys joy to glitter in their sight,   490
When the unmeasur'd firmament bursts to disclose her light,
And all the signs in heav'n are seen that glad the shepherd's heart:
So many fires disclos'd their beams, made by the Trojan part,
Before the face of Ilion, and her bright turrets show'd.
A thousand courts of guard kept fires, and every guard allow'd
Fifty stout men, by whom their horse ate oats and hard white corn,
And all did wilfully expect the silver-throned morn:

THE END OF THE EIGHTH BOOK

BOOK NINE

The Argument

To Agamemnon, urging hopeless flight,
Stand Diomed and Nestor opposite:
By Nestor's counsel, legates are dismiss'd
To Thetis' son, who still denies t' assist.

Another Argument

Iota sings the embassy,
And great Achilles' stern reply.

BOOK NINE

SO HELD the Trojans sleepless guard; the Greeks to flight were giv'n,
The feeble consort of cold fear (strangely infus'd from heav'n).
Grief, not to be endur'd, did wound all Greeks of greatest worth.
And as two lateral-sited winds – the west wind and the north –
Meet at the Thracian sea's black breast, join in a sudden blore,
Tumble together the dark waves, and pour upon the shore
A mighty deal of froth and weed, with which men manure ground:
So Jove and Troy did drive the Greeks, and all their minds confound.
But Agamemnon most of all was tortur'd at his heart;
Who to the voiceful heralds went, and bad them cite, apart,   10
Each Grecian leader severally (not openly proclaim);
In which he labour'd with the first, and all together came.
They sadly sate. The king arose, and pour'd out tears as fast
As from a lofty rock a spring doth his black waters cast;
And deeply sighing, thus bespake the Achives: 'O my friends,
Princes and leaders of the Greeks, heav'n's adverse king extends
His wrath with too much detriment to my so just design,
Since he hath often promis'd me, and bound it with the sign
Of his bent forehead, that this Troy our vengeful hands should race,
And safe return: yet now, engag'd, he plagues us with disgrace,   20
When all our trust to him hath drawn so much blood from our friends.
My glory, nor my brother's wreak, were the proposed ends
For which he drew you to these toils, but your whole country's shame,
Which had been huge, to bear the rape of so divine a dame,
Made in despite of our revenge. And yet not that had mov'd
Our pow'rs to these designs, if Jove had not our drifts approv'd;
Which since we see he did for blood, 'tis desperate fight in us
To strive with him; then let us fly: 'tis flight he urgeth thus.

Long time still silence held them all; at last did Diomed rise:
'Atrides, I am first must cross thy indiscreet advice,   30
As may become me, being a king, in this our martial court.
Be not displeas'd then, for thyself didst broadly misreport
In open field my fortitude, and call'd me faint and weak;
Yet I was silent, knowing the time, loath any rites to break
That appertain'd thy public rule: yet all the Greeks knew well

(Of every age) thou didst me wrong. As thou then didst refel
My valour first of all the host, as of a man dismay'd,
So now, with fit occasion giv'n, I first blame thee – afraid.
Inconstant Saturn's son hath giv'n inconstant spirits to thee,
And with a sceptre over all, an eminent degree.   40
But with a sceptre's sovereign grace, the chief pow'r, fortitude,
To bridle thee, he thought not best thy breast should be endu'd.
Unhappy king, think'st thou the Greeks are such a silly sort,
And so excessive impotent, as thy weak words import?
If thy mind move thee to be gone, the way is open; go:
Mycenian ships enow ride near, that brought thee to this woe.
The rest of Greece will stay, nor stir till Troy be overcome,
With full eversion; or if not, but – doters of their home –
Will put on wings to fly with thee, myself and Sthenelus
Will fight, till (trusting favouring Jove) we bring home Troy with us.'   50
    This all applauded, and admir'd the spirit of Diomed;
When Nestor, rising from the rest, his speech thus seconded:
    'Tydides, thou art questionless our strongest Greek in war,
And gravest in thy counsels too, of all that equal are
In place with thee, and stand on strength; nor is there any one
Can blame or contradict thy speech: and yet thou hast not gone
So far, but we must further go. Thou'rt young, and well mightst be
My youngest son, though still I yield thy words have high degree
Of wisdom in them to our king, since well they did become
Their right in question, and refute inglorious going home.   60
But I, well known thy senior far, will speak, and handle all
Yet to propose which none shall check – no, not our general.
A hater of society, unjust and wild, is he
That loves intestine war, being stuff'd with manless cruelty:
And therefore in persuading peace, and home-flight, we the less
May blame our gen'ral, as one loath to wrap in more distress
His loved soldiers. But because they bravely are resolv'd
To cast lives after toils, before they part in shame involv'd,
Provide we for our honour'd stay: obey black night, and fall
Now to our suppers, then appoint our guards without the wall,   70
And in the bottom of the dike; which guards I wish may stand
Of our brave youth. And, Atreus' son, since thou art in command
Before our other kings, be first in thy command's effect:
It well becomes thee, since 'tis both what all thy peers expect,
And in the royal right of things is no impair to thee.
Nor shall it stand with less than right, that they invited be
To supper by thee; all thy tents are amply stor'd with wine,
Brought daily in Greek ships from Thrace; and to this grace of thine

All necessaries thou hast fit, and store of men to wait:
And many meeting there, thou mayst hear every man's conceit,   80
And take the best. It much concerns all Greeks to use advice
Of gravest nature, since so near our ships our enemies
Have lighted such a sort of fires: with which what man is joy'd?
Look how all bear themselves this night: so live, or be destroy'd.'
    All heard, and follow'd his advice. There was appointed then
Seven captains of the watch, who forth did march with all their men.
The first was famous Thrasymed, adviceful Nestor's son;
Ascalaphus, and Ialmen, and mighty Merion,
Alphareus, and Deipyrus, and lovely Lycomed,
Old Creon's joy. These sev'n bold lords an hundred soldiers led,   90
In every sever'd company, and every man his pike.
Some placed on the rampire's top, and some amidst the dike,
All fires made, and their suppers took. Atrides to his tent
Invited all the peers of Greece, and food sufficient
Appos'd before them, and the peers appos'd their hands to it.
Hunger and thirst being quickly quench'd, to counsel still they sit.
And first spake Nestor, who they thought of late advis'd so well,
A father grave, and rightly wise, who thus his tale did tell:
    'Most high Atrides, since in thee I have intent to end,
From thee will I begin my speech, to whom Jove doth commend   100
The empire of so many men, and puts into thy hand
A sceptre, and establish'd laws, that thou mayst well command,
And counsel all men under thee. It therefore doth behove
Thyself to speak most, since of all thy speeches most will move –
And yet to hear as well as speak, and then perform as well
A free just counsel; in thee still must stick, what others tell.
For me, what in my judgment stands the most convenient
I will advise; and am assur'd, advice more competent
Shall not be given; the general proof that hath before been made
Of what I speak, confirms me still, and now may well persuade,   110
Because I could not then, yet ought, when thou, most royal king,
Ev'n from the tent Achilles' love didst violently bring,
Against my counsel urging thee by all means to relent.
But you, obeying your high mind, would venture the event,
Dishonouring our ablest Greek, a man th' immortals grace:
Again yet let's deliberate, to make him now embrace
Affection to our general good, and bring his force to field:
Both which, kind words and pleasing gifts must make his virtues yield.'
    'O father,' answered the king, 'my wrongs thou tell'st me right;
Mine own offence mine own tongue grants; one man must stand in fight   120
For our whole army; him I wrong'd, him Jove loves from his heart:

He shows it in thus honouring him; who living thus apart,
Proves us but number: for his want makes all our weakness seen.
Yet after my confess'd offence, soothing my hum'rous spleen,
I'll sweeten his affects again with presents infinite:
Which, to approve my firm intent, I'll openly recite:
Seven sacred tripods free from fire, ten talents of fine gold,
Twenty bright cauldrons, twelve young horse, well shap'd and well controll'd,
And victors too; for they have won the prize at many a race.
That man should not be poor, that had but what their winged pace   130
Hath added to my treasury, nor feel sweet gold's defect.
Seven Lesbian ladies he shall have, that were the most select,
And in their needles rarely skill'd: whom, when he took the town
Of famous Lesbos, I did choose; who won the chief renown
For beauty from their whole fair sex, amongst whom I'll resign
Fair Brysis; and I deeply swear (for any fact of mine
That may discourage her receipt) she is untouch'd, and rests
As he resign'd her. To these gifts, if Jove to our requests
Vouchsafe performance, and afford the work for which we wait,
Of winning Troy, with brass and gold he shall his navy freight;   140
And (ent'ring when we be at spoil) that princely hand of his
Shall choose him twenty Trojan dames, excepting Tyndaris,
The fairest Pergamus enfolds; and if we make retreat
To Argos (call'd of all the world the Navel, or chief seat)
He shall become my son-in-law, and I will honour him
Ev'n as Orestes, my sole son, that doth in honours swim.
Three daughters in my well-built court unmarried are, and fair:
Laodice, Chrysothemis that hath the golden hair,
And Iphianassa; of all three the worthiest let him take,
All jointureless to Peleus' court: I will her jointure make –   150
And that so great as never yet did any maid prefer.
Seven cities right magnificent I will bestow on her:
Enope, and Cardamile, Hyra for herbs renown'd,
The fair Aepaea, Pedasus that doth with grapes abound,
Antaea girded with green meads, Phera surnam'd Divine:
All whose bright turrets on the seas in sandy Pylos shine.
Th' inhabitants in flocks and herds are wondrous confluent,
Who like a god will honour him, and him with gifts present,
And to his throne will contribute what tribute he will rate.
All this I gladly will perform, to pacify his hate.   160
Let him be mild and tractable: 'tis for the god of ghosts
To be unrul'd, implacable, and seek the blood of hosts,
Whom therefore men do much abhor: then let him yield to me;
I am his greater, being a king, and more in years than he.'

'Brave king,' said Nestor, 'these rich gifts must make him needs relent:
Choose then fit legates instantly, to greet him at his tent.
But stay; admit my choice of them, and let them straight be gone:
Jove-loved Phoenix shall be chief, then Ajax Telamon,
And prince Ulysses; and on them let these two heralds wait,
Grave Odius and Euribates. Come, lords, take water straight,   170
Make pure your hands, and with sweet words appease Achilles' mind,
Which we will pray the king of gods may gently make inclin'd.'

All lik'd his speech, and on their hands the heralds water shed:
The youths crown'd cups of sacred wine to all distributed.
But having sacrific'd and drunk to every man's content
(With many notes by Nestor given), the legates forward went.
With courtship in fit gestures us'd he did prepare them well,
But most Ulysses, for his grace did not so much excel.
Such rites beseem ambassadors; and Nestor urged these,
That their most honours might reflect enrag'd Aeacides.   180
They went along the shore, and pray'd the god that earth doth bind
In brackish chains, they might not fail, but bow his mighty mind.

The quarter of the Myrmidons they reach'd, and found him set
Delighted with his solemn harp, which curiously was fret
With works conceited; through the verge the bawdrick that embrac'd
His lofty neck was silver twist; this, when his hand laid waste
Aëtion's city, he did choose as his especial prize;
And, loving sacred music well, made it his exercise.
To it he sung the glorious deeds of great heroës dead,
And his true mind, that practice fail'd, sweet contemplation fed.   190
With him alone, and opposite, all silent sat his friend,
Attentive, and beholding him who now his song did end.
Th' ambassadors did forwards press, renown'd Ulysses led,
And stood in view: their sudden sight his admiration bred,
Who with his harp and all arose: so did Menoetius' son
When he beheld them; their receipt Achilles thus begun:

'Health to my lords! Right welcome men assure yourselves you be,
Though some necessity I know doth make you visit me,
Incens'd with just cause 'gainst the Greeks.' This said, a several seat
With purple cushions he set forth, and did their ease intreat;   200
And said: 'Now, friend, our greatest bowl, with wine unmix'd and neat,
Appose these lords; and of the depth let every man make proof:
These are my best-esteemed friends, and underneath my roof.

Patroclus did his dear friend's will; and he that did desire
To cheer the lords (come faint from fight), set on a blazing fire
A great brass pot, and into it a chine of mutton put,
And fat goat's flesh: Automedon held, while he pieces cut

To roast and boil; right cunningly then of a well-fed swine
A huge fat shoulder he cuts out, and spits it wondrous fine;
His good friend made a goodly fire, of which the force once past,   210
He laid the spit low, near the coals, to make it brown at last:
Then sprinkled it with sacred salt, and took it from the racks:
This roasted, and on dresser set, his friend Patroclus takes
Bread in fair baskets; which set on, Achilles brought the meat,
And to divinest Ithacus took his opposed seat
Upon the bench. Then did he will his friend to sacrifice,
Who cast sweet incense in the fire to all the deities.
Thus fell they to their ready food. Hunger and thirst allay'd,
Ajax to Phoenix made a sign as if too long they stay'd
Before they told their legacy. Ulysses saw him wink,   220
And filling the great bowl with wine did to Achilles drink:
'Health to Achilles! But our plights stand not in need of meat,
Who late supp'd at Atrides' tent, though for thy love we eat
Of many things, whereof a part would make a complete feast.
Nor can we joy in these kind rites, that have our hearts oppress'd,
O Prince, with fear of utter spoil: 'tis made a question now
If we can save our fleet or not, unless thyself endow
Thy powers with wonted fortitude. Now Troy and her consorts,
Bold of thy want, have pitch'd their tents close to our fleet and forts,
And made a firmament of fires, and now no more they say   230
Will they be prison'd in their walls, but force their violent way
Ev'n to our ships; and Jove himself hath with his lightnings show'd
Their bold adventures happy signs; and Hector grows so proud
Of his huge strength, borne out by Jove, that fearfully he raves,
Presuming neither men nor gods can interrupt his braves.
Wild rage invades him, and he prays that soon the sacred morn
Would light his fury, boasting then our streamers shall be torn,
And all our naval ornaments fall by his conquering stroke;
Our ships shall burn, and we ourselves lie stifled in the smoke.
And I am seriously afraid heav'n will perform his threats,   240
And that 'tis fatal to us all, far from our native seats,
To perish in victorious Troy. But rise, though it be late,
Deliver the afflicted Greeks from Troy's tumultuous hate.
It will hereafter be thy grief, when no strength can suffice
To remedy th' effected threats of our calamities;
Consider these affairs in time, while thou mayst use thy pow'r,
And have the grace to turn from Greece fate's unrecover'd hour.
O friend, thou know'st thy royal sire forewarn'd what should be done,
That day he sent thee from his court, to honour Atreus' son.
"My son," said he, "the victory let Jove and Pallas use   250

At their high pleasures, but do thou no honour'd means refuse
That may advance her; in fit bounds contain thy mighty mind,
Nor let the knowledge of thy strength be factiously inclin'd,
Contriving mischiefs; be to fame and general good profess'd:
The more will all sorts honour thee; benignity is best."
Thus charg'd thy sire, which thou forgett'st: yet now those thoughts appease
That torture thy great spirit with wrath; which if thou wilt surcease,
The king will merit it with gifts; and if thou wilt give ear,
I'll tell how much he offers thee – yet thou sitt'st angry here.
Seven tripods that no fire must touch, twice ten pans fit for flame;   260
Ten talents of fine gold, twelve horse that ever overcame,
And brought huge prizes from the field with swiftness of their feet.
That man should bear no poor account, nor want gold's quick'ning sweet,
That had but what he won with them; seven worthiest Lesbian dames,
Renown'd for skill in housewifery, and bear the sovereign fames
For beauty, from their general sex; which at thy overthrow
Of well-built Lesbos he did choose, and these he will bestow.
And with these her he took from thee, whom by his state, since then,
He swears he touch'd not, as fair dames use to be touch'd by men.
All these are ready for thee now: and if at length we take,   270
By helps of gods, this wealthy town, thy ships shall burthen make
Of gold and brass at thy desires, when we the spoil divide;
And twenty beauteous Trojan dames thou shalt select beside –
Next Helen, the most beautiful – and when return'd we be
To Argos, be his son-in-law: for he will honour thee
Like his Orestes, his sole son, maintain'd in height of bliss.
Three daughters beautify his court, the fair Chrysothemis,
Laodice, and Iphianesse; of all the fairest take
To Peleus, thy grave father's court, and never jointure make;
He will the jointure make himself, so great, as never sire   280
Gave to his daughter's nuptials: seven cities left entire,
Cardamile, and Enope, and Hyla full of flowers,
Anthaea for sweet meadows prais'd, and Phera deck'd with towers,
The bright Epea, Pedassus that doth god Bacchus please;
All, on the sandy Pylos soil, are seated near the seas.
Th' inhabitants in droves and flocks exceeding wealthy be,
Who, like a god, with worthy gifts will gladly honour thee,
And tribute of especial rate to thy high sceptre pay.
All this he freely will perform, thy anger to allay.
But if thy hate to him be more than his gifts may repress,   290
Yet pity all the other Greeks, in such extreme distress,
Who with religion honour thee: and to their desperate ill
Thou shalt triumphant glory bring, and Hector thou mayst kill,

When pride makes him encounter thee, fill'd with a baneful sprite,
Who vaunts our whole fleet brought not one equal to him in fight.'
    Swift-foot Aeacides replied: 'Divine Laertes' son,
'Tis requisite I should be short, and show what place hath won
Thy serious speech, affirming nought but what you shall approve
Establish'd in my settled heart, that in the rest I move
No murmur nor exception: for like hell mouth I loathe   300
Who holds not in his words and thoughts one indistinguish'd troth.
What fits the freeness of my mind, my speech shall make display'd:
Nor Atreus' son nor all the Greeks shall win me to their aid.
Their suit is wretchedly enforc'd to free their own despairs,
And my life never shall be hir'd with thankless desperate pray'rs;
For never had I benefit, that ever foil'd the foe:
Ev'n share hath he that keeps his tent and he to field doth go;
With equal honour cowards die, and men most valiant,
The much performer, and the man that can of nothing vaunt.
No overplus I ever found, when with my mind's most strife,   310
To do them good, to dangerous fight I have expos'd my life.
But ev'n as to unfeather'd birds the careful dam brings meat,
Which when she hath bestow'd, herself hath nothing left to eat:
So when my broken sleeps have drawn the nights t' extremest length,
And ended many bloody days with still-employed strength,
To guard their weakness, and preserve their wives' contents infract,
I have been robb'd before their eyes. Twelve cities I have sack'd,
Assail'd by sea, eleven by land, while this siege held at Troy:
And of all these, what was most dear, and most might crown the joy
Of Agamemnon, he enjoy'd, who here behind remain'd;   320
Which when he took, a few he gave, and many things retain'd:
Other to optimates and kings he gave, who hold them fast,
Yet mine he forceth: only I sit with my loss disgrac'd.
But so he gain a lovely dame to be his bed's delight,
It is enough; for what cause else do Greeks and Trojans fight?
Why brought he hither such an host? Was it not for a dame?
For fair-hair'd Helen? And doth love alone the hearts inflame
Of the Atrides to their wives, of all the men that move?
Every discreet and honest mind cares for his private love,
As much as they, as I myself lov'd Brisis as my life,   330
Although my captive, and had will to take her for my wife.
Whom since he forc'd, preventing me, in vain he shall prolong
Hopes to appease me, that know well the deepness of my wrong.
But, good Ulysses, with thyself, and all you other kings,
Let him take stomach to repel Troy's fiery threatenings.
Much hath he done without my help: built him a goodly fort,

Cut a dike by it, pitch'd with pales broad, and of deep import;
And cannot all these helps repress this kill-man Hector's fright?
When I was arm'd among the Greeks he would not offer fight
Without the shadow of his walls, but to the Scaean ports,　　　340
Or to the holy beech of Jove come back'd with his consorts,
Where once he stood my charge alone, and hardly made retreat:
And to make new proof of our pow'rs, the doubt is not so great.
To-morrow then, with sacrifice perform'd t' imperial Jove
And all the gods, I'll launch my fleet, and all my men remove:
Which, if thou wilt use so thy sight, or think'st it worth respect,
In forehead of the morn thine eyes shall see, with sails erect
Amidst the fishy Hellespont, help'd with laborious oars.
And if the sea-god send free sail, the fruitful Phthian shores
Within three days we shall attain, where I have store of prize,　　　350
Left, when with prejudice I came to these indignities.
There have I gold as well as here, and store of ruddy brass,
Dames slender, elegantly girt, and steel as bright as glass.
These will I take as I retire, as shares I firmly save,
Though Agamemnon be so base to take the gifts he gave.
Tell him all this, and openly – I on your honours charge –
That others may take shame to hear his lusts command so large.
And if there yet remain a man he hopeth to deceive
(Being dyed in endless impudence), that man may learn to leave
His trust and empire. But alas, though like a wolf he be　　　360
Shameless and rude, he durst not take my prize, and look on me.
I never will partake his works, nor counsels, as before.
He once deceiv'd and injur'd me, and he shall never more
Tie my affections with his words; enough is the increase
Of one success in his deceits: which let him joy in peace,
And bear it to a wretched end. Wise Jove hath reft his brain,
To bring him plagues, and these his gifts, I (as my foes) disdain:
Even in the numbness of calm death, I will revengeful be,
Though ten or twenty times so much he would bestow on me –
All he hath here, or any where; or Orchomen contains,　　　370
To which men bring their wealth for strength; or all the store remains
In circuit of Egyptian Thebes, where much hid treasure lies,
Whose walls contain an hundred ports of so admir'd a size,
Two hundred soldiers may a-front with horse and chariots pass.
Nor, would he amplify all this like sand or dust or grass,
Should he reclaim me, till his wreak pay'd me for all the pains
That with his contumely burn'd like poison in my veins.
Nor shall his daughter be my wife, although she might contend
With golden Venus for her form, or if she did transcend

Blue-ey'd Minerva for her works: let him a Greek select   380
Fit for her, and a greater king. For if the gods protect
My safety to my father's court, he shall choose me a wife.
Many fair Achive princesses of unimpeached life
In Helle and in Pthia live, whose sires do cities hold,
Of whom I can have whom I will. And more – an hundred fold –
My true mind in my country likes to take a lawful wife
Than in another nation, and there delight my life
With those goods that my father got, much rather than die here.
Not all the wealth of well-built Troy, possess'd when peace was there,
All that Apollo's marble fane in stony Pythos holds,   390
I value equal with the life that my free breast enfolds.
Sheep, oxen, tripods, crest-deck'd horse, though lost, may come again:
But when the white guard of our teeth no longer can contain
Our human soul, away it flies; and once gone never more
To her frail mansion any man can her lost pow'rs restore.
And therefore since my mother-queen (fam'd for her silver feet)
Told me two fates about my death in my direction meet:
The one, that if I here remain t'assist our victory,
My safe return shall never live, my fame shall never die:
If my return obtain success, much of my fame decays,   400
But death shall linger his approach, and I live many days.
This being reveal'd, 'twere foolish pride t' abridge my life for praise.
Then with myself I will advise others to hoist their sail,
For 'gainst the height of Ilion you never shall prevail:
Jove with his hand protecteth it, and makes the soldiers bold.
This tell the king in every part, for so grave legates should,
That they may better counsels use, to save their fleet and friends
By their own valours, since this course drown'd in my anger, ends.
Phoenix may in my tent repose, and in the morn steer course
For Phthia, if he think it good; if not, I'll use no force.'   410
    All wond'red at his stern reply: and Phoenix, full of fears
His words would be more weak than just, supplied their wants with tears.
    'If thy return incline thee thus, Peleus' renowned joy,
And thou wilt let our ships be burn'd with harmful fire of Troy,
Since thou art angry, O my son, how shall I after be
Alone in these extremes of death, relinquished by thee?
I, whom thy royal father sent as orderer of thy force,
When to Atrides from his court he left thee for this course,
Yet young, and when in skill of arms thou didst not so abound,
Nor hadst the habit of discourse, that makes men so renown'd.   420
In all which I was set by him t'instruct thee as my son,
That thou might'st speak, when speech was fit, and do, when deeds were done:

Not sit as dumb, for want of words; idle, for skill to move.
I would not then be left by thee, dear son, begot in love,
No, not if god would promise me to raze the prints of time
Carv'd in my bosom and my brows, and grace me with the prime
Of manly youth, as when at first I left sweet Helle's shore,
Deck'd with fair dames, and fled the grudge my angry father bore;
Who was the fair Amyntor call'd, surnam'd Ormenides,
And for a fair-hair'd harlot's sake, that his affects could please,   430
Contemn'd my mother, his true wife; who ceaseless urged me
To use his harlot Clytia, and still would clasp my knee
To do her will, that so my sire might turn his love to hate
Of that lewd dame, converting it to comfort her estate.
At last I was content to prove to do my mother good,
And reconcile my father's love; who straight suspicious stood,
Pursuing me with many a curse, and to the Furies pray'd
No dame might love, nor bring me seed: the deities obey'd
That govern hell, infernal Jove, and stern Proserpiné.
Then durst I in no longer date with my stern father be;   440
Yet did my friends and near allies inclose me with desires
Not to depart; kill'd sheep, boars, beeves; roast them at solemn fires;
And from my father's tuns we drunk exceeding store of wine.
Nine nights they guarded me by turns, their fires did ceaseless shine,
One in the porch of his strong hall, and in the portal one
Before my chamber. But when day beneath the tenth night shone,
I brake my chamber's thick-fram'd doors, and through the hall's guard pass'd,
Unseen of any man or maid. Through Greece then, rich and vast,
I fled to Phthia, nurse of sheep, and came to Peleus' court,
Who entertain'd me heartily, and in as gracious sort   450
As any sire his only son, born when his strength is spent,
And bless'd with great possessions, to leave to his descent.
He made me rich, and to my charge did much command commend.
I dwelt in th' utmost region rich Pthia doth extend,
And govern'd the Dolopians, and made thee what thou art.
O thou that like the gods art fram'd, since, dearest to my heart,
I us'd thee so, thou lov'dst none else; nor anywhere wouldst eat,
Till I had crown'd my knee with thee, and carv'd thee tend'rest meat,
And giv'n thee wine so much, for love, that in thy infancy
(Which still discretion must protect, and a continual eye)   460
My bosom lovingly sustain'd the wine thine could not bear:
Then, now my strength needs thine as much, be mine to thee as dear:
Much have I suffer'd for thy love, much labour'd, wished much,
Thinking, since I must have no heir (the gods' decrees are such),
I would adopt thyself my heir: to thee my heart did give

What any sire could give his son; in thee I hop'd to live.
O mitigate thy mighty spirits: it fits not one that moves
The hearts of all, to live unmov'd; and succour hates for loves.
The gods themselves are flexible, whose virtues, honours, pow'rs,
Are more than thine; yet they will bend their breasts as we bend ours.   470
Perfumes, benign devotions, savours of off'rings burn'd,
And holy rites, the engines are with which their hearts are turn'd
By men that pray to them, whose faith their sins have falsified.
For Prayers are daughters of great Jove; lame, wrinkled, ruddy-ey'd,
And ever following Injury; who, strong and sound of feet,
Flies through the world afflicting men, believing Prayers yet
(To all that love that seed of Jove) the certain blessing get
To have Jove hear, and help them too. But if he shall refuse,
And stand inflexible to them, they fly to Jove, and use
Their pow'rs against him, that the wrongs he doth to them may fall   480
On his own head, and pay those pains whose cure he fails to call.
Then, great Achilles, honour thou this sacred seed of Jove,
And yield to them, since other men of greatest minds they move.
If Agamemnon would not give the selfsame gifts he vows,
But offer other afterwards, and in his still-bent brows
Entomb his honour and his word, I would not thus exhort
(With wrath appeas'd) thy aid to Greece, though plagu'd in heaviest sort.
But much he presently will give, and after yield the rest,
T' assure which he hath sent to thee the men thou lovest best,
And most renown'd of all the host, that they might soften thee.   490
Then let not both their pains and prayers lost and despised be;
Before which, none could reprehend the tumult of thy heart,
But now to rest inexpiate were much too rude a part.
Of ancient worthies we have heard, when they were more displeas'd,
(To their high fames) with gifts and prayers they have been still appeas'd.
For instance, I remember well a fact perform'd of old,
Which to you all, my friends, I'll tell: the Curets wars did hold
With the well-fought Aetolians, where mutual lives had end
About the city Calydon; th' Aetolians did defend
Their flourishing country, which to spoil the Curets did contend.   500
Diana with the golden throne, with Oeneus much incens'd,
Since with his plenteous land's first fruits she was not reverenc'd,
Yet other gods, with hecatombs, had feasts; and she alone
(Great Jove's bright daughter) left unserv'd – or by oblivion,
Or undue knowledge of her dues – much hurt in heart she swore,
And she, enrag'd, excited much: she sent a sylvan boar
From their green groves, with wounding tusks, who usually did spoil
King Oeneus' fields, his lofty woods laid prostrate on the soil,

Rent by the roots trees fresh adorn'd with fragrant apple flow'rs:
Which Meleager (Oeneus' son) slew with assembled pow'rs   510
Of hunters, and of fiercest hounds from many cities brought:
For such he was that with few lives his death could not be bought.
Heaps of dead humans, by his rage, the funeral piles applied.
Yet, slain at last, the goddess stirr'd about his head and hide
A wondrous tumult, and a war betwixt the Curets wrought
And brave Aetolians. All the while fierce Meleager fought,
Ill far'd the Curets: near the walls none durst advance his crest,
Though they were many; but when wrath inflam'd his haughty breast
(Which oft the firm mind of the wise with passion doth infest),
Since 'twixt his mother queen and him arose a deadly strife,   520
He left the court, and privately liv'd with his lawful wife –
Fair Cleopatra, female birth of bright Marpissa's pain
And of Idaeus, who of all terrestrial men did reign
At that time king of fortitude; and for Marpissa's sake,
'Gainst wanton Phoebus, king of flames, his bow in hand did take,
Since he had ravish'd her, his joy; whom her friends after gave
The surname of Alcyone, because they could not save
Their daughter from Alcyone's fate. In Cleopatra's arms
Lay Meleager, feeding on his anger, for the harms
His mother pray'd might fall on him; who for her brother slain   530
By Meleager, griev'd and pray'd the gods to wreak her pain,
With all the horror could be pour'd upon her furious birth.
Still knock'd she with her impious hands the many-feeding earth,
To urge stern Pluto and his queen t'incline their vengeful ears,
Fell on her knees, and all her breast dew'd with her fiery tears,
To make them massacre her son, whose wrath enrag'd her thus:
Erynnis, wand'ring through the air, heard, out of Erebus,
Pray'rs fit for her unpleased mind. Yet Meleager lay
Obscur'd in fury; then the bruit of the tumultuous fray
Rung through the turrets as they scal'd; then came the Aetolian peers   540
To Meleager with low suits, to rise and free their fears:
Then sent they the chief priests of gods, with offer'd gifts t' atone
His differing fury; bade him choose in sweet-soil'd Calydon,
Of the most fat and yieldy soil, what with an hundred steers
Might in an hundred days be plough'd – half that rich vintage bears,
And half of naked earth to plough: yet yielded not his ire.
Then to his lofty chamber-door ascends his royal sire,
With ruthful plaints, shook the strong bars: then came his sisters' cries,
His mother then, and all intreat – yet still more stiff he lies.
His friends, most rev'rend, most esteem'd – yet none impression took,   550
Till the high turrets where he lay, and his strong chamber, shook

With the invading enemy, who now forc'd dreadful way
Along the city; then his wife, in pitiful dismay,
Besought him, weeping, telling him the miseries sustain'd
By all the citizens, whose town the enemy had gain'd:
Men slaughter'd, children bondslaves made, sweet ladies forc'd with lust,
Fires climbing tow'rs, and turning them to heaps of fruitless dust.
These dangers soft'ned his steel heart; up the stout prince arose,
Indu'd his body with rich arms, and freed th' Aetolians' woes,
His smother'd anger giving air, which gifts did not assuage,　　　　　560
But his own peril. And because he did not disengage
Their lives for gifts, their gifts he lost. But for my sake, dear friend,
Be not thou bent to see our plights to these extremes descend,
Ere thou assist us; be not so by thy ill angel turn'd
From thine own honour: it were shame to see our navy burn'd,
And then come with thy timeless aid. For offer'd presents come,
And all the Greeks will honour thee, as of celestial room:
But if without these gifts thou fight, forc'd by thy private woe,
Thou wilt be nothing so renown'd, though thou repel the foe.'

　　Achilles answer'd the last part of his oration thus:　　　　　570
'Phoenix, renown'd and reverend, the honours urg'd on us
We need not: Jove doth honour me, and to my safety sees,
And will whiles I retain a spirit, or can command my knees.
Then do not thou with tears and woes impassion my affects,
Becoming gracious to my foe: nor fits it the respects
Of thy vow'd love, to honour him that hath dishonour'd me,
Lest such loose kindness lose his heart that yet is firm to thee.
It were thy praise to hurt with me the hurter of my state,
Since half my honour and my realm thou mayst participate.
Let these lords then return th' event, and do thou here repose;　　　　　580
And when dark sleep breaks with the day, our counsels shall disclose
The course of our return or stay.' This said, he with his eye
Made to his friend a covert sign, to hasten instantly
A good soft bed, that the old prince, soon as the peers were gone,
Might take his rest. When, soldier-like, brave Ajax Telamon
Spake to Ulysses, as with thought Achilles was not worth
The high direction of his speech, that stood so sternly forth,
Unmov'd with th' other orators; and spake, not to appease
Pelides' wrath, but to depart. His arguments were these:

　　'High-issued Laertiades, let us insist no more　　　　　590
On his persuasion; I perceive the world would end before
Our speeches end in this affair: we must with utmost haste
Return his answer, though but bad: the peers are elsewhere plac'd,
And will not rise till we return. Great Thetis' son hath stor'd

Proud wrath within him, as his wealth, and will not be implor'd,
Rude that he is; nor his friends' love respects, do what they can –
Wherein past all we honour'd him. O unremorseful man!
Another for his brother slain, another for his son,
Accepts of satisfaction; and he the deed hath done
Lives in belov'd society long after his amends,　　　　　　　600
To which his foe's high heart, for gifts, with patience condescends:
But thee a wild and cruel spirit the gods for plague have giv'n –
And for one girl, of whose fair sex we come to offer sev'n,
The most exempt for excellence, and many a better prize.
Then put a sweet mind in thy breast, respect thy own allies,
Though others make thee not remiss: a multitude we are,
Sprung of thy royal family, and our supremest care
Is to be most familiar, and hold most love with thee
Of all the Greeks, how great an host soever here there be.'
　He answer'd: 'Noble Telamon, prince of our soldiers here,　　　　　　　610
Out of thy heart I know thou speak'st, and as thou hold'st me dear:
But still as often as I think how rudely I was us'd,
And like a stranger, for all rites fit for our good refus'd,
My heart doth swell against the man that durst be so profane
To violate his sacred place; not for my private bane,
But since wrack'd virtue's general laws he shameless did infringe,
For whose sake I will loose the reins, and give mine anger swinge,
Without my wisdom's least impeach. He is a fool, and base,
That pities vice-plagu'd minds, when pain, not love of right, gives place.
And therefore tell your king, my lords, my just wrath will not care　　　　　　　620
For all his cares, before my tents and navy charged are
By warlike Hector, making way through flocks of Grecian lives,
Enlight'ned by their naval fire: but when his rage arrives
About my tent, and sable bark, I doubt not but to shield
Them and myself, and make him fly the there-strong-bounded field.'
　This said, each one but kiss'd the cup, and to the ships retir'd,
Ulysses first. Patroclus then the men and maids requir'd
To make grave Phoenix' bed with speed, and see he nothing lacks.
They straight obey'd, and thereon laid the subtile fruit of flax,
And warm sheep-fells for covering: and there the old man slept,　　　　　　　630
Attending till the golden Morn her usual station kept.
Achilles lay in th' inner room of his tent richly wrought,
And that fair lady by his side that he from Lesbos brought,
Bright Diomeda, Phorbas' seed. Patroclus did embrace
The beauteous Iphis, given to him when his bold friend did raze
The lofty Syrus, that was kept in Enyeius' hold.
　Now at the tent of Atreus' son, each man with cups of gold

Receiv'd th' ambassadors return'd; all cluster'd near to know
What news they brought, which first the king would have Ulysses show:
'Say, most praiseworthy Ithacus, the Grecians' great renown,   640
Will he defend us? Or not yet will his proud stomach down?'
    Ulysses made reply: 'Not yet will he appeased be,
But grows more wrathful, prizing light thy offer'd gifts and thee;
And wills thee to consult with us, and take some other course
To save our army and our fleet; and says, with all his force,
The morn shall light him on his way to Phthia's wished soil,
For never shall high-seated Troy be sack'd with all our toil:
Jove holds his hand 'twixt us and it, the soldiers gather heart.'
Thus he replies, which Ajax here can equally impart,
And both these heralds. Phoenix stays, for so was his desire,   650
To go with him, if he thought good; if not, he might retire.'
All wond'red he should be so stern; at last bold Diomed spake:
    'Would god, Atrides, thy request were yet to undertake,
And all thy gifts unoffer'd him; he's proud enough beside,
But this ambassage thou hast sent will make him burst with pride.
But let us suffer him to stay or go at his desire,
Fight when his stomach serves him best, or when Jove shall inspire.
Meanwhile our watch being strongly held, let us a little rest
After our food: strength lives by both, and virtue is their guest.
Then when the rosy-finger'd Morn holds out her silver light,   660
Bring forth thy host, encourage all, and be thou first in fight.'
    The kings admir'd the fortitude that so divinely mov'd
The skilful horseman Diomed, and his advice approv'd.
Then with their nightly sacrifice each took his several tent,
Where all receiv'd the sov'reign gifts soft Somnus did present.

THE END OF THE NINTH BOOK

BOOK TEN

The Argument

Th' Atrides watching, wake the other peers:
And (in the fort, consulting of their fears)
Two kings they send, most stout, and honour'd most,
For royal scouts, into the Trojan host:
Who meeting Dolon (Hector's bribed spy)
Take him, and learn how all the quarters lie.
He told them, in the Thracian regiment,
Of rich king Rhesus and his royal tent,
Striving for safety; but they end his strife,
And rid poor Dolon of a dangerous life.
Then with digressive wiles, they use their force
On Rhesus' life, and take his snowy horse.

Another Argument

Kappa the night exploits applies:
Rhesus' and Dolon's tragedies.

BOOK TEN

T HE OTHER PRINCES at their ships soft-finger'd Sleep did bind,
But not the general; Somnus' silks bound not his labouring mind,
That turn'd, and return'd, many thoughts. And as quick lightnings fly
From well-deck'd Juno's sovereign, out of the thick'ned sky,
Preparing some exceeding rain, or hail, the fruit of cold,
Or down-like snow, that suddenly makes all the fields look old,
Or opes the gulfy mouth of war, with his ensulphur'd hand
In dazzling flashes, pour'd from clouds, on any punish'd land:
So from Atrides' troubled heart, through his dark sorrows, flew
Redoubled sighs; his entrails shook, as often as his view   10
Admir'd the multitude of fires that gilt the Phrygian shade,
And heard the sounds of fifes and shawms, and tumults soldiers made.
But when he saw his fleet and host kneel to his care and love,
He rent his hair up by the roots, as sacrifice to Jove,
Burnt in his fiery sighs, still breath'd out of his royal heart,
And first thought good to Nestor's care his sorrows to impart,
To try if royal diligence, with his approv'd advice,
Might fashion counsels to prevent their threat'ned miseries.

So up he rose, attir'd himself, and to his strong feet tied
Rich shoes, and cast upon his back a ruddy lion's hide,   20
So ample, it his ankles reach'd: then took his royal spear.

Like him was Menelaus pierc'd with an industrious fear,
Nor sat sweet slumber on his eyes, lest bitter fates should quite
The Greeks' high favours, that for him resolv'd such endless fight.
And first a freckled panther's hide hid his broad back athwart;
His head his brazen helm did arm, his able hand his dart;
Then made he all his haste to raise his brother's head as rare,
That he who most excell'd in rule might help t' effect his care.
He found him at his ship's crook'd stern, adorning him with arms,
Who joy'd to see his brother's spirits awak'd without alarms,   30
Well weighing th' importance of the time. And first the younger spake:

'Why, brother, are ye arming thus? Is it to undertake
The sending of some vent'rous Greek t' explore the foe's intent?
Alas! I greatly fear, not one will give that work consent,
Expos'd alone to all the fears that flow in gloomy night:

He that doth this must know death well, in which ends every fright.'
    'Brother,' said he, 'in these affairs we both must use advice;
Jove is against us, and accepts great Hector's sacrifice,
For I have never seen nor heard, in one day, and by one,
So many high attempts well urg'd, as Hector's pow'r hath done   40
Against the hapless sons of Greece, being chiefly dear to Jove –
And without cause, being neither fruit of any goddess' love,
Nor helpful god: and yet I fear the deepness of his hand,
Ere it be 'ras'd out of our thoughts, will many years withstand.
But, brother, hie thee to thy ships, and Idomen dis-ease
With warlike Ajax: I will haste to grave Neleides,
Exhorting him to rise, and give the sacred watch command,
For they will specially embrace incitement at his hand;
And now his son their captain is, and Idomen's good friend
Bold Merion, to whose discharge we did that charge commend.'   50
    'Command'st thou then,' his brother ask'd, 'that I shall tarry here
Attending thy resolv'd approach, or else the message bear,
And quickly make return to thee?' He answer'd: 'Rather stay,
Lest otherwise we fail to meet: for many a different way
Lies through our labyrinthian host; speak ever as you go,
Command strong watch, from sire to son, urge all t' observe the foe,
Familiarly, and with their praise, exciting every eye,
Not with unseason'd violence of proud authority:
We must our patience exercise, and work ourselves with them,
Jove in our births combin'd such care to either's diadem.'   60
    Thus he dismiss'd him, knowing well his charge, before he went
Himself to Nestor, whom he found in bed within his tent:
By him his damask curets hung, his shield, a pair of darts,
His shining casque, his arming waist: in these he led the hearts
Of his apt soldiers to sharp war, not yielding to his years.
He quickly started from his bed, when to his watchful ears
Untimely feet told some approach: he took his lance in hand,
And spake to him: 'Ho, what art thou that walk'st at midnight? Stand.
Is any wanting at the guards? Or lack'st thou any peer?
Speak, come not silent towards me, say what intend'st thou here.'   70
    He answer'd, 'O Neleides, grave honour of our host,
'Tis Agamemnon thou mayst know, whom Jove afflicteth most
Of all the wretched men that live, and will, whilst any breath
Gives motion to my toiled limbs, and bears me up from death.
I walk the round thus, since sweet sleep cannot inclose mine eyes,
Nor shut those organs care breaks ope, for our calamities.
My fear is vehement for the Greeks: my heart (the fount of heat)
With his extreme affects made cold, without my breast doth beat:

And therefore are my sinews struck with trembling: every part
Of what my friends may feel hath act in my dispersed heart.   80
But if thou think'st of any course may to our good redound,
(Since neither thou thyself canst sleep) come, walk with me the round.
In way whereof we may confer, and look to every guard,
Lest watching long, and weariness, with labouring so hard,
Drown their oppressed memories of what they have in charge.
The liberty we give the foe, alas, is over large,
Their camp is almost mix'd with ours, and we have forth no spies
To learn their drifts, who may perchance this night intend surprise.'
      Grave Nestor answer'd: 'Worthy king, let good hearts bear our ill.
Jove is not bound to perfect all this busy Hector's will;   90
But I am confidently giv'n, his thoughts are much dismay'd
With fear, lest our distress incite Achilles to our aid,
And therefore will not tempt his fate, nor ours with further pride.
But I will gladly follow thee, and stir up more beside:
Tydides, famous for his lance, Ulysses, Telamon,
And bold Phyleus' valiant heir: or else if any one
Would haste to call king Idomen, and Ajax, since their sail
Lie so remov'd, with much good speed, it might our haste avail.
But, though he be our honour'd friend, thy brother I will blame,
Not fearing if I anger thee: it is his utter shame   100
He should commit all pains to thee, that should himself employ,
Past all our princes, in the care and cure of our annoy;
And be so far from needing spurs, to these his due respects,
He should apply our spirits himself, with pray'rs and urg'd affects.
Necessity (a law to laws, and not to be endur'd)
Makes proof of all his faculties; not sound, if not enur'd.'
      'Good father,' said the king, 'sometimes you know I have desir'd
You would improve his negligence, too oft to ease retir'd:
Nor is it for defect of spirit, or compass of his brain,
But with observing my estate, he thinks he should abstain   110
Till I commanded, knowing my place, unwilling to assume,
For being my brother, anything might prove he did presume.
But now he rose before me far, and came t' avoid delays:
And I have sent him for the men yourself desir'd to raise.
Come, we shall find them at the guards we plac'd before the fort,
For thither my direction was they should with speed resort.'
      'Why now,' said Nestor, 'none will grudge, nor his just rule withstand;
Examples make excitements strong, and sweeten a command.'
      Thus put he on his arming truss, fair shoes upon his feet,
About him a mandilion, that did with buttons meet,   120
Of purple, large, and full of folds, curl'd with a warmful nap,

A garment that 'gainst cold in nights did soldiers use to wrap:
Then took he his strong lance in hand, made sharp with proved steel,
And went along the Grecian fleet. First at Ulysses' keel
He call'd, to break the silken fumes that did his senses bind;
The voice through th' organs of his ears straight rung about his mind.
Forth came Ulysses, asking him: 'Why stir ye thus so late?
Sustain we such enforcive cause?' He answer'd, 'Our estate
Doth force this perturbation; vouchsafe it, worthy friend,
And come, let us excite one more to counsel of some end   130
To our extremes, by fight or flight.' He back, and took his shield,
And both took course to Diomed; they found him laid in field,
Far from his tent: his armour by, about him was dispread
A ring of soldiers, every man his shield beneath his head,
His spear fix'd by him as he slept, the great end in the ground;
The point, that bristled the dark earth, cast a reflection round
Like pallid lightnings thrown from Jove; thus this heroë lay,
And under him a big ox-hide: his royal head had stay
On arras hangings, rolled up: whereon he slept so fast,
That Nestor stirr'd him with his foot, and chid to see him cast   140
In such deep sleep, in such deep woes, and ask'd him why he spent
All night in sleep, or did not hear the Trojans near his tent,
Their camp drawn close upon their dike, small space 'twixt foes and foes.

  He, starting up, said, 'Strange old man, that never tak'st repose;
Thou art too patient of our toil, have we not men more young,
To be employ'd from king to king? Thine age hath too much wrong.'

  'Said like a king,' replied the sire: 'for I have sons renown'd,
As there are many other men might go this toilsome round;
But you must see, imperious Need hath all at her command:
Now on the eager razor's edge, for life or death we stand.   150
Then go (thou art the younger man), and if thou love my ease,
Call swift-foot Ajax up thyself, and young Phyleides.'

  This said, he on his shoulders cast a yellow lion's hide,
Big, and reach'd earth, then took his spear, and Nestor's will applied:
Rais'd the heroës, brought them both. All met, the round they went,
And found not any captain there asleep or negligent,
But waking, and in arms, give ear to every lowest sound.
And as keen dogs keep sheep in cotes, or folds of hurdles bound,
And grin at every breach of air, envious of all that moves,
Still list'ning when the ravenous beast stalks through the hilly groves;   160
Then men and dogs stand on their guards, and mighty tumults make,
Sleep wanting weight to close one wink: so did the captains wake,
That kept the watch the whole sad night, all with intentive ear
Converted to the enemies' tents, that they might timely hear

If they were stirring to surprise: which Nestor joy'd to see.
'Why so, dear sons, maintain your watch, sleep not a wink,' said he,
'Rather than make your fames the scorn of Trojan perjury.'
This said, he foremost pass'd the dike, the others seconded,
Ev'n all the kings that had been call'd to counsel from the bed:
And with them went Meriones, and Nestor's famous son,   170
For both were call'd by all the kings to consultation.
Beyond the dike they chose a place, near as they could from blood,
Where yet appear'd the falls of some, and whence (the crimson flood
Of Grecian lives being pour'd on earth by Hector's furious chace)
He made retreat, when night repour'd grim darkness in his face.
There sat they down, and Nestor spake: 'O friends, remains not one
That will rely on his bold mind, and view the camp alone
Of the proud Trojans, to approve if any straggling mate
He can surprise near th' utmost tents, or learn the brief estate
Of their intentions for the time, and mix like one of them   180
With their outguards, expiscating, if the renown'd extreme
They force on us, will serve their turns, with glory to retire,
Or still encamp thus far from Troy? This may he well inquire,
And make a brave retreat untouch'd; and this would win him fame
Of all men canopied with heav'n, and every man of name
In all this host shall honour him with an enriching meed:
A black ewe and her sucking lamb (rewards that now exceed
All other best possessions, in all men's choice requests) –
And still be bidden by our kings to kind and royal feasts.'
All reverenc'd one another's worth; and none would silence break,   190
Lest worst should take best place of speech: at last did Diomed speak:
'Nestor, thou ask'st if no man here have heart so well inclin'd
To work this stratagem on Troy: yes, I have such a mind.
Yet if some other prince would join, more probable will be
The strengthen'd hope of our exploit: two may together see
(One going before another still) sly danger every way;
One spirit upon another works, and takes with firmer stay
The benefit of all his pow'rs: for though one knew his course,
Yet might he well distrust himself, which th' other might enforce.'
This offer every man assum'd; all would with Diomed go: 200
The two Ajaces, Merion, and Menelaus too,
But Nestor's son enforc'd it much, and hardy Ithacus,
Who had to every vent'rous deed a mind as venturous.
Amongst all these thus spake the king: 'Tydides, most belov'd,
Choose thy associate worthily: a man the most approv'd
For use and strength in these extremes. Many thou seest stand forth:
But choose not thou by height of place, but by regard of worth,

Lest with thy nice respect of right to any man's degree,
Thou wrong'st thy venture, choosing one least fit to join with thee,
Although perhaps a greater king.' This spake he with suspect   210
That Diomed (for honour's sake) his brother would select.

   Then said Tydides: 'Since thou giv'st my judgment leave to choose,
How can it so much truth forget, Ulysses to refuse,
That bears a mind so most exempt, and vigorous in th' effect
Of all high labours, and a man Pallas doth most respect?
We shall return through burning fire, if I with him combine:
He sets strength in so true a course with counsels so divine.'

   Ulysses, loth to be esteem'd a lover of his praise,
With such exceptions humbled him, as did him higher raise,
And said: 'Tydides, praise me not more than free truth will bear,   220
Nor yet empair me: they are Greeks that give judicial ear.
But come, the morning hastes, the stars are forward in their course;
Two parts of night are past, the third is left t' employ our force.'
Now borrow'd they for haste some arms: bold Thrasymedes lent
Advent'rous Diomed his sword (his own was at his tent),
His shield and helm, tough and well tann'd, without or plume or crest,
And call'd a murrion; archers' heads it used to invest.
Meriones lent Ithacus his quiver and his bow,
His helmet fashion'd of a hide: the workman did bestow
Much labour in it, quilting it with bow-strings; and without,   230
With snowy tusks of white-mouth'd boars 'twas armed round about
Right cunningly: and in the midst, an arming cap was plac'd,
That with the fix'd ends of the tusks his head might not be ras'd.
This, long since, by Autolycus was brought from Eleon,
When he laid waste Amyntor's house, that was Ormenus' son.
In Scandia, to Cytherius, surnan'd Amphydamas,
Autolycus did give this helm: he, when he feasted was
By honour'd Molus, gave it him, as present of a guest:
Molus to his son Merion did make it his bequest.
With this Ulysses arm'd his head; and thus they (both address'd)   240
Took leave of all the other kings: to them a glad ostent,
As they were ent'ring on their way, Minerva did present –
A hernshaw consecrate to her; which they could ill discern
Through sable night, but by her clang they knew it was a hern.
Ulysses joy'd, and thus invok'd: 'Hear me, great seed of Jove,
That ever dost my labours grace with presence of thy love,
And all my motions dost attend; still love me, sacred dame,
Especially in this exploit, and so protect our fame,
We both may safely make retreat, and thriftily employ
Our boldness in some great affair, baneful to them of Troy.'   250

Then pray'd illustrate Diomed: 'Vouchsafe me likewise ear,
O thou unconquer'd queen of arms: be with thy favours near,
As to my royal father's steps thou went'st a bounteous guide,
When th' Achives and the peers of Thebes he would have pacified,
Sent as the Greeks' ambassador, and left them at the flood
Of great Aesopus; whose retreat thou mad'st to swim in blood
Of his enambush'd enemies: and if thou so protect
My bold endeavours, to thy name an heifer, most select,
That never yet was tam'd with yoke, broad-fronted, one year old,
I'll burn in zealous sacrifice, and set the horns in gold.'   260
    The goddess heard, and both the kings their dreadful passage bore
Through slaughter, slaughter'd carcasses, arms and discolour'd gore.
    Nor Hector let his princes sleep, but all to counsel call'd,
And ask'd, 'What one is here will vow, and keep it unappall'd,
To have a gift fit for his deed, a chariot and two horse,
That pass for speed the rest of Greece? What one dares take this course,
For his renown, besides his gifts, to mix amongst the foe,
And learn if still they hold their guards, or with this overthrow
Determine flight, as being too weak to hold us longer war?'
    All silent stood; at last stood forth one Dolon, that did dare   270
This dangerous work, Eumedes' heir, a herald much renown'd:
This Dolon did in gold and brass exceedingly abound,
But in his form was quite deform'd, yet passing swift to run.
Amongst five sisters he was left Eumedes' only son.
And he told Hector, his free heart would undertake t' explore
The Greeks' intentions: 'But,' said he, 'thou shalt be sworn before,
By this thy sceptre, that the horse of great Aeacides
And his strong chariot, bound with brass, thou wilt (before all these)
Resign me as my valour's prize; and so I rest unmov'd
To be thy spy, and not return before I have approv'd   280
(By venturing to Atrides' ship, where their consults are held)
If they resolve still to resist, or fly as quite expell'd.'
    He put his sceptre in his hand, and call'd the thunder's god
(Saturnia's husband) to his oath, those horse should not be rode
By any other man than he, but he for ever joy
(To his renown) their services, for his good done to Troy.
Thus swore he, and forswore himself, yet made base Dolon bold:
Who on his shoulders hung his bow, and did about him fold
A white wolf's hide, and with a helm of weasels' skins did arm
His weasel's head; then took his dart, and never turn'd to harm   290
The Greeks with their related drifts: but being past the troops
Of horse and foot, he promptly runs; and as he runs he stoops
To undermine Achilles' horse. Ulysses straight did see,

And said to Diomed: 'This man makes footing towards thee,
Out of the tents; I know not well, if he be us'd as spy,
Bent to our fleet, or come to rob the slaughter'd enemy.
But let us suffer him to come a little further on,
And then pursue him. If it chance, that we be overgone
By his more swiftness, urge him still to run upon our fleet,
And (lest he 'scape us to the town) still let thy javelin meet　　　300
With all his offers of retreat.' Thus stepp'd they from the plain
Amongst the slaughter'd carcasses. Dolon came on amain,
Suspecting nothing; but once past, as far as mules outdraw
Oxen at plough, being both put on, neither admitted law,
To plough a deep soil'd furrow forth, so far was Dolon past:
Then they pursu'd, which he perceiv'd, and stay'd his speedless haste,
Subtly supposing Hector sent to countermand his spy:
But in a javelin's throw or less, he knew them enemy.
Then laid he on his nimble knees, and they pursu'd like wind.
As when a brace of greyhounds are laid in with hare or hind,　　　310
Close-mouth'd and skill'd to make the best of their industrious course,
Serve either's turn, and set on hard, lose neither ground nor force:
So constantly did Tydeus' son, and his town-razing peer,
Pursue this spy, still turning him, as he was winding near
His covert, till he almost mix'd with their out-courts of guard.
　　Then Pallas prompted Diomed, lest his due worth's reward
Should be impair'd, if any man did vaunt he first did sheath
His sword in him, and he be call'd but second in his death:
Then spake he (threat'ning with his lance): 'Or stay, or this comes on,
And long thou canst not run, before thou be by death outgone.'　　　320
　　This said, he threw his javelin forth: which miss'd (as Diomed would)
Above his right arm making way, the pile stuck in the mould:
He stay'd and trembled, and his teeth did chatter in his head.
They came in blowing, seiz'd him fast; he, weeping, offered
A wealthy ransom for his life, and told them he had brass,
Much gold and iron, that fit for use in many labours was,
From whose rich heaps his father would a wondrous portion give,
If, at the great Achaian fleet, he heard his son did live.
　　Ulysses bad him cheer his heart. 'Think not of death,' said he,
'But tell us true, why runn'st thou forth when others sleeping be?　　　330
Is it to spoil the carcasses? Or art thou choicely sent
T' explore our drifts? Or of thyself seek'st thou some wish'd event?'
　　He trembling answer'd: 'Much reward did Hector's oath propose,
And urg'd me much against my will, t' endeavour to disclose
If you determin'd still to stay, or bent your course for flight,
As all dismay'd with your late foil, and wearied with the fight:

For which exploit, Pelides' horse and chariot he did swear
I only ever should enjoy.' Ulysses smil'd to hear
So base a swain have any hope so high a prize t' aspire,
And said, his labours did affect a great and precious hire: 340
And that the horse Pelides rein'd no mortal hand could use
But he himself, whose matchless life a goddess did produce:
'But tell us, and report but truth, where left'st thou Hector now?
Where are his arms? His famous horse? On whom doth he bestow
The watch's charge? Where sleep the kings? Intend they still to lie
Thus near encamp d? Or turn suffic'd with their late victory?'
   'All this,' said he, 'I'll tell most true. At Ilus' monument
Hector with all our princes sits, t' advise of this event;
Who choose that place remov'd, to shun the rude confused sounds
The common soldiers throw about: but, for our watch, and rounds.   350
Whereof, brave lord, thou mak'st demand; none orderly we keep:
The Trojans that have roofs to save, only abandon sleep,
And privately without command each other they exhort
To make prevention of the worst; and in this slender sort
Is watch and guard maintain'd with us. th' auxiliary bands
Sleep soundly, and commit their cares into the Trojans hands;
For they have neither wives with them, nor children to protect;
The less they need to care, the more, they succour dull neglect.
   'But tell me,' said wise Ithacus, 'are all these foreign pow'rs
Appointed quarters by themselves, or else commix'd with yours?'   360
   'And this,' said Dolon, 'too, my lords, I'll seriously unfold:
The Paeons with the crooked bows, and Cares, quarters hold
Next to the sea; the Leleges and Caucons join'd with them,
And brave Pelasgians; Thimber's mead, remov'd more from the stream,
Is quarter to the Lycians, the lofty Mysian force,
The Phrygians and Meonians, that fight with armed horse.
But what need these particulars? If ye intend surprise
Of any in our Trojan camps, the Thracian quarter lies
Utmost of all, and uncommix'd with Trojan regiments,
That keep the voluntary watch: new pitch'd are all their tents.   370
King Rhesus, Eioneus' son, commands them; who hath steeds
More white than snow, huge and well shap'd; their fiery pace exceeds
The winds in swiftness; these I saw: his chariot is with gold
And pallid silver richly fram'd, and wondrous to behold.
His great and golden armour is not fit a man should wear,
But for immortal shoulders fram'd: come then, and quickly bear
Your happy prisoner to your fleet, or leave him here fast bound
Till your well-urg'd and rich return prove my relation sound.'
   Tydides dreadfully replied: 'Think not of passage thus,

Though of right acceptable news thou hast advertis'd us;   380
Our hands are holds more strict than so: and should we set thee free
For offer'd ransom, for this 'scape, thou still wouldst scouting be
About our ships or do us scathe in plain opposed arms;
But if I take thy life, no way can we repent thy harms.'
   With this, as Dolon reach'd his hand to use a suppliant's part,
And stroke the beard of Diomed, he struck his neck athwart
With his forc'd sword, and both the nerves he did in sunder wound;
And suddenly his head, deceiv'd, fell speaking on the ground:
His weasel's helm they took, his bow, his wolf's skin, and his lance;
Which to Minerva Ithacus did zealously advance   390
With lifted arm into the air; and to her thus he spake:
   'Goddess, triumph in thine own spoils: to thee we first will make
Our invocations, of all powers, thron'd on th' Olympian hill;
Now to the Thracians, and their horse, and beds, conduct us still.'
With this, he hung them up aloft, upon a tamrick bough,
As eyeful trophies: and the sprigs that did about it grow,
He proined from the leafy arms, to make it easier view'd,
When they should hastily retire, and be perhaps pursu'd.
Forth went they, through black blood and arms; and presently aspir'd
The guardless Thracian regiment, fast bound with sleep, and tir'd;   400
Their arms lay by, and triple ranks they, as they slept, did keep,
As they should watch and guard their king; who, in a fatal sleep,
Lay in the midst; their chariot horse, as they coachfellows were,
Fed by them; and the famous steeds, that did their general bear,
Stood next him, to the hinder part of his rich chariot tied.
Ulysses saw them first, and said, 'Tydides, I have spied
The horse that Dolon (whom we slew) assur'd us we should see:
Now use thy strength; now idle arms are most unfit for thee.
Prize thou the horse; or kill the guard, and leave the horse to me.'
   Minerva with the azure eyes breath'd strength into her king,   410
Who fill'd the tent with mixed death: the souls he set on wing
Issu'd in groans, and made air swell into her stormy flood:
Horror and slaughter had one power; the earth did blush with blood.
As when a hungry lion flies with purpose to devour
On flocks unkept, and on their lives doth freely use his pow'r:
So Tydeus son assail'd the foe; twelve souls before him flew;
Ulysses waited on his sword, and ever as he slew,
He drew them by their strengthless heels out of the horses' sight,
That when he was to lead them forth, they should not with affright
Boggle, nor snore, in treading on the bloody carcasses;   420
For being new come, they were unus'd to such stern sights as these.
Through four ranks now did Diomed the king himself attain;

Who (snoring in his sweetest sleep) was like his soldiers slain.
An ill dream, by Minerva sent, that night stood by his head
(Which was Oenides' royal son) – unconquer'd Diomed.

    Meanwhile Ulysses loos'd his horse, took all their reins in hand,
And led them forth: but Tydeus' son did in contention stand
With his great mind, to do some deed of more audacity,
If he should take the chariot, where his rich arms did lie
And draw it by the beam away, or bear it on his back,   430
Or if of more dull Thracian lives he should their bosoms sack.

    In this contention with himself, Minerva did suggest
And bade him think of his retreat, lest from their tempted rest
Some other god should stir the foe, and send him back dismay'd.

    He knew the voice; took horse, and fled; the Trojans' heavenly aid
(Apollo with the silver bow) stood no blind sentinel
To their secure and drowsy host, but did discover well
Minerva following Diomed; and angry with his act,
The mighty host of Ilion he enter'd, and awak'd
The cousin german of the king, a counsellor of Thrace,   440
Hypocoön; who when he rose, and saw the desert place
Where Rhesus' horse did use to stand, and th' other dismal harms,
Men struggling with the pangs of death, he shriek'd out thick alarms,
Call'd 'Rhesus! Rhesus!' but in vain; then still, 'Arm, arm,' he cried.
The noise and tumult was extreme on every startled side
Of Troy's huge host, from whence in throngs all gather'd, and admir'd,
Who could perform such harmful facts, and yet be safe retir'd.

    Now, coming where they slew the scout, Ulysses stay'd the steeds;
Tydides lighted, and the spoils (hung on the tamrick reeds)
He took and gave to Ithacus, and up he got again;   450
Then flew they joyful to their fleet: Nestor did first attain
The sounds the horse-hoofs struck through air, and said: 'My royal peers!
Do I but dote, or say I true? Methinks about mine ears
The sounds of running horses beat. O would to god they were
Our friends thus soon return'd with spoils: but I have hearty fear,
Lest this high tumult of the foe doth their distress intend.'
He scarce had spoke, when they were come: both did from horse descend.
All, with embraces and sweet words, to heaven their worth did raise.
Then Nestor spake: 'Great Ithacus, ev'n heap'd with Grecian praise,
How have you made these horse your prize? Pierc'd you the dangerous host,
Where such gems stand? Or did some god your high attempts accost,
And honour'd you with this reward? Why, they be like the rays
The sun effuseth. I have mix'd with Trojans all my days;
And now, I hope you will not say I always lie abord,
Though an old soldier I confess: yet did all Troy afford

Never the like to any sense that ever I possess'd,
But some good god, no doubt, hath met, and your high valours bless'd.
For he that shadows heaven with clouds loves both as his delights,
And she that supples earth with blood cannot forbear your sights.'

    Ulysses answer'd: 'Honour'd sire, the willing gods can give   470
Horse much more worth than these men yield, since in more power they live:
These horse are of the Thracian breed; their king Tydides slew,
And twelve of his most trusted guard: and of that meaner crew
A scout for thirteenth man we kill'd, whom Hector sent to spy
The whole estate of our designs, if bent to fight or fly.'

    Thus, follow'd with whole troops of friends, they with applauses pass'd
The spacious dike, and in the tent of Diomed they plac'd
The horse without contention, as his deserving's meed:
Which, with his other horse set up, on yellow wheat did feed.
Poor Dolon's spoils Ulysses had; who shrin'd them on his stern,   480
As trophies vow'd to her that sent the good-aboding hern.

    Then enter'd they the mere main sea, to cleanse their honour'd sweat
From off their feet, their thighs and necks: and when their vehement heat
Was calm'd, and their swoln hearts refresh'd, more curious baths they us'd,
Where odorous and dissolving oils they through their limbs diffus'd.
Then, taking breakfast, a big bowl fill'd with the purest wine,
They offer'd to the maiden Queen, that hath the azure eyne.

THE END OF THE TENTH BOOK

BOOK ELEVEN

The Argument

Atrides and his other peers of name
Lead forth their men; whom Eris doth inflame.
Hector (by Iris' charge) takes deedless breath,
Whiles Agamemnon plies the work of death,
Who with the first bears his imperial head.
Himself, Ulysses, and king Diomed,
Euripylus, and Aesculapius' son,
(Enforc'd with wounds) the furious skirmish shun.
Which martial sight, when great Achilles views,
A little his desire of fight renews:
And forth he sends his friend, to bring him word
From old Neleides, what wounded lord
He in his chariot from the skirmish brought:
Which was Machaon. Nestor then besought
He would persuade his friend to wreak their harms,
Or come himself, deck'd in his dreadful arms.

Another Argument

Lamda presents the general
In fight the worthiest man of all.

BOOK ELEVEN

AURORA, out of restful bed, did from bright Tython rise,
　　To bring each deathless essence light and use to mortal eyes;
　　When Jove sent Eris to the Greeks, sustaining in her hand
Stern signs of her designs for war: she took her horrid stand
Upon Ulysses' huge black bark that did at anchor ride
Amidst the fleet, from whence her sounds might ring on every side,
Both to the tents of Telamon, and th' authors of their smarts,
Who held, for fortitude and force, the navy's utmost parts.
　　The red-ey'd goddess seated there thunder'd th' Orthian song,
High, and with horror, through the ears of all the Grecian throng;　　　10
Her verse with spirits invincible did all their breasts inspire,
Blew out all darkness from their limbs, and set their hearts on fire;
And presently was bitter war more sweet a thousand times
Than any choice in hollow keels to greet their native climes.
　　Atrides summon'd all to arms, to arms himself dispos'd:
First on his legs he put bright greaves with silver buttons clos'd,
Then with rich cuirass arm'd his breast, which Cyniras bestow'd
To gratify his royal guest; for even to Cyprus flow'd
Th' unbounded fame of those designs the Greeks propos'd for Troy,
And therefore gave he him those arms, and wish'd his purpose joy.　　　20
Ten rows of azure mix'd with black, twelve golden like the sun,
Twice ten of tin, in beaten paths, did through this armour run.
Three serpents to the gorget crept, that like three rainbows shin'd,
Such as by Jove are fix'd in clouds, when wonders are divin'd.
About his shoulders hung his sword, whereof the hollow hilt
Was fashion'd all with shining bars, exceeding richly gilt;
The scabbard was of silver plate, with golden hangers grac'd;
Then took he up his weighty shield, that round about him cast
Defensive shadows: ten bright zones of gold-affecting brass
Were driven about it; and of tin (as full of gloss as glass)　　　30
Swell'd twenty bosses out of it: in centre of them all
One of black metal had engraven (full of extreme appal)
An ugly gorgon, compassèd with terror and with fear:
At it a silver bawdrick hung, with which he us'd to bear
(Wound on his arm) his ample shield, and in it there was wov'n

An azure dragon, curl'd in folds, from whose one neck was clov'n
Three heads contorted in an orb: then plac'd he on his head
His four-plum'd casque, and in his hands two darts he managed,
Arm'd with bright steel that blaz'd to heaven: then Juno and the Maid
That conquers empires trumpets serv'd to summon out their aid,   40
In honour of the general, and on a sable cloud,
To bring them furious to the field, sate thund'ring out aloud.
    Then all enjoin'd their charioteers to rank their chariot horse
Close to the dike: forth march'd the foot, whose front they did reinforce
With some horse troops: the battle then was all of charioteers,
Lin'd with light horse: but Jupiter disturb'd this form with fears,
And from air's upper region did bloody vapours rain,
For sad ostent much noble life should ere their times be slain.
The Trojan host at Ilus' tomb was in battalia led
By Hector and Polydamas; and old Anchises' seed,   50
Who god-like was esteem'd in Troy; by grave Antenor's race,
Divine Agenor, Polybus, unmarried Acamas,
Proportion'd like the states of heaven: in front of all the field,
Troy's great Priamides did bear his always-equal shield,
Still plying th' ordering of his power. And as amid the sky
We sometimes see an ominous star blaze clear and dreadfully,
Then run his golden head in clouds, and straight appear again:
So Hector otherwhiles did grace the vanguard, shining plain,
Then in the rearguard hid himself, and labour'd everywhere
To order and encourage all: his armour was so clear,   60
And he applied each place so fast, that, like a lightning thrown
Out of the shield of Jupiter, in every eye he shone.
And as upon a rich man's crop of barley or of wheat
(Oppos'd for swiftness at their work), a sort of reapers sweat,
Bear down the furrows speedily, and thick their handfuls fall:
So at the joining of the hosts ran slaughter through them all;
None stoop'd to any fainting thought of foul inglorious flight,
But equal bore they up their heads, and far'd like wolves in fight:
Stern Eris, with such weeping sights, rejoic'd to feed her eyes,
Who only show'd herself in field of all the deities.   70
The other in Olympus tops sate silent, and repin'd,
That Jove to do the Trojans grace should bear so fix'd a mind.
He car'd not, but, enthron'd apart, triumphant sat in sway
Of his free pow'r, and from his seat took pleasure to display
The city so adorn'd with tow'rs, the sea with vessels fill'd,
The splendour of refulgent arms, the killer and the kill'd.
As long as bright Aurora rul'd, and sacred day increas'd,
So long their darts made mutual wounds, and neither had the best:

But when in hill-environ'd vales the timber-feller takes
A sharp-set stomach to his meat, and dinner ready makes,   80
His sinews fainting, and his spirits become surcharg'd and dull,
Time of accustom'd ease arriv'd, his hands with labour full:
Then by their valours Greeks brake through the Trojan ranks, and cheer'd
Their general squadrons through the host; then first of all appear'd
The person of the king himself, and then the Trojans lost
Byanor, by his royal charge, a leader in the host:
Who being slain, his charioteer, Oïleus, did alight,
And stood in skirmish with the king; the king did deadly smite
His forehead with his eager lance, and through his helm it ran,
Enforcing passage to his brain quite through the harden'd pan;   90
His brain mix'd with his clotter'd blood, his body strew'd the ground.
    There left he them, and presently he other objects found:
Isus and Antiphus, two sons king Priam did beget,
One lawful, th' other wantonly; both in one chariot met
Their royal foe; the baser born, Isus, was charioteer,
And famous Antiphus did fight: both which king Peleus' heir,
Whilom in Ida keeping flocks, did deprehend and bind
With pliant osiers, and for prize, them to their sire resign'd.
Atrides with his well-aim'd lance smote Isus on the breast
Above the nipple, and his sword a mortal wound impress'd   100
Beneath the ear of Antiphus; down from their horse they fell.
The king had seen the youths before, and now did know them well,
Rememb'ring them the prisoners of swift Aeacides,
Who brought them to the sable fleet from Ida's foody leas.
    And as a lion having found the furrow of a hind,
Where she hath calv'd two little twins, at will and ease doth grind
Their joints snatch'd in his solid jaws, and crusheth into mist
Their tender lives, their dam, though near, not able to resist,
But shook with vehement fear herself, flies through the oaken chase
From that fell savage, drown'd in sweat, and seeks some covert place: 110
So when with most unmatched strength the Grecian general bent
'Gainst these two princes, none durst aid their native king's descent,
But fled themselves before the Greeks, and where these two were slain,
Pisander and Hippolochus, not able to restrain
Their headstrong horse, the silken reins being from their hands let fall,
Were brought by their unruly guides before the general.
Antimachus begat them both – Antimachus that took
Rich gifts, and gold of Helen's love, and would by no means brook
Just restitution should be made of Menelaus' wealth,
Bereft him, with his ravish'd queen, by Alexander's stealth.   120
Atrides, lion-like, did charge his sons, who on their knees

Fell from their chariot, and besought regard to their degrees,
Who being Antimachus his sons, their father would afford
A worthy ranson for their lives; who in his house did hoard
Much hidden treasure, brass and gold, and steel wrought wondrous choice.
Thus wept they, using smoothing terms, and heard this rugged voice
Breath'd from the unrelenting king: 'If you be of the breed
Of stout Antimachus, that stay'd the honourable deed
The other peers of Ilion in counsel had decreed,
To render Helen and her wealth, and would have basely slain   130
My brother and wise Ithacus, ambassadors t' attain
The most due motion, now receive wreak for his shameful part.'
This said, in poor Pisander's breast he fix'd his wreakful dart,
Who upward spread th' oppressed earth: his brother crouch'd for dread,
And, as he lay, the angry king cut off his arms and head,
And let him like a football lie for every man to spurn.
Then to th' extremest heat of fight he did his valour turn,
And led a multitude of Greeks; where foot did foot subdue,
Horse slaughter'd horse, Need feather'd flight, the batter'd centre flew
In clouds of dust about their ears, rais'd from the horses' hooves,   140
That beat a thunder out of earth, as horrible as Jove's.
The king (persuading speedy chace) gave his persuasions way
With his own valour, slaught'ring still; as in a stormy day
In thick-set woods a ravenous fire wraps in his fierce repair
The shaken trees, and by the roots doth toss them into air:
Even so beneath Atrides' sword flew up Troy's flying heels;
Their horse drew empty chariots, and sought their thund'ring wheels
Some fresh directions through the field, where least the pursuit drives:
Thick fell the Trojans, much more sweet to vultures than their wives.
    Then Jove drew Hector from the darts, from dust, from death and blood,
And from the tumult: still the king firm to the pursuit stood
Till at old Ilus' monument, in midst of all the field,
They reach'd the wild fig-tree, and long'd to make their town their shield.
Yet there they rested not, the king still cried, 'Pursue, pursue',
And all his unreproved hands did blood and dust imbrue.
But when they came to Scaea's ports, and to the beech of Jove,
There made they stand; there every eye, fix'd on each other, strove
Who should outlook his mate amaz'd: through all the field they fled.
And as a lion, when the night becomes most deaf and dead,
Invades ox-herds, affrighting all, that he of one may wreak   160
His dreadful hunger, and his neck he first of all doth break,
Then laps his blood and entrails up: so Agamemnon plied
The manage of the Trojan chace, and still the last man died,
The other fled, a number fell by his imperial hand,

Some grovelling downwards from their horse, some upwards strew'd the sand.
High was the fury of his lance: but having beat them close
Beneath their walls, the both-worlds Sire did now again repose
On fountain-flowing Ida's tops, being newly slid from heav'n,
And held a lightning in his hand: from thence his charge was giv'n
To Iris with the golden wings: 'Thaumantia, fly,' said he,   170
And tell Troy's Hector, that as long as he enrag'd shall see
The soldier-loving Atreus' son amongst the foremost fight,
Depopulating troops of men, so long he must excite
Some other to resist the foe, and he no arms advance.
But when he wounded takes his horse, attain'd with shaft or lance,
Then will I fill his arm with death, even till he reach the fleet,
And peaceful night treads busy day beneath her sacred feet.'

   The wind-foot-swift Thaumantia obey'd, and us'd her wings
To famous Ilion, from the mount enchas'd with silver springs;
And found in his bright chariot the hardy Trojan knight,   180
To whom she spake the words of Jove, and vanish'd from his sight.

   He leap'd upon the sounding earth, and shook his lengthful dart,
And everywhere he breath'd exhorts, and stirr'd up every heart:
A dreadful fight he set on foot, his soldiers straight turn'd head:
The Greeks stood firm, in both the hosts the field was perfected.
But Agamemnon foremost still did all his side exceed,
And would not be the first in name unless the first in deed.

   Now sing, fair presidents of verse, that in the heavens embow'r,
Who first encounter'd with the king, of all the adverse pow'r.
Iphidamas, Antenor's son, ample and bigly set,   190
Brought up in pasture-springing Thrace, that doth soft sheep beget;
In grave Cissaeus' noble house, that was his mother's sire
(Fair Theano), and when his breast was height'ned with the fire
Of gaysome youth, his grandsire gave his daughter to his love,
Who straight his bridal-chamber left; fame with affection strove,
And made him furnish twelve fair ships to lend fair Troy his hand.
His ships he in Percope left, and came to Troy by land:
And now he tried the fame of Greece, encount'ring with the king,
Who threw his royal lance and miss'd. Iphidamas did fling,
And struck him on the arming waist, beneath his coat of brass,   200
Which forc'd him stay upon his arm, so violent it was;
Yet pierc'd it not his well-wrought zone, but when the lazy head
Tried hardness with his silver waist, it turn'd again like lead.
He follow'd, grasping the ground end: but with a lion's wile,
That wrests away a hunter's staff, he caught it by the pile,
And pluck'd it from the caster's hands, whom with his sword he strook
Beneath the ear, and with his wound his timeless death he took:

He fell and slept an iron sleep; wretched young man, he died,
Far from his newly-married wife, in aid of foreign pride,
And saw no pleasure of his love; yet was her jointure great: 210
An hundred oxen gave he her, and vow'd in his retreat
Two thousand head of sheep and goats, of which he store did leave;
Much gave he of his love's first-fruits, and nothing did receive.

　　When Coön (one that for his form might feast an amorous eye,
And elder brother of the slain) beheld this tragedy,
Deep sorrow sat upon his eyes; and (standing laterally,
And to the general undiscern'd) his javelin he let fly,
That 'twixt his elbow and his wrist transfix'd his armless arm:
The bright head shin'd on th' other side. The unexpected harm
Impress'd some horror in the king: yet so he ceas'd not fight,   220
But rush'd on Coön with his lance, who made what haste he might
(Seizing his slaughter'd brother's foot) to draw him from the field,
And call'd the ablest to his aid; when under his round shield
The king's brass javelin, as he drew, did strike him helpless dead,
Who made Iphidamas the block, and cut off Coön's head.

　　Thus under great Atrides' arm Antenor's issue thriv'd,
And to suffice precisest fate, to Pluto's mansion div'd.
He with his lance, sword, mighty stones, pour'd his heroic wreak
On other squadrons of the foe, whiles yet warm blood did break
Through his cleft veins: but when the wound was quite exhaust and crude,
The eager anguish did approve his princely fortitude.
As when most sharp and bitter pangs distract a labouring dame,
Which the divine Ilithiae, that rule the painful frame
Of human child-birth, pour on her – th' Ilithiae that are
The daughters of Saturnia, with whose extreme repair
The woman in her travail strives to take the worst it gives,
With thought it must be, 'tis love's fruit, the end for which she lives,
The mean to make herself new born, what comforts will redound:
So Agamemnon did sustain the torment of his wound.
Then took he chariot, and to fleet bad haste his charioteer,   240
But first pour'd out his highest voice, to purchase every ear:

　　'Princes and leaders of the Greeks, brave friends, now from our fleet
Do you expel this boist'rous sway: Jove will not let me meet
Illustrate Hector, nor give leave that I shall end the day
In fight against the Ilion power: my wound is in my way.'

　　This said, his ready charioteer did scourge his spriteful horse,
That freely to the sable fleet perform'd their fiery course,
To bear their wounded sovereign apart the martial thrust,
Sprinkling their powerful breasts with foam, and snowing on the dust.
When Hector heard of his retreat, thus he for fame contends: 250

'Trojans, Dardanians, Lycians, all my close-fighting friends,
Think what it is to be renown'd: be soldiers all of name:
Our strongest enemy is gone, Jove vows to do us fame:
Then in the Grecian faces drive your one-hoof'd violent steeds,
And far above their best be best, and glorify your deeds.'

    Thus as a dog-giv'n hunter sets upon a brace of boars
His white-tooth'd hounds, puffs, shouts, breathes terms, and on his emprise pours
All his wild art to make them pinch: so Hector urg'd his host
To charge the Greeks, and he himself most bold and active most:
He brake into the heat of fight, as when a tempest raves,   260
Stoops from the clouds, and all on heaps doth cuff the purple waves.

    Who then was first, and last, he kill'd, when Jove did grace his deed?
Asseüs, and Autonous; Opys, and Clytus' seed;
Prince Dolops, and the honour'd sire of sweet Euryalus
(Opheltes); Agelaus next, and strong Hipponous;
Orus, Essymnus, all of name. The common soldiers fell,
As when the hollow flood of air in Zephyr's cheeks doth swell,
And sparseth all the gather'd clouds white Notus' power did draw,
Wraps waves in waves, hurls up the froth, beat with a vehement flaw:
So were the common soldiers wrack'd in troops by Hector's hand.   270
Then ruin had enforc'd such works as no Greeks could withstand,
Then in their fleet they had been hous'd, had not Laertes' son
Stirr'd up the spirit of Diomed, with this impression:

    'Tydides, what do we sustain, forgetting what we are?
Stand by me (dearest in my love), 'twere horrible impair
For our two valours to endure a customary flight,
To leave our navy still engag'd, and but by fits to fight.'

    He answer'd: 'I am bent to stay, and anything sustain:
But our delight to prove us men will prove but short and vain,
For Jove makes Trojans instruments, and virtually then   280
Wields arms himself: our cross affairs are not 'twixt men and men.'

    This said, Thimbraeus with his lance he tumbled from his horse,
Near his left nipple wounding him: Ulysses did enforce
Fair Molion, minion to this king that Diomed subdu'd:
Both sent they thence, till they return'd, who now the king pursu'd
And furrow'd through the thicken'd troops. As when two chased boars
Turn head 'gainst kennels of bold hounds, and race way through their gores:
So (turn'd from flight) the forward kings show'd Trojans backward death;
Nor fled the Greeks but by their wills to get great Hector breath.

    Then took they horse and chariot from two bold city foes,   290
Merops Percosius' mighty sons: their father could disclose,
Beyond all men, hid auguries, and would not give consent
To their egression to these wars: yet wilfully they went,

For Fates, that order sable death, enforc'd their tragedies.
Tydides slew them with his lance, and made their arms his prize;
    Hipporochus, and Hippodus Ulysses reft of light.
But Jove, that out of Ida look'd, then equalis'd the fight;
A Grecian for a Trojan then paid tribute to the Fates;
Yet royal Diomed slew one, even in those even debates,
That was of name more than the rest: Paeon's renowned son,   300
The prince Agastrophus; his lance into his hip did run.
His squire detain'd his horse apart, that hinder'd him to fly;
Which he repented at his heart, yet did his feet apply
His 'scape with all the speed they had, alongst the foremost bands,
And there his loved life dissolv'd. This Hector understands,
And rush'd with clamour on the king, right soundly seconded
With troops of Trojans: which perceiv'd by famous Diomed,
The deep conceit of Jove's high will stiffen'd his royal hair,
Who spake to near-fought Ithacus: 'The fate of this affair
Is bent to us: come, let us stand, and bound his violence.'   310
Thus threw he his long javelin forth, which smote his head's defence
Full on the top, yet pierc'd no skin; brass took repulse with brass:
His helm (with three folds made, and sharp) the gift of Phoebus was.
The blow made Hector take the troop, sunk him upon his hand,
And struck him blind: the king pursu'd before the foremost band
His dart's recovery, which he found laid on the purple plain;
By which time Hector was reviv'd, and taking horse again,
Was far commix'd within his strength, and fled his darksome grave.
He follow'd with his trusty lance, and this elusive brave:
    'Once more be thankful to thy heels, proud dog, for thy escape: 320
Mischief sate near thy bosom now; and now another rape
Hath thy Apollo made of thee, to whom thou well mayst pray,
When through the singing of our darts thou find'st such guarded way.
But I shall meet with thee at length, and bring thy latest hour,
If with like favour any god be fautor of my pow'r:
Meanwhile, some other shall repay what I suspend in thee.'
    This said, he set the wretched soul of Paeon's issue free,
Whom his late wound not fully slew: but Priam's amorous birth
Against Tydides bent his bow, hid with a hill of earth,
Part of the ruinated tomb for honour'd Ilus built: 330
And as the curace of the slain (engrav'n and richly gilt)
Tydides from his breast had spoil'd, and from his shoulders raft
His target and his solid helm, he shot, and his keen shaft
(That never flew from him in vain) did nail upon the ground
The king's right foot: the spleenful knight laugh'd sweetly at the wound,
Crept from his covert, and triumph'd: 'Now art thou maim'd,' said he,

'And would to god my happy hand had so much honour'd me,
To have infix'd it in thy breast as deep as in thy foot,
Ev'n to th' expulsure of thy soul: then blest had been my shoot
Of all the Trojans, who had then breath'd from their long unrests,   340
Who fear thee as the braying goats abhor the king of beasts.'
Undaunted Diomed replied: 'You braver, with your bow,
You slick-hair'd lover, you that hunt and fleer at wenches so,
Durst thou but stand in arms with me, thy silly archery
Would give thee little cause to vaunt; as little suffer I
In this same tall exploit of thine, perform'd when thou wert hid,
As if a woman or a child, that knew not what it did,
Had touch'd my foot: a coward's steel hath never any edge,
But mine (t'assure it sharp) still lays dead carcasses in pledge;
Touch it, it renders lifeless straight: it strikes the fingers' ends   350
Of hapless widows in their cheeks, and children blind of friends:
The subject of it makes earth red, and air with sighs inflames,
And leaves limbs more embrac'd with birds than with enamour'd dames.'

Lance-fam'd Ulysses now came in, and stept before the king,
Kneel'd opposite, and drew the shaft: the eager pain did sting
Through all his body: straight he took his royal chariot there,
And with direction to the fleet did charge his charioteer.

Now was Ulysses desolate; fear made no friend remain.
He thus spake to his mighty mind: 'What doth my state sustain?
If I should fly this odds in fear, that thus comes clust'ring on,   360
'Twere high dishonour; yet 'twere worse to be surpris'd alone:
'Tis Jove that drives the rest to flight, but that's a faint excuse,
Why do I tempt my mind so much? Pale cowards fight refuse.
He that affects renown in war must like a rock be fix'd,
Wound, or be wounded: valour's truth puts no respect betwixt.

In this contention with himself, in flew the shady bands
Of targeteers, who sieg'd him round with mischief-filled hands.
As when a crew of gallants watch the wild muse of a boar,
Their dogs put after in full cry, he rusheth on before;
Whets, with his lather-making jaws, his crooked tusks for blood,   370
And (holding firm his usual haunts) breaks through the deepen'd wood,
They charging, though his hot approach be never so abhorr'd:
So, to assail the Jove-lov'd Greek, the Ilians did accord,
And he made through them: first he hurt, upon his shoulder blade,
Deiops, a blameless man at arms; then sent to endless shade
Thoön and Eunomus; and struck the strong Chersidamas,
As from his chariot he leap'd down, beneath his targe of brass:
Who fell, and crawl'd upon the earth with his sustaining palms,
And left the fight: nor yet his lance left dealing martial alms,

But Socus' brother by both sides, young Carops, did impress: 380
Then princely Socus to his aid made brotherly access,
And (coming near) spake in his charge: 'O great Laertes' son,
Insatiate in sly stratagems, and labours never done,
This hour, or thou shalt boast to kill the two Hypasides,
And prize their arms, or fall thyself, in my resolv'd access.'

  This said, he threw quite through his shield his fell and well-driv'n lance,
Which held way through his curaces, and on his ribs did glance,
Plowing the flesh alongst his sides; but Pallas did repel
All inward passage to his life. Ulysses, knowing well
The wound undeadly (setting back his foot to form his stand), 390
Thus spake to Socus: 'O thou wretch, thy death is in this hand,
That stay'st my victory on Troy: and where thy charge was made
In doubtful terms – or this or that – this shall thy life invade.'

  This frighted Socus to retreat, and in his faint reverse,
The lance betwixt his shoulders fell, and through his breast did pierce.
Down fell he sounding, and the king thus play'd with his misease:

  'O Socus, you that make by birth the two Hypasides,
Now may your house and you perceive death can outfly the flyer:
Ah wretch, thou canst not 'scape my vows: old Hypasus thy sire,
Nor thy well-honour'd mother's hands, in both which lies thy worth, 400
Shall close thy wretched eyes in death, but vultures dig them forth,
And hide them with their darksome wings: but when Ulysses dies,
Divinest Greeks shall tomb my corse with all their obsequies.

  Now from his body and his shield the violent lance he drew,
That princely Socus had infix'd: which drawn, a crimson dew
Fell from his bosom on the earth: the wound did dare him sore.
And when the furious Trojans saw Ulysses' forced gore,
(Encouraging themselves in gross) all his destruction vow'd;
Then he retir'd, and summon'd aid: thrice shouted he aloud
(As did denote a man engag'd), thrice Menelaus' ear 410
Observ'd his aid-suggesting voice: and Ajax being near,
He told him of Ulysses' shouts, as if he were enclos'd
From all assistance, and advis'd their aids might be dispos'd
Against the ring that circled him: lest, charg'd with troops alone
(Though valiant), he might be oppress'd, whom Greece so built upon.

  He led, and Ajax seconded: they found their Jove-lov'd king
Circled with foes. As when a den of bloody lucerns cling
About a goodly palmed hart, hurt with an hunter's bow,
Whose 'scape his nimble feet enforce, whilst his warm blood doth flow,
And his light knees have power to move; but (master'd of his wound, 420
Emboss'd within a shady hill) the lucerns charge him round,
And tear his flesh; when instantly, fortune sends in the pow'rs

Of some stern lion, with whose sight they fly, and he devours:
So charg'd the Ilians Ithacus, many and mighty men:
But then made Menelaus in, and horrid Ajax then,
Bearing a target like a tower: close was his violent stand,
And every way the foe dispers'd; when, by the royal hand,
Kind Menelaus led away the hurt Laertes' son,
Till his fair squire had brought his horse: victorious Telamon
Still plied the foe, and put to sword a young Priamides: 430
Doriclus, Priam's bastard son; then did his lance impress
Pandocus, and strong Pyrasus, Lysander and Palertes.
As when a torrent from the hills, swoln with Saturnian show'rs,
Falls on the fields, bears blasted oaks and wither'd rosy flow'rs,
Loose weeds, and all dispersed filth, into the ocean's force:
So matchless Ajax beat the field, and slaughter'd men and horse.
Yet had not Hector heard of this, who fought on the left wing
Of all the host, near those sweet herbs Scamander's flood doth spring:
Where many foreheads trod the ground, and where the skirmish burn'd
Near Nestor, and king Idomen; where Hector overturn'd   440
The Grecian squadrons, authoring high service with his lance,
And skilful manage of his horse: nor yet the discrepance
He made in death betwixt the hosts had made the Greeks retire,
If fair-hair'd Helen's second spouse had not repress'd the fire
Of bold Machaon's fortitude, who with a three-fork'd head
In his right shoulder wounded him: then had the Grecians dread,
Lest, in his strength declin'd, the foe should slaughter their hurt friend.
Then Crete's king urg'd Neleides his chariot to ascend,
And getting near him, take him in, and bear him to their tents:
'A surgeon is to be preferr'd, with physic ornaments,   450
Before a multitude: his life gives hurt lives native bounds,
With sweet inspersion of fit balms, and perfect search of wounds.'
    Thus spake the royal Idomen: Neleides obey'd,
And to his chariot presently the wounded Greek convey'd,
The son of Aesculapius, the great physician:
To fleet they flew. Cebriones perceiv'd the slaughter done
By Ajax on the other troops, and spake to Hector thus:
'Whiles we encounter Grecians here, stern Telamonius
Is yonder raging, turning up in heaps our horse and men:
I know him by his spacious shield; let us turn chariot then   460
Where both of horse and foot the fight most hotly is propos'd,
In mutual slaughters: hark, their throats from cries are never clos'd.'
    This said, with his shrill scourge he struck the horse, that fast ensu'd,
Stung with his lashes, tossing shields and carcasses imbru'd.
The chariot tree was drown'd in blood, and th' arches by the seat,

Dispurpled from the horses' hoofs, and from the wheelbands' beat.
Great Hector long'd to break the ranks and startle their close fight:
Who horribly amaz'd the Greeks, and plied their sudden fright
With busy weapons, ever wing'd, his lance, sword, weighty stones:
Yet charg'd he other leaders' bands, not dreadful Telamon's,   470
With whom he wisely shunn'd foul blows: but Jove (that weighs above
All human pow'rs) to Ajax' breast divine repressions drove,
And made him shun who shunn'd himself: he ceas'd from fight amaz'd,
Cast on his back his seven-fold shield, and round about him gaz'd,
Like one turn'd wild; look'd on himself in his distract retreat;
Knee before knee did scarcely move. As when from herds of neat
Whole threaves of bores and mongrels chase a lion skulking near,
Loth he should taint the well-priz'd fat of any stall-fed steer,
Consuming all the night in watch; he (greedy of his prey)
Of thrusting on is oft thrust off, so thick the javelins play   480
On his bold charges, and so hot the burning fire-brands shine,
Which he (though horrible) abhors, about his glowing eyne,
And early his great heart retires: so Ajax from the foe,
For fear their fleet should be inflam'd, 'gainst his swoln heart did go.

    As when a dull mill ass comes near a goodly field of corn
Kept from the birds by children's cries, the boys are overborne
By his insensible approach, and simply he will eat;
About whom many wands are broke, and still the children beat,
And still the self-providing ass doth with their weakness bear,
Not stirring till his paunch be full, and scarcely then will steer: 490
So the huge son of Telamon amongst the Trojans far'd,
Bore show'rs of darts upon his shield, yet scorn'd to fly as scar'd,
And so kept softly on his way; nor would he mend his pace
For all their violent pursuits, that still did arm the chase
With singing lances: but at last, when their cur-like presumes
More urg'd the more forborne, his spirits did rarefy their fumes,
And he revok'd his active strength, turn'd head, and did repel
The horse troops that were new made in; 'twixt whom the fight grew fell,
And by degrees he stole retreat, yet with such puissant stay
That none could pass him to the fleet: in both the armies' sway   500
He stood, and from strong hands receiv'd sharp javelins on his shield
Where many stuck, thrown on before; many fell short in field,
Ere the white body they could reach, and stuck, as telling how
They purpos'd to have pierc'd his flesh: his peril pierced now
The eyes of prince Eurypilus, Evemon's famous son,
Who came close on, and with his dart struck duke Apisaon,
Whose surname was Phausiades, ev'n to the concrete blood
That makes the liver: on the earth out gush'd his vital flood.

Eurypilus made in, and eas'd his shoulders of his arms;
Which Paris seeing, he drew his bow, and wreak'd in part the harms   510
Of his good friend Phausiades: his arrow he let fly,
That smote Eurypilus, and brake in his attainted thigh:
Then took he troop, to shun black death, and to the fliers cried:
    'Princes, and leaders of the Greeks, stand, and repulse the tide
Of this our honour-wracking chase; Ajax is drown'd in darts,
I fear past 'scape: turn, honour'd friends, help out his vent'rous parts.'
Thus spake the wounded Greek; the sound cast on their backs their shields,
And rais'd their darts; to whose relief Ajax his person wields.
Then stood he firmly with his friends, retiring their retire,
And thus both hosts indiff'rent join'd, the fight grew hot as fire.   520
    Now had Neleides' sweating steeds brought him and his hurt friend
Amongst their fleet; Aeacides, that wishly did intend
(Standing astern his tall-neck'd ship) how deep the skirmish drew
Amongst the Greeks, and with what ruth the insecution grew,
Saw Nestor bring Machaon hurt, and from within did call
His friend Patroclus, who like Mars, in form celestial,
Came forth with first sound of his voice (first spring of his decay)
And ask'd his princely friend's desire: 'Dear friend,' said he, 'this day
I doubt not will enforce the Greeks to swarm about my knees;
I see unsuffer'd need employ'd in their extremities.   530
Go, sweet Patroclus, and inquire of old Neleides
Whom he brought wounded from the fight; by his back parts I guess
It is Machaon, but his face I could not well descry,
They pass'd me in such earnest speed.' Patroclus presently
Obey'd his friend, and ran to know. They now descended were,
And Nestor's squire Eurymedon the horses did ungear:
Themselves stood near th' extremest shore to let the gentle air
Dry up their sweat, then to the tent; where Hecamed the fair
Set chairs, and for the wounded prince a potion did prepare.
    This Hecamed, by war's hard fate, fell to old Nestor's share,   540
When Thetis' son sack'd Tenedos. She was the princely seed
Of worthy king Arsynous, and by the Greeks decreed
The prize of Nestor, since all men in counsel he surpass'd.
First, a fair table she appos'd, of which the feet were grac'd
With bluish metal, mix'd with black: and on the same she put
A brass fruit dish, in which she serv'd a wholesome onion cut,
For pittance to the potion, and honey newly wrought,
And bread, the fruit of sacred meal: then to the board she brought
A right fair cup, with gold studs driv'n, which Nestor did transfer
From Pylos, on whose swelling sides four handles fixed were,   550
And upon every handle sat a pair of doves of gold,

Some billing, and some pecking meat. Two gilt feet did uphold
The antique body: and withal so weighty was the cup,
That being propos'd brimful of wine, one scarce could lift it up:
Yet Nestor drunk in it with ease, spite of his years' respect.
In this the goddess-like fair dame a potion did confect
With gold old wine of Pramnius, and scrap'd into the wine
Cheese made of goats' milk; and on it spers'd flour exceeding fine:
In this sort for the wounded lord the potion she prepar'd,
And bad him drink; for company, with him old Nestor shar'd.   560

   Thus physically quench'd they thirst, and then their spirits reviv'd
With pleasant conference. And now, Patroclus being arriv'd,
Made stay at th' entry of the tent: old Nestor seeing it,
Rose, and receiv'd him by the hand, and fain would have him sit.
He set that courtesy aside, excusing it with haste,
Since his much-to-be-rev'renced friend sent him to know who pass'd
(Wounded with him in chariot) so swiftly through the shore;
'Whom now,' said he, 'I see and know, and now can stay no more:
You know, good father, our great friend is apt to take offence,
Whose fiery temper will inflame sometimes with innocence.'   570

   He answer'd: 'When will Peleus' son some royal pity show
On his thus wounded countrymen? Ah, is he yet to know
How much affliction tires our host, how our especial aid
(Tainted with lances, at their tents) are miserably laid?
Ulysses, Diomed, our king, Eurypilus, Machaon:
All hurt, and all our worthiest friends, yet no compassion
Can supple thy friend's friendless breast. Doth he reserve his eye
Till our fleet burn, and we ourselves one after other die?
Alas! My forces are not now as in my younger life.
Oh! Would to god I had that strength I used in the strife   580
Betwixt us and the Elians, for oxen to be driv'n,
When Itumonius' lofty soul was by my valour giv'n
As sacrifice to destiny, Hipporocus' strong son,
That dwelt in Elis, and fought first in our contention.
We foraged (as proclaimed foes) a wondrous wealthy boot;
And he, in rescue of his herds, fell breathless at my foot.
All the dorp bores with terror fled; our prey was rich and great,
Twice five and twenty flocks of sheep; as many herds of neat;
As many goats, and nasty swine; an hundred fifty mares,
All sorrel, most with sucking foals; and these soon-monied wares   590
We drave into Neleius' town, fair Pylos, all by night.
My father's heart was glad to see so much good fortune quite
The forward mind of his young son, that us'd my youth in deeds,
And would not smother it in moods. Now drew the sun's bright steeds

Light from the hills; our heralds now accited all that were
Endamag'd by the Elians; our princes did appear;
Our boot was parted; many men th' Epeians much did owe,
That (being our neighbours) they did spoil; afflictions did so flow
On us poor Pyleans though but few. In brake great Hercules
To our sad confines of late years, and wholly did suppress 600
Our hapless princes: twice six sons renown'd Neleius bred;
Only myself am left of all, the rest subdued and dead.
And this was it that made so proud the base Epeian bands,
On their near neighbours, being oppress'd, to lay injurious hands:
A herd of oxen for himself, a mighty flock of sheep,
My sire selected, and made choice of shepherds for their keep:
And from the general spoil he cull'd three hundred of the best:
The Elians ought him infinite, most plagued of all the rest.
Four wager-winning horse he lost, and chariots intervented,
Being led to an appointed race. The prize that was presented 610
Was a religious three-foot urn: Augeas was the king
That did detain them, and dismiss'd their keeper sorrowing
For his lov'd charge, lost with foul words. Then both for words and deeds
My sire being worthily incens'd, thus justly he proceeds
To satisfaction, in first choice of all our wealthy prize:
And as he shar'd much, much he left his subjects to suffice,
That none might be oppress'd with pow'r, or want his portion due:
Thus for the public good we shar'd. Then we to temples drew
Our complete city, and to heav'n we thankful rights did burn
For our rich conquest. The third day ensuing our return, 620
The Elians flew on us in heaps: their general leaders were
The two Moliones, two boys, untrained in the fear
Of horrid war, or use of strength. A certain city shines
Upon a lofty prominent, and in th' extreme confines
Of sandy Pylos, seated where Alpheus' flood doth run,
And call'd Thryessa: this they sieg'd, and gladly would have won;
But, having pass'd through all our fields, Minerva as our spy
Fell from Olympus in the night, and arm'd us instantly:
Nor must'ered she unwilling men, nor unprepar'd for force.
My sire yet would not let me arm, but hid away my horse, 630
Esteeming me no soldier yet; yet shin'd I nothing less
Amongst our gallants, though on foot; Minerva's mightiness
Led me to fight, and made me bear a soldier's worthy name.
　　There is a flood falls into sea, and his crook'd course doth frame
Close to Arena, and is call'd bright Myniaeus stream.
There made we halt: and there the sun cast many a glorious beam
On our bright armours; horse and foot insea'd together there,

Then march'd we on: by fiery noon we saw the sacred clear
Of great Alphaeus, where to Jove we did fair sacrifice:
And to the azure god, that rules the under-liquid skies,   640
We offer'd up a solemn bull; a bull t' Alphaeus' name,
And to the blue-ey'd Maid we burn'd a heifer never tame.
Now was it night; we supp'd and slept about the flood in arms,
The foe laid hard siege to our town, and shook it with alarms:
But for prevention of their spleens, a mighty work of war
Appear'd behind them. For as soon as Phoebus' fiery car
Cast night's foul darkness from his wheels (invoking rev'rend Jove,
And the unconquer'd Maid his birth), we did th' event approve,
And gave them battle: first of all, I slew (the army saw)
The mighty soldier Mulius, Augeas' son-in-law,   650
And spoil'd him of his one-hoof'd horse: his elder daughter was
Bright Agamede, that for skill in simples did surpass
And knew as many kind of drugs as earth's broad centre bred:
Him charg'd I with my brass-arm'd lance, the dust receiv'd him dead:
I (leaping to his chariot) amongst the foremost press'd,
And the great hearted Elians fled frighted, seeing their best
And loftiest soldier taken down, the general of their horse.
I follow'd like a black whirlwind, and did for prize enforce
Full fifty chariots, every one furnish'd with two arm'd men,
Who ate the earth, slain with my lance; and I had slaughter'd then   660
The two young boys, Moliones, if their world-circling sire
(Great Neptune) had not sav'd their lives, and cover'd their retire
With unpierc'd clouds: then Jove bestow'd a haughty victory
Upon us Pyleans. For so long we did the chase apply,
Slaught'ring and making spoil of arms, till sweet Buprasius' soil,
Alesius, and Olenia, were fam'd with our recoil.
For there Minerva turn'd our pow'r, and there the last I slew,
As when our battle join'd, the first: the Pyleans then withdrew
To Pylos from Buprasius. Of all the immortals then,
They most thank'd Jove for victory, Nestor the most of men.   670
Such was I ever, if I were, employ'd with other peers,
And I had honour of my youth, which dies not in my years.
But great Achilles only joys hability of act
In his brave prime, and doth not deign t' impart it where 'tis lack'd.
No doubt he will extremely mourn long after that black hour
Wherein our ruin shall be wrought, and rue his ruthless pow'r.
O friend, my memory revives, the charge Menetius gave
Thy towardness, when thou sett'st forth, to keep out of the grave
Our wounded honour; I myself and wise Ulysses were
Within the room, where every word then spoken we did hear: 680

For we were come to Peleus' court, as we did must'ring pass
Through rich Achaia, where thy sire, renown'd Menoetius, was,
Thyself and great Aeacides, when Peleus the king
To thunder-loving Jove did burn an ox for offering,
In his court-yard: a cup of gold, crown'd with red wine, he held
On th' holy incensory pour'd. You, when the ox was fell'd,
Were dressing his divided limbs, we in the portal stood.
Achilles seeing us come so near, his honourable blood
Was struck with a respective shame, rose, took us by the hands,
Brought us both in, and made us sit, and us'd his kind commands   690
For seemly hospitable rights, which quickly were appos'd.
Then (after needfulness of food) I first of all disclos'd
The royal cause of our repair, mov'd you and your great friend
To consort our renown'd designs: both straight did condescend;
Your fathers knew it, gave consent, and grave instruction
To both your valours. Peleus charg'd his most unequall'd son
To govern his victorious strength, and shine past all the rest
In honour, as in mere main force. Then were thy partings blest
With dear advices from thy sire. "My loved son," said he,
"Achilles by his grace of birth superior is to thee,   700
And for his force more excellent, yet thou more ripe in years:
Then with sound counsels (age's fruits) employ his honour'd years,
Command and overrule his moods; his nature will obey
In any charge discreetly given, that doth his good assay."
   Thus charg'd thy sire, which thou forgett'st; yet now at last approve
(With forced reference of these) th' attraction of his love.
Who knows if sacred influence may bless thy good intent,
And enter with thy gracious words, even to his full consent?
The admonition of a friend is sweet and vehement.
If any oracle he shun, or if his mother queen   710
Hath brought him some instinct from Jove, that fortifies his spleen,
Let him resign command to thee of all his Myrmidons,
And yield by that means some repulse to our confusions,
Adorning thee in his bright arms, that his resembled form
May haply make thee thought himself, and calm this hostile storm:
That so a little we may ease our overcharged hands,
Draw some breath, not expire it all: the foe but faintly stands
Beneath his labours, and your charge being fierce, and freshly giv'n,
They easily from our tents and fleet may to their walls be driv'n.'
   This mov'd the good Patroclus' mind, who made his utmost haste   720
T' inform his friend, and at the fleet of Ithacus he past,
(At which their markets were dispos'd, counsels and martial courts,
And where to th' altars of the gods they made divine resorts)

He met renown'd Eurypilus, Evemon's noble son,
Halting, his thigh hurt with a shaft: the liquid sweat did run
Down from his shoulders and his brows, and from his raging wound
Forth flow'd his melancholy blood; yet still his mind was sound.
His sight in kind Patroclus' breast to sacred pity turn'd,
And (nothing more immartial for true ruth) thus he mourn'd:
'Ah wretched progeny of Greece, princes, dejected kings,   730
Was it your fates to nourish beasts, and serve the outcast wings
Of savage vultures here in Troy? Tell me, Evemon's fame,
Do yet the Greeks withstand his force, whom yet no force can tame,
Or are they hopeless thrown to death by his resistlesss lance?'
'Divine Patroclus,' he replied, 'no more can Greece advance
Defensive weapons, but to fleet they headlong must retire:
For those that to this hour have held our fleet from hostile fire,
And are the bulwarks of our host, lie wounded at their tents,
And Troy's unvanquishable pow'r, still as it toils, augments.
But take me to thy black-stern'd ship, save me, and from my thigh   740
Cut out this arrow; and the blood that is ingor'd and dry
Wash with warm water from the wound: then gentle salves apply,
Which thou know'st best; thy princely friend hath taught thee surgery,
Whom, of all centaurs the most just, Chiron did institute:
Thus to thy honourable hands my ease I prosecute,
Since our physicians cannot help: Machaon at his tent
Needs a physician himself, being leech and patient,
And Podalirius in the field the sharp conflict sustains.'
Strong Menetiades replied: 'How shall I ease thy pains?
What shall we do, Eurypilus? I am to use all haste   750
To signify to Thetis' son occurrents that have past,
At Nestor's honourable suit; but be that work achiev'd,
When this is done, I will not leave thy torments unreliev'd.'
    This said, athwart his back he cast, beneath his breast, his arm,
And nobly help'd him to his tent: his servants seeing his harm,
Dispread ox-hides upon the earth, whereon Machaon lay:
Patroclus cut out the sharp shaft, and clearly wash'd away
With lukewarm water the black blood: then 'twixt his hands he bruis'd
A sharp and mitigatory root, which when he had infus'd
Into the green, well-cleansed wound, the pains he felt before   760
Were well, and instantly allay'd, the wound did bleed no more.

THE END OF THE ELEVENTH BOOK

BOOK TWELVE

The Argument

The Trojans at the trench their pow'rs engage,
Though greeted by a bird of bad presage.
In five parts they divide their pow'r to scale,
And Prince Sarpedon forceth down the pale:
Great Hector from the ports tears out a stone,
And with so dead a strength he sets it gone
At those broad gates the Grecians made to guard
Their tents and ships that, broken and unbarr'd,
They yield way to his pow'r; when all contend
To reach the ships, which all at last ascend.

Another Argument

Mu works the Trojans all the grace,
And doth the Grecian fort deface.

BOOK TWELVE

PATROCLUS thus employ'd in cure of hurt Eurypilus,
   Both hosts are all for other wounds doubly contentious,
   One always labouring to expel, the other to invade.
Nor could the broad dike of the Greeks, nor that strong wall they made
To guard their fleet, be long unrac't; because it was not rais'd
By grave direction of the gods; nor were their deities prais'd
(When they begun) with hecatombs, that then they might be sure
(Their strength being season'd well with heav'n's) it should have force t' endure,
And so the safeguard of their fleet, and all their treasure there,
Infallibly had been confirm'd: when now, their bulwarks were   10
Not only without pow'r of check to their assaulting foe
(Even now, as soon as they were built), but apt to overthrow;
Such as, in very little time, shall bury all their sight,
And thought that ever they were made: as long as the despight
Of great Aeacides held up, and Hector went not down,
And that by those two means stood safe king Priam's sacred town,
So long their rampire had some use (though now it gave some way);
But when Troy's best men suffer'd fate, and many Greeks did pay
Dear for their suff'rance, then the rest home to their country turn'd,
The tenth year of their wars at Troy, and Troy was sack'd and burn'd,   20
And then the gods fell to their fort; then they their pow'rs employ
To ruin their work, and left less of that than they of Troy.
Neptune and Phoebus tumbled down from the Idalian hills
An inundation of all floods, that thence the broad sea fills
On their huge rampire; in one glut, all these together roar'd,
Rhesus, Heptaporus, Rhodius, Scamander (the ador'd),
Caresus, Simois, Grenicus, Aesepus: of them all
Apollo open'd the rough mouths, and made their lusty fall
Ravish the dusty champian, where many a helm and shield,
And half-god race of men, were strew'd: and that all these might yield   30
Full tribute to the heavenly work, Neptune and Phoebus won
Jove to unburthen the black wombs of clouds (fill'd by the sun),
And pour them into all their streams, that quickly they might send
The huge wall swimming to the sea. Nine days their lights did spend
To nights, in tempests; and when all their utmost depth had made,

Jove, Phoebus, Neptune, all came down, and all in state did wade
To ruin of that impious fort: great Neptune went before,
Wrought with his trident, and the stones, trunks, roots of trees he tore
Out of the rampire, toss'd them all into the Hellespont,
Ev'n all the proud toil of the Greeks, with which they durst confront   40
The to-be-shunned deities: and not a stone remain'd
Of all their huge foundations, all with the earth were plain'd.
Which done, again the gods turn'd back the silver-flowing floods,
By that vast channel through whose vaults they pour'd abroad their broods,
And cover'd all the ample shore again with dusty sand:
And this the end was of that wall, where now so many a hand
Was emptied of stones and darts, contending to invade,
Where Clamour spent so high a throat, and where the fell blows made
The new-built wooden turrets groan. And here the Greeks were pent,
Tam'd with the iron whip of Jove, that terrors vehement   50
Shook over them by Hector's hand, who was in every thought,
The terror-master of the field, and like a whirlwind fought,
As fresh as in his morn's first charge. And, as a savage boar
Or lion, hunted long, at last with hounds' and hunters' store
Is compass'd round, they charge him close, and stand (as in a tow'r
They had inchas'd him) pouring on of darts an iron show'r;
His glorious heart yet, nought appall'd, and forcing forth his way,
Here overthrows a troop, and there a running ring doth stay
His utter passage: when again that stay he overthrows,
And then the whole field frees his rage: so Hector wearies blows,   60
Runs out his charge upon the fort; and all his force would force
To pass the dike: which being so deep, they could not get their horse
To venture on, but trample, snore, and on the very brink,
To neigh with spirit, yet still stand off: nor would a human think
The passage safe, or if it were, 'twas less safe for retreat,
The dike being everywhere so deep; and (where 'twas least deep) set
With stakes exceeding thick, sharp, strong, that horse could never pass,
Much less their chariots after them: yet for the foot there was
Some hopeful service, which they wish'd. Polydamas then spake:

    'Hector, and all our friends of Troy, we indiscreetly make   70
Offer of passage with our horse: ye see the stakes, the wall,
Impossible for horse to take; nor can men fight at all,
The place being strait, and much more apt to let us take our bane,
Than give the enemy: and yet, if Jove decree the wane
Of Grecian glory utterly, and so bereave their hearts
That we may freely charge them thus, and then will take our parts,
I would with all speed wish th' assault, that ugly shame might shed
(Thus far from home) these Grecians' bloods. But if they once turn head

And sally on us from their fleet, when in so deep a dike
We shall lie struggling, not a man of all the host is like   80
To live and carry back the news; and therefore be it thus:
Here leave we horse, kept by our men, and all on foot let us
Hold close together, and attend the grace of Hector's guide;
And then they shall not bear our charge, our conquest shall be dyed
In their lives' purples.' This advice pleas'd Hector, for 'twas sound;
Who first obey'd it, and full arm'd betook him to the ground,
And then all left their chariots when he was seen to lead,
Rushing about him, and gave up each chariot and steed
To their directors to be kept, in all procinct of war –
There, and on that side of the dike. And thus the rest prepare   90
Their onset: in five regiments they all their pow'r divide –
Each regiment allow'd three chiefs, of all which, ev'n the pride
Serv'd in great Hector's regiment; for all were set on fire
(Their passage beaten through the wall) with hazardous desire
That they might once but fight at fleet. With Hector captains were
Polydamas and Cebriones, who was his charioteer,
But Hector found that place a worse. Chiefs of the second band
Were Paris and Alcathous, Agenor. The command
The third strong phalanx had was giv'n to th' augur Hellenus,
Deiphobus, that god-like man, and mighty Asius –   100
Even Asius Hertacides, that from Arisba rode
The huge bay horse, and had his house where riv'r Selleës flow'd.
The fourth charge good Aeneas led, and with him were combin'd
Archelochus and Acamas (Antenor's dearest kind,
And excellent at every fight). The fifth brave company
Sarpedon had to charge, who chose, for his command's supply,
Asteropaeus great in arms, and Glaucus, for both these
Were best of all men but himself: but he was fellowless.
     Thus fitted with their well-wrought shields, down the steep dike they go,
And (thirsty of the wall's assault) believe in overthrow,   110
Not doubting but with headlong falls to tumble down the Greeks
From their black navy: in which trust, all on, and no man seeks
To cross Polydamas' advice with any other course,
But Asius Hyrtacides, who (proud of his bay horse)
Would not forsake them; nor his man, that was their manager
(Fool that he was), but all to fleet, and little knew how near
An ill death sat him, and a sure, and that he never more
Must look on lofty Ilion: but looks, and all before
Put on th' all-covering mist of fate, and then did bang upon
The lance of great Deucalides; he fatally rush'd on   120
The left hand way, by which the Greeks, with horse and chariot,

Came usually from field to fleet: close to the gates he got,
Which both unbarr'd and ope he found, that so the easier might
An entry be for any friend that was behind in flight –
Yet not much easier for a foe, because there was a guard
Maintain'd upon it, past his thought; who still put for it hard,
Eagerly shouting, and with him were five more friends of name,
That would not leave him, though none else would hunt that way for fame
(In their free choice) but he himself: Orestes, Iamenus,
And Acamas Asiades, Thoön, Oenomaus,   130
Were those that follow'd Asius: within the gates they found
Two eminently valorous, that from the race renown'd
Of the right valiant Lapithes deriv'd their high descent.
Fierce Leonteus was the one, like Mars in detriment,
The other mighty Polypaet, the great Pirithous' son.
These stood within the lofty gates, and nothing more did shun
The charge of Asius and his friends, than two high hill-bred oaks,
Well rooted in the binding earth, obey the airy strokes
Of wind and weather, standing firm 'gainst every season's spite.
Yet they pour on continu'd shouts, and bear their shields upright,   140
When in the mean space Polypaet and Leonteus cheer'd
Their soldiers to the fleet's defence: but when the rest had heard
The Trojans in attempt to scale, clamour and flight did flow
Amongst the Grecians; and then (the rest dismay'd) these two
Met Asius ent'ring, thrust him back, and fought before their doors:
Nor far'd they then like oaks that stood, but as a brace of boars
Couch'd in their own bred hill, that hear a sort of hunter's shout,
And hounds in hot trail coming on; then from their dens break out,
Traverse their force, and suffer not, in wildness of their way,
About them any plant to stand, but thickets, offering stay,   150
Break through, and rend up by the roots, whet gnashes into air,
Which Tumult fills with shouts, hounds, horns, and all the hot affair
Beats at their bosoms: so their arms rung with assailing blows,
And so they stirr'd them in repulse, right well assur'd that those
Who were within, and on the wall, would add their parts; who knew
They now fought for their tents, fleet, lives, and fames, and therefore threw
Stones from the walls and tow'rs, as thick as when a drift wind shakes
Black clouds in pieces, and plucks snow, in great and plumy flakes,
From their soft bosoms, till the ground be wholly cloth'd in white.
So earth was hid with stones and darts – darts from the Trojan fight,   160
Stones from the Greeks, that on the helms and bossy Trojan shields
Kept such a rapping, it amaz'd great Asius, who now yields
Sighs, beats his thighs, and in a rage his fault to Jove applies.
'O Jove,' said he, 'now clear thou show'st, thou art a friend to lies,

Pretending, in the flight of Greece, the making of it good,
To all their ruins: which I thought could never be withstood.
Yet they, as yellow wasps or bees (that having made their nest
The gasping cranny of a hill) when for a hunter's feast
Hunters come hot and hungry in, and dig for honeycombs,
They fly upon them, strike and sting, and from their hollow homes   170
Will not be beaten, but defend their labour's fruit, and brood:
No more will these be from their port, but either lose their blood
(Although but two against all us) or be our prisoners made.'
All this, to do his action grace, could not firm Jove persuade,
Who for the general counsel stood, and ('gainst his singular brave)
Bestow'd on Hector that day's fame. Yet he and these behave
Themselves thus nobly at this port: but how at other ports,
And all alongst the stony wall, sole force, 'gainst force and forts,
Rag'd in contention 'twixt both hosts, it were no easy thing
(Had I the bosom of a god) to tune to life, and sing.   180
The Trojans fought not of themselves, a fire from heav'n was thrown
That ran amongst them, through the wall, mere added to their own.
The Greeks held not their own: weak Grief went with her wither'd hand,
And dipp'd it deeply in their spirits, since they could not command
Their forces to abide the field, whom harsh Necessity
(To save those ships should bring them home) and their good forts' supply
Drave to th' expulsive fight they made; and this might stoop them more
Than Need itself could elevate, for ev'n gods did deplore
Their dire estates, and all the gods that were their aids in war:
Who (though they could not clear their plights) yet were their friends thus far,
Still to uphold the better sort: for then did Polypaet pass
A lance at Damasus, whose helm was made with cheeks of brass,
Yet had not proof enough; the pile drave through it, and his skull;
His brain in blood drown'd, and the man, so late so spiritful,
Fell now quite spiritless to earth. So emptied he the veins
Of Pylon and Ormenus' lives: and then Leonteus gains
The life's end of Hippomachus, Antimachus's son;
His lance fell at his girdle stead, and with his end begun
Another end: Leonteus left him, and through the press
(His keen sword drawn) ran desperately upon Antiphates,   200
And lifeless tumbled him to earth. Nor could all these lives quench
His fiery spirit, that his flame in Menon's blood did drench,
And rag'd up even to Iamen's, and young Orestes' life;
All heap'd together made their peace, in that red field of strife.
Whose fair arms while the victors spoil'd, the youth of Ilion
(Of which there serv'd the most and best) still boldly built upon
The wisdom of Polydamas, and Hector's matchless strength,

And follow'd, fill'd with wondrous spirit, with wish and hope at length
(The Greeks' wall won) to fire their fleet. But (having passed the dike,
And willing now to pass the wall) this prodigy did strike   210
Their hearts with some deliberate stay: a high-flown eagle soar'd
On their troops' left hand, and sustain'd a dragon all engor'd,
In her strong seres, of wondrous size, and yet had no such check
In life and spirit, but still she fought; and turning back her neck
So stung the eagle's gorge, that down she cast her fervent prey
Amongst the multitude, and took upon the winds her way,
Crying with anguish. When they saw a branded serpent sprawl
So full amongst them from above, and from Jove's fowl let fall,
They took it an ostent from him, stood frighted, and their cause
Polydamas thought just, and spake: 'Hector, you know applause   220
Of humour hath been far from me; nor fits it, or in war
Or in affairs of court, a man employ'd in public care
To blanch things further than their truth, or flatter any pow'r.
And therefore for that simple cause your strength hath oft been sour
To me in counsels, yet again, what shows in my thoughts best,
I must discover: let us cease, and make their flight our rest
For this day's honour, and not now attempt the Grecian fleet;
For this, I fear, will be th' event: the prodigy doth meet
So full with our affair in hand. As this high-flying fowl
Upon the left wing of our host (implying our control)   230
Hover'd above us, and did truss within her golden seres
A serpent so embrew'd, and big, which yet (in all her fears)
Kept life, and fervent spirit to fight, and wrought her own release,
Nor did the eagle's eyrie feed: so though we thus far press
Upon the Grecians, and perhaps may overturn their wall,
Our high minds aiming at their fleet, and that we much appal
Their trussed spirits, yet are they so serpent-like dispos'd
That they will fight, though in our seres, and will at length be loos'd
With all our outcries; and the life of many a Trojan breast
Shall with the eagle fly, before we carry to our nest   240
Them, or their navy.' Thus expounds the augur this ostent,
Whose depth he knows, and these should fear. Hector, with count'nance bent,
Thus answer'd him: 'Polydamas, your depth in augury
I like not; and know passing well, thou dost not satisfy
Thyself in this opinion; or if thou think'st it true,
Thy thoughts the gods blind, to advise and urge that as our due,
That breaks our duties – and to Jove, whose vow and sign to me
Is past directly for our speed; yet light-wing'd birds must be
(By thy advice) our oracles, whose feathers little stay
My serious actions. What care I, if this or th' other way   250

Their wild wings sway them: if the right, on which the sun doth rise,
Or to the left hand, where he sets? 'Tis Jove's high counsel flies
With those wings that shall bear up us, Jove's, that both earth and heav'n,
Both men and gods, sustains and rules; one augury is giv'n
To order all men best of all: fight for thy country's right.
But why fear'st thou our further charge? For though the dangerous fight
Strew all men here about the fleet, yet thou need'st never fear
To bear their rates; thy wary heart will never trust thee where
An enemy's look is, and yet fight; for, if thou dar'st abstain,
Or whisper into any ear an abstinence so vain   260
As thou advisest, never fear that any foe shall take
Thy life from thee, for 'tis this lance.' This said, all forwards make,
Himself the first: yet before him exulting Clamour flew,
And thunder-loving Jupiter from lofty Ida blew
A storm that usher'd their assault, and made them charge like him:
It drave directly on the fleet a dust so fierce and dim,
That it amaz'd the Grecians, but was a grace divine
To Hector and his following troops, who wholly did incline
To him, being now in grace with Jove: and so put boldly on
To raze the rampire, in whose height they fiercely set upon   270
The parapets, and pull'd them down, raz'd every foremost fight,
And all the buttresses of stone that held their tow'rs upright
They tore away with crows of iron, and hop'd to ruin all.

    The Greeks yet stood, and still repair'd the fore-fights of their wall
With hides of oxen, and from thence they pour'd down stones in show'rs
Upon the underminers' heads. Within the foremost tow'rs
Both the Ajaces had command; who answer'd every part
Th' assaulters, and their soldiers, repress'd, and put in heart,
Repairing valour as their wall: spake some fair, some reprov'd,
Whoever made not good his place; and thus they all sorts mov'd: 280
    'O countrymen, now need in aid would have excess be spent:
The excellent must be admir'd, the meanest excellent,
The worst, do well; in changing war all should not be alike,
Nor any idle: which to know, fits all, lest Hector strike
Your minds with frights, as ears with threats; forward be all your hands,
Urge one another: this doubt down, that now betwixt us stands,
Jove will go with us to their walls.' To this effect aloud
Spake both the princes, and as high (with this) th' expulsion flow'd.
And as in winter time, when Jove his cold sharp javelins throws
Amongst us mortals, and is mov'd to white earth with his snows;   290
(The winds asleep) he freely pours, till highest prominents,
Hill tops, low meadows, and the fields that crown with most contents
The toils of men, seaports and shores, are hid, and every place

But floods (that snow's fair tender flakes, as their own brood, embrace):
So both sides cover'd earth with stones, so both for life contend,
To show their sharpness; through the war, uproar stood up on end.
Nor had great Hector and his friends the rampire overrun,
If heav'n's great counsellor, high Jove, had not inflam'd his son
Sarpedon (like the forest's king when he on oxen flies)
Against the Grecians: his round targe he to his arm applies,   300
Brass-leav'd without, and all within, thick ox-hides quilted hard,
The verge nail'd round with rods of gold; and with two darts prepar'd
He leads his people: as ye see a mountain-lion fare,
Long kept from prey; in forcing which, his high mind makes him dare
Assault upon the whole full fold, though guarded never so
With well-arm'd men and eager dogs; away he will not go,
But venture on, and either snatch a prey, or be a prey.
So far'd divine Sarpedon's mind, resolv'd to force his way
Through all the fore-fights, and the wall: yet since he did not see
Others as great as he in name, as great in mind as he,   310
He spake to Glaucus: 'Glaucus, say, why are we honour'd more
Than other men of Lycia in place, with greater store
Of meats and cups, with goodlier roofs, delightsome gardens, walks,
More lands and better, so much wealth that court and country talks
Of us and our possessions, and every way we go,
Gaze on us as we were their gods? This where we dwell is so:
The shores of Xanthus ring of this, and shall we not exceed
As much in merit as in noise? Come, be we great in deed
As well as look; shine not in gold, but in the flames of fight,
That so our neat-arm'd Lycians may say: "See, these are right   320
Our kings, our rulers; these deserve to eat and drink the best;
These govern not ingloriously: these thus exceed the rest,
Do more than they command to do." O friend, if keeping back
Would keep back age from us, and death, and that we might not wrack
In this life's human sea at all, but that deferring now
We shunn'd death ever, nor would I half this vain valour show,
Nor glorify a folly so, to wish thee to advance:
But since we must go, though not here, and that, besides the chance
Propos'd now, there are infinite fates of other sort in death,
Which (neither to be fled nor 'scap'd) a man must sink beneath,   330
Come, try we if this sort be ours: and either render thus
Glory to others, or make them resign the like to us.'

    This motion Glaucus shifted not, but (without words) obey'd;
Foreright went both, a mighty troop of Lycians followed.
Which by Menestheus observ'd, his hair stood up on end,
For at the tow'r where he had charge, he saw Calamity bend

Her horrid brows in their approach. He threw his looks about
The whole fights near, to see what chief might help the misery out
Of his poor soldiers, and beheld where both th' Ajaces fought,
And Teucer, newly come from fleet: whom it would profit nought   340
To call, since tumult on their helms, shield, and upon the ports
Laid such loud claps; for every way, defences of all sorts
Were adding, as Troy took away and Clamour flew so high
Her wings struck heav'n, and drown'd all voice. The two dukes yet so nigh
And at the offer of assault, he to th' Ajaces sent
Thoös the herald with this charge: 'Run to the regiment
Of both th' Ajaces, and call both, for both were better here,
Since here will slaughter, instantly, be more enforc'd than there.
The Lycian captains this way make, who in the fights of stand
Have often show'd much excellence: yet if laborious hand   350
Be there more needful than I hope, at least afford us some:
Let Ajax Telamonius and th' archer Teucer come.'
    The herald hasted, and arriv'd; and both th' Ajaces told,
That Peteus' noble son desir'd their little labour would
Employ itself in succouring him. Both their supplies were best,
Since death assail'd his quarter most: for on it fiercely press'd
The well-prov'd mighty Lycian chiefs. Yet if the service there
Allow'd not both, he pray'd that one part of his charge would bear,
And that was Ajax Telamon, with whom he wish'd would come
The archer Teucer. Telamon left instantly his room   360
To strong Lycomedes, and will'd Ajax Oïliades
With him to make up his supply, and fill with courages
The Grecian hearts till his return, which should be instantly
When he had well reliev'd his friend. With this the company
Of Teucer he took to his aid – Teucer, that did descend
(As Ajax did) from Telamon: with these two did attend
Pandion, that bore Teucer's bow. When to Menestheus' tow'r
They came alongst the wall, they found him, and his heart'ned pow'r
Toiling in making strong their fort; the Lycian princes set
Black-whirlwind-like, with both their pow'rs, upon the parapet.   370
Ajax, and all, resisted them. Clamour amongst them rose:
The slaughter Ajax led, who first the last dear sight did close
Of strong Epicles, that war-friend to Jove's great Lycian son.
Amongst the high munition heap, a mighty marble stone
Lay highest, near the pinnacle; a stone of such a paise
That one of this times' strongest men, with both hands, could not raise.
Yet this did Ajax rouse and throw, and all in sherds did drive
Epicles' four-topp'd casque and skull; who (as ye see one dive
In some deep river) left his height; life left his bones withal.

Teucer shot Glaucus (rushing up yet higher on the wall)   380
Where naked he discern'd his arm, and made him steal retreat
From that hot service, lest some Greek, with an insulting threat,
(Beholding it) might fright the rest. Sarpedon much was griev'd
At Glaucus' parting, yet fought on, and his great heart reliev'd
A little with Alcmaon's blood, surnam'd Thestorides,
Whose life he hurl'd out with his lance; which following through the prease,
He drew from him. Down from the tow'r Alcmaon dead it strook,
His fair arms ringing out his death. Then fierce Sarpedon took
In his strong hand the battlement, and down he tore it quite,
The wall stripp'd naked, and broad way for entry and full fight,   390
He made the many. Against him Ajax and Teucer made;
Teucer the rich belt on his breast did with a shaft invade,
But Jupiter averted death; who would not see his son
Die at the tails of th' Achive ships: Ajax did fetch his run,
And (with his lance) struck through the targe of that brave Lycian king;
Yet kept he it from further pass, nor did it anything
Dismay his mind, although his men stood off from that high way
His valour made them; which he kept, and hop'd that stormy day
Should ever make his glory clear. His men's fault thus he blam'd:
'O Lycians, why are your hot spirits so quickly disinflam'd?   400
Suppose me ablest of you all: 'tis hard for me alone
To ruin such a wall as this, and make confusion
Way to their navy; lend your hands. What many can dispatch,
One cannot think: the noble work of many hath no match.'

The wise king's just rebuke did strike a reverence to his will
Through all his soldiers; all stood in; and 'gainst all th' Achives still
Made strong their squadrons; insomuch, that to the adverse side
The work show'd mighty; and the wall, when 'twas within descried,
No easy service; yet the Greeks could neither free the wall
Of these brave Lycians, that held firm the place they first did scale,   410
Nor could the Lycians from their fort the sturdy Grecians drive,
Nor reach their fleet. But as two men about the limits strive
Of land that toucheth in the field; their measures in their hands,
They mete their parts out curiously, and either stiffly stands,
That so far is his right in law, both hugely set on fire
About a passing little ground: so greedily aspire
Both these foes to their several ends; and all exhaust their most
About the very battlements (for yet no more was lost).

With sword and fire they vex'd for them their targets hugely round
With ox-hides lin'd, and bucklers light, and many a ghastly wound   420
The stern steel gave for that one prize; whereof though some receiv'd
Their portions on their naked backs, yet others were bereav'd

Of brave lives, face-turn'd, through their shields: tow'rs, bulwarks everywhere
Were freckled with the blood of men; nor yet the Greeks did bear
Base back-turn'd faces, nor their foes would therefore be out-fac'd.
But as a spinster poor and just ye sometimes see strait-lac'd
About the weighing of her web, who (careful) having charge
For which she would provide some means, is loth to be too large
In giving, or in taking weight; but ever with her hand
Is doing with the weights and wool, till both in just poise stand: 430
So ev'nly stood it with these foes, till Jove to Hector gave
The turning of the scales; who first against the rampire drave,
And spake so loud that all might hear: 'O stand not at the pale,
Brave Trojan friends, but mend your hands: up, and break through the wall,
And make a bonfire of their fleet.' All heard, and all in heaps
Got scaling-ladders, and aloft. In mean space, Hector leaps
Upon the port, from whose out-part he tore a massy stone;
Thick downwards, upward edg'd it was – it was so huge an one
That two vast yeomen of most strength (such as these times beget)
Could not from earth lift to a cart: yet he did brandish it   440
Alone (Saturnius made it light), and swinging it as nought,
He came before the planky gates, that all for strength were wrought,
And kept the port: two-fold they were, and with two rafters barr'd,
High, and strong lock'd: he rais'd the stone, bent to the hurl so hard,
And made it with so main a strength that all the gates did crack,
The rafters left them, and the folds one from another brake;
The hinges piecemeal flew, and through the fervent little rock
Thunder'd a passage; with his weight th' inwall his breast did knock,
And in rush'd Hector, fierce and grim as any stormy night;
His brass arms round about his breast reflected terrible light.   450
Each arm held up, held each a dart: his presence call'd up all
The dreadful spirits his being held, that to the threaten'd wall
None but the gods might check his way: his eyes were furnaces;
And thus he look'd back, call'd in all: all fir'd their courages,
And in they flow'd: the Grecians fled, their fleet now and their freight
Ask'd all their rescue: Greece went down; Tumult was at his height.

THE END OF THE TWELFTH BOOK

BOOK THIRTEEN

The Argument

Neptune (in pity of the Greeks' hard plight),
Like Calchas, both th' Ajaces doth excite,
And others to repel the charging foe.
Idomeneus bravely doth bestow
His kingly forces, and doth sacrifice
Othryoneus to the Destinies,
With divers others. Fair Deiphobus,
And his prophetic brother Hellenus,
Are wounded. But the great Priamides
(Gathering his forces) heartens their address
Against the enemy; and then the field
A mighty death on either side doth yield.

Another Argument

The Greeks, with Troy's bold power dismay'd,
Are cheer'd by Neptune's secret aid.

BOOK THIRTEEN

JOVE HELPING HECTOR, and his host, thus close to th' Achive fleet,
He let them then their own strengths try, and season there their sweet
With ceaseless toils and grievances. For now he turn'd his face,
Look'd down, and view'd the far-off land of well-rode men in Thrace,
Of the renown'd milk-nourish'd men, the Hippemolgians,
Long-liv'd, most just and innocent, and close-fought Mysians.
Nor turn'd he any more to Troy his ever-shining eyes,
Because he thought not any one of all the deities
(When his care left th' indifferent field) would aid on either side.
But this security in Jove the great Sea-Rector spied,   10
Who sat aloft on th' utmost top of shady Samothrace,
And view'd the fight. His chosen seat stood in so brave a place
That Priam's city, th' Achive ships, all Ida did appear
To his full view; who from the sea was therefore seated there.
He took much ruth to see the Greeks by Troy sustain such ill,
And (mightily incens'd with Jove) stoop'd straight from that steep hill,
That shook as he flew off, so hard his parting press'd the height.
The woods, and all the great hills near, trembled beneath the weight
Of his immortal moving feet: three steps he only took,
Before he far-off Aegas reach'd; but with the fourth, it shook   20
With his dread entry. In the depth of those seas he did hold
His bright and glorious palace, built of never-rusting gold;
And there arriv'd, he put in coach his brazen-footed steeds,
All golden maned, and pac'd with wings; and all in golden weeds
He cloth'd himself. The golden scourge (most elegantly done)
He took, and mounted to his seat: and then the god begun
To drive his chariot through the waves. From whirlpits every way
The whales exulted under him, and knew their king: the sea
For joy did open, and his horse so swift and lightly flew,
The under-axletree of brass no drop of water drew: 30
And thus these deathless coursers brought their king to th' Achive ships.
    'Twixt th' Imber cliffs and Tenedos a certain cavern creeps
Into the deep sea's gulfy breast, and there th' Earth-shaker stay'd
His forward steeds, took them from coach, and heavenly fodder laid
In reach before them. Their brass hoofs he girt with gyves of gold,

Not to be broken, nor dissolv'd, to make them firmly hold
A fit attendance on their king; who went to th' Achive host,
Which, like to tempests or wild flames, the clust'ring Trojans tost,
Insatiably valorous, in Hector's like command,
High sounding and resounding shouts: for hope cheer'd every hand,   40
To make the Greek fleet now their prize, and all the Greeks destroy.
But Neptune, circler of the earth, with fresh heart did employ
The Grecian hands. In strength of voice and body he did take
Calchas' resemblance, and (of all) th' Ajaces first bespake,
Who of themselves were free enough: 'Ajaces! You alone
Sustain the common good of Greece, in ever putting on
The memory of fortitude, and flying shameful flight.
Elsewhere, the desp'rate hands of Troy could give me no affright,
The brave Greeks have withstood their worst: but this our mighty wall
Being thus transcended by their pow'r, grave fear doth much appal   50
My careful spirits, lest we feel some fatal mischief here,
Where Hector, raging like a flame, doth in his charge appear,
And boasts himself the best god's son. Be you conceited so,
And fire so, more than human spirits, that god may seem to do
In your deeds: and, with such thoughts cheer'd, others to such exhort,
And such resistance; these great minds will in as great a sort
Strengthen your bodies, and force check to all great Hector's charge,
Though ne'er so spirit-like, and though Jove still (past himself) enlarge
His sacred actions.' Thus he touch'd with his fork'd sceptre's point
The breasts of both; fill'd both their spirits, and made up every joint   60
With pow'r responsive: when hawk-like, swift, and set sharp to fly,
That fiercely stooping from a rock, inaccessible and high,
Cuts through a field, and sets a fowl (not being of her kind)
Hard, and gets ground still: Neptune so left these two, either's mind
Beyond themselves rais'd. Of both which, Oïleus first discern'd
The masking deity, and said: 'Ajax! Some god hath warn'd
Our pow'rs to fight, and save our fleet. He put on him the hue
Of th' augur Calchas: by his pace, in leaving us, I knew,
Without all question, 'twas a god: the gods are easily known,
And in my tender breast I feel a greater spirit blown   70
To execute affairs of fight; I find my hands so free
To all high motion, and my feet seem feather'd under me.'
This Telamonius thus receiv'd: 'So too, my thoughts, my hands
Burn with desire to toss my lance; each foot beneath me stands
Bare on bright fire to use his speed; my heart is rais'd so high,
That to encounter Hector's self I long insatiately.'
     While these thus talk'd, as overjoy'd with study for the fight
(Which god had stirr'd up in their spirits), the same god did excite

The Greeks that were behind at fleet, refreshing their free hearts
And joints, being ev'n dissolv'd with toil; and (seeing the desp'rate parts   80
Play'd by the Trojans, past their wall) grief struck them, and their eyes
Sweat tears from under their sad lids, their instant destinies
Never supposing they could 'scape. But Neptune stepping in,
With ease stirr'd up the able troops, and did at first begin
With Teucer and Peneleus, th' heroë Leïtus,
Deïpirus, Meriones, and young Antilochus,
All expert in the deeds of arms: 'O youths of Greece,' said he,
'What change is this? In your brave fight I only look'd to see
Our fleet's whole safety; and if you neglect the harmful field,
Now shines the day when Greece to Troy must all her honours yield.   90
O grief! So great a miracle, and horrible to sight,
As now I see, I never thought could have profan'd the light:
The Trojans brave us at our ships, that have been heretofore
Like faint and fearful deer in woods, distracted evermore
With every sound, and yet 'scape not, but prove the torn-up fare
Of lynces, wolves and leopards, as never born to war:
Nor durst these Trojans at first siege, in any least degree
Expect your strength, or stand one shock of Grecian chivalry.
Yet now, far from their walls they dare fight at our fleet maintain,
All by our general's cowardice, that doth infect his men;   100
Who (still at odds with him) for that will needs themselves neglect,
And suffer slaughter in their ships. Suppose there was defect
(Beyond all question) in our king, to wrong Aeacides,
And he, for his particular wreak, from all assistance cease,
We must not cease t' assist ourselves. Forgive our general then,
And quickly too: apt to forgive are all good-minded men.
Yet you (quite void of their good minds) give good, in you quite lost,
For ill in others, though ye be the worthiest of your host.
As old as I am, I would scorn to fight with one that flies,
Or leaves the fight as you do now. The general slothful lies,   110
And you (though slothful too) maintain with him a fight of spleen.
Out, out, I hate ye from my heart, ye rotten-minded men:
In this ye add an ill that's worse than all your sloth's dislikes.
But as I know to all your hearts my reprehension strikes,
So thither let just shame strike too; for while you stand still here
A mighty fight swarms at your fleet, great Hector rageth there,
Hath burst the long bar and the gates.' Thus Neptune rous'd these men,
And round about th' Ajaces did their phalanxes maintain
Their station firm; whom Mars himself (had he amongst them gone)
Could not disparage, nor Jove's Maid, that sets men fiercer on: 120
For now the best were chosen out, and they receiv'd th' advance

Of Hector and his men so full, that lance was lin'd with lance,
Shields thicken'd with opposed shields, targets to targets nail'd:
Helms stuck to helms, and man to man grew, they so close assail'd:
Plum'd casks were hang'd in either's plumes, all join'd so close their stands;
Their lances stood, thrust out so thick by such all-daring hands.
All bent their firm breasts to the point, and made sad fight their joy.
Of both, Troy all in heaps struck first, and Hector first of Troy.
And as a round piece of a rock, which with a winter's flood
Is from his top torn, when a show'r, pour'd from a bursten cloud,   130
Hath broke the natural bond it held within the rough steep rock,
And jumping, it flies down the woods, resounding every shock,
And on, uncheck'd, it headlong leaps, till in a plain it stay;
And then (though never so impell'd) it stirs not any way:
So Hector hereto throated threats, to go to sea in blood,
And reach the Grecian ships and tents, without being once withstood.
But when he fell into the strengths the Grecians did maintain,
And that they fought upon the square, he stood as fetter'd then.
And so the adverse sons of Greece laid on with swords and darts
(Whose both ends hurt), that they repell'd his worst, and he converts   140
His threats, by all means, to retreats; yet made as he retir'd
Only t' encourage those behind; and thus those men inspir'd:

    'Trojans! Dardanians! Lycians! All warlike friends, stand close;
The Greeks can never bear me long, though tow'r-like they oppose.
This lance, be sure, will be their spoil: if ev'n the best of gods,
High-thund'ring Juno's husband, stirs my spirit with true abodes.'

    With this all strengths and minds he mov'd; but young Deiphobus,
Old Priam's son, amongst them all was chiefly virtuous.
He bore before him his round shield, tripp'd lightly through the prease,
At all parts cover'd with his shield: and him Meriones   150
Charg'd with a glitt'ring dart, that took his bull-hide orby shield,
Yet pierc'd it not, but in the top itself did piecemeal yield.

    Deiphobus thrust forth his targe, and fear'd the broken ends
Of strong Meriones his lance, who now turn'd to his friends;
The great heroë scorning much by such a chance to part
With lance and conquest, forth he went to fetch another dart,
Left at his tent. The rest fought on, the clamour heighten'd there
Was most unmeasur'd. Teucer first did flesh the massacre,
And slew a goodly man at arms, the soldier Imbrius,
The son of Mentor, rich in horse; he dwelt at Pedasus   160
Before the sons of Greece sieg'd Troy; from whence he married
Medesicasté, one that sprung of Priam's bastard-bed.
But when the Greek ships (double-oar'd) arriv'd at Ilion,
To Ilion he return'd, and prov'd beyond comparison

Amongst the Trojans; he was lodg'd with Priam, who held dear
His natural sons no more than him: yet him, beneath the ear,
The son of Telamon attain'd, and drew his lance. He fell:
As when an ash on some hill's top (itself topp'd wondrous well)
The steel hews down, and he presents his young leaves to the spoil:
So fell he, and his fair arms groan'd, which Teucer long'd to spoil,   170
And in he ran, and Hector in, who sent a shining lance
At Teucer, who (beholding it) slipp'd by, and gave it chance
On Actor's son, Amphimachus, whose breast it struck; and in
Flew Hector, at his sounding fall, with full intent to win
The tempting helmet from his head; but Ajax with a dart
Reach'd Hector at his rushing in, yet touch'd not any part
About his body; it was hid quite through with horrid brass.
The boss yet of his targe it took, whose firm stuff stay'd the pass,
And he turn'd safe from both the trunks: both which the Grecians bore
From off the field; Amphimachus, Menestheus did restore,   180
And Stichius, to th' Achaian strength: th' Ajaces (that were pleas'd
Still most with most hot services) on Trojan Imbrius seiz'd.
And, as from sharply-bitten hounds a brace of lions force
A new-slain goat, and through the woods bear in their jaws the corse
Aloft, lift up into the air: so up into the skies
Bore both th' Ajaces Imbrius, and made his arms their prize.

 Yet, not content, Oïleades, enrag'd to see there dead
His much-belov'd Amphimachus, he hew'd off Imbrius' head,
Which (swinging round) bowl-like he toss'd amongst the Trojan prease,
And full at Hector's feet it fell. Amphimachus' decease   190
(Being nephew to the god of waves) much vex'd the deity's mind,
And to the ships and tents he march'd, yet more to make inclin'd
The Grecians to the Trojan bane. In hasting to which end,
Idomeneus met with him, returning from a friend,
Whose ham late hurt, his men brought off, and having giv'n command
To his physicians for his cure (much fir'd to put his hand
To Troy's repulse), he left his tent. Him (like Andremon's son,
Prince Thoas, that in Pleuron rul'd, and lofty Calidon,
Th' Aetolian pow'rs, and like a god was of his subjects lov'd)
Neptune encounter'd: and but this his forward spirit mov'd:.   200

 'Idomeneus, prince of Crete! O whither now are fled
Those threats in thee, with which the rest the Trojans menaced?'

 'O Thoas,' he replied, 'no one of all our host stands now
In any question of reproof, as I am let to know –
And why is my intelligence false? We all know how to fight,
And (fear disanimating none) all do our knowledge right.
Nor can our harms accuse our sloth, not one from work we miss:

The great god only works our ill, whose pleasure now it is,
That far from home, in hostile fields, and with inglorious fate,
Some Greeks should perish. But do thou, O Thoas (that of late   210
Hast prov'd a soldier, and was wont, where thou hast sloth beheld,
To chide it, and exhort to pains) now hate to be repell'd,
And set on all men.' He replied, 'I would to heav'n that he
Who ever this day doth abstain from battle willingly,
May never turn his face from Troy, but here become the prey
And scorn of dogs. Come then, take arms, and let our kind assay
Join both our forces; though but two, yet being both combin'd,
The work of many single hands we may perform; we find
That virtue co-augmented thrives in men of little mind,
But we have singly match'd the great.' This said, the god again   220
(With all his conflicts) visited the vent'rous fight of men.
The king turn'd to his tent, rich arms put on his breast, and took
Two darts in hand, and forth he flew; his haste on made him look
Much like a fiery meteor, with which Jove's sulph'ry hand
Opes heaven, and hurls about the air bright flashes, showing aland
Abodes, that ever run before tempest and plagues to men:
So, in his swift pace, show'd his arms; he was encounter'd then
By his good friend Meriones, yet near his tent, to whom
Thus spake the pow'r of Idomen: 'What reason makes thee come,
Thou son of Molus, my most lov'd, thus leaving fight alone?   230
Is 't for some wound? The javelin's head (still sticking in the bone)
Desir'st thou ease of? Bring'st thou news? Or what is it that brings
Thy presence hither? Be assur'd, my spirit needs no stings
To this hot conflict. Of myself thou seest I come, and loth
For any tent's love to deserve the hateful taint of sloth.'

   He answer'd, only for a dart he that retreat did make
(Were any left him at his tent), for that he had, he brake
On proud Deiphobus his shield. 'Is one dart all?' said he.
'Take one and twenty,' if thou like, 'for in my tent they be.
They stand there shining by the walls: I took them as my prize   240
From those false Trojans I have slain. And this is not the guise
Of one that loves his tent, or fights afar off with his foe:
But since I love fight, therefore doth my martial star bestow –
Besides those darts – helms, targets boss'd, and corslets bright as day.'

   'So I,' said Merion,'at my tent and sable bark, may say
I many Trojan spoils retain: but now, not near they be,
To serve me for my present use; and therefore ask I thee,
Not that I lack a fortitude to store me with my own:
For ever in the foremost fights that render men renown,
I fight, when any fight doth stir, and this perhaps may well   250

Be hid to others, but thou know'st, and I to thee appeal.'
  'I know,' replied the king, 'how much thou weigh'st in every worth.
What need'st thou therefore utter this? If we should now choose forth
The worthiest men for ambushes in all our fleet and host –
For ambushes are services that try men's virtues most,
Since there the fearful and the firm will as they are appear,
The fearful alt'ring still his hue, and rests not anywhere,
Nor is his spirit capable of th' ambush constancy,
But riseth, changeth still his place, and croucheth curious
On his bent haunches, half his height scarce seen above the ground,   260
For fear to be seen, yet must see, his heart with many a bound
Off'ring to leap out of his breast, and (ever fearing death)
The coldness of it makes him gnash, and half shakes out his teeth;
Where men of valour neither fear nor ever change their looks,
From lodging th' ambush till it rise, but since there must be strokes,
Wish to be quickly in their midst – thy strength and hand in these
Who should reprove? For if far off, or fighting in the prease,
Thou shouldst be wounded, I am sure the dart that gave the wound
Should not be drawn out of thy back, or make thy neck the ground,
But meet thy belly or thy breast, in thrusting further yet   270
When thou art furthest, till the first, and before him thou get.
But on; like children let not us stand bragging thus, but do –
Lest some hear, and past measure chide, that we stand still and woo.
Go, choose a better dart, and make Mars yield a better chance.'

    This said, Mars-swift Meriones with haste a brazen lance
Took from his tent, and overtook (most careful of the wars)
Idomeneus. And such two in field as harmful Mars
And Terror, his beloved son, that without terror fights,
And is of such strength, that in war the frighter he affrights,
When, out of Thrace, they both take arms against th' Ephyran bands,   280
Or 'gainst the great-soul'd Phlegians, nor favour their own hands,
But give the grace to others still: in such sort to the fight
March'd these two managers of men, in armours full of light.

    And first spake Merion: 'On which part, son of Deucalion,
Serves thy mind to invade the fight? Is t' best to set upon
The Trojans in our battle's aid, the right or left-hand wing?
For all parts I suppose employ'd.' To this the Cretan king
Thus answer'd: 'In our navy's midst are others that assist,
The two Ajaces, Teucer too, with shafts the expertest
Of all the Grecians, and, though small, is great in fights of stand.   290
And these, though huge he be of strength, will serve to fill the hand
Of Hector's self, that Priamist, that studier for blows:
It shall be call'd a deed of height for him (ev'n suff'ring throes

For knocks still) to outlabour them, and bett'ring their tough hands,
Enflame our fleet. If Jove himself cast not his firebrands
Amongst our navy, that affair no man can bring to field:
Great Ajax Telamonius to none alive will yield,
That yields to death, and whose life takes Ceres' nutritions,
That can be cut with any iron, or pash'd with mighty stones.
Not to Aeacides himself he yields for combats set,   300
Though clear he must give place for pace and free swing of his feet.
Since, then, the battle (being our place of most care) is made good
By his high valour, let our aid see all pow'rs be withstood,
That charge the left wing: and to that let us direct our course,
Where quickly feel we this hot foe, or make him feel our force.'
    This order'd, swift Meriones went, and forewent his king,
Till both arriv'd where one enjoin'd. When in the Greeks' left wing
The Trojans saw the Cretan king, like fire in fortitude,
And his attendant in bright arms so gloriously indu'd,
Both cheering the sinister troops, all at the king address'd,   310
And so the skirmish at their sterns on both parts were increas'd –
That as from hollow bustling winds engender'd storms arise,
When dust doth chiefly clog the ways, which up into the skies
The wanton tempest ravisheth, begetting night of day:
So came together both the foes; both lusted to assay,
And work with quick steel either's death. Man's fierce corruptress, Fight,
Set up her bristles in the field, with lances long and light,
Which thick fell foul on either's face: the splendour of the steel,
In new-scour'd curets, radiant casks, and burnish'd shields, did seal
Th' assailer's eyes up. He sustain'd a huge spirit that was glad   320
To see that labour, or in soul that stood not stricken sad.
    Thus these two disagreeing gods, old Saturn's mighty sons,
Afflicted these heroic men with huge oppressions.
Jove honouring Aeacides (to let the Greeks still try
Their want without him) would bestow yet still the victory
On Hector and the Trojan pow'r; yet for Aeacides,
And honour of his mother queen, great goddess of the seas,
He would not let proud Ilion see the Grecians quite destroy'd:
And therefore from the hoary deep he suffer'd so employ'd
Great Neptune in the Grecian aid; who griev'd for them, and storm'd   330
Extremely at his brother Jove. Yet both one goddess form'd,
And one soil bred: but Jupiter precedence took in birth,
And had more knowledge, for which cause the other came not forth
Of his wet kingdom but with care of not being seen t' excite
The Grecian host, and like a man appear'd and made the fight.
So these gods made men's valours great, but equall'd them with war

As harmful as their hearts were good, and stretch'd those chains as far
On both sides as their limbs could bear: in which they were involv'd
Past breach or loosing, that their knees might therefore be dissolv'd.
Then, though a half-grey man he were, Crete's sov'reign did excite   340
The Greeks to blows, and flew upon the Trojans, ev'n to flight:
For he, in sight of all the host, Othryoneus slew,
That from Cabesus with the fame of those wars thither drew
His new-come forces, and requir'd, without respect of dow'r,
Cassandra, fair'st of Priam's race, assuring with his pow'r –
A mighty labour – to expel in their despite from Troy
The sons of Greece. The king did vow (that done) he should enjoy
His goodliest daughter. He, in trust of that fair purchase, fought,
And at him threw the Cretan king a lance, that singled out
This great assumer, whom it struck just in his navel's stead;   350
His brazen curets helping nought resign'd him to the dead.
Then did the conqueror exclaim, and thus insulted then:
    'Othryoneus, I will praise beyond all mortal men
Thy living virtues, if thou wilt now perfect the brave vow
Thou mad'st to Priam, for the wife he promis'd to bestow.
And where he should have kept his word, there we assure thee here,
To give thee for thy princely wife the fairest and most dear
Of our great general's female race, which from his Argive hall
We all will wait upon to Troy, if with our aids and all,
Thou wilt but raze this well-built town. Come, therefore, follow me,   360
That in our ships we may conclude this royal match with thee:
I'll be no jot worse than my word.' With that he took his feet
And dragg'd him through the fervent fight; in which did Asius meet
The victor, to inflict revenge. He came on foot before
His horse, that on his shoulders breath'd, so closely evermore
His coachman led them to his lord: who held a huge desire
To strike the king, but he struck first, and underneath his chin,
At his throat's height, through th' other side his eager lance drave in;
And down he bustled like an oak, a poplar, or a pine,
Hewn down for shipwood, and so lay: his fall did so decline   370
The spirit of his charioteer, that lest he should incense
The victor to impair his spoil, he durst not drive from thence
His horse and chariot: and so pleas'd with that respective part
Antilochus, that for his fear he reach'd him with a dart
About his belly's midst; and down his sad corse fell beneath
The richly-builded chariot, there labouring out his breath.
The horse Antilochus took off; when, griev'd for this event,
Deiphobus drew passing near, and at the victor sent
A shining javelin; which he saw, and shunn'd, with gath'ring round

His body in his all-round shield, at whose top, with a sound,   380
It overflew; yet seizing there, it did not idly fly
From him that wing'd it; his strong hand still drave it mortally
On prince Hypsenor; it did pierce his liver, underneath
The veins it passeth: his shrunk knees submitted him to death.
And then did lov'd Deiphobus miraculously vaunt:
'Now Asius lies not unreveng'd, nor doth his spirit want
The joy I wish it, though it be now ent'ring the strong gate
Of mighty Pluto, since this hand hath sent him down a mate.'
    This glory in him griev'd the Greeks, and chiefly the great mind
Of martial Antilochus, who, though to grief inclin'd,   390
He left not yet his friend, but ran and hid him with his shield;
And to him came two lovely friends, that freed him from the field,
Mecisteus, son of Echius, and the right nobly born
Alastar, bearing him to fleet, and did extremely mourn.
    Idomeneus sunk not yet, but held his nerves entire,
His mind much less deficient, being fed with firm desire
To hide more Trojans in dim night, or sink himself in guard
Of his lov'd countrymen. And then Alcathous prepar'd
Work for his valour, off'ring fate his own destruction.
A great heroë, and had grace to be the loved son   400
Of Aesietes, son-in-law to prince Aeneas' sire,
Hippodamia marrying, who most enflam'd the fire
Of her dear parents' love, and took precedence in her birth
Of all their daughters, and as much exceeded in her worth
(For beauty answer'd with her mind, and both with huswif'ry)
All the fair beauty of young dames that us'd her company;
And therefore (being the worthiest dame) the worthiest man did wed
Of ample Troy. Him Neptune stoop'd beneath the royal force
Of Idomen, his sparkling eyes deluding, and the course
Of his illustrious lineaments so out of nature bound   410
That back nor forward he could stir, but – as he grew to ground –
Stood like a pillar or high tree, and neither mov'd nor fear'd:
When straight the royal Cretan's dart in his mid breast appear'd;
It brake the curets that were proof to every other dart,
Yet now they cleft and rung, the lance stuck shaking in his heart:
His heart with panting made it shake. But Mars did now remit
The greatness of it, and the king, now quitting the brag fit
Of glory in Deiphobus, thus terribly exclaim'd:
    'Deiphobus, now may we think that we are evenly fam'd,
That three for one have sent to Dis. But come, change blows with me;   420
Thy vaunts for him thou slew'st were vain. Come, wretch, that thou may'st see
What issue Jove hath; Jove begot Minos, the strength of Crete;

Minos begot Deucalion; Deucalion did beget
Me Idomen, now Creta's king, that here my ships have brought,
To bring thyself, thy father, friends, all Ilion's pomp to nought.'
　　Deiphobus at two ways stood, in doubt to call some one
(With some retreat) to be his aid, or try the chance alone.
At last, the first seem'd best to him, and back he went to call
Anchises' son to friend; who stood in troop the last of all,
Where still he serv'd: which made him still incense against the king,　　430
That being amongst his best their peer, he grac'd not anything
His wrong'd deserts. Deiphobus spake to him, standing near:
'Aeneas, prince of Troÿans, if any touch appear
Of glory in thee, thou must now assist thy sister's lord,
And one that to thy tend'rest youth did careful guard afford,
Alcathous, whom Creta's king hath chiefly slain to thee,
His right most challenging thy hand: come, therefore, follow me.'
　　This much excited his good mind, and set his heart on fire,
Against the Cretan: who, child-like, dissolv'd not in his ire,
But stood him firm; as when in hills a strength-relying boar,　　440
Alone and hearing hunters come, whom tumult flies before,
Up thrusts his bristles, whets his tusks, sets fire on his red eyes,
And in his brave prepar'd repulse doth dogs and men despise:
So stood the famous-for-his-lance, nor shunn'd the coming charge
That resolute Aeneas brought; yet since the odds was large,
He call'd with good right to his aid war-skill'd Ascalaphus,
Aphareus, Meriones, the strong Deipyrus,
And Nestor's honourable son: 'Come near, my friends,' said he,
'And add your aids to me alone. Fear taints me worthily,
Though firm I stand, and show it not: Aeneas great in fight,　　450
And one that bears youth in his flow'r (that bears the greatest might)
Comes on, with aim direct at me: had I his youthful limb
To bear my mind, he should yield fame, or I would yield it him.'
　　This said, all held, in many souls, one ready helpful mind,
Clapp'd shields and shoulders, and stood close. Aeneas (not inclin'd
With more presumption than the king) call'd aid as well as he –
Divine Agenor, Helen's love, who follow'd instantly,
And all their forces following them, as after bell-wethers
The whole flocks follow to their drink; which sight the shepherd cheers:
Nor was Aeneas' joy less mov'd to see such troops attend　　460
His honour'd person; and all these fought close about his friend.
But two of them, past all the rest, had strong desire to shed
The blood of either: Idomen, and Cytherea's seed.
Aeneas first bestow'd his lance, which th' other seeing shunn'd,
And that, thrown from an idle hand, stuck trembling in the ground.

But Idomen's, discharg'd at him, had no such vain success,
Which Oemomaus' entrails found, in which it did impress
His sharp pile to his fall: his palms tore his returning earth.
Idomeneus straight stepp'd in, and pluck'd his javelin forth,
But could not spoil his goodly arms, they press'd him so with darts.   470
And now the long toil of the fight had spent his vigorous parts,
And made them less apt to avoid the foe that should advance,
Or (when himself advanc'd again) to run and fetch his lance.
And therefore in stiff fights of stand he spent the cruel day:
When coming softly from the slain Deiphobus gave way
To his bright javelin at the king, whom he could never brook,
But then he lost his envy too: his lance yet deadly took
Ascalaphus, the son of Mars; quite through his shoulder flew
The violent head, and down he fell. Nor yet by all means knew
Wide-throated Mars his son was fall'n, but in Olympus' top   480
Sat canopied with golden clouds. Jove's counsel had shut up
Both him and all the other gods from that time's equal task,
Which now about Ascalaphus Strife set: his shining casque
Deiphobus had forc'd from him, but instantly leap'd in
Mars-swift Meriones, and struck, with his long javelin,
The right arm of Deiphobus, which made his hand let fall
The sharp-topp'd helmet, the press'd earth resounding therewithal.
When, vulture-like, Meriones rush'd in again and drew,
From out the low parts of his arm his javelin, and then flew
Back to his friends. Deiphobus (faint with the blood's excess   490
Fall'n from his wound) was carefully convey'd out of the press,
By his kind brother by both sides, Polites, till they gat
His horse and chariot, that were still set fit for his retreat
And bore him now to Ilion. The rest fought fiercely on,
And set a mighty fight on foot. When next Anchises' son
Aphareus Caletorides (that ran upon him) strook
Just in the throat with his keen lance, and straight his head forsook
His upright carriage, and his shield, his helm, and all with him
Fell to the earth, where ruinous death made prize of every limb.

Antilochus (discovering well that Thoön's heart took check)   500
Let fly, and cut the hollow vein that runs up to his neck
Along his back part, quite in twain: down in the dust he fell,
Upwards, and, with extended hands, bade all the world farewell.
Antilochus rush'd nimbly in, and, looking round, made prize
Of his fair arms; in which affair his round-set enemies
Let fly their lances, thundering on his advanced targe,
But could not get his flesh: the god that shakes the earth took charge
Of Nestor's son and kept him safe: who never was away,

But still amongst the thickest foes his busy lance did play,
Observing ever when he might, far off or near, offend.   510
And watching Asius' son, in prease, he spied him, and did send
(Close coming on) a dart at him, that smote in midst his shield,
In which the sharp head of the lance the blue-hair'd god made yield,
Not pleas'd to yield his pupil's life, in whose shield half the dart
Stuck like a truncheon burn'd with fire; on earth lay th' other part.
He, seeing no better end of all, retir'd in fear of worse;
But him Meriones pursu'd, and his lance found full course
To th' other's life: it wounded him betwixt the privy parts
And navel, where (to wretched men, that war's most violent smarts
Must undergo) wounds chiefly vex. His dart Meriones   520
Pursu'd, and Adamas so striv'd with it, and his misease,
As doth a bullock puff and storm, whom in disdained bands
The upland herdsmen strive to cast: so, fall'n beneath the hands
Of his stern foe, Asiades did struggle, pant, and rave,
But no long time; for when the lance was pluck'd out, up he gave
His tortur'd soul. Then Troy's turn came, when with a Thracian sword
The temples of Deipyrus did Hellenus afford
So huge a blow, it struck all light out of his cloudy eyes,
And cleft his helmet; which a Greek, there fighting, made his prize
(It fell so full beneath his feet). Atrides griev'd to see   530
That sight; and, threat'ning, shook a lance at Hellenus, and he
A bow half drew at him; at once out flew both shaft and lance:
The shaft Atrides' curets struck, and far away did glance:
Atrides' dart of Hellenus the thrust-out bow-hand struck,
And through the hand stuck in the bow; Agenor's hand did pluck
From forth the nailed prisoner the javelin quickly out,
And fairly with a little wool, enwrapping round about
The wounded hand, within a scarf he bore it, which his squire
Had ready for him: yet the wound would need he should retire.
    Pisander, to revenge his hurt, right on the king ran he.   540
A bloody fate suggested him, to let him run on thee,
O Menelaus, that he might, by thee, in dangerous war
Be done to death. Both coming on, Atrides' lance did err:
Pisander struck Atrides' shield, that brake at point the dart,
Not running through, yet he rejoic'd as playing a victor's part:
Atrides, drawing his fair sword, upon Pisander flew;
Pisander from beneath his shield his goodly weapon drew –
Two-edg'd, with right sharp steel, and long, the handle olive-tree,
Well polish'd – and to blows they go; upon the top struck he
Atrides' horse-hair'd feather'd helm; Atrides on his brow   550
(Above th' extreme part of the nose) laid such a heavy blow

That all the bones crash'd under it, and out his eyes did drop
Before his feet in bloody dust; he after, and shrunk up
His dying body: which the foot of his triumphing foe
Opened, and stood upon his breast, and off his arms did go,
This insultation us'd the while: 'At length forsake our fleet
Thus (ye false Trojans) to whom war never enough is sweet:
Nor want ye more impieties, with which ye have abus'd
Me, ye bold dogs, that your chief friends so honourably us'd:
Nor fear you hospitable Jove that lets such thunders go: 560
But build upon't, he will unbuild your tow'rs, that clamber so,
For ravishing my goods and wife, in flow'r of all her years,
And without cause; nay, when that fair and liberal hand of hers
Had us'd you so most lovingly; and now again ye would
Cast fire into our fleet, and kill our princes if ye could.
Go to, one day you will be curb'd (though never so ye thirst
Rude war) by war. O father Jove, they say thou art the first
In wisdom of all gods and men; yet all this comes from thee,
And still thou gratifiest these men, how lewd so e'er they be,
Though never they be cloy'd with sins, nor can be satiate,   570
As good men should, with this vile war. Satiety of state,
Satiety of sleep and love, satiety of ease,
Of music, dancing, can find place; yet harsh war still must please
Past all these pleasures, even past these. They will be cloy'd with these
Before their war joys: never war gives Troy satieties.'
    This said, the bloody arms were off, and to his soldiers thrown,
He mixing in first fight again: and then Harpalion,
Kind king Pylemen's son, gave charge; who to those wars of Troy
His loved father followed, nor ever did enjoy
His country's sight again; he struck the targe of Atreus' son   580
Full in the midst; his javelin's steel yet had no power to run
The target through, nor had himself the heart to fetch his lance,
But took him to his strength, and cast on every side a glance,
Lest any his dear sides should dart: but Merion, as he fled,
Sent after him a brazen lance that ran his eager head
Through his right hip, and all along the bladder's region
Beneath the bone; it settled him, and set his spirit gone
Amongst the hands of his best friends; and like a worm he lay
Stretch'd on the earth, with his black blood imbrued and flow'd away.
His corse the Paphlagonians did sadly wait upon   590
(Repos'd in his rich chariot) to sacred Ilion,
The king his father following, dissolv'd in kindly tears,
And no wreak sought for his slain son. But at his slaughterers
Incensed Paris spent a lance (since he had been a guest

To many Paphlagonians) and through the press it press'd.
There was a certain augur's son, that did for wealth excel,
And yet was honest; he was born and did at Corinth dwell:
Who (though he knew his harmful fate) would needs his ship ascend:
His father, Polyidus, oft would tell him that his end
Would either seize him at his house, upon a sharp disease,   600
Or else amongst the Grecian ships, by Trojans slain. Both these
Together he desir'd to shun; but the disease (at last,
And ling'ring death in it) he left, and war's quick stroke embrac'd:
The lance betwixt his ear and cheek ran in, and drave the mind
Of both those bitter fortunes out. Night struck his whole pow'rs blind.

    Thus fought they like the spirit of fire, nor Jove-lov'd Hector knew
How in the fleet's left wing the Greeks his down-put soldiers slew
Almost to victory: the god that shakes the earth so well
Help'd with his own strength, and the Greeks so fiercely did impell.
Yet Hector made the first place good, where both the ports and wall,   610
The thick rank of the Greek shields broke, he enter'd, and did skall,
Where on the gray sea's shore were drawn (the wall being there but slight)
Protesilaus' ships, and those of Ajax, where the fight
Of men and horse were sharpest set. There the Boeotian bands,
Long-rob'd Iaons, Locrians, and (brave men of their hands)
The Phthian and Epeian troops did spritefully assail
The god-like Hector rushing in, and yet could not prevail
To his repulse, though choicest men of Athens there made head:
Amongst whom was Menestheus chief, whom Phidias followed,
Stichius and Bias, huge in strength. Th' Epeian troops were led   620
By Meges' and Philides' cares, Amphion, Dracius.
Before the Phthians Medon march'd, and Meneptolemus;
And these, with the Boeotian pow'rs, bore up the fleet's defence.
Oïleus, by his brother's side, stood close, and would not thence
For any moment of that time: but as through fallow fields
Black oxen draw a well-join'd plough, and either ev'nly yields
His thrifty labour; all heads couch'd so close to earth, they plow
The fallow with their horns, till out the sweat begins to flow,
The stretch'd yokes crack, and yet at last the furrow forth is driv'n:
So toughly stood these to their task, and made their work as ev'n.   630

    But Ajax Telamonius had many helpful men,
That when sweat ran about his knees, and labour flow'd, would then
Help bear his mighty seven-fold shield: when swift Oïleades
The Locrians left, and would not make those murthrous fights of prease,
Because they wore no bright steel casks, nor bristled plumes for show,
Round shields, nor darts of solid ash, but with the trusty bow,
And jacks well quilted with soft wool, they came to Troy, and were,

In their fit place, as confident as those that fought so near,
And reach'd their foes so thick with shafts, that these were they that brake
The Trojan orders first, and then the brave-arm'd men did make   640
Good work with their close fights before. Behind whom, having shot,
The Locrians hid still; and their foes all thought of fight forgot
With shows of those far-striking shafts, their eyes were troubled so:
And then, assur'dly, from the ships and tents th' insulting foe
Had miserably fled to Troy, had not Polydamas
Thus spake to Hector: 'Hector, still impossible 'tis to pass
Good counsel upon you: but say some god prefers thy deeds,
In counsels wouldst thou pass us too? In all things none exceeds.
To some god gives the power of war; to some the sleight to dance;
To some the art of instruments; some doth for voice advance: 650
And that far-seeing god grants some the wisdom of the mind,
Which no man can keep to himself: that, though but few can find,
Doth profit many, that preserves the public weal and state,
And that, who hath, he best can prize: but, for me, I'll relate
Only my censure what's our best. The very crown of war
Doth burn about thee; yet our men, when they have reach'd thus far,
Suppose their valours crown'd, and cease. A few still stir their feet,
And so a few with many fight, spers'd thinly through the fleet.
Retire then, leave speech to the rout, and all thy princes call,
That here in counsels of most weight, we may resolve of all –   660
If having likelihood to believe that god will conquest give,
We shall charge through, or with this grace, make our retreat, and live:
For I must needs affirm, I fear the debt of yesterday
(Since war is such a god of change) the Grecians now will pay.
And since th' insatiate man of war remains at fleet, if there
We tempt his safety, no hour more his hot soul can forbear.'
    This sound stuff Hector lik'd, approv'd, jump'd from his chariot,
And said: 'Polydamas, make good this place, and suffer not
One prince to pass it; I myself will there go, where you see
Those friends in skirmish, and return (when they have heard from me   670
Command that your advice obeys) with utmost speed.' This said,
With day-bright arms, white plume, white scarf, his goodly limbs array'd,
He parted from them, like a hill removing, all of snow:
And to the Trojan peers and chiefs he flew, to let them know
The counsel of Polydamas. All turn'd, and did rejoice,
To haste to Panthus' gentle son, being call'd by Hector's voice.
Who, through the forefights making way, look'd for Deiphobus,
King Hellenus, Asiades, Hyrtasian Asius:
Of whom, some were not to be found unhurt, or undeceas'd,
Some only hurt, and gone from field. As further he address'd,   680

He found within the fight's left wing the fair-hair'd Helen's love,
By all means moving men to blows; which could by no means move
Hector's forbearance, his friends' miss so put his pow'rs in storm,
But thus in wonted terms he chid: 'You with the finest form,
Impostor, woman's man, where are (in your care mark'd) all these?
Deiphobus, King Hellenus, Asius Hyrtacides,
Othryoneus, Acamas? Now haughty Ilion
Shakes to his lowest groundwork: now just ruin falls upon
Thy head. past rescue.' He replied: 'Hector, why chid'st thou now
When I am guiltless? Other times there are for ease, I know,   690
Than these: for she that brought thee forth not utterly left me
Without some portion of thy spirit, to make me brother thee.
But since thou first brought'st in thy force to this our naval fight,
I and my friends have ceaseless fought, to do thy service right.
But all those friends thou seek'st are slain, excepting Hellenus,
(Who parted wounded in his hand) and so Deiphobus;
Jove yet averted death from them. And now lead thou as far
As thy great heart affects; all we will second any war
That thou endurest. And I hope my own strength is not lost;
Though least, I'll fight it to his best; not further fights the most.'   700
    This calm'd hot Hector's spleen; and both turn'd where they saw the face
Of war most fierce: and that was where their friends made good the place
About renown'd Polydamas and god-like Polyphet,
Palmus, Ascanius, Morus, that Hippotion did beget,
And from Ascania's wealthy fields but even the day before
Arriv'd at Troy, that with their aid they kindly might restore
Some kindness they receiv'd from thence: and in fierce fight with these
Phalces and tall Orthaeus stood, and bold Cebriones.
And then the doubt that in advice Polydamas disclos'd,
To fight or fly, Jove took away, and all to fight dispos'd.   710
And as the floods of troubled air to pitchy storms increase
That after thunder sweeps the fields, and ravish up the seas,
Encount'ring with abhorred roars, when the engrossed waves
Boil into foam, and endlessly one after other raves:
So rank'd and guarded th' Ilians march'd, some now, more now, and then
More upon more, in shining steel; now captains, then their men.
And Hector, like man-killing Mars, advanc'd before them all,
His huge round target before him, through thicken'd like a wall,
With hides well couch'd, with store of brass; and on his temples shin'd
His bright helm, on which danc'd his plume: and in this horrid kind,   720
All hid within his world-like shield, he every troop assay'd
For entry, that in his despite stood firm and undismay'd.
Which when he saw, and kept more off, Ajax came stalking then,

And thus provok'd him: 'O good man, why fright'st thou thus our men?
Come nearer; not art's want in war makes us thus navy-bound,
But Jove's direct scourge; his arm'd hand makes our hands give you ground:
Yet thou hop'st, of thyself, our spoil: but we have likewise hands
To hold our own, as you to spoil: and ere thy countermands
Stand good against our ransack'd fleet, your hugely-peopled town
Our hands shall take in, and her tow'rs from all their heights pull down.
And I must tell thee, time draws on, when flying thou shalt cry
To Jove and all the gods to make thy fair-man'd horses fly
More swift than falcons, that their hoofs may rouse the dust, and bear
Thy body, hid, to Ilion.' This said, his bold words were
Confirm'd as soon as spoke; Jove's bird, the high-flown eagle, took
The right hand of their host, whose wings high acclamations strook
From forth the glad breasts of the Greeks. Then Hector made reply:
'Vain-spoken man, and glorious, what hast thou said? Would I
As surely were the son of Jove, and of great Juno born,
Adorn'd like Pallas, and the god that lifts to earth the morn,   740
As this day shall bring harmful light to all your host; and thou
(If thou dar'st stand this lance) the earth before the ships shalt strow,
Thy bosom torn up; and the dogs, with all the fowl of Troy,
Be satiate with thy fat and flesh.' This said, with shouting joy
His first troops follow'd, and the last their shouts with shouts repell'd:
Greece answer'd all, nor could her spirits from all show rest conceal'd.
And to so infinite a height all acclamations strove,
They reach'd the splendours stuck about the unreach'd throne of Jove.

THE END OF THE THIRTEENTH BOOK

BOOK FOURTEEN

The Argument

Atrides, to behold the skirmish, brings
Old Nestor, and the other wounded kings.
Juno (receiving of the Cyprian dame
Her Cestus, whence her sweet enticements came)
Descends to Somnus, and gets him to bind
The pow'rs of Jove with sleep, to free her mind.
Neptune assists the Greeks, and of the foe
Slaughter inflicts a mighty overthrow.
Ajax so sore strikes Hector with a stone,
It makes him spit blood, and his sense sets gone.

Another Argument

In *Xi* with sleep and bed, heav'n's queen
Ev'n Jove himself makes overseen.

BOOK FOURTEEN

NOR WINE, nor feasts, could lay their soft chains on old Nestor's ear
To this high clamour: who requir'd Machaon's thoughts to bear
His care in part, about the cause: 'For methink still,' said he,
'The cry increases. I must needs the watchtow'r mount to see
Which way the flood of war doth drive. Still drink thou wine, and eat
Till fair-hair'd Hecamed hath giv'n a little water heat,
To cleanse the quitture from thy wound.' This said, the goodly shield
Of warlike Thrasimed his son (who had his own in field)
He took, snatch'd up a mighty lance, and so stept forth to view
Cause of that clamour. Instantly, th' unworthy cause he knew –   10
The Grecians wholly put in rout, the Trojans routing still,
Close at the Greeks' backs, their wall raz'd: the old man mourn'd this ill.
And as when with unwieldy waves the great sea forefeels winds,
That both ways murmur, and no way her certain current finds,
But pants and swells confusedly, here goes, and there will stay,
Till on it air casts one firm wind, and then it rolls away:
So stood old Nestor in debate, two thoughts at once on wing
In his discourse, if first to take direct course to the king,
Or to the multitude in fight. At last he did conclude
To visit Agamemnon first: mean time both hosts imbru'd   20
Their steel in one another's blood, nought wrought their healths but harms,
Swords, huge stones, double-headed darts, still thumping on their arms.
And now the Jove-kept kings, whose wounds were yet in cure, did meet
Old Nestor: Diomed, Ithacus, and Atreus' son from fleet,
Bent for the fight, which was far off, the ships being drawn to shore
On heaps at first, till all their sterns a wall was rais'd before;
Which (though not great) it yet suffic'd to hide them, though their men
Were something straited; for whose scope, in form of battle then,
They drew them through the spacious shore, one by another still,
Till all the bosom of the strand their sable bulks did fill,   30
Ev'n till they took up all the space 'twixt both the promontories.
These kings, like Nestor, in desire to know for what those cries
Became so violent, came along (all leaning on their darts)
To see, though not of power to fight; sad and suspicious hearts
Distemp'ring them, and (meeting now Nestor) the king in fear

Cried out: 'O Nestor our renown! Why shows thy presence here,
The harmful fight abandoned? Now Hector will make good
The threatening vow he made (I fear) that, till he had our blood,
And fir'd our fleet, he never more would turn to Ilion.
Nor is it long, I see, before his whole will will be done.   40
O gods, I now see all the Greeks put on Achilles' ire
Against my honour: no mean left to keep our fleet from fire.'

     He answer'd: ''Tis an evident truth, not Jove himself can now
(With all the thunder in his hands) prevent our overthrow.
The wall we thought invincible, and trusted more than Jove,
Is scal'd, raz'd, enter'd, and our pow'rs (driven up) past breathing, prove
A most inevitable fight, both slaughters so commix'd,
That for your life you cannot put your diligent'st thought betwixt
The Greeks and Trojans; and as close their throats cleave to the sky.
Consult we then (if that will serve), for fight advise not I;   50
It fits not wounded men to fight.' Atrides answer'd him:
'If such a wall as cost the Greeks so many a tired limb,
And such a dike be past, and raz'd, that (as yourself said well)
We all esteem'd invincible, and would past doubt repell
The world from both our fleet and us, it doth directly show
That here Jove vows our shames and deaths. I evermore did know
His hand from ours, when he help'd us: and now I see as clear
That (like the blessed gods) he holds our hated enemies dear,
Supports their arms, and pinions ours. Conclude then, 'tis in vain
To strive with him. Our ships drawn up now let us launch again,   60
And keep at anchor till calm night; that then, perhaps, our foes
May calm their storms, and in that time our scape we may dispose:
"It is not any shame to fly from ill, although by night:
Known ill, he better does that flies than he it takes in fight." '

     Ulysses frown'd on him, and said: 'Accurst, why talk'st thou thus?
Would thou hadst led some barbarous host, and not commanded us
Whom Jove made soldiers from our youth, that age might scorn to fly
From any charge it undertakes, and every dazzled eye
The honour'd hand of war might close. Thus wouldst thou leave this town
For which our many miseries felt entitle it our own?   70
Peace, lest some other Greek give ear, and hear a sentence such
As no man's palate should profane – at least that knew how much
His own right weigh'd, and being a prince, and such a prince as bears
Rule of so many Greeks as thou. This counsel loathes mine ears –
Let others toil in light and cries, and we so light of heels
Upon their very noise and groans to hoise away our keels.
Thus we should fit the wish of Troy, that being something near
The victory, we give it clear; and we were sure to bear

A slaughter to the utmost man, for no man will sustain
A stroke, the fleet gone, but at that look still, and wish him slain:　　80
And therefore (prince of men) be sure, thy censure is unfit.'
　　'O Ithacus!' replied the king, 'thy bitter terms have smit
My heart in sunder. At no hand, 'gainst any prince's will
Do I command this; would to god that any man of skill
To give a better counsel would, or old or younger man;
My voice should gladly go with his.' Then Diomed began:
　　'The man not far is, nor shall ask much labour to bring in,
That willingly would speak his thoughts, if spoken they might win
Fit ear, and suffer no impair, that I discover them,
Being youngest of you – since my sire that heir'd a diadem　　90
May make my speech to diadems decent enough, though he
Lies in his sepulchre at Thebes. I boast this pedigree:
Portheus three famous sons begot, that in high Calidon
And Pleuron kept, with state of kings, their habitation.
Agrius, Melus, and the third, the horseman Oeneus,
My father's father, that excell'd in actions generous
The other two; but these kept home, my father being driv'n
With wand'ring and advent'rous spirits; for so the king of heav'n
And th' other gods set down their wills: and he to Argos came,
Where he began the world, and dwelt; there marrying a dame,　　100
One of Adrastus' female race, he kept a royal house,
For he had great demesnes, good land, and being industrious,
He planted many orchard-grounds about his house, and bred
Great store of sheep. Besides all this, he was well qualitied,
And past all Argives for his spear: and these digressive things
Are such as you may well endure, since (being derived from kings,
And kings not poor, nor virtueless) you cannot hold me base,
Nor scorn my words: which oft, though true, in mean men meet disgrace.
However, they are these in short. Let us he seen at fight,
And yield to strong necessity, though wounded, that our sight　　110
May set those men on, that of late have to Achilles' spleen
Been too indulgent, and left blows: but be we only seen,
Not come within the reach of darts, lest wound on wound we lay
(Which reverend Nestor's speech implied), and so far him obey.
　　This counsel gladly all observ'd, went on, Atrides led.
Nor Neptune this advantage lost, but closely followed,
And like an aged man appear'd t' Atrides, whose right hand
He seiz'd, and said: 'Atrides, this doth passing fitly stand
With stern Achilles' wreakful spirit, that he can stand astern
His ship, and both in fight and death the Grecian bane discern,　　120
Since not in his breast glows one spark of any human mind:

But be that his own bane; let god by that loss make him find
How vile a thing he is; for know, the blest gods have not giv'n
Thee ever over, but perhaps the Trojans may from heav'n
Receive that justice. Nay, 'tis sure, and thou shalt see their falls,
Your fleet soon freed, and for fights here, they glad to take their walls.'
This said, he made known who he was, and parted with a cry,
As if ten thousand men had join'd in battle then, so high
His throat flew through the host: and so this great Earth-shaking god
Cheer'd up the Greek hearts, that they wish their pains no period.   130
    Saturnia from Olympus' top saw her great brother there,
And her great husband's brother, too, exciting everywhere
The glorious spirits of the Greeks, which as she joy'd to see,
So, on the fountful Ida's top, Jove's sight did disagree
With her contentment, since she fear'd that his hand would descend,
And check the Sea-god's practices. And this she did contend
How to prevent, which thus seem'd best: to deck her curiously,
And visit the Idalian hill, so that the Lightner's eye
She might enamour with her looks, and his high temples steep
(Even to his wisdom) in the kind and golden juice of sleep.   140
So took she chamber which her son, the god of ferrary,
With firm doors made, being joined close, and with a privy key
That no god could command but Jove, where, enter'd, she made fast
The shining gates, and then upon her lovely body cast
Ambrosia, that first made it clear, and after laid on it
An odorous, rich and sacred oil, that was so wondrous sweet
That ever, when it was but touch'd, it sweeten'd heav'n and earth.
Her body being cleans'd with this, her tresses she let forth,
And comb'd (her comb dipp'd in the oil), then wrapp'd them up in curls:
And thus, her deathless head adorn'd, a heavenly veil she hurls   150
On her white shoulders, wrought by her that rules in housewif'ries,
Who wove it full of antique works, of most divine device.
And this with goodly clasps of gold she fasten'd to her breast,
Then with a girdle, whose rich sphere a hundred studs impress'd,
She girt her small waist. In her ears, tenderly pierc'd, she wore
Pearls, great and orient: on her head, a wreath not worn before
Cast beams out like the sun. At last, she to her feet did tie
Fair shoes, and thus entire attir'd she shin'd in open sky,
Call'd the fair Paphian queen apart from th' other gods, and said:
'Lov'd daughter, should I ask a grace, should I or be obey'd   160
Or wouldst thou cross me, being incens'd, since I cross thee, and take
The Greeks' part, thy hand helping Troy?' She answer'd, 'That shall make
No difference in a different cause: ask, ancient deity,
What most contents thee; my mind stands inclin'd as liberally

To grant it as thine own to ask, provided that it be
A favour fit and in my pow'r.' She, giv'n deceitfully,
Thus said: 'Then give me those two pow'rs, with which both men and gods
Thou vanquishest, Love and Desire. For now the periods
Of all the many-feeding earth, and the original
Of all the gods, Oceanus, and Thetis, whom we call   170
Our mother, I am going to greet: they nurst me in their court,
And brought me up, receiving me in most respectful sort
From Phaea, when Jove under earth and the unfruitful seas
Cast Saturn. These I go to see, intending to appease
Jars grown betwixt them, having long abstain'd from speech and bed.
Which jars could I so reconcile, that in their anger's stead
I could place love, and so renew their first society,
I should their best lov'd be esteem'd, and honour'd endlessly.'
    She answer'd: ''Tis not fit nor just thy will should be denied,
Whom Jove in his embraces holds.' This spoken, she untied   180
And from her odorous bosom took her Ceston, in whose sphere
Were all enticements to delight, all loves, all longings were,
Kind conference, fair speech, whose pow'r the wisest doth inflame:
This, she resigning to her hands, thus urg'd her by her name:
    'Receive this bridle, thus fair wrought, and put it 'twixt thy breasts,
Where all things to be done are done; and whatsoever rests
In thy desire, return with it.' The great-ey'd Juno smil'd,
And put it 'twixt her breasts. Love's queen, thus cunningly beguil'd,
To Jove's court flew. Saturnia (straight stooping from heaven height)
Pieria and Emathia (those countries of delight)   190
Soon reach'd, and to the snowy mounts where Thracian soldiers dwell
Approaching, pass'd their tops untouch'd. From Athos then she fell,
Pass'd all the broad sea, and arriv'd in Lemnos, at the tow'rs
Of godlike Thoas; where she met the prince of all men's pow'rs,
Death's brother Sleep, whose hand she took, and said: 'Thou king of men,
Prince of the gods too, if before thou heard'st my suits, again
Give helpful ear, and through all times I'll offer thanks to thee.
Lay slumber on Jove's fiery eyes, that I may comfort me
With his embraces: for which grace I'll grace thee with a throne
Incorruptible, all of gold, and elegantly done   200
By Mulciber, to which he forg'd a footstool for the ease
Of thy soft feet, when wine and feasts thy golden humours please.'
    Sweet Sleep replied: 'Saturnia, there lives not any god
(Besides Jove) but I would becalm: ay, if it were the flood
That fathers all the deities, the great Oceanus.
But Jove we dare not come more near than he commandeth us.
Now you command me as you did when Jove's great-minded son,

Alcides (having sack'd the town of stubborn Ilion),
Took sail from thence; when by your charge I pour'd about Jove's mind
A pleasing slumber, calming him till thou draw'st up the wind,   210
In all his cruelties, to sea, that set his son ashore
In Cous, far from all his friends; which (waking) vex'd so sore
The supreme godhead, that he cast the gods about the sky,
And me (above them all) he sought: whom he had utterly
Hurl'd from the sparkling firmament, if all-gods-taming Night
(Whom, flying, I besought for aid) had suffer'd his despite,
And not preserv'd me; but his wrath with my offence dispens'd,
For fear t' offend her, and so ceas'd, though never so incens'd:
And now another such escape you wish I should prepare.'

    She answer'd, 'What hath thy deep rest to do with his deep care?   220
As though Jove's love to Ilion in all degrees were such
As 'twas to Hercules his son, and so would storm as much
For their displeasure, as for his! Away, I will remove
Thy fear, with giving thee the dame that thou didst ever love,
One of the fair young Graces born, divine Pasithaë.'

    This started Somnus into joy, who answer'd, 'Swear to me,
By those inviolable springs that feed the Stygian lake,
With one hand touch the nourishing earth, and in the other take
The marble sea, that all the gods of the infernal state
Which circle Saturn, may to us be witnesses, and rate   230
What thou hast vow'd: that with all truth, thou wilt bestow on me
The dame (I grant) I ever lov'd, divine Pasithaë.'

    She swore, as he enjoin'd, in all, and strengthened all his joys,
By naming all th' infernal gods, surnam'd the Titanois.

    The oath thus taken, both took way, and made their quick repair
To Ida from the town and isle, all hid in liquid air.
At Lecton first they left the sea, and there the land they trod:
The fountful nurse of savages, with all her woods, did nod
Beneath their feet: there Somnus stay'd, lest Jove's bright eye should see,
And yet (that he might see to Jove) he climb'd the goodliest tree   240
That all th' Idalian mountain bred, and crown'd her progeny:
A fir it was, that shot past air, and kiss'd the burning sky.
There sate he hid in his dark arms, and in the shape withal
Of that continual prating bird, whom all the deities call
Chalcis, but men Cymmindis name. Saturnia tripp'd apace
Up to the top of Gargarus, and show'd her heav'nly face
To Jupiter; who saw, and lov'd, and with as hot a fire
(Being curious in her tempting view) as when with first desire
(The pleasure of it being stol'n) they mix'd in love and bed.
And (gazing on her still) he said: 'Saturnia, what hath bred   250

This haste in thee from our high court, and whither tends thy gait,
That void of horse and chariot fit for thy sovereign state,
Thou lackiest here?' Her studied fraud replied: 'My journey now
Leaves state and labours to do good. And where in right I owe
All kindness to the sire of gods and our good mother queen
That nurst and kept me curiously, in court (since both have been
Long time at discord), my desire is to atone their hearts;
And therefore go I now to see those earth's extremest parts,
For whose far-seat I spar'd my horse the scaling of this hill,
And left them at the foot of it: for they must taste their fill   260
Of travail with me, that must draw my coach through earth and seas;
Whose far-intended reach, respect and care not to displease
Thy graces, made me not attempt without thy gracious leave.'
     The cloud-compelling god her guile in this sort did receive:
'Juno, thou shalt have after leave, but ere so far thou stray,
Convert we our kind thoughts to love, that now doth every way
Circle with victory my pow'rs: nor yet with any dame
(Woman, or goddess) did his fires my bosom so inflame
As now with thee: not when it lov'd the parts so generous
Ixion's wife had, that brought forth the wise Pyrithous;   270
Nor when the lovely Danaë, Acrisius' daughter, stirr'd
My amorous pow'rs, that Perseus bore, to all men else preferr'd;
Nor when the dame that Phoenix got surpris'd me with her sight,
Who the divine-soul'd Rhadamanth and Minos brought to light;
Nor Semele, that bore to me the joy of mortal men,
The sprightly Bacchus; nor the dame that Thebes renowned then,
Alcmena, that bore Hercules; Latona, so renown'd;
Queen Ceres, with the golden hair, nor thy fair eyes did wound
My entrails to such depth as now, with thirst of amorous ease.'
     The cunning dame seem'd much incens'd, and said, 'What words are these,
Unsufferable Saturn's son? What! Here! In Ida's height!
Desir'st thou this? How fits it us? Or what if in the sight
Of any god thy will were pleas'd, that he the rest might bring
To witness thy incontinence? 'Twere a dishonour'd thing.
I would not show my face in heav'n, and rise from such a bed.
But if love be so dear to thee, thou hast a chamber stead,
Which Vulcan purposely contriv'd with all fit secrecy:
There sleep at pleasure.' He replied: 'I fear not if the eye
Of either god or man observe, so thick a cloud of gold
I'll cast about us, that the sun (who furthest can behold)   290
Shall never find us.' This resolv'd, into his kind embrace
He took his wife: beneath them both fair Tellus strew'd the place
With fresh-sprung herbs, so soft and thick, that up aloft it bore

Their heav'nly bodies: with his leaves did dewy lotus store
Th' Elysian mountain; saffron flow'rs and hyacinths help'd make
The sacred bed, and there they slept: when suddenly there brake
A golden vapour out of air, whence shining dews did fall,
In which they wrapt them close, and slept till Jove was tam'd withal.

    Mean space flew Somnus to the ships, found Neptune out, and said:
'Now cheerfully assist the Greeks, and give them glorious head –   300
At least a little, while Jove sleeps; of whom through every limb
I pour'd dark sleep, Saturnia's love hath so illuded him.'

    This news made Neptune more secure in giving Grecians heart,
And through the first fights thus he stirr'd the men of most desert:

    'Yet, Grecians, shall we put our ships and conquest in the hands
Of Priam's Hector, by our sloth? He thinks so, and commands,
With pride according; all because Achilles keeps away.
Alas, as we were nought but him! We little need to stay
On his assistance, if we would our own strengths call to field,
And mutually maintain repulse. Come on then, all men yield   ‹   310
To what I order; we that bear best arms in all our host,
Whose heads sustain the brightest helms, whose hands are bristled most
With longest lances, let us on. But stay, I'll lead you all;
Nor think I, but great Hector's spirits will suffer some appall,
Though they be never so inspir'd: the ablest of us then,
That on our shoulders worst shields bear, exchange with worser men
That fight with better.' This propos'd, all heard it, and obey'd:
The kings (ev'n those that suffer'd wounds, Ulysses, Diomed
And Agamemnon) helpt'd t'instruct the complete army thus:
To good, gave good arms, worse to worse; yet none were mutinous.   320

    Thus, arm'd with order, forth they flew; the great Earth-shaker led,
A long sword in his sinewy hand, which when he brandished,
It lighten'd still: there was no law for him and it; poor men
Must quake before them. These thus mann'd, illustrious Hector then
His host brought up. The blue-hair'd god and he stretch'd through the prease
A grievous fight, when to the ships and tents of Greece the seas
Brake loose, and rag'd. But when they join'd, the dreadful clamour rose
To such a height, as not the sea, when up the North-spirit blows
Her raging billows, bellows so against the beaten shore;
Nor such a rustling keeps a fire, driven with violent blore,   330
Through woods that grow against a hill; nor so the fervent strokes
Of almost-bursting winds resound against a grove of oaks,
As did the clamour of these hosts, when both the battles clos'd.
Of all which noble Hector first at Ajax' breast dispos'd
His javelin, since so right on him the great-soul'd soldier bore;
Nor miss'd it, but the bawdricks both that his broad bosom wore,

To hang his shield and sword, it struck; both which his flesh preserv'd.
Hector (disdaining that his lance had thus as good as swerv'd)
Trode to his strength; but going off, great Ajax with a stone
(One of the many props for ships that there lay trampled on)   340
Struck his broad breast above his shield, just underneath his throat,
And shook him piecemeal. When the stone sprung back again, and smote
Earth, like a whirlwind gathering dust, with whirring fiercely round,
For fervour of his unspent strength, in settling on the ground;
And as when Jove's bolt by the roots rends from the earth an oak,
His sulphur casting with the blow a strong unsavoury smoke,
And on the fall'n plant none dare look but with amazed eyes
(Jove's thunder being no laughing gam,,) so bow'd strong Hector's thighs,
And so with tost-up heels he fell: away his lance he flung,
His round shield follow'd, then his helm, and out his armour rung.   350
    The Greeks then shouted, and ran in, and hop'd to hale him off,
And therefore pour'd on darts in storms, to keep his aid aloof;
But none could hurt the people's guide, nor stir him from his ground:
Sarpedon, prince of Lycia, and Glaucus, so renown'd,
Divine Agenor, Venus' son, and wise Polydamas,
Rush'd to his rescue, and the rest: no one neglective was
Of Hector's safety; all their shields they couch'd about him close,
Rais'd him from earth, and (giving him, in their kind arms, repose)
From off the labour carried him, to his rich chariot,
And bore him mourning towards Troy: but when the flood they got   360
Of gulfy Xanthus, that was got by deathless Jupiter,
There took they him from chariot, and all besprinkled there
His temples with the stream; he breath'd, look'd up, assay'd to rise,
And on his knees stay'd, spitting blood: again then clos'd his eyes,
And back again his body fell; the main blow had not done
Yet with his spirit. When the Greeks saw worthy Hector gone,
Then thought they of their work, then charg'd with much more cheer the foe,
And then (far first) Oïleades began the overthrow:
He darted Satnius Enops' son, whom famous Naïs bore
(As she was keeping Enops' flocks) on Satnius river's shore,   370
And struck him in his belly's rim, who upwards fell, and rais'd
A mighty skirmish with his fall: and then Panthaedes seiz'd
Prothenor Areilicides with his reveng'ful spear,
On his right shoulder, struck it through, and laid him breathless there.
For which he insolently bragg'd, and cried out: 'Not a dart
From great-soul'd Panthus' son, I think, shall ever vainlier part,
But some Greek's bosom it shall take, and make him give his ghost.'
This brag the Grecians stomach'd much, but Telamonius most,
Who stood most near Prothenor's fall: and out he sent a lance,

Which Panthus' son, declining, scap'd, yet took it to sad chance   380
Archilochus, Antenor's son, whom heav'n did destinate
To that stern end; 'twixt neck and head the javelin wrought his fate,
And ran in at the upper joint of all the back long bone,
Cut both the nerves, and such a load of strength laid Ajax on,
As that small part he seiz'd outweigh'd all th' under limbs, and strook
His heels up so, that head and face the earth's possessions took,
When all the low parts sprung in air; and thus did Ajax quit
Panthaedes' brave: 'Now, Panthus' son, let thy prophetic wit
Consider, and disclose a truth, if this man do not weigh
Even with Prothenor. I conceive, no one of you will say,   390
That either he was base himself, or sprung of any base.
Antenor's brother, or his son, he should be by his face;
One of his race, past question, his likeness shows he is.'
    This spake he, knowing it well enough. The Trojans storm'd at this,
And then slew Acamas (to save his brother yet engag'd)
Boeotius, dragging him to spoil and thus the Greeks enrag'd.
    'O Greeks, ev'n born to bear our darts, yet ever breathing threats,
Not always under tears and toils ye see our fortune sweats,
But sometimes you drop under death: see now your quick among
Our dead, intranc'd with my weak lance, to prove I have ere long   400
Reveng'd my brother: 'tis the wish of every honest man
His brother slain in Mars's field may rest wreak'd in his fane.'
    This stirr'd fresh envy in the Greeks, but urg'd Peneleus most,
Who hurl'd his lance at Acamas; he 'scap't, nor yet it lost
The force he gave it, for it found the flock-rich Phorbas' son,
Ilioneus, whose dear sire (past all in Ilion)
Was lov'd of Hermes, and enrich'd; and to him only bore
His mother this now slaughter'd man. The dart did undergore
His eye-lid, by his eye's dear roots; and out the apple fell,
The eye pierc'd through: nor could the nerve that stays the neck repel   410
His strong-wing'd lance, but neck and all gave way, and down he dropp'd.
Peneleus then unsheath'd his sword, and from the shoulders chopp'd
His luckless head; which down he threw, the helm still sticking on,
And still the lance fix'd in his eye; which not to see alone
Contented him, but up again he snatch'd, and show'd it all,
With this stern brave: 'Ilians, relate brave Ilioneus' fall
To his kind parents, that their roofs their tears may overrun,
For so the house of Promachus, and Alegenor's son,
Must with his wife's eyes overflow, she never seeing more
Her dear lord, though we tell his death, when to our native shore   420
We bring from ruin'd Troy our fleet, and men so long forgone.'
This said, and seen, pale Fear possess'd all those of Ilion,

And ev'ry man cast round his eye, to see where death was not,
That he might flee him. Let not then his grac'd hand be forgot
(O Muses, you that dwell in heav'n) that first imbru'd the field
With Trojan spoil, when Neptune thus had made their irons yield.
   First Ajax Telamonius the Mysian captain slew,
Great Hyrtius Gyrtiades; Antilochus o'erthrew
Phalces and Mermer, to their spoil; Meriones gave end
To Moris and Hippotion; Teucer to fate did send   430
Prothoön and Periphetes; Atrides' javelin chas'd
Duke Hyperenor, wounding him in that part that is plac'd
Betwixt the short ribs and the bones that to the triple gut
Have pertinence; the javelin's head did out his entrails cut,
His forc'd soul breaking through the wound: night's black hand clos'd his eyes;
Then Ajax, great Oïleus' son, had divers victories;
For when Saturnius suffer'd flight, of all the Grecian race
Not one with swiftness of his feet could so enrich a chace.

THE END OF THE FOURTEENTH BOOK

BOOK FIFTEEN

The Argument

Jove waking, and beloved Troy in flight,
Chides Juno, and sends Iris to the fight,
To charge the sea-god to forsake the field,
And Phoebus to invade it with his shield,
Recovering Hector's bruis'd and eras'd pow'rs:
To field he goes, and makes new conquerors,
The Trojans giving now the Grecians chase
Ev'n to their fleet. Then Ajax turns his face,
And feeds, with many Trojan lives, his ire;
Who then brought brands to set the fleet on fire.

Another Argument

Jove sees in *O* his oversight,
Chides Juno, Neptune calls from fight.

BOOK FIFTEEN

THE TROJANS (beat past pale and dike, and numbers prostrate laid)
 All got to chariot, fear-driv'n all, and fear'd as men dismay'd.
 Then Jove on Ida's top awak'd, rose from Saturnia's side,
Stood up, and look'd upon the war, and all inverted spied,
Since he had seen it – th' Ilians now in rout, the Greeks in fight;
King Neptune, with his long sword, chief; great Hector put down quite,
Laid flat in field, and with a crown of princes compassed,
So stopp'd up that he scarce could breathe, his mind's sound habit fled,
And he still spitting blood. Indeed, his hurt was not set on
By one that was the weakest Greek. But him Jove look'd upon   10
With eyes of pity; on his wife with horrible aspect,
To whom he said: 'O thou in ill most cunning architect,
All arts and comments that exceed'st! Not only to enforce
Hector from fight, but with his men to show the Greeks a course.
I fear (as formerly, so now) these ills have with thy hands
Their first fruits sown, and therefore could load all thy limbs with bands.
Forgett'st thou when I hang'd thee up, how to thy feet I tied
Two anvils, golden manacles on thy false wrists implied,
And let thee mercilessly hang from our refined heav'n
Even to earth's vapours; all the gods in great Olympus giv'n   20
To mutinies about thee, yet (though all stood staring on)
None durst dissolve thee; for these hands (had they but seiz'd upon
Thy friend) had headlong thrown him off, from our star-bearing round,
Till he had tumbled out his breath, and piece-meal dash'd the ground.
Nor was my angry spirit calm'd so soon for those foul seas,
On which (inducing northern flaws) thou shipwreck'dst Hercules,
And toss'd him to the Coan shore, that thou shouldst tempt again
My wrath's importance, when thou seest (besides) how grossly vain
My pow'rs can make thy policies: for from their utmost force
I freed my son, and set him safe in Argos, nurse of horse.   30
These I remember to thy thoughts, that thou mayst shun these sleights,
And know how badly bed-sports thrive, procur'd by base deceits.'
 This frighted the offending queen, who with this state excus'd
Her kind unkindness: 'Witness earth and heaven, so far diffus'd,
Thou flood, whose silent-gliding waves the under ground doth bear

(Which is the great'st and gravest oath that any god can swear),
Thy sacred head, those secret joys, that our young bed gave forth
(By which I never rashly swore), that he who shakes the earth
Not by my counsel did this wrong to Hector and his host,
But pitying th' oppressed Greeks, their fleet being nearly lost,   40
Reliev'd their hard condition, yet utterly impell'd
By his free mind: which since I see is so offensive held
To thy high pleasure, I will now advise him not to tread
But where thy tempest-raising feet, O Jupiter, shall lead.'
    Jove laugh'd to hear her so submiss, and said: 'My fair-ey'd love,
If still thus thou and I were one (in counsels held above),
Neptune would still, in word and fact, be ours, if not in heart;
If then thy tongue and heart agree, from hence to heav'n depart,
To call the excellent-in-bows, the Rain-bow, and the Sun,
That both may visit both the hosts – the Grecian army one,   50
And that is Iris; let her haste, and make the sea-god cease
T' assist the Greeks, and to his court retire from war in peace.
Let Phoebus (on the Trojan part) inspire with wonted pow'r
Great Hector's spirits: make his thoughts forget the late stern hour,
And all his anguish, setting on his whole recover'd man
To make good his late grace in fight, and hold in constant wane
The Grecian glories, till they fall in flight before the fleet
Of vex'd Achilles; which extreme will prove the mean to greet
Thee with thy wish, for then the eyes of great Aeacides
(Made witness of the general ill, that doth so near him prease)   60
Will make his own particular look out, and by degrees
Abate his wrath, that through himself for no extremities
Will seem reflected; yet his friend may get of him the grace
To help his country in his arms; and he shall make fit place
For his full presence with his death, which shall be well fore-run:
For I will first renown his life with slaughter of my son
(Divine Sarpedon), and his death great Hector's pow'r shall wreak,
Ending his ends. Then at once, out shall the fury break
Of fierce Achilles: and with that, the flight now felt shall turn,
And then last, till in wrathful flames the long-sieg'd Ilion burn.   70
Minerva's counsel shall become grave mean to this my will,
Which no god shall neglect, before Achilles take his fill
Of slaughter for his slaughter'd friend: even Hector's slaughter, thrown
Under his anger; that these facts may then make fully known
My vow's performance, made of late, and with my bowed head
Confirm'd to Thetis, when her arms embrac'd my knees, and pray'd
That to her city-razing son I would all honour show.'
    This heard, his charge she seem'd t' intend, and to Olympus flew.

But, as the mind of such a man that hath a great way gone,
And either knowing not his way, or then would let alone   80
His purpos'd journey, is distract, and in his vexed mind
Resolves now not to go, now goes, still many ways inclin'd:
So reverend Juno headlong flew, and 'gainst her stomach striv'd.
For (being amongst th' immortal gods, in high heav'n, soon arriv'd,
All rising, welcoming with cups her little absence thence)
She all their courtships overpast with solemn negligence,
Save that which fair-cheek'd Themis show'd, and her kind cup she took:
For first she ran and met with her, and ask'd what troubled look
She brought to heav'n. She thought (for truth) that Jove had terrified
Her spirits strangely, since she went. The fair-arm'd queen replied: 90
    'That truth may easily be suppos'd; you (goddess Themis) know
His old severity and pride; but you bear't out with show,
And like the banquet's arbiter amongst th' immortals fare,
Though well you hear amongst them all how bad his actions are,
Nor are all here, nor anywhere, mortals nor gods (I fear),
Entirely pleas'd with what he does, though thus ye banquet here.'
    Thus took she place, displeasedly, the feast in general
Bewraying privy spleens at Jove; and then (to colour all)
She laugh'd, but merely from her lips: for over her black brows
Her still-bent forehead was not clear'd; yet this her passion's throes   100
Brought forth in spite, being lately school'd: 'Alas, what fools are we
That envy Jove, or that by act, word, thought, can fantasy
Any resistance to his will! He sits far off, nor cares,
Nor moves, but says he knows his strength, to all degrees compares
His greatness, past all other gods, and that in fortitude,
And every other godlike pow'r, he reigns past all indu'd.
For which great eminence all you gods whatever ill he does
Sustain with patience: here is Mars, I think, not free from woes,
And yet he bears them like himself. The great god had a son,
Whom he himself yet justifies, one that from all men won   110
Just surname of their best belov'd, Ascalaphus; yet he
(By Jove's high grace to Troy) is slain.' Mars started horribly
(As Juno knew he would) at this, beat, with his hurl'd out hands,
His brawny thighs, cried out, and said: 'O you that have commands
In these high temples, bear with me, if I revenge the death
Of such a son: I'll to the fleet, and though I sink beneath
The fate of being shot to hell by Jove's fell thunder-stone,
And lie all grim'd amongst the dead with dust and blood, my son
Revenge shall honour.' Then he charg'd Fear and Dismay to join
His horse and chariot; he got arms, that over heav'n did shine: 120
And then a wrath more great and grave in Jove had been prepar'd

Against the gods, than Juno caus'd, if Pallas had not car'd
More for the peace of heaven than Mars; who leap'd out of her throne,
Rapt up her helmet, lance and shield, and made her fane's porch groan
With her egression to his stay, and thus his rage defers:
'Furious and foolish, th' art undone; hast thou for nought thine ears?
Heard'st thou not Juno, being arriv'd from heaven's great king but now?
Or wouldst thou he himself should rise (forc'd with thy rage) to show
The dreadful pow'r she urg'd in him, so justly being stirr'd?
Know (thou most impudent and mad) thy wrath had not inferr'd   130
Mischief to thee, but to us all? His spirit had instantly
Left both the hosts, and turn'd his hands to uproars in the sky.
Guilty and guiltless both to wrack in his high rage had gone:
And therefore (as thou lov'st thyself) cease fury for thy son.
Another, far exceeding him in heart and strength of hand,
Or is, or will be shortly slain. It were a work would stand
Jove in much trouble, to free all from death that would not die.'
     This threat ev'n nail'd him to his throne, when heav'n's chief majesty
Call'd bright Apollo from his fane, and Iris that had place
Of internunciess from the gods, to whom she did the grace   140
Of Jupiter, to this effect: 'It is Saturnius' will
That both, with utmost speed, should stoop to the Idalian hill,
To know his further pleasure there. And this let me advise,
When you arrive, and are in reach of his refulgent eyes,
His pleasure heard, perform it all, of whatsoever kind.'
     Thus mov'd she back, and us'd her throne. Those two outstripp'd the wind,
And Ida (all enchas'd with springs) they soon attain'd, and found
Where far-discerning Jupiter, in his repose, had crown'd
The brows of Gargarus, and wrapt an odoriferous cloud
About his bosom. Coming near, they stood; nor now he show'd   150
His angry countenance, since so soon he saw they made th' access
That his lov'd wife enjoin'd. But first the fair ambassadress
He thus commanded: 'Iris, go to Neptune, and relate
Our pleasure truly, and at large; command him from the fate
Of human war, and either greet the gods' society,
Or the divine sea make his seat. If proudly he deny,
Let better counsels be his guides than such as bid me war
And tempt my charge, though he be strong; for I am stronger far,
And elder born: nor let him dare to boast ev'n state with me,
Whom all gods else prefer in fear.' This said, down hasted she   160
From Ida's top to Ilion; and like a mighty snow,
Or gelid hail, that from the clouds the northern spirit doth blow:
So fell the windy-footed dame; and found with quick repair
The wat'ry god, to whom she said: 'God with the sable hair,

I come from aegis-bearing Jove, to bid thee cease from fight,
And visit heav'n or th' ample seas: which if, in his despite
Or disobedience, thou deniest, he threatens thee to come
(In opposite fight) to field himself, and therefore warns thee home,
His hands eschewing, since his pow'r is far superior,
His birth before thee, and affirms thy lov'd heart should abhor   170
To vaunt equality with him, whom every deity fears.'

He answer'd: 'O unworthy thing! Though he be great, he bears
His tongue too proudly, that ourself, born to an equal share
Of state and freedom, he would force. Three brothers born we are
To Saturn; Rhea brought us forth: this Jupiter and I,
And Pluto, god of under-grounds. The world indifferently
Dispos'd betwixt us, every one his kingdom – I, the seas,
Pluto the black lot, Jupiter the principalities
Of broad heav'n, all the sky and clouds – was sorted out: the earth
And high Olympus common are, and due to either's birth.   180
Why then should I be aw'd by him? Content he his great heart
With his third portion, and not think to amplify his part
With terrors of his stronger hands on me, as if I were
The most ignoble of us all: let him contain in fear
His daughters and his sons, begot by his own person: this
Holds more convenience; they must hear these violent threats of his.'

'Shall I,' said Iris, 'bear from thee an answer so austere?
Or wilt thou change it? Changing minds all noble natures bear:
And well thou know'st, these greatest born the Furies follow still.'

He answer'd: 'Iris, thy reply keeps time, and shows thy skill: 190
O 'tis a most praiseworthy thing, when messengers can tell
(Besides their messages) such things as fit th' occasion well.
But this much grieves my heart and soul, that being in pow'r and state
All ways his equal, and so fix'd by one decree in fate,
He should to me, as under him, ill language give, and chide;
Yet now (though still incens'd) I yield, affirming this beside
(And I enforce it with a threat), that if without consent
Of me, Minerva, Mercury, the queen of regiment,
And Vulcan, he will either spare high Ilion, or not race
Her turrets to the lowest stone, and (with both these) not grace   200
The Greeks as victors absolute, inform him this from me:
His pride and my contempt shall live at endless enmity.'

This said, he left the Greeks, and rush'd into his wat'ry throne,
Much miss'd of all th' heroic host. When Jove discern'd him gone,
Apollo's service he employ'd, and said: 'Lov'd Phoebus, go
To Hector: now th' earth-shaking god hath taken sea, and so
Shrunk from the horrors I denounc'd, which standing, he and all

The under-seated deities, that circle Saturn's fall,
Had heard of me in such a fight as had gone hard for them.
But both for them and me 'tis best that thus they fly th' extreme,   210
That had not pass'd us without sweat. Now then, in thy hands take
My adder-fring'd affrighting shield, which with such terror shake,
That fear may shake the Greeks to flight: besides this, add thy care
(O Phoebus, far-off-shooting god!) that this so sickly fare
Of famous Hector be recur'd; and quickly so excite
His amplest pow'rs, that all the Greeks may grace him with their flight,
Even to their ships, and Hellespont; and then will I devise
All words and facts again for Greece, that largely may suffice
To breath them from their instant toils.' Thus from th' Idean height
(Like air's swift-pigeon-killer) stoop'd the far-shot god of light,   220
And found great Hector sitting up, not stretch'd upon his bed,
Nor wheasing with a stopp'd up spirit, not in cold sweats, but fed
With fresh and comfortable veins, but his mind all his own,
But round about him all his friends, as well as ever known.
And this was with the mind of Jove, that flew to him before
Apollo came; who (as he saw no sign of any sore)
Ask'd (like a cheerful visitant): 'Why in this sickly kind,
Great Hector, sitt'st thou so apart? Can any grief of mind
Invade thy fortitude?' He spake, but with a feeble voice:
'O thou, the best of deities, why (since I thus rejoice   230
By thy so serious benefit) demand'st thou (as in mirth,
And to my face) if I were ill? For (more than what thy worth
Must needs take note of) doth not Fame from all mouths fill thine ears,
That (as my hand at th' Achive fleet was making massacres
Of men, whom valiant Ajax led) his strength struck with a stone
All pow'r of more hurt from my breast? My very soul was gone,
And once to-day I thought to see the house of Dis and Death.'

     'Be strong,' said he, 'for such a spirit now sends the god of breath,
From airy Ida, as shall run through all Greek spirits in thee;
Apollo with the golden sword, the clear far-seer, see –   240
Him who betwixt death and thy life, 'twixt ruin and those tow'rs,
Ere this day oft hath held his shield. Come then, be all thy pow'rs
In wonted vigour: let thy knights with all their horse assay
The Grecian fleet, myself will lead, and scour so clear the way,
That flight shall leave no Greek a rub.' Thus instantly inspir'd
Were all his nerves with matchless strength; and then his friends he fir'd
Against their foes, when (to his eyes) his ears confirm'd the god.
Then, as a goodly headed hart, or goat, bred in the wood,
A rout of country huntsmen chase, with all their hounds in cry,
The beast yet, or the shady woods or rocks excessive high,   250

Keep safe, or our unwieldy fates (that even in hunters sway)
Bar them the poor beast's pulling down, when straight the clamorous fray
Calls out a lion, hugely man'd, and his abhorred view
Turns headlong in unturning flight (though vent'rous) all the crew:
So hitherto the chasing Greeks their slaughter dealt by troops,
But after Hector was beheld range here and there, then stoops
The boldest courage; then their heels took in their dropping hearts,
And then spake Andremonides, a man of far best parts
Of all th' Aetolians, skill'd in darts, strenuous in fights of stand,
And one of whom few of the Greeks could get the better hand   260
(For rhetoric) when they fought with words, with all which, being wise,
Thus spake he to his Grecian friends: 'O mischief! Now mine eyes
Discern no little miracle: Hector escap'd from death,
And all recover'd, when all thought his soul had sunk beneath
The hands of Ajax; but some god hath sav'd and freed again
Him that but now dissolv'd the knees of many a Grecian,
And now I fear will weaken more, for not without the hand
Of him that thunders can his pow'rs thus still the forefight's stand,
Thus still triumphant: hear me then, our troops in quick retreat
Let's draw up to our fleet, and we, that boast ourselves the great,   270
Stand firm and try, if these that raise so high their charging darts
May be resisted: I believe, ev'n this great heart of hearts
Will fear himself to be too bold in charging thorow us.'
     They easily heard him, and obey'd, when all the generous
They call'd t' encounter Hector's charge, and turn'd the common men
Back to the fleet: and these were they that bravely furnish'd then
The fierce forefight: the Ajaces both, the worthy Cretan king,
The Mars-like Meges, Merion, and Teucer. Up then bring
The Trojan chiefs their men in heaps; before whom (amply pac'd)
March'd Hector; and in front of him, Apollo, who had cast   280
About his bright aspect a cloud, and did before him bear
Jove's huge and each-where-shaggy shield, which (to contain in fear
Offending men) the god-smith gave to Jove; with this he led
The Trojan forces. The Greeks stood, a fervent clamour spread
The air on both sides as they join'd; out flew the shafts and darts,
Some falling short, but other some found butts in breasts and hearts.
As long as Phoebus held but out his horrid shield, so long
The darts flew raging either way, and death grew both ways strong.
But when the Greeks had seen his face, and who it was that shook
The bristled targe, knew by his voice, then all their strengths forsook   290
Their nerves and minds; and then look how a goodly herd of neat,
Or wealthy flock of sheep, being close, and dreadless at their meat,
In some black midnight, suddenly (and not a keeper near)

A brace of horrid bears rush in, and then fly here and there
The poor affrighted flocks or herds: so every way dispers'd
The heartless Grecians; so the Sun their headstrong chace revers'd
To headlong flight, and that day rais'd, with all grace, Hector's head.
   Arcesilaus then he slew, and Stichius; Stichius led
Boeotia's brazen-coated men, the other was the friend
Of mighty-soul'd Menestheus. Aeneas brought to end   300
Medon and Janus; Medon was the brother (though but base)
Of swift Oïleades, and dwelt far from his breeding place,
In Phylaca; the other led th' Athenian bands: his sire
Was Spelus, Bucolus's son. Mecistheus did expire
Beneath Polydamas's hand. Polites, Echius slew
Just at the joining of the hosts. Agenor overthrew
Clonius. Bold Deiochus felt Alexander's lance;
It struck his shoulder's upper part, and did his head advance
Quite through his breast, as from the fight he turn'd him for retreat.
   While these stood spoiling of the slain, the Greeks found time to get   310
Beyond the dike, and th' undik'd pales: all scapes they gladly gain'd,
Till all had pass'd the utmost wall, necessity so reign'd.
   Then Hector cried out: 'Take no spoil, but rush on to the fleet,
From whose assault (for spoil or flight) if any man I meet,
He meets his death: nor in the fire of holy funeral
His brother's or his sister's hands shall cast (within our wall)
His loathed body, but without, the throats of dogs shall grave
His manless limbs.' This said, the scourge his forward horses drave
Through every order, and with him all whipp'd their chariots on,
All threatningly, out thund'ring shouts, as earth were overthrown.   320
   Before them march'd Apollo still, and as he march'd, digg'd down
(Without all labour) with his feet, the dike, till with his own
He fill'd it to the top, and made way both for man and horse,
As broad and long as with a lance (cast out to try one's force)
A man could measure. Into this they pour'd whole troops as fast
As numerous, Phoebus still before, for all their haste,
Still shaking Jove's unvalued shield, and held it up to all.
And then, as he had chok'd their dike, he tumbled down their wall.
And look how easily any boy, upon the sea-ebb'd shore,
Makes with a little sand a toy, and cares for it no more,   330
But as he rais'd it childlishly, so in his wanton vein,
Both with his hands and feet he pulls and spurns it down again:
So slight, O Phoebus, thy hands made of that huge Grecian toil,
And their late stand, so well resolv'd, as easily mad'st recoil.
   Thus stood they driv'n up at their fleet, where each heard other's thought,
Exhorted, passing humbly pray'd: all, all the gods besought

(With hands held up to heav'n) for help; 'mongst all, the good old man,
Grave Nestor (for his counsels call'd the Argives' guardian)
Fell on his aged knees, and pray'd, and to the starry host
Stretch'd out his hands for aid to theirs, of all thus moving most: 340
'O father Jove, if ever man of all our host did burn
Fat thighs of oxen or of sheep (for grace of safe return)
In fruitful Argos, and obtain'd the bowing of thy head
For promise of his humble prayers, O now remember him
(Thou merely heav'nly) and clear up the foul brows of this dim
And cruel day; do not destroy our zeal for Trojan pride.'
He pray'd, and heav'n's great counsellor with store of thunder tried
His former grace good, and so heard the old man's hearty prayers.
The Trojans took Jove's sign for them, and pour'd out their affairs
In much more violence on the Greeks, and thought on nought but fight: 350
And as a huge wave of a sea, swoln to his rudest height,
Breaks over both sides of a ship, being all urg'd by the wind,
For that's it makes the wave so proud: in such a borne-up kind
The Trojans overgat the wall; and getting in their horse,
Fought close at fleet, which now the Greeks ascended for their force:
Then from their chariots they with darts, the Greek with bead-hooks fought
(Kept still aboard for naval fights), their heads with iron wrought
In hooks and pikes. Achilles friend, still while he saw the wall
That stood without their fleet afford employment for them all,
Was never absent from the tent of that man-loving Greek,   360
Late-hurt Eurypilus, but sate, and every way did seek
To spend the sharp time of his wound with all the ease he could,
In med'cines and in kind discourse: but when he might behold
The Trojans past the wall, the Greeks flight-driv'n, and all in cries,
Then cried he out, cast down his hands, and beat with grief his thighs.
Then, 'O Eurypilus,' he cried, 'now all thy need of me
Must bear my absence: now a work of more necessity
Calls hence, and I must haste to call Achilles to the field:
Who knows, but (god assisting me) my words may make him yield?
The motion of a friend is strong.' His feet thus took him thence.   370
The rest yet stood their enemies firm, but all their violence
(Though Troy fought there with fewer men) lack'd vigour to repel
Those fewer from their navy's charge; and so, that charge as well
Lack'd force to spoil their fleet or tents. And as a shipwright's line
(Dispos'd by such a hand as learn'd, from th' artizan divine,
The perfect practice of his art) directs or guards so well
The naval timber then in frame, that all the laid-on steel
Can hew no further than may serve to give the timber th' end
Fore-purpos'd by the skilful wright: so both hosts did contend

With such a line or law applied to what their steel would gain.   380
　　At other ships fought other men, but Hector did maintain
His quarrel firm at Ajax' ship; and so did both employ
About one vessel all their toil: nor could the one destroy
The ship with fire, nor force the man, nor that man yet get gone
The other from so near his ship, for god hath brought him on.
　　But now did Ajax with a dart wound deadly in the breast
Caletor, son of Clytius, as he with fire address'd
To burn the vessel; as he fell, the brand fell from his hand.
　　When Hector saw his sister's son lie slaughter'd in the sand,
He call'd to all his friends, and pray'd they would not in that strait   390
Forsake his nephew, but maintain about his corse the fight,
And save it from the spoil of Greece. Then sent he out a lance
At Ajax, in his nephew's wreak, which miss'd, but made the chance
On Lycophron Mestorides, that was the household friend
Of Ajax, born in Cythera, whom Ajax did defend
(Being fled to his protection) for killing of a man
Amongst the god-like Cytherans; the vengeful javelin ran
Quite through his head, above his ear, as he was standing by
His fautor, then astern his ship; from whence his soul did fly,
And to the earth his body fell: the hair stood up on end   400
On Ajax, who to Teucer call'd (his brother), saying: 'Friend,
Our loved consort, whom we brought from Cythera and grac'd
So like our father, Hector's hand hath made him breathe his last.
Where then are all thy death-borne shafts, and that unvalued bow
Apollo gave thee?' Teucer straight his brother's thoughts did know,
Stood near him, and dispatch'd a shaft amongst the Trojan fight:
It struck Pysenor's goodly son, young Clytus, the delight
Of the renown'd Polydamas, the bridle in his hand,
As he was labouring his horse, to please the high command
Of Hector and his Trojan friends, and bring him where the fight   410
Made greatest tumult. But his strife for honour in their sight
Wrought not what sight or wishes help'd; for turning back his look,
The hollow of his neck the shaft came singing on, and strook,
And down he fell; his horses back, and hurried through the field
The empty chariot. Panthus' son made all haste, and withheld
Their loose career, disposing them to Protiaon's son,
Astinous, with special charge to keep them ever on,
And in his sight: so he again amongst the foremost went.
　　At Hector then another shaft incensed Teucer sent,
Which, had it hit him, sure had hurt; and had it hurt him, slain;   420
And had it slain him, it had driv'n all those to Troy again.
　　But Jove's mind was not sleeping now; it wak'd to Hector's fame

And Teucer's infamy, himself (in Teucer's deadly aim)
His well-wrought string dissevering, that serv'd his bravest bow;
His shaft flew quite another way, his bow the earth did strow.
At all which Teucer stood amaz'd, and to his brother cried,
'O prodigy! Without all doubt our angel doth deride
The counsels of our fight; he brake a string my hands put on
This morning, and was newly made, and well might have set gone
A hundred arrows; and beside, he struck out of my hand   430
The bow Apollo gave.' He said: 'Then, good friend, do not stand
More on thy archery, since god (preventer of all grace
Desir'd by Grecians) slights it so. Take therefore in the place
A good large lance, and on thy neck a target cast, as bright;
With which come fight thyself with some, and other some excite,
That without labour at the least (though we prove worser men)
Troy may not brag it took our ships: come, mind our business then.'
    This said, he hasted to his tent, left there his shafts and bow,
And then his double double shield did on his shoulders throw,
Upon his honour'd head he placed his helmet, thickly plum'd,   440
And then his strong and well-pil'd lance in his fair hand assum'd,
Return'd, and boldly took his place by his great brother's side.
    When Hector saw his arrows broke, out to his friends he cried:
'O friends, be yet more comforted! I saw the hands of Jove
Break the great Grecian archer's shafts: 'tis easy to approve
That Jove's power is direct with men, as well in those set high
Upon the sudden, as in those depress'd as suddenly,
And those not put in state at all, as now he takes away
Strength from Greeks, and gives it us; then use it, and assay
With join'd hands this approached fleet. If any bravely buy   450
His fame or fate with wounds or death, in Jove's name let him die.
Who for his country suffers death sustains no shameful thing:
His wife in honour shall survive, his progeny shall spring
In endless summers, and their roofs with patrimony swell;
And all this, though with all their freight the Greek ships we repel.'
    His friends thus cheer'd, on th' other part strong Ajax stirr'd his friends:
'O Greeks,' said he, 'what shame is this, that no man more defends
His fame and safety than to live, and thus be forc'd to shrink:
Now either save your fleet, or die, unless ye vainly think
That you can live, and they destroy'd? Perceives not every ear   460
How Hector heartens up his men, and hath his firebrands here,
Now ready to inflame our fleet? He doth not bid them dance,
That you may take your ease, and see, but to the fight advance.
No counsel can serve us but this: to mix both hands and hearts,
And bear up close; 'tis better much t'expose our utmost parts

To one day's certain life or death, than languish in a war
So base as this, beat to our ships by our inferiors far.'

    Thus rous'd he up their spirits and strengths: to work then both side went,
When Hector, the Phocensian duke, to fields of darkness sent
Fierce Schedius, Perimedes' son; which Ajax did requite   470
With slaughter of Laodamas, that led the foot to fight,
And was Antenor's famous son. Polydamas did end
Otus, surnam'd Cyllenius, whom Phydas made his friend,
Being chief of the Epeians' bands: whose fall when Meges view'd,
He let fly at his feller's life; who (shrinking in) eschew'd
The well-aim'd lance: Apollo's will denied that Panthus' son
Should fall amongst the foremost fights: the dart the mid-breast won
Of Crasmus; Meges won his arms. At Meges Dolops then
Bestow'd his lance; he was the son of Lampus, best of men –
And Lampus of Laomedon, well skill'd in strength of mind.   480
He struck Phylides' shield quite through, whose curets, better lin'd
And hollow'd fitly, sav'd his life: Phyleus left him them,
Who from Epirus brought them home, on that part where the stream
Of famous Seleës doth run; Euphetes did bestow
(Being guest with him) those well-prov'd arms, to wear against the foe,
And now they sav'd his son from death. At Dolops Meges threw
A spear well pil'd, that struck his casque full in the height; off flew
His purple feather, newly made, and in the dust it fell.

    While these thus striv'd for victory, and either's hope serv'd well,
Atrides came to Meges' aid, and (hidden with his side)   490
Let loose a javelin at his foe, that through his back implied
His lusty head, even past his breast; the ground receiv'd his weight.

    While these made into spoil his arms, great Hector did excite
All his allies to quick revenge; and first he wrought upon
Strong Melanippus (that was son to great Hycetaon)
With some reproof. Before these wars he in Percote fed
Clov'n-footed oxen, but did since return where he was bred,
Excell'd amongst the Ilians, was much of Priam lov'd,
And in his court kept as his son; him Hector thus reprov'd:

    'Thus, Melanippus, shall our blood accuse us of neglect?   500
Nor moves it thy lov'd heart (thus urg'd) thy kinsman to protect?
Seest thou not, how they seek his spoil? Come, follow, now no more
Our fight must stand at length, but close: nor leave the close before
We close the latest eye of them, or they the lowest stone
Tear up, and sack the citizens of lofty Ilion.'
He led; he follow'd like a god: and then must Ajax needs
(As well as Hector) cheer his men, and thus their spirits he feeds:
'Good friends, bring but your selves to feel the noble stings of shame

For what ye suffer, and be men: respect each other's fame,
For which who strives in shame's fit fear, and puts on ne'er so far   510
Comes oft'ner off than stick engag'd: these fugitives of war
Save neither life, nor get renown, nor bear more mind than sheep.'
    This short speech fir'd them in his aid, his spirit touch'd them deep,
And turn'd them all before the fleet into a wall of brass:
To whose assault Jove stirr'd their foes, and young Atrides was
Jove's instrument, who thus set on the young Antilochus:
'Antilochus, in all our host, there is not one of us
More young than you, more swift of foot, nor (with both those) so strong.
O would thou wouldst then (for thou canst) one of this lusty throng,
That thus comes skipping out before (whoever, any where)   520
May stick (for my sake) 'twixt both hosts, and leave his bold blood there.'
    He said no sooner, and retir'd, but forth he rush'd before
The foremost fighters, yet his eye did every way explore
For doubt of odds; out flew his lance: the Trojans did abstain
While he was darting, yet his dart he cast not off in vain:
For Melanippus, that rare son of great Hycetaon,
(As bravely he put forth to fight) it fiercely flew upon,
And at the nipple of his breast his breast and life did part.
And then, much like an eager hound, cast off at some young hart
Hurt by the hunters that had left his covert then but new,   530
The great-in-war Antilochus (O Melanippus) flew
On thy torn bosom for thy spoil. But thy death could not lie
Hid to great Hector, who all haste made to thee, and made fly
Antilochus, although in war he were at all parts skill'd:
But as some wild beast, having done some shrewd turn (either kill'd
The herdsman, or the herdsman's dog) and skulks away before
The gather'd multitude makes in: so Nestor's son forbore,
But after him, with horrid cries, both Hector and the rest
Show'rs of tear-thirsty lances pour'd, who having arm'd his breast
With all his friends, he turn'd it then. Then on the ships all Troy,   540
Like raw-flesh-nourish'd lions rush'd, and knew they did employ
Their pow'rs to perfect Jove's high will; who still their spirits enflam'd,
And quench'd the Grecians; one renown'd, the other often sham'd;
For Hector's glory still he stood, and ever went about
To make him cast the fleet such fire as never should go out;
Heard Thetis' foul petition, and wish'd in any wise
The splendour of the burning ships might satiate his eyes.
From him yet the repulse was then to be on Troy conferr'd,
The honour of it giv'n the Greeks; which (thinking on) he stirr'd
(With such addition of his spirit) the spirit Hector bore,   550
To burn the fleet, that of itself was hot enough before.

But now he far'd like Mars himself, so brandishing his lance
As through the deep shades of a hill a raging fire should glance,
Held up to all eyes by a hill; about his lips a foam
Stood, as when th' ocean is enrag'd; his eyes were overcome
With fervour, and resembled flames, set off by his dark brows,
And from his temples his bright helm abhorred lightnings throws.
For Jove, from forth the sphere of stars, to his state put his own,
And all the blaze of both the hosts confin'd in him alone.
And all this was since after this he had not long to live,   560
This lightning flew before his death, which Pallas was to give
(A small time thence, and now prepar'd) beneath the violence
Of great Pelides. In mean time, his present eminence
Thought all things under it: and he still where he saw the stands
Of greatest strength and bravest arm'd, there he would prove his hands,
Or no where, offering to break through. But that pass'd all his pow'r,
Although his will were past all theirs; they stood him like a tow'r
Conjoin'd so firm, that as a rock, exceeding high and great,
And standing near the hoary sea, bears many a boisterous threat
Of high-voic'd winds and billows huge, belch'd on it by the storms: 570
So stood the Greeks great Hector's charge, nor stirr'd their battellous forms.

He (girt in fire, borne for the fleet) still rush'd at every troop,
And fell upon it like a wave, high rais'd, that then doth stoop
Out from the clouds, grows as it stoops, with storms, then down doth come
And cuff a ship, when all her sides are hid in brackish foam,
Strong gales still raging in her sails, her sailors' minds dismay'd,
Death being but little from their lives: so Jove-like Hector fray'd
And plied the Greeks, who knew not what would chance, for all their guards.

And as the baneful king of beasts, leapt in to oxen herds,
Fed in the meadows of a fen, exceeding great, the beasts   580
In number infinite,'mongst whom (their herdsmen wanting breasts
To fight with lions for the price of a black ox's life)
He here and there jumps, first and last, in his bloodthirsty strife,
Chas'd and assaulted; and at length, down in the midst goes one,
And all the rest sperst through the fen: so now all Greece was gone.
So Hector (in a flight from heav'n upon the Grecians cast)
Turn'd all their backs, yet only one his deadly lance laid fast:
Brave Mycenaeus Periphes, Cypraeus' dearest son,
Who of the heaven's-queen-lov'd-king (great Eurysthaeus) won
The grace to greet in embassy the strength of Hercules,   590
Was far superior to his sire in feet, fight, nobleness
Of all the virtues; and all those did such a wisdom guide
As all Mycenae could not match: and this man dignified
(Still making greater his renown) the state of Priam's son.

For his unhappy hasty foot, as he address'd to run,
Stuck in th' extreme ring of his shield, that to his ankles reach'd,
And down he upwards fell; his fall up from the centre fetch'd
A huge sound with his head and helm, which Hector quickly spied,
Ran in, and in his worthy breast his lance's head did hide,
And slew about him all his friends, who could not give him aid: 600
They griev'd, and of his god-like foe fled so extreme afraid.
And now amongst the nearest ships, that first were drawn to shore,
The Greeks were driv'n; beneath whose sides, behind them, and before,
And into them they pour'd themselves, and thence were driv'n again
Up to their tents, and there they stood, not daring to maintain
Their guards more outward, but betwixt the bounds of fear and shame,
Cheer'd still each other, when th' old man, that of the Grecian name
Was call'd the pillar, every man thus by his parents pray'd:

'O friends, be men, and in your minds let others' shames be weigh'd;
Know you have friends besides yourselves: possessions, parents, wives,   610
As well those that are dead to you, as those ye love with lives,
All sharing still their good or bad with yours: by these I pray,
That are not present (and the more should therefore make ye weigh
Their miss of you, as yours of them), that you will bravely stand,
And this forc'd flight you have sustain'd, at length yet countermand.'

Supplies of good words thus supplied the deeds and spirits of all,
And so at last Minerva clear'd the cloud that Jove let fall
Before their eyes: a mighty light flew beaming every way,
As well about their ships as where their darts did hottest play:
Then saw they Hector great in arms, and his associates,   620
As well all those that then abstain'd, as those that help'd the fates,
And all their own fight at the fleet. Nor did it now content
Ajax to keep down like the rest; he up the hatches went,
Stalk'd here and there; and in his hand a huge great head-hook held,
Twelve cubits long, and full of iron: and as a man well skill'd
In horse, made to the martial race, when (of a number more)
He chooseth four, and brings them forth to run them all before
Swarms of admiring citizens, amids their town's high way,
And (in their full career) he leaps from one to one, no stay
Enforc'd on any, nor fails he in either seat or leap: 630
So Ajax with his bead-hook leap'd nimbly from ship to ship,
As actively, commanding all them in their men, as well
As men in them, most terribly exhorting to repel,
To save their navy and their tents. But Hector nothing needs
To stand on exhortations now at home; he strives for deeds.
And look how Jove's great queen of birds (sharp set) looks out for prey,
Knows floods that nourish wild-wing'd fowls, and (from her airy way)

Beholds where cranes, swans, cormorants, have made their foody fall,
Darkens the river with her wings, and stoops amongst them all:
So Hector flew amongst the Greeks, directing his command   640
(In chief) 'gainst one opposite ship, Jove with a mighty hand
Still backing him and all his men: and then again there grew
A bitter conflict at the fleet; you would have said none drew
A weary breath, nor ever would, they laid so freshly on.
And this was it that fir'd them both: the Greeks did build upon
No hope, but what the field would yield; flight, an impossible course.
The Trojans all hope entertain'd that sword and fire should force
Both ships and lives of all the Greeks; and thus, unlike affects
Bred like strenuity in both. Great Hector still directs
His pow'rs against the first near ship. 'Twas that fair bark that brought   650
Protesilaus to those wars, and now, her self to nought,
With many Greek and Trojan lives all spoil'd about her spoil:
One slew another desperately, and close the deadly toil
Was pitch'd on both parts: not a shaft, nor far-off striking dart
Was us'd through all: one fight fell out of one despiteful heart;
Sharp axes, twybills, two-hand swords, and spears with two heads borne,
Were then the weapons; fair short swords, with sanguine hilts still worn,
Had use in like sort; of which last, ye might have numbers view'd
Drop with dissolv'd arms from their hands, as many downright hew'd
From off their shoulders as they fought, their bawdrics cut in twain: 660
And thus the black blood flow'd on earth, from soldiers hurt and slain.
    When Hector once had seiz'd the ship, he clapt his fair broad hand
Fast on the stern, and held it there, and there gave this command:
    'Bring fire, and all together shout; now Jove hath drawn the veil
From such a day as makes amends for all his storms of hail:
By whose blest light we take those ships, that in despite of heav'n
Took sea, and brought us worlds of woe, all since our peers were giv'n
To such a laziness and fear, they would not let me end
Our ling'ring banes, and charge thus home, but keep home and defend.
And so they rul'd the men I led, but though Jove then withheld   670
My natural spirit, now by Jove 'tis freed, and thus impell'd.'
    This more enflam'd them, in so much that Ajax now no more
Kept up, he was so drown'd in darts, a little he forbore
The hatches to a seat beneath, of seven foot long, but thought
It was impossible to 'scape; he sat yet where he fought,
And hurl'd out lances thick as hail at all men that assay'd
To fire the ship; with whom he found his hands so overlaid,
That on his soldiers thus he cried: 'O friends, fight I alone?
Expect ye more walls at your back? Towns rampir'd here are none,
No citizens to take ye in, no help in any kind;   680

We are, I tell you, in Troy's fields, have nought but seas behind,
And foes before, far, far from Greece. For shame, obey commands.
There is no mercy in the wars, your healths lie in your hands.'
   Thus rag'd he, and pour'd out his darts; who ever he espied
Come near the vessel, arm'd with fire, on his fierce dart he died;
All that pleas'd Hector made him mad, all that his thanks would earn,
Of which twelve men, his most resolv'd, lay dead before his stern.

THE END OF THE FIFTEENTH BOOK

BOOK SIXTEEN

The Argument

Achilles, at Patroclus' suit, doth yield
His arms and Myrmidons; which brought to field,
The Trojans fly. Patroclus hath the grace
Of great Sarpedon's death, sprung of the race
Of Jupiter, he having slain the horse
Of Thetis' son (fierce Pedasus); the force
Of Hector doth revenge the much-ru'd end
Of most renown'd Sarpedon, on the friend
Of Thetides, first by Euphorbus harm'd,
And by Apollo's personal pow'r disarm'd.

Another Argument

In *Pi*, Patroclus bears the chance
Of death, impos'd by Hector's lance.

BOOK SIXTEEN

THUS FIGHTING for this well-built ship, Patroclus all that space
Stood by his friend, preparing words to win the Greeks his grace,
With pow'r of uncontained tears: and (like a fountain pour'd
In black streams from a lofty rock) the Greeks, so plagued, deplor'd.
Achilles (ruthful for his tears) said: 'Wherefore weeps my friend,
So like a girl, who though she sees her mother cannot tend
Her childish humours, hangs on her, and would be taken up,
Still viewing her with tear-drown'd eyes, when she has made her stoop.
To nothing liker I can shape thy so unseemly tears.
What causeth them? Hath any ill solicited thine ears,   10
Befall'n my Myrmidons? Or news from loved Phthia brought,
Told only thee, lest I should grieve, and therefore thus hath wrought
On thy kind spirit? Actor's son, the good Menoetius
(Thy father) lives, and Peleus (mine), great son of Aeacus,
Amongst his Myrmidons, whose deaths in duty we should mourn.
Or is it what the Greeks sustain that doth thy stomach turn,
On whom (for their injustice sake) plagues are so justly laid?
Speak, man, let both know either's heart.' Patroclus, sighing, said:
    'O Peleus' son (thou strongest Greek by all degrees that lives),
Still be not angry, our sad state such cause of pity gives.   20
Our greatest Greeks lie at their ships sore wounded: Ithacus,
King Agamemnon, Diomed, and good Eurypilus.
But these, much-med'cine-knowing men (physicians) can recure;
Thou yet unmed'cinable still, though thy wound all endure.
Heav'n bless my bosom from such wrath as thou sooth'st as thy bliss
(Unprofitably virtuous). How shall our progenies,
Born in thine age, enjoy thine aid, when these friends in thy flow'r
Thou leav'st to such unworthy death? O idle, cruel pow'r!
Great Peleus never did beget, nor Thetis bring forth thee;
Thou from the blue sea and her rocks deriv'st thy pedigree.   30
What so declines thee? If thy mind shuns any augury,
Related by thy mother queen, from heaven's foreseeing eye,
And therefore thou forsak'st thy friends, let me go ease their moans
With those brave relics of our host, thy mighty Myrmidons,
That I my bring to field more light to conquest than hath been;

To which end grace me with thine arms, since any shadow seen
Of thy resemblance, all the pow'r of perjur'd Troy will fly,
And our so tired friends will breathe: our fresh-set-on supply
Will easily drive their wearied off.' Thus (foolish man) he su'd
For his sure death; of all whose speech Achilles first renew'd   40
The last part, thus: 'O worthy friend, what have thy speeches been?
I shun the fight for oracles, or what my mother queen
Hath told from Jove? I take no care nor note of one such thing,
But this fit anger stings me still, that the insulting king
Should from his equal take his right, since he exceeds in pow'r.
This (still his wrong) is still my grief: he took my paramour
That all men gave, and whom I won by virtue of my spear,
That (for her) overturn'd a town. This rape he made of her,
And used me like a fugitive, an inmate in a town,
That is no city libertine, nor capable of their gown.   50
But, bear we this, as out of date; 'tis past, nor must we still
Feed anger in our noblest parts; yet thus, I have my will
As well as our great king of men, for I did ever vow
Never to cast off my disdain, till (as it falls out now)
Their miss of me knock'd at my fleet, and told me in their cries
I was reveng'd, and had my wish of all my enemies.
And so of this repeat enough: take thou my fame-blaz'd arms,
And my fight-thirsty Myrmidons lead to these hot alarms.
Whole clouds of Trojans circle us with hateful eminence,
The Greeks shut in a little shore, a sort of citizens   60
Skipping upon them – all because their proud eyes do not see
The radiance of my helmet there, whose beams had instantly
Thrust back, and all these ditches fill'd with carrion of their flesh,
If Agamemnon had been kind; where now they fight as fresh,
As thus far they had put at ease, and at our tents contend –
And may, for the repulsive hand of Diomed doth not spend
His raging darts there, that their death could fright out of our fleet:
Nor from that head of enmity can my poor hearers meet
The voice of great Atrides now: now Hector's only voice
Breaks all the air about both hosts, and with the very noise   70
Bred by his loud encouragements, his forces fill the field,
And fight the poor Achaians down. But on, put thou my shield
Betwixt the fire-plague and our fleet: rush bravely on, and turn
War's tide as headlong on their throats. No more let them ajourn
Our sweet home-turning. But observe the charge I lay on thee
To each least point, that thy rul'd hand may highly honour me,
And get such glory from the Greeks, that they may send again
My most sweet wench, and gifts to boot: when thou hast cast a rein

On these so headstrong citizens and forc'd them from our fleet –
With which grace if the god of sounds thy kind egression greet –   80
Retire, and be not tempted on (with pride, to see thy hand
Rain slaughter'd carcasses on earth) to run forth thy command
As far as Ilion, lest the gods that favour Troy come forth
To thy encounter; for the Sun much loves it, and my worth
(In what thou suffer'st) will be wrong'd, that I would let my friend
Assume an action of such weight without me, and transcend
His friend's prescription. Do not then affect a further fight
Than I may strengthen: let the rest (when thou hast done this right)
Perform the rest. O would to Jove, thou Pallas, and thou Sun,
That not a man hous'd underneath those tow'rs of Ilion,   90
Nor any one of all the Greeks (how infinite a sum
Soever all together make) might live unovercome,
But only we two ('scaping death) might have the thund'ring down
Of every stone stuck in the walls of this so sacred town.'

    Thus spake they only 'twixt themselves. And now the foe no more
Could Ajax stand, being so oppress'd with all the iron store
The Trojans pour'd on; with those darts, and with Jove's will beside,
His pow'rs were cloy'd, and his bright helm did deaf'ning blows abide;
His plume and all head ornaments could never hang in rest,
His arm yet labour'd up his shield, and having done their best,   100
They could not stir him from his stand, although he wrought it out
With short respirings, and with sweat, that ceaseless flow'd about
His reeking limbs, no least time giv'n to take in any breath.
Ill strengthen'd ill; when one was up, another was beneath.

    Now, Muses, you that dwell in heav'n, the dreadful mean inspire
That first enforc'd the Grecian fleet to take in Trojan fire:
First Hector, with his huge broad sword, cut off, at setting on,
The head of Ajax' ashen lance; which Ajax seeing gone,
And that he shook a headless spear (a little while unware),
His wary spirits told him straight the hand of heav'n was there,   110
And trembled under his conceit; which was, that 'twas Jove's deed:
Who, as he poll'd off his dart's head, so, sure, he had decreed
That all the counsels of their war he would poll off like it,
And give the Trojans victory: so trusted he his wit,
And left his darts. And then the ship was heap'd with horrid brands
Of kindling fire, which instantly was seen through all the strands
In unextinguishable flames, that all the ship embrac'd:
And then Achilles beat his thighs, cried out: 'Patroclus, haste;
Make way with horse: I see at fleet a fire of fearful rage.
Arm, arm, lest all our fleet it fire, and all our pow'r engage;   120
Arm quickly, I'll bring up the troops.' To these so dreadful wars

Patroclus, in Achilles' arms, enlighten'd all with stars,
And richly 'ameld, all haste made: he wore his sword, his shield,
His huge-plum'd helm, and two such spears as he could nimbly wield.
But the most fam'd Achilles' spear, big, solid, full of weight,
He only left of all his arms; for that far pass'd the might
Of any Greek to shake but his; Achilles' only ire
Shook that huge weapon, that was given by Chiron to his sire,
Cut from the top of Pelion, to be heroës' deaths.
His steeds Automedon straight join'd, like whóm no man that breathes   130
(Next Peleus' son) Patroclus lov'd; for like him, none so great
He found, in faith, at every fight, nor to out-look a threat.
Automedon did therefore guide (for him) Achilles' steeds:
Xanthius and Balius swift as wind, begotten by the seeds
Of Zephyr and the harpy-born Podarge, in a mead
Close to the wavy ocean, where that fierce harpy fed.
Automedon join'd these before, and with the hindmost geres
He fasten'd famous Pedasus, whom from the massacres
Made by Achilles, when he took Eëtion's wealthy town,
He brought, and (though of mortal race) yet gave him the renown   140
To follow his immortal horse. And now, before his tents,
Himself had seen his Myrmidons, in all habiliments
Of dreadful war. And when ye see (upon a mountain bred)
A den of wolves (about whose hearts unmeasur'd strengths are fed)
New come from currie of a stag, their jaws all blood-besmear'd,
And when from some black water-fount they all together herd,
There having plentifully lapp'd, with thin and thrust-out tongues,
The top and clearest of the spring, go belching from their lungs
The clotter'd gore, look dreadfully, and entertain no dread,
Their bellies gaunt all taken up with being so rawly fed: 150
Then say that such, in strength and look, were great Achilles' men
Now order'd for the dreadful fight: and so with all them then
Their princes and their chiefs did show about their general's friend –
His friend, and all about himself, who chiefly did intend
Th' embattelling of horse and foot. To that siege, held so long,
Twice five and twenty sail he brought; twice five and twenty strong
Of able men was every sail: five colonels he made
Of all those forces, trusty men, and all of pow'r to lead,
But he of pow'r beyond them all. Menesthius was one,
That ever wore discolour'd arms; he was a river's son   160
That fell from heav'n, and good to drink was his delightful stream:
His name, unwearied Sperchius. He lov'd the lovely dame,
Fair Polydora, Peleus' seed, and dear in Borus' sight;
And she, to that celestial flood, gave this Menesthius light,

A woman mixing with a god. Yet Borus bore the name
Of father to Menesthius, he marrying the dame,
And giving her a mighty dow'r; he was the kind descent
Of Perieris. The next man renown'd with regiment
Was strong Eudorus, brought to life by one suppos'd a maid,
Bright Polymela (Phylas' seed) but had the wanton play'd   170
With Argus-killing Mercury, who (fir'd with her fair eyes
As she was singing in the quire of her that makes the cries
In clamorous hunting, and doth bear the crooked bow of gold)
Stole to her bed, in that chaste room that Phebe chaste did hold,
And gave her that swift-warlike son (Eudorus), brought to light
As she was dancing: but as soon as she that rules the plight
Of labouring women, eas'd her throes, and show'd her son the sun,
Strong Echelcaeus, Actor's heir, woo'd earnestly, and won
Her second favour, seeing her with gifts of infinite prize,
And after brought her to his house, where in his grandsire's eyes   180
(Old Phylas) Polymela's son obtain'd exceeding grace,
And found as careful bringing up, as of his natural race
He had descended. The third chief was fair Memalides
Pysandrus, who in skill of darts obtain'd supremest praise
Of all the Myrmidons, except their lord's companion:
The fourth charge aged Phoenix had. The fifth, Alcimedon,
Son of Laercus, and much fam'd. All these digested thus
In fit place, by the mighty son of royal Peleus,
This stern remembrance he gave all: 'You Myrmidons,' said he,
'Lest any of you should forget his threat'nings used to me   190
In this place, and through all the time that my just anger reign'd,
Attempting me with bitter words for being so restrain'd
(For my hot humour) from the fight, remember them, as these:
"Thou cruel son of Peleus, whom she that rules the seas
Did only nourish with her gall, thou dost ungently hold
Our hands against our wills from fight; we will not be controll'd,
But take our ships, and sail for home, before we loiter here,
And feed thy fury." These high words exceeding often were
The threats that in your mutinous troops ye us'd to me for wrath
To be detain'd so from the field: now then, your spleens may bathe   200
In sweat of those great works ye wish'd; now he that can employ
A generous heart, go fight, and fright these bragging sons of Troy.'

  This set their minds and strengths on fire, the speech enforcing well,
Being us'd in time – but being their king's, it much more did impel,
And closer rush'd in all the troops. And as, for buildings high,
The mason lays his stones more thick, against th' extremity
Of wind and weather; and ev'n then, if any storm arise,

He thickens them the more for that, the present act so plies
His honest mind to make sure work: so for the high estate
This work was brought to, these men's minds (according to the rate)   210
Were rais'd, and all their bodies join'd; but their well-spoken king,
With his so timely-thought-on speech more sharp made valour's sting,
And thicken'd so their targets' host, so all their helmets then,
That shields propp'd shields, helms helmets knock'd, and men encourag'd men.
    Patroclus and Automedon did arm before them all,
Two bodies with one mind inform'd; and then the general
Betook him to his private tent, where from a coffer wrought
Most rich and curiously, and given by Thetis, to be brought
In his own ship, top-fill'd with vests, warm robes to check cold wind,
And tapestries, all golden-fring'd, and curl'd with thrumbs behind,   220
He took a most unvalued bowl, in which none drank but he;
Nor he, but to the deities; nor any deity
But Jove himself was serv'd with that; and that he first did cleanse
With sulphur, then with fluences of sweetest water rense;
Then wash'd his hands, and drew himself a mighty bowl of wine,
Which (standing midst the place enclos'd for services divine,
And looking up to heaven and Jove, who saw him well) he pour'd
Upon the place of sacrifice, and humbly thus implor'd:
    'Great Dodonaeus, president of cold Dodonas' towr's;
Divine Pelasgicus, that dwell'st far hence, about whose bow'rs   230
Th' austere prophetic Selli dwell, that still sleep on the ground,
Go bare, and never cleanse their feet – as I before have found
Grace to my vows, and hurt to Greece, so now my prayers intend.
I still stay in the gather'd fleet, but have dismiss'd my friend
Amongst my many Myrmidons to danger of the dart.
O grant his valour my renown, arm with my mind his heart,
That Hector's self may know my friend can work in single war,
And not then only show his hands, so hot and singular,
When my kind presence seconds him: but fight he ne'er so well,
No further let him trust his fight, but, when he shall repel   240
Clamour and danger from our fleet, vouchsafe a safe retreat
To him and all his companies, with fames and arms complete.'
    He pray'd, and heav'n's great counsellor gave satisfying ear
To one part of his orisons, but left the other there:
He let him free the fleet of foes, but safe retreat denied.
Achilles left that outer part, where he his zeal applied,
And turn'd into his inner tent, made fast his cup, and then
Stood forth, and with his mind beheld the foes fight, and his men,
That follow'd his great-minded friend, embattled till they brake
With gallant spirit upon the foe: and as fell wasps, that make   250

Their dwellings in the broad high way, which foolish children use
(Their cottages being near their nests) to anger and abuse
With ever vexing them, and breed (to soothe their childish war)
A common ill to many men, since if a traveller
(That would his journey's end apply, and pass them unassay'd)
Come near and vex them, upon him the children's faults are laid,
For on they fly, as he were such, and still defend their own:
So far'd it with the fervent mind of every Myrmidon,
Who pour'd themselves out of their fleet upon their wanton foes,
That needs would stir them, thrust so near, and cause the overthrows   260
Of many others that had else been never touch'd by them,
Nor would have touch'd. Patroclus then put his wind to the stream,
And thus exhorted: 'Now, my friends, remember you express
Your late urg'd virtue and renown, our great Aeacides,
That he being strong'st of all the Greeks, his eminence may dim
All others likewise in our strengths that far off imitate him.
And Agamemnon now may see his fault as general
As his place high, dishonouring him that so much honours all.'
  Thus made he sparkle their fresh fire, and on they rush'd; the fleet
Fill'd full her hollow sides with sounds, that terribly did greet   270
Th' amazed Trojans, and their eyes did second their amaze
When great Menoetius' son they saw, and his friend's armour blaze;
All troops stood troubled with conceit that Peleus' son was there,
His anger cast off at the ships, and each look'd every where
For some authority to lead the then prepared flight.
Patroclus greeted with a lance the region where the fight
Made strongest tumult, near the ship Protesilaus brought,
And struck Pyrechmen, who before the fair-helm'd Paeons fought,
Led from Amydon, near whose walls the broad-stream'd Axius flows.
Through his right shoulder flew the dart, whose blow struck all the blows   280
In his pow'r from his pow'rless arm, and down he groaning fell:
His men all flying, their leader fled. This one dart did repel
The whole guard placed about the ship, whose fire extinct, half burn'd,
The Paeons left her, and full cry to clamorous flight return'd.
Then spread the Greeks about their ships, triumphant tumult flow'd,
And as from top of some steep hill the Lightner strips a cloud,
And lets a great sky out from heav'n, in whose delightsome light
All prominent foreheads, forests, tow'rs, and temples clear the sight:
So clear'd these Greeks this Trojan cloud, and at their ships and tents
Obtain'd a little time to breathe, but found no present vents   290
To their inclusions; nor did Troy (though these Paeonians fled)
Lose any ground, but from this ship they needfully turn'd head.
  Then every man a man subdu'd; Patroclus in the thigh

Struck Areïlicus; his dart the bone did break and fly
Quite through, and sunk him to the earth. Good Menelaus slew
Accomplish'd Thoas, in whose breast (being nak'd) his lance he threw
Above his shield, and freed his soul. Phylides (taking note
That bold Amphidus bent on him) prevented him, and smote
His thigh's extreme part, where (of man) his fattest muscle lies,
The nerves torn with his lance's pile, and darkness clos'd his eyes.   300
Antilochus Atymnius seiz'd; his steel lance did impress
His first three guts, and loos'd his life. At young Nestorides,
Maris, Atymnius' brother flew, and at him, Thrasimed
(The brother to Antilochus); his eager javelin's head
The muscles of his arm cut out, and shiver'd all the bone;
Night clos'd his eyes, his lifeless corse his brother fell upon,
And so by two kind brothers' hands did two kind brothers bleed,
Both being divine Sarpedon's friends, and were the darting seed
Of Amisodarus, that kept the bane of many men,
Abhorr'd Chimaera, and such bane now caught his childeren.   310
Ajax Oïleades did take Cleobulus alive,
Invading him (stay'd by the press), and at him then let drive
With his short sword, that cut his neck, whose blood warm'd all the steel,
And cold death, with a violent fate, his sable eyes did seal.
Peneleus and Lycon cast together off their darts;
Both miss'd, and both together then went with their swords; in parts
The blade and hilt went, laying on upon the helmet's height.
Peneleus' sword caught Lycon's neck, and cut it thorough quite;
His head hung by the very skin. The swift Meriones
(Pursuing flying Acamas) just as he got access   320
To horse and chariot, overtook, and took him such a blow
On his right shoulder, that he left his chariot, and did strow
The dusty earth; life left his limbs, and night his eyes possess'd.
    Idomenaeus his stern dart at Erymas address'd,
As (like to Acamas) he fled; he cut the sundry bones
Beneath his brain, betwixt his neck and foreparts, and so runs
(Shaking his teeth out) through his mouth, his eyes all drown'd in blood:
So through his nostrils and his mouth (that now dart-open stood)
He breath'd his spirit. Thus had death from every Grecian chief
A chief of Troy. For, as to kids or lambs their cruell'st thief,   330
The wolf, steals in, and when he sees that by the shepherd's sloth
The dams are sperst about the hills, then serves his ravenous tooth
With ease, because his prey is weak: so serv'd the Greeks their foes,
Discerning well how shrieking flight did all their spirits dispose,
Their biding virtues quite forgot; and now the natural spleen
That Ajax bore to Hector still by all means would have been

Within his bosom with a dart: but he, that knew the war
(Well cover'd in a well-lin'd shield), did well perceive how far
The arrows and the javelins reach'd, by being within their sounds
And ominous singings, and observ'd the there-inclining bounds   340
Of conquest, in her aid of him, and so obey'd her change,
Took safest course for him and his, and stood to her as strange.
And as when Jove intends a storm, he lets out of the stars,
From steep Olympus, a black cloud that all heav'n's splendour bars
From men on earth: so from the hearts of all the Trojan host,
All comfort lately found from Jove in flight and cries was lost.
Nor made they any fair retreat; Hector's unruly horse
Would needs retire him; and he left engag'd his Trojan force,
Forc'd by the steepness of the dike, that in ill place they took,
And kept them that would fain have gone. Their horses quite forsook   350
A number of the Trojan kings, and left them in the dike,
Their chariots in their foreteams broke. Patroclus then did strike
While steel was hot, and cheer'd his friends, nor meant his enemies good;
Who when they once began to fly, each way receiv'd a flood,
And chok'd themselves with drifts of dust. And now were clouds begot
Beneath the clouds; with flight and noise the horse neglected not
Their home intendments; and where rout was busiest, there pour'd on
Patroclus most exhorts and threats; and then lay overthrown
Numbers beneath their axle-trees, who (lying in flight's stream)
Made th' after chariots jot and jump, in driving over them.   360

    Th' immortal horse Patroclus rode did pass the dike with ease,
And wish'd the depth and danger more: and Menetiades
As great a spirit had to reach retiring Hector's haste;
But his fleet horse had too much law, and fetch'd him off too fast.
And as in autumn the black earth is loaden with the storms
That Jove in gluts of rain pours down, being angry with the forms
Of judgment in authoris'd men, that in their courts maintain
(With violent office) wrested laws, and (fearing gods nor men)
Exile all justice, for whose faults whole fields are overflown,
And many valleys cut away, with torrents headlong thrown   370
From neighbour mountains, till the sea receive them, roaring in,
And judg'd men's labours then are vain, plagued for their judge's sin:
So now the foul defaults of some all Troy were laid upon;
So like those torrents roar'd they back to windy Ilion;
And so like tempests blew the horse, with ravishing back again
Those hot assailants, all their works at fleet now render'd vain.

    Patroclus (when he had dispers'd the foremost phalanxes)
Call'd back his forces to the fleet, and would not let them press
As they desir'd, too near the town, but 'twixt the ships and flood,

And their steep rampire, his hand steep'd revenge in seas of blood.   380
  Then Pronous was first that fell beneath his fiery lance,
Which struck his bare breast, near his shield. The second, Thestor's chance
(Old Enops' son) did make himself, who shrinking and set close
In his fair seat (even with th' approach Patroclus made) did lose
All manly courage; in so much, that from his hands his reins
Fell flowing down, and his right jaw Patroclus' lance attains,
Struck through his teeth, and there it stuck, and by it to him drew
Dead Thestor to his chariot; it show'd, as when you view
An angler from some prominent rock draw with his line and hook
A mighty fish out of the sea: for so the Greek did pluck   390
The Trojan gaping from his seat; his jaws op'd with the dart,
Which when Patroclus drew, he fell; his life and breast did part,
  Then rush'd he on Euryalus, at whom he hurl'd a stone,
Which strake his head so in the midst, that two were made of one;
Two ways it fell, cleft through his casque: and then Tlepolemus,
Epaltes, Damastorides, Evippus, Echius,
Ipheas, bold Amphoterus, and valiant Erymas,
And Polymelus (by his sire surnam'd Argeadas)
He heap'd upon the much-fed earth. When Jove's most worthy son
(Divine Sarpedon) saw these friends thus stay'd, and others run: 400
  'O shame! Why fly ye?' then he cried; 'now show ye feet enow.
On, keep your way, myself will meet the man that startles you,
To make me understand his name, that flaunts in conquest thus,
And hath so many able knees so soon dissolv'd to us.'
  Down jump'd he from his chariot, down leap'd his foe as light:
And as on some far-looking rock a cast of vultures fight,
Fly on each other, strike and truss, part, meet, and then stick by,
Tug both with crooked beaks and seres, cry, fight, and fight and cry:
So fiercely fought these angry kings and show'd as bitter galls.
  Jove (turning eyes to this stern fight) his wife and sister calls,   410
And much mov'd for the Lycian prince, said: 'O that to my son,
Fate, by this day and man, should cut a thread so nobly spun.
Two minds distract me: if I should now ravish him from fight,
And set him safe in Lycia, or give the Fates their right.'
  'Austere Saturnius,' she replied, 'what unjust words are these?
A mortal long since mark'd by fate wouldst thou immortalise?
Do, but by no god be approv'd: free him, and numbers more
(Sons of immortals) will live free, that death must taste before
These gates of Ilion; every god will have his son a god,
Or storm extremely. Give him then an honest period,   420
In brave fight, by Patroclus' sword, if he be dear to thee,
And grieves thee for his danger'd life: of which, when he is free,

Let Death and Somnus bear him hence, till Lycia's natural womb
Receive him from his brother's hands, and citizens a tomb
And column raise to him; this is the honour of the dead.'

    She said, and her speech rul'd his pow'r: but in his safety's stead,
For sad ostent of his near death, he steep'd his living name
In drops of blood heaven sweat for him, which earth drunk to his fame.

    And now, as this high combat grew to this too humble end,
Sarpedon's death had this state more: 'twas usher'd by his friend   430
And charioteer, brave Thrasimed, whom in his belly's rim
Patroclus wounded with his lance, and endless ended him.

    And then another act of name foreran his princely fate:
His first lance missing, he let fly a second that gave date
Of violent death to Pedasus; who (as he joy'd to die
By his so honourable hand) did (ev'n in dying) neigh.

    His ruin startled th' other steeds, the geres crack'd, and the reins
Strappled his fellows, whose misrule Automedon restrains
By cutting the intangling geres, and so dissundering quite
The brave slain beast; when both the rest obey'd, and went foreright: 440
And then the royal combatants fought for the final stroke,
When Lycia's general miss'd again, his high-rais'd javelin took
Above his shoulder empty way. But no such speedless flight
Patroclus let his spear perform, that on the breast did light
Of his brave foe, where life's strings close about the solid heart,
Impressing a recureless wound; his knees then left their part,
And let him fall, when like an oak, a poplar, or a pine,
New fell'd by arts-men on the hills, he stretcht'd his form divine
Before his horse and chariot. And as a lion leaps
Upon a goodly yellow bull, drives all the herd in heaps,   450
And under his unconquer'd jaws the brave beast sighing dies:
So sigh'd Sarpedon underneath this prince of enemies,
Call'd Glaucus to him (his dear friend), and said: 'Now, friend, thy hands
Much duty owe to fight and arms; now for my love it stands
Thy heart in much hand to approve that war is harmful; now
How active all thy forces are, this one hour's act must show.
First call our Lycian captains up, look round, and bring up all,
And all exhort to stand like friends about Sarpedon's fall;
And spend thyself thy steel for me, for be assur'd no day
Of all thy life, to thy last hour, can clear thy black dismay   460
In woe and infamy for me, if I be taken hence
Spoil'd of mine arms, and thy renown despoil'd of my defence.
Stand firm then, and confirm thy men.' This said, the bounds of death
Concluded all sight to his eyes, and to his nostrils breath.

    Patroclus (though his guard was strong) forc'd way through every doubt,

Climb'd his high bosom with his foot, and pluck'd his javelin out,
And with it drew the film and strings of his yet-panting heart;
And last, together with the pile, his princely soul did part.
    His horse (spoil'd both of guide and king, thick snorting and amaz'd,
And apt to flight) the Myrmidons made nimbly to, and seiz'd.   470
    Glaucus, to hear his friend ask aid of him past all the rest
(Though well he knew his wound uncur'd), confusion fill'd his breast
Not to have good in any pow'r, and yet so much good will.
And laying his hand upon his wound (that pain'd him sharply still,
And was by Teucer's hand set on from their assail'd steep wall,
In keeping hurt from other men), he did on Phoebus call
(The god of med'cines) for his cure. 'Thou king of cures,' said he,
'That art perhaps in Lycia, with her rich progeny,
Or here in Troy, but any where, since thou hast pow'r to hear,
O give a hurt and woeful man (as I am now) thine ear: 480
This arm sustains a cruel wound, whose pains shoot every way,
Afflict this shoulder and this hand, and nothing long can stay
A flux of blood still issuing, nor therefore can I stand
With any enemy in fight, nor hardly make my hand
Support my lance; and here lies dead the worthiest of men,
Sarpedon, worthy son to Jove, whose pow'r could yet abstain
From all aid in this deadly need. Give thou then aid to me
(O king of all aid to men hurt), assuage th' extremity
Of this arm's anguish, give it strength, that by my president
I may excite my men to blows, and this dead corse prevent   490
Of further violence.' He pray'd, and kind Apollo heard,
Allay'd his anguish, and his wound of all the black blood clear'd
That vex'd it so, infus'd fresh pow'rs into his weaken'd mind,
And all his spirits flow'd with joy, that Phoebus stood inclin'd
(In such quick bounty) to his prayers. Then, as Sarpedon will'd,
He cast about his greedy eye, and first of all instill'd
To all his captains all the stings that could inflame their fight
For good Sarpedon. And from them he stretch'd his speedy pace
T' Agenor, Hector, Venus' son, and wise Polydamas;
And (only naming Hector) said: 'Hector, you now forget   500
Your poor auxiliary friends, that in your toils have sweat
Their friendless souls out far from home; Sarpedon, that sustain'd
With justice and his virtues all broad Lycia, hath not gain'd
The like guard for his person here, for yonder dead he lies
Beneath the great Patroclus' lance: but come, let your supplies
(Good friends) stand near him: O disdain to see his corse defil'd
With Grecian fury, and his arms by their oppressions spoil'd.
The Myrmidons are come, enrag'd that such a mighty boot

Of Greeks Troy's darts have made at fleet.' This said, from head to foot
Grief struck their pow'rs past patience, and not to be restrain'd,   510
To hear news of Sarpedon's death, who, though he appertain'd
To other cities, yet to theirs he was the very fort,
And led a mighty people there, of all whose better sort
Himself was best. This made them run in flames upon the foe –
The first man Hector, to whose heart Sarpedon's death did go.

    Patroclus stirr'd the Grecian spirits; and first th' Ajaces thus:
'Now, brothers, be it dear to you to fight and succour us,
As ever heretofore ye did, with men first excellent.
The man lies slain that first did scale and raze the battlement
That crown'd our wall, the Lycian prince. But if we now shall add   520
Force to his corse, and spoil his arms, a prize may more be had
Of many great ones, that for him will put on to the death.'

    To this work, these were prompt enough, and each side ordereth
Those phalanxes that most had rate of resolutions,
The Trojans and the Lycian pow'rs, the Greeks and Myrmidons.
These ran together for the corse, and clos'd with horrid cries,
Their armours thund'ring with the claps laid on about the prize.
And Jove about th' impetuous broil pernicious night pour'd out,
As long as for his loved son pernicious Labour fought.

    The first of Troy the first Greeks foil'd, when not the last indeed   530
Amongst the Myrmidons was slain, the great Agacleus' seed,
Divine Epigeus, that before had exercis'd command
In fair Budaeus; but because he laid a bloody hand
On his own sister's valiant son, to Peleus and his queen
He came for pardon, and obtain'd – his slaughter being the mean
He came to Troy, and so to this. He ventur'd ev'n to touch
The princely carcass, when a stone did more to him, by much;
Sent out of able Hector's hand, it cut his skull in twain,
And struck him dead. Patroclus (griev'd to see his friend so slain)
Before the foremost thrust himself, and as a falcon frays   540
A flock of stares or caddasses: such fear brought his assays
Amongst the Trojans and their friends; and (angry at the heart,
As well as griev'd) for him so slain, another stony dart
As good as Hector's he let fly, that dusted in the neck
Of Sthenelaus, thrust his head to earth first, and did break
The nerves in sunder with his fall; off fell the Trojans too,
Ev'n Hector's self, and all as far as any man can throw
(Provok'd for games, or in the wars to shed an enemy's soul)
A light long dart. The first that turn'd was he that did control
The targetiers of Lycia, Prince Glaucus, who to hell   550
Sent Bathyclaeus, Chalcon's son; he did in Hellas dwell,

And shin'd for wealth and happiness amongst the Myrmidons;
His bosom's midst the javelin struck, his fall gat earth with groans.
The Greeks griev'd, and the Trojans joy'd, for so renown'd a man,
About whom stood the Grecians firm: and then the death began
On Troy's side by Meriones: he slew one great in war,
Laogonus, Onetor's son, the priest of Jupiter,
Created in th' Idean hill. Betwixt his jaw and ear
The dart stuck fast, and loos'd his soul, sad mists of hate and fear
Invading him. Anchises' son dispatch'd a brazen lance   560
At bold Meriones, and hop'd to make an equal chance
On him with bold Laogonus, though under his broad shield
He lay so close. But he discern'd, and made his body yield
So low, that over him it flew, and trembling took the ground;
With which Mars made it quench his thirst; and since the head could wound
No better body, and yet thrown from ne'er the worse a hand,
It turn'd from earth, and look'd awry. Aeneas let it stand,
Much angry at the vain event; and told Meriones,
He scap'd but hardly, nor had cause to hope for such success
Another time, though well he knew his dancing faculty,   570
By whose agility he scap'd; for had his dart gone by
With any least touch, instantly he had been ever slain.

     He answer'd: 'Though thy strength be good, it cannot render vain
The strength of others with thy jests; nor art thou so divine,
But when my lance shall touch at thee, with equal speed to thine,
Death will share with it thy life's pow'rs; thy confidence can shun
No more than mine what his right claims.' Menoetius' noble son
Rebuk'd Meriones, and said: 'What need'st thou use this speech?
Not thy strength is approv'd with words, good friend, nor can we reach
The body, nor make th' enemy yield, with these our counterbraves: 580
We must enforce the binding earth to hold them in her graves.
If you will war, fight. Will you speak? Give counsel. Counsel, blows
Are th' ends of wars and words; talk here the time in vain bestows.'

     He said, and led; and nothing less for any thing he said
(His speech being season'd with such right), the worthy seconded.
And then, as in a sounding vale (near neighbour to a hill)
Wood-sellers make a far-heard noise with chopping, chopping still,
And laying on, on blocks and trees: so they on men laid lode,
And beat like noises into air, both as they struck and trod.
But (past their noise) so full of blood, of dust, of darts, lay smit   590
Divine Sarpedon, that a man must have an excellent wit
That could but know him, and might fail: so from his utmost head
Ev'n to the low plants of his feet, his form was altered,
All thrusting near it every way, as thick as flies in spring

That in a sheep-cote (when new milk assembles them) make wing,
And buzz about the top-full pails. Nor ever was the eye
Of Jove averted from the fight; he view'd, thought ceaselessly
And diversely upon the death of great Achilles' friend:
If Hector there (to wreak his son) should with his javelin end
His life, and force away his arms, or still augment the field.   600
He then concluded that the flight of much more soul should yield
Achilles' good friend more renown, and that ev'n to their gates
He should drive Hector and his host; and so disanimates
The mind of Hector, that he mounts his chariot, and takes flight
Up with him, tempting all to her, affirming his insight
Knew evidently that the beam of Jove's all-ordering scoles
Was then in sinking on their side, surcharg'd with flocks of souls.

    Then not the noble Lycians stay'd, but left their slaughter'd lord
Amongst the corses' common heap; for many more were pour'd
About, and on him, while Jove's hand held out the bitter broil.   610
And now they spoil'd Sarpedon's arms, and to the ships the spoil
Was sent by Menoetiades. Then Jove thus charg'd the Sun:

    'Haste, honour'd Phoebus, let no more Greek violence be done
To my Sarpedon, but his corse of all the sable blood
And javelins purg'd, then carry him far hence to some clear flood,
With whose waves wash, and then embalm each thorough-cleansed limb
With our ambrosia; which perform'd, divine weeds put on him:
And then to those swift mates and twins, sweet Sleep and Death, commit
His princely person, and with speed they both may carry it
To wealthy Lycia, where his friends and brothers will embrace   620
And tomb it in some monument, as fits a prince's place.'

    Then flew Apollo to the fight from the Idalian hill,
At all parts putting into act his great commander's will;
Drew all the darts, wash'd, balm'd the corse; which (deck'd with ornament
By Sleep and Death, those feather'd twins) he into Lycia sent.

    Patroclus then Automedon commands to give his steeds
Large reins, and all way to the chace: so madly he exceeds
The strict commission of his friend, which had he kept, had kept
A black death from him. But Jove's mind hath evermore outstept
The mind of man; who both affrights and takes the victory   630
From any hardiest hand with ease – which he can justify,
Though he himself commands him fight, as now he put this chace
In Menoetiades' mind. How much then weighs the grace,
Patroclus, that Jove gives thee now, in scoles put with thy death,
Of all these great and famous men the honourable breath.

    Of which, Adrestus first he slew, and next Autonous,
Epistora, and Perimus, Pylartes, Elasus,

Swift Melanippus, Molius; all these were overthrown
By him, and all else put in rout, and then proud Ilion
Had stoop'd beneath his glorious hand, he rag'd so with his lance,   640
If Phoebus had not kept the tow'r and help'd the Ilians,
Sustaining ill thoughts 'gainst the prince. Thrice to the prominence
Of Troy's steep wall he bravely leap'd, thrice Phoebus thrust him thence,
Objecting his all-dazzling shield with his resistless hand.
But fourthly, when (like one of heav'n) he would have stirr'd his stand,
Apollo threaten'd him, and said: 'Cease, it exceeds thy fate
(Forward Patroclus) to expugn, with thy bold lance, this state,
Nor under great Achilles' pow'rs (to thine superior far)
Lies Troy's grave ruin.' When he spake, Patroclus left that war,
Leap'd far back, and his anger shunn'd. Hector detain'd his horse   650
Within the Scaean port, in doubt to put his personal force
Amongst the rout, and turn their heads, or shun in Troy the storm.

    Apollo, seeing his suspense, assum'd the goodly form
Of Hector's uncle, Asius, the Phrygian Dymas' son,
Who near the deep Sangarius had habitation,
Being brother to the Trojan queen. His shape Apollo took,
And ask'd of Hector, why his spirit so clear the fight forsook –
Affirming 'twas unfit for him, and wish'd his forces were
As much above his as they mov'd in an inferior sphere:
He should (with shame to him) be gone; and so bad, drive away   660
Against Patroclus, to approve if he that gave them day
Would give the glory of his death to his preferred lance.
So left he him, and to the fight did his bright head advance,
Mix'd with the multitude, and stirr'd foul tumult for the foe.
Then Hector bad Cebriones put on, himself let go
All other Greeks within his reach, and only gave command
To front Patroclus. He at him jump'd down; his strong left hand
A javelin held, his right a stone, a marble sharp, and such
As his large hand had pow'r to gripe, and gave it strength so much
As he could lay to: nor stood long in fear of that huge man   670
That made against him, but full on, with his huge stone he ran,
Discharg'd, and drave it 'twixt the brows of bold Cebriones:
Nor could the thick bone there prepar'd extenuate so th' access,
But out it drave his broken eyes, which in the dust fell down,
And he div'd after; which conceit of diving took the son
Of old Menoetius, who thus play'd upon the other's bane:

    'O heav'ns! For truth, this Trojan was a passing active man;
With what exceeding ease he dives, as if at work he were
Within the fishy seas! This man alone would furnish cheer
For twenty men, though 'twere a storm, to leap out of a sail,   680

And gather oysters for them all; he does it here all well,
And there are many such in Troy.' Thus jested he so near
His own grave death, and then made in to spoil the charioteer,
With such a lion's force, and fate, as (often ruining
Stalls of fat oxen) gets at length a mortal wound to sting
His soul out of that ravenous breast that was so insolent;
And so his life's bliss proves his bane: so deadly confident
Wert thou, Patroclus, in pursuit of good Cebriones,
To whose defence now Hector leap'd. The opposite address
These masters of the cry in war now made, was of the kind   690
Of two fierce kings of beasts, oppos'd in strife about a hind
Slain on the forehead of a hill, both sharp and hungry set,
And to the currie never came but like two deaths they met:
Nor these two entertain'd less mind of mutual prejudice
About the body, close to which, when each had press'd for prize,
Hector the head laid hand upon, which once grip'd, never could
Be forc'd from him; Patroclus then upon the feet got hold,
And he pinch'd with as sure a nail: so both stood tugging there,
While all the rest made eager fight, and grappled every where.
And as the east and south winds strive to make a lofty wood   700
Bow to their greatness, barky elms, wild ashes, beeches bow'd
Ev'n with the earth, in whose thick arms the mighty vapours lie,
And toss by turns, all either way; their leaves at random fly,
Boughs murmur, and their bodies crack, and with perpetual din
The sylvans falter, and the storms are never to begin:
So rag'd the fight, and all from flight pluck'd her forgotten wings;
While some still stuck, still new wing'd shafts flew dancing from their strings,
Huge stones sent after, that did shake the shields about the corse,
Who now (in dust's soft forehead stretch'd) forgat his guiding horse.
    As long as Phoebus turn'd his wheels about the midst of heav'n,   710
So long the touch of either's darts the falls of both made ev'n:
But when his wain drew near the west, the Greeks past measure were
The abler soldiers, and so swept the Trojan tumult clear
From off the body; out of which they drew the hurl'd-in darts,
And from his shoulders stripp'd his arms, and then to more such parts
Patroclus turn'd his striving thoughts, to do the Trojans ill:
Thrice, like the god of war, he charg'd, his voice as horrible,
And thrice nine those three charges slew, but in the fourth assay,
O then, Patroclus, show'd thy last; the dreadful Sun made way
Against that onset, yet the prince discern'd no deity,   720
He kept the press so; and besides, obscur'd his glorious eye
With such felt darkness. At his back he made a sudden stand,
And 'twixt his neck and shoulders laid down-right with either hand

A blow so weighty that his eyes a giddy darkness took,
And from his head his three-plum'd helm the bounding violence shook,
That rung beneath his horses' hoofs, and, like a water-spout,
Was crush'd together with the fall – the plumes that set it out
All spatter'd with black blood and dust, when ever heretofore
It was a capital offence to have or dust or gore
Defile a triple-feather'd helm, but on the head divine   730
And youthful temples of their prince, it us'd untouch'd to shine.
Yet now Jove gave it Hector's hands, the other's death was near.
Besides whose lost and filed helm, his huge long weighty spear,
Well bound with iron, in his hand was shiver'd, and his shield
Fell from his shoulders to his feet, the bawdrick strewing the field.
His curets left him, like the rest, and all this only done
By great Apollo. Then his mind took in confusion;
The vigorous knittings of his joints dissolv'd, and (thus dismay'd)
A Dardan (one of Panthus' sons) and one that overlaid
All Trojans of his place with darts, swift footing, skill, and force,   740
In noble horsemanship, and one that tumbled from their horse,
One after other, twenty men – and when he did but learn
The art of war; nay, when he first did in the field discern
A horse and chariot of his guide: this man, with all these parts
(His name Euphorbus), comes behind, and 'twixt the shoulders darts
Forlorn Patroclus, who yet liv'd, and th' other (getting forth
His javelin) took him to his strength; nor durst he stand the worth
Of thee, Patroclus, though disarm'd, who yet (discomfited
By Phoebus and Euphorbus' wound) the red heap of the dead
He now too late shunn'd, and retir'd. When Hector saw him yield,   750
And knew he yielded with a wound, he scour'd the armed field,
Came close up to him, and both sides struck quite through with his lance.
He fell, and his most weighty fall gave fit tune to his chance,
For which all Greece extremely mourn'd. And as a mighty strife
About a little fount begins and riseth to the life
Of some fell boar, resolv'd to drink, when likewise to the spring
A lion comes, alike dispos'd; the boar thirsts, and his king,
Both proud, and both will first be serv'd; and then the lion takes
Advantage of his sovereign strength, and th' other (fainting) makes
Resign his thirst up with his blood: Patroclus (so enforc'd   760
When he had forc'd so much brave life) was from his own divorc'd.
And thus his great divorcer brav'd: 'Patroclus, thy conceit
Gave thee th' eversion of our Troy, and to thy fleet a freight
Of Trojan ladies, their free lives put all in bands by thee:
But (too much prizer of thy self) all these are propp'd by me,
For these have my horse stretch'd their hoofs to this so long a war,

And I (far best of Troy in arms) keep off from Troy as far,
Even to the last beam of my life, their necessary day.
And here (in place of us and ours) on thee shall vultures prey,
Poor wretch; nor shall thy mighty friend afford thee any aid,　　　770
That gave thy parting much deep charge; and this perhaps he said:
"Martial Patroclus, turn not face, nor see my fleet before
The curets from great Hector's breast, all gilded with his gore,
Thou hew'st in pieces." If thus vain were his far-stretch'd commands,
As vain was thy heart to believe his words lay in thy hands.'

　He, languishing, replied: 'This proves thy glory worse than vain,
That when two gods have giv'n thy hands what their pow'rs did obtain
(They conquering, and they spoiling me both of my arms and mind,
It being a work of ease for them), thy soul should be so blind
To oversee their evident deeds, and take their pow'rs to thee,　　　780
When if the pow'rs of twenty such had dar'd t' encounter me,
My lance had strew'd earth with them all. Thou only dost obtain
A third place in my death, whom first a harmful fate hath slain
Effected by Latona's son; second, and first of men,
Euphorbus. And this one thing more concerns thee; note it then:
Thou shalt not long survive thyself; nay, now Death calls for thee,
And violent Fate; Achilles' lance shall make this good for me.'

　Thus death join'd to his words his end; his soul took instant wing,
And to the house that hath no lights descended sorrowing
For his sad fate, to leave him young, and in his ablest age.　　　790
He dead, yet Hector ask'd him why, in that prophetic rage,
He so forespake him, when none knew but great Achilles might
Prevent his death, and on his lance receive his latest light.
Thus setting on his side his foot, he drew out of his wound
His brazen lance, and upwards cast the body on the ground;
When quickly, while the dart was hot, he charg'd Automedon
(Divine guide of Achilles' steeds) in great contention,
To seize him too: but his so swift and deathless horse, that fetch'd
Their gift to Peleus from the gods, soon rapt him from his reach.

THE END OF THE SIXTEENTH BOOK

BOOK SEVENTEEN

The Argument

A dreadful fight about Patroclus' corse,
Euphorbus slain by Menelaus' force,
Hector in th' armour of Aeacides,
Antilochus relating the decease
Of slain Patroclus to fair Thetis' son,
The body from the striving Trojans won,
Th' Ajaces making good the after field,
Make all the subject that this book doth yield.

Another Argument

In *Rho*, the virtuous hosts maintain
A slaughterous conflict for the same.

BOOK SEVENTEEN

NOR COULD his slaughter rest conceal'd from Menelaus' ear,
    Who flew amongst the foremost fights, and with his targe and spear
    Circled the body, as much griev'd, and with as tender heed
To keep it theirs, as any dam about her first-born seed,
Not proving what the pain of birth would make the love before.
    Nor to pursue his first attaint Euphorbus' spirit forbore.
But, seeing Menelaus chief in rescue of the dead,
Assay'd him thus: 'Atrides, cease, and leave the slaughtered
With his embru'd spoil to the man that first of all our state
And famous succours, in fair fight, made passage to his fate;   10
And therefore suffer me to wear the good name I have won
Amongst the Trojans, lest thy life repay what his hath done.'
    'O Jupiter,' said he, incens'd, 'thou art no honest man
To boast so past thy pow'r to do. Not any lion can,
Nor spotted leopard, nor boar (whose mind is mightiest
In pouring fury from his strength), advance so proud a crest
As Panthus' fighting progeny. But Hyperenor's pride,
That joy'd so little time his youth, when he so vilified
My force in arms, and call'd me worst of all our chivalry,
And stood my worst, might teach ye all to shun this surcuidrie: 20
I think he came not safely home, to tell his wife his acts.
Nor less right of thy insolence my equal fate exacts,
And will obtain me, if thou stay'st; retire then, take advice:
A fool sees nought before 'tis done, and still too late is wise.'
    This mov'd not him, but to the worse, since it renew'd the sting
That his slain brother shot in him, remember'd by the king:
To whom he answer'd: 'Thou shalt pay for all the pains endur'd
By that slain brother; all the wounds sustain'd for him, recur'd
With one, made in thy heart by me. 'Tis true thou mad'st his wife
A heavy widow, when her joys of wedlock scarce had life,   30
And hurt'st our parents with his grief; all which thou gloriest in,
Forespeaking so thy death, that now their grief's end shall begin.
To Panthus, and the snowy hand of Phrontes, I will bring
Those arms, and that proud head of thine; and this laborious thing
Shall ask no long time to perform: nor be my words alone,

But their performance; Strength, and Fight, and Terror thus sets on.'

    This said, he struck his all-round shield; nor shrunk that, but his lance
That turn'd head in it: then the king assail'd the second chance,
First praying to the king of gods, and his dart entry got
(The force much driving back his foe) in low part of his throat,   40
And ran his neck through. Then fell pride and he, and all with gore
His locks, that like the Graces were, and which he ever wore
In gold and silver ribands wrapp'd, were piteously wet.

    As when alone in some choice place a husbandman hath set
The young plant of an olive tree, whose root being ever fed
With plenty of delicious springs, his branches bravely spread,
And all his fresh and lovely head grown curl'd with snowy flow'rs,
That dance and flourish with the winds, that are of gentlest pow'rs;
But when a whirlwind (got aloft) stoops with a sudden gale,
Tears from his head his tender curls, and tosseth therewithal   50
His fix'd root from his hollow mines, it well presents the force
Of Sparta's king, and so the plant, Euphorbus and his corse.
He slain, the king stripp'd off his arms, and with their worthy prize
(All fearing him) had clearly past, if heav'n's fair eye of eyes
Had not, in envy of his acts, to his encounter stirr'd
The Mars-like Hector, to whose pow'rs the rescue he preferr'd
Of those fair arms, and took the shape of Mentas (colonel
Of all the Cicones that near the Thracian Hebrus dwell).
Like him, he thus puts forth his voice: 'Hector, thou scour'st the field
In headstrong pursuit of those horse that hardly are compell'd   60
To take the draught of chariots by any mortal's hand –
The great grandchild of Aeacus hath only their command,
Whom an immortal mother bore. While thou attend'st on these,
The young Atrides, in defence of Menoetiades,
Hath slain Euphorbus.' Thus the god took troop with men again,
And Hector (heartily perplex'd) look'd round, and saw the slain,
Still shedding rivers from his wound: and then took envious view
Of brave Atrides with his spoil, in way to whom he flew
Like one of Vulcan's quenchless flames. Atrides heard the cry
That ever usher'd him, and sigh'd, and said: 'O me, if I   70
Should leave these goodly arms, and him that here lies dead for me,
I fear I should offend the Greeks. If I should stay, and be
Alone with Hector and his men, I may be compass'd in;
Some sleight or other they may use. Many may quickly win
Their wills of one, and all Troy comes ever where Hector leads.
But why (dear mind) dost thou thus talk? When men dare set their heads
Against the gods, as sure they do (that fight with men they love),
Straight one or other plague ensues: it cannot therefore move

The grudge of any Greek that sees I yield to Hector, he
Still fighting with a spirit from heav'n. And yet if I could see   80
Brave Ajax, he and I would stand, though 'gainst a god: and sure
'Tis best I seek him, and then see if we two can procure
This corse's freedom through all these: a little then let rest
The body, and my mind be still; of two bads choose the best.'
    In this discourse, the troops of Troy were in with him, and he
Made such a lion-like retreat, as when the herdsmen see
The royal savage, and come on, with men, dogs, cries and spears,
To clear their horned stall; and then, the kingly heart he bears
(With all his high disdain) falls off: so, from this odds of aid
The golden-hair'd Atrides fled, and in his strength display'd   90
Upon his left hand him he wish'd, extremely busied
About encouraging his men, to whom an extreme dread
Apollo had infus'd: the king reach'd Ajax instantly,
And said: 'Come, friend, let us two haste, and from the tyranny
Of Hector free Patroclus' corse.' He straight and gladly went;
And then was Hector haling off the body, with intent
To spoil the shoulders of the dead, and give the dogs the rest
(His arms he having pris'd before). When Ajax brought his breast
To bar all further spoil, with that he had sure, Hector thought
'Twas best to satisfy his spleen; which temper Ajax wrought   100
With his mere sight, and Hector fled: the arms he sent to Troy,
To make his citizens admire, and pray Jove send him joy.
    Then Ajax gather'd to the corse, and hid it with his targe:
There setting down as sure a foot as, in the tender charge
Of his lov'd whelps, a lion doth; two hundred hunters near,
To give him onset, their more force makes him the more austere,
Drowns all their clamours in his roars, darts, dogs doth all despise,
And lets his rough brows down so low, they cover all his eyes:
So Ajax look'd, and stood, and stay'd for great Priamides.
    When Glaucus Hippolochides saw Ajax thus depress   110
The spirit of Hector, thus he chid: 'O goodly man at arms,
In fight a Paris, why should fame make thee sort 'gainst our harms,
Being such a fugitive? Now mark how well thy boasts defend
Thy city only with her own. Be sure it shall descend
To that proof wholly. Not a man of any Lycian rank
Shall strike one stroke more for thy town, for no man gets a thank
Should he eternally fight here, nor any guard of thee.
How wilt thou (worthless that thou art) keep off an enemy
From our poor soldiers, when their prince, Sarpedon, guest and friend
To thee (and most deservedly) thou flew'st from in his end,   120
And left'st to all the lust of Greece? O gods, a man that was

In life so huge a good to Troy, and to thee such a grace,
In death not kept by thee from dogs? If my friends will do well,
We'll take our shoulders from your walls, and let all sink to hell –
As all will, were our faces turn'd. Did such a spirit breathe
In all you Trojans, as becomes all men that fight beneath
Their country's standard, you would see that such as prop your cause
With like exposure of their lives have all the honour'd laws
Of such a dear confederacy kept to them to a thread –
As now ye might reprise the arms Sarpedon forfeited,   130
By forfeit of your rights to him, would you but lend your hands,
And force Patroclus to your Troy. Ye know how dear he stands
In his love, that of all the Greeks is (for himself) far best,
And leads the best near-fighting men; and therefore would (at least)
Redeem Sarpedon's arms – nay him, whom you have likewise lost.
This body drawn to Ilion would after draw and cost
A greater ransom if you pleas'd: but Ajax startles you;
'Tis his breast bars this right to us: his looks are darts enow
To mix great Hector with his men. And not to blame ye are,
You choose foes underneath your strengths; Ajax exceeds ye far.'   140
    Hector look'd passing sour at this; and answer'd: 'Why dar'st thou
(So under) talk above me so? O friend, I thought till now
Thy wisdom was superior to all th' inhabitants
Of gleby Lycia; but now, impute apparent wants
To that discretion thy words show, to say I lost my ground
For Ajax' greatness: nor fear I the field in combats drown'd,
Nor force of chariots, but I fear a pow'r much better seen,
In right of all war, than all we: that god that holds between
Our victory and us his shield, lets conquest come and go
At his free pleasure, and with fear converts her changes so   150
Upon the strongest; men must fight when his just spirit impels,
Not their vain glories. But come on, make thy steps parallels
To these of mine; and then be judge how deep the work will draw –
If then I spend the day in shifts, or thou canst give such law
To thy detractive speeches then, or if the Grecian host
Holds any that in pride of strength holds up his spirit most,
Whom (for the carriage of this prince, that thou enforcest so)
I make not stoop in his defence. You, friends! Ye hear and know
How much it fits ye to make good this Grecian I have slain,
For ransom of Jove's son, our friend; play then the worthy men,   160
Till I indue Achilles' arms.' This said, he left the fight,
And call'd back those that bore the arms, not yet without his sight,
In convoy of them towards Troy. For them he chang'd his own,
Remov'd from where it rained tears, and sent them back to town.

  Then put he on th' eternal arms that the celestial states
Gave Peleus; Peleus being old, their use appropriates
To his Achilles, that (like him) forsook them not for age.
When he whose empire is in clouds saw Hector bent to wage
War in divine Achilles' arms, he shook his head, and said:
'Poor wretch, thy thoughts are far from Death, though he so near hath laid   170
His ambush for thee. Thou putt'st on those arms as braving him
Whom others fear, hast slain his friend, and from his youthful limb
Torn rudely off his heavenly arms, himself being gentle, kind,
And valiant. Equal measure then thy life in youth must find.
Yet since the justice is so strict, that not Andromache
(In thy denied return from fight) must ever take of thee
Those arms, in glory of thy acts, thou shalt have that frail blaze
Of excellence that neighbours death, a strength ev'n to amaze.'
  To this his sable brows did bow; and he made fit his limb
To those great arms, to fill which up the War-god enter'd him,   180
Austere and terrible: his joints and every part extends
With strength and fortitude; and thus, to his admiring friends,
High Clamour brought him. He so shin'd, that all could think no less,
But he resembled every way great-soul'd Aeacides.
Then every way he scour'd the field, his captains calling on:
Asteropaeus, Eunomus (that foresaw all things done),
Glaucus and Medon, Desinor, and strong Thersilochus,
Phorcis and Mesthles, Chronius, and great Hippothous;
To all these, and their populous troops, these his excitements were:
  'Hear us, innumerable friends, near-bordering nations, hear.   190
We have not call'd you from your towns to fill our idle eye
With number of so many men (no such vain empery
Did ever joy us), but to fight, and of our Trojan wives,
With all their children, manfully to save the innocent lives;
In whose cares we draw all our towns of aiding soldiers dry,
With gifts, guards, victual, all things fit, and hearten their supply
With all like rights; and therefore now let all sides set down this:
Or live, or perish; this of war the special secret is.
In which most resolute design, who ever bears to town
Patroclus (laid dead to his hand) by winning the renown   200
Of Ajax' slaughter, the half-spoil we wholly will impart
To his free use; and to ourself the other half convert:
And so the glory shall be shar'd; ourself will have no more
Than he shall shine in.' This drew all to bring abroad their store
Before the body: every man had hope it would be his,
And forc'd from Ajax. Silly fools, Ajax prevented this
By raising rampiers to his friend with half their carcasses:

And yet his humour was to roar, and fear, and now no less
To startle Sparta's king; to whom he cried out: 'O my friend!
O Menelaus! Ne'er more hope to get off; here's the end   210
Of all our labours: not so much I fear to lose the corse
(For that's sure gone, the fowls of Troy and dogs will quickly force
That piece-meal) as I fear my head, and thine, O Atreus' son.
Hector a cloud brings, will hide all; instant destruction,
Grievous and heavy, comes; O call our peers to aid us; fly.'
   He hasted, and us'd all his voice, sent far and near his cry:
'O princes, chief lights of the Greeks, and you that publicly
Eat with our general and me, all men of charge, O know,
Jove gives both grace and dignity to any that will show
Good minds for only good itself, though presently the eye   220
Of him that rules discern him not. 'Tis hard for me t' espy
(Through all this smoke of burning fight) each captain in his place,
And call assistance to our need. Be then each other's grace,
And freely follow each his next; disdain to let the joy
Of great Aeacides be forc'd to feed the beasts of Troy.'
   His voice was first heard and obey'd by swift Oïleades:
Idomeneus and his mate (renown'd Meriones)
Were seconds to Oïleus' son: but of the rest, whose mind
Can lay upon his voice the names that after these combin'd
In setting up this fight on end? The Trojans first gave on,   230
And as into the sea's vast mouth, when mighty rivers run,
Their billows and the sea resound, and all the utter shore
Rebellows (in her angry shocks) the sea's repulsive roar:
With such sounds gave the Trojans charge; so was their charge repress'd.
One mind fill'd all Greeks, good brass shields close couch'd to every breast,
And on their helms Jove poured down a mighty deal of night
To hide Patroclus. Whom alive, and when he was the knight
Of that grandchild of Aeacus, Saturnius did not hate;
Nor dead, would see him dealt to dogs, and so did instigate
His fellows to his worthy guard. At first the Trojans drave   240
The black-ey'd Grecians from the corse; but not a blow they gave
That came at death. A while they hung about the body's heels,
The Greeks quite gone. But all that while did Ajax whet the steels
Of all his forces, that cut back way to the corse again.
Brave Ajax (that for form and fact, past all that did maintain
The Grecian fame, next Thetis' son) now flew before the first,
And as a sort of dogs and youths are by a boar disperst
About a mountain: so fled these from mighty Ajax, all
That stood in conflict for the corse, who thought no chance could fall
Betwixt them and the prize at Troy. For bold Hippothous   250

(Lethus Pelasgus' famous son) was so adventurous,
That he would stand to bore the corse about the ankle-bone,
Where all the nervy flyers meet, and ligaments in one,
That make the motion of those parts; through which he did convey
The thong or bawdric of his shield, and so was drawing away
All thanks from Hector and his friends; but in their stead he drew
An ill that no man could avert: for Telamonius threw
A lance that struck quite through his helm; his brain came leaping out.
Down fell Letheides, and with him the body's hoisted foot.
Far from Larissa's soil he fell, a little time allow'd   260
To his industrious spirits, to quit the benefits bestow'd
By his kind parents. But his wreak Priamides assay'd,
And threw at Ajax; but his dart (discover'd) pass'd, and stay'd
At Schedius, son of Iphitus, a man of ablest hand
Of all the strong Phocensians, and liv'd with great command,
In Fanopaeus. The fell dart fell through his channel-bone,
Pierc'd through his shoulder's upper part, and set his spirit gone.
When (after his) another flew, the same hand giving wing
To martial Phorcis' startled soul, that was the after spring
Of Phaenops' seed: the javelin struck his curets through, and tore   270
The bowels from the belly's midst. His fall made those before
Give back a little, Hector's self enforc'd to turn his face.
And then the Greeks bestow'd their shouts, took vantage of the chace,
Drew off, and spoil'd Hippothous and Phorcis of their arms.
And then ascended Ilion had shaken with alarms
(Discovering th' impotence of Troy) ev'n past the will of Jove,
And by the proper force of Greece, had Phoebus fail'd to move
Aeneas, in similitude of Periphas (the son
Of grave Epytes) king at arms, and had good service done
To old Anchises, being wise, and ev'n with him in years.   280
But (like this man) the far-seen god to Venus' son appears,
And ask'd him how he would maintain steep Ilion in her height,
In spite of gods (as he presum'd), when men approv'd so slight
All his presumptions, and all theirs, that puff'd him with that pride,
Believing in their proper strengths, and generally supplied
With such unfrighted multitudes? But he well knew that Jove
(Besides their self-conceits) sustain'd their forces with more love
Than theirs of Greece, and yet all that lack'd power to hearten them.
    Aeneas knew the god, and said, it was a shame extreme
That those of Greece should beat them so, and by their cowardice,   290
Not want of man's aid, nor the gods', and this (before his eyes)
A deity stood, ev'n now, and vouch'd, affirming Jove their aid.
And so bade Hector and the rest (to whom all this he said)

Turn head, and not in that quick ease part with the corse to Greece.
     This said, before them all he flew, and all (as of a piece)
Against the Greeks flew. Venus' son Leocritus did end,
Son of Arisbas, and had place of Lycomedes' friend,
Whose fall he friendly pitied: and in revenge, bestow'd
A lance that Apisaon struck so sore that straight he strow'd
The dusty centre, and did stick in that congealed blood   300
That forms the liver. Second man he was to all that stood
In name for arms amongst the troop that from Paeonia came,
Asteropaeus being the first: who was in ruth the same
That Lycomedes was; like whom, he put forth for the wreak
Of his slain friend, but wrought it not, because he could not break
That bulwark made of Grecian shields and bristled wood of spears
Combin'd about the body slain. Amongst whom Ajax bears
The greatest labour, every way exhorting to abide,
And no man fly the corse afoot, nor break their ranks in pride
Of any foremost daring spirit, but each foot hold his stand,   310
And use the closest fight they could. And this was the command
Of mighty Ajax: which observ'd, they steep'd the earth in blood.
The Trojans and their friends fell thick. Nor all the Grecians stood –
Though far the fewer suffer'd fate, for ever they had care
To shun confusion, and the toil that still oppresseth there.
     So set they all the field on fire; with which you would have thought
The sun and moon had been put out, in such a smoke they fought
About the person of the prince. But all the field beside
Fought underneath a lightsome heaven: the sun was in his pride,
And such expansure of his beams he thrust out of his throne   320
That not a vapour durst appear in all that region –
No, not upon the highest hill: there fought they still and breath'd,
Shunn'd danger, cast their darts aloof, and not a sword unsheath'd.
The other plied it, and the war and night plied them as well,
The cruel steel afflicting all; the strongest did not dwell
Unhurt within their iron roofs. Two men of special name,
Antilochus and Thrasimed, were yet unserv'd by fame
With notice of Patroclus' death: they thought him still alive,
In foremost tumult – and might well: for (seeing their fellows thrive
In no more comfortable sort than fight and death would yield)   330
They fought apart; for so their sire, old Nestor, strictly will'd,
Enjoining fight more from the fleet. War here increas'd his heat
The whole day long; continually the labour and the sweat
The knees, calves, feet, hands, faces, smear'd, of men that Mars applied
About the good Achilles' friend. And as a huge ox-hide
A currier gives amongst his men, to supple and extend

With oil till it be drunk withall; they tug, stretch out, and spend
Their oil and liquor liberally, and chafe the leather so
That out they make a vapour breathe, and in their oil doth go;
A number of them set on work, and in an orb they pull,　　　340
That all ways all parts of the hide they may extend at full:
So here and there did both parts hale the corse in little place,
And wrought it always with their sweat; the Trojans hop'd for grace
To make it reach for Ilion, the Grecians to their fleet.
A cruel tumult they stirr'd up, and such as, should Mars see 't
(That horrid hurrier of men), or she that betters him,
Minerva, never so incens'd, they could not disesteem.
So baneful a contention did Jove that day extend
Of men and horse about the slain. Of whom his god-like friend
Had no instruction. So far off, and underneath the wall　　　350
Of Troy, that conflict was maintain'd: which was not thought at all
By great Achilles, since he charg'd, that having set his foot
Upon the ports, he would retire; well knowing Troy no boot
For his assaults without himself, since not by him, as well
He knew, it was to be subdu'd. His mother oft would tell
The mind of mighty Jove therein, oft hearing it in heav'n.
But of that great ill to his friend was no instruction giv'n
By careful Thetis: by degrees must ill events be known.
　　The foes cleft one to other still about the overthrown.
His death with death infected both. Ev'n private Greeks would say　　　360
Either to other: 'Twere a shame for us to go our way,
And let the Trojans bear to Troy the praise of such a prize:
Which let the black earth gasp and drink our blood for sacrifice
Before we suffer: 'tis an act much less infortunate.'
And then would those of Troy resolve: 'Though certainly our fate
Will fell us all together here, of all not turn a face.'
Thus either side his fellow's strength excited past his place,
And thus through all th' unfruitful air an iron sound ascended
Up to the golden firmament, when strange effects contended
In these immortal heav'n-bred horse of great Aeacides;　　　370
Whom (once remov'd from forth the fight) a sudden sense did seize
Of good Patroclus' death, whose hands they oft had undergone,
And bitterly they wept for him: nor could Automedon
With any manage make them stir; oft use the scourge to them,
Oft use his fairest speech, as oft threats never so extreme,
They neither to the Hellespont would bear him, nor the fight:
But still as any tombstone lays his never-stirred weight
On some good man or woman's grave for rites of funeral,
So unremoved stood these steeds, their heads to earth let fall,

And warm tears gushing from their eyes, with passionate desire   380
Of their kind manager; their manes, that flourish'd with the fire
Of endless youth allotted them, fell through the yoky sphere,
Ruthfully ruffled and defil'd. Jove saw their heavy cheer,
And (pitying them) spake to his mind: 'Poor wretched beasts,' said he,
'Why gave we you t' a mortal king, when immortality
And incapacity of age so dignifies your states?
Was it to taste the miseries pour'd out on humans fates?
Of all the miserablest things that breathe and creep on earth,
No one more wretched is than man. And for your deathless birth
Hector must fail to make you prize: is 't not enough he wears   390
And glories vainly in those arms? Your chariots and rich gears
(Besides you) are too much for him. Your knees and spirits again
My care of you shall fill with strength, that so ye may sustain
Automedon, and bear him off. To Troy I still will give
The grace of slaughter, till at fleet their bloody feet arrive,
Till Phoebus drink the western sea, and sacred darkness throws
Her sable mantle 'twixt their points.' Thus in the steeds he blows
Excessive spirit, and through the Greeks and Ilians they rapt
The whirring chariot, shaking off the crumbled centre, wrapt
Amongst their tresses: and with them, Automedon let fly   400
Amongst the Trojans, making way through all as frightfully
As through a jangling flock of geese a lordly vulture beats,
Giv'n way with shrieks by every goose that comes but near his threats:
With such state fled he through the press, pursuing as he fled,
But made no slaughter – nor he could, alone being carried
Upon the sacred chariot. How could he both works do,
Direct his javelin and command his fiery horses too?

   At length he came where he beheld his friend Alcimedon,
That was the good Laercius' (the son of Aemon's) son,
Who close came to his chariot side, and ask'd, 'What god is he   410
That hath so robb'd thee of thy soul, to run thus franticly
Amongst these forefights, being alone, thy fighter being slain,
And Hector glorying in his arms?' He gave these words again:

   'Alcimedon, what man is he, of all the Argive race,
So able as thy self to keep in use of press and pace
These deathless horse, himself being gone that like the gods had th' art
Of their high manage? Therefore take to thy command his part,
And ease me of the double charge which thou hast blam'd with right.'

   He took the scourge and reins in hand, Automedon the fight:
Which Hector seeing, instantly (Aeneas standing near)   420
He told him, he discern'd the horse that mere immortal were,
Address'd to fight with coward guides, and therefore hop'd to make

A rich prize of them, if his mind would help to undertake,
For these two could not stand their charge. He granted, and both cast
Dry solid hides upon their necks, exceeding soundly brast;
And forth thy went, associate with two more god-like men,
Aretus and bold Chronius, nor made they question then
To prize the goodly-crested horse, and safely send to hell
The souls of both their guardians: O fools, that could not tell
They could not work out their return from fierce Automedon　　　430
Without the liberal cost of blood; who first made orison
To father Jove, and then was fill'd with fortitude and strength,
When (counselling Alcimedon to keep at no great length
The horse from him, but let them breathe upon his back, because
He saw th' advance that Hector made, whose fury had no laws
Propos'd to it, but both their lives, and those horse made his prize –
Or his life theirs – he call'd to friend these well-approv'd supplies,
Th' Ajaces and the Spartan king, and said: 'Come, princes, leave
A sure guard with the corse, and then to your kind care receive
Our threaten'd safeties; I discern the two chief props of Troy　　　440
Prepar'd against us: but herein, what best men can enjoy
Lies in the free knees of the gods; my dart shall lead ye all.
The sequel to the care of Jove I leave, whatever fall.'

All this spake good Automedon; then, brandishing his lance,
He threw, and struck Aretus' shield, that gave it enterance
Through all the steel, and (by his belt) his belly's inmost part
It pierc'd, and all his trembling limbs gave life up to his dart.
Then Hector at Automedon a blazing lance let fly,
Whose flight he saw, and falling flat, the compass was too high,
And made it stick beyond in earth, th' extreme part burst, and there　　　450
Mars buried all his violence. The sword then for the spear
Had chang'd the conflict, had not haste sent both th' Ajaces in
(Both serving close their fellow's call) who, where they did begin,
There drew the end: Priamides, Aeneas, Chronius
(In doubt of what such aid might work) left broken-hearted thus
Aretus to Automedon, who spoil'd his arms, and said:

'A little this revives my life, for him so lately dead
(Though by this nothing countervail'd)'; and with his little vent
Of inward grief, he took the spoil, with which he made ascent
Up to his chariot, hands and feet of bloody stains so full,　　　460
That lion-like he look'd, new turn'd from tearing up a bull.

And now another bitter fight about Patroclus grew,
Tear-thirsty, and of toil enough, which Pallas did renew,
Descending from the cope of stars, dismiss'd by sharp-ey'd Jove,
To animate the Greeks; for now inconstant change did move

His mind from what he held of late: and as the purple bow
Jove bends at mortals, when of war he will the signal show,
Or make it a presage of cold, in such tempestuous sort,
That men are of their labours eas'd, but labouring cattle hurt:
So Pallas in a purple cloud involv'd herself, and went   470
Amongst the Grecians; stirr'd up all, but first encouragement
She breath'd in Atreus' younger son, and (for disguise) made choice
Of aged Phoenix' shape, and spake with his unwearied voice:
   'O Menelaus, much defame and equal heaviness
Will touch at thee, if this true friend of great Aeacides
Dogs tear beneath the Trojan walls; and therefore bear thee well,
Toil through the host, and every man with all thy spirit impel.'
   He answer'd: 'O thou long-since born! O Phoenix, that hast won
The honour'd foster-father's name of Thetis' god-like son!
I would Minerva would but give strength to me, and but keep   480
These busy darts off, I would then make in indeed, and steep
My income in their bloods, in aid of good Patroclus; much
His death afflicts me, much: but yet this Hector's grace is such
With Jove, and such a fiery strength and spirit he has, that still
His steel is killing, killing still.' The king's so royal will
Minerva joy'd to hear, since she did all the gods outgo
In his remembrance. For which grace she kindly did bestow
Strength on his shoulders, and did fill his knees as liberally
With swiftness, breathing in his breast the courage of a fly,
Which loves to bite so, and doth bear man's blood so much good will,   490
That still (though beaten from a man) she flies upon him still:
With such a courage Pallas fill'd the black parts near his heart;
And then he hasted to the slain, cast off a shining dart,
And took one Podes, that was heir to old Eëtion,
A rich man, and a strenuous, and by the people done
Much honour – and by Hector too, being consort, and his guest;
And him the yellow-headed king laid hold on at his waist,
In offering flight. His iron pile struck through him, down he fell,
And up Atrides drew his corse. Then Phoebus did impel
The spirit of Hector, Phaenops like, surnam'd Asiades,   500
Whom Hector us'd (of all his guests) with greatest friendliness,
And in Abydus stood his house; in whose form thus he spake:
   'Hector! What man of all the Greeks will any terror make
Of meeting thy strength any more when thou art terrified
By Menelaus? Who before he slew thy friend, was tried
A passing easy soldier; where now (besides his end,
Impos'd by him) he draws him off (and not a man to friend)
From all the Trojans. This friend is Podes, Eëtion's son.'

This hid him in a cloud of grief, and set him foremost on,
And then Jove took his snake-fring'd shield; and Ida cover'd all   510
With sulphury clouds, from whence he let abhorred lightnings fall,
And thunder'd till the mountain shook; and with his dreadful state
He usher'd victory to Troy, to Argos flight and fate.
Peneleus Boeotius was he that foremost fled,
Being wounded in his shoulder's height; but there the lance's head
Struck lightly, glancing to his mouth, because it struck him near,
Thrown from Polydamas: Leïtus next left the fight in fear,
(Being hurt by Hector in his hand) because he doubted sore
His hand in wished fight with Troy would hold his lance no more.

Idomeneus sent a dart at Hector (rushing in,   520
And following Leïtus) that struck his bosom near his chin,
And brake at top; the Ilians for his escape did shout.
When Hector at Deucalides another lance sent out
As in his chariot he stood, it miss'd him narrowly;
For (as it fell) Caeranus drave his speedy chariot by,
And took the Trojan lance himself; he was the charioteer
Of stern Meriones, and first on foot did service there;
Which well he left to govern horse, for saving now his king,
With driving 'twixt him and his death, though thence his own did spring,
Which kept a mighty victory from Troy, in keeping death   530
From his great sovereign: the fierce dart did enter him beneath
His ear, betwixt his jaw and it; drave down, cut through his tongue,
And struck his teeth out; from his hands the horses' reins he flung,
Which now Meriones receiv'd as they bestrew'd the field,
And bade his sovereign scourge away; he saw that day would yield
No hope of victory for them. He fear'd the same, and fled.

Nor from the mighty-minded son of Telamon lay hid
(For all his clouds) high Jove himself, nor from the Spartan king,
They saw him in the victory he still was varying
For Troy; for which sight Ajax said: 'O heav'ns, what fool is he   540
That sees not Jove's hand in the grace now done our enemy?
Not any dart they touch, but takes, from whomsoever thrown,
Valiant or coward; what he wants, Jove adds; not any one
Wants his direction to strike sure; nor ours to miss, as sure:
But come, let us be sure of this, to put the best in ure
That lies in us; which two-fold is: both to fetch off our friend,
And so to fetch him off, as we may likeliest contend
To fetch ourselves off, that our friends surviving may have right
In joy of our secure retreat, as he that fell in fight
Being kept as sure from further wrong: of which perhaps they doubt,   550
And looking this way, grieve for us, not able to work out

Or pass from this man-slaughterer, great Hector and his hands,
That are too hot for men to touch, but that these thirsty sands
Before out fleet will be enforc'd to drink our headlong death.
Which to prevent by all fit means, I would the parted breath
Of good Patroclus to his friend with speed imparted were
By some he loves, for I believe no heavy messenger
Hath yet inform'd him; but alas! I see no man to send;
Both men and horse are hid in mists that every way descend.
O father Jupiter, do thou the sons of Greece release   560
Of this felt darkness; grace this day with fit transparences,
And give the eyes thou giv'st their use, destroy us in the light,
And work thy will with us, since needs thou wilt against us fight.'
    This spake he weeping; and his tears Saturnius pity show'd,
Dispers'd the darkness instantly, and drew away the cloud
From whence it fell: the sun shin'd out, and all the host appear'd;
And then spake Ajax (whose heard prayer his spirits highly cheer'd):
    'Brave Menelaus, look about; and if thou canst descry
Nestor's Antilochus alive, incite him instantly
To tell Achilles that his friend, most dear to him, is dead.'   570
    He said, nor Menelaus stuck at any thing he said
(As loth to do it), but he went. As from the grazier's stall
A lion goes, when overlaid with men, dogs, darts and all,
Not easily losing a fat ox, but strong watch all night held;
His teeth yet watering, oft he comes, and is as oft repell'd,
The adverse darts so thick are pour'd before his brow-hid eyes,
And burning firebrands, which for all his great heart's heat, he flies,
And (grumbling) goes his way betimes: so from Patroclus went
Atrides, much against his mind, his doubts being vehement,
Lest (he gone from his guard) the rest would leave for very fear   580
The person to the spoil of Greece. And yet his guardians were
Th' Ajaces and Meriones, whom much his care did press,
And thus exhort: 'Ajaces both, and you, Meriones,
Now let some true friend call to mind the gentle and sweet nature
Of poor Patroclus; let him think, how kind to every creature
His heart was, living, though now dead.' Thus urg'd the fair-hair'd king,
And parted, casting round his eye. As when upon her wing
An eagle is, whom men affirm to have the sharpest sight
Of all air's region of fowls, and though of mighty height,
Sees yet within her leavy form of humble shrubs, close laid,   590
A light-foot hare, which straight she stoops, trusses, and strikes her dead:
So dead thou struck'st thy charge (O king) through all war's thickets, so
Thou look'dst, and swiftly found'st thy man, exhorting 'gainst the foe,
And heart'ning his plied men to blows, us'd in the war's left wing;

To whom thou saidst: 'Thou god-lov'd man, come here, and hear a thing
Which I wish never were to hear; I think ev'n thy eye sees
What a destruction god hath laid upon the sons of Greece,
And what a conquest he gives Troy, in which the best of men
(Patroclus) lies exanimate, whose person, passing fain,
The Greeks would rescue and bear home; and therefore give thy speed   600
To his great friend, to prove if he will do so good a deed
To fetch the naked person off, for Hector's shoulders wear
His prised arms.' Antilochus was highly griev'd to hear
This heavy news, and stood surpris'd with stupid silence long,
His fair eyes standing full of tears, his voice, so sweet and strong,
Stuck in his bosom; yet all this wrought in him no neglect
Of what Atrides gave in charge: but for that quick effect
He gave Laodocus his arms (his friend that had the guide
Of his swift horse), and then his knees were speedily applied
In his sad message, which his eyes told all the way in tears.   610
Nor would thy generous heart assist his sore-charg'd soldiers
(O Menelaus) in mean time, though left in much distress;
Thou sent'st them god-like Thrasymed, and mad'st thy kind regress
Back to Patroclus, where arriv'd, half breathless thou didst say
To both th' Ajaces: 'I have sent this messenger away
To swift Achilles, who, I fear, will hardly help us now
(Though mad with Hector) – without arms he cannot fight, ye know;
Let us then think of some best mean, both how we may remove
The body and get off ourselves from this vociferous drove
And fate of Trojans.' 'Bravely spoke at all parts,' Ajax said,   620
'O glorious son of Atreus; take thou then straight the dead,
And thou, Meriones. We two, of one mind, as one name,
Will back ye soundly, and on us receive the wild-fire flame
That Hector's rage breathes after you before it come at you.'
    This said, they took into their arms the body – all the show
That might be made to those of Troy, at arm's end bearing it.
Out shriek'd the Trojans when they saw the body borne to fleet,
And rush'd on, as at any boar, gash'd with the hunter's wounds,
A kennel of the sharpest set and sorest bitten hounds
Before their youthful huntsmen haste, and eagerly a while   630
Pursue, as if they were assur'd of their affected spoil.
But when the savage (in his strength as confident as they)
Turns head amongst them, back they fly, and every one his way:
So troop-meal'd Troy pursu'd a while, laying on with swords and darts;
But when th' Ajaces turn'd on them, and made their stand, their hearts
Drunk from their faces all their bloods, and not a man sustain'd
The forechace, nor the after fight. And thus Greece nobly gain'd

The person towards home: but thus the changing war was rack'd
Out to a passing bloody length. For as, once put in act,
A fire invading city roofs is suddenly ingross'd   640
And made a wondrous mighty flame, in which is quickly lost
A house long building, all the while a boist'rous gust of wind
Lumb'ring amongst it: so the Greeks (in bearing off their friend)
More and more foes drew, at their heels a tumult thund'ring still
Of horse and foot. Yet as when mules, in haling from a hill
A beam or mast, through foul deep way, well clapp'd and heartened, close
Lie to their labour, tug and sweat, and passing hard it goes
(Urg'd by their drivers to all haste), so dragg'd they on the corse,
Still both th' Ajaces at their backs, who back still turn'd the force,
Though after it grew still the more: yet as a sylvan hill   650
Thrusts back a torrent that hath kept a narrow channel still,
Till at his oaken breast it beats, but there a check it takes,
That sends it over all the vale with all the stir it makes,
Nor can with all the confluence break through his rooty sides:
In no less firm and brave repulse th' Ajaces curb'd the prides
Of all the Trojans; yet all held the pursuit in his strength,
Their chiefs being Hector, and the son of Venus, who at length
Put all the youths of Greece besides in most amazeful rout,
Forgetting all their fortitudes, distraught, and shrieking out,
A number of their rich arms lost, fall'n from them here and there,   660
About and in the dike; and yet, the war concludes not here.

THE END OF THE SEVENTEENTH BOOK

BOOK EIGHTEEN

The Argument

Achilles mourns, told of Patroclus' end;
When Thetis doth from forth the sea ascend
And comfort him, advising to abstain
From any fight, till her request could gain
Fit arms of Vulcan. Juno yet commands
To show himself. And at the dike he stands
In sight of th' enemy, who with his sight
Flies; and a number perish in the flight.
Patroclus' person (safe brought from the wars)
His soldiers wash. Vulcan the arms prepares.

Another Argument

Sigma continues the alarms,
And fashions the renowned arms.

BOOK EIGHTEEN

T HEY FOUGHT still like the rage of fire. And now Antilochus
Came to Aeacides, whose mind was much solicitous
For that which (as he fear'd) was fall'n. He found him near the fleet
With upright sail-yards, uttering this to his heroic conceit:
'Ay me, why see the Greeks themselves thus beaten from the field,
And routed headlong to their fleet. O let not heaven yield
Effect to what my sad soul fears; that (as I was foretold)
The strongest Myrmidon (next me), when I should still behold
The sun's fair light, must part with it. Past doubt Menoetius' son
Is he on whom that fate is wrought. O wretch, to leave undone   10
What I commanded, that the fleet once freed of hostile fire,
(Not meeting Hector) instantly he should his pow'rs retire.'

   As thus his troubled mind discours'd, Antilochus appear'd,
And told with tears the sad news thus: 'My lord, that must be heard
Which would to heav'n I might not tell: Menoetius' son lies dead,
And for his naked corse (his arms already forfeited,
And worn by Hector) the debate is now most vehement.'

   This said, grief darken'd all his pow'rs. With both his hands he rent
The black mould from the forced earth, and pour'd it on his head,
Smear'd all his lovely face; his weeds (divinely fashioned)   20
All 'fil'd and mangled; and himself he threw upon the shore,
Lay as laid out for funeral, then tumbled round, and tore
His gracious curls; his extasy he did so far extend,
That all the ladies won by him and his now slaughter'd friend
(Afflicted strangely for his plight) came shrieking from the tents,
And fell about him; beat their breasts, their tender lineaments
Dissolv'd with sorrow. And with them wept Nestor's warlike son,
Fell by him, holding his fair hands, in fear he would have done
His person violence; his heart (extremely straiten'd) burn'd,
Beat, swell'd, and sigh'd as it would burst. So terribly he mourn'd   30
That Thetis, sitting in the deeps of her old father's seas,
Heard, and lamented. To her plaints the bright Nereides
Flock'd all, how many those dark gulfs soever comprehend.
There Glauce and Cymodoce and Spyo did attend,
Nesaea and Cymothoa, and calm Amphithoë;

Thalia, Thoa, Panope, and swift Dynamene;
Actaea and Lymnoria, and Halia the fair,
Fam'd for the beauty of her eyes, Amathia for her hair;
Iaera, Proto, Clymene, and curl'd Dexamene;
Pherusa, Doris; and with these the smooth Amphinome;   40
Chaste Galathea so renown'd; and Callianira came
With Doto and Orythia, to cheer the mournful dame;
Apseudes likewise visited; and Callianassa gave
Her kind attendance; and with her Agave grac'd the cave.
Nemertes, Maera followed; Melita, Ianesse,
With Ianira, and the rest of those Nereides
That in the deep seas made abode; all which together beat
Their dewy bosoms, and to all thus Thetis did repeat
Her cause of mourning: 'Sisters, hear how much the sorrows weigh
Whose cries now call'd ye: hapless I brought forth unhappily   50
The best of all the sons of men, who like a well-set plant
In best soils, grew and flourished, and when his spirit did want
Employment for his youth and strength, I sent him with a fleet
To fight at Ilion; from whence his fate-confined feet
Pass all my deity to retire. The court of his high birth,
The glorious court of Peleus, must entertain his worth
Never hereafter. All the life he hath to live with me
Must waste in sorrows; and this son I now am bent to see,
Being now afflicted with some grief, not usually grave,
Whose knowledge and recure I seek.' This said, she left her cave,   60
Which all left with her; swimming forth, the green waves as they swom,
Cleft with their bosoms, curl'd, and gave quick way to Troy. Being come,
They all ascended, two and two, and trod the honour'd shore,
Till where the fleet of Myrmidons (drawn up in heaps) it bore.
There stay'd they at Achilles' ship, and there did Thetis lay
Her fair hand on her son's curl'd head, sigh'd, wept, and bade him say
What grief drew from his eyes those tears: 'Conceal it not,' said she;
'Till this hour thy uplifted hands have all things granted thee.
The Greeks (all thrust up at their sterns) have pour'd out tears enow,
And in them seen how much they miss remission of thy vow.   70
    He said, 'Tis true, Olympius hath done me all that grace:
But what joy have I of it all, when thus thrusts in the place
Loss of my whole self, in my friend? Whom, when his foe had slain,
He spoil'd of those profaned arms that Peleus did obtain
From heaven's high pow'rs, solemnizing thy sacred nuptial bands,
As th' only present of them all; and fitted well their hands,
Being lovely, radiant, marvellous. O would to heaven thy throne,
With these fair deities of the sea, thou still hadst sat upon,

And Peleus had a mortal wife, since by his means is done
So much wrong to thy grieved mind, my death being set so soon,   80
And never suff'ring my return to grace of Peleus' court;
Nor do I wish it, nor to live in any man's resort,
But only that the crying blood for vengeance of my friend,
Mangled by Hector, may be still'd, his foe's death paying his end.'
　　She, weeping, said: 'That hour is near, and thy death's hour then nigh,
Which in thy wish, serv'd of thy foe, succeedeth instantly.'
　　'And instantly it shall succeed,' he answer'd, 'since my fate
Allow'd not to my will a pow'r to rescue (ere the date
Of his late slaughter) my true friend. Far from his friends he died,
Whose wrong therein my eyes had light and right to see denied.   90
Yet now I neither light myself, nor have so spent my light,
That either this friend or the rest (in numbers infinite
Slaughter'd by Hector) I can help, nor grace with wish'd repair
To our dear country, but breathe here unprofitable air,
And only live a load to earth, with all my strength, though none
Of all the Grecians equal it. In counsel many a one
Is my superior. What I have no grace gets; what I want
Disgraceth all. How, then, too soon can hastiest death supplant
My fate-curst life? Her instrument to my indignity
Being that black fiend Contention, who would to god might die   100
To gods and men, and Anger too, that kindles tyranny
In men most wise, being much more sweet than liquid honey is
To men of pow'r, to satiate their watchful enmities;
And like a pliant fume it spreads through all their breasts, as late
It stole stern passage thorough mine, which he did instigate
That is our general. But the fact so long past, the effect
Must vanish with it, though both griev'd, nor must we still respect
Our soothed humours. Need now takes the rule of either's mind.
And when the looser of my friend his death in me shall find,
Let death take all. Send him, ye gods, I'll give him my embrace.   110
Not Hercules himself shunn'd death, though dearest in the grace
Of Jupiter; ev'n him Fate stoop'd, and Juno's cruelty.
And if such fate expect my life, where death strikes, I will lie.
Meantime I wish a good renown, that these deep-breasted dames
Of Ilion and Dardania may for th' extinguish'd flames
Of their friends' lives with both their hands wipe miserable tears
From their so curiously kept cheeks, and be the officers
To execute my sighs on Troy, when (seeing my long retreat
But gather'd strength, and gives my charge an answerable heat)
They well may know 'twas I lay still, and that my being away   120
Presented all their happiness. But any further stay

(Which your much love perhaps may wish) assay not to persuade;
All vows are kept, all pray'rs heard, now free way for fight is made.'
The silver-footed dame replied: 'It fits thee well, my son,
To keep destruction from thy friends; but those fair arms are won
And worn by Hector that should keep thyself in keeping them,
Though their fruition be but short, a long death being near him,
Whose cruel glory they are yet: by all means then forbear
To tread the massacres of war till I again appear
From Mulciber with fit new arms; which, when thy eye shall see   130
The sun next rise, shall enter here, with his first beams and me.'

   Thus to her sisters of the sea she turn'd, and bade them ope
The doors and deeps of Nereus; she in Olympus' top
Must visit Vulcan for new arms, to serve her wreakful son,
And bade inform her father so, with all things further done.

   This said, they underwent the sea, herself flew up to heav'n;
In mean space, to the Hellespont and ships the Greeks were driv'n
In shameful rout; nor could they yet, from rage of Priam's son,
Secure the dead of new assaults, both horse and men made on
With such impression: thrice the feet the hands of Hector seiz'd,   140
And thrice th' Ajaces thump'd him off. With whose repulse displeas'd,
He wreak'd his wrath upon the troops, then to the corse again
Made horrid turnings, crying out of his repulsed men,
And would not quit him quite for death. A lion almost sterv'd
Is not by upland herdsmen driv'n from urging to be serv'd
With more contention than his strength, by those two of a name,
And had perhaps his much prais'd will, if th' airy-footed dame
(Swift Iris) had not stoop'd in haste, ambassadress from heav'n
To Peleus' son, to bid him arm, her message being giv'n
By Juno, kept from all the gods; she thus excited him: 150
'Rise, thou most terrible of men, and save the precious limb
Of thy belov'd, in whose behalf the conflict now runs high
Before the fleet; the either host fells other mutually,
These to retain, those to obtain; amongst whom most of all
Is Hector prompt, he's apt to drag thy friend home, he your pall
Will make his shoulders, his head forc'd; he'll be most famous. Rise,
No more lie idle, set the foe a much more costly prize
Of thy friend's value; then let dogs make him a monument
Where thy name will be grav'n.' He ask'd, 'What deity hath sent
Thy presence hither?' She replied: 'Saturnia; she alone,   160
Not high Jove knowing, nor one god that doth inhabit on
Snowy Olympus.' He again: 'How shall I set upon
The work of slaughter, when mine arms are worn by Priam's son?
How will my goddess-mother grieve, that bade I should not arm

Till she brought arms from Mulciber? But should I do such harm
To her and duty, who is he (but Ajax) that can vaunt
The fitting my breast with his arms? And he is conversant
Amongst the first in use of his, and rampiers of the foe
(Slain near Patroclus) builds to him.' 'All this,' said she, 'we know,
And wish thou only wouldst but show thy person to the eyes   170
Of these hot Ilians, that (afraid of further enterprise)
The Greeks may gain some little breath.' She woo'd, and he was won,
And straight Minerva honour'd him, who Jove's shield clapp'd upon
His mighty shoulders, and his head girt with a cloud of gold,
That cast beams round about his brows. And as when arms enfold
A city in an isle, from thence a fume at first appears
(Being in the day), but when the even her cloudy forehead rears,
Thick show the fires, and up they cast their splendour, that men nigh,
Seeing their distress, perhaps may set ships out to their supply:
So (to show such aid) from his head a light rose, scaling heav'n,   180
And forth the wall he stept and stood, nor brake the precept giv'n
By his great mother (mix'd in fight), but sent abroad his voice,
Which Pallas far-off echoed; who did betwixt them hoise
Shrill tumult to a topless height. And as a voice is heard
With emulous affection, when any town is spher'd
With siege of such a foe as kills men's minds, and for the town
Makes sound his trumpet: so the voice from Thetis' issue thrown
Won emulously th' ears of all. His brazen voice once heard,
The minds of all were startled so, they yielded, and so fear'd
The fair-man'd horses that they flew back, and their chariots turn'd,   190
Presaging in their augurous hearts the labours that they mourn'd
A little after, and their guides a repercussive dread
Took from the horrid radiance of his refulgent head,
Which Pallas set on fire with grace. Thrice great Achilles spake,
And thrice (in heat of all the charge) the Trojans started back:
Twelve men, of greatest strength in Troy, left with their lives exhal'd
Their chariots and their darts to death, with his three summons call'd.
And then the Grecians spritefully drew from the darts the corse,
And hearst it, bearing it to fleet, his friends, with all remorse,
Marching about it. His great friend, dissolving then in tears   200
To see his truly-lov'd return'd so hors'd upon a hearse,
Whom with such horse and chariot he set out safe and whole,
Now wounded with unpitying steel, now sent without a soul,
Never again to be restor'd, never receiv'd but so,
He follow'd mourning bitterly. The sun (yet far to go)
Juno commanded to go down, who in his pow'r's despite
Sunk to the ocean, over earth dispersing sudden night.

And then the Greeks and Trojans both gave up their horse and darts.
The Trojans all to council call'd, ere they refresh'd their hearts
With any supper; nor would sit, they grew so stiff with fear   210
To see (so long from heavy fight) Aeacides appear.
    Polydamas began to speak, who only could discern
Things future by things past, and was vow'd friend to Hector, born
In one night both. He thus advis'd: 'Consider well, my friends,
In this so great and sudden change that now itself extends,
What change is best for us t' oppose. To this stands my command:
Make now the town our strength; not here abide light's rosy hand,
Our wall being far off, and our foe (much greater) still as near.
Till this foe came, I well was pleas'd to keep our watches here;
My fit hope of the fleet's surprise inclin'd me so, but now   220
'Tis stronger guarded; and (their strength increas'd) we must allow
Our own proportionate amends. I doubt exceedingly
That this indifference of fight 'twixt us and th' enemy,
And these bounds we prefix to them, will nothing so confine
Th' uncurb'd mind of Aeacides. The height of his design
Aims at our city, and our wives, and all bars in his way
(Being back'd with less than walls) his pow'r will scorn to make his stay,
And over-run, as over-seen, and not his object. Then
Let Troy be freely our retreat, lest being enforc'd, our men
'Twixt this and that be taken up by vultures, who by night   230
May safe come off, it being a time untimely for his might
To spend at random. That being sure, if next light show us here
To his assaults, each man will wish that Troy his refuge were,
And then feel what he hears not now. I would to heaven mine ear
Were free even now of those complaints that you must after hear,
If ye remove not. If ye yield (though wearied with a fight)
So late and long, we shall have strength in counsel and the night.
And (where we here have no more force than need will force us to,
And which must rise out of our nerves) high ports, tow'rs, walls will do
What wants in us. And in the morn, all arm'd upon our tow'rs,   240
We all will stand out to our foe. Twill trouble all his pow'rs
To come from fleet and give us charge, when his high-crested horse
His rage shall satiate with the toil of this and that way's course,
Vain entry seeking underneath our well-defended walls,
And he be glad to turn to fleet, about his funerals.
For of his entry here at home, what mind will serve his thirst,
Or ever feed him with sack'd Troy? The dogs shall eat him first.'
    At this speech Hector bent his brows, and said, 'This makes not great
Your grace with me, Polydamas, that argue for retreat
To Troy's old prison; have we not enough of those tow'rs yet?   250

And is not Troy yet charg'd enough with impositions set
Upon her citizens to keep our men from spoil without,
But still we must impose within? That houses with our rout,
As well as purses, may be plagued? Before time, Priam's town
Traffick'd with divers-languag'd men, and all gave the renown
Of rich Troy to it, brass and gold abounding: but her store
Is now from every house exhaust, possessions evermore
Are sold out into Phrygia, and lovely Maeonie,
And have been ever since Jove's wrath. And now his clemency
Gives me the mean to quit our want with glory, and conclude   260
The Greeks in sea-bords and our seas, or slack it, and extrude
His offer'd bounty by our flight. Fool that thou art, bewray
This counsel to no common ear, for no man shall obey.
If any will, I'll check his will. But what our self command,
Let all observe: take suppers all, keep watch of every hand.
If any Trojan have some spoil that takes his too much care,
Make him dispose it publicly; 'tis better any fare
The better for him than the Greeks. When light then decks the skies,
Let all arm for a fierce assault. If great Achilles rise,
And will enforce our greater toil, it may rise so to him;   270
On my back he shall find no wings, my spirit shall force my limb
To stand his worst, and give or take; Mars is our common lord,
And the desirous swordman's life he ever puts to sword.'
    This counsel gat applause of all, so much were all unwise.
Minerva robb'd them of their brains, to like the ill advice
The great man gave, and leave the good, since by the meaner given.
All took their suppers, but the Greeks spent all the heavy even
About Patroclus' mournful rites, Pelides leading all
In all the forms of heaviness: he by his side did fall,
And his man-slaughtering hands impos'd into his oft-kiss'd breast;   280
Sighs blew up sighs, and lion-like, grac'd with a goodly crest,
That in his absence being robb'd by hunters of his whelps,
Returns to his so desolate den, and for his wanted helps
Beholding his unlook'd-for wants, flies roaring back again,
Hunts the sly hunter, many a vale resounding his disdain:
So mourn'd Pelides his late loss; so weighty were his moans
Which (for their dumb sounds) now gave words to all his Myrmidons:
'O gods,' said he, 'how vain a vow I made to cheer the mind
Of sad Menoetius, when his son his hand to mine resign'd,
That high tower'd Opus he should see, and leave rac't Ilion   290
With spoil and honour, ev'n with me! But Jove vouchsafes to none
Wish'd passages to all his vows; we both were destinate
To bloody one earth here in Troy, nor any more estate

In my return hath Peleus or Thetis; but because
I last must undergo the ground, I'll keep no funeral laws
(O my Patroclus) for thy corse, before I hither bring
The arms of Hector and his head to thee for offering.
Twelve youths, the most renown'd of Troy, I'll sacrifice beside,
Before thy heap of funeral, to thee unpacified.
In mean time, by our crooked sterns lie, drawing tears from me,   300
And round about thy honour'd corse these dames of Dardanie
And Ilion with the ample breasts (whom our long spears and pow'rs
And labours purchas'd from the rich, and by-us-ruin'd tow'rs,
And cities strong and populous with divers-languag'd men)
Shall kneel, and neither day nor night be licens'd to abstain
From solemn watches, their toil'd eyes held ope with endless tears.'

This passion past, he gave command to his near soldiers
To put a tripod to the fire, to cleanse the fester'd gore
From off the person. They obey'd, and presently did pour
Fresh water in it, kindled wood, and with an instant flame   310
The belly of the tripod girt, till fire's hot quality came
Up to the water. Then they wash'd and fill'd the mortal wound
With wealthy oil of nine years old; then wrapp'd the body round
In largeness of a fine white sheet, and put it then in bed,
When all watch'd all night with their lord, and spent sighs on the dead.

Then Jove ask'd Juno, if at length she had suffic'd her spleen,
Achilles being won to arms? Or if she had not been
The natural mother of the Greeks, she did so still prefer
Their quarrel? She incens'd, ask'd why he still was taunting her
For doing good to those she lov'd, since man to man might show   320
Kind offices, though thrall to death, and though they did not know
Half such deep counsels as disclos'd beneath her far-seeing state –
She reigning queen of goddesses, and being ingenerate
Of one stock with himself, besides the state of being his wife.
And must her wrath, and ill to Troy, continue such a strife
From time to time, 'twixt him and her? This private speech they had,
And now the silver-footed queen had her ascension made
To that incorruptible house, that starry golden court
Of fiery Vulcan, beautiful amongst th' immortal sort;
Which yet the lame god built himself: she found him in a sweat   330
About his bellows, and in haste had twenty tripods beat
To set for stools about the sides of his well-builded hall.
To whose feet little wheels of gold he put, to go withal,
And enter his rich dining room; alone, their motion free
And back again go out alone, miraculous to see.
And thus much he had done of them, yet handles were to add,

For which he now was making studs. And while their fashion had
Employment of his skilful hand, bright Thetis was come near,
Whom first fair well-hair'd Charis saw, that was the nuptial fere
Of famous Vulcan, who the hand of Thetis took, and said:　　　　340
　　'Why, fair-train'd, lov'd, and honour'd dame, are we thus visited
By your kind presence? You, I think, were never here before;
Come near, that I may banquet you, and make you visit more.'
　　She led her in, and in a chair of silver (being the fruit
Of Vulcan's hand) she made her sit: a footstool, of a suit,
Apposing to her crystal feet, and call'd the god of fire.
For Thetis was arriv'd (she said) and entertain'd desire
Of some grace, that his art might grant. 'Thetis to me,' said he,
'Is mighty, and most reverend, as one that nourish'd me
When grief consum'd me, being cast from heav'n by want of shame　　350
In my proud mother, who, because she brought me forth so lame,
Would have me made away, and then I had been much distress'd
Had Thetis and Eurynome in either's silver breast
Not rescu'd me – Eurynome, that to her father had
Reciprocal Oceanus; nine years with them I made
A number of well-arted things, round bracelets, buttons brave,
Whistles and carquenets: my forge stood in a hollow cave,
About which (murmuring with foam) th' unmeasur'd ocean
Was ever beating, my abode known not to god nor man
But Thetis and Eurynome, and they would see me still.　　360
They were my loving guardians; now then the starry hill,
And our particular roof thus grac'd with bright-hair'd Thetis here,
It fits me always to repay, a recompense as dear
To her thoughts as my life to me. Haste, Charis, and appose
Some dainty guest-rites to our friend, while I my bellows loose
From fire, and lay up all my tools.' Then from an anvil rose
Th' unwieldy monster, halted down, and all awry he went.
He took his bellows from the fire, and every instrument
Lock'd safe up in a silver chest. Then with a sponge he drest
His face all over, neck and hands, and all his hairy breast:　　370
Put on his coat, his sceptre took, and then went halting forth,
Handmaids of gold attending him, resembling in all worth
Living young damsels, fill'd with minds and wisdom, and were train'd
In all immortal ministry, virtue and voice contain'd,
And mov'd with voluntary pow'rs: and these still waited on
Their fiery sov'reign; who (not apt to walk) sate near the throne
Of fair-hair'd Thetis, took her hand, and thus he courted her:
　　'For what affair, O fair-train'd queen, rev'rend to me and dear,
Is our court honour'd with thy state, that hast not heretofore

Perform'd this kindness? Speak thy thoughts, thy suit can be no more   380
Than my mind gives me charge to grant, can my pow'r get it wrought,
Or that it have not only pow'r of only act in thought.'
   She thus: 'O Vulcan, is there one of all that are of heav'n,
That in her never-quiet mind Saturnius hath giv'n
So much affliction as to me, whom only he subjects
(Of all the sea-nymphs) to a man, and makes me bear th' affects
Of his frail bed – and all against the freedom of my will?
And he worn to his root with age; from him another ill
Ariseth to me: Jupiter, you know, hath giv'n a son
(The excellent'st of men) to me; whose education   390
On my part well hath answered his own worth, having grown,
As in a fruitful soil a tree that puts not up alone
His body to a naked height, but jointly gives his growth
A thousand branches; yet to him so short a life I brought,
That never I shall see him more return'd to Peleus' court.
And all that short life he hath spent in most unhappy sort.
For first he won a worthy dame, and had her by the hands
Of all the Grecians; yet this dame Atrides countermands,
For which in much disdain he mourn'd, and almost pin'd away;
And yet for this wrong he receiv'd some honour, I must say –   400
The Greeks being shut up at their ships, not suffer'd to advance
A head out of their batter'd sterns; and mighty suppliance
By all their grave men hath been made, gifts, honours, all propos'd
For his reflection; yet he still kept close, and saw enclos'd
Their whole host in this general plague. But now his friend put on
His arms, being sent by him to field, and many a Myrmidon
In conduct of him: all the day they fought before the gates
Of Scaea, and most certainly that day had seen the dates
Of all Troy's honours in her dust, if Phoebus (having done
Much mischief more) the envied life of good Menoetius' son   410
Had not with partial hands enforc'd, and all the honour given
To Hector, who hath priz'd his arms; and therefore I am driven
T'embrace thy knees for new defence to my lov'd son: alas,
His life prefix'd so short a date had need spend that with grace!
A shield then for him, and a helm, fair greaves, and curets such
As may renown thy workmanship, and honour him as much,
I sue for at thy famous hands.' 'Be confident,' said he,
'Let these wants breed thy thoughts no care; I would it lay in me
To hide him from his heavy death, when fate shall seek for him,
As well as with renowned arms to fit his goodly limb;   420
Which thy hands shall convey to him, and all eyes shall admire,
See, and desire again to see thy satisfied desire.'

This said, he left her there, and forth did to his bellows go,
Appos'd them to the fire again, commanding them to blow.
Through twenty holes made to his hearth at once blew twenty pair,
That fir'd his coals, sometimes with soft, sometimes with vehement air
As he will'd, and his work requir'd. Amidst the flame he cast
Tin, silver, precious gold, and brass; and in the stock he plac'd
A mighty anvil; his right hand a weighty hammer held,
His left his tongs. And first he forg'd a strong and spacious shield   430
Adorn'd with twenty several hues, about whose verge he beat
A ring, three-fold and radiant; and on the back he set
A silver handle; five-fold were the equal lines he drew
About the whole circumference, in which his hand did shew
(Directed with a knowing mind) a rare variety:
For in it he represented earth; in it, the sea and sky;
In it, the never-wearied sun, the moon exactly round,
And all those stars with which the brows of ample heaven are crown'd –
Orion, all the Pleiades, and those seven Atlas got,
The close-beam'd Hyades, the Bear, surnam'd the Chariot,   440
That turns about heaven's axle-tree, holds ope a constant eye
Upon Orion, and of all the cressets in the sky
His golden forehead never bows to th' Ocean empery.
    Two cities in the spacious field he built with goodly state,
Of divers-languag'd men: the one did nuptials celebrate,
Observing at them solemn feasts; the brides from forth their bow'rs
With torches usher'd through the streets; a world of paramours
Excited by them, youths and maids, in lovely circles danc'd,
To whom the merry pipe and harp the spriteful sounds advanc'd,
The matrons standing in their doors admiring. Other where   450
A solemn court of law was kept, where throngs of people were:
The case in question was a fine impos'd on one that slew
The friend of him that follow'd it, and for the fine did sue,
Which th' other pleaded he had paid. The adverse part denied,
And openly affirm'd he had no penny satisfied.
Both put it to arbiterment; the people cried 'twas best
For both parts, and th' assistants too gave their dooms like the rest.
The heralds made the people peace: the seniors then did bear
The voiceful heralds' sceptres, sate within a sacred sphere,
On polish'd stones, and gave by turns their sentence. In the court   460
Two talents of gold were cast, for him that judg'd in justest sort.
    The other city other wars employ'd as busily.
Two armies glittering in arms, of one confederacy,
Besieg'd it; and a parley had with those within the town;
Two ways they stood resolv'd: to see the city overthrown,

Or that the citizens should heap in two parts all their wealth,
And give them half. They neither lik'd, but arm'd themselves by stealth;
Left all their old men, wives, and boys behind to man their walls,
And stole out to their enemy's town. The queen of martials
And Mars himself conducted them; both which, being forg'd of gold,   470
Must needs have golden furniture, and men might so behold
They were presented deities. The people Vulcan forg'd
Of meaner metal. When they came where that was to be urg'd
For which they went, within a vale close to a flood, whose stream
Us'd to give all their cattle drink, they there enambush'd them,
And sent two scouts out to descry when th' enemy's herds and sheep
Were setting out: they straight came forth, with two that us'd to keep
Their passage always; both which pip'd, and went on merrily,
Nor dream'd of ambuscados there. The ambush then let fly,
Slew all their white-fleec'd sheep and neat, and by them laid their guard.   480
When those in siege before the town so strange an uproar heard,
Behind, amongst their flocks and herds (being then in counsel set),
They then start up, took horse, and soon their subtle enemy met,
Fought with them on the river's shore, where both gave mutual blows
With well-pil'd darts. Amongst them all, perverse Contention rose,
Amongst them Tumult was enrag'd; amongst them ruinous Fate
Had her red finger; some they took in an unhurt estate,
Some hurt, yet living, some quite slain: and those they tugg'd to them
By both the feet, stripp'd off and took their weeds, with all the stream
Of blood upon them, that their steels had manfully let out.   490
They far'd as men alive indeed, drew dead indeed about.
    To these the fiery artisan did add a new-ear'd field,
Large and thrice plough'd, the soil being soft and of a wealthy yield;
And many men at plough he made, that drave earth here and there,
And turn'd up stitches orderly; at whose end when they were,
A fellow ever gave their hands full cups of luscious wine,
Which emptied, for another stitch the earth they undermine,
And long till th' utmost bound be reach'd of all the ample close:
The soil turn'd up behind the plough all black like earth arose,
Though forg'd of nothing else but gold, and lay in show as light   500
As if it had been plough'd indeed, miraculous to sight.
    There grew by this a field of corn: high, ripe, where reapers wrought,
And let thick handfuls fall to earth; for which some other brought
Bands, and made sheaves. Three binders stood, and took the handfuls reap'd
From boys that gather'd quickly up; and by them armfuls heap'd.
Amongst these at a furrow's end the king stood pleas'd at heart,
Said no word, but his sceptre show'd. And from him, much apart,
His harvest-bailiffs underneath an oak a feast prepar'd:

And having kill'd a mighty ox, stood there to see him shar'd,
Which women for their harvest folks (then come to sup) had dress'd,   510
And many white wheat cakes bestow'd, to make it up a feast.

   He set near this a vine of gold, that crack'd beneath the weight
Of bunches, black with being ripe, to keep which at the height,
A silver rail ran all along, and round about it flow'd
An azure moat; and to this guard a quickset was bestow'd
Of tin, one only path to all, by which the pressmen came
In time of vintage: youths and maids, that bore not yet the flame
Of manly Hymen, baskets bore of grapes and mellow fruit.
A lad that sweetly touch'd a harp, to which his voice did suit,
Center'd the circles of that youth, all whose skill could not do   520
The wanton's pleasure to their minds, that danced, sung, whistled too.

   A herd of oxen then he carv'd, with high rais'd heads, forg'd all
Of gold and tin (for colour mix'd), and bellowing from their stall,
Rush'd to their pastures at a flood that echo'd all their throats,
Exceeding swift and full of reeds; and all in yellow coats
Four herdsmen follow'd, after whom nine mastiffs went. In head
Of all the herd, upon a bull, that deadly bellowed,
Two horrid lions rampt, and seiz'd, and tugg'd off bellowing still;
Both men and dogs came, yet they tore the hide, and lapp'd their fill
Of black blood, and the entrails ate. In vain the men assay'd   530
To set their dogs on: none durst pinch, but cur-like stood and bay'd
In both the faces of their kings, and all their onsets fled.

   Then in a passing pleasant vale the famous artsman fed
(Upon a goodly pasture ground) rich flocks of white-fleec'd sheep,
Built stables, cottages, and cotes, that did the shepherds keep
From wind and weather. Next to these he cut a dancing place,
All full of turnings, that was like the admirable maze
For fair-hair'd Ariadne made by cunning Daedalus;
And in it youths and virgins danc'd, all young and beauteous,
And glewed in another's palms. Weeds that the wind did toss   540
The virgins wore, the youths wov'n coats, that cast a faint dim gloss,
Like that of oil. Fresh garlands too the virgins' temples crown'd;
The youths gilt swords wore at their thighs, with silver bawdrics bound.
Sometimes all wound close in a ring, to which as fast they spun
As any wheel a turner makes, being tried how it will run,
While he is set, and out again as full of speed they wound,
Not one left fast, or breaking hands. A multitude stood round,
Delighted with their nimble sport: to end which two begun
(Midst all) a song, and turning sung the sport's conclusion.
All this he circled in the shield, with pouring round about   550
(In all his rage) the ocean, that it might never out.

This shield thus done, he forg'd for him such curets as outshin'd
The blaze of fire; a helmet then (through which no steel could find
Forc'd passage) he compos'd, whose hue a hundred colours took,
And in the crest a plume of gold, that each breath stirr'd, he stuck.
  All done, he all to Thetis brought, and held all up to her;
She took them all, and, like the hawk surnam'd the osspringer,
From Vulcan to her mighty son, with that so glorious show,
Stoop'd from the steep Olympian hill, hid in eternal snow.

THE END OF THE EIGHTEENTH BOOK

BOOK NINETEEN

The Argument

Thetis presenting armour to her son,
He calls a court, with full reflection
Of all his wrath; takes of the king of men
Free-offer'd gifts. All take their breakfast then;
He (only fasting) arms, and brings abroad
The Grecian host. And (hearing the abode
Of his near death by Xanthus prophesied)
The horse for his so bold presage doth chide.

Another Argument

Tau gives the anger period,
And great Achilles comes abroad.

BOOK NINETEEN

THE MOON AROSE, and from the ocean in her saffron robe
Gave light to all, as well to gods as men of th' under globe.
Thetis stoop'd home, and found the prostrate person of her son
About his friend, still pouring out himself in passion,
A number more being heavy consorts to him in his cares:
Amongst them all Thetis appear'd, and (sacred comforters)
Made these short words: 'Though we must grieve, yet bear it thus, my son:
It was no man that prostrated in this sad fashion
Thy dearest friend; it was a god that first laid on his hand,
Whose will is law: the gods' decrees no human must withstand.   10
Do thou embrace this fabric of a god, whose hand before
Ne'er forg'd the like, and such as yet no human shoulder wore.'
   Thus (setting down), the precious metal of the arms was such
That all the room rung with the weight of every slend'rest touch.
Cold tremblings took the Myrmidons; none durst sustain, all fear'd
T' oppose their eyes. Achilles yet, as soon as they appear'd,
Stern Anger enter'd. From his eyes (as if the day-star rose)
A radiance, terrifying men, did all the state enclose.
At length he took into his hands the rich gift of the god,
And (much pleas'd to behold the art that in the shield he show'd)   20
He brake forth into this applause: 'O mother, these right well
Show an immortal finger's touch; man's hand must never deal
With arms again. Now I will arm; yet (that no honour make
My friend forgotten) I much fear, lest with the blows of flies
His brass-inflicted wounds are fil'd; life gone, his person lies
All apt to putrefaction.' She bade him doubt no harm
Of those offences; she would care to keep the petulant swarm
Of flies (that usually taint the bodies of the slain)
From his friend's person: though a year the earth's top should sustain
His slaughter'd body, it should still rest sound, and rather hold   30
A better state than worse, since time that death first made him cold.
And so bade call a council, to dispose of new alarms,
Where (to the king that was the pastor of that flock in arms)
He should depose all anger, and put on a fortitude
Fit for his arms. All this his pow'rs with dreadful strength indu'd.

She, with her fair hand, still'd into the nostrils of his friend
Red nectar and ambrosia, with which she did defend
The corse from putrefaction. He trod along the shore,
And summon'd all th' heroic Greeks, with all that spent before
The time in exercise with him; the masters, pilots too,   40
Vict'lers, and all: all, when they saw Achilles summon so,
Swarm'd to the council, having long left the laborious wars.
To all these came two halting kings, true servitors of Mars,
Tydides and wise Ithacus, both leaning on their spears,
Their wound still painful, and both these sate first of all the peers.
    The last come was the king of men, sore wounded with the lance
Of Coon Antenorides. All set, the first in utterance
Was Thetis' son, who rose and said: 'Atrides, had not this
Conferr'd most profit to us both, when both our enmities
Consum'd us so, and for a wench – whom when I choos'd for prize   50
(In laying Lyrnessus' ruin'd walls amongst our victories),
I would to heav'n (as first she set her dainty foot aboard)
Diana's hand had tumbled off, and with a javelin gor'd.
For then th' unmeasurable earth had not so thick been gnawn
(In death's convulsions) by our friends, since my affects were drawn
To such distemper. To our foe, and to our foe's chief friend,
Our jar brought profit: but the Greeks will never give an end
To thought of what it prejudic'd them: past things, yet past our aid.
Fit grief for what wrath rul'd in them, must make th' amends repaid
With that necessity of love that now forbids our ire,   60
Which I with free affects obey. 'Tis for the senseless fire
Still to be burning, having stuff; but men must curb rage still,
Being fram'd with voluntary pow'rs as well to check the will
As give it reins. Give you then charge, that for our instant fight
The Greeks may follow me to field, to try if still the night
Will bear out Trojans at our ships. I hope there is some one
Amongst their chief encouragers will thank me to be gone,
And bring his heart down to his knees in that submission.'
    The Greeks rejoic'd to hear the heart of Peleus' mighty son
So qualified. And then the king (not rising from his throne,   70
For his late hurt), to get good ear, thus order'd his reply:
    'Princes of Greece, your states shall suffer no indignity,
If (being far off) ye stand and hear, nor fits it such as stand
At greater distance, to disturb the counsel now in hand
By uproar, in their too much care of hearing. Some, of force,
Must lose some words: for hard it is in such a great concourse
(Though hearers' ears be ne'er so sharp) to touch at all things spoke.
And in assemblies of such trust, how can a man provoke

Fit pow'r to hear, or leave to speak? Best auditors may there
Lose fittest words, and the most vocal orator fit ear.   80
My main end, then, to satisfy Pelides with reply,
My words shall prosecute. To him my speech especially
Shall bear direction. Yet I wish the court in general
Would give fit ear; my speech shall need attention of all.
Oft have our peers of Greece much blam'd my forcing of the prize
Due to Achilles, of which act not I, but destinies,
And Jove himself, and black Erinys (that casts false mists still
Betwixt us and our actions done, both by her pow'r and will)
Are authors: what could I do then? The very day and hour
Of our debate that Fury stole in that act on my pow'r.   90
And more: all things are done by Strife; that ancient seed of Jove,
Ate, that hurts all, perfects all: her feet are soft, and move
Not on the earth; they bear her still aloft men's heads, and there
She harmful hurts them. Nor was I alone her prisoner –
Jove (best of men and gods) hath been. Not he himself hath gone
Beyond her fetters: no, she made a woman put them on.
For when Alcmena was to vent the force of Hercules
In well-wall'd Thebes, thus Jove triumph'd: "Hear, gods and goddesses,
The words my joys urg'd: in this day, Lucina (bringing pain
To labouring women) shall produce into the light of men   100
A man that all his neighbour kings shall in his empire hold,
And vaunt that more than manly race, whose honour'd veins enfold
My eminent blood." Saturnia conceiv'd a present sleight,
And urg'd confirmance of his vaunt, t' infringe it; her conceit
In this sort urg'd: "Thou wilt not hold thy word with this rare man,
Or if thou wilt, confirm it with the oath Olympian,
That whosoever falls this day betwixt a woman's knees,
Of those men's stocks that from thy blood derive their pedigrees,
Shall all his neighbour towns command." Jove (ignorant of fraud)
Took that great oath, which his great ill gave little cause t' applaud.   110
Down from Olympus top she stoop'd, and quickly reach'd the place
In Argos, where the famous wife of Sthenelus (whose race
He fetch'd from Jove, by Perseus) dwelt. She was but seven months gone
With issue, yet she brought it forth; Alcmena's matchless son
Delay'd from light, Saturnia repress'd the teeming throes
Of his great mother. Up to heav'n she mounts again, and shows
(In glory) her deceit to Jove. "Bright-lightning Jove," said she,
"Now th' Argives have an emperor; a son deriv'd from thee
Is born to Persean Sthenelus; Eurystheus his name,
Noble and worthy of the rule thou swor'st to him." This came   120
Close to the heart of Jupiter, and Ate that had wrought

This anger by Saturnia, by her bright hair he caught,
Held down her head, and over her made this infallible vow:
That never to the cope of stars should reascend that brow,
Being so infortunate to all. Thus, swinging her about,
He cast her from the fiery heav'n, who ever since thrust out
Her fork'd sting in th' affairs of men. Jove ever since did grieve,
Since his dear issue Hercules did by his vow achieve
The unjust toils of Eurystheus: thus fares it now with me,
Since under Hector's violence the Grecian progeny   130
Fell so unfitly by my spleen, whose falls will ever stick
In my griev'd thoughts. My weakness yet (Saturnius making sick
The state my mind held) now recur'd, th' amends shall make ev'n weight
With my offence, and therefore rouse thy spirits to the fight
With all thy forces; all the gifts propos'd thee at thy tent
(Last day) by royal Ithacus, my officers shall present;
And (if it like thee) strike no stroke (though never so on thorns
Thy mind stands to thy friend's revenge) till my command adorns
Thy tents and coffers with such gifts as well may let thee know
How much I wish thee satisfied.' He answer'd: 'Let thy vow,   140
Renown'd Atrides, at thy will be kept (as justice would),
Or keep thy gifts; 'tis all in thee. The council now we hold
Is for repairing our main field with all our fortitude.
My fair show made brooks no retreat, nor must delays delude
Our deed's expectance. Yet undone the great work is, all eyes
Must see Achilles in first fight, depeopling enemies,
As well as counsel it in court, that every man set on
May choose his man to imitate my exercise upon.'

    Ulysses answer'd: 'Do not yet, thou man made like the gods,
Take fasting men to field: suppose, that whatsoever odds   150
It brings against them, with full men, thy boundless eminence
Can amply answer; yet refrain to tempt a violence.
The conflict wearing out our men was late, and held as long;
Wherein, though most Jove stood for Troy, he yet made our part strong
To bear that most. But 'twas to bear, and that breeds little heart.
Let wine and bread then add to it; they help the twofold part,
The soul and body in a man, both force and fortitude.
All day men cannot fight, and fast, though never so indu'd
With minds to fight; for that suppos'd, there lurks yet secretly
Thirst, hunger, in th' oppressed joints; which no mind can supply.   160
They take away a marcher's knees. Men's bodies throughly fed,
Their minds share with them in their strength; and (all day combated)
One stirs not, till you call off all. Dismiss them then to meat,
And let Atrides tender here, in sight of all his seat,

The gifts he promis'd. Let him swear before us all, and rise
To that oath, that he never touch'd in any wanton wise
The lady he enforc'd. Besides, that he remains in mind
As chastely satisfied, not touch'd or privily inclin'd
With future vantages. And last, 'tis fit he should approve
All these rites at a solemn feast, in honour of your love,   170
That so you take no mangled law for merits absolute.
And thus the honours you receive, resolving the pursuit
Of your friend's quarrel, well will quit your sorrow for your friend.
And thou, Atrides, in the taste of so severe an end,
Hereafter may on others hold a juster government.
Nor will it aught impair a king to give a sound content
To any subject soundly wrong'd.' 'I joy,' replied the king,
'O Laertiades, to hear thy liberal counselling;
In which is all decorum kept, nor any point lacks touch,
That might be thought on to conclude a reconcilement such   180
As fits example, and us two. My mind yet makes me swear,
Not your impulsion. And that mind shall rest so kind and clear,
That I will not forswear to god. Let then Achilles stay
(Though never so inflam'd for fight), and all men here I pray
To stay, till from my tents these gifts be brought here, and the truce
At all parts finish'd before all. And thou of all I choose,
Divine Ulysses, and command to choose of all your host
Youths of most honour, to present to him we honour most
The gifts we late vow'd, and the dames. Mean space about our tents
Talthybius shall provide a boar, to crown these kind events   190
With thankful sacrifice to Jove, and to the god of light.'
Achilles answer'd: 'These affairs will show more requisite,
Great king of men, some other time, when our more free estates
Yield fit cessation from the war, and when my spleen abates;
But now (to all our shames besides) our friends by Hector slain
(And Jove to friend) lie unfetch'd off. Haste, then, and meat your men,
Though I must still say, my command would lead them fasting forth,
And all together feast at night. Meat will be something worth
When stomachs first have made it way with venting infamy
(And other sorrows late sustain'd) with long'd-for wreaks, that lie   200
Heavy upon them, for right's sake. Before which load be got
From off my stomach, meat nor drink, I vow, shall down my throat,
My friend being dead, who digg'd with wounds, and bor'd through both his feet,
Lies in the entry of my tent, and in the tears doth fleet
Of his associates. Meat and drink have little merit then
To comfort me, but blood and death, and deadly groans of men.'
   The great in counsels yet made good his former counsels thus:

'O Peleus' son, of all the Greeks by much most valorous,
Better and mightier than myself, no little, with thy lance,
I yield thy worth; in wisdom yet no less I dare advance   210
My right above thee, since above in years, and knowing more.
Let then thy mind rest in thy words, we quickly shall have store,
And all satiety of fight; whose steel heaps store of straw,
And little corn upon a floor, when Jove (that doth withdraw,
And join all battles) once begins t' incline his balances
In which he weighs the lives of men. The Greeks you must not press
To mourning with the belly; death hath nought to do with that
In healthful men that mourn for friends. His steel we stumble at,
And fall at, every day you see sufficient store, and fast.
What hour is it that any breathes? We must not use more haste   220
Than speed holds fit for our revenge: nor should we mourn too much.
Who dead is, must be buried; men's patience should be such
That one day's moan should serve one man: the dead must end with death,
And life last with what strengthens life. All those that held their breath
From death in fight, the more should eat, that so they may supply
Their fellows that have stuck in field, and fight incessantly.
Let none expect reply to this, nor stay; for this shall stand
Or fall with some offence to him that looks for new command,
Whoever in dislike holds back. All join then, all things fit
Allow'd for all; set on a charge, at all parts answering it.'   230
    This said, he chose (for noblest youths to bear the presents) these:
The sons of Nestor, and with them renown'd Meriones,
Phylidas, Thoas, Lycomed, and Meges, all which went
(And Melanippus following Ulysses) to the tent
Of Agamemnon. He but spake, and with the word the deed
Had join'd effect: the fitness well was answer'd in the speed.
    The presents added to the dame the general did enforce,
Were twenty cauldrons, tripods seven, twelve young and goodly horse;
Seven ladies excellently seen in all Minerva's skill;
The eighth, Briseis, who had pow'r to ravish every will;   240
Twelve talents of the finest gold, all which Ulysses weigh'd,
And carried first; and after him the other youths convey'd
The other presents, tender'd all in face of all the court.
Up rose the king. Talthybius (whose voice had a report
Like to a god) call'd to the rites; there, having brought the boar,
Atrides with his knife took sey upon the part before;
And lifting up his sacred hands to Jove, to make his vows,
Grave silence struck the complete court, when (casting his high brows
Up to the broad heav'n) thus he spake: 'Now witness Jupiter,
First, highest and thou best of gods, thou earth, that all dost bear,   250

Thou sun, ye Furies under earth, that every soul torment
Whom impious perjury distains – that nought incontinent
In bed, or any other act, to any slend'rest touch
Of my light vows hath wrong'd the dame; and let my plagues be such
As are inflicted by the gods in all extremity
On whomsoever perjur'd men, if godless perjury
In least degree dishonour me.' This said, the bristled throat
Of the submitted sacrifice with ruthless steel he cut;
Which straight into the hoary sea Talthybius cast, to feed
The sea-born nation. Then stood up the half-celestial seed   260
Of fair-hair'd Thetis, strength'ning thus Atrides' innocence:
  'O father Jupiter, from thee descends the confluence
Of all man's ill; for now I see the mighty king of men
At no hand forc'd away my prize, nor first inflam'd my spleen
With any set ill in himself; but thou, the king of gods
(Incens'd with Greece) made that the mean to all their periods,
Which now amend we as we may, and give all suffrages
To what wise Ithacus advis'd. Take breakfasts, and address
For instant conflict.' Thus he rais'd the court, and all took way
To several ships. The Myrmidons the presents did convey   270
T' Achilles fleet, and in his tents dispos'd them, doing grace
Of seat and all rites to the dames, the horses put in place
With others of Aeacides. When (like love's golden queen)
Briseis all in ghastly wounds had dead Patroclus seen,
She fell about him, shrieking out, and with her white hands tore
Her hair, breasts, radiant cheeks; and, drown'd in warm tears, did deplore
His cruel destiny. At length she gat pow'r to express
Her violent passion, and thus spake this like-the-goddesses:
  'O good Patroclus, to my life the dearest grace it had,
I (wretched dame) departing hence, enforc'd and dying sad,   280
Left thee alive, when thou hadst cheer'd my poor captivity;
And now return'd, I find thee dead, misery on misery
Ever increasing with my steps. The lord to whom my sire
And dearest mother gave my life in nuptials, his life's fire
I saw before our city gates extinguish'd; and his fate
Three of my worthy brothers' lives, in one womb generate,
Felt all in that black day of death. And when Achilles' hand
Had slain all these, and ras'd the town Mynetes did command
(All cause of never-ending griefs presented), thou took'st all
On thy endeavour to convert to joy as general,   290
Affirming he that hurt should heal, and thou wouldst make thy friend
(Brave captain that thou wert) supply my vowed husband's end,
And in rich Phthia celebrate, amongst his Myrmidons,

Our nuptial banquets; for which grace, with these most worthy moans
I never shall be satiate, thou ever being kind,
Ever delightsome, one sweet grace fed still with one sweet mind.'

Thus spake she weeping, and with her did th' other ladies moan
Patroclus' fortunes in pretext, but in sad truth their own.

About Aeacides himself the kings of Greece were plac'd,
Entreating him to food; and he entreated them as fast   300
(Still intermixing words and sighs), if any friend were there
Of all his dearest, they would cease, and offer him no cheer
But his due sorrows; for before the sun had left that sky
He would not eat, but of that day sustain th' extremity.

Thus all the kings (in resolute grief and fasting) he dismiss'd;
But both th' Atrides, Ithacus, and war's old martialist,
Idomenaeus and his friend, and Phoenix, these remain'd
Endeavouring comfort, but no thought of his vow'd woe restrain'd –
Nor could, till that day's bloody fight had calm'd his blood; he still
Remember'd something of his friend, whose good was all his ill.   310
Their urging meat, the diligent fashion of his friend renew'd
In that excitement: 'Thou,' said he, 'when this speed was pursued
Against the Trojans, evermore apposedst in my tent
A pleasing breakfast; being so free, and sweetly diligent,
Thou mad'st all meat sweet. Then the war was tearful to our foe,
But now to me, thy wounds so wound me, and thy overthrow.
For which my ready food I fly, and on thy longings feed.
Nothing could more afflict me: fame relating the foul deed
Of my dear father's slaughter, blood drawn from my sole son's heart,
No more could wound me. Cursed man, that in this foreign part   320
(For hateful Helen) my true love, my country, sire and son,
I thus should part with. Scyros now gives education,
O Neoptelemus, to thee (if living yet), from whence
I hop'd, dear friend, thy longer life (safely return'd from hence,
And my life quitting thine) had pow'r to ship him home, and show
His young eyes Phthia, subjects, court – my father being now
Dead, or most short-liv'd, troublous age oppressing him, and fear
Still of my death's news.' These sad words he blew into the ear
Of every visitant, with sighs, all echo'd by the peers,
Rememb'ring who they left at home. All whose so humane tears   330
Jove pitied: and since they all would in the good of one
Be much reviv'd, he thus bespake Minerva: 'Thetis' son
Now, daughter, thou hast quite forgot. O, is Achilles 'care
Extinguish'd in thee? Prostrated in most extreme ill fare
He lies before his high-sail'd fleet, for his dead friend; the rest
Are strength'ning them with meat, but he lies desperately oppress'd

With heartless fasting: go thy ways, and to his breast instil
Red nectar and ambrosia, that fast procure no ill
To his near enterprise.' This spur he added to the free;
And like a harpy (with a voice that shrieks so dreadfully,   340
And feathers that like needles prick) she stoop'd through all the stars
Amongst the Grecians; all whose tents were now fill'd for the wars.
Her seres struck through Achilles' tent, and closely she instill'd
Heaven's most-to-be-desired feast to his great breast, and fill'd
His sinews with that sweet supply, for fear unsavoury fast
Should creep into his knees. Herself the skies again enchas't.

The host set forth, and pour'd his steel waves far out of the fleet.
And as from air the frosty north wind blows a cold thick sleet
That dazzles eyes, flakes after flakes incessantly descending:
So thick helms, curets, ashen darts, and round shields, never ending,   350
Flow'd from the navy's hollow womb; their splendours gave heav'n's eye
His beams again; earth laugh'd to see her face so like the sky,
Arms shin'd so hot, and she such clouds made with the dust she cast –
She thunder'd, feet of men and horse importun'd her so fast.
In midst of all, divine Achilles his fair person arm'd,
His teeth gnash'd as he stood, his eyes so full of fire they warm'd,
Unsuffer'd grief and anger at the Trojans so combin'd.
His greaves first us'd, his goodly curets on his bosom, shin'd,
His sword, his shield that cast a brightness from it like the moon:
And as from sea sailors discern a harmful fire, let run   360
By herdsmen's faults, till all their stall flies up in wrastling flame,
Which being on hills is seen far off; but being alone, none came
To give it quench; at shore no neighbours, and at sea their friends
Driv'n off with tempests: such a fire from his bright shield extends
His ominous radiance, and in heav'n impress'd his fervent blaze.
His crested helmet, grave and high, had next triumphant place
On his curl'd head, and like a star it cast a spurry ray,
About which a bright thick'ned bush of golden hair did play,
Which Vulcan forg'd him for his plume. Thus complete arm'd, he tried
How fit they were, and if his motion could with ease abide   370
Their brave instruction: and so far they were from hind'ring it,
That to it they were nimble wings, and made so light his spirit
That from the earth the princely captain they took up to air.

Then from his armoury he drew his lance, his father's spear,
Huge, weighty, firm, that not a Greek but he himself alone
Knew how to shake; it grew upon the mountain Pelion,
From whose height Chiron hew'd it for his sire, and fatal 'twas
To great-soul'd men – of Pelion surnamed Pelias.
Then from the stable their bright horse Automedon withdraws,

And Alcymus put poitrils on, and cast upon their jaws   380
Their bridles, hurling back the reins, and hung them on the seat.
The fair scourge then Automedon takes up, and up doth get
To guide the horse: the fight's seat last Achilles took behind,
Who look'd so arm'd as if the sun there fall'n from heaven had shin'd,
And terribly thus charg'd his steeds: 'Xanthus and Balius,
Seed of the harpy, in the charge ye undertake of us,
Discharge it not as when Patroclus ye left dead in field,
But when with blood, for this day's fast observ'd, revenge shall yield
Our heart satiety, bring us off.' Thus, since Achilles spake
As if his aw'd steeds understood, 'twas Juno's will to make   390
Vocal the palate of the one, who shaking his fair head
(Which in his mane, let fall to earth, he almost buried),
Thus Xanthus spake: 'Ablest Achilles, now (at least) our care
Shall bring thee off; but not far hence the fatal minutes are
Of thy grave ruin. Nor shall we be then to be reprov'd,
But mightiest fate, and the great god. Nor was thy best belov'd
Spoil'd so of arms by our slow pace, or courage's impair;
The best of gods, Latona's son, that wears the golden hair,
Gave him his death's wound, through the grace he gave to Hector's hand.
We, like the spirit of the west that all spirits can command   400
For pow'r of wing, could run him off: but thou thyself must go,
So fate ordains; god and a man must give thee overthrow.'
This said, the Furies stopp'd his voice. Achilles, far in rage,
Thus answer'd him: 'It fits not thee thus proudly to presage
My overthrow; I know myself it is my fate to fall
Thus far from Phthia; yet that fate shall fail to vent her gall
Till mine vent thousands.' These words us'd, he fell to horrid deeds,
Gave dreadful signal, and forthright made fly his one-hoof'd steeds.

THE END OF THE NINETEENTH BOOK

BOOK TWENTY

The Argument

By Jove's permission, all the gods descend
To aid on both parts. For the Greeks contend
Juno, Minerva, Neptune, Mulciber,
And Mercury. The deities that prefer
The Trojan part are Phoebus, Cyprides,
Phoebe, Latona, and the foe to peace,
With bright Scamander. Neptune in a mist
Preserves Aeneas, daring to resist
Achilles, by whose hand much scathe is done,
Besides the slaughter of old Priam's son
(Young Polydor), whose rescue Hector makes;
Him (flying) Phoebus to his rescue takes,
The rest (all shunning their importun'd fates)
Achilles beats ev'n to the Ilian gates.

Another Argument

In *Upsilon* Strife stirs in heav'n.
The day's grace to the Greeks is giv'n.

BOOK TWENTY

THE GREEKS THUS arm'd, and made insatiate with desire of fight,
About thee, Peleus' son, the foe, in ground of greatest height,
Stood opposite rang'd. Then Jove charg'd Themis from Olympus' top
To call a court; she every way dispers'd, and summon'd up
All deities: not any flood (besides Oceanus)
But made appearance; not a nymph (that arbours odorous,
The heads of floods and flow'ry meadows make their sweet abodes)
Was absent there; but all at his court that is king of gods
Assembled, and in lightsome seats of admirable frame
(Perform'd for Jove by Vulcan) sat. Ev'n angry Neptune came,   10
Nor heard the goddess with unwilling ear, but with the rest
Made free ascension from the sea, and did his state invest
In midst of all, began the council, and inquir'd of Jove
His reason for that session, and on what point did move
His high intention for the foes; he thought the heat of war
Was then near breaking out in flames. To him the Thunderer:
'Thou know'st this council by the rest of those fore-purposes
That still inclin'd me; my cares still must succour the distress
Of Troy, though in the mouth of Fate, yet vow I not to stir
One step from off this top of heav'n, but all th' affair refer   20
To any one. Here I'll hold state, and freely take the joy
Of either's fate: help whom ye please, for 'tis assur'd that Troy
Not one day's conflict can sustain against Aeacides,
If heav'n oppose not. His mere looks threw darts enow t' impress
Their pow'rs with trembling, but when blows sent from his fiery hand
(Thrice heat by slaughter of his friend) shall come and countermand
Their former glories, we have fear, that though Fate keep their wall,
He'll overturn it. Then descend, and cease not till ye all
Add all your aids; mix earth and heav'n together with the fight
Achilles urgeth.' These his words did such a war excite   30
As no man's pow'r could wrastle down; the gods with parted hearts
Departed heav'n, and made earth war. To guide the Grecian darts,
Juno and Pallas, with the god that doth the earth embrace,
And most-for-man's-use Mercury (whom good wise inwards grace)
Were partially and all employ'd; and with them halted down

(Proud of his strength) lame Mulciber, his walkers quite misgrown,
But made him tread exceeding sure. To aid the Ilian side,
The changeable-in-arms went (Mars), and him accompanied
Diana, that delights in shafts, and Phoebus never shorn,
And Aphrodite, laughter-pleas'd, and she of whom was born   40
Still young Apollo, and the flood that runs on golden sands,
Bright Xanthus. All these aided Troy, and till these lent their hands
The Grecians triumph'd in the aid Aeacides did add,
The Trojans trembling with his sight, so gloriously clad
He overshin'd the field, and Mars no harmfuller than he.
He bore the iron stream on clear, but when Jove's high decree
Let fall the gods amongst their troops, the field swell'd, and the light
Grew fierce and horrible. The dame that armies doth excite
Thunder'd with clamour, sometimes set at dike without the wall,
And sometimes on the bellowing shore. On th' other side, the call   50
Of Mars to fight was terrible, he cried out like a storm,
Set on the city's pinnacles; and there he would inform
Sometimes his heart'nings; other times, where Simois pours on
His silver current, at the foot of high Callicolon.
And thus the bless'd gods both sides urg'd; they all stood in the mids,
And brake contention to the hosts. And over all their heads
The gods' king in abhorred claps his thunder rattled out,
Beneath them Neptune toss'd the earth, the mountains round about
Bow'd with affright, and shook their heads: Jove's hill the earthquake felt
(Steep Ida), trembling at her roots, and all her fountains spilt,   60
Their brows all crannied. Troy did nod, the Grecian navy play'd
(As on the sea): th' infernal king, that all things frays, was fray'd,
And leap'd affrighted from his throne; cried out, lest over him
Neptune should rend in two the earth; and so his house, so dim,
So loathsome, filthy, and abhorr'd of all the gods beside,
Should open both to gods and men. Thus all things shook and cried
When this black battle of the gods was joining, thus array'd:
    'Gainst Neptune, Phoebus with wing'd shafts; 'gainst Mars the blue-ey'd Maid;
'Gainst Juno, Phoebe, whose white hands bore singing darts of gold,
Her side arm'd with a sheaf of shafts, and (by the birth twofold   70
Of bright Latona) sister twin to him that shoots so far;
Against Latona, Hermes stood (grave guard, in peace and war,
Of human beings); against the god whose empire is in fire,
The wat'ry godhead, that great flood, to show whose pow'r entire
In spoil as th' other, all his stream on lurking whirlpits trod –
Xanthus by gods, by men Scamander call'd. Thus god 'gainst god
Enter'd the field. Aeacides sustain'd a fervent mind
To cope with Hector; past all these, his spirit stood inclin'd

To glut Mars with the blood of him. And at Aeacides
Apollo set Anchises' son. But first he did impress   80
A more than natural strength in him, and made him feel th' excess
Infus'd from heav'n. Lycaon's shape gave show to his address
(Old Priam's son), and thus he spake: 'Thou counsellor of Troy,
Where now fly out those threats that late put all our peers in joy
Of thy fight with Aeacides? Thy tongue once (steep'd in wine)
Durst vaunt as much.' He answer'd him: 'But why wouldst thou incline
My pow'rs 'gainst that proud enemy, and 'gainst my present heat?
I mean not now to bid him blows; that fear sounds my retreat,
That heretofore discourag'd me, when after he had ras'd
Lyrnessus and strong Pedasus, his still breath'd fury chas'd   90
Our oxen from th' Idaean hill, and set on me; but Jove
Gave strength and knees, and bore me off, that had not walk'd above
This centre now, but propp'd by him. Minerva's hand (that held
A light to this her favourite, whose beams show'd and impell'd
His pow'rs to spoil) had ruin'd me. For these ears heard her cry,
"Kill, kill the seed of Ilion, kill th' Asian Lelegi."
Mere man then must not fight with him that still hath gods to friend,
Averting death on others' darts, and giving his no end
But with the ends of men. If god like fortune in the fight
Would give my forces, not with ease wing'd victory should light   100
On his proud shoulders, nor he 'scape, though all of brass he boasts
His plight consisteth.' He replied: 'Pray thou those gods of hosts,
Whom he implores, as well as he, and his chance may be thine;
Thou cam'st of gods like him: the queen that reigns in Salamine
Fame sounds thy mother, he deriv'd of lower deity,
Old Nereus' daughter bearing him. Bear then thy heart as high,
And thy unwearied steel as right; nor utterly be beat
With only cruelty of words, not proof against a threat.'
    This strengthen'd him, and forth he rush'd, nor could his strength'ning fly
White-wristed Juno, nor his drifts. She every deity   110
Of th' Achive faction call'd to her, and said: 'Ye must have care
(Neptune and Pallas) for the frame of this important war
Ye undertake here; Venus' son (by Phoebus being impell'd)
Runs on Achilles. Turn him back, or see our friend upheld
By one of us. Let not the spirit of Aeacides
Be over-dar'd, but make him know the mightiest deities
Stand kind to him; and that the gods, protectors of these tow'rs
That fight against Greece, and were here before our eminent pow'rs,
Bear no importance. And besides, that all we stoop from heav'n
To curb this fight, that no impair be to his person giv'n   120
By any Trojans, nor their aids, while this day bears the sun.

Hereafter, all things that are wrapp'd in his birth thread, and spun
By Parcas (in that point of time his mother gave him air)
He must sustain. But if report perform not the repair
Of all this to him, by the voice of some immortal state,
He may be fearful (if some god should set on him) that fate
Makes him her minister. The gods, when they appear to men
And manifest their proper forms, are passing dreadful then.'

   Neptune replied: 'Saturnia, at no time let your care
Exceed your reason; 'tis not fit. Where only humans are,   130
We must not mix the hands of gods, our odds is too extreme.
Sit we by, in some place of height, where we may see to them,
And leave the wars of men to men. But if we see from thence
Or Mars or Phoebus enter fight, or offer least offence
To Thetis' son, not giving free way to his conquering rage,
Then comes the conflict to our cares; we soon shall disengage
Achilles, and send them to heav'n, to settle their abode
With equals, flying under-strifes.' This said, the black-hair'd god
Led to the tow'r of Hercules, built circular and high
By Pallas and the Ilians, for fit security   140
To Jove's divine son, 'gainst the whale that drave him from the shore
To th' ample field. There Neptune sat, and all the gods that bore
The Greeks good meaning, casting all thick mantles made of clouds
On their bright shoulders. Th' oppos'd gods sat hid in other shrouds
On top of steep Callicolon, about thy golden sides,
O Phoebus, brandisher of darts; and thine, whose rage abides
No peace in cities. In this state, these gods in council sate,
All ling'ring purpos'd fight, to try who first would elevate
His heavenly weapon. High-thron'd Jove cried out to set them on,
Said all the field was full of men, and that the earth did groan   150
With feet of proud encounterers, burn'd with the arms of men
And barbed horse. Two champions for both the armies then
Met in their midst, prepar'd for blows: divine Aeacides
And Venus' son. Aeneas first stepp'd threat'ning forth the press,
His high helm nodding, and his breast barr'd with a shady shield,
And shook his javelin. Thetis' son did his part to the field.
As when the harmful king of beasts (sore threaten'd to be slain,
By all the country up in arms) at first makes coy disdain
Prepare resistance, but at last when any one hath led
Bold charge upon him with his dart, he then turns yawning head,   160
Fell anger lathers in his jaws, his great heart swells, his stern
Lasheth his strength up, sides and thighs waddled with stripes to learn
Their own pow'r, his eyes glow, he roars, and in he leaps to kill,
Secure of killing: so his pow'r then rous'd up to his will

Matchless Achilles, coming on to meet Anchises' son.
Both near, Achilles thus inquir'd: 'Why stand'st thou thus alone,
Thou son of Venus? Calls thy heart to change of blows with me?
Sure Troy's whole kingdom is propos'd; some one hath promis'd thee
The throne of Priam for my life; but Priam's self is wise,
And (for my slaughter) not so mad to make his throne thy prize.   170
Priam hath sons to second him. Is 't then some piece of land,
Past others fit to set and sow, that thy victorious hand
The Ilians offer for my head? I hope that prize will prove
No easy conquest: once, I think, my busy javelin drove
(With terror) those thoughts from your spleen. Retain'st thou not the time
When single on th' Idaean hill I took thee with the crime
Of runaway, thy oxen left, and when thou hadst no face
That I could see; thy knees bereft it, and Lyrnessus was
The mask for that. Then that mask, too, I open'd to the air
(By Jove and Pallas' help), and took the free light from the fair,   180
Your ladies bearing prisoners. But Jove and th' other gods
Then sav'd thee; yet again I hope they will not add their odds
To save thy wants, as thou presum'st; retire then, aim not at
Troy's throne by me. Fly ere thy soul flies; fools are wise too late.'
    He answer'd him: 'Hope not that words can child-like terrify
My stroke-proof breast. I well could speak in this indecency,
And use tart terms; but we know well what stock us both put out,
Too gentle to bear fruits so rude. Our parents ring about
The world's round bosom; and by fame their dignities are blown
To both our knowledges, by sight neither to either known –   190
Thine to mine eyes, nor mine to thine. Fame sounds thy worthiness
From famous Peleus, the sea-nymph that hath the lovely tress
(Thetis) thy mother; I myself affirm my sire to be
Great-soul'd Anchises, she that holds the Paphian deity
My mother; and of these, this light is now t' exhale the tears
For their lov'd issue – thee or me. Childish, unworthy dares
Are not enough to part our pow'rs; for if thy spirits want
Due excitation (by distrust of that desert I vaunt)
To set up all rests for my life, I'll lineally prove
(Which many will confirm) my race. First, cloud-commanding Jove   200
Was sire to Dardanus that built Dardania; for the walls
Of sacred Ilion spread not yet, these fields, those fair-built halls
Of divers-languag'd men not rais'd; all then made populous
The foot of Ida's fountful hill. This Jove-got Dardanus
Begot king Ericthonius, for wealth past all compares
Of living mortals; in his fens he fed three thousand mares,
All neighing by their tender foals; of which twice six were bred

By lofty Boreas, their dams lov'd by him as they fed.
He took the brave form of a horse that shook an azure mane,
And slept with them. These twice six colts had pace so swift, they ran   210
Upon the top-ayles of corn-ears, nor bent them any whit.
And when the broad back of the sea their pleasure was to sit,
The superficies of his waves they slid upon, their hooves
Nor dipp'd in dank sweat of his brows. Of Ericthonius' loves
Sprang Tros the king of Troÿans; Tros three young princes bred:
Ilus, renown'd Assaracus, and heav'nly Ganymed,
The fairest youth of all that breath'd; whom (for his beauty's love)
The gods did ravish to their state, to bear the cup to Jove.
Ilus begot Laomedon; god-like Laomedon
Got Tithon, Priam, Clytius, Mars-like Hycetaon,   220
And Lampus. Great Assaracus Capys begot. And he,
Anchises. Prince Anchises, me. King Priam, Hector. We
Sprang both of one high family. Thus fortunate men give birth,
But Jove gives virtue; he augments, and he impairs the worth
Of all men; and his will, their rule; he strong'st all strength affords;
Why then paint we (like dames) the face of conflict with our words?
Both may give language that a ship driv'n with a hundred oars
Would overburthen: a man's tongue is voluble, and pours
Words out of all sorts every way; such as you speak you hear.
What then need we vie calumnies, like women that will wear   230
Their tongues out, being once incens'd, and strife for strife to part
(Being on their way) they travel so. From words words may avert;
From virtue, not; it is your steel (divine Aeacides)
Must prove my proof, as mine shall yours.' Thus amply did he ease
His great heart of his pedigree, and sharply sent away
A dart that caught Achilles' shield, and rung so, it did fray
The son of Thetis, his fair hand far-thrusting out his shield,
For fear the long lance had driv'n through. O fool, to think 'twould yield,
And not to know the god's firm gifts want want to yield so soon
To men's poor pow'rs; the eager lance had only conquest won   240
Of two plates, and the shield had five: two forg'd of tin, two brass,
One (that was centre-plate) of gold, and that forbade the pass
Of Anchisiades his lance. Then sent Achilles forth
His lance, that through the first fold struck, where brass of little worth
And no great proof of hides was laid; through all which Pelias ran
His iron head; and after it, his ashen body wan
Pass'd to the earth, and there it stuck, his top on th' other side,
And hung the shield up; which hard down Aeneas pluck'd to hide
His breast from sword blows, shrunk up round, and in his heavy eye
Was much grief shadow'd, much afraid that Pelias struck so nigh.   250

Then prompt Achilles rushing in, his sword drew, and the field
Rung with his voice. Aeneas now left and let hang his shield,
And (all distracted) up he snatch'd a two men's strength of stone,
And either at his shield or cask he set it rudely gone,
Nor car'd where, so it struck a place that put on arms for death.
But he (Achilles came so close) had doubtless sunk beneath
His own death, had not Neptune seen and interpos'd the odds
Of his divine pow'r, uttering this to the Achaian gods:
'I grieve for this great-hearted man; he will be sent to hell,
Ev'n instantly, by Peleus' son, being only mov'd to deal   260
By Phoebus' words. What fool is he! Phoebus did never mean
To add to his great words his guard against the ruin then
Summon'd against him: and what cause hath he to head him on
To others' miseries, he being clear of any trespass done
Against the Grecians? Thankful gifts he oft hath given to us;
Let us then quit him, and withdraw this combat, for if thus
Achilles end him, Jove will rage, since his escape in fate
Is purpos'd – lest the progeny of Dardanus take date –
Whom Jove past all his issue lov'd, begot of mortal dames:
All Priam's race he hates, and this must propagate the names   270
Of Trojans, and their sons' sons rule, to all posterity.'
    Saturnia said: 'Make free your pleasure. Save, or let him die.
Pallas and I have taken many and most public oaths
That th' ill day never shall avert her eye (red with our wroths)
From hated Troy: no, not when all in studied fire she flames
The Greek rage, blowing her last coal.' This nothing turn'd his aims
From present rescue, but through all the whizzing spears he pass'd,
And came where both were combating; when instantly he cast
A mist before Achilles' eyes, drew from the earth and shield
His lance, and laid it at his feet: and then took up and held   280
Aloft the light Anchises' son, who pass'd (with Neptune's force)
Whole orders of heroës' heads, and many a troop of horse
Leap'd over, till the bounds he reach'd of all the fervent broil
Where all the Caucons' quarters lay. Thus (far freed from the toil)
Neptune had time to use these words: 'Aeneas, who was he
Of all the gods, that did so much neglect thy good, and thee,
To urge thy fight with Thetis' son, who in immortal rates
Is better and more dear than thee? Hereafter, lest (past fates)
Hell be thy headlong home, retire; make bold stand never near
Where he advanceth: but his fate once satisfied, then bear   290
A free and full sail: no Greek else shall end thee.' This reveal'd,
He left him, and dispers'd the cloud that all this act conceal'd
From vex'd Achilles: who again had clear light from the skies,

And (much disdaining the escape) said, 'O ye gods, mine eyes
Discover miracles: my lance submitted, and he gone
At whom I sent it with desire of his confusion!
Aeneas sure was lov'd of heav'n; I thought his vaunt from thence
Had flow'd from glory. Let him go; no more experience
Will his mind long for of my hands, he flies them now so clear:
Cheer then the Greeks, and others try.' Thus rang'd he everywhere   300
The Grecian orders; every man (of which the most look'd on
To see their fresh lord shake his lance) he thus put charge upon:

  'Divine Greeks, stand not thus at gaze, but man to man apply
Your several valours: 'tis a task laid too unequally
On me, left to so many men – one man oppos'd to all.
Not Mars, immortal and a god, nor war's she-general
A field of so much fight could chase, and work it out with blows:
But what a man may execute, that all limbs will expose,
And all their strength to th' utmost nerve – though now I lost some play
By some strange miracle, no more shall burn in vain the day   310
To any least beam – all this host I'll ransack, and have hope
Of all; not one (again) will 'scape, whoever gives such scope
To his adventure, and so near dares tempt my angry lance.'

  Thus he excited. Hector then as much strives to advance
The hearts of his men, adding threats, affirming he would stand
In combat with Aeacides. 'Give fear,' said he, 'no hand
Of your great hearts, brave Ilians, for Peleus' talking son;
I'll fight with any god with words; but when their spears put on,
The work runs high, their strength exceeds mortality so far.
And they may make works crown their words, which hold not in the war   320
Achilles makes; his hands have bounds; this word he shall make good,
And leave another to the field: his worst shall be withstood
With sole objection of myself, though in his hands he bear
A rage like fire, though fire itself his raging fingers were
And burning steel flew in his strength.' Thus he incited his;
And they rais'd lances, and to work with mixed courages,
And up flew Clamour; but the heat in Hector Phoebus gave
This temper: 'Do not meet,' said he, 'in any single brave
The man thou threaten'st, but in press; and in thy strength impeach
His violence; for far off or near his sword or dart will reach.'   330

  The god's voice made a difference in Hector's own conceit
Betwixt his and Achilles 'words, and gave such overweight
As weigh'd him back into his strength, and curb'd his flying out.
At all threw fierce Aeacides, and gave a horrid shout.

  The first of all he put to dart was fierce Iphition,
Surnam'd Otryntides, whom Nais the water-nymph made son

To town-destroyer Otrynteus. Beneath the snowy hill
Of Tmolus in the wealthy town of Ide, at his will
Were many able men at arms. He, rushing in, took full
Pelides' lance in his head's midst, that cleft in two his skull.   340
Achilles knew him, one much fam'd, and thus insulted then:
  'Th' art dead, Otryntides, though call'd the terriblest of men;
Thy race runs at Gygaeus lake, there thy inheritance lay,
Near fishy Hillus, and the gulfs of Hermus: but this day
Removes it to the fields of Troy.' Thus left he night to seize
His closed eyes, his body laid in course of all the press,
Which Grecian horse broke with the strakes, nail'd to their chariot wheels.
  Next (through the temples) the burst eyes his deadly javelin seels
Of great-in-Troy Antenor's son, renown'd Demoleon,
A mighty turner of a field. His overthrow set gone   350
Hippodamas, who leap'd from horse, and as he fled before
Aeacides, his turned back he made fell Pelias gore,
And forth he puff'd his flying soul: and as a tortur'd bull
(To Neptune brought for sacrifice) a troop of youngsters pull
Down to the earth, and drag him round about the hallow'd shore
To please the wat'ry deity, with forcing him to roar,
And forth he pours his utmost throat: so bellow'd this slain friend
Of flying Ilion with the breath that gave his being end.
  Then rush'd he on, and in his eye had heavenly Polydore,
Old Priam's son; whom last of all his fruitful princess bore;   360
And for his youth (being dear to him) the king forbade to fight.
Yet (hot of unexperienc'd blood, to show how exquisite
He was of foot, for which of all the fifty sons he held
The special name) he flew before the first heat of the field,
Ev'n till he flew out breath and soul: which, through the back, the lance
Of swift Achilles put in air, and did his head advance
Out at his navel: on his knees the poor prince crying fell,
And gather'd with his tender hands his entrails, that did swell
Quite through the wide wound, till a cloud as black as death conceal'd
Their sight, and all the world from him. When Hector had beheld   370
His brother tumbled so to earth (his entrails still in hand),
Dark sorrow overcast his eyes; not far off could he stand
A minute longer, but like fire he brake out of the throng,
Shook his long lance at Thetis' son, and then came he along
To feed th' encounter: 'O,' said he, 'here comes the man that most
Of all the world destroys my mind, the man by whom I lost
My dear Patroclus; now not long the crooked paths of war
Can yield us any privy scapes: come, keep not off so far,'
He cried to Hector. 'Make the pain of thy sure death as short

As one so desperate of his life hath reason.' In no sort   380
This frighted Hector, who bore close, and said: 'Aeacides,
Leave threats for children; I have pow'r to thunder calumnies
As well as other, and well know thy strength superior far
To that my nerves hold, but the gods (not nerves) determine war.
And yet (for nerves) there will be found a strength of power in mine,
To drive a lance home to thy life; my lance as well as thine
Hath point and sharpness, and 'tis this. Thus brandishing his spear,
He set it flying; which a breath of Pallas back did bear
From Thetis' son to Hector's self, and at his feet it fell.
Achilles us'd no dart, but close flew in, and thought to deal   390
With no strokes but of sure dispatch; but what with all his blood
He labour'd, Phoebus clear'd with ease, as being a god, and stood
For Hector's guard, as Pallas did, Aeacides, for thine.
He rapt him from him, and a cloud of much night cast between
His person and the point oppos'd. Achilles then exclaim'd,
'O see yet more gods are at work; Apollo's hand hath fram'd
(Dog that thou art) thy rescue now: to whom go pay the vows
Thy safety owes him; I shall vent in time those fatal blows
That yet beat in my heart, on thine, if any god remain
My equal fautor. In mean time, my anger must maintain   400
His fire on other Ilians.' Then laid he at his feet
Great Demochus, Philetor's son, and Dryope did greet
With like encounter. Dardanus and strong Laogonus
(Wise Byas' sons) he hurl'd from horse, of one victorious
With his close sword, the other's life he conquer'd with his lance.
    Then Tros, Alastor's son, made in, and sought to 'scape their chance
With free submission. Down he fell, and pray'd about his knees
He would not kill him, but take ruth, as one that destinies
Made to that purpose, being a man born in the self same year
That he himself was: O poor fool, to sue to him to bear   410
A ruthful mind; he well might know he could not fashion him
In ruth's soft mould, he had no spirit to brook that interim
In his hot fury. He was none of these remorseful men,
Gentle and affable, but fierce at all times, and mad then.
    He gladly would have made a pray'r, and still so hugg'd his knee
He could not quit him, till at last his sword was fain to free
His fetter'd knees, that made a vent for his white liver's blood,
That caus'd such pitiful affects, of which it pour'd a flood
About his bosom, which it fill'd, even till it drown'd his eyes,
And all sense fail'd him. Forth then flew this prince of tragedies,   420
Who next stoop'd Mulius, ev'n to death, with his insatiate spear:
One ear it enter'd, and made good his pass to th' other ear.

Echeclus then (Agenor's son), he struck betwixt the brows,
Whose blood set fire upon his sword, that cool'd it till the throes
Of his then labouring brain let out his soul to fixed fate,
And gave cold entry to black death. Deucalion then had state
In these men's beings: where the nerves about the elbow knit,
Down to his hand his spear's steel pierc'd, and brought such pain to it
As led death jointly, whom he saw before his fainting eyes,
And in his neck felt, with a stroke laid on so, that off flies   430
His head: one of the twice twelve bones that all the backbone make
Let out his marrow, when the head he helm and all did take,
And hurl'd amongst the Ilians; the body stretch'd on earth.
　　Rhigmus of fruitful Thrace next fell; he was the famous birth
Of Pireus: his belly's midst the lance took, whose stern force
Quite tumbled him from chariot. In turning back the horse,
Their guider Areithous receiv'd another lance
That threw him to his lord. No end was put to the mischance
Achilles enter'd: but as fire, fall'n in a flash from heav'n,
Inflames the high woods of dry hills, and with a storm is driv'n   440
Through all the sylvan deeps, and raves, till down goes everywhere
The smother'd hill: so every way Achilles and his spear
Consum'd the champain; the black earth flow'd with the veins he tore.
And look how oxen (yok'd and driv'n about the circular floor
Of some fair barn) tread suddenly the thick sheaves, thin of corn,
And all the corn consum'd with chaff: so mix'd and overborne,
Beneath Achilles' one-hoof'd horse, shields, spears and men lay trod,
His axle-tree and chariot wheels all spatter'd with the blood
Hurl'd from the steeds' hoofs and the strakes. Thus to be magnified,
His most inaccessible hands in human blood he dyed.   450

THE END OF THE TWENTIETH BOOK

BOOK TWENTY-ONE

The Argument

In two parts Troy's host parted; Thetis' son
One to Scamander, one to Ilion
Pursues. Twelve lords he takes alive, to end
In sacrifice, for vengeance to his friend.
Asteropaeus dies by his fierce hand,
And Priam's son, Lycaon. Over land
The flood breaks: where, Achilles being engag'd,
Vulcan preserves him, and with spirit enrag'd,
Sets all the champain and the flood on fire;
Contention then doth all the gods inspire.
Apollo in Agenor's shape doth stay
Achilles' fury; and by giving way,
Makes him pursue, till the deceit gives leave,
That Troy in safety might her friends receive.

Another Argument

Phi, at the flood's shore, doth express
The labours of Aeacides.

BOOK TWENTY-ONE

AND NOW THEY reach'd the goodly swelling channel of the flood,
Gulf-eating Xanthus, whom Jove mix'd with his immortal brood:
And there Achilles cleft the host of Ilion: one side fell
On Xanthus, th' other on the town: and that did he impel
The same way that the last day's rage put all the Greeks in rout,
When Hector's fury reign'd; these now Achilles pour'd about
The scatter'd field. To stay the flight, Saturnia cast before
Their hasty feet a standing fog, and then flight's violence bore
The other half full on the flood. The silver-gulfed deep
Receiv'd them with a mighty cry: the billows vast and steep   10
Roar'd at their armours, which the shores did round about resound:
This way and that they swum, and shriek'd, as in the gulfs they drown'd.
And as in fir'd fields locusts rise, as the unwearied blaze
Plies still their rising, till in swarms all rush as in amaze
(For 'scape) into some neighbour flood: so th' Achillean stroke
Here drave the foe; the gulfy flood with men and horse did choke.
   Then on the shore the worthy hid, and left his horrid lance
Amids the tamrisks; then sprite-like did with his sword advance
Up to the river; ill affairs took up his furious brain
For Troy's engagements: every way he doubled slain on slain.   20
A most unmanly noise was made, with those he put to sword,
Of groans and outcries; the flood blush'd to be so much engor'd
With such base souls. And as small fish the swift-finn'd dolphin fly,
Filling the deep pits in the ports, on whose close strength they lie,
And there he swallows them in shoals: so here, to rocks and holes,
About the flood, the Trojans fled; and there most lost their souls,
Even till he tir'd his slaught'rous arm. Twelve fair young princes then
He chose of all to take alive, to have them freshly slain
On that most solemn day of wreak, resolv'd on for his friend.
These led he trembling forth the flood, as fearful of their end   30
As any hind calves: all their hands he pinioned behind
With their own girdles, worn upon their rich weeds, and resign'd
Their persons to his Myrmidons to bear to fleet; and he
Plung'd in the stream again to take more work of tragedy.
He met, then issuing the flood, with all intent of flight,

Lycaon (Dardan Priam's son), whom lately in the night
He had surpris'd as in a wood of Priam's he had cut
The green arms of a wild fig-tree, to make him spokes to put
In naves of his new chariot. An ill then, all unthought,
Stole on him in Achilles' shape, who took him thence, and brought   40
To well-built Lemnos, selling him to famous Jason's son,
From whom a guest then in his house (Imbrius Eëtion)
Redeem'd at high rate, and sent home t' Arisba, whence he fled,
And saw again his father's court; eleven days banqueted
Amongst his friends; the twelfth god thrust his hapless head again
In t' hands of stern Aeacides, who now must send him slain
To Pluto's court, and 'gainst his will. Him when Achilles knew,
Naked of helmet, shield, sword, lance, all which for ease he threw
To earth, being overcome with sweat, and labour wearying
His flying knees, he storm'd, and said: 'O heav'n, a wondrous thing   50
Invades mine eyes: those Ilians that heretofore I slew
Rise from the dark dead quick again; this man Fate makes eschew
Her own steel fingers: he was sold in Lemnos, and the deep
Of all seas 'twixt this Troy and that (that many a man doth keep
From his lov'd country) bars not him; come then, he now shall taste
The head of Pelias, and try if steel will down as fast
As other fortunes, or kind earth can any surer seize
On his sly person, whose strong arms have held down Hercules.

   His thoughts thus mov'd while he stood firm, to see if he he spied
Would offer flight (which first he thought), but when he had descried   60
He was descried, and flight was vain, fearful, he made more nigh,
With purpose to embrace his knees, and now long'd much to fly
His black fate, and abhorred death, by coming in. His foe
Observ'd all this, and up he rais'd his lance as he would throw;
And then Lycaon close ran in, fell on his breast, and took
Achilles' knees, whose lance (on earth now staid) did overlook
His still turn'd back, with thirst to glut his sharp point with the blood
That lay so ready. But that thirst Lycaon's thirst withstood
To save his blood; Achilles' knee in his one hand he knit,
His other held the long lance hard, and would not part with it,   70
But thus besought: 'I kiss thy knees, divine Aeacides!
Respect me, and my fortunes rue; I now present th' access
Of a poor suppliant for thy ruth, and I am one that is
Worthy thy ruth, O Jove's belov'd. First hour my miseries
Fell into any hand, 'twas thine: I tasted all my bread
By thy gift since, O since that hour that thy surprisal led
From forth the fair wood my sad feet, far from my lov'd allies,
To famous Lemnos, where I found a hundred oxen's prize

To make my ransom, for which now I thrice the worth will raise.
This day makes twelve since I arriv'd in Ilion, many days   80
Being spent before in sufferance; and now a cruel fate
Thrusts me again into thy hands. I should haunt Jove with hate,
That with such set malignity gives thee my life again.
There were but two of us for whom Laothoë suffer'd pain –
Laothoë, old Alte's seed – Alte, whose palace stood
In height of upper Pedasus, near Satnius' silver flood,
And rul'd the war-like Lelegi. Whose seed (as many more),
King Priam married, and begot the god-like Polydor,
And me accurs'd: thou slaughter'dst him, and now thy hand on me
Will prove as mortal. I did think, when here I met with thee,   90
I could not 'scape thee; yet give ear, and add thy mind to it:
I told my birth to intimate, though one sire did beget,
Yet one womb brought not into light Hector (that slew thy friend)
And me. O do not kill me then, but let the wretched end
Of Polydor excuse my life. For half our being bred
Brothers to Hector, he (half) paid, no more is forfeited.'
    Thus su'd he humbly; but he heard with this austere reply:
'Fool, urge not ruth nor price to me, till that solemnity
Resolv'd on for Patroclus' death pay all his rites to fate:
Till his death I did grace to Troy, and many lives did rate   100
At price of ransom: but none now of all the brood of Troy
(Whoever Jove throws to my hands) shall any breath enjoy
That death can beat out, specially that touch at Priam's race.
Die, die, my friend. What tears are these? What sad looks spoil thy face?
Patroclus died, that far pass'd thee: nay, seest thou not beside,
Myself, ev'n I, a fair young man, and rarely magnified,
And (to my father, being a king) a mother have, that sits
In rank with goddesses; and yet, when thou hast spent thy spirits,
Death, and as violent a fate, must overtake ev'n me,
By twilight, morn-light, day, high noon, whenever destiny   110
Sets on her man to hurl a lance, or knit out of his string
An arrow that must reach my life.' This said, a-languishing
Lycaon's heart bent like his knees, yet left him strength t' advance
Both hands for mercy as he kneel'd. His foe yet leaves his lance,
And forth his sword flies, which he hid in furrow of a wound
Driv'n through the jointure of his neck; flat fell he on the ground,
Stretch'd with death's pangs, and all the earth imbru'd with timeless blood.
Then grip't Aeacides his heel, and to the lofty flood
Flung (swinging) his unpitied corse, to see it swim and toss
Upon the rough waves, and said: 'Go, feed fat the fish with loss   120
Of thy left blood; they clean will suck thy green wounds, and this saves

Thy mother tears upon thy bed. Deep Xanthus on his waves
Shall hoist thee bravely to a tomb, that in her burly breast
The sea shall open, where great fish may keep thy funeral feast
With thy white fat, and on the waves dance at thy wedding fate,
Clad in black horror, keeping close inaccessible state.
So perish Ilians, till we pluck the brows of Ilion
Down to her feet – you flying still, I flying still upon
Thus in the rear, and (as my brows were fork'd with rabid horns)
Toss ye together. This brave flood, that strengthens and adorns   130
Your city with his silver gulfs, to whom so many bulls
Your zeal hath offer'd, with blind zeal his sacred current gulls
With casting chariots and horse quick to his pray'd-for aid,
Shall nothing profit: perish then, till cruell'st death hath laid
All at the red feet of Revenge for my slain friend, and all
With whom the absence of my hands made yours a festival.'

      This speech great Xanthus more enrag'd, and made his spirit contend
For means to shut up the op't vein against him, and defend
The Trojans in it from his plague. In mean time Peleus' son
(And now with that long lance he hid) for more blood set upon   140
Asteropaeus, the descent of Pelagon, and he
Of broad-stream'd Axius and the dame (of first nativity
To all the daughters that renown'd Acesamenus' seed)
Bright Periboea; whom the flood (arm'd thick with lofty reed)
Compress'd. At her grandchild now went Thetis' great son, whose foe
Stood arm'd with two darts, being set on by Xanthus, anger'd so
For those youths' blood shed in his stream by vengeful Thetis' son,
Without all mercy. Both being near, great Thetides begun
With this high question: 'Of what race art thou, that dar'st oppose
Thy pow'r to mine thus? Cursed wombs they ever did disclose   150
That stood my anger.' He replied: 'What makes thy furies beat,
Talk, and seek pedigrees? Far hence lies my innative seat,
In rich Paeonia. My race from broad-stream'd Axius runs –
Axius, that gives earth purest drink, of all the wat'ry sons
Of great Oceanus, and got the famous-for-his-spear
Pelagonus, that father'd me. And these Paeonians here,
Arm'd with long lances, here I lead: and here th' eleventh fair light
Shines on us since we enter'd Troy: come now, brave man, let's fight.'

      Thus spake he, threat'ning; and to him Pelides made reply
With shaken Pelias; but his foe with two at once let fly   160
(For both his hands were dexterous): one javelin struck the shield
Of Thetis' son, but struck not through (the gold, god's gift, repell'd
The eager point); the other lance fell lightly on the part
Of his fair right hand's cubit; forth the black blood spun, the dart

Glanc'd over, fast'ning on the earth, and there his spleen was spent
That wish'd the body. With which wish Achilles his lance sent,
That quite miss'd, and infix'd itself fast in the steep-up shore.
Even to the midst it enter'd it; himself then fiercely bore
Upon his enemy with his sword. His foe was tugging hard
To get his lance out: thrice he pluck'd, and thrice sure Pelias barr'd   170
His wish'd evulsion. The fourth pluck he bow'd and meant to break
The ashen plant, but (ere that act) Achilles' sword did check
His bent pow'r, and brake out his soul. Full in the navel stead
He ripp'd his belly up, and out his entrails fell, and dead
His breathless body: whence his arms Achilles drew, and said:

    'Lie there, and prove it dangerous to lift up adverse head
Against Jove's sons, although a flood were ancestor to thee:
Thy vaunts urg'd him, but I may vaunt a higher pedigree
(From Jove himself): king Peleus was son to Aeacus,
Infernal Aeacus to Jove, and I to Peleus.   180
Thunder-voic'd Jove far passeth floods, that only murmurs raise
With earth and water, as they run with tribute to the seas:
And his seed theirs exceeds as far. A flood, a mighty flood,
Rag'd near thee now, but with no aid Jove must not be withstood.
King Achelous yields to him, and great Oceanus,
Whence all floods, all the sea, all founts, wells, all deeps humorous,
Fetch their beginnings; yet ev'n he fears Jove's flash, and the crack
His thunder gives, when out of heav'n it tears atwo his rack.'

    Thus pluck'd he from the shore his lance, and left the waves to wash
The wave-sprung entrails, about which fausens and other fish   190
Did shoal, to nibble at the fat which his sweet kidneys hid.
This for himself: now to his men (the well-rode Paeons) did
His rage contend, all which cold fear shook into flight, to see
Their captain slain: at whose maz'd flight (as much enrag'd) flew he,
And then fell all these – Thrasius, Mydon, Astypilus,
Great Ophelestes, Aenius, Mnesus, Thersilochus.
And on these many more had fall'n, unless the angry flood
Had took the figure of a man, and in a whirlpit stood,
Thus speaking to Aeacides: 'Past all, pow'r feeds thy will
(Thou great grandchild of Aeacus), and past all th' art in ill.   200
And gods themselves confederates, and Jove (the best of gods)
All deaths gives thee: all places not. Make my shores periods
To all shore service. In the field, let thy field acts run high,
Not in my waters. My sweet streams choke with mortality
Of men slain by thee. Carcasses so glut me, that I fail
To pour into the sacred sea my waves; yet still assail
Thy cruel forces. Cease, amaze affects me with thy rage,

Prince of the people.' He replied: 'Shall thy command assuage
(Gulf-fed Scamander) my free wrath? I'll never leave pursu'd
Proud Ilion's slaughters, till this hand in her fil'd walls conclude   210
Her flying forces, and hath tried in single fight the chance
Of war with Hector, whose event with stark death shall advance
One of our conquests.' Thus again he like a fury flew
Upon the Trojans, when the flood his sad plaint did pursue
To bright Apollo, telling him he was too negligent
Of Jove's high charge, importuning by all means vehement
His help of Troy, till latest ev'n should her black shadows pour
On earth's broad breast. In all his worst, Achilles yet from shore
Leapt to his midst. Then swell'd his waves, then rag'd, then boil'd again
Against Achilles: up flew all, and all the bodies slain   220
In all his deeps (of which the heaps made bridges to his waves)
He belch'd out, roaring like a bull. The unslain yet he saves
In his black whirlpits vast and deep. A horrid billow stood
About Achilles. On his shield the violence of the flood
Beat so, it drove him back, and took his feet up, his fair palm
Enforc'd to catch into his stay a broad and lofty elm,
Whose roots he toss'd up with his hold, and tore up all the shore;
With this then he repell'd the waves, and those thick arms it bore
He made a bridge to bear him off (for all fell in), when he
Forth from the channel threw himself. The rage did terrify   230
Ev'n his great spirit, and made him add wings to his swiftest feet,
And tread the land. And yet not there the flood left his retreat,
But thrust his billows after him, and black'd them all at top
To make him fear, and fly his charge, and set the broad field ope
For Troy to 'scape in. He sprung out a dart's cast, but came on
Again with a redoubled force; as when the swiftest flown
And strong'st of all fowls (Jove's black hawk, the huntress) stoops upon
A much lov'd quarry: so charg'd he, his arms with horror rung
Against the black waves: yet again he was so urg'd, he flung
His body from the flood, and fled. And after him again   240
The waves flew roaring, as a man that finds a water-vein,
And from some black fount is to bring his streams through plants and groves,
Goes with his mattock, and all checks, set to his course, removes;
When that runs freely, under it the pebbles all give way,
And where it finds a fall, runs swift, nor can the leader stay
His current then; before himself full-pac'd it murmurs on:
So, of Achilles, evermore the strong flood vantage won.
Though most deliver, gods are still above the pow'rs of men.
    As oft as th' able god-like man endeavour'd to maintain
His charge on them that kept the flood (and charg'd, as he would try   250

If all the gods inhabiting the broad unreached sky
Could daunt his spirit), so oft still the rude waves charg'd him round,
Rampt on his shoulders, from whose depth his strength and spirit would bound
Up to the free air, vex'd in soul. And now the vehement flood
Made faint his knees, so overthwart his waves were, they withstood
All the denied dust, which he wish'd, and now was fain to cry,
Casting his eyes to that broad heav'n that late he long'd to try,
And said: 'O Jove, how am I left? No god vouchsafes to free
Me, miserable man; help now, and after torture me
With any outrage. Would to heav'n, Hector (the mightiest   260
Bred in this region) had imbru'd his javelin in my breast
That strong might fall by strong, where now weak water's luxury
Must make my death blush; one heav'n-born shall like a hog-herd die,
Drown'd in a dirty torrent's rage. Yet none of you in heav'n
I blame for this, but she alone by whom this life was giv'n,
That now must die thus. She would still delude me with her tales,
Affirming Phoebus' shafts should end within the Trojan walls
My curs'd beginning.' In this strait, Neptune and Pallas flew
To fetch him off. In men's shapes both close to his danger drew,
And, taking both both hands, thus spake the Shaker of the world: 270
   'Pelides, do not stir a foot, nor these waves, proudly curl'd
Against thy bold breast, fear a jot; thou hast us two thy friends
(Neptune and Pallas), Jove himself approving th' aid we lend.
Tis nothing, as thou fear'st, with fate; she will not see thee drown'd:
This height shall soon down, thine own eyes shall see it set aground.
Be rul'd then, we'll advise thee well; take not thy hand away
From putting all, indifferently, to all that it can lay
Upon the Trojans, till the walls of haughty Ilion
Conclude all in a desperate flight; and when thou hast set gone
The soul of Hector, turn to fleet: our hands shall plant a wreath   280
Of endless glory on thy brows. Thus to the free-from-death
Both made retreat. He (much impell'd by charge the godheads gave)
The field, that now was overcome with many a boundless wave,
He overcame: on their wild breasts they toss'd the carcasses
And arms of many a slaughter'd man. And now the winged knees
Of this great captain bore aloft: against the flood he flies
With full assault, nor could that god make shrink his rescu'd thighs:
Nor shrunk the flood, but as his foe grew powerful, he grew mad,
Thrust up a billow to the sky, and crystal Simois bade
To his assistance: 'Simois! Ho, brother!' out he cried.   290
'Come, add thy current, and resist this man half deified,
Or Ilion he will pull down straight; the Trojans cannot stand
A minute longer. Come, assist, and instantly command

All fountains in thy rule to rise, all torrents to make in,
And stuff thy billows, with whose height engender such a din
(With trees torn up, and justling stones) as so immane a man
May shrink beneath us: whose pow'r thrives, do my pow'r all it can:
He dares things fitter for a god. But nor his form, nor force,
Nor glorious arms shall profit it: all which, and his dead corse,
I vow to roll up in my hands – nay, bury in my mud –   300
Nay, in the very sinks of Troy that, pour'd into my flood,
Shall make him drowning work enough: and being drown'd, I'll set
A sort of such strong filth on him, that Greece shall never get
His bones from it. There, there shall stand Achilles' sepulchre,
And save a burial for his friends.' This fury did transfer
His high-ridg'd billows on the prince, roaring with blood and foam
And carcasses. The crimson stream did snatch into her womb
Surpris'd Achilles; and her height stood, held up by the hand
Of Jove himself. Then Juno cried, and call'd (to countermand
This wat'ry deity) the god that holds command in fire,   310
Afraid lest that gulf-stomach'd flood would satiate his desire
On great Achilles. 'Mulciber! My best-lov'd son!' she cried.
'Rouse thee, for all the gods conceive this flood thus amplified
Is rais'd at thee, and shows as if his waves would drown the sky,
And put out all the sphere of fire; haste, help thy empery:
Light flames deep as his pits. Our self the west wind and the south
Will call out of the sea, and breathe in either's full-charg'd mouth
A storm t' enrage thy fires 'gainst Troy; which shall (in one exhal'd)
Blow flames of sweat about their brows, and make their armours scal'd.
Go thou then, and ('gainst these winds rise) make work on Xanthus' shore,   320
With setting all his trees on fire: and in his own breast pour
A fervor that shall make it burn, nor let fair words or threats
Avert thy fury till I speak, and then subdue the heats
Of all thy blazes.' Mulciber prepar'd a mighty fire,
First in the field us'd, burning up the bodies that the ire
Of great Achilles reft of souls: the quite-drown'd field it dried,
And shrunk the flood up. And as fields that have been long time cloy'd
With catching weather, when their corn lies on the gavill heap,
Are with a constant north wind dried, with which for comfort leap
Their hearts that sow'd them: so this field was dried, the bodies burn'd,   330
And ev'n the flood into a fire as bright as day was turn'd.
Elms, willows, tam'risks were enflam'd; the lote trees, sea-grass reeds,
And rushes, with the galingale roots (of which abundance breeds
About the sweet flood), all were fir'd; the gliding fishes flew
Upwards in flames; the grovelling eels crept upright, all which slew
Wise Vulcan's unresisted spirit. The flood out of a flame

Cried to him: 'Cease, O Mulciber, no deity can tame
Thy matchless virtue: nor would I (since thou art thus hot) strive:
Cease then thy strife; let Thetis' son, with all thy wish'd haste, drive
Ev'n to their gates these Ilians: what toucheth me their aid,   340
Or this contention?' Thus in flames the burning river pray'd:
And as a cauldron, underput with store of fire, and wrought
With boiling of a well-fed brawn, up leaps his wave aloft,
Bavins of sere wood urging it, and spending flames apace,
Till all the cauldron be engirt with a consuming blaze:
So round this flood burn'd, and so sod his sweet and tortur'd streams,
Nor could flow forth, bound in the fumes of Vulcan's fiery beams.
Who (then not mov'd) his mother's ruth by all his means he craves,
And ask'd, why Vulcan should invade and so torment his waves
Past other floods, when his offence rose not to such degree   350
As that of other gods for Troy, and that himself would free
Her wrath to it, if she were pleas'd; and pray'd her, that her son
Might be reflected, adding this, that he would ne'er be won
To help keep off the ruinous day in which all Troy should burn,
Fir'd by the Grecians. This vow heard, she charg'd her son to turn
His fiery spirits to their homes, and said it was not fit
A god should suffer so for men. Then Vulcan did remit
His so unmeasur'd violence, and back the pleasant flood
Ran to his channel. Thus these gods she made friends, th' others stood
At weighty diff'rence; both sides ran together with a sound   360
That earth resounded, and great heav'n about did surrebound.

   Jove heard it, sitting on his hill, and laugh'd to see the gods
Buckle to arms like angry men; and (he pleas'd with their odds)
They laid it freely. Of them all, thump-buckler Mars began,
And at Minerva with a lance of brass he headlong ran,
These vile words ushering his blows: 'Thou dog-fly, what's the cause
Thou mak'st gods fight thus? Thy huge heart breaks all our peaceful laws
With thy insatiate shamelessness. Rememb'rest thou the hour
When Diomed charg'd me – and by thee – and thou with all thy pow'r
Took'st lance thyself, and in all sights rush'd on me with a wound?   370
Now vengeance falls on thee for all.' This said, the shield fring'd round
With fighting adders, borne by Jove, that not to thunder yields,
He clapt his lance on, and this god that with the blood of fields
Pollutes his godhead, that shield pierc'd, and hurt the armed Maid:
But back she leapt, and with her strong hand rapt a huge stone laid
Above the champaign, black and sharp, that did in old time break
Partitions to men's lands; and that she dusted in the neck
Of that impetuous challenger. Down to the earth he sway'd,
And overlaid seven acres land: his hair was all beray'd

With dust and blood mix'd, and his arms rung out. Minerva laugh'd,   380
And thus insulted: 'O thou fool, yet hast thou not been taught
To know mine eminence? Thy strength opposest thou to mine?
So pay thy mother's furies then; who for these aids of thine
(Ever afforded perjur'd Troy, Greece ever left) takes spleen
And vows thee mischief.' Thus she turn'd her blue eyes, when love's queen
The hand of Mars took, and from earth rais'd him with thick-drawn breath,
His spirits not yet got up again. But from the press of death
Kind Aphrodite was his guide. Which Juno seeing, exclaim'd:
'Pallas, see, Mars is help'd from field! "Dog-fly" his rude tongue nam'd
Thyself even now, but that his love, that dog-fly, will not leave   390
Her old consort. Upon her fly.' Minerva did receive
This excitation joyfully, and at the Cyprian flew,
Struck with her hard hand her soft breast, a blow that overthrew
Both her and Mars, and there both lay together in broad field;
When thus she triumph'd. 'So lie all that any succours yield
To these false Trojans 'gainst the Greeks so bold and patient,
As Venus (shunning charge of me); and no less impotent
Be all their aids than hers to Mars, so short work would be made
In our depopulating Troy (this hardiest to invade
Of all earth's cities).' At this wish white-wristed Juno smil'd.   400
Next Neptune and Apollo stood upon the point of field,
And thus spake Neptune: 'Phoebus! Come, why at the lance's end
Stand we two thus?' Twill be a shame for us to re-ascend
Jove's golden house, being thus in field and not to fight. Begin,
For 'tis no graceful work for me: thou hast the younger chin,
I older, and know more. O fool! What a forgetful heart
Thou bear'st about thee, to stand here, press'd to take th' Ilian part,
And fight with me! Forget'st thou then what we two, we alone
(Of all the gods) have suffer'd here, when proud Laomedon
Enjoy'd our service a whole year for our agreed reward?   410
Jove in his sway would have it so, and in that year I rear'd
This broad brave wall about his town, that (being a work of mine)
It might be inexpugnable. This service then was thine,
In Ida (that so many hills and curl'd-head forests crown)
To feed his oxen, crooked-shank'd, and headed like the moon.
But when the much-joy–bringing hours brought term for our reward,
The terrible Laomedon dismiss'd us both, and scar'd
Our high deservings – not alone to hold our promis'd fee,
But give us threats too. Hand and feet he swore to fetter thee
And sell thee as a slave, dismiss'd far hence to foreign isles;   420
Nay more, he would have both our ears. His vow's breach, and reviles,
Made us part angry with him then, and dost thou gratulate now

Such a king's subjects, or with us not their destruction vow,
Ev'n to their chaste wives and their babes?' He answer'd, he might hold
His wisdom little, if with him (a god) for men he would
Maintain contention – wretched men that flourish for a time
Like leaves, eat some of that earth yields, and give earth in their prime
Their whole selves for it. 'Quickly then let us fly fight for them,
Nor show it offer'd: let themselves bear out their own extreme.'

 Thus he retir'd, and fear'd to change blows with his uncle's hands. 430
His sister therefore chid him much (the goddess that commands
In games of hunting), and thus spake: 'Fliest thou, and leav'st the field
To Neptune's glory? And no blows? O fool! Why dost thou wield
Thy idle bow? No more my ears shall hear thee vaunt in skies –
Dares to meet Neptune – but I'll tell thy coward's tongue it lies.'

 He answer'd nothing; yet Jove's wife could put on no such reins,
But spake thus loosely: 'How dar'st thou, dog, whom no fear contains,
Encounter me? 'Twill prove a match of hard condition:
Though the great Lady of the bow and Jove hath set thee down
For lion of thy sex, with gift to slaughter any dame 440
Thy proud will envies, yet some dames will prove th' hadst better tame
Wild lions upon hills than them. But if this question rests
Yet under judgment in thy thoughts, and that thy mind contests,
I'll make thee know it. Suddenly with her left hand she catch'd
Both Cynthia's palms, lock'd fingers fast, and with her right she snatch'd
From her fair shoulders her gilt bow, and (laughing) laid it on
About her ears, and ev'ry way her turnings seiz'd upon,
Till all her arrows scatter'd out, her quiver emptied quite.
And as a dove, that (flying a hawk) takes to some rock her flight,
And in his hollow breasts sits safe, her fate not yet to die: 450
So fled she mourning, and her bow left there. Then Mercury
His opposite thus undertook: 'Latona, at no hand
Will I bide combat; 'tis a work right dangerous to stand
At difference with the wives of Jove. Go, therefore, freely vaunt
Amongst the deities th' hast subdued, and made thy combatant
Yield with plain pow'r.' She answer'd not, but gather'd up the bow
And shafts fall'n from her daughter's side, retiring. Up did go
Diana to Jove's starry hall, her incorrupted veil
Trembling about her, so she shook. Phoebus (lest Troy should fail
Before her fate) flew to her walls, the other deities flew 460
Up to Olympus, some enrag'd, some glad. Achilles slew
Both men and horse of Ilion. And as a city fir'd
Casts up a heat that purples heaven, clamours and shrieks expir'd
In every corner; toil to all, to many misery;
Which fire th' incensed gods let fall: Achilles so let fly

Rage on the Trojans, toils and shrieks as much by him impos'd.
Old Priam in his sacred tow'r stood, and the flight disclos'd
Of his forc'd people, all in rout, and not a stroke return'd,
But fled resistance. His eyes saw in what a fury burn'd
The son of Peleus, and down went weeping from the tow'r   470
To all the port-guards, and their chiefs, told of his flying pow'r,
Commanding th' opening of the ports, but not to let their hands
Stir from them, for Aeacides would pour in with his bands.
'Destruction comes. O shut them strait when we are in,' he pray'd;
'For not our walls, I fear, will check this violent man.' This said,
Off lifted they the bars; the ports hal'd open, and they gave
Safety her entry, with the host; which yet they could not save
Had not Apollo sallied out, and struck destruction
(Brought by Achilles in their necks) back; when they right upon
The ports bore all, dry, dusty, spent, and on their shoulders rode   480
Rabid Achilles with his lance, still glory being the goad
That prick'd his fury. Then the Greeks high-ported Ilion
Had seiz'd, had not Apollo stirr'd Antenor's famous son,
Divine Agenor, and cast in an undertaking spirit
To his bold bosom, and himself stood by to strengthen it,
And keep the heavy hand of death from breaking in. The god
Stood by him, leaning on a beech, and cover'd his abode
With night-like darkness; yet for all the spirit he inspir'd,
When that great city-raser's force his thoughts struck, he retir'd,
Stood, and went on – a world of doubts still falling in his way –   490
When (angry with himself) he said: 'Why suffer I this stay
In this so strong need to go on? If, like the rest, I fly,
'Tis his best weapon to give chase, being swift, and I should die
Like to a coward. If I stand, I fall too. These two ways
Please not my purpose; I would live. What if I suffer these
Still to be routed, and (my feet affording further length)
Pass all these fields of Ilion, till Ida's sylvan strength
And steep heights shroud me, and at ev'n refresh me in the flood,
And turn to Ilion? O my soul! Why drown'st thou in the blood
Of these discourses? If this course that talks of further flight   500
I give my feet, his feet more swift have more odds. Get he sight
Of that pass, I pass least; for pace, and length of pace, his thighs
Will stand out all men. Meet him then, my steel hath faculties
Of pow'r to pierce him; his great breast but one soul holds, and that
Death claims his right in (all men say), but he holds special state
In Jove's high bounty, that's past man, that every way will hold;
And that serves all men, every way.' This last heart made him bold
To stand Achilles, and stirr'd up a mighty mind to blows.

And as a panther (having heard the hounds' trails) doth disclose
Her freckled forehead, and stares forth from out some deep-grown wood   510
To try what strength dares her abroad, and when her fiery blood
The hounds have kindled, no quench serves, of love to live or fear,
Though struck, though wounded, though quite through she feels the mortal spear,
But till the man's close strength she tries, or strews earth with his dart,
She puts her strength out: so it far'd with brave Agenor's heart,
And till Achilles he had prov'd, no thoughts, no deeds once stirr'd
His fixed foot. To his broad breast his round shield he preferr'd,
And up his arm went with his aim, his voice out with this cry:
'Thy hope is too great, Peleus' son, this day to show thine eye
Troy's Ilion at thy foot; O fool! The Greeks with much more woes,   520
More than are suffer'd yet, must buy great Ilion's overthrows.
We are within her many strong, that for our parents' sakes,
Our wives and children, will save Troy, and thou (though he that makes
Thy name so terrible) shalt make a sacrifice to her
With thine own ruins.' Thus he threw, nor did his javelin err,
But struck his foe's leg near his knee; the fervent steel did ring
Against his tin greaves, and leap'd back. The fire's strong-handed king
Gave virtue of repulse, and then Aeacides assail'd
Divine Agenor, but in vain; Apollo's pow'r prevail'd,
And rapt Agenor from his reach, whom quietly he plac'd   530
Without the skirmish, casting mists to save from being chas'd
His tender'd person, and (he gone) to give his soldiers 'scape,
The deity turn'd Achilles still, by putting on the shape
Of him he thirsted; evermore he fed his eye, and fled,
And he with all his knees pursu'd. So cunningly he led,
That still he would be near his reach, to draw his rage with hope,
Far from the conflict, to the flood maintaining still the scope
Of his attraction. In mean time, the other frighted pow'rs
Came to the city, comforted, when Troy and all her tow'rs
Strooted with fillers; none would stand to see who staid without,   540
Who 'scap'd, and who came short: the ports cleft to receive the rout
That pour'd itself in. Every man was for himself, most fleet
Most fortunate; whoever scap'd, his head might thank his feet.

THE END OF THE TWENTY-FIRST BOOK

BOOK TWENTY-TWO

The Argument

All Trojans hous'd but Hector, only he
Keeps field, and undergoes th' extremity.
Aeacides assaulting, Hector flies.
Minerva stays him: he resists, and dies;
Achilles to his chariot doth enforce,
And to the naval station drags his corse.

Another Argument

Hector in *Chi* to death is done
By pow'r of Peleus' angry son.

BOOK TWENTY-TWO

THUS (chas'd like hinds) the Ilians took time to drink and eat,
And to refresh them, getting off the mingled dust and sweat,
And good strong rampires on instead. The Greeks then cast their shields
Aloft their shoulders; and now Fate their near invasion yields
Of those tough walls, her deadly hand compelling Hector's stay
Before Troy at the Scaean ports. Achilles still made way
At Phoebus, who his bright head turn'd, and ask'd: 'Why, Peleus' son,
Pursu'st thou (being a man) a god? Thy rage hath never done.
Acknowledge not thine eyes my state? Esteems thy mind no more
Thy honour in the chase of Troy, but puts my chase before   10
Their utter conquest? They are all now hous'd in Ilion,
While thou hunt'st me. What wishest thou? My blood will never run
On thy proud javelin.' 'It is thou,' replied Aeacides,
'That putt'st dishonour thus on me, thou worst of deities;
Thou turnd'st me from the walls, whose ports had never entertain'd
Numbers now enter'd, over whom thy saving hand hath reign'd,
And robb'd my honour. And all is, since all thy actions stand
Past fear of reckoning: but held I the measure in my hand,
It should afford thee dear-bought scapes.' Thus with elated spirits
(Steed-like, that at Olympus' games wears garlands for his merits,   20
And rattles home his chariot, extending all his pride)
Achilles so parts with the god. When aged Priam spied
The great Greek come, spher'd round with beams, and show'ng as if the star
Surnam'd Orion's hound, that springs in autumn, and sends far
His radiance through a world of stars, of all whose beams his own
Cast greatest splendour, the midnight that renders them most shown
Then being their foil, and on their points cure-passing fevers then
Come shaking down into the joints of miserable men –
As this were fall'n to earth, and shot along the field his rays
Now towards Priam (which he saw in great Aeacides),   30
Out flew his tender voice in shrieks, and with rais'd hands he smit
His rev'rend head, then up to heav'n he cast them, showing it
What plagues it sent him; down again then threw them to his son,
To make him shun them. He now stood without steep Ilion,
Thirsting the combat; and to him thus miserably cried

The kind old king: 'O Hector! Fly this man, this homicide,
That straight will 'stroy thee. He's too strong, and would to heav'n he were
As strong in heav'n's love as in mine. Vultures and dogs should tear
His prostrate carcass, all my woes quench'd with his bloody spirits.
He has robb'd me of many sons, and worthy, and their merits   40
Sold to far islands: two of them (aye me!) I miss but now,
They are not enter'd, nor stay here. Laothoë, O 'twas thou,
O queen of women, from whose womb they breath'd. O did the tents
Detain them only, brass and gold would purchase safe events
To their sad durance: 'tis within. Old Altes (young in fame)
Gave plenty for his daughters dow'r, but if they fed the flame
Of this man's fury, woe is me; woe to my wretched queen.
But in our state's woe, their two deaths will nought at all be seen,
So thy life quit them. Take the town; retire, dear son, and save
Troy's husbands and her wives, nor give thine own life to the grave   50
For this man's glory: pity me – me, wretch, so long alive,
Whom in the door of age Jove keeps, that so he may deprive
My being in fortune's utmost curse, to see the blackest thread
Of this life's miseries: my sons slain, my daughters ravished,
Their resting chambers sack'd, their babes torn from them, on their knees
Pleading for mercy, themselves dragg'd to Grecian slaveries,
(And all this drawn through my red eyes.) Then last of all kneel I
Alone, all helpless at my gates, before my enemy,
That ruthless gives me to my dogs: all the deformity
Of age discover'd and all this thy death (sought wilfully)   60
Will pour on me. A fair young man at all parts it beseems
(Being bravely slain) to lie all gash'd, and wear the worst extremes
Of war's most cruelty; no wound of whatsoever ruth
But is his ornament: but I, a man so far from youth,
White head, white-bearded, wrinkled, pin'd, all shames must show the eye:
Live, prevent this then, this most shame of all men's misery.'
    Thus wept the old king, and tore off his white hair, yet all these
Retir'd not Hector. Hecuba then fell upon her knees,
Stript nak'd her bosom, show'd her breasts, and bad him rev'rence them,
And pity her, if ever she had quieted his exclaim,   70
He would cease hers, and take the town, not tempting the rude field
When all had left it: 'Think,' said she, 'I gave thee life to yield
My life recomfort; thy rich wife shall have no rites of thee,
Nor do thee rites; our tears shall pay thy corse no obsequy,
Being ravish'd from us, Grecian dogs nourish'd with what I nurs'd.'
    Thus wept both these, and to his ruth propos'd the utmost worst
Of what could chance them, yet he stay'd. And now drew deadly near
Mighty Achilles, yet he still kept deadly station there.

Look how a dragon, when she sees a traveller bent upon
Her breeding den, her bosom fed with fell contagion,   80
Gathers her forces, sits him firm, and at his nearest pace
Wraps all her cavern in her folds, and thrusts a horrid face
Out at his entry: Hector so, with unextinguish'd spirit
Stood great Achilles, stirr'd no foot, but at the prominent turret
Bent to his bright shield, and resolv'd to bear fall'n heav'n on it.
Yet all this resolute abode did not so truly fit
His free election, but he felt a much more galling spur
To the performance, with conceit of what he should incur
Ent'ring, like others, for this cause; to which he thus gave way:
  'O me, if I shall take the town, Polydamas will lay   90
This flight and all this death on me, who counsell'd me to lead
My pow'rs to Troy this last black night, when so I saw make head
Incens'd Achilles. I yet stay'd, though (past all doubt) that course
Had much more profited than mine, which being by so much worse
As comes to all our flight and death, my folly now I fear
Hath bred this scandal, all our town now burns my ominous ear
With whispering: "Hector's self-conceit hath cast away his host."
And (this true) this extremity that I rely on most
Is best for me; stay, and retire with this man's life, or die
Here for our city with renown, since all else fled but I.   100
And yet one way cuts both these ways; what if I hang my shield,
My helm and lance here on these walls, and meet in humble field
Renown'd Achilles, offering him Helen and all the wealth,
Whatever in his hollow keels bore Alexander's stealth
For both th' Atrides? For the rest, whatever is possess'd
In all this city, known or hid, by oath shall be confess'd
Of all our citizens; of which one half the Greeks shall have,
One half themselves. But why (lov'd soul) would these suggestions save
Thy state still in me? I'll not sue, nor would he grant, but I
(Mine arms cast off) should be assur'd a woman's death to die.   110
To men of oak and rock, no words; virgins and youths talk thus –
Virgins and youths that love and woo – there's other war with us;
What blows and conflicts urge, we cry: hates and defiances,
And with the garlands these trees bear, try which hand Jove will bless.'
  These thoughts employ'd his stay, and now Achilles comes, now near
His Mars-like presence terribly came brandishing his spear.
His right arm shook it, his bright arms, like day, came glittering on
Like fire-light, or the light of heav'n shot from the rising sun.
This sight outwrought discourse, cold fear shook Hector from his stand:
No more stay now, all ports were left, he fled in fear the hand   120
Of that fear-master, who, hawk-like, air's swiftest passenger,

That holds a timorous dove in chase, and with command doth bear
His fiery onset; the dove hastes, the hawk comes whizzing on,
This way and that he turns and winds, and cuffs the pigeon;
And till he truss it, his great spirit lays hot charge on his wing:
So urg'd Achilles Hector's flight, so still fear's point did sting
His troubled spirit; his knees wrought hard; along the wall he flew
In that fair chariot way that runs beneath the tow'r of view
And Troy's wild fig-tree, till they reach'd where those two mother springs
Of deep Scamander pour'd abroad their silver murmurings: 130
One warm and casts out fumes as fire; the other cold as snow
Or hail dissolv'd. And when the sun made ardent summer glow,
There water's concrete crystal shin'd, near which were cisterns made,
All pav'd and clear, where Trojan wives and their fair daughters had
Laundry for their fine linen weeds in times of cleanly peace,
Before the Grecians brought their siege. These captains noted these,
One flying, th' other in pursuit. A strong man flew before,
A stronger follow'd him by far, and close up to him bore.
Both did their best, for neither now ran for a sacrifice,
Or for the sacrificer's hide (our runners' usual prize).   140
These ran for tame-horse Hector's soul. And as two running steeds,
Back'd in some set race for a game that tries their swiftest speeds
(A tripod, or a woman giv'n for some man's funerals):
Such speed made these men, and on foot ran thrice about the walls.
     The gods beheld them, all much mov'd; and Jove said: 'O ill sight!
A man I love much I see forc'd in most unworthy flight
About great Ilion; my heart grieves, he paid so many vows,
With thighs of sacrificed beeves, both on the lofty brows
Of Ida, and in Ilion's height. Consult we, shall we free
His life from death, or give it now t' Achilles victory?'   150
     Minerva answered: 'Alter Fate? One long since mark'd for death,
Now take from death? Do thou, but know he still shall run beneath
Our other censures.' 'Be it then,' replied the Thunderer,
'My lov'd Tritonia, at thy will; in this I will prefer
Thy free intention, work it all.' Then stoop'd she from the sky
To this great combat. Peleus' son pursued incessantly
Still flying Hector; as a hound that having rous'd a hart,
Although he tappish ne'er so oft, and every shrubby part
Attempts for strength, and trembles in, the hound doth still pursue
So close that not a foot he fails, but hunts it still at view: 160
So plied Achilles Hector's steps; as oft as he assail'd
The Dardan ports and tow'rs for strength (to fetch from thence some aid
With winged shafts), so oft forc'd he amends of pace, and stept
'Twixt him and all his hopes; and still upon the field he kept

His utmost turnings to the town. And yet, as in a dream
One thinks he gives another chase, when such a fain'd extreme
Possesseth both that he in chase the chaser cannot fly,
Nor can the chaser get to hand his flying enemy:
So nor Achilles' chase could reach the flight of Hector's pace,
Nor Hector's flight enlarge itself of swift Achilles' chase.   170
    But how chanc'd this? How, all this time, could Hector bear the knees
Of fierce Achilles with his own, and keep off destinies,
If Phoebus (for his last and best) through all that course hath fail'd
To add his succours to his nerves, and (as his foe assail'd)
Near and within him fed his 'scape? Achilles yet well knew
His knees would fetch him, and gave signs to some friends (making show
Of shooting at him) to forbear, lest they detracted so
From his full glory in first wounds, and in the overthrow
Make his hand last. But when they reach'd, the fourth time, the two founts,
Then Jove his golden scales weigh'd up, and took the last accounts   180
Of fate for Hector, putting in for him and Peleus' son
Two fates of bitter death, of which high heav'n receiv'd the one,
The other hell: so low declin'd the light of Hector's life.
Then Phoebus left him, when war's queen came to resolve the strife
In th' other's knowledge: 'Now,' said she, 'Jove-lov'd Aeacides,
'I hope at last to make renown perform a brave access
To all the Grecians; we shall now lay low this champion's height,
Though never so insatiate was his great heart of fight.
Nor must he 'scape our pursuit still, though all the feet of Jove
Apollo bows into a sphere, soliciting more love   190
To his most favour'd. Breathe thee then, stand firm, myself will haste
And hearten Hector to change blows.' She went, and he stood fast,
Lean'd on his lance, and much was joy'd that single strokes should try
This fadging conflict. Then came close the changed deity
To Hector, like Deiphobus in shape and voice, and said:
    'O brother, thou art too much urg'd to be thus combated
About our own walls; let us stand, and force to a retreat
Th' insulting chaser.' Hector joy'd at this so kind deceit,
And said: 'O good Deiphobus, thy love was most before
(Of all my brothers) dear to me, but now exceeding more   200
It costs me honour, that thus urg'd thou com'st to part the charge
Of my last fortunes; other friends keep town, and leave at large
My rack'd endeavours.' She replied: 'Good brother, 'tis most true,
One after other, king and queen and all our friends did sue
(Ev'n on their knees) to stay me there, such tremblings shake them all
With this man's terror; but my mind so griev'd to see our wall
Girt with thy chases, that to death I long'd to urge thy stay.

Come, fight we, thirsty of his blood; no more let's fear to lay
Cost on our lances, but approve if, bloodied with our spoils,
He can bear glory to their fleet, or shut up all their toils   210
In his one suff'rance on thy lance.' With this deceit she led,
And (both come near) thus Hector spake: 'Thrice I have compassed
This great town, Peleus' son, in flight, with aversation,
That out of fate put off my steps, but now all flight is flown,
The short course set up, death or life. Our resolutions yet
Must shun all rudeness, and the gods before our valour set
For use of victory. And they being worthiest witnesses
Of all vows, since they keep vows best before their deities,
Let vows of fit respect pass both, when conquest hath bestow'd
Her wreath on either. Here I vow no fury shall be show'd,   220
That is not manly, on thy corse; but, having spoil'd thy arms,
Resign thy person; which swear thou.' These fair and temperate terms
Far fled Achilles, his brows bent, and out flew this reply:
    'Hector, thou only pestilence in all mortality
To my sere spirits, never set the point 'twixt thee and me
Any conditions, but as far as men and lions fly
All terms of covenant, lambs and wolves, in so far opposite state
(Impossible t' atone) stand we, till our souls satiate
The god of soldiers; do not dream that our disjunction can
Endure condition. Therefore now, all worth that fits a man   230
Call to thee, all particular parts that fit a soldier,
And they all this include (besides the skill and spirit of war):
Hunger for slaughter, and a hate that eats thy heart to eat
Thy foe's heart. This stirs, this supplies in death the killing heat,
And all this need'st thou. No more flight; Pallas Athenia
Will quickly cast thee to my lance; now, now together draw
All griefs for vengeance, both in me and all my friends late dead
That bled thee, raging with thy lance.' This said, he brandished
His long lance, and away it sung; which, Hector giving view,
Stoop'd low, stood firm (foreseeing it best), and quite it overflew,   240
Fast'ning on earth. Athenia drew it, and gave her friend,
Unseen of Hector. Hector then thus spake: 'Thou want'st thy end,
God-like Achilles. Now I see thou hast not learn'd my fate
Of Jove at all, as thy high words would bravely intimate;
Much tongue affects thee, cunning words well serve thee to prepare
Thy blows with threats, that mine might faint with want of spirit to dare;
But my back never turns with breath, it was not born to bear
Burthens of wounds; strike home before, drive at my breast thy spear,
As mine at thine shall; and try then if heav'ns will favour thee
With 'scape of my lance. O would Jove would take it after me,   250

And make thy bosom take it all; an easy end would crown
Our difficult wars were thy soul fled, thou most bane of our town.'

Thus flew his dart, touch'd at the midst of his vast shield, and flew
A huge way from it; but his heart wrath ent'red with the view
Of that hard 'scape, and heavy thoughts struck through him when he spied
His brother vanish'd, and no lance beside left; out he cried:
'Deiphobus! Another lance.' Lance, nor Deiphobus,
Stood near his call. And then his mind saw all things ominous,
And thus suggested: 'Woe is me, the gods have called, and I
Must meet death here; Deiphobus I well hop'd had been by	260
With his white shield, but our strong walls shield him, and this deceit
Flows from Minerva. Now, O now, ill death comes, no more flight,
No more recovery: O Jove, this hath been otherwise;
Thy bright son and thyself have set the Greeks a greater prize
Of Hector's blood than now, of which (ev'n jealous) you had care;
But fate now conquers; I am hers; and yet not she shall share
In my renown; that life is left to every noble spirit,
And that some great deed shall beget, that all lives shall inherit.'

Thus, forth his sword flew, sharp and broad, and bore a deadly weight,
With which he rush'd in: and look how an eagle from her height	270
Stoops to the rapture of a lamb, or cuffs a timorous hare:
So fell in Hector, and at him Achilles; his mind's fare
Was fierce and mighty, his shield cast a sun-like radiance,
Helm nodded, and his four plumes shook; and when he rais'd his lance,
Up Hesperus rose 'mongst th' evening stars. His bright and sparkling eyes
Look'd through the body of his foe, and sought through all that prise
The next way to his thirsted life. Of all ways, only one
Appear'd to him, and that was where th' unequal winding bone,
That joins the shoulders and the neck, had place, and where there lay
The speeding way to death, and there his quick eye could display	280
The place it sought, ev'n through those arms his friend Patroclus wore
When Hector slew him. There he aim'd, and there his javelin tore
Stern passage quite through Hector's neck; yet miss'd it so his throat,
It gave him pow'r to change some words, but down to earth it got
His fainting body. Then triumph'd divine Aeacides:
'Hector,' said he, 'thy heart suppos'd that in my friend's decease
Thy life was safe, my absent arm not cared for. Fool! He left
One at the fleet that better'd him, and he it is that reft
Thy strong knees thus: and now the dogs and fowls in foulest use
Shall tear thee up, thy corse expos'd to all the Greeks' abuse.'	290

He, fainting, said: 'Let me implore, ev'n by thy knees and soul,
And thy great parents, do not see a cruelty so foul
Inflicted on me: brass and gold receive at any rate,

And quit my person, that the peers and ladies of our state
May tomb it, and to sacred fire turn thy profane decrees.'
    'Dog,' he replied, 'urge not my ruth, by parents, soul, nor knees:
I would to god that any rage would let me eat thee raw,
Sliced into pieces, so beyond the right of any law
I taste thy merits, and believe it flies the force of man
To rescue thy head from the dogs. Give all the gold they can,   300
If ten or twenty times so much as friends would rate thy price
Were tender'd here, with vows of more, to buy the cruelties
I here have vow'd, and after that thy father with his gold
Would free thyself, all that should fail to let thy mother hold
Solemnities of death with thee, and do thee such a grace
To mourn thy whole corse on a bed; which piecemeal I'll deface
With fowls and dogs.' He (dying) said: 'I (knowing thee well) foresaw
Thy now tried tyranny, nor hop'd for any other law
Of nature, or of nations: and that fear forc'd much more
Than death my flight, which never touch'd at Hector's foot before: 310
A soul of iron informs thee; mark what vengeance th' equal fates
Will give me of thee for this rage, when in the Scaean gates
Phoebus and Paris meet with thee.' Thus death's hand clos'd his eyes,
His soul flying his fair limbs to hell, mourning his destinies
To part so with his youth and strength. Thus dead, thus Thetis' son
His prophecy answer'd: 'Die thou now; when my short thread is spun,
I'll bear it as the will of Jove.' This said, his brazen spear
He drew, and stuck by; then his arms (that all imbrued were)
He spoil'd his shoulders of. Then all the Greeks ran in to him
To see his person, and admir'd his terror-stirring limb;   320
Yet none stood by that gave no wound to his so goodly form,
When each to other said: 'O Jove, he is not in the storm
He came to fleet in with his fire, he handles now more soft.'
    'O friends,' said stern Aeacides, 'now that the gods have brought
This man thus down, I'll freely say he brought more bane to Greece
Than all his aiders. Try we then (thus arm'd at every piece,
And girding all Troy with our host) if now their hearts will leave
Their city clear, her clear stay slain, and all their lives receive,
Or hold yet, Hector being no more. But why use I a word
Of any act but what concerns my friend? Dead, undeplor'd,   330
Unsepulchred, he lies at fleet, unthought on: never hour
Shall make his dead state, while the quick enjoys me, and this pow'r
To move these movers. Though in hell men say that such as die
Oblivion seizeth, yet in hell in me shall Memory
Hold all her forms still of my friend. Now, youths of Greece, to fleet
Bear we this body, paeans sing, and all our navy greet

With endless honour; we have slain Hector, the period
Of all Troy's glory, to whose worth all vow'd as to a god.'
    This said, a work not worthy him he set to: of both feet
He bor'd the nerves through from the heel to th' ankle, and then knit   340
Both to his chariot with a thong of whitleather, his head
Trailing the centre. Up he got to chariot, where he laid
The arms repurchas'd, and scourg'd on his horse, that freely flew.
A whirlwind, made of startled dust, drave with them as they drew,
With which were all his black-brown curls knotted in heaps and fil'd.
And there lay Troy's late gracious, by Jupiter exil'd
To all disgrace in his own land, and by his parents seen.
    When (like her son's head) all with dust Troy's miserable queen
Distain'd her temples, plucking off her honour'd hair, and tore
Her royal garments, shrieking out. In like kind Priam bore   350
His sacred person, like a wretch that never saw good day,
Broken with outcries. About both the people prostrate lay,
Held down with clamour, all the town veil'd with a cloud of tears:
Ilion, with all his tops on fire, and all the massacres
Left for the Greeks, could put on looks of no more overthrow
Than now 'fray'd life. And yet the king did all their looks outshow.
The wretched people could not bear his sovereign wretchedness,
Plaguing himself so – thrusting out, and praying all the press
To open him the Dardan ports, that he alone might fetch
His dearest son in; and (all fill'd with rumbling) did beseech   360
Each man by name, thus: 'Loved friends, be you content, let me
(Though much ye grieve) be that poor mean to our sad remedy
Now in our wishes; I will go and pray this impious man
(Author of horrors), making proof if age's reverence can
Excite his pity. His own sire is old like me, and he
That got him to our griefs, perhaps may (for my likeness) be
Mean for our ruth to him. Alas, you have no cause of cares,
Compar'd with me; I many sons, grac'd with their freshest years,
Have lost by him, and all their deaths in slaughter of this one
(Afflicted man) are doubled: this will bitterly set gone   370
My soul to hell. O would to heav'n I could but hold him dead
In these pin'd arms; then tears on tears might fall, till all were shed
In common fortune. Now amaze their natural course doth stop,
And pricks a mad vein.' Thus he mourn'd, and with him all brake ope
Their store of sorrows. The poor queen amongst the women wept,
Turn'd into anguish: 'O my son,' she cried out, 'why still kept
Patient of horrors is my life when thine is vanished?
My days thou glorifiedst; my nights rung of some honour'd deed
Done by thy virtues – joy to me, profit to all our care.

All made a god of thee, and thou mad'st them all that they are: 380
Now under fate, now dead. These two thus vented as they could
Their sorrow's furnace, Hector's wife not having yet been told
So much as of his stay without: she in her chamber close
Sat at her loom; a piece of work, grac'd with a both sides gloss,
Strew'd curiously with varied flowers, her pleasure was; her care,
To heat a cauldron for her lord, to bathe him turn'd from war,
Of which she chief charge gave her maids. Poor dame, she little knew
How much her cares lack'd of his case. But now the clamour flew
Up to her turret: then she shook, her work fell from her hand,
And up she started, call'd her maids; she needs must understand   390
That ominous outcry. 'Come,' said she, 'I hear through all this cry
My mother's voice shriek: to my throat my heart bounds; ecstasy
Utterly alters me: some fate is near the hapless sons
Of fading Priam. Would to god my words' suspicions
No ear had heard yet. O I fear, and that most heartily,
That with some stratagem the son of Peleus hath put by
The wall of Ilion, my lord, and (trusty of his feet)
Obtain'd the chase of him alone; and now the curious heat
Of his still desperate spirit is cool'd. It let him never keep
In guard of others; before all his violent foot must step,   400
Or his place forfeited he held.' Thus fury-like she went,
Two women (as she will'd) at hand, and made her quick ascent
Up to the tow'r and press of men, her spirit in uproar. Round
She cast her greedy eye, and saw her Hector slain, and bound
T' Achilles chariot, manlessly dragg'd to the Grecian fleet.
Black night struck through her; under her, trance took away her feet,
And back she shrunk, with such a sway, then off her head-tire flew,
Her coronet, caul, ribands, veil, that golden Venus threw
On her white shoulders, that high day when warlike Hector won
Her hand in nuptials in the court of king Eëtion,   410
And that great dow'r then given with her. About her, on their knees,
Her husband's sisters, brothers' wives, fell round, and by degrees
Recover'd her. Then, when again her respirations found
Free pass (her mind and spirit met), these thoughts her words did sound:
      'O Hector! O me, cursed dame! Both born beneath one fate,
Thou here, I in Cilician Thebes, where Placus doth elate
His shady forehead in the court where king Eëtion
(Hapless) begot unhappy me; which would he had not done,
To live past thee: thou now art div'd to Pluto's gloomy throne,
Sunk through the coverts of the earth: I, in a hell of moan,   420
Left here thy widow. One poor babe, born to unhappy both,
Whom thou leav'st helpless as he thee; he born to all the wroth

Of woe and labour. Lands left him will others seize upon;
The orphan day of all friends' helps robs every mother's son.
An orphan all men suffer sad; his eyes stand still with tears.
Need tries his father's friends, and fails. Of all his favourers,
If one the cup gives, 'tis not long; the wine he finds in it
Scarce moists his palate: if he chance to gain the grace to sit,
Surviving father's sons repine, use contumelies, strike,
Bid 'Leave us; where's thy father's place?' He (weeping with dislike)   430
Retires to me. To me, alas! Astyanax is he
Born to these miseries. He that late fed on his father's knee,
To whom all knees bow'd, daintiest fare appos'd him, and when sleep
Lay on his temples, his cries still'd (his heart ev'n laid in steep
Of all things precious), a soft bed, a careful nurse's arms
Took him to guardiance: but now as huge a world of harms
Lies on his suff'rance; now thou want'st thy father's hand to friend,
O my Astyanax! O my lord! Thy hand that did defend
These gates of Ilion, these long walls by thy arm measur'd still
Amply and only, yet at fleet thy naked corse must fill   440
Vile worms when dogs are satiate, far from thy parents' care;
Far from those funeral ornaments that thy mind would prepare
(So sudden being the chance of arms), ever expecting death:
Which task (though my heart would not serve t' employ my hands beneath)
I made my women yet perform. Many, and much in price,
Were those integuments they wrought t' adorn thy exequies;
Which, since they fly thy use, thy corse not laid in their attire,
Thy sacrifice they shall be made; these hands in mischievous fire
Shall vent their vanities. And yet (being consecrate to thee)
They shall be kept for citizens, and their fair wives, to see.'   450
    Thus spake she weeping; all the dames endeavouring to cheer
Her desert state (fearing their own), wept with her tear for tear.

THE END OF THE TWENTY-SECOND BOOK

BOOK TWENTY-THREE

The Argument

Achilles orders jousts of exequies
For his Patroclus, and doth sacrifice
Twelve Trojan princes, most lov'd hounds and horse,
And other offerings, to the honour'd corse.
He institutes, besides, a funeral game,
Where Diomed, for horse-race, wins the fame;
For foot, Ulysses; others otherwise
Strive, and obtain; and end the exequies.

Another Argument

Psi sings the rites of the decease
Ordain'd by great Aeacides.

BOOK TWENTY-THREE

THUS MOURN'D all Troy: but when at fleet, and Hellespontus' shore,
    The Greeks arriv'd, each to his ship, only the conqueror
    Kept undispers'd his Myrmidons; and said, 'Lov'd countrymen,
Disjoin not we chariots and horse, but (bearing hard our rein)
With state of both, march soft and close, and mourn about the corse:
'Tis proper honour to the dead. Then take we out our horse,
When with our friends' kind woe our hearts have felt delight to do
A virtuous soul right, and then sup.' This said, all full of woe
Circled the corse. Achilles led, and thrice about him, close
All bore their goodly-coated horse. Amongst all Thetis rose,   10
And stirr'd up a delight in grief, till all their arms with tears,
And all the sands, were wet: so much they lov'd that lord of fears.
Then to the centre fell the prince; and putting in the breast
Of his slain friend his slaught'ring hands, began to all the rest
Words to their tears: 'Rejoice,' said he, 'O my Patroclus, thou
Courted by Dis now: now I pay to thy late overthrow
All my revenges vow'd before; Hector lies slaughter'd here
Dragg'd at my chariot, and our dogs shall all in pieces tear
His hated limbs. Twelve Trojan youths, born of their noblest strains,
I took alive, and (yet enrag'd) will empty all their veins   20
Of vital spirits, sacrific'd before thy heap of fire.'
    This said, (a work unworthy him), he put upon his ire,
And trampled Hector under foot, at his friend's feet. The rest
Disarm'd, took horse from chariot, and all to sleep address'd
At his black vessel. Infinite were those that rested there.
    Himself yet sleeps not, now his spirits were wrought about the cheer
Fit for so high a funeral. About the steel us'd then,
Oxen in heaps lay bellowing, preparing food for men:
Bleating of sheep and goats fill'd air; numbers of white-tooth'd swine
(Swimming in fat) lay singeing there: the person of the slain   30
Was girt with slaughter. All this done, all the Greek kings convey'd
Achilles to the king of men, his rage not yet allay'd
For his Patroclus. Being arriv'd at Agamemnon's tent,
Himself bad heralds put to fire a cauldron, and present
The service of it to the prince, to try if they could win

His pleasure to admit their pains to cleanse the blood soak'd in
About his conquering hands and brows. 'Not by the king of heav'n!'
He swore. 'The laws of friendship damn this false-heart licence giv'n
To men that lose friends: not a drop shall touch me till I put
Patroclus in the funeral pile, before these curls be cut,   40
His tomb erected. 'Tis the last of all care I shall take,
While I consort the careful: yet, for your entreaties' sake,
(And though I loathe food) I will eat: but early in the morn,
Atrides, use your strict command, that loads of wood be borne
To our design'd place, all that fits to light home such a one
As is to pass the shades of death, that fire enough set gone
His person quickly from our eyes, and our diverted men
May ply their business.' This all ears did freely entertain,
And found observance: then they supp'd, with all things fit, and all
Repair'd to tents and rest. The friend the shores maritimal   50
Sought for his bed, and found a place, fair, and upon which play'd
The murmuring billows. There his limbs to rest, not sleep, he laid,
Heavily sighing. Round about (silent, and not too near)
Stood all his Myrmidons, when straight so over-labour'd were
His goodly lineaments with chase of Hector, that beyond
His resolution not to sleep Sleep cast his sudden bond
Over his sense, and loos'd his care. Then of his wretched friend
The soul appear'd; at every part the form did comprehend
His likeness: his fair eyes, his voice, his stature, every weed
His person wore, it fantasied, and stood above his head,   60
This sad speech utt'ring. 'Dost thou sleep? Aeacides, am I
Forgotten of thee? Being alive, I found thy memory
Ever respectful; but now dead, thy dying love abates.
Inter me quickly, enter me in Pluto's iron gates,
For now the souls (the shades) of men, fled from this being, beat
My spirit from rest, and stay my much-desir'd receipt
Amongst souls plac'd beyond the flood. Now every way I err
About this broad-door'd house of Dis. O help then to prefer
My soul yet further. Here I mourn, but had the funeral fire
Consum'd my body, never more my spirit should retire   70
From hell's low region: from thence souls never are retriev'd
To talk with friends here, nor shall I; a hateful fate depriv'd
My being here, that at my birth was fix'd, and to such fate
Ev'n thou, O god-like man, art mark'd; the deadly Ilian gate
Must entertain thy death. O then, I charge thee now, take care
That our bones part not, but as life combin'd in equal fare
Our loving beings, so let death. When from Opunta's tow'rs
My father brought me to your roofs (since 'gainst my will, my pow'rs

Incens'd, and indiscreet at dice, slew fair Amphidamas)
Then Peleus entertain'd me well; then in thy charge I was   80
By his injunction and thy love; and therein let me still
Receive protection. Both our bones provide in thy last will
That one urn may contain, and make the vessel all of gold
That Thetis gave thee, that rich urn.' This said, Sleep ceas'd to hold
Achilles' temples, and the shade thus he receiv'd: 'O friend,
What needed these commands? My care before meant to commend
My bones to thine, and in that urn. Be sure thy will is done.
A little stay yet; let's delight, with some full passion
Of woe enough, either's affects; embrace we.' Opening thus
His greedy arms, he felt no friend: like matter vaporous   90
The spirit vanish'd under earth, and murmur'd in his stoop.
Achilles started; both his hands he clapp'd and lifted up,
In this sort wond'ring: 'O ye gods, I see we have a soul
In th' under-dwellings, and a kind of man-resembling idol:
The soul's seat yet, all matter left, stays with the carcase here.
O friends, hapless Patroclus' soul did all this night appear
Weeping and making moan to me, commanding everything
That I intended towards him, so truly figuring
Himself at all parts, as was strange.' This accident did turn
To much more sorrow, and begat a greediness to mourn   100
In all that heard. When mourning thus, the rosy morn arose:
And Agamemnon through the tents wak'd all, and did dispose
Both men and mules for carriage of matter for the fire.
Of all which work Meriones (the Cretan sov'reign's squire)
Was captain, and abroad they went. Wood-cutting tools they bore
Of all kinds, and well-twisted cords. The mules march all before.
Up hill and down hill, over thwarts and break-neck cliffs they pass'd,
But when the fountful Ida's tops they scal'd with utmost haste,
All fell upon the high-hair'd oaks, and down their curled brows
Fell bustling to the earth; and up went all the boles and boughs,   110
Bound to the mules, and back again they parted the harsh way
Amongst them through the tangling shrubs, and long they thought the day
Till in the plain field all arriv'd, for all the woodmen bore
Logs on their necks; Meriones would have it so: the shore
At last they reach'd yet, and then down their carriages they cast,
And sat upon them, where the son of Peleus had plac'd
The ground for his great sepulchre, and for his friend's, in one.

They rais'd a huge pile, and to arms went every Myrmidon,
Charg'd by Achilles; chariots and horse were harnessed,
Fighters and charioteers got up, and they the sad march led,   120
A cloud of infinite foot behind. In midst of all was borne

Patroclus' person by his peers: on him were all heads shorn,
Ev'n till they cover'd him with curls. Next to him march'd his friend,
Embracing his cold neck all sad, since now he was to send
His dearest to his endless home. Arriv'd all where the wood
Was heap'd for funeral, they sat down. Apart Achilles stood,
And when enough wood was heap'd on, he cut his golden hair,
Long kept for Sperchius the flood, in hope of safe repair
To Phthia by that river's pow'r; but now left hopeless thus
(Enrag'd, and looking on the sea) he cried out: 'Sperchius,   130
In vain my father's piety vow'd (at my implor'd return
To my lov'd country) that these curls should on thy shores be shorn,
Besides a sacred hecatomb, and sacrifice beside
Of fifty wethers, at whose founts, where men have edified
A lofty temple, and perfum'd an altar to thy name.
There vow'd he all these offerings, but fate prevents thy fame,
His hopes not suffering satisfied; and since I never more
Shall see my lov'd soil, my friend's hands shall to the Stygian shore
Convey these tresses.' Thus he put in his friend's hands the hair.
And this bred fresh desire of moan, and in that sad affair   140
The sun had set amongst them all, had Thetis' son not spoke
Thus to Atrides: 'King of men, thy aid I still invoke,
Since thy command all men still hear; dismiss thy soldiers now,
And let them victual; they have mourn'd sufficient, 'tis we owe
The dead this honour; and with us let all the captains stay.'
    This heard, Atrides instantly the soldiers sent away.
The funeral officers remain'd, and heap'd on matter still,
Till of an hundred foot about they made the funeral pile,
In whose hot height they cast the corse, and then they pour'd on tears.
Numbers of fat sheep, and like store of crooked-going steers,   150
They slew before the solemn fire, stripp'd off their hides and dress'd.
Of which Achilles took the fat, and cover'd the deceas'd
From head to foot: and round about he made the officers pile
The beasts nak'd bodies, vessels full of honey and of oil
Pour'd in them, laid upon a bier, and cast into the fire.
Four goodly horse, and of nine hounds, two most in the desire
Of that great prince, and trencher-fed, all fed that hungry flame.
    Twelve Trojan princes last stood forth, young, and of toward fame,
All which (set on with wicked spirits) there struck he, there he slew,
And to the iron strength of fire their noble limbs he threw.   160
    Then breath'd his last sighs, and these words: 'Again rejoice, my friend,
Ev'n in the joyless depth of hell; now give I complete end
To all my vows. Alone thy life sustain'd not violence;
Twelve Trojan princes wait on thee, and labour to incense

Thy glorious heap of funeral. Great Hector I'll excuse;
The dogs shall eat him.' These high threats perform'd not their abuse.
Jove's daughter, Venus, took the guard of noble Hector's corse,
And kept the dogs off, night and day applying sov'reign force
Of rosy balms, that to the dogs were horrible in taste,
And with which she the body fill'd. Renown'd Apollo cast   170
A cloud from heav'n, lest with the sun the nerves and lineaments
Might dry and putrefy. And now some pow'rs denied consents
To this solemnity: the fire (for all the oily fuel
It had injected) would not burn; and then the loving cruel
Studied for help, and standing off, invok'd the two fair winds
(Zephyr and Boreas) to afford the rage of both their kinds
To aid his outrage. Precious gifts his earnest zeal did vow,
Pour'd from a golden bowl much wine, and pray'd them both to blow,
That quickly his friend's corse might burn, and that heap's sturdy breast
Embrace consumption. Iris heard; the winds were at a feast,   180
All in the court of Zephyrus (that boist'rous-blowing air)
Gather'd together. She that wears the thousand-colour'd hair
Flew thither, standing in the porch: they (seeing her) all arose,
Call'd to her; every one desir'd she would awhile repose,
And eat with them. She answer'd: 'No, no place of seat is here;
Retreat calls to the Ocean and Ethiopia, where
A hecatomb is offering now to heav'n, and there must I
Partake the feast of sacrifice; I come to signify
That Thetis' son implores your aids (princes of north and west)
With vows of much fair sacrifice, if each will set his breast   190
Against his heap of funeral, and make it quickly burn.
Patroclus lies there, whose decease all the Achaians mourn.'
   She said, and parted; and out rush'd, with an unmeasur'd roar,
Those two winds, tumbling clouds in heaps, ushers to either's blore,
And instantly they reach'd the sea. Up flew the waves; the gale
Was strong, reach'd fruitful Troy; and full upon the fire they fall.
The huge heap thunder'd. All night long from his chok'd breast they blew
A liberal flame up; and all night swift-foot Achilles threw
Wine from a golden bowl on earth, and steep'd the soil in wine,
Still calling on Patroclus' soul. No father could incline   200
More to a son most dear, nor more mourn at his burned bones,
Than did the great prince to his friend at his combustions,
Still creeping near and near the heap, still sighing, weeping still:
But when the day-star look'd abroad, and promis'd from his hill
Light, which the saffron morn made good, and sprinkled on the seas,
Then languish'd the great pile, then sunk the flames, and then calm peace
Turn'd back the rough winds to their homes, the Thracian billow rings

Their high retreat, ruffled with cuffs of their triumphant wings.
  Pelides then forsook the pile, and to his tired limb
Chose place of rest; where laid, sweet sleep fell to his wish on him –   210
When all the king's guard (waiting then, perceiving will to rise
In that great session) hurried in, and op'd again his eyes
With tumult of their troop, and haste. A little then he rear'd
His troubled person, sitting up, and this affair referr'd
To wish'd commandment of the kings: 'Atrides, and the rest
Of our commanders general, vouchsafe me this request
Before your parting: give in charge the quenching with black wine
Of this heap's reliques, every brand the yellow fire made shine.
And then let search Patroclus' bones, distinguishing them well –
As well ye may; they keep the midst, the rest at random fell   220
About th' extreme part of the pile. Men's bones and horses mix'd
Being found, I'll find an urn of gold t' inclose them; and betwixt
The air and them two kels of fat lay on them, and to rest
Commit them, till mine own bones seal our love, my soul deceas'd.
The sepulchre I have not charg'd to make of too much state,
But of a model something mean, that you of younger fate
(When I am gone) may amplify with such a breadth and height
As fits your judgments and our worths.' This charge receiv'd his weight
In all observance: first they quench'd, with sable wine, the heap
As far as it had fed the flame. The ash fell wondrous deep,   230
In which his consorts, that his life religiously lov'd,
Search'd, weeping, for his bones: which found, they conscionably prov'd
His will made to Aeacides, and what his love did add.
A golden vessel, double fat, contain'd them: all which (clad
In veils of linen, pure and rich) were solemnly convey'd
T'Achilles' tent. The platform then about the pile they laid
Of his fit sepulchre, and rais'd a heap of earth, and then
Offer'd departure. But the prince retain'd there still his men,
Employing them to fetch from fleet rich tripods for his games,
Cauldrons, horse, mules, broad-headed beeves, bright steel, and brighter dames.
  The best at horse-race, he ordain'd a lady for his prize,
Generally praiseful: fair and young, and skill'd in housewif'ries
Of all kind fitting; and withal a trivet, that inclos'd
Twenty-two measures room, with ears. The next prize he propos'd
Was (that which then had high respect) a mare of six years old,
Unhandled, horsed with a mule, and ready to have foal'd.
The third game was a cauldron, new, fair, bright, and could for size
Contain two measures. For the fourth, two talents' quantities
Of finest gold. The fifth game was a great new standing cup,
To set down both ways. These brought in, Achilles then stood up,   250

And said: 'Atrides and my lords, chief horsemen of our host,
These games expect ye. If myself should interpose my most
For our horse-race, I make no doubt but I should take again
These gifts propos'd. Ye all know well of how divine a strain
My horses are, and how eminent. Neptune's gift they are
To Peleus; of his to me. Myself then will not share
In gifts giv'n others, nor my steeds breathe any spirit to shake
Their airy pasterns; so they mourn for their kind guider's sake,
Late lost, that us'd with humorous oil to slick their lofty manes,
Clear water having cleans'd them first, and (his bane being their banes)   260
Those lofty manes now strew the earth, their heads held shaken down.
You then that trust in chariots, and hope with horse to crown
Your conquering temples, gird yourselves; now fame and prize stretch for,
All that have spirits.' This fir'd all: the first competitor
Was king Eumelus, whom the art of horsemanship did grace,
Son to Admetus; next to him rose Diomed to the race,
That under reins rul'd Trojan horse, of late forc'd from the son
Of lord Anchises, himself freed of near confusion
By Phoebus. Next to him set forth the yellow-headed king
Of Lacedaemon, Jove's high seed; and in his managing   270
Podargus and swift Aethe trod, steeds to the king of men –
Aethe giv'n by Echepolus, the Anchisiaden,
A bribe to free him from the war resolv'd for Ilion.
So Delicacy feasted him, whom Jove bestow'd upon
A mighty wealth; his dwelling was in brode Sicyone.
Old Nestor's son, Antilochus, was fourth for chivalry
In this contention: his fair horse were of the Pylian breed,
And his old father (coming near) inform'd him (for good speed)
With good race notes, in which himself could good instruction give:
    'Antilochus, though young thou art, yet thy grave virtues live   280
Belov'd of Neptune and of Jove: their spirits have taught thee all
The art of horsemanship, for which the less thy merits fall
In need of doctrine. Well thy skill can yield a chariot
In all fit turning, yet thy horse their slow feet handle not
As fits thy manage, which makes me cast doubts of thy success.
I well know all these are not seen in art of this address
More than thyself: their horses yet superior are to thine,
For their parts: thine want speed to make discharge of a design
To please an artist. But go on, show but thy art and heart
At all points, and set them against their horse's heart and art;   290
Good judges will not see thee lose. A carpenter's desert
Stands more in cunning than in power. A pilot doth avert
His vessel from the rock and wrack, toss'd with the churlish winds,

By skill not strength. So sorts it here: one charioteer that finds
Want of another's power in horse, must in his own skill set
An overplus of that to that; and so the proof will get
Still, that still rests within a man more grace than pow'r without.
He that in horse and chariots trusts is often hurl'd about
This way and that, unhandsomely, all heav'n wide of his end.
He better skill'd, that rules worse horse, will all observance bend   300
Right on the scope still of a race, bear near, know ever when to rein,
When give rein, as his foe before (well noted in his vein
Of manage, and his steeds' estate) presents occasion.
I'll give the instance now, as plain as if thou saw'st it done:
Here stands a dry stub of some tree, a cubit from the ground
(Suppose the stub of oak or larch, for either are so sound
That neither rots with wet); two stones, white (mark you), white for view,
Parted on either side the stub; and these lay where they drew
The way into a strait, the race betwixt both lying clear.
Imagine them some monument of one long since tomb'd there,   310
Or that they had been lists of race for men of former years,
As now the lists Achilles sets may serve for charioteers
Many years hence. When near to these the race grows, then as right
Drive on them as thy eye can judge; then lay thy bridle's weight
Most of thy left side, thy right horse then switching, all thy throat
(Spent in encouragements) give him, and all the rein let float
About his shoulders: thy near horse will yet be he that gave
Thy skill the prize; and him rein so, his head may touch the nave
Of thy left wheel – but then take care thou runn'st not on the stone
(With wrack of horse and chariot) which so thou bear'st upon.   320
Shipwreck within the hav'n avoid by all means; that will breed
Others delight, and thee a shame. Be wise then, and take heed
(My lov'd son) get but to be first at turning in the course;
He lives not that can cote thee then, not if he back'd the horse
The gods bred, and Adrastus own'd. Divine Arion's speed
Could not outpace thee, or the horse Laomedon did breed,
Whose race is famous, and fed here.' Thus sate Neleides,
When all that could be said, was said. And then Meriones
Set fitly forth his fair-man'd horse. All leap'd to chariot;
And every man then for the start cast in his proper lot.   330
Achilles drew: Antilochus the lot set foremost forth;
Eumelus next; Atrides third; Meriones the fourth.
The fifth and last was Diomed, far first in excellence.
All stood in order and the lists Achilles fix'd far thence
In plain field, and a seat ordain'd fast by, in which he set
Renowned Phoenix, that in grace of Peleus was so great,

To see the race, and give a truth of all their passages.
All start together, scourg'd, and cried, and gave their business
Study and order. Through the field they held a winged pace.
Beneath the bosom of their steeds a dust so dimm'd the race,   340
It stood above their heads in clouds, or like to storms, amaz'd.
Manes flew like ensigns with the wind; the chariots sometimes graz'd,
And sometimes jump'd up to the air; yet still sate fast the men,
Their spirits ev'n panting in their breasts, with fervour to obtain.
But when they turn'd to fleet again, then all men's skills were tried,
Then stretch'd the pasterns of their steeds. Eumelus' horse in pride
Still bore their sov'reign. After them came Diomed's coursers close,
Still apt to leap their chariot, and ready to repose
Upon the shoulders of their king their heads; his back ev'n burn'd
With fire that from their nostrils flew. And then their lord had turn'd   350
The race for him, or giv'n it doubt, if Phoebus had not smit
The scourge out of his hands, and tears of helpless wrath with it
From forth his eyes, to see his horse for want of scourge made slow,
And th' others (by Apollo's help) with much more swiftness go.
     Apollo's spite Pallas discern'd, and flew to Tydeus' son,
His scourge reach'd, and his horse made fresh – then took her angry run
At king Eumelus, brake his gears; his mares on both sides flew,
His draught-tree fell to earth, and him the toss'd up chariot threw
Down to the earth, his elbows torn, his forehead, all his face
Struck at the centre, his speech lost. And then the turned race   360
Fell to Tydides: before all his conquering horse he drave,
And first he glitter'd in the race; divine Athenia gave
Strength to his horse, and fame to him. Next him drave Sparta's king.
Antilochus his father's horse then urg'd with all his sting
Of scourge and voice. 'Run low,' said he, 'stretch out your limbs, and fly.
With Diomed's horse I bid not strive, nor with himself strive I.
Athenia wings his horse, and him renowns. Atrides' steeds
Are they ye must not fail but reach – and soon, lest soon succeeds
The blot of all your fames, to yield in swiftness to a mare,
To female Aethe. What's the cause, ye best that ever were,   370
That thus ye fail us? Be assur'd that Nestor's love ye lose
For ever if ye fail his son: through both your both sides goes
His hot steel, if ye suffer me to bring the last prize home.
Haste, overtake them instantly; we needs must overcome.
This harsh way next us, this my mind will take, this I despise
For peril, this I'll creep through; hard the way to honour lies.
And that take I, and that shall yield.' His horse by all this knew
He was not pleas'd, and fear'd his voice, and for a while they flew;
But straight more clear appear'd the strait Antilochus foresaw:

It was a gasp the earth gave, forc'd by humours cold and raw,   380
Pour'd out of winter's wat'ry breast; met there, and cleaving deep
All that near passage to the lists. This Nestor's son would keep,
And left the roadway, being about; Atrides fear'd, and cried:
'Antilochus, thy course is mad; contain thy horse, we ride
A way most dangerous; turn head, betime take larger field,
We shall be splitted.' Nestor's son with much more scourge impell'd
His horse for this, as if not heard, and got as far before
As any youth can cast a quoit; Atrides would no more;
He back again, for fear himself, his goodly chariot,
And horse together, strew'd the dust, in being so dusty hot   390
Of thirsted conquest. But he chid, at parting, passing sore:

     'Antilochus,' said he, 'a worse than thee earth never bore:
Farewell, we never thought thee wise, that were wise, but not so
Without oaths shall the wreath (be sure) crown thy mad temples; go.'

     Yet he bethought him, and went too, thus stirring up his steeds:
'Leave me not last thus, nor stand vex'd; let these fail in the speeds
Of feet and knees, not you: shall these, these old jades (past the flow'r
Of youth, that you have) pass you?' This the horse fear'd, and more pow'r
Put to their knees, straight getting ground. Both flew, and so the rest;
All came in smokes, like spirits; the Greeks (set to see who did best,   400
Without the race, aloft) now made a new discovery,
Other than that they made at first: Idomeneus' eye
Distinguish'd all; he knew the voice of Diomed, seeing a horse
Of special mark, of colour bay, and was the first in course,
His forehead putting forth a star, round like the moon, and white.
Up stood the Cretan, uttering this: 'Is it alone my sight,
Princes and captains, that discerns another lead the race
With other horse than led of late? Eumelus made most pace
With his fleet mares, and he began the flexure, as we thought.
Now all the field I search, and find nowhere his view; hath nought   410
Befall'n amiss to him? Perhaps he hath not with success
Perform'd his flexure, his reins lost, or seat, or with the tress
His chariot fail'd him, and his mares have outraid with affright:
Stand up, try you your eyes, for mine hold with the second sight.
This seems to me th' Aetolian king, the Tydean Diomed.'

     'To you it seems so,' rusticly Ajax Oïleus said;
'Your words are suited to your eyes. Those mares lead still that led;
Eumelus owes them; and he still holds reins and place that did,
Not fall'n as you hoped: you must prate before us all, though last
In judgment of all: y'are too old, your tongue goes still too fast;   420
You must not talk so. Here are those that better thee, and look
For first place in the censure.' This Idomeneus took

In much disdain, and thus replied: 'Thou best in speeches worst,
Barbarous languag'd; others here might have reprov'd me first,
Not thou, unfitt'st of all. I hold a tripod with thee here,
Or cauldron, and our general make our equal arbiter,
Those horse are first, that when thou pay'st thou then mayst know.' This fir'd
Oileades more, and more than words this quarrel had inspir'd,
Had not Achilles rose, and us'd this pacifying speech:

   'No more: away with words in war. It toucheth both with breach   430
Of that which fits ye. Your deserts should others reprehend,
That give such foul terms: sit ye still, the men themselves will end
The strife betwixt you instantly; and either's own load bear
On his own shoulders. Then to both the first horse will appear,
And which is second.' These words us'd, Tydides was at hand.
His horse ran high, glanc'd on the way, and up they toss'd the sand
Thick on their coachman; on their pace their chariot deck'd with gold
Swiftly attended, no wheel seen, nor wheel's print in the mould
Impress'd behind them. These horse flew a flight, not ran a race.

   Arriv'd, amidst the lists they stood, sweat trickling down apace   440
Their high manes and their prominent breast; and down jump'd Diomed,
Laid up his scourge aloft the seat, and straight his prize was led
Home to his tent: rough Sthenelus laid quick hand on the dame,
And handled trivet, and sent both home by his men. Next came
Antilochus, that won with wiles, not swiftness of his horse,
Precedence of the gold-lock'd king, who yet maintain'd the course
So close, that not the king's own horse gat more before the wheel
Of his rich chariot, that might still the insecution feel
With the extreme hairs of his tail (and that sufficient close
Held to his leader: no great space it let him interpose,   450
Consider'd in so great a field) than Nestor's wily son
Gat of the king, now at his heels, though at the breach he won
A quoit's cast of him, which the king again at th' instant gain'd.
Aethe Agamemnonides that was so richly man'd
Gat strength still as she spent, which words her worth had prov'd with deeds,
Had more ground been allow'd the race, and coted far his steeds,
No question leaving for the prize. And now Meriones
A dart's cast came behind the king, his horse of speed much less,
Himself less skill'd t'importune them, and give a chariot wing.
Admetus' son was last, whose plight Achilles pitying,   460
Thus spake: 'Best man comes last, yet right must see his prize not least:
The second his deserts must bear, and Diomed the best.'

   He said, and all allow'd, and sure the mare had been his own,
Had not Antilochus stood forth, and in his answer shown
Good reason for his interest. 'Achilles,' he replied,

'I should be angry with you much to see this ratified.
Ought you to take from me my right, because his horse had wrong,
Himself being good? He should have us'd (as good men do) his tongue
In pray'r to their pow'rs that bless good (not trusting to his own)
Not to have been in this good last. His chariot overthrown   470
O'erthrew not me. Who's last? Who's first? Men's goodness without these
Is not our question. If his good you pity yet, and please
Princely to grace it, your tents hold a goodly deal of gold,
Brass, horse, sheep, women; out of these your bounty may be bold
To take a much more worthy prize than my poor merit seeks,
And give it here before my face, and all these, that the Greeks
May glorify your liberal hands. This prize I will not yield;
Who bears this (whatsoever man) he bears a tried field.
His hand and mine must change some blows.' Achilles laugh'd, and said:
    'If thy will be, Antilochus, I'll see Eumelus paid   480
Out of my tents; I'll give him th' arms which late I conquer'd in
Asteropaeus, forg'd of brass, and wav'd about with tin;
'Twill be a present worthy him.' This said, Automedon
He sent for them. He went, and brought, and to Admetus' son
Achilles gave them. He, well pleas'd, received. Then arose
Wrong'd Menelaus, much incens'd with young Antilochus.
He bent to speak, a herald took his sceptre, and gave charge
Of silence to the other Greeks; then did the king enlarge
The spleen he prison'd, uttering this: 'Antilochus! Till now
We grant thee wise, but in this act what wisdom utter'st thou?   490
Thou hast disgrac'd my virtue, wrong'd my horse, preferring thine,
Much their inferiors. But go to, princes, nor his nor mine
Judge of with favour; him nor me, lest any Grecian use
This scandal: "Menelaus won with Nestor's son's abuse
The prize in question; his horse worst, himself yet won the best
By pow'r and greatness. Yet because I would not thus contest,
To make parts taking, I'll be judge, and I suppose none here
Will blame my judgment; I'll do right: Antilochus, come near.
Come, noble gentleman, 'tis your place; swear by th' earth-circling god
(Standing before your chariot and horse, and that self rod   500
With which you scourged them in your hand) if both with will and wile
You did not cross my chariot.' He thus did reconcile
Grace with his disgrace, and with wit restor'd him to his wit.
'Now crave I patience, O king. Whatever was unfit,
Ascribe to much more youth in me than you; you more in age,
And more in excellence, know well the outraies that engage
All young men's actions; sharper wits, but duller wisdoms still
From us flow than from you; for which, curb with your wisdom, will.

The prize I thought mine, I yield yours; and, if you please, a prize
Of greater value to my tent I'll send for, and suffice   510
Your will at full, and instantly; for in this point of time,
I rather wish to be enjoin'd your favour's top to climb
Than to be falling all my time from height of such a grace,
O Jove-lov'd king, and of the gods receive a curse in place.'

    This said, he fetch'd his prize to him, and it rejoic'd him so,
That as corn-ears shine with the dew, yet having time to grow,
When fields set all their bristles up: in such a ruff wert thou,
O Menelaus, answering thus: 'Antilochus, I now
(Though I were angry) yield to thee, because I see th' hast wit,
When I thought not; thy youth hath got the mastery of thy spirit.   520
And yet for all this, 'tis more safe not to abuse at all
Great men, than, vent'ring, trust to wit to take up what may fall.
For no man in our host beside had easily calm'd my spleen,
Stirr'd with like tempest. But thyself hast a sustainer been
Of much affliction in my cause: so thy good father too,
And so thy brother, at thy suit; I therefore let all go,
Give thee the game here, though mine own, that all these may discern
King Menelaus bears a mind at no part proud or stern.'

    The king thus calm'd, Antilochus receiv'd, and gave the steed
To lov'd Noëmon to lead thence, and then receiv'd beside   530
The cauldron. Next, Meriones, for fourth game, was to have
Two talents gold. The fifth (unwon) renown'd Achilles gave
To reverend Nestor, being a bowl to set on either end,
Which through the press he carried him. 'Receive,' said he, 'old friend,
This gift, as funeral monument of my dear friend deceas'd,
Whom never you must see again. I make it his bequest
To you, as without any strife obtaining it from all.
Your shoulders must not undergo the churlish whorlbat's fall,
Wrestling is past you, strife in darts, the foot's celerity;
Harsh age in his years fetters you, and honour sets you free.'   540

    Thus gave he it; he took and joy'd, but ere he thank'd, he said:
'Now sure, my honourable son, in all points thou hast play'd
The comely orator. No more must I contend with nerves;
Feet fail, and hands; arms want that strength, that this and that swinge serves
Under your shoulders. Would to heav'n I were so young-chinn'd now,
And strength threw such a many of bones, to celebrate this show,
As when the Epians brought to fire (actively honouring thus)
King Amarynces' funerals in fair Buprasius.
His sons put prizes down for him, where not a man match'd me
Of all the Epians, or the sons of great-soul'd Aetolie;   550
No, nor the Pylians themselves, my countrymen. I beat

Great Clydomedeus, Enops' son, at buffets; at the feat
Of wrestling I laid under me one that against me rose,
Ancaeus, call'd Pleuronius. I made Iphiclus lose
The foot-game to me. At the spear I conquer'd Polidore
And strong Phyleus. Actor's sons (of all men) only bore
The palm at horse-race, conquering with lashing on more horse,
And envying my victory, because (before their course)
All the best games were gone with me. These men were twins; one was
A most sure guide, a most sure guide. The other gave the pass   560
With rod and metal. This was then. But now, young men must wage
These works, and my joints undergo the sad defects of age,
Though then I was another man; at that time I excell'd
Amongst th' heroës. But forth now, let th' other rites be held
For thy deceas'd friend; this thy gift in all kind part I take,
And much it joys my heart that still, for my true kindness' sake,
You give me memory. You perceive in what fit grace I stand
Amongst the Grecians; and to theirs, you set your graceful hand.
The gods give ample recompense of grace again to thee,
For this and all thy favours.' Thus back through the thrust drave he,   570
When he had stay'd out all the praise of old Neleides.

And now for buffets (that rough game) he order'd passages,
Proposing a laborious mule, of six years old, untam'd
And fierce in handling, brought and bound in that place where they gam'd,
And to the conquer'd a round cup; both which he thus proclaims:

'Atrides, and all friends of Greece, two men for these two games
I bid stand forth: who best can strike with high contracted fists
(Apollo giving him the wreath), know all about these lists,
Shall win a mule, patient of toil; the vanquish'd, this round cup.'

This utter'd, Panopeus' son, Epeus, straight stood up,   580
A tall huge man, that to the nail knew that rude sport of hand;
And (seizing the tough mule) thus spake: 'Now let some other stand
Forth for the cup; this mule is mine; at cuffs I boast me best:
Is 't not enough I am no soldier? Who is worthiest
At all works? None – not possible. At this yet this I say,
And will perform this: who stands forth, I'll burst him, I will bray
His bones as in a mortar; fetch surgeons enow to take
His corse from under me.' This speech did all men silent make;
At last stood forth Euryalus, a man god-like, and son
To king Mecisteus, the grandchild of honour'd Talaon.   590
He was so strong, that (coming once to Thebes, when Oedipus
Had like rites solemniz'd for him) he went victorious
From all the Thebans. This rare man Tydides would prepare,
Put on his girdle, oxhide cords, fair wrought, and spent much care

That he might conquer, heart'ned him, and taught him tricks. Both dress'd
Fit for th' affair, both forth were brought, then breast oppos'd to breast,
Fists against fists rose, and they join'd, rattling of jaws was there,
Gnashing of teeth, and heavy blows, dash'd blood out every where.
At length, Epeus spied clear way, rush'd in, and such a blow
Drave underneath the other's ear, that his neat limbs did strow   600
The knock'd earth; no more legs had he, but as a huge fish laid
Near to the cold-weed-gathering shore, is with a north flaw fraid,
Shoots back, and in the black deep hides: so, sent against the ground,
Was foil'd Euryalus, his strength so hid in more profound
Deeps of Epeus; who took up the intranc'd competitor,
About whom rush'd a crowd of friends, that through the blusters bore
His falt'ring knees, he spitting up thick clots of blood, his head
Totter'd of one side, his sense gone – when (to a by-place led)
Thither they brought him the round cup. Pelides then set forth
Prize for a wrestling: to the best a trivet that was worth   610
Twelve oxen, great and fit for fire; the conquer'd was t' obtain
A woman excellent in works, her beauty and her gain
Priz'd at four oxen. Up he stood, and thus proclaim'd: 'Arise,
You wrestlers, that will prove for these.' Out stepp'd the ample size
Of mighty Ajax, huge in strength; to him, Laertes' son,
That crafty one, as huge in sleight. Their ceremony done
Of making ready, forth they stepp'd, catch elbows with strong hands;
And as the beams of some high house crack with a storm, yet stands
The house, being built by well-skill'd men: so crack'd their backbones, wrinch'd
With horrid twitches. In their sides, arms, shoulders (all bepinch'd)   620
Ran thick the wales red with the blood, ready to start out; both
Long'd for the conquest and the prize, yet show'd no play, being loth
To lose both; nor could Ithacus stir Ajax, nor could he
Hale down Ulysses, being more strong than with mere strength to be
Hurl'd from all vantage of his sleight. Tir'd then with tugging play,
Great Ajax Telamonius said: 'Thou wisest man, or lay
My face up, or let me lay thine; let Jove take care for these.'
This said, he hoist him up to air, when Laertiades
His wiles forgat not; Ajax' thigh he struck behind, and flat
He on his back fell; on his breast, Ulysses. Wonder'd at   630
Was this of all; all stood amaz'd. Then the-much-suffering-man
(Divine Ulysses) at next close the Telamonian
A little rais'd from earth – not quite, but with his knee implied
Lock'd legs; and down fell both on earth, close by each other's side,
Both fill'd with dust, but starting up. The third close they had made,
Had not Achilles' self stood up, restraining them, and bade:
'No more tug one another thus, nor moil yourselves; receive

Prize equal; conquest crowns ye both, the lists to others leave.'
　　They heard, and yielded willingly; brush'd off the dust, and on
Put other vests. Pelides then, to those that swiftest run,   640
Propos'd another prize: a bowl, beyond comparison
(Both for the size and workmanship) past all the bowls of earth;
It held six measures, silver all, but had his special worth
For workmanship, receiving form from those ingenious men
Of Sidon: the Phoenicians made choice and brought it then
Along the green sea, giving it to Thoas; by degrees
It came t' Euneus, Jason's son, who young Priamides
(Lycaon) of Achilles' friend bought with it; and this, here,
Achilles made best game for him that best his feet could bear.
For second he propos'd an ox, a huge one and a fat;   650
And half a talent gold for last. These thus he set them at:
　　'Rise, you that will assay for these.' Forth stepp'd Oïleades;
Ulysses answer'd, and the third was one esteem'd past these
For footmanship, Antilochus. All rank'd, Achilles show'd
The race-scope. From the start they glid; Oïleades bestow'd
His feet the swiftest; close to him flew god-like Ithacus;
And as a lady at her loom, being young and beauteous,
Her silk-shuttle close to her breast (with grace that doth inflame,
And her white hand) lifts quick and oft, in drawing from her frame
Her gentle thread, which she unwinds, with ever at her breast   660
Gracing her fair hand: so close still, and with such interest
In all men's likings, Ithacus unwound, and spent the race
By him before; took out his steps, with putting in their place
Promptly and gracefully his own, sprinkled the dust before,
And clouded with his breath his head. So facile he bore
His royal person, that he struck shouts from the Greeks, with thirst
That he should conquer; though he flew, yet 'Come, come, O come first,'
Ever they cried to him, and this ev'n his wise breast did move
To more desire of victory; it made him pray, and prove
Minerva's aid (his fautress still): 'O goddess, hear,' said he,   670
'And to my feet stoop with thy help, now happy fautress be.'
　　She was; and light made all his limbs, and now (both near their crown)
Minerva tripp'd up Ajax' heels, and headlong he fell down
Amids the ordure of the beasts, there negligently left
Since they were slain there; and by this, Minerva's friend bereft
Oïleades of that rich bowl, and left his lips, nose, eyes,
Ruthfully smear'd. The fat ox yet he seiz'd for second prize,
Held by the horn, spit out the tail, and thus spake all besmear'd:
　　'O villainous chance! This Ithacus so highly is endear'd
To this Minerva, that her hand is ever in his deeds: 680

She, like his mother, nestles him, for from her it proceeds
(I know) that I am us'd thus.' This all in light laughter cast,
Amongst whom quick Antilochus laugh'd out his coming last,
Thus wittily: 'Know, all my friends, that all times past, and now,
The gods most honour most-liv'd men. Oïleades ye know
More old than I, but Ithacus is of the foremost race,
First generation of men. Give the old man his grace.
They count him of the green-hair'd eld – they may, or in his flow'r,
For not our greatest flourisher can equal him in pow'r
Of foot-strife, but Aeacides.' Thus sooth'd he Thetis' son,   690
Who thus accepted it: 'Well, youth, your praises shall not run
With unrewarded feet on mine. Your half a talent's prize
I'll make a whole one; take you, sir.' He took, and joy'd. Then flies
Another game forth: Thetis' son set in the lists a lance,
A shield, and helmet, being th' arms Sarpedon did advance
Against Patroclus; and he priz'd. And thus he nam'd the address:
    'Stand forth two the most excellent, arm'd; and before all these
Give mutual onset to the touch and wounds of either's flesh:
Who first shall wound, through other's arms, his blood appearing fresh,
Shall win this sword, silver'd and hatch'd; the blade is right of Thrace,   700
Asteropaeus yielded it. These arms shall part their grace
With either's valour; and the men I'll liberally feast
At my pavilion.' To this game, the first man that address'd
Was Ajax Telamonius; to him, king Diomed;
Both, in oppos'd parts of the press full arm'd, both entered
The lists amids the multitude, put looks on so austere,
And join'd so roughly, that amaze surpris'd the Greeks, in fear
Of either's mischief. Thrice they threw their fierce darts, and clos'd thrice.
Then Ajax struck through Diomed's shield, but did no prejudice;
His curets sav'd him. Diomed's dart still over shoulders flew,   710
Still mounting with the spirit it bore. And now rough Ajax grew
So violent, that the Greeks cried: 'Hold, no more; let them no more;
Give equal prize to either.' Yet the sword propos'd before
For him did best, Achilles gave to Diomed. Then a stone
(In fashion of a sphere) he show'd, of no invention,
But natural, only melted through with iron. 'Twas the bowl
That king Eëtion us'd to hurl: but he, bereft of soul
By great Achilles, to the fleet, with store of other prize,
He brought it; and propos'd it now, both for the exercise
And prize itself. He stood, and said: 'Rise you that will approve   720
Your arms' strengths now in this brave strife: his vigour that can move
This furthest, needs no game but this, for reach he ne'er so far
With large fields of his own in Greece (and so needs for his car,

His plough, or other tools of thrift, much iron), I'll able this
For five revolved years no need shall use his messages
To any town to furnish him, this only bowl shall yield
Iron enough for all affairs.' This said, to try this field,
First Polypaetes issued, next Leontaeus, third
Great Ajax, huge Epeus fourth. Yet he was first that stirr'd
That mine of iron. Up it went, and up he toss'd it so,   730
That laughter took up all the field. The next man that did throw
Was Leontaeus; Ajax third, who gave it such a hand,
That far past both their marks it flew. But now 'twas to be mann'd
By Polypaetes, and as far as at an ox that strays
A herdsman can swing out his goad, so far did he outraise
The stone past all men; all the field rose in a shout to see't.
About him flock'd his friends, and bore the royal game to fleet.
     For archery he then set forth ten axes edg'd two ways,
And ten of one edge. On the shore, far off, he caus'd to raise
A ship-mast, to whose top they tied a fearful dove by th' foot,   740
At which all shot, the game put thus: he that the dove could shoot,
Nor touch the string that fast'ned her, the two-edg'd tools should bear
All to the fleet. Who touch'd the string, and miss'd the dove, should share
The one-edg'd axes. This propos'd, king Teucer's force arose,
And with him rose Meriones; and now lots must dispose
Their shooting first; both which let fall into a helm of brass;
First Teucer's came, and first he shot; and his cross fortune was
To shoot the string, the dove untouch'd: Apollo did envy
His skill, since not to him he vow'd (being god of archery)
A first fall'n lamb. The bitter shaft yet cut in two the cord,   750
That down fell, and the dove aloft up to the welkin soar'd.
The Greeks gave shouts; Meriones first made a hearty vow
To sacrifice a first-fall'n lamb to him that rules the bow,
And then fell to his aim, his shaft being ready nock'd before.
He spied her in the clouds that here, there, everywhere did soar;
Yet at her height he reach'd her side, struck her quite through, and down
The shaft fell at his feet; the dove the mast again did crown.
There hung the head, and all her plumes were ruffled, she stark dead,
And there (far off from him) she fell. The people wondered,
And stood astonish'd, th' archer pleas'd. Aeacides then shows   760
A long lance, and a cauldron new, engrail'd with twenty hues,
Priz'd at an ox. These games were show'd for men at darts, and then
Up rose the general of all, up rose the king of men;
Up rose late-crown'd Meriones. Achilles (seeing the king
Do him this grace) prevents more deed, his royal offering
Thus interrupting: 'King of men, we well conceive how far

Thy worth superior is to all, how much most singular
Thy pow'r is, and thy skill in darts; accept then this poor prize
Without contention, and (your will pleas'd with what I advise)
Afford Meriones the lance.' The king was nothing slow   770
To that fit grace. Achilles then the brass lance did bestow
On good Meriones. The king his present would not save,
But to renown'd Talthybius the goodly cauldron gave.

THE END OF THE TWENTY-THIRD BOOK

BOOK TWENTY-FOUR

The Argument

Jove, entertaining care of Hector's corse,
Sends Thetis to her son for his remorse,
And fit dismission of it. Iris then
He sends to Priam, willing him to gain
His son for ransom. He, by Hermes led,
Gets through Achilles' guards, sleeps deep and dead
Cast on them by his guide. When, with access
And humble suit made to Aeacides,
He gains the body, which to Troy he bears,
And buries it with feasts, buried in tears.

Another Argument

Omega sings the exequies,
And Hector's redemptory prize.

BOOK TWENTY-FOUR

THE GAMES PERFORM'd, the soldiers wholly dispers'd to fleet,
Supper and sleep their only care. Constant Achilles yet
Wept for his friend; nor sleep itself, that all things doth subdue,
Could touch at him. This way and that he turn'd, and did renew
His friend's dear memory, his grace in managing his strength,
And his strength's greatness – how life rack'd into their utmost length
Griefs, battles, and the wraths of seas, in their joint sufferance;
Each thought of which turn'd to a tear. Sometimes he would advance
(In tumbling on the shore) his side, sometimes his face, then turn
Flat on his bosom, start upright. Although he saw the morn   10
Show sea and shore his extasy, he left not till at last
Rage varied his distraction. Horse, chariot, in haste
He call'd for; and (those join'd) the corse was to his chariot tied,
And thrice about the sepulchre he made his fury ride,
Dragging the person. All this past, in his pavilion
Rest seiz'd him, but with Hector's corse his rage had never done,
Still suffering it t' oppress the dust. Apollo yet, even dead,
Pitied the prince, and would not see inhuman tyranny fed
With more pollution of his limbs, and therefore cover'd round
His person with his golden shield, that rude dogs might not wound   20
His manly lineaments (which threat Achilles cruelly
Had us'd in fury). But now heav'n let fall a general eye
Of pity on him; the blest gods persuaded Mercury
(Their good observer) to his stealth; and every deity
Stood pleas'd with it – Juno except, green Neptune, and the Maid
Grac'd with the blue eyes. All their hearts stood hatefully appaid
Long since, and held it as at first to Priam, Ilion,
And all his subjects, for the rape of his licentious son,
Proud Paris, that despis'd these dames in their divine access
Made to his cottage, and prais'd her that his sad wantonness   30
So costly nourish'd. The twelfth morn now shin'd on the delay
Of Hector's rescue, and then spake the deity of the day
Thus to th' immortals: 'Shameless gods, authors of ill ye are,
To suffer ill. Hath Hector's life at all times show'd his care
Of all your rights, in burning thighs of beeves and goats to you?

And are your cares no more of him? Vouchsafe ye not ev'n now
(Ev'n dead) to keep him, that his wife, his mother, and his son,
Father and subjects, may be mov'd to those deeds he hath done,
See'ng you preserve him that serv'd you, and sending to their hands
His person for the rites of fire? Achilles, that withstands   40
All help to others, you can help – one that hath neither heart
Nor soul within him that will move or yield to any part
That fits a man, but lion-like, uplandish, and mere wild,
Slave to his pride, and all his nerves being naturally compil'd
Of eminent strength, stalks out and preys upon a silly sheep:
And so fares this man – that fit ruth that now should draw so deep
In all the world being lost in him, and shame (a quality
Of so much weight that both it helps and hurts excessively
Men in their manners) is not known, nor hath the power to be,
In this man's being. Other men a greater loss than he   50
Have undergone – a son, suppose, or brother of one womb –
Yet, after dues of woes and tears, they bury in his tomb
All their deplorings. Fates have given to all that are true men
True manly patience, but this man so soothes his bloody vein
That no blood serves it; he must have divine-soul'd Hector bound
To his proud chariot, and danc'd in a most barbarous round
About his lov'd friend's sepulchre when he is slain: 'tis vile,
And draws no profit after it. But let him now awhile
Mark but our angers; his is spent; let all his strength take heed
It tempts not our wraths; he begets, in this outrageous deed,   60
The dull earth with his fury's hate. White-wristed Juno said
(Being much incens'd): 'This doom is one that thou wouldst have obey'd,
Thou bearer of the silver bow, that we in equal care
And honour should hold Hector's worth with him that claims a share
In our deservings. Hector suck'd a mortal woman's breast,
Aeacides a goddess's; ourself had interest
Both in his infant nourishment and bringing up with state,
And to the human Peleus we gave his bridal mate,
Because he had th' immortals love. To celebrate the feast
Of their high nuptials, every god was glad to be a guest,   70
And thou fedd'st of his father's cates, touching thy harp in grace
Of that beginning of our friend, whom thy perfidious face
(In his perfection) blusheth not to match with Priam's son,
O thou that to betray and shame art still companion.'
    Jove thus receiv'd her: 'Never give these broad terms to a god.
Those two men shall not be compar'd; and yet of all that trod
The well-pav'd Ilion, none so dear to all the deities
As Hector was, at least to me. For off'rings most of prize

His hands would never pretermit. Our altars ever stood
Furnish'd with banquets fitting us; odours and every good   80
Smok'd in our temples; and for this (foreseeing it) his fate
We mark'd with honour, which must stand; but to give stealth estate
In his deliv'rance, shun we that; nor must we favour one
To shame another. Privily, with wrong to Thetis' son,
We must not work out Hector's right. There is a ransom due,
And open course by laws of arms; in which must humbly sue
The friends of Hector. Which just mean if any god would stay
And use the other, 'twould not serve, for Thetis night and day
Is guardian to him. But would one call Iris hither, I
Would give directions that for gifts the Trojan king should buy   90
His Hector's body, which the son of Thetis shall resign.'

This said, his will was done; the dame that doth in vapours shine,
Dewy and thin, footed with storms, jump'd to the sable seas
'Twixt Samos and sharp Imber's cliffs; the lake groan'd with the press
Of her rough feet, and (plummet-like, put in an ox's horn
That bears death to the raw-fed fish) she div'd, and found forlorn
Thetis, lamenting her son's fate, who was in Troy to have
(Far from his country) his death serv'd. Close to her Iris stood,
And said: 'Rise, Thetis; prudent Jove (whose counsels thirst not blood)
Calls for thee.' Thetis answer'd her with asking: 'What's the cause   100
The great god calls? My sad pow'rs fear'd to break th' immortal laws,
In going, fill'd with griefs, to heav'n. But he sets snares for none
With colour'd counsels; not a word of him but shall be done.'

She said, and took a sable veil – a blacker never wore
A heav'nly shoulder – and gave way. Swift Iris swum before,
About both roll'd the brackish waves. They took their banks, and flew
Up to Olympus, where they found Saturnius (far-of-view)
Spher'd with heav'n's ever-being states. Minerva rose, and gave
Her place to Thetis, near to Jove, and Juno did receive
Her entry with a cup of gold, in which she drank to her,   110
Grac'd her with comfort; and the cup to her hand did refer.
She drank, resigning it. And then the sire of men and gods
Thus entertain'd her: 'Com'st thou up to these our blest abodes,
Fair goddess Thetis, yet art sad, and that in so high kind
As passeth suff'rance? This I know, and tried thee, and now find
Thy will by mine rul'd, which is rule to all worlds' government,
Besides this trial yet, this cause sent down for thy ascent,
Nine days contention hath been held amongst th' immortals here,
For Hector's person and thy son; and some advices were
To have our good spy Mercury steal from thy son the corse: 120
But that reproach I kept far off, to keep in future force

Thy former love and reverence. Haste then, and tell thy son
The gods are angry; and myself take that wrong he hath done
To Hector in worst part of all: the rather, since he still
Detains his person. Charge him then, if he respect my will
For any reason, to resign slain Hector; I will send
Iris to Priam to redeem his son, and recommend
Fit ransom to Achilles' grace; in which right he may joy,
And end his vain grief.' To this charge bright Thetis did employ
Instant endeavour. From heav'n's tops she reach'd Achilles' tent,   130
Found him still sighing, and some friends with all their compliments
Soothing his humour, other some with all contention
Dressing his dinner, all their pains and skills consum'd upon
A huge wool-bearer, slaughter'd there. His rev'rend mother then
Came near, took kindly his fair hand, and ask'd him: 'Dear son, when
Will sorrow leave thee? How long time wilt thou thus eat thy heart,
Fed with no other food, nor rest?' Twere good thou wouldst divert
Thy friend's love to some lady; cheer thy spirits with such kind parts
As she can quit thy grace withal; the joy of thy deserts
I shall not long have; death is near, and thy all-conquering fate,   140
Whose haste thou must not haste with grief, but understand the state
Of things belonging to thy life, which quickly order. I
Am sent from Jove t' advertise thee that every deity
Is angry with thee, himself most, that rage thus reigns in thee
Still to keep Hector. Quit him then, and for fit ransom free
His injur'd person.' He replied: 'Let him come that shall give
The ransom, and the person take. Jove's pleasure must deprive
Men of all pleasures.' This good speech, and many more, the son
And mother us'd, in ear of all the naval station.

    And now to holy Ilion Saturnius Iris sent: 150
'Go, swift-foot Iris, bid Troy's king bear fit gifts, and content
Achilles for his son's release; but let him greet alone
The Grecian navy, not a man excepting such a one
As may his horse and chariot guide, a herald, or one old,
Attending him; and let him take his Hector. Be he bold,
Discourag'd nor with death nor fear; wise Mercury shall guide
His passage till the prince be near. And (he gone) let him ride
Resolv'd, ev'n in Achilles' tent. He shall not touch the state
Of his high person, nor admit the deadliest desperate
Of all about him. For (though fierce) he is not yet unwise,   160
Nor inconsiderate, nor a man past awe of deities,
But passing free and curious to do a suppliant grace.'

    This said, the Rainbow to her feet tied whirlwinds, and the place
Reach'd instantly: the heavy court Clamour and Mourning fill'd,

The sons all set about the sire; and there stood Grief, and still'd
Tears on their garments. In the midst the old king sate, his weed
All wrinkled; head and neck dust fil'd, the princesses his seed,
The princesses his sons' fair wives, all mourning by; the thought
Of friends so many and so good being turn'd so soon to nought
By Grecian hands consum'd their youth, rain'd beauty from their eyes.   170
    Iris came near the king; her sight shook all his faculties,
And therefore spake she soft, and said: 'Be glad, Dardanides.
Of good occurrents, and none ill, am I ambassadress.
Jove greets thee, who in care (as much as he is distant) deigns
Eye to thy sorrows, pitying thee. My embassy contains
This charge to thee from him; he wills thou shouldst redeem thy son,
Bear gifts t' Achilles, cheer him so. But visit him alone;
None but some herald let attend, thy mules and chariot
To manage for thee. Fear nor death let daunt thee; Jove hath got
Hermes to guide thee; who as near to Thetis' son as needs   180
Shall guard thee: and being once with him, nor his nor others' deeds
Stand touch'd with, he will all contain. Nor is he mad, nor vain,
Nor impious; but with all his nerves studious to entertain
One that submits with all fit grace.' Thus vanish'd she like wind.
    He mules and chariot calls, his sons bids see them join'd, and bind
A trunk behind it; he himself down to his wardrobe goes,
Built all of cedar, highly roof'd, and odoriferous,
That much stuff, worth the sight, contain'd. To him he call'd his queen,
Thus greeting her: 'Come, hapless dame, an angel I have seen,
Sent down from Jove, that bade me free our dear son from the fleet   190
With ransom pleasing to our foe. What holds thy judgment meet?
My strength and spirit lays high charge on all my being, to bear
The Greeks' worst, vent'ring through their host.' The queen cried out to hear
His vent'rous purpose, and replied: 'O whither now is fled
The late discretion that renown'd thy grave and knowing head
In foreign and thine own rul'd realms, that thus thou dar'st assay
Sight of that man, in whose brow sticks the horrible decay
Of sons so many and so strong? Thy heart is iron, I think.
If this stern man (whose thirst of blood makes cruelty his drink)
Take, or but see thee, thou art dead. He nothing pities woe,   200
Nor honours age. Without his sight, we have enough to do
To mourn with thought of him; keep we our palace, weep we here,
Our son is past our helps. Those throes, that my deliverers were
Of his unhappy lineaments, told me they should be torn
With black-foot dogs. Almighty fate, that black hour he was born,
Spun, in his springing thread, that end; far from his parents' reach,
This bloody fellow then ordain'd to be their mean, this wretch,

Whose stony liver would to heav'n I might devour, my teeth
My sons' revengers made. Curst Greek, he gave him not his death
Doing an ill work; he alone fought for his country, he   210
Fled not, nor fear'd, but stood his worst, and cursed policy
Was his undoing.' He replied: 'Whatever was his end,
Is not our question; we must now use all means to defend
His end from scandal: from which act dissuade not my just will,
Nor let me nourish in my house a bird presaging ill
To my good actions: 'tis in vain. Had any earthly spirit
Given this suggestion – if our priests or soothsayers, challenging merit
Of prophets – I might hold it false, and be the rather mov'd
To keep my palace; but these ears and these self eyes approv'd
It was a goddess; I will go, for not a word she spake   220
I know was idle. If it were, and that my fate will make
Quick riddance of me at the fleet, kill me, Achilles; come,
When getting to thee, I shall find a happy dying room
On Hector's bosom, when enough thirst of my tears finds there
Quench to his fervour.' This resolv'd, the works most fair and dear
Of his rich screens he brought abroad: twelve veils wrought curiously,
Twelve plain gowns, and as many suits of wealthy tapestry,
As many mantles, horsemen's coats, ten talents of fine gold,
Two tripods, cauldrons four, a bowl whose value he did hold
Beyond all price, presented by th' ambassadors of Thrace.   230
The old king nothing held too dear to rescue from disgrace
His gracious Hector. Forth he came. At entry of his court
The Trojan citizens so press'd, that this opprobrious sort
Of check he us'd: 'Hence, cast-aways; away, ye impious crew!
Are not your griefs enough at home? What come ye here to view?
Care ye for my griefs? Would ye see how miserable I am?
Is 't not enough, imagine ye? Ye might know, ere ye came,
What such a son's loss weigh'd with me. But know this for your pains,
Your houses have the weaker doors: the Greeks will find their gains
The easier for his loss, be sure: but O Troy, ere I see   240
Thy ruin, let the doors of hell receive and ruin me.'

   Thus with his sceptre set he on the crowding citizens,
Who gave back, seeing him so urge. And now he entertains
His sons as roughly: Hellenus, Paris, Hippothous,
Pammon, divine Agathones, renown'd Deiphobus,
Agavus, and Antiphonus, and last, not least in arms,
The strong Polites; these nine sons the violence of his harms
Help'd him to vent in these sharp terms: 'Haste, you infamous brood,
And get my chariot; would to heav'n that all the abject blood
In all your veins had Hector scus'd: O me, accursed man,   250

All my good sons are gone; my light the shades Cimmerian
Have swallow'd from me: I have lost Mestor, surnam'd the fair;
Troilus, that ready knight at arms, that made his field repair
Ever so prompt and joyfully; and Hector, amongst men
Esteem'd god – not from mortal's seed, but of th' eternal strain
He seem'd to all eyes. These are gone; you that survive are base,
Liars and common freebooters: all faulty, not a grace
But in your heels, in all your parts; dancing companions
Ye all are excellent: hence, ye brats; love ye to hear my moans?
Will ye not get my chariot? Command it quickly; fly,   260
That I may perfect this dear work.' This all did terrify,
And straight his mule-drawn chariot came, to which they fast did bind
The trunk with gifts: and then came forth, with an afflicted mind,
Old Hecuba. In her right hand a bowl of gold she bore,
With sweet wine crown'd; stood near, and said: 'Receive this, and implore
(With sacrificing it to Jove) thy safe return. I see
Thy mind likes still to go, though mine dislikes it utterly.
Pray to the black-cloud-gathering god (Idaean Jove) that views
All Troy, and all her miseries, that he will deign to use
His most lov'd bird to ratify thy hopes, that, her broad wing   270
Spread on thy right hand, thou mayst know thy zealous offering
Accepted, and thy safe return confirm'd; but if he fail,
Fail thy intent, though never so it labours to prevail.'
    'This I refuse not,' he replied, 'for no faith is so great
In Jove's high favour, but it must with held-up hands intreat.'
This said, the chambermaid that held the ewer and basin by,
He bad pour water on his hands; when looking to the sky,
He took the bowl, did sacrifice, and thus implor'd: 'O Jove,
From Ida using thy commands, in all deserts above
All other gods, vouchsafe me safe, and pity in the sight   280
Of great Achilles: and for trust to that wish'd grace, excite
Thy swift-wing'd messenger, most strong, most of air's region lov'd,
To soar on my right hand; which sight may firmly see approv'd
Thy former summons, and my speed.' He pray'd, and heav'n's king heard,
And instantly cast from his fist air's all-commanding bird,
The black-wing'd huntress, perfectest of all fowls, which gods call
Percnos, the eagle. And how broad the chamber nuptial
Of any mighty man hath doors, such breadth cast either wing,
Which now she us'd, and spread them wide on right hand of the king.
All saw it, and rejoic'd, and up to chariot he arose,   290
Drave forth, the portal and the porch resounding as he goes.
His friends all follow'd him, and mourn'd as if he went to die;
And bringing him past town to field, all left him, and the eye

Of Jupiter was then his guard, who pitied him, and us'd
These words to Hermes: 'Mercury, thy help hath been profus'd
Ever with most grace, in consorts of travailers distress'd.
Now consort Priam to the fleet: but so, that not the least
Suspicion of him be attain'd, till at Achilles' tent
Thy convoy hath arriv'd him safe.' This charge incontinent
He put in practice. To his feet his feather'd shoes he tied,   300
Immortal, and made all of gold, with which he us'd to ride
The rough sea and th' unmeasur'd earth, and equall'd in his pace
The puffs of wind. Then took he up his rod, that hath the grace
To shut what eyes he lists with sleep, and open them again,
In strongest trances. This he held, flew forth, and did attain
To Troy and Hellespontus strait: then like a fair young prince,
First-down-chinn'd, and of such a grace as makes his looks convince
Contending eyes to view him, forth he went to meet the king.
He, having pass'd the mighty tomb of Ilus, watering
His mules in Xanthus, the dark even fell on the earth; and then   310
Idaeus (guider of the mules) discern'd this grace of men,
And spake afraid to Priamus: 'Beware, Dardanides,
Our states ask counsel: I discern the dangerous access
Of some man near us; now I fear we perish. Is it best
To fly, or kiss his knees, and ask his ruth of men distress'd?'
      Confusion struck the king, cold fear extremely quench'd his veins;
Upright upon his languishing head his hair stood, and the chains
Of strong amaze bound all his pow'rs. To both which then came near
The prince turn'd deity, took his hand, and thus bespake the peer:
      'To what place, father, driv'st thou out through solitary night,   320
When others sleep? Give not the Greeks sufficient cause of fright
To these late travails, being so near, and such vow'd enemies?
Of all which, if with all this load any should cast his eyes
On thy adventures, what would then thy mind esteem thy state –
Thyself old, and thy follower old? Resistance could not rate
At any value; as for me, be sure I mind no harm
To thy grave person, but against the hurt of others arm.
Mine own lov'd father did not get a greater love in me
To his good than thou dost to thine.' He answer'd: 'The degree
Of danger in my course, fair son, is nothing less than that   330
Thou urgest; but some god's fair hand puts in for my safe state,
That sends so sweet a guardian, in this so stern a time
Of night and danger, as thyself, that all grace in his prime
Of body and of beauty show'st, all answer'd with a mind
So knowing, that it cannot be but of some blessed kind
Thou art descended.' 'Not untrue,' said Hermes, 'thy conceit

In all this holds; but further truth relate, if of such weight
As I conceive thy carriage be, and that thy care conveys
Thy goods of most price to more guard? Or go ye all your ways,
Freighted from holy Ilion, so excellent a son   340
As thou hadst (being your special strength) fall'n to destruction,
Whom no Greek better'd for his fight?' 'O, what art thou,' said he,
'Most worthy youth, of what race born, that thus recount'st to me
My wretched son's death with such truth?' 'Now, father,' he replied,
'You tempt me far, in wond'ring how the death was signified
Of your divine son, to a man so mere a stranger here
As you hold me; but I am one that oft have seen him bear
His person like a god in field; and when in heaps he slew
The Greeks, all routed to their fleet, his so victorious view
Made me admire, not feel his hand, because Aeacides,   350
Incens'd, admitted not our fight, myself being of access
To his high person, serving him, and both to Ilion
In one ship sail'd. Besides, by birth I breathe a Myrmidon,
Polyctor (call'd the rich) my sire, declin'd with age like you.
Six sons he hath, and me a seventh, and all those six live now
In Phthia, since all casting lots, my chance did only fall
To follow hither. Now for walk I left my general.
To-morrow all the sun-burn'd Greeks will circle Troy with arms,
The princes rage to be withheld so idly; your alarms
Not giv'n half hot enough, they think, and can contain no more.'   360
He answer'd: 'If you serve the prince, let me be bold t' implore
This grace of thee, and tell me true, lies Hector here at fleet,
Or have the dogs his flesh?' He said, 'Nor dogs nor fowl have yet
Touch'd at his person; still he lies at fleet, and in the tent
Of our great captain, who indeed is much too negligent
Of his fit usage: but though now twelve days have spent their heat
On his cold body, neither worms with any taint have eat,
Nor putrefaction perish'd it; yet ever when the morn
Lifts her divine light from the sea, unmercifully borne
About Patroclus' sepulchre, it bears his friend's disdain,   370
Bound to his chariot; but no fits of further outrage reign
In his distemper: you would muse to see how deep a dew
Ev'n steeps the body, all the blood wash'd off, no slend'rest show
Of gore or quitture, but his wounds all clos'd, though many were
Open'd about him. Such a love the blest immortals bear,
Ev'n dead, to thy dear son, because his life show'd love to them.'

   He joyful answer'd: 'O my son, it is a grace supreme
In any man to serve the gods. And I must needs say this:
For no cause (having season fit) my Hector's hands would miss

Advancement to the gods with gifts, and therefore do not they   380
Miss his remembrance after death. Now let an old man pray
Thy graces to receive this cap, and keep it for my love;
Nor leave me till the gods and thee have made my prayers approve
Achilles' pity, by thy guide brought to his princely tent.'

    Hermes replied: 'You tempt me now, old king, to a consent
Far from me, though youth aptly errs. I secretly receive
Gifts, that I cannot broadly vouch? Take graces that will give
My lord dishonour, or what he knows not, or will esteem
Perhaps unfit? Such briberies perhaps at first may seem
Sweet and secure, but futurely they still prove sour, and breed   390
Both fear and danger. I could wish thy grave affairs did need
My guide to Argos, either shipp'd or lackeying by thy side,
And would be studious in thy guard, so nothing could be tried
But care in me to keep thee safe, for that I could excuse
And vouch to all men.' These words past, he put the deeds in use
For which Jove sent him; up he leapt to Priam's chariot,
Took scourge and reins, and blew in strength to his free steeds, and got
The naval tow'rs and deep dike straight. The guards were all at meat;
Those he enslumber'd, op'd the ports, and in he safely let
Old Priam with his wealthy prize. Forthwith they reach'd the tent   400
Of great Achilles. Large and high, and in his most ascent
A shaggy roof of seedy reeds mown from the meads, a hall
Of state they made their king in it, and strengthen'd it withal
Thick with fir rafters; whose approach was let in by a door
That had but one bar, but so big that three men evermore
Rais'd it to shut, three fresh take down; which yet Aeacides
Would shut and ope himself. And this with far more ease
Hermes set ope, ent'ring the king; then leap'd from horse, and said:

    'Now know, old king, that Mercury (a god) hath giv'n this aid
To thy endeavour, sent by Jove; and now away must I: 410
For men must envy thy estate, to see a deity
Affect a man thus: enter thou, embrace Achilles' knee,
And by his sire, son, mother, pray his ruth and grace to thee.'

    This said, he high Olympus reach'd. The king then left his coach
To grave Idaeus, and went on, made his resolv'd approach,
And enter'd in a goodly room, where with his princes, sate
Jove-lov'd Achilles at their feast; two only kept the state
Of his attendance, Alcimus and lord Automedon.
At Priam's entry, a great time Achilles gaz'd upon
His wonder'd-at approach, nor ate; the rest did nothing see,   420
While close he came up, with his hands fast holding the bent knee
Of Hector's conqueror, and kiss'd that large man-slaught'ring hand,

That much blood from his sons had drawn. And as in some strange land,
And great man's house, a man is driv'n (with that abhorr'd dismay
That follows wilful bloodshed still, his fortune being to slay
One whose blood cries aloud for his) to plead protection
In such a miserable plight as frights the lookers on:
In such a stupified estate Achilles sate to see,
So unexpected, so in night, and so incredibly,
Old Priam's entry; all his friends one on another star'd　　　430
To see his strange looks, seeing no cause. Thus Priam then prepar'd
His son's redemption: 'See in me, O god-like Thetis' son,
Thy aged father, and perhaps even now being outrun
With some of my woes: neighbour foes (thou absent) taking time
To do him mischief, no mean left to terrify the crime
Of his oppression; yet he hears thy graces still survive,
And joys to hear it, hoping still to see thee safe arrive
From ruin'd Troy. But I (curs'd man) of all my race shall live
To see none living. Fifty sons the deities did give
My hopes to live in, all alive when near our trembling shore　　　440
The Greek ships harbour'd, and one womb nineteen of those sons bore.
Now Mars a number of their knees hath strengthless left, and he
That was (of all) my only joy, and Troy's sole guard, by thee
(Late fighting for his country) slain, whose tender'd person now
I come to ransom. Infinite is that I offer you,
Myself conferring it, expos'd alone to all your odds,
Only imploring right of arms. Achilles, fear the gods,
Pity an old man, like thy sire, different in only this,
That I am wretcheder, and bear that weight of miseries
That never man did, my curs'd lips enforc'd to kiss that hand　　　450
That slew my children.' This mov'd tears; his father's name did stand
(Mention'd by Priam) in much help, to his compassion,
And mov'd Aeacides so much he could not look upon
The weeping father. With his hand he gently put away
His grave face; calm remission now did mutually display
Her pow'r in either's heaviness: old Priam to record
His son's death, and his deathsman see, his tears and bosom pour'd
Before Achilles. At his feet he laid his rev'rend head;
Achilles' thoughts now with his sire, now with his friend, were fed.
Betwixt both sorrow fill'd the tent. But now Aeacides　　　460
(Satiate at all parts with the ruth of their calamities)
Starts up, and up he rais'd the king. His milk-white head and beard
With pity he beheld, and said: 'Poor man, thy mind is scar'd
With much affliction; how durst thy person thus alone
Venture on his sight, that hath slain so many a worthy son,

And so dear to thee? Thy old heart is made of iron. Sit,
And settle we our woes, though huge, for nothing profits it.
Cold mourning wastes but our lives' heats. The gods have destinate
That wretched mortals must live sad. 'Tis the immortal state
Of deity that lives secure. Two tuns of gifts there lie   470
In Jove's gate, one of good, one ill, that our mortality
Maintain, spoil, order; which when Jove doth mix to any man,
One while he frolics, one while mourns. If of his mournful can
A man drinks only, only wrongs he doth expose him to.
Sad hunger, in th' abundant earth, doth toss him to and fro,
Respected nor of gods nor men. The mix'd cup Peleus drank.
Ev'n from his birth, heav'n blest his life; he liv'd not that could thank
The gods for such rare benefits as set forth his estate.
He reign'd among his Myrmidons most rich, most fortunate,
And (though a mortal) had his bed deck'd with a deathless dame.   480
And yet with all this good, one ill god mix'd, that takes all name
From all that goodness – his name now (whose preservation here
Men count the crown of their most good) not bless'd with pow'r to bear
One blossom but myself; and I, shaken as soon as blown.
Nor shall I live to cheer his age, and give nutrition
To him that nourish'd me. Far off my rest is set in Troy,
To leave thee restless and thy seed. Thyself that did enjoy
(As we have heard) a happy life – what Lesbos doth contain
(In times past being a bless'd man's seat), what the unmeasur'd main
Of Hellespontus, Phrygia holds, are all said to adorn   490
Thy empire, wealth and sons enow; but when the gods did turn
Thy blest state to partake with bane, war and the bloods of men
Circled thy city, never clear – sit down and suffer then,
Mourn not inevitable things; thy tears can spring no deeds
To help thee, nor recall thy son; impatience ever breeds
Ill upon ill, makes worst things worse, and therefore sit.' He said:
'Give me no seat, great seed of Jove, when yet unransomed
Hector lies riteless in thy tents; but deign with utmost speed
His resignation, that these eyes may see his person freed,
And thy grace satisfied with gifts. Accept what I have brought,   500
And turn to Phthia; 'tis enough thy conquering hand hath fought
Till Hector falter'd under it, and Hector's father stood
With free humanity safe.' He frown'd and said: 'Give not my blood
Fresh cause of fury; I know well I must resign thy son,
Jove by my mother utter'd it, and what besides is done,
I know as amply; and thyself, old Priam, I know too
Some god hath brought thee: for no man durst use a thought to go
On such a service. I have guards, and I have gates to stay

Easy accesses; do not then presume thy will can sway,
Like Jove's will, and incense again my quench'd blood: lest nor thou   510
Nor Jove gets the command of me.' This made the old king bow,
And down he sate in fear. The prince leap'd like a lion forth,
Automedon and Alcimus attending; all the worth
Brought for the body, they took down and brought in; and with it
Idaeus (herald to the king); a coat embroider'd yet,
And two rich cloaks, they left to hide the person. Thetis' son
Call'd out his women to anoint and quickly overrun
The corse with water, lifting it in private to the coach,
Lest Priam saw, and his cold blood embrac'd a fiery touch
Of anger, at the turpitude profaning it, and blew   520
Again his wrath's fire to his death. This done, his women threw
The coat and cloak on, but the corse Achilles' own hand laid
Upon a bed, and with his friends to chariot it convey'd.
For which forc'd grace (abhorring so from his free mind) he wept,
Cried out for anger, and thus pray'd: 'O friend, do not except
Against this favour to our foe (if in the deep thou hear),
And that I give him to his sire; he gave fair ransom. Dear
In my observance is Jove's will; and whatsoever part
Of all these gifts by any mean I fitly may convert
To thy renown here, and will there, it shall be pour'd upon   530
Thy honour'd sepulchre.' This said, he went, and what was done,
Told Priam, saying: 'Father, now thy will's fit rites are paid,
Thy son is giv'n up; in the morn thine eyes shall see him laid
Deck'd in thy chariot on his bed: in mean space let us eat.
The rich-hair'd Niobe found thoughts that made her take her meat,
Though twelve dear children she saw slain: six daughters, six young sons.
The sons incens'd Apollo slew, the maids' confusions
Diana wrought, since Niobe her merits durst compare
With great Latona's, arguing, that she did only bear
Two children, and herself had twelve; for which, those only two   540
Slew all her twelve. Nine days they lay steep'd in their blood: her woe
Found no friend to afford them fire; Saturnius had turn'd
Humans to stones. The tenth day yet the good celestials burn'd
The trunks themselves; and Niobe, when she was tir'd with tears,
Fell to her food, and now with rocks and wild hills mix'd she bears
(In Sypilus) the gods' wraths still, in that place where 'tis said
The goddess fairies use to dance about the funeral bed
Of Achelous, where (though turn'd with cold grief to a stone)
Heav'n gives her heat enough to feel, what plague comparison
With his pow'rs (made by earth) deserves: affect not then too far   550
With grief like a god, being a man; but for a man's life care,

And take fit food: thou shalt have time beside to mourn thy son.
He shall be tearful, thou being full; not here, but Ilion
Shall find thee weeping-rooms enow.' He said, and so arose,
And caus'd a silver-fleec'd sheep kill'd; his friends' skills did dispose
The flaying, cutting of it up, and cookly spitted it,
Roasted, and drew it artfully. Automedon, as fit,
Was for the reverend server's place, and all the brown joints serv'd
On wicker vessels to the board; Achilles' own hands carv'd,
And close they fell to. Hunger stanch'd, talk and observing time   560
Was us'd of all hands; Priam sate amaz'd to see the prime
Of Thetis' son, accomplish'd so with stature, looks, and grace,
In which the fashion of a god he thought had chang'd his place.
Achilles fell to him as fast, admir'd as much his years
(Told in his grave and good aspect); his speech even charm'd his ears,
So order'd, so material. With this food feasted too,
Old Priam spake thus: 'Now (Jove's seed) command that I may go,
And add to this feast grace of rest: these lids ne'er clos'd mine eyes
Since under thy hands fled the soul of my dear son; sighs, cries
And woes all use from food and sleep have taken; the base courts   570
Of my sad palace made my beds, where all the abject sorts
Of sorrow I have varied, tumbled in dust, and hid –
No bit, no drop of sustenance touch'd.' Then did Achilles bid
His men and women see his bed laid down, and covered
With purple blankets, and on them an arras coverlid,
Waistcoats of silk plush laying by. The women straight took lights,
And two beds made with utmost speed, and all the other rites
Their lord nam'd, us'd, who pleasantly the king in hand thus bore:
    'Good father, you must sleep without, lest any counsellor
Make his access in depth of night, as oft their industry   580
Brings them t' impart our war-affairs, of whom should any eye
Discern your presence, his next steps to Agamemnon fly,
And then shall I lose all these gifts. But go to, signify
(And that with truth) how many days you mean to keep the state
Of Hector's funerals, because so long would I rebate
Mine own edge, set to sack your town, and all our host contain
From interruption of your rites.' He answer'd: 'If you mean
To suffer such rites to my son, you shall perform a part
Of most grace to me. But you know with how dismay'd a heart
Our host took Troy, and how much fear will therefore apprehend   590
Their spirits to make out again, so far as we must send
For wood to raise our heap of death, unless I may assure
That this your high grace will stand good, and make their pass secure;
Which if you seriously confirm, nine days I mean to mourn,

The tenth, keep funeral and feast, th' eleventh raise and adorn
My son's fit sepulchre. The twelfth (if we must needs) we'll fight.'
   'Be it,' replied Aeacides. 'Do Hector all this right;
I'll hold war back those whole twelve days; of which, to free all fear,
Take this my right hand.' This confirm'd, the old king rested there,
His herald lodg'd by him, and both in forepart of the tent –   600
Achilles in an inmost room of wondrous ornament,
Whose side bright-cheek'd Briseis warm'd. Soft sleep tam'd gods and men,
All but most useful Mercury; sleep could not lay one chain
On his quick temples, taking care for getting off again
Engaged Priam undiscern'd of those that did maintain
The sacred watch. Above his head he stood with this demand:
   'O father, sleep'st thou so secure still lying in the hand
Of so much ill, and being dismiss'd by great Aeacides?
'Tis true thou hast redeem'd the dead, but for thy life's release
(Should Agamemnon hear thee here) three times the price now paid   610
Thy sons' hands must repay for thee.' This said, the king, afraid,
Starts from his sleep, Idaeus call'd; and (for both) Mercury
The horse and mules (before loos'd) join'd so soft and curiously,
That no ear heard, and thorough the host drave; but when they drew
To gulfy Xanthus' bright-wav'd stream, up to Olympus flew
Industrious Mercury. And now the saffron morning rose,
Spreading her white robe over all the world, when (full of woes)
They scourg'd on with the corse to Troy, from whence no eye had seen
(Before Cassandra) their return. She (like love's golden queen,
Ascending Pergamus) discern'd her father's person nigh,   620
His herald, and her brother's corse, and then she cast this cry
Round about Troy: 'O Troÿans, if ever ye did greet
Hector return'd from fight alive, now look ye out, and meet
His ransom'd person. Then his worth was all your city's joy,
Now do it honour.' Out all rush'd, woman nor man in Troy
Was left: a most unmeasur'd cry took up their voices. Close
To Scaea's ports they met the corse, and to it headlong goes
The reverend mother, the dear wife, upon it strow their hair,
And he entranced. Round about the people broke the air
In lamentations, and all day had stay'd the people there,   630
If Priam had not cried: 'Give way, give me but leave to bear
The body home, and mourn your fills.' Then cleft the press, and gave
Way to the chariot. To the court herald Idaeus drave,
Where on a rich bed they bestow'd the honour'd person, round
Girt it with singers that the woe with skilful voices crown'd.
A woeful elegy they sung, wept singing, and the dames
Sigh'd as they sung. Andromache the downright prose exclaims

Began to all; she on the neck of slaughter'd Hector fell,
And cried out: 'O my husband! Thou in youth bad'st youth farewell,
Left'st me a widow, thy sole son an infant. Ourselves curs'd   640
In our birth, made him right our child, for all my care that nurs'd
His infancy will never give life to his youth; ere that
Troy from her top will be destroy'd. Thou guardian of our state,
Thou ev'n of all her strength the strength, thou that in care wert past
Her careful mothers of their babes, being gone, how can she last?
Soon will the swoln fleet fill her womb with all their servitude,
Myself with them, and thou with me (dear son) in labours rude
Shalt be employ'd, sternly survey'd by cruel conquerors,
Or, rage not suffering life so long, some one whose hate abhors
Thy presence (putting him in mind of his sire slain by thine,   650
His brother, son, or friend) shall work thy ruin before mine,
Toss'd from some tow'r, for many Greeks have eat earth from the hand
Of thy strong father: in sad fight his spirit was too much mann'd,
And therefore mourn his people – we, thy parents (my dear lord)
For that thou mak'st endure a woe, black and to be abhorr'd.
Of all yet thou hast left me worst, not dying in thy bed,
And reaching me thy last-rais'd hand, in nothing counselled,
Nothing commanded by that pow'r thou hadst of me, to do
Some deed for thy sake: O for these will never end my woe,
Never my tears cease.' Thus wept she, and all the ladies clos'd   660
Her passion with a general shriek. Then Hecuba dispos'd
Her thoughts in like words: 'O my son, of all mine much most dear;
Dear while thou liv'st too even to gods: and after death they were
Careful to save thee. Being best, thou most wert envied;
My other sons Achilles sold; but thee he left not, dead.
Imber and Samos, the false ports of Lemnos, entertain'd
Their persons; thine, no port but death, nor there in rest remain'd
Thy violated corse, the tomb of his great friend was spher'd
With thy dragg'd person; yet from death he was not therefore rear'd.
But (all his rage us'd) so the gods have tender'd thy dead state;   670
Thou liest as living, sweet and fresh as he that felt the fate
Of Phoebus' holy shafts.' These words the queen us'd for her moan,
And next her, Helen held that state of speech and passion.
      'O Hector, all my brothers more were not so lov'd of me
As thy most virtues. Not my lord I held so dear as thee,
That brought me hither; before which, I would I had been brought
To ruin, for what breeds that wish (which is the mischief wrought
By my access) yet never found one harsh taunt, one word's ill
From thy sweet carriage. Twenty years do now their circles fill
Since my arrival, all which time thou didst not only bear   680

Thyself without check, but all else, that my lord's brothers were,
Their sisters' lords, sisters themselves, the queen my mother-in-law
(The king being never but most mild), when thy man's spirit saw
Sour and reproachful, it would still reprove their bitterness
With sweet words and thy gentle soul. And therefore thy decease
I truly mourn for, and myself curse as the wretched cause,
All broad Troy yielding me not one that any human laws
Of pity or forgiveness mov'd t' entreat me humanly,
But only thee; all else abhorr'd me for my destiny.'
    These words made ev'n the commons mourn, to whom the king said: 'Friends,
Now fetch wood for our funeral fire, nor fear the foe intends
Ambush, or any violence; Achilles gave his word
At my dismission, that twelve days he would keep sheath'd his sword,
And all men's else. Thus oxen, mules, in chariots straight they put,
Went forth, and an unmeasur'd pile of sylvan matter cut,
Nine days employ'd in carriage, but when the tenth morn shin'd
On wretched mortals, then they brought the fit-to-be-divin'd
Forth to be burn'd: Troy swum in tears. Upon the pile's most height
They laid the person, and gave fire: all day it burn'd, all night;
But when th' eleventh morn let on earth her rosy fingers shine,   700
The people flock'd about the pile, and first with blackish wine
Quench'd all the flames. His brothers then and friends the snowy bones
Gather'd into an urn of gold, still pouring on their moans.
Then wrapt they in soft purple veils the rich urn; digg'd a pit,
Grav'd it; ramm'd up the grave with stones; and quickly built to it
A sepulchre. But while that work and all the funeral rites
Were in performance, guards were held at all parts, days and nights,
For fear of false surprise before they had impos'd the crown
To these solemnities. The tomb advanc'd once, all the town
In Jove-nurs'd Priam's court partook a passing sumptuous feast;   710
And so horse-taming Hector's rites gave up his soul to rest.

Thus far the Ilian ruins I have laid
Open to English eyes. In which (repaid
With thine own value) go, unvalued book,
Live, and be lov'd. If any envious look
Hurt thy clear fame, learn that no state more high
Attends on virtue than pin'd envy's eye.
Would thou wert worth it that the best doth wound
Which this age feeds, and which the last shall bound.

Thus, with labour enough (though with more comfort in the merits of my divine author), I have brought my translation of his *Iliads* to an end. If, either therein, or in the harsh utterance or matter of my Comment before, I have, for haste, scattered with my burthen (less than fifteen weeks being the whole time that the last twelve books translation stood me in), I desire my present will and (I doubt not) ability (if God give life) to reform and perfect all hereafter, may be ingenuously accepted for the absolute work – the rather, considering the most learned, with all their helps and time, have been so often, and unanswerably, miserably taken halting. In the mean time, that most assistful and unspeakable spirit, by whose thrice sacred conduct and inspiration I have finished this labour, diffuse the fruitful horn of his blessings through these goodness-thirsting watchings: without which, utterly dry and bloodless is whatsoever mortality soweth.

But where our most diligent Spondanus ends his work with a prayer to be taken out of these Maeanders and Euripian rivers (as he terms them) of ethnic and profane writers (being quite contrary to himself at the beginning), I thrice humbly beseech the most dear and divine mercy (ever most incomparably preferring the great light of his truth in his direct and infallible Scriptures) I may ever be enabled, by resting wondering in his right comfortable shadows in these, to magnify the clearness of his almighty appearance in the other.

And with this salutation of Poesy given by our Spondanus in his Preface to these *Iliads* – ("All hail saint-sacred Poesy, that, under so much gall of fiction, such abundance of honey doctrine, hast hidden, not revealing them to the unworthy worldly, wouldst thou but so much make me that amongst thy novices I might be numbered, no time should ever come near my life that could make me forsake thee") I will conclude with this my daily and nightly prayer, learned of the most learned Simplicius: –

Supplico tibi, Domine, Pater, et dux rationis nostrae, ut nostrae nobilitatis
recordemur qua tu nos ornasti; et ut tu nobis praesto sis ut iis qui
per sese moventur; ut et a corporis contagio brutorumque
affectuum repurgemur, eosque superemus et regamus,
et, sicut decet, pro instrumentis iis utamur. Deinde
ut nobis adjumento sis, ad accuratam rationis
nostrae correctionem, et conjunctionem cum
iis qui vere sunt per lucem veritatis.
Et tertium, Salvatori supplex oro,
ut ab oculis animorum nostrorum
caliginem prorsus abstergas, ut
(quod apud Homerum est)
norimus bene qui Deus,
aut mortalis, habendus.
Amen.

FINIS

THE ODYSSEY

THE EPISTLE DEDICATORY

TO THE MOST WORTHILY HONOURED,
MY SINGULAR GOOD LORD, ROBERT,
EARL OF SOMERSET, LORD CHAMBERLAIN, ETC.

I have adventured, right noble Earl, out of my utmost and ever-vowed service to your virtues, to entitle their merits to the patronage of Homer's English life, whose wished natural life the great Macedon would have protected as the spirit of his empire,

> That he to his unmeasur'd mighty acts
> Might add a fame as vast; and their extracts,
> In fires as bright and endless as the stars,
> His breast might breathe and thunder out his wars.
> But that great monarch's love of fame and praise
> Receives an envious cloud in our foul days;
> For since our great ones cease themselves to do
> Deeds worth their praise, they hold it folly too
> To feed their praise in others. But what can,
> Of all the gifts that are, be given to man
> More precious than Eternity and Glory,
> Singing their praises in unsilenced story?
> Which no black day, no nation, nor no age,
> No change of time or fortune, force nor rage,
> Shall ever rase ? All which the monarch knew,
> Where HOMER lived entitled, would ensue:
> > *Cujus de gurgite vivo*
> *Combibit arcanos vatum omnis turba furores, &c.*
> From whose deep fount of life the thirsty rout
> Of Thespian prophets have lien sucking out
> Their sacred rages. And as th'influent stone
> Of Father Jove's great and laborious son
> Lifts high the heavy irons and far implies
> The wide orbs that the needle rectifies,
> In virtuous guide of every sea-driven course,
> To all aspiring his one boundless force:

So from one HOMER all the holy fire
That ever did the hidden heat inspire
In each the Muse came clearly sparkling down,
And must for him compose one flaming crown.
  He, at Jove's table set, fills out to us
Cups that repair age sad and ruinous,
And gives it built of an eternal stand
With his all-sinewy Odyssean hand,
Shifts time and fate, puts death in life's free state,
And life doth into ages propagate.
He doth in men the Gods' affects inflame,
His fuel Virtue blown by Praise and Fame;
And, with the high soul's first impression driv'n,
Breaks through rude chaos, earth, the seas, and heav'n,
The nerves of all things hid in nature lie
Naked before him, all their harmony
Tun'd to his accents, that in beasts breathe minds.
What fowls, what floods, what earth, what air, what winds,
What fires ethereal, what the Gods conclude
In all their counsels, his Muse makes indued
With varied voices that even rocks have moved.
And yet for all this, naked Virtue loved,
Honours without her he as abject prizes,
And foolish Fame, derived from thence, despises.
When from the vulgar taking glorious bound
Up to the mountain where the Muse is crown'd,
He sits and laughs to see the jaded rabble
Toil to his hard heights, t'all access unable, &c

And that your Lordship may in his face take view of his mind, the first words
of his Iliads is μῆνιν, wrath; the first word of his Odysseys, ἄνδρα, man:
contracting in either word his each work's proposition. In one *predominant
perturbation*; in the other *overruling wisdom*. In one the body's fervour and
fashion of outward fortitude to all possible height of heroical action; in the
other the mind's inward, constant, and unconquered empire, unbroken, unaltered, with any most insolent and tyrannous infliction. To many most sovereign
praises is this poem entitled; but to that grace, in chief, which sets on the crown
both of poets and orators; τὸ τὰ μικρὰ μεγάλως, καὶ τὰ κοινὰ καίνως: that is, *Parva
magne dicere; pervulgata nove; jejuna plene* – To speak things little greatly; things
common rarely; things barren and empty fruitfully and fully. The return of a
man into his country is his whole scope and object; which in itself, your
Lordship may well say, is jejune and fruitless enough, affording nothing
feastful, nothing magnificent. And yet even this doth the divine inspiration

render vast, illustrious, and of miraculous composure. And for this, my Lord, is this poem preferred to his *Iliads*; for therein much magnificence, both of person and action, gives great aid to his industry; but in this are these helps exceeding sparing or nothing; and yet is the structure so elaborate and pompous that the poor plain groundwork, considered together, may seem the naturally rich womb to it, and produce it needfully. Much wondered at, therefore, is the censure of Dionysius Longinus (a man otherwise affirmed grave and of elegant judgment), comparing Homer in his *Iliads* to the Sun rising, in his *Odysseys* to his descent or setting, or to the ocean robbed of his æsture, many tributary floods and rivers of excellent ornament withheld from their observance. When this his work so far exceeds the ocean, with all his court and concourse, that all his sea is only a serviceable stream to it. Nor can it be compared to any one power to be named in nature, being an entirely well-sorted and digested confluence of all; where the most solid and grave is made as nimble and fluent as the most airy and fiery, the nimble and fluent as firm and well-bounded as the most grave and solid. And, taking all together, of so tender impression, and of such command to the voice of the Muse, that they knock heaven with her breath, and discover their foundations as low as hell. Nor is this all-comprising Poesy fantastic or mere fictive; but the most material and doctrinal illations of truth, both for all manly information of manners in the young, all prescription of justice, and even Christian piety, in the most grave and high governed. To illustrate both which, in both kinds, with all height of expression, the Poet creates both a body and a soul in them. Wherein, if the body (being the letter or history) seems fictive, and beyond possibility to bring into act, the sense then and allegory, which is the soul, is to be sought, which intends a more eminent expressure of Virtue for her loveliness, and of Vice for her ugliness, in their several effects, going beyond the life, than my art within life can possibly delineate. Why then is fiction to this end so hateful to our true ignorants? Or why should a poor chronicler of a Lord Mayor's naked truth (that peradventure will last his year) include more worth with our modern wizards than Homer for his naked Ulysses clad in eternal fiction? But this proser Dionysius, and the rest of these grave and reputatively learned – that dare undertake for their gravities the headstrong censure of all things, and challenge the understanding of these toys in their childhoods; when even these childish vanities retain deep and most necessary learning enough in them to make them children in their ages, and teach them while they live – are not in these absolute divine infusions allowed either voice or relish: for *Qui poeticas ad fores accedit, &c.* (says the divine philosopher), he that knocks at the gates of the Muses, *sine Musarum furore*, is neither to be admitted entry, nor a touch at their thresholds: his opinion of entry ridiculous, and his presumption impious. Nor must Poets themselves (might I a little insist on these contempts, not tempting too far your Lordship's Ulyssean patience) presume to these doors without the truly genuine and peculiar induction. There being in poesy a twofold rapture – or alienation of soul, as the above-said teacher terms it – one *insania*, a disease of the mind, and a mere madness, by which the infected is thrust beneath all the degrees of humanity: et *ex homine, brutum quodammodo redditur* (for which poor Poesy, in this diseased and impostorous age, is so barbarously vilified) – the other is, *divinus furor*, by which the sound and divinely healthful *supra hominis naturam erigitur, et in Deum transit.* One a perfection directly infused from God; the other an infection obliquely and degenerately proceeding from man. Of the divine fury, my Lord, your Homer hath ever been both first and last instance; being pronounced absolutely, τὸν σοφώτατον, καὶ τὸν θειότατον ποιητήν, 'THE MOST WISE AND MOST DIVINE POET'. Against whom whosoever shall open his profane mouth may worthily receive answer with this of his divine defender – Empedocles, Heraclitus, Protagoras, Epicharmus, &c. being of HOMER's part – τίς οὖν, &c.; who against such an army, and the general HOMER, dares attempt the assault but he must be reputed ridiculous? And yet against this host, and this invincible commander, shall we have every *besogne* and fool a leader. The common herd, I assure myself, ready to receive it on their horns, Their infected leaders,

> Such men as sideling ride the ambling Muse,
> Whose saddle is as frequent as the stews.
> Whose raptures are in every pageant seen,
> In every wassail-rhyme and dancing green;
> When he that writes by any beam of truth
> Must dive as deep as he, past shallow youth.
> Truth dwells in gulfs, whose deeps hide shades so rich
> That Night sits muffled there in clouds of pitch,
> More dark than Nature made her, and requires,
> To clear her tough mists, heaven's great fire of fires,
> To whom the sun itself is but a beam.
> For sick souls then – but rapt in foolish dream –
> To wrestle with these heaven-strong mysteries,
> What madness is it? When their light serves eyes
> That are not worldly in their least aspect,
> But truly pure, and aim at heaven direct.
> Yet these none like but what the brazen head
> Blatters abroad, no sooner born but dead.

Holding, then, in eternal contempt, my Lord, those short-lived bubbles, eternize your virtue and judgment with the Grecian monarch; esteeming, not as the least of your new-year's presents,

HOMER, three thousand years dead, now reviv'd,
Even from that dull death that in life he liv'd;
When none conceited him, none understood
That so much life in so much death as blood
Conveys about it could mix. But when death
Drunk up the bloody mist that human breath
Pour'd round about him – poverty and spite
Thick'ning the hapless vapour – then truth's light
Glimmer'd about his poem; the pinch'd soul
(Amidst the mysteries it did enrol)
Brake powerfully abroad. And as we see
The sun all hid in clouds, at length got free,
Through some forced covert, over all the ways,
Near and beneath him, shoots his vented rays
Far off, and sticks them in some little glade,
All woods, fields, rivers, left besides in shade;
So your Apollo, from that world of light
Closed in his poem's body, shot to sight
Some few forced beams, which near him were not seen,
(As in his life or country) Fate and spleen
Clouding their radiance; which when Death had clear'd,
To far-off regions his free beams appear'd;
In which all stood and wonder'd, striving which
His birth and rapture should in right enrich.
    Twelve labours of your Thespian Hercules
I now present your Lordship; do but please
To lend life means till th' other twelve receive
Equal achievement; and let Death then reave
My life now lost in our patrician loves,
That knock heads with the herd; in whom there moves
One blood, one soul, both drown'd in one set height
Of stupid envy and mere popular spite.
Whose loves with no good did my least vein fill;
And from their hates I fear as little ill.
Their bounties nourish not when most they feed,
But, where there is no merit or no need
Rain into rivers still, and are such show'rs
As bubbles spring and overflow the flow'rs.
Their worse parts and worst men their best suborns,
Like winter cows whose milk runs to their horns.
And as litigious clients' books of law
Cost infinitely; taste of all the awe
Bench'd in our kingdom's policy, piety, state;

Earn all their deep explorings; satiate
All sorts there thrust together by the heart
With thirst of wisdom spent on either part;
Horrid examples made of Life and Death
From their fine stuff woven; yet when once the breath
Of sentence leaves them, all their worth is drawn
As dry as dust, and wears like cobweb lawn:
So these men set a price upon their worth,
That no man gives but those that trot it forth
Through Need's foul ways, feed Humours with all cost
Though Judgment starves in them; rout, State engrost
(At all tobacco benches, solemn tables,
Where all that cross their envies are their fables)
In their rank faction; shame and death approved
Fit penance for their opposites; none loved
But those that rub them; not a reason heard
That doth not soothe and glorify their preferr'd
Bitter opinions. When, would Truth resume
The cause to his hands, all would fly in fume
Before his sentence; since the innocent mind
Just God makes good, to whom their worst is wind.
For, that I freely all my thoughts express,
My conscience is my thousand witnesses;
And to this stay my constant comforts vow,
You for the world I have, or God for you.

CERTAIN ANCIENT GREEK EPIGRAMS TRANSLATED

All stars are drunk up by the fiery sun,
And in so much a flame lies shrunk the moon.
HOMER's all-liv'd name all names leaves in death,
Whose splendour only Muses' bosoms breathe.

ANOTHER

Heaven's fires shall first fall darken'd from his sphere,
Grave Night the light weed of the Day shall wear,
Fresh streams shall chase the sea, tough ploughs shall tear
Her fishy bottoms, men in long date dead
Shall rise and live, before Oblivion shed
Those still-green leaves that crown great HOMER's head.

ANOTHER

The great Mæonides doth only write,
And to him dictates the great God of Light.

ANOTHER

Seven kingdoms strove in which should swell the womb
That bore great HOMER, whom Fame freed from tomb;
Argos, Chios, Pylos, Smyrna, Colophone,
The learn'd Athenian, and Ulyssean throne.

ANOTHER

Art thou of Chios? No. Of Salamine?
As little. Was the Smyrnean country thine?
Nor so. Which then? Was Cuma's? Colophone?
Nor one nor other. Art thou, then, of none
That Fame proclaims thee? None. Thy reason call.
If I confess of one I anger all.

BOOK ONE

The Argument

The gods in council sit, to call
Ulysses from Calypso's thrall,
And order their high pleasures thus:
Grey Pallas to Telemachus
(In Ithaca) her way addrest;
And did her heavenly limbs invest
In Mentas' likeness, that did reign
King of the Taphians, in the main
Whose rough waves near Leucadia run,
Advising wise Ulysses' son
To seek his father, and address
His course to young Tantalides
That govern'd Sparta. Thus much said,
She shew'd she was heaven's martial Maid,
And vanish'd from him. Next to this,
The banquet of the wooers is.

Another Argument

Alpha   The deities sit;
      The Man retired;
    The Ulyssean wit
      By Pallas fired.

BOOK ONE

THE MAN, O Muse, inform, that many a way
Wound with his wisdom to his wished stay;
That wandered wondrous far, when he the town
Of sacred Troy had sack'd and shivered down;
The cities of a world of nations,
With all their manners, minds, and fashions,
He saw and knew; at sea felt many woes,
Much care sustained, to save from overthrows
Himself and friends in their retreat for home;
But so their fates he could not overcome,   10
Though much he thirsted it. O men unwise,
They perish'd by their own impieties,
That in their hunger's rapine would not shun
The oxen of the lofty-going Sun,
Who therefore from their eyes the day bereft
Of safe return. These acts, in some part left,
Tell us, as others, deified seed of Jove.
   Now all the rest that austere death outstrove
At Troy's long siege at home safe anchor'd are,
Free from the malice both of sea and war;   20
Only Ulysses is denied access
To wife and home. The grace of goddesses,
The reverend nymph Calypso, did detain
Him in her caves past all the race of men
Enflam'd to make him her lov'd lord and spouse.
And when the gods had destin'd that his house,
Which Ithaca on her rough bosom bears,
(The point of time wrought out by ambient years)
Should be his haven, Contention still extends
Her envy to him, even amongst his friends.   30
All gods took pity on him; only he,
That girds earth in the cincture of the sea,
Divine Ulysses ever did envy,
And made the fix'd port of his birth to fly.
   But he himself solemnized a retreat

To th' Aethiops, far dissunder'd in their seat,
(In two parts parted, at the sun's descent,
And underneath his golden orient,
The first and last of men) t' enjoy their feast
Of bulls and lambs, in hecatombs address'd;   40
At which he sat, given over to delight.
    The other gods in heav'n's supremest height
Were all in council met; to whom began
The mighty father both of god and man
Discourse, inducing matter that inclined
To wise Ulysses, calling to his mind
Faultful Aegisthus, who to death was done
By young Orestes, Agamemnon's son.
His memory to the immortals then
Mov'd Jove thus deeply: 'O how falsely men   50
Accuse us gods as authors of their ill,
When by the bane their own bad lives instil
They suffer all the miseries of their states,
Past our inflictions, and beyond their fates.
As now Aegisthus, past his fate, did wed
The wife of Agamemnon, and (in dread
To suffer death himself) to shun his ill,
Incurred it by the loose bent of his will,
In slaughtering Atrides in retreat.
Which we foretold him would so hardly set   60
To his murderous purpose, sending Mercury
That slaughter'd Argus, our considerate spy,
To give him this charge: "Do not wed his wife,
Nor murder him; for thou shalt buy his life
With ransom of thine own, imposed on thee
By his Orestes, when in him shall be
Atrides' self renew'd, and but the prime
Of youth's spring put abroad, in thirst to climb
His haughty father's throne by his high acts."
These words of Hermes wrought not into facts   70
Aegisthus' powers; good counsel he despised,
And to that good his ill is sacrificed.'
    Pallas, whose eyes did sparkle like the skies,
Answer'd: 'O sire! Supreme of deities,
Aegisthus pass'd his fate and had desert
To warrant our infliction; and convert
May all the pains such impious men inflict
On innocent sufferers to revenge as strict,

Their own hearts eating. But that Ithacus,
Thus never meriting, should suffer thus,   80
I deeply suffer. His more pious mind
Divides him from these fortunes, though unkind
Is piety to him, giving him a fate
More suffering than the most unfortunate,
So long kept friendless in a sea-girt soil,
Where the sea's navel is a sylvan isle,
In which the goddess dwells that doth derive
Her birth from Atlas, who of all alive
The motion and the fashion doth command
With his wise mind, whose forces understand   90
The inmost deeps and gulfs of all the seas,
Who (for his skill of things superior) stays
The two steep columns that prop earth and heav'n.
His daughter 'tis, who holds this homeless-driv'n
Still mourning with her, evermore profuse
Of soft and winning speeches, that abuse
And make so languishingly, and possest
With so remiss a mind her loved guest,
Manage the action of his way for home.
Where he, though in affection overcome,   100
In judgment yet more longs to show his hopes,
His country's smoke leap from her chimney tops,
And death asks in her arms. Yet never shall
Thy lov'd heart be converted on his thrall,
Austere Olympius. Did not ever he,
In ample Troy, thy altars gratify,
And Grecians' fleet make in thy offerings swim?
O Jove, why still then burns thy wrath to him?'
    The Cloud-assembler answer'd: 'What words fly,
Bold daughter, from thy pale of ivory?   110
As if I ever could cast from my care
Divine Ulysses, who exceeds so far
All men in wisdom, and so oft hath given
To all th' immortals throned in ample heaven
So great and sacred gifts? But his decrees,
That holds the earth in with his nimble knees,
Stand to Ulysses' longings so extreme,
For taking from the god-foe Polypheme
His only eye – a Cyclop, that excell'd
All other Cyclops, with whose burden swell'd   120
The nymph Thoosa, the divine increase

Of Phorcys' seed, a great god of the seas.
She mix'd with Neptune in his hollow caves,
And bore this Cyclop to that god of waves.
For whose lost eye, th' Earth-shaker did not kill
Erring Ulysses, but reserves him still
In life for more death. But use we our pow'rs,
And round about us cast these cares of ours,
All to discover how we may prefer
His wish'd retreat, and Neptune make forbear   130
His stern eye to him, since no one god can,
In spite of all, prevail, but 'gainst a man.'
    To this, this answer made the grey-eyed Maid:
'Supreme of rulers, since so well apaid
The blessed gods are all then, now, in thee,
To limit wise Ulysses' misery,
And that you speak as you referred to me
Prescription for the means, in this sort be
Their sacred order: let us now address
With utmost speed our swift Argicides,   140
To tell the nymph that bears the golden tress
In th' isle Ogygia, that 'tis our will
She should not stay our loved Ulysses still,
But suffer his return; and then will I
To Ithaca, to make his son apply
His sire's inquest the more, infusing force
Into his soul, to summon the concourse
Of curl'd-head Greeks to council, and deter
Each wooer, that hath been the slaughterer
Of his fat sheep and crooked-headed beeves,   150
From more wrong to his mother; and their leaves
Take in such terms, as fit deserts so great.
To Sparta then, and Pylos, where doth beat
Bright Amathus, the flood and epithet
To all that kingdom, my advice shall send
The spirit-advanc'd prince, to the pious end
Of seeking his lost father, if he may
Receive report from Fame where rests his stay,
And make, besides, his own successive worth
Known to the world, and set in action forth.'   160
    This said, her wing'd shoes to her feet she tied,
Formed all of gold, and all eternified,
That on the round earth or the sea sustain'd
Her ravish'd substance swift as gusts of wind.

Then took she her strong lance with steel made keen,
Great, massy, active, that whole hosts of men,
Though all heroës, conquers, if her ire
Their wrongs inflame, back'd by so great a sire.
Down from Olympus' tops she headlong div'd,
And swift as thought in Ithaca arriv'd,   170
Close at Ulysses' gates; in whose first court
She made her stand, and, for her breast's support,
Leaned on her iron lance, her form impress'd
With Mentas' likeness, come as being a guest.
There found she those proud wooers, that were then
Set on those ox-hides that themselves had slain,
Before the gates, and all at dice were playing.
To them the heralds, and the rest obeying,
Fill'd wine and water – some still as they play'd,
And some for solemn supper's state purvey'd,   180
With porous sponges, cleansing tables, serv'd
With much rich feast; of which to all they carv'd.
     god-like Telemachus amongst them sat,
Griev'd much in mind; and in his heart begat
All representment of his absent sire,
How, come from far-off parts, his spirits would fire
With those proud wooers' sight, with slaughter parting
Their bold concourse, and to himself converting
The honours they usurp'd, his own commanding.
     In this discourse, he first saw Pallas standing,   190
Unbidden entry; up rose, and address'd
His pace right to her, angry that a guest
Should stand so long at gate; and, coming near,
Her right hand took, took in his own her spear,
And thus saluted: 'Grace to your repair,
Fair guest, your welcome shall be likewise fair.
Enter, and, cheer'd with feast, disclose th' intent
That caused your coming.' This said, first he went,
And Pallas follow'd. To a room they came,
Steep, and of state; the javelin of the dame   200
He set against a pillar vast and high,
Amidst a large and bright-kept armory,
Which was, besides, with woods of lances grac'd
Of his grave father's. In a throne he plac'd
The man-turn'd goddess, under which was spread
A carpet, rich and of deviceful thread,
A footstool staying her feet; and by her chair

Another seat (all garnish'd wondrous fair,
To rest or sleep on in the day) he set,
Far from the prease of wooers, lest at meat   210
The noise they still made might offend his guest,
Disturbing him at banquet or at rest,
Even to his combat with that pride of theirs,
That kept no noble form in their affairs.
And these he set far from them, much the rather
To question freely of his absent father.

   A table fairly-polish'd then was spread,
On which a reverend officer set bread,
And other servitors all sorts of meat
(Salads, and flesh, such as their haste could get)   220
Serv'd with observance in. And then the sewer
Pour'd water from a great and golden ewer,
That from their hands t' a silver cauldron ran.
Both wash'd, and seated close, the voiceful man
Fetch'd cups of gold, and set by them, and round
Those cups with wine with all endeavour crown'd.

   Then rush'd in the rude wooers, themselves plac'd;
The heralds water gave; the maids in haste
Serv'd bread from baskets. When, of all prepar'd
And set before them, the bold wooers shar'd,   230
Their pages plying their cups past the rest.
But lusty wooers must do more than feast;
For now, their hungers and their thirsts allay'd,
They call'd for songs and dances; those, they said,
Were th' ornaments of feast. The herald straight
A harp, carv'd full of artificial sleight,
Thrust into Phemius', a learn'd singer's, hand,
Who, till he much was urg'd, on terms did stand,
But after, play'd and sung with all his art.

   Telemachus to Pallas then (apart,   240
His ear inclining close, that none might hear)
In this sort said: 'My guest, exceeding dear,
Will you not sit incens'd with what I say?
These are the cares these men take: feast and play.
Which eas'ly they may use, because they eat,
Free and unpunish'd, of another's meat –
And of a man's, whose white bones wasting lie
In some far region, with th' incessancy
Of show'rs pour'd down upon them, lying ashore,
Or in the seas wash'd naked. Who, if he wore   250

Those bones with flesh and life and industry,
And these might here in Ithaca set eye
On him return'd, they all would wish to be
Either past other in celerity
Of feet and knees, and not contend t' exceed
In golden garments. But his virtues feed
The fate of ill death; nor is left to me
The least hope of his life's recovery,
No, not if any of the mortal race
Should tell me his return; the cheerful face   260
Of his return'd day never will appear.
But tell me, and let truth your witness bear,
Who, and from whence you are? What city's birth?
What parents? In what vessel set you forth?
And with what mariners arriv'd you here?
I cannot think you a foot passenger.
Recount then to me all, to teach me well
Fit usage for your worth, and if it fell
In chance now first that you thus see us here,
Or that in former passages you were   270
My father's guest. For many men have been
Guests to my father. Studious of men
His sociable nature ever was.'
On him again the grey-eyed Maid did pass
This kind reply: 'I'll answer passing true
All thou hast ask'd: my birth his honour drew
From wise Anchialus. The name I bear
Is Mentas, the commanding islander
Of all the Taphians studious in the art
Of navigation, having touch'd this part   280
With ship and men, of purpose to maintain
Course through the dark seas t' other-languag'd men;
And Temesis sustains the city's name
For which my ship is bound, made known by fame
For rich in brass, which my occasions need,
And therefore bring I shining steel in stead,
Which their use wants, yet makes my vessel's freight,
That near a plough'd field rides at anchor's weight,
Apart this city, in the harbour call'd
Rhethrus, whose waves with Neius' woods are wall'd.   290
Thy sire and I were ever mutual guests,
At either's house still interchanging feasts.
I glory in it. Ask, when thou shalt see

Laertes, th' old heroë, these of me,
From the beginning. He, men say, no more
Visits the city, but will needs deplore
His son's believed loss in a private field,
One old maid only at his hands to yield
Food to his life, as oft as labour makes
His old limbs faint – which, though he creeps, he takes   300
Along a fruitful plain, set all with vines,
Which husbandman-like, though a king, he proins.
But now I come to be thy father's guest;
I hear he wanders, while these wooers feast.
And (as th' immortals prompt me at this hour)
I'll tell thee, out of a prophetic pow'r
(Not as profess'd a prophet, nor clear seen
At all times what shall after chance to men),
What I conceive, for this time, will be true:
The gods' inflictions keep your sire from you.   310
Divine Ulysses yet abides, not dead
Above earth, nor beneath, nor buried
In any seas, as you did late conceive,
But, with the broad sea sieged, is kept alive
Within an isle by rude and upland men,
That in his spite his passage home detain.
Yet long it shall not be before he tread
His country's dear earth, though solicited,
And held from his return, with iron chains;
For he hath wit to forge a world of trains,   320
And will, of all, be sure to make good one
For his return, so much relied upon.
But tell me, and be true: art thou indeed
So much a son, as to be said the seed
Of Ithacus himself? Exceeding much
Thy forehead and fair eyes at his form touch;
For oftentimes we met, as you and I
Meet at this hour, before he did apply
His pow'rs for Troy, when other Grecian states
In hollow ships were his associates.   330
But, since that time, mine eyes could never see
Renown'd Ulysses, nor met his with me.'

    The wise Telemachus again replied:
'You shall with all I know be satisfied.
My mother certain says I am his son;
I know not, nor was ever simply known

By any child the sure truth of his sire.
But would my veins had took in living fire
From some man happy, rather than one wise,
Whom age might see seiz'd of what youth made prize. 340
But he whoever of the mortal race
Is most unblest, he holds my father's place.
This, since you ask, I answer.' She, again:
'The gods sure did not make the future strain
Both of thy race and days obscure to thee,
Since thou wert born so of Penelope.
The style may by thy after acts be won,
Of so great sire the high undoubted son.
     Say truth in this then: what's this feasting here?
What all this rout? Is all this nuptial cheer, 350
Or else some friendly banquet made by thee?
For here no shots are, where all sharers be.
Past measure contumeliously this crew
Fare through thy house; which should th' ingenuous view
Of any good or wise man come and find
(Impiety seeing play'd in every kind),
He could not but through ev'ry vein be mov'd.'
     Again Telemachus: 'My guest much loved,
Since you demand and sift these sights so far,
I grant 'twere fit a house so regular, 360
Rich, and so faultless once in government,
Should still at all parts the same form present
That gave it glory while her lord was here.
But now the gods, that us displeasure bear,
Have otherwise appointed, and disgrace
My father most of all the mortal race.
For whom I could not mourn so were he dead,
Amongst his fellow captains slaughtered
By common enemies, or in the hands
Of his kind friends had ended his commands, 370
After he had egregiously bestow'd
His power and order in a war so vow'd,
And to his tomb all Greeks their grace had done,
That to all ages he might leave his son
Immortal honour; but now Harpies have
Digg'd in their gorges his abhorred grave.
Obscure, inglorious, death hath made his end,
And me, for glories, to all griefs contend.
Nor shall I any more mourn him alone,

The gods have giv'n me other cause of moan.   380
For look how many optimates remain
In Samos, or the shores Dulichian,
Shady Zacynthus, or how many bear
Rule in the rough brows of this island here:
So many now my mother and this house
At all parts make defamed and ruinous;
And she her hateful nuptials nor denies
Nor will dispatch their importunities,
Though she beholds them spoil still as they feast
All my free house yields, and the little rest   390
Of my dead sire in me perhaps intend
To bring ere long to some untimely end.'
   This Pallas sigh'd and answer'd: 'O,' said she,
'Absent Ulysses is much miss'd by thee,
That on these shameless suitors he might lay
His wreakful hands. Should he now come, and stay
In thy court's first gates, arm'd with helm and shield,
And two such darts as I have seen him wield,
When first I saw him in our Taphian court,
Feasting, and doing his desert's disport;   400
When from Ephyrus he return'd by us
From Ilus, son to centaur Mermerus,
To whom he travell'd through the watery dreads,
For bane to poison his sharp arrows' heads
That death, but touch'd, caus'd; which he would not give,
Because he fear'd the gods that ever live
Would plague such death with death; and yet their fear
Was to my father's bosom not so dear
As was thy father's love (for what he sought
My loving father found him to a thought);   410
If such as then Ulysses might but meet
With these proud wooers, all were at his feet
But instant dead men, and their nuptials
Would prove as bitter as their dying galls.
But these things in the gods' knees are repos'd –
If his return shall see with wreak inclos'd
These in his house, or he return no more.
And therefore I advise thee to explore
All ways thyself, to set these wooers gone;
To which end give me fit attention: 420
Tomorrow into solemn council call
The Greek heroës, and declare to all

(The gods being witness) what thy pleasure is.
Command to towns of their nativity
These frontless wooers. If thy mother's mind
Stands to her second nuptials so inclin'd,
Return she to her royal father's tow'rs,
Where th' one of these may wed her, and her dow'rs
Make rich, and such as may consort with grace
So dear a daughter of so great a race.   430
And thee I warn as well (if thou as well
Wilt hear and follow): take thy best-built sail,
With twenty oars mann'd, and haste t' inquire
Where the abode is of thy absent sire,
If any can inform thee, or thine ear
From Jove the fame of his retreat may hear;
For chiefly Jove gives all that honours men.
    To Pylos first be thy addression then,
To god-like Nestor; thence to Sparta haste,
To gold-lock'd Menelaus, who was last   440
Of all the brass-arm'd Greeks that sail'd from Troy;
And try from both these, if thou canst enjoy
News of thy sire's return'd life anywhere,
Though sad thou suffer'st in his search a year.
If of his death thou hear'st, return thou home,
And to his memory erect a tomb,
Performing parent-rites of feast and game,
Pompous, and such as best may fit his fame;
And then thy mother a fit husband give.
These past, consider how thou mayst deprive   450
Of worthless life these wooers in thy house,
By open force or projects enginous.
Things childish fit not thee; th' art so no more.
Hast thou not heard how all men did adore
Divine Orestes, after he had slain
Aegisthus murdering by a treacherous train
His famous father? Be then, my most lov'd,
Valiant and manly, every way approv'd
As great as he. I see thy person fit,
Noble thy mind, and excellent thy wit,   460
All given thee so to use and manage here
That even past death they may their memories bear.
In mean time I'll descend to ship and men,
That much expect me. Be observant then
Of my advice, and careful to maintain

In equal acts thy royal father's reign.'
    Telemachus replied: 'You ope, fair guest,
A friend's heart in your speech, as well express'd
As might a father serve t' inform his son;
All which sure place have in my memory won.   470
Abide yet, though your voyage calls away,
That, having bath'd, and dignified your stay
With some more honour, you may yet beside
Delight your mind by being gratified
With some rich present taken in your way,
That, as a jewel, your respect may lay
Up in your treasury, bestow'd by me,
As free friends use to guests of such degree.'
    'Detain me not,' said she, 'so much inclin'd
To haste my voyage. What thy loved mind   480
Commands to give at my return this way,
Bestow on me, that I directly may
Convey it home; which more of price to me
The more it asks my recompense to thee.'
    This said, away grey-eyed Minerva flew,
Like to a mounting lark; and did endue
His mind with strength and boldness, and much more
Made him his father long for than before;
And weighing better who his guest might be,
He stood amaz'd, and thought a deity   490
Was there descended, to whose will he fram'd
His powers at all parts, and went so inflam'd
Amongst the wooers, who were silent set,
To hear a poet sing the sad retreat
The Greeks perform'd from Troy; which was from thence
Proclaim'd by Pallas, pain of her offence.
    When which divine song was perceiv'd to bear
That mournful subject by the listening ear
Of wise Penelope, Icarius' seed,
Who from an upper room had given it heed,   500
Down she descended by a winding stair,
Not solely, but the state in her repair
Two maids of honour made. And when this queen
Of women stoop'd so low, she might be seen
By all her wooers. In the door, aloof,
Entering the hall grac'd with a goodly roof,
She stood, in shade of graceful veils implied
About her beauties; on her either side,

Her honour'd women. When, to tears mov'd, thus
She chid the sacred singer: 'Phemius,   510
You know a number more of these great deeds
Of gods and men, that are the sacred seeds
And proper subjects of a poet's song,
And those due pleasures that to men belong,
Besides these facts that furnish Troy's retreat.
Sing one of those to these, that round your seat
They may with silence sit, and taste their wine;
But cease this song, that through these ears of mine
Conveys deserv'd occasion to my heart
Of endless sorrows, of which the desert   520
In me unmeasur'd is past all these men,
So endless is the memory I retain,
And so desertful is that memory
Of such a man as hath a dignity
So broad it spreads itself through all the pride
Of Greece and Argos.' To the queen replied
Inspired Telemachus: 'Why thus envies
My mother him that fits societies
With so much harmony, to let him please
His own mind in his will to honour these?   530
For these ingenious and first sort of men,
That do immediately from Jove retain
Their singing raptures, are by Jove as well
Inspir'd with choice of what their songs impel;
Jove's will is free in it, and therefore theirs.
Nor is this man to blame, that the repairs
The Greeks make homeward sings; for his fresh muse
Men still most celebrate that sings most news.
    And therefore in his note your ears employ:
For not Ulysses only lost in Troy   540
The day of his return, but numbers more
The deadly ruins of his fortunes bore.
Go you then in, and take your work in hand,
Your web, and distaff; and your maids command
To ply their fit work. Words to men are due,
And those reproving counsels you pursue –
And most to me of all men, since I bear
The rule of all things that are manag'd here.'
She went amaz'd away, and in her heart
Laid up the wisdom Pallas did impart   550
To her lov'd son so lately, turn'd again

Up to her chamber, and no more would reign
In manly counsels. To her women she
Applied her sway, and to the wooers he
Began new orders, other spirits bewray'd
Than those in spite of which the wooers sway'd.
And (whiles his mother's tears still wash'd her eyes,
Till grey Minerva did those tears surprise
With timely sleep, and that her wooers did rouse
Rude tumult up through all the shady house,   560
Dispos'd to sleep because their widow was)
Telemachus this new-giv'n spirit did pass
On their old insolence: 'Ho! You that are
My mother's wooers! Much too high ye bear
Your petulant spirits; sit, and while ye may
Enjoy me in your banquets, see ye lay
These loud notes down, nor do this man the wrong,
Because my mother hath dislik'd his song,
To grace her interruption. 'Tis a thing
Honest, and honour'd too, to hear one sing   570
Numbers so like the gods in elegance
As this man flows in. By the morn's first light
I'll call ye all before me in a court,
That I may clearly banish your resort,
With all your rudeness, from these roofs of mine.
Away, and elsewhere in your feasts combine.
Consume your own goods, and make mutual feast
At either's house. Or if ye still hold best,
And for your humours' more sufficed fill,
To feed, to spoil, because unpunish'd still,   580
On other findings, spoil; but here I call
Th' eternal gods to witness, if it fall
In my wish'd reach once to be dealing wreaks
By Jove's high bounty, these your present checks
To what I give in charge shall add more reins
To my revenge hereafter; and the pains
Ye then must suffer shall pass all your pride
Ever to see redress'd, or qualified.'
    At this all bit their lips, and did admire
His words sent from him with such phrase and fire;   590
Which so much mov'd them that Antinous,
Eupitheus' son, cried out: 'Telemachus!
The gods, I think, have rapt thee to this height
Of elocution, and this great conceit

Of self-ability. We all may pray
That Jove invest not in this kingdom's sway
Thy forward forces, which I see put forth
A hot ambition in thee for thy birth.'

    'Be not offended,' he replied, 'if I
Shall say, I would assume this empery,   600
If Jove gave leave. You are not he that sings:
The rule of kingdoms is the worst of things.
Nor is it ill at all to sway a throne;
A man may quickly gain possession
Of mighty riches, make a wondrous prize
Set of his virtues; but the dignities
That deck a king, there are enough beside
In this circumfluous isle that want no pride
To think them worthy of, as young as I,
And old as you are. An ascent so high   610
My thoughts affect not. Dead is he that held
Desert of virtue to have so excell'd.
But of these turrets I will take on me
To be the absolute king, and reign as free
As did my father over all his hand
Left here in this house slaves to my command.'

    Eurymachus, the son of Polybus,
To this made this reply: 'Telemachus!
The girlond of this kingdom let the knees
Of deity run for; but the faculties   620
This house is seized of, and the turrets here,
Thou shalt be lord of, nor shall any bear
The least part off of all thou dost possess,
As long as this land is no wilderness,
Nor ruled by outlaws. But give these their pass,
And tell me, best of princes, who he was
That guested here so late? From whence? And what
In any region boasted he his state?
His race? His country? Brought he any news
Of thy returning father? Or for dues   630
Of moneys to him made he fit repair?
How suddenly he rush'd into the air,
Nor would sustain to stay and make him known!
His port show'd no debauch'd companion.'

    He answer'd: 'The return of my lov'd sire
Is past all hope; and should rude Fame inspire

From any place a flattering messenger
With news of his survival, he should bear
No least belief off from my desperate love.
Which if a sacred prophet should approve,   640
Call'd by my mother for her care's unrest,
It should not move me. For my late fair guest,
He was of old my father's, touching here
From sea-girt Taphos, and for name doth bear
Mentas, the son of wise Anchialus,
And governs all the Taphians studious
Of navigation.' This he said, but knew
It was a goddess. These again withdrew
To dances and attraction of the song;
And while their pleasures did the time prolong,   650
The sable ev'n descended, and did steep
The lids of all men in desire of sleep.
    Telemachus into a room built high
Of his illustrious court, and to the eye
Of circular prospect, to his bed ascended,
And in his mind much weighty thought contended.
Before him Euryclea (that well knew
All the observance of a handmaid's due,
Daughter to Opis Pisenorides)
Bore two bright torches; who did so much please   660
Laërtes in her prime, that for the price
Of twenty oxen, he made merchandise
Of her rare beauties; and love's equal flame
To her he felt as to his nuptial dame,
Yet never durst he mix with her in bed,
So much the anger of his wife he fled.
She, now grown old, to young Telemachus
Two torches bore, and was obsequious
Past all his other maids, and did apply
Her service to him from his infancy.   670
His well-built chamber reach'd, she op'd the door,
He on his bed sat, the soft weeds he wore
Put off, and to the diligent old maid
Gave all; who fitly all in thick folds laid,
And hung them on a beam-pin near the bed,
That round about was rich embroidered.
Then made she haste forth from him, and did bring
The door together with a silver ring,

And by a string a bar to it did pull.
He, laid, and cover'd well with curled wool   680
Wov'n in silk quilts, all night employ'd his mind
About the task that Pallas had design'd.

THE END OF THE FIRST BOOK

BOOK TWO

The Argument

Telemachus to court doth call
The wooers, and commands them all
To leave his house; and taking then
From wise Minerva ship and men,
And all things fit for him beside
That Euryclea could provide
For sea-rites, till he found his sire,
He hoists sail; when heav'n stoops his fire.

Another Argument

Beta   The old Maid's store
        The voyage cheers.
      The ship leaves shore,
        Minerva steers.

BOOK TWO

N OW WHEN with rosy fingers, th' early born
And thrown through all the air, appear'd the Morn,
Ulysses' lov'd son from his bed appear'd,
His weeds put on, and did about him gird
His sword that thwart his shoulders hung, and tied
To his fair feet fair shoes, and all parts plied
For speedy readiness; who, when he trod
The open earth, to men show'd like a god.
   The heralds then he straight charg'd to consort
The curl'd-head Greeks, with loud calls, to a court.   10
They summon'd; th' other came in utmost haste.
Who all assembled, and in one heap plac'd,
He likewise came to council, and did bear
In his fair hand his iron-headed spear.
Nor came alone, nor with men troops prepar'd,
But two fleet dogs made both his train and guard.
Pallas supplied with her high wisdom's grace,
That all men's wants supplies, state's painted face.
His ent'ring presence all men did admire;
Who took seat in the high throne of his sire,   20
To which the grave peers gave him reverend way.
Amongst whom, an Egyptian heroë
(Crooked with age, and full of skill) begun
The speech to all; who had a loved son
That with divine Ulysses did ascend
His hollow fleet to Troy; to serve which end,
He kept fair horse, and was a man at arms,
And in the cruel Cyclops' stern alarms
His life lost by him in his hollow cave,
Whose entrails open'd his abhorred grave,   30
And made of him, of all Ulysses' train,
His latest supper, being latest slain;
His name was Antiphus. And this old man,
This crooked-grown, this wise Egyptian,
Had three sons more; of which one riotous

A wooer was, and call'd Eurynomus;
The other two took both his own wish'd course.
Yet both the best fates weigh'd not down the worse,
But left the old man mindful still of moan;
Who, weeping, thus bespake the session: 40

  'Hear, Ithacensians, all I fitly say:
Since our divine Ulysses' parting day
Never was council call'd, nor session,
And now by whom is this thus undergone?
Whom did necessity so much compel,
Of young or old? Hath any one heard tell
Of any coming army, that he now
May openly take boldness to avow,
First having heard it? Or will any here
Some motion for the public good prefer?   50
Some worth of note there is in this command;
And, methinks, it must be some good man's hand
That's put to it, that either hath direct
Means to assist, or, for his good affect,
Hopes to be happy in the proof he makes;
And that Jove grant, whate'er he undertakes.'

  Telemachus (rejoicing much to hear
The good hope and opinion men did bear
Of his young actions) no longer sat,
But long'd t' approve what this man pointed at,   60
And make his first proof in a cause so good;
And in the council's chief place up he stood;
When straight Pisenor (herald to his sire,
And learn'd in counsels) felt his heart on fire
To hear him speak, and put into his hand
The sceptre that his father did command;
Then, to the old Egyptian turn'd, he spoke:

  'Father, not far he is that undertook
To call this council; whom you soon shall know.
Myself, whose wrongs my griefs will make me show,   70
Am he that author'd this assembly here.
Nor have I heard of any army near,
Of which, being first told, I might iterate,
Nor for the public good can aught relate,
Only mine own affairs all this procure,
That in my house a double ill endure:
One, having lost a father so renown'd,
Whose kind rule once with your command was crown'd;

The other is, what much more doth augment
His weighty loss, the ruin imminent   80
Of all my house by it, my goods all spent.
And of all this the wooers, that are sons
To our chief peers, are the confusions,
Importuning my mother's marriage
Against her will; nor dares their blood's bold rage
Go to Icarius', her father's, court,
That, his will ask'd in kind and comely sort,
He may endow his daughter with a dow'r,
And, she consenting, at his pleasure's pow'r
Dispose her to a man that, thus behav'd,   90
May have fit grace, and see her honour sav'd;
But these, in none but my house, all their lives
Resolve to spend, slaught'ring my sheep and beeves,
And with my fattest goats lay feast on feast,
My generous wine consuming as they list.
A world of things they spoil, here wanting one
That, like Ulysses, quickly could set gone
These peace-plagues from his house, that spoil like war;
Whom my powers are unfit to urge so far,
Myself immartial. But, had I the pow'r,   100
My will should serve me to exempt this hour
From out my life-time. For, past patience,
Base deeds are done here, that exceed defence
Of any honour. Falling is my house,
Which you should shame to see so ruinous.
Reverence the censures that all good men give,
That dwell about you; and for fear to live
Exposed to heaven's wrath (that doth ever pay
Pains for joys forfeit) even by Jove I pray,
Or Themis, both which pow'rs have to restrain   110
Or gather councils, that ye will abstain
From further spoil, and let me only waste
In that most wretched grief I have embrac'd
For my lost father. And though I am free
From meriting your outrage, yet if he,
Good man, hath ever with a hostile heart
Done ill to any Greek, on me convert
Your like hostility, and vengeance take
Of his ill on my life, and all these make
Join in that justice; but to see abus'd   120
Those goods that do none ill but being ill us'd,

Exceeds all right. Yet better 'tis for me
My whole possessions and my rents to see
Consum'd by you, than lose my life and all;
For on your rapine a revenge may fall,
While I live; and so long I may complain
About the city, till my goods again,
Oft ask'd, may be with all amends repaid.
But in the mean space your misrule hath laid
Griefs on my bosom, that can only speak,   130
And are denied the instant power of wreak.'
    This said, his sceptre 'gainst the ground he threw,
And tears still'd from him; which mov'd all the crew,
The court struck silent, not a man did dare
To give a word that might offend his ear.
Antinous only in this sort replied:
    'High spoken, and of spirit unpacified,
How have you sham'd us in this speech of yours!
Will you brand us for an offence not ours?
Your mother, first in craft, is first in cause.   140
Three years are past, and near the fourth now draws,
Since first she mock'd the peers Achaian.
All she made hope, and promis'd every man,
Sent for us ever, left love's show in nought,
But in her heart conceal'd another thought
Besides, as curious in her craft, her loom
She with a web charg'd, hard to overcome,
And thus bespake us: 'Youths, that seek my bed,
Since my divine spouse rests amongst the dead,
Hold on your suits but till I end, at most,   150
This funeral weed, lest what is done be lost.
Besides, I purpose, that when th' austere fate
Of bitter death shall take into his state
Laertes the heroë, it shall deck
His royal corse, since I should suffer check
In ill report of every common dame,
If one so rich should show in death his shame.'
This speech she used; and this did soon persuade
Our gentle minds. But this a work she made
So hugely long, undoing still in night,   160
By torches, all she did by day's broad light,
That three years her deceit div'd past our view,
And made us think that all she feign'd was true.
But when the fourth year came, and those sly hours

That still surprise at length dames' craftiest pow'rs,
One of her women, that knew all, disclos'd
The secret to us, that she still unloos'd
Her whole day's fair affair in depth of night.
And then no further she could force her sleight,
But, of necessity, her work gave end.   170
And thus by me doth every other friend,
Professing love to her, reply to thee,
That ev'n thyself, and all Greeks else, may see
That we offend not in our stay, but she.
To free thy house then, send her to her sire,
Commanding that her choice be left entire
To his election, and one settled will.
Nor let her vex with her illusions still
Her friends that woo her, standing on her wit,
Because wise Pallas hath given wills to it   180
So full of art, and made her understand
All works in fair skill of a lady's hand.
But (for her working mind) we read of none
Of all the old world, in which Greece hath shown
Her rarest pieces, that could equal her:
Tyro, Alcmena and Mycena were
To hold comparison in no degree,
For solid brain, with wise Penelope.
And yet, in her delays of us, she shows
No prophet's skill with all the wit she owes;   190
For all this time thy goods and victuals go
To utter ruin; and shall ever so,
While thus the gods her glorious mind dispose.
Glory herself may gain, but thou shalt lose
Thy longings ev'n for necessary food;
For we will never go where lies our good,
Nor any other where, till this delay
She puts on all, she quits with th' endless stay
Of some one of us, that to all the rest
May give free farewell with his nuptial feast.'   200

    The wise young prince replied: 'Antinous!
I may by no means turn out of my house
Her that hath brought me forth and nourish'd me.
Besides, if quick or dead my father be
In any region, yet abides in doubt;
And 'twill go hard, my means being so run out,
To tender to Icarius again,

If he again my mother must maintain
In her retreat, the dow'r she brought with her.
And then a double ill it will confer,   210
Both from my father and from god on me,
When, thrust out of her house, on her bent knee,
My mother shall the horrid Furies raise
With imprecations, and all men dispraise
My part in her exposure. Never then
Will I perform this counsel. If your spleen
Swell at my courses, once more I command
Your absence from my house; some other's hand
Charge with your banquets; on your own goods eat,
And either other mutually intreat,   220
At either of your houses, with your feast.
But if ye still esteem more sweet and best
Another's spoil, so you still wreakless live,
Gnaw, vermin-like, things sacred, no laws give
To your devouring; it remains that I
Invoke each ever-living deity,
And vow, if Jove shall deign in any date
Pow'r of like pains for pleasure so past rate,
From thenceforth look, where ye have revell'd so
Unwreak'd, your ruins all shall undergo.'   230
    Thus spake Telemachus; t' assure whose threat,
Far-seeing Jove upon their pinions set
Two eagles from the high brows of a hill,
That, mounted on the winds, together still
Their strokes extended; but arriving now
Amidst the council, over every brow
Shook their thick wings and, threat'ning death's cold fears,
Their necks and cheeks tore with their eager seres;
Then, on the court's right-hand away they flew,
Above both court and city. With whose view,   240
And study what events they might foretell,
The council into admiration fell.
The old heroë Halitherses then,
The son of Nestor, that of all old men,
His peers in that court, only could foresee
By flight of fowls man's fixed destiny,
'Twixt them and their amaze this interpos'd:
    'Hear, lthacensians, all your doubts disclos'd.
The wooers most are touch'd in this ostent,
To whom are dangers great and imminent;   250

For now not long more shall Ulysses bear
Lack of his most lov'd, but fills some place near,
Addressing to these wooers fate and death.
And many more this mischief menaceth
Of us inhabiting this famous isle.
Let us consult yet, in this long forewhile,
How to ourselves we may prevent this ill.
Let these men rest secure, and revel still,
Though they might find it safer, if with us
They would in time prevent what threats them thus,   260
Since not without sure trial I foretell
These coming storms, but know their issue well.
For to Ulysses all things have event,
As I foretold him, when for Ilion went
The whole Greek fleet together, and with them
Th' abundant-in-all-counsels took the stream.
I told him that, when much ill he had pass'd,
And all his men were lost, he should at last,
The twentieth year, turn home, to all unknown;
All which effects are to perfection grown.'   270
    Eurymachus, the son of Polybus,
Opposed this man's presage, and answer'd thus:
    'Hence, great in years, go prophesy at home;
Thy children teach to shun their ills to come.
In these superior far to thee am I.
A world of fowls beneath the sun-beams fly
That are not fit t' inform a prophecy.
Besides, Ulysses perish'd long ago;
And would thy fates to thee had destin'd so,
Since so thy so much prophecy had spar'd   280
Thy wronging of our rights, which, for reward
Expected home with thee, hath summon'd us
Within the anger of Telemachus.
But this I will presage, which shall be true:
If any spark of anger chance t' ensue
Thy much old art in these deep auguries,
In this young man incensed by thy lies,
Even to himself his anger shall confer
The greater anguish, and thine own ends err
From all their objects; and, besides, thine age   290
Shall feel a pain, to make thee curse presage
With worthy cause, for it shall touch thee near.
But I will soon give end to all our fear,

Preventing whatsoever chance can fall,
In my suit to the young prince for us all,
To send his mother to her father's house,
That he may sort her out a worthy spouse,
And such a dow'r bestow, as may befit
One lov'd to leave her friends and follow it.
Before which course be, I believe that none   300
Of all the Greeks will cease th' ambition
Of such a match. For, chance what can to us,
We no man fear, no not Telemachus,
Though ne'er so greatly spoken. Nor care we
For any threats of austere prophecy,
Which thou, old dotard, vaunt'st of so in vain.
And thus shalt thou in much more hate remain;
For still the gods shall bear their ill expense,
Nor ever be dispos'd by competence,
Till with her nuptials she dismiss our suits;   310
Our whole lives' days shall sow hopes for such fruits.
Her virtues we contend to, nor will go
To any other, be she never so
Worthy of us, and all the worth we owe.'

　　He answer'd him: 'Eurymachus, and all
Ye generous wooers, now, in general,
I see your brave resolves, and will no more
Make speech of these points – and much less implore.
It is enough, that all the Grecians here,
And all the gods besides, just witness bear   320
What friendly premonitions have been spent
On your forbearance, and their vain event.
Yet, with my other friends, let love prevail
To fit me with a vessel free of sail,
And twenty men, that may divide to me
My ready passage through the yielding sea.
For Sparta, and Amathoan Pylos' shore,
I now am bound, in purpose to explore
My long-lack'd father, and to try if fame
Or Jove, most author of man's honour'd name,   330
With his return and life may glad mine ear,
Though toil'd in that proof I sustain a year.
If dead I hear him, nor of more state, here
Retir'd to my lov'd country, I will rear
A sepulchre to him, and celebrate
Such royal parent-rites as fits his state –

And then my mother to a spouse dispose.'
   This said, he sat; and to the rest arose
Mentor, that was Ulysses' chosen friend,
To whom, when he set forth, he did commend   340
His complete family, and whom he will'd
To see the mind of his old sire fulfill'd,
All things conserving safe till his retreat.
Who, tender of his charge, and seeing so set
In slight care of their king his subjects there,
Suffering his son so much contempt to bear,
Thus gravely, and with zeal, to him began:
   'No more let any sceptre-bearing man
Benevolent or mild or human be,
Nor in his mind form acts of piety,   350
But ever feed on blood, and facts unjust
Commit, ev'n to the full swing of his lust,
Since of divine Ulysses no man now,
Of all his subjects, any thought doth show.
All whom he govern'd, and became to them,
Rather than one that wore a diadem,
A most indulgent father. But, for all
That can touch me, within no envy fall
These insolent wooers, that in violent kind
Commit things foul by th' ill wit of the mind,   360
And with the hazard of their heads devour
Ulysses' house, since his returning hour
They hold past hope. But it affects me much,
Ye dull plebeians, that all this doth touch
Your free states nothing; who, struck dumb, afford
These wooers not so much wreak as a word,
Though few, and you with only number might
Extinguish to them the profaned light.'
   Evenor's son, Leocritus, replied:
'Mentor the railer, made a fool with pride,   370
What language giv'st thou that would quiet us
With putting us in storm, exciting thus
The rout against us? Who, though more than we,
Should find it is no easy victory
To drive men, habited in feast, from feasts –
No, not if Ithacus himself such guests
Should come and find so furnishing his court,
And hope to force them from so sweet a fort.
His wife should little joy in his arrive,

Though much she wants him; for, where she alive   380
Would hers enjoy, there death should claim his rights.
He must be conquer'd that with many fights.
Thou speak'st unfit things. To their labours then
Disperse these people; and let these two men,
Mentor and Halitherses, that so boast
From the beginning to have govern'd most
In friendship of the father, to the son
Confirm the course he now affects to run.
But my mind says, that if he would but use
A little patience, he should here hear news   390
Of all things that his wish would understand,
But no good hope for of the course in hand.'

   This said, the council rose; when every peer
And all the people in dispersion were
To houses of their own, the wooers yet
Made to Ulysses' house their old retreat.

   Telemachus, apart from all the prease,
Prepar'd to shore, and, in the aged seas
His fair hands wash'd, did thus to Pallas pray:
'Hear me, O goddess, that but yesterday   400
Didst deign access to me at home, and lay
Brave charge on me to take ship, and inquire
Along the dark seas for mine absent sire!
Which all the Greeks oppose; amongst whom most
Those that are proud still at another's cost,
Past measure, and the civil rights of men,
My mother's wooers, my repulse maintain.'

   Thus spake he praying; when close to him came
Pallas, resembling Mentor both in flame
Of voice and person, and advis'd him thus :   410

   'Those wooers well might know, Telemachus,
Thou wilt not ever weak and childish be,
If to thee be instill'd the faculty
Of mind and body that thy father grac'd,
And if, like him, there be in thee enchas'd
Virtue to give words works, and works their end.
This voyage, that to them thou didst commend,
Shall not so quickly, as they idly ween,
Be vain, or giv'n up, for their opposite spleen.
But, if Ulysses nor Penelope   420
Were thy true parents, I then hope in thee
Of no more urging thy attempt in hand;

For few, that rightly bred on both sides stand,
Are like their parents, many that are worse –
And most few, better. Those then that the nurse
Or mother call true born, yet are not so,
Like worthy sires much less are like to grow.
But thou show'st now that in thee fades not quite
Thy father's wisdom; and that future light
Shall therefore show thee far from being unwise,   430
Or touch'd with stain of bastard cowardice.
Hope therefore says, that thou wilt to the end
Pursue the brave act thou didst erst intend.
But for the foolish wooers, they bewray
They neither counsel have nor soul, since they
Are neither wise nor just, and so must needs
Rest ignorant how black above their heads
Fate hovers holding death, that one sole day
Will make enough to make them all away.
For thee, the way thou wishest shall no more   440
Fly thee a step; I, that have been before
Thy father's friend, thine likewise now will be,
Provide thy ship myself, and follow thee.
Go thou then home, and soothe each wooer's vein,
But under hand fit all things for the main:
Wine in as strong and sweet casks as you can,
And meal, the very marrow of a man,
Which put in good sure leather sacks, and see
That with sweet food sweet vessels still agree.
I from the people straight will press for you   450
Free voluntaries; and, for ships, enow
Sea-circled Ithaca contains, both new
And old-built; all which I'll exactly view,
And choose what one soever most doth please;
Which rigg'd, we'll straight launch, and assay the seas.'
This spake Jove's daughter, Pallas; whose voice heard,
No more Telemachus her charge deferr'd,
But hasted home, and, sad at heart, did see
Amidst his hall th' insulting wooers flea
Goats, and roast swine. 'Mongst whom Antinous,   460
Careless, discovering in Telemachus
His grudge to see them, laugh'd, met, took his hand,
And said: 'High-spoken, with the mind so mann'd!
Come, do as we do, put not up your spirits
With these low trifles, nor our loving merits

In gall of any hateful purpose steep,
But eat egregiously, and drink as deep.
The things thou think'st on, all at full shall be
By th' Achives thought on, and perform'd to thee:
Ship, and choice oars, that in a trice will land   470
Thy hasty fleet on heav'nly Pylos' sand,
And at the fame of thy illustrous sire.'
He answer'd: 'Men whom pride did so inspire,
Are not fit consorts for an humble guest;
Nor are constrain'd men merry at their feast.
Is't not enough, that all this time ye have
Op'd in your entrails my chief goods a grave,
And, while I was a child, made me partake?
My now more growth more grown my mind doth make,
And, hearing speak more judging men than you,   480
Perceive how much I was misgovern'd now.
I now will try if I can bring ye home
An ill fate to consort you, if it come
From Pylos, or amongst the people here.
But thither I resolve, and know that there
I shall not touch in vain. Nor will I stay,
Though in a merchant's ship I steer my way;
Which shows in your sights best, since me ye know
Incapable of ship, or men to row.'
     This said, his hand he coyly snatch'd away   490
From forth Antinous' hand. The rest the day
Spent through the house with banquets, some with jests,
And some with railings, dignifying their feasts.
To whom a jest-proud youth the wit began:
     'Telemachus will kill us every man.
From Sparta to the very Pylian sand,
He will raise aids to his impetuous hand.
O he affects it strangely! Or he means
To search Ephyra's fat shores, and from thence
Bring deathful poisons, which amongst our bowls   500
Will make a general shipwrack of our souls.'
     Another said: 'Alas, who knows but he
Once gone, and erring like his sire at sea,
May perish like him, far from aid of friends,
And so he makes us work? For all the ends
Left of his goods here we shall share, the house
Left to his mother and her chosen spouse.'
     Thus they; while he a room ascended, high

And large, built by his father, where did lie
Gold and brass heap'd up, and in coffers were   510
Rich robes, great store of odorous oils, and there
Stood tuns of sweet old wines along the wall,
Neat and divine drink, kept to cheer withall
Ulysses' old heart, if he turn'd again
From labours fatal to him to sustain.
The doors of plank were, their close exquisite,
Kept with a double key, and day and night
A woman lock'd within; and that was she
Who all trust had for her sufficiency,
Old Euryclea, one of Opis' race,   520
Son to Pisenor, and in passing grace
With grey Minerva; her the prince did call,
And said: 'Nurse! Draw me the most sweet of all
The wine thou keep'st, next that which for my sire
Thy care reserves, in hope he shall retire.
Twelve vessels fill me forth, and stop them well.
Then into well-sew'd sacks of fine ground meal
Pour twenty measures. Nor to any one
But thee thyself let this design be known.
All this see got together; I it all   530
In night will fetch off, when my mother shall
Ascend her high room, and for sleep prepare.
Sparta and Pylos I must see, in care
To find my father.' Out Euryclea cried,
And ask'd with tears: 'Why is your mind applied,
Dear son, to this course? Whither will you go?
So far off leave us – and beloved so,
So only, and the sole hope of your race?
Royal Ulysses, far from the embrace
Of his kind country, in a land unknown   540
Is dead; and, you from your lov'd country gone,
The wooers will with some deceit assay
To your destruction, making then their prey
Of all your goods. Where in your own y'are strong,
Make sure abode. It fits not you so young
To suffer so much by the aged seas,
And err in such a wayless wilderness.'
    'Be cheer'd, lov'd nurse,' said he, 'for not without
The will of god go my attempts about.
Swear therefore, not to wound my mother's ears   550
With word of this, before from heav'n appears

Th' eleventh or twelfth light, or herself shall please
To ask of me, or hears me put to seas,
Lest her fair body with her woe be wore.'

    To this the great oath of the gods she swore;
Which having sworn, and of it every due
Perform'd to full, to vessels wine she drew,
And into well-sew'd sacks pour'd foody meal.
In mean time he, with cunning to conceal
All thought of this from others, himself bore   560
In broad house, with the wooers, as before.

    Then grey-eyed Pallas other thoughts did own,
And like Telemachus trod through the town,
Commanding all his men in th' even to be
Aboard his ship. Again then question'd she
Noemon, famed for aged Phronius' son,
About his ship; who all things to be done
Assured her freely should. The sun then set,
And sable shadows slid through every street,
When forth they launch'd, and soon aboard did bring   570
All arms, and choice of every needful thing
That fits a well-rigg'd ship. The goddess then
Stood in the port's extreme part, where her men,
Nobly appointed, thick about her came,
Whose every breast she did with spirit enflame.
Yet still fresh projects laid the grey-eyed dame.

    Straight to the house she hasted, and sweet sleep
Pour'd on each wooer; which so laid in steep
Their drowsy temples, that each brow did nod,
As all were drinking, and each hand his load,   580
The cup, let fall. All start up, and to bed,
Nor more would watch, when sleep so surfeited
Their leaden eyelids. Then did Pallas call
Telemachus, in body, voice and all
Resembling Mentor, from his native nest,
And said, that all his arm'd men were addrest
To use their oars, and all expected now
He should the spirit of a soldier show.
'Come then,' said she, 'no more let us defer
Our honour'd action.' Then she took on her   590
A ravish'd spirit, and led as she did leap;
And he her most haste took out step by step.

    Arrived at sea and ship, they found ashore
The soldiers that their fashion'd-long hair wore;

To whom the prince said: 'Come my friends, let's bring
Our voyage's provision; every thing
Is heap'd together in our court; and none –
No not my mother, nor her maids – but one
Knows our intention.' This express'd, he led,
The soldiers close together followed;   600
And all together brought aboard their store.
Aboard the prince went; Pallas still before
Sat at the stern, he close to her, the men
Up hasted after. He and Pallas then
Put from the shore. His soldiers then he bad
See all their arms fit; which they heard, and had.

  A beechen mast, then, in the hollow base
They put, and hoisted, fix'd it in his place
With cables; and with well-wreath'd halsers hoise
Their white sails, which grey Pallas now employs   610
With full and fore-gales through the dark deep main.
The purple waves, so swift cut, roar'd again
Against the ship sides, that now ran and plow'd
The rugged seas up. Then the men bestow'd
Their arms about the ship, and sacrifice
With crown'd wine-cups to th' endless deities
They offer'd up. Of all yet thron'd above,
They most observ'd the grey-eyed seed of Jove;
Who, from the evening till the morning rose,
And all day long, their voyage did dispose.   620

THE END OF THE SECOND BOOK

BOOK THREE

The Argument

Telemachus, and heav'n's wise dame
That never husband had, now came
To Nestor; who his either guest
Received at the religious feast
He made to Neptune on his shore,
And there told what was done before
The Trojan turrets, and the state
Of all the Greeks since Ilion's fate.
This book these three of greatest place
Doth serve with many a varied grace.
Which past, Minerva takes her leave.
Whose state when Nestor doth perceive,
With sacrifice he makes it known,
Where many a pleasing rite is shown.
Which done, Telemachus hath gain'd
A chariot of him; who ordain'd
Pisistratus, his son, his guide
To Sparta; and when starry-eyed
The ample heav'n began to be,
All house-rites to afford them free,
In Pheris, Diocles did please,
His surname Ortilochides.

Another Argument

Gamma   Ulysses' son
            With Nestor lies,
        To Sparta gone;
            Thence Pallas flies.

BOOK THREE

THE SUN now left the great and goodly lake,
     And to the firm heav'n bright ascent did make,
     To shine as well upon the mortal birth,
Inhabiting the plow'd life-giving earth,
As on the ever-treaders-upon-death.
And now to Pylos, that so garnisheth
Herself with buildings, old Neleus' town,
The prince and goddess come had strange sights shown;
For, on the marine shore, the people there
To Neptune, that the azure locks doth wear,   10
Beeves that were wholly black gave holy flame.
Nine seats of state they made to his high name;
And every seat set with five hundred men,
And each five hundred was to furnish then
With nine black oxen every sacred seat.
These of the entrails only pleas'd to eat,
And to the god enflam'd the fleshy thighs.
     By this time Pallas with the sparkling eyes,
And he she led, within the haven bore,
Struck sail, cast anchor, and trod both the shore,   20
She first, he after. Then said Pallas: 'Now
No more befits thee the least bashful brow;
T' embolden which this act is put on thee,
To seek thy father both at shore and sea,
And learn in what clime he abides so close,
Or in the power of what Fate doth repose.
     Come then, go right to Nestor; let us see
If in his bosom any counsel be,
That may inform us. Pray him not to trace
The common courtship, and to speak in grace   30
Of the demanders, but to tell the truth;
Which will delight him, and commend thy youth
For such prevention; for he loves no lies,
Nor will report them, being truly wise.'
     He answer'd: 'Mentor! How, alas, shall I

Present myself? How greet his gravity?
My youth by no means that ripe form affords
That can digest my mind's instinct in words
Wise, and beseeming th' ears of one so sage.
Youth of most hope blush to use words with age.'   40
    She said: 'Thy mind will some conceit impress,
And something god will prompt thy towardness;
For, I suppose, thy birth, and breeding too,
Were not in spite of what the gods could do.'
    This said, she swiftly went before, and he
Her steps made guides, and follow'd instantly.
When soon they reach'd the Pylian throngs and seats
Where Nestor with his sons sat; and the meats
That for the feast serv'd, round about them were
Adherents dressing, all their sacred cheer   50
Being roast and boil'd meats. When the Pylians saw
These strangers come, in thrust did all men draw
About their entry, took their hands, and pray'd
They both would sit; their entry first assay'd
By Nestor's son, Pisistratus. In grace
Of whose repair, he gave them honour'd place
Betwixt his sire and brother Thrasymed,
Who sat at feast on soft fells that were spread
Along the sea sands, carv'd, and reach'd to them
Parts of the inwards, and did make a stream   60
Of spritely wine into a golden bowl;
Which to Minerva with a gentle soul
He gave, and thus spake: 'Ere you eat, fair guest,
Invoke the seas' king, of whose sacred feast
Your travel hither makes ye partners now;
When, sacrificing as becomes, bestow
This bowl of sweet wine on your friend, that he
May likewise use these rites of piety;
For I suppose his youth doth prayers use,
Since all men need the gods. But you I choose   70
First in this cup's disposure, since his years
Seem short of yours, who more like me appears.'
Thus gave he her the cup of pleasant wine;
And since a wise and just man did design
The golden bowl first to her free receipt,
Ev'n to the goddess it did add delight,
Who thus invok'd: 'Hear thou, whose vast embrace
Enspheres the whole earth, nor disdain thy grace

To us that ask it in performing this:
To Nestor first, and these fair sons of his,					80
Vouchsafe all honour; and, next them, bestow
On all these Pylians, that have offer'd now
This most renowned hecatomb to thee,
Remuneration fit for them, and free;
And lastly deign Telemachus and me,
The work perform'd for whose effect we came,
Our safe return, both with our ship and fame.'
Thus prayed she; and herself herself obey'd,
In th' end performing all for which she pray'd.
And now, to pray, and do as she had done,					90
She gave the fair round bowl t' Ulysses' son.

　　The meat then dress'd and drawn, and serv'd t' each guest,
They celebrated a most sumptuous feast.
When, appetite to wine and food allay'd,
Horse-taming Nestor then began, and said:
　　'Now life's desire is serv'd, as far as fare,
Time fits me to enquire what guests these are.
Fair guests, what are ye? And for what coast tries
Your ship the moist deeps? For fit merchandise,
Or rudely coast ye, like our men of prise,					100
The rough seas tempting, desperately erring,
The ill of others in their good conferring?'

　　The wise prince now his boldness did begin,
For Pallas' self had harden'd him within,
By this device of travel to explore
His absent father; which two girlonds wore:
His good by manage of his spirits; and then
To gain him high grace in th' accounts of men.
　　'O Nestor, still in whom Neleus lives,
And all the glory of the Greeks survives,					110
You ask from whence we are, and I relate:
From Ithaca (whose seat is situate
Where Neius, the renowned mountain, rears
His haughty forehead, and the honour bears
To be our sea-mark) we assay'd the waves.
The business, I must tell, our own good craves,
And not the public. I am come t' enquire
If, in the fame that best men doth inspire
Of my most-suffering father, I may hear
Some truth of his estate now, who did bear					120
The name, being join'd in fight with you alone,

To even with earth the height of Ilion.
Of all men else that any name did bear,
And fought for Troy, the several ends we hear;
But his death Jove keeps from the world unknown,
The certain fame thereof being told by none –
If on the continent by enemies slain,
Or with the waves eat of the ravenous main.
For his love 'tis that to your knees I sue,
That you would please, out of your own clear view,   130
T' assure his sad end, or say, if your ear
Hath heard of the unhappy wanderer,
To too much sorrow whom his mother bore.
You then by all your bounties I implore,
(If ever to you deed or word hath stood
By my good father promis'd, render'd good
Amongst the Trojans, where ye both have tried
The Grecian suff'rance) that in nought applied
To my respect or pity you will glose,
But uncloth'd truth to my desires disclose.'   140
    'O my much-lov'd,' said he, 'since you renew
Remembrance of the miseries that grew
Upon our still-in-strength-opposing Greece
Amongst Troy's people, I must touch a piece
Of all our woes there, either in the men
Achilles brought by sea and led to gain
About the country, or in us that fought
About the city, where to death were brought
All our chief men, as many as were there.
There Mars-like Ajax lies; Achilles there;   150
There the in-counsel-like-the-gods, his friend;
There my dear son Antilochus took end,
Past measure swift of foot, and staid in fight.
A number more that ills felt infinite;
Of which to reckon all, what mortal man,
If five or six years you should stay here, can
Serve such enquiry? You would back again,
Affected with unsufferable pain,
Before you heard it. Nine years sieg'd we them,
With all the depth and sleight of stratagem   160
That could be thought. Ill knit to ill past end.
Yet still they toil'd us; nor would yet Jove send
Rest to our labours, nor will scarcely yet.
But no man lived, that would in public set

His wisdom by Ulysses' policy,
As thought his equal; so excessively
He stood superior all ways. If you be
His son indeed, mine eyes even ravish me
To admiration. And in all consent
Your speech puts on his speech's ornament.   170
Nor would one say, that one so young could use,
Unless his son, a rhetoric so profuse.
And while we liv'd together, he and I
Never in speech maintain'd diversity;
Nor sat in counsel but, by one soul led,
With spirit and prudent counsel furnished
The Greeks at all hours, that with fairest course,
What best became them they might put in force.
But when Troy's high tow'rs we had levell'd thus,
We put to sea, and god divided us.   180
And then did Jove our sad retreat devise:
For all the Greeks were neither just nor wise,
And therefore many felt so sharp a fate,
Sent from Minerva's most pernicious hate;
Whose mighty father can do fearful things.
By whose help she betwixt the brother kings
Let fall contention; who in council met
In vain, and timeless, when the sun was set,
And all the Greeks call'd, that came charg'd with wine.
Yet then the kings would utter their design,   190
And why they summon'd. Menelaus, he
Put all in mind of home, and cried, 'To sea.'
But Agamemnon stood on contraries,
Whose will was, they should stay and sacrifice
Whole hecatombs to Pallas, to forego
Her high wrath to them. Fool, that did not know
She would not so be won; for not with ease
Th' eternal gods are turn'd from what they please.
So they, divided, on foul language stood.
The Greeks in huge rout rose, their wine-heat blood   200
Two ways affecting. And, that night's sleep too,
We turn'd to studying either other's woe;
When Jove besides made ready woes enow.
Morn came, we launch'd, and in our ships did stow
Our goods, and fair-girt women. Half our men
The people's guide, Atrides, did contain,
And half, being now aboard, put forth to sea.

A most free gale gave all ships prosperous way.
god settled then the huge whale-bearing lake,
And Tenedos we reach'd; where, for time's sake,   210
We did divine rites to the gods. But Jove,
Inexorable still, bore yet no love
To our return, but did again excite
A second sad contention, that turn'd quite
A great part of us back to sea again,
Which were: th' abundant-in-all-counsels man,
Your matchless father who, to gratify
The great Atrides, back to him did fly.
But I fled all, with all that follow'd me,
Because I knew god studied misery,   220
To hurl amongst us. With me likewise fled
Martial Tydides. I the men he led
Gat to go with him. Winds our fleet did bring
To Lesbos, where the yellow-headed king,
Though late, yet found us, as we put to choice
A tedious voyage: if we sail should hoise
Above rough Chius, left on our left hand,
To th' isle of Psyria; or that rugged land
Sail under, and for windy Mimas steer.
We ask'd of god that some ostent might clear   230
Our cloudy business, who gave us sign,
And charge, that all should, in a middle line,
The sea cut for Euboea, that with speed
Our long-sustain'd infortune might be freed.
Then did a whistling wind begin to rise,
And swiftly flew we through the fishy skies,
Till to Geraestus we in night were brought;
Where, through the broad sea since we safe had wrought,
At Neptune's altars many solid thighs
Of slaughter'd bulls we burn'd for sacrifice.   240

    The fourth day came, when Tydeus' son did greet
The haven of Argos with his complete fleet.
But I for Pylos straight steer'd on my course,
Nor ever left the wind his foreright force,
Since god fore-sent it first. And thus I came,
Dear son, to Pylos, uninform'd by fame,
Nor know one sav'd by Fate or overcome.
Whom I have heard of since, set here at home,
As fits, thou shalt be taught, nought left unshown.
    The expert spear-men, every Myrmidon,   250

Led by the brave heir of the mighty-soul'd
Unpeer'd Achilles, safe of home got hold;
Safe Philoctetes, Paean's famous seed;
And safe Idomeneus his men led
To his home, Crete, who fled the armed field,
Of whom yet none the sea from him withheld.
  Atrides you have both heard, though ye be
His far-off dwellers, what an end had he –
Done by Aegisthus to a bitter death;
Who miserably paid for forced breath,   260
Atrides leaving a good son, that dyed,
In blood of that deceitful parricide,
His wreakful sword. And thou my friend, as he
For this hath his fame, the like spirit in thee
Assume at all parts. Fair and great, I see,
Thou art in all hope. Make it good to th' end,
That after-times as much may thee commend.'
  He answer'd: 'O thou greatest grace of Greece,
Orestes made that wreak his master-piece,
And him the Greeks will give a master-praise,   270
Verse finding him to last all after-days.
And would to god the gods would favour me
With his performance, that my injury
Done by my mother's wooers, being so foul,
I might revenge upon their every soul;
Who, pressing me with contumelies, dare
Such things as past the power of utt'rance are.
But heav'n's great pow'rs have graced my destiny
With no such honour. Both my sire and I
Are born to suffer everlastingly.'   280
  'Because you name those wooers, friend,' said he,
'Report says many such, in spite of thee,
Wooing thy mother, in thy house commit
The ills thou nam'st. But say: proceedeth it
From will in thee to bear so foul a foil,
Or from thy subjects' hate, that wish thy spoil,
And will not aid thee, since their spirits rely,
Against thy rule, on some grave augury?
What know they, but at length thy father may
Come, and with violence their violence pay –   290
Or he alone, or all the Greeks with him?
But if Minerva now did so esteem
Thee, as thy father in times past, whom past

All measure she with glorious favours grac'd
Amongst the Trojans, where we suffer'd so
(O, I did never see in such clear show,
The gods so grace a man, as she to him,
To all our eyes, appear'd in all her trim) –
If so, I say, she would be pleased to love,
And that her mind's care thou so much couldst move,   300
As did thy father, every man of these
Would lose in death their seeking marriages.'

   'O father,' answer'd he, 'you make amaze
Seize me throughout. Beyond the height of phrase
You raise expression; but 'twill never be,
That I shall move in any deity
So blest an honour. Not by any means,
If hope should prompt me, or blind confidence
(The god of fools), or every deity
Should will it; for 'tis past my destiny.'   310

   The burning-eyed dame answer'd: 'What a speech
Hath pass'd the teeth-guard Nature gave to teach
Fit question of thy words before they fly!
god easily can (when to a mortal eye
He's furthest off) a mortal satisfy,
And does the more still. For thy car'd-for sire,
I rather wish that I might home retire,
After my suff'rance of a world of woes
Far off, and then my glad eyes might disclose
The day of my return, than straight retire,   320
And perish standing by my household fire
As Agamemnon did, that lost his life
By false Aegisthus, and his falser wife.

   For death to come at length, 'tis due to all;
Nor can the gods themselves, when fate shall call
Their most lov'd man, extend his vital breath
Beyond the fix'd bounds of abhorred death.'

   'Mentor!' said he, 'let's dwell no more on this,
Although in us the sorrow pious is.
No such return as we wish fates bequeath   330
My erring father, whom a present death
The deathless have decreed. I'll now use speech
That tends to other purpose, and beseech
Instruction of grave Nestor, since he flows
Past shore in all experience, and knows
The sleights and wisdoms, to whose heights aspire

Others, as well as my commended sire,
Whom fame reports to have commanded three
Ages of men, and doth in sight to me
Show like th' immortals: 'Nestor, the renown   340
Of old Neleius, make the clear truth known,
How the most great in empire, Atreus' son,
Sustain'd the act of his destruction.
Where then was Menelaus? How was it
That false Aegisthus, being so far unfit
A match for him, could his death so enforce?
Was he not then in Argos, or his course
With men so left, to let a coward breathe
Spirit enough to dare his brother's death?'
    'I'll tell thee truth in all, fair son,' said he: 350
'Right well was this event conceiv'd by thee.
If Menelaus in his brother's house
Had found the idle liver with his spouse,
Arriv'd from Troy, he had not liv'd, nor dead
Had the digg'd heap pour'd on his lustful head,
But fowls and dogs had torn him in the fields,
Far off of Argos; not a dame it yields
Had given him any tear, so foul his fact
Show'd even to women. Us Troy's wars had rack'd
To every sinew's sufferance, while he   360
In Argos' uplands liv'd, from those works free,
And Agamemnon's wife with force of word
Flatter'd and soften'd, who, at first, abhorr'd
A fact so infamous. The heav'nly dame
A good mind had, but was in blood to blame.
There was a poet, to whose care the king
His queen committed, and in every thing,
When he from Troy went, charg'd him to apply
Himself in all guard to her dignity.
But when strong Fate so wrapt-in her effects   370
That she resolv'd to leave her fit respects,
Into a desert isle her guardian led
(There left), the rapine of the vultures fed.
Then brought he willing home his will's won prize,
On sacred altars offer'd many thighs,
Hung in the gods' fanes many ornaments,
Garments and gold, that he the vast events
Of such a labour to his wish had brought,
As neither fell into his hope nor thought.

At last, from Troy sail'd Sparta's king and I,   380
Both holding her untouch'd. And, that his eye
Might see no worse of her, when both were blown
To sacred Sunium, of Minerva's town
The goodly promontory, with his shafts severe
Augur Apollo slew him that did steer
Atrides' ship, as he the stern did guide,
And she the full speed of her sail applied.
He was a man that nations of men
Excell'd in safe guide of a vessel, when
A tempest rush'd in on the ruffled seas;   390
His name was Phrontis Onetorides.
And thus was Menelaus held from home,
Whose way he thirsted so to overcome,
To give his friend the earth, being his pursuit,
And all his exsequies to execute.
But sailing still the wine-hued seas, to reach
Some shore for fit performance, he did fetch
The steep mount of the Malians; and there,
With open voice, offended Jupiter
Proclaim'd the voyage his repugnant mind,   400
And pour'd the puffs out of a shrieking wind,
That nourish'd billows heighten'd like to hills,
And with the fleet's division fulfils
His hate proclaim'd, upon a part of Crete
Casting the navy, where the sea-waves meet
Rough Jardanus, and where the Cydons live.
    There is a rock, on which the sea doth drive,
Bare, and all broken, on the confines set
Of Gortys, that the dark seas likewise fret;
And hither sent the South a horrid drift   410
Of waves against the top, that was the left
Of that torn cliff as far as Phaestus' strand.
A little stone the great sea's rage did stand.
The men here driven 'scap'd hard the ships' sore shocks,
The ships themselves being wrack'd against the rocks,
Save only five, that blue forecastles bore,
Which wind and water cast on Egypt's shore.
When he (there vict'ling well, and store of gold
Aboard his ships brought) his wild way did hold,
And t' other-languag'd men was forced to roam.   420
Mean space Aegisthus made sad work at home,
And slew his brother, forcing to his sway

Atrides' subjects, and did seven years lay
His yoke upon the rich Mycenian state.
But in the eighth, to his affrighting fate,
Divine Orestes home from Athens came,
And what his royal father felt, the same
He made the false Aegisthus groan beneath.
Death evermore is the reward of death.

  Thus having slain him, a sepulchral feast   430
He made the Argives for his lustful guest,
And for his mother whom he did detest.
The selfsame day upon him stole the king
Good-at-a-martial-shout, and goods did bring,
As many as his freighted fleet could bear.
But thou, my son, too long by no means err,
Thy goods left free for many a spoilful guest,
Lest they consume some, and divide the rest,
And thou, perhaps, besides, thy voyage lose.
To Menelaus yet thy course dispose,   440
I wish and charge thee; who but late arriv'd
From such a shore and men, as to have liv'd
In a return from them he never thought,
And whom black whirlwinds violently brought
Within a sea so vast, that in a year
Not any fowl could pass it anywhere,
So huge and horrid was it. But go thou
With ship and men (or, if thou pleasest now
To pass by land, there shall be brought for thee
Both horse and chariot, and thy guides shall be   450
My sons themselves) to Sparta the divine,
And to the king whose looks like amber shine.
Intreat the truth of him, nor loves he lies;
Wisdom in truth is, and he's passing wise.'

  This said, the sun went down, and up rose night,
When Pallas spake: 'O father, all good right
Bear thy directions. But divide we now
The sacrifices' tongues, mix wines, and vow
To Neptune and the other ever-blest,
That, having sacrific'd, we may to rest.   460
The fit hour runs now, light dives out of date,
At sacred feasts we must not sit too late.'

  She said; they heard; the herald water gave;
The youths crown'd cups with wine, and let all have
Their equal shares, beginning from the cup

Their parting banquet. All the tongues cut up,
The fire they gave them sacrific'd, and rose,
Wine, and divine rites us'd, to each dispose.
Minerva and Telemachus desir'd
They might to ship be, with his leave, retir'd.   470
     He, mov'd with that, provok'd thus their abodes:
'Now Jove forbid, and all the long-liv'd gods,
Your leaving me, to sleep aboard a ship –
As I had drunk of poor Penia's whip,
Even to my nakedness, and had nor sheet
Nor covering in my house, that warm nor sweet
A guest nor I myself had means to sleep;
Where I both weeds and wealthy coverings keep
For all my guests. Nor shall fame ever say
The dear son of the man Ulysses lay   480
All night a-shipboard here while my days shine,
Or in my court whiles any son of mine
Enjoys survival, who shall guests receive,
Whomever my house hath a nook to leave.'
     'My much-lov'd father,' said Minerva, 'well
All this becomes thee. But persuade to dwell
This night with thee thy son Telemachus,
For more convenient is the course for us,
That he may follow to thy house and rest,
And I may board our black-sail, that address'd   490
At all parts I may make our men, and cheer
All with my presence, since of all men there
I boast myself the senior; th' others are
Youths, that attend in free and friendly care
Great-soul'd Telemachus, and are his peers
In fresh similitude of form and years.
For their confirmance, I will therefore now
Sleep in our black bark. But when light shall show
Her silver forehead, I intend my way
Amongst the Caucons, men that are to pay   500
A debt to me, nor small, nor new. For this,
Take you him home; whom in the morn dismiss,
With chariot and your sons, and give him horse
Ablest in strength, and of the speediest course.'
     This said, away she flew, form'd like the fowl
Men call the ossifrage; when every soul
Amaze invaded; even th' old man admir'd,
The youth's hand took, and said: 'O most desir'd,

My hope says thy proof will no coward show,
Nor one unskill'd in war, when deities now　　　　510
So young attend thee, and become thy guides –
Nor any of the heav'n-hous'd states besides
But Tritogeneia's self, the seed of Jove,
The great-in-prey, that did in honour move
So much about thy father, amongst all
The Grecian army. Fairest queen, let fall
On me like favours! Give me good renown!
Which as on me, on my lov'd wife let down,
And all my children. I will burn to thee
An ox right bred, broad-headed and yoke-free,　　　　520
To no man's hand yet humbled. Him will I,
His horns in gold hid, give thy deity.'
　　Thus pray'd he, and she heard; and home he led
His sons, and all his heaps of kindered.
Who ent'ring his court royal, every one
He marshall'd in his several seat and throne.
And every one, so kindly come, he gave
His sweet-wine cup; which none was let to have
Before his 'leventh year landed him from Troy;
Which now the butleress had leave t' employ,　　　　530
Who therefore pierc'd it, and did give it vent.
Of this the old duke did a cup present
To every guest; made his Maid many a prayer
That wears the shield fring'd with his nurse's hair,
And gave her sacrifice. With this rich wine
And food suffic'd, sleep all eyes did decline,
And all for home went; but his court alone
Telemachus, divine Ulysses' son,
Must make his lodging, or not please his heart.
　　A bed, all chequer'd with elaborate art,　　　　540
Within a portico that rung like brass,
He brought his guest to; and his bedfere was
Pisistratus, the martial guide of men,
That liv'd, of all his sons, unwed till then.
Himself lay in a by-room, far above,
His bed made by his barren wife, his love.
　　The rosy-finger'd morn no sooner shone,
But up he rose, took air, and sat upon
A seat of white and goodly polish'd stone,
That such a gloss as richest ointments wore　　　　550
Before his high gates; where the counsellor

That match'd the gods (his father) used to sit,
Who now, by fate forc'd, stoop'd as low as it.
And here sat Nestor, holding in his hand
A sceptre; and about him round did stand,
As early up, his sons' troop: Perseus,
The god-like Thrasymed, and Aretus,
Echephron, Stratius, the sixth and last
Pisistratus, and by him (half embrac'd
Still as they came) divine Telemachus;   560
To these spake Nestor, old Gerenius.

   'Haste, loved sons, and do me a desire,
That, first of all the gods, I may aspire
To Pallas' favour, who vouchsaf'd to me
At Neptune's feast her sight so openly.
Let one to field go, and an ox with speed
Cause hither brought, which let the herdsman lead;
Another to my dear guest's vessel go,
And all his soldiers bring, save only two;
A third the smith that works in gold command   570
(Laertius) to attend, and lend his hand,
To plate the both horns round about with gold;
The rest remain here close. But first, see told
The maids within, that they prepare a feast,
Set seats through all the court, see straight address'd
The purest water, and get fuel fell'd.'

   This said, not one but in the service held
Officious hand. The ox came led from field;
The soldiers troop'd from ship; the smith he came,
And those tools brought that serv'd the actual frame   580
His art conceiv'd; brought anvil, hammers brought,
Fair tongs, and all, with which the gold was wrought.
Minerva likewise came, to set the crown
On that kind sacrifice, and make 't her own.

   Then th' old knight Nestor gave the smith the gold,
With which he straight did both the horns infold,
And trimm'd the offering so, the goddess joy'd.
About which thus were Nestor's sons employ'd:
Divine Echephron and fair Stratius
Held both the horns. The water odorous,   590
In which they wash'd what to the rites was vow'd,
Aretus, in a cauldron all bestrow'd
With herbs and flow'rs, serv'd in from th' holy room
Where all were drest, and whence the rites must come.

And after him a hallow'd virgin came,
That brought the barley-cake, and blew the flame.
The axe, with which the ox should both be fell'd
And cut forth, Thrasymed stood by and held.
Perseus the vessel held that should retain
The purple liquor of the off'ring slain.　　　　　　　　600

　　Then wash'd the pious father, then the cake
(Of barley, salt and oil made) took, and brake,
Ask'd many a boon of Pallas, and the state
Of all the offering did initiate,
In three parts cutting off the hair, and cast
Amidst the flame. All th' invocation past,
And all the cake broke, manly Thrasymed
Stood near and sure, and such a blow he laid
Aloft the offering, that to earth he sunk,
His neck-nerves sunder'd, and his spirits shrunk.　　　　610
Out shriek'd the daughters, daughter-in-laws, and wife
Of three-aged Nestor, who had eldest life
Of Clymen's daughters, chaste Eurydice.
The ox on broad earth then laid laterally
They held, while duke Pisistratus the throat
Dissolv'd, and set the sable blood afloat,
And then the life the bones left. Instantly
They cut him up; apart flew either thigh,
That with the fat they dubb'd, with art alone
The throat-brisk and the sweetbread pricking on.　　　　620
Then Nestor broil'd them on the coal-turn'd wood,
Pour'd black wine on; and by him young men stood,
That spits fine-pointed held, on which, when burn'd
The solid thighs were, they transfix'd, and turn'd
The innards, cut in cantles; which, the meat
Vow'd to the gods consum'd, they roast and eat.

　　In mean space, Polycaste (call'd the fair,
Nestor's young'st daughter) bath'd Ulysses' heir;
Whom having cleans'd, and with rich balms bespread,
She cast a white shirt quickly o'er his head,　　　　　630
And then his weeds put on; when forth he went,
And did the person of a god present,
Came, and by Nestor took his honour'd seat,
This pastor of the people. Then, the meat
Of all the spare parts roasted, off they drew,
Sat, and fell to. But soon the temperate few
Rose, and in golden bowls fill'd others' wine.

Till, when the rest felt thirst of feast decline,
Nestor his sons bad fetch his high-man'd horse,
And them in chariot join, to run the course   640
The prince resolv'd. Obey'd as soon as heard
Was Nestor by his sons, who straight prepar'd
Both horse and chariot. She that kept the store
Both bread and wine, and all such viands more
As should the feast of Jove-fed kings compose,
Purvey'd the voyage. To the rich coach rose
Ulysses' son, and close to him ascended
The duke Pisistratus, the reins intended,
And scourg'd, to force to field; who freely flew,
And left the town that far her splendour threw,   650
Both holding yoke, and shook it all the day.
But now the sun set, dark'ning every way,
When they to Pheris came, and in the house
Of Diocles (the son t' Orsilochus,
Whom flood Alpheus got) slept all that night;
Who gave them each due hospitable rite.
But when the rosy-finger'd morn arose,
They went to coach, and did their horse inclose,
Drave forth the forecourt, and the porch that yields
Each breath a sound, and to the fruitful fields   660
Rode scourging still their willing flying steeds,
Who strenuously perform'd their wonted speeds –
Their journey ending just when sun went down
And shadows all ways through the earth were thrown.

THE END OF THE THIRD BOOK

BOOK FOUR

The Argument

Received now in the Spartan court,
Telemachus prefers report
To Menelaus of the throng
Of wooers with him, and their wrong.
Atrides tells the Greeks' retreat,
And doth a prophecy repeat
That Proteus made, by which he knew
His brother's death; and then doth show
How with Calypso lived the sire
Of his young guest. The wooers conspire
Their prince's death; whose treach'ry known,
Penelope in tears doth drown.
Whom Pallas by a dream doth cheer,
And in similitude appear
Of fair Iphthima, known to be
The sister of Penelope.

Another Argument

Delta   Here of the sire
    The son doth hear.
  The wooers conspire,
    The mother's fear.

BOOK FOUR

IN LACEDAEMON now, the nurse of whales,
These two arriv'd, and found at festivals,
With mighty concourse, the renowned king,
His son and daughter jointly marrying.
Alector's daughter he did give his son,
Strong Megapenthes, who his life begun
By Menelaus' bondmaid, whom he knew
In years when Helen could no more renew
In issue like divine Hermione,
Who held in all fair form as high degree   10
As golden Venus. Her he married now
To great Achilles' son, who was by vow
Betroth'd to her at Troy. And thus the gods
To constant loves give nuptial periods –
Whose state here past, the Myrmidons' rich town
(Of which she shar'd in the imperial crown)
With horse and chariots he resign'd her to.
Mean space, the high huge house with feast did flow
Of friends and neighbours, joying with the king.
Amongst whom did a heavenly poet sing,   20
And touch his harp. Amongst whom likewise danc'd
Two who, in that dumb motion advanc'd,
Would prompt the singer what to sing and play.
All this time in the outer court did stay,
With horse and chariot, Telemachus
And Nestor's noble son Pisistratus.
Whom Eteoneus, coming forth, descried,
And, being a servant to the king most tried
In care and his respect, he ran and cried:
'Guests, Jove-kept Menelaus – two such men   30
As are for form of high Saturnius' strain.
Inform your pleasure, if we shall unclose
Their horse from coach, or say they must dispose
Their way to some such house as may embrace
Their known arrival with more welcome grace?'

He, angry, answer'd: 'Thou didst never show
Thyself a fool, Boethides, till now;
But now, as if turn'd child, a childish speech
Vents thy vain spirits. We ourselves now reach
Our home by much spent hospitality   40
Of other men, nor know if Jove will try
With other after-wants our state again;
And therefore from our feast no more detain
Those welcome guests, but take their steeds from coach,
And with attendance guide in their approach.'
    This said, he rush'd abroad, and call'd some more
Tried in such service, that together bore
Up to the guests, and took their steeds that swet
Beneath their yokes from coach, at mangers set,
Wheat and white barley gave them mix'd, and plac'd   50
Their chariot by a wall so clear, it cast
A light quite thorough it. And then they led
Their guests to the divine house, which so fed
Their eyes at all parts with illustrious sights,
That admiration seized them. Like the lights
The sun and moon gave, all the palace threw
A lustre through it. Satiate with whose view,
Down to the king's most-bright-kept baths they went,
Where handmaids did their services present,
Bath'd, balm'd them, shirts and well-napt weeds put on,   60
And by Atrides' side set each his throne.
Then did the handmaid-royal water bring,
And to a laver, rich and glittering,
Of massy gold, pour'd; which she plac'd upon
A silver cauldron, into which might run
The water as they wash'd. Then set she near
A polish'd table, on which all the cheer
The present could afford a reverend dame,
That kept the larder, set. A cook then came,
And divers dishes borne thence serv'd again,   70
Furnish'd the board with bowls of gold. And then,
His right hand given the guests, Atrides said:
'Eat, and be cheerful. Appetite allay'd,
I long to ask of what stock ye descend;
For not from parents whose race nameless end
We must derive your offspring. Men obscure
Could get none such as you. The portraiture
Of Jove-sustain'd and sceptre-bearing kings

Your either person in his presence brings.'
An ox's fat chine then they up did lift,   80
And set before the guests; which was a gift,
Sent as an honour to the king's own taste.
They saw yet 'twas but to be eaten plac'd,
And fell to it. But food and wine's care past,
Telemachus thus prompted Nestor's son
(His ear close laying, to be heard of none):
    'Consider, thou whom most my mind esteems,
The brass-work here, how rich it is in beams,
And how, besides, it makes the whole house sound;
What gold, and amber, silver, ivory, round   90
Is wrought about it. Out of doubt, the hall
Of Jupiter Olympius hath of all
This state the like. How many infinites
Take up to admiration all men's sights!'
    Atrides overheard, and said: 'Lov'd son,
No mortal must affect contention
With Jove, whose dwellings are of endless date.
Perhaps of men some one may emulate,
Or none, my house or me; for I am one
That many a grave extreme have undergone,   100
Much error felt by sea, and till th' eighth year
Had never stay, but wander'd far and near,
Cyprus, Phoenicia, and Sidonia,
And fetch'd the far-off Ethiopia,
Reach'd the Erembi of Arabia,
And Libya, where with horns ewes yean their lambs –
Which every full year ewes are three times dams –
Where neither king nor shepherd want comes near
Of cheese, or flesh, or sweet milk; all the year
They ever milk their ewes. And here while I   110
Err'd, gath'ring means to live, one murderously,
Unwares, unseen, bereft my brother's life,
Chiefly betray'd by his abhorred wife.
So hold I, not enjoying, what you see.
And of your fathers, if they living be,
You must have heard this, since my sufferings were
So great and famous, from this palace here
(So rarely-well-built, furnished so well,
And substanced with such a precious deal
Of well-got treasure) banish'd by the doom   120
Of fate, and erring as I had no home.

And now I have, and use it, not to take
Th' entire delight it offers, but to make
Continual wishes, that a triple part
Of all it holds were wanting, so my heart
Were eas'd of sorrows taken for their deaths
That fell at Troy, by their revived breaths.
And thus sit I here weeping, mourning still
Each least man lost; and sometimes make mine ill,
In paying just tears for their loss, my joy.   130
Sometimes I breathe my woes, for in annoy
The pleasure soon admits satiety.
But all these men's wants wet not so mine eye,
Though much they move me, as one sole man's miss,
For which my sleep and meat even loathsome is
In his renew'd thought, since no Greek hath won
Grace for such labours as Laërtes' son
Hath wrought and suffer'd, to himself nought else
But future sorrows forging, to me hells
For his long absence, since I cannot know   140
If life or death detain him; since such woe
For his love, old Laërtes, his wise wife
And poor young son sustains, whom new with life
He left as sireless.' This speech grief to tears –
Pour'd from the son's lids on the earth, his ears
Told of the father – did excite; who kept
His cheeks dry with his red weed as he wept,
His both hands used therein. Atrides then
Began to know him, and did strife retain,
If he should let himself confess his sire,   150
Or with all fitting circumstance enquire
    While this his thoughts disputed, forth did shine,
Like to the golden-distaff-deck'd divine,
From her bed's high and odoriferous room,
Helen. To whom, of an elaborate loom,
Adresta set a chair; Alcippe brought
A piece of tapestry of fine wool wrought;
Phylo a silver cabinet conferr'd,
Given by Alcandra, nuptially endear'd
To lord Polybius, whose abode in Thebes   160
Th' Egyptian city was, where wealth in heaps
His famous house held, out of which did go,
In gift t' Atrides, silver bathtubs two,
Two tripods, and of fine gold talents ten.

His wife did likewise send to Helen then
Fair gifts, a distaff that of gold was wrought,
And that rich cabinet that Phylo brought,
Round, and with gold ribb'd, now of fine thread full,
On which extended (crown'd with finest wool,
Of violet gloss) the golden distaff lay.   170

    She took her state-chair, and a footstool's stay
Had for her feet; and of her husband thus
Ask'd to know all things: 'Is it known to us,
King Menelaus, whom these men commend
Themselves for, that our court now takes to friend?
I must affirm, be I deceived or no,
I never yet saw man nor woman so
Like one another, as this man is like
Ulysses' son. With admiration strike
His looks my thoughts, that they should carry now   180
Power to persuade me thus, who did but know,
When newly he was born, the form they bore.
But 'tis his father's grace, whom more and more
His grace resembles, that makes me retain
Thought that he now is like Telemachus, then
Left by his sire, when Greece did undertake
Troy's bold war for my impudency's sake.'

    He answer'd: 'Now wife, what you think I know;
The true cast of his father's eye doth show
In his eye's order. Both his head and hair,   190
His hands and feet, his very father's are.
Of whom, so well remember'd, I should now
Acknowledge for me his continual flow
Of cares and perils, yet still patient.
But I should too much move him, that doth vent
Such bitter tears for that which hath been spoke,
Which, shunning soft show, see how he would cloak,
And with his purple weed his weepings hide.'

    Then Nestor's son, Pisistratus, replied:
'Great pastor of the people, kept of god,   200
He is Ulysses' son, but his abode
Not made before here, and he modest too,
He holds it an indignity to do
A deed so vain, to use the boast of words,
Where your words are on wing; whose voice affords
Delight to us as if a god did break
The air amongst us, and vouchsafe to speak.

But me my father, old duke Nestor, sent
To be his consort hither, his content
Not to be heighten'd so as with your sight,   210
In hope that therewith words and actions might
Inform his comforts from you, since he is
Extremely grieved and injured by the miss
Of his great father; suffering even at home,
And few friends found to help him overcome
His too weak suff'rance, now his sire is gone –
Amongst the people not afforded one
To check the miseries that mate him thus.
And this the state is of Telemachus.'
  'O gods,' said he, 'how certain, now, I see   220
My house enjoys that friend's son, that for me
Hath undergone so many willing fights!
Whom I resolved, past all the Grecian knights,
To hold in love, if our return by seas
The far-off Thunderer did ever please
To grant our wishes. And to his respect
A palace and a city to erect,
My vow had bound me; whither bringing then
His riches and his son and all his men
From barren Ithaca (some one sole town   230
Inhabited about him batter'd down),
All should in Argos live. And there would I
Ease him of rule, and take the empery
Of all on me. And often here would we,
Delighting, loving either's company,
Meet and converse; whom nothing should divide
Till death's black veil did each all over hide.
But this perhaps hath been a mean to take
Ev'n god himself with envy, who did make
Ulysses therefore only the unblest,   240
That should not reach his loved country's rest.'
  These woes made every one with woe in love.
Ev'n Argive Helen wept, the seed of Jove;
Ulysses' son wept, Atreus' son did weep,
And Nestor's son his eyes in tears did steep –
But his tears fell not from the present cloud
That from Ulysses was exhaled, but flow'd
From brave Antilochus' remember'd due,
Whom the renown'd son of the Morning slew;
Which yet he thus excus'd: 'O Atreus' son,   250

Old Nestor says, there lives not such a one
Amongst all mortals as Atrides is
For deathless wisdom. 'Tis a praise of his,
Still giv'n in your remembrance, when at home
Our speech concerns you. Since then overcome
You please to be with sorrow, ev'n to tears,
That are in wisdom so exempt from peers,
Vouchsafe the like effect in me excuse,
If it be lawful. I affect no use
Of tears thus after meals – at least at night;   260
But when the morn brings forth, with tears, her light,
It shall not then impair me to bestow
My tears on any worthy's overthrow.
It is the only rite that wretched men
Can do dead friends, to cut hair, and complain.
But death my brother took, whom none could call
The Grecian coward, you best knew of all.
I was not there, nor saw, but men report
Antilochus excell'd the common sort
For footmanship, or for the chariot race,   270
Or in the fight for hardy hold of place.'
　　'O friend,' said he, 'since thou hast spoken so,
At all parts as one wise should say and do,
And like one far beyond thyself in years,
Thy words shall bounds be to our former tears.
O he is questionless a right-born son,
That of his father hath not only won
The person but the wisdom; and that sire
Complete himself that hath a son entire.
Jove did not only his full fate adorn,   280
When he was wedded, but when he was born.
As now Saturnius, through his life's whole date,
Hath Nestor's bliss raised to as steep a state,
Both in his age to keep in peace his house,
And to have children wise and valorous.
But let us not forget our rear feast thus.
Let some give water here. Telemachus!
The morning shall yield time to you and me
To do what fits, and reason mutually.'
　　This said, the careful servant of the king,   290
Asphalion, pour'd on th' issue of the spring
And all to ready feast set ready hand.
But Helen now on new device did stand,

Infusing straight a medicine to their wine,
That drowning cares and angers, did decline
All thought of ill. Who drunk her cup could shed
All that day not a tear, no not if dead
That day his father or his mother were,
Not if his brother, child, or chiefest dear,
He should see murder'd then before his face.   300
Such useful medicines, only borne in grace
Of what was good, would Helen ever have.
And this juice to her Polydamna gave
The wife of Thoön, an Egyptian born,
Whose rich earth herbs of medicine do adorn
In great abundance. Many healthful are,
And many baneful. Every man is there
A good physician out of Nature's grace,
For all the nation sprung of Paeon's race.
     When Helen then her medicine had infus'd,   310
She bad pour wine to it, and this speech us'd:
     'Atrides, and these good men's sons, great Jove
Makes good and ill one after other move,
In all things earthly; for he can do all.
The woes past, therefore, he so late let fall,
The comforts he affords us let us take;
Feast and, with fit discourses, merry make.
Nor will I other use. As then our blood
Griev'd for Ulysses since he was so good,
Since he was good, let us delight to hear   320
How good he was, and what his sufferings were –
Though every fight and every suffering deed
Patient Ulysses underwent, exceed
My woman's pow'r to number or to name.
But what he did and suffer'd, when he came
Amongst the Trojans, where ye Grecians all
Took part with suff'rance, I in part can call
To your kind memories – how with ghastly wounds
Himself he mangled, and the Trojan bounds,
Thrust thick with enemies, adventur'd on,   330
His royal shoulders having cast upon
Base abject weeds, and enter'd like a slave.
Then, beggar-like, he did of all men crave,
And such a wretch was, as the whole Greek fleet
Brought not besides. And thus through every street
He crept discovering, of no one man known.

And yet through all this difference, I alone
Smoked his true person, talk'd with him; but he
Fled me with wiles still. Nor could we agree,
Till I disclaim'd him quite; and so (as mov'd   340
With womanly remorse of one that prov'd
So wretched an estate, whate'er he were)
Won him to take my house. And yet ev'n there,
Till freely I, to make him doubtless, swore
A powerful oath, to let him reach the shore
Of ships and tents before Troy understood,
I could not force on him his proper good.
But then I bath'd and sooth'd him, and he then
Confess'd, and told me all; and, having slain
A number of the Trojan guards, retired,   350
And reach'd the fleet, for sleight and force admired.
Their husbands' deaths by him the Trojan wives
Shriek'd for; but I made triumphs for their lives,
For then my heart conceiv'd, that once again
I should reach home; and yet did still retain
Woe for the slaughters Venus made for me,
When both my husband, my Hermione,
And bridal room, she robb'd of so much right,
And drew me from my country with her sleight,
Though nothing under heaven I here did need,   360
That could my fancy or my beauty feed.'
   Her husband said: 'Wife! What you please to tell
Is true at all parts, and becomes you well;
And I myself, that now may say have seen
The minds and manners of a world of men,
And groat heroës, measuring many a ground,
Have never, by these eyes that light me, found
One with a bosom so to be belov'd,
As that in which th' accomplish'd spirit mov'd
Of patient Ulysses. What, brave man,   370
He both did act and suffer, when he won
The town of Ilion, in the brave-built horse,
When all we chief states of the Grecian force
Were hous'd together, bringing death and fate
Amongst the Trojans, you, wife, may relate;
For you, at last, came to us; god, that would
The Trojans' glory give, gave charge you should
Approach the engine; and Deiphobus,
The godlike, follow'd. Thrice ye circled us

With full survey of it; and often tried   380
The hollow crafts that in it were implied.
When all the voices of their wives in it
You took on you with voice so like and fit,
And every man by name so visited,
That I, Ulysses, and king Diomed,
(Set in the midst, and hearing how you call'd
Tydides and myself) as half appall'd
With your remorseful plaints, would passing fain
Have broke own silence, rather than again
Endure, respectless, their so moving cries.   390
But Ithacus our strongest fantasies
Contain'd within us from the slenderest noise,
And every man there sat without a voice.
Anticlus only would have answer'd thee,
But his speech Ithacus incessantly
With strong hand held in, till, Minerva's call
Charging thee off, Ulysses sav'd us all.'

Telemachus replied: 'Much greater is
My grief, for hearing this high praise of his.
For all this doth not his sad death divert,   400
Nor can, though in him swell'd an iron heart.
Prepare, and lead then, if you please, to rest:
Sleep, that we hear not, will content us best.'

Then Argive Helen made her handmaid go,
And put fair bedding in the portico,
Lax purple blankets on rugs warm and soft,
And cast an arras coverlet aloft.

They torches took, made haste, and made the bed;
When both the guests were to their lodgings led
Within a portico without the house.   410
Atrides, and his large-train-wearing spouse,
The excellent of women, for the way,
In a retired receit, together lay.
The morn arose; the king rose, and put on
His royal weeds, his sharp sword hung upon
His ample shoulders, forth his chamber went,
And did the person of a god present.

Telemachus accosts him, who begun
Speech of his journey's proposition:

'And what, my young Ulyssean heroë,   420
Provoked thee on the broad back of the sea
To visit Lacedaemon the divine?

Speak truth: some public good, or only thine?'
   'I come,' said he, 'to hear if any fame
Breath'd of my father to thy notice came.
My house is sack'd, my fat works of the field
Are all destroy'd; my house doth nothing yield
But enemies, that kill my harmless sheep
And sinewy oxen, nor will ever keep
Their steels without them. And these men are they   430
That woo my mother, most inhumanly
Committing injury on injury.
To thy knees therefore I am come, t' attend
Relation of the sad and wretched end
My erring father felt, if witness'd by
Your own eyes, or the certain news that fly
From others' knowledges. For, more than is
The usual heap of human miseries,
His mother bore him to. Vouchsafe me then,
Without all ruth of what I can sustain,   440
The plain and simple truth of all you know.
Let me beseech so much, if ever vow
Was made, and put in good effect to you,
At Troy, where suff'rance bred you so much smart,
Upon my father good Ulysses' part,
And quit it now to me (himself in youth)
Unfolding only the unclosed truth.'
   He, deeply sighing, answer'd him: 'O shame,
That such poor vassals should affect the fame
To share the joys of such a worthy's bed!   450
As when a hind, her calves late farrowed,
To give suck enters the bold lion's den,
He roots of hills and herby vallies then
For food (there feeding) hunting, but at length
Returning to his cavern, gives his strength
The lives of both the mother and her brood
In deaths indecent: so the wooers' blood
Must pay Ulysses' pow'rs as sharp an end.
O would to Jove, Apollo, and thy friend
The wise Minerva, that thy father were   460
As once he was, when he his spirits did rear
Against Philomelides, in a fight
Perform'd in well-built Lesbos, where downright
He strook the earth with him, and gat a shout
Of all the Grecians! O, if now full out

He were as then, and with the wooers cop'd,
Short-liv'd they all were, and their nuptials hop'd
Would prove as desperate. But, for thy demand
Enforc'd with prayers, I'll let thee understand
The truth directly, nor decline a thought,   470
Much less deceive or soothe thy search in ought.
But what the old and still-true-spoken god,
That from the sea breathes oracles abroad,
Disclos'd to me, to thee I'll all impart,
Nor hide one word from thy solicitous heart.

   I was in Egypt, where a mighty time
The gods detain'd me, though my natural clime
I never so desir'd, because their homes
I did not greet with perfect hecatombs.
For they will put men evermore in mind,   480
How much their masterly commandments bind.

   There is, besides, a certain island, call'd
Pharos, that with the high-wav'd sea is wall'd,
Just against Egypt, and so much remote
As in a whole day, with a fore-gale smote,
A hollow ship can sail. And this isle bears
A port most portly, where sea-passengers
Put in still for fresh water, and away
To sea again. Yet here the gods did stay
My fleet full twenty days; the winds, that are   490
Masters at sea, no prosp'rous puff would spare
To put us off; and all my victuals here
Had quite corrupted, as my men's minds were,
Had not a certain goddess giv'n regard,
And pitied me in an estate so hard;
And 'twas Idothea, honour'd Proteus' seed,
That old seafarer. Her mind I made bleed
With my compassion, when (walk'd all alone,
From all my soldiers, that were ever gone
About the isle on fishing with hooks bent –   500
Hunger their bellies on her errand sent)
She came close to me, spake, and thus began:

   "Of all men thou art the most foolish man,
Or slack in business, or stay'st here of choice,
And dost in all thy suff'rances rejoice,
That thus long liv'st detain'd here, and no end
Canst give thy tarriance? Thou dost much offend
The minds of all thy fellows." I replied:

    "Whoever thou art of the deified,
I must affirm, that no way with my will   510
I make abode here; but, it seems, some ill
The gods, inhabiting broad heav'n, sustain
Against my getting off. Inform me then,
For godheads all things know, what god is he
That stays my passage from the fishy sea?"

    "Stranger," said she, "I'll tell thee true: there lives
An old seafarer in these seas, that gives
A true solution of all secrets here,
Who deathless Proteus is, th' Egyptian peer,
Who can the deeps of all the seas exquire,   520
Who Neptune's priest is, and, they say, the sire
That did beget me. Him if any way
Thou couldst inveigle, he would clear display
Thy course from hence, and how far off doth lie
Thy voyage's whole scope through Neptune's sky,
Informing thee, O god-preserv'd, beside,
If thy desires would so be satisfied,
Whatever good or ill hath got event,
In all the time thy long and hard course spent
Since thy departure from thy house." This said,   530
Again I answer'd: "Make the sleights display'd
Thy father useth, lest his foresight see,
Or his foreknowledge taking note of me,
He flies the fixt place of his us'd abode.
'Tis hard for man to countermine with god."

    She straight replied: "I'll utter truth in all:
When heaven's supremest height the sun doth skall,
The old Sea-tell-truth leaves the deeps, and hides
Amidst a black storm, when the West wind chides,
In caves still sleeping. Round about him sleep   540
(With short feet swimming forth the foamy deep)
The sea-calves, lovely Halosydnes call'd,
From whom a noisome odour is exhal'd,
Got from the whirlpools, on whose earth they lie.
Here, when the morn illustrates all the sky,
I'll guide, and seat thee in the fittest place
For the performance thou hast now in chace.
In mean time, reach thy fleet, and choose out three
Of best exploit, to go as aids to thee.

    But now I'll show thee all the old god's sleights   550
He first will number, and take all the sights

Of those his guard, that on the shore arrives.
When having view'd, and told them forth by fives,
He takes place in their midst, and there doth sleep,
Like to a shepherd 'midst his flock of sheep.
In his first sleep, call up your hardiest cheer,
Vigour and violence, and hold him there,
In spite of all his strivings to be gone.
He then will turn himself to every one
Of all things that in earth creep and respire,   560
In water swim, or shine in heavenly fire.
Yet still hold you him firm, and much the more
Press him from passing. But when, as before,
When sleep first bound his pow'rs, his form ye see,
Then cease your force, and th' old heroë free,
And then demand, which heav'n-born it may be
That so afflicts you, hindering your retreat
And free sea-passage to your native seat."

    This said, she div'd into the wavy seas,
And I my course did to my ships address,   570
That on the sands stuck; where arriv'd, we made
Our supper ready. Then th' ambrosian shade
Of night fell on us, and to sleep we fell.
Rosy Aurora rose; we rose as well,
And three of them on whom I most relied
For firm at every force, I choos'd, and hied
Straight to the many-river-served seas,
And all assistance ask'd the deities.

    Mean time Idothea the sea's broad breast
Embrac'd, and brought for me, and all my rest,   580
Four of the sea-calves' skins but newly flay'd,
To work a wile which she had fashioned
Upon her father. Then, within the sand
A covert digging, when these calves should land,
She sat expecting. We came close to her;
She plac'd us orderly, and made us wear
Each one his calf's skin. But we then must pass
A huge exploit. The sea-calves' savour was
So passing sour, they still being bred at seas,
It much afflicted us; for who can please   590
To lie by one of these same sea-bred whales?
But she preserves us, and to memory calls
A rare commodity; she fetch'd to us
Ambrosia, that an air most odorous

Bears still about it, which she 'nointed round
Our either nostrils, and in it quite drown'd
The nasty whale-smell. Then the great event
The whole morn's date, with spirits patient,
We lay expecting. When bright noon did flame,
Forth from the sea in shoals the sea-calves came,   600
And orderly, at last lay down and slept
Along the sands. And then th' old sea-god crept
From forth the deeps, and found his fat calves there,
Survey'd, and number'd, and came never near
The craft we used, but told us five for calves.
His temples then dis-eas'd with sleep he salves
And in rush'd we, with an abhorred cry,
Cast all our hands about him manfully;
And then th' old forger all his forms began:
First was a lion with a mighty mane,   610
Then next a dragon, a pied panther then,
A vast boar next, and suddenly did strain
All into water. Last he was a tree,
Curl'd all at top, and shot up to the sky.
    We, with resolv'd hearts, held him firmly still,
When th' old one (held too straight for all his skill
To extricate) gave words, and question'd me:
    "Which of the gods, O Atreus' son," said he,
"Advis'd and taught thy fortitude this sleight,
To take and hold me thus in my despite?   620
What asks thy wish now?" I replied. "Thou know'st.
Why dost thou ask? What wiles are these thou show'st?
I have within this isle been held for wind
A wondrous time, and can by no means find
An end to my retention. It hath spent
The very heart in me. Give thou then vent
To doubts thus bound in me. Ye gods know all –
Which of the godheads doth so foully fall
On my addression home, to stay me here,
Avert me from my way, the fishy clear   630
Barr'd to my passage?" He replied: "Of force,
If to thy home thou wishest free recourse,
To Jove and all the other deities
Thou must exhibit solemn sacrifice;
And then the black sea for thee shall be clear,
Till thy lov'd country's settled reach. But where
Ask these rites thy performance? 'Tis a fate

To thee and thy affairs appropriate,
That thou shalt never see thy friends, nor tread
Thy country's earth, nor see inhabited   640
Thy so magnificent house, till thou make good
Thy voyage back to the Egyptian flood,
Whose waters fell from Jove, and there hast giv'n
To Jove, and all gods hous'd in ample heav'n,
Devoted hecatombs, and then free ways
Shall open to thee, clear'd of all delays."
    This told he; and, methought, he brake my heart,
In such a long and hard course to divert
My hope for home, and charge my back retreat
As far as Egypt. I made answer yet: 650
    "Father, thy charge I'll perfect; but before,
Resolve me truly, if their natural shore
All those Greeks, and their ships, do safe enjoy,
That Nestor and myself left, when from Troy
We first raised sail? Or whether any died
At sea a death unwish'd? Or, satisfied,
When war was past, by friends embrac'd, in peace
Resign'd their spirits?" He made answer: "Cease
To ask so far. It fits thee not to be
So cunning in thine own calamity.   660
Nor seek to learn what learn'd thou shouldst forget.
Men's knowledges have proper limits set,
And should not prease into the mind of god.
But 'twill not long be, as my thoughts abode,
Before thou buy this curious skill with tears.
Many of those, whose states so tempt thine ears,
Are stoop'd by death, and many left alive,
One chief of which in strong hold doth survive,
Amidst the broad sea. Two, in their retreat,
Are done to death. I list not to repeat   670
Who fell at Troy, thyself was there in fight.
But in return swift Ajax lost the light,
In his long-oar'd ship. Neptune, yet, awhile
Sav'd him unwrack'd to the Gyraean isle,
A mighty rock removing from his way.
And surely he had 'scap'd the fatal day,
In spite of Pallas, if to that foul deed
He in her fane did (when he ravished
The Trojan prophetess) he had not here
Adjoin'd an impious boast, that he would bear,   680

Despite the gods, his ship safe through the waves
Then rais'd against him. These his impious braves
When Neptune heard, in his strong hand he took
His massy trident, and so soundly strook
The rock Gyraean, that in two it cleft;
Of which one fragment on the land he left,
The other fell into the troubled seas,
At which first rush'd Ajax Oïliades,
And split his ship, and then himself afloat
Swum on the rough waves of the world's vast moat,   690
Till having drunk a salt cup for his sin,
There perish'd he. Thy brother yet did win
The wreath from death, while in the waves they strove,
Afflicted by the reverend wife of Jove.
But when the steep mount of the Malian shore
He seem'd to reach, a most tempestuous blore,
Far to the fishy world that sighs so sore,
Straight ravish'd him again as far away
As to th' extreme bounds where the Agrians stay,
Where first Thyestes dwelt, but then his son   700
Aegisthus Thyestiades liv'd. This done,
When his return untouch'd appear'd again,
Back turn'd the gods the wind, and set him then
Hard by his house. Then, full of joy, he left
His ship, and close t' his country earth he cleft,
Kiss'd it, and wept for joy, pour'd tear on tear,
To set so wishedly his footing there.
But see, a sentinel that all the year
Crafty Aegisthus in a watchtow'r set
To spy his landing, for reward as great   710
As two gold talents, all his pow'rs did call
To strict remembrance of his charge, and all
Discharg'd at first sight, which at first he cast
On Agamemnon, and with all his haste
Inform'd Aegisthus. He an instant train
Laid for his slaughter: twenty chosen men
Of his plebeians he in ambush laid;
His other men he charged to see purvey'd
A feast; and forth, with horse and chariots grac'd,
He rode t' invite him, but in heart embrac'd   720
Horrible welcomes, and to death did bring,
With treacherous slaughter, the unwary king,
Receiv'd him at a feast, and, like an ox

Slain at his manger, gave him bits and knocks.
No one left of Atrides' train, nor one
Saved to Aegisthus, but himself alone,
All strew'd together there the bloody court."
This said, my soul he sunk with his report;
Flat on the sands I fell, tears spent their store,
I light abhorr'd, my heart would live no more.   730

    When dry of tears, and tired of tumbling there,
Th' old Tell-truth thus my daunted spirits did cheer:
    "No more spend tears nor time, O Atreus' son;
With ceaseless weeping never wish was won.
Use uttermost assay to reach thy home,
And all unwares upon the murderer come,
For torture, taking him thyself alive;
Or let Orestes, that should far out-strive
Thee in fit vengeance, quickly quit the light
Of such a dark soul, and do thou the rite   740
Of burial to him with a funeral feast."

    With these last words I fortified my breast,
In which again a generous spring began
Of fitting comfort, as I was a man;
But, as a brother, I must ever mourn.
Yet forth I went, and told him the return
Of these I knew; but he had named a third,
Held on the broad sea, still with life inspir'd,
Whom I besought to know, though likewise dead,
And I must mourn alike. He answered: 750

    "He is Laertes' son; whom I beheld
In nymph Calypso's palace, who compell'd
His stay with her, and, since he could not see
His country earth, he mourn'd incessantly.
For he had neither ship instruct with oars,
Nor men to fetch him from those stranger shores.
Where leave we him, and to thy self descend,
Whom not in Argos fate nor death shall end,
But the immortal ends of all the earth,
So ruled by them that order death by birth,   760
The fields Elysian, fate to thee will give,
Where Rhadamanthus rules, and where men live
A never-troubled life, where snow nor show'rs,
Nor irksome winter spends his fruitless pow'rs,
But from the ocean Zephyr still resumes
A constant breath, that all the fields perfumes.

Which, since thou marriedst Helen, are thy hire,
And Jove himself is by her side thy sire."

    This said, he dived the deepsome watery heaps;
I and my tried men took us to our ships,   770
And worlds of thoughts I varied with my steps.

    Arriv'd and shipp'd, the silent solemn night
And sleep bereft us of our visual light.
At morn, masts, sails rear'd, we sat, left the shores,
And beat the foamy ocean with our oars.

    Again then we the Jove-fall'n flood did fetch,
As far as Egypt, where we did beseech
The gods with hecatombs; whose angers ceas'd,
I tomb'd my brother that I might be blest.

    All rites perform'd, all haste I made for home,   780
And all the prosp'rous winds about were come.
I had the passport now of every god,
And here clos'd all these labours' period.

    Here stay then till th' eleventh or twelfth day's light,
And I'll dismiss thee well, gifts exquisite
Preparing for thee, chariot, horses three,
A cup of curious frame to serve for thee
To serve th' immortal gods with sacrifice,
Mindful of me while all suns light thy skies.'

    He answer'd: 'Stay me not too long time here,   790
Though I could sit attending all the year.
Nor should my house, nor parents, with desire,
Take my affections from you, so on fire
With love to hear you are my thoughts; but so
My Pylian friends I shall afflict with woe,
Who mourn even this stay. Whatsoever be
The gifts your grace is to bestow on me,
Vouchsafe them such as I may bear and save
For your sake ever. Horse I list not have,
To keep in Ithaca, but leave them here,   800
To your soil's dainties, where the broad fields bear
Sweet cypers grass, where men-fed lote doth flow,
Where wheat-like spelt, and wheat itself, doth grow,
Where barley, white and spreading like a tree;
But Ithaca hath neither ground to be,
For any length it comprehends, a race
To try a horse's speed, nor any place
To make him fat in; fitter far to feed
A cliff-bred goat, than raise or please a steed.

Of all isles, Ithaca doth least provide   810
Or meads to feed a horse, or ways to ride.'
He, smiling, said: 'Of good blood art thou, son.
What speech, so young! What observation
Hast thou made of the world! I well am pleas'd
To change my gifts to thee, as being confess'd
Unfit; indeed, my store is such I may.
Of all my house-gifts then, that up I lay
For treasure there, I will bestow on thee
The fairest, and of greatest price to me.
I will bestow on thee a rich carv'd cup,   820
Of silver all, but all the brims wrought up
With finest gold; it was the only thing
That the heroical Sidonian king
Presented to me, when we were to part
At his receipt of me, and 'twas the art
Of that great artist that of heav'n is free –
And yet ev'n this will I bestow on thee.'
    This speech thus ended, guests came, and did bring
Muttons, for presents, to the godlike king,
And spirit-prompting wine, that strenuous makes.   830
Their riband-wreathed wives brought fruit and cakes.
    Thus in this house did these their feast apply.
And in Ulysses' house activity
The wooers practis'd: tossing of the spear,
The stone, and hurling; thus delighted, where
They exercised such insolence before,
Even in the court that wealthy pavements wore.
Antinous did still their strifes decide,
And he that was in person deified
Eurymachus, both ringleaders of all,   840
For in their virtues they were principal.
    These by Noemon, son to Phronius,
Were sided now, who made the question thus:
    'Antinous! Does any friend here know
When this Telemachus returns, or no,
From sandy Pylos? He made bold to take
My ship with him; of which I now should make
Fit use myself, and sail in her as far
As spacious Elis, where of mine there are
Twelve delicate mares, and under their sides go   850
Laborious mules, that yet did never know
The yoke, nor labour; some of which should bear

The taming now, if I could fetch them there.'
This speech the rest admir'd, nor dream'd that he
Neleïan Pylos ever thought to see,
But was at field about his flocks' survey –
Or thought his herdsmen held him so away.
Eupitheus' son, Antinous, then replied:
'When went he, or with what train dignified
Of his selected Ithacensian youth?   860
Press'd men or bond men were they? Tell the truth.
Could he effect this? Let me truly know.
To gain thy vessel did he violence show,
And used her 'gainst thy will? Or had her free,
When fitting question he had made with thee?'
 Noemon answer'd: 'I did freely give
My vessel to him. Who deserves to live
That would do other, when such men as he
Did in distress ask? He should churlish be
That would deny him. Of our youth the best   870
Amongst the people, to the interest
His charge did challenge in them, giving way,
With all the tribute all their powers could pay.
Their captain, as he took the ship, I knew;
Who Mentor was, or god – a deity's show
Mask'd in his likeness. But, to think 'twas he,
I much admire, for I did clearly see,
But yester-morning, god-like Mentor here:
Yet th' other evening he took shipping there,
And went for Pylos.' Thus went he for home,   880
And left the rest with envy overcome;
Who sat, and pastime left. Eupitheus' son,
Sad, and with rage his entrails overrun,
His eyes like flames, thus interpos'd his speech:
'Strange thing! An action of how proud a reach
Is here committed by Telemachus!
A boy, a child, and we, a sort of us,
Vow'd 'gainst his voyage, yet admit it thus!
With ship and choice youth of our people too!
But let him on, and all his mischief do,   890
Jove shall convert upon himself his pow'rs,
Before their ill presum'd he brings on ours.
Provide me then a ship, and twenty men
To give her manage, that, against again
He turns for home, on th' Ithacensian seas

Or cliffy Samian, I may interprease,
Way-lay, and take him, and make all his craft
Sail with his ruin for his father sav'd.'

    This all applauded, and gave charge to do;
Rose, and to greet Ulysses' house did go.   900
But long time pass'd not, ere Penelope
Had notice of their far-fetch'd treachery.
Medon the herald told her, who had heard
Without the hall how they within conferr'd,
And hasted straight to tell it to the queen;
Who, from the entry having Medon seen,
Prevents him thus: 'Now herald, what affair
Intend the famous wooers, in your repair?
To tell Ulysses' maids that they must cease
From doing our work, and their banquets dress?   910
I would to heav'n, that, leaving wooing me,
Nor ever troubling other company,
Here might the last feast be, and most extreme,
That ever any shall address for them.
They never meet but to consent in spoil,
And reap the free fruits of another's toil.
O did they never, when they children were,
What to their fathers was Ulysses, hear?
Who never did 'gainst any one proceed
With unjust usage, or in word or deed?   920
'Tis yet with other kings another right,
One to pursue with love, another spite;
He still yet just, nor would, though might, devour,
Nor to the worst did ever taste of pow'r.
But their unrul'd acts show their minds' estate.
Good turns received once, thanks grow out of date.'

    Medon, the learn'd in wisdom, answer'd her:
'I wish, O queen, that their ingratitudes were
Their worst ill towards you; but worse by far,
And much more deadly, their endeavours are,   930
Which Jove will fail them in. Telemachus
Their purpose is, as he returns to us,
To give their sharp steels in a cruel death;
Who now is gone to learn, if fame can breathe
News of his sire, and will the Pylian shore,
And sacred Sparta, in his search explore.'

    This news dissolv'd to her both knees and heart.
Long silence held her ere one word would part,

Her eyes stood full of tears, her small soft voice
All late use lost; that yet at last had choice　　　　940
Of wonted words, which briefly thus she us'd:
　　'Why left my son his mother? Why refus'd
His wit the solid shore, to try the seas,
And put in ships the trust of his distress,
That are at sea to men unbridled horse,
And run, past rule, their far-engaged course,
Amidst a moisture past all mean unstaid?
No need compell'd this. Did he it afraid
To live and leave posterity his name?'
　　'I know not,' he replied, 'if th' humour came　　　　950
From current of his own instinct, or flow'd
From others' instigations; but he vow'd
Attempt to Pylos, or to see descried
His sire's return, or know what death he died.'
　　This said, he took him to Ulysses' house
After the wooers; the Ulyssean spouse,
Run through with woes, let torture seize her mind,
Nor in her choice of state chairs stood inclin'd
To take her seat, but th' abject threshold chose
Of her fair chamber for her loath'd repose,　　　　960
And mourn'd most wretch-like. Round about her fell
Her handmaids, join'd in a continuate yell.
From every corner of the palace, all
Of all degrees tun'd to her comfort's fall
Their own dejections; to whom her complaint
She thus enforc'd: 'The gods, beyond constraint
Of any measure, urge these tears on me;
Nor was there ever dame of my degree
So past degree griev'd. First, a lord so good,
That had such hardy spirits in his blood,　　　　970
That all the virtues was adorn'd withal,
That all the Greeks did their superior call,
To part with thus, and lose! And now a son,
So worthily belov'd, a course to run
Beyond my knowledge; whom rude tempests have
Made far from home his most inglorious grave!
Unhappy wenches, that no one of all
(Though in the reach of every one must fall
His taking ship) sustain'd the careful mind
To call me from my bed, who this design'd　　　　980
And most vow'd course in him had either stay'd,

How much soever hasted, or dead laid
He should have left me. Many a man I have,
That would have call'd old Dolius my slave
(That keeps my orchard, whom my father gave
At my departure), to have run, and told
Laertes this, to try if he could hold
From running through the people, and from tears,
In telling them of these vow'd murderers
That both divine Ulysses' hope, and his,   990
Resolv'd to end in their conspiracies.'
    His nurse then, Euryclea, made reply:
'Dear sovereign, let me with your own hands die,
Or cast me off here, I'll not keep from thee
One word of what I know. He trusted me
With all his purpose, and I gave him all
The bread and wine for which he pleas'd to call.
But then a mighty oath he made me swear,
Not to report it to your royal ear
Before the twelfth day either should appear,   1000
Or you should ask me when you heard him gone.
Impair not then your beauties with your moan,
But wash, and put untearstain'd garments on;
Ascend your chamber with your ladies here,
And pray the seed of goat-nurs'd Jupiter,
Divine Athenia, to preserve your son,
And she will save him from confusion.
Th' old king, to whom your hopes stand so inclin'd
For his grave counsels, you perhaps may find
Unfit affected, for his age's sake.   1010
But heaven-kings wax not old, and therefore make
Fit prayers to them; for my thoughts never will
Believe the heavenly pow'rs conceit so ill
The seed of righteous Arcesiades,
To end it utterly, but still will please
In some place evermore some one of them
To save, and deck him with a diadem,
Give him possession of erected tow'rs,
And far-stretch'd fields, crown'd all of fruits and flow'rs.'
This eas'd her heart, and dried her humorous eyes,   1020
When having wash'd, and weeds of sacrifice
Pure and unstain'd with her distrustful tears,
Put on, with all her women-ministers
Up to a chamber of most height she rose,

And cakes of salt and barley did impose
Within a wicker basket; all which broke
In decent order, thus she did invoke:
   'Great virgin of the goat-preserved god,
If ever the inhabited abode
Of wise Ulysses held the fatted thighs   1030
Of sheep and oxen, made thy sacrifice
By his devotion, hear me, nor forget
His pious services, but safe see set
His dear son on these shores, and banish hence
These wooers past all mean in insolence.'
   This said, she shriek'd, and Pallas heard her prayer.
The wooers broke with tumult all the air
About the shady house; and one of them,
Whose pride his youth had made the more extreme,
Said: 'Now the many-wooer-honour'd queen   1040
Will surely satiate her delayful spleen,
And one of us in instant nuptials take.
Poor dame, she dreams not what design we make
Upon the life and slaughter of her son.'
   So said he, but so said was not so done;
Whose arrogant spirit in a vaunt so vain
Antinous chid, and said: 'For shame, contain
These braving speeches. Who can tell who hears?
Are we not now in reach of others' ears?
If our intentions please us, let us call   1050
Our spirits up to them, and let speeches fall.
By watchful danger men must silent go.
What we resolve on, let's not say, but do.'
This said, he choos'd out twenty men, that bore
Best reck'ning with him, and to ship and shore
All hasted, reach'd the ship, launch'd, rais'd the mast,
Put sails in, and with leather loops made fast
The oars. Sails hoisted, arms their men did bring,
All giving speed and form to everything.
Then to the high deeps their rigg'd vessel driv'n,   1060
They supp'd, expecting the approaching ev'n.
   Mean space, Penelope her chamber kept
And bed, and neither ate, nor drank, nor slept,
Her strong thoughts wrought so on her blameless son,
Still in contention, if he should be done
To death, or 'scape the impious wooers' design.
Look how a lion, whom men-troops combine

To hunt, and close him in a crafty ring,
Much varied thought conceives, and fear doth sting
For urgent danger: so fared she, till sleep   1070
All juncture of her joints and nerves did steep
In his dissolving humour; when, at rest,
Pallas her favours varied, and address'd
An idol, that Iphthima did present
In structure of her every lineament,
Great-soul'd Icarius' daughter, whom for spouse
Eumelus took, that kept in Pheris' house.
This to divine Ulysses' house she sent,
To try her best mean how she might content
Mournful Penelope, and make relent   1080
The strict addiction in her to deplore.
This idol, like a worm, that less or more
Contracts or strains her, did itself convey,
Beyond the wards or windings of the key,
Into the chamber, and, above her head
Her seat assuming, thus she comforted
Distress'd Penelope: 'Doth sleep thus seize
Thy pow'rs, affected with so much dis-ease?
The gods, that nothing troubles, will not see
Thy tears nor griefs, in any least degree,   1090
Sustain'd with cause, for they will guard thy son
Safe to his wish'd and native mansion,
Since he is no offender of their states,
And they to such are firmer than their fates.'

    The wise Penelope receiv'd her thus,
Bound with a slumber most delicious,
And in the port of dreams: 'O sister, why
Repair you hither, since so far off lie
Your house and household? You were never here
Before this hour, and would you now give cheer   1100
To my so many woes and miseries,
Affecting fitly all the faculties
My soul and mind hold, having lost before
A husband, that of all the virtues bore
The palm amongst the Greeks, and whose renown
So ample was that fame the sound hath blown
Through Greece and Argos to her very heart?
And now again, a son, that did convert
My whole pow'rs to his love, by ship is gone –
A tender plant, that yet was never grown   1110

To labour's taste, nor the commerce of men –
For whom more than my husband I complain,
And lest he should at any suff'rance touch
(Or in the sea, or by the men so much
Estrang'd to him that must his consorts be)
Fear and chill tremblings shake each joint of me.
Besides, his danger sets on foes profess'd
To way-lay his return, that have address'd
Plots for his death.' The scarce-discerned dream
Said: 'Be of comfort, nor fears so extreme   1120
Let thus dismay thee; thou hast such a mate
Attending thee, as some at any rate
Would wish to purchase, for her pow'r is great;
Minerva pities thy delights' defeat,
Whose grace hath sent me to foretell thee these.'

    'If thou,' said she, 'be of the goddess's,
And heardst her tell thee these, thou mayst as well
From her tell all things else. Deign then to tell,
If yet the man to all misfortunes born,
My husband, lives, and sees the sun adorn   1130
The darksome earth, or hides his wretched head
In Pluto's house, and lives amongst the dead?'

    'I will not,' she replied, 'my breath exhale
In one continu'd and perpetual tale –
Lives he or dies he. 'Tis a filthy use,
To be in vain and idle speech profuse.'
This said, she through the keyhole of the door
Vanish'd again into the open blore.
Icarius' daughter started from her sleep,
And Joy's fresh humour her lov'd breast did steep,   1140
When now so clear, in that first watch of night,
She saw the seen dream vanish from her sight.

    The wooers' ship the sea's moist waves did ply,
And thought the prince a haughty death should die.
There lies a certain island in the sea,
'Twixt rocky Samos and rough Ithaca,
That cliffy is itself, and nothing great,
Yet holds convenient havens that two ways let
Ships in and out, call'd Asteris; and there
The wooers hop'd to make their massacre.   1150

                    THE END OF THE FOURTH BOOK

BOOK FIVE

A second court on Jove attends;
Who Hermes to Calypso sends,
Commanding her to clear the ways
Ulysses sought; and she obeys.
When Neptune saw Ulysses free,
And so in safety plough the sea,
Enrag'd, he ruffles up the waves,
And splits his ship. Leucothea saves
His person yet, as being a dame
Whose godhead govern'd in the frame
Of those seas' tempers. But the mean,
By which she curbs dread Neptune's spleen,
Is made a jewel, which she takes
From off her head, and that she makes
Ulysses on his bosom wear;
About his neck she ties it there,
And, when he is with waves beset,
Bids wear it as an amulet,
Commanding him, that not before
He touch'd upon Phaeacia's shore
He should not part with it, but then
Return it to the sea again,
And cast it from him. He performs,
Yet after this bides bitter storms,
And in the rocks sees death engrav'd,
But on Phaeacia's shore is sav'd.

Another Argument

Epsilon   Ulysses builds
    A ship, and gains
  The glassy fields,
    Pays Neptune pains.

BOOK FIVE

AURORA ROSE from highborn Tithon's bed,
That men and gods might be illustrated,
And then the deities sat. Imperial Jove,
That makes the horrid murmur beat above,
Took place past all, whose height for ever springs,
And from whom flows th' eternal power of things.
 Then Pallas, mindful of Ulysses, told
The many cares that in Calypso's hold
He still sustain'd, when he had felt before
So much affliction, and such dangers more.   10
 'O father,' said she, 'and ye ever-blest,
Give never king hereafter interest
In any aid of yours, by serving you,
By being gentle, human, just, but grow
Rude and for ever scornful of your rights,
All justice ordering by their appetites,
Since he that rul'd as it in right behov'd,
That all his subjects as his children lov'd,
Finds you so thoughtless of him and his birth.
Thus, men begin to say, ye rule in earth,   20
And grudge at what ye let him undergo,
Who yet the least part of his suff'rance know:
Thrall'd in an island, shipwrack'd in his tears,
And in the fancies that Calypso bears,
Bound from his birthright, all his shipping gone,
And of his soldiers not retaining one.
And now his most-lov'd son's life doth inflame
Their slaught'rous envies, since his father's fame
He puts in pursuit, and is gone as far
As sacred Pylos, and the singular   30
Dame-breeding Sparta.' This, with this reply,
The Cloud-assembler answer'd: 'What words fly
Thine own remembrance, daughter? Hast not thou
The counsel giv'n thyself, that told thee how
Ulysses shall with his return address

His wooers' wrongs? And, for the safe access
His son shall make to his innative port,
Do thou direct it, in as curious sort
As thy wit serves thee – it obeys thy pow'rs –
And in their ship return the speedless wooers.'   40

Then turn'd he to his issue Mercury,
And said: 'Thou hast made good our embassy
To th' other statists. To the nymph then now,
On whose fair head a tuft of gold doth grow,
Bear our true-spoken counsel, for retreat
Of patient Ulysses; who shall get
No aid from us, nor any mortal man,
But in a patch'd-up skiff (built as he can,
And suffering woes enough) the twentieth day
At fruitful Scheria let him breathe his way,   50
With the Phaeacians, that half deities live,
Who like a god will honour him, and give
His wisdom clothes, and ship, and brass, and gold,
More than for gain of Troy he ever told;
Where, at the whole division of the prey,
If he a saver were, or got away
Without a wound, if he should grudge, 'twas well.
But th' end shall crown all; therefore fate will deal
So well with him, to let him land, and see
His native earth, friends, house and family.'   60

Thus charg'd he; nor Argicides denied,
But to his feet his fair wing'd shoes he tied,
Ambrosian, golden, that in his command
Put either sea or the unmeasur'd land
With pace as speedy as a puft of wind.
Then up his rod went, with which he declin'd
The eyes of any waker, when he pleas'd,
And any sleeper, when he wish'd, dis-eas'd.

This took, he stoop'd Pieria, and thence
Glid through the air, and Neptune's confluence   70
Kiss'd as he flew, and check'd the waves as light
As any sea-mew in her fishing flight,
Her thick wings sousing in the savory seas.
Like her, he pass'd a world of wilderness;
But when the far-off isle he touch'd, he went
Up from the blue sea to the continent,
And reach'd the ample cavern of the queen,
Whom he within found – without seldom seen.

A sun-like fire upon the hearth did flame,
The matter precious, and divine the frame;   80
Of cedar cleft and incense was the pile,
That breathed an odour round about the isle.
Herself was seated in an inner room,
Whom sweetly sing he heard, and at her loom
About a curious web, whose yarn she threw
In with a golden shuttle. A grove grew
In endless spring about her cavern round,
With odorous cypress, pines and poplars, crown'd,
Where hawks, sea-owls, and long-tongu'd bitterns bred,
And other birds their shady pinions spread –   90
All fowls maritimal; none roosted there
But those whose labours in the waters were.
A vine did all the hollow cave embrace,
Still green, yet still ripe bunches gave it grace.
Four fountains, one against another, pour'd
Their silver streams, and meadows all enflower'd
With sweet balm-gentle and blue violets hid,
That deck'd the soft breasts of each fragrant mead.
Should any one, though he immortal were,
Arrive and see the sacred objects there,   100
He would admire them, and be overjoy'd;
And so stood Hermes' ravish'd pow'rs employ'd.
    But having all admir'd, he enter'd on
The ample cave, nor could be seen unknown
Of great Calypso (for all deities are
Prompt in each other's knowledge, though so far
Sever'd in dwellings) but he could not see
Ulysses there within; without was he
Set sad ashore, where 'twas his use to view
Th' unquiet sea, sigh'd, wept, and empty drew   110
His heart of comfort. Plac'd here in her throne,
That beams cast up to admiration,
Divine Calypso question'd Hermes thus:
    'For what cause, dear and much-esteem'd by us,
Thou golden-rod-adorned Mercury,
Arriv'st thou here? Thou hast not used t' apply
Thy passage this way. Say, whatever be
Thy heart's desire, my mind commands it thee,
If in my means it lie, or power of fact.
But first, what hospitable rites exact,   120
Come yet more near, and take.' This said, she set

A table forth, and furnish'd it with meat
Such as the gods taste; and serv'd in with it
Vermilion nectar. When with banquet fit
He had confirm'd his spirits, he thus express'd
His cause of coming: 'Thou hast made request,
Goddess of goddesses, to understand
My cause of touch here; which thou shalt command,
And know with truth: Jove caused my course to thee
Against my will, for who would willingly   130
Lackey along so vast a lake of brine,
Near to no city that the pow'rs divine
Receives with solemn rites and hecatombs?
But Jove's will ever all law overcomes –
No other god can cross or make it void –
And he affirms, that one the most annoy'd
With woes and toils of all those men that fought
For Priam's city, and to end hath brought
Nine years in the contention, is with thee.
For in the tenth year, when the victory   140
Was won to give the Greeks the spoil of Troy,
Return they did profess, but not enjoy,
Since Pallas they incens'd – and she the waves,
By all the winds' pow'r, that blew ope their graves.
And there they rested. Only this poor one
This coast both winds and waves have cast upon;
Whom now forthwith he wills thee to dismiss,
Affirming that th' unaltered destinies
Not only have decreed he shall not die
Apart his friends, but of necessity   150
Enjoy their sights before those fatal hours,
His country earth reach, and erected tow'rs.'
This struck a love-check'd horror through her pow'rs;
When, naming him, she this reply did give:
'Insatiate are ye gods, past all that live,
In all things you affect; which still converts
Your pow'rs to envies. It afflicts your hearts
That any goddess should, as you obtain
The use of earthly dames, enjoy the men,
And most in open marriage. So ye far'd,   160
When the delicious-finger'd Morning shar'd
Orion's bed; you easy-living states
Could never satisfy your emulous hates,
Till in Ortygia the precise-liv'd dame,

Gold-thron'd Diana, on him rudely came,
And with her swift shafts slew him. And such pains,
When rich-hair'd Ceres pleas'd to give the reins
To her affections, and the grace did yield
Of love and bed amidst a three-cropp'd field,
To her Iasion, he paid angry Jove,   170
Who lost no long time notice of their love,
But with a glowing lightning was his death.
And now your envies labour underneath
A mortal's choice of mine, whose life I took
To liberal safety when his ship Jove strook,
With red-hot flashes, piecemeal in the seas,
And all his friends and soldiers succourless
Perish'd but he. Him, cast upon this coast
With blasts and billows, I, in life given lost,
Preserv'd alone, lov'd, nourish'd, and did vow   180
To make him deathless, and yet never grow
Crooked, or worn with age, his whole life long.
But since no reason may be made so strong
To strive with Jove's will, or to make it vain –
No not if all the other gods should strain
Their pow'rs against it – let his will be law,
So he afford him fit means to withdraw,
As he commands him, to the raging main.
But means from me he never shall obtain,
For my means yield nor men, nor ship, nor oars,   190
To set him off from my so envied shores.
But if my counsel and good will can aid
His safe pass home, my best shall be assay'd.'

    'Vouchsafe it so,' said heav'n's ambassador,
'And deign it quickly. By all means abhor
T' incense Jove's wrath against thee, that with grace
He may hereafter all thy wish embrace.'

    Thus took the Argus-killing god his wings.
And since the reverend nymph these awful things
Receiv'd from Jove, she to Ulysses went;   200
Whom she ashore found, drown'd in discontent,
His eyes kept never dry he did so mourn,
And waste his dear age for his wish'd return;
Which still without the cave he us'd to do,
Because he could not please the goddess so.
At night yet, forc'd, together took their rest
The willing goddess and th' unwilling guest;

But he all day in rocks, and on the shore,
The vex'd sea view'd, and did his fate deplore.
Him, now, the goddess coming near bespake: 210
    'Unhappy man, no more discomfort take
For my constraint of thee, nor waste thine age;
I now will passing freely disengage
Thy irksome stay here. Come then, fell thee wood,
And build a ship, to save thee from the flood.
I'll furnish thee with fresh wave, bread, and wine
Ruddy and sweet, that will the piner pine,
Put garments on thee, give thee winds foreright,
That every way thy home-bent appetite
May safe attain to it, if so it please   220
At all parts all the heav'n-housed deities,
That more in pow'r are, more in skill, than I,
And more can judge what fits humanity.'
    He stood amaz'd at this strange change in her,
And said: 'O goddess, thy intents prefer
Some other project than my parting hence,
Commanding things of too high consequence
For my performance, that myself should build
A ship of power, my home-assays to shield
Against the great sea of such dread to pass;   230
Which not the best-built ship that ever was
Will pass exulting, when such winds as Jove
Can thunder up their trims and tacklings prove.
But could I build one, I would ne'er aboard,
Thy will oppos'd – nor, won, without thy word,
Giv'n in the great oath of the gods to me,
Not to beguile me in the least degree.'
    The goddess smil'd, held hard his hand, and said:
'O y' are a shrewd one, and so habited
In taking heed, thou know'st not what it is   240
To be unwary, nor use words amiss.
How hast thou charm'd me, were I ne'er so sly!
Let earth know then, and heav'n, so broad, so high,
And th' under-sunk waves of th' infernal stream
(Which is an oath as terribly supreme
As any god swears) that I had no thought
But stood with what I spake, nor would have wrought,
Nor counsell'd, any act against thy good,
But ever diligently weigh'd, and stood
On those points in persuading thee, that I   250

Would use myself in such extremity
For my mind simple is, and innocent,
Not given by cruel sleights to circumvent,
Nor bear I in my breast a heart of steel,
But with the sufferer willing suff'rance feel.'
This said, the grace of goddesses led home,
He trac'd her steps; and, to the cavern come,
In that rich throne, whence Mercury arose,
He sat. The nymph herself did then appose,
For food and beverage, to him all best meat   260
And drink, that mortals use to taste and eat.
Then sat she opposite, and for her feast
Was nectar and ambrosia address'd
By handmaids to her. Both, what was prepar'd,
Did freely fall to. Having fitly far'd,
The nymph Calypso this discourse began:
    'Jove-bred Ulysses, many-witted man!
Still is thy home so wish'd? So soon, away?
Be still of cheer, for all the worst I say.
But if thy soul knew what a sum of woes,   270
For thee to cast up, thy stern fates impose,
Ere to thy country earth thy hopes attain,
Undoubtedly thy choice would here remain,
Keep house with me, and be a liver ever.
Which, methinks, should thy house and thee dissever,
Though for thy wife there thou art set on fire,
And all thy days are spent in her desire,
And though it be no boast in me to say
In form and mind I match her every way.
Nor can it fit a mortal dame's compare,   280
T' affect those terms with us that deathless are.'
    The great-in-counsels made her this reply:
'Renown'd and to-be-reverenc'd deity!
Let it not move thee, that so much I vow
My comforts to my wife, though well I know
All cause myself why wise Penelope
In wit is far inferior to thee,
In feature, stature, all the parts of show,
She being a mortal, an immortal thou,
Old ever growing, and yet never old.   290
Yet her desire shall all my days see told,
Adding the sight of my returning day,
And natural home. If any god shall lay

His hand upon me as I pass the seas,
I'll bear the worst of what his hand shall please,
As having giv'n me such a mind as shall
The more still rise the more his hand lets fall.
In wars and waves my sufferings were not small;
I now have suffer'd much, as much before.
Hereafter let as much result, and more.'   300

    This said, the sun set, and earth shadows gave;
When these two (in an in-room of the cave,
Left to themselves) left love no rites undone.
The early Morn up, up he rose, put on
His in and out weed. She herself enchaces
Amidst a white robe, full of all the graces,
Ample, and pleated thick like fishy scales;
A golden girdle then her waist impales,
Her head a veil decks, and abroad they come.
And now began Ulysses to go home.   310

    A great axe first she gave, that two ways cut,
In which a fair well-polish'd helm was put,
That from an olive bough receiv'd his frame;
A planer then. Then led she, till they came
To lofty woods that did the isle confine.
The fir tree, poplar, and heav'n-scaling pine,
Had there their offspring. Of which, those that were
Of driest matter, and grew longest there,
He choos'd for lighter sail. This place thus shown,
The nymph turn'd home. He fell to felling down,   320
And twenty trees he stoop'd in little space,
Plan'd, used his plumb, did all with artful grace.
In mean time did Calypso wimbles bring.
He bor'd, clos'd, nail'd, and order'd every thing,
And look how much a ship-wright will allow
A ship of burden (one that best doth know
What fits his art), so large a keel he cast,
Wrought up her decks, and hatches, side-boards, mast,
With willow watlings arm'd her to resist
The billows' outrage, added all she miss'd,   330
Sail-yards, and stern for guide. The nymph then brought
Linen for sails, which with dispatch he wrought,
Gables and halsters, tacklings. All the frame
In four days' space to full perfection came.
The fifth day, they dismiss'd him from the shore,
Weeds neat and odorous gave him, victuals' store,

Wine, and strong waters, and a prosp'rous wind,
To which, Ulysses, fit-to-be-divin'd,
His sails expos'd, and hoised. Off he gat;
And cheerful was he. At the stern he sat,   340
And steer'd right artfully, nor sleep could seize
His eyelids. He beheld the Pleiades;
The Bear, surnam'd the Wain, that round doth move
About Orion, and keeps still above
The billowy ocean; the slow-setting star
Boötes call'd, by some the waggoner.
    Calypso warn'd him he his course should steer
Still to his left hand. Seventeen days did clear
The cloudy night's command in his moist way,
And by the eighteenth light he might display   350
The shady hills of the Phaeacian shore,
For which, as to his next abode, he bore.
The country did a pretty figure yield,
And look'd from off the dark seas like a shield.
    Imperious Neptune, making his retreat
From th' Aethiopian earth, and taking seat
Upon the mountains of the Solymi,
From thence, far off discovering, did descry
Ulysses his fields ploughing. All on fire
The sight straight set his heart, and made desire   360
Of wreak run over, it did boil so high.
When, his head nodding, 'O impiety,'
He cried out, 'now the gods' inconstancy
Is most apparent, altering their designs
Since I the Aethiops saw, and here confines
To this Ulysses' fate, his misery:
The great mark, on which all his hopes rely,
Lies in Phaeacia. But I hope he shall
Feel woe at height, ere that dead calm befall.'
This said, he begging gather'd clouds from land,   370
Frighted the seas up, snatch'd into his hand
His horrid trident, and aloft did toss,
Of all the winds, all storms he could engross;
All earth took into sea with clouds, grim night
Fell tumbling headlong from the cope of light,
The East and South winds justled in the air,
The violent Zephyr, and North making-fair,
Roll'd up the waves before them. And then bent
Ulysses' knees, then all his spirit was spent.

In which despair, he thus spake: 'Woe is me!   380
What was I born to, man of misery!
Fear tells me now, that all the goddess said
Truth's self will author, that fate would be paid
Grief's whole sum due from me, at sea, before
I reach'd the dear touch of my country's shore.
With what clouds Jove heav'n's heighten'd forehead binds!
How tyrannize the wraths of all the winds!
How all the tops he bottoms with the deeps,
And in the bottoms all the tops he steeps!
Thus dreadful is the presence of our death.   390
Thrice four times blest were they that sunk beneath
Their fates at Troy, and did to nought contend
But to renown Atrides with their end!
I would to god, my hour of death and fate
That day had held the power to terminate;
When showers of darts my life bore undepress'd
About divine Aeacides deceased!
Then had I been allotted to have died,
By all the Greeks with funerals glorified
(Whence death, encouraging good life, had grown),   400
Where now I die by no man mourn'd nor known.'
     This spoke, a huge wave took him by the head,
And hurl'd him o'er board; ship and all it laid
Inverted quite amidst the waves, but he
Far off from her sprawl'd, strow'd about the sea,
His stern still holding broken off, his mast
Burst in the midst, so horrible a blast
Of mix'd winds struck it. Sails and sail-yards fell
Amongst the billows; and himself did dwell
A long time under water, nor could get   410
In haste his head out, wave with wave so met
In his depression; and his garments too,
Giv'n by Calypso, gave him much to do,
Hind'ring his swimming; yet he left not so
His drenched vessel, for the overthrow
Of her nor him, but gat at length again,
Wrestling with Neptune, hold of her; and then
Sat in her bulk, insulting over death,
Which, with the salt stream prest to stop his breath,
He 'scap'd, and gave the sea again to give   420
To other men. His ship so striv'd to live,
Floating at randon, cuff'd from wave to wave.

As you have seen the North wind when he drave
In autumn heaps of thorn-fed grasshoppers
Hither and thither, one heap this way bears,
Another that, and makes them often meet
In his confus'd gales: so Ulysses' fleet
The winds hurl'd up and down; now Boreas
Toss'd it to Notus, Notus gave it pass
To Eurus, Eurus Zephyr made pursue   430
The horrid tennis. This sport call'd the view
Of Cadmus' daughter, with the narrow heel,
Ino Leucothea, that first did feel
A mortal dame's desires, and had a tongue,
But now had th' honour to be nam'd among
The marine godheads. She with pity saw
Ulysses justled thus from flaw to flaw,
And like a cormorant in form and flight,
Rose from a whirlpool, on the ship did light,
And thus bespake him: 'Why is Neptune thus   440
In thy pursuit extremely furious,
Oppressing thee with such a world of ill,
Ev'n to thy death? He must not serve his will,
Though 'tis his study. Let me then advise
As my thoughts serve; thou shalt not be unwise
To leave thy weeds and ship to the commands
Of these rude winds, and work out with thy hands
Pass to Phaeacia, where thy austere fate
Is to pursue thee with no more such hate.
Take here this tablet, with this riband strung,   450
And see it still about thy bosom hung;
By whose eternal virtue never fear
To suffer thus again, nor perish here.
But when thou touchest with thy hand the shore,
Then take it from thy neck, nor wear it more,
But cast it far off from the continent,
And then thy person far ashore present.'
    Thus gave she him the tablet; and again
Turn'd to a cormorant, div'd, past sight, the main.
    Patient Ulysses sigh'd at this, and stuck   460
In the conceit of such fair-spoken luck,
And said: 'Alas! I must suspect ev'n this,
Lest any other of the deities
Add sleight to Neptune's force, to counsel me
To leave my vessel, and so far off see

The shore I aim at. Not with thoughts too clear
Will I obey her, but to me appear
These counsels best: as long as I perceive
My ship not quite dissolv'd, I will not leave
The help she may afford me, but abide,   470
And suffer all woes till the worst be tried.
When she is split, I'll swim. No miracle can,
Past near and clear means, move a knowing man.'

     While this discourse employ'd him, Neptune rais'd
A huge, a high, and horrid sea, that seiz'd
Him and his ship, and toss'd them through the lake.
As when the violent winds together take
Heaps of dry chaff, and hurl them every way:
So his long wood-stack Neptune strook astray.

     Then did Ulysses mount on rib, perforce,   480
Like to a rider of a running horse,
To stay himself a time, while he might shift
His drenched weeds, that were Calypso's gift.
When putting straight Leucothea's amulet
About his neck, he all his forces set
To swim, and cast him prostrate to the seas.
When powerful Neptune saw the ruthless prease
Of perils siege him thus, he mov'd his head,
And this betwixt him and his heart he said:

     'So, now feel ills enow, and struggle so,   490
Till to your Jove-lov'd islanders you row.
But my mind says, you will not so avoid
This last task too, but be with suff'rance cloy'd.'

     This said, his rich-man'd horse he mov'd, and reach'd
His house at Aegas. But Minerva fetch'd
The winds from sea, and all their ways but one
Barr'd to their passage; the bleak North alone
She set to blow, the rest she charg'd to keep
Their rages in, and bind themselves in sleep.
But Boreas still flew high to break the seas,   500
Till Jove-bred Ithacus the more with ease
The navigation-skill'd Phaeacian states
Might make his refuge, death and angry fates
At length escaping. Two nights yet, and days,
He spent in wrestling with the sable seas;
In which space, often did his heart propose
Death to his eyes. But when Aurora rose,
And threw the third light from her orient hair,

The winds grew calm, and clear was all the air,
Not one breath stirring. Then he might descry,   510
Rais'd by the high seas, clear, the land was nigh.
And then, look how to good sons that esteem
Their father's life dear (after pains extreme,
Felt in some sickness that hath held him long
Down to his bed, and with affections strong
Wasted his body, made his life his load,
As being inflicted by some angry god),
When on their pray'rs they see descend at length
Health from the heav'ns, clad all in spirit and strength,
The sight is precious: so, since here should end   520
Ulysses' toils, which therein should extend
Health to his country (held to him his sire,
And on which long for him disease did tire),
And then, besides, for his own sake to see
The shores, the woods so near, such joy had he
As those good sons for their recover'd sire.
Then labour'd feet and all parts to aspire
To that wish'd continent; which when as near
He came, as Clamour might inform an ear,
He heard a sound beat from the sea-bred rocks,   530
Against which gave a huge sea horrid shocks,
That belch'd upon the firm land weeds and foam,
With which were all things hid there, where no room
Of fit capacity was for any port,
Nor from the sea for any man's resort,
The shores, the rocks, the cliffs, so prominent were.
'O,' said Ulysses then, 'now Jupiter
Hath giv'n me sight of an unhoped-for shore –
Though I have wrought these seas so long, so sore –
Of rest yet no place shows the slend'rest prints,   540
The rugged shore so bristled is with flints,
Against which every way the waves so flock,
And all the shore shows as one eminent rock,
So near which 'tis so deep, that not a sand
Is there for any tired foot to stand,
Nor fly his death-fast-following miseries,
Lest, if he land, upon him fore-right flies
A churlish wave, to crush him 'gainst a cliff,
Worse than vain rend'ring all his landing strife.
And should I swim to seek a hav'n elsewhere,   550
Or land less way-beat, I may justly fear

I shall be taken with a gale again,
And cast a huge way off into the main;
And there the great Earth-shaker (having seen
My so near landing, and again his spleen
Forcing me to him) will some whale send out
(Of which a horrid number here about
His Amphitrite breeds) to swallow me.
I well have prov'd, with what malignity
He treads my steps.' While this discourse he held,   560
A curs'd surge 'gainst a cutting rock impell'd
His naked body, which it gash'd and tore,
And had his bones broke, if but one sea more
Had cast him on it. But she prompted him,
That never fail'd, and bade him no more swim
Still off and on, but boldly force the shore,
And hug the rock that him so rudely tore;
Which he with both hands sigh'd and clasp'd, till past
The billow's rage was; when 'scap'd, back so fast
The rock repuls'd it, that it reft his hold,   570
Sucking him from it, and far back he roll'd.
And as the polypus that (forc'd from home
Amidst the soft sea, and near rough land come
For shelter 'gainst the storms that beat on her
At open sea, as she abroad doth err)
A deal of gravel and sharp little stones
Needfully gathers in her hollow bones:
So he forc'd hither by the sharper ill,
Shunning the smoother, where he best hop'd, still
The worst succeeded; for the cruel friend,   580
To which he cling'd for succour, off did rend
From his broad hands the soaken flesh so sore,
That off he fell, and could sustain no more.
Quite under water fell he; and, past fate,
Hapless Ulysses there had lost the state
He held in life, if, still the grey-eyed Maid
His wisdom prompting, he had not assay'd
Another course, and ceas'd t' attempt that shore,
Swimming and casting round his eye t' explore
Some other shelter. Then the mouth he found   590
Of fair Callicoë's flood, whose shores were crown'd
With most apt succours; rocks so smooth they seem'd
Polish'd of purpose; land that quite redeem'd
With breathless coverts th' others' blasted shores.

The flood he knew, and thus in heart implores:
'King of this river, hear! Whatever name
Makes thee invok'd, to thee I humbly frame
My flight from Neptune's furies. Reverend is
To all the ever-living deities
What erring man soever seeks their aid.   600
To thy both flood and knees a man dismay'd
With varied suff'rance sues. Yield then some rest
To him that is thy suppliant profess'd.'
This, though but spoke in thought, the godhead heard,
Her current straight stay'd, and her thick waves clear'd
Before him, smooth'd her waters, and, just where
He pray'd half-drown'd, entirely sav'd him there.
     Then forth he came, his both knees falt'ring, both
His strong hands hanging down, and all with froth
His cheeks and nostrils flowing, voice and breath   610
Spent to all use, and down he sunk to death.
The sea had soak'd his heart through; all his veins
His toils had rack'd t' a labouring woman's pains.
Dead weary was he. But when breath did find
A pass reciprocal, and in his mind
His spirit was recollected, up he rose,
And from his neck did th' amulet unloose,
That Ino gave him; which he hurl'd from him
To sea. It sounding fell, and back did swim
With th' ebbing waters, till it straight arriv'd   620
Where Ino's fair hand it again receiv'd.
Then kiss'd he th' humble earth, and on he goes,
Till bulrushes show'd place for his repose;
Where laid, he sigh'd, and thus said to his soul:
'O me, what strange perplexities control
The whole skill of thy pow'rs in this event!
What feel I? If till care-nurse night be spent
I watch amidst the flood, the sea's chill breath
And vegetant dews I fear will be my death,
So low brought with my labours. Towards day   630
A passing sharp air ever breathes at sea.
If I the pitch of this next mountain scale,
And shady wood, and in some thicket fall
Into the hands of sleep, though there the cold
May well be check'd, and healthful slumbers hold
Her sweet hand on my pow'rs, all care allay'd,
Yet there will beasts devour me. Best appaid

Doth that course make me yet; for there some strife,
Strength, and my spirit, may make me make for life;
Which, though impair'd, may yet be fresh applied,   640
Where peril possible of escape is tried.
But he that fights with heav'n, or with the sea,
To indiscretion adds impiety.'

    Thus to the woods he hasted; which he found
Not far from sea, but on far-seeing ground,
Where two twin underwoods he enter'd on,
With olive-trees and oil-trees overgrown;
Through which the moist force of the loud-voic'd wind
Did never beat, nor ever Phoebus shin'd,
Nor shower beat through, they grew so one in one,   650
And had, by turns, their pow'r t' exclude the sun.
Here enter'd our Ulysses, and a bed
Of leaves huge, and of huge abundance, spread
With all his speed. Large he made it, for there
For two or three men ample coverings were,
Such as might shield them from the winter's worst,
Though steel it breath'd, and blew as it would burst.

    Patient Ulysses joy'd, that ever day
Show'd such a shelter. In the midst he lay,
Store of leaves heaping high on every side.   660
And as in some outfield a man doth hide
A kindled brand, to keep the seed of fire,
No neighbour dwelling near, and his desire
Serv'd with self store he else would ask of none,
But of his fore-spent sparks rakes th' ashes on:
So this out-place Ulysses thus receives,
And thus nak'd, virtue's seed lies hid in leaves.
Yet Pallas made him sleep as soon as men
Whom delicacies all their flatteries deign,
And all that all his labours could comprise   670
Quickly concluded in his closed eyes.

THE END OF THE FIFTH BOOK

BOOK SIX

The Argument

Minerva in a vision stands
Before Nausicaa; and commands
She to the flood her weeds should bear,
For now her nuptial day was near.
Nausicaa her charge obeys,
And then with other virgins plays.
Their sports make wak'd Ulysses rise,
Walk to them, and beseech supplies
Of food and clothes. His naked sight
Puts th' other maids, afraid, to flight;
Nausicaa only boldly stays,
And gladly his desire obeys.
He, furnished with her favours shown,
Attends her and the rest to town.

Another Argument

Zeta   Here olive leaves
       T' hide shame began.
   The maid receives
       The naked man.

BOOK SIX

THE MUCH-SUSTAINING, patient, heav'nly man,
 Whom toil and sleep had worn so weak and wan,
 Thus won his rest. In mean space Pallas went
To the Phaeacian city, and descent
That first did broad Hyperia's lands divide,
Near the vast Cyclops, men of monstrous pride,
That prey'd on those Hyperians, since they were
Of greater power; and therefore longer there
Divine Nausithous dwelt not, but arose,
And did for Scheria all his pow'rs dispose,   10
Far from ingenious art-inventing men.
But there did he erect a city then,
First drew a wall round, then he houses builds,
And then a temple to the gods, the fields
Lastly dividing. But he, stoop'd by fate,
Div'd to th' infernals; and Alcinous sate
In his command, a man the gods did teach
Commanding counsels. His house held the reach
Of grey Minerva's project, to provide
That great-soul'd Ithacus might be supplied   20
With all things fitting his return. She went
Up to the chamber, where the fair descent
Of great Alcinous slept: a maid, whose parts
In wit and beauty wore divine deserts.
Well deck'd her chamber was; of which the door
Did seem to lighten, such a gloss it bore
Betwixt the posts, and now flew ope to find
The goddess entry. Like a puft of wind
She reach'd the virgin bed; near which there lay
Two maids, to whom the Graces did convey   30
Figure and manners. But above the head
Of bright Nausicaa did Pallas tread
The subtle air, and put the person on
Of Dymas' daughter, from comparison
Exempt in business naval. Like his seed

Minerva look'd now; whom one year did breed
With bright Nausicaa, and who had gain'd
Grace in her love, yet on her thus complain'd:
      'Nausicaa, why bred thy mother one
So negligent in rites so stood upon   40
By other virgins? Thy fair garments lie
Neglected by thee, yet thy nuptials nigh;
When rich in all attire both thou shouldst be,
And garments give to others honouring thee,
That lead thee to the temple. Thy good name
Grows amongst men for these things; they inflame
Father and reverend mother with delight.
Come, when the day takes any wink from night,
Let's to the river, and repurify
Thy wedding garments. My society   50
Shall freely serve thee for thy speedier aid,
Because thou shalt no more stand on the maid.
The best of all Phaeacia woo thy grace,
Where thou wert bred, and ow'st thyself a race.
Up, and stir up to thee thy honour'd sire,
To give thee mules and coach, thee and thy tire,
Veils, girdles, mantles, early to the flood
To bear in state. It suits thy high-born blood,
And far more fits thee, than to foot so far,
For far from town thou knowst the bath-founts are.'   60
      This said, away blue-ey'd Minerva went
Up to Olympus, the firm continent
That bears in endless being the deified kind,
That's neither sous'd with showers, nor shook with wind,
Nor chill'd with snow, but where serenity flies
Exempt from clouds, and ever-beamy skies
Circle the glittering hill, and all their days
Give the delights of blessed deity praise.
And hither Pallas flew, and left the maid,
When she had all that might excite her said.   70
Straight rose the lovely Morn, that up did raise
Fair-veil'd Nausicaa, whose dream her praise
To admiration took; who no time spent
To give the rapture of her vision vent
To her lov'd parents, whom she found within:
Her mother set at fire, who had to spin
A rock, whose tincture with sea-purple shin'd,
Her maids about her. But she chanced to find

Her father going abroad, to council call'd
By his grave Senate. And to him exhal'd   80
Her smother'd bosom was: 'Lov'd sire,' said she,
'Will you not now command a coach for me,
Stately and complete, fit for me to bear
To wash at flood the weeds I cannot wear
Before repurified? Yourself it fits
To wear fair weeds, as every man that sit
In place of council. And five sons you have,
Two wed, three bachelors, that must be brave
In every day's shift, that they may go dance;
For these three last with these things must advance   90
Their states in marriage, and who else but I,
Their sister, should their dancing rites supply?'
     This general cause she show'd, and would not name
Her mind of nuptials to her sire, for shame.
He understood her yet, and thus replied:
'Daughter! Nor these, nor any grace beside,
I either will deny thee, or defer,
Mules, nor a coach, of state and circular,
Fitting at all parts. Go, my servants shall
Serve thy desires, and thy command in all.'   100
     The servants then commanded soon obey'd,
Fetch'd coach, and mules join'd in it. Then the maid
Brought from the chamber her rich weeds, and laid
All up in coach; in which her mother plac'd
A maund of victuals, varied well in taste,
And other junkets. Wine she likewise fill'd
Within a goat-skin bottle, and distill'd
Sweet and moist oil into a golden cruse,
Both for her daughter's and her handmaids' use,
To soften their bright bodies, when they rose   110
Cleans'd from their cold baths. Up to coach then goes
Th' observed maid, takes both the scourge and reins,
And to her side her handmaid straight attains.
Nor these alone, but other virgins, grac'd
The nuptial chariot. The whole bevy plac'd,
Nausicaa scourg'd to make the coach-mules run,
That neigh'd, and pac'd their usual speed, and soon
Both maids and weeds brought to the river side,
Where baths for all the year their use supplied,
Whose waters were so pure they would not stain,   120
But still ran fair forth, and did more remain

Apt to purge stains, for that purg'd stain within,
Which by the water's pure store was not seen.
   These, here arriv'd, the mules uncoach'd, and drave
Up to the gulfy river's shore, that gave
Sweet grass to them. The maids from coach then took
Their clothes, and steep'd them in the sable brook;
Then put them into springs, and trod them clean
With cleanly feet, adventuring wagers then,
Who should have soonest and most cleanly done.   130
When having throughly cleans'd, they spread them on
The flood's shore, all in order. And then, where
The waves the pebbles wash'd, and ground was clear,
They bath'd themselves, and all with glittering oil
Smooth'd their white skins, refreshing then their toil
With pleasant dinner by the river's side,
Yet still watch'd when the sun their clothes had dried.
Till which time, having din'd, Nausicaa
With other virgins did at stool-ball play,
Their shoulder-reaching head-tires laying by.   140
Nausicaa, with the wrists of ivory,
The liking stroke struck, singing first a song,
As custom order'd, and amidst the throng
Made such a show, and so past all was seen,
As when the chaste-born, arrow-loving queen,
Along the mountains gliding, either over
Spartan Taygetus, whose tops far discover,
Or Eurymanthus, in the wild boar's chace,
Or swift-hoov'd hart, and with her Jove's fair race,
The field nymphs, sporting; amongst whom, to see   150
How far Diana had priority,
Though all were fair, for fairness yet of all
As both by head and forehead being more tall,
Latona triumph'd, since the dullest sight
Might eas'ly judge whom her pains brought to light:
Nausicaa so, whom never husband tam'd,
Above them all in all the beauties flam'd.
But when they now made homewards, and array'd,
Ordering their weeds disorder'd as they play'd,
Mules and coach ready, then Minerva thought   160
What means to wake Ulysses might be wrought,
That he might see this lovely-sighted maid,
Whom she intended should become his aid,
Bring him to town, and his return advance.

Her mean was this, though thought a stool-ball chance:
The queen now, for the upstroke, struck the ball
Quite wide off th' other maids, and made it fall
Amidst the whirlpools. At which out shriek'd all,
And with the shriek did wise Ulysses wake;
Who, sitting up, was doubtful who should make   170
That sudden outcry, and in mind thus striv'd:
'On what a people am I now arriv'd?
At civil hospitable men, that fear
The gods? Or dwell injurious mortals here,
Unjust and churlish? Like the female cry
Of youth it sounds. What are they? Nymphs bred high
On tops of hills, or in the founts of floods,
In herby marshes, or in leafy woods?
Or are they high-spoke men I now am near?
I'll prove, and see.' With this, the wary peer   180
Crept forth the thicket, and an olive bough
Broke with his broad hand, which he did bestow
In covert of his nakedness, and then
Put hasty head out. Look how from his den
A mountain lion looks, that, all embru'd
With drops of trees, and weather-beaten-hu'd,
Bold of his strength, goes on, and in his eye
A burning furnace glows, all bent to prey
On sheep, or oxen, or the upland hart,
His belly charging him, and he must part   190
Stakes with the herdsman in his beast's attempt,
Even where from rape their strengths are most exempt:
So wet, so weather-beat, so stung with need,
Even to the home-fields of the country's breed
Ulysses was to force forth his access,
Though merely naked; and his sight did press
The eyes of soft-hair'd virgins. Horrid was
His rough appearance to them; the hard pass
He had at sea stuck by him. All in flight
The virgins scatter'd, frighted with this sight,   200
About the prominent windings of the flood.
All but Nausicaa fled; but she fast stood,
Pallas had put a boldness in her breast,
And in her fair limbs tender fear compress'd.
And still she stood him, as resolv'd to know
What man he was, or out of what should grow
His strange repair to them. And here was he

Put to his wisdom; if her virgin knee
He should be bold, but kneeling, to embrace,
Or keep aloof, and try with words of grace,   210
In humblest suppliance, if he might obtain
Some cover for his nakedness, and gain
Her grace to show and guide him to the town.
The last he best thought, to be worth his own,
In weighing both well: to keep still aloof,
And give with soft words his desires their proof,
Lest, pressing so near as to touch her knee,
He might incense her maiden modesty.
This fair and fil'd speech then shew'd this was he:
    'Let me beseech, O queen, this truth of thee: 220
Are you of mortal, or the deified, race?
If of the gods, that th' ample heav'ns embrace,
I can resemble you to none above
So near as to the chaste-born birth of Jove,
The beamy Cynthia. Her you full present,
In grace of every godlike lineament,
Her goodly magnitude, and all th' address
You promise of her very perfectness.
If sprung of humans, that inhabit earth,
Thrice blest are both the authors of your birth,   230
Thrice blest your brothers, that in your deserts
Must, even to rapture, bear delighted hearts,
To see, so like the first trim of a tree,
Your form adorn a dance. But most blest he,
Of all that breathe, that hath the gift t' engage
Your bright neck in the yoke of marriage,
And deck his house with your commanding merit.
I have not seen a man of so much spirit –
Nor man, nor woman I did ever see –
At all parts equal to the parts in thee.   240
T' enjoy your sight, doth admiration seize
My' eyes, and apprehensive faculties.
Lately in Delos (with a charge of men
Arrived, that render'd me most wretched then,
Now making me thus naked) I beheld
The burthen of a palm, whose issue swell'd
About Apollo's fane, and that put on
A grace like thee; for earth had never none
Of all her sylvan issue so adorn'd.
Into amaze my very soul was turn'd,   250

To give it observation: as now thee
To view, O virgin, a stupidity
Past admiration strikes me, join'd with fear
To do a suppliant's due, and press so near,
As to embrace thy knees. Nor is it strange,
For one of fresh and firmest spirit would change
T' embrace so bright an object. But, for me,
A cruel habit of calamity
Prepar'd the strong impression thou hast made;
For this last day did fly night's twentieth shade   260
Since I, at length, escap'd the sable seas;
When in the mean time th' unrelenting prease
Of waves and stern storms toss'd me up and down,
From th' isle Ogygia. And now god hath thrown
My wrack on this shore, that perhaps I may
My miseries vary here; for yet their stay,
I fear, heav'n hath not order'd, though before
These late afflictions, it hath lent me store.
O queen, deign pity then, since first to you
My fate importunes my distress to vow.   270
No other dame, nor man, that this earth own,
And neighbour city, I have seen or known.
The town then show me; give my nakedness
Some shroud to shelter it, if to these seas
Linen or woollen you have brought to cleanse.
god give you, in requital, all th' amends
Your heart can wish, a husband, family,
And good agreement. Nought beneath the sky
More sweet, more worthy is, than firm consent
Of man and wife in household government.   280
It joys their wishers well, their enemies wounds,
But to themselves the special good redounds.'

   She answer'd: 'Stranger! I discern in thee
Nor sloth nor folly reigns; and yet I see
Th' art poor and wretched. In which I conclude,
That industry nor wisdom make endu'd
Men with those gifts that make them best to th' eye;
Jove only orders man's felicity.
To good and bad his pleasure fashions still
The whole proportion of their good and ill.   290
And he perhaps hath form'd this plight in thee,
Of which thou must be patient, as he free.
But after all thy wand'rings, since thy way

Both to our earth and near our city lay,
As being expos'd to our cares to relieve,
Weeds, and what else a human hand should give
To one so suppliant and tam'd with woe,
Thou shalt not want. Our city I will show,
And tell our people's name: this neighbour town,
And all this kingdom, the Phaeacians own.   300
And (since thou seem'dst so fain to know my birth,
And mad'st a question, if of heav'n or earth)
This earth hath bred me, and my father's name
Alcinous is, that in the power and frame
Of this isle's rule is supereminent.'
  Thus, passing him, she to the virgins went,
And said: 'Give stay both to your feet and fright.
Why thus disperse ye for a man's mere sight?
Esteem you him a Cyclop, that long since
Made use to prey upon our citizens?   310
This man no moist man is, nor wat'rish thing,
That's ever flitting, ever ravishing
All it can compass; and, like it, doth range
In rape of women, never stay'd in change;
This man is truly manly, wise, and stay'd,
In soul more rich the more to sense decay'd,
Who nor will do, nor suffer to be done,
Acts lewd and abject; nor can such a one
Greet the Phaeacians with a mind envious.
Dear to the gods they are, and he is pious.   320
Besides, divided from the world we are,
The out-part of it, billows circular
The sea revolving round about our shore;
Nor is there any man that enters more
Than our own countrymen, with what is brought
From other countries. This man, minding nought
But his relief, a poor unhappy wretch,
Wrack'd here, and hath no other land to fetch,
Him now we must provide for. From Jove come
All strangers, and the needy of a home,   330
Who any gift, though ne'er so small it be,
Esteem as great, and take it gratefully.
And therefore, virgins, give the stranger food
And wine; and see ye bathe him in the flood,
Near to some shore to shelter most inclin'd.
To cold-bath-bathers hurtful is the wind,

Not only rugged making th' outward skin,
But by his thin powers pierceth parts within.'

　　This said, their flight in a return they set,
And did Ulysses with all grace entreat,　　　　　　　　　340
Show'd him a shore, wind-proof and full of shade,
By him a shirt and outer mantle laid,
A golden jug of liquid oil did add,
Bad wash and all things as Nausicaa bad.

　　Divine Ulysses would not use their aid,
But thus bespake them: 'Every lovely maid,
Let me entreat to stand a little by,
That I, alone, the fresh flood may apply
To cleanse my bosom of the sea-wrought brine,
And then use oil, which long time did not shine　　　　350
On my poor shoulders. I'll not wash in sight
Of fair-hair'd maidens. I should blush outright,
To bathe all bare by such a virgin light.'

　　They mov'd, and mus'd a man had so much grace,
And told their mistress what a man he was.

　　He cleans'd his broad soil'd shoulders, back, and head,
Yet never tam'd, but now had foam and weed
Knit in the fair curls. Which dissolv'd, and he
Slick'd all with sweet oil, the sweet charity
The untouch'd virgin show'd in his attire　　　　　　　360
He cloth'd him with. Then Pallas put a fire,
More than before, into his sparkling eyes,
His late soil set off with his soon fresh guise.
His locks, cleans'd, curl'd the more, and match'd, in pow'r
To please an eye, the hyacinthian flow'r.
And as a workman, that can well combine
Silver and gold, and make both strive to shine,
As being by Vulcan, and Minerva too,
Taught how far either may be urg'd to go
In strife of eminence, when work sets forth　　　　　　370
A worthy soul to bodies of such worth,
No thought reproving th' act, in any place,
Nor art no debt to nature's liveliest grace:
So Pallas wrought in him a grace as great
From head to shoulders, and ashore did seat
His goodly presence. To which such a guise
He show'd in going, that it ravish'd eyes.
All which continu'd, as he sat apart,
Nausicaa's eye struck wonder through her heart,

Who thus bespake her consorts: 'Hear me, you   380
Fair-wristed virgins! This rare man, I know,
Treads not our country earth against the will
Of some god thron'd on the Olympian hill.
He show'd to me, till now, not worth the note,
But now he looks as he had godhead got.
I would to heaven my husband were no worse,
And would be call'd no better, but the course
Of other husbands pleas'd to dwell out here.
Observe and serve him with our utmost cheer.'

   She said; they heard, and did. He drunk and eat   390
Like to a harpy, having touch'd no meat
A long before time. But Nausicaa now
Thought of the more grace she did lately vow,
Had horse to chariot join'd, and up she rose,
Up cheer'd her guest, and said: 'Guest, now dispose
Yourself for town, that I may let you see
My father's court, where all the peers will be
Of our Phaeacian state. At all parts, then,
Observe to whom and what place y' are t' attain –
Though I need usher you with no advice,   400
Since I suppose you absolutely wise.
While we the fields pass, and men's labours there,
So long, in these maids' guides, directly bear
Upon my chariot (I must go before
For cause that after comes, to which this more
Be my induction); you shall then soon end
Your way to town, whose tow'rs you see ascend
To such a steepness. On whose either side
A fair port stands, to which is nothing wide
An enterer's passage; on whose both hands ride   410
Ships in fair harbours; which once past, you win
The goodly marketplace (that circles in
A fane to Neptune, built of curious stone,
And passing ample) where munition,
Gables, and masts, men make, and polish'd oars;
For the Phaeacians are not conquerors
By bows nor quivers; oars, masts, ships they are
With which they plough the sea, and wage their war.
And now the cause comes why I lead the way,
Not taking you to coach: the men that sway   420
In work of those tools that so fit our state,
Are rude mechanicals, that rare and late

Work in the marketplace; and those are they
Whose bitter tongues I shun, who straight would say
(For these vile vulgars are extremely proud,
And foully-languag'd) 'What is he, allow'd
To coach it with Nausicaa, so large set,
And fairly? Where were these two met?
He shall be sure her husband. She hath been
Gadding in some place, and, of foreign men   430
Fitting her fancy, kindly brought him home
In her own ship. He must, of force, be come
From some far region; we have no such man.
It may be, praying hard, when her heart ran
On some wish'd husband, out of heav'n some god
Dropp'd in her lap; and there lies she at road
Her complete life time. But, in sooth, if she,
Ranging abroad, a husband such as he
Whom now we saw, laid hand on, she was wise;
For none of all our nobles are of prize   440
Enough for her; he must beyond sea come,
That wins her high mind, and will have her home.
Of our peers many have importun'd her,
Yet she will none.' Thus these folks will confer
Behind my back; or, meeting, to my face
The foul-mouth rout dare put home this disgrace.
And this would be reproaches to my fame,
For ev'n myself just anger would inflame,
If any other virgin I should see,
Her parents living, keep the company   450
Of any man to any end of love,
Till open nuptials should her act approve.
And therefore hear me, guest, and take such way,
That you yourself may compass, in your stay,
Your quick deduction by my father's grace,
And means to reach the root of all your race.

    We shall, not far out of our way to town,
A never-fell'd grove find, that poplars crown,
To Pallas sacred, where a fountain flows,
And round about the grove a meadow grows,   460
In which my father holds a manor house,
Deck'd all with orchards, green and odorous,
As far from town as one may hear a shout.
There stay, and rest your foot-pains, till full out
We reach the city; where, when you may guess

We are arriv'd, and enter our access
Within my father's court, then put you on
For our Phaeacian state; where, to be shown
My father's house, desire. Each infant there
Can bring you to it; and yourself will clear   470
Distinguish it from others, for no shows
The city buildings make compar'd with those
That king Alcinous' seat doth celebrate.
In whose roofs, and the court (where men of state
And suitors sit and stay) when you shall hide,
Straight pass it, ent'ring further, where abide
My mother, with her withdrawn housewiferies,
Who still sits in the fire-shine, and applies
Her rock, all purple, and of pompous show,
Her chair plac'd 'gainst a pillar, all a-row   480
Her maids behind her set; and to her here
My father's dining throne looks, seated where
He pours his choice of wine in, like a god.
This view once past, for th' end of your abode,
Address suit to my mother, that her mean
May make the day of your redition seen,
And you may frolic straight, though far away
You are in distance from your wished stay.
For, if she once be won to wish you well,
Your hope may instantly your passport seal,   490
And thenceforth sure abide to see your friends,
Fair house, and all to which your heart contends.'

   This said, she used her shining scourge, and lash'd
Her mules, that soon the shore left where she wash'd,
And, knowing well the way, their pace was fleet,
And thick they gather'd up their nimble feet.
Which yet she temper'd so, and used her scourge
With so much skill, as not to over-urge
The foot behind, and make them straggle so
From close society. Firm together go   500
Ulysses and her maids. And now the sun
Sunk to the waters, when they all had won
The never-fell'd and sound-exciting wood,
Sacred to Pallas; where the godlike good
Ulysses rested, and to Pallas pray'd:

   'Hear me, of goat-kept Jove th' unconquer'd Maid!
Now throughly hear me, since in all the time
Of all my wrack, my prayers could never climb

Thy far-off ears, when noiseful Neptune toss'd
Upon his wat'ry bristles my emboss'd   510
And rock-torn body. Hear yet now, and deign
I may of the Phaeacian state obtain
Pity and grace.' Thus pray'd he, and she heard,
By no means yet expos'd to sight appear'd
For fear t' offend her uncle, the supreme
Of all the sea-gods, whose wrath still extreme
Stood to Ulysses, and would never cease
Till with his country shore he crown'd his peace.

THE END OF THE SIXTH BOOK

BOOK SEVEN

The Argument

Nausicaa arrives at town,
And then Ulysses. He makes known
His suit to Arete, who view
Takes of his vesture, which she knew,
And asks him from whose hands it came.
He tells, with all the hapless frame
Of his affairs in all the while
Since he forsook Calypso's isle.

Another Argument

Eta   The honour'd minds
            And welcome things
        Ulysses finds
            In Scheria's kings.

BOOK SEVEN

THUS PRAY'D the wise and god-observing man.
    The maid, by free force of her palfreys, won
    Access to town, and the renowned court
Reach'd of her father; where, within the port,
She stay'd her coach, and round about her came
Her brothers, made as of immortal frame,
Who yet disdain'd not, for her love, mean deeds,
But took from coach her mules, brought in her weeds.
And she ascends her chamber, where purvey'd
A quick fire was by her old chambermaid,   10
Eurymedusa, th' Aperaean born,
And brought by sea from Apera t' adorn
The court of great Alcinous, because
He gave to all the blest Phaeacians laws,
And, like a heav'n-born pow'r in speech, acquir'd
The people's ears. To one then so admir'd,
Eurymedusa was esteem'd no worse
Than worth the gift; yet now, grown old, was nurse
To ivory-arm'd Nausicaa, gave heat
To all her fires, and dress'd her privy meat.   20
    Then rose Ulysses, and made way to town;
Which ere he reach'd, a mighty mist was thrown
By Pallas round about him, in her care
Lest, in the sway of envies popular,
Some proud Phaeacian might foul language pass,
Justle him up, and ask him what he was.
    Ent'ring the lovely town yet, through the cloud
Pallas appear'd, and like a young wench show'd
Bearing a pitcher, stood before him so
As if objected purposely to know   30
What there he needed; whom he question'd thus:
    'Know you not, daughter, where Alcinous,
That rules this town, dwells? I, a poor distress'd
Mere stranger here, know none I may request
To make this court known to me.' She replied:

'Strange father, I will see you satisfied
In that request. My father dwells just by
The house you seek for; but go silently,
Nor ask nor speak to any other; I
Shall be enough to show your way. The men   40
That here inhabit do not entertain
With ready kindness strangers, of what worth
Or state soever, nor have taken forth
Lessons of civil usage or respect
To men beyond them. They, upon their pow'rs
Of swift ships building, top the wat'ry tow'rs,
And Jove hath giv'n them ships, for sail so wrought
They cut a feather, and command a thought.'

    This said, she usher'd him, and after he
Trod in the swift steps of the deity.   50
The free-sail'd seamen could not get a sight
Of our Ulysses yet, though he forthright
Both by their houses and their persons past,
Pallas about him such a darkness cast.
By her divine pow'r and her reverend care,
She would not give the town-born cause to stare.

    He wonder'd, as he past, to see the ports;
The shipping in them; and for all resorts
The goodly market-steads; and aisles beside
For the heroës; walls so large and wide;   60
Rampires so high, and of such strength withal,
It would with wonder any eye appal.

    At last they reach'd the court, and Pallas said:
'Now, honour'd stranger, I will see obey'd
Your will, to show our ruler's house: 'tis here,
Where you shall find kings celebrating cheer.
Enter amongst them, nor admit a fear.
More bold a man is, he prevails the more,
Though man nor place he ever saw before.

    You first shall find the queen in court, whose name   70
Is Arete, of parents born the same
That was the king her spouse; their pedigree
I can report. The great Earth-shaker, he
Of Periboea (that her sex out-shone,
And youngest daughter was t' Eurymedon,
Who of th' unmeasur'd-minded giants sway'd
Th' imperial sceptre, and the pride allay'd
Of men so impious with cold death, and died

Himself soon after) got the magnified
In mind Nausithous, who the kingdom's state   80
First held in supreme rule. Nausithous gat
Rhexenor and Alcinous, now king.
Rhexenor (whose seed did no male fruit spring,
And whom the silver-bow-grac'd Phoebus slew
Young in the court) his shed blood did renew
In only Arete, who now is spouse
To him that rules the kingdom in this house,
And is her uncle king Alcinous,
Who honours her past equal. She may boast
More honour of him than the honour'd most   90
Of any wife in earth can of her lord,
How many more soever realms afford
That keep house under husbands. Yet no more
Her husband honours her, than her blest store
Of gracious children. All the city cast
Eyes on her as a goddess, and give taste
Of their affections to her in their pray'rs,
Still as she decks the streets; for all affairs
Wrapt in contention she dissolves to men.
Whom she affects, she wants no mind to deign   100
Goodness enough. If her heart stand inclin'd
To your dispatch, hope all you wish to find,
Your friends, your longing family, and all
That can within your most affections fall.'

    This said, away the grey-eyed goddess flew
Along th' untam'd sea, left the lovely hue
Scheria presented, out flew Marathon,
And ample-streeted Athens lighted on;
Where to the house, that casts so thick a shade,
Of Erectheus she ingression made.   110

    Ulysses to the lofty-builded court
Of king Alcinous made bold resort;
Yet in his heart cast many a thought, before
The brazen pavement of the rich court bore
His enter'd person. Like heav'n's two main lights,
The rooms illustrated both days and nights.
On every side stood firm a wall of brass,
Ev'n from the threshold to the inmost pass,
Which bore a roof up that all sapphire was.
The brazen thresholds both sides did enfold   120
Silver pilasters, hung with gates of gold

Whose portal was of silver; over which
A golden cornice did the front enrich.
On each side, dogs, of gold and silver fram'd,
The house's guard stood; which the deity lam'd
With knowing inwards had inspired, and made
That death nor age should their estates invade.

   Along the wall stood every way a throne,
From th' entry to the lobby, every one
Cast over with a rich-wrought cloth of state;   130
Beneath which the Phaeacian princes sate
At wine and food, and feasted all the year.
Youths forg'd of gold at every table there
Stood holding flaming torches, that in night
Gave through the house each honour'd guest his light.

   And, to encounter feast with housewif'ry,
In one room fifty women did apply
Their several tasks. Some apple-colour'd corn
Ground in fair querns, and some did spindles turn,
Some work in looms; no hand least rest receives,   140
But all had motion, apt as aspen leaves.
And from the weeds they wove, so fast they laid,
And so thick thrust together thread by thread,
That th' oil, of which the wool had drunk his fill,
Did with his moisture in light dews distill.

   As much as the Phaeacian men excell'd
All other countrymen in art to build
A swift-sail'd ship: so much the women there
For work of webs past other women were.
Past mean, by Pallas' means, they understood   150
The grace of good works; and had wits as good.

   Without the hall, and close upon the gate,
A goodly orchard-ground was situate,
Of near ten acres; about which was led
A lofty quickset. In it flourished
High and broad fruit trees, that pomegranates bore,
Sweet figs, pears, olives; and a number more
Most useful plants did there produce their store,
Whose fruits the hardest winter could not kill,
Nor hottest summer wither. There was still   160
Fruit in his proper season all the year.
Sweet Zephyr breath'd upon them blasts that were
Of varied tempers. These he made to bear
Ripe fruits, these blossoms. Pear grew after pear,

Apple succeeded apple, grape the grape,
Fig after fig came; time made never rape
Of any dainty there. A spritely vine
Spread here his root, whose fruit a hot sunshine
Made ripe betimes; here grew another green.
Here some were gathering, here some pressing seen.   170
A large-allotted several each fruit had;
And all th' adorn'd grounds their appearance made
In flower and fruit, at which the king did aim
To the precisest order he could claim.
    Two fountains grac'd the garden; of which, one
Pour'd out a winding stream that over-run
The grounds for their use chiefly, th' other went
Close by the lofty palace gate, and lent
The city his sweet benefit. And thus
The gods the court deck'd of Alcinous.   180
    Patient Ulysses stood a while at gaze,
But, having all observed, made instant pace
Into the court; where all the peers he found,
And captains of Phaeacia, with cups crown'd,
Offering to sharp-ey'd Hermes, to whom last
They us'd to sacrifice, when sleep had cast
His inclination through their thoughts. But these
Ulysses past, and forth went; nor their eyes
Took note of him, for Pallas stopp'd the light
With mists about him, that unstay'd he might   190
First to Alcinous and Arete,
Present his person; and, of both them, she
By Pallas' counsel was to have the grace
Of foremost greeting. Therefore his embrace
He cast about her knee. And then off flew
The heav'nly air that hid him; when his view
With silence and with admiration strook
The court quite through; but thus he silence broke:
    'Divine Rhexenor's offspring, Arete,
To thy most honour'd husband and to thee   200
A man whom many labours have distress'd
Is come for comfort, and to every guest –
To all whom heav'n vouchsafe delightsome lives,
And after to your issue that survives
A good resignment of the goods ye leave,
With all the honour that yourselves receive
Amongst your people. Only this of me

Is the ambition, that I may but see
(By your vouchsaf'd means, and betimes vouchsaf'd)
My country earth, since I have long been left   210
To labours and to errors barr'd from end,
And far from benefit of any friend.'

   He said no more, but left them dumb with that,
Went to the hearth, and in the ashes sat,
Aside the fire. At last their silence brake,
And Echinëus, th' old heroë, spake –
A man that all Phaeacians pass'd in years,
And in persuasive eloquence all the peers,
Knew much, and us'd it well; and thus spake he:
   'Alcinous! It shews not decently,   220
Nor doth your honour what you see admit,
That this your guest should thus abjectly sit,
His chair the earth, the hearth his cushion,
Ashes as if appos'd for food. A throne,
Adorn'd with due rites, stands you more in hand
To see his person plac'd in, and command
That instantly your heralds fill in wine,
That to the god that doth in lightnings shine
We may do sacrifice; for he is there,
Where these his reverend suppliants appear.   230
Let what you have within be brought abroad,
To sup the stranger. All these would have show'd
This fit respect to him, but that they stay
For your precedence, that should grace the way.'

   When this had added to the well-inclin'd
And sacred order of Alcinous' mind,
Then of the great-in-wit the hand he seiz'd,
And from the ashes his fair person rais'd,
Advanc'd him to a well-adorned throne,
And from his seat rais'd his most loved son,   240
Laodamas, that next himself was set,
To give him place. The handmaid then did get
An ewer of gold, with water fill'd, which plac'd
Upon a cauldron, all with silver grac'd,
She pour'd out on their hands. And then was spread
A table, which the butler set with bread,
As others serv'd with other food the board,
In all the choice the present could afford.
Ulysses meat and wine took; and then thus
The king the herald call'd: 'Pontonous!   250

Serve wine through all the house, that all may pay
Rites to the Lightner, who is still in way
With humble suppliants, and them pursues
With all benign and hospitable dues.'

   Pontonous gave act to all he will'd,
And honey-sweetness-giving-minds wine fill'd,
Disposing it in cups for all to drink.
All having drunk what either's heart could think
Fit for due sacrifice, Alcinous said:
'Hear me, ye dukes that the Phaeacians lead,   260
And you our counsellors, that I may now
Discharge the charge my mind suggests to you,
For this our guest: feast past, and this night's sleep,
Next morn, our senate summon'd, we will keep
Justs, sacred to the gods, and this our guest
Receive in solemn court with fitting feast;
Then think of his return, that, under hand
Of our deduction, his natural land
(Without more toil or care, and with delight,
And that soon giv'n him, how far hence dissite   270
Soever it can be) he may ascend;
And in the mean time without wrong attend,
Or other want, fit means to that ascent.
What, after, austere fates shall make th' event
Of his life's thread, now spinning, and began
When his pain'd mother freed his root of man,
He must endure in all kinds. If some god
Perhaps abides with us in his abode,
And other things will think upon than we,
The gods' wills stand, who ever yet were free   280
Of their appearance to us, when to them
We offer'd hecatombs of fit esteem,
And would at feast sit with us, even where we
Order'd our session. They would likewise be
Encount'rers of us, when in way alone
About his fit affairs went any one.
Nor let them cloak themselves in any care
To do us comfort; we as near them are,
As are the Cyclops, or the impious race
Of earthy giants, that would heav'n outface.'   290

   Ulysses answer'd; 'Let some other doubt
Employ your thoughts than what your words give out;
Which intimate a kind of doubt that I

Should shadow in this shape a deity.
I bear no such least semblance, or in wit,
Virtue, or person. What may well befit
One of those mortals, whom you chiefly know
Bears up and down the burthen of the woe
Appropriate to poor man, give that to me;
Of whose moans I sit in the most degree,   300
And might say more, sustaining griefs that all
The gods consent to, no one 'twixt their fall
And my unpitied shoulders letting down
The least diversion. Be the grace then shown,
To let me taste your free-giv'n food in peace.
Through greatest grief the belly must have ease.
Worse than an envious belly nothing is.
It will command his strict necessities,
Of men most griev'd in body or in mind,
That are in health, and will not give their kind   310
A desperate wound. When most with cause I grieve,
It bids me still, "Eat, man, and drink, and live,
And this makes all forgot." Whatever ill
I ever bear, it ever bids me fill.
But this ease is but forc'd, and will not last,
Till what the mind likes be as well embrac'd;
And therefore let me wish you would partake
In your late purpose; when the morn shall make
Her next appearance, deign me but the grace,
Unhappy man, that I may once embrace   320
My country earth. Though I be still thrust at
By ancient ills, yet make me but see that,
And then let life go, when withal I see
My high-roof'd large house, lands, and family.'

    This all approv'd; and each will'd every one,
Since he hath said so fairly, set him gone.

    Feast past and sacrifice, to sleep all vow
Their eyes at either's house. Ulysses now
Was left here with Alcinous, and his queen,
The all-lov'd Arete. The handmaids then   330
The vessel of the banquet took away;
When Arete set eye on his array,
Knew both his out and under weed, which she
Made with her maids, and mus'd by what means he
Obtain'd their wearing; which she made request
To know, and wings gave to these speeches: 'Guest,

First let me ask what and from whence you are?
And then, who grac'd you with the weeds you wear?
Said you not lately, you had err'd at seas,
And thence arrived here?' Laertiades   340
To this thus answer'd: 'Tis a pain, O queen,
Still to be opening wounds wrought deep and green,
Of which the gods have open'd store in me;
Yet your will must be serv'd. Far hence, at sea,
There lies an isle that bears Ogygia's name,
Where Atlas' daughter, the ingenious dame,
Fair-hair'd Calypso lives – a goddess grave,
And with whom men nor gods society have.
Yet I, past man unhappy, liv'd alone,
By heav'n's wrath forc'd, her house companion.   350
For Jove had with a fervent lightning cleft
My ship in twain, and far at black sea left
Me and my soldiers; all whose lives I lost.
I in mine arms the keel took, and was toss'd
Nine days together up from wave to wave.
The tenth grim night, the angry deities drave
Me and my wrack on th' isle in which doth dwell
Dreadful Calypso; who exactly well
Receiv'd and nourish'd me, and promise made
To make me deathless, nor should age invade   360
My pow'rs with his deserts through all my days.
All mov'd not me, and therefore, on her stays,
Sev'n years she made me lie; and there spent I
The long time, steeping in the misery
Of ceaseless tears the garments I did wear,
From her fair hand. The eighth revolved year
(Or by her chang'd mind, or by charge of Jove)
She gave provok'd way to my wish'd remove,
And in a many-jointed ship, with wine
Dainty in savour, bread, and weeds divine,   370
Sign'd, with a harmless and sweet wind, my pass.
Then seventeen days at sea I homeward was,
And by the eighteenth the dark hills appear'd
That your earth thrusts up. Much my heart was cheer'd –
Unhappy man, for that was but a beam,
To show I yet had agonies extreme
To put in suff'rance, which th' Earth-shaker sent,
Crossing my way with tempests violent,
Unmeasur'd seas up-lifting, nor would give

The billows leave to let my vessel live   380
The least time quiet, that even sigh'd to bear
Their bitter outrage; which at last did tear
Her sides in pieces, set on by the winds.
I yet through-swum the waves that your shore binds
Till wind and water threw me up to it;
When, coming forth, a ruthless billow smit
Against huge rocks, and an accessless shore,
My mangl'd body. Back again I bore,
And swum till I was fall'n upon a flood,
Whose shores, methought, on good advantage stood   390
For my receipt, rock-free and fenc'd from wind;
And this I put for, gathering up my mind.
Then the divine night came, and treading earth,
Close by the flood that had from Jove her birth,
Within a thicket I repos'd, when round
I ruffled up fall'n leaves in heap, and found,
Let fall from heav'n, a sleep interminate.
And here my heart, long time excruciate,
Amongst the leaves I rested all that night,
Ev'n till the morning and meridian light.   400
The sun declining then, delightsome sleep
No longer laid my temples in his steep,
But forth I went, and on the shore might see
Your daughter's maids play. Like a deity
She shin'd above them; and I pray'd to her,
And she in disposition did prefer
Noblesse, and wisdom, no more low than might
Become the goodness of a goddess' height.
Nor would you therefore hope, suppos'd distrest
As I was then, and old, to find the least   410
Of any grace from her, being younger far.
With young folks wisdom makes her commerce rare.
Yet she in all abundance did bestow
Both wine, that makes the blood in humans grow,
And food, and bath'd me in the flood, and gave
The weeds to me which now ye see me have.
This through my griefs I tell you, and 'tis true.'
   Alcinous answer'd: 'Guest! My daughter knew
Least of what most you give her; nor became
The course she took, to let with every dame   420
Your person lackey; nor hath with them brought
Yourself home too, which first you had besought.'

'O blame her not,' said he, 'heroical lord,
Nor let me hear against her worth a word.
She faultless is, and wish'd I would have gone
With all her women home; but I alone
Would venture my receipt here, having fear
And reverend awe of accidents that were
Of likely issue: both your wrath to move,
And to enflame the common people's love   430
Of speaking ill, to which they soon give place.
We men are all a most suspicious race.'
     'My guest,' said he, 'I use not to be stirr'd
To wrath too rashly; and where are preferr'd
To men's conceits things that may both ways fail,
The noblest ever should the most prevail.
Would Jove our father, Pallas, and the Sun,
That, were you still as now, and could but run
One fate with me, you would my daughter wed,
And be my son-in-law, still vow'd to lead   440
Your rest of life here! I a house would give,
And household goods; so freely you would live,
Confin'd with us. But 'gainst your will shall none
Contain you here, since that were violence done
To Jove our father. For your passage home,
That you may well know we can overcome
So great a voyage, thus it shall succeed:
Tomorrow shall our men take all their heed,
While you securely sleep, to see the seas
In calmest temper, and, if that will please,   450
Show you your country and your house ere night,
Though far beyond Euboea be that sight.
And this Euboea, as our subjects say
That have been there and seen, is far away,
Farthest from us of all the parts they know
And made the trial when they help'd to row
The gold-lock'd Rhadamanth, to give him view
Of earth-born Tityus; whom their speeds did show
In that far-off Euboea, the same day
They set from hence; and home made good their way   460
With ease again, and him they did convey.
Which I report to you, to let you see
How swift my ships are, and how matchlessly
My young Phaeacians with their oars prevail,
To beat the sea through, and assist a sail.'

This cheer'd Ulysses, who in private pray'd:
'I would to Jove our father, what he said
He could perform at all parts; he should then
Be glorified for ever, and I gain
My natural country.' This discourse they had,   470
When fair-arm'd Arete her handmaids bad
A bed make in the portico, and ply
With clothes, the covering tapestry,
The blankets purple; well-napp'd waistcoats too,
To wear for more warmth. What these had to do,
They torches took and did. The bed purvey'd,
They moved Ulysses for his rest, and said:
    'Come guest, your bed is fit, now frame to rest.'
Motion of sleep was gracious to their guest,
Which now he took profoundly, being laid   480
Within a loop-hole tower, where was convey'd
The sounding portico. The king took rest
In a retir'd part of the house, where dress'd
The queen her self a bed, and trundlebed,
And by her lord repos'd her reverend head.

THE END OF THE SEVENTH BOOK

BOOK EIGHT

The Argument

The peers of the Phaeacian state
A council call, to consolate
Ulysses with all means for home.
The council to a banquet come,
Invited by the king. Which done,
Assays for hurling of the stone
The youths make with the stranger king.
Demodocus, at feast, doth sing
Th' adultery of the god of arms
With her that rules in amorous charms;
And after sings the entercourse
Of acts about th' Epaean horse.

Another Argument

Theta   The council's frame
             At fleet applied;
          In strifes of game
             Ulysses tried.

BOOK EIGHT

NOW WHEN the rosy-finger'd Morn arose,
The sacred pow'r Alcinous did dispose
Did likewise rise; and, like him, left his ease
The city-razer Laertiades.
The council at the navy was design'd;
To which Alcinous with the sacred mind
Came first of all. On polish'd stones they sate,
Near to the navy. To increase the state,
Minerva took the herald's form on her
(That served Alcinous), studious to prefer   10
Ulysses' suit for home. About the town
She made quick way, and fill'd with the renown
Of that design the ears of every man,
Proclaiming thus: 'Peers Phaeacensian!
And men of council, all haste to the court,
To hear the stranger that made late resort
To king Alcinous, long time lost at sea,
And is in person like a deity.'
    This all their pow'rs set up, and spirit instill'd,
And straight the court and seats with men were fill'd.   20
The whole state wonder'd at Laertes' son,
When they beheld him. Pallas put him on
A supernatural and heav'nly dress,
Enlarg'd him with a height, and goodliness
In breast and shoulders, that he might appear
Gracious and grave and reverend, and bear
A perfect hand on his performance there
In all the trials they resolv'd t' impose.
    All met and gather'd in attention close,
Alcinous thus bespake them: 'Dukes and lords,   30
Hear me digest my hearty thoughts in words.
This stranger here, whose travels found my court,
I know not, nor can tell if his resort
From east or west comes; but his suit is this –
That to his country earth we would dismiss

His hither-forced person – and doth bear
The mind to pass it under every peer;
Whom I prepare and stir up, making known
My free desire of his deduction.
Nor shall there ever any other man   40
That tries the goodness Phaeacensian
In me, and my court's entertainment, stay,
Mourning for passage, under least delay.
Come then, a ship into the sacred seas,
New-built, now launch we; and from out our prease
Choose two and fifty youths, of all, the best
To use an oar. All which see straight impress'd,
And in their oar-bound seats. Let others hie
Home to our court, commanding instantly
The solemn preparation of a feast,   50
In which provision may for any guest
Be made at my charge. Charge of these low things
I give our youth. You, sceptre-bearing kings,
Consort me home, and help with grace to use
This guest of ours; no one man shall refuse.
   Some other of you haste, and call to us
The sacred singer, grave Demodocus,
To whom hath god giv'n song that can excite
The heart of whom he listeth with delight.'
This said, he led. The sceptre-bearers lent   60
Their free attendance; and with all speed went
The herald for the sacred man in song.
Youths two and fifty, chosen from the throng,
Went, as was will'd, to the untam'd sea's shore;
Where come, they launch'd the ship, the mast it bore
Advanc'd, sails hoised, every seat his oar
Gave with a leather thong. The deep moist then
They further reach'd. The dry streets flow'd with men
That troop'd up to the king's capacious court,
Whose porticos were chok'd with the resort,   70
Whose walls were hung with men, young, old, thrust there
In mighty concourse; for whose promis'd cheer
Alcinous slew twelve sheep, eight white-tooth'd swine,
Two crook-haunch'd beeves; which flay'd and dress'd, divine
The show was of so many a jocund guest,
All set together at so set a feast.
To whose accomplish'd state the herald then
The lovely singer led; who past all men

The muse affected, gave him good and ill,
His eyes put out, but put in soul at will.   80
His place was given him in a chair all grac'd
With silver studs, and 'gainst a pillar plac'd;
Where, as the centre to the state, he rests,
And round about the circle of the guests.
The herald on a pin above his head
His soundful harp hung, to whose height he led
His hand for taking of it down at will;
A board set by with food, and forth did fill
A bowl of wine, to drink at his desire.
The rest then fell to feast, and, when the fire   90
Of appetite was quench'd, the muse inflam'd
The sacred singer. Of men highliest fam'd
He sung the glories, and a poem penn'd,
That in applause did ample heaven ascend.
Whose subject was, the stern contention
Betwixt Ulysses and great Thetis' son,
As, at a banquet sacred to the gods,
In dreadful language they express'd their odds.
When Agamemnon sat rejoic'd in soul
To hear the Greek peers jar in terms so foul;   100
For augur Phoebus in presage had told
The king of men (desirous to unfold
The war's perplex'd end, and being therefore gone
In heavenly Pythia to the porch of stone)
That then the end of all griefs should begin
'Twixt Greece and Troy, when Greece (with strife to win
That wish'd conclusion) in her kings should jar,
And plead if force or wit must end the war.
     This brave contention did the poet sing,
Expressing so the spleen of either king,   110
That his large purple wood Ulysses held
Before his face and eyes, since thence distill'd
Tears uncontain'd; which he obscur'd, in fear
To let th' observing presence note a tear.
But when his sacred song the mere divine
Had given an end, a goblet crown'd with wine
Ulysses, drying his wet eyes, did seize,
And sacrific'd to those gods that would please
T' inspire the poet with a song so fit
To do him honour, and renown his wit.   120
His tears then stay'd. But when again began,

By all the kings' desires, the moving man,
Again Ulysses could not choose but yield
To that soft passion, which again, withheld,
He kept so cunningly from sight, that none,
Except Alcinous himself alone,
Discern'd him mov'd so much. But he sat next,
And heard him deeply sigh; which his pretext
Could not keep hid from him. Yet he conceal'd
His utterance of it, and would have it held   130
From all the rest, brake off the song, and this
Said to those oar-affecting peers of his:

     'Princes and peers! We now are satiate
With sacred song that fits a feast of state,
With wine and food. Now then to field, and try
In all kinds our approv'd activity,
That this our guest may give his friends to know,
In his return, that we as little owe
To fights and wrestlings, leaping, speed of race,
As these our court-rites; and commend our grace   140
In all to all superior.' Forth he led,
The peers and people troop'd up to their head.
Nor must Demodocus be left within;
Whose harp the herald hung upon the pin,
His hand in his took, and abroad he brought
The heavenly poet, out the same way wrought
That did the princes, and what they would see
With admiration, with his company
They wish'd to honour. To the place of game
These throng'd; and after routs of other came,   150
Of all sort, infinite. Of youths that strove,
Many and strong rose to their trial's love.
Up rose Acroneus, and Ocyalus,
Elatreus, Prymneus, and Anchialus,
Nauteus, Eretmeus, Thoön, Proreus,
Ponteus, and the strong Amphialus,
Son to Tectonides Polyneus.
Up rose to these the great Euryalus,
In action like the Homicide of War.
Naubolides, that was for person far   160
Past all the rest, but one he could not pass,
Nor any thought improve, Laodamas.
Up Anabesineus then arose;
And three sons of the sceptre-state, and those

Were Halius, the fore-prais'd Laodamas,
And Clytoneus, like a god in grace.
These first the foot-game tried, and from the lists
Took start together. Up the dust in mists
They hurl'd about, as in their speed they flew;
But Clytoneus first of all the crew   170
A stitch's length in any fallow field
Made good his pace when, where the judges yield
The prize and praise, his glorious speed arriv'd.
Next, for the boist'rous wrestling game they striv'd,
At which Euryalus the rest outshone.
At leap Amphialus. At the hollow stone
Elatreus excell'd. At buffets, last,
Laodamas, the king's fair son, surpass'd.

When all had striv'd in these assays their fill,
Laodamas said: 'Come friends, let's prove what skill   180
This stranger hath attain'd to in our sport.
Methinks, he must be of the active sort –
His calves, thighs, hands, and well-knit shoulders show
That nature disposition did bestow
To fit with fact their form. Nor wants he prime,
But sour affliction, made a mate with time,
Makes time the more seen. Nor imagine I
A worse thing to enforce debility
Than is the sea, though nature ne'er so strong
Knits one together.' 'Nor conceive you wrong,'   190
Replied Euryalus, 'but prove his blood
With what you question.' In the midst then stood
Renown'd Laodamas, and prov'd him thus:

'Come, stranger father, and assay with us
Your pow'rs in these contentions. If your show
Be answer'd with your worth, 'tis fit that you
Should know these conflicts. Nor doth glory stand
On any worth more, in a man's command,
Than to be strenuous both of foot and hand.
Come then, make proof with us, discharge your mind   200
Of discontentments; for not far behind
Comes your deduction; ship is ready now,
And men, and all things.' 'Why,' said he, 'dost thou
Mock me, Laodamas, and these strifes bind
My powers to answer? I am more inclin'd
To cares than conflict. Much sustain'd I have,
And still am suffering. I come here to crave,

In your assemblies, means to be dismiss'd,
And pray both kings and subjects to assist.'
    Euryalus an open brawl began,   210
And said: 'I take you, sir, for no such man
As fits these honour'd strifes. A number more
Strange men there are that I would choose before.
To one that loves to lie a-shipboard much,
Or is the prince of sailors, or to such
As traffic far and near, and nothing mind
But freight, and passage, and a foreright wind,
Or to a victualler of a ship, or men
That set up all their pow'rs for rampant gain,
I can compare, or hold you like to be: 220
But, for a wrestler, or of quality
Fit for contentions noble, you abhor
From worth of any such competitor.'
Ulysses, frowning, answer'd: 'Stranger, far
Thy words are from the fashions regular
Of kind, or honour. Thou art in thy guise
Like to a man that authors injuries.
I see the gods to all men give not all
Manly addiction – wisdom, words that fall,
Like dice, upon the square still. Some man takes   230
Ill form from parents, but god often makes
That fault of form up with observ'd repair
Of pleasing speech, that makes him held for fair,
That makes him speak securely, makes him shine
In an assembly with a grace divine.
Men take delight to see how ev'nly lie
His words asteep in honey modesty.
Another, then, hath fashion like a god,
But in his language he is foul and broad.
And such art thou. A person fair is giv'n,   240
But nothing else is in thee sent from heav'n;
For in thee lurks a base and earthy soul,
And th' hast compell'd me, with a speech most foul,
To be thus bitter. I am not unseen
In these fair strifes, as thy words overween,
But in the first rank of the best I stand;
At least I did, when youth and strength of hand
Made me thus confident, but now am worn
With woes and labours, as a human born
To bear all anguish. Suffer'd much I have.   250

The war of men, and the inhuman wave,
Have I driv'n through at all parts. But with all
My waste in sufferance, what yet may fall
In my performance, at these strifes I'll try.
Thy speech hath mov'd, and made my wrath run high.'
   This said, with robe and all, he grasp'd a stone,
A little graver than was ever thrown
By these Phaeacians in their wrestling rout,
More firm, more massy; which, turn'd round about,
He hurried from him with a hand so strong   260
It sung, and flew, and over all the throng
That at the others' marks stood, quite it went;
Yet down fell all beneath it, fearing spent
The force that drave it flying from his hand,
As it a dart were, or a walking wand;
And far past all the marks of all the rest
His wing stole way; when Pallas straight impress'd
A mark at fall of it, resembling then
One of the navy-giv'n Phaeacian men,
And thus advanc'd Ulysses: 'One, though blind,   270
O stranger, groping, may thy stone's fall find;
For not amidst the rout of marks it fell,
But far before all. Of thy worth think well,
And stand in all strifes. No Phaeacian here
This bound can either better or come near.'
Ulysses joy'd to hear that one man yet
Us'd him benignly, and would truth abet
In those contentions; and then thus smooth
He took his speech down: 'Reach me that now, youth,
You shall, and straight, I think, have one such more,   280
And one beyond it too. And now, whose core
Stands sound and great within him, since ye have
Thus put my spleen up, come again and brave
The guest ye tempted with such gross disgrace,
At wrestling, buffets, whirlbat, speed of race.
At all or either, I except at none,
But urge the whole state of you; only one
I will not challenge in my forced boast,
And that's Laodamas, for he's mine host.
And who will fight, or wrangle, with his friend?   290
Unwise he is, and base, that will contend
With him that feeds him, in a foreign place,
And takes all edge off from his own sought grace.

None else except I here, nor none despise,
But wish to know, and prove his faculties,
That dares appear now. No strife ye can name
Am I unskill'd in; reckon any game
Of all that are, as many as there are
In use with men. For archery I dare
Affirm myself not mean. Of all a troop   300
I'll make the first foe with mine arrow stoop,
Though with me ne'er so many fellows bend
Their bows at mark'd men, and affect their end.
Only was Philoctetes with his bow
Still my superior, when we Greeks would show
Our archery against our foes of Troy.
But all, that now by bread frail life enjoy,
I far hold my inferiors. Men of old,
None now alive shall witness me so bold
To vaunt equality with, such men as these –   310
Oechalian Eurytus, Hercules,
Who with their bows durst with the gods contend,
And therefore caught Eurytus soon his end,
Nor died at home, in age, a reverend man,
But by the great incensed Delphian
Was shot to death, for daring competence
With him in all an archer's excellence.
A spear I'll hurl as far as any man
Shall shoot a shaft. How at a race I can
Bestir my feet, I only yield to fear,   320
And doubt to meet with my superior here.
So many seas so too much have misus'd
My limbs for race, and therefore have diffus'd
A dissolution through my loved knees.'
    This said, he still'd all talking properties;
Alcinous only answer'd: 'O my guest,
In good part take we what you have been press'd
With speech to answer. You would make appear
Your virtues therefore, that will still shine where
Your only look is. Yet must this man give   330
Your worth ill language, when he does not live
In sort of mortals (whencesoe'er he springs,
That judgment hath to speak becoming things)
That will deprave your virtues. Note then now
My speech, and what my love presents to you,
That you may tell heroës, when you come

To banquet with your wife and birth at home,
(Mindful of our worth) what deservings Jove
Hath put on our parts likewise, in remove
From sire to son, as an inherent grace   340
Kind, and perpetual. We must needs give place
To other countrymen, and freely yield
We are not blameless in our fights of field,
Buffets, nor wrestlings; but in speed of feet,
And all the equipage that fits a fleet,
We boast us best; for table ever spread
With neighbour feasts, for garments varied,
For poesy, music, dancing, baths, and beds.
And now, Phaeacians, you that bear your heads
And feet with best grace in enamouring dance,   350
Enflame our guest here, that he may advance
Our worth past all the world's to his home friends,
As well for the unmatch'd grace that commends
Your skill in footing of a dance, as theirs
That fly a race best. And so, all affairs,
At which we boast us best, he best may try,
As sea-race, land-race, dance, and poesy.
Some one with instant speed to court retire,
And fetch Demodocus his soundful lyre.'
  This said the god-grac'd king; and quick resort   360
Pontonous made for that fair harp to court.
  Nine of the lot-choos'd public rulers rose,
That all in those contentions did dispose,
Commanding a most smooth ground, and a wide,
And all the people in fair game aside.
  Then with the rich harp came Pontonous,
And in the midst took place Demodocus.
About him then stood forth the choice young men,
That on man's first youth made fresh entry then,
Had art to make their natural motion sweet,   370
And shook a most divine dance from their feet,
That twinkled starlike, mov'd as swift and fine,
And beat the air so thin, they made it shine.
Ulysses wonder'd at it, but amaz'd
He stood in mind to hear the dance so phras'd.
For as they danc'd, Demodocus did sing
The bright-crown'd Venus' love with Battle's King;
As first they closely mixed in th' house of fire,
What worlds of gifts won her to his desire;

Who then the night-and-day-bed did defile   380
Of good king Vulcan. But in little while
The Sun their mixture saw, and came and told.
The bitter news did by his ears take hold
Of Vulcan's heart. Then to his forge he went,
And in his shrewd mind deep stuff did invent.
His mighty anvil in the stock he put,
And forg'd a net that none could loose or cut,
That when it had them it might hold them fast.
Which having finish'd, he made utmost haste
Up to the dear room where his wife he woo'd,   390
And, madly wrath with Mars, he all bestrow'd
The bed, and bedposts, all the beam above
That cross'd the chamber; and a circle strove
Of his device to wrap in all the room.
And 'twas as pure, as of a spider's loom
The woof before 'tis wov'n. No man nor god
Could set his eye on it, a sleight so odd
His art show'd in it. All his craft bespent
About the bed, he feign'd as if he went
To well-built Lemnos, his most loved town   400
Of all towns earthly; nor left this unknown
To golden-bridle-using Mars, who kept
No blind watch over him, but, seeing stepp'd
His rival so aside, he hasted home,
With fair-wreath'd Venus' love stung, who was come
New from the court of her most mighty sire.
Mars enter'd, wrung her hand, and the retire
Her husband made to Lemnos told, and said:
'Now, love, is Vulcan gone, let us to bed;
He's for the barbarous Sintians.' Well appay'd   410
Was Venus with it, and afresh assay'd
Their old encounter. Down they went, and straight
About them cling'd the artificial sleight
Of most wise Vulcan; and were so ensnar'd,
That neither they could stir their course prepar'd
In any limb about them, nor arise.
And then they knew they would no more disguise
Their close conveyance, but lay, forc'd, stone still.
Back rush'd the both-foot-cook'd, but straight in skill,
From his near scout-hole turn'd, nor ever went   420
To any Lemnos, but the sure event
Left Phoebus to discover, who told all.

Then home hopp'd Vulcan, full of grief and gall,
Stood in the portal, and cried out so high,
That all the gods heard: 'Father of the sky
And every other deathless god,' said he,
'Come all, and a ridiculous object see,
And yet not sufferable neither. Come,
And witness how, when still I step from home,
Lame that I am, Jove's daughter doth profess   430
To do me all the shameful offices,
Indignities, despites, that can be thought;
And loves this all-things-making-come-to-nought,
Since he is fair forsooth, foot-sound, and I
Took in my brain a little, legg'd awry;
And no fault mine, but all my parent's fault,
Who should not get, if mock me with my halt.
But see how fast they sleep, while I, in moan,
Am only made an idle looker-on.
One bed their turn serves, and it must be mine;   440
I think yet, I have made their self-loves shine.
They shall no more wrong me, and none perceive.
Nor will they sleep together, I believe,
With too hot haste again. Thus both shall lie
In craft, and force, till the extremity
Of all the dow'r I gave her sire (to gain
A dogged set-fac'd girl, that will not stain
Her face with blushing, though she shame her head)
He pays me back. She's fair, but was no maid.'
   While this long speech was making, all were come   450
To Vulcan's wholly-brazen-founded home,
Earth-shaking Neptune, useful Mercury,
And far-shot Phoebus. No she-deity,
For shame, would show there. All the give-good gods
Stood in the portal, and past periods
Gave length to laughters, all rejoic'd to see
That which they said, that no impiety
Finds good success at th' end. 'And now,' said one,
'The slow outgoes the swift. Lame Vulcan, known
To be the slowest of the gods, outgoes   460
Mars the most swift. And this is that which grows
To greatest justice: that adult'ry's sport,
Obtain'd by craft, by craft of other sort
(And lame craft too) is plagu'd, which grieves the more,
That sound limbs turning lame the lame restore.'

This speech amongst themselves they entertain'd,
When Phoebus thus ask'd Hermes: 'Thus enchain'd
Wouldst thou be, Hermes, to be thus disclos'd,
Though with thee golden Venus were repos'd?'

He soon gave that an answer: 'O,' said he,   470
'Thou king of archers, would 'twere thus with me.
Though thrice so much shame, nay, though infinite
Were pour'd about me, and that every light,
In great heav'n shining, witness'd all my harms,
So golden Venus slumber'd in mine arms.'

The gods again laugh'd; even the Wat'ry State
Wrung out a laughter, but propitiate
Was still for Mars, and pray'd the god of fire
He would dissolve him, offering the desire
He made to Jove to pay himself, and said,   480
All due debts should be by the gods repaid.

'Pay me no words,' said he. 'Where deeds lend pain,
Wretched the words are giv'n for wretched men.
How shall I bind you in th' immortals' sight,
If Mars be once loos'd, nor will pay his right?'

'Vulcan,' said he, 'if Mars should fly, nor see
Thy right repaid, it should be paid by me.'

'Your word, so giv'n, I must accept,' said he.
Which said, he loos'd them. Mars then rush'd from sky
And stoop'd cold Thrace. The laughing deity   490
For Cyprus was, and took her Paphian state,
Where she a grove, ne'er cut, had consecrate,
All with Arabian odours fum'd, and hath
An altar there, at which the Graces bathe,
And with immortal balms besmooth her skin,
Fit for the bliss immortals solace in,
Deck her in to-be-studied attire,
And apt to set beholders' hearts on fire.

This sung the sacred muse, whose notes and words
The dancers' feet kept as his hands his chords.   500
Ulysses much was pleased, and all the crew.

This would the king have varied with a new
And pleasing measure, and performed by
Two, with whom none would strive in dancery;
And those his sons were, that must therefore dance
Alone, and only to the harp advance,
Without the words. And this sweet couple was
Young Halius and divine Laodamas;

Who danc'd a ball dance. Then the rich-wrought ball,
That Polybus had made, of purple all,   510
They took to hand. One threw it to the sky
And then danc'd back; the other, capering high,
Would surely catch it ere his foot touch'd ground,
And up again advanc'd it, and so found
The other cause of dance; and then did he
Dance lofty tricks, till next it came to be
His turn to catch, and serve the other still.
When they had kept it up to either's will,
They then danc'd ground tricks, oft mix'd hand in hand,
And did so gracefully their change command,   520
That all the other youth that stood at pause,
With deaf'ning shouts, gave them the great applause.
   Then said Ulysses: 'O, past all men here
Clear, not in pow'r, but in desert as clear,
You said your dancers did the world surpass,
And they perform it clear, and to amaze.'
   This won Alcinous' heart, and equal prize
He gave Ulysses, saying: 'Matchless wise,
Princes and rulers, I perceive our guest,
And therefore let our hospitable best   530
In fitting gifts be giv'n him: twelve chief kings
There are that order all the glorious things
Of this our kingdom; and, the thirteenth, I
Exist, as crown to all. Let instantly
Be thirteen garments giv'n him, and of gold
Precious and fine, a talent. While we hold
This our assembly, be all fetch'd, and giv'n,
That to our feast prepar'd, as to his heav'n,
Our guest may enter. And, that nothing be
Left unperform'd that fits his dignity,   540
Euryalus shall here conciliate
Himself with words and gifts, since past our rate
He gave bad language.' This did all commend
And give in charge; and every king did send
His herald for his gift. Euryalus,
Answering for his part, said: 'Alcinous,
Our chief of all, since you command, I will
To this our guest by all means reconcile,
And give him this entirely-metall'd sword,
The handle massy silver, and the board   550
That gives it cover all of ivory,

New, and in all kinds worth his quality.'
   This put he straight into his hand, and said:
'Frolic, O guest and father; if words fled
Have been offensive, let swift whirlwinds take
And ravish them from thought. May all gods make
Thy wife's sight good to thee, in quick retreat
To all thy friends, and best-lov'd breeding-seat,
Their long miss quitting with the greater joy;
In whose sweet vanish all thy worst annoy.'   560
   'And frolic thou to all height, friend,' said he,
'Which heav'n confirm with wish'd felicity;
Nor ever give again desire to thee
Of this sword's use, which with affects so free,
In my reclaim, thou hast bestow'd on me.'
   This said, athwart his shoulders he put on
The right fair sword; and then did set the sun.
When all the gifts were brought – which back again
(With king Alcinous in all the train)
Were by the honour'd heralds borne to court,   570
Which his fair sons took, and from the resort
Laid by their reverend mother – each his throne
Of all the peers (which yet were overshone
In king Alcinous' command) ascended;
Whom he to pass as much in gifts contended,
And to his queen said: 'Wife! See brought me here
The fairest cabinet I have, and there
Impose a well-cleans'd in and outer weed.
A cauldron heat with water, that with speed
Our guest well bath'd, and all his gifts made sure,   580
It may a joyful appetite procure
To his succeeding feast, and make him hear
The poet's hymn with the securer ear.
To all which I will add my bowl of gold,
In all frame curious, to make him hold
My memory always dear, and sacrifice
With it at home to all the deities.'
   Then Arete her maids charg'd to set on
A well-sized cauldron quickly. Which was done,
Clear water pour'd in, flame made so entire,   590
It gilt the brass, and made the water fire.
In mean space, from her chamber brought the queen
A wealthy cabinet, where, pure and clean,
She put the garments, and the gold bestow'd

By that free state, and then the other vow'd
By her Alcinous, and said: 'Now, guest,
Make close and fast your gifts, lest, when you rest
A-shipboard sweetly, in your way you meet
Some loss, that less may make your next sleep sweet.'

This when Ulysses heard, all sure he made,   600
Enclosed and bound safe; for the saving trade
The reverend-for-her-wisdom, Circe, had
In foreyears taught him. Then the handmaid bad
His worth to bathing; which rejoic'd his heart,
For since he did with his Calypso part,
He had no hot baths; none had favour'd him,
Nor been so tender of his kingly limb.
But all the time he spent in her abode,
He lived respected as he were a god.

Cleans'd then and balm'd, fair shirt and robe put on,   610
Fresh come from bath, and to the feasters gone,
Nausicaa, that from the gods' hands took
The sovereign beauty of her blessed look,
Stood by a well-carv'd column of the room,
And through her eye her heart was overcome
With admiration of the port impress'd
In his aspect, and said: 'god save you, guest!
Be cheerful, as in all the future state
Your home will show you in your better fate.
But yet, ev'n then, let this remember'd be,   620
Your life's price I lent, and you owe it me.'

The varied-in-all-counsels gave reply:
'Nausicaa! Flower of all this empery!
So Juno's husband, that the strife for noise
Makes in the clouds, bless me with strife of joys,
In the desir'd day that my house shall show,
As I, as to a goddess there shall vow
To thy fair hand that did my being give,
Which I'll acknowledge every hour I live.'

This said, Alcinous plac'd him by his side.   630
Then took they feast, and did in parts divide
The several dishes, fill'd out wine, and then
The striv'd-for-for-his-worth of worthy men,
And reverenc'd-of-the-state, Demodocus,
Was brought in by the good Pontonous.
In midst of all the guests they gave him place,
Against a lofty pillar, when this grace

The grac'd-with-wisdom did him: from the chine,
That stood before him, of a white-tooth'd swine,
Being far the daintiest joint, mixed through with fat,   640
He carv'd to him, and sent it where he sat
By his old friend the herald, willing thus:
'Herald, reach this to grave Demodocus.
Say, I salute him, and his worth embrace.
Poets deserve, past all the human race,
Reverend respect and honour, since the queen
Of knowledge, and the supreme worth in men,
The muse, informs them, and loves all their race.'
    This reach'd the herald to him, who the grace
Receiv'd encourag'd; which, when feast was spent,   650
Ulysses amplified to this ascent:
    'Demodocus! I must prefer you far,
Past all your sort, if or the muse of war,
Jove's daughter, prompts you, that the Greeks respects,
Or if the Sun, that those of Troy affects.
For I have heard you, since my coming, sing
The fate of Greece to an admired string:
How much our suff'rance was, how much we wrought,
How much the actions rose to when we fought –
So lively forming, as you had been there,   660
Or to some free relater lent your ear.
Forth then, and sing the wooden horse's frame,
Built by Epeus, by the martial dame
Taught the whole fabric; which, by force of sleight,
Ulysses brought into the city's height,
When he had stuff'd it with as many men
As levell'd lofty Ilion with the plain.
With all which if you can as well enchant,
As with expression quick and elegant
You sung the rest, I will pronounce you clear   670
Inspired by god, past all that ever were.'
    This said, ev'n stirr'd by god up, he began,
And to his song fell, past the form of man,
Beginning where the Greeks a-shipboard went,
And every chief had set on fire his tent,
When th' other kings, in great Ulysses' guide,
In Troy's vast market place the horse did hide,
From whence the Trojans up to Ilion drew
The dreadful engine. Where sat all arew
Their kings about it, many counsels giv'n   680

How to dispose it. In three ways were driv'n
Their whole distractions. First, if they should feel
The hollow wood's heart, search'd with piercing steel;
Or from the battlements drawn higher yet
Deject it headlong; or that counterfeit
So vast and novel set on sacred fire,
Vow'd to appease each anger'd godhead's ire.
On which opinion, they thereafter saw,
They then should have resolved, th' unalter'd law
Of fate presaging, that Troy then should end,   690
When th' hostile horse she should receive to friend;
For therein should the Grecian kings lie hid,
To bring the fate and death they after did.

  He sung, besides, the Greeks' eruption
From those their hollow crafts, and horse forgone;
And how they made depopulation tread
Beneath her feet so high a city's head.
In which affair, he sung in other place
That of that ambush some man else did race
The Ilion towers than Laertiades;   700
But here he sung that he alone did seize,
With Menelaus, the ascended roof
Of prince Deiphobus, and Mars-like proof
Made of his valour, a most dreadful fight
Daring against him; and there vanquish'd quite,
In little time, by great Minerva's aid,
All Ilion's remnant, and Troy level laid.
This the divine expressor did so give
Both act and passion, that he made it live,
And to Ulysses' facts did breathe a fire   710
So deadly quick'ning, that it did inspire
Old death with life, and render'd life so sweet
And passionate, that all there felt it fleet;
Which made him pity his own cruelty,
And put into that ruth so pure an eye
Of human frailty, that to see a man
Could so revive from death, yet no way can
Defend from death, his own quick pow'rs it made
Feel there death's horrors, and he felt life fade
In tears his feeling brain swet; for, in things   720
That move past utt'rance, tears ope all their springs.
Nor are there in the pow'rs that all life bears
More true interpreters of all than tears.

And as a lady mourns her sole-lov'd lord,
That's fall'n before his city by the sword,
Fighting to rescue from a cruel fate
His town and children, and in dead estate,
Yet panting, seeing him, wraps him in her arms,
Weeps, shrieks, and pours her health into his arms,
Lies on him, striving to become his shield   730
From foes that still assail him, spears impell'd
Through back and shoulders, by whose points embru'd,
They raise and lead him into servitude,
Labour, and languor; for all which the dame
Eats down her cheeks with tears, and feeds life's flame
With miserable suff'rance: so this king
Of tear-swet anguish op'd a boundless spring;
Nor yet was seen to any one man there
But king Alcinous, who sat so near
He could not 'scape him, sighs, so choked, so brake   740
From all his tempers; which the king did take
Both note and grave respect of, and thus spake:
'Hear me, Phaeacian counsellors and peers,
And cease Demodocus; perhaps all ears
Are not delighted with his song, for, ever
Since the divine Muse sung, our guest hath never
Contain'd from secret mournings. It may fall,
That something sung he hath been griev'd withal,
As touching his particular. Forbear,
That feast may jointly comfort all hearts here,   750
And we may cheer our guest up; 'tis our best
In all due honour. For our reverend guest
Is all our celebration, gifts, and all,
His love hath added to our festival.
A guest, and suppliant too, we should esteem
Dear as our brother; one that doth but dream
He hath a soul, or touch but at a mind
Deathless and manly, should stand so inclin'd.
Nor cloak you longer with your curious wit,
Lov'd guest, what ever we shall ask of it.   760
It now stands on your honest state to tell,
And therefore give your name, nor more conceal
What of your parents, and the town that bears
Name of your native, or of foreigners
That near us border, you are call'd in fame.
There's no man living walks without a name,

Noble nor base, but had one from his birth
Impos'd as fit as to be borne. What earth,
People, and city, own you, give to know.
Tell but our ships all, that your way must show.   770
For our ships know th' expressed minds of men;
And will so most intentively retain
Their scopes appointed, that they never err,
And yet use never any man to steer,
Nor any rudders have, as others need.
They know men's thoughts and whither tends their speed,
And there will set them; for you cannot name
A city to them, nor fat soil, that fame
Hath any notice giv'n, but well they know,
And will fly to them, though they ebb and flow   780
In blackest clouds and nights; and never bear
Of any wrack or rock the slend'rest fear.
But this I heard my sire Nausithous say
Long since, that Neptune, seeing us convey
So safely passengers of all degrees,
Was angry with us; and upon our seas
A well-built ship we had, near harbour come
From safe deduction of some stranger home,
Made in his flitting billows stick stone still;
And dimm'd our city, like a mighty hill   790
With shade cast round about it. This report
The old king made; in which miraculous sort,
If god had done such things, or left undone,
At his good pleasure be it. But now, on,
And truth relate us, both from whence you err'd,
And to what clime of men would be transferr'd,
With all their fair towns, be they as they are,
If rude, unjust, and all irregular,
Or hospitable, bearing minds that please
The mighty deity. Which one of these   800
You would be set at, say, and you are there.
And therefore what afflicts you? Why, to hear
The fate of Greece and Ilion, mourn you so?
The gods have done it; as to all they do
Destine destruction, that from thence may rise
A poem to instruct posterities.
Fell any kinsman before Ilion?
Some worthy sire-in-law, or like-near son,
Whom next our own blood and self-race we love?

Or any friend perhaps, in whom did move   810
A knowing soul, and no unpleasing thing?
Since such a good one is no underling
To any brother; for, what fits true friends,
True wisdom is, that blood and birth transcends.

THE END OF THE EIGHTH BOOK

BOOK NINE

The Argument

Ulysses here is first made known;
Who tells the stern contention
His powers did 'gainst the Cicons try;
And thence to the Lotophagi
Extends his conquest; and from them
Assays the Cyclop Polypheme,
And, by the crafts his wits apply,
He puts him out his only eye.

Another Argument

Iota   The strangely fed
      Lotophagi;
    The Cicons fled;
      The Cyclop's eye.

BOOK NINE

ULYSSES THUS resolv'd the king's demands:
    'Alcinous, in whom this empire stands,
    You should not of so natural right disherit
Your princely feast, as take from it the spirit.
To hear a poet, that in accent brings
The gods' breasts down, and breathes them as he sings,
Is sweet, and sacred; nor can I conceive,
In any common-weal, what more doth give
Note of the just and blessed empery,
Than to see comfort universally   10
Cheer up the people, when in every roof
She gives observers a most human proof
Of men's contents. To see a neighbour's feast
Adorn it through; and thereat hear the breast
Of the divine muse; men in order set;
A wine-page waiting; tables crown'd with meat,
Set close to guests that are to use it skill'd;
The cup-boards furnish'd, and the cups still fill'd;
This shows, to my mind, most humanely fair.
Nor should you, for me, still the heav'nly air,   20
That stirr'd my soul so; for I love such tears
As fall from fit notes, beaten through mine ears
With repetitions of what heav'n hath done,
And break from hearty apprehension
Of god and goodness, though they show my ill.
And therefore doth my mind excite me still,
To tell my bleeding moan; but much more now,
To serve your pleasure, that to over-flow
My tears with such cause may by sighs be driv'n,
Though ne'er so much plagued I may seem by heav'n.   30
    And now my name; which way shall lead to all
My miseries after, that their sounds may fall
Through your ears also, and show (having fled
So much affliction) first, who rests his head
In your embraces, when, so far from home,

I knew not where t' obtain it resting room.
    I am Ulysses Laertiades,
The fear of all the world for policies,
For which my facts as high as heav'n resound.
I dwell in Ithaca, earth's most renown'd,   40
All over-shadow'd with the shake-leaf hill,
Tree-famed Neritus; whose near confines fill
Islands a-number, well inhabited,
That under my observance taste their bread:
Dulichius, Samos, and the full-of-food
Zacynthus, likewise grac'd with store of wood.
But Ithaca, though in the seas it lie,
Yet lies she so aloft she casts her eye
Quite over all the neighbour continent;
Far northward situate, and, being lent   50
But little favour of the morn and sun,
With barren rocks and cliffs is over-run,
And yet of hardy youths a nurse of name;
Nor could I see a soil, where'er I came,
More sweet and wishful. Yet, from hence was I
Withheld with horror by the deity,
Divine Calypso, in her cavy house,
Enflam'd to make me her sole lord and spouse.
Circe Aeaea too, that knowing dame,
Whose veins the like affections did enflame,   60
Detain'd me likewise. But to neither's love
Could I be tempted; which doth well approve,
Nothing so sweet is as our country's earth,
And joy of those from whom we claim our birth.
Though roofs far richer we far off possess,
Yet, from our native, all our more is less.
    To which as I contended, I will tell
The much-distress-conferring facts that fell
By Jove's divine prevention, since I set
From ruin'd Troy my first foot in retreat.   70
    From Ilion ill winds cast me on the coast
The Cicons hold, where I employ'd mine host
For Ismarus, a city built just by
My place of landing; of which victory
Made me expugner. I depeopled it,
Slew all the men, and did their wives remit,
With much spoil taken; which we did divide,
That none might need his part. I then applied

All speed for flight; but my command therein,
Fools that they were, could no observance win   80
Of many soldiers, who, with spoil fed high,
Would yet fill higher, and excessively
Fell to their wine, gave slaughter on the shore
Clov'n-footed beeves and sheep in mighty store.
In mean space, Cicons did to Cicons cry,
When, of their nearest dwellers, instantly
Many and better soldiers made strong head,
That held the continent, and managed
Their horse with high skill, on which they would fight,
When fittest cause serv'd, and again alight,   90
With soon seen vantage, and on foot contend.
Their concourse swift was, and had never end;
As thick and sudden 'twas, as flowers and leaves
Dark spring discovers, when she light receives.
And then began the bitter fate of Jove
To alter us unhappy, which ev'n strove
To give us suff'rance. At our fleet we made
Enforced stand; and there did they invade
Our thrust-up forces; darts encounter'd darts,
With blows on both sides, either making parts   100
Good upon either, while the morning shone,
And sacred day her bright increase held on –
Though much out-match'd in number; but as soon
As Phoebus westward fell, the Cicons won
Much hand of us; six proved soldiers fell
Of every ship; the rest they did compel
To seek of flight escape from death and fate.
   Thence sad in heart we sail'd; and yet our state
Was something cheer'd, that (being o'er-match'd so much
In violent number) our retreat was such   110
As saved so many – our dear loss the less,
That they surviv'd, so like for like success.
Yet left we not the coast, before we call'd
Home to our country earth the souls exhal'd
Of all the friends the Cicons overcame.
Thrice call'd we on them by their several name,
And then took leave. Then from the angry North
Cloud-gathering Jove a dreadful storm call'd forth
Against our navy, cover'd shore and all
With gloomy vapours. Night did headlong fall   120
From frowning heav'n. And then hurl'd here and there

Was all our navy; the rude winds did tear
In three, in four parts, all their sails; and down
Driv'n under hatches were we, press'd to drown.
Up rush'd we yet again, and with tough hand
(Two days, two nights entoil'd) we gat near land,
Labours and sorrows eating up our minds.
The third clear day yet, to more friendly winds
We masts advanc'd, we white sails spread, and sate.
Forewinds and guides again did iterate   130
Our ease and home-hopes; which we clear had reach'd,
Had not, by chance, a sudden north-wind fetch'd,
With an extreme sea, quite about again
Our whole endeavours, and our course constrain
To giddy round, and with our bow'd sails greet
Dreadful Maleia, calling back our fleet
As far forth as Cythera. Nine days more
Adverse winds toss'd me; and the tenth the shore,
Where dwelt the blossom-fed Lotophagi,
I fetch'd, fresh water took in, instantly   140
Fell to our food a-shipboard, and then sent
Two of my choice men to the continent
(Adding a third, a herald) to discover
What sort of people were the rulers over
The land next to us; where the first they met
Were the Lotophagi, that made them eat
Their country diet, and no ill intent
Hid in their hearts to them; and yet th' event
To ill converted it, for, having eat
Their dainty viands, they did quite forget   150
(As all men else that did but taste their feast)
Both countrymen and country, nor address'd
Any return t' inform what sort of men
Made fix'd abode there, but would needs maintain
Abode themselves there, and eat that food ever.
I made out after, and was feign to sever
Th' enchanted knot by forcing their retreat,
That striv'd, and wept, and would not leave their meat
For heav'n itself. But, dragging them to fleet,
I wrapt in sure bands both their hands and feet,   160
And cast them under hatches, and away
Commanded all the rest without least stay,
Lest they should taste the lote too, and forget
With such strange raptures their despis'd retreat.

All then aboard, we beat the sea with oars,
And still with sad hearts sail'd by out-way shores,
Till th' out-law'd Cyclops' land we fetch'd, a race
Of proud-liv'd loiterers, that never sow,
Nor put a plant in earth, nor use a plow,
But trust in god for all things; and their earth,   170
Unsown, unplow'd, gives every offspring birth
That other lands have: wheat and barley, vines
That bear in goodly grapes delicious wines;
And Jove sends showers for all. No counsels there,
Nor counsellors, nor laws; but all men bear
Their heads aloft on mountains, and those steep,
And on their tops too; and their houses keep
In vaulty caves, their households govern'd all
By each man's law, impos'd in several,
Nor wife, nor child aw'd but as he thinks good,   180
None for another caring. But there stood
Another little isle, well stor'd with wood,
Betwixt this and the entry; neither nigh
The Cyclops' isle, nor yet far off doth lie.
Men's want it suffer'd, but the men's supplies
The goats made with their inarticulate cries.
Goats beyond number this small island breeds,
So tame, that no access disturbs their feeds;
No hunters, that the tops of mountains scale,
And rub through woods with toil, seek them at all.   190
Nor is the soil with flocks fed down, nor plow'd,
Nor ever in it any seed was sow'd.
Nor place the neighbour Cyclops their delights
In brave vermilion-prow-deck'd ships, nor wrights
Useful, and skilful in such works as need
Perfection to those traffics that exceed
Their natural confines, to fly out and see
Cities of men, and take in mutually
The prease of others; to themselves they live,
And to their island that enough would give   200
A good inhabitant, and time of year
Observe to all things art could order there.
There, close upon the sea, sweet meadows spring,
That yet of fresh streams want no watering
To their soft burthens, but of special yield
Your vines would be there, and your common field
But gentle work make for your plow, yet bear

A lofty harvest when you came to shear;
For passing fat the soil is. In it lies
A harbour so opportune, that no ties,   210
Halsers, or cables need, nor anchors cast.
Whom storms put in there are with stay embrac'd,
Or to their full wills safe, or winds aspire
To pilots' uses their more quick desire.
At entry of the hav'n, a silver ford
Is from a rock-impressing fountain pour'd,
All set with sable poplars. And this port
Were we arrived at, by the sweet resort
Of some god guiding us, for 'twas a night
So ghastly dark all port was past our sight,   220
Clouds hid our ships, and would not let the moon
Afford a beam to us, the whole isle won
By not an eye of ours. None thought the blore,
That then was up, shov'd waves against the shore,
That then to an unmeasured height put on;
We still at sea esteem'd us, till alone
Our fleet put in itself. And then were strook
Our gather'd sails; our rest ashore we took,
And day expected. When the morn gave fire,
We rose, and walk'd, and did the isle admire –   230
The nymphs, Jove's daughters, putting up a herd
Of mountain goats to us, to render cheer'd
My fellow soldiers. To our fleet we flew,
Our crooked bows took, long-pil'd darts, and drew
Ourselves in three parts out; when, by the grace
That god vouchsaf'd, we made a gainful chace.
Twelve ships we had, and every ship had nine
Fat goats allotted [it], ten only mine.
Thus all that day, ev'n till the sun was set,
We sat and feasted, pleasant wine and meat   240
Plenteously taking; for we had not spent
Our ruddy wine a-shipboard; supplement
Of large sort each man to his vessel drew,
When we the sacred city overthrew
That held the Cicons. Now then saw we near
The Cyclops' late-prais'd island, and might hear
The murmur of their sheep and goats, and see
Their smokes ascend. The sun then set, and we,
When night succeeded, took our rest ashore.
And when the world the morning's favour wore,   250

I call'd my friends to council, charging them
To make stay there, while I took ship and stream,
With some associates, and explor'd what men
The neighbour isle held: if of rude disdain,
Churlish and tyrannous, or minds bewray'd
Pious and hospitable. Thus much said,
I boarded, and commanded to ascend
My friends and soldiers; to put off, and lend
Way to our ship. They boarded, sat, and beat
The old sea forth, till we might see the seat   260
The greatest Cyclop held for his abode,
Which was a deep cave, near the common road
Of ships that touch'd there, thick with laurels spread,
Where many sheep and goats lay shadowed;
And, near to this, a hall of torn-up stone,
High built with pines, that heav'n and earth attone,
And lofty-fronted oaks; in which kept house
A man in shape immane, and monsterous,
Fed all his flocks alone, nor would afford
Commerce with men, but had a wit abhorr'd,   270
His mind his body answ'ring. Nor was he
Like any man that food could possibly
Enhance so hugely, but, beheld alone,
Show'd like a steep hill's top, all overgrown
With trees and brambles; little thought had I
Of such vast objects. When, arriv'd so nigh,
Some of my lov'd friends I made stay aboard,
To guard my ship, and twelve with me I shor'd,
The choice of all. I took besides along
A goat-skin flagon of wine, black and strong,   280
That Maro did present, Evantheus' son,
And priest to Phoebus, who had mansion
In Thracian Ismarus (the town I took);
He gave it me, since I (with reverence strook
Of his grave place), his wife and children's good
Freed all of violence. Amidst a wood,
Sacred to Phoebus, stood his house; from whence
He fetch'd me gifts of varied excellence;
Seven talents of fine gold; a bowl all fram'd
Of massy silver; but his gift most fam'd   290
Was twelve great vessels, fill'd with such rich wine
As was incorruptible and divine.
He kept it as his jewel, which none knew

But he himself, his wife, and he that drew.
It was so strong, that never any fill'd
A cup, where that was but by drops instill'd,
And drunk it off, but 'twas before allay'd
With twenty parts in water; yet so sway'd
The spirit of that little, that the whole
A sacred odour breath'd about the bowl.   300
Had you the odour smelt and scent it cast,
It would have vex'd you to forbear the taste.
But then, the taste gain'd too, the spirit it wrought
To dare things high set up an end my thought.
      Of this a huge great flagon full I bore,
And in a good large knapsack victuals' store,
And long'd to see this heap of fortitude,
That so illiterate was and upland rude
That laws divine nor human he had learn'd.
With speed we reach'd the cavern; nor discern'd   310
His presence there, his flocks he fed at field.
      Ent'ring his den, each thing beheld did yield
Our admiration; shelves with cheeses heap'd;
Sheds stuff'd with lambs and goats, distinctly kept,
Distinct the biggest, the more mean distinct,
Distinct the youngest. And in their precinct,
Proper and placeful, stood the troughs and pails
In which he milk'd; and what was giv'n at meals,
Set up a-creaming, in the evening still
All scouring bright as dew upon the hill.   320
      Then were my fellows instant to convey
Kids, cheeses, lambs a-shipboard, and away
Sail the salt billow. I thought best not so,
But better otherwise; and first would know,
What guest-gifts he would spare me. Little knew
My friends on whom they would have prey'd. His view
Prov'd after, that his innards were too rough
For such bold usage. We were bold enough
In what I suffer'd; which was there to stay,
Make fire and feed there, though bear none away.   330
There sat we, till we saw him feeding come,
And on his neck a burthen lugging home,
Most highly huge, of sere-wood, which the pile
That fed his fire supplied all supper-while.
Down by his den he threw it, and up rose
A tumult with the fall. Afraid, we close

Withdrew ourselves, while he into a cave
Of huge receipt his high-fed cattle drave,
All that he milk'd; the males he left without
His lofty roofs, that all bestrow'd about   340
With rams and buck-goats were. And then a rock
He lift aloft, that damm'd up to his flock
The door they enter'd; 'twas so hard to wield,
That two and twenty waggons, all four-wheel'd,
(Could they be loaded, and have teams that were
Proportion'd to them) could not stir it there.
Thus making sure, he kneel'd and milk'd his ewes,
And braying goats, with all a milker's dues;
Then let in all their young. Then quick did dress
His half milk up for cheese, and in a press   350
Of wicker press'd it; put in bowls the rest,
To drink and eat, and serve his supping feast.
    All works dispatch'd thus, he began his fire;
Which blown, he saw us, and did thus inquire:
'Ho! Guests! What are ye? Whence sail ye these seas?
Traffic, or rove ye, and like thieves oppress
Poor strange adventurers, exposing so
Your souls to danger, and your lives to woe?'
    This utter'd he, when fear from our hearts took
The very life, to be so thunder-strook   360
With such a voice, and such a monster see;
But thus I answer'd: 'Erring Grecians, we
From Troy were turning homewards, but by force
Of adverse winds, in far diverted course,
Such unknown ways took, and on rude seas toss'd,
As Jove decreed, are cast upon this coast.
Of Agamemnon, famous Atreus' son,
We boast ourselves the soldiers; who hath won
Renown that reacheth heav'n, to overthrow
So great a city, and to ruin so   370
So many nations. Yet at thy knees lie
Our prostrate bosoms, forced with pray'rs to try
If any hospitable right, or boon
Of other nature, such as have been won
By laws of other houses, thou wilt give.
Reverence the gods, thou great'st of all that live.
We suppliants are; and hospitable Jove
Pours wreak on all whom pray'rs want pow'r to move,
And with their plagues together will provide

That humble guests shall have their wants supplied.'   380
    He cruelly answer'd: 'O thou fool,' said he,
'To come so far, and to importune me
With any god's fear, or observed love!
We Cyclops care not for your goat-fed Jove,
Nor other bless'd ones; we are better far.
To Jove himself dare I bid open war
To thee, and all thy fellows, if I please.
But tell me, where's the ship that by the seas
Hath brought thee hither? If far off, or near,
Inform me quickly.' These his temptings were;   390
But I too much knew not to know his mind,
And craft with craft paid, telling him the wind
(Thrust up from sea by him that shakes the shore)
Had dash'd our ships against his rocks, and tore
Her ribs in pieces close upon his coast,
And we from high wrack saved, the rest were lost.
    He answer'd nothing, but rush'd in, and took
Two of my fellows up from earth, and strook
Their brains against it. Like two whelps they flew
About his shoulders, and did all embrue   400
The blushing earth. No mountain lion tore
Two lambs so sternly, lapp'd up all their gore
Gush'd from their torn-up bodies, limb by limb
(Trembling with life yet) ravish'd into him.
Both flesh and marrow-stuffed bones he eat,
And even th' uncleans'd entrails made his meat.
We, weeping, cast our hands to heav'n, to view
A sight so horrid. Desperation flew,
With all our after lives, to instant death,
In our believ'd destruction. But when breath   410
The fury of his appetite had got,
Because the gulf his belly reach'd his throat,
Man's flesh and goat's milk laying layer on layer,
Till near chok'd up was all the pass for air,
Along his den, amongst his cattle, down
He rush'd, and streak'd him; when my mind was grown
Desperate to step in, draw my sword, and part
His bosom where the strings about the heart
Circle the liver, and add strength of hand –
But that rash thought, more stay'd, did countermand,   420
For there we all had perish'd, since it pass'd
Our pow'rs to lift aside a log so vast

As barr'd all outscape; and so sigh'd away
The thought all night, expecting active day.
Which come, he first of all his fire enflames,
Then milks his goats and ewes, then to their dams
Lets in their young, and, wondrous orderly,
With manly haste dispatch'd his houswif'ry.
Then to his breakfast, to which other two
Of my poor friends went; which eat, out then go   430
His herds and fat flocks, lightly putting by
The churlish bar, and clos'd it instantly;
For both those works with ease as much he did,
As you would ope and shut your quiver lid.

    With storms of whistlings then his flock he drave
Up to the mountains; and occasion gave
For me to use my wits, which to their height
I striv'd to screw up, that a vengeance might
By some means fall from thence, and Pallas now
Afford a full ear to my neediest vow.   440
This then my thoughts preferr'd: a huge club lay
Close by his milk-house, which was now in way
To dry and season, being an olive-tree
Which late he fell'd, and, being green, must be
Made lighter for his manage. 'Twas so vast,
That we resembled it to some fit mast,
To serve a ship of burthen that was driv'n
With twenty oars, and had a bigness giv'n
To bear a huge sea. Full so thick, so tall,
We judg'd this club; which I, in part, hew'd small,   450
And cut a fathom off. The piece I gave
Amongst my soldiers, to take down, and shave;
Which done, I sharpen'd it at top, and then,
Harden'd in fire, I hid it in the den
Within a nasty dunghill reeking there,
Thick, and so moist it issu'd everywhere.
Then made I lots cast by my friends to try
Whose fortune served to dare the bored-out eye
Of that man-eater; and the lot did fall
On four I wish'd to make my aid of all,   460
And I the fifth made, chosen like the rest.

    Then came the ev'n, and he came from the feast
Of his fat cattle, drave in all, nor kept
One male abroad; if or his memory slept,
By god's direct will, or of purpose was

His driving in of all then, doth surpass
My comprehension. But he clos'd again
The mighty bar, milk'd, and did still maintain
All other observation as before.
His work all done, two of my soldiers more   470
At once he snatch'd up, and to supper went.
Then dar'd I words to him, and did present
A bowl of wine, with these words: 'Cyclop! Take
A bowl of wine, from my hand, that may make
Way for the man's flesh thou hast eat, and show
What drink our ship held; which in sacred vow
I offer to thee to take ruth on me
In my dismission home. Thy rages be
Now no more sufferable. How shall men,
Mad and inhuman that thou art, again   480
Greet thy abode, and get thy actions grace,
If thus thou ragest, and eat'st up their race.'
    He took, and drunk, and vehemently joy'd
To taste the sweet cup; and again employ'd
My flagon's pow'rs, entreating more, and said:
'Good guest, again afford my taste thy aid,
And let me know thy name, and quickly now,
That in thy recompense I may bestow
A hospitable gift on thy desert,
And such a one as shall rejoice thy heart.   490
For to the Cyclops too the gentle earth
Bears generous wine, and Jove augments her birth,
In store of such, with show'rs; but this rich wine
Fell from the river, that is mere divine,
Of nectar and ambrosia.' This again
I gave him, and again; nor could the fool abstain,
But drunk as often. When the noble juice
Had wrought upon his spirit, I then gave use
To fairer language, saying: 'Cyclop! Now,
As thou demand'st, I'll tell thee my name; do thou   500
Make good thy hospitable gift to me.
My name is No-Man; No-Man each degree
Of friends, as well as parents, call my name.'
He answer'd, as his cruel soul became:
'No-Man! I'll eat thee last of all thy friends;
And this is that in which so much amends
I vow'd to thy deservings. Thus shall be
My hospitable gift made good to thee.'

This said, he upwards fell, but then bent round
His fleshy neck; and Sleep, with all crowns crown'd,   510
Subdu'd the savage. From his throat brake out
My wine, with man's flesh gobbets, like a spout,
When, loaded with his cups, he lay and snor'd;
And then took I the club's end up, and gor'd
The burning coal-heap, that the point might heat;
Confirm'd my fellow's minds, lest fear should let
Their vow'd assay, and make them fly my aid.
Straight was the olive-lever I had laid
Amidst the huge fire to get hardening, hot,
And glow'd extremely, though 'twas green; which got   520
From forth the cinders, close about me stood
My hardy friends; but that which did the good
Was god's good inspiration, that gave
A spirit beyond the spirit they us'd to have;
Who took the olive spar, made keen before,
And plung'd it in his eye, and up I bore,
Bent to the top close, and help'd pour it in,
With all my forces. And as you have seen
A ship-wright bore a naval beam, he oft
Thrusts at the auger's froofe, works still aloft,   530
And at the shank help others, with a cord
Wound round about to make it sooner bor'd,
All plying the round still: so into his eye
The fiery stake we labour'd to imply.
Out gush'd the blood that scalded; his eye-ball
Thrust out a flaming vapour, that scorch'd all
His brows and eye-lids; his eye-strings did crack,
As in the sharp and burning rafter brake.
And as a smith to harden any tool,
Broad axe or mattock, in his trough doth cool   540
The red-hot substance, that so fervent is
It makes the cold wave straight to seethe and hiss:
So sod and hiss'd his eye about the stake.
He roar'd withal, and all his cavern brake
In claps like thunder. We did frighted fly,
Dispers'd in corners. He from forth his eye
The fixed stake pluck'd; after which the blood
Flow'd freshly forth; and mad, he hurl'd the wood
About his hovel. Out he then did cry
For other Cyclops, that in caverns by   550
Upon a windy promontory dwell'd;

Who, hearing how impetuously he yell'd,
Rush'd every way about him, and inquir'd,
What ill afflicted him, that he exspir'd
Such horrid clamours, and in sacred night
To break their sleeps so? Ask'd him, if his fright
Came from some mortal that his flocks had driv'n?
Or if by craft or might his death were giv'n?
He answer'd from his den: 'By craft, nor might,
No-Man hath giv'n me death.' They then said right,   560
'If no man hurt thee, and thyself alone,
That which is done to thee by Jove is done;
And what great Jove inflicts no man can fly.
Pray to thy father yet, a deity,
And prove, from him if thou canst help acquire.'
    Thus spake they, leaving him; when all on fire
My heart with joy was, that so well my wit
And name deceiv'd him; whom now pain did split,
And groaning up and down he groping tried
To find the stone; which found, he put aside,   570
But in the door sat, feeling if he could
(As his sheep issu'd) on some man lay hold –
Esteeming me a fool, that could devise
No stratagem to 'scape his gross surprise.
But I, contending what I could invent
My friends and me from death so imminent
To get deliver'd, all my wiles I wove
(Life being the subject) and did this approve:
Fat fleecy rams, most fair and great, lay there,
That did a burden like a violet bear.   580
These, while this learn'd-in-villany did sleep,
I yok'd with osiers cut there, sheep to sheep,
Three in a rank, and still the mid sheep bore
A man about his belly; the two more
March'd on his each side for defence. I then,
Choosing myself the fairest of the den,
His fleecy belly under-crept, embrac'd
His back, and in his rich wool wrapt me fast
With both my hands, arm'd with as fast a mind.
And thus each man hung, till the morning shin'd;   590
Which come, he knew the hour, and let abroad
His male-flocks first; the females unmilk'd stood
Bleating and braying, their full bags so sore
With being unemptied, but their shepherd more

With being unsighted, which was cause his mind
Went not a-milking. He, to wreak inclin'd,
The backs felt, as they pass'd, of those male dams –
Gross fool, believing we would ride his rams!
Nor ever knew that any of them bore
Upon his belly any man before.   600
The last ram came to pass him, with his wool
And me together loaded to the full,
For there did I hang; and that ram he stay'd,
And me withal had in his hands, my head
Troubled the while, not causelessly, nor least.
This ram he grop'd, and talk'd to: 'Lazy beast!
Why last art thou now? Thou hast never us'd
To lag thus hindmost, but still first hast bruis'd
The tender blossom of a flower, and held
State in thy steps, both to the flood and field;   610
First still at fold at ev'n, now last remain?
Dost thou not wish I had mine eye again,
Which that abhorr'd man No-Man did put out,
Assisted by his execrable rout,
When he had wrought me down with wine? But he
Must not escape my wreak so cunningly.
I would to heav'n thou knew'st, and could but speak,
To tell me where he lurks now! I would break
His brain about my cave, strew'd here and there,
To ease my heart of those foul ills, that were   620
Th' inflictions of a man I priz'd at nought.'
    Thus let he him abroad; when I, once brought
A little from his hold, myself first loos'd,
And next my friends. Then drave we, and dispos'd,
His straight-legg'd fat fleece-bearers over land,
Ev'n till they all were in my ship's command;
And to our lov'd friends show'd our pray'd-for sight,
Escap'd from death. But, for our loss, outright
They brake in tears; which with a look I stay'd,
And bade them take our boot in. They obey'd,   630
And up we all went, sat, and used our oars.
But having left as far the savage shores
As one might hear a voice, we then might see
The Cyclop at the hav'n; when instantly
I stay'd our oars, and this insultance us'd:
'Cyclop! Thou shouldst not have so much abus'd
Thy monstrous forces, to oppose their least

Against a man immartial, and a guest,
And eat his fellows. Thou mightst know there were
Some ills behind, rude swain, for thee to bear,   640
That fear'd not to devour thy guests, and break
All laws of humans. Jove sends therefore wreak,
And all the gods, by me.' This blew the more
His burning fury; when the top he tore
From off a huge rock, and so right a throw
Made at our ship, that just before the prow
It overflew and fell, miss'd mast and all
Exceeding little; but about the fall
So fierce a wave it rais'd, that back it bore
Our ship so far, it almost touch'd the shore.   650
A bead-hook then, a far-extended one,
I snatch'd up, thrust hard, and so set us gone
Some little way; and straight commanded all
To help me with their oars, on pain to fall
Again on our confusion. But a sign
I with my head made, and their oars were mine
In all performance. When we off were set
(Than first, twice further), my heart was so great,
It would again provoke him, but my men
On all sides rush'd about me, to contain,   660
And said: 'Unhappy! Why will you provoke
A man so rude, that with so dead a stroke,
Giv'n with his rock-dart, made the sea thrust back
Our ship so far, and near had forc'd our wrack?
Should he again but hear your voice resound,
And any word reach, thereby would be found
His dart's direction, which would, in his fall,
Crush piece-meal us, quite split our ship and all,
So much dart wields the monster.' Thus urg'd they
Impossible things, in fear; but I gave way   670
To that wrath which so long I held depress'd,
By great necessity conquer'd, in my breast:

    'Cyclop! If any ask thee, who impos'd
Th' unsightly blemish that thine eye enclos'd,
Say that Ulysses, old Laertes' son,
Whose seat is Ithaca, and who hath won
Surname of city-raser, bored it out.'

    At this, he bray'd so loud, that round about
He drave affrighted echoes through the air,
And said: 'O beast! I was premonish'd fair,   680

By aged prophecy, in one that was
A great and good man, this should come to pass;
And how 'tis prov'd now! Augur Telemus,
Surnam'd Eurymides (that spent with us
His age in augury, and did exceed
In all presage of truth) said all this deed
Should this event take, author'd by the hand
Of one Ulysses, who I thought was mann'd
With great and goodly personage, and bore
A virtue answerable; and this shore   690
Should shake with weight of such a conqueror;
When now a weakling came, a dwarfy thing,
A thing of nothing; who yet wit did bring,
That brought supply to all, and with his wine
Put out the flame where all my light did shine.
Come, land again, Ulysses, that my hand
May guest-rites give thee, and the great command,
That Neptune hath at sea, I may convert
To the deduction where abides thy heart,
With my solicitings; whose son I am,   700
And whose fame boasts to bear my father's name.
Nor think my hurt offends me, for my sire
Can soon repose in it the visual fire,
At his free pleasure; which no power beside
Can boast, of men, or of the deified.'
   I answer'd: 'Would to god I could compel
Both life and soul from thee, and send to hell
Those spoils of nature! Hardly Neptune then
Could cure thy hurt, and give thee all again.'
   Then flew fierce vows to Neptune, both his hands   710
To star-born heav'n cast: 'O thou that all lands
Gird'st in thy ambient circle, and in air
Shak'st the curl'd tresses of thy sapphire hair,
If I be thine, or thou mayst justly vaunt
Thou art my father, hear me now, and grant
That this Ulysses, old Laertes' son,
That dwells in Ithaca, and name hath won
Of city-ruiner, may never reach
His natural region. Or if to fetch
That, and the sight of his fair roofs and friends,   720
Be fatal to him, let him that amends
For all his miseries, long time and ill,
Smart for, and fail of; nor that fate fulfill,

Till all his soldiers quite are cast away
In others' ships. And when, at last, the day
Of his sole-landing shall his dwelling show,
Let detriment prepare him wrongs enow.'
   Thus pray'd he Neptune; who, his sire, appear'd,
And all his pray'r to every syllable heard.
But then a rock, in size more amplified   730
Than first, he ravish'd to him, and implied
A dismal strength in it, when, wheel'd about,
He sent it after us; nor flew it out
From any blind aim, for a little pass
Beyond our fore-deck from the fall there was,
With which the sea our ship gave back upon,
And shrunk up into billows from the stone,
Our ship again repelling near as near
The shore as first. But then our rowers were,
Being warn'd, more arm'd, and stronglier stemm'd the flood
That bore back on us, till our ship made good
The other island, where our whole fleet lay,
In which our friends lay mourning for our stay,
And every minute look'd when we should land.
Where, now arriv'd, we drew up to the sand,
The Cyclops' sheep dividing, that none there
Of all our privates might be wrung, and bear
Too much on pow'r. The ram yet was alone
By all my friends made all my portion
Above all others; and I made him then   750
A sacrifice for me and all my men
To cloud-compelling Jove that all commands,
To whom I burn'd the thighs; but my sad hands
Receiv'd no grace from him, who studied how
To offer men and fleet to overthrow. ·
   All day, till sun-set, yet we sat and eat,
And liberal store took in of wine and meat.
The sun then down, anal place resign'd to shade,
We slept. Morn came, my men I rais'd, and made
All go aboard, weigh anchor, and away.   760
They boarded, sat, and beat the aged sea,
And forth we made sail, sad for loss before,
And yet had comfort since we lost no more.

THE END OF THE NINTH BOOK

BOOK TEN

Ulysses now relates to us
The grace he had with Aeolus,
Great guardian of the hollow winds;
Which in a leather bag he binds,
And gives Ulysses; all but one,
Which Zephyr was, who fill'd alone
Ulysses' sails. The bag once seen,
While he slept, by Ulysses' men,
They thinking it did gold enclose,
To find it, all the winds did loose,
Who back flew to their guard again.
Forth sail'd he, and did next attain
To where the Laestrygonians dwell;
Where he elev'n ships lost, and fell
On the Aeaean coast, whose shore
He sends Eurylochus t' explore,
Dividing with him half his men;
Who go, and turn no more again,
All, save Eurylochus, to swine
By Circe turn'd. Their stays incline
Ulysses to their search; who got
Of Mercury an antidote,
Which *moly* was, 'gainst Circe's charms,
And so avoids his soldiers' harms.
A year with Circe all remain,
And then their native forms regain.
On utter shores a time they dwell,
While Ithacus descends to hell.

Another Argument

Kappa   Great Aeolus
                And Circe, friends
            Finds Ithacus;
                And hell descends.

BOOK TEN

TO THE AEOLIAN ISLAND we attain'd,
        That swum about still on the sea, where reign'd
        The god-lov'd Aeolus Hippotades.
A wall of steel it had, and in the seas
A wave-beat-smooth rock moved about the wall.
Twelve children in his house imperial
Were born to him; of which six daughters were,
And six were sons, that youth's sweet flower did bear.
His daughters to his sons he gave as wives;
Who spent in feastful comforts all their lives,   10
Close seated by their sire and his grave spouse.
Past number were the dishes that the house
Made ever savour; and still full the hall
As long as day shin'd; in the night-time, all
Slept with their chaste wives, each his fair carv'd bed
Most richly furnish'd; and this life they led.
    We reach'd the city and fair roofs of these,
Where, a whole month's time, all things that might please
The king vouchsaf'd us; of great Troy inquir'd,
The Grecian fleet, and how the Greeks retir'd.   20
To all which I gave answer as behov'd.
    The fit time come when I dismission mov'd,
He nothing would deny me, but address'd
My pass with such a bounty, as might best
Teach me contentment; for he did enfold
Within an ox-hide, flay'd at nine years old,
All th' airy blasts that were of stormy kinds.
Saturnius made him steward of his winds,
And gave him power to raise and to assuage.
And these he gave me, curb'd thus of their rage,   30
Which in a glittering silver band I bound,
And hung up in my ship, enclos'd so round
That no egression any breath could find;
Only he left abroad the Western wind,
To speed our ships and us with blasts secure.

But our securities made all unsure;
Nor could he consummate our course alone,
When all the rest had got egression;
Which thus succeeded: nine whole days and nights
We sail'd in safety; and the tenth, the lights   40
Borne on our country earth we might descry,
So near we drew; and yet even then fell I,
Being overwatch'd, into a fatal sleep,
For I would suffer no man else to keep
The foot that ruled my vessel's course, to lead
The faster home. My friends then envy fed
About the bag I hung up, and suppos'd
That gold and silver I had there enclos'd,
As gift from Aeolus, and said: 'O heav'n!
What grace and grave price is by all men giv'n   50
To our commander! Whatsoever coast
Or town he comes to, how much he engrost
Of fair and precious prey, and brought from Troy!
We the same voyage went, and yet enjoy
In our return these empty hands for all.
This bag, now, Aeolus was so liberal
To make a guest-gift to him; let us try
Of what consists the fair-bound treasury,
And how much gold and silver it contains.'
Ill counsel present approbation gains.   60
They op'd the bag, and out the vapours brake,
When instant tempest did our vessel take,
That bore us back to sea, to mourn anew
Our absent country. Up amaz'd I flew,
And desperate things discours'd: if I should cast
Myself to ruin in the seas, or taste
Amongst the living more moan, and sustain?
Silent, I did so, and lay hid again
Beneath the hatches, while an ill wind took
My ships back to Aeolia, my men strook   70
With woe enough. We pump'd and landed then,
Took food, for all this; and of all my men
I took a herald to me, and away
Went to the court of Aeolus, where they
Were feasting still: he, wife, and children, set
Together close. We would not at their meat
Thrust in, but humbly on the threshold sat.
He then, amaz'd, my presence wonder'd at,

And call'd to me: 'Ulysses! How thus back
Art thou arriv'd here? What foul spirit brake   80
Into thy bosom, to retire thee thus?
We thought we had deduction curious
Given thee before, to reach thy shore and home.
Did it not like thee?' I, ev'n overcome
With worthy sorrow, answer'd: 'My ill men
Have done me mischief, and to them hath been
My sleep th' unhappy motive; but do you,
Dearest of friends, deign succour to my vow.
Your pow'rs command it.' Thus endeavour'd I
With soft speech to repair my misery.   90
The rest with ruth sat dumb. But thus spake he:
'Avaunt, and quickly quit my land of thee,
Thou worst of all that breathe. It fits not me
To convoy, and take in, whom heav'ns expose.
Away, and with thee go the worst of woes,
That seek'st my friendship, and the gods thy foes.'
   Thus he dismiss'd me sighing. Forth we sail'd,
At heart afflicted. And now wholly fail'd
The minds my men sustain'd, so spent they were
With toiling at their oars, and worse did bear   100
Their growing labours – and they caused their grought
By self-will'd follies – nor now ever thought
To see their country more. Six nights and days
We sail'd; the seventh we saw fair Lamos raise
Her lofty towers, the Laestrigonian state
That bears her ports so far disterminate;
Where shepherd shepherd calls out, he at home
Is call'd out by the other that doth come
From charge abroad, and then goes he to sleep,
The other issuing; he whose turn doth keep   110
The night observance hath his double hire,
Since day and night in equal length expire
About that region, and the night's watch weigh'd
At twice the day's ward, since the charge that's laid
Upon the nights-man (besides breach of sleep)
Exceeds the days-man's; for one oxen keep,
The other sheep. But when the hav'n we found
(Exceeding famous, and environ'd round
With one continuate rock, which so much bent
That both ends almost met, so prominent   120
They were, and made the hav'n's mouth passing strait),

Our whole fleet in we got; in whose receit
Our ships lay anchor'd close. Nor needed we
Fear harm on any stays, tranquillity
So purely sat there, that waves great nor small
Did ever rise to any height at all.
And yet would I no entry make, but stay'd
Alone without the hav'n, and thence survey'd,
From out a lofty watch-tower raised there,
The country round about; nor anywhere   130
The work of man or beast appear'd to me,
Only a smoke from earth break I might see.
I then made choice of two, and added more,
A herald for associate, to explore
What sort of men liv'd there. They went, and saw
A beaten way, through which carts us'd to draw
Wood from the high hills to the town, and met
A maid without the port, about to get
Some near spring-water. She the daughter was
Of mighty Laestrigonian Antiphas,   140
And to the clear spring call'd Artacia went,
To which the whole town for their water sent.
To her they came, and ask'd who govern'd there,
And what the people whom he order'd were?
She answer'd not, but led them through the port,
As making haste to show her father's court.
Where enter'd, they beheld, to their affright,
A woman like a mountain-top in height,
Who rush'd abroad, and from the counsel place
Call'd home her horrid husband Antiphas.   150
Who, deadly minded, straight he snatch'd up one,
And fell to supper. Both the rest were gone,
And to the fleet came. Antiphas a cry
Drave through the city; which heard, instantly
This way and that innumerable sorts,
Not men, but giants, issued through the ports,
And mighty flints from rocks tore, which they threw
Amongst our ships; through which an ill noise flew
Of shiver'd ships, and life-expiring men,
That were, like fishes, by the monsters slain,   160
And borne to sad feast. While they slaughter'd these,
That were engag'd in all th' advantages
The close-mouth'd and most dead-calm hav'n could give,
I, that without lay, made some means to live,

My sword drew, cut my cables, and to oars
Set all my men; and, from the plagues those shores
Let fly amongst us, we made haste to fly,
My men close working as men loth to die.
My ship flew freely off; but theirs that lay
On heaps in harbours could enforce no way   170
Through these stern fates that had engag'd them there.
Forth our sad remnant sail'd, yet still retain'd
The joys of men, that our poor few remain'd.

   Then to the isle Aeaea we attain'd,
Where fair-hair'd, dreadful, eloquent Circe reign'd,
Aeaeta's sister both by dame and sire,
Both daughters to heav'n's man-enlightning fire,
And Perse, whom Oceanus begat.
The ship-fit port here soon we landed at,
Some god directing us. Two days, two nights,   180
We lay here pining in the fatal spights
Of toil and sorrow; but the next third day
When fair Aurora had inform'd, quick way
I made out of my ship, my sword and lance
Took for my surer guide, and made advance
Up to a prospect; I assay to see
The works of men, or hear mortality
Expire a voice. When I had climb'd a height,
Rough and right hardly accessible, I might
Behold from Circe's house, that in a grove   190
Set thick with trees stood, a bright vapour move.
I then grew curious in my thought to try
Some fit inquiry, when so spritely fly
I saw the yellow smoke; but my discourse
A first retiring to my ship gave force,
To give my men their dinner, and to send
(Before th' adventure of myself) some friend.
Being near my ship, of one so desolate
Some god had pity, and would recreate
My woes a little, putting up to me   200
A great and high-palm'd hart, that (fatally,
Just in my way, itself to taste a flood)
Was then descending; the sun heat had sure
Importun'd him, besides the temperature
His natural heat gave. Howsoever, I
Made up to him, and let my javelin fly,
That struck him through the mid-part of his chine,

And made him, braying, in the dust confine
His flying forces. Forth his spirit flew;
When I stept in, and from the death's wound drew   210
My shrewdly-bitten lance; there let him lie
Till I, of cut-up osiers, did imply
A withe a fathom long, with which his feet
I made together in a sure league meet,
Stoop'd under him, and to my neck I heav'd
The mighty burden, of which I receiv'd
A good part on my lance, for else I could
By no means with one hand alone uphold
(Join'd with one shoulder) such a deathful load.
And so, to both my shoulders, both hands stood   220
Needful assistants; for it was a deer
Goodly-well-grown. When (coming something near
Where rode my ships) I cast it down, and rear'd
My friends with kind words; whom by name I cheer'd,
In note particular, and said: 'See friends,
We will not yet to Pluto's house; our ends
Shall not be hasten'd, though we be declin'd
In cause of comfort, till the day design'd
By Fate's fix'd finger. Come, as long as food
Or wine lasts in our ship, let's spirit our blood,   230
And quit our care and hunger both in one.'

     This said, they frolick'd, came, and look'd upon
With admiration the huge-bodied beast;
And when their first-serv'd eyes had done their feast,
They wash'd, and made a to-be-striv'd-for meal
In point of honour. On which all did dwell
The whole day long. And, to our venison's store,
We added wine till we could wish no more.

     Sun set, and darkness up, we slept till light
Put darkness down; and then did I excite   240
My friends to counsel, uttering this: 'Now, friends,
Afford unpassionate ear; though ill fate lends
So good cause to your passion, no man knows
The reason whence and how the darkness grows;
The reason how the morn is thus begun;
The reason how the man-enlight'ning sun
Dives under earth; the reason how again
He rears his golden head. Those counsels, then,
That pass our comprehension, we must leave
To him that knows their causes, and receive   250

Direction from him in our acts, as far
As he shall please to make them regular,
And stoop them to our reason. In our state
What then behoves us? Can we estimate,
With all our counsels, where we are? Or know
(Without instruction, past our own skills) how,
Put off from hence, to steer our course the more?
I think we cannot. We must then explore
These parts for information; in which way
We thus far are: last morn I might display   260
(From off a high-rais'd cliff) an island lie
Girt with th' unmeasur'd sea, and is so nigh
That in the midst I saw the smoke arise
Through tufts of trees. This rests then to advise,
Who shall explore this?' This struck dead their hearts,
Rememb'ring the most execrable parts
That Laestrigonian Antiphas had play'd,
And that foul Cyclop that their fellows bray'd
Betwixt his jaws; which mov'd them so, they cried.
But idle tears had never wants supplied;   270
I in two parts divided all, and gave
To either part his captain. I must have
The charge of one; and one of godlike look,
Eurylochus, the other. Lots we shook,
Put in a casque together, which of us
Should lead th' attempt; and 'twas Eurylochus.
He freely went, with two and twenty more;
All which took leave with tears, and our eyes wore
The same wet badge of weak humanity.
These in a dale did Circe's house descry,   280
Of bright stone built, in a conspicuous way.
Before her gates hill-wolves and lions lay;
Which with her virtuous drugs so tame she made,
That wolf nor lion would one man invade
With any violence, but all arose,
Their huge long tails wagg'd, and in fawns would close,
As loving dogs, when masters bring them home
Relics of feast, in all observance come,
And soothe their entries with their fawns and bounds,
All guests still bringing some scraps for their hounds: 290
So on these men the wolves and lions ramp'd,
Their horrid paws set up. Their spirits were damp'd
To see such monstrous kindness, stay'd at gate,

And heard within the goddess elevate
A voice divine, as at her web she wrought,
Subtle, and glorious, and past earthly thought,
As all the housewif'ries of deities are.
To hear a voice so ravishingly rare,
Polites (one exceeding dear to me,
A prince of men, and of no mean degree   300
In knowing virtue, in all acts whose mind
Discreet cares all ways us'd to turn and wind)
Was yet surpris'd with it, and said: 'O friends,
Some one abides within here, that commends
The place to us, and breathes a voice divine,
As she some web wrought, or her spindle's twine
She cherish'd with her song; the pavement rings
With imitation of the tunes she sings.
Some woman, or some goddess, 'tis. Assay
To see with knocking.' Thus said he, and they   310
Both knock'd, and call'd; and straight her shining gates
She open'd, issuing, bade them in to cates.
Led, and unwise, they follow'd – all but one,
Which was Eurylochus, who stood alone
Without the gates, suspicious of a sleight.
They enter'd, she made sit; and her deceit
She cloak'd with thrones, and goodly chairs of state;
Set herby honey, and the delicate
Wine brought from Smyrna, to them; meal and cheese;
But harmful venoms she commix'd with these,   320
That made their country vanish from their thought.
Which eat, she touch'd them with a rod that wrought
Their transformation far past human wonts;
Swine's snouts, swine's bodies took they, bristles, grunts,
But still retain'd the souls they had before,
Which made them mourn their bodies' change the more.
She shut them straight in sties, and gave them meat:
Oak-mast, and beech, and cornel fruit, they eat,
Grovelling like swine on earth, in foulest sort.
Eurylochus straight hasted the report   330
Of this his fellows' most remorseful fate;
Came to the ships, but so excruciate
Was with his woe, he could not speak a word,
His eyes stood full of tears, which show'd how stor'd
His mind with moan remain'd. We all admir'd,
Ask'd what had chanc'd him, earnestly desir'd

He would resolve us. At the last, our eyes
Enflam'd in him his fellows' memories,
And out his grief burst thus: 'You will'd; we went
Through those thick woods you saw, when a descent   340
Show'd us a fair house in a lightsome ground,
Where, at some work, we heard a heavenly sound
Breathed from a goddess', or a woman's, breast.
They knock'd, she op'd her bright gates, each her guest
Her fair invitement made; nor would they stay,
Fools that they were, when she once led the way.
I enter'd not, suspecting some deceit,
When all together vanish'd, nor the sight
Of any one (though long I look'd) mine eye
Could any way discover.' Instantly,   350
My sword and bow reach'd, I bad show the place,
When down he fell, did both my knees embrace,
And pray'd with tears thus: 'O thou kept of god,
Do not thyself lose, nor to that abode
Lead others rashly; both thyself and all
Thou ventur'st thither, I know well must fall
In one sure ruin. With these few then fly;
We yet may shun the others' destiny.'

   I answer'd him: 'Eurylochus! Stay thou
And keep the ship then, eat and drink; I now   360
Will undertake th' adventure; there is cause
In great Necessity's unalter'd laws.'
This said, I left both ship and seas, and on
Along the sacred valleys all alone
Went in discovery, till at last I came
Where of the main-medicine-making dame
I saw the great house; where encounter'd me
The golden-rod-sustaining Mercury,
Even ent'ring Circe's doors. He met me in
A young man's likeness, of the first-flower'd chin,   370
Whose form hath all the grace of one so young.
He first call'd to me, then my hand he wrung,
And said: 'Thou no-place-finding-for-repose,
Whither, alone, by these hill-confines goes
Thy erring foot? Th' art entering Circe's house,
Where, by her med'cines, black and sorcerous,
Thy soldiers all are shut in well-arm'd sties,
And turn'd to swine. Art thou arrived with prize
Fit for their ransoms? Thou com'st out no more,

If once thou ent'rest, like thy men before   380
Made to remain here. But I'll guard thee free,
And save thee in her spite. Receive of me
This fair and good receipt; with which once arm'd,
Enter her roofs, for th' art to all proof charm'd
Against the ill day. I will tell thee all
Her baneful counsel: with a festival
She'll first receive thee, but will spice thy bread
With flow'ry poisons; yet unaltered
Shall thy firm form be, for this remedy
Stands most approv'd 'gainst all her sorcery,   390
Which thus particularly shun: when she
Shall with her long rod strike thee, instantly
Draw from thy thigh thy sword, and fly on her
As to her slaughter. She, surpris'd with fear
And love, at first will bid thee to her bed.
Nor say the goddess nay, that welcomed
Thou may'st with all respect be, and procure
Thy fellows' freedoms. But before, make sure
Her favours to thee; and the great oath take
With which the blessed gods assurance make   400
Of all they promise, that no prejudice
(By stripping thee of form and faculties)
She may so much as once attempt on thee.'
This said, he gave his antidote to me,
Which from the earth he pluck'd, and told me all
The virtue of it, with what deities call
The name it bears; and *moly* they impose
For name to it. The root is hard to loose
From hold of earth by mortals, but god's pow'r
Can all things do. 'Tis black, but bears a flow'r   410
As white as milk. And thus flew Mercury
Up to immense Olympus, gliding by
The sylvan island. I made back my way
To Circe's house, my mind of my assay
Much thought revolving. At her gates I stay'd
And call'd; she heard, and her bright doors display'd,
Invited, led; I follow'd in, but trac'd
With some distraction. In a throne she plac'd
My welcome person; of a curious frame
'Twas, and so bright I sat as in a flame,   420
A foot-stool added. In a golden bowl
She then suborn'd a potion, in her soul

Deform'd things thinking; for amidst the wine
She mix'd her man-transforming medicine;
Which when she saw I had devour'd, she then
No more observ'd me with her soothing vein,
But struck me with her rod, and to her sty
Bad 'Out, away, and with thy fellows lie.'
I drew my sword, and charg'd her, as I meant
To take her life. When out she cried, and bent   430
Beneath my sword her knees, embracing mine,
And, full of tears, said: 'Who, of what high line,
Art thou the issue? Whence? What shores sustain
Thy native city? I amaz'd remain
That, drinking these my venoms, th' art not turn'd.
Never drunk any this cup but he mourn'd
In other likeness, if it once had pass'd
The ivory bounders of his tongue and taste.
All but thyself are brutishly declin'd.
Thy breast holds firm yet, and unchanged thy mind.   440
Thou canst be therefore none else but the man
Of many virtues, Ithacensian,
Deep-soul'd Ulysses, who, I oft was told
By that sly god that bears the rod of gold,
Was to arrive here in retreat from Troy.
Sheathe then thy sword, and let my bed enjoy
So much a man, that when the bed we prove,
We may believe in one another's love.'
    I then: 'O Circe, why entreat'st thou me
To mix in any human league with thee,   450
When thou my friends hast beasts turn'd, and thy bed
Tender'st to me, that I might likewise lead
A beast's life with thee, soften'd, naked stripp'd,
That in my blood thy banes may more be steep'd?
I never will ascend thy bed before
I may affirm, that in heav'n's sight you swore
The great oath of the gods, that all attempt
To do me ill is from your thoughts exempt.'
    I said, she swore, when, all the oath-rites said,
I then ascended her adorned bed,   460
But thus prepar'd: four handmaids serv'd her there
That daughters to her silver fountains were,
To her bright-sea-observing sacred floods,
And to her uncut consecrated woods.
One deck'd the throne-tops with rich cloths of state,

And did with silks the foot-pace consecrate.
Another silver tables set before
The pompous throne, and golden dishes' store
Serv'd in with several feast. A third fill'd wine.
The fourth brought water, and made fuel shine   470
In ruddy fires beneath a womb of brass.
Which heat, I bath'd; and odorous water was
Disperpled lightly on my head and neck,
That might my late heart-hurting sorrows check
With the refreshing sweetness; and, for that,
Men sometimes may be something delicate.
Bath'd, and adorn'd, she led me to a throne
Of massy silver, and of fashion
Exceeding curious. A fair foot-stool set,
Water appos'd, and every sort of meat   480
Set on th' elaborately-polish'd board,
She wish'd my taste employ'd, but not a word
Would my ears taste of taste; my mind had food
That must digest, eye meat would do me good.
Circe (observing that I put no hand
To any banquet, having countermand
From weightier cares the light cates could excuse)
Bowing her near me, these wing'd words did use:
    'Why sits Ulysses like one dumb, his mind
Lessening with languors? Nor to food inclin'd,   490
Nor wine? Whence comes it? Out of any fear
Of more illusion? You must needs forbear
That wrongful doubt, since you have heard me swear.'
    'O Circe!' I replied, 'what man is he,
Aw'd with the rights of true humanity,
That dares taste food or wine, before he sees
His friends redeem'd from their deformities?
If you be gentle, and indeed incline
To let me taste the comfort of your wine,
Dissolve the charms that their forc'd forms enchain,   500
And show me here my honour'd friends like men.'
    This said, she left her throne, and took her rod,
Went to her sty, and let my men abroad,
Like swine of nine years old. They opposite stood,
Observ'd their brutish form, and look'd for food;
When, with another med'cine, every one
All over smear'd, their bristles all were gone,
Produc'd by malice of the other bane,

And every one, afresh, look'd up a man,
Both younger than they were, of stature more,   510
And all their forms much goodlier than before.
All knew me, cling'd about me, and a cry
Of pleasing mourning flew about so high
The horrid roof resounded; and the queen
Herself was mov'd to see our kind so keen,
Who bad me now bring ship and men ashore,
Our arms and goods in caves hid, and restore
Myself to her, with all my other men.
I granted, went, and op'd the weeping vein
In all my men; whose violent joy to see   520
My safe return was, passing kindly, free
Of friendly tears, and miserably wept.
You have not seen young heifers (highly kept,
Fill'd full of daisies at the field, and driv'n
Home to their hovels, all so spritely giv'n
That no room can contain them, but about
Bace by the dams, and let their spirits out
In ceaseless bleating) of more jocund plight
Than my kind friends, ev'n crying out with sight
Of my return so doubted; circled me   530
With all their welcomes, and as cheerfully
Dispos'd their rapt minds, as if there they saw
Their natural country, cliffy Ithaca,
And even the roofs where they were bred and born,
And vow'd as much, with tears: 'O your return
As much delights us as in you had come
Our country to us, and our natural home.
But what unhappy fate hath reft our friends?'
I gave unlook'd for answer, that amends
Made for their mourning, bad them first of all   540
Our ship ashore draw, then in caverns stall
Our foody cattle, hide our mutual prize,
'And then,' said I, 'attend me, that your eyes
In Circe's sacred house may see each friend
Eating and drinking banquets out of end.'
    They soon obey'd; all but Eurylochus,
Who needs would stay them all, and counsell'd thus:
    'O wretches! Whither will ye? Why are you
Fond of your mischiefs, and such gladness show
For Circe's house, that will transform ye all   550
To swine, or wolves, or lions? Never shall

Our heads get out, if once within we be,
But stay compell'd by strong necessity.
So wrought the Cyclop, when t' his cave our friends
This bold one led on, and brought all their ends
By his one indiscretion.' I for this
Thought with my sword (that desperate head of his
Hewn from his neck) to gash upon the ground
His mangled body, though my blood was bound
In near alliance to him. But the rest   560
With humble suit contain'd me, and request,
That I would leave him with my ship alone,
And to the sacred palace lead them on.'
    I led them; nor Eurylochus would stay
From their attendance on me, our late fray
Struck to his heart so. But mean time, my men,
In Circe's house, were all, in several bain,
Studiously sweeten'd, smug'd with oil, and deck'd
With in and out weeds, and a feast secret
Serv'd in before them; at which close we found   570
They all were set, cheer'd, and carousing round.
When mutual sight had, and all thought on, then
Feast was forgotten, and the moan again
About the house flew, driv'n with wings of joy.
But then spake Circe: 'Now, no more annoy.
I know myself what woes by sea and shore,
And men unjust, have plagu'd enough before
Your injur'd virtues. Here then feast as long,
And be as cheerful, till ye grow as strong
As when ye first forsook your country earth.   580
Ye now fare all like exiles; not a mirth
Flash'd in amongst ye but is quench'd again
With still-renew'd tears, though the beaten vein
Of your distresses should, methink, be now
Benumb with suff'rance.' We did well allow
Her kind persuasions, and the whole year stay'd
In varied feast with her. When now array'd
The world was with the spring, and orby hours
Had gone the round again through herbs and flow'rs,
The months absolv'd in order, till the days   590
Had run their full race in Apollo's rays,
My friends remember'd me of home, and said,
If ever fate would sign my pass, delay'd
It should be now no more. I heard them well,

Yet that day spent in feast, till darkness fell,
And sleep his virtues through our vapours shed,
When I ascended sacred Circe's bed,
Implored my pass, and her performed vow
Which now my soul urg'd, and my soldiers now
Afflicted me with tears to get them gone.   600
All these I told her, and she answer'd these:
'Much skill'd Ulysses Laertiades!
Remain no more against your wills with me,
But take your free way; only this must be
Perform'd before you steer your course for home:
You must the way to Pluto overcome,
And stern Persephone, to form your pass,
By th' aged Theban soul Tiresias,
The dark-brow'd prophet, whose soul yet can see
Clearly and firmly; grave Persephone,   610
Ev'n dead, gave him a mind, that he alone
Might sing truth's solid wisdom, and not one
Prove more than shade in his comparison.'

  This broke my heart; I sunk into my bed,
Mourn'd, and would never more be comforted
With light, nor life. But having now express'd
My pains enough to her in my unrest,
That so I might prepare her ruth, and get
All I held fit for an affair so great,
I said: 'O Circe, who shall steer my course   620
To Pluto's kingdom? Never ship had force
To make that voyage.' The divine-in-voice
Said: 'Seek no guide; raise you your mast, and hoise
Your ship's white sails, and then sit you at peace,
The fresh North Spirit shall waft ye through the seas.
But, having past the ocean, you shall see
A little shore, that to Persephone
Puts up a consecrated wood, where grows
Tall firs, and sallows that their fruits soon loose.
Cast anchor in the gulfs, and go alone   630
To Pluto's dark house, where to Acheron
Cocytus runs, and Pyriphlegethon –
Cocytus born of Styx, and where a rock
Of both the met floods bears the roaring shock.
The dark heroë, great Tiresias,
Now coming near, to gain propitious pass,
Dig of a cubit every way a pit,

And pour, to all that are deceas'd, in it
A solemn sacrifice. For which, first take
Honey and wine, and their commixtion make,   640
Then sweet wine neat, and thirdly water pour,
And lastly add to these the whitest flour.
Then vow to all the weak necks of the dead
Offerings a-number; and, when thou shalt tread
The Ithacensian shore, to sacrifice
A heifer never-tam'd, and most of prize,
A pile of all thy most esteemed goods
Enflaming to the dear streams of their bloods;
And, in secret rites, to Tiresias vow
A ram coal-black at all parts, that doth flow   650
With fat and fleece, and all thy flocks doth lead.
When the all-calling nation of the dead
Thou thus hast pray'd to, offer on the place
A ram and ewe all black, being turn'd in face
To dreadful Erebus, thyself aside
The flood's shore walking. And then, gratified
With flocks of souls of men and dames deceas'd
Shall all thy pious rites be. Straight address'd
See then the offering that thy fellows slew,
Flay'd, and impos'd in fire; and all thy crew   660
Pray to the state of either deity,
Grave Pluto, and severe Persephone.
Then draw thy sword, stand firm, nor suffer one
Of all the faint shades of the dead and gone
T' approach the blood, till thou hast heard their king,
The wise Tiresias, who thy offering
Will instantly do honour, thy home ways,
And all the measure of them by the seas,
Amply unfolding.' This the goddess told;
And then the Morning in her throne of gold   670
Survey'd the vast world; by whose orient light
The nymph adorn'd me with attires as bright,
Her own hands putting on both shirt and weed,
Robes fine and curious, and upon my head
An ornament that glitter'd like a flame,
Girt me in gold; and forth betimes I came
Amongst my soldiers, rous'd them all from sleep,
And bad them now no more observance keep
Of ease and feast, but straight a-shipboard fall,
For now the goddess had inform'd me all.   680

Their noble spirits agreed; nor yet so clear
Could I bring all off, but Elpenor there
His heedless life left. He was youngest man
Of all my company, and one that won
Least fame for arms, as little for his brain;
Who (too much steep'd in wine, and so made fain
To get refreshing by the cool of sleep,
Apart his fellows, plung'd in vapours deep,
And they as high in tumult of their way)
Suddenly wak'd and (quite out of the stay   690
A sober mind had given him) would descend
A huge long ladder, forward, and on end
Fell from the very roof, full pitching on
The dearest joint his head was placed upon,
Which quite dissolv'd, let loose his soul to hell.
I to the rest, and Circe's means did tell
Of our return, as crossing clean the hope
I gave them first, and said: 'You think the scope
Of our endeavours now is straight for home.
No, Circe otherwise design'd, whose doom   700
Enjoin'd us first to greet the dreadful house
Of austere Pluto and his glorious spouse,
To take the counsel of Tiresias,
The reverend Theban, to direct our pass.'
    This brake their hearts, and grief made tear their hair.
But grief was never good at great affair;
It would have way yet. We went woeful on
To ship and shore, where was arriv'd as soon
Circe unseen, a black ewe and a ram
Binding for sacrifice, and, as she came,   710
Vanish'd again unwitness'd by our eyes;
Which griev'd not us, nor check'd our sacrifice,
For who would see god, loath to let us see,
This way or that bent? Still his ways are free.

THE END OF THE TENTH BOOK

BOOK ELEVEN

The Argument

Ulysses' way to Hell appears,
Where he the grave Tiresias hears;
Enquires his own and others' fates;
His mother sees, and th' after states
In which were held by sad decease
Heroës, and Heroësses,
A number that at Troy wag'd war,
As Ajax that was still at jar
With Ithacus, for th' arms he lost,
And with the great Achilles' ghost.

Another Argument

Lamba   Ulysses here
        Invokes the dead.
    The lives appear
        Hereafter led.

BOOK ELEVEN

ARRIV'D now at our ship, we launch'd, and set
  Our mast up, put forth sail, and in did get
  Our late-got cattle. Up our sails, we went,
My wayward fellows mourning now th' event.
A good companion yet, a foreright wind,
Circe (the excellent utterer of her mind)
Supplied our murmuring consorts with, that was
Both speed and guide to our adventurous pass.
All day our sails stood to the winds, and made
Our voyage prosp'rous. Sun then set, and shade   10
All ways obscuring, on the bounds we fell
Of deep Oceanus, where people dwell
Whom a perpetual cloud obscures outright,
To whom the cheerful sun lends never light –
Nor when he mounts the star-sustaining heav'n,
Nor when he stoops earth, and sets up the ev'n –
But night holds fix'd wings, feather'd all with banes,
Above those most unblest Cimmerians.
Here drew we up our ship, our sheep withdrew,
And walk'd the shore till we attain'd the view   20
Of that sad region Circe had foreshow'd.
And then the sacred offerings to be vow'd
Eurylochus and Persimedes bore;
When I my sword drew, and earth's womb did gore
Till I a pit digg'd of a cubit round,
Which with the liquid sacrifice we crown'd,
First honey mix'd with wine, then sweet wine neat,
Then water pour'd in, last the flour of wheat.
Much I importuned then the weak-neck'd dead,
And vow'd, when I the barren soil should tread   30
Of cliffy Ithaca, amidst my hall
To kill a heifer, my clear best of all,
And give in off'ring, on a pile compos'd
Of all the choice goods my whole house enclos'd;
And to Tiresias himself, alone,

A sheep coal-black, and the selectest one
Of all my flocks. When to the pow'rs beneath,
The sacred nation that survive with death,
My pray'rs and vows had done devotions fit,
I took the off'rings, and upon the pit					40
Bereft their lives. Out gush'd the sable blood,
And round about me fled out of the flood
The souls of the deceas'd. There cluster'd then
Youths and their wives, much-suffering aged men,
Soft tender virgins that but new came there
By timeless death, and green their sorrows were.
There men at arms, with armours all embrew'd,
Wounded with lances, and with falchions hew'd,
In numbers, up and down the ditch, did stalk,
And threw unmeasur'd cries about their walk,					50
So horrid that a bloodless fear surpris'd
My daunted spirits. Straight then I advis'd
My friends to flay the slaughter'd sacrifice,
Put them in fire, and to the deities,
Stern Pluto and Persephone, apply
Exciteful prayers. Then drew I from my thigh
My well-edg'd sword, stept in, and firmly stood
Betwixt the prease of shadows and the blood,
And would not suffer any one to dip
Within our off'ring his unsolid lip,					60
Before Tiresias that did all control.
The first that press'd in was Elpenor's soul,
His body in the broad-way'd earth as yet
Unmourn'd, unburied by us, since we swet
With other urgent labours. Yet his smart
I wept to see, and ru'd it from my heart,
Enquiring how he could before me be
That came by ship? He, mourning, answer'd me:
'In Circe's house, the spite some spirit did bear,
And the unspeakable good liquor there,					70
Hath been my bane; for, being to descend
A ladder much in height, I did not tend
My way well down, but forwards made a proof
To tread the rounds, and from the very roof
Fell on my neck, and brake it; and this made
My soul thus visit this infernal shade.
And here, by them that next thyself are dear,
Thy wife and father, that a little one

Gave food to thee, and by thy only son
At home behind thee left, Telemachus,   80
Do not depart by stealth, and leave me thus,
Unmourn'd, unburied, lest neglected I
Bring on thyself th' incensed deity.
I know that, sail'd from hence, thy ship must touch
On th' isle Aeaea; where vouchsafe thus much,
Good king, that, landed, thou wilt instantly
Bestow on me thy royal memory
To this grace, that my body, arms and all,
May rest consum'd in fiery funeral;
And on the foamy shore a sepulchre   90
Erect to me, that after times may hear
Of one so hapless. Let me these implore,
And fix upon my sepulchre the oar
With which alive I shook the aged seas,
And had of friends the dear societies.'
   I told the wretched soul I would fulfill
And execute to th' utmost point his will;
And, all the time we sadly talk'd, I still
My sword above the blood held when aside
The idol of my friend still amplified   100
His plaint, as up and down the shades he err'd.
Then my deceased mother's soul appear'd,
Fair daughter of Autolycus the great,
Grave Anticlaea, whom, when forth I set
For sacred Ilion, I had left alive.
Her sight much moved me, and to tears did drive
My note of her decease; and yet not she
(Though in my ruth she held the highest degree)
Would I admit to touch the sacred blood,
Till from Tiresias I had understood   110
What Circe told me. At the length did land
Theban Tiresias' soul, and in his hand
Sustain'd a golden sceptre, knew me well,
And said: 'O man unhappy, why to hell
Admitt'st thou dark arrival, and the light
The sun gives leav'st, to have the horrid sight
Of this black region, and the shadows here?
Now sheathe thy sharp sword, and the pit forbear,
That I the blood may taste, and then relate
The truth of those acts that affect thy fate.'   120
   I sheath'd my sword, and left the pit, till he,

The black blood tasting, thus instructed me:
'Renown'd Ulysses! All unask'd I know
That all the cause of thy arrival now
Is to enquire thy wish'd retreat for home;
Which hardly god will let thee overcome,
Since Neptune still will his opposure try,
With all his laid-up anger, for the eye
His lov'd son lost to thee. And yet through all
Thy suff'ring course (which must be capital),   130
If both thine own affections, and thy friends',
Thou wilt contain, when thy access ascends
The three-fork'd island, having 'scaped the seas,
Where ye shall find fed on the flow'ry leas
Fat flocks and oxen, which the Sun doth own,
To whom are all things as well heard as shown,
And never dare one head of those to slay,
But hold unharmful on your wished way,
Though through enough affliction, yet secure
Your fates shall land ye; but presage says sure,   140
If once ye spoil them, spoil to all thy friends,
Spoil to thy fleet, and if the justice ends
Short of thyself, it shall be long before,
And that length forc'd out with inflictions store,
When, losing all thy fellows, in a sail
Of foreign built (when most thy fates prevail
In thy deliv'rance) thus th' event shall sort:
Thou shalt find shipwrack raging in thy port,
Proud men, thy goods consuming and thy wife
Urging with gifts, give charge upon thy life.   150
But all these wrongs revenge shall end to thee,
And force or cunning set with slaughter free
Thy house of all thy spoilers. Yet again
Thou shalt a voyage make, and come to men
That know no sea, nor ships, nor oars that are
Wings to a ship, nor mix with any fare
Salt's savoury vapour. Where thou first shalt land,
This clear-giv'n sign shall let thee understand,
That there those men remain: assume ashore
Up to thy royal shoulder a ship oar,   160
With which, when thou shalt meet one on the way
That will in country admiration say,
'What dost thou with that wan upon thy neck?'
There fix that wan thy oar, and that shore deck

With sacred rites to Neptune; slaughter there
A ram, a bull, and (who for strength doth bear
The name of husband to a herd) a boar.
And, coming home, upon thy natural shore
Give pious hecatombs to all the gods,
Degrees observ'd. And then the periods   170
Of all thy labours in the peace shall end
Of easy death; which shall the less extend
His passion to thee, that thy foe, the sea,
Shall not enforce it, but death's victory
Shall chance in only-earnest-pray-vow'd age,
Obtain'd at home, quite emptied of his rage,
Thy subjects round about thee rich and blest.
And here hath Truth summ'd up thy vital rest.'
    I answer'd him: 'We will suppose all these
Decreed in deity; let it likewise please   180
Tiresias to resolve me, why so near
The blood and me my mother's soul doth bear,
And yet nor word nor look vouchsafe her son?
Doth she not know me?' 'No,' said he, 'nor none
Of all these spirits, but myself alone,
Knows anything till he shall taste the blood.
But whomsoever you shall do that good,
He will the truth of all you wish unfold;
Who you envy it to will all withhold.'
    Thus said the kingly soul, and made retreat   190
Amidst the inner parts of Pluto's seat,
When he had spoke thus by divine instinct.
Still I stood firm, till to the blood's precinct
My mother came, and drunk; and then she knew
I was her son, had passion to renew
Her natural plaints, which thus she did pursue:
'How is it, O my son, that you alive
This deadly-darksome region underdive?
'Twixt which and earth so many mighty seas
And horrid currents interpose their prease,   200
Oceanus in chief? Which none (unless
More help'd than you) on foot now can transgress.
A well-built ship he needs that ventures there.
Com'st thou from Troy but now, enforc'd to err
All this time with thy soldiers? Nor hast seen,
Ere this long day, thy country and thy queen?'
    I answer'd, that a necessary end

To this infernal state made me contend,
That from the wise Tiresias' Theban soul
I might an oracle involv'd unroll;   210
For I came nothing near Achaia yet,
Nor on our lov'd earth happy foot had set,
But, mishaps suff'ring, err'd from coast to coast,
Ever since first the mighty Grecian host
Divine Atrides led to Ilion,
And I his follower to set war upon
The rapeful Trojans; and so pray'd she would
The fate of that ungentle death unfold,
That forc'd her thither; if some long disease,
Or that the spleen of her that arrows please,   220
Diana, envious of most eminent dames,
Had made her th' object of her deadly aims?
My father's state and son's I sought, if they
Kept still my goods, or they became the prey
Of any other, holding me no more
In power of safe return? Or if my store
My wife had kept, together with her son?
If she her first mind held, or had been won
By some chief Grecian from my love and bed?
    All this she answer'd, that affliction fed   230
On her blood still at home, and that to grief
She all the days and darkness of her life
In tears had consecrate. That none possess'd
My famous kingdom's throne, but th' interest
My son had in it still he held in peace,
A court kept like a prince, and his increase
Spent in his subjects' good, administ'ring laws
With justice, and the general applause
A king should merit, and all call'd him king.
My father kept the upland, labouring,   240
And shunn'd the city, used no sumptuous beds,
Wonder'd-at furnitures, nor wealthy weeds,
But in the winter strew'd about the fire
Lay with his slaves in ashes, his attire
Like to a beggar's; when the summer came,
And autumn all fruits ripen'd with his flame,
Where grape-charg'd vines made shadows most abound,
His couch with fall'n leaves made upon the ground,
And here lay he, his sorrow's fruitful state
Increasing as he faded for my fate;   250

And now the part of age that irksome is
Lay sadly on him. And that life of his
She led, and perish'd in, not slaughter'd by
The dame that darts lov'd, and her archery,
Nor by disease invaded, vast and foul,
That wastes the body, and sends out the soul
With shame and horror; only in her moan,
For me and my life, she consum'd her own.

    She thus; when I had great desire to prove
My arms the circle where her soul did move.   260
Thrice prov'd I, thrice she vanish'd like a sleep,
Or fleeting shadow, which struck much more deep
The wounds my woes made, and made ask her why
She would my love to her embraces fly,
And not vouchsafe that ev'n in hell we might
Pay pious Nature her unalter'd right,
And give vexation here her cruel fill?
'Should not the queen here, to augment the ill
Of every suff'rance, which her office is,
Enforce thy idol to afford me this?'   270

    'O son,' she answer'd, 'of the race of men
The most unhappy, our most equal queen
Will mock no solid arms with empty shade,
Nor suffer empty shades again t' invade
Flesh, bones and nerves; nor will defraud the fire
Of his last dues, that, soon as spirits expire
And leave the white bone, are his native right,
When, like a dream, the soul assumes her flight.
The light then of the living with most haste,
O son, contend to. This thy little taste   280
Of this state is enough; and all this life
Will make a tale fit to be told thy wife.'

    This speech we had; when now repair'd to me
More female spirits, by Persephone
Driv'n on before her. All th' heroës' wives
And daughters, that led there their second lives,
About the black blood throng'd. Of whom yet more
My mind impell'd me to inquire, before
I let them altogether taste the gore,
For then would all have been dispers'd, and gone   290
Thick as they came. I therefore one by one
Let taste the pit, my sword drawn from my thigh,
And stand betwixt them made, when, severally,

All told their stocks. The first that quench'd her fire
Was Tyro, issued of a noble sire.
She said she sprung from pure Salmoneus' bed,
And Cretheus, son of Aeolus, did wed,
Yet the divine flood Enipeus lov'd,
Who much the most fair stream of all floods mov'd.
Near whose streams Tyro walking, Neptune came,   300
Like Enipeus, and enjoy'd the dame.
Like to a hill, the blue and shaky flood
Above th' immortal and the mortal stood,
And hid them both, as both together lay,
Just where his current falls into the sea.
Her virgin waist dissolv'd, she slumber'd then.
But when the god had done the work of men,
Her fair hand gently wringing, thus he said:
'Woman! Rejoice in our combined bed,
For when the year hath run his circle round   310
(Because the gods' loves must in fruit abound)
My love shall make, to cheer thy teeming moans,
Thy one dear burden bear two famous sons;
Love well, and bring them up. Go home, and see
That, though of more joy yet I shall be free,
Thou dost not tell, to glorify thy birth,
Thy love is Neptune, shaker of the earth.'
This said, he plung'd into the sea; and she,
Begot with child by him, the light let see
Great Pelias and Neleus, that became   320
In Jove's great ministry of mighty fame.
Pelias in broad Iolcus held his throne,
Wealthy in cattle; th' other royal son
Rul'd sandy Pylos. To these issue more
This queen of women to her husband bore,
Aeson, and Pheres, and Amythaon
That for his fight on horseback stoop'd to none.
    Next her, I saw admir'd Antiope,
Asopus' daughter, who (as much as she
Boasted attraction of great Neptune's love)   330
Boasted to slumber in the arms of Jove,
And two sons likewise at one burden bore
To that her all-controlling paramour,
Amphion and fair Zethus, that first laid
Great Thebes' foundations, and strong walls convey'd
About her turrets, that seven ports enclos'd.

For though the Thebans much in strength repos'd,
Yet had not they the strength to hold their own
Without the added aids of wood and stone.

  Alcmena next I saw, that famous wife   340
Was to Amphitryo, and honour'd life
Gave to the lion-hearted Hercules,
That was of Jove's embrace the great increase.

  I saw, besides, proud Creon's daughter there,
Bright Megara, that nuptial yoke did wear
With Jove's great son, who never field did try
But bore to him the flower of victory.

  The mother then of Oedipus I saw,
Fair Epicasta, that, beyond all law,
Her own son married, ignorant of kind,   350
And he, as darkly taken in his mind,
His mother wedded, and his father slew.
Whose blind act heav'n expos'd at length to view,
And he in all-lov'd Thebes the supreme state
With much moan manag'd, for the heavy fate
The gods laid on him. She made violent flight
To Pluto's dark house from the loathed light,
Beneath a steep beam strangled with a cord,
And left her son, in life, pains as abhorr'd
As all the Furies pour'd on her in hell.   360
Then saw I Chloris, that did so excel
In answering beauties, that each part had all.
Great Neleus married her, when gifts not small
Had won her favour, term'd by name of dow'r.
She was of all Amphion's seed the flow'r –
Amphion, call'd Iasides, that then
Ruled strongly Myniaean Orchomen,
And now his daughter rul'd the Pylian throne,
Because her beauty's empire overshone.
She brought her wife-aw'd husband, Neleus,   370
Nestor much honour'd, Periclymenus,
And Chromius, sons with sovereign virtues grac'd
But after brought a daughter that surpass'd,
Rare-beautied Pero, so for form exact
That nature to a miracle was rack'd
In her perfections, blaz'd with th' eyes of men,
That made of all the country's hearts a chain,
And drew them suitors to her. Which her sire
Took vantage of, and, since he did aspire

To nothing more than to the broad-brow'd herd   380
Of oxen, which the common fame so rear'd,
Own'd by Iphiclus, not a man should be
His Pero's husband, that from Phylace
Those never-yet-driv'n oxen could not drive.
Yet these a strong hope held him to achieve,
Because a prophet, that had never err'd,
Had said, that only he should be preferr'd
To their possession. But the equal fate
Of god withstood his stealth; inextricate
Imprisoning bands, and sturdy churlish swains   390
That were the herdsmen, who withheld with chains
The stealth-attempter; which was only he
That durst abet the act with prophecy,
None else would undertake it, and he must –
The king would needs a prophet should be just.
But when some days and months expired were,
And all the hours had brought about the year,
The prophet did so satisfy the king
(Iphiclus, all his cunning questioning)
That he enfranchis'd him; and, all worst done,   400
Jove's counsel made th' all-safe conclusion.

   Then saw I Leda, link'd in nuptial chain
With Tyndarus, to whom she did sustain
Sons much renown'd for wisdom: Castor one,
That pass'd for use of horse comparison,
And Pollux, that excell'd in whirlbat fight;
Both these the fruitful earth bore, while the light
Of life inspir'd them; after which, they found
Such grace with Jove, that both liv'd under ground,
By change of days; life still did one sustain,   410
While th' other died; the dead then liv'd again,
The living dying; both of one self date
Their lives and deaths made by the gods and fate.

   Iphimedia after Leda came,
That did derive from Neptune too the name
Of father to two admirable sons.
Life yet made short their admirations,
Who god-opposed Otus had to name,
And Ephialtes far in sound of fame.
The prodigal earth so fed them, that they grew   420
To most huge stature, and had fairest hue
Of all men but Orion, under heav'n.

At nine years old nine cubits they were driv'n
Abroad in breadth, and sprung nine fathoms high.
They threaten'd to give battle to the sky,
And all th' immortals. They were setting on
Ossa upon Olympus, and upon
Steep Ossa leavy Pelius, that ev'n
They might a highway make with lofty heav'n;
And had perhaps perform'd it, had they liv'd　　　　430
Till they were striplings; but Jove's son depriv'd
Their limbs of life, before th' age that begins
The flow'r of youth, and should adorn their chins.

　　Phaedra and Procris, with wise Minos' flame,
Bright Ariadne, to the offering came,
Whom whilom Theseus made his prise from Crete,
That Athens' sacred soil might kiss her feet,
But never could obtain her virgin flow'r,
Till in the sea-girt Dia, Dian's pow'r
Detain'd his homeward haste, where (in her fane,　　　440
By Bacchus witness'd) was the fatal wane
Of her prime glory. Maera, Clymene,
I witness'd there; and loath'd Eriphyle,
That honour'd gold more than she lov'd her spouse.

　　But all th' heroësses in Pluto's house
That then encounter'd me, exceeds my might
To name or number, and ambrosian night
Would quite be spent, when now the formal hours
Present to sleep our all-disposed pow'rs,
If at my ship, or here. My home-made vow　　　450
I leave for fit grace to the gods and you.'

　　This said, the silence his discourse had made
With pleasure held still through the house's shade,
When white-arm'd Arete this speech began:
'Phaeacians! How appears to you this man,
So goodly person'd, and so match'd with mind?
My guest he is, but all you stand combin'd
In the renown he doth us. Do not then
With careless haste dismiss him, nor the main
Of his dispatch to one so needy maim;　　　460
The gods' free bounty gives us all just claim
To goods enow.' This speech the oldest man
Of any other Phaeacensian,
The grave heroë, Echineus, gave
All approbation, saying: 'Friends! Ye have

The motion of the wise queen in such words
As have not miss'd the mark, with which accords
My clear opinion. But Alcinous
In word and work must be our rule.' He thus;
And then Alcinous said: 'This then must stand,   470
If while I live I rule in the command
Of this well-skill'd-in-navigation state:
Endure then, guest, though most importunate
Be your affects for home. A little stay
If your expectance bear, perhaps it may
Our gifts make more complete. The cares of all
Your due deduction asks; but principal
I am therein the ruler.' He replied:
'Alcinous, the most duly glorified,
With rule of all, of all men, if you lay   480
Commandment on me of a whole year's stay,
So all the while your preparations rise,
As well in gifts as time, ye can devise
No better wish for me; for I shall come
Much fuller-handed, and more honour'd, home,
And dearer to my people, in whose loves
The richer evermore the better proves.'

    He answer'd: 'There is argu'd in your sight
A worth that works not men for benefit,
Like prowlers or impostors; of which crew,   490
The gentle black earth feeds not up a few,
Here and there wanderers, blanching tales and lies,
Of neither praise nor use. You move our eyes
With form, our minds with matter, and our ears
With elegant oration, such as bears
A music in the order'd history
It lays before us. Not Demodocus
With sweeter strains hath us'd to sing to us
All the Greek sorrows, wept out in your own.
But say, of all your worthy friends, were none   500
Objected to your eyes that consorts were
To Ilion with you, and serv'd destiny there?
This night is passing long, unmeasur'd, none
Of all my household would to bed yet; on,
Relate these wondrous things. Were I with you,
If you would tell me but your woes, as now,
Till the divine Aurora show'd her head,
I should in no night relish thought of bed.'

   'Most eminent king,' said he, 'times all must keep;
There's time to speak much, time as much to sleep.   510
But would you hear still, I will tell you still,
And utter more, more miserable, ill
Of friends than yet, that 'scaped the dismal wars,
And perish'd homewards, and in household jars
Wag'd by a wicked woman. The chaste queen
No sooner made these lady ghosts unseen,
Here and there fitting, but mine eye-sight won
The soul of Agamemnon, Atreus' son,
Sad, and about him all his train of friends,
That in Aegisthus' house endur'd their ends   520
With his stern fortune. Having drunk the blood,
He knew me instantly, and forth a flood
Of springing tears gush'd; out he thrust his hands,
With will t' embrace me, but their old commands
Flow'd not about him, nor their weakest part.
I wept to see, and moan'd him from my heart,
And ask'd: 'O Agamemnon! King of men!
What sort of cruel death hath render'd slain
Thy royal person? Neptune in thy fleet
Heav'n and his hellish billows making meet,   530
Rousing the winds? Or have thy men by land
Done thee this ill, for using thy command,
Past their consents, in diminution
Of those full shares their worths by lot had won
Of sheep or oxen? Or of any town,
In covetous strife, to make their rights thine own
In men or women prisoners?' He replied:
'By none of these in any right I died,
But by Aegisthus and my murderous wife
(Bid to a banquet at his house) my life   540
Hath thus been reft me, to my slaughter led
Like to an ox pretended to be fed.
So miserably fell I, and with me
My friends lay massacred, as when you see
At any rich man's nuptials, shot, or feast,
About his kitchen white-tooth'd swine lie dress'd.
The slaughters of a world of men thine eyes,
Both private, and in prease of enemies,
Have personally witness'd; but this one
Would all thy parts have broken into moan,   550
To see how strew'd about our cups and cates,

As tables set with feast so we with fates,
All gash'd and slain lay, all the floor embru'd
With blood and brain. But that which most I ru'd,
Flew from the heavy voice that Priam's seed,
Cassandra, breath'd, whom she that wit doth feed
With baneful crafts, false Clytemnestra, slew,
Close sitting by me; up my hands I threw
From earth to heav'n, and tumbling on my sword
Gave wretched life up; when the most abhorr'd,   560
By all her sex's shame, forsook the room,
Nor deign'd, though then so near this heavy home,
To shut my lips, or close my broken eyes.
Nothing so heap'd is with impieties
As such a woman that would kill her spouse
That married her a maid, when to my house
I brought her, hoping of her love in heart,
To children, maids, and slaves. But she (in th' art
Of only mischief hearty) not alone
Cast on herself this foul aspersion,   570
But loving dames, hereafter, to their lords
Will bear, for good deeds, her bad thoughts and words.'
    'Alas,' said I, 'that Jove should hate the lives
Of Atreus' seed so highly for their wives!
For Menelaus' wife a number fell,
For dangerous absence thine sent thee to hell.'
    'For this,' he answer'd, 'be not thou more kind
Than wise to thy wife. Never all thy mind
Let words express to her. Of all she knows,
Curbs for the worst still in thyself repose.   580
But thou by thy wife's wiles shalt lose no blood,
Exceeding wise she is, and wise in good.
Icarius' daughter, chaste Penelope,
We left a young bride, when for battle we
Forsook the nuptial peace, and at her breast
Her first child sucking, who by this hour, blest
Sits in the number of surviving men.
And his bliss she hath, that she can contain,
And her bliss thou hast, that she is so wise.
For, by her wisdom, thy returned eyes   590
Shall see thy son, and he shall greet his sire
With fitting welcomes; when in my retire,
My wife denies mine eyes my son's dear sight,
And, as from me, will take from him the light,

Before she adds one just delight to life,
Or her false wit one truth that fits a wife.
For her sake therefore let my harms advise,
That though thy wife be ne'er so chaste and wise,
Yet come not home to her in open view,
With any ship or any personal show,   600
But take close shore disguis'd, nor let her know,
For 'tis no world to trust a woman now.
But what says fame? Doth my son yet survive,
In Orchomen, or Pylos? Or doth live
In Sparta with his uncle? Yet I see
Divine Orestes is not here with me.'
    I answer'd, asking: 'Why doth Atreus' son
Enquire of me, who yet arriv'd where none
Could give to these news any certain wings?
And 'tis absurd to tell uncertain things.'   610
    Such sad speech pass'd us; and as thus we stood,
With kind tears rendering unkind fortunes good,
Achilles' and Patroclus' soul appear'd,
And his soul, of whom never ill was heard,
The good Antilochus, and the soul of him
That all the Greeks pass'd both for force and limb,
Excepting the unmatch'd Aeacides,
Illustrious Ajax. But the first of these
That saw, acknowledg'd, and saluted me,
Was Thetis' conquering son, who (heavily   620
His state here taking) said: 'Unworthy breath!
What act yet mightier imagineth
Thy vent'rous spirit? How dost thou descend
These under regions, where the dead man's end
Is to be look'd on, and his foolish shade?'
    I answer'd him: 'I was induced t' invade
These under parts, most excellent of Greece,
To visit wise Tiresias, for advice
Of virtue to direct my voyage home
To rugged Ithaca; since I could come   630
To note in no place where Achaia stood,
And so lived ever, tortur'd with the blood
In man's vain veins. Thou therefore, Thetis' son,
Hast equall'd all, that ever yet have won
The bliss the earth yields, or hereafter shall.
In life thy eminence was ador'd of all,
Ev'n with the gods; and now, ev'n dead, I see

Thy virtues propagate thy empery
To a renew'd life of command beneath;
So great Achilles triumphs over death.'   640
This comfort of him this encounter found:
'Urge not my death to me, nor rub that wound.
I rather wish to live in earth a swain,
Or serve a swain for hire, that scarce can gain
Bread to sustain him, than, that life once gone,
Of all the dead sway the imperial throne.
But say, and of my son some comfort yield,
If he goes on in first fights of the field,
Or lurks for safety in the obscure rear?
Or of my father if thy royal ear   650
Hath been advertis'd, that the Phthian throne
He still commands, as greatest Myrmidon?
Or that the Phthian and Thessalian rage
(Now feet and hands are in the hold of age)
Despise his empire? Under those bright rays,
In which heav'n's fervour hurls about the days,
Must I no more shine his revenger now,
Such as of old the Ilion overthrow
Witness'd my anger, th' universal host
Sending before me to this shady coast,   660
In fight for Grecia. Could I now resort
(But for some small time) to my father's court,
In spirit and power as then, those men should find
My hands inaccessible, and of fire my mind,
That durst with all the numbers they are strong
Unseat his honour, and suborn his wrong.'
    This pitch still flew his spirit, though so low,
And this I answer'd thus: 'I do not know
Of blameless Peleus any least report,
But of your son, in all the utmost sort,   670
I can inform your care with truth, and thus:
    From Scyros princely Neoptolemus
By fleet I convey'd to the Greeks, where he
Was chief at both parts, when our gravity
Retir'd to council, and our youth to fight.
In council still so fiery was conceit
In his quick apprehension of a cause,
That first he ever spake, nor pass'd the laws
Of any grave stay, in his greatest haste.
None would contend with him, that counsell'd last,   680

Unless illustrious Nestor, he and I
Would sometimes put a friendly contrary
On his opinion. In our fights, the prease
Of great or common, he would never cease,
But far before fight ever. No man there,
For force, he forced. He was slaughterer
Of many a brave man in most dreadful fight.
But one and other whom he reft of light,
In Grecian succour, I can neither name,
Nor give in number. The particular fame   690
Of one man's slaughter yet I must not pass:
Eurypylus Telephides he was,
That fell beneath him, and with him the falls
Of such huge men went, that they show'd like whales
Rampired about him. Neoptolemus
Set him so sharply, for the sumptuous
Favours of mistresses he saw him wear;
For past all doubt his beauties had no peer
Of all that mine eyes noted, next to one,
And that was Memnon, Tithon's Sun-like son.   700
Thus far, for fight in public, may a taste
Give of his eminence. How far surpass'd
His spirit in private, where he was not seen,
Nor glory could be said to praise his spleen,
This close note I excerpted. When we sat
Hid in Epeus' horse, no optimate
Of all the Greeks there had the charge to ope
And shut the stratagem but I. My scope
To note then each man's spirit in a strait
Of so much danger, much the better might   710
Be hit by me than others, as, provok'd,
I shifted place still, when in some I smok'd
Both privy tremblings and close vent of tears,
In him yet not a soft conceit of theirs
Could all my search see, either his wet eyes
Ply'd still with wipings, or the goodly guise
His person all ways put forth, in least part,
By any tremblings, show'd his touch'd-at heart.
But ever he was urging me to make
Way to their sally, by his sign to shake   720
His sword hid in his scabbard, or his lance
Loaded with iron, at me. No good chance
His thoughts to Troy intended. In th' event,

High Troy depopulate, he made ascent
To his fair ship, with prise and treasure store,
Safe, and no touch away with him he bore
Of far-off-hurl'd lance, or of close-fought sword,
Whose wounds for favours war doth oft afford,
Which he (though sought) miss'd in war's closest wage.
In close fights Mars doth never fight, but rage.'   730
    This made the soul of swift Achilles tread
A march of glory through the herby mead,
For joy to hear me so renown his son;
And vanish'd stalking. But with passion
Stood th' other souls struck, and each told his bane.
Only the spirit Telamonian
Kept far off, angry for the victory
I won from him at fleet, though arbitry
Of all a court of war pronounced it mine,
And Pallas' self. Our prise were th' arms divine   740
Of great Aeacides, propos'd t' our fames
By his bright mother, at his funeral games.
I wish to heav'n I ought not to have won,
Since for those arms so high a head so soon
The base earth cover'd: Ajax, that of all
The host of Greece had person capital,
And acts as eminent, excepting his
Whose arms those were, in whom was nought amiss.
I tried the great soul with soft words, and said:
'Ajax! Great son of Telamon, array'd   750
In all our glories! What! Not dead resign
Thy wrath for those curst arms? The pow'rs divine
In them forg'd all our banes in thine own one;
In thy grave fall our tow'r was overthrown.
We mourn, for ever maim'd, for thee as much
As for Achilles; nor thy wrong doth touch,
In sentence, any but Saturnius' doom,
In whose hate was the host of Greece become
A very horror; who express'd it well
In signing thy fate with this timeless hell.   760
Approach then, king of all the Grecian merit,
Repress thy great mind, and thy flamy spirit,
And give the words I give thee worthy ear.'
    All this no word drew from him, but less near
The stern soul kept; to other souls he fled,
And glid along the river of the dead.

Though anger mov'd him, yet he might have spoke,
Since I to him. But my desires were strook
With sight of other souls. And then I saw
Minos, that minister'd to Death a law,   770
And Jove's bright son was. He was set, and sway'd
A golden sceptre; and to him did plead
A sort of others, set about his throne,
In Pluto's wide-door'd house; when straight came on
Mighty Orion, who was hunting there
The herds of those beasts he had slaughter'd here
In desert hills on earth. A club he bore,
Entirely steel, whose virtues never wore.

    Tityus I saw, to whom the glorious earth
Open'd her womb, and gave unhappy birth.   780
Upwards, and flat upon the pavement, lay
His ample limbs, that spread in their display
Nine acres' compass. On his bosom sat
Two vultures, digging, through his caul of fat,
Into his liver with their crooked beaks;
And each by turns the concrete entrail breaks,
As smiths their steel beat, set on either side.
Nor doth he ever labour to divide
His liver and their beaks, nor with his hand
Offer them off, but suffers by command   790
Of th' angry Thund'rer, off'ring to enforce
His love Latona, in the close recourse
She used to Pytho through the dancing land,
Smooth Panopaeus. I saw likewise stand,
Up to the chin amidst a liquid lake,
Tormented Tantalus, yet could not slake
His burning thirst. Oft as his scornful cup
Th' old man would taste, so oft 'twas swallow'd up,
And all the black earth to his feet descried
(Divine pow'r plaguing him) the lake still dried.   800
About his head, on high trees clust'ring hung
Pears, apples, granates, olives ever young,
Delicious figs, and many fruit trees more
Of other burden; whose alluring store
When th' old soul striv'd to pluck, the winds from sight,
In gloomy vapours made them vanish quite.

    There saw I Sisyphus in infinite moan,
With both hands heaving up a massy stone,
And on his tip-toes racking all his height,

To wrest up to a mountain-top his freight;   810
When prest to rest it there, his nerves quite spent,
Down rush'd the deadly quarry, the event
Of all his torture new to raise again;
To which straight set his never-rested pain.
The sweat came gushing out from every pore,
And on his head a standing mist he wore,
Reeking from thence, as if a cloud of dust
Were rais'd about it. Down with these was thrust
The idol of the force of Hercules;
But his firm self did no such fate oppress,   820
He feasting lives amongst th' immortal states,
White-ankled Hebe and himself made mates
In heavenly nuptials – Hebe, Jove's dear race
And Juno's whom the golden sandals grace.
About him flew the clamours of the dead
Like fowls, and still stoop'd cuffing at his head.
He with his bow, like Night, stalk'd up and down,
His shaft still nock'd, and hurling round his frown
At those vex'd hoverers, aiming at them still,
And still, as shooting out desire to still.   830
A horrid bawdrick wore he thwart his breast,
The thong all gold, in which were forms impress'd,
Where art and miracle drew equal breaths,
In bears, boars, lions, battles, combats, deaths.
Who wrought that work did never such before,
Nor so divinely will do ever more.
Soon as he saw, he knew me, and gave speech:
'Son of Laertes, high in wisdom's reach,
And yet unhappy wretch, for in this heart,
Of all exploits achiev'd by thy desert,   840
Thy worth but works out some sinister fate,
As I in earth did. I was generate
By Jove himself, and yet past mean oppress'd
By one my far inferior, whose proud hest
Impos'd abhorred labours on my hand.
Of all which one was, to descend this strand,
And hale the dog from thence. He could not think
An act that danger could make deeper sink.
And yet this depth I drew, and fetch'd as high,
As this was low, the dog. The deity   850
Of sleight and wisdom, as of downright pow'r,
Both stoop'd and raised, and made me conqueror.'

This said, he made descent again as low
As Pluto's court; when I stood firm, for show
Of more heroës of the times before,
And might perhaps have seen my wish of more
(As Theseus and Pirithous, deriv'd
From roots of deity) but before th' achiev'd
Rare sight of these, the rank-soul'd multitude
In infinite flocks rose, venting sounds so rude   860
That pale fear took me, lest the gorgon's head
Rush'd in amongst them, thrust up, in my dread,
By grim Persephone. I therefore sent
My men before to ship, and after went.
Where, boarded, set, and launch'd, th' ocean wave
Our oars and forewinds speedy passage gave.

THE END OF THE ELEVENTH BOOK

BOOK TWELVE

The Argument

He shows from Hell his safe retreat
To th' isle Aeaea, Circe's seat;
And how he scap'd the Sirens' calls,
With th' erring rocks, and waters' falls,
That Scylla and Charybdis break;
The Sun's stol'n herds, and his sad wreak
Both of Ulysses' ship and men,
His own head 'scaping scarce the pain.

Another Argument

Mu   The rocks that err'd;
        The Sirens' call;
        The Sun's stol'n herd;
        The soldiers' fall.

BOOK TWELVE

OUR SHIP now past the straits of th' ocean flood,
    She plow'd the broad sea's billows, and made good
    The isle Aeaea, where the palace stands
Of th' early riser with the rosy hands,
Active Aurora, where she loves to dance,
And where the Sun doth his prime beams advance.
  When here arrived, we drew her up to land,
And trod ourselves the re-saluted sand,
Found on the shore fit resting for the night,
Slept, and expected the celestial light.   10
  Soon as the white-and-red-mix'd-finger'd dame
Had gilt the mountains with her saffron flame,
I sent my men to Circe's house before,
To fetch deceas'd Elpenor to the shore.
  Straight swell'd the high banks with fell'd heaps of trees,
And, full of tears, we did due exsequies
To our dead friend. Whose corse consum'd with fire
And honour'd arms, whose sepulchre entire
And over that a column rais'd, his oar,
Curiously carv'd to his desire before,   20
Upon the top of all his tomb we fix'd.
Of all rites fit his funeral pile was mix'd.
  Nor was our safe ascent from hell conceal'd
From Circe's knowledge; nor so soon reveal'd
But she was with us, with her bread and food,
And ruddy wine, brought by her sacred brood
Of woods and fountains. In the midst she stood,
And thus saluted us: 'Unhappy men,
That have, inform'd with all your senses, been
In Pluto's dismal mansion! You shall die   30
Twice now, where others, that mortality
In her fair arms holds, shall but once decease.
But eat and drink out all conceit of these,
And this day dedicate to food and wine,
The following night to sleep. When next shall shine

The cheerful morning, you shall prove the seas.
Your way, and every act ye must address,
My knowledge of their order shall design,
Lest with your own bad counsels ye incline
Events as bad against ye, and sustain,   40
By sea and shore, the woeful ends that reign
In wilful actions.' Thus did she advise,
And, for the time, our fortunes were so wise
To follow wise directions. All that day
We sat and feasted. When his lower way
The sun had enter'd, and the ev'n the high,
My friends slept on their cables; she and I
(Led by her fair hand to a place apart,
By her well-sorted) did to sleep convert
Our timid powers; when all things fate let fall   50
In our affair she ask'd; I told her all.
To which she answer'd: 'These things thus took end.
And now to those that I inform attend,
Which you rememb'ring, god himself shall be
The blessed author of your memory.

    First to the Sirens ye shall come, that taint
The minds of all men, whom they can acquaint
With their attractions. Whomsoever shall,
For want of knowledge mov'd, but hear the call
Of any Siren, he will so despise   60
Both wife and children, for their sorceries,
That never home turns his affection's stream,
Nor they take joy in him, nor he in them.
The Sirens will so soften with their song
(Shrill, and in sensual appetite so strong)
His loose affections, that he gives them head.
And then observe: they sit amidst a mead,
And round about it runs a hedge or wall
Of dead men's bones, their wither'd skins and all
Hung all along upon it; and these men   70
Were such as they had fawn'd into their fen,
And then their skins hung on their hedge of bones.
Sail by them therefore, thy companions
Beforehand causing to stop every ear
With sweet soft wax, so close that none may hear
A note of all their charmings. Yet may you,
If you affect it, open ear allow
To try their motion; but presume not so

To trust your judgment, when your senses go
So loose about you, but give straight command   80
To all your men, to bind you foot and hand
Sure to the mast, that you may safe approve
How strong in instigation to their love
Their rapting tunes are. If so much they move,
That, spite of all your reason, your will stands
To be enfranchis'd both of feet and hands,
Charge all your men before to slight your charge,
And rest so far from fearing to enlarge
That much more sure they bind you. When your friends
Have outsail'd these, the danger that transcends   90
Rests not in any counsel to prevent,
Unless your own mind finds the tract and bent
Of that way that avoids it. I can say
That in your course there lies a twofold way,
The right of which your own, taught, present wit,
And grace divine, must prompt. In general yet
Let this inform you: near these Sirens' shore
Move two steep rocks, at whose feet lie and roar
The black sea's cruel billows; the bless'd gods
Call them the Rovers. Their abhorr'd abodes   100
No bird can pass – no, not the doves, whose fear
Sire Jove so loves that they are said to bear
Ambrosia to him, can their ravine 'scape,
But one of them falls ever to the rape
Of those sly rocks; yet Jove another still
Adds to the rest, that so may ever fill
The sacred number. Never ship could shun
The nimble peril wing'd there, but did run
With all her bulk, and bodies of her men,
To utter ruin. For the seas retain   110
Not only their outrageous testure there,
But fierce assistants of particular fear
And supernatural mischief they expire,
And those are whirlwinds of devouring fire
Whisking about still. Th' Argive ship alone,
Which bore the care of all men, got her gone,
Come from Areta. Yet perhaps ev'n she
Had wrack'd at those rocks, if the deity
That lies by Jove's side, had not lent her hand
To their transmission, since the man that mann'd   120
In chief that voyage, she in chief did love.

Of these two spiteful rocks, the one doth shove
Against the height of heav'n her pointed brow.
A black cloud binds it round, and never show
Lends to the sharp point; not the clear blue sky
Lets ever view it, not the summer's eye,
Not fervent autumn's. None that death could end
Could ever scale it, or, if up, descend,
Though twenty hands and feet he had for hold,
A polish'd ice-like glibness doth enfold   130
The rock so round, whose midst a gloomy cell
Shrouds so far westward that it sees to hell.
From this keep you as far as from his bow
An able young man can his shaft bestow.
For here the whuling Scylla shrouds her face,
That breathes a voice at all parts no more base
Than are a newly-kitten'd kitling's cries,
Herself a monster yet of boundless size,
Whose sight would nothing please a mortal's eyes –
No, nor the eyes of any god, if he   140
(Whom nought should fright) fell foul on her, and she
Her full shape show'd. Twelve foul feet bear about
Her ugly bulk. Six huge long necks look out
Of her rank shoulders; every neck doth let
A ghastly head out; every head three set,
Thick thrust together, of abhorred teeth,
And every tooth stuck with a sable death.
    She lurks in midst of all her den, and streaks
From out a ghastly whirlpool all her necks;
Where, gloting round her rock, to fish she falls;   150
And up rush dolphins, dogfish, somewhiles whales,
If got within her when her rapine feeds;
For ever-groaning Amphitrite breeds
About her whirlpool an unmeasur'd store.
No sea-man ever boasted touch of shore
That there touch'd with his ship, but still she fed
Of him and his, a man for every head
Spoiling his ship of. You shall then descry
The other humbler rock, that moves so nigh
Your dart may mete the distance. It receives   160
A huge wild fig-tree, curl'd with ample leaves,
Beneath whose shades divine Charybdis sits,
Supping the black deeps – thrice a day her pits
She drinking all dry, and thrice a day again

All up she belches, baneful to sustain.
When she is drinking, dare not near her draught,
For not the force of Neptune, if once caught,
Can force your freedom. Therefore in your strife
To 'scape Charybdis, labour all for life
To row near Scylla, for she will but have　　　　170
For her six heads six men; and better save
The rest, than all make off'rings to the wave.'

　　This need she told me of my loss, when I
Desir'd to know, if that Necessity,
When I had 'scaped Charybdis' outrages,
My powers might not revenge, though not redress.
She answer'd: 'O unhappy! Art thou yet
Enflam'd with war, and thirst to drink thy sweat?
Not to the gods give up both arms and will?
She deathless is, and that immortal ill　　　　180
Grave, harsh, outrageous, not to be subdu'd,
That men must suffer till they be renew'd.
Nor lives there any virtue that can fly
The vicious outrage of their cruelty.
Shouldst thou put arms on, and approach the rock,
I fear six more must expiate the shock.
Six heads six men ask still. Hoise sail, and fly,
And, in thy flight, aloud on Cratis cry
(Great Scylla's mother, who expos'd to light
The bane of men) and she will do such right　　190
To thy observance, that she down will tread
Her daughter's rage, nor let her show a head.

　　From thenceforth then, for ever past her care,
Thou shalt ascend the isle triangular,
Where many oxen of the Sun are fed,
And fatted flocks. Of oxen fifty head
In every herd feed, and their herds are seven;
And of his fat flocks is their number even.
Increase they yield not, for they never die.
There every shepherdess a deity –　　　　　200
Fair Phaëthusa and Lampetië
The lovely nymphs are that their guardians be,
Who to the daylight's lofty-going flame
Had gracious birthright from the heav'nly dame,
Still-young Neaera; who (brought forth and bred)
Far off dismiss'd them, to see duly fed
Their father's herds and flocks in Sicily.

These herds and flocks if to the deity
Ye leave, as sacred things, untouch'd, and on
Go with all fit care of your home, alone,   210
(Though through some suff'rance) you yet safe shall land
In wished Ithaca. But if impious hand
You lay on those herds to their hurts, I then
Presage sure ruin to thy ship and men.
If thou escap'st thyself, extending home
Thy long'd-for landing, thou shalt loaded come
With store of losses, most exceeding late,
And not consorted with a saved mate.'

   This said, the golden-thron'd Aurora rose,
She her way went, and I did mine dispose   220
Up to my ship, weigh'd anchor, and away;
When reverend Circe help'd us to convey
Our vessel safe, by making well inclin'd
A seaman's true companion, a forewind,
With which she fill'd our sails; when, fitting all
Our arms close by us, I did sadly fall
To grave relation what concern'd in fate
My friends to know, and told them that the state
Of our affairs' success, which Circe had
Presag'd to me alone, must yet be made   230
To one nor only two known, but to all;
That, since their lives and deaths were left to fall
In their elections, they might life elect,
And give what would preserve it fit effect.

   I first inform'd them, that we were to fly
The heav'nly-singing Sirens' harmony,
And flow'r-adorned meadow; and that I
Had charge to hear their song, but fetter'd fast
In bands, unfavour'd, to th' erected mast,
From whence, if I should pray, or use command,   240
To be enlarg'd, they should with much more band
Contain my strugglings. This I simply told
To each particular, nor would withhold
What most enjoin'd mine own affection's stay,
That theirs the rather might be taught t' obey.

   In mean time flew our ships, and straight we fetch'd
The Sirens' isle, a spleenless wind so stretch'd
Her wings to waft us, and so urg'd our keel.
But having reach'd this isle, we could not feel
The least gasp of it, it was stricken dead,   250

And all the sea in prostrate slumber spread,
The Sirens' devil charm'd all. Up then flew
My friends to work, struck sail, together drew
And under hatches stow'd them, sat and plied
The polish'd oars, and did in curls divide
The white-head waters. My part then came on:
A mighty waxen cake I set upon,
Chopp'd it in fragments with my sword, and wrought
With strong hand every piece till all were soft.
The great power of the sun, in such a beam   260
. As then flew burning from his diadem,
To liquefaction help'd us. Orderly
I stopp'd their ears; and they as fair did ply
My feet and hands with cords, and to the mast
With other halsers made me soundly fast.
    Then took they seat, and forth our passage strook;
The foamy sea beneath their labour shook.
    Row'd on in reach of an erected voice,
The Sirens soon took note, without, our noise,
Tun'd those sweet accents that made charms so strong,   270
And these learn'd numbers made the Sirens' song:
'Come here, thou worthy of a world of praise,
That dost so high the Grecian glory raise,
Ulysses! Stay thy ship, and that song hear
That none pass'd ever but it bent his ear,
But left him ravish'd, and instructed more
By us, than any ever heard before.
For we know all things whatsoever were
In wide Troy labour'd; whatsoever there
The Grecians and the Trojans both sustain'd   280
By those high issues that the gods ordain'd.
And whatsoever all the earth can show
T' inform a knowledge of desert, we know.'
    This they gave accent in the sweetest strain
That ever open'd an enamour'd vein;
When my constrain'd heart needs would have mine ear
Yet more delighted, force way forth, and hear.
To which end I commanded with all sign
Stern looks could make (for not a joint of mine
Had pow'r to stir) my friends to rise, and give   290
My limbs free way. They freely striv'd to drive
Their ship still on; when, far from will to loose,
Eurylochus and Perimedes rose

To wrap me surer, and oppress'd me more
With many a halser than had use before.
When, rowing on without the reach of sound,
My friends unstopp'd their ears, and me unbound,
And that isle quite we quitted. But again
Fresh fears employ'd us. I beheld a main
Of mighty billows, and a smoke ascend,   300
A horrid murmur hearing. Every friend
Astonish'd sat; from every hand his oar
Fell quite forsaken; with the dismal roar
Were all things there made echoes; stone still stood
Our ship itself, because the ghastly flood
Took all men's motions from her in their own.
I through the ship went, labouring up and down
My friends' recover'd spirits. One by one
I gave good words, and said: that well were known
These ills to them before, I told them all,   310
And that these could not prove more capital
Than those the Cyclops block'd us up in, yet
My virtue, wit, and heav'n-help'd counsels set
Their freedoms open. I could not believe
But they remember'd it, and wish'd them give
My equal care and means now equal trust.
The strength they had for stirring up they must
Rouse and extend, to try if Jove had laid
His pow'rs in theirs up, and would add his aid
To 'scape ev'n that death. In particular then,   320
I told our pilot, that past other men
He most must bear firm spirits, since he sway'd
The continent that all our spirits convey'd,
In his whole guide of her. He saw there boil
The fiery whirlpools that to all our spoil
Inclos'd a rock, without which he must steer,
Or all our ruins stood concluded there.
   All heard me and obey'd, and little knew
That, shunning that rock, six of them should rue
The wrack another hid. For I conceal'd   330
The heavy wounds, that never would be heal'd,
To be by Scylla open'd; for their fear
Would then have robb'd all of all care to steer,
Or stir an oar, and made them hide beneath,
When they and all had died an idle death.
But then ev'n I forgot to shun the harm

Circe forewarn'd; who will'd I should not arm,
Nor show myself to Scylla, lest in vain
I ventur'd life. Yet could not I contain,
But arm'd at all parts, and two lances took,   340
Up to the foredeck went, and thence did look
That rocky Scylla would have first appear'd,
And taken my life with the friends I fear'd.

     From thence yet no place could afford her sight,
Though through the dark rock mine eye threw her light,
And ransack'd all ways. I then took a strait
That gave myself, and some few more, receipt
'Twixt Scylla and Charybdis; whence we saw
How horridly Charybdis' throat did draw
The brackish sea up, which when all abroad   350
She spit again out, never cauldron sod
With so much fervour, fed with all the store
That could enrage it; all the rock did roar
With troubled waters; round about the tops
Of all the steep crags flew the foamy drops.
But when her draught the sea and earth dissunder'd,
The troubled bottoms turn'd up, and she thunder'd,
Far under shore the swart sands naked lay;
Whose whole stern sight the startled blood did bay
From all our faces. And while we on her   360
Our eyes bestow'd thus to our ruin's fear,
Six friends had Scylla snatch'd out of our keel,
In whom most loss did force and virtue feel.
When looking to my ship, and lending eye
To see my friends' estates, their heels turn'd high,
And hands cast up, I might discern, and hear
Their calls to me for help, when now they were
To try me in their last extremities.
And as an angler med'cine for surprise
Of little fish sits pouring from the rocks,   370
From out the crook'd horn of a fold-bred ox,
And then with his long angle hoists them high
Up to the air, then slightly hurls them by,
When helpless sprawling on the land they lie:
So easily Scylla to her rock had rapt
My woeful friends, and so unhelp'd entrapp'd
Struggling they lay beneath her violent rape;
Who in their tortures, desp'rate of escape,
Shriek'd as she tore, and up their hands to me

Still threw for sweet life. I did never see,   380
In all my suff'rance ransacking the seas,
A spectacle so full of miseries.
     Thus having fled these rocks (these cruel dames
Scylla, Charybdis), where the king of flames
Hath offerings burn'd to him our ship put in,
The island that from all the earth doth win
The epithet *Faultless*, where the broad-of-head
And famous oxen for the Sun are fed,
With many fat flocks of that high-gone god.
Set in my ship, mine ear reach'd where we rode   390
The bellowing of oxen, and the bleat
Of fleecy sheep, that in my memory's seat
Put up the forms that late had been impress'd
By dread Aeaean Circe, and the best
Of souls and prophets, the blind Theban seer,
The wise Tiresias, who was grave decreer
Of my return's whole means; of which this one
In chief he urg'd – that I should always shun
The island of the man-delighting Sun.
When, sad at heart for our late loss, I pray'd   400
My friends to hear fit counsel (though dismay'd
With all ill fortunes) which was giv'n to me
By Circe's and Tiresias' prophecy –
That I should fly the isle where was ador'd
The comfort of the world, for ills abhorr'd
Were ambush'd for us there; and therefore will'd
They should put off and leave the isle. This kill'd
Their tender spirits; when Eurylochus
A speech that vex'd me utter'd, answering thus:
     'Cruel Ulysses! Since thy nerves abound   410
In strength, the more spent, and no toils confound
Thy able limbs, as all beat out of steel,
Thou ablest us too, as unapt to feel
The teeth of labour and the spoil of sleep,
And therefore still wet waste us in the deep,
Nor let us land to eat, but madly now
In night put forth, and leave firm land to strow
The sea with errors. All the rabid flight
Of winds that ruin ships are bred in night.
Who is it that can keep off cruel death,   420
If suddenly should rush out th' angry breath
Of Notus, or the eager-spirited West,

That cuff ships dead, and do the gods their best?
Serve black night still with shore, meat, sleep and ease,
And offer to the Morning for the seas.'
       This all the rest approv'd, and then knew I
That past all doubt the devil did apply
His slaught'rous works. Nor would they be withheld;
I was but one, nor yielded but compell'd.
But all that might contain them I assay'd,   430
A sacred oath on all their powers I laid,
That if with herds or any richest flocks
We chanc'd t' encounter, neither sheep nor ox
We once should touch, nor (for that constant ill
That follows folly) scorn advice and kill,
But quiet sit us down and take such food
As the immortal Circe had bestow'd.
       They swore all this in all severest sort;
And then we anchor'd in the winding port
Near a fresh river, where the long'd-for shore   440
They all flew out to, took in victuals store,
And, being full, thought of their friends, and wept
Their loss by Scylla, weeping till they slept.
       In night's third part, when stars began to stoop,
The Cloud-assembler put a tempest up.
A boist'rous spirit he gave it, drave out all
His flocks of clouds, and let such darkness fall
That earth and seas, for fear, to hide were driv'n,
For with his clouds he thrust out night from heav'n.
       At morn we drew our ships into a cave,   450
In which the nymphs that Phoebus' cattle drave
Fair dancing-rooms had, and their seats of state.
I urged my friends then, that, to shun their fate,
They would observe their oath, and take the food
Our ship afforded, nor attempt the blood
Of those fair herds and flocks, because they were
The dreadful god's that all could see and hear.
       They stood observant, and in that good mind
Had we been gone; but so adverse the wind
Stood to our passage, that we could not go.   460
For one whole month perpetually did blow
Impetuous Notus, not a breath's repair
But his and Eurus' ruled in all the air.
As long yet as their ruddy wine and bread
Stood out amongst them, so long not a head

Of all those oxen fell in any strife
Amongst those students for the gut and life;
But when their victuals fail'd they fell to prey,
Necessity compell'd them then to stray
In rape of fish and fowl; whatever came   470
In reach of hand or hook, the belly's flame
Afflicted to it. I then fell to pray'r,
And (making to a close retreat repair,
Free from both friends and winds) I wash'd my hands
And all the gods besought, that held commands
In liberal heav'n, to yield some mean to stay
Their desp'rate hunger, and set up the way
Of our return restrain'd. The gods, instead
Of giving what I pray'd for – power of deed –
A deedless sleep did on my lids distill,   480
For mean to work upon my friends their fill.
For whiles I slept there wak'd no mean to curb
Their headstrong wants; which he that did disturb
My rule in chief at all times, and was chief
To all the rest in counsel to their grief,
Knew well, and of my present absence took
His fit advantage, and their iron strook
At highest heat. For, feeling their desire
In his own entrails, to allay the fire
That famine blew in them, he thus gave way   490
To that affection: 'Hear what I shall say,
Though words will staunch no hunger. Every death
To us poor wretches that draw temporal breath
You know is hateful; but, all know, to die
The death of famine is a misery
Past all death loathsome. Let us, therefore, take
The chief of this fair herd, and offerings make
To all the deathless that in broad heav'n live,
And in particular vow, if we arrive
In natural Ithaca, to straight erect   500
A temple to the haughty-in-aspect,
Rich and magnificent, and all within
Deck it with relics many and divine.
If yet he stands incens'd, since we have slain
His high-brow'd herd, and therefore will sustain
Desire to wrack our ship, he is but one,
And all the other gods that we atone
With our divine rites will their suffrage give

To our design'd return, and let us live.
If not, and all take part, I rather crave   510
To serve with one sole death the yawning wave,
Than in a desert island lie and starve,
And with one pin'd life many deaths observe.'
    All cried 'He counsels nobly,' and all speed
Made to their resolute driving; for the feed
Of those coal-black, fair, broad-brow'd, sun-lov'd beeves
Had place close by our ships. They took the lives
Of sense, most eminent; about their fall
Stood round, and to the states celestial
Made solemn vows, but other rites their ship   520
Could not afford them; they did, therefore, strip
The curl'd-head oak of fresh young leaves, to make
Supply of service for their barley-cake.
And on the sacredly enflam'd, for wine,
Pour'd purest water, all the parts divine
Spitting and roasting, all the rites beside
Orderly using. Then did light divide
My low and upper lids; when, my repair
Made near my ship, I met the delicate air
Their roast exhal'd; out instantly I cried,   530
And said: 'O Jove, and all ye deified,
Ye have oppress'd me with a cruel sleep,
While ye conferr'd on me a loss as deep
As death descends to. To themselves alone
My rude men left ungovern'd, they have done
A deed so impious, I stand well assur'd,
That you will not forgive, though ye procur'd.'
    Then flew Lampetië with the ample robe
Up to her father with the golden globe,
Ambassadress t' inform him that my men   540
Had slain his oxen. Heart-incensed then,
He cried: 'Revenge me, Father, and the rest
Both ever-living and for ever blest!
Ulysses' impious men have drawn the blood
Of those my oxen that it did me good
To look on, walking all my starry round,
And when I trod earth all with meadows crown'd.
Without your full amends I'll leave heav'n quite,
Dis and the dead adorning with my light.'
    The Cloud-herd answer'd: 'Son! Thou shalt be ours, 550
And light those mortals in that mine of flow'rs!

My red-hot flash shall graze but on their ship,
And eat it, burning, in the boiling deep.'
    This by Calypso I was told, and she
Inform'd it from the verger Mercury.
    Come to our ship, I chid and told by name
Each man how impiously he was to blame.
But chiding got no peace, the beeves were slain!
When straight the gods forewent their following pain
With dire ostents. The hides the flesh had lost   560
Crept all before them. As the flesh did roast,
It bellow'd like the ox itself alive.
And yet my soldiers did their dead beeves drive
Through all these prodigies in daily feasts.
Six days they banqueted and slew fresh beasts;
And when the seventh day Jove reduc'd, the wind
That all the month rag'd and so in did bind
Our ship and us, was turn'd and calmed, and we
Launch'd, put up masts, sails hoised, and to sea.
    The island left so far that land nowhere   570
But only sea and sky had power t' appear,
Jove fixed a cloud above our ship, so black
That all the sea it darken'd. Yet from wrack
She ran a good free time, till from the West
Came Zephyr ruffling forth, and put his breast
Out in a singing tempest, so most vast
It burst the cables that made sure our mast;
Our masts came tumbling down, our cattle down
Rush'd to the pump, and by our pilot's crown
The main-mast pass'd his fall, pash'd all his skull,   580
And all this wrack but one flaw made at full;
Off from the stern the sternsman diving fell,
And from his sinews flew his soul to hell.
Together all this time Jove's thunder chid,
And through and through the ship his lightning glid,
Till it embrac'd her round; her bulk was fill'd
With nasty sulphur, and her men were kill'd,
Tumbled to sea, like sea-mews swum about,
And there the date of their return was out.
    I toss'd from side to side still, till all broke   590
Her ribs were with the storm, and she did choke
With let-in surges; for the mast torn down
Tore her up piecemeal, and for me to drown
Left little undissolv'd. But to the mast

There was a leather thong left, which I cast
About it and the keel, and so sat tost
With baneful weather, till the West had lost
His stormy tyranny. And then arose
The South, that bred me more abhorred woes;
For back again his blasts expell'd me quite   600
On ravenous Charybdis. All that night
I totter'd up and down, till light and I
At Scylla's rock encounter'd, and the nigh
Dreadful Charybdis. As I drave on these,
I saw Charybdis supping up the seas,
And had gone up together, if the tree
That bore the wild figs had not rescu'd me;
To which I leap'd, and left my keel, and high
Clamb'ring upon it did as close imply
My breast about it as a reremouse could;   610
Yet might my feet on no stub fasten hold
To ease my hands, the roots were crept so low
Beneath the earth, and so aloft did grow
The far-spread arms that, though good height I gat,
I could not reach them. To the main bole flat
I, therefore, still must cling, till up again
She belch'd my mast, and after that amain
My keel came tumbling. So at length it chanc'd
To me, as to a judge that long advanc'd
To judge a sort of hot young fellows' jars,   620
At length time frees him from their civil wars,
When glad he riseth and to dinner goes:
So time, at length, releas'd with joys my woes,
And from Charybdis' mouth appear'd my keel.
To which, my hand now loos'd and now my heel,
I altogether with a huge noise dropp'd,
Just in her midst fell, where the mast was propp'd,
And there row'd off with owers of my hands.
god and man's Father would not from her sands
Let Scylla see me, for I then had died   630
That bitter death that my poor friends supplied.
    Nine days at sea I hover'd – the tenth night
In th' isle Ogygia, where, about the bright
And right renown'd Calypso, I was cast
By pow'r of deity; where I lived embrac'd
With love and feasts. But why should I relate
Those kind occurrents? I should iterate

What I in part to your chaste queen and you
So late imparted. And, for me to grow
A talker-over of my tale again,   640
Were past my free contentment to sustain.'

THE END OF THE TWELFTH BOOK

BOOK THIRTEEN

The Argument

Ulysses (shipp'd, but in the ev'n,
With all the presents he was giv'n,
And sleeping then) is set next morn
In full scope of his wish'd return,
And treads unknown his country shore,
Whose search so many winters wore.
The ship (returning, and arriv'd
Against the city) is depriv'd
Of form, and, all her motion gone,
Transform'd by Neptune to a stone.
   Ulysses (let to know the strand
Where the Phaeacians made him land)
Consults with Pallas, for the life
Of every wooer of his wife.
His gifts she hides within a cave,
And him into a man more grave,
All hid in wrinkles, crooked, gray,
Transform'd; who so goes on his way.

Another Argument

Nu   Phaeacia
        Ulysses leaves;
     Whom Ithaca,
        Unwares, receives.

BOOK THIRTEEN

HE SAID; and silence all their tongues contain'd
In admiration, when with pleasure chain'd
Their ears had long been to him. At last brake
Alcinous silence, and in this sort spake
To th' Ithacensian, Laertes' son:
'O Ithacus! However over-run
With former suff'rings in your way for home,
Since 'twas, at last, your happy fate to come
To my high-roof'd and brass-foundation'd house,
I hope such speed and pass auspicious   10
Our loves shall yield you, that you shall no more
Wander, nor suffer, homewards, as before.

    You then, whoever that are ever grac'd
With all choice of authoris'd pow'r to taste
Such wine with me as warms the sacred rage,
And is an honorary given to age,
With which ye likewise hear divinely sing,
In honour's praise, the poet of the king,
I move, by way of my command, to this:
That where in an elaborate chest there lies   20
A present for our guest, attires of price,
And gold engrav'n with infinite device,
I wish that each of us should add beside
A tripod, and a cauldron, amplified
With size, and metal of most rate, and great;
For we, in council of taxation met,
Will from our subjects gain their worth again;
Since 'tis unequal one man should sustain
A charge so weighty, being the grace of all,
Which borne by many is a weight but small.'   30

    Thus spake Alcinous, and pleas'd the rest;
When each man clos'd with home and sleep his feast.
But when the colour-giving light arose,
All to the ship did all their speeds dispose,
And wealth, that honest men makes, brought with them.

All which ev'n he that wore the diadem
Stow'd in the ship himself, beneath the seats
The rowers sat in, stooping, lest their lets
In any of their labours he might prove.
Then home he turn'd, and after him did move   40
The whole assembly to expected feast.
Among whom he a sacrifice address'd,
And slew an ox, to weather-wielding Jove,
Beneath whose empire all things are, and move.

   The thighs then roasting, they made glorious cheer,
Delighted highly; and amongst them there
The honour'd-of-the-people us'd his voice,
Divine Demodocus. Yet, through this choice
Of cheer and music, had Ulysses still
An eye directed to the eastern hill,   50
To see him rising that illustrates all:
For now into his mind a fire did fall
Of thirst for home. And as in hungry vow
To needful food a man at fixed plow
(To whom the black ox all day long hath turn'd
The stubborn fallows up, his stomach burn'd
With empty heat and appetite to food,
His knees afflicted with his spirit-spent blood)
At length the long-expected sun-set sees,
That he may sit to food, and rest his knees: 60
So to Ulysses set the friendly light
The sun afforded, with as wish'd a sight.
Who straight bespake that oar-affecting state,
But did in chief his speech appropriate
To him by name, that with their rule was crown'd.

   'Alcinous, of all men most renown'd,
Dismiss me with as safe pass as you vow
(Your off'ring past), and may the gods to you
In all contentment use as full a hand;
For now my landing here and stay shall stand   70
In all perfection with my heart's desire,
Both my so safe deduction to aspire,
And loving gifts; which may the gods to me
As blest in use make as your acts are free,
Ev'n to the finding firm in love and life,
With all desir'd event, my friends and wife.
When, as myself shall live delighted there,
May you with your wives rest as happy here,

Your sons and daughters, in particular state,
With every virtue render'd consummate;   80
And, in your general empire, may ill never
Approach your land, but good your good quit ever.'

This all applauded, and all jointly cried:
'Dismiss the stranger! He hath dignified
With fit speech his dismission.' Then the king
Thus charg'd the herald: 'Fill for offering
A bowl of wine; which through the whole large house
Dispose to all men, that, propitious
Our father Jove made with our pray'rs, we may
Give home our guest in full and wished way.'   90

This said, Pontonous commix'd a bowl
Of such sweet wine as did delight the soul.
Which making sacred to the blessed gods,
That hold in broad heav'n their supreme abodes,
godlike Ulysses from his chair arose,
And in the hands of th' empress did impose
The all-round cup; to whom, fair spoke, he said:

'Rejoice, O queen, and be your joys repaid
By heav'n, for me, till age and death succeed;
Both which inflict their most unwelcome need   100
On men and dames alike. And first, for me,
I must from hence, to both: live you here free,
And ever may all living blessings spring,
Your joy in children, subjects, and your king.'

This said, divine Ulysses took his way;
Before whom the unalterable sway
Of king Alcinous' virtue did command
A herald's fit attendance to the strand,
And ship appointed. With him likewise went
Handmaids, by Arete's injunction sent.   110
One bore an out-and in-weed, fair and sweet,
The other an embroider'd cabinet,
The third had bread to bear, and ruddy wine;
All which, at sea and ship arriv'd, resign
Their freight conferr'd. With fair attendants then,
The sheets and bedding of the man of men –
Within a cabin of the hollow keel,
Spread and made soft, that sleep might sweetly seal
His restful eyes – he enter'd, and his bed
In silence took. The rowers ordered   120
Themselves in several seats, and then set gone

The ship, the cable from the hollow stone
Dissolv'd and weigh'd up, all together, close
Then beat the sea. His lids in sweet repose
Sleep bound so fast, it scarce gave way to breath,
Inexcitable, next of all to death.
And as amids a fair field four brave horse
Before a chariot, stung into their course
With fervent lashes of the smarting scourge,
That all their fire blows high, and makes them urge   130
To utmost speed the measure of their ground:
So bore the ship aloft her fiery bound;
About whom rush'd the billows black and vast,
In which the sea-roars burst. As firm as fast
She ply'd her course yet; nor her winged speed
The falcon-gentle could for pace exceed;
So cut she through the waves, and bore a man
Ev'n with the gods in counsels, that began
And spent his former life in all misease,
Battles of men, and rude waves of the seas,   140
Yet now securely slept, forgetting all.
And when heav'n's brightest star, that first doth call
The early morning out, advanc'd her head,
Then near to Ithaca the billow-bred
Phaeacian ship approach'd. There is a port,
That th' aged sea-god Phorcys makes his fort,
Whose earth the Ithacensian people own,
In which two rocks inaccessible are grown
Far forth into the sea, whose each strength binds
The boist'rous waves in from the high-flown winds   150
On both the out-parts so, that all within
The well-built ships, that once their harbour win
In his calm bosom, without anchor rest,
Safe, and unstirr'd. From forth the hav'n's high crest
Branch the well-brawn'd arms of an olive-tree;
Beneath which runs a cave from all sun free,
Cool and delightsome, sacred to th' access
Of nymphs whose surnames are the Naiades;
In which flew humming bees, in which lay thrown
Stone cups, stone vessels, shittles all of stone,   160
With which the nymphs their purple mantles wove,
In whose contexture art and wonder strove;
In which pure springs perpetually ran;
To which two entries were: the one for man,

On which the North breath'd; th' other for the gods,
On which the South; and that bore no abodes
For earthy men, but only deathless feet
Had there free way. This port these men thought meet
To land Ulysses, being the first they knew;
Drew then their ship in, but no further drew   170
Than half her bulk reach'd, by such cunning hand
Her course was manag'd. Then her men took land,
And first brought forth Ulysses, bed, and all
That richly furnish'd it, he still in thrall
Of all-subduing sleep. Upon the sand
They set him softly down; and then the strand
They strew'd with all the goods he had, bestow'd
By the renown'd Phaeacians, since he show'd
So much Minerva. At the olive root
They drew them then in heap, most far from foot   180
Of any traveller, lest, ere his eyes
Resum'd their charge, they might be others' prise.
    These then turn'd home; nor was the sea's supreme
Forgetful of his threats, for Polypheme
Bent at divine Ulysses, yet would prove
(Ere their performance) the decree of Jove:
    'Father! No more the gods shall honour me,
Since men despise me, and those men that see
The light in lineage of mine own lov'd race.
I vow'd Ulysses should, before the grace   190
Of his return, encounter woes enow
To make that purchase dear; yet did not vow
Simply against it, since thy brow had bent
To his reduction, in the fore-consent
Thou hadst vouchsaf'd it; yet, before my mind
Hath full pow'r on him, the Phaeacians find
Their own minds' satisfaction with his pass,
So far from suff'ring what my pleasure was,
That ease and softness now is habited
In his secure breast, and his careless head   200
Return'd in peace of sleep to Ithaca,
The brass and gold of rich Phaeacia
Rocking his temples, garments richly wov'n,
And worlds of prise, more than was ever strov'n
From all the conflicts he sustain'd at Troy,
If safe he should his full share there enjoy.'
    The Shower-dissolver answer'd: 'What a speech

Hath pass'd thy palate, O thou great in reach
Of wrackful empire! Far the gods remain
From scorn of thee, for 'twere a work of pain   210
To prosecute with ignominies one
That sways our ablest and most ancient throne.
For men, if any so beneath in pow'r
Neglect thy high will, now, or any hour
That moves hereafter, take revenge to thee,
Soothe all thy will, and be thy pleasure free.'
    'Why then,' said he, 'thou blacker of the fumes
That dim the sun, my licens'd pow'r resumes
Act from thy speech; but I observe so much
And fear thy pleasure, that I dare not touch   220
At any inclination of mine own,
Till thy consenting influence be known.
But now this curious-built Phaeacian ship,
Returning from her convoy, I will strip
Of all her fleeting matter, and to stone
Transform and fix it, just when she hath gone
Her full time home, and jets before their prease
In all her trim, amids the sable seas,
That they may cease to convoy strangers still,
When they shall see so like a mighty hill   230
Their glory stick before their city's grace,
And my hands cast a mask before her face.'
    'O friend,' said Jove, 'it shows to me the best
Of all earth's objects, that their whole prease, dress'd
In all their wonder, near their town shall stand,
And stare upon a stone, so near the land,
So like a ship, and dam up all their lights,
As if a mountain interpos'd their sights.'
    When Neptune heard this, he for Scheria went,
Whence the Phaeacians took their first descent.   240
Which when he reach'd, and, in her swiftest pride,
The water-treader by the city's side
Came cutting close, close he came swiftly on,
Took her in violent hand, and to a stone
Turn'd all her sylvan substance; all below
Firm'd her with roots, and left her. This strange show
When the Phaeacians saw, they stupid stood,
And ask'd each other, who amids the flood
Could fix their ship so in her full speed home,
And quite transparent make her bulk become?   250

    Thus talk'd they; but were far from knowing how
These things had issue. Which their king did show,
And said: 'O friends, the ancient prophecies
My father told to me, to all our eyes
Are now in proof. He said, the time would come
When Neptune, for our safe conducting home
All sorts of strangers, out of envy fir'd,
Would meet our fairest ship as she retir'd,
And all the goodly shape and speed we boast
Should like a mountain stand before us lost,   260
Amids the moving waters; which we see
Perform'd in full end to our prophecy.
Hear then my counsel, and obey me then:
Renounce henceforth our convoy home of men,
Whoever shall hereafter greet our town;
And to th' offended deity's renown
Twelve chosen oxen let us sacred make,
That he may pity us, and from us take
This shady mountain. They, in fear, obey'd,
Slew all the beeves, and to the godhead pray'd,   270
The dukes and princes all ensphering round
The sacred altar; while whose tops were crown'd,
Divine Ulysses, on his country's breast
Laid bound in sleep, now rose out of his rest,
Nor (being so long remov'd) the region knew.
Besides which absence, yet Minerva threw
A cloud about him, to make strange the more
His safe arrival, lest upon his shore
He should make known his face, and utter all
That might prevent th' event that was to fall.   280
Which she prepar'd so well, that not his wife,
Presented to him, should perceive his life –
No citizen, no friend, till righteous fate
Upon the wooers' wrongs were consummate.
Through which cloud all things show'd now to the king
Of foreign fashion; the enflower'd spring
Amongst the trees there, the perpetual waves,
The rocks, that did more high their foreheads raise
To his rapt eye than naturally they did,
And all the hav'n, in which a man seem'd hid   290
From wind and weather, when storms loudest chid.
    He therefore, being risen, stood and view'd
His country earth; which, not perceiv'd, he ru'd,

And, striking with his hurl'd-down hands his thighs,
He mourn'd, and said: 'O me! Again where lies
My desert way? To wrongful men and rude,
And with no laws of human right endu'd?
Or are they human, and of holy minds?
What fits my deed with these so many kinds
Of goods late giv'n? What with myself will floods   300
And errors do? I would to god, these goods
Had rested with their owners, and that I
Had fall'n on kings of more regality,
To grace out my return, that lov'd indeed,
And would have giv'n me consorts of fit speed
To my distresses' ending! But, as now,
All knowledge flies me, where I may bestow
My labour'd purchase. Here they shall not stay,
Lest what I car'd for others make their prey.
O gods! I see the great Phaeacians then   310
Were not all just and understanding men,
That land me elsewhere than their vaunts pretended,
Assuring me my country should see ended
My miseries told them, yet now eat their vaunts.
O Jove! Great guardian of poor suppliants,
That others sees, and notes too, shutting in
All in thy plagues, that most presume on sin,
Revenge me on them. Let me number now
The goods they gave, to give my mind to know
If they have stol'n none, in their close retreat.'   320

    The goodly cauldrons then, and tripods, set
In sev'ral ranks from out the heap, he told,
His rich wrought garments too, and all his gold,
And nothing lack'd; and yet this man did mourn
The but suppos'd miss of his home-return –
And creeping to the shore, with much complaint,
Minerva (like a shepherd, young and quaint,
As king's sons are, a double mantle cast
Athwart his shoulders, his fair goers grac'd
With fitted shoes, and in his hand a dart)   330
Appear'd to him, whose sight rejoic'd his heart;
To whom he came, and said: 'O friend! Since first
I meet your sight here, be all good the worst
That can join our encounter. Fare you fair,
Nor with adverse mind welcome my repair,
But guard these goods of mine, and succour me.

As to a god I offer pray'rs to thee,
And low access make to thy loved knee.
Say truth, that I may know, what country then,
What common people live here, and what men?   340
Some famous isle is this? Or gives it vent,
Being near the sea, to some rich continent?'
    She answer'd: 'Stranger, whatsoe'er you are,
Y' are either foolish, or come passing far,
That know not this isle, and make that doubt trouble,
For 'tis not so exceedingly ignoble,
But passing many know it; and so many,
That of all nations there abides not any,
From where the morning rises and the sun,
To where the ev'n and night their courses run,   350
But know this country. Rocky 'tis, and rough,
And so for use of horse unapt enough,
Yet with sad barrenness not much infested,
Since clouds are here in frequent rains digested,
And flow'ry dews. The compass is not great,
The little yet well-fill'd with wine and wheat.
It feeds a goat and ox well, being still
Water'd with floods, that ever over-fill
With heav'n's continual showers; and wooded so,
It makes a spring of all the kinds that grow.   360
And therefore, stranger, the extended name
Of this dominion makes access by fame
From this extreme part of Achaia
As far as Ilion, and 'tis Ithaca.'
    This joy'd him much, that so unknown a land
Turn'd to his country. Yet so wise a hand
He carried, ev'n of this joy, flown so high,
That other end he put to his reply
Than straight to show that joy, and lay abroad
His life to strangers. Therefore he bestow'd   370
A veil on truth; for evermore did wind
About his bosom a most crafty mind,
Which thus his words show'd: 'I have far at sea,
In spacious Crete, heard speak of Ithaca,
Of which myself, it seems, now reach the shore,
With these my fortunes; whose whole value more
I left in Crete amongst my children there,
From whence I fly for being the slaughterer
Of royal Idomen's most loved son,

Swift-foot Orsilochus, that could out-run   380
Profess'd men for the race. Yet him I slew,
Because he would deprive me of my due
In Trojan prise; for which I suffer'd so
(The rude waves piercing) the redoubled woe
Of mind and body in the wars of men.
Nor did I gratify his father then
With any service, but, as well as he
Sway'd in command of other soldiery,
So, with a friend withdrawn, we waylaid him,
When gloomy night the cope of heav'n did dim,   390
And no man knew; but, we lodged close, he came,
And I put out to him his vital flame.
Whose slaughter having author'd with my sword,
I instant flight made, and straight fell aboard
A ship of the renown'd Phoenician state;
When pray'r, and pay at a sufficient rate,
Obtain'd my pass of men in her command;
Whom I enjoin'd to set me on the land
Of Pylos, or of Elis the divine,
Where the Epeians in great empire shine.   400
But force of weather check'd that course to them,
Though (loath to fail me) to their most extreme
They spent their willing pow'rs. But, forc'd from thence,
We err'd, and put in here, with much expence
Of care and labour, and in dead of night,
When no man there serv'd any appetite
So much as with the memory of food,
Though our estates exceeding needy stood.
But, going ashore, we lay; when gentle sleep
My weary powers invaded, and from ship   410
They fetching these my riches, with just hand
About me laid them, while upon the sand
Sleep bound my senses; and for Sidon they
(Put off from hence) made sail, while here I lay,
Left sad alone.' The goddess laugh'd, and took
His hand in hers, and with another look
(Assuming then the likeness of a dame,
Lovely and goodly, expert in the frame
Of virtuous housewif'ries) she answer'd thus:
    'He should be passing sly, and covetous   420
Of stealth, in men's deceits, that coted thee
In any craft, though any god should be

Ambitious to exceed in subtilty.
Thou still-wit-varying wretch! Insatiate
In over-reaches! Not secure thy state
Without these wiles, though on thy native shore
Thou sett'st safe footing, but upon thy store
Of false words still spend, that ev'n from thy birth
Have been thy best friends? Come, our either worth
Is known to either. Thou of men art far,   430
For words and counsels, the most singular,
But I above the gods in both may boast
My still-tried faculties. Yet thou hast lost
The knowledge ev'n of me, the seed of Jove,
Pallas Athenia, that have still out-strove
In all thy labours their extremes, and stood
Thy sure guard ever, making all thy good
Known to the good Phaeacians, and receiv'd.
And now again I greet thee, to see weav'd
Fresh counsels for thee, and will take on me   440
The close reserving of these goods for thee,
Which the renown'd Phaeacian states bestow'd
At thy deduction homewards, only mov'd
With my both spirit and counsel. All which grace
I now will amplify, and tell what case
Thy household stands in, uttering all those pains
That of mere need yet still must wrack thy veins.
Do thou then freely bear, nor one word give
To man nor dame to show thou yet dost live,
But silent suffer over all again   450
Thy sorrows past, and bear the wrongs of men.'
   'Goddess,' said he, 'unjust men, and unwise,
That author injuries and vanities,
By vanities and wrongs should rather be
Bound to this ill-abearing destiny,
Than just and wise men. What delight hath heav'n,
That lives unhurt itself, to suffer giv'n
Up to all domage those poor few that strive
To imitate it, and like the deities live?
But where you wonder that I know you not   460
Through all your changes, that skill is not got
By sleight or art, since thy most hard-hit face
Is still distingtush'd by thy free-giv'n grace;
And therefore, truly, to acknowledge thee
In thy encounters, is a mastery

In men most knowing; for to all men thou
Tak'st several likeness. All men think they know
Thee in their wits; but, since thy seeming view
Appears to all, and yet thy truth to few,
Through all thy changes to discern thee right   470
Asks chief love to thee, and inspired light.
But this I surely know, that, some years past,
I have been often with thy presence grac'd,
All time the sons of Greece waged war at Troy;
But when fate's full hour let our swords enjoy
Our vows in sack of Priam's lofty town,
Our ships all boarded, and when god had blown
Our fleet in sunder, I could never see
The seed of Jove, nor once distinguish'd thee
Boarding my ship, to take one woe from me.   480
But only in my proper spirit involv'd,
Err'd here and there, quite slain, till heav'n dissolv'd
Me, and my ill; which chanc'd not, till thy grace
By open speech confirm'd me, in a place
Fruitful of people, where, in person, thou
Didst give me guide, and all their city show;
And that was the renown'd Phaeacian earth.
Now then, even by the author of thy birth,
Vouchsafe my doubt the truth (for far it flies
My thoughts that thus should fall into mine eyes   490
Conspicuous Ithaca, but fear I touch
At some far shore, and that thy wit is such
Thou dost delude me) is it sure the same
Most honour'd earth that bears my country's name?'
     'I see,' said she, 'thou wilt be ever thus
In every worldly good incredulous,
And therefore have no more the pow'r to see
Frail life more plagu'd with infelicity
In one so eloquent, ingenious, wise.
Another man, that so long miseries   500
Had kept from his lov'd home, and thus return'd
To see his house, wife, children, would have burn'd
In headlong lust to visit. Yet t' inquire
What states they hold, affects not thy desire,
Till thou hast tried if in thy wife there be
A sorrow wasting days and nights for thee
In loving tears, that then the sight may prove
A full reward for either's mutual love.

But I would never credit in you both
Least cause of sorrow, but well knew the troth   510
Of this thine own return, though all thy friends,
I knew as well, should make returnless ends;
Yet would not cross mine uncle Neptune so
To stand their safeguard, since so high did go
His wrath for thy extinction of the eye
Of his lov'd son. Come then, I'll show thee why
I call this isle thy Ithaca, to ground
Thy credit on my words: this hav'n is own'd
By th' aged sea-god Phorcys, in whose brow
This is the olive with the ample bough;   520
And here, close by, the pleasant-shaded cave
That to the fount-nymphs th' Ithacensians gave,
As sacred to their pleasures. Here doth run
The large and cover'd den, where thou hast done
Hundreds of offerings to the Naiades.
Here Mount Neritus shakes his curled tress
Of shady woods.' This said, she clear'd the cloud
That first deceiv'd his eyes; and all things show'd
His country to him. Glad he stood with sight
Of his lov'd soil, and kiss'd it with delight.   530
And instantly to all the nymphs he paid
(With hands held up to heav'n) these vows, and said:
     'Ye nymphs the Naiades, great seed of Jove,
I had conceit that never more should move
Your sight in these spheres of my erring eyes,
And therefore, in the fuller sacrifice
Of my heart's gratitude, rejoice, till more
I pay your names in off'rings as before,
Which here I vow, if Jove's benign descent,
The mighty Pillager, with life convent   540
My person home, and to my sav'd decease
Of my loved son's sight add the sweet increase.'
'Be confident,' said Pallas, 'nor oppress
Thy spirits with care of these performances,
But these thy fortunes let us straight repose
In this divine cave's bosom, that may close
Reserve their value; and we then may see
How best to order other acts to thee.'
     Thus enter'd she the light-excluding cave,
And through it sought some inmost nook to save   550
The gold, the great brass, and robes richly wrought,

Giv'n to Ulysses. All which in he brought,
Laid down in heap; and she impos'd a stone
Close to the cavern's mouth. Then sat they on
The sacred olive's root, consulting how
To act th' insulting wooers' overthrow;
When Pallas said: 'Examine now the means
That best may lay hands on the impudence
Of those proud wooers, that have now three years
Thy roof's rule sway'd, and been bold offerers   560
Of suit and gifts to thy renowned wife,
Who for thy absence all her desolate life
Dissolves in tears till thy desir'd return;
Yet all her wooers, while she thus doth mourn,
She holds in hope, and every one affords
(In fore-sent message) promise; but her words
Bear other utterance than her heart approves.'
       'O gods,' said Ithacus, 'it now behoves
My fate to end me in the ill decease
That Agamemnon underwent, unless   570
You tell me, and in time, their close intents.
Advise then means to the reveng'd events
We both resolve on. Be thyself so kind
To stand close to me, and but such a mind
Breathe in my bosom, as when th' Ilion tow'rs
We tore in cinders. O if equal pow'rs
Thou wouldst enflame amids my nerves as then,
I could encounter with three hundred men –
Thy only self, great goddess, had to friend
In those brave ardours thou wert wont t' extend!'   580
       'I will be strongly with thee,' answer'd she,
'Nor must thou fail, but do thy part with me.
When both whose pow'rs combine, I hope the bloods
And brains of some of these that waste thy goods
Shall strew thy goodly pavements. Join we then:
I first will render thee unknown to men,
And on thy solid lineaments make dry
Thy now smooth skin; thy bright-brown curls imply
In hoary mattings; thy broad shoulders clothe
In such a cloak as every eye shall loathe;   590
Thy bright eyes blear and wrinkle; and so change
Thy form at all parts, that thou shalt be strange
To all the wooers, thy young son, and wife.
But to thy herdsman first present thy life,

That guards thy swine, and wisheth well to thee,
That loves thy son and wife Penelope.
Thy search shall find him set aside his herd,
That are with taste-delighting acorns rear'd,
And drink the dark-deep water of the spring,
Bright Arethusa, the most nourishing   600
Raiser of herds. There stay, and, taking seat
Aside thy herdsman, of the whole state treat
Of home occurrents, while I make access
To fair-dame-breeding Sparta for regress
Of lov'd Telemachus, who went in quest
Of thy lov'd fame, and liv'd the welcome guest
Of Menelaus.' The much-knower said:
    'Why wouldst not thou, in whose grave breast is bred
The art to order all acts, tell in this
His error to him? Let those years of his   610
Amids the rude seas wander, and sustain
The woes there raging, while unworthy men
Devour his fortunes?' 'Let not care extend
Thy heart for him,' said she, 'myself did send
His person in thy search, to set his worth,
By good fame blown, to such a distance forth.
Nor suffers he in any least degree
The grief you fear, but all variety
That Plenty can yield in her quiet'st fare,
In Menelaus' court, doth sit and share.   620
In whose return from home, the wooers yet
Lay bloody ambush, and a ship have set
To sea, to intercept his life, before
He touch again his birth's attempted shore.
All which, my thoughts say, they shall never do,
But rather, that the earth shall overgo
Some one at least of these love-making men,
By which thy goods so much impair sustain.'
Thus using certain secret words to him,
She touch'd him with her rod; and every limb   630
Was hid all over with a wither'd skin;
His bright eyes blear'd; his brow curls white and thin;
And all things did an aged man present.
Then, for his own weeds, shirt and coat, all rent,
Tann'd, and all sootiëd with noisome smoke,
She put him on; and, over all, a cloak
Made of a stag's huge hide, of which was worn

The hair quite off; a scrip, all patch'd and torn,
Hung by a cord, oft broke and knit again;
And with a staff did his old limbs sustain.   640
Thus having both consulted of th' event,
They parted both; and forth to Sparta went
The gray-eyed goddess, to see all things done
That appertain'd to wise Ulysses' son.

THE END OF THE THIRTEENTH BOOK

BOOK FOURTEEN

The Argument

Ulysses meets amids the field
His swain Eumaeus; who doth yield
Kind guest-rites to him, and relate
Occurrents of his wrong'd estate.

Another Argument

Xi   Ulysses feigns
        For his true good.
    His pious swain's
        Faith understood.

BOOK FOURTEEN

BUT HE the rough way took from forth the port,
　　Through woods and hill tops, seeking the resort
　　Where Pallas said divine Eumaeus liv'd;
Who of the fortunes, that were first achiev'd
By god-like Ithacus in household rights,
Had more true care than all his prosylites.
He found him sitting in his cottage door,
Where he had rais'd to every airy blore
A front of great height, and in such a place
That round ye might behold, of circular grace   10
A walk so wound about it; which the swain
(In absence of his far-gone sovereign)
Had built himself, without his queen's supply,
Or old Laertes', to see safely lie
His housed herd. The inner part he wrought
Of stones, that thither his own labours brought,
Which with an hedge of thorn he fenc'd about,
And compass'd all the hedge with pales cleft out
Of sable oak, that here and there he fix'd
Frequent and thick. Within his yard he mix'd   20
Twelve styes to lodge his herd; and every stye
Had room and use for fifty swine to lie;
But those were females all. The male swine slept
Without doors ever; nor was their herd kept
Fair like the females, since they suffer'd still
Great diminution, he being forc'd to kill
And send the fattest to the dainty feasts
Affected by th' ungodly wooing guests.
Their number therefore but three hundred were
And sixty. By them mastiffs, as austere   30
As savage beasts, lay ever, their fierce strain
Bred by the herdsman, a mere prince of men,
Their number four. Himself was then applied
In cutting forth a fair-hu'd ox's hide,
To fit his feet with shoes. His servants held

Guard of his swine; three, here and there, at field,
The fourth he sent to city with a sow,
Which must of force be offer'd to the vow
The wooers made to all satiety,
To serve which still they did those off'rings ply.   40
The fate-born-dogs-to-bark took sudden view
Of Odyssëus, and upon him flew
With open mouth. He, cunning to appal
A fierce dog's fury, from his hand let fall
His staff to earth, and sat him careless down.
And yet to him had one foul wrong been shown
Where most his right lay, had not instantly
The herdsman let his hide fall, and his cry
(With frequent stones flung at the dogs) repell'd,
This way and that, their eager course they held;   50
When through the entry pass'd, he thus did mourn:
    'O father! How soon had you near been torn
By these rude dogs, whose hurt had branded me
With much neglect of you! But deity
Hath giv'n so many other sighs and cares
To my attendant state, that well unwares
You might be hurt for me, for here I lie
Grieving and mourning for the majesty
That, godlike, wonted to be ruling here,
Since now I fat his swine for others' cheer,   60
Where he, perhaps, errs hungry up and down,
In countries, nations, cities, all unknown
If any where he lives yet, and doth see
The sun's sweet beams. But, father, follow me,
That, cheer'd with wine and food, you may disclose
From whence you truly are, and all the woes
Your age is subject to.' This said, he led
Into his cottage, and of osiers spread
A thicken'd hurdle, on whose top he strow'd
A wild goat's shaggy skin, and then bestow'd   70
His own couch on it, that was soft and great.
    Ulysses joy'd to see him so entreat
His uncouth presence, saying: 'Jove requite,
And all th' immortal gods, with that delight
Thou most desir'st, thy kind receipt of me,
O friend to human hospitality!'
    Eumaeus answer'd: 'Guest! If one much worse
Arriv'd here than thyself, it were a curse

To my poor means, to let a stranger taste
Contempt for fit food. Poor men, and unplac'd   80
In free seats of their own, are all from Jove
Commended to our entertaining love.
But poor is th' entertainment I can give,
Yet free and loving. Of such men as live
The lives of servants, and are still in fear
Where young lords govern, this is all the cheer
They can afford a stranger. There was one
That used to manage this now desert throne,
To whom the gods deny return, that show'd
His curious favour to me, and bestow'd   90
Possessions on me, a most wished wife,
A house, and portion, and a servant's life
Fit for the gift a gracious king should give;
Who still took pains himself, and god made thrive
His personal endeavour, and to me
His work the more increas'd, in which you see
I now am conversant. And therefore much
His hand had help'd me, had heav'n's will been such
He might have here grown old. But he is gone,
And would to god the whole succession   100
Of Helen might go with him, since for her
So many men died, whose fate did confer
My liege to Troy, in Agamemnon's grace,
To spoil her people, and her turrets rase!'

    This said, his coat to him he straight did gird,
And to his styes went, that contain'd his herd;
From whence he took out two, slew both, and cut
Both fairly up; a fire enflam'd, and put
To spit the joints; which roasted well, he set
With spit and all to him, that he might eat   110
From thence his food in all the singeing heat,
Yet dredg'd it first with flour; then fill'd his cup
With good sweet wine; sat then, and cheer'd him up:
'Eat now, my guest, such lean swine as are meat
For us poor swains; the fat the wooers eat,
In whose minds no shame, no remorse, doth move,
Though well they know the bless'd gods do not love
Ungodly actions, but respect the right,
And in the works of pious men delight.
But these are worse than impious, for those   120
That vow t' injustice, and profess them foes

To other nations, enter on their land,
And Jupiter (to show his punishing hand
Upon th' invaded, for their penance then)
Gives favour to their foes, though wicked men,
To make their prey on them; who, having freight
Their ships with spoil enough, weigh anchor straight,
And each man to his house (and yet ev'n these
Doth pow'rful fear of god's just vengeance seize,
Even for that prize in which they so rejoice)   130
But these men, knowing (having heard the voice
Of god by some means) that sad death hath reft
The ruler here, will never suffer left
Their unjust wooing of his wife, nor take
Her often answer, and their own roofs make
Their fit retreats, but (since uncheck'd they may)
They therefore will make still his goods their prey,
Without all spare or end. There is no day
Nor night, sent out from god, that ever they
Profane with one beast's blood, or only two,   140
But more make spoil of; and the wrongs they do
In meat's excess to wine as well extend,
Which as excessively their riots spend,
Yet still leave store, for sure his means were great,
And no heroë, that hath choicest seat
Upon the fruitful neighbour continent,
Or in this isle itself, so opulent
Was as Ulysses; no, nor twenty such,
Put altogether, did possess so much.
    Whose herds and flocks I'll tell to every head: 150
Upon the continent he daily fed
Twelve herds of oxen, no less flocks of sheep,
As many herds of swine, stalls large and steep,
And equal sorts of goats, which tenants there,
And his own shepherds, kept. Then fed he here
Eleven fair stalls of goats, whose food hath yield
In the extreme part of a neighbour field.
Each stall his herdsman hath, an honest swain,
Yet every one must every day sustain
The load of one beast (the most fat, and best   160
Of all the stall-fed) to the wooers' feast.
And I, for my part, of the swine I keep
(With four more herdsmen) every day help steep
The wooers' appetites in blood of one,

The most select our choice can full upon.'
   To this Ulysses gave good ear, and fed,
And drunk his wine, and vex'd, and ravished
His food for mere vexation. Seeds of ill
His stomach sow'd, to hear his goods go still
To glut of wooers. But, his dinner done,   170
And stomach fed to satisfaction,
He drunk a full bowl, all of only wine,
And gave it to the guardian of his swine,
Who took it, and rejoic'd; to whom he said:
   'O friend, who is it that, so rich, hath paid
Price for thy service, whose commended pow'r,
Thou sayst, to grace the Grecian conqueror,
At Ilion perish'd? Tell me. It may fall
I knew some such. The great god knows, and all
The other deathless godheads, if I can,   180
Far having travell'd, tell of such a man.'
   Eumaeus answer'd: 'Father, never one,
Of all the strangers that have touch'd upon
This coast, with his life's news could ever yet
Of queen, or lov'd son, any credit get.
These travellers, for clothes, or for a meal,
At all adventures, any lie will tell.
Nor do they trade for truth. Not any man,
That saw the people Ithacensian,
Of all their sort, and had the queen's supplies,   190
Did ever tell her any news but lies.
She graciously receives them yet, inquires
Of all she can, and all in tears expires.
It is th' accustom'd law, that women keep,
Their husbands elsewhere dead, at home to weep.
But do thou quickly, father, forge a tale,
Some coat or cloak to keep thee warm withal,
Perhaps some one may yield thee; but for him,
Vultures and dogs have torn from every limb
His porous skin, and forth his soul is fled,   200
His corse at sea to fishes forfeited,
Or on the shore lies hid in heaps of sand,
And there hath he his ebb, his native strand
With friends' tears flowing. But to me past all
Were tears created, for I never shall
Find so humane a royal master more,
Whatever sea I seek, whatever shore.

Nay, to my father or my mother's love
Should I return, by whom I breathe and move,
Could I so much joy offer; nor these eyes   210
(Though my desires sustain extremities
For their sad absence) would so fain be blest
With sight of their lives, in my native nest,
As with Ulysses dead; in whose last rest,
O friend, my soul shall love him. He's not here,
Nor do I name him like a flatterer,
But as one thankful for his love and care
To me a poor man – in the rich so rare.
And be he past all shores where sun can shine,
I will invoke him as a soul divine.'   220
   'O friend,' said he, 'to say, and to believe,
He cannot live, doth too much license give
To incredulity; for, not to speak
At needy random, but my breath to break
In sacred oath, Ulysses shall return.
And when his sight recomforts those that mourn
In his own roofs, then give me cloak and coat,
And garments worthy of a man of note.
Before which, though need urg'd me never so,
I'll not receive a thread, but naked go.   230
No less I hate him than the gates of hell,
That poorness can force an untruth to tell.
Let Jove then (heav'n's chief god) just witness bear,
And this thy hospitable table here,
Together with unblam'd Ulysses' house,
In which I find receipt so gracious,
What I affirm'd of him shall all be true.
This instant year thine eyes ev'n here shall view
Thy lord Ulysses. Nay, ere this month's end,
Return'd full home, he shall revenge extend   240
To every one, whose ever deed hath done
Wrong to his wife and his illustrious son.'
   'O father,' he replied, 'I'll neither give
Thy news reward, nor doth Ulysses live.
But come, enough of this, let's drink and eat,
And never more his memory repeat.
It grieves my heart to be remember'd thus
By any one of one so glorious.
But stand your oath in your assertion strong,
And let Ulysses come, for whom I long,   250

For whom his wife, for whom his aged sire,
For whom his son consumes his godlike fire,
Whose chance I now must mourn, and ever shall.
Whom when the gods had brought to be as tall
As any upright plant, and I had said
He would amongst a court of men have sway'd
In counsels, and for form have been admir'd
Ev'n with his father, some god misinspir'd,
Or man took from him his own equal mind,
And pass'd him for the Pylian shore to find   260
His long-lost father. In return from whence,
The wooers' pride way-lays his innocence,
That of divine Arcesius all the race
May fade to Ithaca, and not the grace
Of any name left to it. But leave we
His state, however, if surpris'd he be,
Or if he 'scape. And may Saturnius' hand
Protect him safely to his native land.
Do thou then, father, show your griefs, and cause
Of your arrival here; nor break the laws   270
That truth prescribes you, but relate your name,
And of what race you are, your father's fame,
And native city's; ship and men unfold,
That to this isle convey'd you, since I hold
Your here arrival was not all by shore,
Nor that your feet your aged person bore.'

   He answer'd him: 'I'll tell all strictly true,
If time, and food, and wine enough, accrue
Within your roof to us, that freely we
May sit and banquet. Let your business be   280
Discharg'd by others; for, when all is done,
I cannot easily, while the year doth run
His circle round, run over all the woes,
Beneath which, by the course the gods dispose,
My sad age labours. First, I'll tell you then,
From ample Crete I fetch my native strain;
My father wealthy, whose house many a life
Brought forth and bred besides by his true wife,
But me a bond-maid bore, his concubine.
Yet tender'd was I as his lawful line   290
By him of whose race I my life profess,
Castor his name, surnamed Hylacides –
A man, in fore-times, by the Cretan state,

For goods, good children, and his fortunate
Success in all acts, of no mean esteem.
But death-conferring fates have banish'd him
To Pluto's kingdom. After whom, his sons
By lots divided his possessions,
And gave me passing little; yet bestow'd
A house on me, to which my virtues woo'd   300
A wife from rich men's roofs; nor was borne low,
Nor last in fight, though all nerves fail me now.
But I suppose that you, by thus much seen,
Know by the stubble what the corn hath been.
For, past all doubt, affliction past all mean
Hath brought my age on; but, in seasons past,
Both Mars and Pallas have with boldness grac'd,
And fortitude, my fortunes, when I chus'd
Choice men for ambush, press'd to have produc'd
Ill to mine enemies; my too vent'rous spirit   310
Set never death before mine eyes, for merit,
But, far the first advanc'd still, still I strook
Dead with my lance whoever overtook
My speed of foot. Such was I then for war.
But rustic actions ever fled me far,
And household thrift, which breeds a famous race.
In oar-driv'n ships did I my pleasures place,
In battles, light darts, arrows, sad things all,
And into others' thoughts with horror fall.
    But what god put into my mind, to me   320
I still esteem'd as my felicity.
As men of several metals are address'd,
So several forms are in their souls impress'd.

    Before the sons of Greece set foot in Troy,
Nine times, in chief, I did command enjoy
Of men and ships against our foreign foe,
And all I fitly wish'd succeeded so.
Yet after this, I much exploit achiev'd,
When straight my house in all possessions thriv'd.
Yet after that, I great and reverend grew   330
Amongst the Cretans, till the Thunderer drew
Our forces out in his foe-Troy decrees –
A hateful service that dissolv'd the knees
Of many a soldier. And to this was I,
And famous Idomen, enjoin'd t' apply
Our ships and pow'rs. Nor was there to be heard

One reason for denial, so preferr'd
Was the unreasonable people's rumour.
Nine years we therefore fed the martial humour,
And in the tenth, de-peopling Priam's town,   340
We sail'd for home. But god had quickly blown
Our fleet in pieces; and to wretched me
The counsellor Jove did much mishap decree,
For only one month I had leave t' enjoy
My wife and children, and my goods t' employ.
But, after this, my mind for Egypt stood,
When nine fair ships I rigg'd forth for the flood,
Mann'd them with noble soldiers, all things fit
For such a voyage soon were won to it.
Yet six days after stay'd my friends in feast,   350
While I in banquets to the gods address'd
Much sacred matter for their sacrifice.
The seventh, we boarded; and the northern skies
Lent us a frank and passing prosperous gale,
'Fore which we bore as free and easy sail
As we had back'd a full and frolic tide;
Nor felt one ship misfortune for her pride,
But safe we sat, our sailors and the wind
Consenting in our convoy. When heav'n shin'd
In sacred radiance of the fifth fair day,   360
To sweetly-water'd Egypt reach'd our way,
And there we anchor'd; where I charg'd my men
To stay aboard, and watch. Dismissing then
Some scouts to get the hill-tops, and discover,
They (to their own intemperance given over)
Straight fell to forage the rich fields, and thence
Enforce both wives and infants, with th' expence
Of both their bloods. When straight the rumour flew
Up to the city. Which heard, up they drew
By day's first break, and all the field was fill'd   370
With foot and horse, whose arms did all things gild.
And then the lightning-loving deity cast
A foul flight on my soldiers – nor stood fast
One man of all – about whom Mischief stood,
And with his stern steel drew in streams the blood
The greater part fed in their dissolute veins;
The rest were sav'd, and made enthralled swains
To all the basest usages there bred.
And then, ev'n Jove himself supplied my head

With saving counsel, though I wish'd to die,   380
And there in Egypt with their slaughters lie;
So much grief seiz'd me; but Jove made me yield,
Dishelm my head, take from my neck my shield,
Hurl from my hand my lance, and to the troop
Of horse the king led instantly made up,
Embrace, and kiss his knees; whom pity won
To give me safety, and (to make me shun
The people's outrage, that made in amain,
All jointly fired with thirst to see me slain)
He took me to his chariot, weeping, home,   390
Himself with fear of Jove's wrath overcome,
Who yielding souls receives, and takes most ill
All such as well may save yet love to kill.
Seven years I sojourn'd here, and treasure gat
In good abundance of th' Egyptian state,
For all would give; but when th' eighth year began,
A knowing fellow (that would gnaw a man
Like to a vermin, with his hellish brain,
And many an honest soul ev'n quick had slain,
Whose name was Phoenix) close accosted me,   400
And with insinuations, such as he
Practis'd on others, my consent he gain'd
To go into Phoenicia, where remain'd
His house, and living. And with him I liv'd
A complete year; but when were all arriv'd
The months and days, and that the year again
Was turning round, and every season's reign
Renew'd upon us, we for Libya went,
When, still inventing crafts to circumvent,
He made pretext, that I should only go   410
And help convey his freight; but thought not so,
For his intent was to have sold me there,
And made good gain for finding me a year.
Yet him I follow'd, though suspecting this,
For, being aboard his ship, I must be his
Of strong necessity. She ran the flood
(Driv'n with a northern gale, right free, and good)
Amids the full stream, full on Crete. But then
Jove plotted death to him and all his men,
For (put off quite from Crete, and so far gone   420
That shore was lost, and we set eye on none,
But all show'd heav'n and sea) above our keel

Jove pointed right a cloud as black as hell,
Beneath which all the sea hid, and from whence
Jove thunder'd as his hand would never thence,
And thick into our ship he threw his flash,
That 'gainst a rock, or flat, her keel did dash
With headlong rapture. Of the sulphur all
Her bulk did savour; and her men let fall
Amids the surges, on which all lay tost　　　　　430
Like sea-gulls, round about her sides, and lost.
And so god took all home-return from them.
But Jove himself, though plung'd in that extreme,
Recover'd me by thrusting on my hand
The ship's long mast. And, that my life might stand
A little more up, I embrac'd it round,
And on the rude winds, that did ruins sound,
Nine days we hover'd. In the tenth black night
A huge sea cast me on Thesprotia's height,
Where the heroë Phidon, that was chief　　　　　440
Of all the Thesprots, gave my wrack relief,
Without the price of that redemption
That Phoenix fish'd for. Where the king's lov'd son
Came to me, took me by the hand, and led
Into his court my poor life, surfeited
With cold and labour; and because my wrack
Chanc'd on his father's shore, he let not lack
My plight or coat or cloak, or anything
Might cherish heat in me. And here the king
Said he receiv'd Ulysses as his guest,　　　　　450
Observ'd him friend-like, and his course address'd
Home to his country, showing there to me
Ulysses' goods, a very treasury
Of brass, and gold, and steel of curious flame.
And to the tenth succession of his name
He laid up wealth enough, to serve beside
In that king's house, so hugely amplified
His treasure was. But from his court the king
Affirm'd him shipp'd for the Dodonean spring,
To hear, from out the high-hair'd oak of Jove,　　　　　460
Counsel from him for means to his remove
To his lov'd country, whence so many a year
He had been absent; if he should appear
Disguis'd, or manifest; and further swore
In his mid court, at sacrifice, before

These very eyes, that he had ready there
Both ship and soldiers, to attend and bear
Him to his country. But, before, it chanc'd
That a Thesprotian ship was to be launch'd
For the much-corn-renown'd Dulichian land,   470
In which the king gave to his men command
To take, and bring me under tender hand
To king Acastus. But in ill design
Of my poor life did their desires combine,
So far forth, as might ever keep me under
In fortune's hands, and tear my state in sunder.
And when the water-treader far away
Had left the land, then plotted they the day
Of my long servitude, and took from me
Both coat and cloak, and all things that might be   480
Grace in my habit, and in place put on
These tatter'd rags, which now you see upon
My wretched bosom. When heav'n's light took sea,
They fetch'd the field-works of fair Ithaca,
And in the arm'd ship, with a well-wreath'd cord,
They straitly bound me, and did all disboard
To shore to supper, in contentious rout.
Yet straight the gods themselves took from about
My pressed limbs the bands, with equal ease,
And I, my head in rags wrapp'd, took the seas,   490
Descending by the smooth stern, using then
My hands for oars, and made from these bad men
Long way in little time. At last, I fetch'd
A goodly grove of oaks, whose shore I reach'd,
And cast me prostrate on it. When they knew
My thus-made 'scape, about the shores they flew,
But, soon not finding, held it not their best
To seek me further, but return'd to rest
Aboard their vessel. Me the gods lodg'd close,
Conducting me into the safe repose   500
A good man's stable yielded. And thus fate
This poor hour added to my living date.'

    'O wretch of guests,' said he, 'thy tale hath stirr'd
My mind to much ruth, both how thou hast err'd,
And suffer'd, hearing in such good parts shown.
But, what thy chang'd relation would make known
About Ulysses, I hold neither true,
Nor will believe. And what need'st thou pursue

A lie so rashly, since he sure is so
As I conceive, for which my skill shall go?   510
The safe return my king lacks cannot be,
He is so envied of each deity,
So clear, so cruelly. For not in Troy
They gave him end, nor let his corpse enjoy
The hands of friends (which well they might have done,
He manag'd arms to such perfection,
And should have had his sepulchre, and all,
And all the Greeks to grace his funeral,
And this had giv'n a glory to his son
Through all times future), but his head is run   520
Unseen, unhonour'd, into Harpies' maws.
For my part, I'll not meddle with the cause;
I live a separate life amongst my swine,
Come at no town for any need of mine,
Unless the circularly-witted queen
(When any far-come guest is to be seen
That brings her news) commands me bring a brawn,
About which (all things being in question drawn,
That touch the king) they sit, and some are sad
For his long absence, some again are glad   530
To waste his goods unwreak'd, all talking still.
But, as for me, I nourish'd little will
T' inquire or question of him, since the man
That feign'd himself the fled Aetolian,
For slaught'ring one, through many regions stray'd,
In my stall, as his diversory, stay'd.
Where well entreating him, he told me then,
Amongst the Cretans, with king Idomen,
He saw Ulysses at his ship's repair,
That had been brush'd with the enraged air;   540
And that in summer, or in autumn, sure,
With all his brave friends and rich furniture,
He would be here; and nothing so, nor so.
But thou, an old man, taught with so much woe
As thou hast suffer'd, to be season'd true,
And brought by his fate, do not here pursue
His gratulations with thy cunning lies.
Thou canst not soak so through my faculties,
For I did never either honour thee
Or give thee love, to bring these tales to me,   550
But in my fear of hospitable Jove

Thou didst to this pass my affections move.'
'You stand exceeding much incredulous,'
Replied Ulysses, 'to have witness'd thus
My word and oath, yet yield no trust at all.
But make we now a covenant here, and call
The dreadful gods to witness, that take seat
In large Olympus: if your king's retreat
Prove made, ev'n hither, you shall furnish me
With cloak and coat, and make my passage free   560
For lov'd Dulichius; if, as fits my vow,
Your king return not, let your servants throw
My old limbs headlong from some rock most high,
That other poor men may take fear to lie.'

      The herdsman, that had gifts in him divine,
Replied: 'O guest, how shall this fame of mine
And honest virtue, amongst men, remain
Now and hereafter, without worthy stain,
If I, that led thee to my hovel here,
And made thee fitting hospitable cheer,   570
Should after kill thee, and thy loved mind
Force from thy bones? Or how should stand inclin'd
With any faith my will t' importune Jove
In any prayer hereafter for his love?

      Come, now 'tis supper's hour, and instant haste
My men will make home, when our sweet repast
We'll taste together.' This discourse they held
In mutual kind, when from a neighbour field
His swine and swine-herds came, who in their cotes
Inclos'd their herds for sleep, which mighty throats   580
Laid out in ent'ring. Then the god-like swain
His men enjoin'd thus: 'Bring me to be slain
A chief swine female for my stranger guest,
When all together we will take our feast,
Refreshing now our spirits, that all day take
Pains in our swine's good, who may therefore make
For our pains with them all amends with one,
Since others eat our labours, and take none.'
This said, his sharp steel hew'd down wood, and they
A passing fat swine haled out of the sty,   590
Of five years old, which to the fire they put.
When first Eumaeus from the front did cut
The sacred hair, and cast it in the fire,
Then pray'd to heav'n; for still before desire

Was serv'd with food, in their so rude abodes,
Not the poor swine-herd would forget the gods;
Good souls they bore, how bad soever were
The habits that their bodies' parts did bear.
When all the deathless deities besought,
That wise Ulysses might be safely brought   600
Home to his house; then with a log of oak
Left lying by, high lifting it, a stroke
He gave so deadly it made life expire.
Then cut the rest her throat, and all in fire
They hid and sing'd her, cut her up; and then,
The master took the office from the men,
Who on the altar did the parts impose
That served for sacrifice, beginning close
About the belly, thorough which he went,
And (all the chief fat gathering) gave it vent   610
(Part dredg'd with flour) into the sacred flame;
Then cut they up the joints, and roasted them,
Drew all from spit, and serv'd in dishes all.
Then rose Eumaeus (who was general
In skill to guide each act his fit event)
And, all in sev'n parts cut, the first part went
To service of the nymphs and Mercury,
To whose names he did rites of piety
In vows particular; and all the rest
He shared to every one, but his lov'd guest   620
He grac'd with all the chine, and of that king,
To have his heart cheer'd, set up every string.
Which he observing said: 'I would to Jove,
Eumaeus, thou liv'dst in his worthy love
As great as mine, that giv'st to such a guest
As my poor self of all thy goods the best.'

   Eumaeus answer'd: 'Eat, unhappy wretch,
And to what here is at thy pleasure reach.
This I have, this thou want'st; thus god will give,
Thus take away, in us, and all that live.   630
To his will's equal centre all things fall,
His mind he must have, for he can do all.'

   Thus having eat, and to his wine descended,
Before he serv'd his own thirst, he commended
The first use of it in fit sacrifice
(As of his meat) to all the deities,
And to the city-raser's hand applied

The second cup, whose place was next his side.
Mesaulius did distribute the meat
(To which charge was Eumaeus solely set,   640
In absence of Ulysses, by the queen
And old Laertes), and this man had been
Bought by Eumaeus, with his faculties
Employ'd then in the Taphian merchandise.
    But now, to food appos'd, and order'd thus,
All fell. Desire suffic'd, Mesaulius
Did take away. For bed then next they were,
All throughly satisfied with complete cheer.
The night then came, ill, and no taper shin'd;
Jove rain'd her whole date; th' ever-wat'ry wind   650
Zephyr blew loud; and Laertiades
(Approving kind Eumaeus' carefulness
For his whole good) made far about assay,
To get some cast-off cassock (lest he lay
That rough night cold) of him, or any one
Of those his servants; when he thus begun:
    'Hear me, Eumaeus, and my other friends,
I'll use a speech that to my glory tends,
Since I have drunk wine past my usual guise.
Strong wine commands the fool and moves the wise,
Moves and impels him too to sing and dance,   660
And break in pleasant laughters, and, perchance,
Prefer a speech too that were better in.
But when my spirits once to speak begin,
I shall not then dissemble. Would to heav'n,
I were as young, and had my forces driv'n
As close together, as when once our pow'rs
We led to ambush under th' Ilion tow'rs!
Where Ithacus and Menelaus were
The two commanders, when it pleas'd them there   670
To take myself for third, when to the town
And lofty walls we led; we couch'd close down,
All arm'd, amids the osiers and the reeds,
Which oftentimes th' o'er-flowing river feeds.
The cold night came, and th' icy northern gale
Blew bleak upon us, after which did fall
A snow so cold, it cut as in it beat
A frozen water, which was all concrete
About our shields like crystal. All made fain
Above our arms to clothe, and clothe again.   680

And so we made good shift, our shields beside
Clapp'd close upon our clothes, to rest and hide
From all discovery. But I, poor fool,
Left my weeds with my men, because so cool
I thought it could not prove; which thought my pride
A little strengthen'd, being loath to hide
A goodly glittering garment I had on;
And so I follow'd with my shield alone,
And that brave weed. But when the night near ended
Her course on earth, and that the stars descended,   690
I jogg'd Ulysses, who lay passing near,
And spake to him, that had a nimble ear,
Assuring him, that long I could not lie
Amongst the living, for the fervency
Of that sharp night would kill me, since as then
My evil angel made me with my men
Leave all weeds but a fine one. "But I know
'Tis vain to talk; here wants all remedy now."
    This said, he bore that understanding part
In his prompt spirit that still show'd his art   700
In fight and counsel, saying (in a word,
And that low whisper'd) "Peace, lest you afford
Some Greek note of your softness." No word more,
But made as if his stern austerity bore
My plight no pity; yet, as still he lay
His head reposing on his hand, gave way
To this invention: "Hear me friends, a dream
(That was of some celestial light a beam)
Stood in my sleep before me, prompting me
With this fit notice: 'We are far,' said he,   710
'From out our fleet. Let one go then, and try
If Agamemnon will afford supply
To what we now are strong.' " This stirr'd a speed
In Thoas to th' affair, whose purple weed
He left for haste; which then I took, and lay
In quiet after, till the dawn of day.
    This shift Ulysses made for one in need,
And would to heav'n, that youth such spirit did feed
Now in my nerves, and that my joints were knit
With such a strength as made me then held fit   720
To lead men with Ulysses! I should then
Seem worth a weed that fits a herdsman's men,
For two respects: to gain a thankful friend,

And to a good man's need a good extend.'
   'O father,' said Eumaeus,' thou hast shown
Good cause for us to give thee good renown,
Not using any word that was not freed
From all least ill. Thou, therefore, shalt not need
Or coat or other thing, that aptly may
Beseem a wretched suppliant for defray   730
Of this night's need. But, when her golden throne
The Morn ascends, you must resume your own,
For here you must not dream of many weeds,
Or any change at all. We serve our needs
As you do yours: one back, one coat. But when
Ulysses' loved son returns, he then
Shall give you coat and cassock, and bestow
Your person where your heart and soul is now.'
   This said, he rose, made near the fire his bed,
Which all with goats' and sheep skins he bespread,   740
All which Ulysses with himself did line.
With whom, besides, he changed a gaberdine,
Thick-lined, and soft, which still he made his shift
When he would dress him 'gainst the horrid drift
Of tempest, when deep winter's season blows.
Nor pleas'd it him to lie there with his sows,
But while Ulysses slept there, and close by
The other younkers, he abroad would lie,
And therefore arm'd him. Which set cheerful fare
Before Ulysses' heart, to see such care   750
Of his goods taken, how far off soever
His fate his person and his wealth should sever.
First then, a sharp-edg'd sword he girt about
His well-spread shoulders, and (to shelter out
The sharp west wind that blew) he put him on
A thick-lin'd jacket, and yet cast upon
All that the large hide of a goat, well fed.
A lance then took he, with a keen steel head,
To be his keep-off both 'gainst men and dogs.
And thus went he to rest with his male hogs,   760
That still abroad lay underneath a rock,
Shield to the north-wind's ever-eager shock.

THE END OF THE FOURTEENTH BOOK

BOOK FIFTEEN

The Argument

Minerva to his native seat
Exhorts Ulysses' son's retreat,
In bed and waking. He receives
Gifts of Atrides, and so leaves
The Spartan court. And, going aboard,
Doth favourable way afford
To Theoclymenus, that was
The Argive augur, and sought pass,
Fled for a slaughter he had done.
    Eumaeus tells Laertes' son
How he became his father's man,
Being sold by the Phoenician
For some agreed-on faculties,
From forth the Syrian Isle made prise.
    Telemachus, arriv'd at home,
Doth to Eumaeus' cottage come.

Another Argument

Omicron   From Sparta's strand
              Makes safe access
           To his own land
              Ulyssides.

BOOK FIFTEEN

IN LACEDAEMON, large, and apt for dances,
  Athenian Pallas her access advances
  Up to the great-in-soul Ulysses' seed,
Suggesting his return now fit for deed.
She found both him and Nestor's noble son
In bed, in front of that fair mansion,
Nestorides surpris'd with pleasing sleep,
But on the watch Ulysses' son did keep;
Sleep could not enter, cares did so excite
His soul, through all the solitary night,   10
For his lov'd father. To him, near, she said:
  'Telemachus! 'Tis time that now were stay'd
Thy foreign travels, since thy goods are free
For those proud men that all will eat from thee,
Divide thy whole possessions, and leave
Thy too-late presence nothing to receive.
Incite the shrill-voiced Menelaus then,
To send thee to thy native seat again,
While thou mayst yet find in her honour strong
Thy blameless mother 'gainst thy father's wrong.   20
For both the father, and the brothers too,
Of thy lov'd mother, will not suffer so
Extended any more her widow's bed,
But make her now her richest wooer wed,
Eurymachus, who chiefly may augment
Her gifts, and make her jointure eminent.
And therefore haste thee, lest, in thy despite,
Thy house stand empty of thy native right.
For well thou know'st what mind a woman bears;
The house of him, whoever she endears   30
Herself in nuptials to, she sees increas'd,
The issue of her first lov'd lord deceas'd
Forgotten quite, and never thought on more.
In thy return then, the re-counted store
Thou find'st reserv'd, to thy most trusted maid

Commit in guard, till heav'n's pow'rs have purvey'd
A wife, in virtue and in beauty's grace
Of fit sort for thee, to supply her place.
And this note more I'll give thee, which repose
In sure remembrance: the best sort of those   40
That woo thy mother watchful scouts address,
Both in the straits of th' Ithacensian seas,
And dusty Samos, with intent t' invade
And take thy life, ere thy return be made.
Which yet I think will fail, and some of them
That waste thy fortunes taste of that extreme
They plot for thee. But keep off far from shore,
And day and night sail, for a fore-right blore
Whoever of th' immortals that vow guard
And 'scape to thy return, will see prepar'd.   50
As soon as thou arriv'st, dismiss to town
Thy ship and men, and first of all make down
To him that keeps thy swine, and doth conceive
A tender care to see thee well survive.
There sleep; and send him to the town, to tell
The chaste Penelope, that safe and well
Thou liv'st in his charge, and that Pylos' sands
The place contain'd from whence thy person lands.'
    Thus she to large Olympus made ascent.
When with his heel a little touch he lent   60
To Nestor's son, whose sleep's sweet chains he loos'd,
Bad rise, and see in chariot inclos'd
Their one-hoof'd horse, that they might straight be gone.
    'No such haste,' he replied. 'Night holds her throne,
And dims all way to course of chariot.
The Morn will soon get up. Nor see forgot
The gifts with haste, that will, I know, be rich,
And put into our coach with gracious speech
By lance-fam'd Menelaus. Not a guest
Shall touch at his house, but shall store his breast   70
With fit mind of an hospitable man,
To last as long as any daylight can
His eyes recomfort, in such gifts as he
Will proofs make of his hearty royalty.'
    He had no sooner said, but up arose
Aurora, that the golden hills repose.
And Menelaus, good-at-martial-cries,
From Helen's bed rais'd, to his guest applies

His first appearance. Whose repair made known
T' Ulysses' lov'd son, on his robe was thrown 80
About his gracious body, his cloak cast
Athwart his ample shoulders, and in haste
Abroad he went, and did the king accost:
  'Atrides, guarded with heav'n's deified host,
Grant now remission to my native right,
My mind now urging mine own house's sight.'
'Nor will I stay,' said he, 'thy person long,
Since thy desires to go are grown so strong.
I should myself be angry to sustain
The like detention urg'd by other men. 90
Who loves a guest past mean, past mean will hate;
The mean in all acts bears the best estate.
A like ill 'tis, to thrust out such a guest
As would not go, as to detain the rest.
We should a guest love, while he loves to stay,
And, when he likes not, give him loving way.
Yet suffer so, that we may gifts impose
In coach to thee; which ere our hands inclose,
Thine eyes shall see, lest else our loves may glose.
Besides, I'll cause our women to prepare 100
What our house yields, and merely so much fare
As may suffice for health. Both well will do,
Both for our honour and our profit too.
And, serving strength with food, you after may
As much earth measure as will match the day.
If you will turn your course from sea, and go
Through Greece and Argos (that myself may so
Keep kind way with thee) I'll join horse, and guide
T' our human cities. Nor ungratified
Will any one remit us; some one thing 110
Will each present us, that along may bring
Our pass with love, and prove our virtues blaz'd:
A cauldron, or a tripod, richly braz'd,
Two mules, a bowl of gold, that hath his price
Heighten'd with emblems of some rare device.'
  The wise prince answer'd: 'I would gladly go
Home to mine own, and see that govern'd so
That I may keep what I for certain hold,
Not hazard that for only hoped-for gold.
I left behind me none so all ways fit 120
To give it guard, as mine own trust with it.

Besides, in this broad course which you propose,
My father seeking I myself may lose.'
    When this the shrill-voic'd Menelaus heard,
He charg'd his queen and maids to see prepar'd
Breakfast, of what the whole house held for best.
To him rose Eteoneus from his rest,
Whose dwelling was not far off from the court,
And his attendance his command did sort
With kindling fires, and furth'ring all the roast,   130
In act of whose charge heard no time he lost.
    Himself then to an odorous room descended,
Whom Megapenthe and his queen attended.
Come to his treasury, a two-ear'd cup
He choos'd of all, and made his son bear up
A silver bowl. The queen then taking stand
Aside her chest, where by her own fair hand
Lay vests of all hues wrought, she took out one
Most large, most artful, chiefly fair, and shone
Like to a star, and lay of all the last.   140
    Then through the house with either's gift they pass'd
When to Ulysses' son Atrides said:
    'Telemachus, since so entirely sway'd
Thy thoughts are with thy vow'd return now tender'd,
May Juno's thund'ring husband see it render'd
Perfect at all parts, action answering thought.
Of all the rich gifts in my treasure sought,
I give thee here the most in grace and best:
A bowl but silver, yet the brim's compress'd
With gold, whose fabric his desert doth bring   150
From Vulcan's hand, presented by the king
And great heroë of Sidonia's state,
When at our parting he did consummate
His whole housekeeping. This do thou command.'
    This said, he put the round bowl in his hand,
And then his strong son Megapenthe plac'd
The silver cup before him, amply grac'd
With work and lustre. Helen (standing by,
And in her hand the robe, her housewif'ry)
His name rememb'ring, said: 'And I present,   160
Lov'd son, this gift to thee, the monument
Of the so-many-loved Helen's hands,
Which, at the knitting of thy nuptial bands,
Present thy wife. In mean space, may it lie

By thy lov'd mother; but to me apply
Thy pleasure in it, and thus take thy way
To thy fair house, and country's wished stay.'
Thus gave she to his hands the veil, and he
The acceptation author'd joyfully.
Which in the chariot's chest Pisistratus   170
Plac'd with the rest, and held miraculous.

   The yellow-headed king then led them all
To seats and thrones, plac'd in his spacious hall.
The hand-maid water brought, and gave it stream
From out a fair and golden ewer to them,
From whose hands to a silver cauldron fled
The troubled wave. A bright board then she spread,
On which another reverend dame set bread;
To which more servants store of victuals serv'd.
Eteonaeus was the man that carv'd,   180
And Megapenthe fill'd them all their wine.
All fed and drank, till all felt care decline
For those refreshings. Both the guests did go
To horse and coach, and forth the portico
A little issu'd, when the yellow king
Brought wine himself, that, with an offering
To all the gods, they might their journey take.
He stood before the gods, and thus he spake:

   'Farewell, young princes! To grave Nestor's ear
This salutation from my gratitude bear: 190
That I profess, in all our Ilion wars,
He stood a careful father to my cares.'

   To whom the wise Ulyssides replied:
'With all our utmost shall be signified,
Jove-kept Atrides, your right royal will;
And would to god, I could as well fulfill
Mine own mind's gratitude, for your free grace,
In telling to Ulysses, in the place
Of my return, in what accomplish'd kind
I have obtain'd the office of a friend   200
At your deservings; whose fair end you crown
With gifts so many, and of such renown!'

   His wish, that he might find in his retreat
His father safe return'd (to so repeat
The king's love to him) was saluted thus:
An eagle rose, and in her seres did truss
A goose, all white, and huge, a household one,

Which men and women, crying out upon,
Pursu'd, but she, being near the guests, her flight
Made on their right hand, and kept still fore-right   210
Before their horses; which observ'd by them,
The spirits in all their minds took joys extreme,
Which Nestor's son thus question'd: 'Jove-kept king,
Yield your grave thoughts, if this ostentful thing
(This eagle and this goose) touch us or you?'

    He put to study, and not knowing how
To give fit answer, Helen took on her
Th' ostent's solution, and did this prefer:

    'Hear me, and I will play the prophet's part,
As the immortals cast it in my heart,   220
And as, I think, will make the true sense known:
As this Jove's bird, from out the mountains flown
(Where was her eyrie, and whence rose her race)
Truss'd up this goose, that from the house did graze,
So shall Ulysses, coming from the wild
Of seas and sufferings, reach, unreconcil'd,
His native home, where ev'n this hour he is,
And on those house-fed wooers those wrongs of his
Will shortly wreak, with all their miseries.'

    'O,' said Telemachus, 'if Saturnian Jove   230
To my desires thy dear presage approve,
When I arrive, I will perform to thee
My daily vows, as to a deity.'

    This said, he used his scourge upon the horse,
That through the city freely made their course
To field, and all day made that first speed good.
But when the sun set, and obscureness stood
In each man's way, they ended their access
At Pheras, in the house of Diocles,
Son to Orsilochus, Alpheus' seed,   240
Who gave them guest-rites; and sleep's natural need
They that night serv'd there. When Aurora rose,
They join'd their horse, took coach, and did dispose
Their course for Pylos; whose high city soon
They reach'd. Nor would Telemachus be won
To Nestor's house, and therefore order'd thus
His speech to Nestor's son, Pisistratus:

    'How shall I win thy promise to a grace
That I must ask of thee? We both embrace
The names of bed-fellows, and in that name   250

Will glory as an adjunct of our fame;
Our fathers' friendship, our own equal age,
And our joint travel, may the more engage
Our mutual concord. Do not then assay,
My god-lov'd friend, to lead me from my way
To my near ship, but take a course direct
And leave me there, lest thy old sire's respect,
In his desire to love me, hinder so
My way for home, that have such need to go.'
     This said, Nestorides held all discourse   260
In his kind soul, how best he might enforce
Both promise and performance; which, at last,
He vow'd to venture, and directly cast
His horse about to fetch the ship and shore.
Where come, his friends' most lovely gifts he bore
Aboard the ship, and in her hind-deck plac'd
The veil that Helen's curious hand had grac'd,
And Menelaus' gold, and said: 'Away,
Nor let thy men in any least date stay,
But quite put off, ere I get home and tell   270
The old duke you are pass'd; for passing well
I know his mind to so exceed all force
Of any pray'r, that he will stay your course,
Himself make hither, all your course call back,
And, when he hath you, have no thought to rack
Him from his bounty, and to let you part
Without a present, but be vex'd at heart
With both our pleadings, if we once but move
The least repression of his fiery love.'
     Thus took he coach, his fair-man'd steeds scourg'd on
Along the Pylian city, and anon
His father's court reach'd; while Ulysses' son
Bade board, and arm; which with a thought was done.
     His rowers set, and he rich odours firing
In his hind-deck, for his secure retiring,
To great Athenia, to his ship came flying
A stranger, and a prophet, as relying
On wished passage, having newly slain
A man at Argos, yet his race's vein
Flow'd from Melampus, who in former date   290
In Pylos liv'd, and had a huge estate,
But fled his country, and the punishing hand
Of great-soul'd Neleus, in a foreign land,

From that most famous mortal having held
A world of riches, nor could be compell'd
To render restitution in a year.
In mean space, living as close prisoner
In court of Phylacus, and for the sake
Of Neleus' daughter, mighty cares did take,
Together with a grievous langour sent   300
From grave Erinnys, that did much torment
His vexed conscience; yet his life's expense
He 'scap'd, and drave the loud-voic'd oxen thence,
To breed-sheep Pylos, bringing vengeance thus
Her foul demerit to great Neleus,
And to his brother's house reduc'd his wife.
Who yet from Pylos did remove his life
For feed-horse Argos, where his fate set down
A dwelling for him, and in much renown
Made govern many Argives, where a spouse   310
He took to him, and built a famous house.
There had he born to him Antiphates,
And forceful Mantius. To the first of these
Was great Oïcleus born: Oïcleus gat
Amphiaräus, that the popular state
Had all their health in, whom ev'n from his heart
Jove lov'd, and Phoebus in the whole desert
Of friendship held him; yet not bless'd so much
That age's threshold he did ever touch,
But lost his life by female bribery.   320
Yet two sons author'd his posterity,
Alcmaeon, and renown'd Amphilochus.
Mantius had issue Polyphidius,
And Clytus, but Aurora ravish'd him,
For excellence of his admired limb,
And interested him amongst the gods.
His brother knew men's good and bad abodes
The best of all men, after the decease
Of him that perish'd in unnatural peace
At spacious Thebes. Apollo did inspire   330
His knowing soul with a prophetic fire.
Who, angry with his father, took his way
To Hyperesia; where, making stay,
He prophesied to all men, and had there
A son call'd Theoclymenus, who here
Came to Telemachus, and found aboard

Himself at sacrifice, whom in a word
He thus saluted: 'O friend, since I find,
Ev'n here at ship, a sacrificing mind
Inform your actions, by your sacrifice,   340
And by that worthy choice of deities
To whom you offer, by yourself, and all
These men that serve your course maritimal,
Tell one that asks the truth, nor give it glose,
Both who, and whence, you are? From what seed rose
Your royal person? And what city's tow'rs
Hold habitation to your parents' pow'rs?'

     He answer'd: 'Stranger! The sure truth is this:
I am of Ithaca; my father is
(Or was) Ulysses, but austere death now   350
Takes his state from him; whose event to know,
Himself being long away, I set forth thus
With ship and soldiers.' Theoclymenus
As freely said: 'And I to thee am fled
From forth my country, for a man struck dead
By my unhappy hand, who was with me
Of one self-tribe, and of his pedigree
Are many friends and brothers, and the sway
Of Achive kindred reacheth far away.
From whom, because I fear their spleens suborn   360
Blood, and black fate against me (being born
To be a wand'rer among foreign men)
Make thy fair ship my rescue, and sustain
My life from slaughter. Thy deservings may
Perform that mercy, and to them I pray.'

     'Nor will I bar,' said he, 'thy will to make
My means and equal ship thy aid, but take
(With what we have here, in all friendly use)
Thy life from any violence that pursues.'

     Thus took he in his lance, and it extended   370
Aloft the hatches, which himself ascended.
The prince took seat at stern, on his right hand
Set Theoclymenus, and gave command
To all his men to arm, and see made fast
Amidst the hollow keel the beechen mast
With able halsers, hoise sail, launch; which soon
He saw obey'd. And then his ship did run
A merry course; blue-eyed Minerva sent
A fore-right gale, tumultuous, vehement,

Along the air, that her way's utmost yield   380
The ship might make, and plough the brackish field.
    Then set the sun, and night black'd all the ways.
The ship, with Jove's wind wing'd, where th' Epian sways,
Fetch'd Pheras first, then Elis the divine,
And then for those isles made, that sea-ward shine
For form and sharpness like a lance's head,
About which lay the wooers ambushed;
On which he rush'd, to try if he could 'scape
His plotted death, or serve her treach'rous rape.
    And now return we to Eumaeus' shed,   390
Where, at their food with others marshalled,
Ulysses and his noble herdsman sate.
To try if whose love's curious estate
Stood firm to his abode, or felt it fade,
And so would take each best cause to persuade
His guest to town, Ulysses thus contends:
    'Hear me, Eumaeus, and ye other friends.
Next morn to town I covet to be gone,
To beg some others' alms, not still charge one.
Advise me well then, and as well provide   400
I may be fitted with an honest guide,
For through the streets, since need will have it so,
I'll tread, to try if any will bestow
A dish of drink on me, or bit of bread,
Till to Ulysses' house I may he led;
And there I'll tell all-wise Penelope news,
Mix with the wooers' pride, and, since they use
To fare above the full, their hands excite
To some small feast from out their infinite:
For which I'll wait, and play the servingman,   410
Fairly enough, command the most they can.
For I will tell thee, note me well, and hear,
That, if the will be of heav'n's messenger,
(Who to the works of men, of any sort,
Can grace infuse, and glory) nothing short
Am I of him, that doth to most aspire
In any service, as to build a fire,
To cleave sere wood, to roast or boil their meat,
To wait at board, mix wine, or know the neat,
Or any work, in which the poor-call'd worst   420
To serve the rich-call'd best in fate are forc'd.'
    He, angry with him, said: 'Alas, poor guest,

Why did this counsel ever touch thy breast?
Thou seek'st thy utter spoil beyond all doubt,
If thou giv'st venture on the wooers' rout,
Whose wrong and force affects the iron heav'n,
Their light delights are far from being giv'n
To such grave servitors. Youths richly trick'd
In coats or cassocks, locks divinely slick'd,
And looks most rapting, ever have the gift   430
To taste their crown'd cups, and full trenchers shift.
Their tables ever like their glasses shine,
Loaded with bread, with varied flesh, and wine.
And thou go thither? Stay, for here do none
Grudge at thy presence, nor myself, nor one
Of all I feed. But when Ulysses' son
Again shall greet us, he shall put thee on
Both coat and cassock, and thy quick retreat
Set where thy heart and soul desire thy seat.'
   Industrious Ulysses gave reply: 440
'I still much wish, that heav'n's chief deity
Lov'd thee as I do, that hast eas'd my mind
Of woes and wand'rings never yet confin'd.
Nought is more wretched in a human race,
Than country's want, and shift from place to place.
But for the baneful belly men take care
Beyond good counsel, whosoever are
In compass of the wants it undergoes
By wand'rings, losses, or dependent woes.
Excuse me therefore, if I err'd at home;   450
Which since thou wilt make here, as overcome
With thy command for stay, I'll take on me
Cares appertaining to this place, like thee.
Does then Ulysses' sire, and mother, breathe,
Both whom he left in th' age next door to death?
Or are they breathless, and descended where
The dark house is, that never day doth clear?'
   'Laertes lives,' said he, 'but every hour
Beseecheth Jove to take from him the pow'r
That joins his life and limbs; for with a moan   460
That breeds a marvel he laments his son
Depriv'd by death, and adds to that another
Of no less depth for that dead son's dead mother,
Whom he a virgin wedded, which the more
Makes him lament her loss, and doth deplore

Yet more her miss, because her womb the truer
Was to his brave son, and his slaughter slew her.
Which last love to her doth his life engage,
And makes him live an undigested age.
O such a death she died as never may   470
Seize any one that here beholds the day,
That either is to any man a friend,
Or can a woman kill in such a kind.
As long as she had being, I would be
A still inquirer (since 'twas dear to me,
Though death to her, to hear his name) when she
Heard of Ulysses, for I might be bold –
She brought me up, and in her love did hold
My life compar'd with long-veil'd Ctimene,
Her youngest issue (in some small degree   480
Her daughter yet preferr'd), a brave young dame.
And when of youth the dearly-loved flame
Was lighted in us, marriage did prefer
The maid to Samos; whence was sent for her
Infinite riches, when the queen bestow'd
A fair new suit, new shoes, and all, and vow'd
Me to the field, but passing loath to part,
As loving me more than she lov'd her heart.
And these I want now; but their business grows
Upon me daily, which the gods impose,   490
To whom I hold all, give account to them,
For I see none left to the diadem
That may dispose all better. So, I drink
And eat of what is here; and whom I think
Worthy or reverend, I have given to, still,
These kinds of guest-rites; for the household ill
(Which, where the queen is, riots) takes her quite
From thought of these things. Nor is it delight
To hear, from her plight, of or work or word;
The wooers spoil all. But yet my men will board   500
Her sorrows often, with discourse of all,
Eating and drinking of the festival
That there is kept, and after bring to field
Such things as servants make their pleasures yield.
    'O me, Eumaeus,' said Laertes' son,
'Hast thou then err'd so of a little one,
Like me, from friends and country? Pray thee say,
And say a truth, doth vast Destruction lay

Her hand upon the wide-way'd seat of men,
Where dwelt thy sire and reverend mother then,　　　510
That thou art spar'd there? Or else, set alone
In guard of beeves or sheep, set th' enemy on,
Surpris'd and shipp'd, transferr'd, and sold thee here?
He that bought thee paid well, yet bought not dear.'
　'Since thou enquir'st of that, my guest,' said he,
'Hear and be silent, and, mean space, sit free
In use of these cups to thy most delights;
Unspeakable in length now are the nights.
Those that affect sleep yet, to sleep have leave,
Those that affect to hear, their hearers give.　　　520
But sleep not ere your hour; much sleep doth grieve.
Whoever lists to sleep, away to bed,
Together with the morning raise his head,
Together with his fellows break his fast,
And then his lord's herd drive to their repast.
We two, still in our tabernacle here
Drinking and eating, will our bosoms cheer
With memories and tales of our annoys.
Betwixt his sorrows every human joys,
He most, who most hath felt and furthest err'd.　　　530
And now thy will to act shall be preferr'd.
　There is an isle above Ortygia,
If thou hast heard, they call it Syria,
Where, once a day, the sun moves backward still.
'Tis not so great as good, for it doth fill
The fields with oxen, fills them still with sheep,
Fills roofs with wine, and makes all corn there cheap.
No dearth comes ever there, nor no disease
That doth with hate us wretched mortals seize,
But when men's varied nations, dwelling there　　　540
In any city, enter th' aged year,
The silver-bow-bearer, the Sun, and she
That bears as much renown for archery,
Stoop with their painless shafts, and strike them dead,
As one would sleep, and never keep the bed.
In this isle stand two cities, betwixt whom
All things that of the soil's fertility come
In two parts are divided. And both these
My father rul'd, Ctesius Ormenides,
A man like the immortals. With these states　　　550
The cross-biting Phoenicians traffick'd rates

Of infinite merchandise in ships brought there,
In which they then were held exempt from peer.
   There dwelt within my father's house a dame,
Born a Phoenician, skilful in the frame
Of noble housewif'ries, right tall and fair.
Her the Phoenician great-wench-net-layer
With sweet words circumvented, as she was
Washing her linen. To his amorous pass
He brought her first, shor'd from his ship to her,   560
To whom he did his whole life's love prefer,
Which of these breast-exposing dames the hearts
Deceives, though fashion'd of right honest parts.
He ask'd her after, what she was, and whence?
She, passing presently, the excellence
Told of her father's turrets, and that she
Might boast herself sprung from the progeny
Of the rich Sidons, and the daughter was
Of the much-year-revenu'd Arybas;
But that the Taphian pirates made their prise,   570
As she return'd from her field-housewif'ries,
Transferr'd her hither, and, at that man's house
Where now she lived, for value precious
Sold her to th' owner. He that stole her love
Bade her again to her birth's sent remove,
To see the fair roofs of her friends again,
Who still held state, and did the port maintain
Herself reported. She said: 'Be it so,
So you, and all that in your ship shall row,
Swear to return me in all safety hence.'   580
   All swore. Th' oath past, with every consequence,
She bade: 'Be silent now, and not a word
Do you, or any of your friends, afford,
Meeting me afterward in any way,
Or at the washing-fount, lest some display
Be made, and told the old man, and he then
Keep me strait bound, to you and to your men
The utter ruin plotting of your lives.
Keep in firm thought then every word that strives
For dangerous utterance. Haste your ship's full freight   590
Of what you traffic for, and let me straight
Know by some sent friend she hath nil in hold,
And with myself I'll bring thence all the gold
I can by all means finger; and, beside,

I'll do my best to see your freight supplied
With some well-weighing burthen of mine own.
For I bring up in house a great man's son,
As crafty as myself, who will with me
Run every way along, and I will be
His leader, till your ship hath made him sure.   600
He will an infinite great price procure,
Transfer him to what languag'd men ye may.'
    This said, she gat her home, and there made stay
A whole year with us, goods of great avail
Their ship enriching. Which now fit for sail,
They sent a messenger t' inform the dame;
And to my father's house a fellow came,
Full of Phoenician craft, that to be sold
A tablet brought, the body all of gold,
The verge all amber. This had ocular view   610
Both by my honour'd mother and the crew
Of her house-handmaids, handled, and the price
Bent, ask'd, and promis'd. And while this device
Lay thus upon the forge, this jeweller
Made privy signs, by winks and wiles, to her
That was his object; which she took, and he,
His sign seeing noted, hied to ship. When she
(My hand still taking, as she us'd to do
To walk abroad with her) convey'd me so
Abroad with her, and in the portico   620
Found cups, with tasted viands, which the guests
That us'd to flock about my father's feasts
Had left. They gone (some to the council court,
Some to hear news amongst the talking sort),
Her theft three bowls into her lap convey'd,
And forth she went. Nor was my wit so stay'd
To stay her, or myself. The sun went down,
And shadows round about the world were flown,
When we came to the hav'n in which did ride
The swift Phoenician ship; whose fair broad side   630
They boarded straight, took us up; and all vent
Along the moist waves. Wind Saturnius sent.
Six days we day and night sail'd; but when Jove
Put up the sev'nth day, she that shafts doth love
Shot dead the woman, who into the pump
Like to a dop-chick div'd, and gave a thump
In her sad settling. Forth they cast her then

To serve the fish and sea-calves, no more men;
But I was left there with a heavy heart;
When wind and water drave them quite apart   640
Their own course, and on Ithaca they fell,
And there poor me did to Laertes sell.
And thus these eyes the sight of this isle prov'd.'
    'Eumaeus,' he replied, 'thou much hast mov'd
The mind in me with all things thou hast said,
And all the suff'rance on thy bosom laid.
But, truly, to thy ill hath Jove join'd good,
That one whose veins are serv'd with human blood
Hath bought thy service, that gives competence
Of food, wine, cloth to thee; and sure th' expence   650
Of thy life's date here is of good desert,
Whose labours not to thee alone impart
Sufficient food and housing, but to me;
Where I through many a heap'd humanity
Have hither err'd, where, though like thee not sold,
Nor stay'd like thee yet, nor nought needful hold.'
    This mutual speech they us'd, nor had they slept
Much time before the much-near Morning leapt
To her fair throne. And now struck sail the men
That serv'd Telemachus, arriv'd just then   660
Near his lov'd shore; where now they stoop'd the mast,
Made to the port with oars, and anchor cast,
Made fast the ship, and then ashore they went,
Dress'd supper, fill'd wine; when (their appetites spent)
Telemachus commanded they should yield
The ship to th' owner, while himself at field
Would see his shepherds; when light drew to end
He would his gifts see, and to town descend,
And in the morning at a feast bestow
Rewards for all their pains. 'And whither now,'   670
Said Theoclymenus, 'my loved son,
Shall I address myself? Whose mansion,
Of all men, in this rough-hewn isle, shall I
Direct my why to? Or go readily
To thy house and thy mother?' He replied:
'Another time I'll see you satisfied
With my house entertainment, but as now
You should encounter none that could bestow
Your fit entreaty, and (which less grace were)
You could not see my mother, I not there;   680

For she's no frequent object, but apart
Keeps from her wooers, woo'd with her desert,
Up in her chamber, at her housewif'ry.
But I'll name one to whom you shall apply
Direct repair, and that's Eurymachus,
Renown'd descent to wise Polybius,
A man whom th' Ithacensians look on now
As on a god, since he of all that woo
Is far superior man, and likest far
To wed my mother, and as circular   690
Be in that honour as Ulysses was.
But heav'n-hous'd Jove knows the yet hidden pass
Of her disposure, and on them he may
A blacker sight bring than her nuptial day.'

  As this he utter'd, on his right hand flew
A saker, sacred to the god of view,
That in his talons truss'd and plumed a dove;
The feathers round about the ship did rove,
And on Telemachus fell; whom th' augur then
Took fast by th' hand, withdrew him from his men,   700
And said: 'Telemachus! This hawk is sent
From god; I knew it for a sure ostent
When first I saw it. Be you well assur'd,
There will no wooer be by heav'n endur'd
To rule in Ithaca above your race,
But your pow'rs ever fill the regal place.'

  'I wish to heav'n,' said he, 'thy word might stand.
Thou then shouldst soon acknowledge from my hand
Such gifts and friendship as would make thee, guest,
Met and saluted as no less than blest.'   710

  This said, he call'd Piraeus, Clytus' son,
His true associate, saying: 'Thou hast done
(Of all my followers to the Pylian shore)
My will in chief in other things, once more
Be chiefly good to me; take to thy house
This loved stranger, and be studious
T' embrace and greet him with thy greatest fare,
Till I myself come and take off thy care.'

  The famous-for-his-lance said: 'If your stay
Take time for life here, this man's care I'll lay   720
On my performance, nor what fits a guest
Shall any penury withhold his feast.'

  Thus took he ship, bade them board, and away.

They boarded, sat, but did their labour stay
Till he had deck'd his feet, and reach'd his lance.
They to the city; he did straight advance
Up to his sties, where swine lay for him store,
By whose side did his honest swine-herd snore,
Till his short cares his longest nights had ended,
And nothing worse to both his lords intended.   730

THE END OF THE FIFTEENTH BOOK

BOOK SIXTEEN

The Argument

The prince at field, he sends to town
Eumaeus, to make truly known
His safe return. By Pallas' will,
Telemachus is giv'n the skill
To know his father. Those that lay
In ambush, to prevent the way
Of young Ulyssides for home,
Retire, with anger overcome.

Another Argument

Pi To his most dear
   Ulysses shows.
  The wise son here
   His father knows.

BOOK SIXTEEN

ULYSSES and divine Eumaeus rose
　　Soon as the morning could her eyes unclose,
　　Made fire, brake fast, and to their pasture send
The gather'd herds, on whom their swains attend.
The self-tire barking dogs all fawn'd upon,
Nor bark'd, at first sight of Ulysses' son.
The whinings of their fawnings yet did greet
Ulysses' ears, and sounds of certain feet,
Who thus bespake Eumaeus: 'Sure some friend,
Or one well-known, comes, that the mastiffs spend　　10
Their mouths no louder. Only some one near
They whine, and leap about, whose feet I hear.'
　　Each word of this speech was not spent, before
His son stood in the entry of the door.
Out rush'd amaz'd Eumaeus, and let go
The cup to earth, that he had labour'd so,
Cleans'd for the neat wine, did the prince surprise,
Kiss'd his fair forehead, both his lovely eyes,
Both his white hands, and tender tears distill'd.
There breath'd no kind-soul'd father that was fill'd　　20
Less with his son's embraces, that had liv'd
Ten years in far-off earth, now new retriev'd,
His only child too, gotten in his age,
And for whose absence he had felt the rage
Of griefs upon him, than for this divin'd
So-much-for-form was this divine-for-mind;
Who kiss'd him through, who grew about him kissing,
As fresh from death 'scaped. Whom so long time missing,
He wept for joy, and said: 'Thou yet art come,
Sweet light, sweet sun-rise, to thy cloudy home.　　30
O, never I look'd, when once shipp'd away
For Pylos' shores, to see thy turning day.
Come, enter, lov'd son, let me feast my heart
With thy sweet sight, new come, so far apart.
Nor, when you lived at home, would you walk down

Often enough here, but stay'd still at town;
It pleas'd you then to cast such forehand view
About your house on that most damned crew.'

   'It shall be so then, friend,' said he, 'but now
I come to glad mine eyes with thee, and know   40
If still my mother in her house remain,
Or if some wooer hath aspir'd to gain
Of her in nuptials; for Ulysses' bed,
By this, lies all with spiders' cobwebs spread,
In penury of him that should supply it.'

   'She still,' said he, 'holds her most constant quiet,
Aloft thine own house, for the bed's respect,
But, for her lord's sad loss, sad nights and days
Obscure her beauties, and corrupt their rays.'

   This said, Eumaeus took his brazen spear,   50
And in he went; when, being enter'd near
Within the stony threshold, from his seat
His father rose to him, who would not let
Th' old man remove, but drew him back and press'd
With earnest terms his sitting, saying: 'Guest,
Take here your seat again, we soon shall get
Within our own house here some other seat.
Here's one will fetch it.' This said, down again
His father sat, and to his son his swain
Strew'd fair green osiers, and impos'd thereon   60
A good soft sheepskin, which made him a throne.

   Then he appos'd to them his last-left roast,
And in a wicker basket bread engross'd,
Fill'd luscious wine, and then took opposite seat
To the divine Ulysses. When, the meat
Set there before them, all fell to, and eat.
When they had fed, the prince said: 'Pray thee say,
Whence comes this guest? What seaman gave him ray
To this our isle? I hope these feet of his
Could walk no water. Who boasts he he is?'   70

   'I'll tell all truly, son: from ample Crete
He boasts himself, and says, his erring feet
Have many cities trod, and god was he
Whose finger wrought in his infirmity.
But, to my cottage, the last 'scape of his
Was from a Thesprot's ship. Whate'er he is,
I'll give him you, do what you please; his vaunt
Is, that he is, at most, a suppliant.'

   'Eumaeus,' said the prince, 'to tell me this,
You have afflicted my weak faculties,   80
For how shall I receive him to my house
With any safety, that suspicious
Of my young forces (should I be assay'd
With any sudden violence) may want aid
To shield myself? Besides, if I go home,
My mother is with two doubts overcome –
If she shall stay with me, and take fit care
For all such guests as there seek guestive fare,
Her husband's bed respecting, and her fame
Amongst the people; or her blood may frame   90
A liking to some wooer, such as best
May bed her in his house, not giving least.
And thus am I unsure of all means free
To use a guest there, fit for his degree.
But, being thy guest, I'll be his supply
For all weeds, such as mere necessity
Shall more than furnish, fit him with a sword,
And set him where his heart would have been shor'd;
Or, if so pleas'd, receive him in thy shed,
I'll send thee clothes, I vow, and all the bread   100
His wish would eat, that to thy men and thee
He be no burthen. But that I should be
His mean to my house, where a company
Of wrong-professing wooers wildly live,
I will in no sort author, lest they give
Foul use to him, and me as gravely grieve.
For what great act can any one achieve
Against a multitude, although his mind
Retain a courage of the greatest kind?
For all minds have not force in one degree.'   110
   Ulysses answer'd: 'O friend, since 'tis free
For any man to change fit words with thee,
I'll freely speak: methinks, a wolfish pow'r
My heart puts on to tear and to devour,
To hear your affirmation, that, in spite
Of what may fall on you, made opposite,
Being one of your proportion, birth, and age,
These wooers should in such injustice rage.
What should the cause be? Do you wilfully
Endure their spoil? Or hath your empery   120
Been such amongst your people, that all gather

In troop, and one voice (which ev'n god doth father)
And vow your hate so, that they suffer them?
Or blame your kinsfolk's faiths, before th' extreme
Of your first stroke hath tried them, whom a man,
When strifes to blows rise, trusts, though battle ran
In huge and high waves? Would to heav'n my spirit
Such youth breath'd, as the man that must inherit
Yet-never-touch'd Ulysses, or that he,
But wandering this way, would but come, and see   130
What my age could achieve (and there is fate
For hope yet left, that he may recreate
His eyes with such an object); this my head
Should any stranger strike off, if stark dead
I struck not all, the house in open force
Ent'ring with challenge! If their great concourse
Did over-lay me, being a man alone,
(Which you urge for yourself) be you that one,
I rather in mine own house wish to die
One death for all, than so indecently   140
See evermore deeds worse than death applied,
Guests wrong'd with vile words and blow-giving pride,
The women-servants dragg'd in filthy kind
About the fair house, and in corners blind
Made serve the rapes of ruffians, food devour'd
Idly and rudely, wine exhaust, and pour'd
Through throats profane; and all about a deed
That's ever wooing, and will never speed.'

    'I'll tell you, guest, most truly,' said his son,
'I do not think that all my people run   150
One hateful course against me; nor accuse
Kinsfolks that I in strifes of weight might use;
But Jove will have it so, our race alone
(As if made singular) to one and one
His hand confining. Only to the king,
Jove-bred Arcesius, did Laertes spring;
Only to old Laertes did descend
Ulysses; only to Ulysses' end
Am I the adjunct, whom he left so young,
That from me to him never comfort sprung.   160
And to all these now, for their race, arise
Up in their house a brood of enemies.
As many as in these isles bow men's knees,
Samos, Dulichius, and the rich-in-trees

Zacynthus, or in this rough isle's command,
So many suitors for the nuptials stand,
That ask my mother, and, mean space, prefer
Their lusts to all spoil, that dishonour her.
Nor doth she, though she loathes, deny their suits,
Nor they denials take, though taste their fruits.   170
But all this time the state of all things there
Their throats devour, and I must shortly bear
A part in all. And yet the periods
Of these designs lie in the knees of gods.
Of all loves then, Eumaeus, make quick way
To wise Penelope, and to her say
My safe return from Pylos, and alone
Return thou hither, having made it known.
Nor let, besides my mother, any ear
Partake thy message, since a number bear   180
My safe return displeasure.' He replied:

  'I know, and comprehend you. You divide
Your mind with one that understands you well.
But, all in one yet, may I not reveal
To th' old hard-fated Arcesiades
Your safe return? Who, through his whole distress
Felt for Ulysses, did not yet so grieve,
But with his household he had will to live,
And serv'd his appetite with wine and food,
Survey'd his husbandry, and did his blood   190
Some comforts fitting life; but since you took
Your ship for Pylos, he would never brook
Or wine or food, they say, nor cast an eye
On any labour, but sits weeping by,
And sighing out his sorrows, ceaseless moans
Wasting his body, turn'd all skin and bones.'

  'More sad news still,' said he, 'yet, mourn he still;
For if the rule of all men's works be will,
And his will his way goes, mine stands inclin'd
T' attend the home-turn of my nearer kind.   200
Do then what I enjoin; which giv'n effect,
Err not to field to him, but turn direct,
Entreating first my mother, with most speed,
And all the secrecy that now serves need,
To send this way their store-house guardian,
And she shall tell all to the aged man.'

  He took his shoes up, put them on, and went.

Nor was his absence hid from Jove's descent,
Divine Minerva, who took straight to view
A goodly woman's shape, that all works knew.   210
And, standing in the entry, did prefer
Her sight t' Ulysses; but, though meeting her,
His son Telemachus nor saw nor knew.
The gods' clear presences are known to few.
Yet, with Ulysses, ev'n the dogs did see,
And would not bark, but, whining lovingly,
Fled to the stall's far side; when she her eyne
Mov'd to Ulysses. He knew her design,
And left the house, pass'd the great sheep-cote's wall,
And stood before her. She bade utter all   220
Now to his son, nor keep the least unloos'd,
That, all the wooers' deaths being now dispos'd,
They might approach the town, affirming she
Not long would fail t' assist to victory.

     This said, she laid her golden rod on him,
And with his late-worn weeds grac'd every limb,
His body straighten'd, and his youth instill'd,
His fresh blood call'd up, every wrinkle fill'd
About his broken eyes, and on his chin
The brown hair spread. When his whole trim wrought in,
She issu'd, and he enter'd to his son,
Who stood amaz'd, and thought some god had done
His house that honour, turn'd away his eyes,
And said: 'Now guest, you grace another guise
Than suits your late show. Other weeds you wear,
And other person. Of the starry sphere
You certainly present some deathless god.
Be pleased, that to your here vouchsaf'd abode
We may give sacred rites, and offer gold,
To do us favour.' He replied: 'I hold   240
No deified state. Why put you thus on me
A god's resemblance? I am only he
That bears thy father's name; for whose lov'd sake
Thy youth so grieves, whose absence makes thee take
Such wrongs of men.' Thus kiss'd he him, nor could
Forbear those tears that in such mighty hold
He held before, still held, still issuing ever;
And now, the shores once broke, the springtide never
Forbore earth from the cheeks he kiss'd. His son,
By all these violent arguments not won   250

To credit him his father, did deny
His kind assumpt, and said, some deity
Feign'd that joy's cause, to make him grieve the more;
Affirming, that no man, whoever wore
The garment of mortality, could take,
By any utmost pow'r his soul could make,
Such change into it, since, at so much will,
Not Jove himself could both remove and fill
Old age with youth, and youth with age so spoil,
In such an instant. 'You wore all the soil　　　　　260
Of age but now, and were old; and but now
You bear that young grace that the gods endow
Their heav'n-born forms withal.' His father said:
'Telemachus! Admire, nor stand dismay'd,
But know thy solid father; since within
He answers all parts that adorn his skin.
There shall no more Ulysseses come here.
I am the man, that now this twentieth year
(Still under suff'rance of a world of ill)
My country earth recover. 'Tis the will　　　　　270
The prey-professor Pallas puts in act,
Who put me thus together, thus distract
In aged pieces as ev'n now you saw,
This youth now rend'ring. 'Tis within the law
Of her free pow'r. Sometimes to show me poor,
Sometimes again thus amply to restore
My youth and ornaments, she still would please.
The gods can raise, and throw men down, with ease.'
　　This said, he sat; when his Telemachus pour'd
Himself about him; tears on tears he shower'd,　　　　　280
And to desire of moan increas'd the cloud.
Both wept and howl'd, and laid out shrieks more loud
Than or the bird-bone-breaking eagle rears,
Or brood-kind vulture with the crooked seres,
When rustic hands their tender eyries draw,
Before they give their wings their full-plum'd law.
But miserably pour'd they from beneath
Their lids their tears, while both their breasts did breathe
As frequent cries; and, to their fervent moan,
The light had left the skies, if first the son　　　　　290
Their dumb moans had not vented, with demand
What ship it was that gave the natural land
To his bless'd feet? He then did likewise lay

Hand on his passion, and gave these words way:
   'I'll tell thee truth, my son: the men that bear
Much fame for shipping, my reducers were
To long-wish'd Ithaca, who each man else
That greets their shore give pass to where he dwells.
The Phaeacensian peers, in one night's date,
While I fast slept, fetch'd th' Ithacensian state,   300
Grac'd me with wealthy gifts, brass, store of gold,
And robes fair wrought; all which have secret hold
In caves that by the god's advice I chus'd.
And now Minerva's admonitions us'd
For this retreat, that we might here dispose
In close discourse the slaughters of our foes.
Recount the number of the wooers then,
And let me know what name they hold with men,
That my mind may cast over their estates
A curious measure, and confer the rates   310
Of our two pow'rs and theirs, to try if we
Alone may propagate to victory
Our bold encounters of them all, or prove
The kind assistance of some others' love.'
   'O father,' he replied, 'I oft have heard
Your counsels and your force of hand preferr'd
To mighty glory, but your speeches now
Your vent'rous mind exceeding mighty show.
Ev'n to amaze they move me; for, in right
Of no fit counsel, should be brought to fight   320
Two men 'gainst th' able faction of a throng.
No one two, no one ten, no twice ten, strong
These wooers are, but more by much. For know,
That from Dulichius there are fifty two,
All choice young men; and every one of these
Six men attend. From Samos cross'd the seas
Twice twelve young gallants. From Zacynthus came
Twice ten. Of Ithaca, the best of name,
Twice six. Of all which all the state they take
A sacred poet and a herald make.   330
Their delicacies two, of special sort
In skill of banquets, serve. And all this port
If we shall dare t' encounter, all thrust up
In one strong roof, have great care lest the cup
Your great mind thirsts exceeding bitter taste,
And your retreat commend not to your haste

Your great attempt, but make you say, you buy
Their pride's revenges at a price too high.
And therefore, if you could, 'twere well you thought
Of some assistant. Be your spirit wrought   340
In such a man's election, as may lend
His succours freely, and express a friend.'
    His father answer'd: 'Let me ask of thee;
Hear me, consider, and then answer me:
Think'st thou, if Pallas and the king of skies
We had to friend, would their sufficiencies
Make strong our part? Or that some other yet
My thoughts must work for?' 'These,' said he, 'are set
Aloft the clouds, and are found aids indeed,   350
As pow'rs not only that these men exceed,
But bear of all men else the high command,
And hold of gods an overruling hand.'
    'Well then,' said he, 'not these shall sever long
Their force and ours in fights assur'd and strong.
And then 'twixt us and them shall Mars prefer
His strength, to stand our great distinguisher,
When in mine own roofs I am forced to blows.
But when the day shall first her fires disclose,
Go thou for home, and troop up with the woo'rs,
Thy will with theirs join'd, pow'r with their rude pow'rs;
And after shall the herdsman guide to town
My steps, my person wholly overgrown
With all appearance of a poor old swain,
Heavy, and wretched. If their high disdain
Of my vile presence make them my desert
Affect with contumelies, let thy lov'd heart
Beat in fix'd confines of thy bosom still,
And see me suffer, patient of their ill.
Ay, though they drag me by the heels about
Mine own free earth, and after hurl me out,   370
Do thou still suffer. Nay, though with their darts
They beat and bruise me, bear. But these foul parts
Persuade them to forbear, and by their names
Call all with kind words, bidding, for their shames,
Their pleasures cease. If yet they yield not way,
There breaks the first light of their fatal day.
In mean space, mark this: when the chiefly wise
Minerva prompts me, I'll inform thine eyes
With some giv'n sign, and then all th' arms that are

Aloft thy roof in some near room prepare   380
For speediest use. If those brave men inquire
Thy end in all, still rake up all thy fire
In fair cool words, and say: 'I bring them down
To scour the smoke off, being so overgrown
That one would think all fumes that ever were
Breath'd since Ulysses' loss, reflected here.
These are not like the arms he left behind,
In way for Troy. Besides, Jove prompts my mind
In their remove apart thus with this thought,
That if in height of wine there should be wrought   390
Some harsh contention 'twixt you, this apt mean
To mutual bloodshed may be taken clean
From out your reach, and all the spoil prevented
Of present feast, perhaps ev'n then presented
My mother's nuptials to your long kind vows.
Steel itself, ready, draws a man to blows.'
Thus make their thoughts secure; to us alone
Two swords, two darts, two shields left; which see done
Within our readiest reach, that at our will
We may resume, and charge, and all their skill   400
Pallas and Jove, that all just counsels breathe,
May darken with secureness to their death.
And let me charge thee now, as thou art mine,
And as thy veins mine own true blood combine:
Let, after this, none know Ulysses near,
Not any one of all the household there,
Not here the herdsman, not Laertes be
Made privy, nor herself Penelope,
But only let thyself and me work out
The women's thoughts of all things borne about   410
The wooers' hearts; and then thy men approve,
To know who honours, who with rev'rence love,
Our well-weigh'd memories, and who is won
To fail thy fit right, though my only son.'
    'You teach,' said he, 'so punctually now
As I knew nothing, nor were sprung from you.
I hope, hereafter, you shall better know
What soul I bear, and that it doth not let
The least loose motion pass his natural seat.
But this course you propose will prove, I fear,   420
Small profit to us; and could wish your care
Would weigh it better, as too far about.

For time will ask much, to the sifting out
Of each man's disposition by his deeds;
And, in the mean time, every wooer feeds
Beyond satiety, nor knows how to spare.
The women yet, since they more easy are
For our inquiry, I would wish you try,
Who right your state, who do it injury.
The men I would omit, and these things make   430
Your labour after. But, to undertake
The wooers' war, I wish your utmost speed,
Especially if you could cheer the deed
With some ostent from Jove.' Thus, as the sire
Consented to the son, did here expire
Their mutual speech. And now the ship was come,
That brought the young prince and his soldiers home.
The deep hav'n reach'd, they drew the ship ashore,
Took all their arms out, and the rich gifts bore
To Clitius' house. But to Ulysses' court   440
They sent a herald first, to make report
To wise Penelope, that safe at field
Her son was left; yet, since the ship would yield
Most haste to her, he sent that first, and them
To comfort with his utmost the extreme
He knew she suffer'd. At the court now met
The herald and the herdsman, to repeat
One message to the queen. Both whom arriv'd
Within the gates, both to be foremost striv'd
In that good news. The herald, he for haste   450
Amongst the maids bestow'd it, thinking plac'd
The queen amongst them. 'Now,' said he, 'O queen,
Your lov'd son is arriv'd.' And then was seen
The queen herself, to whom the herdsman told
All that Telemachus enjoin'd he should;
All which discharg'd, his steps he back bestows,
And left both court and city for his sows.
The wooers then grew sad, soul-vex'd, and all
Made forth the court; when by the mighty wall
They took their several seat, before the gates.   460
To whom Eurymachus initiates
Their utter'd grievance: 'O,' said he, 'my friends,
A work right great begun, as proudly ends.
We said Telemachus should never make
His voyage good, nor this shore ever take

For his return's receipt; and yet we fail,
And he performs it. Come, let's man a sail,
The best in our election, and bestow
Such soldiers in her as can swiftest row,
To tell our friends that way-lay his retreat   470
'Tis safe perform'd, and make them quickly get
Their ship for Ithaca.' This was not said
Before Amphinomus in port display'd
The ship arriv'd, her sails then under-stroke,
And oars resum'd; when, laughing, thus he spoke:
    'Move for no messenger. These men are come.
Some god hath either told his turning home,
Or they themselves have seen his ship gone by,
Had her in chase, and lost her.' Instantly
They rose, and went to port; found drawn to land   480
The ship, the soldiers taking arms in hand.
The wooers themselves to council went in throng,
And not a man besides, or old or young,
Let sit amongst them. Then Eupitheus' son,
Antinous, said: 'See what the gods have done!
They only have deliver'd from our ill
The men we waylaid. Every windy hill
Hath been their watch-tower, where by turns they stood
Continual sentinel. And we made good
Our work as well, for, sun once set, we never   490
Slept wink ashore all night, but made sail ever,
This way and that, ev'n till the morning kept
Her sacred station, so to intercept
And take his life, for whom our ambush lay;
And yet hath god to his return giv'n way.
But let us prosecute with counsels here
His necessary death, nor any where
Let rest his safety; for if he survive,
Our sails will never in wish'd hav'ns arrive,
Since he is wise, hath soul and counsel too,   500
To work the people, who will never do
Our faction favour. What we then intend
Against his person, give we present end,
Before he call a council, which, believe,
His spirit will haste, and point where it doth grieve,
Stand up amongst them all, and urge his death
Decreed amongst us. Which complaint will breathe
A fire about their spleens, and blow no praise

On our ill labours. Lest they therefore raise
Pow'r to exile us from our native earth,   510
And force our lives' societies to the birth
Of foreign countries, let our speeds prevent
His coming home to this austere complaint,
At field and far from town, or in some way
Of narrow passage, with his latest day
Shown to his forward youth, his goods and lands
Left to the free division of our hands,
The moveables made all his mother's dow'r,
And his, whoever fate affords the pow'r
To celebrate with her sweet Hymen's rites.   520
Or if this please not, but your appetites
Stand to his safety, and to give him seat
In his whole birthright, let us look to eat
At his cost never more, but every man
Haste to his home, and wed with whom he can
At home, and there lay first about for dow'r,
And then the woman give his second pow'r
Of nuptial liking, and, for last, apply
His purpose with most gifts and destiny.'

    This silence caus'd; whose breach, at last, begun   530
Amphinomus, the much renowned son
Of Nisus surnam'd Aretiades,
Who from Dulichius full of flow'ry leas
Led all the wooers, and in chief did please
The queen with his discourse, because it grew
From roots of those good minds that did endue
His goodly person; who, exceeding wise,
Us'd this speech: 'Friends, I never will advise
The prince's death; for 'tis a damned thing
To put to death the issue of a king.   540
First, therefore, let's examine, what applause
The gods will give it: if the equal laws
Of Jove approve it, I myself will be
The man shall kill him, and this company
Exhort to that mind; if the gods remain
Adverse, and hate it, I advise, refrain.'

    This said Amphinomus, and pleas'd them all;
When all arose, and in Ulysses' hall
Took seat again. Then to the queen was come
The wooers' plot, to kill her son at home,   550
Since their abroad design had miss'd success,

The herald Medon (who the whole address
Knew of their counsels) making the report.
The goddess of her sex, with her fair sort
Of lovely women, at the large hall's door
(Her bright cheeks clouded with a veil she wore)
Stood, and directed to Antinous
Her sharp reproof, which she digested thus:
   'Antinous! Compos'd of injury!
Plotter of mischief! Though reports that fly   560
Amongst our Ithacensian people say
That thou, of all that glory in their sway,
Art best in words and counsels, th' art not so.
Fond, busy fellow, why plott'st thou the woe
And slaughter of my son, and dost not fear
The presidents of suppliants, when the ear
Of Jove stoops to them? 'Tis unjust to do
Slaughter for slaughter, or pay woe for woe.
Mischief for kindness, death for life sought, then,
Is an injustice to be loath'd of men.   570
Serves not thy knowledge to remember when
Thy father fled to us? Who (mov'd to wrath
Against the Taphian thieves) pursu'd with scathe
The guiltless Thesprots; in whose people's fear,
Pursuing him for wreak, he landed here,
They after him, professing both their prize
Of all his chiefly valued faculties
And more priz'd life. Of all whose bloodiest ends
Ulysses curb'd them, though they were his friends.
Yet thou, like one that no law will allow   580
The least true honour, eat'st his house up now
That fed thy father, woo'st for love his wife,
Whom thus thou griev'st, and seek'st her sole son's life!
Cease, I command thee, and command the rest
To see all thought of these foul fashions ceas'd.'
   Eurymachus replied: 'Be confident,
Thou all-of-wit-made, the most fam'd descent
Of king Icarius. Free thy spirits of fear.
There lives not any one, nor shall live here
Now, nor hereafter, while my life gives heat   590
And light to me on earth, that dares intreat
With any ill touch thy well-lov'd son,
But here I vow, and here will see it done,
His life shall stain my lance. If on his knees

The city-raser, Laertiades,
Hath made me sit, put in my hand his food,
And held his red wine to me, shall the blood
Of his Telemachus on my hand lay
The least pollution, that my life can stay?
No! I have ever charg'd him not to fear   600
Death's threat from any. And, for that most dear
Love of his father, he shall ever be
Much the most lov'd of all that live to me.
Who kills a guiltless man from man may fly,
From god his searches all escapes deny.'
     Thus cheer'd his words, but his affections still
Fear'd not to cherish foul intent to kill
Ev'n him whose life to all lives he preferr'd.
     The queen went up, and to her love appear'd
Her lord so freshly, that she wept, till sleep   610
(By Pallas forc'd on her) her eyes did steep
In his sweet humour. When the ev'n was come,
The godlike herdsman reach'd the whole way home.
Ulysses and his son for supper drest
A year-old swine, and ere their host and guest
Had got their presence, Pallas had put by
With her fair rod Ulysses' royalty,
And render'd him an aged man again,
With all his vile integuments, lest his swain
Should know him in his trim, and tell his queen,   620
In these deep secrets being not deeply seen.
     He seen, to him the prince these words did use:
'Welcome, divine Eumaeus! Now what news
Employs the city? Are the wooers come
Back from their scout dismay'd? Or here at home
Will they again attempt me?' He replied:
'These touch not my care. I was satisfied
To do, with most speed, what I went to do;
My message done, return. And yet, not so
Came my news first; a herald (met with there)   630
Forestall'd my tale, and told how safe you were.
Besides which merely necessary thing,
What in my way chanc'd I may over-bring,
Being what I know, and witness'd with mine eyes.
Where the Hermaean sepulchre doth rise
Above the city, I beheld take port
A ship, and in her many a man of sort;

Her freight was shields and lances; and methought
They were the wooers; but, of knowledge, nought
Can therein tell you.' The prince smil'd, and knew   640
They were the wooers, casting secret view
Upon his father. But what they intended
Fled far the herdsman; whose swain's labours ended,
They dress'd the supper, which, past want, was eat.
When all desire suffic'd of wine and meat,
Of other human wants they took supplies
At Sleep's soft hand, who sweetly clos'd their eyes.

THE END OF THE SIXTEENTH BOOK

BOOK SEVENTEEN

The Argument

Telemachus, return'd to town,
Makes to his curious mother known,
In part, his travels. After whom
Ulysses to the court doth come,
In good Eumaeus' guide, and press'd
To witness of the wooers' feast;
Whom, though twice ten years did bestow
In far-off parts, his dog doth know.

Another Argument

Rho   Ulysses shows
       Through all disguise.
    Whom his dog knows;
       Who knowing dies.

BOOK SEVENTEEN

BUT WHEN air's rosy birth, the Morn, arose,
　　Telemachus did for the town dispose
　　His early steps; and took to his command
His fair long lance, well sorting with his hand,
Thus parting with Eumaeus: 'Now, my friend,
I must to town, lest too far I extend
My mother's moan for me, who, till her eyes
Mine own eyes witness, varies tears and cries
Through all extremes. Do then this charge of mine,
And guide to town this hapless guest of thine,　　　　　10
To beg elsewhere his further festival.
Give they that please, I cannot give to all,
Mine own wants take up for myself my pain.
If it incense him, he the worst shall gain.
The lovely truth I love, and must be plain.'
　　'Alas, friend,' said his father, 'nor do I
Desire at all your further charity.
'Tis better beg in cities than in fields,
And take the worst a beggar's fortune yields.
Nor am I apt to stay in swine-sties more,　　　　　　20
However; ever the great chief before
The poor ranks must to every step obey.
But go; your man in my command shall sway,
Anon yet too, by favour, when your fires
Have comforted the cold heat age expires,
And when the sun's flame hath besides corrected
The early air abroad, not being protected
By these my bare weeds from the morning's frost,
Which (if so much ground is to be engross'd
By my poor feet as you report) may give　　　　　　30
Too violent charge to th' heat by which I live.'
　　This said, his son went on with spritely pace,
And to the wooers studied little grace.
Arriv'd at home, he gave his javelin stay
Against a lofty pillar, and bold way

Made further in. When having so far gone
That he transcended the fair porch of stone,
The first by far that gave his entry eye
Was nurse Euryclea: who th' embrodery
Of stools there set was giving cushions fair;   40
Who ran upon him, and her rapt repair
Shed tears for joy. About him gather'd round
The other maids, his head and shoulders crown'd
With kisses and embraces. From above
The queen herself came, like the queen of love,
Or bright Diana; cast about her son
Her kind embraces, with effusion
Of loving tears; kiss'd both his lovely eyes,
His cheeks, and forehead; and gave all supplies
With this entreaty: 'Welcome, sweetest light!   50
I never had conceit to set quick sight
On thee thus soon, when thy lov'd father's fame
As far as Pylos did thy spirit inflame,
In that search ventur'd all unknown to me.
O say, by what pow'r cam'st thou now to be
Mine eyes' dear object?' He return'd reply:
'Move me not now, when you my 'scape descry
From imminent death, to think me fresh entrapp'd,
The fear'd wound rubbing, felt before I 'scap'd.
Double not needless passion on a heart   60
Whose joy so green is, and so apt t' invert;
But pure weeds putting on, ascend and take
Your women with you, that ye all may make
Vows of full hecatombs in sacred fire
To all the godheads, if their only sire
Vouchsafe revenge of guest-rites wrong'd, which he
Is to protect as being their deity.
My way shall be directed to the hall
Of common concourse, that I thence may call
A stranger, who from off the Pylian shore   70
Came friendly with me; whom I sent before
With all my soldiers, but in chief did charge
Piraeus with him, wishing him t' enlarge
His love to him at home, in best affair,
And utmost honours, till mine own repair.'
     Her son thus spoken, his words could not bear
The wings too easily through her either ear,
But putting pure weeds on, made vows entire

Of perfect hecatombs in sacred fire
To all the deities, if their only sire   80
Vouchsaf'd revenge of guest-rites wrong'd, which he
Was to protect as being their deity.

  Her son left house, in his fair hand his lance,
His dogs attending, and, on every glance
His looks cast from them, Pallas put a grace
That made him seem of the celestial race.
Whom, come to concourse, every man admir'd.
About him throng'd the wooers, and desir'd
All good to him in tongues, but in their hearts
Most deep ills threaten'd to his most deserts.   90
Of whose huge rout once free, he cast glad eye
On some that, long before his infancy,
Were with his father great and gracious,
Grave Halitherses, Mentor, Antiphus;
To whom he went, took seat by them, and they
Inquir'd of all things since his parting day.
To them Piraeus came, and brought his guest
Along the city thither, whom not least
The prince respected, nor was long before
He rose and met him. The first word yet bore   100
Piraeus from them both, whose haste besought
The prince to send his women to see brought
The gifts from his house that Atrides gave,
Which his own roofs, he thought, would better save.

  The wise prince answer'd: 'I can scarce conceive
The way to these works. If the wooers reave
By privy stratagem my life at home,
I rather wish Piraeus may become
The master of them, than the best of these.
But, if I sow in their fields of excess   110
Slaughter and ruin, then thy trust employ,
And to me joying bring thou those with joy.'

  This said, he brought home his grief-practis'd guest;
Where both put off, both oil'd, and did invest
Themselves in rich robes, wash'd, and sate, and eat.
His mother, in a fair chair taking seat
Directly opposite, her loom applied;
Who, when her son and guest had satisfied
Their appetites with feast, said: 'O my son,
You know that ever since your sire was won   120
To go in Agamemnon's guide to Troy,

Attempting sleep, I never did enjoy
One night's good rest, but made my quiet bed
A sea blown up with sighs, with tears still shed
Embrew'd and troubled; yet, though all your miss
In your late voyage hath been made for this,
That you might know th' abode your father made,
You shun to tell me what success you had.
Now then, before the insolent access
The wooers straight will force on us, express						130
What you have heard.' 'I will,' said he, 'and true.
We came to Pylos, where the studious due
That any father could afford his son
(But new arriv'd from some course he had run
To an extreme length, in some voyage vow'd)
Nestor, the pastor of the people, show'd
To me arriv'd, in turrets thrust up high,
Where not his brave sons were more lov'd than I.
Yet of th' unconquer'd ever-sufferer,
Ulysses, never he could set his ear,						140
Alive or dead, from any earthy man.
But to the great Lacedaemonian,
Atrides, famous for his lance, he sent,
With horse and chariots, me, to learn th' event
From his relation; where I had the view
Of Argive Helen, whose strong beauties drew,
By wills of gods, so many Grecian states,
And Trojans, under such laborious fates.
Where Menelaus ask'd me, what affair
To Lacedaemon render'd my repair.						150
I told him all the truth, who made reply:
'O deed of most abhorr'd indecency!
A sort of impotents attempt his bed
Whose strength of mind hath cities levelled!
As to a lion's den, when any hind
Hath brought her young calves, to their rest inclin'd,
When he is ranging hills and herby dales,
To make of feeders there his festivals,
But, turning to his luster, calves and dam
He shows abhorr'd death, in his anger's flame:						160
So, should Ulysses find this rabble hous'd
In his free turrets, courting his espous'd,
Foul death would fall them. O, I would to Jove,
Phoebus, and Pallas, that, when he shall prove

The broad report of his exhausted store
True with his eyes, his nerves and sinews wore
That vigour then that in the Lesbian tow'rs,
Provok'd to wrestle with the iron pow'rs
Philomelides vaunted, he approv'd;
When down he hurl'd his challenger, and mov'd   170
Huge shouts from all the Achives then in view.
If, once come home, he all those forces drew
About him there to work, they all were dead,
And should find bitter his attempted bed.
But what you ask and sue for, I, as far
As I have heard the true-spoke mariner,
Will tell directly, nor delude your ear:
He told me that an island did ensphere,
In much discomfort, great Laertes' son;
And that the nymph Calypso, overrun   180
With his affection, kept him in her caves,
Where men, nor ship of pow'r to brook the waves,
Were near his convoy to his country's shore,
And where herself importun'd evermore
His quiet stay; which not obtain'd, by force
She kept his person from all else recourse.'
     This told Atrides, which was all he knew.
Nor stay'd I more, but from the gods there blew
A prosperous wind, that set me quickly here.'
     This put his mother quite from all her cheer;   190
When Theoclymenus the augur said:
     'O woman honour'd with Ulysses' bed,
Your son, no doubt, knows clearly nothing more;
Hear me yet speak, that can the truth uncore,
Nor will be curious. Jove then witness bear,
And this thy hospitable table here,
With this whole household of your blameless lord,
That at this hour his royal feet are shor'd
On his lov'd country earth, and that ev'n here
Coming, or creeping, he will see the cheer   200
These wooers make, and in his soul's field sow
Seeds that shall thrive to all their overthrow.
This, set a-shipboard, I knew sorted thus,
And cried it out to your Telemachus.'
     Penelope replied: 'Would this would prove,
You well should witness a most friendly love,
And gifts such of me, as encount'ring Fame

Should greet you with a blessed mortal's name.'
This mutual speech past, all the wooers were
Hurling the stone, and tossing of the spear,   210
Before the palace, in the paved court,
Where otherwhiles their petulant resort
Sat plotting injuries. But when the hour
Of supper enter'd, and the feeding pow'r
Brought sheep from field, that fill'd up every way
With those that us'd to furnish that purvey,
Medon, the herald (who of all the rest
Pleas'd most the wooers, and at every feast
Was ever near) said: 'You whose kind consort
Make the fair branches of the tree our court,   220
Grace it within now, and your suppers take.
You that for health, and fair contention's sake,
Will please your minds, know, bodies must have meat;
Play's worse than idleness in times to eat.'

     This said, all left, came in, cast by on thrones
And chairs their garments. Their provisions
Were sheep, swine, goats, the chiefly great and fat,
Besides an ox that from the herd they gat.
And now the king and herdsman, from the field,
In good way were to town; 'twixt whom was held   230
Some walking conference, which thus begun
The good Eumaeus: 'Guest, your will was won,
Because the prince commanded, to make way
Up to the city, though I wish'd your stay,
And to have made you guardian of my stall;
But I, in care and fear of what might fall
In after-anger of the prince, forbore.
The checks of princes touch their subjects sore.
But make we haste, the day is nearly ended,
And cold airs still are in the ev'n extended.'   240

     'I know't,' said he, 'consider all; your charge
Is giv'n to one that understands at large.
Haste then. Hereafter, you shall lead the way;
Afford your staff too, if it fit your stay,
That I may use it, since you say our pass
Is less friend to a weak foot than it was.'

     Thus cast he on his neck his nasty scrip,
All patch'd and torn; a cord, that would not slip
For knots and bracks about the mouth of it,
Made serve the turn; and then his swain did fit   250

His forc'd state with a staff. Then plied they hard
Their way to town, their cottage left in guard
To swains and dogs. And now Eumaeus led
The king along, his garments to a thread
All bare, and burn'd, and he himself hard bore
Upon his staff, at all parts like a poor
And sad old beggar. But when now they got
The rough highway, their voyage wanted not
Much of the city, where a fount they reach'd,
From whence the town their choicest water fetch'd,   260
That ever overflow'd, and curious art
Was shown about it; in which three had part,
Whose names Neritus and Polyctor were,
And famous Ithacus. It had a sphere
Of poplar, that ran round about the wall;
And into it a lofty rock let fall
Continual supply of cool clear stream.
On whose top, to the nymphs that were supreme
In those parts' loves, a stately altar rose,
Where every traveller did still impose   270
Devoted sacrifice. At this fount found
These silly travellers a man renown'd
For guard of goats, which now he had in guide,
Whose huge-stor'd herd two herdsmen kept beside,
For all herds it excell'd, and bred a feed
For wooers only. He was Dolius' seed,
And call'd Melanthius. Who casting eye
On these two there, he chid them terribly,
And so past mean, that ev'n the wretched fate
Now on Ulysses he did irritate.   280
His fume to this effect he did pursue:
'Why so, 'tis now at all parts passing true,
That ill leads ill, good evermore doth train
With like his like. Why, thou unenvied swain,
Whither dost thou lead this same victless leaguer,
This bane of banquets, this most nasty beggar,
Whose sight doth make one sad, it so abhors?
Who, with his standing in so many doors,
Hath broke his back; and all his beggary tends
To beg base crusts, but to no manly ends,   290
As asking swords, or with activity
To get a cauldron. Wouldst thou give him me,
To farm my stable, or to sweep my yard,

And bring browse to my kids, and that preferr'd,
He should be at my keeping for his pains
To drink as much whey as his thirsty veins
Would still be swilling (whey made all his fees);
His monstrous belly would oppress his knees.
But he hath learn'd to lead base life about,
And will not work, but crouch among the rout   300
For broken meat to cram his bursten gut.
Yet this I'll say, and he will find it put
In sure effect, that if he enters where
Ulysses' roofs cast shade, the stools will there
About his ears fly, all the house will throw,
And rub his ragged sides with cuffs enow.'

    Past these reviles, his manless rudeness spurn'd
Divine Ulysses; who at no part turn'd
His face from him, but had his spirit fed
With these two thoughts: if he should strike him dead 310
With his bestowed staff, or at his feet
Make his direct head and the pavement meet.
But he bore all, and entertain'd a breast
That in the strife of all extremes did rest.

    Eumaeus, frowning on him, chid him yet,
And, lifting up his hands to heav'n, he set
This bitter curse at him: 'O you that bear
Fair name to be the race of Jupiter,
Nymphs of these fountains! If Ulysses ever
Burn'd thighs to you, that, hid in fat, did never   320
Fail your acceptance, of or lamb or kid,
Grant this grace to me: let the man thus hid
Shine through his dark fate, make some god his guide,
That, to thee, goatherd, this same palate's pride
Thou driv'st afore thee, he may come and make
The scatterings of the earth, and overtake
Thy wrongs, with forcing thee to ever err
About the city, hunted by his fear.
And in the mean space may some slothful swains
Let lousy sickness gnaw thy cattle's veins.'   330

    'O gods!' replied Melanthius. 'What a curse
Hath this dog bark'd out, and can yet do worse!
This man shall I have giv'n into my hands,
When in a well-built ship to far-off lands
I shall transport him, that, should I want here,
My sale of him may find me victuals there.

And, for Ulysses, would to heav'n his joy
The silver-bearing-bow god would destroy
This day, within his house, as sure as he
The day of his return shall never see.'   340
  This said, he left them going silent on;
But he out-went them, and took straight upon
The palace royal, which he enter'd straight,
Sat with the wooers, and his trencher's freight
The carvers gave him of the flesh there vented,
But bread the reverend butleress presented.
He took against Eurymachus his place,
Who most of all the wooers gave him grace.
And now Ulysses and his swain got near,
When round about them visited their ear   350
The hollow harp's delicious-stricken string,
To which did Phemius, near the wooers, sing.
  Then by the hand Ulysses took his swain,
And said: 'Eumaeus, one may here see plain,
In many a grace, that Laertiades
Built here these turrets, and, 'mongst others these,
His whole court arm'd with such a goodly wall,
The cornice and the cope majestical,
His double gates and turrets, built too strong
For force or virtue ever to expugn.   360
I know the feasters in it now abound,
Their cates cast such a savour; and the sound
The harp gives argues an accomplish'd feast.
The gods made music banquet's dearest guest.'
  'These things,' said he,' your skill may tell with ease,
Since you are grac'd with greater knowledges.
But now consult we how these works shall sort,
If you will first approach this praised court,
And see these wooers, I remaining here;
Or I shall enter, and yourself forbear?   370
But be not you too tedious in your stay,
Lest thrust ye be and buffeted away.
Brain hath no fence for blows; look to 't, I pray.'
  'You speak to one that comprehends,' said he.
'Go you before, and here adventure me.
I have of old been used to cuffs and blows;
My mind is harden'd, having borne the throes
Of many a sour event in waves and wars,
Where knocks and buffets are no foreigners.

And this same harmful belly by no mean   380
The greatest abstinent can ever wean.
Men suffer much bane by the belly's rage;
For whose sake ships in all their equipage
Are arm'd, and set out to th' untamed seas,
Their bulks full fraught with ills to enemies.'
Such speech they chang'd; when in the yard there lay
A dog call'd Argus, which, before his way
Assum'd for Ilion, Ulysses bred,
Yet stood his pleasure then in little stead,
As being too young, but, growing to his grace,   390
Young men made choice of him for every chace,
Or of their wild goats, of their hares, or harts.
But, his king gone, and he now past his parts,
Lay all abjectly on the stable's store,
Before the ox-stall, and mules' stable door,
To keep the clothes cast from the peasants' hands,
While they laid compass on Ulysses' lands,
The dog, with ticks (unlook'd to) overgrown.
But by this dog no sooner seen but known
Was wise Ulysses; who new enter'd there,   400
Up went his dog's laid ears, and, coming near,
Up he himself rose, fawn'd, and wagg'd his stern,
Couch'd close his ears, and lay so; nor discern
Could ever more his dear-lov'd lord again.
Ulysses saw it, nor had power t' abstain
From shedding tears; which (far-off seeing his swain)
He dried from his sight clean; to whom he thus
His grief dissembled: 'Tis miraculous,
That such a dog as this should have his lair
On such a dunghill, for his form is fair.   410
And yet I know not if there were in him
Good pace or parts, for all his goodly limb,
Or he lived empty of those inward things,
As are those trencher-beagles tending kings,
Whom for their pleasure's or their glory's sake,
Or fashion, they into their favours take.'
   'This dog,' said he, 'was servant to one dead
A huge time since. But if he bore his head,
For form and quality, of such a height
As when Ulysses, bound for th' Ilion fight,   420
Or quickly after, left him, your rapt eyes
Would then admire to see him use his thighs

In strength and swiftness. He would nothing fly,
Nor anything let 'scape. If once his eye
Seiz'd any wild beast, he knew straight his scent;
Go where he would, away with him he went.
Nor was there ever any savage stood
Amongst the thickets of the deepest wood
Long time before him, but he pull'd him down,
As well by that true hunting to be shown   430
In such vast coverts, as for speed of pace
In any open lawn. For in deep chace
He was a passing wise and well-nos'd hound.
And yet is all this good in him uncrown'd
With any grace here now, nor he more fed
Than any errant cur. His king is dead,
Far from his country; and his servants are
So negligent they lend his hound no care.
Where masters rule not, but let men alone,
You never there see honest service done.   440
That man's half virtue Jove takes quite away,
That once is sun-burnt with the servile day.'
    This said, he enter'd the well-builded towers,
Up bearing right upon the glorious wooers,
And left poor Argus dead; his lord's first sight
Since that time twenty years bereft his light.
    Telemachus did far the first behold
Eumaeus enter, and made signs he should
Come up to him. He, noting, came, and took
On earth his seat. And then the master cook   450
Served in more banquet; of which part he set
Before the wooers, part the prince did get;
Who sate alone, his table plac'd aside,
To which the herald did the bread divide.
    After Eumaeus, enter'd straight the king,
Like to a poor and heavy aged thing,
Bore hard upon his staff, and was so clad
As would have made his mere beholder sad.
Upon the ashen floor his limbs he spread,
And 'gainst a cypress threshold stay'd his head,   460
The tree wrought smooth, and in a line direct
Tried by the plumb and by the architect.
The prince then bade the herdsman give him bread,
The finest there, and see that prostrated
At-all-parts plight of his giv'n all the cheer

His hands could turn to: 'Take,' said he, 'and bear
These cates to him, and bid him beg of all
These wooers here, and to their festival
Bear up with all the impudence he can;
Bashful behaviour fits no needy man.'   470

   He heard, and did his will. 'Hold guest,' said he,
'Telemachus commends these cates to thee,
Bids thee bear up, and all these wooers implore.
Wit must make impudent whom fate makes poor.'

   'O Jove,' said he, 'do my poor pray'rs the grace
To make him blessed'st of the mortal race,
And every thought now in his generous heart
To deeds that further my desires convert.'

   Thus took he in with both his hands his store,
And in the uncouth scrip, that lay before   480
His ill-shod feet, repos'd it; whence he fed
All time the music to the feasters play'd.
Both jointly ending, then began the wooers
To put in old act their tumultuous pow'rs;
When Pallas standing close did prompt her friend,
To prove how far the bounties would extend
Of those proud wooers, so to let him try
Who most, who least, had learn'd humanity.
However, no thought touch'd Minerva's mind
That any one should 'scape his wreak design'd.   490
He handsomely became all, crept about
To every wooer, held a forc'd hand out,
And all his work did in so like a way
As he had practis'd begging many a day.
And though they knew all beggars could do this,
Yet they admir'd it as no deed of his
(Though far from thought of other), used expense
And pity to him, who he was, and whence,
Inquiring mutually. Melanthius then:
'Hear me, ye wooers of the far-fam'd queen,   500
About this beggar. I have seen before
This face of his; and know for certain more,
That this swain brought him hither. What he is,
Or whence he came, flies me.' Reply to this
Antinous made, and mock'd Eumaeus thus:

   'O thou renowned herdsman, why to us
Brought'st thou this beggar? Serves it not our hands,
That other land-leapers, and cormorands,

Profane poor knaves, lie on us, unconducted,
But you must bring them? So amiss instructed   510
Art thou in course of thrift, as not to know
Thy lord's goods wrack'd in this their overflow?
Which think'st thou nothing, that thou call'st in these?'

    Eumaeus answer'd: 'Though you may be wise,
You speak not wisely. Who calls in a guest
That is a guest himself? None call to feast
Other than men that are of public use,
Prophets or poets, whom the gods produce,
Physicians for men's ills, or architects.
Such men the boundless earth affords respects   520
Bounded in honour, and may call them well.
But poor men who calls? Who doth so excel
In others' good to do himself an ill?
But all Ulysses' servants have been still
Eyesores in your way more than all that woo,
And chiefly I. But what care I for you,
As long as these roofs hold as thralls to none
The wise Penelope and her godlike son?'

    'Forbear,' said he,* 'and leave this tongue's bold ill.
Antinous uses to be crossing still,   530
And give sharp words; his blood that humour bears,
To set men still together by the ears.
But,' turning then t' Antinous, 'O,' said he,
'You entertain a father's care of me,
To turn these eating guests out. 'Tis advice
Of needful use for my poor faculties.
But god doth not allow this; there must be
Some care of poor men in humanity.
What you yourselves take, give; I not envy,
But give command that hospitality   540
Be giv'n all strangers. Nor shall my pow'rs fear,
If this mood in me reach my mother's ear –
Much less the servants', that are here to see
Ulysses' house kept in his old degree.
But you bear no such mind, your wits more cast
To fill yourself than let another taste.'

    Antinous answer'd him: 'Brave spoken man,
Whose mind's free fire see check'd no virtue can!

* Telemachus

If all we wooers here would give as much
As my mind serves, his largess should be such   550
As would for three months serve his far-off way
From troubling your house with more cause of stay.'

   This said, he took a stool up, that did rest,
Beneath the board, his spangled feet at feast,
And offer'd at him; but the rest gave all,
And fill'd his fulsome scrip with festival.
And so Ulysses for the present was,
And for the future, furnish'd, and his pass
Bent to the door to eat – yet could not leave
Antinous so, but said: 'Do you too give,   560
Lov'd lord; your presence makes a show to me
As you not worst were of the company,
But best, and so much that you seem the king,
And therefore you should give some better thing
Than bread, like others. I will spread your praise
Through all the wide world, that have in my days
Kept house myself, and trod the wealthy ways
Of other men even to the title Blest;
And often have I giv'n an erring guest
(How mean soever) to the utmost gain   570
Of what he wanted, kept whole troops of men,
And had all other comings in, with which
Men live so well, and gain the fame of rich.
Yet Jove consum'd all; he would have it so;
To which, his mean was this: he made me go
Far off, for Egypt, in the rude consort
Of all-ways-wand'ring pirates; where, in port,
I bade my lov'd men draw their ships ashore,
And dwell amongst them; sent out some t' explore
Up to the mountains, who, intemperate,   580
And their inflam'd bloods bent to satiate,
Forag'd the rich fields, hal'd the women thence,
And unwean'd children, with the foul expence
Both of their fames and bloods. The cry then flew
Straight to the city, and the great fields grew
With horse and foot, and flam'd with iron arms;
When Jove (that breaks the thunder in alarms)
An ill flight cast amongst my men, not one
Inspir'd with spirit to stand, and turn upon
The fierce pursuing foe; and therefore stood   590
Their ill fate thick about them, some in blood,

And some in bondage, toils led by constraint
Fast'ning upon them. Me along they sent
To Cyprus with a stranger prince they met,
Dmetor Iasides, who th' imperial seat
Of that sweet island sway'd in strong command.
And thus feel I here need's contemned hand.'

'And what god sent,' said he, 'this suffering bane
To vex our banquet? Stand off, nor profane
My board so boldly, lest I show thee here   600
Cyprus and Egypt made more sour than there.
You are a saucy set-faced vagabond.
About with all you go, and they, beyond
Discretion, give thee, since they find not here
The least proportion set down to their cheer.
But every fountain hath his under-floods.
It is no bounty to give others' goods.'

'O gods,' replied Ulysses, 'I see now,
You bear no soul in this your goodly show.
Beggars at your board, I perceive, should get   610
Scarce salt from your hands, if themselves brought meat,
Since sitting where another's board is spread,
That flows with feast, not to the broken bread
Will your allowance reach.' 'Nay then,' said he,
And look'd austerely, 'if so saucy be
Your suffer'd language, I suppose that clear
You shall not 'scape without some broken cheer.'

Thus rapt he up a stool, with which he smit
The king's right shoulder, 'twixt his neck and it.
He stood him like a rock. Antinous' dart   620
Not stirr'd Ulysses; who in his great heart
Deep ills projected, which, for time yet, close
He bound in silence, shook his head, and went
Out to the entry, where he then gave vent
To his full scrip, sat on the earth, and eat,
And talk'd still to the wooers: 'Hear me yet,
Ye wooers of the queen. It never grieves
A man to take blows, where for sheep, or beeves,
Or other main possessions, a man fights;
But for his harmful belly this man smites,   630
Whose love to many a man breeds many a woe.
And if the poor have gods, and furies too,
Before Antinous wear his nuptial wreath,
He shall be worn upon the dart of death.'

'Harsh guest,' said he, 'sit silent at your meat,
Or seek your desperate plight some safer seat,
Lest by the hands or heels youths drag your years,
And rend your rotten rags about your ears.'

This made the rest as highly hate his folly,
As he had violated something holy.					640
When one, ev'n of the proudest, thus began:

'Thou dost not nobly, thus to play the man
On such an errant wretch. O, ill dispos'd!
Perhaps some sacred godhead goes enclos'd
Even in his abject outside; for the gods
Have often visited these rich abodes
Like such poor stranger pilgrims, since their pow'rs
(Being always shapeful) glide through towns and tow'rs,
Observing, as they pass still, who they be
That piety love, and who impiety.'					650

This all men said, but he held sayings cheap.
And all this time Telemachus did heap
Sorrow on sorrow on his beating heart,
To see his father stricken; yet let part
No tear to earth, but shook his head, and thought
As deep as those ills that were after wrought.

The queen now, hearing of her poor guest's stroke,
Said to her maid (as to her wooer she spoke),
'I wish the famous-for-his-bow, the Sun,
Would strike thy heart so.' Her wish, thus begun,					660
Her lady, fair Eurynome, pursu'd
Her execration, and did thus conclude:
'So may our vows call down from heav'n his end,
And let no one life of the rest extend
His life till morning.' 'O Eurynome,'
Replied the queen, 'may all gods speak in thee,
For all the wooers we should rate as foes,
Since all their weals they place in others' woes!
But this Antinous we past all should hate,
As one resembling black and cruel fate.					670
A poor strange wretch begg'd here, compell'd by need,
Ask'd all, and every one gave in his deed,
Fill'd his sad scrip, and eas'd his heavy wants;
Only this man bestow'd unmanly taunts,
And with a cruel blow, his force let fly,
'Twixt neck and shoulders show'd his charity.'
These minds, above, she and her maids did show,

While, at his scrip, Ulysses sat below.
In which time she Eumaeus call'd, and said:
'Go, good Eumaeus, and see soon convey'd   680
The stranger to me; bid him come and take
My salutations for his welcome's sake,
And my desire serve, if he hath not heard
Or seen distress'd Ulysses, who hath err'd
Like such a man, and therefore chance may fall
He hath by him been met and spoke withal?'
     'O queen,' said he, 'I wish to heav'n your ear
Were quit of this unreverend noise you hear
From these rude wooers, when I bring the guest;
Such words your ear would let into your breast   690
As would delight it to your very heart.
Three nights and days I did my roof impart
To his fruition (for he came to me
The first of all men since he fled the sea)
And yet he had not given a perfect end
To his relation of what woes did spend
The spite of fate on him; but as you see
A singer, breathing out of deity
Love-kindling lines, when all men seated near
Are rapt with endless thirst to ever hear: 700
So sweeten'd he my bosom at my meat,
Affirming that Ulysses was in Crete,
Where first the memories of Minos were,
A guest to him there dwelling then, as dear
As his true father; and from thence came he
Tired on with sorrows, toss'd from sea to sea,
To cast himself in dust, and tumble here,
At wooers' feet, for blows and broken cheer.
But of Ulysses, where the Thesprots dwell,
A wealthy people, Fame, he says, did tell   710
The still survival; who his native light
Was bound for now, with treasure infinite.'
     'Call him,' said she, 'that he himself may say
This over to me. We shall soon have way
Giv'n by the wooers; they, as well at gate
As set within doors, use to recreate
Their high-fed spirits. As their humours lead
They follow – and may well, for still they tread
Uncharg'd ways here, their own wealth lying unwasted
In poor-kept houses, only something tasted   720

Their bread and wine is by their household swains,
But they themselves let loose continual reins
To our expenses, making slaughter still
Of sheep, goats, oxen, feeding past their fill,
And vainly lavishing our richest wine –
All these extending past the sacred line,
For here lives no man like Ulysses now
To curb these ruins. But should he once show
His country light his presence, he and his
Would soon revenge these wooers' injuries.'   730

This said, about the house, in echoes round,
Her son's strange sneezings made a horrid sound;
At which the queen yet laugh'd, and said: 'Go call
The stranger to me. Heard'st thou not, to all
My words last utter'd, what a sneezing brake
From my Telemachus? From whence I make
This sure conclusion: that the death and fate
Of every wooer here is near his date.
Call, then, the guest, and if he tell as true
What I shall ask him, coat, cloak, all things new,   740
These hands shall yield him.' This said, down he went,
And told Ulysses, that the queen had sent
To call him to her, that she might enquire
About her husband what her sad desire
Urg'd her to ask; and, if she found him true,
Both coat and cassock (which he needed) new
Her hands would put on him; and that the bread,
Which now he begg'd amongst the common tread,
Should freely feed his hunger now from her,
Who all he wish'd would to his wants prefer.'   750

His answer was: 'I will with fit speed tell
The whole truth to the queen; for passing well
I know her lord, since he and I have shar'd
In equal sorrows. But I much am scar'd
With this rude multitude of wooers here,
The rage of whose pride smites heav'n's brazen sphere.
Of whose rout when one struck me for no fault,
Telemachus nor none else turn'd th' assault
From my poor shoulders. Therefore, though she haste,
Beseech the queen her patience will see past   760
The day's broad light, and then may she enquire.
'Tis but my closer pressing to the fire
In th' evening's cold, because my weeds, you know,

Are passing thin; for I made bold to show
Their bracks to you, and pray'd your kind supply.'
    He heard, and hasted; and met instantly
The queen upon the pavement in his way,
Who ask'd: 'What! Bring'st thou not? What cause of stay
Find his austere supposes? Takes he fear
Of th' unjust wooers? Or thus hard doth bear   770
On any other doubt the house objects?
He does me wrong, and gives too nice respects
To his fear'd safety.' 'He does right,' said he,
'And what he fears should move the policy
Of any wise one, taking care to shun
The violent wooers. He bids bide, till sun
Hath hid his broad light. And, believe it, queen,
'Twill make your best course, since you two, unseen,
May pass th' encounter – you to speak more free,
And he your ear gain less distractedly.'   780
    'The guest is wise,' said she, 'and well doth give
The right thought use. Of all the men that live,
Life serves none such as these proud wooers are,
To give a good man cause to use his care.'
    Thus, all agreed, amongst the wooers goes
Eumaeus to the prince, and, whisp'ring close,
Said: 'Now, my love, my charge shall take up me
(Your goods and mine). What here is, you must see
In fit protection. But, in chief, regard
Your own dear safeguard; whose state study hard,   790
Lest suff'rance seize you. Many a wicked thought
Conceal these wooers; whom just Jove see brought
To utter ruin, ere it touch at us.'
    'So chance it, friend,' replied Telemachus,
'Your bever taken, go. In first of day
Come, and bring sacrifice the best you may.
To me and to th' immortals be the care
Of whatsoever here the safeties are.'
    This said, he sat in his elaborate throne.
Eumaeus (fed to satisfaction)   800
Went to his charge, left both the court and walls
Full of secure and fatal festivals,
In which the wooers' pleasures still would sway.
And now begun the ev'n's near-ending day.

THE END OF THE SEVENTEENTH BOOK

BOOK EIGHTEEN

The Argument

Ulysses and rogue Irus fight.
Penelope vouchsafes her sight
To all her wooers; who present
Gifts to her, ravish'd with content.
A certain parlé then we sing
Betwixt a wooer and the king.

Another Argument

Sigma   The beggar's glee,
       The king's high fame.
     Gifts giv'n to see
       A virtuous dame.

BOOK EIGHTEEN

THERE CAME a common beggar to the court,
 Who in the city begg'd of all resort,
 Excell'd in madness of the gut, drunk, ate
Past intermission, was most hugely great,
Yet had no fibres in him nor no force,
In sight a man, in mind a living corse.
His true name was Arnaeus, for his mother
Impos'd it from his birth, and yet another
The city youth would give him (from the course
He after took, deriv'd out of the force   10
That need held on him, which was up and down
To run on all men's errands through the town),
Which sounded Irus. When whose gut was come,
He needs would bar Ulysses his own home,
And fell to chiding him: 'Old man,' said he,
'Your way out of the entry quickly see
Be with fair language taken, lest your stay
But little longer see you dragg'd away.
See, sir, observe you not how all these make
Direct signs at me, charging me to take   20
Your heels, and drag you out? But I take shame.
Rise yet, y' are best, lest we two play a game
At cuffs together.' He bent brows, and said:
'Wretch! I do thee no ill, nor once upbraid
Thy presence with a word, nor, what mine eye
By all hands sees thee giv'n, one thought envy.
Nor shouldst thou envy others. Thou may'st see
The place will hold us both, and seem'st to me
A beggar like myself; which who can mend?
The gods give most to whom they least are friend. 30
The chief goods gods give, is in good to end.
But to the hands' strife, of which y' are so free,
Provoke me not, for fear you anger me,
And lest the old man, on whose scorn you stood,
Your lips and bosom make shake hands in blood.

I love my quiet well, and more will love
Tomorrow than to day. But if you move
My peace beyond my right, the war you make
Will never after give you will to take
Ulysses' house into your begging walk.'   40

  'O gods,' said he, 'how volubly doth talk
This eating gulf! And how his fume breaks out,
As from an old crack'd ov'n! Whom I will clout
So bitterly, and so with both hands mall
His chaps together, that his teeth shall fall
As plain seen on the earth as any sow's,
That ruts the cornfields, or devours the mows.
Come, close we now, that all may see what wrong
An old man tempts that takes at cuffs a young.'

  Thus in the entry of those lofty tow'rs   50
These two, with all spleen, spent their jarring pow'rs.
Antinous took it, laugh'd, and said: 'O friends,
We never had such sport! This guest contends
With this vast beggar at the buffets' fight.
Come, join we hands, and screw up all their spite.'

  All rose in laughters, and about them bore
All the ragg'd rout of beggars at the door.
Then moved Antinous the victor's hire
To all the wooers thus: 'There are now at fire
Two breasts of goat; both which let law set down   60
Before the man that wins the day's renown,
With all their fat and gravy. And of both
The glorious victor shall prefer his tooth,
To which he makes his choice of, from us all,
And ever after banquet in our hall,
With what our boards yield; not a beggar more
Allow'd to share, but all keep out at door.'
This he proposed; and this they all approv'd.
To which Ulysses answer'd: 'O most lov'd,
By no means should an old man, and one old   70
In chief with sorrows, be so over-bold
To combat with his younger; but, alas,
Man's own-ill-working belly needs will pass
This work upon me, and enforce me, too,
To beat this fellow. But then, you must do
My age no wrong, to take my younger's part,
And play me foul play, making your strokes' smart
Help his to conquer; for you easily may

With your strengths crush me. Do then right, and lay
Your honours on it in your oaths, to yield   80
His part no aid, but equal leave the field.'
   All swore his will. But then Telemachus
His father's scoffs with comforts serious
Could not but answer, and made this reply:
   'Guest! If thine own pow'rs cheer thy victory,
Fear no man's else that will not pass it free.
He fights with many that shall touch but thee.
I'll see thy guest-right paid. Thou here art come
In my protection; and to this the sum
Of all these wooers (which Antinous are   90
And King Eurymachus) conjoin their care.'
   Both vow'd it; when Ulysses, laying by
His upper weed, his inner beggary
Near show'd his shame, which he with rags prevented
Pluck'd from about his thighs, and so presented
Their goodly sight, which were so white and great,
And his large shoulders were to view so set
By his bare rags, his arms, his breast and all,
So broad and brawny – their grace natural
Being kept by Pallas, ever standing near –   100
That all the wooers his admirers were
Beyond all measure, mutual whispers driv'n
Through all their cluster, saying: 'Sure as heav'n
Poor Irus pull'd upon him bitter blows.
Through his thin garment what a thigh he shows!'
   They said; but Irus felt. His coward mind
Was mov'd at root. But now he needs must find
Facts to his brags; and forth at all parts fit
The servants brought him, all his arteries smit
With fears and tremblings. Which Antinous saw,   110
And said: 'Nay, now too late comes fear. No law
Thou shouldst at first have giv'n thy braggart vein,
Nor should it so have swell'd, if terrors strain
Thy spirits to this pass, for a man so old,
And worn with penuries that still lay hold
On his ragg'd person. Howsoever, take
This vow from me for firm: that if he make
Thy forces stoop, and prove his own supreme,
I'll put thee in a ship, and down the stream
Send thee ashore where King Echetus reigns   120
(The roughest tyrant that the world contains),

And he will slit thy nostrils, crop each ear,
Thy shame cut off, and give it dogs to tear.'
This shook his nerves the more. But both were now
Brought to the lists, and up did either throw
His heavy fists – Ulysses in suspense,
To strike so home that he should fright from thence
His coward soul, his trunk laid prostrate there,
Or let him take more leisure to his fear,
And stoop him by degrees. The last show'd best,   130
To strike him slightly, out of fear the rest
Would else discover him. But, peace now broke,
On his right shoulder Irus laid his stroke.
Ulysses struck him just beneath the ear,
His jawbone broke, and made the blood appear;
When straight he strew'd the dust, and made his cry
Stand for himself; with whom his teeth did lie,
Spit with his blood out; and against the ground
His heels lay sprawling. Up the hands went round
Of all the wooers, all at point to die   140
With violent laughters. Then the king did ply
The beggar's feet, and dragg'd him forth the hall,
Along the entry, to the gates and wall;
Where leaving him, he put into his hand
A staff, and bade him there use his command
On swine and dogs, and not presume to be
Lord of the guests, or of the beggary,
Since he of all men was the scum and curse;
And so bade please with that, or fare yet worse.
Then cast he on his scrip, all patch'd and rent,   150
Hung by a rotten cord, and back he went
To greet the entry's threshold with his seat.

     The wooers throng'd to him, and did entreat
With gentle words his conquest, laughing still,
Pray'd Jove and all the gods to give his will
What most it wish'd him and would joy him most,
Since he so happily had clear'd their coast
Of that unsavoury morsel; whom they vow'd
To see with all their utmost haste bestow'd
Aboard a ship, and for Epirus sent   160
To King Echetus, on whose throne was spent
The worst man's seat that breath'd. And thus was grac'd
Divine Ulysses, who with joy embrac'd
Ev'n that poor conquest. Then was set to him

The goodly goat's breast promis'd (that did swim
In fat and gravy) by Antinous.
And from a basket, by Amphinomus,
Were two breads giv'n him; who, besides, renown'd
His banquet with a golden goblet crown'd,
And this high salutation: 'Frolic, guest,   170
And be those riches that you first possest
Restored again with full as many joys,
As in your poor state I see now annoys.'
     'Amphinomus,' said he, 'you seem to me
Exceeding wise, as being the progeny
Of such a father as authentic fame
Hath told me was so, one of honour'd name,
And great revenues in Dulichius,
His fair name Nisus. He is blazon'd thus,
And you to be his son, his wisdom heiring,   180
As well as wealth, his state in nought impairing.
To prove which, always, let me tell you this
(As warning you to shun the miseries
That follow full states, if they be not held
With wisdom still at full, and so compell'd
To courses that abode not in their brows,
By too much swing, their sudden overthrows):
Of all things breathing, or that creep on earth,
Nought is more wretched than a human birth.
Bless'd men think never they can cursed be,   190
While any power lasts to move a knee.
But when the bless'd gods make them feel that smart,
That fled their faith so, as they had no heart
They bear their suff'rings, and, what well they might
Have clearly shunn'd, they then meet in despite.
The mind of man flies still out of his way,
Unless god guide and prompt it every day.
I thought me once a blessed man with men,
And fashion'd me to all so counted then,
Did all injustice like them, what for lust   200
Or any pleasure never so unjust,
I could by pow'r or violence obtain,
And gave them both in all their pow'rs the rein,
Bold of my fathers and my brothers still;
While which held good, my arts seem'd never ill.
And thus is none held simply good or bad,
But as his will is either miss'd or had.

All goods god's gifts man calls, howe'er he gets them,
And so takes all, what price soe'er god sets them,
Says nought how ill they come, nor will control   210
That ravine in him, though it cost his soul.
And these parts here I see these wooers play,
Take all that falls, and all dishonours lay
On that man's queen, that, tell your friends, doth bear
No long time's absence, but is passing near.
Let god then guide thee home, lest he may meet
In his return thy undeparted feet;
For when he enters, and sees men so rude,
The quarrel cannot but in blood conclude.'

    This said, he sacrific'd, then drunk, and then   220
Referr'd the giv'n bowl to the guide of men;
Who walk'd away, afflicted at his heart,
Shook head, and fear'd that these facts would convert
To ill in th' end; yet had not grace to fly –
Minerva stay'd him, being ordain'd to die
Upon the lance of young Ulyssides.

    So down he sat; and then did Pallas please
T' incline the queen's affections to appear
To all the wooers, to extend their cheer
To th' utmost lightning that still ushers death,   230
And made her put on as the painted sheath,
That might both set her wooers' fancies high,
And get her greater honour in the eye
Ev'n of her son and sovereign than before.
Who laughing yet, to show her humour bore
No serious appetite to that light show,
She told Eurynome, that not till now
She ever knew her entertain desire
To please her wooers' eyes, but oft on fire
She set their hate, in keeping from them still;   240
Yet now she pleased t' appear, though from no will
To do them honour, vowing she would tell
Her son that of them that should fit him well
To make use of; which was, not to converse
Too freely with their pride, nor to disperse
His thoughts amongst them, since they us'd to give
Good words, but through them ill intents did drive.

    Eurynome replied: 'With good advise
You vow his counsel, and your open guise.
Go then, advise your son, nor keep more close   250

Your cheeks, still drown'd in your eyes' overflows,
But bathe your body, and with balms make clear
Your thicken'd count'nance. Uncomposed cheer,
And ever mourning, will the marrow wear.
Nor have you cause to mourn; your son hath now
Put on that virtue which in chief your vow
Wish'd, as your blessing at his birth, might deck
His blood and person.' 'But forbear to speak
Of baths, or balmings, or of beauty, now,'
The queen replied, 'lest, urging comforts, you   260
Discomfort much, because the gods have won
The spoil of my looks since my lord was gone.
But these must serve. Call hither then to me
Hippodamia and Autonoë,
That those our train additions may supply
Our own deserts. And yet, besides, not I,
With all my age, have learn'd the boldness yet
T' expose myself to men, unless I get
Some other gracers.' This said, forth she went
To call the ladies, and much spirit spent   270
To make their utmost speed, for now their queen
Would both herself show, and make them be seen.

　　But now Minerva other projects laid,
And through Icarius' daughter's veins convey'd
Sweet sleep's desire; in whose soft fumes involv'd
She was as soon as laid, and quite dissolv'd
Were all her lineaments. The goddess then
Bestow'd immortal gifts on her, that men
Might wonder at her beauties; and the beams
That glister in the deified supremes   280
She clear'd her mourning count'nance up withal.
Ev'n such a radiance as doth round empall
Crown'd Cytherea, when her order'd places
Conduct the bevy of the dancing Graces,
She added to her own, more plump, more high,
And fairer than the polish'd ivory,
Rend'ring her parts and presence. This grace done,
Away the deity flew; and up did run
Her lovely-wristed ladies, with a noise
That blew the soft chains from her sleeping joys;   290
When she her fair eyes wip'd, and, gasping, said:

　　'O me unblest! How deep a sweet sleep spread
His shades about me! Would Diana pleas'd

To shoot me with a death no more diseas'd,
As soon as might be, that no more my moan
Might waste my blood in weepings never done,
For want of that accomplish'd virtue spher'd
In my lov'd lord, to all the Greeks preferr'd!'

Then she descended with her maids, and took
Place in the portal; whence her beamy look   300
Reach'd ev'ry wooer's heart; yet cast she on
So thin a veil, that through it quite there shone
A grace so stol'n, it pleas'd above the clear,
And sunk the knees of every wooer there,
Their minds so melted in love's vehement fires,
That to her bed she heighten'd all desires.

The prince then coming near, she said: 'O son,
Thy thoughts and judgments have not yet put on
That constancy in what becomes their good,
Which all expect in thee. Thy younger blood   310
Did sparkle choicer spirits; but, arriv'd
At this full growth, wherein their form hath thriv'd
Beyond the bounds of childhood, and when now,
Beholders should affirm "This man doth grow
Like to the rare son of his matchless sire –
His goodliness, his beauty, and his fire
Of soul aspired to," thou mak'st nothing good
Thy fate, nor fortune, nor thy height of blood,
In manage of thy actions. What a deed
Of foul desert hath thy gross suff'rance freed   320
Beneath thine own roof! A poor stranger here
Us'd most unmanly! How will this appear
To all the world, when Fame shall trumpet out,
That thus, and thus, are our guests beat about
Our court unrighted? 'Tis a blaze will show
Extremely shameful to your name and you.'

'I blame you not, O mother,' he replied,
'That this clear wrong sustain'd by me, you chide;
Yet know I both the good and bad of all,
Being past the years in which young errors fall.   330
But, all this known, skill is not so exact
To give, when once it knows, things fit their fact.
I well may doubt the prease of strangers here,
Who, bent to ill, and only my nerves near,
May do it in despite. And yet the jar
Betwixt our guest and Irus was no war

Wrought by the wooers; nor our guest sustain'd
Wrong in that action, but the conquest gain'd.
And would to Jove, Minerva, and the Sun,
That all your wooers might serve contention   340
For such a purchase as the beggar made,
And wore such weak heads! Some should death invade,
Strew'd in the entry, some embrue the hall,
Till every man had vengeance capital,
Settled like Irus at the gates, his head
Every way nodding, like one forfeited
To reeling Bacchus, knees nor feet his own,
To bear him where he's better lov'd or known.'

    Their speeches giv'n this end, Eurymachus
Began his courtship, and express'd it thus: 350

    'Most wise Icarius' daughter! If all those,
That did for Colchos' vent'rous sail dispose
For that rich purchase, had before but seen
Earth's richer prize in th' Ithacensian queen,
They had not made that voyage, but to you
Would all their virtues and their beings vow.
Should all the world know what a worth you store,
Tomorrow than today and next light, more
Your court should banquet, since to all dames you
Are far preferr'd, both for the grace of show,   360
In stature, beauty, form in every kind
Of all parts outward, and for faultless mind.'

    'Alas,' said she, 'my virtue, body, form,
The gods have blasted with that only storm
That ravish'd Greece to Ilion, since my lord,
For that war shipp'd, bore all my goods aboard.
If he, return'd, should come and govern here
My life's whole state, the grace of all things there
His guide would heighten, as the spirit it bore,
Which dead in me lives, giv'n him long before.   370
A sad course I live now; heav'n's stern decree
With many an ill hath numb'd and deaded me.
He took life with him, when he took my hand
In parting from me to the Trojan strand,
These words my witness: "Woman! I conceive
That not all th' Achives bound for Troy shall leave
Their native earth their safe returned bones,
Fame saying that Troy trains up approved sons
In deeds of arms, brave putters-off of shafts,

For winging lances masters of their crafts,   380
Unmatched riders, swift of foot, and straight
Can arbitrate a war of deadliest weight.
Hope then can scarce fill all with life's supply,
And of all any failing, why not I?
Nor do I know, if god hath marshall'd me
Amongst the safe-return'd, or his decree
Hath left me to the thraldom order'd there.
However, all cares be thy burthens here,
My sire and mother tend as much as now;
I further off, more near in cares be you.   390
Your son to man's state grown, wed whom you will
And, you gone, his care let his household fill."
Thus made my lord his will, which heav'n sees prov'd
Almost at all parts; for the sun remov'd
Down to his set, ere long will lead the night
Of those abhorred nuptials, that should fright
Each worthy woman, which her second are
With any man that breathes, her first lord's care
Dead, because he to flesh and blood is dead;
Which, I fear, I shall yield to, and so wed   400
A second husband; and my reason is,
Since Jove hath taken from me all his bliss.
Whom god gives over they themselves forsake,
Their griefs their joys, their god their devil, make.
And 'tis a great grief, nor was seen till now
In any fashion of such men as woo
A good and wealthy woman, and contend
Who shall obtain her, that those men should spend
Her beeves and best sheep, as their chiefest ends,
But rather that herself and all her friends   410
They should with banquets and rich gifts entreat.
Their life is death that live with other's meat.'

    Divine Ulysses much rejoic'd to hear
His queen thus fish for gifts, and keep in cheer
Their hearts with hope that she would wed again,
Her mind yet still her first intent retain.

    Antinous saw the wooers won to give,
And said: 'Wise queen, by all your means receive
Whatever bounty any wooer shall use.
Gifts freely given 'tis folly to refuse.   420
For know, that we resolve not to be gone
To keep our own roofs, till of all some one,

Whom best you like, your long-woo'd love shall win.'
　　This pleas'd the rest, and every one sent in
His present by the herald. First had place
Antinous' gift: a robe of special grace,
Exceeding full and fair, and twenty hues
Changed lustre to it; to which choice of shows,
Twelve massy plated buttons, all of gold,
Enrich'd the substance, made to fairly hold　　　　　　430
The robe together, all lac'd down before,
Where keeps and catches both sides of it wore.
　　Eurymachus a golden tablet gave,
In which did art her choicest works engrave;
And round about an amber verge did run,
That cast a radiance from it like the sun.
　　Eurydamas two servants had, that bore
Two goodly earrings, whose rich hollows wore
Three pearls in either, like so many eyes,
Reflecting glances radiant as the skies.　　　　　　440
　　The king Pisander, great Polyctor's heir,
A casket gave, exceeding rich and fair.
　　The other other wealthy gifts commended
To her fair hand; which took, and straight ascended
This goddess of her sex her upper state,
Her ladies all her gifts elaborate
Up bearing after. All to dancing then
The wooers went, and song's delightful strain;
In which they frolick'd, till the evening came,
And then rais'd sable Hesperus his flame.　　　　　　450
When, for their lights within, they set up there
Three lamps, whose wicks were wood exceeding sere,
And passing porous; which they caus'd to burn,
Their matter ever minister'd by turn
Of several handmaids. Whom Ulysses seeing
Too conversant with wooers, ill agreeing
With guise of maids, advis'd in this fair sort:
'Maids of your long-lack'd king, keep you the port
Your queen's chaste presence bears. Go up to her,
Employ your looms or rocks, and keep ye there;　　　　460
I'll serve to feed these lamps, should these lords' dances
Last till Aurora cheer'd us with her glances.
They cannot weary me, for I am one
Born to endure when all men else have done.'
　　They wantonly brake out in laughters all,

Look'd on each other, and to terms did fall
Cheek-proud Melantho, who was Dolius' seed,
Kept by the queen, that gave her dainty bread
Fit for her daughter; and yet won not so
Her heart to her to share in any woe   470
She suffer'd for her lord, but she was great
With great Eurymachus, and her love's heat
In his bed quench'd. And this choleric thing
Bestow'd this railing language on the king:
    'Base stranger, you are taken in your brain,
You talk so wildly. Never you again
Can get where you were born, and seek your bed
In some smith's hovel, or the marketstead,
But here you must take confidence to prate
Before all these; for fear can get no state   480
In your wine-hardy stomach. Or 'tis like
To prove your native garb, your tongue will strike
On this side of your mouth still, being at best.
Is the man idle-brain'd for want of rest?
Or proud because he beat the roguish beggar?
Take heed, sir, lest some better man beleager
Your ears with his fists, and set headlong hence
Your bold abode here, with your blood's expence.'
    He, looking sternly on her, answer'd her:
'Dog! What broad language giv'st thou? I'll prefer   490
Your usage to the prince, that he may fall
Foul on your fair limbs till he tell them all.'
    This fray'd the wenches, and all straight got gone
In fear about their business, every one
Confessing he said well. But he stood now
Close by the cressets, and did looks bestow
On all men there, his brain employ'd about
Some sharper business than to dance it out,
Which had not long to go. Nor therefore would
Minerva let the wooers' spleens grow cold   500
With too good usage of him, that his heart
Might fret enough, and make his choler smart.
Eurymachus provok'd him first, and made
His fellow laugh, with a conceit he had
Fetch'd far from what was spoken long before,
That his poor form perhaps some deity bore.
'It well may chance,' said he, 'some god doth bear
This man's resemblance; for, thus standing near

The glistering torches, his slick'd head doth throw
Beams round about it as those cressets do,   510
For not a hair he hath to give it shade.
Say, will thy heart serve t' undertake a trade
For fitting wages? Should I take thee hence
To walk my grounds, and look to every fence,
Or plant high trees, thy hire should raise thy forces,
Food store, and clothes. But these same idle courses
Thou art so prompt in that thou wilt not work,
But forage up and down, and beg, and lurk
In every house whose roofs hold any will
To feed such fellows. That thy gut may fill,   520
Gives end to all thy being.' He replied:
    'I wish at any work we two were tried,
In height of spring-time, when heav'n's lights are long;
I a good crook'd scythe that were sharp and strong,
You such another, where the grass grew deep,
Up by day-break, and both our labours keep
Up till slow darkness eas'd the labouring light,
Fasting all day, and not a crumb till night;
We then should prove our either workmanship.
Or if, again, beeves that the goad or whip   530
Were apt t' obey before a tearing plow,
Big lusty beasts, alike in bulk and brow,
Alike in labour, and alike in strength,
Our task four acres, to be till'd in length
Of one sole day; again then you should try
If the dull glebe before the plow should fly,
Or I a long stitch could bear clean and ev'n.
Or lastly, if the guide of earth and heav'n
Should stir stern war up, either here or there,
And that at this day I had double spear   540
And shield, and steel casque fitting for my brows
At this work likewise, 'midst the foremost blows,
Your eyes should note me, and get little cause
To twit me with my belly's sole applause.
But you affect t' affect with injury,
Your mind ungentle, seem in valour high,
Because 'gainst few, and those not of the best,
Your conversation hath been still profess'd.
But if Ulysses, landed on his earth,
And enter'd on the true right of his birth,   550
Should come and front ye, straight his ample gates

Your feet would hold too narrow for your fates.'
　　He frowned, raged, call'd him wretch, and vow'd
To be his death, since he durst prove so proud
Amongst so many, to tell him so home
What he affected; ask'd, if overcome
With wine he were, or, as his minion said,
Talk'd still so idly, and were palsied
In his mind's instruments, or was proud because
He gat from Irus off with such applause?   560
With all which, snatching up a stool, he threw;
When old Ulysses to the knees withdrew
Of the Dulichian lord, Amphinomus,
As if he fear'd him – his dart missing thus
His aged object – and his page's hand
(A boy that waited on his cup's command,
Now holding of an ew'r to him) he smit.
Down fell the sounding ew'r, and after it
The guiltless page lay sprawling in the dust,
And crying out. When all the wooers thrust   570
A tumult up amongst them, wishing all
The rogue had perish'd in some hospital,
Before his life there stirr'd such uproars up,
And with rude speeches spice their pleasures' cup.
And all this for a beggar to fulfil
A filthy proverb: 'Good still yields to ill.'
　　The prince cried out on them, to let the bad
Obscure the good so; told them they were mad,
Abus'd their banquet, and affirm'd some god
Tried mast'ries with them; bade them take their load   580
Of food and wine, sit up, or fall to bed
At their free pleasures; and since he gave head
To all their freedoms, why should they mistake
Their own rich humours for a beggar's sake?
　　All bit their lips to be so taken down,
And taught the course that should have been their own,
Admir'd the prince, and said he bravely spoke.
But Nisus' son then struck the equal stroke,
And said: 'O friends, let no man here disdain
To put up equal speeches, nor maintain   590
With serious words an humour, nor with stroke
A stranger in another's house provoke,
Nor touch the meanest servant, but confine
All these dissensions in a bowl of wine;

Which fill us, cup-bearer, that having done
Our nightly sacrifice, we may atone
Our pow'rs with sleep, resigning first the guest
Up to the prince, that holds all interest
In his disposure here, the house being his
In just descent, and all the faculties.'   600

    This all approv'd; when noble Mulius,
Herald in chief to lord Amphinomus,
The wine distributed with reverend grace
To every wooer; when the gods giv'n place
With service fit, they serv'd themselves, and took
Their parting cups, till, when they all had shook
The angry humour off, they bent to rest,
And every wooer to several roofs address'd.

THE END OF THE EIGHTEENTH BOOK

BOOK NINETEEN

The Argument

Ulysses and his son eschew
Offending of the wooers' view
With any armour. His birth's seat,
Ulysses tells his queen, is Crete.
Euryclea the truth yet found,
Discover'd by a scar-healed wound,
Which in Parnassus' tops a boar,
Struck by him in his chase, did gore.

Another Argument

Tau   The king, still hid
      By what he said,
    By what he did
      Informs his maid.

BOOK NINETEEN

YET DID divine Ulysses keep his roof,
And with Minerva plotted still the proof
Of all the wooers' deaths; when thus his son
He taught with these fore-counsels: 'We must run
A close course with these arms, and lay them by,
And to the wooers make so fair a sky
As it would never thunder. Let me then,
That you may well retain, repeat again
What in Eumaeus' cottage I advis'd:
If when they see no leisure exercis'd   10
In fetching down your arms, and ask what use
Your mind will give them, say, 'tis their abuse
With smoke and rust that makes you take them down,
This not being like the armory well known
To be the leavings of Laertes' son
Consorting the design for Ilion;
Your eyes may see how much they are infected,
As all fires' vapours ever since reflected
On those sole arms. Besides, a graver thought
Jove graves within you, lest, their spirits wrought   20
Above their pitch with wine, they might contend
At some high banquet, and to wounds transcend,
Their feast inverting; which, perhaps, may be
Their nuptial feast with wise Penelope.
The ready weapon, when the blood is up,
Doubles the uproar heighten'd by the cup.
Wrath's means for act curb all the ways ye can.
As loadstones draw the steel, so steel draws man.
Retain these words; nor what is good think, thus
Receiv'd at second hand, superfluous.'   30
    The son, obeying, did Euryclea call,
And bade her shut in th' outer porches all
The other women, till himself brought down
His father's arms, which all were overgrown
By his neglect with rust, his father gone,

And he too childish to spend thoughts upon
Those manly implements; but he would now
Reform those young neglects, and th' arms bestow
Past reach of smoke. The loving nurse replied:
  'I wish, O son, your pow'rs would once provide   40
For wisdom's habit, see your household were
In thrifty manage, and tend all things there.
But if these arms must down, and every maid
Be shut in outer rooms, who else should aid
Your work with light?' He answer'd: 'This my guest.
There shall no one in my house taste my feast,
Or join in my nave, that shall idly live,
However far hence he his home derive.'
  He said, and his words stood. The doors she shut
Of that so well-fill'd house. And th' other put   50
Their thoughts in act; best shields, helms, sharpen'd lances,
Brought down; and Pallas before both advances
A golden cresset, that did cast a light
As if the day sat in the throne of night.
  When, half amaz'd, the prince said: 'O my father,
Mine eyes my soul's pow'rs all in wonder gather,
For though the walls and goodly wind-beams here,
And all these pillars that their heads so rear,
And all of fir, they seem yet all of fire.
Some god is surely with us.' His wise sire   60
Bade peace, and keep the counsels of the gods,
Nor ask a word: 'These pow'rs, that use abodes
Above the stars, have pow'r from thence to shine
Through night and all shades to earth's inmost mine.
Go thou for sleep, and leave me here to wake
The women and the queen, whose heart doth ache
To make inquiry for myself of me.'
  He went to sleep where lights did endlessly
Burn in his night-rooms; where he feasted rest,
Till day's fair weed did all the world invest.   70
Thus was divine Ulysses left alone
With Pallas, plotting foul confusion
To all the wooers. Forth then came the queen;
Phoebe, with golden Cytherea seen,
Her port presented. Whom they set a chair
Aside the fire, the fashion circular,
The substance silver and rich elephant;
Whose fabric did the cunning finger vaunt

Of great Icmalius, who besides had done
A footstool for her that did suit her throne,   80
On which they cast an ample skin, to be
The cushion for her other royalty.
And there she sat; about whom came her maids,
Who brought upon a table store of breads,
And bowls that with the wooers' wine were crown'd.
The embers then they cast upon the ground
From out the lamps, and other fuel added,
That still with cheerful flame the sad house gladded.
　　Melantho seeing still Ulysses there,
Thus she held out her spleen: 'Still, stranger, here?   90
Thus late in night? To see what ladies do?
Avaunt you, wretch; hence, go without doors, go;
And quickly, too, lest ye be singed away
With burning firebrands.' He, thus seeing their fray
Continu'd by her with such spleen, replied:
　　'Minion! What makes your angry blood thus chide
My presence still? Is it because you see
I shine not in your wanton bravery,
But wear these rags? It fits the needy fate
That makes me beg thus of the common state.   100
Such poor souls, and such beggars, yet are men;
And ev'n my mean means means had to maintain
A wealthy house, and kept a manly press,
Was counted blessed, and the poor access
Of any beggar did not scorn, but feed
With often hand, and any man of need
Reliev'd as fitted; kept my servants, too,
Not few, but did with those additions go
That call choice men "The Honest", who are styl'd
The rich, the great. But what such great ones build   110
Jove oft pulls down, as thus he ruin'd me;
His will was such, which is his equity.
And therefore, woman, bear you fitting hand
On your behaviour, lest your spirit thus mann'd,
And cherish'd with your beauties, when they wane,
Comes down, your pride now being then your bane;
And in the mean space shun the present danger,
Lest your bold fashion breed your sovereign's anger,
Or lest Ulysses come, of whom ev'n yet
Hope finds some life in fate. Or, be his seat   120
Amongst the merely ruin'd, yet his son,

Whose life's heat Phoebus saves, is such a one
As can discover who doth well deserve
Of any woman here his years now serve.'

    The queen gave ear, and thus suppress'd the flame:
'Thou quite without a brow, past female shame,
I hear thy monstrous boldness, which thy head
Shall pay me pains for. Thou hast heard it said,
And from myself too, and at every part
Thy knowledge serves thee, that to ease my heart   130
So punish'd in thy witness, my desire
Dwelt on this stranger, that I might inquire
My lost friend's being. But 'tis ever tried,
Both man and god are still forgot with pride.
Eurynome, bring here this guest a seat
And cushion on it, that we two may treat
Of the affair in question. Set it near,
That I may softly speak, yet he well hear.'

    She did this little freely; and he sat
Close by the queen, who ask'd him, whence, and what   140
He was himself? And what th' inhabited place
Where liv'd his parents? Whence he fetch'd his race?

    'O woman,' he replied, 'with whom no man,
That moves in earth's unbounded circle, can
Maintain contention for true honour giv'n,
Whose fame hath reach'd the fairly-flowing heav'n,
Who, like a never-ill-deserving king,
That is well spoke of, first for worshipping,
And striving to resemble god in empire;
Whose equal hand impartially doth temper   150
Greatness and goodness; to whom therefore bears
The black earth store of all grain, trees confers
Cracking with burthen, long-liv'd herds creates,
All which the sea with her sorts emulates;
And all this feeds beneath his powerful hand
Men valiant, many, making strong his land
With happy lives led; nothing else the cause
Of all these blessings but well-order'd laws:
Like such a king are you, in love, in fame,
And all the bliss that deifies a dame.   160
And therefore do not mix this with a moan
So wretched as is now in question;
Ask not my race nor country, lest you fill
My heart yet fuller with repeated ill;

For I must follow it with many tears,
Though 'tis not seemly to sit wounding ears
In public roofs with our particular life.
Time's worst expense is still-repeated grief.
I should be irksome to your ladies here,
And you yourself would say you urg'd your ear   170
To what offends it, my still-broken eyne
Supposing wounded with your too-much wine.'
   'Stranger,' said she, 'you fear your own excess
With giving me too great a nobleness.
The gods my person, beauty, virtue too,
Long since subverted, when the Ilion woe
The Greek design attempted; in which went
My praise and honour. In his government
Had I deserv'd your utmost grace, but now
Sinister deity makes dishonour woo,   180
In show of grace, my ruin. All the peers –
Sylvan Zacynthus' and Dulichius' spheres,
Samos and Ithaca – strange strifes have shown
To win me, spending on me all mine own;
Will wed me, in my spite; and these are those
That take from me all virtue to dispose
Or guest or suppliant, or take any course
Amongst my heralds, that should all disburse,
To order anything. Though I need none
To give me grief at home, abroad errs one   190
That my veins shrink for, whom these holding gone,
Their nuptials hasten, and find me as slow.
Good spirits prompted me to make a show
Of undertaking a most curious task,
That an unmeasur'd space of time would ask;
Which they enduring long would often say,
"When ends thy work?" I soon had my delay,
And pray'd their stay; for though my lord were dead,
His father's life yet matter ministred
That must employ me; which, to tell them true,   200
Was that great work I nam'd. For now near drew
Laertes' death, and on my hand did lie
His funeral-robe, whose end, being now so nigh,
I must not leave, and lose so much begun,
The rather lest the Greek dames might be won
To tax mine honour, if a man so great
Should greet his grave without his winding sheet.

Pride made them credulous, and I went on;
When whatsoever all the day had done
I made the night help to undo again,   210
Though oil and watch it cost, and equal pain.
Three years my wit secur'd me undiscern'd,
Yet, when the fourth came, by my maids discern'd,
False careless wenches, how they were deluded;
When, by my light discern'd, they all intruded,
Us'd threat'ning words, and made me give it end.
And then could I to no more length extend
My linger'd nuptials; not a counsel more
Was to be stood upon; my parents bore
Continual hand on me to make me wed;   220
My son grew angry that so ruined
His goods were by them. He is now a man
Wise in a great degree, and one that can
Himself give order to his household fare –
And Jove give equal glory to his care.
But thus you must not pass me; I must know,
It may be for more end, from whence doth grow
Your race and you; for I suppose you none
Sprung of old oak, or justled out of stone.'

He answer'd: 'O Ulysses' reverend wife!   230
Yet hold you purpose to inquire my life?
I'll tell you, though it much afflict me more
Than all the sorrows I have felt before –
As worthily it may, since so long time
As I have wander'd from my native clime
Through human cities, and in suff'rance still,
To rip all wounds up, though of all their ill
I touch but part, must actuate all their pain.
But, ask you still, I'll tell, though still sustain.

In middle of the sable sea there lies   240
An isle call'd Crete, a ravisher of eyes,
Fruitful, and mann'd with many an infinite store;
Where ninety cities crown the famous shore,
Mix'd with all-languag'd men. There Greeks survive,
There the great-minded Eteocretans live,
There the Dorensians never out of war,
The Cydons there, and there the singular
Pelasgian people. There doth Cnossus stand,
That mighty city, where had most command
Great Jove's disciple, Minos, who nine years   250

Conferr'd with Jove, both great familiars
In mutual counsels. And this Minos' son,
The mighty-minded king Deucalion,
Was sire to me and royal Idomen,
Who with Atrides went to Ilion then,
My elder brother and the better man,
My name Aëthon. At that time began
My knowledge of Ulysses, whom my home
Receiv'd with guest-rites. He was thither come
By force of weather, from the Malean coast   260
But new got off, where he the navy lost,
Then under sail for Troy, and wind-bound lay
Long in Amnisus, hardly got away
From horrid storms, that made him anchor there,
In hav'ns that sacred to Lucina were,
Dreadful and dangerous, in whose bosom crept
Lucina's cavern. But in my roof slept
Ulysses, shor'd in Crete; who first inquir'd
For royal Idomen, and much desir'd
To taste his guest-rites, since to him had been   270
A welcome guest my brother Idomen.
The tenth or 'leventh light on Ulysses shin'd
In stay at Crete, attending then the wind
For threaten'd Ilion. All which time my house
With love and entertainments curious
Embrac'd his person, though a number more
My hospitable roofs receiv'd before.
His men I likewise call'd, and from the store
Allow'd them meal and heat-exciting wine,
And oxen for their slaughter, to confine   280
In my free hand the utmost of their need.
Twelve days the Greeks stay'd, ere they got them freed,
A gale so bitter blew out of the north,
That none could stand on earth, being tumbled forth
By some stern god. But on the thirteenth day
The tempest ceas'd, and then went Greeks their way.'
      Thus many tales Ulysses told his wife,
At most but painting, yet most like the life;
Of which her heart such sense took through her ears,
It made her weep as she would turn to tears.   290
And as from off the mountains melts the snow,
Which Zephyr's breath conceal'd, but was made flow
By hollow Eurus, which so fast pours down,

That with their torrent floods have overflown:
So down her fair cheeks her kind tears did glide,
Her miss'd lord mourning, set so near her side.
　　Ulysses much was mov'd to see her mourn;
Whose eyes yet stood as dry as iron or horn
In his untroubled lids, which in his craft
Of bridling passion he from issue sav'd.   300
　　When she had given her moan so many tears,
That now 'twas satiate, her yet loving fears
Ask'd thus much further: 'You have thus far tried
My love's credulity, but if gratified
With so long stay he was with you, you can
Describe what weed he wore, what kind of man
Both he himself was, and what followers
Observ'd him there.' 'Alas,' said he, 'the years
Have grown so many since – this making now
Their twentieth revolution – that my show   310
Of these slight notes will set my memory sore;
But, to my now remembrance, this he wore:
A double purple robe, drawn close before
With golden buttons, plaited thick, and bore
A facing where a hundred colours shin'd.
About the skirts a hound a freckled hind
In full course hunted; on the foreskirts, yet,
He pinch'd and pull'd her down, when with her feet,
And all her force, she struggled hard for flight.
Which had such life in gold, that to the sight   320
It seem'd the hind itself for every hue,
The hound and all so answering the view,
That all admir'd all. I observ'd beside
His inner weed, so rarely beautified
That dumb amaze it bred, and was as thin
As any dry and tender onion skin;
As soft 'twas, too, and glister'd like the sun.
The women were to loving wonder won
By him and by his weeds. But, by the way,
You must excuse me, that I cannot say   330
He brought this suit from home, or had it there
Sent for some present, or, perhaps, elsewhere
Receiv'd it for his guest-gift; for your lord
Had friends not few, the fleet did not afford
Many that had not fewer. I bestow'd
A well-edg'd sword on him, a robe that flow'd

In folds and fulness, and did reach his feet,
Of richest purple; brought him to his fleet
With all my honour; and besides, to add
To all this sifted circumstance, he had　　　　　　340
A herald there, in height a little more
Put from the earth, that thicker shoulders wore,
A swarth complexion and a curled head,
His name Eurybates; and much in stead
He stood your king, employ'd in most command,
Since most of all his mind could understand.'
　　When all these signs she knew for chiefly true,
Desire of moan upon her beauties grew,
And yet, ev'n that desire suffic'd, she said:
　　'Till this, my guest, a wretched state array'd　　　350
Your ill-us'd person, but from this hour forth
You shall be honour'd, and find all the worth
That fits a friend. Those weeds these hands bestow'd
From my wardrobe, those gold buttons sew'd
Before for closure and for ornament.
But never more must his return present
The person that gave those adornments state;
And therefore, under an abhorred fate,
Was he induc'd to feed the common fame,
To visit vile Troy, ay too vile to name.'　　　　　360
　　'No more yet mourn,' said he, 'nor thus see pin'd
Your lovely person. Weeping wastes the mind.
And yet I blame you not; for any dame
That weds one young, and brings to him his name,
Whatever man he is, will mourn his loss.
Much more respectful then must show your woes
That weep thus for Ulysses, who, fame says,
Was equal with the gods in all his ways.
But where no cause is there must be no moan;
And therefore hear me, my relation　　　　　　370
Shall lay the clear truth naked to your view:
I heard amongst the Thesprots for most true,
That lord Ulysses liv'd, and stood just now
On his return for home; that wealth did flow
In his possession, which he made not known,
But begg'd amongst the people, since alone
He quite was left, for all his men were lost
In getting off from the Trinacrian coast;
Jove and the Sun was wroth with them for rape

Made of his oxen, and no man let 'scape   380
The rugged deeps of Neptune; only he,
The ship's keel only keeping, was by sea
Cast on the fair Phaeacian continent,
Where men survive that are the gods' descent,
And like a god receiv'd him, gave him heaps
Of wealthy gifts, and would conduct his steps
Themselves safe home; which he might long ago
His pleasure make, but profit would not so.
He gather'd going, and had mighty store
Of gold in safeguard; so beyond the shore   390
That common sails kept, his high food of wit
Bore glorious top, and all the world for it
Hath far exceeded. All this Phaedon told,
That doth the sceptre of Thesprotia hold,
Who swore to me, in household sacrifice,
The ship was launch'd, and men to man the prise,
That soon should set him on his country earth;
Show'd me the goods, enough to serve the birth
That in the tenth age of his seed should spring,
Yet in his court contain'd. But then the king,   400
Your husband, for Dodona was in way,
That from th' oraculous oak he might display
Jove's will what course for home would best prevail,
To come in pomp, or bear a secret sail.
But me the king dispatch'd in course before,
A ship then bound for the Dulichian shore.
So thus you see his safety whom you mourn;
Who now is passing near, and his return
No more will punish with delays, but see
His friends and country. All which truth to thee   410
I'll seal with sacred oath. Be witness, Jove,
Thou first and best of all the thron'd above!
And thou house of the great Laertes' heir,
To whose high roofs I tender my repair,
That what I tell the queen event shall crown!
This year Ulysses shall possess his own,
Nay ere the next month ends shall here arrive,
Nay, ere it enters, here abide alive!'

　　'O may this prove,' said she, 'gifts, friendship then
Should make your name the most renown'd of men.   420
But 'tis of me receiv'd, and must so sort,
That nor my lord shall ever see his court,

Nor you gain your deduction thence, for now
The alter'd house doth no such man allow
As was Ulysses, if he ever were,
To entertain a reverend passenger,
And give him fair dismission. But, maids, see
Ye bathe his feet, and then with tapestry,
Best sheets and blankets, make his bed, and lay
Soft waistcoats by him, that, lodg'd warm, he may   430
Ev'n till the golden-seated morning's ray
Enjoy good rest; and then, with her first light,
Bathe, and give alms, that cherish'd appetite
He may apply within our hall, and sit
Safe by Telemachus. Or, if th' unfit
And harmful mind of any be so base
To grieve his age again, let none give grace
Of doing any deed he shall command,
How wroth soever, to his barbarous hand.
For how shall you, guest, know me for a dame   440
That pass so far, nay, turn and wind the fame
Of other dames for wisdom, and the frame
Of household usage, if your poor thin weeds
I let draw on you want, and worser deeds,
That may, perhaps, cause here your latest day?
The life of man is short and flies away.
And if the ruler's self of households be
Ungentle, studying inhumanity,
The rest prove worse, but he bears all the blame;
All men will, living, vow against his name   450
Mischiefs and miseries, and, dead, supply
With bitter epitaphs his memory.
But if himself be noble, noble things
Doing and knowing, all his underlings
Will imitate his noblesse, and all guests
Give it, in many, many interests.'

   'But, worthiest queen,' said he, 'where you command
Baths and rich beds for me, I scorn to stand
On such state now, nor ever thought it yet,
Since first I left the snowy hills of Crete.   460
When once I fell a-shipboard those thoughts fled;
I love to take now, as long since, my bed.
Though I began the use with sleepless nights,
I many a darkness with right homely rites
Have spent ere this hour, and desir'd the morn

Would come, and make sleep to the world a scorn.
Nor run these dainty baths in my rude head;
Nor any handmaid, to your service bred,
Shall touch my ill-kept feet, unless there live
Some poor old drudge here, that hath learn'd to give   470
Old men good usage, and no work will fly,
As having suffer'd ill as much as I.
But if there live one such in your command,
I will not shame to give my foot her hand.'

    She gave this answer: 'O my loved guest,
There never enter'd these kind roofs for rest
Stranger or friend that so much wisdom laid
In gage for guest-rites, as your lips have paid.
There lives an old maid in my charge that knows
The good you speak of by her many woes;   480
That nourish'd and brought up, with curious care,
Th' unhappy man, your old familiar,
Ev'n since his mother let him view the light,
And oft hath felt in her weak arms his weight;
And she, though now much weaker, shall apply
Her maiden service to your modesty.
Euryclea, rise, and wash the feet of one
That is of one age with your sovereign gone,
Such hands, such feet hath, though of alter'd grace.
Much grief in men will bring on change apace.'   490

    She, from her aged slumber wak'd, did clear
Her heavy eyes, and instantly, to hear
Her sovereign's name, had work enough to dry
Her cheeks from tears, and to his memory
These moans did offer: 'O my son,' said she,
'I never can take grief enough for thee,
Whom goodness hurts, and whom even Jove's high spleen,
Since thou art Jove-like, hates the most of men.
For none hath offer'd him so many thighs,
Nor such whole hecatombs of sacrifice,   500
Fat and selected, as thy zeal hath done;
For all, but praying that thy noble son
Thy happy age might see at state of man.
And yet hath Jove with mists Cimmerian
Put out the light of his returning day.
And as yourself, O father, in your way
Took these fair roofs for hospitable rites,
Yet find, for them, our dogged women's spites:

So he, in like course, being driv'n to proof,
Long time ere this, what such a royal roof　　　510
Would yield his miseries, found such usage there.
And you, now flying the foul language here,
And many a filthy fact of our fair dames,
Fly me like them, and put on causeless shames
To let me cleanse your feet. For not the cause
The queen's command yields is the pow'r that draws
My will to wash your feet, but what I do
Proceeds from her charge and your reverence too,
Since I in soul am stricken with a ruth
Of your distresses, and past show of truth,　　　520
Your strangeness claiming little interest
In my affections. And yet many a guest
Of poor condition hath been harbour'd here,
But never any did so right appear
Like king Ulysses as yourself, for state
Both of your stature, voice, and very gait.'
　'So all have said,' said he, 'that ever yet
Had the proportions of our figures met
In their observances; so right your eye
Proves in your soul your judging faculty.'　　　530
　Thus took she up a cauldron brightly scour'd,
To cleanse his feet in; and into it pour'd
Store of cold wave, which on the fire she set
And therein bath'd, being temperately heat,
Her sovereign's feet. Who turn'd him from the light,
Since suddenly he doubted her conceit,
So rightly touching at his state before,
A scar now seeing on his foot, that bore
An old note, to discern him, might descry
The absolute truth; which, witness'd by her eye,　　　540
Was straight approv'd. He first receiv'd this sore
As in Parnassus' tops a white-tooth'd boar
He stood in chase withal, who struck him there,
At such time as he lived a sojourner
With his grandsire, Autolycus; who th' art
Of theft and swearing (not out of the heart,
But by equivocation) first adorn'd
Your witty man withal, and was suborn'd
By Jove's descent, ingenious Mercury,
Who did bestow it, since so many a thigh　　　550
Of lambs and kids he had on him bestow'd

In sacred flames, who therefore when he vow'd
Was ever with him. And this man impos'd
Ulysses' name, the light being first disclos'd
To his first sight then, when his grandsire came
To see the then preferrer of his fame,
His loved daughter. The first supper done,
Euryclea put in his lap her son,
And pray'd him to bethink and give his name,
Since that desire did all desires inflame.   560

   'Daughter and son-in-law,' said he, 'let then
The name that I shall give him stand with men.
Since I arriv'd here at the hour of pain,
In which mine own kind entrails did sustain
Moan for my daughter's yet unended throes,
And when so many men's and women's woes,
In joint compassion met of human birth,
Brought forth t' attend the many-feeding earth,
Let Odyssëus be his name, as one
Expos'd to just constraint of all men's moan.   570
When here at home he is arriv'd at state
Of man's first youth, he shall initiate
His practis'd feet in travel made abroad,
And to Parnassus, where mine own abode
And chief means lie, address his way, where I
Will give him from my open'd treasury
What shall return him well, and fit the fame
Of one that had the honour of his name.'

   For these fair gifts he went, and found all grace
Of hands and words in him and all his race.   580
Amphithea, his mother's mother, too,
Applied her to his love, withal, to do
In grandame's welcomes, both his fair eyes kist,
And brows; and then commanded to assist
Were all her sons by their respected sire
In furnishing a feast, whose ears did fire
Their minds with his command; who home straight led
A five-years-old male ox, fell'd, slew, and flay'd,
Gather'd about him, cut him up with art,
Spitted, and roasted, and his every part   590
Divided orderly. So all the day
They spent in feast; no one man went his way
Without his fit fill. When the sun was set,
And darkness rose, they slept, till day's fire het

Th' enlighten'd earth; and then on hunting went
Both hounds and all Autolycus' descent.
In whose guide did divine Ulysses go,
Climb'd steep Parnassus, on whose forehead grow
All sylvan offsprings round. And soon they reach'd
The concaves, whence air's sounding vapours fetch'd   600
Their loud descent. As soon as any sun
Had from the ocean, where his waters run
In silent deepness, rais'd his golden head,
The early huntsmen all the hill had spread,
Their hounds before them on the searching trail –
They near, and ever eager to assail,
Ulysses brandishing a lengthful lance,
Of whose first flight he long'd to prove the chance.
    Then found they lodg'd a boar of bulk extreme,
In such a queach as never any beam   610
The sun shot pierc'd, nor any pass let find
The moist impressions of the fiercest wind,
Nor any storm the sternest winter drives,
Such proof it was; yet all within lay leaves
In mighty thickness; and through all this flew
The hounds' loud mouths. The sounds the tumult threw,
And all together, rous'd the boar, that rush'd
Amongst their thickest, all his bristles push'd
From forth his rough neck, and with flaming eyes
Stood close, and dar'd all. On which horrid prise   620
Ulysses first charg'd; whom above the knee
The savage struck, and ras'd it crookedly
Along the skin, yet never reach'd the bone.
Ulysses' lance yet through him quite was thrown,
At his right shoulder ent'ring, at his left
The bright head passage to his keenness cleft,
And show'd his point gilt with the gushing gore.
Down in the dust fell the extended boar,
And forth his life flew. To Ulysses round
His uncle drew; who, woeful for his wound,   630
With all art bound it up, and with a charm
Stay'd straight the blood, went home, and, when the harm
Receiv'd full cure, with gifts, and all event
Of joy and love to his lov'd home they sent
Their honour'd nephew; whose return his sire
And reverend mother took with joys entire,
Enquir'd all passages, all which he gave

In good relation, nor of all would save
His wound from utterance; by whose scar he came
To be discover'd by this aged dame.   640

   Which when she cleansing felt, and noted well,
Down from her lap into the cauldron fell
His weighty foot, that made the brass resound,
Turn'd all aside, and on th' embrewed ground
Spilt all the water. Joy and grief together
Her breast invaded, and of weeping weather
Her eyes stood full; her small voice stuck within
Her part expressive, till at length his chin
She took and spake to him: 'O son,' said she,
'Thou art Ulysses, nor canst other be;   650
Nor could I know thee yet, till all my king
I had gone over with the warmed spring.'

   Then look'd she for the queen to tell her all;
And yet knew nothing sure, though nought could fall
In compass of all thoughts to make her doubt,
Minerva that distraction struck throughout
Her mind's rapt forces that she might not tell.
Ulysses, noting yet her aptness well,
With one hand took her chin, and made all show
Of favour to her, with the other drew   660
Her offer'd parting closer, ask'd her why
She, whose kind breast had nurs'd so tenderly
His infant life, would now his age destroy,
Though twenty years had held him from the joy
Of his loved country? But, since only she,
god putting her in mind, now knew 'twas he,
He charg'd her silence, and to let no ear
In all the court more know his being there,
Lest, if god gave into his wreakful hand
Th' insulting wooers' lives, he did not stand   670
On any partial respect with her,
Because his nurse, and to the rest prefer
Her safety therefore, but, when they should feel
His punishing finger, give her equal steel.

   'What words,' said she, 'fly your retentive pow'rs?
You know you lock your counsels in your tow'rs
In my firm bosom, and that I am far
From those loose frailties. Like an iron bar,
Or bolt of solid'st stone, I will contain,
And tell you this besides: that if you gain,   680

By god's good aid, the wooers' lives in yours,
What dames are here their shameless paramours,
And have done most dishonour to your worth,
My information well shall paint you forth.'
    'It shall not need,' said he; 'myself will soon,
While thus I mask here, set on every one
My sure observance of the worst and best.
Be thou then silent, and leave god the rest.'
This said, the old dame for more water went,
The rest was all upon the pavement spent   690
By known Ulysses' foot. More brought, and he
Supplied beside with sweetest ointments, she
His seat drew near the fire, to keep him warm,
And with his piec'd rags hiding close his harm.
The queen came near, and said: 'Yet, guest, afford
Your further patience, till but in a word
I'll tell my woes to you; for well I know
That rest's sweet hour her soft foot orders now,
When all poor men, how much soever griev'd,
Would gladly get their woe-watch'd pow'rs reliev'd.   700
But god hath giv'n my grief a heart so great
It will not down with rest, and so I set
My judgment up to make it my delight.
All day I mourn, yet nothing let the right
I owe my charge both in my work and maids;
And when the night brings rest to others' aids,
I toss my bed, Distress, with twenty points,
Slaught'ring the pow'rs that to my turning joints
Convey the vital heat. And as all night
Pandareus' daughter, poor Edone, sings,   710
Clad in the verdure of the yearly springs,
When she for Itylus, her loved son,
By Zethus' issue in his madness done
To cruel death, pours out her hourly moan,
And draws the ears to her of every one:
So flows my moan that cuts in two my mind,
And here and there gives my discourse the wind,
Uncertain whether I shall with my son
Abide still here the safe possession
And guard of all goods, rev'rence to the bed   720
Of my lov'd lord, and to my far-off-spread
Fame with the people, putting still in use,
Or follow any best Greek I can choose

To his fit house, with treasure infinite,
Won to his nuptials. While the infant plight
And want of judgment kept my son in guide,
He was not willing with my being a bride,
Nor with my parting from his court; but now,
Arriv'd at man's state, he would have me vow
My love to some one of my wooers here,   730
And leave his court, offended that their cheer
Should so consume his free possessions.
To settle then a choice in these my moans,
Hear and expound a dream that did engrave
My sleeping fancy: twenty geese I have,
All which, methought, mine eye saw tasting wheat
In water steep'd, and joy'd to see them eat;
When straight a crook-beak'd eagle from a hill
Stoop'd, and truss'd all their necks, and all did kill;
When, all left scatter'd on the pavement there,   740
She took her wing up to the gods' fair sphere.
I, ev'n amid my dream, did weep and mourn
To see the eagle, with so shrewd a turn,
Stoop my sad turrets; when, methought, there came
About my mournings many a Grecian dame,
To cheer my sorrows; in whose most extreme
The hawk came back, and on the prominent beam
That cross'd my chamber fell, and us'd to me
A human voice, that sounded horribly,
And said: "Be confident, Icarius' seed,   750
This is no dream, but what shall chance indeed.
The geese the wooers are; the eagle, I,
Was heretofore a fowl, but now imply
Thy husband's being, and am come to give
The wooers death, that on my treasure live."
With this sleep left me, and my waking way
I took, to try if any violent prey
Were made of those my fowls, which well enough
I, as before, found feeding at their trough
Their yoted wheat.' 'O woman,' he replied,   760
'Thy dream can no interpretation bide
But what the eagle made, who was your lord,
And said himself would sure effect afford
To what he told you; that confusion
To all the wooers should appear, and none
Escape the fate and death he had decreed.'

She answer'd him: 'O guest, these dreams exceed
The art of man t' interpret; and appear
Without all choice or form; nor ever were
Perform'd to all at all parts. But there are   770
To these light dreams, that like thin vapours fare,
Two two-leav'd gates, the one of ivory,
The other horn. Those dreams that Fantasy
Takes from the polish'd ivory port, delude
The dreamer ever, and no truth include;
Those that the glittering horn-gate lets abroad,
Do evermore some certain truth abode.
But this my dream I hold of no such sort
To fly from thence; yet, whichsoever port
It had access from, it did highly please   780
My son and me. And this my thoughts profess:
That day that lights me from Ulysses' court
Shall both my infamy and curse consort.
I therefore purpose to propose them now,
In strong contention, Ulysses his bow;
Which he that easily draws, and from his draft
Shoots through twelve axes (as he did his shaft,
All set up in a row, and from them all
His stand-far-off kept firm), my fortunes shall
Dispose, and take me to his house from hence,   790
Where I was wed a maid, in confluence
Of feast and riches; such a court here then
As I shall ever in my dreams retain.'

'Do not,' said he, 'defer the gameful prize,
But set to task their importunities
With something else than nuptials; for your lord
Will to his court and kingdom be restor'd
Before they thread those steels, or draw his bow.'

'O guest,' replied Penelope, 'would you
Thus sit and please me with your speech, mine ears   800
Would never let mine eyelids close their spheres!
But none can live without the death of sleep.
Th' immortals in our mortal memories keep
Our ends and deaths by sleep, dividing so,
As by the fate and portion of our woe,
Our times spent here, to let us nightly try
That while we live, as much live as we die.
In which use I will to my bed ascend,
Which I bedew with tears, and sigh past end

Through all my hours spent, since I lost my joy   810
For vile, lewd, never-to-be-named Troy.
Yet there I'll prove for sleep, which take you here,
Or on the earth, if that your custom were,
Or have a bed dispos'd for warmer rest.'
Thus left she with her ladies her old guest,
Ascended her fair chamber, and her bed,
Whose sight did ever duly make her shed
Tears for her lord; which still her eyes did steep,
Till Pallas shut them with delightsome sleep.

THE END OF THE NINETEENTH BOOK

BOOK TWENTY

The Argument

Ulysses, in the wooers' beds
Resolving first to kill the maids,
That sentence giving off, his care
For other objects doth prepare.

Another Argument

Psi   Jove's thunder chides,
        But cheers the king,
    The wooers' prides
        Discomfiting.

BOOK TWENTY

ULYSSES in the entry laid his head,
 And under him an oxhide newly flay'd,
 Above him sheep fells store; and over those
Eurynome cast mantles. His repose
Would bring no sleep yet, studying the ill
He wish'd the wooers; who came by him still
With all their wenches, laughing, wantoning,
In mutual lightness; which his heart did sting,
Contending two ways: if, all patience fled,
He should rush up and strike those strumpets dead,   10
Or let that night be last, and take th' extreme
Of those proud wooers, that were so supreme
In pleasure of their high-fed fantasies.
His heart did bark within him to surprise
Their sports with spoils; no fell she-mastiff can,
Amongst her whelps, fly eag'rer on a man
She doth not know, yet scents him something near,
And fain would come to please her tooth, and tear,
Than his disdain, to see his roof so fil'd
With those foul fashions, grew within him wild   20
To be in blood of them. But, finding best
In his free judgment to let passion rest,
He chid his angry spirit, and beat his breast,
And said: 'Forbear, my mind, and think on this:
There hath been time when bitter agonies
Have tried thy patience. Call to mind the day
In which the Cyclop, which pass'd manly sway
Of violent strength, devour'd thy friends; thou then
Stood'st firmly bold, till from that hellish den
Thy wisdom brought thee off, when nought but death   30
Thy thoughts resolved on.' This discourse did breathe
The fiery boundings of his heart, that still
Lay in that aesture, without end his ill
Yet manly suff'ring. But from side to side
It made him toss apace. You have not tried

A fellow roasting of a pig before
A hasty fire, his belly yielding store
Of fat and blood, turn faster, labour more
To have it roast, and would not have it burn,
Than this and that way his unrest made turn   40
His thoughts and body, would not quench the fire,
And yet not have it heighten his desire
Past his discretion, and the fit enough
Of haste and speed, that went to all the proof
His well-laid plots and his exploits requir'd,
Since he, but one, to all their deaths aspir'd.

    In this contention Pallas stoop'd from heav'n,
Stood over him, and had her presence giv'n
A woman's form, who sternly thus began:
'Why, thou most sour and wretched-fated man   50
Of all that breathe, yet liest thou thus awake?
The house in which thy cares so toss and take
Thy quiet up is thine; thy wife is there
And such a son, as if thy wishes were
To be suffic'd with one they could not mend.'

    'Goddess,' said he, 'tis true; but I contend
To right their wrongs, and, though I be but one,
To lay unhelp'd and wreakful hand upon
This whole resort of impudents, that here
Their rude assemblies never will forbear.   60
And yet a greater doubt employs my care,
That if their slaughters in my reaches are,
And I perform them, Jove and you not pleas'd,
How shall I fly their friends? And would stand seis'd
Of counsel to resolve this care in me.'

    'Wretch,' she replied, 'a friend of worse degree
Might win thy credence, that a mortal were,
And us'd to second thee, though nothing near
So pow'rful in performance nor in care;
Yet I, a goddess, that have still had share   70
In thy achievements, and thy person's guard,
Must still be doubted by thy brain, so hard
To credit anything above thy pow'r –
And that must come from heav'n – if every hour
There be not personal appearance made,
And aid direct giv'n, that may sense invade.
I'll tell thee, therefore, clearly: if there were
Of divers-languag'd men an army here

Of fifty companies, all driving hence
Thy sheep and oxen, and with violence   80
Offer'd to charge us, and besiege us round,
Thou shouldst their prey reprise, and them confound.
Let sleep then seize thee. To keep watch all night
Consumes the spirits, and makes dull the sight.'
Thus pour'd the goddess sleep into his eyes,
And reascended the Olympian skies.

    When care-and-lineament-resolving sleep
Had laid his temples in his golden steep,
His wise-in-chaste-wit-worthy wife did rise,
First sitting up in her soft bed, her eyes   90
Open'd with tears, in care of her estate,
Which now her friends resolv'd to terminate
To more delays, and make her marry one.
Her silent tears then ceas'd, her orison
This queen of women to Diana made:

    'Rev'rend Diana, let thy darts invade
My woeful bosom, and my life deprive,
Now at this instant, or soon after drive
My soul with tempests forth, and give it way
To those far-off dark vaults, where never day   100
Hath pow'r to shine, and let them cast it down
Where refluent Oceanus doth crown
His curled head, where Pluto's orchard is,
And entrance to our after miseries.
As such stern whirlwinds ravish'd to that stream
Pandareus' daughters, when the gods to them
Had reft their parents, and them left alone,
Poor orphan children, in their mansion;
Whose desolate life did love's sweet queen incline
To nurse with pressed milk and sweetest wine;   110
Whom Juno deck'd beyond all other dames
With wisdom's light, and beauty's moving flames;
Whom Phoebe goodliness of stature render'd;
And to whose fair hands wise Minerva tender'd
The loom and needle in their utmost skill;
And while love's empress scaled th' Olympian hill
To beg of lightning-loving Jove (since he
The means to all things knows, and doth decree
Fortunes, infortunes, to the mortal race)
For those poor virgins, the accomplish'd grace   120
Of sweetest nuptials, the fierce Harpies prey'd

On every good and miserable maid,
And to the hateful Furies gave them all
In horrid service: yet may such fate fall
From steep Olympus on my loathed head,
Or fair-chair'd Phoebe strike me instant dead,
That I may undergo the gloomy shore
To visit great Ulysses' soul, before
I soothe my idle blood and wed a worse.
And yet, beneath how desperate a curse   130
Do I live now! It is an ill that may
Be well endur'd, to mourn the whole long day,
So night's sweet sleeps, that make a man forget
Both bad and good, in some degree would let
My thoughts leave grieving; but, both day and night,
Some cruel god gives my sad memory sight.
This night, methought, Ulysses grac'd my bed
In all the goodly state with which he led
The Grecian army; which gave joys extreme
To my distress, esteeming it no dream,   140
But true indeed; and that conceit I had,
That when I saw it false I might be mad,
Such cruel fates command in my life's guide.'

    By this the morning's orient dews had dyed
The earth in all her colours; when the king,
In his sweet sleep, suppos'd the sorrowing
That she us'd waking in her plaintive bed
To be her mourning, standing by his head,
As having known him there; who straight arose,
And did again within the hall dispose   150
The carpets and the cushions, where before
They served the seats. The hide without the door
He carried back; and then, with held-up hands,
He pray'd to him that heav'n and earth commands:

    'O father Jove, if through the moist and dry
You, willing, brought me home, when misery
Had punish'd me enough by your free dooms,
Let some of these within those inner rooms,
Startled with horror of some strange ostent,
Come here, and tell me that great Jove hath bent   160
Threat'nings without at some lewd men within.'

    To this his pray'r Jove shook his sable chin,
And thunder'd from those pure clouds that, above
The breathing air, in bright Olympus move.

Divine Ulysses joy'd to hear it roar.
Report of which a woman miller bore
Straight to his ears; for near to him there ground
Mills for his corn, that twice six women found
Continual motion, grinding barley meal,
And wheat, man's marrow. Sleep the eyes did seal　　　170
Of all the other women, having done
Their usual task; which yet this dame alone
Had scarce given end to, being, of all the rest,
Least fit for labour. But when these sounds press'd
Her ears, above the rumbling of her mill,
She let that stand, look'd out, and heav'n's steep hill
Saw clear and temperate; which made her (unware
Of giving any comfort to his care
In that strange sign he pray'd for) thus invoke:
　　'O king of men and gods, a mighty stroke　　　180
Thy thund'ring hand laid on the cope of stars,
No cloud in all the air; and therefore wars
Thou bidst to some men in thy sure ostent!
Perform to me, poor wretch, the main event;
And make this day the last, and most extreme,
In which the wooers' pride shall solace them
With whorish banquets in Ulysses' roof,
That, with sad toil to grind them meal enough,
Have quite dissolv'd my knees. Vouchsafe, then, now
Thy thunders may their latest feast foreshow.'　　　190
　　This was the boon Ulysses begg'd of Jove,
Which, with his thunder, through his bosom drove
A joy, that this vaunt breath'd: 'Why now these men,
Despite their pride, will Jove make pay me pain.'
　　By this had other maids than those that lay
Mix'd with the wooers, made a fire like day
Amidst the hearth of the illustrious hall;
And then the prince, like a celestial,
Rose from his bed, to his embalm'd feet tied
Fair shoes, his sword about his breast applied,　　　200
Took to his hand his sharp-pil'd lance, and met,
Amidst the entry, his old nurse, that set
His haste at sudden stand; to whom he said:
　　'O, my lov'd nurse, with what grace have you laid
And fed my guest here? Could you so neglect
His age, to lodge him thus? Though all respect
I give my mother's wisdom, I must yet

Affirm it fail'd in this; for she hath set
At much more price a man of much less worth,
Without his person's note, and yet casts forth   210
With ignominious hands, for his form sake,
A man much better.' 'Do not faulty make,
Good son, the faultless. He was giv'n his seat
Close to her side, and food till he would eat,
Wine till his wish was serv'd; for she requir'd
His wants, and will'd him all things he desir'd;
Commanded her chief maids to make his bed,
But he, as one whom sorrow only fed
And all infortune, would not take his rest
In bed, and coverings fit for any guest,   220
But in the entry, on an ox's hide
Never at tanner's, his old limbs implied
In warm sheep-fells; yet over all we cast
A mantle, fitting for a man more grac'd.'

  He took her answer, left the house, and went,
Attended with his dogs, to sift th' event
Of private plots, betwixt him and his sire
In common counsel. Then the crew entire
Of all the household maids Euryclea bad
Bestir them through the house, and see it clad   230
In all best form; gave all their parts; and one
She set to furnish every seat and throne
With needleworks, and purple clothes of state;
Another set to scour and cleanse the plate;
Another all the tables to make proud
With porous sponges; others she bestow'd
In all speed to the spring, to fetch from thence
Fit store of water; all at all expense
Of pains she will'd to be, for this to all
Should be a day of common festival,   240
And not a wooer now should seek his home
Elsewhere than there, but all were bid to come
Exceeding early, and be raised to heav'n
With all the entertainment could be giv'n.

  They heard with greedy ears, and everything
Put straight in practice. Twenty to the spring
Made speed for water; many in the house
Took pains; and all were both laborious
And skill'd in labour; many fell to fell
And cleave their wood; and all did more than well.   250

Then troop'd the lusty wooers in, and then
Came all from spring; at their heels loaded men
With slaughter'd brawns, of all the herd the prize,
That had been long fed up in several sties;
Eumaeus and his men convey'd them there.
He, seeing now the king, began to cheer,
And thus saluted him: 'How now, my guest?
Have yet your virtues found more interest
In these great wooers' good respects? Or still
Pursue they you with all their wonted ill?'   260

'I would to heav'n, Eumaeus,' he replied,
'The deities once would take in hand their pride,
That such unseemly fashions put in frame
In others' roofs, as show no spark of shame.'

Thus these; and to these came Melanthius,
Great guardian of the most egregious
Rich wooers' herds, consisting all of goats,
Which he, with two more, drave, and made their cotes
The sounding porticos of that fair court.
Melanthius, seeing the king, this former sort   270
Of upland language gave: 'What? Still stay here,
And dull these wooers with thy wretched cheer?
Not gone for ever yet? Why, now I see
This strife of cuffs betwixt the beggary,
That yesterday assay'd to get thee gone,
And thy more roguery, needs will fall upon
My hands to arbitrate. Thou wilt not hence
Till I set on thee; thy ragg'd impudence
Is so fast-footed. Are there not beside
Other great banquetants, but you must ride   280
At anchor still with us?' He nothing said,
But thought of ill enough, and shook his head.

Then came Philoetius, a chief of men,
That to the wooers' all-devouring den
A barren steer drave, and fat goats; for they
In custom were with traffickers by sea,
That who they would sent, and had utterance there.
And for these likewise the fair porches were
Hurdles and sheep-pens, as in any fair.
Philoetius took note in his repair   290
Of seen Ulysses, being a man as well
Giv'n to his mind's use as to buy and sell,
Or do the drudg'ry that the blood desir'd,

And, standing near Eumaeus, this enquir'd:
'What guest is this that makes our house of late
His entertainer? Whence claims he the state
His birth in this life holds? What nation?
What race? What country stands his speech upon?
O'er-hardly portion'd by the terrible fates,
The structure of his lineaments relates   300
A king's resemblance in his pomp of reign,
Ev'n thus in these rags. But poor erring men,
That have no firm home, but range here and there
As need compels, god keeps in this earth's sphere
As under water, and this tune he sings,
When he is spinning ev'n the cares of kings.'
    Thus coming to him, with a kind of fear
He took his hand, and, touch'd exceeding near
With mere imagination of his worth,
This salutation he sent loudly forth: 310
    'Health, father stranger! In another world
Be rich and happy, though thou here art hurl'd
At feet of never such insulting need.
O Jove, there lives no one god of thy seed
More ill to man than thou. Thou tak'st no ruth –
When thou thyself hast got him in most truth –
To wrap him in the straits of most distress,
And in the curse of others' wickedness.
My brows have swet to see it, and mine eyes
Broke all in tears, when this being still the guise   320
Of worthiest men, I have but only thought,
That down to these ills was Ulysses wrought,
And that, thus clad, even he is error-driv'n,
If yet he lives and sees the light of heav'n.
But, if now dead, and in the house of hell,
O me! O good Ulysses, that my weal
Did ever wish, and when, but half a man
Amongst the people Cephallenian,
His bounty to his oxen's charge preferr'd
One in that youth; which now is grown a herd   330
Unspeakable for number, and feed there
With their broad heads, as thick as of his ear
A field of corn is to a man. Yet these
Some men advise me that this noted prease
Of wooers may devour, and wish me drive
Up to their feasts with them, that neither give

His son respect, though in his own free roof,
Nor have the wit to fear th' infallible proof
Of heav'nly vengeance, but make offer now
The long-lack'd king's possessions to bestow   340
In their self-shares. Methinks the mind in me
Doth turn as fast as in a flood or sea
A raging whirlpit doth, to gather in
To fishy death those swimmers in their sin;
Or feeds a motion as circular
To drive my herds away. But while the son
Bears up with life, 'twere heinous wrong to run
To other people with them, and to trust
Men of another earth. And yet more just
It were to venture their laws, the main right   350
Made still their masters, than at home lose quite
Their right and them, and sit and grieve to see
The wrong authoriz'd by their gluttony.
And I had long since fed, and tried th' event
With other proud kings, since more insolent
These are than can be borne, but that ev'n still
I had a hope that this, though born to ill,
Would one day come from some coast, and their last
In his roofs strew with ruins red and vast.'

'Herdsman,' said he, 'because thou art in show   360
Nor lewd nor indiscreet, and that I know
There rules in thee an understanding soul,
I'll take all oath, that in thee shall control
All doubt of what I swear: be witness, Jove,
That sway'st the first seat of the thron'd above,
This hospitable table, and this house,
That still hold title for the strenuous
Son of Laertes, that – if so you please –
Your eyes shall witness Laertiades
Arriv'd at home, and all these men that reign   370
In such excesses here shall here lie slain!'

He answer'd: 'Stranger! Would just Jove would sign
What you have sworn! In your eyes' beams should shine
What pow'rs I manage, and how these my hands
Would rise and follow where he first commands.'

So [too] Eumaeus, praying all the sky
That wise Ulysses might arrive and try.

Thus while they vow'd, the wooers sat as hard
On his son's death, but had their counsels scarr'd,

For on their left hand did an eagle soar,   380
And in her seres a fearful pigeon bore.
Which seen, Amphinomus presag'd: 'O friends,
Our counsels never will receive their ends
In this man's slaughter. Let us therefore ply
Our bloody feast, and make his oxen die.'

   Thus came they in, cast off on seats their cloaks,
And fell to giving sacrificing strokes
Of sheep and goats, the chiefly fat and great,
Slew fed-up swine, and from the herd a neat.

   The innards roasted, they dispos'd betwixt   390
Their then observers, wine in flagons mix'd.

   The bowls Eumaeus brought, Philoetius bread,
Melanthius fill'd the wine. Thus drank and fed
The feastful wooers. Then the prince, in grace
Of his close project, did his father place
Amidst the paved entry, in a seat
Seemless and abject, a small board and meat
Of th' only innards; in a cup of gold
Yet sent him wine, and bade him now drink bold,
All his approaches he himself would free   400
'Gainst all the wooers, since he would not see
His court made popular, but that his sire
Built it to his use. Therefore all the fire
Blown in the wooers' spleens he bade suppress,
And that in hands nor words they should digress
From that set peace his speech did then proclaim.
They bit their lips and wonder'd at his aim
In that brave language; when Antinous said:
'Though this speech, Grecians, be a mere upbraid,
Yet this time give it pass. The will of Jove   410
Forbids the violence of our hands to move,
But of our tongues we keep the motion free,
And, therefore, if his further jollity
Tempt our encounter with his braves, let's check
His growing insolence, though pride to speak
Fly passing high with him.' The wise prince made
No more spring of his speech, but let it fade.

   And now the heralds bore about the town
The sacred hecatomb; to whose renown
The fair-hair'd Greeks assembled, and beneath   420
Apollo's shady wood the holy death
They put to fire; which made enough, they drew,

Divided all, that did in th' end accrue
To glorious satisfaction. Those that were
Disposers of the feast did equal cheer
Bestow on wretched Laertiades,
With all the wooers' souls, it so did please
Telemachus to charge them. And for these
Minerva would not see the malices
The wooers bore too much contain'd, that so　　　　　430
Ulysses' mov'd heart yet might higher flow
In wreakful anguish. There was wooing there,
Amongst the rest, a gallant that did bear
The name of one well-learn'd in jests profane,
His name Ctesippus, born a Samian;
Who, proud because his father was so rich,
Had so much confidence as did bewitch
His heart with hope to wed Ulysses' wife;
And this man said: 'Hear me, my lords in strife
For this great widow. This her guest did share　　　　　440
Ev'n feast with us, with very comely care
Of him that order'd it; for 'tis not good
Nor equal to deprive guests of their food,
And specially whatever guest makes way
To that house where Telemachus doth sway;
And therefore I will add to his receipt
A gift of very hospitable weight,
Which he may give again to any maid
That bathes his grave feet, and her pains see paid,
Or any servant else that the divine　　　　　450
Ulysses' lofty battlements confine.'
　　Thus snatch'd he with a valiant hand, from out
The poor folks' common basket, a neat's foot,
And threw it at Ulysses; who his head
Shrunk quietly aside, and let it shed
His malice on the wall – the suffering man
A laughter raising most Sardinian,
With scorn and wrath mix'd, at the Samian.
Whom thus the prince reproved: 'Your valour won
Much grace, Ctesippus, and hath eas'd your mind　　　　　460
With mighty profit, yet you see it find
No mark it aim'd at; the poor stranger's part
Himself made good enough, to 'scape your dart.
But should I serve thee worthily, my lance
Should strike thy heart through, and, in place t'advance

Thyself in nuptials with his wealth, thy sire
Should make thy tomb here, that the foolish fire
Of all such valours may not dare to show
These foul indecencies to me. I now
Have years to understand my strength, and know   470
The good and bad of things, and am no more
At your large suff'rance, to behold my store
Consum'd with patience, see my cattle slain,
My wine exhausted, and my bread in vain
Spent on your license; for to one then young
So many enemies were match too strong.
But let me never more be witness to
Your hostile minds, nor those base deeds ye do;
For, should ye kill me in my offer'd wreak,
I wish it rather, and my death would speak   480
Much more good of me, than to live and see
Indignity upon indignity,
My guests provok'd with bitter words and blows,
My women servants dragg'd about my house
To lust and rapture.' This made silence seize
The house throughout; till Damastorides
At length the calm brake, and said: 'Friend, forbear
To give a just speech a disdainful ear;
The guest no more touch, nor no servant here.
Myself will to the prince and queen commend   490
A motion grateful, if they please to lend
Grateful receipt. As long as any hope
Left wise Ulysses any passage ope
To his return in our conceits, so long
The queen's delays to our demands stood strong
In cause and reason, and our quarrels thus
With guests, the queen, or her Telemachus,
Set never foot amongst our liberal feast;
For should the king return, though thought deceas'd,
It had been gain to us, in finding him,   500
To lose his wife. But now, since nothing dim
The days break out that show he never more
Shall reach the dear touch of his country shore,
Sit by your mother, in persuasion
That now it stands her honour much upon
To choose the best of us, and, who gives most,
To go with him home. For so, all things lost
In sticking on our haunt so, you shall clear

Recover in our no more concourse here,
Possess your birthright wholly, eat and drink,   510
And never more on our disgraces think.'
    'By Jove, no, Agelaus! For I swear
By all my father's sorrows, who doth err
Far off from Ithaca, or rests in death,
I am so far from spending but my breath
To make my mother any more defer
Her wished nuptials, that I'll counsel her
To make her free choice; and besides will give
Large gifts to move her. But I fear to drive
Or charge her hence; for god will not give way   520
To any such course, if I should assay.'
    At this, Minerva made for foolish joy
The wooers mad, and rous'd their late annoy
To such a laughter as would never down.
They laugh'd with others' cheeks, ate meat o'erflown
With their own bloods, their eyes stood full of tears
For violent joys; their souls yet thought of fears,
Which Theoclymenus express'd, and said:
    'O wretches! Why sustain ye, well apaid,
Your imminent ill? A night, with which death sees   530
Your heads and faces hides beneath your knees;
Shrieks burn about you; your eyes thrust out tears;
These fixed walls, and that main beam that bears
The whole house up, in bloody torrents fall;
The entry full of ghosts stands; full the hall
Of passengers to hell; and under all
The dismal shades; the sun sinks from the poles;
And troubled air pours bane about your souls.'
    They sweetly laugh'd at this. Eurymachus
To mocks dispos'd, and said: 'This new-come-t'us   540
Is surely mad, conduct him forth to light
In th' open market-place; he thinks 'tis night
Within the house.' 'Eurymachus,' said he,
'I will not ask for any guide of thee.
I both my feet enjoy, have ears and eyes,
And no mad soul within me; and with these
Will I go forth the doors, because I know
That imminent mischief must abide with you,
Which not a man of all the wooers here
Shall fly or 'scape. Ye all too highly bear   550
Your uncurb'd heads. Impieties ye commit,

And every man affect with forms unfit.'
This said, he left the house, and took his way
Home to Piraeus; who as free as day
Was of his welcome. When the wooers' eyes
Chang'd looks with one another, and, their guise
Of laughters still held on, still eas'd their breasts
Of will to set the prince against his guests,
Affirming that of all the men alive
He worst luck had, and prov'd it worst to give   560
Guests entertainment; for he had one there,
A wandering hunter out of provender,
An errant beggar every way, yet thought
(He was so hungry) that he needed nought
But wine and victuals, nor knew how to do,
Nor had a spirit to put a knowledge to,
But liv'd an idle burthen to the earth.
   Another then stepp'd up, and would lay forth
His lips in prophecy, thus: 'But, would he heal
His friends' persuasions, he should find it were   570
More profit for him to put both aboard
For the Sicilian people, that afford
These feet of men good price; and this would bring
Good means for better guests.' These words made win
To his ears idly, who had still his eye
Upon his father, looking fervently
When he would lay his long-withholding hand
On those proud wooers. And, within command
Of all this speech that pass'd, Icarius' heir,
The wise Penelope, her royal chair   580
Had plac'd of purpose. Their high dinner then
With all-pleas'd palates these ridiculous men
Fell sweetly to, as joying they had slain
Such store of banquet. But there did not reign
A bitterer banquet-planet in all heav'n
Than that which Pallas had to that day driv'n,
And, with her able friend now, meant t' appose,
Since they till then were in deserts so gross.

THE END OF THE TWENTIETH BOOK

BOOK TWENTY-ONE

The Argument

Penelope proposeth now
To him that draws Ulysses' bow
Her instant nuptials. Ithacus
Eumaeus and Philoetius
Gives charge for guarding of the gates;
And he his shaft shoots through the plates.

Another Argument

Phi   The nuptial vow
      And game rehears'd,
    Drawn is the bow,
      The steels are pierc'd.

BOOK TWENTY-ONE

P ALLAS, THE GODDESS with the sparkling eyes,
    Excites Penelope t' object the prize,
     The bow and bright steels, to the wooers' strength;
And here began the strife and blood at length.
She first ascended by a lofty stair
Her utmost chamber; of whose door her fair
And half-transparent hand receiv'd the key,
Bright, brazen, bitted passing curiously,
And at it hung a knob of ivory.
And this did lead her where was strongly kept   10
The treasure royal; in whose store lay heapt
Gold, brass, and steel, engrav'n with infinite art –
The crooked bow, and arrowy quiver part
Of that rich magazine. In the quiver were
Arrows a-number, sharp and sighing gear.
The bow was giv'n by kind Eurytides –
Iphitus, fashion'd like the deities –
To young Ulysses, when within the roof
Of wise Orsilochus their pass had proof
Of mutual meeting in Messena; where   20
Ulysses claim'd a debt, to whose pay were
The whole Messenian people bound, since they
From Ithaca had forc'd a wealthy prey
Of sheep and shepherds. In their ships they thrust
Three hundred sheep together; for whose just
And instant rendry old Laertes sent
Ulysses his ambassador, that went
A long way in the ambassy, yet then
Bore but the foremost prime of youngest men,
His father sending first to that affair   30
His gravest counsellors, and then his heir.
Iphitus made his way there, having lost
Twelve female horse, and mules, commended most
For use of burthen; which were after cause
Of death and fate to him; for, past all laws

Of hospitality, Jove's mighty son,
Skill'd in great acts, was his confusion
Close by his house, though at that time his guest,
Respecting neither the apposed feast
And hospitable table, that in love   40
He set before him, nor the voice of Jove,
But, seizing first his mares, he after slew
His host himself. From those mares' search now grew
Ulysses known t' Iphitus; who that bow
At their encounter did in love bestow,
Which great Eurytus' hand had borne before
(Iphitus' father), who at death's sad door,
In his steep turrets, left it to his son.
Ulysses gave him a keen falchion,
And mighty lance. And thus began they there   50
Their fatal loves; for after never were
Their mutual tables to each other known,
Because Jove's son th' unworthy part had shown
Of slaughtering this god-like loving man,
Eurytus' son, who with that bow began
And ended love t' Ulysses; who so dear
A gift esteem'd it, that he would not bear
In his black fleet that guest-rite to the war,
But, in fit memory of one so far
In his affection, brought it home, and kept   60
His treasure with it; where till now it slept.

  And now the queen of women had intent
To give it use, and therefore made ascent
Up all the stairs' height to the chamber door,
Whose shining leaves two bright pilasters bore
To such a close when both together went
It would resist the air in their consent.
The ring she took then, and did draw aside
A bar that ran within, and then implied
The key into the lock, which gave a sound,   70
The bolt then shooting, as in pasture ground
A bull doth low, and make the valleys ring;
So loud the lock humm'd when it loos'd the spring,
And ope the doors flew. In she went, along
The lofty chamber, that was boarded strong
With heart of oak, which many years ago
The architect did smooth and polish so
That now as then he made it freshly shine,

And tried the evenness of it with a line.
    There stood in this room presses that enclos'd   80
Robes odoriferous, by which repos'd
The bow was upon pins; nor from it far
Hung the round quiver glittering like a star;
Both which her white extended hand took down.
Then sat she low, and made her lap a crown
Of both those relics, which she wept to see,
And cried quite out with loving memory
Of her dear lord; to whose worth paying then
Kind debts enow, she left, and to the men
Vow'd to her wooing, brought the crooked bow   90
And shaft-receiving quiver, that did flow
With arrows beating sighs up where they fell.
Then, with another chest, replete as well
With games won by the king, of steel and brass,
Her maids attended. Past whom making pass
To where her wooers were, she made her stay
Amids the fair hall door, and kept the ray
Of her bright count'nance hid with veils so thin,
That though they seem'd t' expose, they let love in;
Her maids on both sides stood; and thus she spake: 100
    'Hear me, ye wooers, that a pleasure take
To do me sorrow, and my house invade
To eat and drink, as if 'twere only made
To serve your rapines: my lord long away,
And you allow'd no colour for your stay
But his still absence, striving who shall frame
Me for his wife, and since 'tis made a game,
I here propose divine Ulysses' bow
For that great masterpiece to which ye vow.
He that can draw it with least show to strive,   110
And through these twelve axe-heads an arrow drive,
Him will I follow, and this house forego
That nourish'd me a maid, now furnish'd so
With all things fit, and which I so esteem
That I shall still live in it in my dream.'
This said, she made Eumaeus give it them.
He took and laid it by, and wept for woe;
And like him wept Philoetius, when the bow
Of which his king was bearer he beheld.
Their tears Antinous' manhood much refell'd,   120
And said: 'Ye rustic fools, that still each day

Your minds give over to this vain dismay!
Why weep ye, wretches, and the widow's eyes
Tempt with renew'd thought, that would otherwise
Depose her sorrows, since her lord is dead,
And tears are idle? Sit, and eat your bread,
Nor whisper more a word; or get ye gone,
And weep without doors. Let this bow alone
To our out-match'd contention. For I fear
The bow will scarce yield draught to any here;   130
Here no such man lives as Laertes' son
Amongst us all. I knew him; thought puts on
His look's sight now, methinks, though then a child.'
    Thus show'd his words doubt, yet his hopes instill'd
His strength the stretcher of Ulysses' string,
And his steels' piercer. But his shaft must sing
Through his pierc'd palate first; whom so he wrong'd
In his free roof, and made the rest ill-tongu'd
Against his virtues. Then the sacred heat
That spirited his son did further set   140
Their confidence on fire, and said: 'O friends,
Jove hath bereft my wits. The queen intends,
Though I must grant her wise, ere long to leave
Ulysses' court, and to her bed receive
Some other lord; yet, notwithstanding, I
Am forced to laugh, and set my pleasures high
Like one mad sick. But, wooers, since ye have
An object for your trials now so brave
As all the broad Achaian earth exceeds,
As sacred Pylos, as the Argive breeds,   150
As black Epirus, as Mycena's birth,
And as the more fam'd Ithacensian earth,
All which, yourselves well know, and oft have said
(For what need hath my mother of my aid
In her advancement?) tender no excuse
For least delay, nor too much time profuse
In stay to draw this bow, but draw it straight,
Shoot, and the steels pierce; make all see how slight
You make these poor bars to so rich a prize.
No eagerer yet? Come on. My faculties   160
Shall try the bow's strength, and the pierced steel.
I will not for my rev'rend mother feel
The sorrows that I know will seize my heart,
To see her follow any, and depart

From her so long-held home, but first extend
The bow and arrow to their tender'd end.
For I am only to succeed my sire
In guard of his games, and let none aspire
To their besides possession.' This said,
His purple robe he cast off; by he laid　　　　170
His well-edg'd sword; and first, a several pit
He digg'd for every axe, and strengthen'd it
With earth close ramm'd about it; on a row
Set them, of one height, by a line he drew
Along the whole twelve; and so orderly
Did every deed belonging (yet his eye
Never before beholding how 'twas done)
That in amaze rose all his lookers-on.
Then stood he near the door, and prov'd to draw
The stubborn bow. Thrice tried, and thrice gave law　　　　180
To his uncrown'd attempts, the fourth assay
With all force off'ring, which a sign gave stay
Giv'n by his father; though he show'd a mind
As if he stood right heartily inclin'd
To perfect the exploit, when all was done
In only drift to set the wooers on.
His weakness yet confess'd, he said: 'O shame!
I either shall be ever of no name,
But prove a wretch; or else I am too young,
And must not now presume on pow'rs so strong　　　　190
As sinews yet more growing may engraft,
To turn a man quite over with a shaft.
Besides, to men whose nerves are best prepar'd,
All great adventures at first proof are hard.
But come, you stronger men, attempt this bow,
And let us end our labour.' Thus, below
A well-join'd board he laid it, and close by
The brightly-headed shaft; then thron'd his thigh
Amidst his late-left seat. Antinous then
Bade all arise, but first, who did sustain　　　　200
The cup's state ever, and did sacrifice
Before they ate still; and that man bade rise,
Since on the other's right hand he was plac'd,
Because he held the right hand's rising, grac'd
With best success still. This discretion won
Supreme applause; and first rose Oenops' son,
Liodes, that was priest to all the rest,

Sat lowest with the cup still, and their jest
Could never like, but ever was the man
That check'd their follies; and he now began   210
To taste the bow, the sharp shaft took, tugg'd hard
And held aloft, and, till he quite had marr'd
His delicate tender fingers, could not stir
The churlish string; who therefore did refer
The game to others, saying, that same bow,
In his presage, would prove the overthrow
Of many a chief man there; nor thought the fate
Was any whit austere, since death's short date
Were much the better taken, than long life
Without the object of their amorous strife,   220
For whom they had burn'd out so many days
To find still other, nothing but delays
Obtaining in them; and affirm'd that now
Some hop'd to have her, but when that tough bow
They all had tried, and seen the utmost done,
They must rest pleas'd to cease; and now some one
Of all their other fair-veil'd Grecian dames
With gifts, and dow'r, and hymeneal flames,
Let her love light to him that most will give,
And whom the nuptial destiny did drive.'   230
     Thus laid he on the well-join'd polish'd board
The bow and bright-pil'd shaft, and then restor'd
His seat his right. To him Antinous
Gave bitter language, and reprov'd him thus:
     'What words, Liodes, pass thy speech's guard –
That 'tis a work to bear, and set so hard
They set up my disdain! This bow must end
The best of us, since thy arms cannot lend
The string least motion? Thy mother's throes
Brought never forth thy arms to draught of bows,   240
Or knitting shafts off. Though thou canst not draw
The sturdy plant, thou art to us no law.
Melanthius! Light a fire, and set thereat
A chair and cushions, and that mass of fat
That lies within bring out, that we may set
Our pages to this bow, to see it het
And suppled with the suet, and then we
May give it draught, and pay this great decree
Utmost performance.' He a mighty fire
Gave instant flame, put into act th' entire   250

Command laid on him, chair and cushions set;
Laid on the bow, which straight the pages het,
Chaf'd, suppled with the suet to their most.
And still was all their unctuous labour lost,
All wooers' strengths too indigent and poor
To draw that bow; Antinous' arms it tore,
And great Eurymachus', the both clear best,
Yet both it tir'd, and made them glad to rest.
Forth then went both the swains, and after them
Divine Ulysses; when, being past th' extreme   260
Of all the gates, with winning words he tried
Their loves, and this ask'd: 'Shall my counsels hide
Their depths from you? My mind would gladly know,
If suddenly Ulysses had his vow
Made good for home, and had some god to guide
His steps and strokes to wreak these wooers' pride,
Would your aids join on his part, or with theirs?
How stand your hearts affected?' They made pray'rs
That some god would please to return their lord,
He then should see how far they would afford   270
Their lives for his. He, seeing their truth, replied:
'I am your lord, through many a suff'rance tried,
Arriv'd now here, whom twenty years have held
From forth my country. Yet are not conceal'd
From my sure knowledge your desires to see
My safe return. Of all the company
Now serving here besides, not one but you
Mine ear hath witness'd willing to bestow
Their wishes of my life, so long held dead.
I therefore vow, which shall be perfected,   280
That if god please beneath my hand to leave
These wooers lifeless, ye shall both receive
Wives from that hand, and means, and near to me
Have houses built to you, and both shall be
As friends and brothers to my only son.
And, that ye well may know me, and be won
To that assurance, the infallible sign
The white-tooth'd boar gave, this mark'd knee of mine,
When in Parnassus he was held in chase
By me, and by my famous grandsire's race,   290
I'll let you see.' Thus sever'd he his weed
From that his wound; and every word had deed
In their sure knowledges. Which made them cast

Their arms about him, his broad breast embrac'd,
His neck and shoulders kiss'd. And him as well
Did those true pow'rs of human love compel
To kiss their heads and hands, and to their moan
Had set the free light of the cheerful sun,
Had not Ulysses broke the ruth, and said:
   'Cease tears and sorrows, lest we prove display'd   300
By some that issue from the house, and they
Relate to those within. Take each his way,
Not all together in, but one by one,
First I, then you; and then see this be done:
The envious wooers will by no means give
The offer of the bow and arrow leave
To come at me; 'spite then their pride, do thou,
My good Eumaeus, bring both shaft and bow
To my hand's proof; and charge the maids before,
That instantly they shut in every door,   310
That they themselves (if any tumult rise
Beneath my roofs by any that envies
My will to undertake the game) may gain
No passage forth, but close at work contain
With all free quiet, or at least constrain'd.
And therefore, my Philoetius, see maintain'd,
When close the gates are shut, their closure fast,
To which end be it thy sole work to cast
Their chains before them.' This said, in he led,
Took first his seat; and then they seconded   320
His entry with their own. Then took in hand
Eurymachus the bow, made close his stand
Aside the fire, at whose heat here and there
He warm'd and suppled it, yet could not steer
To any draught the string, with all his art;
And therefore swell'd in him his glorious heart,
Affirming, that himself and all his friends
Had cause to grieve, not only that their ends
They miss'd in marriage, since enough besides
Kind Grecian dames there lived to be their brides   330
In Ithaca, and other bordering towns,
But that to all times future their renowns
Would stand disparag'd, if Ulysses' bow
They could not draw, and yet his wife would woo.
   Antinous answer'd: that there could ensue
No shame at all to them, for well he knew

That this day was kept holy to the Sun
By all the city, and there should be done
No such profane act, therefore bade lay by
The bow for that day; but the mastery   340
Of axes that were set up still might stand,
Since that no labour was, nor any hand
Would offer to invade Ulysses' house,
To take, or touch with surreptitious
Or violent hand, what there was left for use.
He therefore bade the cup-bearer infuse
Wine to the bowls, that so with sacrifice
They might let rest the shooting exercise,
And in the morning make Melanthius bring
The chief goats of his herd, that to the king   350
Of bows and archers they might burn the thighs
For good success, and then attempt the prize.

    The rest sat pleas'd with this. The heralds straight
Pour'd water on their hands; each page did wait
With his crown'd cup of wine, serv'd every man
Till all were satisfied. And then began
Ulysses' plot of his close purpose thus:

    'Hear me, ye much renown'd Eurymachus,
And king Antinous, in chief, who well,
And with decorum sacred, doth compel   360
This day's observance, and to let lay down
The bow all this light, giving gods their own.
The morning's labour god the more will bless,
And strength bestow where he himself shall please.
Against which time let me presume to pray
Your favours with the rest, that this assay
May my old arms prove, trying if there lie
In my poor pow'rs the same activity
That long since crown'd them, or if needy fare
And desolate wand'ring have the web worn bare   370
Of my life's thread at all parts, that no more
Can furnish these affairs as heretofore.'
This het their spleens past measure, blown with fear
Lest his loath'd temples would the garland wear
Of that bow's draught – Antinous using speech
To this sour purpose: 'Thou most arrant wretch
Of all guests breathing, in no least degree
Grac'd with a human soul, it serves not thee
To feast in peace with us, take equal share

Of what we reach to, sit, and all things hear   380
That we speak freely – which no begging guest
Did ever yet – but thou must make request
To mix with us in merit of the queen.
But wine inflames thee, that hath ever been
The bane of men, whoever yet would take
Th' excess it offers and the mean forsake.
Wine spoil'd the centaur, great Eurytion,
In guest-rites with the mighty-minded son
Of bold Ixion, in his way to war
Against the Lapithes; who, driv'n as far   390
As madness with the bold effects of wine,
Did outrage to his kind host, and decline
Other heroës from him feasted there
With so much anger that they left their cheer,
And dragg'd him forth the fore-court, slit his nose,
Cropp'd both his ears, and, in the ill-dispose
His mind then suffer'd, drew the fatal day
On his head with his host; for thence the fray
Betwixt the Centaurs and the Lapithes
Had mortal act. But he for his excess   400
In spoil of wine far'd worst himself, as thou
For thy large cups, if thy arms draw the bow,
My mind foretells shalt fear; for not a man
Of all our consort, that in wisdom can
Boast any fit share, will take prayers then,
But to Echetus, the most stern of men,
A black sail freight with thee, whose worst of ill,
Be sure, is past all ransom. Sit then still,
Drink temp'rately, and never more contend
With men your youngers.' This the queen did end   410
With her defence of him, and told his foe
It was not fair nor equal t' overcrow
The poorest guest her son pleas'd t' entertain
In his free turrets with so proud a strain
Of threats and bravings; asking if he thought,
That if the stranger to his arms had brought
The stubborn bow down, he should marry her,
And bear her home? And said, himself should err
In no such hope; nor of them all the best
That griev'd at any good she did her guest   420
Should banquet there, since it in no sort show'd
Noblesse in them, nor paid her what she ow'd

Her own free rule there. This Eurymachus
Confirm'd and said: 'Nor feeds it hope in us,
Icarius' daughter, to solemnize rites
Of nuptials with thee, nor in noblest sights
It can show comely, but to our respects
The rumour both of sexes and of sects
Amongst the people would breed shame and fear,
Lest any worst Greek said: 'See, men that were　　　　430
Of mean deservings well presume t' aspire
To his wife's bed, whom all men did admire
For fame and merit, could not draw his bow,
And yet his wife had foolish pride to woo –
When straight an errant beggar comes and draws
The bow with ease, performing all the laws
The game besides contain'd.' And this would thus
Prove both indignity and shame to us.'

　　　The queen replied: 'The fame of men, I see,
Bears much price in your great suppos'd degree;　　　　440
Yet who can prove amongst the people great,
That of one so esteem'd of them the seat
Doth so defame and ruin? And beside,
With what right is this guest thus vilified
In your high censures, when the man in blood
Is well compos'd and great, his parents good?
And therefore give the bow to him, to try
His birth and breeding by his chivalry.
If his arms draw it, and that Phoebus stands
So great a glory to his strength, my hands　　　　450
Shall add this guerdon: every sort of weed,
A two-edg'd sword, and lance to keep him freed
From dogs and men hereafter, and dismiss
His worth to what place tends that heart of his.'

　　　Her son gave answer: that it was a wrong
To his free sway in all things that belong
To guard of that house, to demand the bow
Of any wooer, and the use bestow
Upon the stranger; for the bow was his
To give or to withhold; no masteries　　　　460
Of her proposing giving any pow'r
T' impair his right in things for any wooer,
Or any that rough Ithaca affords,
Any that Elis; of which no man's words
Nor pow'rs should curb him, stood he so inclin'd,

To see the bow in absolute gift resign'd
To that his guest to bear and use at will,
And therefore bade his mother keep her still
Amongst her women at her rock and loom;
Bows were for men; and this bow did become   470
Past all men's his disposure, since his sire
Left it to him, and all the house entire.'

    She stood dismay'd at this, and in her mind
His wise words laid up, standing so inclin'd
As he had will'd, with all her women going
Up to her chamber, there her tears bestowing,
As every night she did, on her lov'd lord,
Till sleep and Pallas her fit rest restor'd.

    The bow Eumaeus took, and bore away;
Which up in tumult, and almost in fray,   480
Put all the wooers, one enquiring thus:

    'Whither, rogue abject, wilt thou bear from us
That bow propos'd? Lay down, or I protest
Thy dogs shall eat thee, that thou nourishest
To guard thy swine; amongst whom, left of all,
Thy life shall leave thee, if the festival
We now observe to Phoebus, may our zeals
Grace with his aid, and all the deities else.'

    This threat made good Eumaeus yield the bow
To his late place, not knowing what might grow   490
From such a multitude. And then fell on
Telemachus with threats, and said: 'Set gone
That bow yet further; 'tis no servant's part
To serve too many masters; raise your heart
And bear it off, lest, though your younger, yet
With stones I pelt you to the field with it.
If you and I close, I shall prove too strong.
I wish as much too hard for all this throng
The gods would make me, I should quickly send
Some after with just sorrow to their end,   500
They waste my victuals so, and ply my cup,
And do me such shrewd turns still.' This put up
The wooers all in laughters, and put down
Their angers to him, that so late were grown
So grave and bloody; which resolved that fear
Of good Eumaeus, who did take and bear
The king the bow; call'd nurse, and bade her make
The doors all sure, that if men's tumults take

The ears of some within, they may not fly,
But keep at work still close and silently.   510
    These words put wings to her, and close she put
The chamber door. The court gates then were shut
By kind Philoetius, who straight did go
From out the hall, and in the portico
Found laid a cable of a ship, compos'd
Of spongy bulrushes; with which he clos'd,
In winding round about them, the court gates,
Then took his place again, to view the fates
That quickly follow'd. When he came, he saw
Ulysses viewing, ere he tried to draw,   520
The famous bow, which every way he mov'd,
Up and down turning it; in which he prov'd
The plight it was in, fearing, chiefly, lest
The horns were eat with worms in so long rest.
But what his thoughts intended turning so,
And keeping such a search about the bow,
The wooers little knowing fell to jest,
And said: 'Past doubt he is a man profess'd
In bowyers' craft, and sees quite through the wood;
Or something, certain, to be understood   530
There is in this his turning of it still.
A cunning rogue he is at any ill.'
    Then spake another proud one: 'Would to heav'n
I might, at will, get gold till he hath giv'n
That bow his draught!' With these sharp jests did these
Delightsome woo'rs their fatal humours please.
But when the wise Ulysses once had laid
His fingers on it, and to proof survey'd
The still sound plight it held, as one of skill
In song and of the harp, doth at his will,   540
In tuning of his instrument, extend
A string out with his pin, touch all, and lend
To every well-wreath'd string his perfect sound,
Struck all together: with such ease drew round
The king the bow. Then twang'd he up the string,
That as a swallow in the air doth sing
With no continu'd tune, but, pausing still,
Twinks out her scatter'd voice in accents shrill:
So sharp the string sung when he gave it touch,
Once having bent and drawn it. Which so much   550
Amaz'd the wooers, that their colours went

And came most grievously. And then Jove rent
The air with thunder; which at heart did cheer
The now-enough-sustaining traveller,
That Jove again would his attempt enable.
Then took he into hand, from off the table,
The first drawn arrow – and a number more
Spent shortly on the wooers – but this one
He measured by his arm, as if not known
The length were to him, nock'd it then, and drew;   560
And through the axes, at the first hole, flew
The steel-charg'd arrow; which when he had done
He thus bespake the prince: 'You have not won
Disgrace yet by your guest; for I have strook
The mark I shot at, and no such toil took
In wearying the bow with fat and fire
As did the wooers. Yet reserv'd entire,
Thank heav'n, my strength is, and myself am tried,
No man to be so basely vilified
As these men pleas'd to think me. But free way   570
Take that and all their pleasures; and while day
Holds her torch to you, and the hour of feast
Hath now full date, give banquet, and the rest,
Poem and harp, that grace a well-fill'd board.'

  This said, he beckon'd to his son; whose sword
He straight girt to him, took to hand his lance,
And complete arm'd did to his sire advance.

THE END OF THE TWENTY-FIRST BOOK

BOOK TWENTY-TWO

The Argument

The wooers in Minerva's sight
Slain by Ulysses; all the light
And lustful housewives by his son
And servants are to slaughter done.

Another Argument

Chi   The end of pride,
   And lawless lust,
  Is wretched tried
   With slaughters just.

BOOK TWENTY-TWO

THE UPPER RAGS that wise Ulysses wore
Cast off, he rusheth to the great hall door
With bow and quiver full of shafts, which down
He pour'd before his feet, and thus made known
His true state to the wooers: 'This strife thus
Hath harmless been decided; now for us
There rests another mark, more hard to hit,
And such as never man before hath smit;
Whose full point likewise my hands shall assay,
And try if Phoebus will give me his day.'   10
He said, and off his bitter arrow thrust
Right at Antinous, that struck him just
As he was lifting up the bowl, to show
That 'twixt the cup and lip much ill may grow.
Death touch'd not at his thoughts at feast; for who
Would think that he alone could perish so
Amongst so many, and he best of all?
The arrow in his throat took full his fall,
And thrust his head far through the other side.
Down fell his cup, down he, down all his pride;   20
Straight from his nostrils gush'd the human gore
And, as he fell, his feet far overbore
The feastful table, all the roast and bread
About the house strew'd. When his highborn head
The rest beheld so low, up rush'd they all,
And ransack'd every corner of the hall
For shields and darts; but all fled far their reach.
Then fell they foul on him with terrible speech,
And told him it should prove the dearest shaft
That ever pass'd him, and that now was sav'd   30
No shift for him but sure and sudden death;
For he had slain a man whose like did breathe
In no part of the kingdom, and that now
He should no more for games strive with his bow,
But vultures eat him there. These threats they spent,

Yet every man believ'd that stern event
Chanc'd 'gainst the author's will. O fools, to think
That all their rest had any cup to drink
But what their great Antinous began!

He, frowning, said: 'Dogs, see in me the man   40
Ye all held dead at Troy. My house it is
That thus ye spoil, and thus your luxuries
File with my womens' rapes; in which ye woo
The wife of one that lives, and no thought show
Of man's fit fear, or god's, your present fame,
Or any fair sense of your future name;
And, therefore, present and eternal death
Shall end your base life.' This made fresh fears breathe
Their former boldness. Every man had eye
On all the means, and studied ways to fly   50
So deep deaths imminent. But seeing none,
Eurymachus began with suppliant moan
To move his pity, saying: 'If you be
This isle's Ulysses, we must all agree,
In grant of your reproof's integrity,
The Greeks have done you many a wrong at home,
At field as many. But of all the sum
Lies here contract in death; for only he
Impos'd the whole ill-offices that we
Are now made guilty of, and not so much   60
Sought his endeavours, or in thought did touch
At any nuptials, but a greater thing
Employ'd his forces; for to be our king
Was his chief object; his sole plot it was
To kill your son, which Jove's hand would not pass,
But set it to his own most merited end.
In which, end your just anger, nor extend
Your stern wreak further; spend your royal powers
In mild ruth of your people; we are yours,
And whatsoever waste of wine or food   70
Our liberties have made, we'll make all good
In restitutions. Call a court, and pass
A fine of twenty oxen, gold, and brass,
On every head, and raise your most rates still,
Till you are pleas'd with your confessed fill.
Which if we fail to tender, all your wrath
It shall be justice in our bloods to bathe.'

'Eurymachus,' said he, 'if you would give

All that your fathers hoard, to make ye live,
And all that ever you yourselves possess,   80
Or shall by any industry increase,
I would not cease from slaughter, till your bloods
Had bought out your intemperance in my goods.
It rests now for you that you either fight
That will 'scape death, or make your way by flight.
In whose best choice, my thoughts conceive, not one
Shall shun the death your first hath undergone.'
    This quite dissolv'd their knees. Eurymachus,
Enforcing all their fears, yet counsell'd thus:
    'O friends! This man, now he hath got the bow   90
And quiver by him, ever will bestow
His most inaccessible hands at us,
And never leave, if we avoid him thus,
Till he hath strewn the pavement with us all;
And, therefore, join we swords, and on him fall
With tables forc'd up, and borne in oppos'd
Against his sharp shafts; when, being round enclos'd
By all our onsets, we shall either take
His horrid person, or for safety make
His rage retire from out the hall and gates;   100
And then, if he escape, we'll make our states
Known to the city by our general cry.
And thus this man shall let his last shaft fly
That ever this hand vaunted.' Thus he drew
His sharp-edg'd sword, and with a table flew
In on Ulysses, with a terrible throat
His fierce charge urging. But Ulysses smote
The board, and cleft it through from end to end
Borne at his breast, and made his shaft extend
His sharp head to his liver, his broad breast   110
Pierc'd at his nipple; when his hand releas'd
Forthwith his sword, that fell and kiss'd the ground,
With cups and victuals lying scatter'd round
About the pavement; amongst which his brow
Knock'd the imbru'd earth, while in pains did flow
His vital spirits, till his heels shook out
His feastful life, and hurl'd a throne about
That way-laid death's convulsions in his feet;
When from his tender eyes the light did fleet.
    Then charg'd Amphinomus with his drawn blade   120
The glorious king, in purpose to have made

His feet forsake the house; but his assay
The prince prevented, and his lance gave way
Quite through his shoulder, at his back, his breast
The fierce pile letting forth. His ruin press'd
Groans from the pavement, which his forehead strook.

   Telemachus his long lance then forsook –
Left in Amphinomus – and to his sire
Made fiery pass, not staying to acquire
His lance again, in doubt that, while he drew   130
The fixed pile, some other might renew
Fierce charge upon him, and his unarm'd head
Cleave with his back-drawn sword; for which he fled
Close to his father, bade him arm, and he
Would bring him shield and javelins instantly,
His own head arming, more arms laying by
To serve the swine-herd and the oxen-herd.
Valour well arm'd is ever most preferr'd.

   'Run then,' said he, 'and come before the last
Of these auxiliary shafts are past,   140
For fear lest, left alone, they force my stand
From forth the ports.' He flew, and brought to hand
Eight darts, four shields, four helms. His own parts then
First put in arms, he furnish'd both his men,
That to their king stood close; but he, as long
As he had shafts to friend, enough was strong
For all the wooers, and some one man still
He made make ev'n with earth, till all a hill
Had raised in th' ev'n-floor'd hall. His last shaft spent,
He set his bow against a beam, and went   150
To arm at all parts, while the other three
Kept off the wooers, who, unarm'd, could be
No great assailants. In the well-built wall
A window was thrust out, at end of all
The house's entry; on whose outer side
There lay a way to town, and in it wide
And two-leav'd folds were forg'd, that gave fit mean
For flyers out; and therefore, at it then
Ulysses placed Eumaeus in close guard;
One only pass ope to it, which (prepar'd   160
In this sort by Ulysses 'gainst all pass)
By Agelaus' tardy memory was
In question call'd, who bade some one ascend
At such a window, and bring straight to friend

The city with his clamour, that this man
Might quickly shoot his last. 'This no one can
Make safe access to,' said Melanthius,
'For 'tis too near the hall's fair doors, whence thus
The man afflicts ye; for from thence there lies
But one strait passage to it, that denies   170
Access to all, if any one man stand,
Being one of courage, and will countermand
Our offer to it. But I know a way
To bring you arms, from where the king doth lay
His whole munition – and believe there is
No other place to all the armories
Both of himself and son.' This said, a pair
Of lofty stairs he climb'd, and to th' affair
Twelve shields, twelve lances brought, as many casques
With horsehair plumes; and set to bitter tasks   180
Both son and sire. Then shrunk Ulysses' knees,
And his lov'd heart, when thus in arms he sees
So many wooers, and their shaken darts;
For then the work show'd as it ask'd more parts
To safe performance, and he told his son
That or Melanthius or his maids had done
A deed that foul war to their hands conferr'd.

   'O father,' he replied, 'tis I have err'd
In this caus'd labour: I, and none but I,
That left the door ope of your armoury.   190
But some, it seems, hath set a sharper eye
On that important place. Eumaeus! Haste
And shut the door, observing who hath pass'd
To this false action: any maid, or one
That I suspect more, which is Dolius' son.'

   While these spake thus, Melanthius went again
For more fair arms; whom the renowned swain
Eumaeus saw, and told Ulysses straight
It was the hateful man that his conceit
Before suspected, who had done that ill;   200
And, being again there, ask'd if he should kill,
If his power serv'd, or he should bring the swain
To him, t' inflict on him a several pain
For every forfeit he had made his house.

   He answer'd: 'I and my Telemachus
Will here contain these proud ones in despite,
How much soever these stolen arms excite

Their guilty courages, while you two take
Possession of the chamber. The doors make
Sure at your back, and then, surprising him,   210
His feet and hands bind, wrapping every limb
In pliant chains; and with a halter cast
Above the wind-beam – at himself made fast –
Aloft the column draw him; where alive
He long may hang, and pains enough deprive
His vexed life before his death succeed.'
This charge, soon heard, as soon they put to deed,
Stole on his stealth, and at the further end
Of all the chamber saw him busily bend
His hands to more arms, when they, still at door,   220
Watch'd his return. At last he came, and bore
In one hand a fair helm, in th' other held
A broad and ancient rusty-rested shield,
That old Laertes in his youth had worn,
Of which the cheek-bands had with age been torn.
They rush'd upon him, caught him by the hair,
And dragg'd him in again; whom, crying out,
They cast upon the pavement, wrapp'd about
With sure and pinching cords both foot and hand,
And then, in full act of their king's command,   230
A pliant chain bestow'd on him, and hal'd
His body up the column, till he scal'd
The highest wind-beam; where made firmly fast,
Eumaeus on his just infliction pass'd
This pleasurable cavil: 'Now you may
All night keep watch here, and the earliest day
Discern, being hung so high, to rouse from rest
Your dainty cattle to the wooers' feast.
There, as befits a man of means so fair,
Soft may you sleep, nought under you but air;   240
And so long hang you.' Thus they left him there,
Made fast the door, and with Ulysses were
All arm'd in th' instant. Then they all stood close,
Their minds fire breath'd in flames against their foes,
Four in th' entry fighting all alone,
When from the hall charged many a mighty one.
    But to them then Jove's seed, Minerva, came,
Resembling Mentor both in voice and frame
Of manly person. Passing well apaid
Ulysses was, and said: 'Now, Mentor, aid   250

'Gainst these odd mischiefs; call to memory now
My often good to thee, and that we two
Of one year's life are.' Thus he said, but thought
It was Minerva, that had ever brought
To her side safety. On the other part,
The wooers threaten'd; but the chief in heart
Was Agelaus, who to Mentor spake:

   'Mentor! Let no words of Ulysses make
Thy hand a fighter on his feeble side
'Gainst all us wooers; for we firm abide   260
In this persuasion, that when sire and son
Our swords have slain, thy life is sure to run
One fortune with them. What strange acts hast thou
Conceit to form here? Thy head must bestow
The wreak of theirs on us. And when thy pow'rs
Are taken down by these fierce steels of ours,
All thy possessions, in doors and without,
Must raise on heap with his, and all thy rout
Of sons and daughters in thy turrets bleed
Wreak offerings to us, and our town stand freed   270
Of all charge with thy wife.' Minerva's heart
Was fired with these braves, the approv'd desert
Of her Ulysses chiding, saying: 'No more
Thy force nor fortitude as heretofore
Will gain thee glory, when nine years at Troy
White-wristed Helen's rescue did employ
Thy arms and wisdom, still and ever us'd,
The bloods of thousands through the field diffus'd
By thy vast valour. Priam's broad-way'd town
By thy grave parts was sack'd and overthrown;   280
And now, amongst thy people and thy goods,
Against the wooers' base and petulant bloods
Stint'st thou thy valour, rather mourning here
Than manly fighting? Come, friend, stand we near,
And note my labour, that thou may'st discern
Amongst thy foes how Mentor's nerves will earn
All thy old bounties.' This she spake, but stay'd
Her hand from giving each-way-often-sway'd
Uncertain conquest to his certain use,
But still would try what self-pow'rs would produce   290
Both in the father and the glorious son.

   Then on the wind-beam that along did run
The smoky roof, transform'd, Minerva sat,

Like to a swallow, sometimes cuffing at
The swords and lances, rushing from her seat,
And up and down the troubled house did beat
Her wing at every motion. And as she
Had rous'd Ulysses, so the enemy
Damastor's son excited, Polybus,
Amphimedon, and Demoptolemus,   300
Eurynomus, and Polyetorides;
For these were men that of the wooing prease
Were most egregious, and the clearly best
In strength of hand of all the desperate rest
That yet surviv'd, and now fought for their souls;
Which straight swift arrows sent among the fowls.
But first, Damastor's son had more spare breath
To spend on their excitements ere his death,
And said: that now Ulysses would forbear
His dismal hand, since Mentor's spirit was there,   310
And blew vain vaunts about Ulysses' ears;
In whose trust he would cease his massacres,
Rest him, and put his friend's huge boasts in proof;
And so was he beneath the entry's roof
Left with Telemachus, and th' other two.
'At whom,' said he, 'discharge no darts, but throw
All at Ulysses, rousing his faint rest;
Whom if we slaughter, by our interest
In Jove's assistance, all the rest may yield
Our pow'rs no care, when he strews once the field.'   320
    As he then will'd, they all at random threw
Where they suppos'd he rested; and then flew
Minerva after every dart, and made
Some strike the threshold, some the walls invade,
Some beat the doors, and all acts render'd vain
Their grave steel offer'd. Which escap'd, again
Came on Ulysses, saying: 'O that we
The wooers' troop with our joint archery
Might so assail, that where their spirits dream
On our deaths first, we first may slaughter them!'   330
    Thus the much-sufferer said; and all let fly,
When every man struck dead his enemy.
Ulysses slaughter'd Demoptolemus.
Euryades by young Telemachus
His death encounter'd. Good Eumaeus slew
Elatus. And Philoetius overthrew

Pisander. All which tore the paved floor
Up with their teeth. The rest retir'd before
Their second charge to inner rooms; and then
Ulysses follow'd, from the slaughter'd men   340
Their darts first drawing. While which work was done,
The wooers threw with huge contention
To kill them all; when with her swallow wing
Minerva cuff'd, and made their javelins ring
Against the doors and thresholds, as before.
Some yet did graze upon their marks. One tore
The prince's wrist, which was Amphimedon,
Th' extreme part of the skin but touch'd upon.
Ctesippus over good Eumaeus' shield
His shoulder's top did taint; which yet did yield   350
The lance free pass, and gave his hurt the ground.
    Again then charged the wooers, and girt round
Ulysses with their lances; who turn'd head,
And with his javelin struck Eurydamas dead.
Telemachus dislif'd Amphimedon;
Eumaeus, Polybus; Philoetius won
Ctesippus' bosom with his dart, and said,
In quittance of the jester's part he play'd,
The neat's foot hurling at Ulysses: 'Now,
Great son of Polytherses, you that vow   360
Your wit to bitter taunts, and love to wound
The heart of any with a jest, so crown'd
Your wit be with a laughter, never yielding
To fools in folly, but your glory building
On putting down in fooling, spitting forth
Puff'd words at all sorts, cease to scoff at worth,
And leave revenge of vile words to the gods,
Since their wits bear the sharper edge by odds;
And, in the mean time, take the dart I drave,
For that right hospitable foot you gave   370
Divine Ulysses, begging but his own.'
    Thus spake the black-ox-herdsman; and straight down
Ulysses struck another with his dart –
Damastor's son. Telemachus did part,
Just in the midst, the belly of the fair
Evenor's son, his fierce pile taking air
Out at his back. Flat fell he on his face,
His whole brows knocking, and did mark the place.
    And now man-slaught'ring Pallas took in hand

Her snake-fring'd shield, and on that beam took stand   380
In her true form, where swallow-like she sat.
And then, in this way of the house and that,
The wooers, wounded at the heart with fear,
Fled the encounter, as, in pastures where
Fat herds of oxen feed, about the field
(As if wild madness their instincts impell'd)
The high-fed bullocks fly, whom in the spring,
When days are long, gad-bees or breezes sting.
Ulysses and his son the flyers chas'd,
As when, with crooked beaks and seres, a cast   390
Of hill-bred eagles, cast off at some game,
That yet their strengths keep, but (put up) in flame
The eagle stoops; from which along the field
The poor fowls make wing, this and that way yield
Their hard-flown pinions, then the clouds assay
For 'scape or shelter, their forlorn dismay
All spirit exhaling, all wings' strength to carry
Their bodies forth, and, truss'd up, to the quarry
Their falc'ners ride in, and rejoice to see
Their hawks perform a flight so fervently: 400
So, in their flight, Ulysses with his heir
Did stoop and cuff the wooers, that the air
Broke in vast sighs, whose heads they shot and cleft,
The pavement boiling with the souls they reft.
    Liodes, running to Ulysses, took
His knees, and thus did on his name invoke:
'Ulysses! Let me pray thee, to my place
Afford the reverence, and to me the grace,
That never did or said to any dame
Thy court contain'd, or deed or word to blame,   410
But others so affected I have made
Lay down their insolence; and, if the trade
They kept with wickedness have made them still
Despise my speech, and use their wonted ill,
They have their penance by the stroke of death,
Which their desert divinely warranteth.
But I am priest amongst them, and shall I,
That nought have done worth death, amongst them die?
From thee this proverb then will men derive:
Good turns do never their mere deeds survive.'   420
    He, bending his displeased forehead, said:
'If you be priest among them, as you plead,

Yet you would marry, and with my wife too,
And have descent by her. For all that woo
Wish to obtain – which they should never do,
Dames' husbands living. You must therefore pray,
Of force and oft, in court here, that the day
Of my return for home might never shine;
The death to me wish'd therefore shall be thine.'

This said, he took a sword up that was cast   430
From Agelaus, having struck his last,
And on the priest's mid neck he laid a stroke
That struck his head off, tumbling as he spoke.

Then did the poet Phemius (whose surname
Was call'd Terpiades, who thither came
Forced by the wooers) fly death; but being near
The court's great gate, he stood, and parted there
In two his counsels: either to remove
And take the altar of Herceian Jove
(Made sacred to him, with a world of art   440
Engrav'n about it, where were wont t' impart
Laertes and Ulysses many a thigh
Of broad-brow'd oxen to the deity),
Or venture to Ulysses, clasp his knee,
And pray his ruth. The last was the decree
His choice resolv'd on. 'Twixt the royal throne
And that fair table that the bowl stood on
With which they sacrific'd, his harp he laid
Along the earth, the king's knees hugg'd, and said:

'Ulysses! Let my pray'rs obtain of thee   450
My sacred skill's respect, and ruth to me!
It will hereafter grieve thee to have slain
A poet, that doth sing to gods and men.
I of myself am taught, for god alone
All sorts of song hath in my bosom sown,
And I, as to a god, will sing to thee;
Then do not thou deal like the priest with me.
Thine own lov'd son Telemachus will say,
That not to beg here, nor with willing way
Was my access to thy high court address'd,   460
To give the wooers my song after feast,
But, being many, and so much more strong,
They forc'd me hither, and compell'd my song.'

This did the prince's sacred virtue hear,
And to the king, his father, said: 'Forbear

To mix the guiltless with the guilty's blood.
And with him likewise let our mercies save
Medon the herald, that did still behave
Himself with care of my good from a child,
If by Eumaeus yet he be not kill'd,   470
Or by Philoetius, nor your fury met,
While all this blood about the house it swet.'

  This Medon heard, as lying hid beneath
A throne set near, half dead with fear of death;
A new-flay'd oxhide, as but there thrown by,
His serious shroud made, he lying there to fly.
But hearing this he quickly left the throne,
His oxhide cast as quickly, and as soon
The prince's knees seiz'd, saying: 'O my love,
I am not slain, but here alive and move.   480
Abstain yourself, and do not see your sire
Quench with my cold blood the unmeasur'd fire
That flames in his strength, making spoil of me,
His wrath's right, for the wooers' injury.'

  Ulysses smiled, and said: 'Be confident
This man hath sav'd and made thee different,
To let thee know, and say, and others see,
Good life is much more safe than villany.
Go then, sit free without from death within,
This much-renowned singer from the sin   490
Of these men likewise quit. Both rest you there,
While I my house purge as it fits me here.'

  This said, they went and took their seat without
At Jove's high altar, looking round about,
Expecting still their slaughter; when the king
Search'd round the hall, to try life's hidden wing
Made from more death. But all laid prostrate there
In blood and gore he saw. Whole shoals they were,
And lay as thick as in a hollow creek
Without the white sea, when the fishers break   500
Their many-meshed draught-net up, there lie
Fish frisking on the sands, and fain the dry
Would for the wet change, but th' all-seeing beam
The sun exhales hath suck'd their lives from them:
So one by other sprawl'd the wooers there.
Ulysses and his son then bid appear
The nurse Euryclea, to let her hear

His mind in something fit for her affair.
　　He op'd the door, and call'd, and said: 'Repair,
Grave matron long since born, that art our spy　　　　　510
To all this house's servile housewif'ry;
My father calls thee, to impart some thought
That asks thy action.' His word found in nought
Her slack observance, who straight op'd the door
And enter'd to him, when himself before
Had left the hall. But there the king she view'd
Amongst the slain, with blood and gore imbru'd.
And as a lion skulking all in night,
Far-off in pastures, and come home, all dight
In jaws and breast-locks with an ox's blood　　　　　520
New feasted on him, his looks full of mood:
So look'd Ulysses, all his hands and feet
Freckled with purple. When which sight did greet
The poor old woman (such works being for eyes
Of no soft temper) out she brake in cries,
Whose vent, though throughly open'd, he yet clos'd,
Call'd her more near, and thus her plaints compos'd:
'Forbear, nor shriek thus, but vent joys as loud.
It is no piety to bemoan the proud,
Though ends befall them moving ne'er so much;　　　　530
These are the portions of the gods to such.
Men's own impieties in their instant act
Sustain their plagues, which are with stay but wrack'd.
But these men gods nor men had in esteem,
Nor good nor bad had any sense in them.
Their lives directly ill were, therefore, cause
That death in these stern forms so deeply draws.
Recount, then, to me those licentious dames
That lost my honour and their sex's shames.'
　　'I'll tell you truly,' she replied: 'There are　　　　540
Twice five-and-twenty women here that share
All work amongst them; whom I taught to spin,
And bear the just bands that they suffer'd in.
Of all which only there were twelve that gave
Themselves to impudence and light behave,
Nor me respecting, nor herself – the queen.
And for your son he hath but lately been
Of years to rule; nor would his mother bear
His empire where her women's labours were.

But let me go and give her notice now   550
Of your arrival. Sure some god doth show
His hand upon her in this rest she takes,
That all these uproars bears and never wakes.'
'Nor wake her yet,' said he, 'but cause to come
Those twelve light women to this outer room.'
    She made all utmost haste to come and go,
And bring the women he had summon'd so.
    Then both his swains and son he bade go call
The women to their aid, and clear the hall
Of those dead bodies, cleanse each board and throne   560
With wetted sponges. Which with fitness done,
He bade take all the strumpets 'twixt the wall
Of his first court and that room next the hall,
In which the vessel of the house were scour'd,
And in their bosoms sheath their every sword,
Till all their souls were fled, and they had then
Felt 'twas but pain to sport with lawless men.
    This said, the women came all drown'd in moan,
And weeping bitterly. But first was done
The bearing thence the dead; all which beneath   570
The portico they stow'd, where death on death
They heap'd together. Then took all the pains
Ulysses will'd. His son yet and the swains
With paring-shovels wrought. The women bore
Their parings forth, and all the clotter'd gore.
The house then cleans'd, they brought the women out,
And put them in a room so wall'd about
That no means serv'd their sad estates to fly.
Then said Telemachus: 'These shall not die
A death that lets out any wanton blood,   580
And vents the poison that gave lust her food,
The body cleansing, but a death that chokes
The breath, and altogether that provokes
And seems as bellows to abhorred lust,
That both on my head pour'd depraves unjust,
And on my mother's, scandalling the court
With men debauch'd in so abhorr'd a sort.'
This said, a halser of a ship they cast
About a cross-beam of the roof, which fast
They made about their necks, in twelve parts cut,   590
And hal'd them up so high they could not put

Their feet to any stay. As which was done,
Look how a mavis, or a pigeon,
In any grove caught with a springe or net,
With struggling pinions 'gainst the ground doth beat
Her tender body, and that then strait bed
Is sour to that swing in which she was bred:
So striv'd these taken birds, till every one
Her pliant halter had enforc'd upon
Her stubborn neck, and then aloft was haul'd   600
To wretched death. A little space they sprawl'd,
Their feet fast moving, but were quickly still.

    Then fetch'd they down Melanthius, to fulfill
The equal execution; which was done
In portal of the hall, and thus begun:
They first slit both his nostrils, cropp'd each ear,
His members tugg'd off, which the dogs did tear
And chop up bleeding sweet; and, while red-hot
The vice-abhorring blood was, off they smote
His hands and feet; and there that work had end.   610
Then wash'd they hands and feet that blood had stain'd,
And took the house again. And then the king,
Euryclea calling, bade her quickly bring
All-ill-expelling brimstone, and some fire,
That with perfumes cast he might make entire
The house's first integrity in all.
And then his timely will was, she should call
Her queen and ladies; still yet charging her
That all the handmaids she should first confer.

    She said he spake as fitted; but, before,   620
She held it fit to change the weeds he wore,
And she would others bring him, that not so
His fair broad shoulders might rest clad and show
His person to his servants, was to blame.

    'First bring me fire,' said he. She went, and came
With fire and sulphur straight; with which the hall
And of the huge house all rooms capital
He throughly sweeten'd. Then went nurse to call
The handmaid servants down; and up she went
To tell the news, and will'd them to present   630
Their service to their sov'reign. Down they came
Sustaining torches all, and pour'd a flame
Of love about their lord, with welcomes home,
With huggings of his hands, with laboursome

Both heads' and foreheads' kisses, and embraces,
And plied him so with all their loving graces
That tears and sighs took up his whole desire;
For now he knew their hearts to him entire.

THE END OF THE TWENTY SECOND BOOK

BOOK TWENTY-THREE

The Argument

Ulysses to his wife is known,
A brief sum of his travels shown.
Himself, his son, and servants go
T' approve the wooers' overthrow.

Another Argument

Psi For all annoys
    Sustain'd before,
  The true wife's joys
    Now made the more.

BOOK TWENTY-THREE

THE SERVANTS thus inform'd, the matron goes
Up where the queen was cast in such repose,
Affected with a fervent joy to tell
What all this time she did with pain conceal.
Her knees revok'd their first strength, and her feet
Were borne above the ground with wings to greet
The long-griev'd queen with news her king was come;
And, near her, said: 'Wake, leave this withdrawn room,
That now your eyes may see at length, though late,
The man return'd, which all the heavy date   10
Your woes have rack'd out, you have long'd to see.
Ulysses is come home, and hath set free
His court of all your wooers, slaughtering all
For wasting so his goods with festival,
His house so vexing, and for violence done
So all ways varied to his only son.'
She answer'd her: 'The gods have made thee mad,
Of whose pow'r now thy pow'rs such proof have had.
The gods can blind with follies wisest eyes,
And make men foolish, so to make them wise.   20
For they have hurt ev'n thy grave brain, that bore
An understanding spirit heretofore.
Why hast thou wak'd me to more tears, when moan
Hath turn'd my mind with tears into her own?
Thy madness much more blameful, that with lies
Thy haste is laden, and both robs mine eyes
Of most delightsome sleep, and sleep of them,
That now had bound me in his sweet extreme,
T' embrace my lids and close my visual spheres.
I have not slept so much this twenty years,   30
Since first my dearest sleeping-mate was gone
For that too-ill-to-speak-of Ilion.
Hence, take your mad steps back. If any maid
Of all my train besides a part had play'd
So bold to wake, and tell mine ears such lies,

I had return'd her to her housewif'ries
With good proof of my wrath to such rude dames.
But go, your years have sav'd their younger blames.'

　　She answer'd her: 'I nothing wrong your ear,
But tell the truth. Your long-miss'd lord is here,   40
And with the wooers' slaughter his own hand,
In chief exploit, hath to his own command
Reduc'd his house; and that poor guest was he
That all those wooers wrought such injury.
Telemachus had knowledge long ago
That 'twas his father, but his wisdom so
Observ'd his counsels, to give surer end
To that great work to which they did contend.'

　　This call'd her spirits to their conceiving places;
She sprung for joy from blames into embraces   50
Of her grave nurse, wip'd every tear away
From her fair cheeks, and then began to say
What nurse said over thus: 'O nurse, can this
Be true thou say'st? How could that hand of his
Alone destroy so many? They would still
Troop all together. How could he then kill
Such numbers so united?' 'How,' said she,
'I have not seen nor heard, but certainly
The deed is done. We sat within in fear,
The doors shut on us, and from thence might hear   60
The sighs and groans of every man he slew,
But heard nor saw more, till at length there flew
Your son's voice to mine ear, that call'd to me,
And bade me then come forth, and then I see
Ulysses standing in the midst of all
Your slaughter'd wooers, heap'd up like a wall,
One on another round about his side.
It would have done you good to have descried
Your conquering lord all smear'd with blood and gore
So like a lion. Straight, then, off they bore   70
The slaughter'd carcasses, that now before
The forecourt gates lie, one on another pil'd.
And now your victor all the hall, defil'd
With stench of hot death, is perfuming round,
And with a mighty fire the hearth hath crown'd.
Thus, all the death remov'd, and every room
Made sweet and sightly, that yourself should come
His pleasure sent me. Come, then, take you now

Your mutual fills of comfort. Grief on you
Hath long and many suff'rings laid; which length,   80
Which many suff'rings, now your virtuous strength
Of uncorrupted chasteness hath conferr'd
A happy end to. He that long hath err'd
Is safe arriv'd at home; his wife, his son,
Found safe and good; all ill that hath been done
On all the doers' heads, though long prolong'd,
His right hath wreak'd, and in the place they wrong'd.'
    She answer'd: 'Do not you now laugh and boast
As you had done some great act, seeing most
Into his being; for you know he won   90
(Ev'n through his poor and vile condition)
A kind of prompted thought that there was plac'd
Some virtue in him fit to be embrac'd –
By all the house, but most of all by me,
And by my son that was the progeny
Of both our loves. And yet it is not he,
For all the likely proofs ye plead to me.
Some god hath slain the wooers in disdain
Of the abhorred pride he saw so reign
In those base works they did. No man alive,   100
Or good or bad, whoever did arrive
At their abodes once, ever could obtain
Regard of them; and therefore their so vain
And vile deserts have found as vile an end.
But for Ulysses, never will extend
His wish'd return to Greece, nor he yet lives.'
    'How strange a queen are you,' said she, 'that gives
No truth your credit; that your husband, set
Close in his house at fire, can purchase yet
No faith of you, but that he still is far   110
From any home of his! Your wit's at war
With all credulity ever! And yet now
I'll name a sign shall force belief from you:
I bath'd him lately, and beheld the scar
That still remains a mark too ocular
To leave your heart yet blinded; and I then
Had run and told you, but his hand was fain
To close my lips from th' acclamation
My heart was breathing, and his wisdom won
My still retention, till he gave me leave   120
And charge to tell you this. Now then receive

My life for gage of his return; which take
In any cruel fashion, if I make
All this not clear to you.' 'Lov'd nurse,' said she,
'Though many things thou know'st, yet these things be
Veil'd in the counsels th' uncreated gods
Have long time mask'd in; whose dark periods
'Tis hard for thee to see into. But come,
Let's see my son, the slain, and him by whom
They had their slaughter.' This said, down they went; 130
When, on the queen's part, divers thoughts were spent:
If, all this giv'n no faith, she still should stand
Aloof, and question more, or his hugg'd hand
And loved head she should at first assay
With free-giv'n kisses. When her doubtful way
Had pass'd the stony pavement, she took seat
Against her husband, in the opposite heat
The fire then cast upon the other wall.
Himself set by the column of the hall,
His looks cast downwards, and expected still 140
When her incredulous and curious will
To shun ridiculous error, and the shame
To kiss a husband that was not the same,
Would down, and win enough faith from his sight.
She silent sat, and her perplexed plight
Amaze encounter'd. Sometimes she stood clear
He was her husband; sometimes the ill wear
His person had put on transform'd him so
That yet his stamp would hardly current go.

 Her son, her strangeness seeing, blam'd her thus: 150
'Mother, ungentle mother! Tyrannous
In this too curious modesty you show!
Why sit you from my father, nor bestow
A word on me t' enquire and clear such doubt
As may perplex you? Found man ever out
One other such a wife that could forbear
Her lov'd lord's welcome home, when twenty year
In infinite suff'rance he had spent apart.
No flint so hard is as a woman's heart.'

 'My son,' said she, 'amaze contains my mind, 160
Nor can I speak and use the common kind
Of those enquiries, nor sustain to see
With opposite looks his count'nance. If this be
My true Ulysses now return'd, there are

Tokens betwixt us of more fitness far
To give me argument he is my lord;
And my assurance of him may afford
My proofs of joy for him from all these eyes
With more decorum than object their guise
To public notice.' The much-sufferer brake   170
In laughter out, and to his son said: 'Take
Your mother from the prease, that she may make
Her own proofs of me, which perhaps may give
More cause to the acknowledgments that drive
Their show thus off. But now, because I go
So poorly clad, she takes disdain to know
So loath'd a creature for her loved lord.
Let us consult, then, how we may accord
The town to our late action. Some one slain
Hath made the all-left slaught'rer of him fain   180
To fly his friends and country; but our swords
Have slain a city's most supportful lords,
The chief peers of the kingdom; therefore see
You use wise means t' uphold your victory.'

　'See you to that, good father,' said the son,
'Whose counsels have the sov'reign glory won
From all men living. None will strive with you,
But with unquestion'd garlands grace your brow,
To whom our whole alacrities we vow
In free attendance. Nor shall our hands leave   190
Your onsets needy of supplies to give
All the effects that in our pow'rs can fall.'
'Then this,' said he, 'to me seems capital
Of all choice courses: bathe we first, and then
Attire we freshly, all our maids and men
Enjoining likewise to their best attire.
The sacred singer then let touch his lyre,
And go before us all in graceful dance,
That all without, to whose ears shall advance
Our cheerful accents, or of travellers by,   200
Or firm inhabitants, solemnity
Of frolic nuptials may imagine here.
And this perform we, lest the massacre
Of all our wooers be divulg'd about
The ample city, ere ourselves get out
And greet my father in his grove of trees;
Where, after, we will prove what policies

Olympius shall suggest to overcome
Our latest toils, and crown our welcome home.'
   This all obey'd; bath'd, put on fresh attire   210
Both men and women did. Then took his lyre
The holy singer, and set thirst on fire
With songs and faultless dances; all the court
Rung with the footings that the numerous sport
From jocund men drew and fair-girdled dames;
Which heard abroad, thus flew the common fames:
   'This sure the day is when the much-woo'd queen
Is richly wed. O wretch, that hath not been
So constant as to keep her ample house
Till th' utmost hour had brought her foremost spouse.'   220
   Thus some conceiv'd, but little knew the thing.
And now Eurynome had bath'd the king,
Smooth'd him with oils, and he himself attir'd
In vestures royal. Her part then inspir'd,
The goddess Pallas deck'd his head and face
With infinite beauties, gave a goodly grace
Of stature to him, a much plumper plight
Through all his body breath'd, curls soft and bright
Adorn'd his head withal, and made it show
As if the flowery hyacinth did grow   230
In all his pride there, in the general trim
Of every lock and every curious limb.
Look how a skilful artizan, well seen
In all arts metalline, as having been
Taught by Minerva and the god of fire,
Doth gold with silver mix so that entire
They keep their self-distinction, and yet so
That to the silver from the gold doth flow
A much more artificial lustre than his own,
And thereby to the gold itself is grown   240
A greater glory than if wrought alone,
Both being stuck off by either's mixtion:
So did Minerva her's and his combine;
He more in her, she more in him, did shine.
Like an immortal from the bath he rose,
And to his wife did all his grace dispose,
Encount'ring thus her strangeness: 'Cruel dame,
Of all that breathe, the gods past steel and flame
Have made thee ruthless. Life retains not one
Of all dames else that bears so overgrown   250

A mind with abstinence, as twenty years
To miss her husband, drown'd in woes and tears,
And at his coming keep aloof, and fare
As of his so long absence and his care
No sense had seiz'd her. Go, nurse, make a bed,
That I alone may sleep; her heart is dead
To all reflection!' To him thus replied
The wise Penelope: 'Man half deified,
'Tis not my fashion to be taken straight
With bravest men, nor poorest use to slight.   260
Your mean appearance made not me retire,
Nor this your rich show makes me now admire,
Nor moves at all; for what is all to me
If not my husband? All his certainty
I knew at parting; but, so long apart,
The outward likeness holds no full desert
For me to trust to. Go, nurse, see address'd
A soft bed for him, and the single rest
Himself affects so. Let it be the bed
That stands within our bridal chamber-stead,   270
Which he himself made. Bring it forth from thence,
And see it furnish'd with magnificence.'

  This said she to assay him, and did stir
Ev'n his establish'd patience, and to her;
Whom thus he answer'd: 'Woman! Your words prove
My patience strangely. Who is it can move
My bed out of his place? It shall oppress
Earth's greatest understander; and, unless
Ev'n god himself come, that can easily grace
Men in their most skills, it shall hold his place;   280
For man, he lives not that (as not most skill'd,
So not most young) shall easily make it yield,
If, building on the strength in which he flows,
He adds both levers too and iron crows.
For in the fixture of the bed is shown
A masterpiece, a wonder; and 'twas done
By me, and none but me, and thus was wrought:
There was an olive-tree that had his growth
Amidst a hedge, and was of shadow proud,
Fresh, and the prime age of his verdure show'd,   290
His leaves and arms so thick that to the eye
It show'd a column for solidity.
To this had I a comprehension

To build my bridal bow'r; which all of stone,
Thick as the tree of leaves, I rais'd, and cast
A roof about it nothing meanly grac'd,
Put glu'd doors to it, that op'd art enough.
Then from the olive every broad-leav'd bough
I lopp'd away; then fell'd the tree, and then
Went over it both with my axe and plane,   300
Both govern'd by my line. And then I hew'd
My curious bedstead out; in which I shew'd
Work of no common hand. All this begun,
I could not leave till to perfection
My pains had brought it; took my wimble, bor'd
The holes, as fitted, and did last afford
The varied ornament, which show'd no want
Of silver, gold, and polish'd elephant.
An oxhide dyed in purple then I threw
Above the cords. And thus to curious view   310
I hope I have objected honest sign
To prove I author nought that is not mine.
But if my bed stand unremov'd or no,
O woman, passeth human wit to know.'
This sunk her knees and heart, to hear so true
The signs she urg'd; and first did tears ensue
Her rapt assurance; then she ran and spread
Her arms about his neck, kiss'd oft his head,
And thus the curious stay she made excus'd:
    'Ulysses! Be not angry that I us'd   320
Such strange delays to this, since heretofore
Your suff'ring wisdom hath the garland wore
From all that breathe; and 'tis the gods that thus,
With mutual miss so long afflicting us,
Have caused my coyness; to our youths envied
That wish'd society that should have tied
Our youths and years together; and since now
Judgment and duty should our age allow
As full joys therein as in youth and blood,
See all young anger and reproof withstood   330
For not at first sight giving up my arms,
My heart still trembling lest the false alarms
That words oft strike up should ridiculize me.
Had Argive Helen known credulity
Would bring such plagues with it, and her again,
As authoress of them all, with that foul stain

To her and to her country, she had stay'd
Her love and mixture from a stranger's bed;
But god impell'd her to a shameless deed
Because she had not in herself decreed,   340
Before th' attempt, that such acts still were shent
As simply in themselves as in th' event.
By which not only she herself sustains,
But we, for her fault, have paid mutual pains.
Yet now, since these signs of our certain bed
You have discover'd, and distinguished
From all earth's others, no one man but you
Yet ever getting of it th' only show,
Nor one of all dames but myself and she
My father gave, old Actor's progeny,   350
Who ever guarded to ourselves the door
Of that thick-shaded chamber, I no more
Will cross your clear persuasion, though till now
I stood too doubtful and austere to you.'

    These words of hers, so justifying her stay,
Did more desire of joyful moan convey
To his glad mind than if at instant sight
She had allow'd him all his wishes' right.
He wept for joy, t' enjoy a wife so fit
For his grave mind, that knew his depth of wit,   360
And held chaste virtue at a price so high.
And as sad men at sea when shore is nigh,
Which long their hearts have wish'd, their ship quite lost
By Neptune's rigour, and they vex'd and toss'd
'Twixt winds and black waves, swimming for their lives,
A few escaped, and that few that survives
All drench'd in foam and brine, crawl up to land,
With joy as much as they did worlds command:
So dear to this wife was her husband's sight,
Who still embrac'd his neck – and had, till light   370
Display'd her silver ensign, if the dame
That bears the blue sky intermix'd with flame
In her fair eyes had not infix'd her thought
On other joys, for loves so hardly brought
To long'd-for meeting; who th' extended night
Withheld in long date, nor would let the light
Her wing-hoov'd horse join – Lampus, Phaëton,
Those ever colts that bring the morning on
To worldly men – but, in her golden chair,

Down to the ocean by her silver hair   380
Bound her aspirings. Then Ulysses said:
'O wife! Nor yet are my contentions stay'd.
A most unmeasur'd labour long and hard
Asks more performance – to it being prepared
By grave Tiresias, when down to hell
I made dark passage, that his skill might tell
My men's return and mine. But come, and now
Enjoy the sweet rest that our fates allow.'
     'The place of rest is ready,' she replied,
'Your will at full serve, since the deified   390
Have brought you where your right is to command.
But since you know, god making understand
Your searching mind, inform me what must be
Your last set labour; since 'twill fall to me,
I hope, to hear it after, tell me now.
The greatest pleasure is before to know.'
'Unhappy!' said Ulysses. 'To what end
Importune you this labour? It will lend
Nor you nor me delight, but you shall know
I was commanded yet more to bestow   400
My years in travel, many cities more
By sea to visit; and when first for shore
I left my shipping, I was will'd to take
A naval oar in hand, and with it make
My passage forth till such strange men I met
As knew no sea, nor ever salt did eat
With any victuals, who the purple beaks
Of ships did never see, nor that which breaks
The waves in curls, which is a fan-like oar,
And serves as wings with which a ship doth soar.   410
To let me know, then, when I was arriv'd
On that strange earth where such a people liv'd,
He gave me this for an unfailing sign:
When any one, that took that oar of mine
Borne on my shoulder, for a corn-cleanse fan,
I met ashore, and show'd to be a man
Of that land's labour, there had I command
To fix mine oar, and offer on that strand
T' imperial Neptune, whom I must implore,
A lamb, a bull, and sow-ascending boar;   420
And then turn home, where all the other gods
That in the broad heav'n made secure abodes

I must solicit – all my curious heed
Giv'n to the several rites they have decreed –
With holy hecatombs; and then, at home,
A gentle death should seize me that would come
From out the sea, and take me to his rest
In full ripe age, about me living blest
My loving people; to which, he presag'd,
The sequel of my fortunes were engag'd.'   430
   'If then,' said she, 'the gods will please t' impose
A happier being to your fortune's close
Than went before, your hope gives comfort strength
That life shall lend you better days at length.'
   While this discourse spent mutual speech, the bed
Eurynome and nurse had made, and spread
With richest furniture, while torches spent
Their parcel-gilt thereon. To bed then went
The aged nurse; and, where their sovereigns were,
Eurynome, the chambermaid, did bear   440
A torch, and went before them to their rest;
To which she left them and for hers address'd.
The king and queen then now, as newly wed,
Resum'd the old laws of th' embracing bed.
   Telemachus and both his herdsmen then
Dissolv'd the dances both to maids and men;
Who in their shady roofs took timely sleep.
The bride and bridegroom having ceas'd to keep
Observed love-joys, from their fit delight
They turn'd to talk. The queen then did recite   450
What she had suffer'd by the hateful rout
Of harmful wooers, who had eat her out
So many oxen and so many sheep,
How many tun of wine their drinking deep
Had quite exhausted. Great Ulysses then,
Whatever slaughters he had made of men,
Whatever sorrows he himself sustain'd,
Repeated amply; and her ears remain'd
With all delight attentive to their end,
Nor would one wink sleep till he told her all,   460
Beginning where he gave the Cicons fall;
From thence his pass to the Lotophagi;
The Cyclop's acts, the putting out his eye,
And wreak of all the soldiers he had eat,
No least ruth shown to all they could entreat;

His way to Aeolus; his prompt receipt
And kind dismission; his enforc'd retreat
By sudden tempest to the fishy main,
And quite distraction from his course again;
His landing at the Laestrigonian port,   470
Where ships and men in miserable sort
Met all their spoils, his ship and he alone
Got off from the abhorr'd confusion;
His pass to Circe, her deceits and arts;
His thence descension to th' infernal parts;
His life's course of the Theban prophet learn'd,
Where all the slaughter'd Grecians he discern'd
And loved mother; his astonish'd ear
With what the Sirens' voices made him hear;
His 'scape from th' erring rocks, which Scylla was,   480
And rough Charybdis, with the dangerous pass
Of all that touch'd there; his Sicilian
Offence given to the Sun; his every man
Destroy'd by thunder vollied out of heav'n,
That split his ship; his own endeavours driv'n
To shift for succours on th' Ogygian shore,
Where nymph Calypso such affection bore
To him in his arrival, that with feast
She kept him in her caves, and would have blest
His welcome life with an immortal state   490
Would he have stay'd and liv'd her nuptial mate –
All which she never could persuade him to;
His pass to the Phaeacians spent in woe;
Their hearty welcome of him, as he were
A god descended from the starry sphere;
Their kind dismission of him home with gold,
Brass, garments, all things his occasions would.

   This last word used, sleep seiz'd his weary eye
That salves all care to all mortality.

   In mean space Pallas entertain'd intent   500
That when Ulysses thought enough time spent
In love-joys with his wife, to raise the day,
And make his grave occasions call away.
The Morning rose, and he; when thus he said:
'O queen, now satiate with afflictions laid
On both our bosoms – you oppressed here
With cares for my return, I everywhere
By Jove and all the other deities toss'd

Ev'n till all hope of my return was lost –
And both arriv'd at this sweet hav'n, our bed,   510
Be your care us'd to see administ'red
My house-possessions left. Those sheep that were
Consum'd in surfeits by your wooers here,
I'll forage to supply with some; and more
The suffering Grecians shall be made restore,
Ev'n till our stalls receive their wonted fill.
And now, to comfort my good father's ill
Long suffer'd for me, to the many-tree'd
And ample vineyard grounds it is decreed
In my next care that I must haste and see   520
His long'd-for presence. In the mean time, be
Your wisdom us'd, that since, the sun ascended,
The fame will soon be through the town extended
Of those I here have slain, yourself got close
Up to your chamber, see you there repose,
Cheer'd with your women, and nor look afford
Without your court, nor any man a word.'
   This said, he arm'd, to arms both son and swain
His pow'r commanding, who did entertain
His charge with spirit, op'd the gates and out,   530
He leading all. And now was hurl'd about
Aurora's ruddy fire, through all whose light
Minerva led them through the town from sight.

THE END OF THE TWENTY-THIRD BOOK

BOOK TWENTY-FOUR

The Argument

By Mercury the wooers' souls
Are usher'd to th' infernal pools.
Ulysses with Laertes met,
The people are in uproar set
Against them, for the wooers' ends;
Whom Pallas stays and renders friends.

Another Argument
Omega   The uproar's fire,
        The people's fall:
        The grandsire, sire,
          And son, to all.

BOOK TWENTY-FOUR

CYLLENIAN HERMES with his golden rod
The wooers' souls, that yet retain'd abode
Amidst their bodies, call'd in dreadful rout
Forth to th' infernals; who came murmuring out.
And, as amidst the desolate retreat
Of some vast cavern, made the sacred seat
Of austere spirits, bats with breasts and wings
Clasp fast the walls, and each to other clings,
But, swept off from their coverts, up they rise
And fly with murmurs in amazeful guise   10
About the cavern: so these, grumbling, rose
And flock'd together. Down before them goes
None-hurting Mercury to Hell's broad ways,
And straight to those straits where the ocean stays
His lofty current in calm deeps they flew.
Then to the snowy rock they next withdrew,
And to the close of Phoebus' orient gates,
The nation then of dreams, and then the states
Of those souls' idols that the weary dead
Gave up in earth, which in a flow'ry mead   20
Had habitable situation.
And there they saw the soul of Thetis' son,
Of good Patroclus, brave Antilochus,
And Ajax, the supremely strenuous
Of all the Greek host next Peleïon;
All which assembled about Maia's son.
And to them, after, came the mournful ghost
Of Agamemnon, with all those he lost
In false Aegisthus' court. Achilles then
Beholding there that mighty king of men,   30
Deplor'd his plight, and said: 'O Atreus' son!
Of all heroës, all opinion
Gave thee for Jove's most lov'd, since most command
Of all the Greeks he gave thy eminent hand
At siege of Ilion, where we suffer'd so.

And is the issue this, that first in woe
Stern Fate did therefore set thy sequel down?
None borne past others' fates can pass his own.
I wish to heav'n that in the height of all
Our pomp at Ilion Fate had sign'd thy fall,   40
That all the Greeks might have advanc'd to thee
A famous sepulchre, and Fame might see
Thy son giv'n honour in thy honour'd end!
But now a wretched death did Fate extend
To thy confusion and thy issue's shame.'
    'O Thetis' son,' said he, 'the vital flame
Extinct at Ilion, far from th' Argive fields,
The style of "blessed" to thy virtue yields.
About thy fall the best of Greece and Troy
Were sacrific'd to slaughter – thy just joy   50
Conceiv'd in battle with some worth forgot
In such a death as great Apollo shot
At thy encounters. Thy brave person lay
Hid in a dusty whirlwind, that made way
With human breaths spent in thy ruin's state.
Thou, great, wert greatly valued in thy fate.
All day we fought about thee; nor at all
Had ceas'd our conflict, had not Jove let fall
A storm that forc'd off our unwilling feet.
But, having brought thee from the fight to fleet,   60
Thy glorious person, bath'd and balm'd, we laid
Aloft a bed; and round about thee paid
The Greeks warm tears to thy deplor'd decease,
Quite daunted, cutting all their curls' increase.
Thy death drave a divine voice through the seas
That started up thy mother from the waves;
And all the marine godheads left their caves,
Consorting to our fleet her rapt repair.
The Greeks stood frighted to see sea and air
And earth combine so in thy loss's sense –   70
Had taken ship and fled for ever thence,
If old much-knowing-Nestor had not stay'd
Their rushing off, his counsels having sway'd
In all times former with such cause their courses;
Who bade contain themselves, and trust their forces,
For all they saw was Thetis come from sea,
With others of the wat'ry progeny,
To see and mourn for her deceased son;

Which stay'd the fears that all to flight had won.
And round about thee stood th' old sea-god's seeds   80
Wretchedly mourning, their immortal weeds
Spreading upon thee. All the sacred Nine
Of deathless Muses paid thee dues divine,
By varied turns their heavenly voices venting,
All in deep passion for thy death consenting.
And then of all our army not an eye
You could have seen undrown'd in misery,
The moving muse so ruled in every mind –
Full seventeen days and nights our tears confin'd
To celebration of thy mourned end;   90
Both men and gods did in thy moan contend.
The eighteenth day we spent about thy heap
Of dying fire. Black oxen, fattest sheep
We slew past number. Then the precious spoil,
Thy corse, we took up, which with floods of oil
And pleasant honey we embalm'd; and then
Wrapp'd thee in those robes that the gods did rain;
In which we gave thee to the hallow'd flame.
To which a number of heroical name,
All arm'd, came rushing in in desperate plight,   100
As press'd to sacrifice their vital right
To thy dead ruins while so bright they burn'd.
Both foot and horse brake in, and fought and mourn'd
In infinite tumult. But when all the night
The rich flame lasted, and that wasted quite
Thy body was with the enamour'd fire,
We came in early morn, and an entire
Collection made of every ivory bone,
Which wash'd in wine, and giv'n fit unction,
A two-ear'd bowl of gold thy mother gave,   110
By Bacchus giv'n her, and did form receive
From Vulcan's famous hand, which, O renown'd
Great Thetis' son, with thy fair bones we crown'd,
Mix'd with the bones of Menoetiades
And brave Antilochus; who, in decease
Of thy Patroclus, was thy favour's dear.
About thee then a matchless sepulchre
The sacred host of the Achaians rais'd
Upon the Hellespont, where most it seiz'd,
For height and conspicuity, the eyes   120
Of living men and their posterities.

Thy mother then obtain'd the gods' consent
To institute an honour'd game, that spent
The best approvement of our Grecian fames.
In whose praise I must say that many games
About heroës' sepulchres mine eyes
Have seen perform'd, but these bore off the prize
With miracles to me from all before.
In which thy silver-footed mother bore
The institution's name, but thy deserts,   130
Being great with heav'n, caus'd all the eminent parts.
And thus, through all the worst effects of fate
Achilles' fame ev'n death shall propagate.
While any one shall lend the light an eye,
Divine Aeacides shall never die.
But wherein can these comforts be conceiv'd
As rights to me, when, having quite achiev'd
An end with safety, and with conquest, too,
Of so unmatch'd a war, what none could do
Of all our enemies there, at home a friend   140
And wife have given me inglorious end?'
     While these thus spake, the Argus-killing spy
Brought near Ulysses' noble victory
To their renew'd discourse, in all the ends
The wooers suffer'd, and show'd those his friends.
Whom now amaze invaded with the view,
And made give back; yet Agamemnon knew
Melanthius' heir, much-fam'd Amphimedon,
Who had in Ithaca guest-favours shown
To great Atrides; who first spake, and said: 150
     'Amphimedon! What suff'rance hath been laid
On your alive parts that hath made you make
This land of darkness the retreat you take,
So all together, all being like in years,
Nor would a man have choos'd, of all the peers
A city honours, men to make a part
More strong for any object? Hath your smart
Been felt from Neptune, being at sea – his wrath
The winds and waves exciting to your scathe?
Or have offensive men impos'd this fate,   160
Your oxen driving, or your flock's estate?
Or for your city fighting and your wives,
Have deaths untimely seiz'd your best-tim'd lives?
Inform me truly. I was once your guest,

When I and Menelaus had profess'd
First arms for Ilion, and were come ashore
On Ithaca, with purpose to implore
Ulysses' aid, that city-rasing man,
In wreak of the adulterous Phrygian.
Retain not you the time? A whole month's date   170
We spent at sea, in hope to instigate
In our arrival old Laertes' son,
Whom hardly yet to our design we won.'
   The soul made answer: 'Worthiest king of men,
I well remember every passage then
You now reduce to thought, and will relate
The truth in whole form of our timeless fate:
   'We woo'd the wife of that long-absent king,
Who (though her second marriage were a thing
Of most hate to her) she would yet deny   180
At no part our affections, nor comply
With any in performance, but decreed,
In her delays, the cruel fates we feed.
Her craft was this: she undertook to weave
A funeral garment destin'd to receive
The corse of old Laertes – being a task
Of infinite labour, and which time would ask.
In midst of whose attempt she caus'd our stay
With this attraction: "Youths, that come in way
Of honour'd nuptials to me, though my lord   190
Abide amongst the dead, yet cease to board
My choice for present nuptials, and sustain,
Lest what is past me of this web be vain,
Till all receive perfection. 'Tis a weed
Dispos'd to wrap in at his funeral need
The old Laertes; who, possessing much,
Would, in his want of rites as fitting, touch
My honour highly with each vulgar dame."
Thus spake she, and persuaded; and her frame
All day she labour'd, her day's work not small,   200
But every night-time she unwrought it all,
Three years continuing this imperfect task;
But when the fourth year came her sleights could mask
In no more covert, since her trusted maid
Her whole deceit to our true note betray'd.
With which surpris'd, she could no more protract
Her work's perfection, but gave end exact

To what remain'd, wash'd up, and set thereon
A gloss so bright that like the sun and moon
The whole work show'd together. And when now   210
Of mere necessity her honour'd vow
She must make good to us, ill fortune brought
Ulysses home, who yet gave none one thought
Of his arrival, but far off at field
Liv'd with his herdsman, nor his trust would yield
Note of his person, but liv'd there as guest,
Ragg'd as a beggar in that life profess'd.
At length Telemachus left Pylos' sand,
And with a ship fetch'd soon his native land,
When yet not home he went, but laid his way   220
Up to his herdsman where his father lay,
And where both laid our deaths. To town then bore
The swine-herd and his king, the swain before.
Telemachus in other ways bestow'd
His course home first, t' associate us that woo'd.
The swain the king led after, who came on
Ragged and wretched, and still lean'd upon
A borrow'd staff. At length he reach'd his home,
Where (on the sudden and so wretched come)
Nor we nor much our elders once did dream   230
Of his return there, but did wrongs extreme
Of words and blows to him; all which he bore
With that old patience he had learn'd before.
But when the mind of Jove had rais'd his own,
His son and he fetch'd all their armour down,
Fast lock'd the doors, and, to prepare their use,
He will'd his wife, for first mean, to produce
His bow to us to draw; of which no one
Could stir the string. Himself yet set upon
The deadly strength it held, drew all with ease,   240
Shot through the steels, and then began to seize
Our armless bosoms, striking first the breast
Of King Antinous, and then the rest
In heaps turn'd over; hopeful of his end
Because some god, he knew, stood firm his friend.
Nor prov'd it worse with him, but all in flood
The pavement straight blush'd with our vital blood.
And thus our souls came here, our bodies laid
Neglected in his roofs, no word convey'd
To any friend to take us home and give   250

Our wounds fit balming, nor let such as live
Entomb our deaths, and for our fortunes shed
Those tears and dead-rites that renown the dead.'
    Atrides' ghost gave answer: 'O bless'd son
Of old Laertes, thou at length hast won
With mighty virtue thy unmatched wife.
How good a knowledge, how untouch'd a life,
Hath wise Penelope! How well she laid
Her husband's rights up, whom she lov'd a maid!
For which her virtues shall extend applause   260
Beyond the circles frail mortality draws,
The deathless in this vale of death comprising
Her praise in numbers into infinites rising.
The daughter Tyndarus begat begot
No such chaste thoughts, but cut the virgin knot
That knit her spouse and her with murderous swords.
For which posterities shall put hateful words
To notes of her that all her sex defam'd,
And for her ill shall ev'n the good be blam'd.'
    To this effect these these digressions made   270
In hell, earth's dark and ever-hiding shade.
    Ulysses and his son, now past the town,
Soon reach'd the field elaborately grown
By old Laertes' labour when, with cares
For his lost son, he left all court affairs,
And took to this rude upland, which with toil
He made a sweet and habitable soil.
Where stood a house to him, about which ran,
In turnings thick and labyrinthian,
Poor hovels, where his necessary men   280
That did those works (of pleasure to him then)
Might sit, and eat, and sleep. In his own house
An old Sicilian dame lived, studious
To serve his sour age with her cheerful pains.
    Then said Ulysses to his son and swains:
'Go you to town, and for your dinner kill
The best swine ye can choose; myself will still
Stay with my father, and assay his eye
If my acknowledg'd truth it can descry,
Or that my long time's travel doth so change   290
My sight to him that I appear as strange.'
Thus gave he arms to them, and home they hied.
Ulysses to the fruitful field applied

His present place; nor found he Dolius there,
His sons, or any servant, anywhere
In all that spacious ground; all gone from thence
Were dragging bushes to repair a fence,
Old Dolius leading all. Ulysses found
His father far above in that fair ground,
Employ'd in proining of a plant, his weeds   300
All torn and tatter'd, fit for homely deeds,
But not for him. Upon his legs he wore
Patch'd boots to guard him from the bramble's gore;
His hands had thorn-proof hedging mittens on;
His head a goat-skin casque; through all which shone
His heart giv'n over to abjectest moan.

    Him when Ulysses saw consum'd with age,
And all the ensigns on him that the rage
Of grief presented, he brake out in tears;
And, taking stand then where a tree of pears   310
Shot high his forehead over him, his mind
Had much contention, if to yield to kind,
Make straight way to his father, kiss, embrace,
Tell his return, and put on all the face
And fashion of his instant-told return;
Or stay th' impulsion, and the long day burn
Of his quite loss giv'n in his father's fear
A little longer, trying first his cheer
With some free dalliance, th' earnest being so near.

    This course his choice preferr'd, and forth he went –   320
His father then his aged shoulders bent
Beneath what years had stoop'd, about a tree
Busily digging: 'O, old man,' said he,
'You want no skill to dress and deck your ground,
For all your plants doth order'd distance bound.
No apple, pear or olive, fig or vine,
Nor any plot or quarter you confine
To grass or flow'rs stands empty of your care,
Which shows exact in each peculiar;
And yet (which let not move you) you bestow   330
No care upon yourself, though to this show
Of outward irksomeness to what you are
You labour with an inward froward care,
Which is your age, that should wear all without
More neat and cherishing. I make no doubt
That any sloth you use procures your lord

To let an old man go so much abhorr'd
In all his weeds; nor shines there in your look
A fashion and a goodliness so took
With abject qualities to merit this   340
Nasty entreaty. Your resemblance is
A very king's, and shines through this retreat.
You look like one that having wash'd and eat
Should sleep securely, lying sweet and neat.
It is the ground of age, when cares abuse it,
To know life's end, and, as 'tis sweet, so use it.
    But utter truth, and tell what lord is he
That rates your labour and your liberty?
Whose orchard is it that you husband thus?
Or quit me this doubt, for if Ithacus   350
This kingdom claims for his, the man I found
At first arrival here is hardly sound
Of brain or civil, not enduring stay
To tell nor hear me my inquiry out
Of that my friend, if still he bore about
His life and being, or were div'd to death,
And in the house of him that harboureth
The souls of men. For once he liv'd my guest;
My land and house retaining interest
In his abode there; where there sojourn'd none   360
As guest from any foreign region
Of more price with me. He deriv'd his race
From Ithaca, and said his father was
Laertes, surnamed Arcesiades.
I had him home, and all the offices
Perform'd to him that fitted any friend,
Whose proof I did to wealthy gifts extend:
Seven talents gold; a bowl all silver, set
With pots of flow'rs; twelve robes that had no pleat;
Twelve cloaks, or mantles, of delicious dye;   370
Twelve inner weeds; twelve suits of tapestry.
I gave him likewise women skill'd in use
Of loom and needle, freeing him to choose
Four the most fair.' His father, weeping, said:
    'Stranger! The earth to which you are convey'd
Is Ithaca, by such rude men possess'd,
Unjust and insolent, as first address'd
To your encounter; but the gifts you gave
Were giv'n, alas, to the ungrateful grave.

If with his people, where you now arrive,   380
Your fate had been to find your friend alive,
You should have found like guest-rites from his hand,
Like gifts, and kind pass to your wished land.
But how long since receiv'd you for your guest
Your friend, my son, who was th' unhappiest
Of all men breathing, if he were at all?
O born when fates and ill-aspects let fall
A cruel influence for him! Far away
From friends and country destined to allay
The sea-bred appetites, or left ashore,   390
To be by fowls and upland monsters tore,
His life's kind authors nor his wealthy wife
Bemoaning, as behov'd, his parted life,
Nor closing, as in honour's course it lies
To all men dead, in bed his dying eyes.
But give me knowledge of your name and race.
What city bred you? Where the anchoring-place
Your ship now rides at lies that shored you here?
And where your men? Or, if a passenger
In other keels you came, who (giving land   400
To your adventures here, some other strand
To fetch in further course) have left to us
Your welcome presence?' His reply was thus:
    'I am of Alybande, where I hold
My name's chief house, to much renown extoll'd.
My father Aphidantes, fam'd to spring
From Polypemon, the Molossian king.
My name Eperitus. My taking land
On this fair isle was ruled by the command
Of god or fortune, quite against consent   410
Of my free purpose, that in course was bent
For th' isle Sicania. My ship is held
Far from the city, near an ample field.
And for Ulysses, since his pass from me
'Tis now five years. Unbless'd by destiny,
That all this time hath had the fate to err –
Though at his parting good birds did augur
His putting off, and on his right hand flew,
Which to his passage my affection drew,
His spirit joyful; and my hope was now   420
To guest with him and see his hand bestow
Rites of our friendship.' This a cloud of grief

Cast over all the forces of his life.
With both his hands the burning dust he swept
Up from the earth, which on his head he heap'd,
And fetch'd a sigh, as in it life were broke.
Which griev'd his son, and gave so smart a stroke
Upon his nostrils with the inward stripe,
That up the vein rose there; and weeping ripe
He was to see his sire feel such woe   430
For his dissembled joy; which now let go,
He sprung from earth, embrac'd and kiss'd his sire,
And said: 'O father! He of whom y' enquire
Am I myself, that, from you twenty years,
Is now returned. But do not break in tears,
For now we must not forms of kind maintain,
But haste and guard the substance. I have slain
All my wife's wooers, so revenging now
Their wrong so long time suffer'd. Take not you
The comfort of my coming then to heart   440
At this glad instant, but, in proved desert
Of your grave judgment, give moan glad suspense,
And on the sudden put this consequence
In act as absolute, as all time went
To ripening of your resolute assent.'
    All this haste made not his staid faith so free
To trust his words; who said: 'If you are he,
Approve it by some sign.' 'This scar then see,'
Replied Ulysses, 'giv'n me by the boar
Slain in Parnassus, I being sent before,   450
By your's and by my honour'd mother's will,
To see your sire Autolycus fulfil
The gifts he vow'd at giving of my name.
I'll tell you, too, the trees, in goodly frame
Of this fair orchard, that I ask'd of you
Being yet a child, and follow'd for your show
And name of every tree. You gave me then
Of fig-trees forty, apple-bearers ten,
Pear-trees thirteen, and fifty ranks of vine –
Each one of which a season did confine   460
For his best eating. Not a grape did grow
That grew not there, and had his heavy brow
When Jove's fair daughters, the all-ripening Hours,
Gave timely date to it.' This charg'd the pow'rs
Both of his knees and heart with such impression

Of sudden comfort, that it gave possession
Of all to trance, the signs were all so true,
And did the love that gave them so renew.
He cast his arms about his son and sunk,
The circle slipping to his feet, so shrunk   470
Were all his age's forces with the fire
Of his young love rekindled. The old sire
The son took up quite lifeless. But his breath
Again respiring, and his soul from death
His body's pow'r recov'ring, out he cried,
And said: 'O Jupiter! I now have tried
That still there live in heav'n remembering gods
Of men that serve them, though the periods
They set on their appearances are long
In best men's sufferings, yet as sure as strong   480
They are in comforts, be their strange delays
Extended never so from days to days.
Yet see the short joys or the soon-mix'd fears
Of helps withheld by them so many years!
For if the wooers now have paid the pain
Due to their impious pleasures, now again
Extreme fear takes me, lest we straight shall see
The Ithacensians here in mutiny,
Their messengers dispatch'd to win to friend
The Cephallenian cities.' 'Do not spend   490
Your thoughts on these cares,' said his suffering son,
'But be of comfort, and see that course run
That best may shun the worst. Our house is near,
Telemachus and both his herdsmen there
To dress our supper with their utmost haste;
And thither haste we.' This said, forth they pass'd,
Came home, and found Telemachus at feast
With both his swains; while who had done, all dress'd
With baths and balms and royally array'd
The old king was by his Sicilian maid.   500
By whose side Pallas stood, his crook'd-age straight'ning,
His flesh more plumping, and his looks enlight'ning.
Who issuing then to view, his son admir'd
The gods' aspects into his form inspir'd,
And said: 'O father, certainly some god
By your addression in this state hath stood,
More great, more reverend rend'ring you by far
At all your parts than of yourself you are!'

'I would to Jove,' said he, 'the Sun, and she
That bears Jove's shield, the state had stood with me   510
That help'd me take in the well-builded tow'rs
Of strong Nericus (the Cephalian pow'rs
To that fair city leading) two days past,
While with the wooers thy conflict did last,
And I had then been in the wooers' wreak!
I should have help'd thee so to render weak
Their stubborn knees, that in thy joy's desert
Thy breast had been too little for thy heart.'

    This said, and supper order'd by their men,
They sat to it, old Dolius entering then,   520
And with him, tried with labour, his sons came,
Call'd by their mother, the Sicilian dame
That brought them up and dress'd their father's fare;
As whose age grew, with it increas'd her care
To see him serv'd as fitted. When thus set
These men beheld Ulysses there at meat,
They knew him, and astonish'd in the place
Stood at his presence; who, with words of grace,
Call'd to old Dolius, saying: 'Come, and eat,
And banish all astonishment. Your meat   530
Hath long been ready, and ourselves made stay,
Expecting ever when your wished way
Would reach amongst us.' This brought fiercely on
Old Dolius from his stand; who ran upon,
With both his arms abroad, the king, and kiss'd
Of both his rapt up hands the either wrist,
Thus welcoming his presence: 'O my love,
Your presence here, for which all wishes strove,
No one expected. Ev'n the gods have gone
In guide before you to your mansion.   540
Welcome, and all joys to your heart contend.
Knows yet Penelope? Or shall we send
Some one to tell her this?' 'She knows,' said he,
'What need these troubles, father, touch at thee?'

    Then came the sons of Dolius, and again
Went over with their father's entertain,
Welcom'd, shook hands, and then to feast sat down.
About which while they sat, about the town
Fame flew, and shriek'd about the cruel death
And fate the wooers had sustain'd beneath   550
Ulysses' roofs. All heard; together all

From hence and thence met in Ulysses' hall,
Short-breath'd and noiseful, bore out all the dead
To instant burial, while their deaths were spread
To other neighbour cities where they liv'd,
From whence in swiftest fisher-boats arriv'd
Men to transfer them home. In mean space here
The heavy nobles all in counsel were;
Where, met in much heap, up to all arose
Extremely griev'd Eupitheus so to lose   560
His son Antinous, who first of all
By great Ulysses' hand had slaught'rous fall.
Whose father, weeping for him, said: 'O friends,
This man hath author'd works of dismal ends,
Long since conveying in his guide to Troy
Good men, and many that did ships employ,
All which are lost, and all their soldiers dead;
And now the best men Cephallenia bred
His hand hath slaughter'd. Go we then (before
His 'scape to Pylos, or the Elian shore   570
Where rule the Epeans) 'gainst his horrid hand.
For we shall grieve, and infamy will brand
Our fames for ever, if we see our sons
And brothers end in these confusions,
Revenge left uninflicted. Nor will I
Enjoy one day's life more, but grieve and die
With instant onset; nor should you survive
To keep a base and beastly name alive.
Haste, then, lest flight prevent us.' This with tears
His griefs advis'd, and made all sufferers   580
In his affliction. But by this was come
Up to the council from Ulysses' home –
When sleep had left them, which the slaughters there
And their self-dangers from their eyes in fear
Had two nights intercepted – those two men
That just Ulysses saved out of the slain,
Which Medon and the sacred singer were.
These stood amidst the council; and the fear
The slaughter had impress'd in either's look
Stuck still so ghastly, that amaze it strook   590
Through every there beholder. To whose ears
One thus enforc'd, in his fright, cause of theirs:
    'Attend me, Ithacensians! This stern fact
Done by Ulysses was not put in act

Without the gods' assistance. These self eyes
Saw one of the immortal deities
Close by Ulysses, Mentor's form put on
At every part. And this sure deity shone
Now near Ulysses, setting on his bold
And slaught'rous spirit, now the points controll'd   600
Of all the wooers' weapons, round about
The arm'd house whisking, in continual rout
Their party putting, till in heaps they fell.'
This news new fears did through their spirits impel,
When Halitherses (honour'd Mastor's son,
Who of them all saw only what was done
Present and future), the much-knowing man
And aged heroë, this plain course ran
Amongst their counsels: 'Give me likewise ear,
And let me tell ye, friends, that these ills bear   610
On your malignant spleens their sad effects,
Who not what I persuaded gave respects,
Nor what the people's pastor, Mentor, said –
That you should see your issues' follies stay'd
In those foul courses, by their petulant life
The goods devouring, scandalling the wife
Of no mean person, who, they still would say,
Could never more see his returning day.
Which yet appearing now, now give it trust,
And yield to my free counsels: do not thrust   620
Your own safe persons on the acts your sons
So dearly bought, lest their confusions
On your lov'd heads your like addictions draw.'
     This stood so far from force of any law
To curb their loose attempts, that much the more
They rush'd to wreak, and made rude tumult roar.
The greater part of all the court arose;
Good counsel could not ill designs dispose.
Eupitheus was persuader of the course,
Which, complete arm'd, they put in present force;   630
The rest sat still in council. These men met
Before the broad town, in a place they set
All girt in arms, Eupitheus choosing chief
To all their follies, who put grief to grief,
And in his slaughter'd son's revenge did burn.
But Fate gave never feet to his return,
Ordaining there his death. Then Pallas spake

To Jove her father, with intent to make
His will high arbiter of th' act design'd,
And ask'd of him what his unsearched mind   640
Held undiscover'd? If with arms and ill
And grave encounter he would first fulfil
His sacred purpose, or both parts combine
In peaceful friendship? He ask'd: 'Why incline
These doubts thy counsels? Hast not thou decreed
That Ithacus should come and give his deed
The glory of revenge on these and theirs?
Perform thy will; the frame of these affairs
Have this fit issue: when Ulysses' hand
Hath reach'd full wreak, his then renown'd command   650
Shall reign for ever, faithful truces strook
'Twixt him and all; for every man shall brook
His sons' and brothers' slaughters, by our mean
To send Oblivion in, expunging clean
The character of enmity in them all,
As in best leagues before. Peace, festival,
And riches in abundance, be the state
That crowns the close of wise Ulysses' fate.'
This spurr'd the free, who from heav'n's continent
To th' Ithacensian isle made straight descent.   660
Where, dinner past, Ulysses said: 'Some one
Look out to see their nearness.' Dolius' son
Made present speed abroad, and saw them nigh,
Ran back and told, bade arm; and instantly
Were all in arms. Ulysses' part was four,
And six more sons of Dolius; all his pow'r
Two only more, which were his aged sire
And like-year'd Dolius, whose lives' slaked fire
All white had left their heads, yet, driv'n by need,
Made soldiers both of necessary deed.   670
And now, all girt in arms, the ports set wide,
They sallied forth, Ulysses being their guide;
And to them in the instant Pallas came,
In form and voice like Mentor, who a flame
Inspir'd of comfort in Ulysses' heart
With her seen presence. To his son, apart,
He thus then spake: 'Now, son, your eyes shall see,
Expos'd in slaughterous fight the enemy,
Against whom who shall best serve will be seen.

Disgrace not then your race, that yet hath been   680
For force and fortitude the foremost tried
Of all earth's offsprings.' His true son replied:
'Yourself shall see, lov'd father, if you please,
That my deservings shall in nought digress
From best fame of our race's foremost merit.'
The old king sprung for joy to hear his spirit,
And said: 'O lov'd immortals, what a day
Do your clear bounties to my life display!
I joy, past measure, to behold my son
And nephew close in such contention   690
Of virtues martial.' Pallas, standing near,
Said: 'O my friend! Of all supremely dear,
Seed of Arcesius, pray to Jove and her
That rules in arms, his daughter, and a dart,
Spritefully brandish'd, hurl at th' adverse part.'
    This said, he pray'd; and she a mighty force
Inspir'd within him, who gave instant course
To his brave-brandish'd lance, which struck the brass
That cheek'd Eupitheus' casque, and thrust his pass
Quite through his head; who fell, and sounded falling,   700
His arms the sound again from earth recalling.
    Ulysses and his son rush'd on before,
And with their both-way-headed darts did gore
Their enemies' breasts so thick, that all had gone
The way of slaughter, had not Pallas thrown
Her voice betwixt them, charging all to stay
And spare expense of blood. Her voice did fray
The blood so from their faces that it left
A greenish paleness; all their hands it reft
Of all their weapons, falling thence to earth;   710
And to the common mother of their birth,
The city, all fled, in desire to save
The lives yet left them. Then Ulysses gave
A horrid shout, and like Jove's eagle flew
In fiery pursuit, till Saturnius threw
His smoking lightning 'twixt them, that had fall
Before Minerva, who then out did call
Thus to Ulysses: 'Born of Jove! Abstain
From further bloodshed. Jove's hand in the slain
Hath equall'd in their pains their prides to thee.   720
Abstain, then, lest you move the deity.'

Again then 'twixt both parts the seed of Jove,
Athenian Pallas, of all future love
A league compos'd, and for her form took choice
Of Mentor's likeness both in limb and voice.

THE END OF THE TWENTY-FOURTH BOOK

So wrought divine Ulysses through his woes,
So crown'd the light with him his mother's throes,
As through his great renowner I have wrought,
And my safe sail to sacred anchor brought.
Nor did the Argive ship more burthen feel,
That bore the care of all men in her keel,
Than my adventurous bark; the Colchian fleece
Not half so precious as this soul of Greece,
In whose songs I have made our shores rejoice,
And Greek itself vail to our English voice.   10
Yet this inestimable pearl will all
Our dunghill chanticleers but obvious call,
Each modern scraper this gem scratching by,
His oat preferring far. Let such let lie.
So scorn the stars the clouds, as true-soul'd men
Despise deceivers. For, as clouds would fain
Obscure the stars, yet (regions left below
With all their envies) bar them but of show,
For they shine ever, and will shine, when they
Dissolve in sinks, make mire, and temper clay: 20
So puff'd impostors (our muse-vapours) strive,
With their self-blown additions, to deprive
Men solid of their full, though infinite short
They come in their compare, and false report
Of levelling or touching at their light,
That still retain their radiance, and clear right,
And shall shine ever, when, alas, one blast
Of least disgrace tears down th' impostor's mast,
His tops and tacklings, his whole freight, and he
Confiscate to the fishy monarchy,   30
His trash, by foolish Fame brought now, from hence
Giv'n to serve mackerel forth, and frankincense.
Such then, and any too soft-eyed to see,
Through works so solid, any worth, so free
Of all the learn'd professions, as is fit
To praise at such price, let him think his wit
Too weak to rate it, rather than oppose
With his poor pow'rs ages and hosts of foes.

TO THE RUINS OF TROY AND GREECE

Troy rac't, Greece wrack't, who mourns? Ye both may boast,
Else th' Iliads and Odysseys had been lost!

AD DEUM

The Only True God (betwixt Whom and me
I only bound my comfort, and agree
With all my actions) only truly knows,
And can judge truly, me, with all that goes
To all my faculties. In Whose free Grace
And Inspiration I only place
All means to know (with my means, study, prayer,
In and from His Word taken) stair by stair,
In all continual contentation, rising
To knowledge of His Truth, and practising   10
His Will in it, with my sole Saviour's Aid,
Guide, and Enlight'ning; nothing done, nor said,
Nor thought, that good is, but acknowledg'd by
His Inclination, Skill, and Faculty.
By which, to find the way out to His Love
Past all the worlds, the sphere is where doth move
My studies, pray'rs, and pow'rs; no pleasure taken
But sign'd by His, for which, my blood forsaken,
My soul I cleave to, and what (in His Blood
That hath redeem'd, cleansed, taught her) fits her good.   20

DEO OPT. MAX. GLORIA

FINIS